GREAT
LOVE
STORIES
OF THE WORLD

GREAT
LOVE
STORIES
OF THE WORLD

GALLERY BOOKS

First published in Great Britain in 1932 by
George G. Harrap & Co. Ltd

This edition published in 1990 by Gallery Books
An imprint of W.H. Smith Publishers Inc.
112 Madison Avenue
New York 10016

By arrangement with Octopus Books Limited

ISBN 0-8317-3978-9

Printed in Czechoslovakia

PREFACE

"IT is a remarkable fact," writes Mr G. K. Chesterton, "when we consider how much happiness love has doubtless given to mankind as a whole, that mankind has never pointed to any great historical example of a hero and heroine wedded in a way entirely worthy of them; of a great man and a great woman, united by a great love, that was entirely supreme and satisfying, as in the tradition of the gigantic loves of Eden." It is true that, if we name over the most famous lovers either in history or in fiction, we shall be hard put to find a pair whose story is the story of a happy marriage. Dido and Aeneas, Antony and Cleopatra, Paolo and Francesca, Launcelot and Guinevere, Romeo and Juliet, Dante and Beatrice—we shall look in vain for names of lovers as famous as these whose happiness was secure from disaster. Even the gods, as we find them in the Greek and Roman legends, never achieved in their loves that monotony of bliss described in the tag of the fairy-tales, "They married and lived happily ever after." Zeus himself knew what it was to be miserable with Hera. Was he not on one occasion so angry with her that he hung her from heaven with anvils tied to her feet? The love of Aphrodite for Adonis, like the love of Apollo for Daphne, had a sorrowful ending. Princes and men of genius, again, have not been conspicuously more successful in their loves than the gods. Or, perhaps, it might be nearer the truth to say that the world remembers more vividly the stories of those who loved unhappily than the stories of those who were as fortûnate as they were faithful in their love.

By a curious paradox, the ordinary man, when young and in love, dreams of an existence as free from the shadow of disaster as the pavements of heaven; but in literature he finds himself drawn to tales in which love is subjected to all the injuries of fate—misunderstanding, despair, faithlessness, separation, death. It is as though the perfect love that men desire in life were too undramatic to content them in literature.

It has often been said that perfection is necessarily uninteresting—possibly because the human mind can scarcely conceive it except as a negation—and the record of a perfect marriage, unflawed by faults of character, peril, or tragedy, would in most hands be too wanting in variety to keep us spellbound for long. We read most eagerly when we are in a state of suspense, and we could feel no suspense in following the fortunes of a perfect man and a perfect woman who lived a perfect life in a perfect world. Everybody knows how pleasant Utopias are to dream about, and how dull to read about, and a Utopia of love, if described at length, would be as tedious as any other. Robert Browning himself, whose marriage was almost as near being perfect as can be imagined, did not take a perfect marriage as the theme of his greatest book. *The Ring and the Book,* on the contrary, is a story of tragic suffering as dark as *Othello* or as *Romeo and Juliet*—a story of a world more cruel indeed than we find in either of these plays. After the appearance of *The Ring and the Book* Carlyle met Browning and made a characteristic effort to compliment him on his work. "It is a wonderful book," he declared, "one of the most wonderful poems ever written. I re-read it all through—all made out of an Old Bailey story that might have been told in ten lines and only wants forgetting." It is strange that Carlyle did not realize that without the "Old Bailey" element in Pompilia's story she would not have been a memorable figure in literature. If she and Count Guido, having married, had lived happily ever after, she would by now be as far sunk in oblivion as nearly every other woman who has ever lived or been written about. Literature, like journalism, is not mainly a chronicle of the impeccable lives of impeccable people, but turns for its subjects rather to what in human destiny is symbolized by war, earthquake, storm, and shipwreck. Its real subject it might be said, is the human soul at strife with evil, or entangled in circumstances, but this strife, this struggle with circumstances, is necessary in order to awaken our interest and enlist our sympathy.

Even among the fairy-tales that we read in the nursery we prefer those stories in which the lives of the young and beautiful are free from any suspicion of idyllic perfection. We insist that Cinderella, Beauty, and all the rest of our heroines must live happily ever after; but if they lived happily before as well, we should not trouble to read about them twice. And in the sentimental love stories that are the fairy-tales of the grown-up, those heroes and heroines are the most popular who do not reach the shore of safety till after many a severe and perilous struggle. Sentimental novelists are often accused of a lack of realism in not prolonging the sufferings of their heroes and heroines after marriage, but it is difficult to believe that everybody is miserable after marriage. All that we can be sure of is that those who are so are easier to write stories about than the others.

The Greeks are said by many non-Greeks to have taken a joyous view of life, but even they compounded their love-stories of elements by no means joyous. Paris and Helen, Aegistheus and Clytemnestra, Phaedra and Hippolytus, Medea and Jason—these are all names in a long legend of disaster. If the Trojans had won the war with the Greeks, and if Hector and Andromache had both survived into a happy old age, would a Trojan poet have celebrated their happiness as movingly as a Greek poet has celebrated the sorrow of their parting? It is true that Homer rewarded the faithfulness of Penelope by a happy ending to her trouble; but, in regard to this, he is at variance with other Greek story-tellers who have it that Penelope proved faithless and that she was cast off by Ulysses on his return. It was, I fancy, in the decadence of the ancient literature that the love-story with the idyllically happy ending became popular. It is then that we find a Greek novelist giving "Daphnis and Chloe" just such a cheerful ending as magazine-readers love to-day. It is then that the Africo-Latin Apuleius writes the perfect version of the story of Cupid and Psyche, telling how Jupiter at the last summons her into the palace of Heaven and, taking a pot of immortality, says to her, "Hold, Psyche, and drink to the end thou mayest be immortal, and that Cupid may never depart from thee but be thine everlasting husband." "Cupid and Psyche" is the prototype of hundreds of thousands of love-stories that have since been written—stories of love long imperilled and at last rewarded. In Christian Europe, on the other hand, the love-story with the happy ending has flourished as exuberantly in the noblest periods of literature as in times of decadence—in the age of Shakespeare, for example, as in the 'Nineties.

The chief difficulty of any one who sets out to compile an anthology of love-stories lies in the fact that very few of the great books of the world are predominantly love-stories, and that those which can be so described are as a rule too long to be fitted into an anthology. The great epics of the ancient world contain love-stories, but Helen is no more than a fleeting presence on the *Iliad*, and the love of Dido and Aeneas in Virgil is only an incident soon over. Similarly the great sagas and story-cycles are written on the assumption that love is of man's life a thing apart, and that the main business of life is other than amorous. There are no more resplendent stories of love between man and woman than are to be found in *Morte d'Arthur,* but even *Morte d'Arthur*, through which love flows as rivers flow through a magical landscape, cannot be confined within the definition of a love-story.

When we come to the prose fiction of the last two centuries, we find that the greatest writers have, as a rule, been the most expansive and that the most memorable lovers have been characters, not in short stories, but in long novels, Clarissa Harlowe, Elizabeth Bennet, Lucy Snowe, Beatrix Esmond, Richard Feverel, Bathsheba Everdene—to name a few characters in English literature—are figures more real to us and more unforgettable than any of whom we catch a hurried glimpse in stories that are over in a few pages. To say this is not to disparage the short story in comparison with the novel. The short story has as unquestionable a place in literature as the short poem. At the same time, we are most deeply interested in the emotions of those characters with whom we are most deeply intimate, and it is only a rare writer of short stories who can give us a sense of deep intimacy with his characters within the limits of his art. Tchehov can certainly do so. He can take a casual cup out of the ocean of life and the ocean itself moves restlessly before our imaginations. But even he cannot in his short stories create a character whom we know as intimately in a variety of aspects as we know Anna Karenina.

When I undertook to compile this anthology of love-stories, I naturally inquired of all sorts of people belonging to all sorts of countries what they considered to be the greatest love-stories in their particular languages. I was astonished by the number of those who either could not remember a great love-story in their literature or could remember it only in the form of an epic or a novel. Some of them even said, "We have no love-stories." I ultimately found that, in order to include what seemed to me the best stories of the kind, I should have to go beyond the confines of the short story, properly so called, and admit narratives such as are commonly and contradictorily described as long short stories. "Launcelot and Guinevere" would only be ruined if it were hacked and hewed in order to be compressed into a small space while Turgenev's "First Love" is as long as a short novel, and "Dante and Beatrice" is a book—the *Vita Nuova* with the verse omitted. It may be thought that I might well have gone still further in the direction of admitting longish stories and made room for so comparatively short a novel as *Manon Lescaut*. But to admit novels was beyond the purpose of the anthology which would otherwise have swelled far beyond the size of a single volume.

In so far as I have followed any principle in choosing the stories—and I have obeyed no iron principle—I have attempted in the first place to bring together as many of the famous love-stories in literature as could be found in good prose versions of tolerable length. There are stories that have been made famous in poetry, in drama, and in opera, or, at least, that have become a part of the imaginative life of man through treatment in poetry and music; and some of these stories have been included, not only for their own sake, but because they have become the themes of poets and musicians of genius. For example "Carmen" is read with a heightened eagerness by many people because it provided Bizet with the book for his opera. Not that such stories necessarily owe their eminence to the fact that they inspired poets and composers; it was, as a rule, because of their inherent excellence that poets and composers were attracted to them.

Most of the older stories in this volume, indeed, have been handed down for centuries as part of the common imaginative heritage of Europe. Such stories have survived not only as marvellous legends, but as mirrors of a beauty and a sorrow that have been since the beginning of time and that will be to the end.

It may seem a little inconsistent—or even extremely inconsistent—to draw on the Greek and Roman poets for a number of these stories and at the same time to have rigidly excluded the stories of the English poets. It was decided, however, to confine the anthology to stories in prose; and as Homer and Virgil are to be found in English prose as well as in their original verse, it would have been a merely pedantic consistency to refuse to borrow from them.

And, as I have not scrupled to mingle original prose with prose that has been translated from verse, so I have not hesitated to introduce fact when it seemed as moving and as entertaining as fiction. The story of Launcelot and Guinevere casts a spell on the imagination, as does Cobbett, as he prowls outside the house all night throwing stones at the dogs in order to keep them from disturbing his wife's sleep, albeit on a lower plane. I wish, indeed, I had been able to include more of those historical stories that have become legendary. But, for the most part, they exist only piecemeal, sometimes merely in a few scattered sentences; and I could find no consecutive version of them.

As regards the definition of 'love-story' by which I have been guided in choosing these stories, I may say it has been wide enough to include almost any kind of preference, temporary or lifelong, of a human being (or divine person) of one sex for a human being (or divine person) of the other. Since fiction became the principal reading of mankind, every kind of relationship between men and women, noble and trivial, has been used as

9

a subject of story-tellers, from the flirtations of Simla to the self-sacrificing devotion of the heroines of Turgenev. Love-stories, again, obviously show marked variations between one country and another; and nationality can be discovered in love-stories as in drinks. It is arguable that the typical English love-story of the nineteenth century which ends with wedding-bells, was the natural product of a country in which, theoretically at least, most people married for love. In countries, on the other hand, in which marriages of convenience are the rule, and in which it is, therefore, not taken for granted that a wedding is the end of a perfect love-story, it seems reasonable to expect that novelists will more frequently choose as their theme a passion that ends, rather than a passion that ends in, marriage. Realists assure us that, in fact, marriages of convenience are on the whole as happy as marriages for love, and as little likely to be disrupted; and Dr Johnson was firmly of this opinion. But the theory of the marriage for love as the happy marriage was dominant in the English imagination in the golden age of the novel, and colours the greater part of English fiction till recent times.

On the other hand, whatever may be the difference between the love-stories of one age or country and those of another, I doubt whether these differences go very deep. It was the most anti-feminist period of the history of Greece that bequeathed to us the story of the Faithful Wife of Susa; and the ideal of heroic fidelity comes down to us from beyond Homer. It was the custom toward the end of the nineteenth century in some circles to complain that man had always made of woman his doll and his dickybird, and to assume that women were then only emerging from slavery; but, if women were a subject race socially, they move in the ancient literatures with the nobility and dignity of godlike spirits, and if they love as slaves, it is not as the slaves of society but as the slaves of destiny. The fact that the ancient love-stories still move us is a proof that, in essentials, love has changed but little since savagery became tempered with gentleness. The sorrows of Deirdre touch us more nearly than the sorrows of the heroine of the latest novel. While everything changes, nothing changes.

Count Keyserling prophesies apprehensively in one of his books that, if civilization continues along its present lines, love will disappear from the earth; and he assures us that the women of Europe are now rapidly tranforming themselves into a race of Amazons. The human being of the future, however, has always been an odious person, because the prophets, even when they imagined perfection, left human nature with its subtle and infinite variety out of account. There is little evidence in contemporary literature of this coming Amazonian change. More novels are being written than used to be written about passing sexual adventures in contrast with love. When a kind of ready-made psychology comes in at the door, love flies out at the window. At the same time, such literature of our time as is likely to last contains no omens of the approach of an age which will be unable to understand how, for love of each other, Romeo and Juliet died; or how, because of a beautiful woman, armies perished and a city went down in ashes; or even how Beauty, through piety and pity, loved a Beast and was rewarded with a Prince.

The chief difference between modern and ancient times, in the matter of love-stories, lies, indeed, not in the exclusion of the old themes, but in an extension of the subject-matter so as to include not only heroic and passionate love, but the very minutiae of love and even the faint and temporary mutual attractions of men and women incapable of profundity either of passion or of affection. But the stories that hold the imagination of men are the same to-day as they have always been; and even Rudel, who loved the Lady of Tripoli whom he had never seen and who thought his life blessed for having set eyes on her, though but for a moment, before he died, is a symbolic figure of an ideal love that men will understand in their hearts till the last of the race have vanished from the earth.

ROBERT LYND

CONTENTS

Preface

ENGLAND

SCOTLAND

WALES

IRELAND

UNITED STATES

FRANCE

GERMANY

AUSTRIA

SWITZERLAND

SPAIN

GEORGIA

POLAND

RUSSIA

CONTENTS

ENGLAND

LAUNCELOT AND GUENEVER[1]

Sir Thomas Malory

HOW TRUE LOVE IS LIKENED TO SUMMER

AND thus it passed on from Candelmass until after Easter, that the month
of May was come, when every lusty heart beginneth to blossom, and to
bring forth fruit; for like as herbs and trees bring forth fruit and flourish
in May, in like wise every lusty heart that is in any manner a lover springeth
and flourisheth in lusty deeds. For it giveth unto all lovers courage, that
lusty month of May, in something to constrain him to some manner of
thing more in that month than in any other month, for divers causes. For
then all herbs and trees renew a man and woman, and likewise lovers call
again to their mind old gentleness and old service, and many kind deeds
that were forgotten by negligence. For like as winter rasure doth alway
arase and deface green summer, so fareth it by unstable love in man and
woman. For in many persons there is no stability; for we may see all day,
for a little blast of winter's rasure, anon we shall deface and lay apart true
love for little or naught, that cost much thing; this is no wisdom nor stability, but it is feebleness of nature and great disworship, whomsoever
useth this. Therefore, like as May month flowereth and flourisheth in many
gardens, so in like wise let every man of worship flourish his heart in this
world, first unto God, and next unto the joy of them that he promised his
faith unto; for there was never worshipful man or worshipful woman, but
they loved one better than another; and worship in arms may never be
foiled, but first reserve the honour to God, and secondly the quarrel must
come of thy lady: and such love I call virtuous love.

But nowadays men can not love seven night but they must have all
their desires: that love may not endure by reason; for where they be soon
accorded and hasty heat, soon it cooleth. Right so fareth love nowadays,
soon hot soon cold: this is no stability. But the old love was not so; men
and women could love together seven years, and no licours lusts were

---

[1] From *Morte d'Arthur*.

between them, and then was love, truth, and faithfulness: and lo, in like wise was used love in King Arthur's days. Wherefore I liken love nowadays unto summer and winter; for like as the one is hot and the other cold, so fareth love nowadays; therefore all ye that be lovers call unto your remembrance the month of May, like as did Queen Guenever, for whom I make here little a mention, that while she lived she was a true lover, and therefore she had a good end.

OF SIR LAUNCELOT AND DAME GUENEVER THE FRENCH BOOK TELLETH

In May when every lusty heart flourisheth and bourgeoneth, for as the season is lusty to behold and comfortable, so man and woman rejoice and gladden of summer coming with his fresh flowers: for winter with his rough winds and blasts causeth a lusty man and woman to cower, and sit fast by the fire. So in this season, as in the month of May, it befell a great anger and unhap that stinted not till the flower of chivalry of all the world was destroyed and slain; and all was long upon two unhappy knights, the which were named Sir Agravaine and Sir Mordred, that were brethren unto Sir Gawaine. For this Sir Agravaine and Sir Mordred had ever a privy hate unto the queen Dame Guenever and to Sir Launcelot, and daily and nightly they ever watched upon Sir Launcelot.

So it mishapped, Sir Gawaine and all his brethren were in King Arthur's chamber; and then Sir Agravaine said thus openly, and not in no counsel, that many knights might hear it: I marvel that we all be not ashamed both to see and to know how Sir Launcelot lieth daily and nightly by the queen, and all we know it so; and it is shamefully suffered of us all, that we all should suffer so noble a king as King Arthur is so to be shamed.

Then spake Sir Gawaine, and said: Brother Sir Agravaine, I pray you and charge you move no such matters no more afore me, for wit you well, said Sir Gawaine, I will not be of your counsel. So God me help, said Sir Gaheris and Sir Gareth, we will not be knowing, brother Agravaine, of your deeds. Then will I, said Sir Mordred. I lieve well that, said Sir Gawaine, for ever unto all unhappiness, brother Sir Mordred, thereto will ye grant; and I would that ye left all this, and made you not so busy, for I know, said Sir Gawaine, what will fall of it. Fall of it what fall may, said Sir Agravaine, I will disclose it to the King. Not by my counsel, said Sir Gawaine, for an there rise war and wrack betwixt Sir Launcelot and us, wit you well brother, there will many kings and great lords hold with Sir Launcelot. Also, brother Sir Agravaine, said Sir Gawaine, ye must remember how ofttimes Sir Launcelot hath rescued the king and the queen;

and the best of us all had been full cold at the heart-root had not Sir Launcelot been better than we, and that hath he proved himself full oft. And as for my part, said Sir Gawaine, I will never be against Sir Launcelot for one day's deed, when he rescued me from King Carados of the Dolorous Tower, and slew him, and saved my life. Also, brother Sir Agravaine and Sir Mordred, in like wise Sir Launcelot rescued you both, and threescore and two, from Sir Turquin. Methinketh brother, such kind deeds and kindness should be remembered. Do as ye list, said Sir Agravaine, for I will hide it no longer. With these words came to them King Arthur. Now brother, stint your noise, said Sir Gawaine. We will not, said Sir Agravaine and Sir Mordred. Will ye so? said Sir Gawaine; then God speed you, for I will not hear your tales nor be of your counsel. No more will I. said Sir Gareth and Sir Gaheris, for we will never say evil by that man; for, because, said Sir Gareth, Sir Launcelot made me knight, by no manner owe I to say ill of him: and therewithal they three departed, making great dole. Alas, said Sir Gawaine and Sir Gareth, now is this realm wholly mischieved, and the noble fellowship of the Round Table shall be disparpled: so they departed.

And then Sir Arthur asked them what noise they made. My lord, said Agravaine, I shall tell you that I may keep no longer. Here is I, and my brother Sir Mordred, brake unto my brothers Sir Gawaine, Sir Gaheris, and to Sir Gareth, how this we know all, that Sir Launcelot holdeth your queen, and hath done long; and we be your sister's sons, and we may suffer it no longer, and all we wot that ye should be above Sir Launcelot; and ye are the king that made him knight, and therefore we will prove it, that he is a traitor to your person.

If it be so, said Sir Arthur, wit you well he is none other, but I would be loath to begin such a thing but I might have proofs upon it; for Sir Launcelot is an hardy knight, and all ye know he is the best knight among us all; and but if he be taken with the deed, he will fight with him that bringeth up the noise, and I know no knight that is able to match him. Therefore an it be sooth as ye say, I would he were taken with the deed. For as the French book saith, the king was full loath thereto, that any noise should be upon Sir Launcelot and his queen; for the king had a deeming, but he would not hear of it, for Sir Launcelot had done so much for him and the queen so many times, that wit ye well the King loved him passingly well. My lord, said Sir Agravaine, ye shall ride to-morn a-hunting, and doubt ye not Sir Launcelot will not go with you. Then when it draweth toward night, ye may send the queen word that ye will lie out all that night, and so may ye send for your cooks, and then upon pain of death we shall

.ke him that night with the queen, and outher we shall bring him to you dead or quick. I will well, said the king; then I counsel you, said the King, take with you sure fellowship. Sir, said Agravaine, my brother, Sir Mordred, and I, will take with us twelve knights of the Round Table. Beware, said King Arthur, for I warn you ye shall find him wight. Let us deal, said Sir Agravaine and Sir Mordred.

So on the morn King Arthur rode a-hunting, and sent word to the queen that he would be out all that night. Then Sir Agravaine and Sir Mordred gat to them twelve knights, and hid themself in a chamber in the Castle of Carlisle, and these were their names: Sir Colgrevance, Sir Mador de la Porte, Sir Gingaline, Sir Meliot de Logris, Sir Petipase of Winchelsea, Sir Galleron of Galway, Sir Melion of the Mountain, Sir Astamore, Sir Gromore Somir Joure, Sir Curselaine, Sir Florence, Sir Lovel. So these twelve knights were with Sir Mordred and Sir Agravaine, and all they were of Scotland, outher of Sir Gawaine's kin, either well-willers to his brethren.

So when the night came, Sir Launcelot told Sir Bors how he would go that night and speak with the queen. Sir, said Sir Bors, ye shall not go this night by my counsel. Why? said Sir Launcelot. Sir, said Sir Bors, I dread me ever of Sir Agravaine, that waiteth you daily to do you shame and us all; and never gave my heart against no going, that ever ye went to the queen, so much as now; for I mistrust that the king is out this night from the queen because peradventure he hath lain some watch for you and the queen, and therefore I dread me sore of treason. Have ye no dread, said Sir Launcelot, for I shall go and come again, and make no tarrying. Sir, said Sir Bors, that me repenteth, for I dread me sore that your going out this night shall wrath us all. Fair nephew, said Sir Launcelot, I marvel much why ye say this, sithen the queen hath sent for me; and wit ye well I will not be so much a coward, but she shall understand I will see her good grace. God speed you well, said Sir Bors, and send you sound and safe again.

So Sir Launcelot departed, and took his sword under his arm, and so in his mantle that noble knight put himself in great jeopardy; and so he passed till he came to the queen's chamber, and then Sir Launcelot was lightly put into the chamber. And then, as the French book saith, the queen and Launcelot were together. And whether they were abed or at other manner of disports, me list not hereof make no mention, for love that time was not as is now-a-days. But thus as they were together, there came Sir Agravaine and Sir Mordred, with twelve knights with them of the Round Table, and they said with crying voice: Traitor-knight, Sir Launcelot du Lake, now art thou taken. And thus they cried with a loud voice, that all the court might hear it; and they all fourteen were armed at all points as they should fight in a battle. Alas, said Queen Guenever, now are we mischieved both. Madam, said Sir Launcelot, is there here any armour within your chamber, that I might cover my poor body withal? An if there be any give it me, and I shall soon stint their malice, by the grace of God. Truly, said the queen, I have none armour, shield, sword, nor spear; wherefore I dread me sore our long love is come to a mischievous end, for I hear by their noise there be many noble knights, and well I wot they be surely armed; against them ye may make no resistance. Wherefore ye are likely to be slain, and then shall I be brent. For an ye might escape them, said the queen, I would not doubt but that ye would rescue me in what danger that ever I stood in. Alas, said Sir Launcelot, in all my life thus was I never bestead, that I should be thus shamefully slain for lack of mine armour.

But ever in one Sir Agravaine and Sir Mordred cried: Traitor-knight, come out of the queen's chamber, for wit thou well thou art so beset that thou shalt not escape. O Jesu mercy, said Sir Launcelot, this shameful cry and noise I may not suffer, for better were death at once than thus to endure this pain. Then he took the queen in his arms, and kissed her, and said: Most noble Christian queen, I beseech you as ye have been ever my special good lady, and I at all times your true poor knight unto my power, and as I never failed you in right nor in wrong sithen the first day King Arthur made me knight, that ye will pray for my soul if that I here be slain; for well I am assured that Sir Bors, my nephew, and all the remnant of my kin, with Sir Lavaine and Sir Urre, that they will not fail you to rescue you from the fire; and therefore, mine own lady, recomfort yourself, whatsomever come of me, that ye go with Sir Bors, my nephew, and Sir Urre, and they all will do you all the pleasure that they can or may, that ye shall live like a queen upon my lands. Nay Launcelot, said the queen, wit thou well I will never live after thy days, but an thou be slain I will take my death as meekly for Jesu Christ's sake as ever did any Christian queen. Well, madam, said Launcelot, sith it is so that the day is come that our love must depart, wit you well I shall sell my life as dear as I may; and a thousandfold, said Sir Launcelot, I am more heavier for you than for myself. And now I had liefer than to be lord of all Christendom, that I had sure armour upon me, that men might speak of my deeds or ever I were slain. Truly, said the queen, I would an it might please God that they would take me and slay me, and suffer you to escape. That shall never be, said Sir Launcelot, God defend me from such a shame, but Jesu be Thou my shield and mine armour!

21

And therewith Sir Launcelot wrapped his mantle about his arm well and surely; and by then they had gotten a great form out of the hall, and therewithal they rashed at the door. Fair lords, said Sir Launcelot, leave your noise and your rashing, and I shall set upon this door, and then may ye do with me what it liketh you. Come off then, said they all, and do it, for it availeth thee not to strive against us all; and therefore let us into this chamber, and we shall save thy live until thou come to King Arthur. Then Launcelot unbarred the door, and with his left hand he held it open a little, so that but one man might come in at once; and so there came striding a good knight, a much man and large, and his name was Colgrevance of Gore, and he with a sword struck at Sir Launcelot mightily; and he put aside the stroke, and gave him such a buffet upon the helmet, that he fell grovelling dead within the chamber door. And then Sir Launcelot with great might drew that dead knight within the chamber door; and Sir Launcelot with help of the queen and her ladies was lightly armed in Sir Colgrevance's armour.

And ever stood Sir Agravaine and Sir Mordred crying: Traitor-knight, come out of the queen's chamber. Leave your noise, said Sir Launcelot unto Sir Agravaine, for wit you well, Sir Agravaine, ye shall not prison me this night; and therefore an ye do by my counsel, go ye all from this chamber door, and make not such crying and such manner of slander as ye do; for I promise you by my knighthood, an ye will depart and make no more noise, I shall as to-morn appear afore you all before the king, and then let it be seen which of you all, outher else ye all, that will accuse me of treason; and there I shall answer you as a knight should, that hither I came to the queen for no manner of mal engin, and that will I prove and make it good upon you with my hands. Fie on thee, traitor, said Sir Agravaine and Sir Mordred, we will have thee maugre thy head, and slay thee if we list; for we let thee wit we have the choice of King Arthur to save thee or to slay thee. Ah sirs, said Sir Launcelot, is there none other grace with you? then keep yourself.

So then Sir Launcelot set all open the chamber door, and mightily and knightly he strode in amongst them; and anon at the first buffet he slew Sir Agravaine. And twelve of his fellows after, within a little while after, he laid them cold to the earth, for there was none of the twelve that might stand Sir Launcelot one buffet. Also Sir Launcelot wounded Sir Mordred, and he fled with all his might. And then Sir Launcelot returned again unto the queen, and said: Madam, now wit you well all our true love is brought to an end, for now will King Arthur ever be my foe; and therefore, madam, an it like you that I may have you with me, I shall save you from all manner

22

adventures dangerous. That is not best, said the queen; meseemeth now ye have done so much harm, it will be best ye hold you still with this. And if ye see that as to morn they will put me unto the death, then may ye rescue me as ye think best. I will well, said Sir Launcelot, for have ye no doubt, while I am living I shall rescue you. And then he kissed her, and either gave other a ring; and so there he left the queen, and went until his lodging.

So Sir Launcelot came to Sir Bors, and told him how he had sped, and in what adventure he had been, and how he had escaped.

Then Sir Bors called unto him Sir Lionel, Sir Ector de Maris, Sir Blamore de Ganis, Sir Bleoberis de Ganis, Sir Gahalantine, Sir Galihodin, Sir Galihud, Sir Menadeuke, Sir Villiers the Valiant, Sir Hebes le Renoumes, Sir Lavaine, Sir Urre of Hungary, Sir Nerounes, Sir Plenorius. These two knights Sir Launcelot made, and the one he won upon a bridge, and therefore they would never be against him. And Harry le Fise du Lake, and Sir Selises of the Dolorous Tower, and Sir Melias de Lile, and Sir Bellangere le Beuse, that was Sir Alisander's son Le Orphelin, because his mother Alice le Beale Pellerin and she was kin unto Sir Launcelot, and he held with him. So there came Sir Palomides and Sir Safere, his brother, to hold with Sir Launcelot, and Sir Clegis of Sadok, and Sir Dinas, Sir Clarious of Cleremont. So these two-and-twenty knights drew them together, and by then they were armed on horseback, and promised Sir Launcelot to do what he would. Then there fell to them, what of North Wales and of Cornwall, for Sir Lamorak's sake and for Sir Tristam's sake, to the number of a fourscore knights.

And then that noble knight Sir Launcelot told them all how he was hard bestead in the queen's chamber, and how and in what manner he escaped from them. And therefore, said Sir Launcelot, wit you well, my fair lords, I am sure there nis but war unto me and mine. And for because I have slain this night these knights, I wot well, as is Sir Agravaine Sir Gawaine's brother, and at the least twelve of his fellows, for this cause now I am sure of mortal war, for these knights were sent and ordained by King Arthur to betray me. And therefore the king will in his heat and malice judge the queen to the fire, and that may I not suffer, that she should be brent for my sake; for an I may be heard and suffered and so taken, I will fight for the queen, that she is a true lady unto her lord; but the king in his heat I dread me will not take me as I ought to be taken.

My lord, Sir Launcelot, said Sir Bors, by mine advice ye shall take the woe with the weal, and take it in patience, and thank God of it. And sithen it is fallen as it is, I counsel you keep yourself, for an ye will yourself, there is no fellowship of knights christened that shall do you wrong. Also I will counsel you my lord, Sir Launcelot, than an my lady, Queen Guenever, be in distress, insomuch as she is in pain for your sake, that ye knightly rescue her; an ye did otherwise, all the world will speak of you shame to the world's end. Insomuch as ye were taken with her, whether ye did right or wrong, it is now your part to hold with the queen, that she be not slain and put to a mischievous death, for an she so die the shame shall be yours. Jesu defend me from shame, said Sir Launcelot, and keep and save my lady the queen from villainy and shameful death, and that she never be destroyed in my default; wherefore my fair lords, my kin, and my friends, said Sir Launcelot, what will ye do? Then they said all: We will do as ye will do. I put this to you, said Sir Launcelot, that if my lord Arthur by evil counsel will to-morn in his heat put my lady the queen to the fire there to be brent, now I pray you counsel me what is best to do. Then they said all at once with one voice: Sir, us thinketh best that ye knightly rescue the queen, insomuch as she shall be brent it is for your sake; and it is to suppose, an ye might be handled, ye should have the same death, or a more shamefuler death. And Sir, we say all, that ye have many times rescued her from death for other men's quarrels, us seemeth it is more your worship that ye rescue the queen from this peril, insomuch she hath it for your sake.

Then Sir Launcelot stood still, and said: My fair lords, wit you well I would be loath to do that thing that should dishonour you or my blood, and wit you well I would be loath that my lady, the queen, should die a shameful death; but an it be so that ye will counsel me to rescue her, I must do much harm or I rescue her; and peradventure I shall there destroy some of my best friends, that should much repent me; and peradventure there be some, an they could well bring it about, or disobey my lord King Arthur, they would soon come to me, the which I were loath to hurt. And if so be that I rescue her, where shall I keep her? That shall be the least care of us all, said Sir Bors. How did the noble knight Sir Tristam, by your good will? kept not he with him la Beale Isoud near three year in Joyous Gard? he which was done by your elders' device, and that same place is your own; and in likewise may ye do an ye list, and take the queen lightly away, if it so be the king will judge her to be brent; and in Joyous Gard ye may keep her long enough until the heat of the king be past. And then shall ye bring again the queen to the king with great worship; and then peradventure ye shall have thank for her bringing home, and love and thank where other shall have maugre.

So to make short tale, they were all consented that for better other for worse, if so were that the queen were on that morn brought to the fire, shortly they all would rescue her. And so by the advice of Sir Launcelot, they put them all in an embushment in a wood, as nigh Carlisle as they might, and there they abode still, to wit what the king would do.

Now turn we again unto Sir Mordred, that when he was escaped from the noble knight, Sir Launcelot, he anon gat his horse and mounted upon him, and rode unto King Arthur, sore wounded and smitten, and all forbled; and there he told the king all how it was, and how they were all slain save himself all only. Jesu mercy, how, may this be? said the king; took ye him in the queen's chamber? Yea, so God me help, said Sir Mordred, there we found him unarmed, and there he slew Colgrevance, and armed him in his armour; and all this he told the king from the beginning to the ending. Jesu mercy, said the king, he is a marvellous knight of prowess. Alas, me sore repenteth, said the king, that ever Sir Launcelot should be against me. Now I am sure the noble fellowship of the Round Table is broken for ever, for with him will many a noble knight hold; and now it is fallen so, said the king, that I may not with my worship, but the queen must suffer the death. So then there was made great ordinance in this heat that the queen must be judged to the death. And the law was such in those days that whatsomever they were, of what estate or degreee, if they were found guilty of treason, there should be none other remedy but death; and outher the men or the taking with the deed should be causer of their hasty judgment. And right so was it ordained for Queen Guenever, because Sir Mordred was escaped sore wounded, and the death of thirteen knights of the Round Table. These proofs and experiences caused King Arthur to command the queen to the fire there to be brent.

Then spake Sir Gawaine, and said: My lord Arthur, I would counsel you not to be over-hasty, but that ye would put it in respite, this judgment of my lady the queen, for many causes. One it is, though it were so that Sir Launcelot were found in the queen's chamber, yet it might be that he came thither for none evil; for ye know my lord, said Sir Gawaine, that the queen is much beholden unto Sir Launcelot, more than unto any other knight, for ofttimes he hath saved her life, and done battle for her when all the court refused the queen; and peradventure she sent for him for goodness and for none evil, to reward him for his good deeds that he had done to her in times past. And peradventure my lady, the queen, sent for him to that intent that Sir Launcelot should come to her good grace privily and secretly, weening to her that it was best so to do, in eschewing and dreading of slander; for ofttimes we do so many things that we ween it be for the best, and yet peradventure it turneth so the worst. For I dare say, said Sir Gawaine, my lady, your queen, is to you both good and true;

25

and as for Sir Launcelot, said Sir Gawaine, I dare say he will make it good upon any knight living that will put upon himself villainy or shame, and in like wise he will make good for my lady, Dame Guenever.

That I believe well, said King Arthur, but I will not that way with Sir Launcelot, for he trusteth so much upon his hands and his might that he doubteth no man; and therefore for my queen he shall never fight more, for she shall have the law. And if I may get Sir Launcelot, wit you well he shall have a shameful death. Jesu defend, said Sir Gawaine, that I may never see it. Why say ye so? said King Arthur; forsooth ye have no cause to love Sir Launcelot, for this night last past he slew your brother, Sir Agravaine, a full good knight, and almost he had slain your brother, Sir Mordred, and also there he slew thirteen noble knights; and also, Sir Gawaine, remember ye he slew two sons of yours, Sir Florence and Sir Lovel. My lord, said Sir Gawaine, of all this I have knowledge, of whose deaths I repent me sore; but insomuch I gave them warning and told my brethren and my sons aforehand what would fall in the end, insomuch they would not do by my counsel, I will not meddle me thereof, nor revenge me nothing of their deaths; for I told them it was no boot to strive with Sir Launcelot. Howbeit I am sorry of the death of my brethren and of my sons, for they are the causers of their own death; for ofttimes I warned my brother Sir Agravaine, and I told him the perils the which be now fallen.

Then said the noble King Arthur to Sir Gawaine: Dear nephew, I pray you make you ready in your best armour, with your brethren, Sir Gaheris and Sir Gareth, to bring my queen to the fire, there to have her judgment and receive the death. Nay, my most noble lord, said Sir Gawaine, that will I never do; for wit you well I will never be in that place where so noble a queen as is my lady, Dame Guenever, shall take a shameful end. For wit you well, said Sir Gawaine, my heart will never serve me to see her die; and it shall never be said that ever I was of your counsel of her death.

Then said the king to Sir Gawaine; Suffer your brothers Sir Gaheris and Sir Gareth to be there. My lord, said Sir Gawaine, wit you well they will be loath to be there present, because of many adventures the which be like there to fall, but they are young and full unable to say you nay. Then spake Sir Gaheris, and the good knight Sir Gareth, unto Sir Arthur; Sir, ye may well command us to be there, but wit you well it shall be sore against our will; but an we be there by your strait commandment ye shall plainly hold us there excused; we will be there in peaceable wise, and bear none harness of war upon us. In the name of God, said the king, then make youready, for she shall soon have her judgment anon. Alas, said Sir Gawaine, that ever I should endure to see this woful day. So Sir Gawaine turned him

26

and wept heartily, and so he went into his chamber; and then the queen was led forth without Carlisle, and there she was despoiled unto her smock. And so then her ghostly father was brought to her, to be shriven of her misdeeds. Then was there weeping, and wailing, and wringing of hands, of many lords and ladies, but there were but few in comparison that would any bear armour for to strength the death of the queen.

Then was there one that Sir Launcelot had sent unto that place for to espy what time the queen should go unto her death; and anon as he saw the queen despoiled unto her smock, and so shriven, then he gave Sir Launcelot warning. Then was there but spurring and plucking up of horses, and right so they came to the fire. And who that stood against them, there were they slain; there might none withstand Sir Launcelot, so all that bare arms and withstood them, there were they slain, full many a noble knight. For there was slain Sir Belliance le Orgulous, Sir Segwarides, Sir Griflet, Sir Brandiles, Sir Aglovale, Sir Tor; Sir Gauter, Sir Gillimer, Sir Reynolds' three brethren; Sir Damas, Sir Priamus, Sir Kay the Stranger, Sir Driant, Sir Lambegus, Sir Herminde; Sir Pertilope, Sir Perimones, two brethren that were called the Green Knight and the Red Knight. And so in this rushing and hurling, as Sir Launcelot thrang here and there, it mishapped him to slay Gaheris and Sir Gareth, the noble knight, for they were unarmed and unware. For as the French book saith, Sir Launcelot smote Sir Gareth and Sir Gaheris upon the brain-pans, wherethrough they were slain in the field; howbeit in very truth Sir Launcelot saw them not, and so were they found dead among the thickest of the press.

Then when Sir Launcelot had thus done, and slain and put to flight all that would withstand him, then he rode straight unto Dame Guenever, and made a kirtle and a gown to be cast upon her; and then he made her to be set behind him, and prayed her to be of good cheer. Wit you well the queen was glad that she was escaped from the death. And then she thanked God and Sir Launcelot; and so he rode his way with the queen, as the French book saith, unto Joyous Gard, and there he kept her as a noble knight should do; and many great lords and some kings sent Sir Launcelot many good knights, and many noble knights drew unto Sir Launcelot. When this was known openly, that King Arthur and Sir Launcelot were at debate, many knights were glad of their debate, and many were full heavy of their debate.

So turn we again unto King Arthur, that when it was told him how and in what manner of wise the queen was taken away from the fire, and when he heard of the death of his noble knights, and in especial of Sir Gaheris and Sir Gareth's death, then the king swooned for pure sorrow. And when he awoke of his swoon, then he said: Alas, that ever I bare crown upon my head! for now have I lost the fairest fellowship of noble knights that ever held Christian king together. Alas, my good knights be slain away from me: now within these two days I have lost forty knights, and also the noble fellowship of Sir Launcelot and his blood, for now I may never hold them together no more with my worship. Alas that ever this war began. Now fair fellows, said the king, I charge you that no man tell Sir Gawaine of the death of his two brethren; for I am sure, said the king, when Sir Gawaine heareth tell that Sir Gareth is dead he will go right out of his mind. Mercy Jesu, said the king, why slew he Sir Gareth and Sir Gaheris, for I dare say as for Sir Gareth he loved Sir Launcelot above all men earthly. That is truth, said some knights, but they were slain in the hurtling as Sir Launcelot thrang in the thick of the press; and as they were unarmed he smote them and wist not whom that he smote, and so unhappily they were slain. The death of them, said Arthur, will cause the greatest mortal war that ever was; I am sure, wist Sir Gawaine that Sir Gareth were slain, I should never have rest of him till I had destroyed Sir Launcelot's kin and himself both, outher else he to destroy me. And therefore, said the king, wit you well my heart was never so heavy as it is now, and much more I am sorrier for my good knights' loss than for the loss of my fair queen; for queens I might have enow, but such a fellowship of good knights shall never be together in no company. And now I dare say, said King Arthur, there was never Christian king held such a fellowship together; and alas that ever Sir Launcelot and I should be at debate. Ah Agravaine, Agravaine, said the king, Jesu forgive it thy soul, for thine evil will, that thou and thy brother Sir Mordred hadst unto Sir Launcelot, hath caused all this sorrow: and ever among these complaints the king wept and swooned.

Then there came one unto Sir Gawaine, and told him how the queen was led away with Sir Launcelot, and nigh a twenty-four knights slain. O Jesu defend my brethren, said Sir Gawaine, for full well wist I that Sir Launcelot would rescue her, outher else he would die in that field; and to say the truth he had not been a man of worship had he not rescued the queen that day, insomuch she should have been brent for his sake. And as in that, said Sir Gawaine, he hath done but knightly, and as I would have done myself an I had stood in like case. But where are my brethren? said Sir Gawaine, I marvel I hear not of them. Truly, said that man, Sir Gareth and Sir Gaheris be slain. Jesu defend, said Sir Gawaine, for all the world I would not that they were slain, and in especial my good brother, Sir Gareth. Sir, said the man, he is slain, and that is great pity. Who slew him? said Sir Gawaine. Sir, said the man, Launcelot slew them both. That may

I not believe, said Sir Gawaine, that ever he slew my brother, Sir Gareth; for I dare say my brother Gareth loved him better than me, and all his brethren, and the king both. Also I dare say, an Sir Launcelot had desired my brother, Sir Gareth, with him he would have been with him against the king and us all, and therefore I may never believe that Sir Launcelot slew my brother. Sir, said this man, it is noised that he slew him.

Alas, said Sir Gawaine, now is my joy gone. And then he fell down and swooned, and long he lay there as he had been dead. And then, when he arose of his swoon, he cried out sorrowfully, and said: Alas! And right so Sir Gawaine ran to the king, crying and weeping: O King Arthur, mine uncle, my good brother Sir Gareth is slain, and so is my brother Sir Gaheris, the which were two noble knights. Then the king wept, and he both; and so they fell a-swooning. And when they were revived then spake Sir Gawaine: Sir, I will go see my brother, Sir Gareth. Ye may not see him, said the king, for I caused him to be interred, and Sir Gaheris both; for I well understood that he would make over-much sorrow, and the sight of Sir Gareth should have caused your double sorrow. Alas, my lord, said Sir Gawaine, how slew he my brother, Sir Gareth? Mine own good lord I pray you tell me. Truly, said the king, I shall tell you how it is told me, Sir Launcelot slew him and Sir Gaheris both. Alas, said Sir Gawaine, they bare none arms against him, neither of them both. I wot not how it was, said the king, but as it is said, Sir Launcelot slew them both in the thickest of the press and knew them not; and therefore let us shape a remedy for to revenge their deaths.

My king, my lord, and mine uncle, said Sir Gawaine, wit you well now I shall make you a promise that I shall hold by my knighthood, that from this day I shall never fail Sir Launcelot until the one of us have slain the other. And therefore I require you, my lord and king, dress you to the war, for wit you well I will be revenged upon Sir Launcelot; and therefore, as ye will have my service and my love, now haste you thereto, and assay your friends. For I promise unto God, said Sir Gawaine, for the death of my brother, Sir Gareth, I shall seek Sir Launcelot throughout seven kings' realms, but I shall slay him or else he shall slay me. Ye shall not need to seek him so far, said the king, for as I hear say, Sir Launcelot will abide me and you in the Joyous Gard; and much people draweth unto him, as I hear say. That may I believe, said Sir Gawaine; but my lord, he said, assay your friends, and I will assay mine. It shall be done, said the king, and as I suppose I shall be big enough to draw him out of the biggest tower of his castle.

So then the king sent letters and writs throughout all England, both in the length and the breadth, for to assummon all his knights. And so unto Arthur drew many knights, dukes, and earls, so that he had a great host. And when they were assembled, the king informed them how Sir Launcelot had bereft him his queen. Then the king and all his host made them ready to lay siege about Sir Launcelot, where he lay within Joyous Gard. Thereof heard Sir Launcelot, and purveyed him of many good knights, for with him held many knights; and some for his own sake, and some for the queen's sake. Thus they were on both parties well furnished and garnished of all manner of thing that longed to the war. But King Arthur's host was so big that Sir Launcelot would not abide him in the field, for he was full loath to do battle against the king; but Sir Launcelot drew him to his strong castle with all manner of victual, and as many noble men as he might suffice within the town and the castle. Then came King Arthur with Sir Gawaine with an huge host, and laid a siege all about Joyous Gard, both at the town and at the castle, and there they made strong war on both parties. But in no wise Sir Launcelot would ride out, nor go out of his castle, of long time; neither he would none of his good knights to issue out, neither none of the town nor of the castle, until fifteen weeks were past.

I leave here of this tale and overskip great books telling of the communication between King Arthur and Sir Launcelot, and how King Arthur reproved him; and of a grievous battle.

This war was noised through all Christendom, and at the last it was noised afore the Pope; and he considering the great goodness of King Arthur, and of Sir Launcelot, that was called the most noblest knight of the world, wherefore the Pope called unto him a noble clerk that at that time was there present; the French book saith, it was the Bishop of Rochester; and the Pope gave him bulls under lead unto King Arthur of England, charging him upon pain of interdicting of all England, that he take his queen Dame Guenever unto him again, and accord with Sir Launcelot.

So when the Bishop was come to Joyous Gard, there he shewed Sir Launcelot how the Pope had written to Arthur and unto him, and there he told him the perils if he withheld the queen from the king. It was never in my thought, said Launcelot, to withhold the queen from my lord Arthur; but, insomuch she should have been dead for my sake, meseemeth it was my part to save her life, and put her from that danger, till better recover might come. And now I thank God, said Sir Launcelot, that the Pope hath made her peace; for God knoweth, said Sir Launcelot, I will be a thousand-fold more gladder to bring her again, than ever I was of her taking away;

with this, I may be sure to come safe and go safe, and that the queen shall have her liberty as she had before; and never for no thing that hath been surmised afore this time, she never from this day stand in no peril. For else, said Sir Launcelot, I dare adventure me to keep her from an harder shour than ever I kept her. It shall not need you, said the Bishop, to dread so much; for wit you well, the Pope must be obeyed, and it were not the Pope's worship nor my poor honesty to wit you distressed, neither the queen, neither in peril nor shamed. And then he shewed Sir Launcelot all his writing, both from the Pope and from King Arthur. This is sure enough, said Sir Launcelot, for full well I dare trust my lord's own writing and his seal, for he was never ashamed of his promise. Therefore, said Sir Launcelot unto the Bishop, ye shall ride unto the king afore, and recommend me unto his good grace, and let him have knowledging that this same day eight days, by the grace of God, I myself shall bring my lady, Queen Guenever, unto him. And then say ye unto my most redoubted king, that I will say largely for the queen, that I shall none except for dread nor fear, but the king himself, and my lord Sir Gawaine; and that is more for the king's love than for himself.

So the Bishop departed and came to the king at Carlisle, and told him all how Sir Launcelot answered him; and then the tears brast out of the king's eyen. Then Sir Launcelot purveyed him an hundred knights, and all were clothed in green velvet, and their horses trapped to their heels; and every knight held a branch of olive in his hand, in tokening of peace. And the queen had four-and-twenty gentlewomen following her in the same wise; and Sir Launcelot had twelve coursers following him, and on every courser sat a young gentleman, and all they were arrayed in green velvet, with sarps of gold about their quarters, and the horse trapped in the same wise down to the heels, with many ouches, y-set with stones and pearls in gold, to the number of a thousand. And she and Sir Launcelot were clothed in white cloth of gold tissue; and right so as ye have heard, as the French book maketh mention, he rode with the queen from Joyous Gard to Carlisle. And so Sir Launcelot rode throughout Carlisle, and so in the castle, that all men might behold; and wit you well there was many a weeping eye. And then Sir Launcelot himself alighted and avoided his horse, and took the queen, and so led her where King Arthur was in his seat: and Sir Gawaine sat afore him, and many other great lords. So when Sir Launcelot saw the king and Sir Gawaine, then he led the queen by the arm, and then he kneeled down, and the queen both. Wit you well then was there many bold knights there with King Arthur that wept as tenderly as though they had seen all their kin afore them. So the king sat still, and said no word. And when Sir Launcelot saw his countenance, he arose and pulled up the queen with him, and thus he spake full knightly.

My most redoubted king, ye shall understand, by the Pope's commandment and yours, I have brought to you my lady the queen, as right requireth; and if there be any knight, of whatsomever degree that he be except your person, that will say or dare say but that she is true and clean to you, I here myself, Sir Launcelot du Lake, will make it good upon his body, that she is a true lady unto you; but liars ye have listened, and that hath caused debate betwixt you and me. For time hath been, my lord Arthur, that ye have been greatly pleased with me when I did battle for my lady, your queen; and full well ye know, my most noble king, that she hath been put to great wrong or this time; and sithen it pleased you at many times that I should fight for her, meseemeth, my good lord, I had more cause to rescue her from the fire, insomuch she should have been brent for my sake. For they that told you those tales were liars, and so it fell upon them; for by likelihood had not the might of God been with me, I might never have endured fourteen knights, and they armed and afore purposed, and I unarmed and not purposed. For I was sent for unto my lady your queen, I wot not for what cause, but I was not so soon within the chamber door, but anon Sir Agravaine and Sir Mordred called me traitor and recreant knight. They called thee right, said Sir Gawaine. My lord Sir Gawaine, said Launcelot, in their quarrel they proved themselves not in the right. Well well, Sir Launcelot, said the king, I have given thee no cause to do to me as thou hast done, for I have worshipped thee and thine more than any of all my knights.

My good lord, said Sir Launcelot, so ye be not displeased, ye shall understand I and mine have done you oft better service than any other knights have done, in many divers places; and where ye have been full hard bestead divers times, I have myself rescued you from many dangers; and ever unto my power I was glad to please you, and my lord Sir Gawaine; both in jousts, and tournaments, and in battles set, both on horseback and on foot, I have often rescued you, and my lord Sir Gawaine, and many more of your knights in many divers places. For now I will make avaunt, said Sir Launcelot, I will that ye all wit that yet I found never no manner of knight but that I was overhard for him, an I had done my utterance, thanked be God; howbeit I have been matched with good knights, as Sir Tristram and Sir Lamorak, but ever I had a favour unto them and a deeming what they were. And I take God to record, said Sir Launcelot, I never was wroth nor greatly heavy with no good knight an I saw him busy about to win worship; and glad I was ever when I found any knight that might endure me on horseback and on foot: howbeit Sir Carados of the Dolorous Tower was a full noble knight and a passing strong man, and that wot ye, my lord Sir Gawaine; for he might well be called a noble knight when he by fine force pulled you out of your saddle, and bound you overthwart afore him to his saddle bow; and there, my lord Sir Gawaine, I rescued you, and slew him afore your sight. Also I found his brother, Sir Turquin, in likewise leading Sir Gaheris, your brother, bounden afore him; and there I rescued your brother and slew that Turquin, and delivered three-score-and-four of my lord Arthur's knights out of his prison. And now I dare say, said Sir Launcelot, I met never with so strong knights, nor so well fighting, as with Sir Carados and Sir Turquin, for I fought with them to the uttermost. And therefore, said Sir Launcelot unto Sir Gawaine, meseemeth ye ought of right to remember this; for, an I might have your good will, I would trust to God to have my lord Arthur's good grace.

The king may do as he will, said Sir Gawaine, but wit thou well, Sir Launcelot, thou and I shall never be accorded while we live. Then Sir Launcelot sighed, and therewith the tears fell on his cheeks.

And then Sir Launcelot said unto Guenever, in hearing of the king and them all: Madam, now I must depart from you and this noble fellowship for ever; and sithen it is so, I beseech you to pray for me, and say me well; and if ye be hard bestead by any false tongues, lightly my lady send me word, and if any knight's hands may deliver you by battle, I shall deliver you. And therewithal Sir Launcelot kissed the queen; and then he said all openly: Now let see what he be in this place that dare say the queen is not true unto my lord Arthur, let see who will speak an he dare speak. And therewith he brought the queen to the king, and then Sir Launcelot took his leave and departed; and there was neither king, duke, nor earl, baron nor knight, lady nor gentlewoman, but all they wept as people out of their mind, except Sir Gawaine. And when the noble Sir Launcelot took his horse to ride out of Carlisle, there was sobbing and weeping for pure dole of his departing; and so he took his way unto Joyous Gard. And then ever after he called it the Dolorous Gard. And thus departed Sir Launcelot from the court for ever.

I leave here of this tale and overskip great books telling how Sir Launcelot passed over the sea, and how he made great lords of the knights that went with him; how King Arthur and Sir Gawaine made a great host ready to go over sea to make war on Sir Launcelot; what message Sir Gawaine sent to Sir Launcelot; and how King Arthur laid siege to Benwick, and other matters; how Sir Launcelot and Sir Gawaine did battle together, and how

Sir Gawaine was overthrown and hurt; of the sorrow that King Arthur made for the war, and of another battle where also Sir Gawaine had the worse; and I tell how Sir Mordred presumed and took on him to be King of England, and would have married the queen, his father's wife.

As Sir Mordred, King Arthur being over the sea, was ruler of all England, he did do make letters as though that they came from beyond the sea, and the letters specified that King Arthur was slain in battle with Sir Launcelot. Wherefore Sir Mordred made a parliament, and called the lords together, and there he made them to choose him king; and so was he crowned at Canterbury, and held there a feast for fifteen days; and afterward he drew him unto Winchester, and there he took the Queen Guenever, and said plainly that he would wed her which was his uncle's wife and his father's wife. And so he made ready for the feast, and a day prefixed that they should be wedded; wherefore Queen Guenever was passing heavy. But she durst not discover her heart, but spake fair, and agreed to Sir Mordred's will. Then she desired of Sir Mordred for to go to London, to buy all manner of things that longed unto the wedding. And because of her fair speech Sir Mordred trusted her well enough, and gave her leave to go. And so when she came to London she took the Tower of London, and suddenly in all haste possible she stuffed it with all manner of victual, and well garnished it with men, and so kept it.

Then when Sir Mordred wist and understood how he was beguiled, he was passing wroth out of measure. And a short tale for to make, he went and laid a mighty siege about the Tower of London, and made many great assaults thereat, and threw many great engines unto them, and shot great guns. But all might not prevail Sir Mordred, for Queen Guenever would never, for fair speech nor for foul, would never trust to come in his hands again.

Then came the Bishop of Canterbury, the which was a noble clerk and an holy man, and thus he said to Sir Mordred: Sir, what will ye do? will ye first displease God and sithen shame yourself, and all knighthood? Is not King Arthur your uncle, no farther but your mother's brother, and on her himself King Arthur begat you upon his own sister, therefore how may you wed your father's wife? Sir, said the noble clerk, leave this opinion or I shall curse you with book and bell and candle. Do thou thy worst, said Sir Mordred, wit thou well I shall defy thee. Sir, said the Bishop, and wit you well I shall not fear me to do that me ought to do. Also where ye noise where my lord Arthur is slain, and that is not so, and therefore ye will make a foul work in this land. Peace, thou false priest, said Sir Mordred, for an thou chafe me any more I shall make strike off thy head. So the

Bishop departed and did the cursing in the most orgulist wise that might be done. And then Sir Mordred sought the Bishop of Canterbury, for to have slain him. Then the Bishop fled, and took part of his goods with him, and went nigh unto Glastonbury; and there he was as priest hermit in a chapel, and lived in poverty and in holy prayers, for well he understood that mischievous war was at hand.

Then Sir Mordred sought on Queen Guenever by letters and sonds, and by fair means and foul means, for to have her to come out of the Tower of London; but all this availed not, for she answered him shortly, openly and privily, that she had liefer slay herself than to be married with him. Then came word to Sir Mordred that King Arthur had araised the siege for Sir Launcelot, and he was coming homeward with a great host, to be avenged upon Sir Mordred; wherefore Sir Mordred made write writs to all the barony of this land, and much people drew to him. For then was the common voice among them that with Arthur was none other life but war and strife, and with Sir Mordred was great joy and bliss. Thus was Sir Arthur depraved, and evil said of. And many there were that King Arthur had made up of nought, and given them lands, might not then say him a good word. Lo ye all Englishmen, see ye not what a mischief here was! for he that was the most king and knight of the world, and most loved the fellowship of noble knights, and by him they were all upholden, now might not these Englishmen hold them content with him. Lo thus was the old custom and usage of this land; and also men say that we of this land have not yet lost nor forgotten that custom and usage. Alas, this is a great default of us Englishmen, for there may no thing please us no term. And so fared the people at that time, they were better pleased with Sir Mordred than they were with King Arthur; and much people drew unto Sir Mordred and said they would abide with him for better and for worse. And so Sir Mordred drew with a great host to Dover, for there he heard say that Sir Arthur would arrive, and so he thought to beat his own father from his lands; and the most part of all England held with Sir Mordred, the people were so new-fangle.

And so as Sir Mordred was at Dover with his host, there came King Arthur with a great navy of ships, and galleys, and carracks. And there was Sir Mordred ready awaiting upon his landing, to let his own father to land upon the land that he was king over. Then there was launching of great boats and small, and full noble men of arms; and there was much slaughter of gentle knights, and many a full bold baron was laid full low, on both parties. But King Arthur was so courageous that there might no manner of knights let him to land, and his knights fiercely followed him;

and so they landed maugre Sir Mordred and all his power, and put Sir Mordred aback, that he fled and all his people.

So when this battle was done, King Arthur let bury his people that were dead. And then was noble Sir Gawaine found in a great boat, lying more than half dead. When Sir Arthur wist that Sir Gawaine was laid so low, he went unto him; and there the king made sorrow out of measure, and took Sir Gawaine in his arms, and thrice he there swooned. And then when he awaked, he said: Alas, Sir Gawaine, my sister's son, here now thou liest, the man in the world that I loved most; and now is my joy gone, for now, my nephew Sir Gawaine, I will discover me unto your person: in Sir Launcelot and you I most had my joy, and mine affiance, and now have I lost my joy of you both; wherefore all mine earthly joy is gone from me. Mine uncle King Arthur, said Sir Gawaine, wit you well my death-day is come, and all is through mine own hastiness and wilfulness; for I am smitten upon the old wound the which Sir Launcelot gave me, on the which I feel well I must die; and had Sir Launcelot been with you as he was, this unhappy war had never begun; and of all this am I causer, for Sir Launcelot and his blood, through their prowess, held all your cankered enemies in subjection and daunger. And now, said Sir Gawaine, ye shall miss Sir Launcelot. But alas, I would not accord with him, and therefore, said Sir Gawaine, I pray you, fair uncle, that I may have paper, pen, and ink, that I may write to Sir Launcelot a cedle with mine own hands.

And then when paper and ink was brought, then Gawaine was set up weakly by King Arthur, for he was shriven a little to-fore; and then he wrote thus, as the French book maketh mention: Unto Sir Launcelot, flower of all noble knights that ever I heard of or saw by my days, I, Sir Gawaine, King Lot's son of Orkney, sister's son unto the noble King Arthur, send thee greeting, and let thee have knowledge that the tenth day of May I was smitten upon the old wound that thou gavest me afore the city of Benwick, and through the same wound that thou gavest me I am come to my death-day. And I will that all the world wit, that I, Sir Gawaine, knight of the Table Round, sought my death, and not through thy deserving, but it was mine own seeking; wherefore I beseech thee, Sir Launcelot, to return again unto this realm, and see my tomb, and pray some prayer more or less for my soul. And this same day that I wrote this cedle, I was hurt to the death in the same wound, the which I had of they hand, Sir Launcelot; for of a more nobler man might I not be slain. Also Sir Launcelot, for all the love that ever was betwixt us, make no tarrying, but come over the sea in all haste, that thou mayest with thy noble knights rescue that noble king that made thee knight, that is my lord Arthur; for he is full straitly bestead with a false traitor, that is my half-brother, Sir Mordred; and he hath let crown him king, and would have wedded my lady Queen Guenever, and so had he done had she not put herself in the Tower of London. And so the tenth day of May last past, my lord Arthur and we all landed upon them at Dover; and there we put that false traitor, Sir Mordred to flight, and there it misfortuned me to be stricken upon thy stroke. And at the date of this letter was written, but two hours and a half afore my death, written with mine own hand, and so subscribed with part of my heart's blood. And I require thee, most famous knight of the world, that thou wilt see my tomb. And then Sir Gawaine wept, and King Arthur wept; an then they swooned both. And when they awaked both, the king made Sir Gawaine to receive his Saviour. And then Sir Gawaine prayed the king for to send for Sir Launcelot, and to cherish him above all other knights.

And so at the hour of noon Sir Gawaine yielded up the spirit; and then the king let inter him in a chapel within Dover Castle; and there yet all men may see the skull of him, and the same wound is seen that Sir Launcelot gave him in battle. Then was it told the king that Sir Mordred had pight a new field upon Barham Down. And upon the morn the king rode thither to him, and there was a great battle betwixt them, and much people was slain on both parties; but at the last Sir Arthur's party stood best, and Sir Mordred and his party fled unto Canterbury.

Then were they condescended that King Arthur and Sir Mordred should meet betwixt both their hosts, and every each of them should bring fourteen persons; and they came with this word unto Arthur. Then said he: I am glad that this is done: and so he went into the field. And when Arthur should depart, he warned all his host that an they see any sword drawn: Look ye come on fiercely, and slay that traitor, Sir Mordred, for I in no wise trust him. In like wise Sir Mordred warned his host that: An ye see any sword drawn, look that ye come on fiercely, and so slay all that ever before you standeth; for in no wise I will not trust for this treaty, for I know well my father will be avenged on me. And so they met as their appointment was, and so they were agreed and accorded thoroughly; and wine was fetched, and they drank. Right soon came an adder out of a little heath bush, and it stung a knight on the foot. And when the knight felt him stung, he looked down and saw the adder, and then he drew his sword to slay the adder, and thought of none other harm. And when the host on both parties saw that sword drawn, then they blew beams, trumpets, and horns, and shouted grimly. And so both hosts dressed them together. And King Arthur took his horse, and said: Alas this unhappy day! and so rode to his party. And Sir Mordred in like wise. And never was there seen a more dolefuller battle in no Christian land; for there was but rushing and riding, foining and striking, and many a grim word was there spoken either to other, and many a deadly stroke. But ever King Arthur rode throughout the battle of Sir Mordred many times, and did full nobly as a noble king should, and at all times he fainted never: and Sir Mordred that day put him in devoir, and in great peril. And thus they fought all the long day, and never stinted till the noble knights were laid to the cold earth; and ever they fought still till it was near night, and by that time was there an hundred thousand laid dead upon the down. Then was Arthur wroth out of measure, when he saw his people so slain from him.

Then the king looked about him, and then was he ware, of all his host and of all his good knights, were left no more alive but two knights; that one was Sir Lucan the Butler, and his brother Sir Bedivere, and they were full sore wounded. Jesu mercy, said the king, where are all my noble knights become? Alas that ever I should see this doleful day, for now, said Arthur, I am come to mine end. But would to God that I wist where were that traitor Sir Mordred, that hath caused all this mischief. Then was King Arthur ware where Sir Mordred leaned upon his sword among a great heap of dead men. Now give me my spear, said Arthur unto Sir Lucan, for yonder I have espied the traitor that all this woe hath wrought. Sir, let him be, said Sir Lucan, for he is unhappy; and if ye pass this unhappy day ye shall be right well revenged upon him. Good lord, remember ye of your night's dream, and what the spirit of Sir Gawaine told you this night, yet God of his great goodness hath preserved you hitherto. There- fore, for God's sake, my lord, leave off by this, for blessed be God ye have won the field, for here we be three alive, and with Sir Mordred is none alive; and if ye leave off now this wicked day of destiny is past. Tide me death, betide me life, saith the king, now I see him yonder alone he shall never escape mine hands, for at a better avail shall I never have him. God speed you well, said Sir Bedivere.

Then the king gat his spear in both his hands, and ran toward Sir Mor- dred, crying: Traitor, now is thy death-day come. And when Sir Mordred heard Sir Arthur, he ran until him with his sword drawn in his hand. And there King Arthur smote Sir Mordred under the shield, with a foin of his spear, throughout the body, more than a fathom. And when Sir Mordred felt that he had his death wound he thrust himself with the might that he had up to the bur of King Arthur's spear. And right so he smote his father Arthur, with his sword holden in both his hands, on the side of the head, that the sword pierced the helmet and the brain-pan, and therewithal Sir

Mordred fell stark dead to the earth; and the noble Arthur fell in a swoon to the earth, and there he swooned ofttimes. And Sir Lucan the Butler and Sir Bedivere ofttimes heaved him up. And so weakly they led him betwixt them both, to a little chapel not far from the seaside. And when the king was there he thought him well eased.

Then heard they people cry in the field. Now go thou, Sir Lucan, said the King, and do me to wit what betokens that noise in the field. So Sir Lucan departed, for he was grievously wounded in many places. And so as he yede, he saw and hearkened by the moonlight, how that pillers and robbers were come into the field, to pill and to rob many a full noble knight of brooches, and beads, of many a good ring, and of many a rich jewel; and who that were not dead all out, there they slew them for their harness and their riches. When Sir Lucan understood this work, he came to the king as soon as he might, and told him all what he had heard and seen. Therefore by my rede, said Sir Lucan, it is best that we bring you to some town. I would it were so, said the king.

But I may not stand, mine head works so. Ah Sir Launcelot, said King Arthur, this day have I sore missed thee; alas, that ever I was against thee, for now have I my death, whereof Sir Gawaine me warned in my dream. Then Sir Lucan took up the king the one part, and Sir Bedivere the other part, and in the lifting the king swooned; and Sir Lucan fell in a swoon with the lift, that the part of his guts fell out of his body, and therewith the noble knight's heart brast. And when the king awoke, he beheld Sir Lucan, how he lay foaming at the mouth, and part of his guts lay at his feet. Alas, said the king, this is to me a full heavy sight, to see this noble duke so die for my sake, for he would have holpen me, that had more need of help than I. Alas, he would not complain him, his heart was so set to help me; now Jesu have mercy on his soul! Then Sir Bedivere wept for the death of his brother. Leave this mourning and weeping, said the king, for all this will not avail me, for wit thou well an I might live myself, the death of Sir Lucan would grieve me evermore; but my time hieth fast, said the king. Therefore, said Arthur unto Sir Bedivere, take thou Excalibur, my good sword, and go with it to yonder water side, and when thou comest there I charge thee throw my sword in that water, and come again and tell me what thou there seest. My lord, said Bedivere, your commandment shall be done, and lightly bring you word again.

So Sir Bedivere departed, and by the way he beheld that noble sword, that the pommel and the haft was all of precious stone; and then he said to himself: If I throw this rich sword in the water, thereof shall never come good, but harm and loss. And then Sir Bedivere hid Excalibur under a tree. And so, as soon as he might, he came again unto the king, and said he had been at the water, and had thrown the sword in the water. What saw thou there? said the king. Sir, he said, I saw nothing but waves and winds. That is untruly said of thee, said the king, therefore go thou lightly again, and do my commandment; as thou art to me lief and dear, spare not, but throw it in. Then Sir Bedivere returned again, and took the sword in his hand; and then him thought sin and shame to throw away that noble sword, and so eft he hid the sword, and returned again, and told to the king that he had been at the water, and done his commandment. What saw thou there? said the king. Sir, he said, I saw nothing but the waters wap and waves wan. Ah, traitor untrue, said King Arthur, now hast thou betrayed me twice. Who would have weened that, thou that hast been to me so lief and dear? and thou art named a noble knight, and would betray me for the richness of the sword. But now go again lightly, for thy long tarrying putteth me in great jeopardy of my life, for I have taken cold. And but if thou do now as I bid thee, if ever I may see thee, I shall slay thee with mine own hands; for thou wouldst for my rich sword see me dead.

Then Sir Bedivere departed, and went to the sword, and lightly took it up, and went to the water side; and there he bound the girdle about the hilts, and then he threw the sword as far into the water as he might; and there came an arm and an hand above the water and met it, and caught it, and so shook it thrice and brandished, and then vanished away the hand with the sword in the water. So Sir Bedivere came again to the king, and told him what he saw. Alas, said the king, help me hence, for I dread me I have tarried over long. Then Sir Bedivere took the king upon his back, and so went with him to that water side. And when they were at the water side, even fast by the bank hoved a little barge with many fair ladies in it, and among them all was a queen, and all they had black hoods, and all they wept and shrieked when they saw King Arthur. Now put me into the barge, said the king, And so he did softly; and there received him three queens with great mourning; and so they set them down, and in one of their laps King Arthur laid his head. And then that queen said: Ah, dear brother, why have ye tarried so long from me? alas, this wound on your head hath caught over-much cold. And so then they rowed from the land, and Sir Bedivere beheld all those ladies go from him. Then Sir Bedivere cried: Ah my lord Arthur, what shall become of me, now ye go from me and leave me here alone among mine enemies? Comfort thyself, said the king, and do as well as thou mayst, for in me is no trust for to trust in; for I will into the vale of Avilion to heal me of my grievous wound: and if thou hear never more of me, pray for my soul. But ever the queens and ladies wept and shrieked, that it was pity to hear. And as soon as Sir Bedivere had lost the sight of the barge, he wept and wailed, and so took the forest; and so he went all that night, and in the morning he was ware betwixt two holts hoar, of a chapel and an hermitage.

Then was Sir Bedivere glad, and thither he went; and when he came into the chapel, he saw where lay an hermit grovelling on all four, there fast by a tomb was new graven. When the hermit saw Sir Bedivere he knew him well, for he was but little to-fore Bishop of Canterbury, that Sir Mordred flemed. Sir, said Bedivere, what man is there interred that ye pray so fast for? Fair son. said the hermit, I wot not verily, but by deeming. But this night, at midnight, here came a number of ladies, and brought hither a dead corpse, and prayed me to bury him; and here they offered an hundred tapers, and they gave me an hundred besants. Alas, said Sir Bedivere, that was my lord King Arthur, that here lieth buried in this chapel. Then Sir Bedivere swooned; and when he awoke he prayed the hermit he might abide with him still there, to live with fasting and prayers. For from hence will I never go, said Sir Bedivere, by my will, but all the days of my life here to pray for my lord Arthur. Ye are welcome to me, said the hermit, for I know ye better than ye ween that I do. Ye are the bold Bedivere, and the full noble duke, Sir Lucan the Butler, was your brother. Then Sir Bedivere told the hermit all as ye have heard to-fore. So there bode Sir Bedivere with the hermit that was to-fore Bishop of Canterbury, and there Sir Bedivere put upon him poor clothes, and served the hermit full lowly in fasting and in prayers.

And when Queen Guenever understood that King Arthur was slain, and all the noble knights, Sir Mordred and all the remnant, then the queen stole away, and five ladies with her, and so she went to Almesbury; and there she let make herself a nun, and ware white clothes and black, and great penance she took, as ever did sinful lady in this land, and never creature could make her merry; but lived in fasting, prayers, and alms-deeds, that all manner of people marvelled how virtuously she was changed. Now leave we Queen Guenever in Almesbury, a nun in white clothes and black, and there she was Abbess and ruler as reason would; and turn we from her, and speak we of Sir Launcelot du Lake.

Now when Sir Launcelot heard of the death of King Arthur, and of Sir Gawaine, and other matters, he came into England. And so he passed over the sea till he came to Dover, and there he landed with seven kings, and the number was hideous to behold. Then Sir Launcelot spered of men of Dover where was King Arthur become. The the people told him how that he was slain, and Sir Mordred and an hundred thousand died on a day; and how Sir Mordred gave King Arthur there the first battle at his landing, and there was Good Sir Gawaine slain; and on the morn Sir Mordred fought with the king upon Barham Down, and there the king put Sir Mordred to the worse. Alas, said Sir Launcelot, this is the heaviest tidings that ever came to me. Now, fair sirs, said Sir Launcelot, shew me the tomb of Sir Gawaine. And then certain people of the town brought him into the castle of Dover, and shewed him the tomb. Then Sir Launcelot kneeled down and wept, and prayed heartily for his soul. And that night he made a dole, and all they that would come had as much flesh, fish, wine, and ale, and every man and woman had twelve pence, come who would. Thus with his own hand dealt he this money, in a mourning gown; and ever he wept, and prayed them to pray for the soul of Sir Gawaine. And on the morn all the priests and clerks that might be gotten in the country were there, and sang mass of Requiem; and there offered first Sir Launcelot, and he offered an hundred pound; and then the seven kings offered forty pound apiece; and also there was a thousand knights, and each of them offered a pound; and the offering dured from morn till night, and Sir Launcelot lay two nights on his tomb in prayers and weeping.

Then on the third day Sir Launcelot called the kings, dukes, earls, barons, and knights, and said thus: My fair lords, I thank you all of your coming into this country with me, but we came too late, and that shall repent me while I live, but against death may no man rebel. But sithen it is so, said Sir Launcelot, I will myself ride and seek my lady, Queen Guenever, for as I hear say she hath had great pain and much disease; and I heard say that she is fled into the west. Therefore ye all shall abide me here, and but if I come again within fifteen days, then take your ships and your fellowship, and depart into your country, for I will do as I say to you.

Then came Sir Bors de Ganis, and said: My lord Sir Launcelot, what think ye for to do, now, to ride in this realm? wit ye well ye shall find few friends. Be as be may, said Sir Launcelot, keep you still here, for I will forth on my journey, and no man nor child shall go with me. So it was no boot to strive, but he departed and rode westerly, and there he sought a seven or eight days; and at the last he came to a nunnery, and then was Queen Guenever ware of Sir Launcelot as he walked in the cloister. And when she saw him there she swooned thrice, that all the ladies and gentlewomen had work enough to hold the queen up. So when she might speak, she called the ladies and gentlewomen to her, and said: Ye marvel, fair ladies, why I make this fare. Truly, she said, it is for the sight of yonder knight that yonder standeth; wherefore I pray you all call him to me.

When Sir Launcelot was brought to her, then she said to all the ladies: Through this man and me hath all this war been wrought, and the death of the most noblest knight of the world; for through our love that we have loved together is my most noble lord slain. Therefore, Sir Launcelot, wit thou well I am set in such a plight to get my soul-heal; and yet I trust through God's grace that after my death to have a sight of the blessed face of Christ, and at domesday to sit on his right side, for as sinful as ever I was are saints in heaven. Therefore, Sir Launcelot, I require thee and beseech thee heartily, for all the love that ever was betwixt us, that thou never see me more in the visage; and I command thee, on God's behalf, that thou forsake my company, and to thy kingdom thou turn again, and keep well thy realm from war and wrack; for as well as I have loved thee, mine heart will not serve me to see thee, for through thee and me is the flower of kings and knights destroyed; therefore, Sir Launcelot, go to thy realm, and there take thee a wife, and live with her with joy and bliss; and I pray thee heartily, pray for me to our Lord that I may amend my misliving. Now, sweet madam, said Sir Launcelot, would ye that I should now return unto my country, and there to wed a lady? Nay, madam, wit you well that shall I never do, for I shall never be so false to you of that I have promised; but the same destiny that ye have taken you to, I will take me unto, for to please Jesu, and ever for you I cast me specially to pray. If thou wilt do so, said the queen, hold thy promise, but I may never believe but that thou wilt turn to the world again. Well, madam, said he, ye say as pleaseth you, yet wist you me never false of my promise, and God defend but I should forsake the world as ye have done. For in the quest of the Sangreal I had forsaken the vanities of the world had not your lord been. And if I had done so at that time, with my heart, will, and thought, I had passed all the knights that were in the Sangreal except Sir Galahad, my son. And therefore, lady, sithen ye have taken you to perfection, I must needs take me to perfection, of right. For I take record of God, in you I have had mine earthly joy; and if I had found you now so disposed, I had cast me to have had you into mine own realm.

So Sir Launcelot came to the hermitage where the Archbishop of Canterbury was, and took the habit on him. And he endured such penance, in prayers, and fasting, that took no force what pain he endured, that the noblest knight of the world took such abstinence that he waxed full lean. And thus upon a night, there came a vision to Sir Launcelot, and charged him, in remission of his sins, to haste him unto Almesbury: And by then thou come there, thou shalt find Queen Guenever dead. And therefore take thy fellows with thee, and purvey them of an horse bier, and fetch thou the corpse of her, and bury her by her husband, the noble King Arthur. So this avision came to Sir Launcelot thrice in one night.

Then Sir Launcelot rose up or day, and told the hermit. It were well done, said the hermit, that ye made you ready, and that you disobey not the avision. Then Sir Launcelot took his eight fellows with him, and on foot they yede from Glastonbury to Almesbury, the which is little more than thirty mile. And thither they came within two days, for they were weak and feeble to go. And when Sir Launcelot was come to Almesbury within the nunnery, Queen Guenever died but half an hour afore. And the ladies told Sir Launcelot that Queen Guenever told them all or she passed, that Sir Launcelot had been priest near a twelvemonth. And hither he cometh as fast as he may to fetch my corpse; and beside my lord, King Arthur, he shall bury me. Wherefore the queen said in hearing of them all: I beseech Almighty God that I may never have power to see Sir Launcelot with my worldly eyen; and thus, said all the ladies, was ever her prayer these two days, till she was dead. Then Sir Launcelot saw her visage, but he wept not greatly, but sighed. And so he did all the observance of the service himself, both the dirige, and on the morn he sang mass. And there was ordained an horse bier; and so with an hundred torches ever brenning about the corpse of the queen, and ever Sir Launcelot with his eight fellows went about the horse bier, singing and reading many an holy orison, and frankincense upon the corpse incensed. Thus Sir Launcelot and his eight fellows went on foot from Almesbury unto Glastonbury.

And when they were come to the chapel and the hermitage, there she had a dirige, with great devotion. And on the morn the hermit that sometime was Bishop of Canterbury sang the mass of Requiem with great devotion. And Sir Launcelot was the first that offered, and then also his eight fellows. And then she was wrapped in cered cloth of Raines, from the top to the toe, in thirtyfold; and after she was put in a web of lead, and then in a coffin of marble. And when she was put in the earth Sir Launcelot swooned, and lay long still, while the hermit came and awaked him, and said: Ye be to blame, for ye displease God with such manner of sorrow-making. Truly, said Sir Launcelot, I trust I do not displease God, for He knoweth mine intent. For my sorrow was not, nor is not, for any rejoicing of sin, but my sorrow may never have end. For when I remember of her beauty, and of her noblesse, that was both with her king and with her, so when I saw his corpse and her corpse so lie together, truly mine heart would not serve to sustain my careful body. Also when I remember me how by my default, mine orgule, and my pride that they were both laid full low, that were peerless that ever was living of Christian people, wit you well, said Sir Launcelot, this remembered, of their kindness and mine unkindness, sank so to mine heart, that I might not sustain myself. So the French book maketh mention.

Then Sir Launcelot began to sicken, and after died, and his body was borne to Joyous Gard for to be buried. And they kept Sir Launcelot's corpse aloft fifteen days, and then they buried it with great devotion. And then at leisure they went all with the Bishop of Canterbury to his hermitage, and there they were together more than a month. Then Sir Constantine, that was Sir Cador's son of Cornwall, was chosen king of England. And he was a full noble knight, and worshipfully he ruled this realm. And then this King Constantine sent for the Bishop of Canterbury, for he heard say where he was. And so he was restored unto his Bishopric, and left that hermitage. And Sir Bedivere was there ever still hermit to his life's end. Then Sir Bors de Ganis, Sir Ector de Maris, Sir Gahalantine, Sir Galihud, Sir Galihodin, Sir Blamore, Sir Bleoberis, Sir Villiars le Valiant, Sir Clarrus of Clermont, all these knights drew them to their countries. Howbeit King Constantine would have had them with him, but they would not abide in this realm. And there they all lived in their countries as holy men. And some English books make mention that they went never out of England after the death of Sir Launcelot, but that was but favour of makers. For the French book maketh mention, and is autho- rised, that Sir Bors, Sir Ector, Sir Blamore, and Sir Bleoberis, went into the Holy Land thereas Jesu Christ was quick and dead, and anon as they had stablished their lands. For the book saith, so Sir Launcelot commanded them for to do, or ever he passed out of this world. And these four knights did many battles upon the miscreants or Turks. And there they died upon a Good Friday for God's sake.

A PERFECT HUSBAND[1]

William Cobbett

I BEGAN my young marriage days in and near Philadelphia. At one of those times to which I have just alluded, in the middle of the burning hot month of July, I was greatly afraid of fatal consequences to my wife for want of sleep, she not having, after the great danger was over, had any sleep for more than forty-eight hours. All great cities, in hot countries,

---

[1] From *Advice to Young Men.*

45

are, I believe, full of dogs; and they, in the very hot weather, keep up, during the night, a horrible barking and fighting and howling. Upon the particular occasion to which I am adverting, they made a noise so terrible and so unremitted, that it was next to impossible that even a person in full health and free from pain should obtain a minute's sleep. I was, about nine in the evening, sitting by the bed: "I do think," said she, "that I could go to sleep now, if it were not for the dogs." Downstairs I went, and out I sallied, in my shirt and trousers, and without shoes and stockings; and, going to a heap of stones lying beside the road, set to work upon the dogs, going backward and forward, and keeping them at two or three hundred yards' distance from the house. I walked thus the whole night, barefooted, lest the noise of my shoes might possibly reach her ears; and I remember that the bricks of the causeway were, even in the night, so hot as to be disagreeable to my feet. My exertions produced the desired effect: a sleep of several hours was the consequence; and, at eight o'clock in the morning, off went I to a day's business which was to end at six in the evening.

THE BOOTS AT THE HOLLY-TREE INN[1]

Charles Dickens

WHERE had he been in his time? he repeated, when I asked him the question. Lord, he had been everywhere! And what had he been? Bless you, he had been everything you could mention a'most!

Seen a good deal? Why, of course he had. I should say so, he could assure me, if I only knew about a twentieth part of what had come in *his* way. Why, it would be easier for him, he expected, to tell what he hadn't seen than what he had. Ah! A deal, it would.

What was the curiousest thing he had seen? Well! He didn't know. He couldn't momently name what was the curiousest thing he had seen, —unless it was a Unicorn,—and he see *him* once at a Fair. But supposing a young gentleman not eight year old was to run away with a fine young woman of seven, might I think *that* a queer start? Certainly. Then that was a start as he himself had had his blessed eyes on, and he had cleaned the shoes they run away in—and they was so little that he couldn't get his hand into 'em.

Master Harry Walmers' father, you see, he lived at the Elmses, down

---

[1] From *Christmas Stories*.

away by Shooter's Hill there, six or seven miles from Lunnon. He was a gentleman of spirit, and good-looking, and held his head up when he walked, and had what you may call Fire about him. He wrote poetry, and he rode, and he ran and he cricketed, and he danced, and he acted, and he done it all equally beautiful. He was uncommon proud of Master Harry as was his only child; but he didn'r spoil him neither. He was a gentleman that had a will of his own and a eye of his own, and that would be minded. Consequently, though he made quite a companion of the fine bright boy, and was delighted to see him so fond of reading his fairy books, and was never tired of hearing him say my name is Norval, or hearing him sing his songs about Young May Moons is beaming love, and When he as adores thee has left but the name, and that; still he kept the command over the child, and the child *was* a child, and it's to be wished more of 'em was!

How did Boots happen to know all this? Why, through being under-gardener. Of course he couldn't be under-gardener, and be always about, in the summer-time, near the windows on the lawn, a-mowing, and sweep-ing, and weeding, and pruning, and this and that without getting ac-quainted with the ways of the family. Even supposing Master Harry hadn't come to him one morning early, and said, "Cobbs, how should you spell Norah, if you was asked?" and then began cutting it in print all over the fence.

He couldn't say he had taken particular notice of children before that; but really it was pretty to see them two mites a going about the place toge-ther, deep in love. And the courage of the boy! Bless your soul, he'd have throwed off his little hat, and tucked up his little sleeves, and gone in at a Lion, he would, if they had happened to meet one, and she had been frightened of him. One day he stops, along with her, where Boots was hoeing weeds in the gravel, and says, speaking up, "Cobbs," he says, "I like *you*." "Do you, Sir? I'm proud to hear it." "Yes, I do, Cobbs. Why do I like you, do you think, Cobbs?" "Don't know, Master Harry, I am sure." "Because Norah likes you, Cobbs." "Indeed, Sir? That's very grati-fying." "Gratifying, Cobbs? It's better than millions of the brightest diamonds to be liked by Norah." "Certainly, Sir," "You're going away, ain't you, Cobbs?" "Yes, Sir," "Would you like another situation, Cobbs?" "Well, Sir, I shouldn't object, if it was a good 'un." "Then, Cobbs," says he, "you shall be our Head Gardener when we are married." And he tucks her, in her little sky-blue mantle, under his arm, and walks away.

Boots could assure me that it was better than a picter, and equal to a play, to see them babies, with their long, bright, curling hair, their spark-ling eyes, and their beautiful light tread, a rambling about the garden, deep in love. Boots was of opinion that the birds believed they was birds, and kept up with 'em, singing to please 'em. Sometimes they would creep under the Tulip-tree, and would sit there with their arms round one another's necks, and their soft cheeks touching, a reading about the Prince and the Dragon, and the good and bad enchanters, and the king's fair daughter. Sometimes he would hear them planning about having a house in a forest, keeping bees and a cow, and living entirely on milk and honey. Once he came upon them by the pond, and heard Master Harry say, "Adorable Norah, kiss me, and say you love me to distraction, or I'll jump in head-foremost." And Boots made no question he would have done it if she hadn't complied. One the whole, Boots said it had a tendency to make him feel as if he was in love himself—only he didn't exactly know who with.

"Cobbs," said Master Harry, one evening, when Cobbs was watering the flowers, "I am going on a visit, this present Mid-summer, to my grandmamma's at York."

"Are you indeed, Sir? I hope you'll have a pleasant time. I am going into Yorkshire, myself, when I leave here."

"Are you going to your grandmamma's, Cobbs?"

"No, Sir. I haven't got such a thing."

"Not as a grandmamma, Cobbs?"

"No, Sir."

The boy looked on at the watering of the flowers for a little while, and then said, "I shall be very glad indeed to go, Cobbs,—Norah's going."

"You'll be all right then, Sir," says Cobbs, "with your beautiful sweetheart by your side."

"Cobbs," returned the boy, flushing, "I never let anybody joke about it, when I can prevent them."

"It wasn't a joke, Sir," says Cobbs, with humility,—"wasn't so meant."

"I am glad of that, Cobbs, because I like you, you know, and you're going to live with us.—Cobbs!"

"Sir."

"What do you think my grandmamma gives me when I go down there?"

"I couldn't so much as make a guess, Sir."

"A Bank of England five-pound note, Cobbs.'

"Whew!" says Cobbs, "that's a spanking sum of money, Master Harry."

"A person could do a good deal with such a sum of money as that,— couldn't a person, Cobbs?"

"I believe you, Sir!"

"Cobbs," said the boy, "I'll tell you a secret. At Norah's house, they have been joking her about me, and pretending to laugh at our being engaged,—pretending to make game of it, Cobbs!"

"Such, Sir," says Cobbs "is the depravity of human natur."

The boy, looking exactly like his father, stood for a few minutes with his glowing face towards the sunset, and then departed with, "Good-night, Cobbs. I'm going in."

If I was to ask Boots how it happened that he was a going to leave that place just at that present time, well, he couldn't rightly answer me. He did suppose he might have stayed there till now if he had been anyways inclined. But, you see, he was younger then, and he wanted change. That's what he wanted—change. Mr Walmers, he said to him when he gave him notice of his intentions to leave, "Cobbs," he says, "have you anything to complain of? I make the inquiry because if I find that any of my people really has anythink to complain of, I wish to make it right if I can." "No, Sir," says Cobbs; "thanking you, Sir, I find myself as well sitiwated here as I could hope to be anywheres. The truth is, Sir, that I'm a going to seek my fortun'." "O, indeed, Cobbs!" he says; "I hope you may find it." And Boots could assure me—which he did, touching his hair with his bootjack, as a salute in the way of his present calling—that he hadn't found it yet.

Well, Sir! Boots left the Elmses when his time was up, and Master Harry, he went down to the old lady's at York, which old lady would have given that child the teeth out of her head (if she had had any), she was so wrapped up in him. What does that Infant do,—for Infant you may call him and be within the mark,—but cut away from that old lady's with his Norah, on a expedition to go to Gretna Green and be married!

Sir, Boots was at this identical Holly-Tree Inn (having left it several times since to better himself, but always come back through one thing or another), when, one summer afternoon, the coach drives up, and out of the coach gets them two children. The Guard says to our Governor, "I don't quite make out these little passengers, but the young gentleman's words was, that they was to be brought here." The young gentleman gets out; hands his lady out; gives the Guard something for himself; says to our Governor, "We're to stop here to-night, please. Sitting-room and two bedrooms will be required. Chops and cherry-pudding for two!" and tucks her, in her little sky-blue mantle, under his arm, and walks into the house much bolder than Brass.

Boots leaves me to judge what the amazement of that establishment was, when these two tiny creatures all alone by themselves was marched into the Angel,—much more so, when he, who had seen them without their seeing him, give the Governor his views of the expedition

49

they was upon. "Cobbs," says the Governor, "if this is so, I must set off myself to York, and quiet their friends' minds. In which case you must keep your eye upon 'em, and humour 'em, till I come back. But before I take these measures, Cobbs, I should wish you to find from themselves whether your opinion is correct." "Sir, to you," says Cobbs, "that shall be done directly."

So Boots goes upstairs to the Angel, and there he finds Master Harry on a e-normous, sofa,—immense at any time, but looking like the Great Bed of Ware, compared with him,—a drying the eyes of Miss Norah, with his pocket-hankecher. Their little legs was entirely off the ground, of course, and it really is not possible for Boots to express to me how small them children looked.

"It's Cobbs! It's Cobbs!" cried Master Harry, and comes running to him, and catching hold of his hand. Miss Norah comes running to him on t'other side and catching hold of his t'other hand, and they both jump for joy.

"I see you a getting out, Sir," says Cobbs. "I thought it was you. I thought I couldn't be mistaken in your height and figure. What's the object of your journey, Sir?—Matrimonial?"

"We are going to be married, Cobbs, at Gretna Green," returned the boy. "We have run away on purpose. Norah has been in rather low spirits, Cobbs; but she'll be happy, now we have found you to be our friend."

"Thank you, Sir, and thank *you*, Miss," says Cobbs, "for your good opinion. *Did* you bring any luggage with you, Sir?"

If I will believe Boots when he gives me his word and honour upon it, the lady had got a parasol, a smelling-bottle, a round and a half of cold buttered toast, eight peppermint drops, and a hair-brush,—seemingly a doll's. The gentleman had got about half-a-dozen yards of string, a knife, three or four sheets of writing-paper folded up surprising small, a orange, and a Chaney mug with his name upon it.

"What may be the exact natur of your plans, Sir?" says Cobbs.

"To go on," replied the boy,—which the courage of that boy was something wonderful!—"in the morning, and be married to-morrow."

"Just so, Sir," says Cobbs. "Would it meet your views, Sir, if I was to acompany you?"

When Cobbs said this, they both jumped for joy again, and cried out, "Oh, yes, yes, Cobbs! Yes!"

"Well, Sir," says Cobbs. "If you will excuse my having the freedom to give an opinion, what I should recommend would be this. I'm acquainted

50

with a pony, Sir, which, put in a pheayton that I could borrow, would take you and Mrs Harry Walmers, Junior, (myself driving, if you approved,) to the end of your journey in a very short space of time. I am not altogether sure, Sir, that this pony will be at liberty to-morrow, but even if you had to wait over to-morrow for him, it might be worth your while. As to the small account here, Sir, in case you was to find yourself running at all short, that don't signify; because I'm a part proprietor of this inn, and it could stand over."

Boots assures me that when they clapped their hands, and jumped for joy again, and called him "Good Cobbs!" and "Dear Cobbs!" and bent across him to kiss one another in the delight of their confiding hearts, he felt himself the meanest rascal for deceiving 'em that ever was born.

"Is there anything you want just at present, Sir?" says Cobbs, mortally ashamed of himself.

"We should like some cakes after dinner," answered Master Harry, folding his arms, putting out one leg, and looking straight at him, "and two apples,—and jam. With dinner we should like to have toast-and-water. But Norah has always been accustomed to half a glass of currant wine at dessert. And so have I."

"It shall be ordered at the bar, Sir," says Cobbs; and away he went.

Boots has the feeling as fresh upon him at this minute of speaking as he had then, that he would far rather have had it out in half-a-dozen rounds with the Governor than have combined with him; and that he wished with all his heart there was any impossible place where those two babies could make an impossible marriage, and live impossibly happy ever afterwards. However, as it couldn't be, he went into the Governor's plans, and the Governor set off for York in half an hour.

The way in which the women of that house—without exception—every one of 'em—married *and* single—took to that boy when they heard the story, Boots considers surprising. It was as much as he could do to keep 'em from dashing into the room and kissing him. They climbed up all sorts of places, at the risk of their lives, to look at him through a pane of glass. They was seven deep at the keyhole. They was out of their minds about him and his bold spirit.

In the evening, Boots went into the room to see how the runaway couple was getting on. The gentleman was on the window-seat, supporting the lady in his arms. She had tears upon her face, and was lying, very tired and half asleep, with her head upon his shoulder.

"Mrs Harry Walmers, Junior, fatigued, Sir?" says Cobbs.

"Yes, she is tired, Cobbs; but she is not used to be away from home, and she has been in low spirits again. Cobbs, do you think you could bring a biffin, please?"

"I ask your pardon, Sir," says Cobbs. "What was it you—?"

"I think a Norfolk biffin would rouse her, Cobbs. She is very fond of them."

Boots withdrew in search of the required restorative, and, when he brought it in, the gentleman handed it to the lady, and fed her with a spoon, and took a little himself; the lady being heavy with sleep, and rather cross. "What should you think, Sir," says Cobbs, "of a chamber candlestick?" The gentleman approved; the chambermaid went first, up the great staircase; the lady, in her sky-blue mantle, followed, gallantly escorted by the gentleman; the gentleman embraced her at her door, and retired to his own apartment, where Boots softly locked him up.

Boots couldn't but feel with increased acuteness what a base deceiver he was, when they consulted him at breakfast (they had ordered sweet milk-and-water, and toast and currant jelly, overnight) about the pony. It really was as much as he could do, he don't mind confessing to me, to look them two young things in the face, and think what a wicked old father of lies he had grown up to be. Howsomever, he went on a lying like a Trojan about the pony. He told 'em that it did so unfort'nately happen that the pony was half clipped, you see, and that he couldn't be taken out in that state, for fear it should strike to his inside. But that he'd be finished clipping in the course of the day, and that to-morrow morning at eight o'clock the pheayton would be ready. Boots's view of the whole case, looking back on it in my room, is, that Mrs Harry Walmers, Junior, was beginning to give in. She hadn't had her hair curled when she went to bed, and she didn't seem quite up to brushing it herself, and its getting in her eyes put her out. But nothing put out Master Harry. He sat behind his breakfast-cup, a tearing away at the jelly, as if he had been his own father.

After breakfast, Boots is inclined to consider that they drawed soldiers, —at least, he knows that many such was found in the fireplace, all on horseback. In the course of the morning, Master Harry rang the bell,— it was surprising how that there boy did carry on,—and said, in a sprightly way, "Cobbs, is there any good walks in this neighbourhood?"

"Yes, Sir," says Cobbs. "There's Love-lane."

"Get out with you, Cobbs!"—that was that there boy's expression— "you're joking."

"Begging your pardon, Sir," says Cobbs, "there really is Love-lane.

And a pleasant walk it is, and proud shall I be to show it to yourself and Mrs Harry Walmers, Junior."

"Norah, dear," said Master Harry, "this is curious. We really ought to see Love-lane. Put on your bonnet, my sweetest darling, and we will go there with Cobbs."

Boots leaves me to judge what a Beast he felt himself to be, when that young pair told him, as they all three jogged along together, that they had made up their minds to give him two thousand guineas a year as head-gardener, on accounts of his being so true a friend to 'em. Boots could have wished at the moment that the earth would have opened and swallowed him up, he felt so mean, with their beaming eyes a looking at him, and believing him. Well, Sir, he turned the conversation as well as he could, and he took 'em down Love-lane to the water-meadows, and there Master Harry would have drowned himself in half a moment more, a getting out a water-lily for her,—but nothing daunted that boy. Well, Sir, they was tired out. All being so new and strange to 'em, they was tired as tired could be. And they laid down on a bank of daisies, like the children in the wood, leastways meadows, and fell asleep.

Boots don't know—perhaps I do,—but never mind, it don't signify either way—why it made a man fit to make a fool of himself to see them two pretty babies a lying there in the clear still sunny day, not dreaming half so hard when they was asleep as they done when they was awake. But, Lord! when you come to think of yourself, you know, and what a game you have been up to ever since you was in your own cradle, and what a poor sort of a chap you are, and how it's always either Yesterday with you, or else To-morrow, and never To-day, that's where it is!

Well, Sir, they woke up at last, and then one thing was getting pretty clear to Boots, namely, that Mrs Harry Walmerses, Junior's, temper was on the move. When Master Harry took her round the waist, she said he "teased her so"; and when he says, "Norah, my young May Moon, your Harry tease you?" she tells him, "Yes; and I want to go home!"

A biled fowl, and baked bread-and-butter pudding, brought Mrs Walmers up a little; but Boots could have wished, he must privately own to me, to have seen her more sensible of the woice of love, and less abandoning of herself to currants. However, Master Harry, he kept up, and his noble heart was as fond as ever. Mrs Walmer turned very sleepy about dusk, and began to cry. Therefore, Mr Walmers went off to bed as per yesterday; and Master Harry ditto repeated.

About eleven or twelve at night comes back the Governor in a chaise, along with Mr Walmers and a elderly lady. Mr Walmers looks amused and very serious, both at once, and says to our missis, "We are much indebted to you, ma'am, for your kind care of our little children, which we can never sufficiently acknowledge. Pray, ma'am, where is my boy?" Our missis says, "Cobss has the dear child in charge, Sir. Cobbs, show Forty!" Then he says to Cobbs, "Ah, Cobbs, I am glad to see *you!* I understood you was here!" And Cobbs says, "Yes, Sir. Your most obedient, Sir."

I may be surprised to hear Boots say it, perhaps; but Boots assures me that his heart beat like a hammer, going upstairs. "I beg your pardon, Sir," says he, while unlocking the door; "I hope you are not angry with Master Harry. For Master Harry is a fine boy, Sir, and will do you credit and honour." And Boots signifies to me, that, if the fine boy's father had contradicted him in the daring state of mind in which he then was, he thinks he should have "fetched him a crack," and taken the consequences.

But Mr Walmers only says, "No, Cobbs. No, my good fellow. Thank you!" And, the door being opened, goes in.

Boots goes in too, holding the light, and he sees Mr Walmers go up to the bedside, bend gently down, and kiss the little sleeping face. Then he stands looking at it for a minute, looking wonderfully like it (they do say he ran away with Mrs Walmers); and then he gently shakes the little shoulder.

"Harry, my dear boy! Harry!"

Master Harry starts up and looks at him. Looks at Cobbs too. Such is the honour of that mite, that he looks at Cobbs, to see whether he has brought him into trouble.

"I am not angry, my child. I only want you to dress yourself and come home."

"Yes, pa."

Master Harry dresses himself quickly. His breast begins to swell when he has nearly finished, and it swells more and more as he stands, at last, a looking at his father: his father standing a looking at him, the quiet image of him.

"Please may I"—the spirit of that little creatur, and the way he kept his rising tears down!—"please, dear pa—may I—kiss Norah before I go?"

"You may, my child."

So he takes Master Harry in his hand, and Boots leads the way with the candle, and they come to that other bedroom, where the elderly lady is seated by the bed, and poor little Mrs Harry Walmers, Junior, is fast asleep. There the father lifts the child up to the pillow, and he lays his little face down for an instant by the little warm face of poor unconscious little Mrs Harry Walmers, Junior, and gently draws it to him,—a sight so touching to the chambermaids who are peeping through the door, that one of them calls out, "It's a shame to part 'em!" But this chambermaid was always, as Boots informs me, a soft-hearted one. Not that there was any harm in that girl. Far from it.

Finally, Boots says, that's all about it. Mr Walmers drove away in the chaise, having hold of Master Harry's hand. The elderly lady and Mrs Harry Walmers, Junior, that was never to be (she married a Captain long afterwards, and died in India), went off next day. In conclusion, Boots put it to me whether I hold with him in two opinions: firstly, that there are not many couples on their way to be married who are half as innocent of guile as those two children; secondly, that it would be a jolly good thing for a great many couples on their way to be married, if they could only be stopped in time, and brought back separately.

A DIVERSION PLAYED ON A PENNY-WHISTLE[1]

George Meredith

AWAY with Systems! Away with a corrupt World! Let us breathe the air of the Enchanted Island.

Golden lie the meadows; golden run the streams; red gold is on the pine-stems. The sun is coming down to earth, and walks the fields and the waters.

The sun is coming down to earth, and the fields and the waters shout to him golden shouts. He comes, and his heralds run before him, and touch the leaves of oaks and planes and beeches lucid green, and the pine-stems redder gold; leaving brightest footprints upon thickly-weeded banks where the foxglove's last upperbells incline, and bramble-shoots wander amid moist rich herbage. The plumes of the woodland are alight; and beyond them, over the open, 'tis a race with the long-thrown shadows; a race across the heaths and up the hills, till, at the farthest bourne of mounted eastern cloud, the heralds of the sun lay rosy fingers and rest.

Sweet are the shy recesses of the woodland. The ray treads softly there. A film athwart the pathway quivers many-hued against the purple shade

---

[1] From *The Ordeal of Richard Feverel*. Reprinted by permission of Messrs Constable and Co., Ltd., London, and Messrs Charles Scribner's Sons, New York.

fragrant with warm pines, deep moss-beds, feathery ferns. The little brown squirrel drops tail, and leaps; the inmost bird is startled to a chance tuneless note. From silence into silence things move.

Peeps of the revelling splendour above and around enliven the conscious full heart within. The flaming West, the crimson heights, shower their glories through voluminous leafage. But these are bowers where deep bliss dwells, imperial joy, that owes no fealty to yonder glories, in which the young lamb gambols and the spirits of men are glad. Descend, great Radiance! embrace creation with beneficent fire, and pass from us! You and the vice-regal light that succeeds to you and all heavenly pageants, are the ministers and the slaves of the throbbing content within.

For this is the home of the enchantment. Here, secluded from vexed shores, the prince and princess of the island meet; here like darkling nightingales they sit, and into eyes and ears and hands pour endless ever-fresh treasures of their souls.

Roll on, grinding wheels of the world: cries of ships going down in a calm, groans of a System which will not know its rightful hour of exultation, complain to the universe. You are not heard here.

He calls her by her name, Lucy: and she, blushing at her great boldness, as called him by his, Richard. Those two names are the key notes of the wonderful harmonies the angels sing aloft.

"Lucy! my beloved!"

"O Richard!"

Out in the world there, on the skirts of the woodland, a sheep-boy pipes to meditative eve on a penny-whistle.

Love's musical instrument is as old, and as poor: it has but two stops; and yet, you see, the cunning musician does thus much with it!

Other speech they have little; light foam playing upon waves of feeling, and of feeling compact, that bursts only when the sweeping volume is too wild, and is no more than their sigh of tenderness spoken.

Perhaps love played his tune so well because their natures had unblunted edges, and were keen for bliss, confiding in it as natural food. To gentlemen and ladies he fine-draws upon the viol, ravishingly; or blows into the mellow bassoon; or rouses the heroic ardours of the trumpet; or, it may be, commands the whole Orchestra for them. And they are pleased. He is still the cunning musician. They languish, and taste ecstasy: but it is, however sonorous, an earthly concert. For them the spheres move not to two notes. They have lost, or forfeited and never known, the first supersensual spring of the ripe senses into passion; when they carry the soul with them, and have the privileges of spirits to walk disembodied, boundlessly to feel. Or one has it, and the other is a dead body. Ambrosia let them eat, and drink the nectar: here sit a couple to whom Love's simple bread and water is a finer feast.

Pipe, happy sheep-boy, Love! Irradiated angels, unfold your wings and lift your voices!

They have outflown philosophy. Their instinct has shot beyond the ken of science. They were made for their Eden.

"And this divine gift was in store for me!"

So runs the internal outcry of each, clasping each: it is their recurring refrain to the harmonies. How it illumined the years gone by and suffused the living Future!

"You for me: I for you!"

"We are born for each other!"

They believe that the angels have been busy about them from their cradles. The celestial host have worthily striven to bring them together. And, O victory! O wonder! after toil and pain, and difficulties exceeding, the celestial hosts have succeeded!

"Here we two sit who are written above as one!"

Pipe, happy Love! pipe on to these dear innocents! The tide of colour has ebbed from the upper sky. In the West the sun of sunken fire draws back; and the stars leap forth, and tremble, and retire before the advancing moon, who slips the silver train of cloud from her shoulders, and, with her foot upn the pine-tops, surveys heaven.

"Lucy, did you never dream of meeting me?"

"O Richard! yes; for I remembered you."

"Lucy! and did you pray that we might meet?"

"I did!"

Young as when she looked upon the lovers in Paradise, the fair Immortal journeys onward. Fronting her, it is not night but veiled day. Full half the sky is flushed. Not darkness, not day, but the nuptials of the two.

"My own! my own for ever! You are pledged to me? Whisper!"

He hears the delicious music.

"And you are mine?"

A soft beam travels to the fern-covert under the pinewood where they sit, and for answer he has her eyes: turned to him an instant, timidly fluttering over the depths of his, and then downcast; for through her eyes her soul is naked to him.

"Lucy! my bride! my life!"

The night-jar spins his dark monotony on the branch of the pine. The soft beam travels round them, and listens to their hearts. Their lips are locked.

57

Pipe no more, Love, for a time! Pipe as you will you cannot express their first kiss; nothing of its sweetness and of the sacredness of it nothing. St Cecilia up aloft, before the silver organ pipes of Paradise, pressing fingers upon all the notes of which Love is but one, from her you may hear it.

So Love is silent. Out in the world there, on the skirts of the woodland, the self-satisfied sheep-boy delivers a last complacent squint down the length of his penny-whistle, and with a flourish correspondingly awry, he also marches into silence, hailed by supper. The woods are still. There is heard but the night-jar spinning on the pine-branch, circled by moon-light.

MRS JOHNSON[1]

Alice Meynell

THIS paper shall not be headed "Tetty." What may be graceful enough freedom with the wives of other men shall be prohibited in the case of Johnson's, she with whose name no writer until now has scrupled to take freedoms whereto all graces were lacking. "Tetty" it should not be, if for no other reason, for this—that the chance of writing "Tetty" as a title is a kind of facile literary opportunity; it shall be denied. The Essay owes thus much amends of deliberate care to Dr Johnson's wife. But, indeed, the reason is graver. What wish would he have had but that the language in the making wherof he took no ignoble part should somewhere, at some time, treat his only friend with ordinary honour?

Men who would trust Dr Johnson with their orthodoxy, with their vocabulary, and with the most intimate vanity of their human wishes, refuse, with every mark of insolence, to trust him in regard to his wife. On that one point no reverence is paid to him, no deference, no respect, not so much as the credit due to our common sanity. Yet he is not reviled on account of his Thrale—nor, indeed, is his Thrale now seriously re-proached for her Piozzi. It is true that Macaulay, preparing himself and his reader " in his well-known way" (as a rustic of Mr Hardy's might have it) for the recital of her second marriage, says that it would have been well if she had been laid beside the kind and generous Thrale when, in the prime

---

[1] From *Essays*. Reprinted by permission of Mr Wilfrid Meynell.

of her life, he died. But Macaulya has not left us heirs to his indignation. His well-known way was to exhaust those possibilities of effect in which the commonplace is so rich. And he was permitted to point his paragraphs as he would, not only by calling Mrs Thrale's attachment to her second husband "a degrading passion" but by summoning a chorus of "all London" to the same purpose. She fled, he tells us, from the laughter and hisses of her countrymen and countrywomen to a land where she was unknown. Thus when Macaulay chastises Mrs Elizabeth Porter for marrying Johnson, he is not inconsistent, for he· pursues Mrs Thrale with equal rigour for her audacity in keeping gaiety and grace in her mind and manners longer than Macaulay liked to see such ornaments added to the charm of twice "married brows."

It is not so with succeeding essayists. One of these minor biographers is so gentle as to call the attachment of Mrs Thrale and Piozzi "a mutual affection." He adds, "No one who has had some experience of life will be inclined to condemn Mrs Thrale." But there is no such courtesy, even from him, for Mrs Johnson. Neither to him nor to any other writer has it yet occurred that if England loves her great Englishman's memory, she owes not only courtesy, but gratitude, to the only woman who loved him while there was yet time.

Not a thought of that debt has stayed the alacrity with which a caricature has been acclaimed as the only possible portrait of Mrs Johnson. Garrick's school reminiscences would probably have made a much more charming woman grotesque. Garrick is welcome to his remembrances; we may even reserve for ourselves the liberty of envying those who heard him. But honest laughter should not fall into that tone of common antithesis which seems to say, "See what are the absurdities of the great! Such is life! On this one point we, even we, are wiser than Dr Johnson—we know how grotesque was his wife. We know something of the privacies of her toilet-table. We are able to compare her figure with the figures we, unlike him in his youth, have had the opportunity of admiring—the figures of the well-bred and well-dressed." It is a sorry success to be able to say so much.

But in fact such a triumph belongs to no man. When Samuel Johnson, at twenty-six, married his wife, he gave the dull an advantage over himself which none but the dullest will take. He chose, for love, a woman who had the wit to admire him at first meeting, and in spite of first sight. "That," she said to her daughter, "is the most sensible man I ever met." He was penniless. She had what was no mean portion for those times and those conditions; and, granted that she was affected, and provincial, and short, and all the rest with which she is charged, she was probably not without suitors; nor do her defects or faults seem to have been those of an unadmired or neglected woman. Next, let us remember what was the aspect of Johnson's form and face, even in his twenties, and how little he could have touched the senses of a widow fond of externals. This one loved him, accepted him, made him happy, gave to one of the noblest of all English hearts the one love of its sombre life. And English literature has had no better phrase for her than Macaulay's—"She accepted, with a readiness which did her little honour, the addresses of a suitor who might have been her son."

Her readiness did her incalculable honour. But it is at last worth remembering that Johnson had first done her incalculable honour. No one has given to man or woman the right to judge as to the worthiness of her who received it. The meanest man is generally allowed his own counsel as to his own wife; one of the greatest of men has been denied it. "The lover," says Macaulay, "continued to be under the illusions of the wedding day till the lady died." What is so graciously said is not enough. He was under those "illusions" until he too died, when he had long passed her latest age, and was therefore able to set right that balance of years which has so much irritated the impertinent. Johnson passed from this life twelve years older than she, and so for twelve years his constant eyes had to turn backwards to dwell upon her. Time gave him a younger wife.

And here I will put into Mrs Johnson's mouth, that mouth to which no one else has ever attributed any beautiful sayings, the words of Marceline Desbordes-Valmore to the young husband she loved: "Older than thou! Let me never see thou knowest it. Forget it! I will remember it, to die before thy death."

Macaulay, in his unerring effectiveness, uses Johnson's short sight for an added affront to Mrs Johnson. The bridegroom was too weak of eyesight "to distinguish ceruse from natural bloom." Nevertheless, he saw well enough, when he was old, to distinguish Mrs Thrale's dresses. He reproved her for wearing a dark dress; it was unsuitable, he said, for her size; a little creature should show gay colours "like an insect." We are not called upon to admire his wife; why, then, our taste being thus uncompromised, do we not suffer him to admire her? It is the most gratuitous kind of intrusion. Moreover, the biographers are eager to permit that touch of romance and grace in his relations to Mrs Thrale, which they officially deny in the case of Mrs Johnson. But the difference is all on the other side. He would not have bidden his wife dress like an insect. Mrs Thrale was to him "the first of womankind" only because his wife was dead.

Beauclerc, we learn, was wont to cap Garrick's mimicry of Johnson's

lovemaking by repeating the words of Johnson himself in after years—
"It was a love-match on both sides." And obviously he was as strange
a lover as they said. Who doubted it? Was there any other woman in
England to give such a suitor the opportunity of an eternal love? "A life
radically wretched," was the life of this master of Letters; but she, who
has received nothing in return except ignominy from these unthankful
Letters, had been alone to make it otherwise. Well for him that he married
so young as to earn the ridicule of all the biographers in England; for
by doing so he most happily possessed his wife for nearly twenty years.
I have called her his only friend. So indeed she was, though he had followers,
disciples, rivals, competitors, and companions, many degrees of admirers,
a biographer, a patron, and a public. He had also the houseful of sad old
women who quarrelled under his beneficent protection. But what friend
had he? He was 'solitary' from the day she died.

Let us consider under what solemn conditions and in what immortal
phrase the word 'solitary' stands. He wrote it, all Englishmen know
where. He wrote it in the hour of that melancholy triumph when he had
been at last set free from the dependence upon hope. He hoped no more,
and he needed not to hope. The 'notice' of Lord Chesterfield had been
too long deferred; it was granted at last, when it was a flattery which
Johnson's court of friends would applaud. But not for their sake was it
welcome. To no living ear would he bring it and report it with delight.

He was indifferent, he was known. The sensitiveness to pleasure was
gone, and the sensitiveness to pain, slight, and neglect would thenceforth
be suffered to rest; no man in England would put that to proof again. No
man in England, did I say? But indeed, that is not so. No slight to him, to
his person, or to his fame could have had power to cause him pain more
sensibly than the customary, habitual, ready-made ridicule that has been
cast by posterity upon her whom he loved for twenty years, prayed for
during thirty-two years more, who satisfied one of the saddest human
hearts, but to whom the world, assiduous to admire him, hardly accords
human dignity. He wrote praises of her manners and of her person for her
tomb. But her epitaph, that does not name her, is in the greatest of English
prose. What was favour to him? "I am indifferent... I am known...I am
solitary, and cannot impart it."

THE SCRUPULOUS FATHER[1]

George Gissing

IT WAS market day in the little town; at one o'clock a rustic company
besieged the table of the Greyhound, lured by savoury odours and the
frothing of amber ale. Apart from three frequenters of the ordinary, in
a small room prepared for overflow, sat two persons of a different stamp
—a middle-aged man, bald, meagre, unimpressive, but wholly respectable
in bearing and apparel, and a girl, evidently his daughter, who had the
look of the latter twenties, her plain dress harmonising with a subdued
charm of feature and a timidity of manner not ungraceful. Whilst waiting
for their meal they conversed in 'an undertone; their brief remarks and
ejaculations told of a long morning's ramble from the seaside resort some
miles away; in their quiet fashion they seemed to have enjoyed themselves,
and dinner at an inn evidently struck them as something of an escapade.
Rather awkwardly the girl arranged a handful of wild flowers which she
had gathered, and put them for refreshment into a tumbler of water;
when a woman entered with viands, silence fell upon the two; after hesi-
tations and mutual glances, they began to eat with nervous appetite.

Scarcely was their modest confidence restored, when in the doorway
sounded a virile voice, gaily humming, and they became aware of a tall
young, man, red-headed, anything but handsome, flushed and perspiring
from the sunny road, his open jacket showed a blue cotton shirt without
waistcoat, in his hand was a shabby straw hat, and thick dust covered his
boots. One would have judged him a tourist of the noisier class, and his
rather loud "Good morning!" as he entered the room seemed a serious
menace to privacy; on the other hand, the rapid buttoning of his coat, and
the quiet choice of a seat as far as possible from the two guests whom his
arrival disturbed, indicated a certain tact. His greeting had met with the
merest murmur of reply; their eyes on their plates, father and daughter
resolutely disregarded him; yet he ventured to speak again.

"They're busy here to-day. Not a seat to be had in the other room."

It was apologetic in intention, and not rudely spoken. After a moment's
delay the bald, respectable man made a curt response.

"This room is public, I believe."

The intruder held his peace. But more than once he glanced at the girl,

---

[1] From *The House of Cobwebs*. Reprinted by permission of Mr A. C. Gissing, Messrs
Constable and Co., Ltd., London, and Messrs E. P. Dutton and Co., Inc., New York.

and after each furtive scrutiny his plain visage manifested some disturbance, a troubled thoughtfulness. His one look at the mute parent was from beneath contemptuous eyebrows.

Very soon another guest appeared, a massive agricultural man, who descended upon a creaking chair and growled a remark about the hot weather. With him the red-haired pedestrian struck into talk. Their topic was beer. Uncommonly good, they agreed, the local brew, and each called for a second pint. What, they asked in concert, would England be without her ale? Shame on the base traffickers who enfeebled or poisoned this noble liquor! And how cool it was—ah! The right sort of cellar! He of the red hair hinted at a third pewter.

These two were still but midway in their stout attack on meat and drink, when father and daughter, having exchanged a few whispers, rose to depart. After leaving the room, the girl remembered that she had left her flowers behind; she durst not return for them, and, knowing her father would dislike to do so, said nothing about the matter.

"A pity!" exlaimed Mr Whiston (that was his respectable name) as they strolled away. "It looked at first as if we should have such a nice quiet dinner."

"I enjoyed it all the same," replied his companion, whose name was Rose.

"That abominable habit or drinking!" added Mr Whiston austerely. He himself had quaffed water, as always. "Their ale, indeed! See the coarse, gross creatures it produces!"

He shuddered. Rose, however, seemed less consentient than usual. Her eyes were on the ground; her lips were closed with a certain firmness. When she spoke, it was on quite another subject.

They were Londoners. Mr Whiston held the position of draughtsman in the office of a geographical publisher; though his income was small, he had always practised a rigid economy, and the possession of a modest private capital put him beyond fear of reverses. Profoundly conscious of social limits, he felt it a subject for gratitude that there was nothing to be ashamed of in his calling, which he might fairly regard as a profession, and he nursed this sense of respectability as much on his daughter's behalf as on his own. Rose was an only child; her mother had been dead for years; her kinsfolk on both sides laid claim to the title of gentlefolk, but supported it on the narrowest margin of independence. The girl had grown up in an atmosphere unfavourable to mental development, but she had received a fairly good education, and nature had dowered her with intelligence. A sense of her father's conscientiousness and of his truh affection forbade her to criticise openly the principles on which he had directed her life; hence a habit of solitary meditation, which half fostered, yet half opposed, the gentle diffidence of Rose's character.

Mr Whiston shrank from society, ceaselessly afraid of receiving less than his due; privately, meanwhile, he deplored the narrowness of the social opportunities granted to his daughter, and was for ever forming schemes for her advantage—schemes which never passed beyond the stage of nervous speculation. They inhabited a little house in a western suburb, a house illumined with every domestic virtue; but scarcely a dozen persons crossed the threshold within a twelvemonth. Rose's two or three friends were, like herself, mistrustful of the world. One of them had lately married after a very long engagement, and Rose still trembled from the excitement of that occasion, still debated fearfully with herself on the bride's chances of happiness. Her own marriage was an event so inconceivable that merely to glance at the thought appeared half immodest and wholly irrational.

Every winter Mr Whiston talked of new places which he and Rose would visit when the holidays came round; every summer he shrank from the thought of adventurous novelty, and ended by proposing a return to the same western seaside-town, to the familiar lodgings. The climate suited neither him nor his daughter, who both needed physical as well as moral bracing; but they only thought of this on finding themselves at home again with another long year of monotony before them. And it was so good to feel welcome, respected; to receive the smiling reverences of tradesfolk; to talk with just a little well-bred condescension, sure that it would be appreciated. Mr Whiston savoured these things, and Rose in this respect was not wholly unlike him.

To-day was the last of their vacation. The weather had been magnificent throughout; Rose's cheeks were more than touched by the sun, greatly to the advantage of her unpretending comeliness. She was a typical English maiden, rather tall, shapely rather than graceful, her head generally bent, her movements always betraying the diffidence of solitary habit. The lips were her finest feature, their perfect outline indicating sweetness without feebleness of character. Such a girl is at her best towards the stroke of thirty. Rose had begun to know herself; she needed only opportunity to act upon her knowledge.

A train would take them back to the seaside. At the railway station Rose seated herself on a shaded part of the platform, whilst her father, who was exceedingly short of sight, peered over publications on the bookstall. Rather tired after her walk, the girl was dreamily tracing a pattern with the point of her parasol, when some one advanced and stood immediately in front of her. Startled, she looked up, and recognised the red-haired stranger of the inn.

"You left these flowers in a glass of water on the table. I hope I'm not doing a rude thing in asking whether they were left by accident."

He had the flowers in his hand, their stems carefully protected by a piece of paper. For a moment Rose was incapable of replying; she looked at the speaker; she felt her cheeks burn; in utter embarrassment she said she knew not what.

"Oh!—thank you! I forgot them. It's very kind."

Her hand touched his as she took the bouquet from him. Without another word the man turned and strode away.

Mr Whiston had seen nothing of this. When he approached, Rose held up the flowers with a laugh.

"Wasn't it kind? I forgot them, you know, and some one from the inn came looking for me."

"Very good of them, very," replied her father graciously. "A very nice inn, that. We'll go again—some day. One likes to encourage such civility; it's rare nowadays."

He of the red hair travelled by the same train, though not in the same carriage. Rose caught sight of him at the seaside station. She was vexed with herself for having so scantily acknowledged his kindness; it seemed to her that she had not really thanked him at all; how absurd, at her age, to be incapable of common self-command! At the same time she kept thinking of her father's phrase "coarse, gross creatures," and it vexed her even more than her own ill behaviour. The stranger was certainly not coarse, far from gross. Even his talk about beer (she remembered every word of it) had been amusing rather than offensive. Was he a 'gentleman'? The question agitated her; it involved so technical a definition, and she felt so doubtful as to the reply. Beyond doubt he had acted in a gentlemanly way; but his voice lacked something. Coarse? Gross? No, no, no! Really, her father was very severe, not to say uncharitable. But perhaps he was thinking of the heavy agricultural man; oh, he must have been!

Of a sudden she felt very weary. At the lodgings she sat down in her bedroom, and gazed through the open window at the sea. A sense of discouragement, hitherto almost unknown, had fallen upon her; it spoilt the blue sky and the soft horizon. She thought rather drearily of the town-ward journey to-morrow, of her home in the suburbs, of the endless mono-tony that awaited her. The flowers lay on her lap; she smelt them, dreamed over them. And then—strange incongruity—she thought of beer!

Between tea and supper she and her father rested on the beach. Mr

Whiston was reading. Rose pretended to turn the leaves of a book. Of a sudden, as unexpectedly to herself as to her companion, she broke silence.

"Don't you think, father, that we are too much afraid of talking with strangers?"

"Too much afraid?"

Mr Whiston was puzzled. He had forgotten all about the incident at the dinner-table.

"I mean—what harm is there in having a little conversation when one is away from home? At the inn to-day, you know, I can't help thinking we were rather—pernaps a little too silent."

"My dear Rose, did you want to talk about beer?"

She reddened, but answered all the more emphatically.

"Of course not. But, when the first gentleman came in, wouldn't it have been natural to exchange a few friendly words? I'm sure he wouldn't have talked of beer to *us*."

"The *gentleman*? I saw no gentleman, my dear. I suppose he was a small clerk, or sometning of the sort, and he had no business whatever to address us."

"Oh, but he only said good morning, and apologised for sitting at our table. He needn't have apologised at all."

"Precisely. That is just what I mean," said Mr Whiston with self-satisfaction. "My dear Rose, if I had been alone, I might perhaps have talked a little, but with you it was impossible. One cannot be too careful A man like that will take all sorts of liberties. One has to keep such people at a distance."

A moment's pause, then Rose spoke with unusual decision—

"I feel quite sure, father, tnat he would not have taken liberties. It seems to me that he knew quite well how to behave himself."

Mr Whiston grew still more puzzled. He closed his book to meditate this new problem.

"One has to lay down rules," fell from him at length, sententiously. "Our position, Rose, as I have often explained, is a delicate one. A lady in circumstances such as yours cannot exercise too much caution. Your natural associates are in the world of wealth; unhappily, I cannot make you wealthy. We have to guard our self-respect, my dear child. Really, it is not *safe* to talk with strangers—least of all at an inn. And you have only to remember tnat disgusting conversation about beer!"

Rose said no more. Her father pondered a little, felt that he had delivered his soul, and resumed the book.

The next morning they were early at the station to secure good places

66

for the long journey to London. Up to almost the last moment it seemed that they would have a carriage to themselves. Then the door suddenly opened, a bag was flung on to the seat, and after it came a hot, panting man, a red-haired man, recognised immediately by both the travellers.

"I thought I'd missed it!" ejaculated the intruder merrily.

Mr Whiston turned his head away, disgust transforming his countenance. Rose sat motionless, her eyes cast down. And the stranger mopped his forehead in silence.

He glanced at her; he glanced again and again; and Rose was aware of every look. It did not occur to her to feel offended. On the contrary, she fell into a mood of tremulous pleasure, enhanced by every turn of the stranger's eyes in her direction. At him she did not look, yet she saw him. Was it a coarse face? she asked herself. Plain, perhaps but decidedly not vulgar. The red hair, she thought, was not disagreebly red; she didn't dislike that shade of colour. He was humming a tune; it seemed to be his habit, and it argued healthy cheerfulness. Meanwhile Mr Whiston sat stiffly in his corner, staring at the landscape, a model of respectable mutteness.

At the first stop another man entered. This time, unmistakably, a commercial traveller. At once a dialogue sprang up between him and Rufus. The traveller complained that all the smoking compartments were full.

"Why," exclaimed Rufus, with a laugh, "that reminds me that I wanted a smoke. I never thought about it till now; jumped in here in a hurry."

The traveller's 'line' was tobacco; they talked tobacco—Rufus with much gusto. Presently the conversation took a wider scope.

"I envy you," cried Rufus, "always travelling about. I'm in a beastly office, and get only a fortnight off once a year. I enjoy it, I can tell you! Time's up to-day, worse luck! I've a good mind to emigrate. Can you give me a tip about the colonies?"

He talked of how he had spent his holiday. Rose missed not a word, and her blood pulsed in sympathy with the joy of freedom which he expressed. She did not mind his occasional slang; the tone was manly and right-hearted; it evinced a certain simplicity of feeling by no means common in men, whether gentle or other. At a certain moment the girl was impelled to steal a glimpse of his face. After all, was it really so plain? The features seemed to her to have a certain refinement which she had not noticed before.

"I'm going to try for a smoker," said the man of commerce, as the train slackened into a busy station.

Rufus hesitated. His eye wandered.

67

"I think I shall stay where I am," he ended by saying.

In that same moment, for the first time, Rose met his glance. She saw that his eyes did not at once avert themselves; they had a singular expression, a smile which pleaded pardon for its audacity. And Rose, even whilst turning away, smiled in response.

The train stopped. The commercial traveller alighted. Rose, leaning towards her father, whispered that she was thirsty; would he get her a glass of milk or of lemonade? Though little disposed to rush on such errands, Mr Whiston had no choice but to comply; he sped at once for the refreshment-room.

And Rose knew what would happen; she knew perfectly. Sitting rigid, her eyes on vacancy, she felt the approach of the young man, who for the moment was alone with her. She saw him at her side: she heard his voice.

"I can't help it. I want to speak to you. May I?"

Rose faltered a reply.

"It was so kind to bring the flowers. I didn't thank you properly."

"It's now or never," pursued the young man in rapid, excited tones. "Will you let me tell you my name? Will you tell me yours?"

Rose's silence consented. The daring Rufus rent a page from a pocketbook, scribbled his name and address, gave it to Rose. He rent out another page, offered it to Rose with the pencil, and in a moment had secured the precious scrap of paper in his pocket. Scarce was the transaction completed when a stranger jumped in. The young man bounded to his own corner, just in time to see the return of Mr Whiston, glass in hand.

During the rest of the journey Rose was in the strangest state of mind. She did not feel in the least ashamed of herself. It seemed to her that what had happened was wholly natural and simple. The extraordinary thing was that she must sit silent and with cold countenance at the distance of a few feet from a person with whom she ardently desired to converse. Sudden illumination had wholly changed the aspect of life. She seemed to be playing a part in a gotesque comedy rather than living in a world of grave realities. Her father's dignified silence struck her as intolerably absurd. She could have burst into laughter; at moments she was indignant, irritated, tremulous with the spirit of revolt. She detected a glance of frigid superiority with which Mr Whiston chanced to survey the other occupants of the compartment. It amazed her. Never had she seen her father in such an alien light. He bent forward and addressed to her some commonplace remark; she barely deigned a reply. Her views of conduct, of character, had undergone an abrupt and extraordinary change. Having justified without shadow of argument her own incredible proceeding, she judged everything and everybody by some new standard, mysteriously attained. She was no longer the Rose Whiston of yesterday. Her old self seemed an object of compassion. She felt an unspeakable happiness, and at the same time an encroaching fear.

The fear predominated; when she grew aware of the streets of London looming on either hand it became a torment, an anguish. Small-folded, crushed within her palm, the piece of paper with its still unread inscription seemed to burn her. Once, twice, thrice she met the look of her friend. He smiled cheerily, bravely, with evident purpose of encouragement. She knew his face better than that of any oldest acquaintance; she saw in it a manly beauty. Only by a great effort of self-control could she refrain from turning aside to unfold and read what he had written. The train slackened speed, stopped. Yes, it was London. She must arise and go. Once more their eyes met. Then, without recollection of any interval, she was on the Metropolitan Railway, moving towards her suburban home.

A severe headache sent her early to bed. Beneath her pillow lay a scrap of paper with a name and address she was not likely to forget. And through the night of broken slumbers Rose suffered a martyrdom. No more self-glorification! All her courage gone, all her new vitality! She saw herself with the old eyes, and was shame-stricken to the very heart.

Whose the fault? Towards dawn she argued it with the bitterness of misery. What a life was hers in this little world of choking respectabilities! Forbidden this, forbidden that; permitted—the pride of ladyhood. And she was not a lady, after all. What lady would have permitted herself to exchange names and addresses with a strange man in a railway carriage—furtively, too, escaping her father's observation? If not a lady, what *was* she? It meant the utter failure of her breeding and education. The sole end for which she had lived was frustrate. A common, vulgar young woman—well mated, doubtless, with an impudent clerk, whose noisy talk was of beer and tobacco!

This arrested her. Stung to the defence of her friend, who, clerk though he might be, was neither impudent nor vulgar, she found herself driven back upon self-respect. The battle went on for hours; it exhausted her; it undid all the good effects of sun and sea, and left her flaccid, pale.

"I'm afraid the journey yesterday was too much for you," remarked Mr Whiston, after observing her as she sate mute the next evening.

"I shall soon recover," Rose answered coldly.

The father meditated with some uneasiness. He had not forgotten Rose's singular expression of opinion after their dinner at the inn. His affection made him sensitive to changes in the girl's demeanour. Next summer they must really find a more bracing resort. Yes, yes; clearly Rose needed bracing. But she was always better when the cool days came round.

On the morrow it was his daughter's turn to feel anxious. Mr Whiston all at once wore a face of indignant severity. He was absentminded; he sat at table with scarce a word; he had little nervous movements, and subdued mutterings as of wrath. This continued on a second day, and Rose began to suffer an intolerable agitation. She could not help connecting her father's strange behaviour with the secret which tormented her heart.

Had something happened? Had her friend seen Mr Whiston, or written to him?

She had awaited with tremors every arrival of the post. It was probable —more than probable—that *he* would write to her; but as yet no letter came. A week passed, and no letter came. Her father was himself again; plainly she had mistaken the cause of his perturbation. Ten days, and no letter came.

It was Saturday afternoon. Mr Whiston reached home at tea-time. The first glance showed his daughter that trouble and anger once more beset him. She trembled, and all but wept, for suspense had overwrought her nerves.

"I find myself obliged to speak to you on a very disagreeable subject,"— thus began Mr Whiston over the tea-cups—"a very unpleasant subject indeed. My one consolation is that it will probably settle a little argument we had down at the seaside."

As his habit was when expressing grave opinions (and Mr Whiston seldom expressed any other), he made a long pause and ran his fingers through his thin beard. The delay irritated Rose to the last point of endurance.

"The fact is," he proceeded at length, "a week ago I received a most extraordinary letter—the most impudent letter I ever read in my life. It came from that noisy, beer-drinking man who intruded upon us at the inn—you remember. He began by explaining who he was, and—if you can believe it—had the impertinence to say that he wished to make my acquaintance! An amazing letter! Naturally, I left it unanswered—the only dignified thing to do. But the fellow wrote again, asking if I had received his proposal. I now replied, briefly and severely, asking him, first, how he came to know my name; secondly, what reason I had given him for supposing that I desired to meet him again. His answer to this was even more outrageous than the first offence. He bluntly informed me that in order to discover my name and address he had followed us home that day from Paddington Station! As if this was not bad enough, he went on to—really, Rose, I feel I must apologise to you, but the fact is I seem to have no choice but to tell you what he said. The fellow tells me, really, that he wants to know *me* only that he may come to know *you!* My first idea was to go with this letter to the police. I am not sure that I shan't do so even yet; most certainly I shall if he writes again. The man may be crazy—he may be dangerous. Who knows but he may come lurking around the house? I felt obliged to warn you of this unpleasant possibility."

Rose was stirring her tea; also she was smiling. She continued to stir and to smile, without consciousness of either performance.

"You make light of it?" exclaimed her father solemnly.

"O father, of course I am sorry you have had this annoyance."

So little was there of manifest sorrow in the girl's tone and countenance that Mr Whiston gazed at her rather indignantly. His pregnant pause gave birth to one of those admonitory axioms which had hitherto ruled his daughter's life.

"My dear, I advise you never to trifle with questions of propriety. Could there possibly be a better illustration of what I have so often said— that in self-defence we are bound to keep strangers at a distance?"

"Father——"

Rose began firmly, but her voice failed.

"You were going to say, Rose?"

She took her courage in both hands.

"Will you allow me to see the letters?"

"Certainly. There can be no objection to that."

He threw from his pocket the three envelopes, held them to his daughter. With shaking hand Rose unfolded the first letter; it was written in clear commercial character, and was signed "Charles James Burroughs." When she had read all, the girl said quietly——

"Are you quite sure, father, that these letters are impertinent?"

Mr Whiston stopped in the act of finger-combing his beard.

"What doubt can there be of it?"

"They seem to me," proceeded Rose nervously, "to be very respectful and very honest."

"My dear, you astound me! Is it respectful to force one's acquaintance upon an unwilling stranger? I really don't understand you. Where is your sense of propriety, Rose? A vulgar, noisy fellow, who talks of beer and tobacco—a petty clerk! And he has the audacity to write to me that he wants to—to make friends with my daughter! Respectful? Honest? Really!"

When Mr Whiston became sufficiently agitated to lose his decorous gravity, he began to splutter, and at such moments he was not impressive. Rose kept her eyes cast down. She felt her strength once more, the strength of a wholly reasonable and half-passionate revolt against that tyrannous propriety which Mr Whiston worshipped.

"Father——"

"Well, my dear?"

"There is only one thing I dislike in these letters—and that is a falseg hood."

"I don't understand."

Rose was flushing. Her nerves grew tense; she had wrought herself to a simple audacity which overcame small embarrassments.

"Mr Burroughs says that he followed us home from Paddington to discover our address. That is not true. He asked me for my name and address in the train, and gave me his."

The father gasped.

"He *asked*——? You *gave*——?"

"It was whilst you were away in the refreshment-room," proceeded the girl, with singular self-control, in a voice almost matter-of-fact. "I ought to tell you, at the same time, that it was Mr Burroughs who brought me the flowers from the inn, when I forgot them. You didn't see him give them to me in the station."

The father stared.

"But, Rose, what does all this mean? You—you overwhelm me! Go on, please. What next?"

"Nothing, father."

And of a sudden the girl was so beset with confusing emotions that she hurriedly quitted her chair and vanished from the room.

Before Mr Whiston returned to his geographical drawing on Monday morning, he had held long conversations with Rose, and still longer with himself. Not easily could he perceive the justice of his daughter's quarrel with propriety; many days were to pass, indeed, before he would consent to do more than make inquiries about Charles James Burroughs, and to permit that aggressive young man to give a fuller account of himself in writing. It was by silence that Rose prevailed. Having defended herself against the charge of immodesty, she declined to urge her own inclination or the rights of Mr Burroughs; her mute patience did not lack its effect with the scrupulous but tender parent.

"I am willing to admit, my dear," said Mr Whiston one evening, *à propos* of nothing at all, "that the falsehood in that young man's letter gave proof of a certain delicacy."

"Thank you, father," replied Rose, very quietly and simply.

It was next morning that the father posted a formal, proper, self-respecting note of invitation, which bore results.

A LONG-AGO AFFAIR[1]

John Galsworthy

HUBERT MARSLAND, the landscape painter, returning from a day's sketching on the river in the summer of 1921, had occasion to stay the progress of his two-seater about ten miles from London for a minor repair, and while his car was being seen to, strolled away from the garage to have a look at a house where he had often spent his holidays as a boy. Walking through a gateway and passing a large gravel-pit on his left, he was soon opposite the house, which stood back a little in its grounds. Very much changed! More pretentious, not so homely as when his Uncle and Aunt lived there, and he used to play cricket on this warren opposite, where the cricket ground, it seemed, had been turned into a golf course. It was late— the dinner-hour, nobody playing, and passing on to the links he stood digesting the geography. Here must have been where the old pavilion was. And there—still turfed—where he had made that particularly nice stroke to leg, when he went in last and carried his bat for thirteen. Thirty-nine years ago—his sixteenth birthday. How vividly he remembered his new pads! A. P. Lucas had played against them and only made thirty-two—one founded one's style on A. P. Lucas in those days—feet in front of the bat, and pointed a little forward, elegant; you never saw it now, and a good thing too—one could sacrifice too much to style! Still, the tendency was all the other way; style was too much 'off,' perhaps!

He stepped back into then sun and sat down on the grass. Peaceful— very still! The haze of the distant downs was visible between his Uncle's old house and the next; and there was the clump of elms on the far side behind which the sun would be going down just as it used to then. He pressed the palms of his hands to the turf. A glorious summer—something like that summer of long ago. And warmth from the turf, or perhaps from the past, crept into his heart and made it ache a little. Just here he must have sat, after his innings, at Mrs Monteith's feet peeping out of a flounced dress.

---

[1] From *Caravan*, by permission of Messrs William Heinemann, Ltd., and from *Captures*, copyright 1923, by Messrs Charles Scribner's Sons. By permission of the publishers.

Lord! The fools boys were! How headlong and uncalculating their devotions! A softness in voice and eyes, a smile, a touch or two—and they were slaves! Young fools, but good young fools. And, standing behind her chair—he could see him now—that other idol Captain MacKay, with his face of browned ivory—just the colour of that elephant's tusk his Uncle had, which had gone so yellow—and his perfect black moustache, his white tie, check suit, carnation, spats, Malacca cane— all so fascinating! Mrs Monteith, "the grass widow" they had called her! He remembered the look in people's eyes, the tone in their voices. Such a pretty woman! He had 'fallen for her' at first sight, as the Yanks put it—her special scent, her daintiness, her voice! And that day on the river, when she made much of him, and Captain MacKay attended Evelyn Curtiss so assiduously that he was expected to propose. Quaint period! They used the word courting then, wore full skirts, high stays; and himself a blue elastic belt round his white flannelled waist. And in the evening afterwards, his Aunt had said with an arch smile: "Good-night, *silly* boy!" Silly boy indeed, with a flower the grass widow had dropped pressed by his cheek into his pillow! What folly! And that next Sunday—looking forward to Church—passionately brushing his top hat; all through the service spying at her creamy profile, two pews in front on the left, between goat-bearded old Hallgrave her Uncle, and her pink, broad, white-haired Aunt; scheming to get near her when she came out, lingering, lurking, getting just a smile and the rustle of her flounces. Ah, ha! A little went a long way then! And the last day of his holidays and its nights with the first introduction to reality. Who said the Victorian Age was innocent?

Marsland put his palm up to his cheek. No! the dew was not yet falling! And his mind lightly turned and tossed his memories of women, as a man turns and tosses hay to air it; but nothing remembered gave him quite the feeling of that first experience.

His Aunt's dance! His first white waistcoat, bought *ad hoc*, from the local tailor, his tie laboriously imitating the hero—Captain MacKay's. All came back with such freshness in the quiet of the warren—the expectancy, the humble shy excitement, the breathless asking for a dance, the writing "Mrs Monteith" twice on his little gilt-edged programme with its tiny tasselled white pencil; her slow-moving fan, her smile. And the first dance when it came; what infinite care not to tread on her white satin toes; what a thrill when her arm pressed his in the crush—such holy rapture, about all the first part of the evening, with yet another dance to come! If only he could have twirled her and 'reversed' like his pattern, Captain MacKay! Then delirium growing as the second dance came near, making him cut his partner—the cool grass-scented air out on the dark terrace, with the chafers booming by, and in the starshine the poplars wondrously tall; the careful adjustment of his tie and waistcoat, the careful polishing of his hot face! A long breath then, and into the house to find her! Ballroom, supper-room, stairs, library, billiard-room, all drawn blank—"Estudiantina" going on and on, and he a wandering, whitewaistcoated young ghost. Ah! The conservatory—and the hurrying there! And then the moment which had always been, was even now, such a blurred confused impression. Smothered voices from between a clump of flowers: "I saw her." "Who was the man?" A glimpse, gone past in a flash, of an ivory face, a black moustache! And then her voice: "Hubert"; and her hot hand clasping his, drawing him to her; her scent, her face smiling, very set! A rustling behind the flowers, those people spying; and suddenly her lips on his cheek, the kiss sounding in his ears, her voice saying very softly: "Hubert, dear boy!" The rustle receded, ceased. What a long silent minute, then, among the ferns and blossoms in the dusk with her face close to his, pale, perturbed, before she led him out into the light, while he was slowly realising that she had made use of him to shelter her. A boy—not old enough to be her lover, but old enough to save her name and that of Captain MacKay! Her kiss—the last of many—but not upon *his* lips, *his* cheeks! Hard work realising that! A boy—of no account—a boy, who in a day would be at school again, kissed that *he* and *she* might renew their intrigue unsuspected!

How had he behaved the rest of that evening of romance bedrabbled? He hardly knew. Betrayed with a kiss! Two idols in the dust! And did they care what he was feeling? Not they! All they cared for was to cover up their tracks with him! But somehow—somehow—he had never shown her that he knew. Only, when their dance was over, and some one came and took her for the next, he escaped up to his little room, tore off his gloves, his waistcoat; lay on the bed, thought bitter thoughts. A boy! There he had stayed, with the thrum of the music in his ears, till at last it died away for good and the carriages were gone, and the night was quiet.

Squatting on the warren grass, still warm and dewless, Marsland rubbed his knees. Nothing like boys for generosity! And, with a little smile, he thought of his Aunt next morning, half-arch and half-concerned: "It isn't nice, dear, to sit out in dark corners, and—well, perhaps it wasn't your fault, but still, it isn't nice—not—quite——" and of how suddenly she had stopped, looking in his face, where his lips were curling in his first ironic laugh. She had never forgiven him that laugh—thinking him a cynical

75

young Lothario? And Marsland thought: "Live and learn! Wonder what became of those two? Victorian Age! Hatches were battened down in those days! But, innocent—my hat!"

Ah! The sun was off, dew falling. He got up, rubbing his knees to take the stiffness out of them. Pigeons in the wood beyond were calling. A window in his Uncle's old home blazed like a jewel in the sun's last rays between the poplar trees. Heh! dear—a little long-ago affair!

RED[1]

W. Somerset Maugham

THE skipper thrust his hand into one of his trousers pockets and with difficulty, for they were not at the sides but in front and he was a portly man, pulled out a large silver watch. He looked at it and then looked again at the declining sun. The Kanaka at the wheel gave him a glance, but did not speak. The skipper's eyes rested on the island they were approaching. A white line of foam marked the reef. He knew there was an opening large enough to get his ship through, and when they came a little nearer he counted on seeing it. They had nearly an hour of daylight still before them. In the lagoon the water was deep and they could anchor comfortably. The chief of the village which he could already see among the coco-nut trees was a friend of the mate's, and it would be pleasant to go ashore for the night. The mate came forward at that minute and the skipper turned to him.

"We'll take a bottle of booze along with us and get some girls in to dance," he said.

"I don't see the opening," said the mate.

He was a Kanaka, a handsome, swarthy fellow, with somewhat the look of a later Roman emperor, inclined to stoutness; but his face was fine and clean-cut.

"I'm dead sure there's one right here," said the captain, looking through his glasses. "I can't understand why I can't pick it up. Send one of the boys up the mast to have a look."

The mate called one of the crew and gave him the order. The captain watched the Kanaka climb and waited for him to speak. But the Kanaka

---

[1] From *The Trembling of a Leaf*. Reprinted by permission of Messrs William Heinemann, Ltd., London, and Messrs Doubleday, Doran and Company, Inc., New York (Copyright 1921).

shouted down that he could see nothing but the unbroken line of foam. The captain spoke Samoan like a native, and he cursed him freely.

"Shall he stay up there?" asked the mate.

"What the hell good does that do?" answered the captain. "The blame fool can't see worth a cent. You bet your sweet life I'd find the opening if I was up there."

He looked at the slender mast with anger. It was all very well for a native who had been used to climbing up coco-nut trees all his life. He was fat and heavy.

"Come down," he shouted. "You're no more use than a dead dog. We'll just have to go along the reef till we find the opening."

It was a seventy-ton schooner with paraffin auxiliary, and it ran, when there was no head wind, between four and five knots an hour. It was a bedraggled object; it had been painted white a very long time ago, but it was now dirty, dingy, and mottled. It smelt strongly of paraffin and of the copra which was its usual cargo. They were within a hundred feet of the reef now and the captain told the steersman to run along it till they came to the opening. But when they had gone a couple of miles he realized that they had missed it. He went about and slowly worked back again. The white foam of the reef continued without interruption and now the sun was setting. With a curse at the stupidity of the crew the skipper resigned himself to waiting till next morning.

"Put her about," he said. "I can't anchor here."

They went out to sea a little and presently it was quite dark. They anchored. When the sail was furled the ship began to roll a good deal. They said in Apia that one day she would roll right over; and the owner, a German-American who managed one of the largest stores, said that no money was big enough to induce him to go out in her. The cook, a Chinese in white trousers, very dirty and ragged, and a thin white tunic, came to say that supper was ready, and when the skipper went into the cabin he found the engineer already seated at table. The engineer was a long, lean man with a scraggy neck. He was dressed in blue overalls and a sleeveless jersey which showed his thin arms tattooed from elbow to wrist.

"Hell, having to spend the night outside," said the skipper.

The engineer did not answer, and they ate their supper in silence. The cabin was lit by a dim oil lamp. When they had eaten the canned apricots with which the meal finished the Chink brought them a cup of tea. The skipper lit a cigar and went on the upper deck. The island now was only a darker mass against the night. The stars were very bright. The only sound was the ceaseless breaking of the surf. The skipper sank into a deck-chair and smoked idly. Presently three or four members of the crew came up and sat down. One of them had a banjo and another a concertina. They began to play, and one of them sang. The native song sounded strange on these instruments. Then to the singing a couple began to dance. It was a barbaric dance savage and primeval, rapid, with quick movements of the hands and feet and contortions of the body; it was sensual, sexual even, but sexual without passion. It was very animal, direct, weird without mystery, natural in short, and one might almost say childlike. At last they grew tired. They stretched themselves on the deck and slept, and all was silent. The skipper lifted himself heavily out of his chair and clambered down the companion. He went into his cabin and got out of his clothes. He climbed into his bunk and lay there. He panted a little in the heat of the night.

But next morning, when the dawn crept over the tranquil sea, the opening in the reef which had eluded them the night before was seen a little to the east of where they lay. The schooner entered the lagoon. There was not a ripple on the surface of the water. Deep down among the coral rocks you saw little coloured fish swim. When he had anchored his ship the skipper ate his breakfast and went on deck. The sun shone from an unclouded sky, but in the early morning the air was grateful and cool. It was Sunday, and there was a feeling of quietness, a silence as though nature were at rest, which gave him a peculiar sense of comfort. He sat, looking at the wooded coast, and felt lazy and well at ease. Presently a slow smile moved his lips and he threw the stump of his cigar into the water.

"I guess I'll go ashore," he said. "Get the boat out."

He climbed stiffly down the ladder and was rowed to a little cove. The coco-nut trees came down to the water's edge, not in rows, but spaced out with an ordered formality. They were like a ballet of spinsters, elderly but flippant, standing in affected attitudes with the simpering graces of a bygone age. He sauntered idly through them, along a path that could be just seen winding its tortuous way, and it led him presently to a broad creek. There was a bridge across it, but a bridge constructed of single trunks of coco-nut trees, a dozen of them, placed end to end and supported where they met by a forked branch driven into the bed of the creek. You walked on a smooth, round surface, narrow and slippery, and there was no support for the hand. To cross such a bridge required sure feet and a stout heart. The skipper hesitated. But he saw on the other side, nestling among the trees, a white man's house; he made up his mind and, rather gingerly, began to walk. He watched his feet carefully, and where one trunk joined on to the next and there was a difference of level, he tottered

78

a little. It was with a gasp of relief that he reached the last tree and finally set his feet on the firm ground of the other side. He had been so intent on the difficult crossing that he never noticed any one was watching him, and it was with surprise that he heard himself spoken to.

"It takes a bit of nerve to cross these bridges when you're not used to them."

He looked up and saw a man standing in front of him. He had evidently come out of the house which he had seen.

"I saw you hesitate," the man continued, with a smile on his lips, "and I was watching to see you fall in."

"Not on your life," said the captain, who had now recovered his confidence.

"I've fallen in myself before now. I remember, one evening I came back from shooting, and I fell in, gun and all. Now I get a boy to carry my gun for me."

He was a man no longer young, with a small beard, now somewhat grey, and a thin face. He was dressed in a singlet, without arms, and a pair of duck trousers. He wore neither shoes nor socks. He spoke English with a slight accent.

"Are you Neilson?" asked the skipper.

"I am."

"I've heard about you. I thought you lived somewheres round here."

The skipper followed his host into the little bungalow and sat down heavily in the chair which the other motioned him to take. While Neilson went out to fetch whisky and glasses he took a look round the room. It filled him with amazement. He had never seen so many books. The shelves reached from floor to ceiling on all four walls, and they were closely packed. There was a grand piano littered with music, and a large table on which books and magazines lay in disorder. The room made him feel embarrassed. He remembered that Neilson was a queer fellow. No one knew very much about him, although he had been in the islands for so many years, but those who knew him agreed that he was queer. He was a Swede.

"You've got one big heap of books here," he said, when Neilson returned.

"They do no harm," answered Neilson with a smile.

"Have you read them all?" asked the skipper.

"Most of them."

"I'm a bit of a reader myself. I have the *Saturday Evening Post* sent me regler."

Neilson poured his visitor a good stiff glass of whisky and gave him a cigar. The skipper volunteered a little information.

79

"I got in last night, but I couldn't find the opening, so I had to anchor outside. I never been this run before, but my people had some stuff they wanted to bring over here. Gray, d'you know him?"

"Yes, he's got a store a little way along."

"Well, there was a lot of canned stuff that he wanted over, an' he's got some copra. They thought I might just as well come over as lie idle at Apia. I run between Apia and Pago-Pago mostly, but they've got small-pox there just now, and there's nothing stirring."

He took a drink of his whisky and lit a cigar. He was a taciturn man, but there was something in Neilson that made him nervous, and his nervousness made him talk. The Swede was looking at him with large dark eyes in which there was an expression of faint amusement.

"This is a tidy little place you've got here."

"I've done my best with it."

"You must do pretty well with your trees. They look fine. With copra at the price it is now. I had a bit of a plantation myself once, in Upolu it was, but I had to sell it."

He looked round the room again, where all those books gave him a feeling of sometnihg incomprehensible and hostile.

"I guess you must find it a bit lonesome here though," he said.

"I've got used to it. I've been here for twenty-five years."

Now the captain could think of nothing more to say, and he smoked in silence. Neilson had apparently no wish to break it. He looked at his guest with a meditative eye. He was a tall man, more than six feet high, and very stout. His face was red and blotchy, with a network of little purple veins on the cheeks, and his features were sunk into its fatness. His eyes were bloodshot. His neck was buried in rolls of fat. But for a fringe of long curly hair, nearly white, at the back of his head, he was quite bald; and that immense, shiny surface of forehead, which might have given him a false look of intelligence, on the contrary gave him one of peculiar imbe-cility. He wore a blue flannel shirt, open at the neck and showing his fat chest covered with a mat of reddish hair, and a very old pair of blue serge trousers. He sat in his chair in a heavy ungainly attitude, his great belly thrust forward and his fat legs uncrossed. All elasticity had gone from his limbs. Neilson wondered idly what sort of man he had been in his youth. It was almost impossible to imagine that this creatuer of vast bulk had ever been a boy who ran about. The skipper finished his whisky, and Neilson pushed the bottle towards him.

"Help yourself."

The skipper leaned forward and with his great hand seized it.

"And how come you in these parts anyways?" he said.

"Oh, I came out to the islands for my health. My lungs were bad and they said I hadn't a year to live. You see they were wrong."

"I meant, how come you to settle down right here?"

"I am a sentimentalist."

"Oh!"

Neilson knew that the skipper had not an idea what he meant, and he looked at him with an ironical twinkle in his dark eyes. Perhaps just because the skipper was so gross and dull a man the whim seized him to talk further.

"You were too busy keeping your balance to notice, when you crossed the bridge, but this spot is generally considered rather pretty."

"It's a cute little house you've got here."

"Ah, that wasn't here when I first came. There was a native hut, with its beehive roof and its pillars, overshadowed by a great tree with red flowers; and the croton bushes, their leaves yellow and red and golden, made a pied fence around it. And then all about were the coco-nut trees, as fanciful as women, and as vain. They stood at the water's edge and spent all day looking at their reflections. I was a young man then—Good Heavens, it's a quarter of a century ago—and I wanted to enjoy all the loveliness of the world in the short time allotted to me before I passed into the darkness. I thought it was the most beautiful spot I had ever seen. The first time I saw it I had a catch at my heart, and I was afraid I was going to cry. I wasn't more than twenty-five, and though I put the best face I could on it, I didn't want to die. And somehow it seemed to me that the very beauty of this place made it easier for me to accept my fate. I felt when I came here that all my past life had fallen away, Stockholm and its University, and then Bonn: it all seemed the life of somebody else, as though now at last I had achieved the reality which our doctors of philosophy—I am one myself, you know—had discussed so much. 'A year,' I cried to myself. 'I have a year. I will spend it here and then I am content to die.'"

"We are foolish and sentimental and melodramatic at twenty-five, but if we weren't perhaps we should be less wise at fifty."

"Now drink, my friend. Don't let the nonsense I talk interfere with you."

He waved his thin hands toward the bottle, and the skipper finished what remained in his glass.

"You ain't drinking nothin'," he said, reaching for the whisky.

"I am of a sober habit," smiled the Swede. "I intoxicate myself in ways which I fancy are more subtle. But perhaps that is only vanity. Anyhow, the effects are more lasting and the results less deleterious."

"They say there's deal of cocaine taken in the States now," said the captain.

Neilson chuckled.

"But I do not see a white man often," he continued, "and for once I don't think a drop of whisky can do me any harm."

He poured himself out a little, added some soda, and took a sip.

"And presently I found out why the spot had such an unearthly loveliness. Here love had tarried for a moment like a migrant bird that happens on a ship in mid-ocean and for a little while folds its tired wings. The fragrance of a beautiful passion hovered over it like the fragrance of hawthorn in May in the meadows of my home. It seems to me that the places where men have loved or suffered keep about them always some faint aroma of something that has not wholly died. It is as though they had acquired a spiritual significance which mysteriously affects those who pass. I wish I could make myself clear." He smiled a little. "Though I cannot imagine that if I did you would understand."

He paused.

"I think this place was beautiful because here I had been loved beautifully." And now he shrugged his shoulders. "But perhaps it is only that my aesthetic sense is gratified by the happy conjunction of young love and a suitable setting."

Even a man less thick-witted than the skipper might have been forgiven if he were bewildered by Neilson's words. For he seemed faintly to laugh at what he said. It was as though he spoke from emotion which his intellect found ridiculous. He had said himself that he was a sentimentalist, and when sentimentality is joined with scepticism there is often the devil to pay.

He was silent for an instant and looked at the captain with eyes in which there was a sudden perplexity.

"You know, I can't help thinking that I've seen you before somewhere or other," he said.

"I couldn't say as I remember you," returned the skipper.

"I have a curious feeling as though your face were familiar to me. It's been puzzling me for some time. But I can't situate my recollection in any place or at any time."

The skipper massively shrugged his heavy shoulders.

"It's thirty years since I first came to the islands. A man can't figure on remembering all the folk he meets in a while like that."

82

The Swede shook his head.

"You know how one sometimes has the feeling that a place one has never been to before is strangely familiar. That's how I seem to see you." He gave a whimsical smile. "Perhaps I knew you in some past existence. Perhaps, perhaps you were the master of a galley in ancient Rome and I was a slave at the oar. Thirty years have you been here?"

"Every bit of thirty years."

"I wonder if you knew a man called Red?"

"Red?"

"That is the only name I've ever known him by. I never knew him personally. I never even set eyes on him. And yet I seem to see him more clearly than many men, my brothers, for instance, with whom I passed my daily life for many years. He lives in my imagination with the distinctness of a Paolo Malatesta or a Romeo. But I daresay you have never read Dante or Shakespeare?"

"I can't say as I have," said the captain.

Neilson, smoking a cigar, leaned back in his chair and looked vacantly at the ring of smoke which floated in the still air. A smile played on his lips, but his eyes were grave. Then he looked at the captain. There was in his gross obesity something extraordinarily repellent. He had the plethoric self-satisfaction of the very fat. It was an outrage. It set Neilson's nerves on edge. But the contrast between the man before him and the man he had in mind was pleasant.

"It appears that Red was the most comely thing you ever saw. I've talked to quite a number of people who knew him in those days, white men, and they all agree that the first time you saw him his beauty just took your breath away. They called him Red on account of his flaming hair. It had a natural wave and he wore it long. It must have been of that wonderful colour that the pre-Raphaelites raved over. I don't think he was vain of it, he was much too ingenuous for that, but no one could have blamed him if he had been. He was tall, six feet and an inch or two—in the native house that used to stand here was the mark of his height cut with a knife on the central trunk that supported the roof—and he was made like a Greek god, broad in the shoulders and thin in the flanks; he was like Apollo, with just that soft roundness which Praxiteles gave him, and that suave, feminine grace which has in it something troubling and mysterious. His skin was dazzling white, milky, like satin; his skin was like a woman's."

"I had kind of a white skin myself when I was a kiddie," said the skipper, with a twinkle in his bloodshot eyes.

But Neilson paid no attention to him. He was telling his story now and interruption made him impatient.

"And his face was just as beautiful as his body. He had large blue eyes, very dark, so that some say they were black, and unlike most red-haired people he had dark eyebrows and long dark lashes. His features were perfectly regular and his mouth was like a scarlet wound. He was twenty."

On these words the Swede stopped with a certain sense of the dramatic. He took a sip of whisky.

"He was unique. There never was any one more beautiful. There was no more reason for him than for a wonderful blossom to flower on a wild plant. He was a happy accident of nature.

"One day he landed at that cove into which you must have put this morning. He was an American sailor, and he had deserted from a man-of-war in Apia. He had induced some good-humoured native to give him a passage on a cutter that happened to be sailing from Apia to Safoto, and he had been put ashore here in a dug-out. I do not know why he deserted. Perhaps life on a man-of-war with its restrictions irked him, perhaps he was in trouble and perhaps it was the South Seas and these romantic islands that got into his bones. Every now and then they take a man strangely, and he finds himself like a fly in a spider's web. It may be that there was a softness of fibre in him, and these green hills with their soft airs, this blue sea, took the northern strength from him as Delilah took the Nazarite's. Anyhow, he wanted to hide himself, and he thought he would be safe in this secluded nook till his ship had sailed from Samoa.

"There was a native hut at the cove and as he stood there, wondering where exactly he should turn his steps, a young girl came out and invited him to enter. He knew scarcely two words of the native tongue and she as little English. But he understood well enough what her smiles meant, and her pretty gestures, and he followed her. He sat down on a mat and she gave him slices of pine-apple to eat. I can speak of Red only from hearsay, but I saw the girl three years after he first met her, and she was scarcely nineteen then. You cannot imagine how exquisite she was. She had the passionate grace of the hibiscus and the rich colour. She was rather tall, slim, with the delicate features of her race, and large eyes like pools of still water under the palm trees; her hair, black and curling, fell down her back, and she wore a wreath of scented flowers. Her hands were lovely. They were so small, so exquisitely formed, they gave your heartstrings a wrench. And in those days she laughed easily. Her smile was so delightful that it made your knees shake. Her skin was like a field of ripe corn on a summer day. Good Heavens, how can I describe her? She was too beautiful to be real.

"And these two young things, she was sixteen and he was twenty, fell in love with one another at first sight. That is the real love, not the love that comes from sympathy, common interests, or intellectual community, but love pure and simple. That is the love that Adam felt for Eve when he awoke and found her in the garden gazing at him with dewy eyes. That is the love that draws the beasts to one another, and the Gods. That is the love that makes the world a miracle. That is the love which gives life its pregnant meaning. You have never heard of the wise, cynical French duke who said that with two lovers there is always one who loves and one who lets himself be loved; it is a bitter truth to which most of us have to resign ourselves; but now and then there are two who love and two who let themselves be loved. Then one might fancy that the sun stands still at it stood when Joshua prayed to the God of Israel.

"And even now after all these years, when I think of these two, so young, so fair, so simple, and of their love, I feel a pang. It tears my heart just as my heart is torn when on certain nights I watch the full moon shining on the lagoon from an unclouded sky. There is always pain in the contemplation of perfect beauty.

"They were children. She was good and sweet and kind. I know nothing of him, and I like to think that then at all events he was ingenuous and frank. I like to think that his soul was as comely as his body. But I daresay he had no more soul than the creatures of the woods and forests who made pipes from reeds and bathed in the mountain streams when the world was young, and you might catch sight of little fauns galloping through the glade on the back of a bearded centaur. A soul is a troublesome possession and when man developed it he lost the Garden of Eden.

"Well, when Red came to the island it had recently been visited by one of those epidemics which the white man has brought to the South Seas, and one-third of the inhabitants had died. It seems that the girl had lost all her near kin and she lived now in the house of distant cousins. The household consisted of two ancient crones, bowed and wrinkled, two younger women, and a man and a boy. For a few days he stayed there. But perhaps he felt himself too near the shore, with the possibility that he might fall in with white men who would reveal his hiding-place; perhaps the lovers could not bear that the company of others should rob them for an instant of the delight of being together. One morning they set out, the pair of them, with the few things that belonged to the girl, and walked along a grassy path under the coco-nuts, till they came to the creek you see.

They had to cross the bridge you crossed, and the girl laughed gleefully because he was afraid. She held his hand till they came to the end of the first tree, and then his courage failed him and he had to go back. He was obliged to take off all his clothes before he could risk it, and she carried them over for him on her head. They settled down in the empty hut that stood here. Whether she had any rights over it (land tenure is a complicated business in the islands), or whether the owner had died during the epidemic, I do not know, but anyhow no one questioned them, and they took possession. Their furniture consisted of a couple of grass mats on which they slept, a fragment of looking-glass, and a bowl or two. In this pleasant land that is enough to start housekeeping on.

"They say that happy people have no history, and certainly a happy love has none. They did nothing all day long and yet the days seemed all too short. The girl had a native name, but Red called her Sally. He picked up the easy language very quickly, and he used to lie on the mat for hours while she chattered gaily to him. He was a silent fellow, and perhaps his mind was lethargic. He smoked incessantly the cigarettes which she made him out of the native tobacco and pandanus leaf, and he watched her while with deft fingers she made grass mats. Often natives would come in and tell long stories of the old days when the island was disturbed by tribal wars. Sometimes he would go fishing on the reef, and bring home a basketful of coloured fish. Sometimes at night he would go out with a lantern to catch lobster. There were plantains round the hut and Sally would roast them for their frugal meal. She knew how to make delicious messes from coconuts, and the bread-fruit tree by the side of the creek gave them its fruit. On feast-days they killed a little pig and cooked it on hot stones. They bathed together in the creek; and in the evening they went down to the lagoon and paddled about in a dugout, with its great out-rigger. The sea was deep blue, wine-coloured at sundown, like the sea of Homeric Greece; but in the lagoon the colour had an infinite variety, aquamarine and amethyst and emerald; and the setting sun turned it for a short moment to liquid gold. Then there was the colour of the coral, brown, white, pink, red, purple; and the shapes it took were marvellous. It was like a magic garden, and the hurrying fish were like butterflies. It strangely lacked reality. Among the coral were pools with a floor of white sand and here, where the water was dazzling clear, it was very good to bathe. Then, cool and happy, they wandered back in the gloaming over the soft grass road to the creek, walking hand in hand, and now the mynah birds filled the coco-nut trees with their clamour. And then the night, with that great sky shining with gold, that seemed to stretch more widely than the skies of Europe, and the soft airs that blew gently through the open hut, the long night again was all too short. She was sixteen and he was barely twenty. The dawn crept in among the wooden pillars of the hut and looked at those lovely children sleeping in one another's arms. The sun hid behind the great tattered leaves of the plantains so that it might not disturb them, and then, with playful malice, shot a golden ray, like the out-stretched paw of a Persian cat, on their faces. They opened their sleepy eyes and they smiled to welcome another day. The weeks lengthened into months, and a year passed. They seemed to love one another as—I hesitate to say passionately, for passion has in its always a shade of sadness, a touch of bitterness of anguish, but as wholeheartedly, as simply and naturally as on that first day on which, meeting, they had recognized that a god was in them.

"If you had asked them I have no doubt that they would have thought it impossible to suppose their love could ever cease. Do we not know that the essential element of love is a belief in its own eternity? And yet perhaps in Red there was already a very little seed, unknown to himself and unsuspected by the girl, which would in time have grown to weariness. For one day one of the natives from the cove told them that some way down the coast at the anchorage was a British whaling-ship.

" 'Gee,' he said, 'I wonder if I could make a trade of some nuts and plantains for a pound or two of tobacco.'

"The pandanus cigarettes that Sally made him with untiring hands were strong and pleasant enough to smoke, but they left him unsatisfied; and he yearned on a sudden for real tobacco, hard, rank, and pungent. He had not smoked a pipe for many months. His mouth watered at the thought of it. One would have thought some premonition of harm would have made Sally seek to dissuade him, but love possessed her so completely that it never occurred to her any power on earth could take him from her. They went up into the hills together and gathered a great basket of wild oranges, green, but sweet and juicy; and they picked plantains from around the hut, and coco-nuts from their trees, and bread-fruit and mangoes; and they carried them down to the cove. They loaded the unstable canoe with them, and Red and the native boy who had brought them the news of the ship paddled along outside the reef.

"It was the last time she ever saw him.

"Next day the boy came back alone. He was all in tears. This is the story he told. When after their long paddle they reached the ship and Red hailed it, a white man looked over the side and told them to come on board. They took the fruit they had brought with them and Red piled it up on the deck. The white man and he began to talk, and they seemed to come to some agreement. One of them went below and brought up tobacco. Red took some at once and lit a pipe. The boy imitated the zest with which he blew a great cloud of smoke from his mouth. Then they said something to him and he went into the cabin. Throught the open door the boy, watching curiously, saw a bottle brought out and glasses. Red drank and smoked. They seemed to ask him something, for he shook his head and laughed. The man, the first man who had spoken to them, laughed too, and he filled Red's glass once more. They went on talking and drinking, and presently, growing tired of watching a sight that meant nothing to him, the boy curled himself up on the deck and slept. He was awakened by a kick; and, jumping to his feet, he saw that the ship was slowly sailing out of the lagoon. He caught sight of Red seated at the table, with his head resting heavily on his arms, fast asleep. He made a movement towards him, intending to wake him, but a rough hand seized his arm, and a man, with a scowl and words which he did not understand, pointed to the side. He shouted to Red, but in a moment he was seized and flung overboard. Helpless, he swam round to his canoe which was drifting a little way off, and pushed it on to the reef. He climbed in and, sobbing all the way, paddled back to shore.

"What had happened was obvious enough. The whaler, by desertion or sickness, was short of hands, and the captain when Red came aboard had asked him to sign on; on his refusal he had made him drunk and kidnapped him.

"Sally was beside herself with grief. For three days she screamed and cried. The natives did what they could to comfort her, but she would not be comforted. She would not eat. And then, exhausted, she sank into a sullen apathy. She spent long days at the cove, watching the lagoon, in the vain hope that Red somehow or other would manage to escape. She sat on the white sand, hour after hour, with the tears running down her cheeks, and at night dragged herself wearily back across the creek to the little hut where she had been happy. The people with whom she had lived before Red came to the island wished her to return to them, but she would not; she was convinced that Red would come back, and she wanted him to find her where he had left her. Four months later she was delivered of a still-born child, and the old woman who had come to help her through her confinement remained with her in the hut. All joy was taken from her life. If her anguish with time became less intolerable it was replaced by a settled melancholy. You would not have thought that among these people, whose emotions, though so violent, are very transient, a woman could be found capable of so enduring a passion. She never lost the profound conviction that sooner or later Red would come back. She watched for him, and every time some one crossed this slender little bridge of coco-nut trees she looked. It might at last be he."

Neilson stopped talking and gave a faint sigh.

"And what happened to her in the end?" asked the skipper.

Neilson smiled bitterly.

"Oh, three years afterwards she took up with another white man."

The skipper gave a fat, cynical chuckle.

"That's generally what happens to them," he said.

The Swede shot him a look of hatred. He did not know why that gross, obese man excited in him so violent a repulsion. But his thoughts wandered and he found his mind filled with memories of the past. He went back five-and-twenty years. It was when he first came to the island, weary of Apia, with its heavy drinking, its gambling and coarse sensuality, a sick man, trying to resign himself to the loss of the career which had fired his imagination with ambitious thoughts. He set behind him resolutely all his hopes of making a great name for himself and strove to content himself with the few poor months of careful life which was all that he could count on. He was boarding with a half-caste trader who had a store a couple of miles along the coast at the edge of a native village; and one day, wandering aimlessly along the grassy paths of the coco-nut groves, he had come upon the hut in which Sally lived. The beauty of the spot had filled him with a rapture so great that it was almost painful, and then he had seen Sally. She was the loveliest creature he had ever seen, and the sadness in those dark, magnificent eyes of hers affected him strangely. The Kanakas were a handsome race, and beauty was not rare among them, but it was the beauty of shapely animals. It was empty. But those tragic eyes were dark with mystery, and you felt in them the bitter complexity of the groping, human soul. The trader told him the story and it moved him.

"Do you think he'll ever come back?" asked Neilson.

"No fear. Why, it'll be a couple of years before the ship is paid off, and by then he'll have forgotten all about her. I bet he was pretty mad when he woke up and found he'd been shanghaied, and I shouldn't wonder but he wanted to fight somebody. But he'd got to grin and bear it, and I guess in a month he was thinking it the best thing that had ever happened to him that he got away from the island."

But Neilson could not get the story out of his head. Perhaps because he was sick and weakly, the radiant health of Red appealed to his imagination. Himself an ugly man, insignificant of appearance, he prized very highly comeliness in others. He had never been passionately in love, and certainly he had never been passionately loved. The mutual attraction of those two young things gave him a singular delight. It had the ineffable beauty of the Absolute. He went again to the little hut by the creek. He had a gift for languages and an energetic mind, accustomed to work, and he had already given much time to the study of the local tongue. Old habit was strong in him and he was gathering together material for a paper on the Samoan speech. The old crone who shared the hut with Sally invited him to come in and sit down. She gave him *hava* to drink and cigarettes to smoke. She was glad to have some one to chat with and while she talked he looked at Sally. She reminded him of the Psyche in the museum at Naples. Her features had the same clear purity of line, and though she had borne a child she had still a virginal aspect.

It was not till he had seen her two or three times that he induced her to speak. Then it was only to ask him if he had seen in Apia a man called Red. Two years had passed since his disappearance, but it was plain that she still thought of him incessantly.

It did not take Neilson long to discover that he was in love with her. It was only by an effort of will now that he prevented himself from going every day to the creek, and when he was not with Sally his thoughts were. At first, looking upon himself as a dying man, he asked only to look at her, and occasionally hear her speak, and his love gave him a wonderful happiness. He exulted in its purity. He wanted nothing from her but the opportunity to weave around her graceful person a web of beautiful fancies. But the open air, the equable temperature, the rest, the simple fare, began to have an unexpected effect on his health. His temperature did not soar at night to such alarming heights, he coughed less and began to put on weight; six months passed without his having a haemorrhage; and on a sudden he saw the possibility that he might live. He had studied his disease carefully, and the hope dawned upon him that with great care he might arrest its course. It exhilarated him to look forward once more to the future. He made plans. It was evident that any active life was out of the question, but he could live on the islands, and the small income he had, insufficient elsewhere, would be ample to keep him. He could grow coco-nuts; that would give him an occupation; and he would send for his books and a piano; but his quick mind saw that in all this he was merely trying to conceal from himself the desire which obsessed him.

He wanted Sally. He loved not only her beauty, but that dim soul which he divined behind her suffering eyes. He would intoxicate her with his passion. In the end he would make her forget. And in an ecstasy of surrender he fancied himself giving her too the happiness which he had

90

thought never to know again, but had now so miraculously achieved.

He asked her to live with him. She refused. He had expected that and did not let it depress him, for he was sure that sooner or later she would yield. His love was irresistible. He told the old woman of his wishes, and found somewhat to his surprise that she and the neighbours, long aware of them, were strongly urging Sally to accept his offer. After all, every native was glad to keep house for a white man, and Neilson according to the standards of the island was a rich one. The trader with whom he boarded went to her and told her not to be a fool; such an opportunity would not come again, and after so long she could not still believe that Red would ever return. The girl's resistance only increased Neilson's desire, and what had been a very pure love now became an agonizing passion. He was determined that nothing should stand in his way. He gave Sally no peace. At last, worn out by his persistence and the persuasions, by turns pleading and angry, of every one around her, she consented. But the day after when, exultant, he went to see her he found that in the night she had burnt down the hut in which she and Red had lived together. The old crone ran towards him full of angry abuse of Sally, but he waved her aside; it did not matter; they would build a bungalow on the place where the hut had stood. A European house would really be more convenient if he wanted to bring out a piano and a vast number of books.

And so the little wooden house was built in which he had now lived for many years, and Sally became his wife. But after the first few weeks of rapture, during which he was satisfied with what she gave him, he had known little happiness. She had yielded to him, through weariness, but she had only yielded what she set no store on. The soul which he had dimly glimpsed escaped him. He knew that she cared nothing for him. She still loved Red, and all the time she was waiting for his return. At a sign from him, Neilson knew that, notwithstanding his love, his tenderness, his sympathy, his generosity, she would leave him without a moment's hesitation. She would never give a thought to his distress. Anguish seized him and he battered at that impenetrable self of hers which sullenly resisted him. His love became bitter. He tried to melt her heart with kindness, but it remained as hard as before; he feigned indifference, but she did not notice it. Sometimes he lost his temper and abused her, and then she wept silently. Sometimes he thought she was nothing but a fraud, and that soul simply an invention of his own, and that he could not get into the sanctuary of her heart because there was no sanctuary there. His love became a prison from which he longed to escape, but he had not the strength merely to open the door— that was all it needed—and walk out into the open air. It was

91

torture and at last he became numb and hopeless. In the end the fire burnt itself out and, when he saw her eyes rest for an instant on the slender bridge, it was no longer rage that filled his heart but impatience. For many years now they had lived together bound by the ties of habit and convenience, and it was with a smile that he looked back on his old passion. She was an old woman, for the women on the islands age quickly, and if he had no love for her any more he had tolerance. She left him alone. He was contented with his piano and his books.

His thoughts led him to a desire for words.

"When I look back now and reflect on that brief passionate love of Red and Sally, I think that perhaps they should thank the ruthless fate that separated them when their love seemed still to be at its height. They suffered, but they suffered in beauty. They were spared the real tragedy of love."

"I don't know exactly as I get you," said the skipper.

"The tragedy of love is not death or separation. How long do you think it would have been before one or other of them ceased to care? Oh, it is dreadfully bitter to look at a woman whom you have loved with all your heart and soul, so that you felt you could not bear to let her out of your sight, and realize that you would not mind if you never saw her again. The tragedy of love is indifference."

But while he was speaking a very extraordinary thing happened. Though he had been addressing the skipper he had not been talking to him, he had been putting his thoughts into words for himself, and with his eyes fixed on the man in front of him he had not seen him. But now an image presented itself to them, an image not of the man he saw, but of another man. It was as though he were looking into one of those distorting mirrors that make you extraordinarily squat or outrageously elongate, but here exactly the opposite took place, and in the obese, ugly old man he caught the shadowy glimpse of a stripling. He gave him now a quick, searching scrutiny. Why had a haphazard stroll brought him just to this place? A sudden tremor of his heart made him slightly breathless. An absurd suspicion seized him. What had occurred to him was impossible, and yet it might be a fact.

"What is your name?" he asked abruptly.

The skipper's face puckered and he gave a cunning chuckle. He looked then malicious and horribly vulgar.

"It's such a damned long time since I heard it that I almost forget it myself. But for thirty years now in the islands they've always called me Red."

His huge form shook as he gave a low, almost silent laugh. It was obscene. Neilson shuddered. Red was hugely amused, and from his blood-shot eyes tears ran down his cheeks.

Neilson gave a gasp, for at that moment a woman came in. She was a native, a woman of somewhat commanding presence, stout without being corpulent, dark, for the natives grow darker with age, with very grey hair. She wore a black Mother Hubbard, and its thinness showed her heavy breasts. The moment had come.

She made an observation to Neilson about some household matter and he answered. He wondered if his voice sounded as unnatural to her as it did to himself. She gave the man who was sitting in the chair by the window an indifferent glance, and went out of the room. The moment had come and gone.

Neilson for a moment could not speak. He was strangely shaken. Then he said:

"I'd be very glad if you'd stay and have a bit of dinner with me. Pot luck."

"I don't think I will," said Red. "I must go after this fellow Gray. I'll give him his stuff and then I'll get away. I want to be back in Apia to-morrow."

"I'll send a boy along with you to show you the way."

"That'll be fine."

Red heaved himself out of his chair, while the Swede called one of the boys who worked on the plantation. He told him where the skipper wanted to go, and the boy stepped along the bridge. Red prepared to follow him.

"Don't fall in," said Neilson.

"Not on your life."

Neilson watched him make his way across and when he had disappeared among the coco-nuts he looked still. Then he sank heavily in his chair. Was that the man who had prevented him from being happy? Was that the man whom Sally had loved all these years and for whom she had waited so desperately? It was grotesque. A sudden fury seized him so that he had an instinct to spring up and smash everything around him. He had been cheated. They had seen each other at last and had not known it. He began to laugh, mirthlessly, and his laughter grew till it became hysterical. The Gods had played him a cruel trick. And he was old now.

At last Sally came in to tell him dinner was ready. He sat down in front of her and tried to eat. He wondered what she would say if he told her now that the fat old man sitting in the chair was the lover whom she remembered still with the passionate abandonment of her youth. Years ago, when he hated her because she made him so unhappy, he would have been glad to tell her. He wanted to hurt her then as she hurt him, because his hatred was only love. But now he did not care. He shrugged his shoulders listlessly.

"What did that man want?" she asked presently.

He did not answer at once. She was old too, a fat old native woman. He wondered why he had ever loved her so madly, He had laid at her feet all the treasures of his soul, and she had cared nothing for them. Waste, what waste! And now, when he looked at her, he felt only contempt. His patience was at last exhausted. He answered her question.

"He's the captain of a schooner. He's come from Apia."

"Yes."

"He brought me news from home. My eldest brother is very ill and I must go back."

"Will you be gone long?"

He shrugged his shoulders.

THE ETERNAL MOMENT[1]

E. M. Forster

I

"DO YOU see that mountain just behind Elizabeth's toque? A young man fell in love with me there so nicely twenty years ago. Bob your head a minute, would you, Elizabeth, kindly."

"Yes'm," said Elizabeth, falling forward on the box like an unstiffened doll. Colonel Leyland put on his pince-nez, and looked at the mountain where the young man had fallen in love.

"Was he a nice young man?" he asked, smiling though he lowered his voice a little on account of the maid.

"I never knew. But it is a very gratifying incident to remember at my age. Thank you, Elizabeth."

"May one ask who he was?"

"A porter," answered Miss Raby in her usual tones. "Not even a certi-

---

[1] From *The Eternal Moment and Other Stories*. Reprinted by permission of Messrs Sidgwick and Jackson, Ltd., London, and Messrs Harcourt, Brace and Company, Inc., New York (Copyright, 1928).

ficated guide. A male person who was hired to carry the luggage, which he dropped."

"Well! well! What did you do?"

"What a young lady should. Screamed and thanked him not to insult me. Ran, which was quite unnecessary, fell, sprained my ankle, screamed again; and he had to carry me half a mile, so penitent that I thought he would fling me over a precipice. In that state we reached a certain Mrs Harbottle, at sight of whom I burst into tears. But she was so much stupider than I was, that I recovered quickly."

"Of course you said it was all your own fault?"

"I trust I did," she said more seriously. "Mrs Harbottle, who, like most people, was always right, had warned me against him; we had had him for expeditions before."

"Ah! I see."

"I doubt whether you do. Hitherto he had known his place. But he was too cheap: he gave us more than our money's worth. That, as you know, is an ominous sign in a low-born person".

"But how was this your fault?"

"I encouraged him: I greatly preferred him to Mrs Harbottle. He was handsome and what I call agreeable; and he wore beautiful clothes. We lagged behind, and he picked me flowers. I held out my hand for them— instead of which he seized it and delivered a love oration which he had prepared out of *I promessi Sposi*."

"Ah! an Italian."

They were crossing the frontier at that moment. On the little bridge amid fir trees were two poles, one painted red, white, and green, and the other black and yellow.

"He lived in Italia Irredenta," said Miss Raby. "But we were to fly to the Kingdom. I wonder what would have happened if we had."

"Good Lord!" said Colonel Leyland, in sudden disgust. On the box Elizabeth trembled.

"But it might have been a most successful match."

She was in the habit of talking in this mildly conventional way. Colonel Leyland, who made allowances for her brilliancy, managed to exclaim: "Rather! yes, rather!"

She turned on him with: "Do you think I'm laughing at him?"

He looked a little bewildered, smiled, and did not reply. Their carriage was now crawling round the base of the notorious mountain. The road was built over the debris which had fallen and which still fell from its sides; and it had scarred the pine woods with devastating rivers of white stone. But farther up, Miss Raby remembered, on its gentler eastern slope, it possessed tranquil hollows, and flower-clad rocks, and a most tremendous view. She had not been quite as facetious as her companion supposed. The incident, certainly, had been ludicrous. But she was somehow able to laugh at it without laughing much at the actors or the stage.

"I had rather he made me a fool than that I thought he was one," she said, after a long pause.

"Here is the Custom House," said Colonel Leyland, changing the subject.

They had come to the land of *Ach* and *Ja*. Miss Raby sighed; for she loved the Latins, as every one must who is not pressed for time. But Colonel Leyland, a military man, respected Teutonia.

"They still talk Italian for seven miles," she said, comforting herself like a child.

"German is the coming language," answered Colonel Leyland. "All the important books on any subject are written in it."

"But all the books on any important subject are written in Italian. Elizabeth—tell me an important subject."

"Human nature, ma'am," said the maid, half shy, half impertinent.

"Elizabeth is a novelist, like her mistress," said Colonel Leyland. He turned away to look at the scenery, for he did not like being entangled in a mixed conversation. He noted that the farms were more prosperous, that begging had stopped, that the women were uglier and the men more rotund, that more nourishing food was being eaten outside the wayside inns.

"Colonel Leyland, shall we go to the Grand Hôtel des Alpes, to the Hôtel de Londres, to the Pension Liebig, to the Pension Atherley-Simon, to the Pension Belle Vue, to the Pension Old England, or to the Albergo Biscione?"

"I suppose you would prefer the Biscione."

"I really shouldn't mind the Grand Hôtel des Alpes. The Biscione people own both. I hear. They have become quite rich."

"You should have a splendid reception—if such people know what gratitude is."

For Miss Raby's novel, *The Eternal Moment*, which had made her reputation, had also made the reputation of Vorta.

"Oh, I was properly thanked. Signor Cantù wrote to me about three years after I had published. The letter struck me as a little pathetic, though it was very prosperous: I don't like transfiguring people's lives. I wonder whether they live in their old house or in the new one."

Colonel Leyland had come to Vorta to be with Miss Raby; but he was very willing that they should be in different hotels. She, indifferent to such subtleties, saw no reason why they should not stop under the same roof, just as she could not see why they should not travel in the same carriage. On the other hand, she hated anything smart. He had decided on the Grand Hôtel des Alpes, and she was drifting towards the Biscione, when the tiresome Elizabeth said, "My friend's lady is staying at the Alpes."

"Oh! if Elizabeth's friend is there that settles it: we'll all go."

"Very well'm," said Elizabeth, studiously avoiding even the appearance of gratitude. Colonel Leyland's face grew severe over the want of discipline.

"You spoil her," he murmured, when they had all descended to walk up a hill.

"There speaks the military man."

"Certainly I have had too much to do with Tommies to enter into what you call 'human relations.' A little sentimentality, and the whole army would go to pieces."

"I know; but the whole world isn't an army. So why should I pretend I'm an officer. You remind me of my Anglo-Indian friends, who were so shocked when I would be pleasant to some natives. They proved, quite conclusively, that it would never do for them, and have never seen that the proof didn't apply. The unlucky people here are always trying to lead the lucky; and it must be stopped. You've been unlucky: all your life you've had to command men, and exact prompt obedience and other unprofitable virtues. I'm lucky: I needn't do the same—and I won't."

"Don't then," he said smiling. "But take care that the world isn't an army after all. And take care, besides, that you aren't being unjust to the unlucky people: we're fairly kind to your beloved lower orders, for instance."

"Of course," she said dreamily, as if he had made her no concession. "It's becoming usual. But they see through it. They, like ourselves, know that only one thing in the world is worth having."

"Ah! yes," he sighed. "It's a commercial age."

"No!" exclaimed Miss Raby, so irritably that Elizabeth looked back to see what was wrong. "You are stupid. Kindness and money are both quite easy to part with. The only thing worth giving away is yourself. Did you ever give yourself away?"

"Frequently."

"I mean, did you ever, intentionally, make a fool of yourself before your inferiors?"

"Intentionally, never." He saw at last what she was driving at. It was her pleasure to pretend that such self-exposure was the only possible basis of true intercourse, the only gate in the spiritual barrier that divided class from class. One of her books had dealt with the subject; and very agreeable reading it made. "What about you?" he added playfully.

"I've never done it properly. Hitherto I've never felt a really big fool; but when I do, I hope I shall show it plainly."

"May I be there?"

"You might not like it," she replied. "I may feel it at any moment and in mixed company. Anything might set me off."

"Behold Vorta!" cried the driver, cutting short the sprightly conversation. He and Elizabeth and the carriage had reached the top of the hill. The black woods ceased; and they emerged into a valley whose sides were emerald lawns, rippling and doubling and merging each into each, yet always with an upward trend, so that it was 2000 feet to where the rock burst out of the grass and made great mountains, whose pinnacles were delicate in the purity of evening.

The driver, who had the gift of repetition, said: "Vorta! Vorta!"

Far up the valley was a large white village, tossing on undulating meadows like a ship in the sea, and at its prow, breasting a sharp incline, stood a majestic tower of new grey stone. As they looked at the tower it became vocal and spoke magnificently to the mountains, who replied.

They were again informed that this was Vorta, and that that was the new campanile—like the campanile of Venice, only finer—and that the sound was the sound of the campanile's new bell.

"Thank you; exactly," said Colonel Leyland while Miss Raby rejoiced that the village had made such use of its prosperity. She had feared to return to the place she had loved so well, lest she should find something new. It had never occurred to her that the new thing might be beautiful. The architect had indeed gone south for his inspiration, and the tower which stood among the mountains was akin to the tower which had once stood beside the lagoons. But the birthplace of the bell it was impossible to determine, for there is no nationality in sound.

They drove forward into the lovely scene, pleased and silent. Approving tourists took them for a well-matched couple. There was indeed nothing offensively literary in Miss Raby's kind angular face; and Colonel Leyland's profession had made him neat rather than aggressive. They did very well for a cultured and refined husband and wife, who had spent their lives admiring the beautiful things with which the world is filled·

As they approached, other churches, hitherto unnoticed, replied—tiny churches, ugly churches, churches painted pink with towers like pumpkins, churches hidden altogether in the glades of a wood or the folds of a meadow—till the evening air was full of little voices, with the great voice sing-ing in their midst. Only the English church, lately built in the Early English style, kept chaste silence.

The bells ceased, and all the little churches receded into darkness. Instead, there was a sound of dressing-gongs, and a vision of tired tourists hurrying back for dinner. A landau, with Pension Atherley-Simon upon it, was trotting to meet the diligence, which was just due. A lady was talking to her mother about an evening dress. Young men with rackets were talking to young men with alpenstocks. Then, across the darkness, a fiery finger wrote Grand Hôtel des Alpes.

"Behold the electric light!" said the driver, hearing his passengers exclaim.

Pension Belle Vue started out against a pinewood, and from the brink of the river the Hôtel de Londres replied. Pensions Liebig and Lorelei were announced in green and amber respectively. The Old-England appeared in scarlet. The illuminations covered a large area, for the best hotels stood outside the village, in elevated or romantic situations. This display took place every evening in the season, but only while the diligence arrived. As soon as the last tourist was suited, the lights went out, and the hotel-keepers, cursing or rejoicing, retired to their cigars.

"Horrible!" said Miss Raby.

"Horrible people!" said Colonel Leyland.

The Hôtel des Alpes was an enormous building, which, being made of wood, suggested a distended chalet. But this impression was corrected by a costly and magnificient view terrace, the squared stones of which were visible for miles, and from which, as from some great reservoir, asphalt paths trickled over the adjacent country. Their carriage, having ascended a private drive, drew up under a vaulted portico of pitch-pine, which opened on to this terrace on one side, and into the covered lounge on the other. There was a whirl of officials—men with gold braid, smarter men with more gold braid, men smarter still with no gold braid. Elizabeth assumed an arrogant air, and carried a small straw basket with difficulty. Colonel Leyland became every inch a soldier. Miss Raby, whom, in spite of long experience, a large hotel always flustered, was hurried into an expensive bedroom, and advised to dress herself immediately if she wished to partake of table d'hôte.

As she came up the staircase she had seen the dining-room filling with English and Americans and with rich hungry Germans. She liked company but to-night she was curiously depressed. She seemed to be confronted with an unpleasing vision, the outlines of which were still obscure.

"I will eat in my room," she told Elizabeth. "Go to your dinner: I'll do the unpacking."

She wandered round looking at the list of rules, the list of prices, the list of excursions, the red plush sofa, the jugs and basins on which was lithographed a view of the mountains. Where amid such splendour was there a place for Signor Cantù with his china-bowled pipe, and for Signora Cantù with her snuff-coloured shawl?

When the waiter at last brought up her dinner she asked after her host and hostess.

He replied, in cosmopolitan English, that they were both well.

"Do they live here, or at the Biscione?"

"Here, why yes. Only poor tourists go to the Biscione."

"Who lives there, then?"

"The mother of Signor Cantù. She is unconnected," he continued like one who has learnt a lesson, "she is unconnected absolutely with us. Fifteen years back, yes. But now, where is the Biscione? I beg you contradict if we are spoken about together."

Miss Raby said quietly: "I have made a mistake. Would you kindly give notice that I shall not want my room, and say that the luggage is to be taken, immediately, to the Biscione."

"Certainly! certainly!" said the waiter, who was well trained. He added with a vicious snort, "You will have to pay."

"Undoubtedly," said Miss Raby.

The elaborate machinery which had so recently sucked her in began to disgorge her. The trunks were carried down, the vehicle in which she had arrived was recalled. Elizabeth, white with indignation, appeared in the hall. She paid for beds in which they had not slept, and for food which they had never eaten. Amidst the whirl of gold-laced officials, who hoped even in that space of time to have established a claim to be tipped, she moved towards the door. The guests in the lounge observed her with amusement, concluding that she had found the hotel too dear.

"What is it? Whatever is it? Are you not comfortable?" Colonel Leyland in his evening dress ran after her.

"Not that; I've made a mistake. This hotel belongs to the son; I must go to the Biscione. He's quarrelled with the old people: I think the father's dead."

"But really—if you are comfortable here——"

"I must find out to-night whether it is true. And I must also"—her voice quivered—"find out whether it is my fault."

"How in the name of goodness——"

100

"I shall bear it if it is," she continued gently. "I am too old to be a tragedy queen as well as an evil genius."

"What does she mean? Whatever does she mean?" he murmured, as he watched the carriage lights descending the hill. "What harm has she done? What harm is there for that matter? Hotel-keepers always quarrel: it's no business of ours." He ate a good dinner in silence. Then his thoughts were turned by the arrival of his letters from the post office.

DEAREST EDWIN,

It is with greatest diffidence that I write you, and I know you will believe me when I say that I do not write from curiosity. I only require an answer to one plain question. Are you engaged to Miss Raby or no? Fashions have altered even since my young days. But, for all that an engagement is still an engagement, and should be announced at once, to save all parties discomfort. Though your health has broken down and you have abandoned your profession, you can still protect the family honour.

"Drivel!" exclaimed Colonel Leyland. Acquaintance with Miss Raby had made his sight keener. He recognized in this part of his sister's letter nothing but an automatic conventionality. He was no more moved by its perusal than she had been by its composition.

As for the maid whom the Bannons mentioned to me, she is not a chaperone—nothing but a sop to throw in the eyes of the world. I am not saying a word against Miss Raby, whose books we always read. Literary people are always unpractical, and we are confident that she does not know. Perhaps I do not think her the wife for you; but that is another matter.

My babes, who all send love (so does Lionel), are at present an unmitigated joy. One's only anxiety is for the future, when the crushing expenses of good education will have to be taken into account.

Your loving NELLY.

How could he explain the peculiar charm of relations between himself and Miss Raby? There had never been a word of marriage, and would probably never be a word of love. If, instead of seeing each other frequently, they should come to see each other always it would be as sage companions, familiar with life, not as egoistic lovers, craving for infinities of passion which they had no right to demand and no power to supply. Neither professed to be a virgin soul, or to be ignorant of the other's limitations and inconsistencies. They scarcely even made allowances for each other. Toleration implies reserve; and the greatest safeguard of unruffled intercourse is knowledge. Colonel Leyland had courage of no mean order: he cared little for the opinion of people whom he understood. Nelly and Lionel and their babes were welcome to be shocked or displeased. Miss Raby was an authoress, a kind of Radical; he a soldier, a kind of aristocrat. But the time for their activities was passing; he was ceasing to fight, she to write. They could pleasantly spend together their autumn. Nor might they prove the worst companions for a winter.

He was too delicate to admit, even to himself, the desirability of marrying two thousand a year. But it lent an unacknowledged perfume to his thoughts. He tore Nelly's letter into little pieces, and dropped them into the darkness out of the bedroom window.

"Funny lady!" he murmured, as he looked towards Vorta, trying to detect the campanile in the growing light of the moon. "Why have you gone to be uncomfortable? Why will you interfere in the quarrels of people who can't understand you, and whom you don't understand? How silly you are to think you've caused them. You think you've written a book which has spoilt the place and made the inhabitants corrupt and sordid. I know just how you think. So you will make yourself unhappy, and go about trying to put right what never was right. Funny lady!"

Close below him he could now see the white fragments of his sister's letter. In the valley the campanile appeared, rising out of wisps of silvery vapour.

"Dear lady!" he whispered, making towards the village a little movement with his hands.

II

Miss Raby's first novel, *The Eternal Moment*, was written round the idea that man does not live by time alone, that an evening gone may become like a thousand ages in the courts of heaven—the idea that was afterwards expounded more philosophically by Maeterlinck. She herself now declared that it was a tiresome, affected book, and that the title suggested the dentist's chair. But she had written it when she was feeling young and happy; and that, rather than maturity, is the hour in which to formulate a creed. As years pass, the conception may become more solid, but the desire and the power to impart to others are alike weakened. It did not altogether displease her that her earliest work had been her most ambitious.

By a strange fate, the book made a great sensation, especially in the unimaginative circles. Idle people interpreted it to mean that there was no harm in wasting time, vulgar people that there was no harm in being fickle, pious people interpreted it as an attack on morality. The authoress became well known in society, where her enthusiasm for the lower classes only lent her an additional charm. That very year Lady Anstey, Mrs Heriot, the Marquis of Bamburgh, and many others, penetrated to Vorta, where the scene of the book was laid.

They returned enthusiastic. Lady Anstey exhibited her water-colour drawings; Mrs Heriot, who photographed, wrote an article in *The Strand*; while *The Nineteenth Century* published a long description of the place by the Marquis of Bamburgh, entitled "The Modern Peasant, and his Relations with Roman Catholicism."

Thanks to these efforts, Vorta became a rising place, and people who liked being off the beaten track went there, and pointed out the way to others. Miss Raby, by a series of trivial accidents, had never returned to the village whose rise was so intimately connected with her own. She had heard from time to time of its progress. It had also been whispered that an inferior class of tourists was finding it out, and, fearing to find something spoilt, she had at last a certain diffidence in returning to scenes which had given her so much pleasure. Colonel Leyland persuaded her; he wanted a cool healthy spot for the summer, where he could read and talk and find walks suitable for an athletic invalid. Their friends laughed; their acquaintances gossiped; their relatives were furious. But he was courageous and she was indifferent. They had accomplished the expedition under the scanty ægis of Elizabeth.

Her arrival was saddening. It displeased her to see the great hotels in a great circle, standing away from the village where all life should have centred. Their illuminated titles, branded on the tranquil evening slopes, still danced in her eyes. And the monstrous Hôtel des Alpes haunted her like a nightmare. In her dreams she recalled the portico, the ostentatious lounge, the polished walnut bureau, the vast rack for the bedroom keys, the panoramic bedroom crockery, the uniform of the officials, and the smell of smart people—which is to some nostrils quite as depressing as the smell of poor ones. She was not enthusiastic over the progress of civilization, knowing by Eastern experiences that civilization rarely puts her best foot foremost, and is apt to make the barbarians immoral and vicious before her compensating qualities arrive. And here there was no question of progress: the world had more to learn from the village than the village from the world.

At the Biscione, indeed, she had found little change—only the pathos of a survival. The old landlord had died, and the old landlady was ill in bed, but the antique spirit had not yet departed. On the timbered front was still painted the dragon swallowing the child—the arms of the Visconti, from whom the Cantùs might well be descended. For there was something about the little hotel which compelled a sympathetic guest to believe, for a time at all events, in aristocracy. The great manner, only to be obtained without effort, ruled throughout. In each bedroom were three or four beautiful things—a little piece of silk tapestry, a fragment of rococo carving, some blue tiles, framed and hung upon the white-washed wall. There were pictures in the sitting-rooms and on the stairs—eighteenth century pictures in the style of Carlo Dolci and the Caracci—a blue robed Mater Dolorosa, a fluttering saint, a magnanimous Alexander with a receding chin. A debased style—so the superior person and the textbook say. Yet, at times, it may have more freshness and significance than a newly purchased Fra Angelico. Miss Raby, who had visited dukes in their residences without a perceptible tremor, felt herself blatant and modern when she entered the Albergo Biscione. The most trivial things—the sofa cushions, the table cloths, the cases for the pillows—though they might be made of poor material and be aesthetically incorrect, inspired her with reverence and humility. Through this cleanly, gracious dwelling there had once moved Signor Cantù with his china-bowled pipe, Signora Cantù in her snuff-coloured shawl, and Bartolommeo Cantù, now proprietor of the Grand Hôtel des Alpes.

She sat down to breakfast next morning in a mood which she tried to attribute to her bad night and her increasing age. Never, she thought, had she seen people more unattractive and more unworthy than her fellow guests. A black-browed woman was holding forth on patriotism and the duty of English tourists to present an undivided front to foreign nations. Another woman kept up a feeble, lament, like a dribbling tap which never gathers flow yet never quite ceases, complaining of the food, the charges, the noise, the clouds, the dust. She liked coming here herself, she said; but she hardly liked to recommend it to her friends: it was the kind of hotel one felt like that about. Males were rare, and in great demand; a young one was describing, amid fits of laughter, the steps he had taken to astonish the natives.

Miss Raby was sitting opposite the famous fresco, which formed the only decoration of the room. It had been discovered during some repairs; and, though the surface had been injured in places, the colours were still bright. Signora Cantù attributed it now to Titian, now to Giotto, and declared that no one could interpret its meaning; professors and artists had puzzled themselves in vain. This she said because it pleased her to say it; the meaning was perfectly clear, and had been frequently explained to her.

Those four figures were sibyls, holding prophecies of the Nativity. It was uncertain for what original reason they had been painted high up in the mountains, at the extreme boundary of Italian art. Now, at all events, they were an invaluable source of conversation; and many an acquaintance had been opened, and argument averted, by their timely presence on the wall.

"Aren't those saints cunning!" said an American lady, following Miss Raby's glance.

The lady's father muttered something about superstition. They were a lugubrious couple, lately returned from the Holy Land, where they had been cheated shamefully, and their attitude towards religion had suffered in consequence.

Miss Raby said, rather, sharply, that the saints were sibyls.

"But I don't recall sibyls," said the lady, "either in the N. T. or the O."

"Inventions of the priests to deceive the peasantry," said the father sadly. "Same as their churches; tinsel pretending to be gold, cotton pretending to be silk, stucco pretending to be marble; same as their processions, same as their—[he swore]—campaniles."

"My father," said the lady, bending forward, "he does suffer so from insomnia. Fancy a bell every morning at six!"

"Yes, ma'am; you profit. We've stopped it."

"Stopped the early bell ringing?" cried Miss Raby.

People looked up to see who she was. Some one whispered that she wrote.

He replied that he had come up all these feet for rest, and that if he did not get it he would move on to another centre. The English and American visitors had co-operated, and forced the hotel-keepers to take action. Now the priests rang a dinner bell, which was endurable. He believed that "corperation" would do anything: it had been the same with the peasants,

"How did the tourists interfere with the peasants?" asked Miss Raby, getting very hot, and trembling all over.

"We said the same; we had come for a rest, and we would have it. Every week they got drunk and sang till two. Is that a proper way to go on, anyhow?"

"I remember," said Miss Raby, "that some of them did get drunk. But I also remember how they sang."

"Quite so. Till two," he retorted.

They parted in mutual irritation. She left him holding forth on the necessity of a new universal religion of the open air. Over his head stood the four sibyls, gracious for all their clumsiness and crudity, each offering

105

a tablet inscribed with concise promise of redemption. If the old religions had indeed become insufficient for humanity, it did not seem probable that an adequate substitute would be produced in America.

It was too early to pay her promised visit to Signora Cantù. Nor was Elizabeth, who had been rude overnight and was now tiresomely penitent, a possible companion. There were a few tables outside the inn, at which some women sat, drinking beer. Pollarded chestnuts shaded them; and a low wooden balustrade fenced them off from the village street. On this balustrade Miss Raby perched, for it gave her a view of the campanile. A critical eye could discover plenty of faults in its architecture. But she looked at it all with increasing pleasure, in which was mingled a certain gratitude.

The German waitress came out and suggested very civilly that she should find a more comfortable seat. This was the place where the lower classes ate; would she not go to the drawing-room?

"Thank you, no; for how many years have you classified your guests according to their birth?"

"For many years. It was necessary," replied the admirable woman. She returned to the house full of meat and common sense, one of the many signs that the Teuton was gaining on the Latin in this debatable valley.

A grey-haired lady came out next, shading her eyes from the sun, and crackling *The Morning Post*. She glanced at Miss Raby pleasantly, blew her nose, apologized for speaking, and spoke as follows:

"This evening, I wonder if you know, there is a concert in aid of the stained-glass window for the English Church. Might I persuade you to take tickets? As has been said, it is so important that English people should have a rallying point, is it not?"

"Most important," said Miss Raby; "but I wish the rallying point could be in England."

The grey-haired lady smiled. Then she looked puzzled. Then she realized that she had been insulted, and crackling *The Morning Post*, departed.

"I have been rude," thought Miss Raby dejectedly. "Rude to a lady as silly and as grey-haired as myself. This is not a day on which I ought to talk to people."

Her life had been successful, and on the whole happy. She was unaccustomed to that mood, which is termed depressed, but which certainly gives visions of wider, if greyer, horizons. That morning her outlook altered. She walked through the village, scarcely noticing the mountains by which it was still surrounded, or the unaltered radiance of its sun. But she was fully conscious of something new; of the indefinable corruption which is produced by the passage of a large number of people.

Even at that time the air was heavy with meat and drink, to which was added dust and tobacco smoke and the smell of tired horses. Carriages were huddled against the church, and underneath the campanile a woman guarding a stack of bicycles. The season had been bad for climbing; and groups of young men in smart Norfolk suits were idling up and down, waiting to be hired as guides. Two large inexpensive hotels stood opposite the post office; and in front of them innumerable little tables surged out into the street. Here, from an early hour in the morning, eating had gone on, and would continue till a late hour at night. The customers, chiefly German, refreshed themselves with cries and with laughter, passing their arms round the waists of their wives. Then, rising heavily, they departed in single file towards some view-point, whereon a red flag indicated the possibility of another meal. The whole population was employed, even down to the little girls, who worried the guests to buy picture-postcards and edelweiss. Vorta had taken to the tourist trade.

A village must have some trade; and this village had always been full of virility and power. Obscure and happy, its splendid energies had found employment in wresting a livelihood out of the earth, whence had come a certain dignity, and kindliness, and love for other men. Civilization did not relax these energies, but it had diverted them; and all the precious qualities, which might have helped to heal the world, had been destroyed. The family affection, the affection for the commune, the sane pastoral virtues—all had perished while the campanile which was to embody them was being built. No villain had done this thing: it was the work of ladies and gentlemen who were good and rich and often clever—who, if they thought about the matter at all, thought that they were conferring a benefit, moral as well as commercial, on any place in which they chose to stop.

Never before had Miss Raby been conscious of such universal misdoing. She returned to the Biscione shattered and exhausted, remembering that terrible text in which there is much semblance of justice: "But woe to him through whom the offence cometh."

Signora Cantù, somewhat over-excited, was lying in a dark room on the ground floor. The walls were bare; for all the beautiful things were in the rooms of her guests whom she loved as a good queen might love her subjects—and the walls were dirty also, for this was Signora Cantù's own room. But no palace had so fair a ceiling; for from the wooden beams were suspended a whole dowry of copper vessels—pails, cauldrons, water pots, of every colour from lustrous black to the palest pink. It pleased the old lady to look up at these tokens of prosperity. An American lady had lately departed without them, more puzzled than angry.

The two women had little in common; for Signora Cantù was an inflexible aristocrat. Had she been a great lady of the great century, she would have gone speedily to the guillotine, and Miss Raby would have howled approval. Now, with her scanty hair in curl-papers and the snuff-coloured shawl spread over her, she entertained the distinguished authoress with accounts of other distinguished people who had stopped, and might again stop, at the Biscione. At first her tone was dignified. But before long she proceeded to village news, and a certain bitterness began to show itself. She chronicled deaths with a kind of melancholy pride. Being old herself, she liked to meditate on the fairness of Fate, which had not spared her contemporaries, and often had not spared her juniors. Miss Raby was unaccustomed to extract such consolation. She too was growing old, but it would have pleased her better if others could have remained young. She remembered few of these people well, but deaths were symbolical, just as the death of a flower may symbolize the passing of all the spring.

Signora Cantù then went on to her own misfortunes, beginning with an account of a landslip, which had destroyed her little farm. A landslip, in that valley, never hurried. Under the green coat of turf water would collect, just as an abscess is formed under the skin. There would be a lump on the sloping meadow, then the lump would break and discharge a slowly moving stream of mud and stones. Then the whole area seemed to be corrupted; on every side the grass cracked and doubled into fantastic creases, the trees grew awry, the barns and cottages collapsed, all the beauty turned gradually to indistinguishable pulp, which slid downwards till it was washed away by some stream.

From the farm they proceeded to other grievances, over which Miss Raby became almost too depressed to sympathize. It was a bad season; the guests did not understand the ways of the hotel; the servants did not understand the guests; she was told she ought to have a concierge. But what was the good of a concierge?

"I have no idea." said Miss Raby, feeling that no concierge would ever restore the fortunes of the Biscione.

"They say he would meet the diligence and entrap the new arrivals. What pleasure should I have from guests I entrapped?"

"The other hotels do it," said Miss Raby, sadly.

"Exactly. Every day a man comes down from the Alpes."

There was an awkward silence. Hitherto they had avoided mentioning that name.

"He takes them all," she continued, in a burst of passion. "My son takes all my guests. He has taken all the English nobility, and the best Americans, and all my old Milanese friends. He slanders me up and down the valley, saying that the drains are bad. The hotel-keepers will not recommend me; they send on their guests to him, because he pays them five per cent. for every one they send. He pays the drivers, he pays the porters, he pays the guides. He pays the band, so that it hardly ever plays down in the village. He even pays the little children to say my drains are bad. He and his wife and his concierge, they mean to ruin me, they would like to see me die."

"Don't—don't say these things, Signora Cantù." Miss Raby began to walk about the room, speaking, as was her habit, what was true rather than what was intelligible. "Try not to be so angry with your son. You don't know what he had to contend with. You don't know who led him into it. Some one else may be to blame. And whoever it may be—you will remember them in your prayes."

"Of course I am a Christian!" exclaimed the angry old lady. "But he will not ruin me. I seem poor, but he has borrowed—too much. That hotel will fail!"

"And perhaps," continued Miss Raby, "there is not much wickedness in the world. Most of the evil we see is the result of little faults—of stupidity or vanity."

"And I even know who led him into it—his wife, and the man who is now his concierge."

"This habit of talking, of self expression—it seems so pleasant and necessary—yet it does harm——"

They were both interrupted by an uproar in the street. Miss Raby opened the window; and a cloud of dust, heavy with petrol, entered. A passing motor-car had twitched over a table. Much beer had been spilt, and a little blood.

Signora Cantù sighed peevishly at the noise. Her ill-temper had exhausted her, and she lay motionless, with closed eyes. Over her head two copper vases clinked gently in the sudden gust of wind. Miss Raby had been on the point of a great dramatic confession, of a touching appeal for forgiveness. Her words were ready. But she looked at those closed eyes, that suffering enfeebled frame, and she knew that she had no right to claim the luxury of pardon.

It seemed to her that with this interview her life had ended. She had done all that was possible. She had done much evil. It only remained for her to fold her hands and to wait, till her ugliness and her incompetence went the way of beauty and strength. Before her eyes there arose the pleasant face of Colonel Leyland, with whom she might harmlessly conclude her days. He would not be stimulating, but it did not seem desirable that she should be stimulated. It would be better if her faculties did close, if the senseless activity of her brain and her tongue were gradually numbed. For the first time in her life, she was tempted to become old.

Signora Cantù was still speaking of her son's wife and concierge; of the vulgarity of the former and the ingratitude of the latter, whom she had been kind to long ago, when he first wandered up from Italy, an obscure boy. Now he had sided against her. Such was the reward of charity.

"And what is his name?" asked Miss Raby absently.

"Feo Ginori," she replied. "You would not remember him. He used to carry——"

From the new campanile there burst a flood of sound to which the copper vessels vibrated responsively. Miss Raby lifted her hands, not to her ears but to her eyes. In her enfeebled state, the throbbing note of the bell had the curious effect of blood returning into frozen veins.

"I remember that man perfectly," she said at last; "and I shall see him this afternoon."

III

Miss Raby and Elizabeth were seated together in the lounge of the Hôtel des Alpes. They had walked up from the Biscione to see Colonel Leyland. But he, apparently, had walked down there to see them, and the only thing to do was to wait, and to justify the wait be ordering some refreshment. So Miss Raby had afternoon tea, while Elizabeth behaved like a perfect lady over an ice, occasionally turning the spoon upside down in the mouth when she saw that no one was looking. The underwaiters were clearing cups and glasses off the marble-topped tables, and the gold-laced officials were rearranging the wicker chairs into seductive groups of three and two. Here and there the visitors lingered among their crumbs, and the Russian Prince had fallen asleep in a prominent and ungraceful position. But most people had started for a little walk before dinner, or had gone to play tennis, or had taken a book under a tree. The weather was delightful, and the sun had so far declined that its light had become spiritualized, suggesting new substance as well as new colour in everything on which it fell. From her seat Miss Raby could see the great precipices under which they had passed the day before; and beyond those precipices she could see Italy—the Val d'Aprile, the Val Senese, and the mountains she had named "The Beasts of the South." All day those mountains were insignificant—distant chips of white or grey stone. But the evening sun transfigured them, and they would sit up like purple bears against the southern sky.

"It is a sin you should not be out, Elizabeth. Find your friend if you can, and make her go with you. If you see Colonel Leyland, tell him I am here."

"Is that all, ma'am?" Elizabeth was fond of her eccentric mistress, and her heart had been softened by the ice. She saw that Miss Raby did not look well. Possibly the course of love was running roughly. And indeed gentlemen must be treated with tact, especially when both parties are getting on.

"Don't give pennies to the children: that is the only other thing."

The guests had disappeared, and the number of officials visibly diminished. From the hall behind came the genteel sniggers of those two most vile creatures, a young lady behind the bureau and a young man in a frock coat who shows new arrivals to their rooms. Some of the porters joined them, standing at a suitable distance. At last only Miss Raby, the Russian Prince, and the concierge were left in the lounge.

The concierge was a competent European of forty or so, who spoke all languages fluently, and some well. He was still active, and had evidently once been muscular. But either his life or his time of life had been unkind to his figure: in a few years he would certainly be fat. His face was less easy to decipher. He was engaged in the unquestioning performance of his duty, and that is not a moment for self revelation. He opened the windows, he filled the match-boxes, he flicked the little tables with a duster, always keeping an eye on the door in case anyone arrived without luggage, or left without paying. He touched an electric bell, and a waiter flew up and cleared away Miss Raby's tea things. He touched another bell, and sent an underling to tidy up some fragments of paper which had fallen out of a bedroom widnow. Then "Excuse me, madam!" and he had picked up Miss Raby's handkerchief with a slight bow. He seemed to bear her no grudge for her abrupt departure of the preceding evening. Perhaps it was into his hand that she had dropped a tip. Perhaps he did not remember she had been there.

The gesture with which he returned the handkerchief troubled her with vague memories. Before she could thank him he was back in the doorway, standing sideways, so that the slight curve of his stomach was outlined against the view. He was speaking to a youth of athletic but melancholy appearance, who was fidgeting in the portico without. "I told you the percentage," she heard. "If you had agreed to it, I would have

111

recommended you. Now it is too late. I have enough guides." Our generosity benefits more people than we suppose. We tip the cabman, and something goes to the man who whistled for him. We tip the man who lights up the stalactite grotto with magnesium wire, and something goes to the boatman who brought us there. We tip the waiter in the restaurant, and something goes off the waiter's wages. A vast machinery, whose very existence we seldom realize, promotes the distribution of our wealth. When the concierge returned, Miss Raby asked: "And what is the percentage?"

She asked with definite intention of disconcerting him, not because she was unkind, but because she wished to discover what qualities, if any, lurked beneath that civil efficient exterior. And the spirit of her inquiry was sentimental rather than scientific.

With an educated man she would have succeeded. In attempting to reply to her question, he would have revealed something. But the concierge had no reason to pay even lip service to logic. He replied: "Yes, madam! this is perfect weather, both for our visitors and for the hay," and hurried to help a bishop, who was selecting a picture postcard.

Miss Raby, instead of moralizing on the inferior resources of the lower classes, acknowledged a defeat. She watched the man spreading out the postcards, helpful yet not obtrusive, alert yet deferential. She watched him make the bishop buy more than he wanted. This was the man who had talked of love to her upon the mountain. But hitherto he had only revealed his identity by chance gestures bequeathed to him at birth. Intercourse with the gentle classes had required new qualities—civility, omniscience, imperturbability. It was the old answer: the gentle classes were responsible for him. It is inevitable, as well as desirable, that we should bear each other's burdens.

It was absurd to blame Feo for his worldliness—for his essential vulgarity. He had not made himself. It was even absurd to regret his transformation from an athlete: his greasy stoutness, his big black kisscurl, his waxed moustache, his chin which was dividing and propagating itself like some primitive form of life. In England, nearly twenty years before, she had altered his figure as well as his character. He was one of the products of *The Eternal Moment*.

A great tenderness overcame her—the sadness of an unskilful demiurge, who makes a world and beholds that it is bad. She desired to ask pardon of her creatures, even though they were too poorly formed to grant it. The longing to confess, which she had suppressed that morning beside the bed of Signora Cantù, broke out again with the violence of a physical desire. Whe the bishop had gone she renewed the conversation, though on different lines, saying: "Yes, it is beautiful weather. I have just been enjoying a walk up from the Biscione. I am stopping there!"

He saw that she was willing to talk, and replied pleasantly: "The Biscione must be a very nice hotel: many people speak well of it. The fresco is very beautiful." He was too shrewd to object to a little charity.

"What lots of new hotels there are!" She lowered her voice in order not to rouse the Prince, whose presence weighed on her curiously.

"Oh, madam! I should indeed think so. When I was a lad—excuse me one moment."

An American girl, who was new to the country, came up with her hand full of coins, and asked him hopelessly "whatever they were worth." He explained, and gave her change: Miss Raby was not sure that he gave her right change.

"When I was a lad——" He was again interrupted, to speed two parting guests. One of them tipped him; he said "Thank you.". The other did not tip him; he said "Thank you," all the same but not in the same way. Obviously he had as yet no recollections of Miss Raby.

"When I was a lad, Vorta was a poor little place."

"But a pleasant place?"

"Very pleasant, madam."

"Kouf!" said the Russian Prince, suddenly waking up and startling them both. He clapped on a felt hat, and departed at full speed for a constitutional. Miss Raby and Feo were left together.

It was then she ceased to hesitate, and determined to remind him that they had met before. All day she had sought for a spark of life, and it might be summoned by pointing to that other fire which she had discerned, far back in the travelled distance, high up in the mountains of youth. What he would do, if he also discerned it, she did not know; but she hoped that he would become alive, that he at all events would escape the general doom which she had prepared for the place and the people. And what she would, do, during their joint contemplation, she did not even consider.

"This is my second visit," she said boldly. "I stayed at the Biscione twenty years ago."

He showed the first sign of emotion: *that* reference to the Biscione annoyed him.

"I was told I should find you up here," continued Miss Raby. "I remember you very well. You used to take us over the passes."

She watched his face intently. She did not expect it to relax into an expansive smile. "Ah!" he said, taking off his peaked cap, "I remember you perfectly, madam. What a pleasure, if I may say so, to meet you again!"

"I am pleased, too," said the lady, looking at him doubtfully.

"You and another lady, madam, was it not? Miss——"

"Mrs Harbottle."

"To be sure; I carried your luggage. I often remember your kindness."

She looked up. He was standing near an open window, and the whole of fairyland stretched behind him. Her sanity forsook her, and she said gently: "Will you misunderstand me, if I say I that never forgotten your kindness either?"

He replied. "The kindness was yours, madam; I only did my duty."

"Duty?" she cried; "what about duty?"

"You and Miss Harbottle were such generous ladies. I well remember how grateful I was: you always paid me above the tariff fare——"

Then she realized that he had forgotten everything; forgotten her, forgotten what had happened, even forgotten what he was like when he was young.

"Stop being polite," she said coldly. "You were not polite when I saw you last."

"I am very sorry," he exclaimed, suddenly alarmed.

"Turn round. Look at the mountains."

"Yes, yes." His fishy eyes blinked nervously. He fiddled with his watch chain which lay in a furrow of his waistcoat. He ran away to warn some poorly dressed children off the view-terrace. When he returned she still insisted.

"I must tell you," she said, in calm, businesslike tones. "Look at that great mountain, round which the road goes south. Look half-way up on its eastern side—where the flowers are. It was there that you once gave yourself away."

He gaped at her in horror. He remembered. He was inexpressibly shocked.

It was at that moment Colonel Leyland returned. She walked up to him, saying, "This is the man I spoke of yesterday."

"Good afternoon; what man?" said Colonel Leyland fussily. He saw that she was flushed, and concluded that some one had been rude to her. Since their relations were somewhat anomalous, he was all the more particular that she should be treated with respect.

"The man who fell in love with me when I was young."

"It is untrue!" cried the wretched Feo, seeing at once the trap that had been laid for him. "The lady imagined it. I swear, sir—I meant nothing. I was a lad. It was before I learnt behaviour. I had even forgotten it. She reminded me. She has disturbed me."

"Good Lord!" said Colonel Leyland. "Good Lord!"

"I shall lose my place, sir; and I have a wife and children. I shall be ruined."

"Sufficient!" cried Colonel Leyland. "Whatever Miss Raby's intentions may be, she does not intend to ruin you."

"You have misunderstood me, Feo," said Miss Raby gently.

"How unlucky we have been missing each other," said Colonel Leyland, in trembling tones that were meant to be nonchalant. "Shall we go a little walk before dinner? I hope that you are stopping."

She did not attend. She was watching Feo. His alarm had subsided; and he revealed a new emotion, even less agreeable to her. His shoulders straightened, he developed an irresistible smile, and when he saw that she was looking and that Colonel Leyland was not, he winked at her.

It was a ghastly sight, perhaps the most hopelessly depressing of all the things she had seen at Vorta. But its effect on her was memorable. It evoked a complete vision of that same man as he had been twenty years before. She could see him to the smallest detail of his clothes or his hair, the flowers in his hand, the graze on his wrist, the heavy bundle that he had loosed from his back, so that he might speak as a freeman. She could hear his voice, neither insolent nor diffident, never threatening, never apologizing, urging her first in the studied phrases he had learnt from books, the, as his passion grew, becoming incoherent, crying that she must believe him, that she must love him in return, that she must fly with him to Italy where they would live for ever, always happy, always young. She had cried out then, as a young lady should, and had thanked him not to insult her. And now, in her middle age, she cried out again, because the sudden shock and the contrast had worked a revelation. "Don't think I'm in love with you now!" she cried.

For she realized that only now was she not in love with him: that the incident upon the mountain had been one of the great moments of her life—perhaps the greatest, certainly the most enduring: that she had drawn unacknowledged power and inspiration from it, just as trees draw vigour from a subterranean spring, Never again could she think of it as a half-humorous episode in her development. There was more reality in it than in all the years of success and varied achievement which had followed, and which it had rendered possible. For all her correct behaviour and lady-like display, she had been in love with Feo, and she had never loved so greatly again. A presumptuous boy had taken her to the gates of heaven; and, though she would not enter with him, the eternal remembrance of the vision had made life seem endurable and good.

Colonel Leyland, by her side, babbled respectabilities, trying to pass the situation off as normal. He was saving her, for he liked her very much, and it pained him when she was foolish. But her last remark to Feo had frightened him; and he began to feel that he must save himself. They were no longer alone. The bureau lady and the young gentleman were listening breathlessly, and the porters were tittering at the discomfiture of their superior. A French lady had spead amongst the guests the agreeable news that an Englishman had surprised his wife making love to the concierge. On the terrace outside, a mother waved away her daughters. The bishop was preparing, very leisurely, for a walk.

But Miss Raby was oblivious. "How little I know!" she said. "I never knew till now that I had loved him and that it was a mere chance—a little catch, a kink—that I never told him so."

It was her habit to speak out; and there was no present passion to disturb or prevent her. She was still detached, looking back at a fire upon the mountains, marvelling at its increased radiance, but too far off to feel its heat. And by speaking out she believed, pathetically enough, that she was making herself intelligible. Her remark seemed inexpressibly coarse to Colonel Leyland.

"But these beautiful thoughts are a poor business, are they not?" she continued, addressing Feo, who was losing his gallant air, and becoming bewildered. "They're hardly enough to grow old on. I think I would give all my imagination, all my skill with words, if I could recapture one crude fact, if I could replace one single person whom I have broken."

"Quite so, madam," he responded, with downcast eyes.

"If only I could find some one here who would understand me, to whom I could confess, I think I should be happier. I have done so much harm in Vorta, dear Feo——"

Feo raised his eyes. Colonel Leyland struck his stick on the parquetry floor.

"——and at last I thought I would speak to you, in case you understood me. I remembered that you had once been very gracious to me—yes, gracious: there is no other word. But I have harmed you also: how could you understand?"

"Madam, I understand perfectly," said the concierge, who had recovered a little, and was determined to end the distressing scene, in which his reputation was endangered, and his vanity aroused only to be rebuffed. "It is you who are mistaken. You have done me no harm at all. You have benefited me."

"Precisely," said Colonel Leyland. "That is the conclusion of the whole matter. Miss Raby has been the making of Vorta."

116

"Exactly, sir. After the lady's book, foreigners come, hotels are built, we all grow richer. When I first came here, I was a common ignorant porter who carried luggage over the passes; I worked, I found opportunities, I was pleasing to the visitors—and now!" He checked himself suddenly. "Of course I am still but a poor man. My wife and children——"

"Children!" cried Miss Raby, suddenly seeing a path of salvation. "What children have you?"

"Three dear little boys," he replied, without enthusiasm.

"How old is the youngest?"

"Madam, five."

"Let me have that child," she said impressively, "and I will bring him up. He shall live among rich people. He shall see that they are not the vile creatures he supposes, always clamouring for respect and deference and trying to buy them with money. Rich people are good: they are capable of sympathy and love: they are fond of the truth; and when they are with each other they are clever. Your boy shall learn this, and he shall try to teach it to you. And when he grows up, if God is good to him he shall teach the rich: he shall teach them not to be stupid to the poor. I have tried myself, and people buy my books and say that they are good, and smile and lay them down. But I know this: so long as the stupidity exists, not only our charities and missions and schools, but the whole of our civilization, are vain."

It was painful for Colonel Leyland to listen to such phrases. He made one more effort to rescue Miss Raby. "*Je vous prie de ne pas—*" he began gruffly, and then stopped, for he remembered that the concierge must know French. But Feo was not attending, nor, of course had he attended to the lady's prophecies. He was wondering if he could persuade his wife to give up the little boy, and, if he did, how much they dare ask from Miss Raby without repulsing her.

"That will be my pardon," she continued, "if out of the place where I have done so much evil I bring some good. I am tired of memories, though they have been very beautiful. Now, Feo, I want you to give me something else: a living boy. I shall always puzzle you; and I cannot help it. I have changed so much since we met, and I have changed you also. We are both new people. Remember that; for I want to ask you one question before we part, and I cannot see why you shouldn't answer it. Feo! I want you to attend."

"I beg your pardon, madam," said the concierge, rousing himself from his calculations. "Is there anything I can do for you?"

"Answer 'yes' or 'no'; that day when you said you were in love with me—was it true?"

It was doubtful whether he could have answered, whether he had now any opinion about that day at all. But he did not make the attempt. He saw again that he was menaced by an ugly, withered, elderly woman, who was trying to destroy his reputation and his domestic peace. He shrank towards Colonel Leyland, and faltered: "Madam, you must excuse me, but I had rather you did not see my wife; she is so sharp. You are most kind about my little boy; but, madam, no, she would never permit it."

"You have insulted a lady!" shouted the colonel, and made a chivalrous movement of attack. From the hall behind came exclamations of horror and expectancy. Some one ran for the manager.

Miss Raby interposed, saying, "He will never think me respectable." She looked at the dishevelled Feo, fat, perspiring, and unattractive, and smiled sadly at her own stupidity, not at his. It was useless to speak to him again; her talk had scared away his competence and his civility, and scarcely anything was left. He was hardly more human than a frightened rabbit. "Poor man," she murmured, "I have only vexed him. But I wish he would have given me the boy. And I wish he would have answered my question, if only out of pity. He does not know the sort of thing that keeps me alive." She was looking at Colonel Leyland, and so discovered that he too was discomposed. It was her peculiarity that she could only attend to the person she was speaking with, and forgot the personality of the listeners. "I have been vexing you as well: I am very silly."

"It is a little late to think about me," said Colonel Leyland grimly.

She remembered their conversation of yesterday, and understood him at once. But for him she had no careful explanation, no tender pity. Here was a man who was well born and well educated, who had all those things called advantages, who imagined himself full of insight and cultivation and knowledge of mankind. And he had proved himself to be at the exact spiritual level of the man who had no advantages, who was poor and had been made vulgar, whose early virtue had been destroyed by circumstance, whose manliness and simplicity had perished in serving the rich. If Colonel Leyland also believed that she was now in love with Feo, she would not exert herself to undeceive him. Nor indeed would she have found it possible.

From the darkening valley there rose up the first strong singing note of the campanile, and she turned from the men towards it with a motion of love. But that day was not to close without the frustration of every hope. The sound inspired Feo to make conversation and, as the mountains reverberated, he said: "Is it not unfortunate, sir? A gentleman went to

118

see our fine new tower this morning and he believes that the land is slipping from underneath, and that it will fall. Of course it will not harm us
up here."

His speech was successful. The stormy scene came to an abrupt and
placid conclusion. Before they had realized it, she had taken up her *Baedeker*
and left them, with no tragic gesture. In that moment of final failure, there
had been vouchsafed to her a vision of herself, and she saw that she had
lived worthily. She was conscious of a triumph over experience and
earthly facts, a triumph magnificent, cold, hardly human, whose existence
no one but herself would ever surmise. From the view-terrace she looked
down on the perishing and perishable beauty of the valley, and, though she
loved it no less, it seemed to be infinitely distant, like a valley in a star.
At that moment, if kind voices had called her from the hotel, she would not
have returned. "I suppose this is old age," she thought. "It's not so very
dreadful."

No one did call her. Colonel Leyland would have liked to do so; for
he knew she must be unhappy. But she had hurt him too much; she had
exposed her thoughts and desires to a man of another class. Not only she,
but he himself and all their eqhals, were degraded by it. She had discovered
their nakedness to the alien.

People came in to dress for dinner and for the concert. From the hall
there pressed out a stream of excited servants filling the lounge as an
operatic chorus fills the stage, and announcing the approach of the manager. It was impossible to pretend that nothing had happened. The scandal
would be immense, and must be diminished as it best might.

Much as Colonel Leyland disliked touching people he took Feo by the
arm, and then quickly raised his finger to his forehead.

"Exactly, sir," whispered the conceirge. "Of course we understand—
Oh, thank you, sir, thank you very much: thank you very much indeed!'

THE FOX[1]

D. H. Lawrence

THE two girls were usually known by their surnames, Banford and March.
They had taken the farm together, intending to work it all by themselves:
that is, they were going to rear chickens, make a living by poultry, and

---

[1] From *The Ladybird.* Reprinted by permission of the executors, Messrs Martin Secker,
Ltd., London, and Messrs A. A. Knopf. Inc., New York.

add to this by keeping a cow, and raising one or two young beasts. Unfortunately, things did not turn out well.

Banford was a small, thin, delicate thing with spectacles. She, however, was the principal investor, for March had little or no money. Banford's father, who was a tradesman in Islington, gave his daughter the start, for her health's sake, and because he loved her, and because it did not look as if she would marry. March was more robust. She had learned carpentry and joinery at the evening classes in Islington. She would be the man about the place. They had, moreover, Banford's old grandfather living with them at the start. He had been a farmer. But unfortunately the old man died after he had been at Bailey Farm for a year. Then the two girls were left alone.

They were neither of them young: that is, they were near thirty. But they certainly were not old. They set out quite gallantly with their enterprise. They had numbers of chickens, black Leghorns and white Leghorns, Plymouths and Wyandottes; also some ducks; also two heifers in the fields. One heifer, unfortunately, refused absolutely to stay in the Bailey Farm closes. No matter how March made up the fences, the heifer was out, wild in the woods, or trespassing on the neighbouring pasture, and March and Banford were away, flying after her, with more haste than success. So this heifer they sold in despair. Then, just before the other beast was expecting her first calf, the old man died, and the girls, afraid of the coming event, sold her in a panic, and limited their attentions to fowl and ducks.

In spite of a little chagrin, it was a relief to have no more cattle on hand. Life was not made merely to be slaved away. Both girls agreed in this. The fowls were quite enough trouble. March had set up her carpenter's bench at the end of the open shed. Here she worked, making coops and doors and other appurtenances. The fowls were housed in the bigger building, which had served as barn and cowshed in old days. They had a beautiful home, and should have been perfectly content. Indeed, they looked well enough. But the girls were disgusted at their tendency to strange illnesses, at their exacting way of life, and at their refusal, obstinate refusal to lay eggs.

March did most of the outdoor work. When she was out and about, in her puttees and breeches, her belted coat and her loose cap, she looked almost like some graceful, loose-balanced young man, for her shoulders were straight, and her movements easy and confident, even tinged with a little indifference, or irony. But her face was not a man's face, ever. The wisps of her crisp dark hair blew about her as she stooped, her eyes were big and wide and dark, when she looked up again, strange, startled, shy, and sardonic at once. Her mouth, too, was almost pinched as if in pain and irony. There was something odd and unexplained about her. She would stand balanced on one hip, looking at the fowls pattering about in the obnoxious fine mud of the sloping yard, and calling to her favourite white hen, which came in answer to her name. But there was an almost satirical flicker in March's big dark eyes as she looked at her three-toed flock pottering about under her gaze, and the same slight dangerous satire in her voice as she spoke to the favoured Patty, who pecked at March's boot by way of friendly demonstration.

Fowls did not flourish at Bailey Farm, in spite of all that March did for them. When she provided hot food for them in the morning, according to rule, she noticed that it made them heavy and dozy for hours. She expected to see them lean against the pillars of the shed in their languid processes of digestion. And she knew quite well that they ought to be busily scratching and foraging about, if they were to come to any good. So she decided to give them their hot food at night, and let them sleep on it. Which she did. But it made no difference.

War conditions, again, were very unfavourable to poultry keeping. Food was scarce and bad. And when the Daylight Saving Bill was passed, the fowls obstinately refused to go to bed as usual, about nine o'clock in the summer time. That was late enough, indeed, for there was no peace till they were shut up and asleep. Now they cheerfully walked around without so much as glancing at the barn, until ten o'clock or later. Both Banford and March disbelieved in living for work alone. They wanted to read or take a cycle-ride in the evening, or perhaps March wished to paint curvilinear swans on porcelain, with green background, or else make a marvellous fire-screen by processes of elaborate cabinet work. For she was a creature of odd whims and unsatisfied tendencies. But from all these things she was prevented by the stupid fowls.

One evil there was greater than any other. Bailey Farm was a little homestead, with ancient wooden barn and low-gabled farm-house, lying just one field removed from the edge of the wood. Since the war the fox was a demon. He carried off the hens under the very noses of March and Banford. Banford would start and stare through her big spectacles with all her eyes, as another squawk and flutter took place at her heels. Too late! Another white Leghorn gone. It was disheartening.

They did what they could to remedy it. When it became permitted to shoot foxes, they stood sentinel with their guns, the two of them, at the favoured hours. But it was no good. The fox was too quick for them. So another year passed, and another, and they were living on their losses as Banford said. They let their farm-house one summer, and retired to live in a railway-carriage that was deposited as a sort of out-house in a corner of the field. This amused them, and helped their finances. None the less, things looked dark.

Although they were usually the best of friends, because Banford, though nervous and delicate, was a warm, generous soul, and March, though so odd and absent in herself, had a strange magnanimity, yet, in the long solitude, they were apt to become a little irritable with one another, tired of one another. March had four-fifths of the work to do, and though she did not mind, there seemed no relief, and it made her eyes flash curiously sometimes. Then Banford, feeling more nerve-worn than ever, would become despondent, and March would speak sharply to her. They seemed to be losing ground, somehow, losing hope as the months went by. There alone in the fields by the wood, with the wide country stretching hollow and dim to the round hills of the White Horse, in the far distance, they seemed to have to live too much off themselves. There was nothing to keep them up-and no hope.

The fox really exasperated them both. As soon as they had let the fowls out, in the early summer mornings, they had to take their guns and keep guard: and then again, as soon as evening began to mellow, they must go once more. And he was so sly. He slid along in the deep grass; he was difficult as a serpent to see. And he seemed to circumvent the girls deliberately. Once or twice March had caught sight of the white tip of his brush, or the ruddy shadow of him in the deep grass, and she had let fire at him. But he made no account of this.

One evening March was standing with her back to the sunset, her gun under her arm, her hair pushed under her cap. She was half watching, half musing. It was her constant state. Her eyes were keen and observant, but her inner mind took no notice of what she saw. She was always lapsing into this odd, rapt state, her mouth rather screwed up. It was a question whether she was there, actually conscious present, or not.

The trees on the wood-edge were a darkish, brownish green in the full light—for it was the end of August. Beyond, the naked, copper-like shafts and limbs of the pine-trees shone in the air. Nearer the rough grass, with its long brownish stalks all agleam, was full of light. The fowls were round about—the ducks were still swimming on the pond under the pine-trees. March looked at it all, saw it all, and did not see it. She heard Banford speaking to the fowls in the distance—and she did not hear. What was she thinking about? Heaven knows. Her consciousness was, as it were, held back.

She lowered her eyes, and suddenly saw the fox. He was looking up at her. His chin was pressed down, and his eyes were looking up. They met her eyes. And he knew her. She was spell-bound—she knew he knew her. So he looked into her eyes, and her soul failed her. He knew her, he was not daunted.

She struggled, confusedly she came to herself, and saw him making off, with slow leaps over some fallen boughs, slow, impudent jumps. Then he glanced over his shoulder, and ran smoothly away. She saw his brush held smooth like a feather, she saw his white buttocks twinkle. And he was gone, softly, soft as the wind.

She put her gun to her shoulder, but even then pursed her mouth, knowing it was nonsense to pretend to fire. So she began to walk slowly after him, in the direction he had gone, slowly, pertinaciously. She expected to find him. In her heart she was determined to find him. What she would do when she saw him again she did not consider. But she was determined to find him. So she walked abstractedly about on the edge of the wood, with wide, vivid dark eyes, and a faint flush in her cheeks. She did not think. In strange mindlessness she walked hither and thither.

At last she became aware that Banford was calling her. She made an effort of attention, turned, and gave some sort of screaming call in answer. Then again she was striding off towards the homestead. The red sun was setting, the fowls were retiring towards their roost. She watched them, white creatures, black creatures, gathering to the barn. She watched them spellbound, without seeing them. But her automatic intelligence told her when it was time to shut the door.

She went indoors to supper, which Banford had set on the table. Banford chatted easily. March seemed to listen, in her distant, manly way. She answered a brief word now and then. But all the time she was as if spellbound. And as soon as supper was over, she rose again to go out, without saying why.

She took her gun again and went to look for the fox. For he had lifted his eyes upon her, and his knowing look seemed to have entered her brain. She did not so much think of him: she was possessed by him. She saw his dark, shrewd, unabashed eye looking into her, knowing her. She felt him invisibly master her spirit. She knew the way he lowered his chin as he looked up, she knew his muzzle, the golden brown, and the greyish white. And again, she saw him glance over his shoulder at her, half inviting, half contemptuous and cunning. So she went, with her great startled eyes glowing, her gun under her arm, along the wood edge. Meanwhile the night fell, and a great moon rose above the pine-trees. And again Banford was calling.

123

So she went indoors. She was silent and busy. She examined her gun, and cleaned it, musing abstractedly by the lamplight. Then she went out again, under the great moon, to see if everything was right. When she saw the dark crests of the pine-trees against the blood-red sky, again her heart beat to the fox, the fox.. She wanted to follow him, with her gun.

It was some days before she mentioned the affair to Banford. Then suddenly one evening she said:

"The fox was right at my feet on Saturday night."

"Where?" said Banford, her eyes opening behind her spectacles.

"When I stood just above the pond."

"Did you fire?" cried Banford.

"No, I didn't."

"Why not?"

"Why, I was too much surprised, I suppose."

It was the same old, slow, laconic way of speech March always had. Banford stared at her friend for a few moments.

"You saw him?" she cried.

"Oh yes! He was looking up at me, cool as anything."

"I tell you," cried Banford—"the cheek! They're not afraid of us, Nellie."

"Oh no," said March.

"Pity you didn't get a shot at him," said Banford.

"Isn't it a pity! I've been looking for him ever since. But I don't suppose he'll come so near again."

"I don't suppose he will," said Banford.

And she proceeded to forget about it, except that she was more indignant than ever at the impudence of the beggar. March also was not conscious that she thought of the fox. But whenever she fell into her half-musing, when she was half rapt and half intelligently aware of what passed under her vision, then it was the fox which somehow dominated her unconsciousness, possessed the blank half of her musing. And so it was for weeks, and months. No matter whether she had been climbing the trees for the apples, or beating down the last of the damsons, or whether she had been digging out the ditch from the duck-pond, or clearing out the barn, when she had finished, or when she straightened herself, and pushed the wisps of hair away again from her forehead, and pursed up her mouth again in an odd, screwed fashion, much too old for her years, there was sure to come over her mind the old spell of the fox, as it came when he was looking at her. It was as if she could smell him at these times. And it always recurred, at unexpected moments, just as she was going to sleep at night, or just as she was pouring the water into the tea-pot to make

124

tea—it was the fox, it came over her like a spell.

So the months passed. She still looked for him unconsciously when she went towards the wood. He had become a settled effect in her spirit, a state permanently established, not continuous, but always recurring. She did not know what she felt or thought: only the state came over her, as when he looked at her.

The months passed, the dark evenings came, heavy, dark November, when March went about in high boots, ankle deep in mud, when the night began to fall at four o'clock, and the day never properly dawned. Both girls dreaded these times. They dreaded the almost continuous darkness that enveloped them on their desolate little farm near the wood. Banford was physically afraid. She was afraid of tramps, afraid lest some one should come prowling round. March was not so much afraid as uncomfortable, and disturbed. She felt discomfort and gloom in all her physique.

Usually the two girls had tea in the sitting-room. March lighted a fire at dusk, and put on the wood she had chopped and sawed during the day. Then the long evening was in front, dark, sodden, black outside, lonely and rather oppressive inside, a little dismal. March was content not to talk, but Banford could not keep still. Merely listening to the wind in the pines outside, or the drip of water, was too much for her.

One evening the girls had washed up the tea-things in the kitchen, and March had put on her house-shoes, and taken up a roll of crochet-work, which she worked at slowly from time to time. So she lapsed into silence. Banford stared at the red fire, which, being of wood, needed constant attention. She was afraid to begin to read too early, because her eyes would not bear any strain. So she sat staring at the fire, listening to the distant sounds, sound of cattle lowing, of a dull, heavy moist wind, of the rattle of the evening train on the little railway not far off. She was almost fascinated by the red glow of the fire.

Suddenly both girls started, and lifted their heads. They heard a foot-step—distinctly a footstep. Banford recoiled in fear. March stood listening. Then rapidly she approached the door that led into the kitchen. At the same time they heard the footsteps approach the back door. They waited a second. The back door opened softly. Banford gave a loud cry. A man's voice said softly:

"Hello!"

March recoiled, and took a gun from a corner.

"What do you want?" she cried, in a sharp voice.

Again the soft, softly-vibrating man's voice said:

"Hello! What's wrong?"

"I shall shoot!" cried March. "What do you want?"

"Why, what's wrong? What's wrong?" came the soft, wondering, rather scared voice: and a young soldier, with his heavy kit on his back, advanced into the dim light.

"Why," he said, "who lives here then?"

"We live here," said March. "What do you want?"

"Oh!" came the long, melodious, wonder-note from the young soldier. "Doesn't William Grenfel live here then?"

"No—you know he doesn't."

"Do I? Do I? I don't, you see. He *did* live here, because he was my grandfather, and I lived here myself five years ago. What's become of him then?"

The young man—or youth, for he would not be more than twenty—now advanced and stood in the inner doorway. March, already under the influence of his strange, soft, modulated voice, stared at him spellbound. He had a ruddy, roundish face, with fairish hair, rather long, flattened to his forehead with sweat. His eyes were blue, and very bright and sharp. On his cheeks, on the fresh ruddy skin were fine, fair hairs, like a down, but sharper. It gave him a slightly glistening look. Having his heavy sack on his shoulders, he stooped, thrusting his head forward. His hat was loose in one hand. He stared brightly, very keenly from girl to girl, particularly at March, who stood pale, with great dilated eyes, in her belted coat and puttees, her hair knotted in a big crisp knot behind. She still had the gun in her hand. Behind her, Banford, clinnging to the sofa-arm, was shrinking away, with half-averted heart.

"I thought my grandfather still lived here? I wonder if he's dead."

"We've been here for three years," said Banford, who was beginning to recover her wits, seeing something boyish in the round head with its rather long sweaty hair.

"Three years! You don't say so! And you don't know who was here before you?"

"I know it was an old man, who lived by himself."

"Ay! Yes, that's him! And what became of him, then?"

"He died. I know he died."

"Ay! He's dead then!"

The youth stared at them without changing colour or expression. If he had any expression, besides a slight baffled look of wonder, it was one of sharp curiosity concerning the two girls; sharp, impersonal curiosity, the curiosity of that round young head.

But to March he was the fox. Whether it was the thrusting forward

126

of his head, or the glisten of fine whitish hairs on the ruddy cheek-bones, or the bright, keen eyes, that can never be said: but the boy was to her the fox, and she could not see him otherwise.

"How is it you didn't know if your grandfather was alive or dead?" asked Banford, recovering her natural sharpness.

"Ay, that's it," replied the softly-breathing youth. "You see I joined up in Canada, and I hadn't heard for three or four years. I ran away to Canada."

"And now have you just come from France?"

"Well—from Salonika really."

There was a pause, nobody knowing quite what to say.

"So you've nowhere to go now?" said Banford rather lamely.

"Oh, I know some people in the village. Anyhow, I can go to the Swan."

"You came on the train, I suppose. Would you like to sit down a bit?"

"Well—I don't mind."

He gave an odd little groan as he swung off his kit. Banford looked at March.

"Put the gun down," she said. "We'll make a cup of tea."

"Ay," said the youth. "We've seen enough of rifles."

He sat down rather tired on the sofa, leaning forward.

March rcovered her presence of mind, and went into the kitchen. There she heard the soft young voice musing:

"Well, to think I should come back and find it like this!" He did not seem sad, not at all—only rather interestedly surprised.

"And what a difference in the place, eh?" he continued, looking round the room.

"You see a difference, do you?" said Banford.

"Yes—don't I?"

His eyes were unnaturally clear and bright, though it was the brightness of abundant health.

March was busy in the kitchen preparing another meal. It was about seven o'clock. All the time, while she was active, she was attending to the youth in the sitting-room, not so much listening to what he said as feeling the soft run of his voice. She primmed up her mouth tighter and tighter, puckering as if it were sewed, in her effort to keep her will uppermost. Yet her large eyes dilated and glowed in spite of her; she lost herself. Rapidly and carelessly she prepared the meal, cutting large chunks of bread and margarine—for there was no butter. She racked her brain to think of something else to put on the tray—she had only bread, margarine, and jam, and the larder was bare. Unable to conjure anything up, she went into the sitting-room with her tray.

127

She did not want to be noticed. Above all, she did not want him to look at her. But when she came in, and was busy setting the table just behind him, he pulled himself up from his sprawling, and turned and looked over his shoulder. She became pale and wan.

The youth watched her as she bent over the table, looked at her slim, well-shaped legs, at the belted coat dropping around her thighs, at the knot of dark hair, and his curiosity, vivid and widely alert, was again arrested by her.

The lamp was shaded with a dark-green shade, so that the light was thrown downwards and the upper half of the room was dim. His face moved bright under the light, but March loomed shadowy in the distance.

She turned around, but kept her eyes sideways, dropping and lifting her dark lashes. Her mouth unpuckered as she said to Banford:

"Will you pour out?"

Then she went into the kitchen again.

"Have your tea where you are, will you?" said Banford to the youth—"unless you'd rather come to the table."

"Well," said he, "I'm nice and comfortable here, aren't I? I will have it here, if you don't mind."

"There's nothing but bread and jam," she said. And she put his plate on a stool by him. She was very happy now, waiting on him. For she loved company. And now she was no more afraid of him than if he were her own younger brother. He was such a boy.

"Nellie," he called. "I've poured you a cup out."

March appeared in the doorway, took her cup, and sat down in a corner, as far from the light as possible. She was very sensitive in her knees. Having no skirts to cover them, and being forced to sit with them boldly exposed, she suffered. She shrank and shrank, trying not to be seen. And the youth, sprawling low on the couch, glanced up at her, with long steady, penetrating looks, till she was almost ready to disappear. Yet she held her cup balanced, she drank her tea, screwed up her mouth, and held her head averted. Her desire to be invisible was so strong that it quite baffled the youth. He felt he could not see her distinctly. She seemed like a shadow within the shadow. And ever his eyes came back to her, searching, unremitting, with unconscious fixed attention.

Meanwhile he was talking softly and smoothly to Banford, who loved nothing so much as gossip, and who was full of perky interest, like a bird. Also he ate largely and quickly and voraciously, so that March had to cut more chunks of bread and margarine, for the roughness of which Banford apologised.

"Oh well," said March, suddenly speaking, "if there's no butter to put on it, it's no good trying to make dainty pieces."

Again the youth watched her, and he laughed, with a sudden, quick laugh, showing his teeth and wrinkling his nose.

"It isn't, is it?" he answered, in his soft, near voice.

It appeared he was Cornish by birth and upbringing. When he was twelve years old he had come to Bailey Farm with his grandfather, with whom he had never agreed very well. So he had run away to Canada, and worked far away in the West. Now he was here—and that was the end of it.

He was very curious about the girls, to find out exactly what they were doing. His questions were those of a farm youth; acute, practical, a little mocking. He was very much amused by their attitude to their losses: for they were amusing on the score of heifers and fowls.

"Oh well," broke in March, "we don't believe in living for nothing but work."

"Don't you?" he answered. And again the quick young laugh came over his face. He kept his eyes steadily on the obscure woman in the corner.

"But what will you do when you've used up all your capital?" he said.

"Oh, I don't know," answered March laconically. "Hire ourselves out for land-workers, I suppose."

"Yes, but there won't be any demand for women land-workers now the War's over," said the youth.

"Oh, we'll see. We shall hold on a bit longer yet," said March, with a plangent, half-sad, half-ironical infference.

"There wants a man about the place," said the youth softly.

Banford burst out laughing.

"Take care what you say," she interrupted. "We consider ourselves quite efficient."

"Oh," came March's slow plangent voice, "it isn't a case of efficiency, I'm afraid. If you're going to do farming you must be at it from morning till night, and you might as well be a beast yourself."

"Yes, that's it," said the youth. "You aren't willing to put yourselves into it."

"We aren't," said March, "and we know it."

"We want some of our time for ourselves," said Banford.

The youth threw himself back on the sofa, his face tight with laughter, and laughed silently but thoroughly. The calm scorn of the girls tickled him tremendously.

"Yes," he said, "but why did you begin then?"

"Oh," said March, "we had a better opinion of the nature of fowls then than we have now."

"Of Nature altogether, I'm afraid," said Banford. "Don't talk to me about Nature."

Again the face of the youth tightened with delighted laughter.

"You haven't a very high opinion of fowls and cattle, have you?" he said.

"Oh no—quite a low one," said March.

He laughed out.

"Neither fowls nor heifers," said Banford, "nor goats not the weather."

The youth broke into a sharp yap of laughter, delighted. The girls began to laugh too, March turning aside her face and wrinkling her mouth in amusement.

"Oh, well," said Banford, "we don't mind, do we, Nellie?"

"No," said March, "we don't mind."

The youth was very pleased. He had eaten and drunk his fill. Banford began to question him. His name was Henry Grenfel—no, he was not called Harry, always Henry. He countinued to answer with courteous simplicity, grave and charming. March, who was not included, cast long, slow glances at him from her recess, as he sat there on the sofa, his hands clasping his knees, his face under the lamp bright and alert, turned to Banford. She became almost peaceful at last. He was identified with the fox—and he was here in full presence. There in the shadow of her corner she gave herself up to a warm, relaxed peace, almost like sleep, accepting the spell that was on her. But she wished to remain hidden. She was only fully at peace whilst he forgot her, talking to Banford. Hidden in the shadow of the corner, she need not any more be divided in herself, trying to keep up two planes of consciousness. She could at last lapse into the odour of the fox.

For the youth, sitting before the fire in his uniform, sent a faint but distinct odour into the room, indefinable, but something like a wild creature. March no longer tried to reserve herself from it. She was still and soft in her corner like a passive creature in its cave.

At last the talk dwindled. The youth relaxed his clasp of his knees, pulled himself together a little, and looked round. Again he became aware of the silent, half-invisible woman in the corner.

"Well," he said unwillingly, "I suppose I'd better be going, or they'll be in bed at the Swan."

"I'm afraid they're in bed anyhow," said Banford, "They've all got this influenza."

"Have they!" he exclaimed. And he pondered. "Well," he continued, "I shall find a place somewhere."

"I'd say you could stay here, only—" Banford began. He turned and watched her, holding his head forward.

"What?" he asked.

"Oh, well," she said, "propriety, I suppose." She was rather confused.

"It wouldn't be improper, would it?" he said, gently surprised.

"Not as far as we're concerned," said Banford.

"And not as far as *I'm* concerned," he said, with grave naiveté. "After all, it's my own home, in a way."

Banford smiled at this.

"It's what the village will have to say," she said.

There was a moment's blank pause.

"What do you say, Nellie?" asked Banford.

"I don't mind," said March, in her distinct tone. "The village doesn't matter to me, anyhow."

"No," said the youth, quick and soft. "Why should it? I mean, what should they say?"

"Oh, well," came March's pangent, laconic voice, "they'll easily find something to say. But it makes no difference what they say. We can look after ourselves."

"Of course you can," said the youth.

"Well then, stop if you like," said Banford. "The spare room is quite ready."

His face shone with pleasure.

"If you're quite sure it isn't troubling you too much," he said, with that soft courtesy which distinguished him.

"Oh, it's no trouble," they both said.

He looked, smiling with delight, from one to another.

"It's awfully nice not to have to turn out again, isn't it?" he said gratefully.

"I suppose it is," said Banford.

March disappeared to attend to the room. Banford was as pleased and thoughtful as if she had her own young brother home from France. It gave her just the same kind of gratification to attend on him, to get out the bath for him, and everything. Her natural warmth and kindliness had now an outlet. And the youth luxuriated in her sisterly attention. But it puzzled him slightly to know that March was silently working for him too. She was so curiously silent and obliterated. It seemed to him he had not really seen her. He felt he should not know her if he met her in the road.

That night March dreamed vividly. She dreamed she heard a singing outside which she could not understand, a singing that roamed round the house, in the fields, and in the darkness. It moved her so that she felt she must weep. She went out, and suddenly she knew it was the fox singing. He was very yellow and bright, like corn. She went nearer to him but he ran away and ceased singing. He seemed near, and she wanted to touch him. She stretched out her hand, but suddenly he bit her wrist, and at the same instant, as she drew back, the fox, turning round to bound away, whisked his brush across her face, and it seemed his brush was on fire, for it seared and burned her mouth with a great pain. She awoke with the pain of it, and lay trembling as if she were really seared.

In the morning, however, she only remembered it as a distant memory. She arose and was busy preparing the house and attending to the fowls. Banford flew into the village on her bicycle to try and buy food. She was a hospitable soul. But alas in the year 1918 there was not much food to buy. The youth came downstairs in his shirt-sleeves. He was young and fresh, but he walked with his head thrust forward, so that his shoulders seemed raised and round, as if he had a slight curvature of the spine. It must have been only a manner of bearing himself, for he was young and vigorous. He washed himself and went outside, whilst the women were preparing breakfast.

He saw everything, and examined everything. His curiosity was quick and insatiable. He compared the state of things with that which he remembered before, and cast over in his mind the effect of the changes. He watched the fowls and the ducks, to see their condition; he noticed the flight of wood-pigeons overhead: they were very numerous; he saw the few apples high up, which March had not been able to reach; he remarked that they had borrowed a draw-pump, presumably to empty the big soft-water cistern which was on the north side of the house.

"It's a funny, dilapidated old place," he said to the girls, as he sat at breakfast.

His eyes were wise and childish, with thinking about things. He did not say much, but ate largely. March kept her face averted. She, too, in the early morning could not be aware of him, though something about the glint of his khaki reminded her of the brilliance of her dream-fox.

During the day the girls went about their business. In the morning he attended to the guns, shot a rabbit and a wild duck that was flying high towards the wood. That was a great addition to the empty larder. The girls felt that already he had earned his keep. He said nothing about leaving, however. In the afternoon he went to the village. He came back at tea-time.

He had the same alert, forward-reaching look on his roundish face. He hung his hat on a peg with a little swinging gesture. He was thinking about something.

"Well," he said to the girls, as he sat at table. "What am I going to do?"

"How do you mean—what are you going to do?" said Banford.

"Where am I going to find a place in the village to stay?" he said.

"I don't know," said Banford. "Where do you think of staying?"

"Well,"—he hesitated—"at the Swan the've got this flu, and at the Plough and Harrow they've got the soldiers who are collecting the hay for the army: besides, in the private houses, there's ten men and a corporal altogether billeted in the village, they tell me. I'm not sure where I could get a bed."

He left the matter to them. He was rather calm about it. March sat with her elbows on the table, her two hands supporting her chin, looking at him unconsciously. Suddenly he lifted his clouded blue eyes, and unthinking looked straight into March's eyes. He was startled as well as she. He, too, recoiled a little. March felt the same sly, taunting, knowing spark leap out of his eyes, as he turned his head aside, and fall into her soul, as it had fallen from the dark eyes of the fox. She pursed her mouth as if in pain, as if asleep too.

"Well, I don't know," Banford was saying. She seemed reluctant, as if she were afraid of being imposed upon. She looked at March. But, with her weak, troubled sight, she only saw the usual semi-abstraction on her friend's face. "Why don't you speak, Nellie?" she said.

But March was wide-eyed and silent, and the youth, as if fascinated, was watching her without moving his eyes.

"Go on—answer something," said Banford. And March turned her head slightly aside, as if coming to consciousness, or trying to come to consciousness.

"What do you expect me to say?" she asked automatically.

"Say what you think," said Banford.

"It's all the same to me," said March.

And again there was silence. A pointed light seemed to be on the boy's eyes, penetrating like a needle.

"So it is to me," said Banford. "You can stop on here if you like."

A smile like a cunning little flame came over his face, suddenly and involuntarily. He dropped his head quickly to hide it, and remained with his head dropped, his face hidden.

"You can stop on here if you like. You can please yourself, Henry," Banford concluded.

Still he did not reply, but remained with his head dropped. Then he lifted his face. It was bright with a curious light, as if exultant, and his eyes were strangely clear as he watched March. She turned her face aside, her mouth suffering as if wounded, and her consciousness dim.

Banford became a little puzzled. She watched the steady, pellucid gaze of the youth's eyes as he looked at March, with the invisible smile gleaming on his face. She did not know how he was smiling, for no feature moved. It seemed only in the gleam, almost the glitter of the fine hairs on his cheeks. Then he looked with quite a changed look at Banford.

"I'm sure," he said in his soft, courteous voice, "you're awfully good. You're too good. You don't want to be bothered with me, I'm sure."

"Cut a bit of bread, Nellie," said Banford uneasily, adding: "It's no bother, if you like to stay. It's like having my own brother here for a few days. He's a boy like you are."

"That's awfully kind of you," the lad repeated. "I should like to stay ever so much, if you're sure I'm not a trouble to you."

"No, of course you're no trouble. I tell you, it is a pleasure to have somebody in the house besides ourselves," said warm-hearted Banford.

"But Miss March?" he said in his soft voice, looking at her.

"Oh; it's quite all right as far as I'm concerned," said March vaguely. His face beamed, and he almost rubbed his hands with pleasure.

"Well then," he said. "I should love it, if you'd let me pay my board and help with the work."

"You've no need to talk about board," said Banford.

One or two days went by, and the youth stayed on at the farm. Banford was quite charmed by him. He was so soft and courteous in speech, not wanting to say much himself, preferring to hear what she had to say, and to laugh in his quick, half-mocking way. He helped readily with the work —but not too much. He loved to be out alone with the gun in his hands, to watch, to see. For his sharp-eyed, impersonal curiosity was insatiable, and he was most free when he was quite alone, half-hidden, watching.

Particularly he watched March. She was a strange character to him. Her figure, like a graceful young man's, piqued him. Her dark eyes made something rise in his soul, with a curious elate excitement, when he looked into them, an excitement he was afraid to let be seen, it was so keen and secret. And then her odd, shrewd speech made him laugh outright. He felt he must go further, he was inevitably impelled. But he put away the thought of her and went off towards the wood's edge with the gun.

The dusk was falling as he came home, and with the dusk, a fine, late November rain. He saw the fire-light leaping in the window of the sitting-room, a leaping light in the little cluster of the dark buildings. And he thought to himself it would be a good thing to have this place for his own. And then the thought entered him shewdly: why not marry March? He stood still in the middle of the field for some moments, the dead rabbit hanging still in his hand, arrested by his thought. His mind waited in amazement—it seemed to calculate—and then he smiled curiously to himself in acquiescence. Why not? Why not indeed? It was a food idea. What if it was rather ridiculous? What did it matter? What if she was older than he? It didn't matter. When he thought of her dark, startled, vulnerable eyes he smiled subtly to himself. He was older than she, really. He was master of her.

He scarcely admitted his intention even to himself. He kept it as a secret even from himself. It was all too uncertain as yet. He would have to see how things went. Yes, he would have to see how things went. If he wasn't careful, she would just simply mock at the idea. He knew, sly and subtle as he was, that if he went to her plainly and said: "Miss March, I love you and want you to marry me," her inevitable answer would be: "Get out. I don't want any of that tomfoolery." This was her attitude to men and their "tomfoolery". If he was not careful she would turn round on him with her savage, sardonic ridicule, and dismiss him from the farm and from her own mind for ever. He would have to go gently. He would have to catch her as you catch a deer or a woodcock when you go out shooting. It's no good walking out into the forest and saying to the deer: "Please fall to my gun." No, it is a slow, subtle battle. When you really go out to get a deer, you gather yourself together, you coil yourself inside yourself, and you advance secretly, before dawn, into the mountains. It is not so much what you do, when you go out hunting, as how you feel. You have to be subtle and cunning and absolutely fatally ready. It becomes like a fate. Your own fate overtakes and determines the fate of the deer you are hunting. First of all, even before you come in sight of your quarry, there is a strange battle, like mesmerism. Your own soul, as a hunter, has gone out to fasten on the soul of the deer, even before you see any deer. And the soul of the deer fights to escape. Even before the deer has any wind of you, it is so. It is a subtle, profound battle of wills which takes place in the invisible. And it is a battle never finished till your bullet goes home. When you are *really* worked up to the true pitch, and you come at last into range, you don't then aim as you do when you are firing at a bottle. It is your own *will* which carries the bullet into the heart of your quarry. The bullet's flight home is a sheer projection of your own fate into the fate of the deer. It happens like a supreme wish, a supreme act of volition, not as a dodge of cleverness.

He was a huntsman in spirit, not a farmer, and not a soldier stuck in a regiment. And it was as a young hunter that he wanted to bring down March as his quarry, to make her his wife. So he gathered himself subtly together, seemed to withdraw into a kind of invisibility. He was not quite sure how he would go on. And March was suspicious as a hare. So he remained in appearance just the nice, odd stranger-youth, staying for a fortnight on the place.

He had been sawing logs for the fire in the afternoon. Darkness came very early. It was still a cold, raw mist. It was getting almost too dark to see. A pile of short sawed logs lay beside the trestle. March came to carry them indoors, or into the shed, as he was busy sawing the last log. He was working in his shirt-sleeves, and did not notice her approach; she came unwillingly, as if shy. He saw her stooping to the bright-ended logs, and he stopped sawing. A fire like lightning flew down his legs in the nerves.

"March?" he said, in his quiet, young voice.

She looked up from the logs she was piling.

"Yes!" she said.

He looked down on her in the dusk. He could see her not too distinctly.

"I wanted to ask you something," he said.

"Did you? What was it?" she said. Already the fright was in her voice. But she was too much mistress of herself.

"Why"— his voice seemed to draw out soft and subtle, it penetrated her nerves—"why, what do you think it is?"

She stood up, placed her hands on her hips, and stood looking at him transfixed, without answering. Again he burned with a sudden power.

"Well," he said and his voice was so soft it seemed rather like a subtle touch, like the merest touch of a cat's paw, a feeling rather than a sound. "Well—I wanted to ask you to marry me."

March felt rather than heard him. She was trying in vain to turn aside her face. A great relaxation seemed to have come over her. She stood silent, her head slightly on one side. He seemed to be bending towards her, invisibly smiling. It seemed to her fine sparks came out of him.

Then very suddenly she said:

"Don't try any of your tomfoolery on me."

A quiver went over his nerves. He had missed. He waited a moment to collect himself again. Then he said, putting all the strange softness into his voice, as if he were imperceptibly stroking her:

"Why, it's not tomfoolery. It's not tomfoolery. I mean it. I mean it. What makes you disbelieve me?"

He sounded hurt. And his voice had such a curious power over her;

making her feel loose and relaxed. She struggled somewhere for her own power. She felt for a moment that she was lost—lost—lost. The word seemed to rock in her as if she were dying. Suddenly again she spoke.

"You don't know what you're talking about," she said, in a brief and transient stroke of scorn. "What nonsense! I'm old enough to be your mother."

"Yes, I do know what I'm talking about. Yes, I do," he persisted softly, as if he were producing his voice in her blood. "I know quite well what I'm talking about. You're not old enough to be my mother. That isn't true. And what does it matter even if it was. You can marry me whatever age we are. What is age to me? And what is age to you? Age is nothing."

A swoon went over her as he concluded. He spoke rapidly—in the rapid Cornish fashion—and his voice seemed to sound in her somewhere where she was helpless against it. "Age is nothing!" The soft, heavy insistence of it made her sway dimly out there in the darkness. She could not answer.

A great exultance leaped like fire over his limbs. He felt he had won.

"I want to marry you, you see. Why shouldn't I?" he proceeded, soft and rapid. He waited for her to answer. In the dusk he saw her almost phosphorescent. Her eye-lids were dropped, her face half-averted and unconscious. She seemed to be in his power. But he waited, watchful. He dared not yet touch her.

"Say then," he said, "say then you'll marry me. Say—say!" He was softly insistent.

"What?" she asked, faint, from a distance, like one in pain. His voice was now unthinkably near and soft. He drew very near to her.

"Say yes."

"Oh, I can't," she wailed helplessly, half-articulate, as if semi-conscious, and as if in pain, like one who dies. "How can I?"

"You can," he said softly, laying his hand gently on her shoulder as she stood with her head averted and dropped, dazed. "You can. Yes, you can. What makes you say you can't? You can. You can." And with awful softness he bent forward and just touched her neck with his mouth and his chin.

"Don't!" she cried, with a faint mad cry like hysteria, starting away and facing round on him. "What do you mean?" But she had no breath to speak with. It was as if she was killed.

"I mean what I say," he persisted softly and cruelly. "I want you to marry me. I want you to marry me. You know that, now, don't you? You know that, now? Don't you? Don't you?"

"What?" she said.

"Know," he replied.

"Yes," she said. "I know you say so."

"And you know I mean it, don't you?"

"I know you say so."

"You believe me?" he said.

She was silent for some time. Then she pursed her lips.

"I don't know what I believe," she said.

"Are you out there?" came Banford's voice, calling from the house.

"Yes, we're bringing in the logs," he answered.

"I thought you'd gone lost," said Banford disconsolately. "Hurry up, do, and come and let's have tea. The kettle's boiling."

He stooped at once, to take an armful of little logs and carry them into the kitchen, where they were piled in a corner. March also helped, filling her arms and carrying the logs on her breasts as if they were some heavy child. The night had fallen cold.

When the logs were all in, the two cleaned their boots noisily on the scraper outside, then rubbed them on the mat. March shut the door and took off her felt hat—her farm-girl hat. Her thick, crisp black hair was loose, her face was pale and strained. She pushed back her hair vaguely, and washed her hands. Banford came hurrying into the dimly-lighted kitchen, to take from the oven the scones she was keeping hot.

"Whatever have you been doing all this time?" she asked fretfully. "I thought you were never coming in. And it's ages since you stopped sawing. What were you doing out there?"

"Well," said Henry, "we had to stop that hole in the barn, to keep the rats out."

"Why I could see you standing there in the shed. I could see your shirt-sleeves," challenged Banford.

"Yes, I was just putting the saw away."

They went in to tea. March was quite mute. Her face was pale and strained and vague. The youth, who always had the same ruddy, self-contained look on his face, as though he were keeping himself to himself, had come to tea in his shirt-sleeves as if he were at home. He bent over his plate as he ate his food.

"Aren't you cold?" said Banford spitefully. "In your shirt-sleeves."

He looked up at her, with his chin near his plate, and his eyes very clear, pellucid, and unwavering as he watched her.

"No, I'm not cold," he said with his usual soft courtesy. "It's much warmer in here than it is outside, you see."

138

"I hope it is," said Banford, feeling nettled by him. He had a strange suave assurance, and a wide-eyed bright look that got on her nerves this evening.

"But perhaps," he said softly and courteously, "you don't like me coming to tea without my coat. I forgot that."

"Oh, I don't mind," said Banford; although she *did.*

"I'll go and get it, shall I?" he said.

March's dark eyes turned slowly down to him.

"No, don't you bother," she said in her queer, twanging tone. "If you feel all right as you are, stop as you are." She spoke with a crude authority.

"Yes," said he, "I *feel* all right, if I'm not rude."

"It's usually considered rude," said Banford. "But we don't mind."

"Go along, 'considered rude'," ejaculated March. "Who considers it rude?"

"Why you do, Nellie, in anybody else," said Banford, bridling a little behind her spectacles, and feeling her food stick in her throat.

But March had again gone vague and unheeding, chewing her food as if she did not know she was eating at all. And the youth looked from one to another, with bright, watchful eyes.

Banford was offended. For all his suave courtesy and soft voice, the youth seemed to her impudent. She did not like to look at him. She did not like to meet his clear, watchful eyes, she did not like to see the strange glow in his face, his cheeks with their delicate fine hair, and his ruddy skin that was quite dull and yet which seemed to burn with a curious heat of life. It made her feel a little ill to look at him: the quality of his physical presence was too penetrating, too hot.

After tea the evening was very quiet. The youth rarely went into the village. As a rule he read: he was a great reader in his own hours. That is, when he did begin, he read absorbedly. But he was not very eager to begin. Often he walked about the fields and along the hedges alone in the dark at night, prowling with a queer instinct for the night, and listening to the wild sounds.

To-night, however, he took a Captain Mayne Reid book from Banford's shelf and sat down with knees wide apart and immersed himself in his story. His brownish fair hair was long, and lay on his head like a thick cap, combed sideways. He was still in his shirt-sleeves, and bending forward under the lamp-light, with his knees stuck wide apart and the book in his hand and his whole figure absorbed in the rather strenuous business of reading, he gave Banford's sitting-room the look of a lumber-camp. She resented this. For on her sitting-room floor she had a red Turkey rug and dark stain round, the fire-place had fashionable green tiles, the piano stood open with the latest dance-music: she played quite well: and on the walls were March's hand-painted swans and water-lilies. Moreover, with the logs nicely, tremulously burning in the grate, the thick curtains drawn, the doors all shut, and the pine-trees hissing and shuddering in the wind outside, it was cosy, it was refined and nice. She resented the big, raw, long-legged youth sticking his khaki knees out and sitting there with his soldier's shirt-cuffs buttoned on his thick red wrists. From time to time he turned a page, and from time to time he gave a sharp look at the fire, setting the logs. Then he immersed himself again in the intense and isolated business of reading.

March, on the far side of the table, was spasmodically crochetting. Her mouth was pursed in an odd way, as when she had dreamed the fox's brush burned it, her beautiful, crisp black hair strayed in wisps. But her whole figure was miles away. In a sort of semi-dream she seemed to be hearing the fox singing round the house in the wind, singing wildly and sweetly and like a madness. With red but well-shaped hands she slowly crochetted the white cotton, very slowly, awkwardly.

Banford was also trying to read, sitting in her low chair. But between those two she felt fidgetty. She kept moving and looking round and listening to the wind, and glancing secretly from one to the other of her companions. March, seated on a straight chair, with her knees in their close breeches crossed, and slowly, laboriously crochetting, was also a trial.

"Oh dear!" said Banford. "My eyes are bad to-night." And she pressed her fingers on her eyes.

The youth looked up at her with his clear, bright look, but did not speak.

"Are they, Jill?" said March absently.

Then the youth began to read again, and Banford perforce returned to her book. But she could not keep still. After a while she looked up at March, and a queer, almost malignant little smile was on her thin face.

"A penny for them, Nell," she said suddenly.

March looked round with big, startled black eyes, and went pale as if with terror. She had been listening to the fox singing so tenderly, as he wandered round the house.

"What?" she said vaguely.

"A penny for them," said Banford sarcastically. "Or twopence, if they're as deep as all that."

The youth was watching with bright, clear eyes from beneath the lamp.

"Why," came March's vague voice, "what do you want to waste your money for?"

"I thought it would be well spent," said Banford.

"I wasn't thinking of anything except the way the wind was blowing," said March.

"Oh dear," replied Banford, "I could have had as original thoughts as that myself. I'm afraid I *have* wasted my money this time."

"Well, you needn't pay," said March.

The youth suddenly laughed. Both women looked at him: March rather surprised-looking, as if she had hardly known he was there.

"Why, do you ever pay up on these occasions?" he asked.

"Oh yes," said Banford. "We always do. I've sometimes had to pass a shilling a week to Nellie, in the winter time. It costs much less in summer."

"What, paying for each other's thoughts?" he laughed.

"Yes, when we've absolutely come to the end of everything else."

He laughed quickly, wrinkling his nose sharply like a puppy and laughing with quick pleasure, his eyes shining.

"It's the first time I ever heard of that," he said.

"I guess you'd hear of it often enough if you stayed a winter on Bailey Farm," said Banford lamentably.

"Do you get so tired, then?" he asked.

"So bored," said Banford.

"Oh!" he said gravely. "But why should you be bored?"

"Who wouldn't be bored?" said Banford.

"I'm sorry to hear that," he said gravely.

"You must be, if you were hoping to have a lively time here," said Banford.

He looked at her long and gravely.

"Well," he said, with his odd, young seriousness, "it's quite lively enough for me."

"I'm glad to hear it," said Banford.

And she returned to her book. In her thin, frail hair were already many threads of grey, though she was not yet thirty. The boy did not look down, but turned his eyes to March, who was sitting with pursed mouth laboriously crochetting, her eyes wide and absent. She had a warm, pale, fine skin, and a delicate nose. Her pursed mouth looked shrewish. But the shrewish look was contradicted by the curious lifted arch of her dark brows, and the wideness of her eyes; a look of startled wonder and vagueness. She was listening again for the fox, who seemed to have wandered farther off into the night.

From under the edge of the lamp-light the boy sat with his face looking up, watching her silently, his eyes round and very clear and intent.

141

Banford, biting her fingers irritably, was glancing at him under her hair. He sat there perfectly still, his ruddy face tilted up from the low level under the light, on the edge of the dimness, and watching with perfect abstract intentness. March suddenly lifted her great, dark eyes from her crochetting, and saw him. She started, giving a little exclamation.

"There he is!" she cried, involuntarily, as if terribly startled.

Banford looked around in amazement, sitting up straight.

"Whatever has got you, Nellie?" she cried.

But March, her face flushed a delicate rose colour, was looking away to the door.

"Nothing! Nothing!" she said crossly. "Can't one speak?"

"Yes, if you speak sensibly," said Banford. "Whatever did you mean?"

"I don't know what I meant," cried March testily.

"Oh Nellie, I hope you aren't going jumpy and nervy. I feel I can't stand another *thing!* Whoever did you mean? Did you mean Henry?" cried poor, frightened Banford.

"Yes, I suppose so," said March laconically. She would never confess to the fox.

"Oh dear, my nerves are all gone for to-night," wailed Banford.

At nine o'clock March brought in a tray with bread and cheese and tea—Henry had confessed that he liked a cup of tea. Banford drank a glass of milk, and ate a little bread. And soon she said:

"I'm going to. bed, Nellie. I'm all nerves to-night. Are you coming?"

"Yes, I'm coming the minute I've taken the tray away," said March.

"Don't be long then," said Banford fretfully. "Good night, Henry. You'll see the fire is safe, if you come up last, won't you?"

"Yes, Miss Banford, I'll see it's safe," he replied in his reassuring way.

March was lighting the candle to go to the kitchen. Banford took her candle and went upstairs. When March came back to the fire, she said to him:

"I suppose we can trust you to put out the fire and everything?" She stood there with her hand on her hip, and one knee loose, her head averted shyly, as if she could not look at him. He had his face lifted, watching her.

"Come and sit down a minute," he said softly.

"No, I'll be going, Jill will be waiting, and she'll get upset if I don't come."

"What made you jump like that this evening?" he asked.

"When did I jump?" she retorted, looking at him.

"Why, just now you did," he said. "When you cried out."

142

"Oh," she said. "Then!—Why, I thought you were the fox!" And her face screwed into a queer smile, half ironic.

"The fox! Why the fox!" he asked softly.

"Why, one evening last summer when I was out with the gun I saw the fox in the grass nearly at my feet, looking straight up at me. I don't know—I suppose he made an impression on me." She turned aside her head again, and let one foot stray loose, self-consciously.

"And did you shoot him?" asked the boy.

"No, he gave me such a start, staring straight at me as he did, and then stopping to look back at me over his shoulder with a laugh on his face."

"A laugh on his face!" repeated Henry, also laughing. "He frightened you, did he?"

"No, he didn't frighten me. He made an impression on me, that's all."

"And you thought I was the fox, did you?" he laughed, with the same queer, quick little laugh, like a puppy wrinkling its nose.

"Yes, I did, for the moment," she said. "Perhaps he'd been in my mind without my knowing."

"Perhaps you think I've come to steal your chickens or something," he said, with the same young laugh.

But she only looked at him with a wide, dark, vacant eye.

"It's the first time," he said, "that I've ever been taken for a fox. Won't you sit down for a minute?" His voice was very soft and cajoling.

"No," she said. "Jill will be waiting." But still she did not go, but stood with one foot loose and her face turned aside, just outside the circle of light.

"But won't you answer my question?" he said, lowering his voice still more.

"I don't know what question you mean."

"Yes, you do. Of course you do. I mean the question of you marrying me."

"No, I shan't answer that question" she said flatly.

"Won't you?" The queer, young laugh came on his nose again. "Is it because I'm like the fox? Is that why?" And still he laughed.

She turned and looked at him with a long, slow look.

"I wouldn't let that put you against me," he said. "Let me turn the lamp low, and come and sit down a minute."

He put his red hand under the glow of the lamp, and suddenly made the light very dim. March stood there in the dimness quite shadowy, but unmoving. He rose silently to his feet, on his long legs. And now his voice was extraordinarily soft and suggestive, hardly audible.

143

"You'll stay a moment," he said. "Just a moment." And he put his hand on her shoulder. She turned her face from him. "I'm sure you don't really think I'm like the fox," he said, with the same softness and with a suggestion of laughter in his tone, a subtle mockery. "Do you now?"

And he drew her gently towards him and kissed her neck, softly. She winced and trembled and hung away. But his strong, young arm held her, and he kissed her softly again, still on the neck, for her face was averted.

"Won't you answer my question? Won't you now?" came his soft, lingering voice. He was trying to draw her near to kiss her face. And he kissed her cheek softly, near the ear.

At that moment Banford's voice was heard calling fretfully, crossly from upstairs.

"There's Jill!" cried March, starting and drawing erect.

And as she did so, quick as lightning he kissed her on the mouth, with a quick brushing kiss. It seemed to burn through her every fibre. She gave a queer little cry.

"You will, won't you? You will?" he insisted softly.

"Nellie! *Nellie!* Whatever are you so long for?" came Banford's faint cry from the outer darkness.

But he held her fast, and was murmuring with that intolerable softness and insistency:

"You will, won't you? Say yes! Say yes!"

March, who felt as if the fire had gone through her and scathed her, as if she could do no more, murmured:

"Yes! Yes! Anything you like! Anything you like! Only let me go! Only let me go! Jill's calling."

"You know you've promised," he said insidiously.

"Yes! Yes! I do!" Her voice suddenly rose into a shrill cry. "All right, Jill, I'm coming."

Startled, he let her go, and she went straight upstairs.

In the morning at breakfast, after he had looked round the place and attended to the stock and thought to himself that one could live easily enough here, he said to Banford:

"Do you know what, Miss Banford?"

"Well, what?" said the good-natured, nervy Banford. He looked at March, who was spreading jam on her bread.

"Shall I tell?" he said to her.

She looked up at him, and a deep pink colour flushed over her face.

"Yes, if you mean Jill," she said. "I hope you won't go talking all over the village, that's all." And she swallowed her dry bread with difficulty.

144

"Whatever is coming?" said Banford, looking up with wide, tired, slightly reddened eyes. She was a thin, frail little thing, and her hair, which was delicate and thin, was bobbed, so it hung softly by her worn face in its faded brown and grey.

"Why, what do you think?" he said, smiling like one who has a secret.

"How do I know!" said Banford.

"Can't you guess?" he said, making bright eyes, and smiling, pleased with himself.

"I'm sure I can't. What's more, I'm not going to try."

"Nellie and I are going to be married."

Banford put down her knife out of her thin, delicate fingers, as if she would never take it up to eat any more. She stared with blank, reddened eyes.

"You what?" she exclaimed.

"We're going to get married. Aren't we, Nellie?" and he turned to March.

"You say so, anyway," said March laconically. But again she flushed with an agonised flush. She, too, could swallow no more.

Banford looked at her like a bird that has been shot: a poor, little sick bird. She gazed at her with all her wounded soul in her face, at the deep-flushed March.

"Never!" she exclaimed, helpless.

"It's quite right," said the bright and gloating youth.

Banford turned aside her face, as if the sight of the food on the table made her sick. She sat like this for some moments, as if she were sick. Then, with one hand on the edge of the table, she rose to her feet.

"I'll *never* believe it, Nellie," she cried. "It's absolutely impossible!"

Her plaintive, fretful voice had a thread of hot anger and despair.

"Why? Why shouldn't you believe it" asked the youth, with all his soft, velvety impertinence in his voice.

Banford looked at him from her wide, vague eyes, as if he were some creature in a museum.

"Oh," she said languidly, "because she can never be such a fool. She can't lose her self-respect to such an extent." Her voice was cold and plaintive, drifting.

"In what way will she lose her self-respect?" asked the boy.

Banford looked at him with vague fixity from behind her spectacles.

"If she hasn't lost it already," she said.

He became very red, vermilion, under the slow, vague stare from behind the spectacles.

"I don't see it at all," he said.

"Probably you don't. I shouldn't expect you would," said Banford, with that straying mild tone of remoteness which made her words even more insulting.

He sat stiff in his chair, staring with hot, blue eyes from his scarlet face. An ugly look came on his brow.

"My word, she doesn't know what she's letting herself in for," said Banford, in her plaintive, drifting, insulting voice.

"What has it got to do with you, anyway?" said the youth, in a temper.

"More than it has to do with you, probably," she replied, plaintive and venomous.

"Oh, has it! I don't see that at all," he jerked out.

"No, you wouldn't," she answered, drifting.

"Anyhow," said March, pushing back her chair and rising uncouthly. "It's no good arguing about it." And she seized the bread and the teapot, and strode away to the kitchen.

Banford let her fingers stray across her brow and along her hair, like one bemused. Then she turned and went away upstairs.

Henry sat stiff and sulky in his chair, with his face and his eyes on fire. March came and went, clearing the table. But Henry sat on, stiff with temper. He took no notice of her. She had regained her composure and her soft, even, creamy complexion. But her mouth was pursed up. She glanced at him each time as she came to take things from the table, glanced from her large, curious eyes, more in curiosity than anything. Such a long, red-faced, sulky boy! That was all he was. He seemed as remote from her as if his red face were a red chimney-pot on a cottage across the fields, and she looked at him just as objectively, as remotely.

At length he got up and stalked out into the fields wth the gun. He came in only at dinner-time, with the devil still in his face, but his manner quite polite. Nobody said anything particular; they sat each one at the sharp corner of a triangle, in obstinate remoteness. In the afternoon he went out again at once with the gun. He came in at nightfall with a rabbit and a pigeon. He stayed in all the evening, but hardly opened his mouth. He was in the devil of a temper, feeling he had been insulted.

Banford's eyes were red, she had evidently been crying. But her manner was more remote and supercilious then ever; the way she turned her head if he spoke at all, as if he were some tramp or inferior intruder of that sort, made his blue eyes go almost black with rage. His face looked sulkier. But he never forgot his polite intonation, if he opened his mouth to speak.

March seemed to flourish in this atmosphere. She seemed to sit between the two antagonists with a little wicked smile on her face, enjoying herself. There was even a sort of complacency in the way she laboriously crochetted this evening.

When he was in bed, the youth could hear the two women talking and arguing in their room. He sat up in bed and strained his ears to hear what they said. But he could hear nothing, it was too far off. Yet he could hear the soft, plaintive drip of Banford's voice, and March's deeper note.

The night was quiet, frosty. Big stars were snapping outside beyond the ridge-tops of the pine-trees. He listened and listened. In the distance he heard a fox yelping: and the dogs from the farms barking in answer. But it was not that he wanted to hear. It was what the two women were saying.

He got stealthily out of bed, and stood by his door. He could hear no more than before. Very, very carefully he began to lift the door latch. After quite a time he had his door open. Then he stepped stealthily out into the passage. The old oak planks were cold under his feet, and they creaked preposterously. He crept very, very gently up the one step, and along by the wall, till he stood outside their door. And there he held his breath and listened. Banford's voice:

"No, I simply couldn't stand it. I should be dead in a month. Which is just what he would be aiming at, of course. That would just be his game, to see me in the churchyard. No, Nellie, if you were to do such a thing as to marry him, you could never stop here. I couldn't, I couldn't live in the same house with him. Oh-h! I feel quite sick with the smell of his clothes. And his red face simply turns me over. I can't eat my food when he's at the table. What a fool I was ever to let him stop. One ought *never* to try to do a kind action. It always flies back in your face like a boomerang."

"Well, he's only got two more days," said March.

"Yes, thank heaven. And when he's gone, he'll never come in this house again. I feel so bad while he's here. And I know, I know he's only counting what he can get out of you. I *know* that's all it is. He's just a good-for-nothing, who doesn't want to work, and who thinks he'll live on us. But he won't live on me. If you're such a fool, then it's your own lookout. Mrs Burgess knew him all the time he was here. And the old man could never get him to do any steady work. He was off with the gun on every occasion, just as he is now. Nothing but the gun! Oh, I do hate it! You don't know what you're doing, Nellie, you don't. If you marry him he'll just make a fool of you. He'll go off and leave you stranded. I know he will if he can't get Bailey Farm out of us—and he's not going to, while

I live. While I live he's never going to set foot here. I know what it would be. He'd soon think he was master of both of us, as he thinks he's master of you already."

"But he isn't," said Nellie.

"He thinks he is, anyway. And that's what he wants: to come and be master here. Yes, imagine it! That's what we've got the place together for, is it, to be bossed and bullied by a hateful red-faced boy, a beastly labourer. Oh, we did make a mistake when we let him stop. We ought never to have lowered ourselves. And I've had such a fight with all the people here, not to be pulled down to their level. No, he's not coming here. And then you see—if he can't have the place, he'll run off to Canada or somewhere again, as if he'd never known you. And here you'll be, absolutely ruined and made a fool of. I know I shall never have any peace of mind again."

"We'll tell him he can't come here. We'll tell him that," said March.

"Oh, don't you bother; I'm going to tell him that, and other things as well, before he goes. He's not going to have all his own way while I've got the strength left to speak. Oh, Nellie, he'll despise you, he'll despise you, like the awful little beast he is, if you give way to him. I'd no more trust him than I'd trust a cat not to steal. He's deep, he's deep, and he's bossy, and he's selfish through and through, as cold as ice. All he wants is to make use of you. And when you're no more use to him, then I pity you."

"I don't think he's as bad as all that," said March.

"No, because he's been playing up to you. But you'll find out, if you see much more of him. Oh, Nellie, I can't bear to think of it."

"Well, it won't hurt you, Jill, darling."

"Won't it! Won't it! I shall never know a moment's peace again while I live, nor a moment's happiness. No, Nellie—" and Banford began to weep bitterly.

The boy outside could hear the stifled sound of the woman's sobbing, and could hear March's soft, deep, tender voice comforting, with wonderful gentleness and tenderness, the weeping woman.

His eyes were so round and wide that he seemed to see the whole night, and his ears were almost jumping off his head. He was frozen stiff. He crept back to bed, but felt as if the top of his head was coming off. He could not sleep. He could not keep still. He rose, quietly dressed himself, and crept out on to the landing once more. The women were silent. He went softly downstairs and out to the kitchen.

Them he put on his boots and his overcoat, and took the gun. He did not think to go away from the farm. No, he only took the gun. As softly as possible he unfastened the door and went out into the frosty December night. The air was still, the stars bright, the pine-trees seemed to bristle audibly in the sky. He went stealthily away down a fence-side, looking for something to shoot. At the same time he remembered that he ought not to shoot and frighten the women.

So he prowled round the edge of the gorse cover, and through the grove of tall old hollies, to the woodside. There he skirted the fence, peering through the darkness with dilated eyes that seemed to be able to grow black and full of sight in the dark, like a cat's. An owl was slowly and mournfully whooing round a great oak-tree. He stepped stealthily with his gun, listening, listening, watching.

As he stood under the oaks of the wood-edge he heard the dogs from the neighbouring cottage up the hill yelling suddenly and startlingly, and the wakened dogs from the farms around barking answer. And suddenly, it seemed to him England was little and tight, he felt the landscape was constricted even in the dark, and that there were too many dogs in the night, making a noise like a fence of sound, like the network of English hedges netting the view. He felt the fox didn't have a chance. For it must be the fox that had started all this hullabaloo.

Why not watch for him, anyhow! He would, no doubt, be coming sniffing round. The lad walked downhill where the farmstead with its few pine-trees crouched blackly. In the angle of the long shed, in the black dark, he crouched down. He knew the fox would be coming. It seemed to him it would be the last of the foxes in this loudly-barking, thick-voiced England, tight with innumerable little houses.

He sat a long time with his eyes fixed unchanging upon the open gateway, where a little light seemed to fall from the stars or from the horizon, who knows. He was sitting on a log in a dark corner with the gun across his knees. The pine-trees snapped. Once a chicken fell off its perch in the barn with a loud crawk and cackle and commotion that startled him, and he stood up, watching with all his eyes, thinking it might be a rat. But he *felt* it was nothing. So he sat down again with the gun on his knees and his hands tucked in to keep them warm, and his eyes fixed unblinking on the pale reach of the open gateway. He felt he could smell the hot, sickly, rich smell of live chickens on the cold air.

And then—a shadow. A sliding shadow in the gateway. He gathered all his vision into a concentrated spark, and saw the shadow of the fox, the fox creeping on his belly through the gate. There he went, on his belly like a snake. The boy smiled to himself and brought the gun to his shoulder. He knew quite well what would happen. He knew the fox would go to where the fowl-door was boarded up, and sniff there. He knew he would lie there for a minute, sniffing the fowls within. And then he would start again prowling under the edge of the old barn, waiting to get in.

The fowl-door was at the top of a slight incline. Soft, soft as a shadow the fox slid up this incline, and crouched with his nose to the boards. And at the same moment there was the awful crash of a gun reverberating between the old buildings, as if all the night had gone smash. But the boy watched keenly. He saw even the white belly of the fox as the beast beat his paws in death. So he went forward.

There was a commotion everywhere. The fowls were scuffling and crawking, the ducks were quark-quarking, the pony had stamped wildly to his feet. But the fox was on his side, struggling in his last tremors. The boy bent over him and smelt his foxy smell.

There was a sound of a window opening upstairs, then March's voice calling:

"Who is it?"

"It's me," said Henry; "I've shot the fox."

"Oh, goodness! You nearly frightened us to death."

"Did I? I'm awfully sorry."

"Whatever made you get up?"

"I heard him about."

"And have you shot him?"

"Yes, he's here," and the boy stood in the yard holding up the warm, dead brute. "You can't see, can you? Wait a minute." And he took his flash-light from his pocket, and flashed it on to the dead animal. He was holding it by the brush. March saw, in the middle of the darkness, just the reddish fleece and the white belly and the white underneath of the pointed chin, and the queer, dangling paws. She did not know what to say.

"He's a beauty," he said. "He will make you a lovely fur."

"You don't catch me wearing a fox fur," she replied.

"Oh!" he said. And he switched off the light.

"Well, I should think you'll come in and go to bed again now," she said.

"Probably I shall. What time is it?"

"What time is it, Jill?" called March's voice. It was a quarter to one.

That night March had another dream. She dreamed that Banford was dead, and that she, March, was sobbing her heart out. Then she had to put Banford into her coffin. And the coffin was the rough wood-box in

150

which the bits of chopped wood were kept in the kitchen, by the fire. This was the coffin, and there was no other, and March was in agony and dazed bewilderment, looking for something to line the box with, something to make it soft with, something to cover up the poor, dead darling. Because she couldn't lay her in there just in her white, thin nightdress, in the horrible wood-box. So she hunted and hunted, and picked up thing after thing, and threw it aside in the agony of dream-frustration. And in her dream-despair all she could find that would do was a fox-skin. She knew that it wasn't right, that this was not what she should have. But it was all she could find. And so she folded the brush of the fox, and laid her darling Jill's head on this, and she brought round the skin of the fox and laid it on the top of the body, so that it seemed to make a whole ruddy, fiery coverlet, and she cried and cried, and woke to find the tears streaming down her face.

The first thing that both she and Banford did in the morning was to go out to see the fox. Henry had hung it up by the heels in the shed, with its poor brush falling backwards. It was a lovely dog-fox in its prime, with a handsome, thick, winter coat: a lovely golden-red colour, with grey as it passed to the belly, and belly all white, and a great full brush with a delicate black and grey and pure white tip.

"Poor brute!" said Banford. "If it wasn't such a thieving wretch, you'd feel sorry for it."

March said nothing, but stood with her foot trailing aside, one hip out; her face was pale and her eyes big and black, watching the dead animal that was suspended upside down. White and soft as snow his belly: white and soft as snow. She passed her hand softly down it. And his wonderful black-glinted brush was full and frictional, wonderful. She passed her hand down this also, and quivered. Time after time she took the full fur of that thick tail between her fingers, and passed her hand slowly downward. Wonderful, sharp, thick splendour of a tail. And he was dead! She pursed her lips, and her eyes went black and vacant. Then she took the head in her hand.

Henry was sauntering up, so Banford walked rather pointedly away. March stood there bemused, with the head of the fox in her hand. She was wondering, wondering, wondering over his long fine muzzle. For some reason it reminded her of a spoon or a spatula. She felt she could not understand it. The beast was a strange beast to her, incomprehensible, out of her range. Wonderful silver whiskers he had, like ice-threads. And pricked ears with hair inside. But that long, long slender spoon of a nose!— and the marvellous white teeth beneath! It was to thrust forward and bite with, deep, deep into the living prey, to bite and bite the blood.

"He's a beauty, isn't he?" said Henry, standing by.

"Oh yes, he's a fine big fox. I wonder how many chickens he's responsible for," she replied.

"A good many. Do you think he's the same one you saw in the summer?"

"I should think very likely he is," she replied.

He watched her, but he could make hothing of her. Partly she was so shy and virgin, and partly she was so grim, matter-of-fact, shrewish. What she said seemed to him so different from the look of her big, queer, dark eyes.

"Are you going to skin him?" she asked.

"Yes, when I've had breakfast, and got a board to peg him on."

"My word, what a strong smell he's got! Pooo! It'll take some washing off one's hands. I don't know why I was so silly as to handle him." And she looked at her right hand, that had passed dowh his belly, and along his tail, and had even got a tiny streak of blood from one dark place in his fur.

"Have you seen the chickens when they smell him, how frightened they are?" he said.

"Yes, aren't they!"

"You must mind you don't get some of his fleas."

"Oh, fleas!" she replied, nonchalant.

Later in the day she saw the fox's skin nailed flat on a board, as if crucified. It gave her an uneasy feeling.

The boy was angry. He went about with his mouth shut, as if he had swallowed part of his chin. But in behaviour he was polite and affable. He did not say anything about his intention. And he left March alone.

That evening they sat in the dining-room. Banford wouldn't have him in her sitting-room any more. There was a very big log on the fire. And everybody was busy. Banford had letters to write, March was sewing a dress, and he was mending some little contrivance.

Banford stopped her letter-writing from time to time to look round and rest her eyes. The boy had his head down, his face hidden over his job.

"Let's see," said Banford. "What train do you go by, Henry?"

He looked up straight at her.

"The morning train. In the morning," he said.

"What, the eight-ten or the eleven-twenty?"

"The eleven-twenty, I suppose," he said.

"That is the day after to-morrow?" said Banford.

"Yes, the day after to-morrow."

"Mm!" murmured Banford, and she returned to her writing. But as she was licking her envelope, she asked:

"And what plans have you made for the future, if I may ask?"

"Plans?" he said, his face very bright and angry.

"I mean about you and Nellie, if you are going on with this business. When do you expect the wedding to come off?" She spoke in a jeering tone.

"Oh, the wedding," he replied. "I don't know."

"Don't you know anything?" said Banford. "Are you going to clear out on Friday and leave things no more settled than they are?"

"Well, why shouldn't I? We can always write letters."

"Yes, of course you can. But I wanted to know because of this place. If Nellie is going to get married all of a sudden, I shall have to be looking round for a new partner."

"Couldn't she stay on here if she were married?" he said. He knew quite well what was coming.

"Oh," said Banford, "this is no place for a married couple. There's not enough work to keep a man going, for one thing. And there's no money to be made. It's quite useless your thinking of staying on here if you marry. Absolutely!"

"Yes, but I wasn't thinking of staying on here," he said.

"Well, that's what I want to know. And what about Nellie, then? How long is *she* going to be here with me, in that case?"

The two antagonists looked at one another.

"That I can't say," he answered.

"Oh, go along," she cried petulantly. "You must have some idea what you are going to do, if you ask a woman to marry you. Unless it's all a hoax."

"Why should it be a hoax? I am going back to Canada."

"And taking her with you?"

"Yes, certainly."

"You hear that, Nellie?" said Banford.

March, who had had her head bent over her sewing, now looked up with a sharp, pink blush on her face, and a queer, sardonic laugh in her eyes and on her twisted mouth.

"That's the first time I've heard that I was going to Canada," she said.

"Well, you have to hear it for the first time, haven't you?" said the boy.

"Yes, I suppose I have," she said nonchalantly. And she went back to her sewing.

"You're quite ready, are you, to go to Canada? Are you, Nellie?" asked Banford.

March looked up again. She let her shoulders go slack, and let her hand that held the needle lie loose in her lap.

"It depends on *how* I'm going," she said. "I don't think I want to go jammed up in the steerage, as a soldier's wife. I'm afraid I'm not used to that way."

The boy watched her with bright eyes.

"Would you rather stay over here while I go first?" he asked.

"I would, if that's the only alternative," she replied.

"That's much the wisest. Don't make it any fixed engagement," said Banford. "Leave yourself free to go or not after he's got back and found you a place, Nellie. Anything else is madness, madness."

"Don't you think," said the youth, "we ought to get married before I go—and then go together, or separate, according to how it happens?"

"I think it's a terrible idea," cried Banford.

But the boy was watching March.

"What do you think?" he asked her.

She let her eyes stray vaguely into space.

"Well, I don't know," she said. "I shall have to think about it."

"Why?" he asked, pertinently.

"Why?" she repeated his question in a mocking way, and looked at him laughing, though her face was pink again. "I should think there's plenty of reasons why."

He watched her in silence. She seemed to have escaped him. She had got into league with Banford against him. There was again the queer sardonic look about her; she would mock stoically at everything he said or which life offered.

"Of course," he said, "I don't want to press you to do anything you don't wish to do."

"I should think not, indeed," cried Banford indignantly.

At bedtime Banford said plaintively to March:

"You take my hot bottle up for me, Nellie, will you."

"Yes, I'll do it," said March, with the kind of willing unwillingness she so often showed towards her beloved but uncertain Jill.

The two women went upstairs. After a time March called from the top of the stairs: "Good night, Henry. I shan't be coming down. You'll see to the lamp and the fire, won't you?"

The next day Henry went about with the cloud on his brow and his young cub's face shut up tight. He was cogitating all the time. He had wanted March to marry him and go back to Canada with him. And he had been sure she would do it. Why he wanted her he didn't know. But he did want her. He had set his mind on her. And he was convulsed with a youth's fury at being thwarted. To be thwarted, to be thwarted! It made him so furious inside that he did not know what to do with himself. But he kept himself in hand. Because even now things might turn out differently. She might come over to him. Of course she might. It was her business to do so.

Things drew to a tension again towards evening. He and Banford had avoided each other all day. In fact, Banford went in to the little town by the 11.20 train. It was market day. She arrived back on the 4.25. Just as the night was falling Henry saw her little figure in a dark-blue coat and a dark-blue tam-o'shanter hat crossing the first meadow from the station. He stood under one of the wild pear-trees, with the old dead leaves round his feet. And he watched the little blue figure advancing persistently over the rough winter-ragged meadow. She had her arms full of parcels, and advanced slowly, frail thing she was, but with that devilish little certainty which he so detested in her. He stood invisible under the pear-tree, watching her every step. And if looks could have affected her, she would have felt a log of iron on each of her ankles as she made her way forward. "You're a nasty little thing, you are," he was saying softly, across the distance. "You're a nasty little thing. I hope you'll be paid back for all the harm you've done me for nothing. I hope you will—you nasty little thing. I hope you'll have to pay for it. You will, if wishes are anything. You nasty little creature that you are."

She was toiling slowly up the slope. But if she had been slipping back at every step towards the Bottomless Pit, he would not have gone to help her with her parcels. Aha, there went March, striding with her long, land stride, in her breeches and her short tunic! Striding down hill at a great pace, and even running a few steps now and then, in her great solicitude and desire to come to the rescue of the little Banford. The boy watched her with rage in his heart. See her leap a ditch, and run, run as if a house was on fire, just to get to that creeping, dark little object down there! So, the Banford just stood still and waited. And March strode up and took *all* the parcels except a bunch of yellow chrysanthemums. These the Banford still carried—yellow chrysanthemums!

"Yes, you look well, don't you," he said softly into the dusk air. "You look well, pottering up there with a bunch of flowers, you do. I'd make you eat them for your tea, if you hug them so tight. And I'd give them you for breakfast again, I would. I'd give you flowers. Nothing but flowers."

He watched the progress of the two women. He could hear their voices:

March always outspoken and rather scolding in her tenderness, Banford murmuring rather vaguely. They were evidently good friends. He could not hear what they said till they came to the fence of the home meadow, which they must climb. Then he saw March manfully climbing over the bars with all her packages in her arms, and on the still air he heard Banford's fretful:

"Why don't you let me help you with the parcels?" She had a queer, plaintive hitch in her voice. Then came March's robust and reckless.

"Oh, I can manage. Don't you bother about me. You've all you can do to get yourself over."

"Yes, that's all very well," said Banford fretfully. "You say *Don't you bother about me*, and then all the while you feel injured because nobody thinks of you."

"When do I feel injured?" said March.

"Always. You always feel injured. Now you're feeling injured because I won't have that boy to come and live on the farm."

"I'm not feeling injured at all," said March.

"I know you are. When he's gone you'll sulk over it. I know you will."

"Shall I?" said March. "We'll see."

"Yes, we *shall* see, unfortunately. I can't think how you can make yourself so cheap. I can't *imagine* how you can lower yourself like it."

"I haven't lowered myself," said March.

"I don't know what you call it, then. Letting a boy like that come so cheeky and impudent and make a mug of you. I don't know what you think of yourself. How much respect do you think he's going to have for you afterwards? My word, I wouldn't be in your shoes, if you married him."

"Of course you wouldn't. My boots are a good bit too big for you, and not half dainty enough'" said March, with rather a miss-fire sarcasm.

"I thought you had too much pride, really I did. A woman's got to hold herself high, especially with a youth like that. Why, he's impudent. Even the way he forced himself on us at the start."

"We asked him to stay," said March.

"Not till he'd almost forced us to. And then he's so cocky and self-assured. My word, he puts my back up. I simply can't imagine how you can let him treat you so cheaply."

"I don't let him treat me cheaply," said March. "Don't you worry yourself, nobody's going to treat me cheaply. And even you aren't, either." She had a tender defiance, and a certain fire in her voice.

"Yes, it's sure to come back to me" said Banford bitterly. "That's always the end of it. I believe you only do it to spite me."

They went now in silence up the steep, grassy slope and over the brow, through the gorse-bushes. On the other side of the hedge the boy followed in the dusk, at some little distance. Now and then, through the huge ancient hedge of hawthorn, risen into trees, he saw the two dark figures creeping up the hill. As he came to the top of the slope he saw the homestead dark in the twilight, with a huge old peartree leaning from the near gable, and a little yellow light twinkling in the small side windows of the kitchen. He heard the clink of the latch and saw the kitchen door open into light as the two women went indoors. So, they were at home.

And so!—this was what they thought of him. It was rather in his nature to be a listener, so he was not at all surprised whatever he heard. The things people said about him always missed him personally. He was only rather surprised at the women's way with one another. And he disliked the Banford with an acid dislike. And he felt drawn to the March again He felt again irresistibly drawn to her. He felt there was a secret bond, a secret thread between him and her, something very exclusive, which shut out everybody else and made him and her possess each other in secret.

He hoped again that she would have him. He hoped with his blood suddenly firing up that she would agree to marry him quite quickly: at Christmas, very likely. Christmas was not far off. He wanted, whatever else happened, to snatch her into a hasty marriage and a consummation with him. Then for the future, they could arrange later. But he hoped it would happen as he wanted it. He hoped that to-night she would stay a little while with him, after Banford had gone upstairs. He hoped he could touch her soft, creamy cheek, her strange, frightened face. He hoped he could look into her dilated, frightened dark eyes, quite near. He hoped he might even put his hand on her bosom and feel her soft breasts under her tunic. His heart beat deep and powerful as he thought of that. He wanted very much to do so. He wanted to make sure of her soft woman's breasts under her tunic. She always kept the brown linen coat buttoned so close up to her throat. It seemed to him like some perilous secret, that her soft woman's breasts must be buttoned up in that uniform. It seemed to him, moreover, that they were so much softer, tenderer, more lovely and lovable, shut up in that tunic, than were the Banford's breasts, under her soft blouses and chiffon dresses. The Banford would have little iron breasts, he said to himself. For all her frailty and fretfulness and delicacy, she would have tiny iron breasts. But March under her crude, fast, workman's tunic, would have soft, white breasts, white and unseen. So he told himself, and his blood burned.

When he went in to tea, he had a surprise. He appeared at the inner door, his face very ruddy and vivid and his blue eyes shining, dropping his head forward as he came in, in his usual way, and hesitating in the doorway to watch the inside of the room, keenly and cautiously, before he entered. He was wearing a long-sleeved waistcoat. His face seemed extraordinarily like a piece of the out-of-doors come indoors: as hollyberries do. In his second of pause in the doorway he took in the two women sitting at table, at opposite ends, saw them sharply. And to his amazement March was dressed in a dress of dull, green silk crape. His mouth came open in surprise. If she had suddenly grown a moustache he could not have been more surprised.

"Why," he said, "do you wear a dress, then?"

She looked up, flushed a deep rose colour, and twisting her mouth with a smile, said:

"Of course I do. What else do you expect me to wear, but a dress?"

"A land girl's uniform, of course," he said.

"Oh," she cried, nonchalant, "that's only for this dirty, mucky work about here."

"Isn't it your proper dress, then?" he said.

"No, not indoors it isn't," she said. But she was blushing all the time as she poured out his tea. He sat down in his chair at table, unable to take his eyes off her. Her dress was a perfectly simple slip of bluey-green crape, with a line of gold stitching round the top and round the sleeves, which came to the elbow. It was cut just plain and round at the top, and showed her white, soft throat. Her arms he knew, strong and firm muscled, for he had often seen her with her sleeves rolled up. But he looked her up and down, up and down.

Banford, at the other end of the table, said not a word, but piggled with the sardine on her plate. He had forgotten her existence. He just simply stared at March, while he ate his bread and margarine in huge mouthfuls, forgetting even his tea.

"Well, I never knew anything make such a difference!" he murmured, across his mouthfuls.

"Oh goodness!" cried March, blushing still more. "I might be a pink monkey!"

And she rose quickly to her feet and took the teapot to the fire, to the kettle. And as she crouched on the hearth with her green slip about her, the boy stared more wide-eyed than ever. Through the crape her woman's form seemed soft and womanly. And when she stood up and walked he saw her legs move soft within her modernly short skirt. She had on black silk stockings, and small patent shoes with little gold buckles.

No, she was another being. She was something quite different. Seeing her always in the hard-cloth breeches, wide on the hips, buttoned on the knee, strong as armour, and in the brown puttees and thick boots it had never occurred to him that she had a woman's legs and feet. Now it came upon him. She had a woman's soft, skirted legs, and she was accessible. He blushed to the roots of his hair, shoved his nose in his tea-cup and drank his tea with a little noise that made Banford simply squirm: and strangely, suddenly he felt a man, no longer a youth. He felt a man, with all a man's grave weight of responsibility. A curious quietness, and gravity came over his soul. He felt a man, quiet, with a little of the heaviness of male destiny upon him.

She was soft and accessible in her dress. The thought went home in him like an everlasting responsibility.

"Oh, for goodness sake, say something somebody," cried Banford fretfully. "It might be a funeral." The boy looked at her, and she could not bear his face.

"A funeral," said March, with a twisted smile. "Why, that breaks my dream."

Suddenly she had thought of Banford in the wood-box for a coffin.

"What, have you been dreaming of a wedding?" said Banford sarcastically.

"Must have been," said March.

"Whose wedding?" asked the boy.

"I can't remember," said March.

She was shy and rather awkward that evening, in spite of the fact that, wearing a dress, her bearing was much more subdued than in her uniform She felt unpeeled and rather exposed. She felt almost improper.

They talked desultorily about Henry's departure next morning, and made the trivial arrangement. But of the matter on their minds, none of them spoke. They were rather quiet and friendly this evening; Banford had practically nothing to say. But inside herself she seemed still, perhaps kindly.

At nine o'clock March brought in the tray with the everlasting tea and a little cold meat which Banford had managed to procure. It was the last supper, so Banford did not want to be disagreeable. She felt a bit sorry for the boy, and felt she must be as nice as she could.

He wanted her to go to bed. She was usually the first. But she sat on in her chair under the lamp, glancing at her book now and then, and staring into the fire. A deep silence had come into the room. It was broken by March asking, in a rather small tone:

"What time is it, Jill?"

"Five past ten," said Banford, looking at her wrist.

And then not a sound. The boy had looked up from the book he was holding between his knees. His rather wide, cat-shaped face had its obstinate look, his eyes were watchful.

"What about bed?" said March at last.

"I'm ready when you are," said Banford.

"Oh, very well," said March. "I'll fill your bottle."

She was as good as her word. When the hot-water bottle was ready, she lit a candle and went upstairs with it. Banford remained in her chair, listening acutely. March came downstairs again.

"There you are, then," she said. "Are you going up?"

"Yes, in a minute," said Banford. But the minute passed, and she sat on in her chair under the lamp.

Henry, whose eyes were shining like a cat's as he watched from under his brows, and whose face seemed wider, more chubbed and cat-like with unalterable obstinacy, now rose to his feet to try his throw.

"I think I'll go and look if I can see the she-fox," he said. "She may be creeping round. Won't you come as well for a minute, Nellie, and see if we see anything?"

"Me!" cried March, looking up with her startled, wondering face.

"Yes. Come on," he said. It was wonderful how soft and warm and coaxing his voice could be, how near. The very sound of it made Banford's blood boil. "Come on for a minute," he said, looking down into her uplifted, unsure face.

And she rose to her feet as if drawn up by his young, ruddy face that was looking down on her.

"I should think you're never going out at this time of night, Nellie!" cried Banford.

"Yes, just for a minute," said the boy, looking round on her, and speaking with an odd, sharp yelp in his voice.

March looked from one to the other, as if confused, vague. Banford rose to her feet for battle.

"Why, it's ridiculous. It's bitter cold. You'll catch your death in that thin frock. And in those slippers. You're not going to do any such thing."

There was a moment's pause. Banford turtled up like a little fighting cock, facing March and the boy.

"Oh, I don't think you need worry yourself," he replied. "A moment under the stars won't do anybody any damage. I'll get the rug of the sofa in the dining-room. You're coming, Nellie."

His voice had so much anger and contempt and fury in it as he spoke to Banford: and so much tenderness and proud authority as he spoke to March, that the latter answered:

"Yes, I'm coming."

And she turned with him to the door.

Banford, standing there in the middle of the room, suddenly burst into a long wail and a spasm of sobs. She covered her face with her poor, thin hands, and her thin shoulders shook in an agony of weeping. March looked back from the door.

"Jill!" she cried in a frantic tone, like some one just coming awake. And she seemed to start towards her darling.

But the boy had March's arm in his grip, and she could not move. She did not know why she could not move. It was as in a dream when the heart strains and the body cannot stir.

"Never mind," said the boy softly. "Let her cry. Let her cry. She will have to cry sooner or later. And the tears will relieve her feelings. They will do her good."

So he drew March slowly through the doorway. But her last look was back to the poor little figure which stood in the middle of the room with covered face and thin shoulders shaken with bitter weeping.

In the dining-room he picked up the rug and said:

"Wrap yourself up in this."

She obeyed—and they reached the kitchen door, he holding her soft and firm by the arm, though she did not know it. When she saw the night outside she started back.

"I must go back to Jill," she said. "I *must*! Oh yes, I must."

Her tone sounded final. The boy let go of her and she turned indoors. But he seized her again and arrested her.

"Wait a minute," he said. "Wait a minute. Even if you go, you're not going yet."

"Leave go! Leave go!" she cried. "My place is at Jill's side. Poor little thing, she's sobbing her heart out."

"Yes," said the boy bitterly. "And your heart too, and mine as well."

"Your heart?" asked March. He still gripped her and detained her.

"Isn't it as good as her heart?" he said. "Or do you think it's not?"

"Your heart?" she said again, incredulous.

"Yes, mine! Mine! Do you think I haven't got a heart?" And with his hot grasp he took her hand and pressed it under his left breast. "There's my heart," he said, "if you don't believe in it."

It was wonder which made her attend. And then she felt the deep, heavy, powerful stroke of his heart, terrible, like something from beyond. It was like something from beyond, something awful from outside, signalling to her. And the signal paralysed her. It beat upon her very soul, and made her helpless. She forgot Jill. She could not think of Jill any more. She could not think of her. That terrible signalling from outside!

The boy put his arm round her waist.

"Come with me," he said gently. "Come and let us say what we've got to say."

And he drew her outside, closed the door. And she went with him darkly down the garden path. That he should have a beating heart! And that he should have his arm round her, outside the blanket! She was too confused to think who he was or what he was.

He took her to a dark corner of the shed, where there was a tool-box with a lid, long and low.

"We'll sit here a minute," he said.

And obediently she sat down by his side.

"Give me your hand," he said.

She gave him both her hands, and he held them between his own. He was young, and it made him tremble.

"You'll marry me. You'll marry me before I go back, won't you?" he pleaded.

"Why, aren't we both a pair of fools?" she said.

He had put her in the corner, so that she should not look out and see the lighted window of the house, across the dark yard and garden. He tried to keep her all there inside the shed with him.

"In what way a pair of fools?" he said. "If you go back to Canada with me, I've got a job and a good wage waiting for me, and it's a nice place near the mountains. Why shouldn't you marry me? Why shouldn't we marry? I should like to have you there with me. I should like to feel I'd got somebody there, at the back of me, all my life."

"You'd easily find somebody else who'd suit you better," she said.

"Yes, I might easily find another girl. I know I could. But not one I really wanted. I've never met one I really wanted, for good. You see, I'm thinking of all my life. If I marry, I want to feel it's for all my life. Other girls: well, they're just girls, nice enough to go a walk with now and then. Nice enough for a bit of play. But when I think of my life, then I should be very sorry to have to marry one of them, I should indeed."

"You mean they wouldn't make you a good wife."

162

"Yes, I mean that. But I don't mean they wouldn't make their duty by me. I mean—I don't know what I mean. Only when I think of my life, and of you, then the two things go together."

"And what if they didn't?" she said, with her odd, sardonic touch.

"Well, I think they would."

They sat for some time silent. He held her hands in his, but he did not make love to her. Since he had realized that she was a woman, and vulnerable, accessible, a certain heaviness had possessed his soul. He did not want to make love to her. He shrank from any such performance, almost with fear. She was a woman, and vulnerable, accessible to him finally, and he held back from that which was ahead, almost with dread. It was a kind of darkness he knew he would enter finally, but of which he did not want as yet even to think. She was the woman, and he was responsible for the strange vulnerability he had suddenly realised in her.

"No," she said at last, "I'm a fool. I know I'm a fool."

"What for?" he asked.

"To go on with this business."

"Do you mean me?" he asked.

"No, I mean myself. I'm making a fool of myself, and a big one."

"Why, because you don't want to marry me, really?"

"Oh, I don't know whether I'm against it, as a matter of fact. That's just it, I don't know."

He looked at her in the darkness, puzzled. He did not in the least know what she meant.

"And don't you know whether you like to sit here with me this minute, or not?" he asked.

"No, I don't really. I don't know whether I wish I was somewhere else, or whether I like being here, I don't know, really."

"Do you wish you were with Miss Banford? Do you wish you'd gone to bed with her?" he asked, as a challenge.

She waited a long time before she answered:

"No," she said at last. "I don't wish that."

"And do you think you would spend all your life with her—when your hair goes white, and you are old?" he said.

"No," she said, without much hesitation. "I don't see Jill and me two old women together."

"And don't you think when I'm an old man and you're an old woman, we might be together still, as we are now?" he said.

"Well, not as we are now," she replied. "But I could imagine—no, I can't. I can't imagine you an old man. Besides, it's dreadful!"

"What, to be an old man?"

"Yes, of course."

"Not when the time comes," he said. "But it hasn't come. Only it will. And when it does, I should like to think you'd be there as well."

"Sort of old age pensioners," she said drily.

Her kind of witless humour alway startled him. He never knew what she meant. Probably she didn't quite know herself.

"No," he said, hurt.

"I don't know why you harp on old age," she said. "I'm not ninety."

"Did anybody ever say you were?" he asked, offended.

They were silent for some time, pulling different ways in the silence.

"I don't want you to make fun of me," he said.

"Don't you?" she replied, enigmatic.

"No, because just this minute I'm serious. And when I'm serious I believe in not making fun of it."

"You mean nobody else must make fun of you," she replied.

"Yes, I mean that. And I mean I don't believe in making fun of it myself. When it comes over me so that I'm serious, then—there it is, I don't want it to be laughed at."

She was silent for some time. Then she said, in a vague, almost pained voice:

"No, I'm not laughing at you."

A hot wave rose in his heart.

"You believe me, do you?" he asked.

"Yes, I believe you," she replied, with a twang of her old tired nonchalance, as if she gave in because she was tired. But he didn't care. His heart was hot and clamorous.

"So you agree to marry me before I go?—perhaps at Christmas?"

"Yes, I agree."

"There!" he exclaimed. "That's settled it."

And he sat silent, unconscious, with all the blood burning in all his veins, like fire in all the branches and twigs of him. He only pressed her two hands to his chest, without knowing. When the curious passion began to die down, he seemed to come awake to the world.

"We'll go in, shall we?" he said: as if he realised it was cold.

She rose without answering.

"Kiss me before we go, now you've said it," he said.

And he kissed her gently on the mouth, with a young, frightened kiss. It made her feel so young, too, and frightened, and wondering: and tired, as if she were going to sleep.

They went indoors. And in the sitting-room, there, crouched by the fire like a queer little witch, was Banford. She looked round with reddened eyes as they entered, but did not rise. He thought she looked frightened, unnatural, crouching there and looking round at them. Evil he thought her look was, and he crossed his fingers.

Banford saw the ruddy, elate face of the youth: he seemed strangely tall and bright and looming. And March had a delicate look on her face; she wanted to hide her face, to screen it, to let it not be seen.

"You've come at last," said Banford uglily.

"Yes, we've come," said he.

"You've been long enough for anything," she said.

"Yes, we have. We've settled it. We shall marry as soon as possible," he replied.

"Oh, you've settled it, have you! Well, I hope you won't live to repent it," said Banford.

"I hope so too," he replied.

"Are you going to bed *now*, Nellie?" said Banford.

"Yes, I'm going now."

"Then for goodness sake come along."

March looked at the boy. He was glancing with his very bright eyes at her and at Banford. March looked at him wistfully. She wished she could stay with him. She wished she had married him already, and it was all over. For oh, she felt suddenly so safe with him. She felt so strangely safe and peaceful in his presence. If only she could sleep in his shelter, and not with Jill. She felt afraid of Jill. In her dim, tender state, it was agony to have to go with Jill and sleep with her. She wanted the boy to save her. She looked again at him.

And he, watching with bright eyes, divined something of what she felt. It puzzled and distressed him that she must go with Jill.

"I shan't forget what you've promised," he said, looking clear into her eyes, right into her eyes, so that he seemed to occupy all herself with his queer, bright look.

She smiled to him, faintly, gently. She felt safe again—safe with him.

But in spite of all the boy's precautions, he had a set-back. The morning he was leaving the farm he got March to accompany him to the market-town, about six miles away, where they went to the registrar and had their names stuck up as two people who were going to marry. He was to come at Christmas, and the wedding was to take place then. He hoped in the spring to be able to take March back to Canada with him, now the war was really over. Though he was so young, he had saved some money.

165

"You never have to be without *some* money at the back of you, if you can help it," he said.

So she saw him off in the train that was going West: his camp was on Salisbury Plain. And with big, dark eyes she watched him go, and it seemed as if everything real in life was retreating as the train retreated with his queer, chubby, ruddy face, that seemed so broad across the cheeks, and which never seemed to change its expression, save when a cloud of sulky anger hung on the brow, or the bright eyes fixed themselves in their stare. This was what happened now. He leaned there out of the carriage window as the train drew off, saying good-bye and staring back at her, but his face quite unchanged. There was no emotion on his face. Only his eyes tightened and became fixed and intent in their watching like a cat's when suddenly she sees something and stares. So the boy's eyes stared fixedly as the train drew away, and she was left feeling intensely forlorn. Failing his physical presence, she seemed to have nothing of him. And she had nothing of anything. Only his face was fixed in her mind: the full, ruddy, unchanging cheeks, and the straight snout of a nose, and the two eyes staring above. All she could remember was how he suddenly wrinkled his nose when he laughed, as a puppy does when he is playfully growling. But him, himself, and what he was—she knew nothing, she had nothing of him when he left her.

On the ninth day after he had left her he received this letter.

Dear Henry,

I have been over it all again in my mind, this business of me and you, and it seems to be impossible. When you aren't there I see what a fool I am. When you are there you seem to blind me to things as they actually are. You make me see things all unreal, and I don't know what. Then when I am alone again with Jill I seem to come to my own senses and realise what a fool I am making of myself, and how I am treating you unfairly. Because it must be unfair to you for me to go on with this affair when I can't feel in my heart that I really love you. I know people talk a lot of stuff and nonsense about love, and I don't want to do that. I want to keep to plain facts and act in a sensible way. And that seems to me what I'm not doing. I don't see on what grounds I am going to marry you. I know I am not head over heels in love with you, as I have fancied myself to be with fellows when I was a young fool of a girl. You are an absolute stranger to me, and it seems to me you will always be one. So on what grounds am I going to marry you? When I think of Jill, she is ten times more real to me. I know her and I'm awfully fond of her, and I hate myself for a beast if I ever hurt her little finger. We have a life together. And even if it can't last for ever, it is a life while it does last. And it might last as long as either of us lives. Who knows how long we've got to live? She is a delicate little thing, perhaps nobody but me knows how delicate. And as for me, I feel I might fall down the well any day. What I don't seem to see at all is you. When I think of what I've been and what I've done with you, I'm afraid I am a few screws loose. I should be sorry to think that softening of the brain is setting in so soon, but that is what it seems like. You are such an absolute stranger, and so different from what I'm used to, and we don't seem to have a thing in common. As for love, the very word seems impossible. I know what love means even in Jill's case, and I know that in this affair with you it's an absolute impossibility. And then going to Canada. I'm sure I must have been clean off my chump when I promised such a thing. It makes me feel fairly frightened of myself. I feel I might do something really silly, that I wasn't responsible for—and end my days in a lunatic asylum. You may think that's all I'm fit for after the way I've gone on, but it isn't a very nice thought for me. Thank goodness Jill is here, and her being here makes me feel sane again, else I don't know what I might do; I might have an accident with the gun one evening. I love Jill and she makes me feel safe and sane, with her loving anger against me for being such a fool. Well, what I want to say is, won't you let us cry the whole thing off? I can't marry you, and really, I won't do such a thing if it seems to me wrong. It is all a great mistake. I've made a complete fool of myself, and all I can do is to apologise to you and ask you please forget it, and please to take no further notice of me. Your fox skin is nearly ready, and seems all right. I will post it to you if you will let me know if this address is still right, and if you will accept my apology for the awful and lunatic way I have behaved with you, and then let the matter rest.

Jill sends her kindest regards. Her mother and father are staying with us over Christmas.

Yours very sincerely,

ELLEN MARCH

The boy read this letter in camp as he was cleaning his kit. He set his He said nothing and saw nothing and felt nothing but a livid rage that was quite unreasoning. Balked! Balked again! Balked! He wanted the woman, he had fixed like doom upon having her. He felt that was his doom, his destiny, and his reward, to have this woman. She was his heaven and hell on earth, and he would have none elsewhere. Sightless with rage and thwarted madness he got through the morning. Save that in his mind he was lurking and scheming towards an issue, he would have committed some insane act. Deep in himself he felt like roaring and howling and gnashing his teeth and breaking things. But he was too intelligent. He knew society was on top of him and he must scheme. So with his teeth bitten together, and his nose curiously slightly lifted, like some creature that is vicious, and his eyes fixed and staring, he went through the morning's affairs drunk with

167

anger and suppression. In his mind was one thing—Banford. He took no heed of all March's outpouring: none. One thorn rankled, stuck in his mind. Banford. In his mind, in his soul, in his whole being, one thorn rankling to insanity. And he would have to get it out. He would have to get the thorn of Banford out of his life, if he died for it.

With this one fixed idea in his mind, he went to ask for twenty-four hours' leave of absence. He knew it was not due to him. His consciousness was supernaturally keen. He knew where he must go—he must go to the captain. But how could he get at the captain? In that great camp of wooden huts and tents he had no idea where his captain was.

But he went to the officers' canteen. There was his captain standing talking with three other officers. Henry stood in the doorway at attention.

"May I speak to Captain Berryman?" The captain was Cornish like himself.

"What do you want?" called the captain.

"May I speak to you, Captain?"

"What do you want?" replied the Captain, not stirring from among his group of fellow officers.

Henry watched his superior for a minute without speaking.

"You won't refuse me, sir, will you?" he asked gravely.

"It depends what it is."

"Can I have twenty-four hour's leave?"

"No, you've no business to ask."

"I know I haven't. But I must ask you."

"You've had your answer."

"Don't send me away, Captain."

There was something strange about the boy as he stood there so everlasting in the doorway. The Cornish captain felt the strangeness at once, and eyed him shrewdly.

"Why, what's afoot?" he said, curious.

"I'm in trouble about something. I must go to Blewbury," said the boy.

"Blewbury, eh? After the girls?"

"Yes, it is a woman, Captain." And the boy, as he stood there with his head reaching forward a little, went suddenly terribly pale, or yellow, and his lips seemed to give off pain. The captain saw and paled a little also. He turned aside.

"Go on, then," he said. "But for God's sake don't cause any trouble of any sort."

"I won't, Captain, thank you."

He was gone. The captain, upset, took a gin and bitters. Henry managed to hire a bicycle. It was twelve o'clock when he left the camp. He had sixty miles of wet and muddy cross-roads to ride. But he was in the saddle and down the road without a thought of food.

At the farm, March was busy with a work she had had some time in hand. A bunch of Scotch fir-trees stood at the end of the open shed, on a little bank where ran the fence between two of the gorse-shaggy meadows. The farthest of these trees was dead—it had died in the summer, and stood with all its needles brown and sere in the air. It was not a very big tree. And it was absolutely dead. So March determined to have it, although they were not allowed to cut any of the timber. But it would make such splendid firing, in these days of scarce fuel.

She had been giving a few stealthy chops at the trunk for a week or more, every now and then hacking away for five minutes, low down, near the ground, so no one should notice. She had not tried the saw, it was such hard work, alone. Now the tree stood with a great yawning gap in his base, perched as it were on one sinew, and ready to fall. But he did not fall.

It was late in the damp December afternoon, with cold mists creeping out of the woods and up the hollows, and darkness waiting to sink in from above. There was a bit of yellowness where the sun was fading away beyond the low woods of the distance. March took her axe and went to the tree. The small thud-thud of her blows resounded rather ineffectual about the wintry homestead. Banford came out wearing her thick coat, but with no hat on her head, so that her thin, bobbed hair blew on the uneasy wind that sounded in the pines and in the wood.

"What I'm afraid of," said Banford, "is that it will fall on the shed and we shall have another job repairing that."

"Oh, I don't think so," said March, straightening herself and wiping her arm over her hot brow. She was flushed red, her eyes were very wide-open and queer, her upper lip lifted away from her two white, front teeth with a curious, almost rabbit-look.

A little stout man in a black overcoat and a bowler hat came pottering across the yard. He had a pink face and a white beard and smallish, pale-blue eyes. He was not very old, but nervy, and he walked with little short steps.

"What do you think, Father?" said Banford. "Don't you think it might hit the shed in falling?"

"Shed, no!" said the old man. "Can't hit the shed. Might as well say the fence."

"The fence doesn't matter," said March, in her high voice.

"Wrong as usual, am I!" said Banford, wiping her straying hair from her eyes.

The tree stood as it were on one spelch of itself, leaning, and creaking in the wind. It grew on the bank of a little dry ditch between the two meadows. On the top of the bank straggled one fence, running to the bushes uphill. Several trees clustered there in the corner of the field near the shed and near the gate which led into the yard. Towards this gate, horizontal across the weary meadows, came the grassy, rutted approach from the high road. There trailed another ricketty fence, long split poles joining the short, thick, wide-apart uprights. The three people stood at the back of the tree, in the corner of the shed meadow, just above the yard gate. The house, with its two gables and its porch, stood tidy in a little grassed garden across the yard. A little, stout, rosy-faced woman in a little red woollen shoulder shawl had come and taken her stand in the porch.

"Isn't it down yet," she cried, in a high little voice.

"Just thinking about it," called her husband. His tone towards the two girls was always rather mocking and satirical. March did not want to go on with her hitting while he was there. As for him, he wouldn't lift a stick from the ground if he could help it, complaining, like his daughter, of rheumatics in his shoulder. So the three stood there a moment silent in the cold afternoon, in the bottom corner near the yard.

They heard the far-off taps of a gate, and craned to look. Away across, on the green horizontal approach, a figure was just swinging on to a bicycle again, and lurching up and down over the grass, approaching.

"Why, it's one of our boys—it's Jack," said the old man.

"Can't be," said Banford.

March craned her head to look. She alone recognised the khaki figure. She flushed, but said nothing.

"No, it isn't Jack, I don't think," said the old man, staring with little round blue eyes under his white lashes.

In another moment the bicycle lurched into sight, and the rider dropped off at the gate. It was Henry, his face wet and red and spotted with mud. He was altogether a muddy sight.

"Oh!" cried Banford, as if afraid. "Why, it's Henry!"

"What!" muttered the old man. He had a thick, rapid, muttering way of speaking, and was slightly deaf. "What? What? Who is it? Who is it, do you say? That young fellow? That young fellow of Nellie's? Oh! Oh!" And the satiric smile came on his pink face and white eyelashes.

Henry, pushing the wet hair off his steaming brow, had caught sight of them and heard what the old man said. His hot, young face seemed to flame in the cold light.

"Oh, are you all there!" he said, giving his sudden, puppy's little laugh.

He was so hot and dazed with cycling he hardly knew where he was. He leaned the bicycle against the fence and climbed over into the corner on to the bank, without going into the yard.

"Well, I must say, we weren't expecting *you*," said Banford laconically.

"No, I suppose not," said he, looking at March.

She stood aside, slack, with one knee drooped and the axe resting its head loosely on the ground. Her eyes were wide and vacant, and her upper lip lifted from her teeth in that helpless, fascinated rabbit-look. The moment she saw his glowing, red face it was all over with her. She was as helpless as if she had been bound. The moment she saw the way his head seemed to reach forward.

"Well, who is it? Who is it, anyway?" asked the smiling, satiric old man in his muttering voice.

"Why, Mr Grenfel, whom you've heard us tell about, Father," said Banford coldly.

"Heard you tell about, I should think so. Heard of nothing else practically," muttered the elderly man, with his queer little jeering smile on his face. "How do you do," he added, suddenly reaching out his hand to Henry.

The boy shook hands just as startled. Then the two men fell apart.

"Cycled over from Salisbury Plain, have you?" asked the old man.

"Yes."

"Hm! Longish ride. How long d'it take you, eh? Some time, eh? Several hours, I suppose."

"About four."

"Eh? Four! Yes, I should have thought so. When are you going back, then?"

"I've got till to-morrow evening."

"Till to-morrow evening, eh? Hm! Girls weren't expecting you, were they?"

And the old man turned his pale-blue, round little eyes under their white lashes mockingly towards the girls. Henry also looked around. He had become a little awkward. He looked at March, who was still staring away into the distance as if to see where the cattle were. Her hand was on the pommel of the axe, whose head rested loosely on the ground.

"What were you doing there?" he asked in his soft, courteous voice. "Cutting a tree down?"

March seemed not to hear, as if in trance.

"Yes," said Banford. "We've been at it for over a week."

"Oh! And have you done it all by yourselves then?"

"Nellie's done it all, I've done nothing," said Banford.

"Really! You must have worked quite hard," he said, addressing himself in a curious gentle tone direct to March. She did not answer, but remained half averted staring away towards the woods above as if in a trance.

"*Nellie!*" cried Banford sharply. "Can't you answer?"

"What—me?" cried March, starting round, and looking from one to the other. "Did anyone speak to me?"

"Dreaming!" muttered the old man, turning aside to smile. "Must be in love, eh, dreaming in the day-time!"

"Did you say anything to me?" said March, looking at the boy as from a strange distance, her eyes wide and doubtful, her face delicately flushed.

"I said you must have worked hard at the tree," he replied courteously.

"Oh that! Bit by bit. I thought it would have come down by now."

"I'm thankful it hasn't come down in the night, to frighten us to death," said Banford.

"Let me just finish it for you, shall I?" said the boy.

March slanted the axe-shaft in his direction.

"Would you like to?" she said.

"Yes, if you wish it," he said.

"Oh, I'm thankful when the thing's down, that's all," she replied, nonchalant.

"Which way is it going to fall?" said Banford. "Will it hit the shed?"

"No, it won't hit the shed," he said. "I should think it will fall there——quite clear. Though it might give a twist and catch the fence."

"Catch the fence!" cried the old man. "What, catch the fence! When it's leaning at that angle? Why, it's further off than the shed. It won't catch the fence."

"No," said Henry. "I don't suppose it will. It has plenty of room to fall quite clear, and I suppose it will fall clear."

"Won't tumble backwards on top of *us*, will it?" asked the old man, sarcastic.

"No, it won't do that," said Henry, taking off his short overcoat and his tunic. "Ducks! Ducks! Go back!"

A line of four brown-speckled ducks led by a brown-and-green drake were stemming away downhill from the upper meadow, coming like boats running on a ruffled sea, cockling their way top speed downwards towards the fence and towards the little group of people, and cackling as excitedly as if they brought news of the Spanish Armada.

"Silly things! Silly things!" cried Banford, going forward to turn them off. But they came eagerly towards her, opening their yellow-green beaks

172

and quacking as if they were so excited to say something.

"There's no food. There's nothing here. You must wait a bit," said Banford to them. "Go away. Go away. Go round to the yard."

They didn't go, so she climbed the fence to swerve them round under the gate and into the yard. So off they waggled in an excited string once more, wagging their rumps like the stems of little gondolas, ducking under the bar of the gate. Banford stood on the top of the bank, just over the fence, looking down on the other three.

Henry looked up at her, and met her queer, round-pupilled, weak eyes staring behind her spectacles. He was perfectly still. He looked away, up at the weak, leaning tree. And as he looked into the sky, like a huntsman who is watching a flying bird, he thought to himself: "If the tree falls in just such a way, and spins just so much as it falls, then the branch there will strike her exactly as she stands on top of that bank."

He looked at her again. She was wiping the hair from her brow again, with that perpetual gesture. In his heart he had decided her death. A terrible still force seemed in him, and a power that was just his. If he turned even a hair's breadth in the wrong direction, he would lose the power.

"Mind yourself, Miss Banford," he said. And his heart held perfectly still, in the terrible pure will that she should not move.

"Who, me, mind myself?" she cried, her father's jeering tone in her voice. "Why, do you think you might hit me with the axe?"

"No, it's just possible the tree might, though," he answered soberly. But the tone of his voice seemed to her to imply that he was only being falsely solicitous, and trying to make her move because it was his will to move her.

"Absolutely impossible," she said.

He heard her. But he held himself icy still, lest he should lose his power.

"No, it's just possible. You'd better come down this way."

"Oh, all right. Let us see some crack Canadian tree felling," she retorted.

"Ready, then," he said, taking the axe, looking round to see he was clear.

There was a moment of pure, motionless suspense, when the world seemed to stand still. Then suddenly his form seemed to flash up enormously tall and fearful, he gave two swift, flashing blows, in immediate succession, the tree was severed, turning slowly, spinning strangely in the air and coming down like a sudden darkness on the earth. No one saw what was happening except himself. No one heard the strange little cry which the Banford gave as the dark end of the bough swooped down, down on her. No one saw her crouch a little and receive the blow on the back of the neck. No one saw her flung outwards and laid, a little twitching heap, at the foot of the fence. No one except the boy. And he watched with intense bright eyes, as he would watch a wild goose he had shot. Was it winged, or dead? Dead!

Immediately he gave a loud cry. Immediately March gave a wild shriek that went far, far down the afternoon. And the father started a strange bellowing sound.

The boy leapt the fence and ran to the figure. The back of the neck and head was a mass of blood, of horror. He turned it over. The body was quivering with little convulsions. But she was dead really. He knew it, that it was so. He knew it in his soul and his blood. The inner necessity of his life was fulfilling itself, it was he who was to live. The thorn was drawn out of his bowels. So he put her down gently. She was dead.

He stood up. March was standing there petrified and absolutely motionless. Her face was dead white, her eyes big black pools. The old man was scrambling horribly over the fence.

"I'm afraid it's killed her," said the boy.

The old man was making curious, blubbering noises as he huddled over the fence. "What!" cried March, starting electric.

"Yes, I'm afraid," repeated the boy.

March was coming forward. The boy was over the fence before she reached it.

"What do you say, killed her?" she asked in a sharp voice.

"I'm afraid so," he answered softly.

She went still whiter, fearful. The two stood facing one another. Her black eyes gazed on him with the last look of resistance. And then in a last agonised failure she began to grizzle, to cry in a shivery little fashion of a child that doesn't want to cry, but which is beaten from within, and gives that little first shudder of sobbing which is not yet weeping, dry and fearful.

He had won. She stood there absolutely helpless, shuddering her dry sobs and her mouth trembling rapidly. And then, as in a child, with a little crash came the tears and the blind agony of sightless weeping. She sank down on the grass, and sat there with her hands on her breast and her face lifted in sightless, convulsed weeping. He stood above her, looking down on her, mute, pale, and everlasting seeming. He never moved, but looked down on her. And among all the torture of the scene, the torture of his own heart and bowels, he was glad, he had won.

After a long time he stooped to her and took her hands.

"Don't cry," he said softly. "Don't cry."

She looked up at him with tears running from her eyes, a senseless look

174

of helplessness and submission. So she gazed on him as if sightless, yet looking up to him. She would never leave him again. He had won her. And he knew it and was glad, because he wanted her for his life. His life must have her. And now he had won her. It was what his life must have.

But if he had won her, he had not yet got her. They were married at Christmas as he had planned, and he got again ten days' leave. They went to Cornwall, to his own village, on the sea. He realised that it was awful for her to be at the farm any more.

But though she belonged to him, though she lived in his shadow, as if she could not be away from him, she was not happy. She did not want to leave him: and yet she did not feel free with him. Everything around her seemed to watch her, seemed to press on her. He had won her, he had her with him, she was his wife. And she—she belonged to him, she knew it. But she was not glad. And he was still foiled. He realised that though he was married to her and possessed her in every possible way, apparently, and though she *wanted* him to possess her, she wanted it, she wanted nothing else, now, still he did not quite succeed.

Something was missing. Instead of her soul swaying with new life, it seemed to droop, to bleed, as if it were wounded. She would sit for a long time with her hand in his, looking away at the sea. And in her dark, vacant eyes was a sort of wound, and her face looked a little peaked. If he spoke to her, she would turn to him with a faint new smile, the strange, quivering little smile of a woman who has died in the old way of love, and can't quite rise to the new way. She still felt she ought to *do* something, to strain herself in some direction. And there was nothing to do, and no direction in which to strain herself. And she could not quite accept the submergence which his new love put upon her. If she was in love, she ought to *exert* herself, in some way, loving. She felt the weary need of our day to *exert* herself in love. But she knew that in fact she must no more exert herself in love. He would not have the love which exerted itself towards him. It made his brow go black. No, he wouldn't let her exert her love towards him. No, she had to be passive, to acquiesce, and to be submerged under the surface of love. She had to be like the seaweeds she saw as she peered down from the boat, swaying forever delicately under water, with all their delicate fibrils put tenderly out upon the flood, sensitive, utterly sensitive and receptive within the shadowy sea, and never, never rising and looking forth above water while they lived. Never. Never looking forth from the water until they died, only then washing, corpses, upon the surface. But while they lived, always submerged, always beneath the wave. Beneath the wave they might have powerful roots, stronger than iron;

they might be tenacious and dangerous in their soft waving within the flood. Beneath the water they might be stronger, more indestructible than resistant oak trees are on land. But it was always under-water, always under-water. And she, being a woman, must be like that.

And she had been so used to the very opposite. She had had to take all the thought for love and for life, and all the responsibility. Day after day she had been responsible for the coming day, for the coming year: for her dear Jill's health and happiness and well-being. Verily, in her own small way, she had felt herself responsible for the well-being of the world. And this had been her great stimulant, this grand feeling that, in her own small sphere, she was responsible for the well-being of the world.

And she had failed. She knew that, even in her small way, she had failed. She had failed to satisfy her own feeling of responsibility. It was so difficult. It seemed so grand and easy at first. And the more you tried, the more difficult it became. It had seemed so easy to make one beloved creature happy. And the more you tried, the worse the failure. It was terrible. She had been all her life reaching, reaching, and what she reached for seemed so near, until she had stretched to her utmost limit. And then it was always beyond her.

Always beyond her, vaguely, unrealisably beyond her, and she was left with nothingness at last. The life she reached for, the happiness she reached for, the well-being she reached for all slipped back, became unreal, the further she stretched her hand. She wanted some goal, some finality— and there was none. Always this ghastly reaching, reaching, striving for something that might be just beyond. Even to make Jill happy. She was glad Jill was dead. For she had realised she could never make her happy. Jill would always be fretting herself thinner and thinner, weaker and weaker. Her pains grew worse instead of less. It would be so for ever. She was glad she was dead.

And if Jill had married a man it would have been just the same. The woman striving, striving to make the man happy, striving within her own limits for the well-being of the world. And always achieving failure. Little, foolish successes in money or in ambition. But at the very point where she most wanted success, in the anguished effort to make some one beloved human being happy and perfect, there the failure was almost catastrophic. You wanted to make your beloved happy, and his happiness seemed always achievable If only you did just this, that, and the other. And you did this, that, and the other, in all good faith, and every time the failure became a little more ghastly. You could love yourself to ribbons, and strive and strain yourself to the bone, and things would go from bad to worse, bad to worse, as far as happiness went. The awful mistake of happiness.

Poor March, in her good will and her responsibility, she had strained herself till it seemed to her that the whole of life and everything was only a horrible abyss of nothingness. The more you reached after the fatal flower of happiness, which trembles so blue and lovely in a crevice just beyond your grasp, the more fearfully you become aware of the ghastly and awful gulf of the precipice below you, into which you will inevitably plunge, as into the bottomless pit, if you reach any further. You pluck flower after flower—it is never *the* flower. The flower itself—its calyx is a horrible gulf, it is the bottomless pit.

That is the whole history of the search for happiness, whether it be your own or somebody else's that you want to win. It ends, and it always ends, in the ghastly sense of bottomless nothingness into which you will inevitably fall if you strain any further.

And women?—what goal can any woman conceive, except happiness? Just happiness, for herself and the whole world. That, and nothing else. And so, she assumes the responsibility, and sets off towards her goal. She can see it there, at the foot of the rainbow. Or she can see it a little way beyond, in the blue distance. Not far, not far.

But the end of the rainbow is a bottomless gulf down which you can fall forever without arriving, and the blue distance is a void pit which can swallow you and all your efforts into its emptiness, and still be no emptier. You and all your efforts. So, the illusion of attainable happiness!

Poor March, she had set off so wonderfully towards the blue goal. And the further and further she had gone, the more fearful had become the realisation of emptiness. An agony, an insanity at last.

She was glad it was over. She was glad to sit on the shore and look westwards over the sea, and know the great strain had ended. She would never strain for love and happiness any more. And Jill was safely dead. Poor Jill, poor Jill. It must be sweet to be dead.

For her own part, death was not her destiny. She would have to leave her destiny to the boy. But then, the boy. He wanted more than that. He wanted her to give herself without defences, to sink and become submerged in him. And she—she wanted to sit still, like a woman on the last milestone, and watch. She wanted to see, to know, to understand. She wanted to be alone: with him at her side.

And he! He did not want her to watch any more, to see any more, to understand any more. He wanted to veil her woman's spirit, as Orientals veil the woman's face. He wanted her to commit herself to him, and to put her independent spirit to sleep. He wanted to take away from her all her effort, all that seemed her very *raison d'être*. He wanted to make her submit, yield, blindly pass away out of all her strenuous consciousness. He wanted to take away her consciousness, and make her just his woman. Just his woman.

And she was so tired, like a child that wants to go to sleep, but which fights against sleep as if sleep were death. She seemed to stretch her eyes wider in the obstinate effort and tension of keeping awake. She *would* keep awake. She *would* know. She *would* consider and judge and decide. She *would* have the reins of her own life between her own hands. She *would* be an independent woman, to the last. But she was so tired, so tired of everything. And sleep seemed near. And there was such rest in the boy.

Yet there, sitting in a niche of the high, wild cliffs of West Cornwall, looking over the westward sea, she stretched her eyes wider and wider. Away to the West, Canada, America. She *would* know and she *would* see what was ahead. And the boy, sitting beside her, staring down at the gulls, had a cloud between his brows and the strain of discontent in his eyes. He wanted her asleep, at peace in him. He wanted her at peace, asleep in him. And *there* she was, dying with the strain of her own wakefulness. Yet she would not sleep: no, never. Sometimes he thought bitterly that he ought to have left her. He ought never to have killed Banford. He should have left Banford and March to kill one another.

But that was only impatience: and he knew it. He was waiting, waiting to go west. He was aching almost in torment to leave England, to go west, to take March away. To leave this shore! He believed that as they crossed the seas, as they left this England which he so hated, because in some way it seemed to have stung him with poison, she would go to sleep. She would close her eyes at last, and give in to him.

And then he would have her, and he would have his own life at last. He chafed, feeling he hadn't got his own life. He would never have it till she yielded and slept in him. Then he would have all his own life as a young man and a male, and she would have all her own life as a woman and a female. Ther would be no more of this awful straining. She would not be a man any more, an independent woman with a man's responsibility. Nay, even the responsibility for her own soul she would have to commit to him. He knew it was so, and obstinately held out against her, waiting for her surrender.

"You'll feel better when once we get over the seas to Canada over there," he said to her as they sat among the rocks on the cliff.

She looked away to the sea's horizon, as if it were not real. Then she looked round at him, with the strained, strange look of a child that is struggling against sleep.

"Shall I?" she said.

"Yes," he answered quietly.

And her eyelids dropped with the slow motion, sleep weighing them unconscious. But she pulled them open again to say:

"Yes, I may. Y can't tell. I can't tell what it will be like over there."

"If only we could go soon!" he said, with pain in his voice.

A DILL PICKLE[1]

Katherine Mansfield

AND then, after six years, she saw him again. He was seated at one of those little bamboo tables decorated with a Japanese vase of paper daffodils. There was a tall plate of fruit in front of him, and very carefully, in a way she recognized immediately as his 'special' way, he was peeling an orange.

He must have felt that shock of recognition in her for he looked up and met her eyes. Incredible! He didn't know her! She smiled; he frowned. She came towards him. He closed his eyes an instant, but opening them his face lit up as though he had struck a match in a dark room. He laid down the orange and pushed back his chair, and she took her little warm hand out of her muff and gave it to him.

"Vera!" he exclaimed. "How strange. Really, for a moment I didn't know you. Won't you sit down? You've had lunch? Won' tyou have some coffee?"

She hesitated, but of course she meant to.

"Yes, I'd like some coffee." And she sat down opposite him.

"You've changed. You've changed very much," he said, staring at her with that eager, lighted look. "You look so well. I've never seen you look so well before."

"Really?" She raised her veil and unbuttoned her high fur collar. "I don't feel very well. I can't bear this weather, you know."

"Ah, no. You hate the cold...."

"Loathe it." She shuddered. "And the worst of it is that the older one grows...."

He interrupted her. "Excuse me," and tapped on the table for the waitress. "Please bring some coffee and cream." To her: "You are sure you won't eat anything? Some fruit, perhaps. The fruit here is very good."

---

[1] From *Bliss and Other Stories*. Reprinted by permission of Messrs Constable and Co., Ltd., London, and Messrs Alfred A. Knopf, Inc., New York

"No, thanks. Nothing."

"Then that's settled." And smiling just a hint too broadly he took up the orange again. "You were saying—the older one grows——"

"The colder," she laughed. But she was thinking how well she remembered that trick of his—the trick of interrupting her—and how it used to exasperate her six years ago. She used to feel then as though he, quite suddenly, in the middle of what she was saying, put his hand over her lips, turned from her, attended to something different, and then took his hand away, and with just the same slightly too broad smile, gave her his attention again.... Now we are ready. That is settled.

"The colder!" He echoed her words, laughing too. "Ah, ah. You still say the same things. And there is another thing about you that is not changed at all—your beautiful voice—your beautiful way of speaking." Now he was very grave; he leaned towards her, and she smelled the warm, stinging scent of the orange peel. "You have only to say one word and I would know your voice among all other voices. I don't know what it is—I've often wondered—that makes your voice such a—haunting memory.... Do you remember that first afternoon we spent together at Kew Gardens? You were so surprised because I did not know the names of any flowers. I am still just as ignorant for all your telling me. But whenever it is very fine and warm, and I see some bright colours— it's awfully strange—I hear your voice saying: 'Geranium, marigold, and verbena.' And I feel those three words are all I recall of some forgotten, heavenly language.... You remember that afternoon?"

"Oh, yes, very well." She drew a long, soft breath, as though the paper daffodils between them were almost too sweet to bear. Yet, what had remained in her mind of that particular afternoon was an absurd scene over the tea table. A great many people taking tea in a Chinese pagoda, and he behaving like a maniac about the wasps—waving them away, flapping at them with his straw hat, serious and infuriated out of all proportion to the occasion. How delighted the sniggering tea drinkers had been. And how she had suffered.

But now, as he spoke, the memory faded. His was the truer. Yes, it had been a wonderful afternoon, full of geranium and marigold and verbena, and—warm sunshine. Her thoughts lingered over the last two words as though she sang them.

In the warmth, as it were, another memory unfolded. She saw herself sitting on a lawn. He lay beside her, and suddenly, after a long silence, he rolled over and put his head in her lap.

"I wish," he said, in a low, troubled voice, "I wish that I had taken

180

poison and were about to die—here now!"

At that moment a little girl in a white dress, holding a long, dripping water-lily, dodged from behind a bush, stared at them, and dodged back again. But he did not see. She leaned over him.

"Ah, why do you say that? I could not say that."

But he gave a kind of soft moan, and taking her hand he held it to his cheek.

"Because I know I am going to love you too much—far too much. And I shall suffer so terribly, Vera, because you never, never will love me."

He was certainly far better looking now than he had been then. He had lost all that dreamy vagueness and indecision. Now he had the air of a man who has found his place in life, and fills it with a confidence and an assurance which was, to say the least, impressive. He must have made money, too. His clothes were admirable, and at that moment he pulled a Russian cigarette case out of his pocket.

"Won't you smoke?"

"Yes, I will." She hovered over them. "They look very good."

"I think they are. I get them made for me by a little man in St. James's Street. I don't smoke very much. I'm not like you—but when I do, they must be delicious, very fresh cigarettes. Smoking isn't a habit with me; it's a luxury—like perfume. Are you still so fond of perfumes? Ah, when I was in Russia..."

She broke in: "You've really been to Russia?"

"Oh, yes. I was there for over a year. Have you forgotten how we used to talk of going there?"

"No, I've not forgotten."

He gave a strange half laugh and leaned back in his chair. "Isn't it curious. I have really carried out all those journeys that we planned. Yes, I have been to all those places that we talked of, and stayed in them long enough to—as you used to say, 'air oneself' in them. In fact, I have spent the last three years of my life travelling all the time. Spain, Corsica, Siberia, Russia, Egypt. The only country left is China, and I mean to go there, too, when the War is over."

As he spoke, so lightly, tapping the end of his cigarette against the ash-tray, she felt the strange beast that had slumbered so long within her bosom stir, stretch itself, yawn, prick up its ears, and suddenly bound to its feet, and fix its longing, hungry stare upon those far-away places. But all she said was, smiling gently: "How I envy you."

He accepted that. "It has been," he said. "very wonderful—especially Russia. Russia was all that we had imagined, and far, far more. I even spent some days on a river boat on the Volga. Do you remember that boatman's song that you used to play?"

"Yes." It began to play in her mind as she spoke.

"Do you ever play it now?"

"No, I've no piano."

He was amazed at that. "But what has become of your beautiful piano?"

She made a little grimace. "Sold. Ages ago."

"But you were so fond of music," he wondered.

"I've no time for it now," said she.

He let it go at that. "That river life," he went on, "is something quite special. After a day or two you cannot realize that you have ever known another. And it is not necessary to know the language—the life of the boat creates a bond between you and the people that's more than sufficient. You eat with them, pass the day with them, and in the evening there is that endless singing."

She shivered, hearing the boatman's song break out again loud and tragic, and seeing the boat floating on the darkening river with melancholy trees on either side.... "Yes, I should like that," said she, stroking her muff.

"You'd like almost everything about Russian life," he said warmly. "It's so informal, so impulsive, so free without question. And then the peasants are so splendid. They are such human beings—yes, that is it. Even the man who drives your carriage has—has some real part in what is happening. I remember the evening a party of us, two friends of mine and the wife of one of them, went for a picnic by the Black Sea. We took supper and champagne and ate and drank on the grass. And while we were eating the coachman came up. 'Have a dill pickle,' he said. He wanted to share with us. That seemed to me so right, so—you know what I mean?"

And she seemed at that moment to be sitting on the grass beside the mysteriously Black Sea, black as velvet, and rippling against the banks in silent, velvet waves. She saw the carriage drawn up to one side of the road, and the little group on the grass, their faces and hands white in the moonlight. She saw the pale dress of the woman outspread and her folded parasol, lying on the grass like a huge pearl crochet hook. Apart from them, with his supper in a cloth on his knees, sat the coachman. "Have a dill pickle," said he, and although she was not certain what a dill pickle was, she saw the greenish glass jar with a red chili like a parrot's beak glimmering through. She sucked in her cheeks; the dill pickle was terribly sour.... "Yes, I know perfectly what you mean," she said.

In the pause that followed they looked at each other. In the past when they had looked at each other like that they had felt such a boundless un-

182

derstanding between them that their souls had, as it were, put their arms round each other and dropped into the same sea, content to be drowned, like mournful lovers. But now, the surprising thing was that it was he who held back. He who said:

"What a marvellous listener you are. When you look at me with those wild eyes I feel that I could tell you things that I would never breathe to another human being."

Was there just a hint of mockery in his voice or was it her fancy? She could not be sure.

"Before I met you," he said, "I had never spoken of myself to anybody, How well I remember one night, the night that I brought you the little Christmas-tree, telling you all about my childhood. And of how I was so miserable that I ran away and lived under a cart in our yard for two days without being discovered. And you listened, and your eyes shone, and I felt that you had even made the little Christmas-tree listen too, as in a fairy story."

But of that evening she had remembered a little pot of caviare. It had cost seven and sixpence. He could not get over it. Think of it—a tiny jar like that costing seven and sixpence. While she ate it he watched her, delighted and shocked.

"No, really, that is eating money. You could not get seven shillings into a little pot that size. Only think of the profit they must make...." And he had begun some immensely complicated calculations.... But now good-bye to the caviare. The Christmas-tree was on the table, and the little boy lay under the cart with his head pillowed on the yard dog.

"The dog was called Bosun," she cried delightfully.

But he did not follow, "Which dog? Had you a dog? I don't remember a dog at all."

"No, no. I mean the yard dog when you were a little boy." He laughed and snapped the cigarette case to.

"Was he? Do you know I had forgotten that. It seems such ages ago. I cannot believe that it is only six years. After I had recognized you to-day —I had to take such a leap—I had to take a leap over my whole life to get back to that time. I was such a kid then." He drummed on the table. "I've often thought how I must have bored you. And now I understand so perfectly why you wrote to me as you did—although at the time that letter nearly finished my life. I found it again the other day, and I couldn't help laughing as I read it. It was so clever—such a true picture of me." He glanced up. "You're not going?"

She had buttoned her collar again and drawn down her veil.

"Yes, I am afraid I must," she said, and managed a smile. Now she knew that he had been mocking.

"Ah, no, please," he pleaded. "Don't go just for a moment," and he caught up one of her gloves from the table and clutched at it as if that would hold her. "I see so few people to talk to nowadays, that I have turned into a sort of barbarian," he said. "Have I said something to hurt you?"

"Not a bit," she lied. But as she watched him draw her glove through his fingers, gently, gently, her anger really did die down, and besides, at the moment he looked more like himself of six years ago....

"What I really wanted then," he said softly, "was to be a sort of carpet —to make myself into a sort of carpet for you to walk on so that you need not be hurt by the sharp stones and the mud that you hated so. It was nothing more positive than that—nothing more selfish. Only I did desire, eventually, to turn into a magic carpet and carry you away to all those lands you longed to see." As he spoke she lifted her head as though she drank something; the strange beast in her bosom began to purr....

"I felt that you were more lonely than anybody else in the world," he went on, "and yet, perhaps, that you were the only person in the world who was really, truly alive. Born out of your time," he murmured, stroking the glove, "fated."

Ah, God! What had she done! How had she dared to throw away her happiness like this. This was the only man who had ever understood her. Was it too late? Could it be too late? *She* was that glove that he held in his fingers....

"And then the fact that you had no friends and never had made friends with people. How I understood that, for neither had I. Is it just the same now?"

"Yes," she breathed. "Just the same. I am as alone as ever."

"So am I." he laughed gently, "just the same."

Suddenly with a quick gesture he handed her back the glove and scraped his chair on the floor. "But what seemed to me so mysterious then is perfectly plain to me now. And to you, too, of course.... It simply was that we were such egoists, so self-engrossed, so wrapped up in ourselves that we hadn't a corner in our hearts for anybody else. Do you know," he cried, naive and hearty, and dreadfully like another side of that old self again, "I began studying a Mind System when I was in Russia, and I found that we were not peculiar at all. It's quite a well known form of..."

She had gone. He sat there, thunder-struck, astounded beyond words. ... And then he asked the waitress for the bill.

"But the cream has not been touched," he said. "Please do not charge me for it."

184

SCOTLAND

MARY, QUEEN OF SCOTS[1]

Sir Walter Scott

MARY STEWART, the Queen Dowager of France, and the hereditary Queen of Scotland, was accounted the most beautiful and accomplished woman of her time. Her countenance was lovely; she was tall, well-formed, elegant in all her motions, skilled in the exercises of riding and dancing, and possessed of all the female accomplishments which were in fashion at that period. Her education in France had been carefully attended to. She was mistress of several languages, and understood state affairs in which her husband had often followed her advice. The beauty of Mary was enhanced by her great condescension, ans by the good-humour and gaiety which she sometimes carried to the verge of excess. Her youth, for she was only eighteen when she returned to Scotland, increased the liveliness of her disposition. The Catholic religion, in which she had been strictly educated, was a great blemish in the eyes of her people; but on the whole the nation expected her return with more hope and joy than Mary herself entertained at the thought of exchanging the fine climate of France, and the gaieties of its court, for the rough tempests and turbulent politics of her native country.

Mary set sail from France 15th August 1561. Occupied with anxious forebodings, the Queen remained on the deck of her galley, gazing on the coasts of France, and when they vanished from her eyes, she exclaimed in sorrow, "Farewell, farewell, happy France; I shall never see thee more!"

She arrived at Leith on the 19th August, where little or no preparation had been made for her honourable reception. Such of the nobles as were in the capital hastened, however, to wait upon their young Queen, and convey her to Holyrood, the palace of her ancestors. Horses were provided to bring her and her train to Edinburgh; but they were wretched ponies, and had such tattered furniture and accoutrements that poor Mary, when she thought of the splendid palfreys and rich appointments at the court of France, could not forbear shedding tears. The people were, however, in their way, rejoiced to see her; and about two hundred citizens of Edin-

---

[1] From *Tales of a Grandfather*.

burgh, each doing his best upon a three-stringed fiddle, played under her window all night, by way of welcome, a noisy serenade, which deprived her of sleep after her fatigue. She took it as it was meant nevertheless, and expressed her thanks to the perpetrators of this mistuned and mistimed concert. Mary had immediately after her arrival a specimen of the religious zeal of her Reformed subjects. She had ordered mass to be performed by a Popish ecclesiastic in her own chapel, but the popular indignation was so much excited, that but for the interference of her natural brother, the Prior of St Andrews, the priest would have been murdered on his own altar.

Mary behaved with admirable prudence at this early period of her reign. She enchanted the common people by her grace and condescension, and while she sat in council, usually employed in some female work, she gained credit for her wisdom among the statemen whom she consulted. She was cautious of attempting anything contrary to the religion of her subjects, though different from her own; and guided by the advice of the Prior of St Andrews, and of the sagacious Maitland, she made rapid progress in the affections of her people. With similar prudence, the Queen maintained all the usual intercourse of civility with Elizabeth; and while she refused to abandon her title to the crown of England, in the case of Elizabeth dying without heirs of her body, she expressed her anxious wish to live on the best terms with her sister sovereign, and her readiness to relinquish, during the life of the English Queen, any right of inheritance to the English crown. Elizabeth was silenced if not satisfied; and there continued to be a constant communication of apparent friendship between the two sovereigns, and an exchange of letters, compliments, and occasionally of presents, becoming their rank, with much profession of mutual kindness. But there was one important class of persons to whom Mary's form of religion was so obnoxious that they could not be gained to any favourable thoughts of her. These were the preachers of the Reformed faith, who exclaimed against the Queen, even in the pulpit, with an indecent violence unfitting that place, and never spoke of her but as one hardened in resistance to the voice of true Christian instruction. John Knox himself introduced such severe expressions into his sermons, that Queen Mary condescended to expostulate with him personally. Nevertheless, though the language of these rough Reformers was too vehement, it must be owned that their suspicions of Mary's sincerity were natural. The Queen uniformly declined to ratify the religious system adopted by the Parliament in 1560, or the confiscation of the Church lands. She always seemed to consider the present state of things as a temporary arrangement, to which she wasindeed willing to submit for the time, but with the reservation that it should be subjected to alterations when there was a fitting opportunity. Her brother, however, who was at this time her principal counsellor, and her best friend, used his influence with the Protestant clergy in her behalf.

The first troublesome affair in Queen Mary's reign seems to have arisen from her attachment to this brother and his interest. She had created him Earl of Mar, but it was her purpose to confer on him, instead of this title, that of Earl of Moray, and with it great part of the large estates belonging to that northern earldom.

This exchange, however, could not be made, without giving offence to the Earl of Huntly, head of the most powerful family in the North, who had possessed himself of a considerable part of those domains which had belonged to the earldom of Moray. This Earl of Huntly was a brave man, and possessed of very great power in the northern counties. He was one of the few remaining peers who continued attached to the Catholic religion.

The Earl of Mar was, on his part, determined to break the strength of this great opponent; and Queen Mary, who appears also to have feared Huntly's power, and the use which he seemed disposed to make of it, undertook a personal journey to the north of Scotland, to enforce obedience to her commands.

The young Queen advanced northward at the head of a small army, encamping in the fields, or accepting such miserable lodgings as the houses of the smaller gentry afforded. It was, however a scene which awoke her natural courage, and, marching at the head of her soldiery, such was her spirit, that she publicly wished she had been a man, to sleep all night in the fields, and to walk armed with a jack and skull-cap of steel, a good Glasgow buckler at her back, and a broadsword by her side.

Huntly easily assembled a considerable host, and advanced towards Aberdeen. The purpose of his enterprise was, perhaps, an attack rather upon the Queen's counsellors than on her person. But her brother, who had now exchanged his title of Mar for that of Moray, was an excellent soldier. He drew up the men he could trust on an eminence called the hill of Fare. He did not allow the northern clans to mix their doubtful succours with this resolute battalion, and the event showed the wisdom of his precaution. Huntly approached, and encountered the northern troops, his allies and neighbours, who offered little or no resistance. They fled tumultuously towards Moray's main body, pursued by the Gordons, who threw away their spears, drew their swords, and advanced in disorder, as to an assured victory. In this tumult they encountered the resistance of Moray's firm battalion of spearmen, who received the attack in close order, and with determined resolution. The Gordons were repulsed in their turn; and those clans who had before fled, seeing they were about to lose the day, returned, fell upon the Gordons, and completed Moray's victory. Huntly, a bulky man, and heavily armed, fell from horseback in the flight, and was trodden to death.

Moray was placed in possession of the estates belonging to his new earldom, and the Queen returned.

Thus far the reign of Mary had been eminently prosperous; but a fatal crisis approached. She had no children, and her subjects were desirous that she should marry a second husband. Queen Elizabeth had declared her own resolution never to marry, and Mary of Scotland was the next heir to the English crown. It was both prudent and natural that in forming a new marriage Mary should desire to have the advice and approbation of the princess to whose realm she or her children might hope to succeed.

Elizabeth was one of the wisest Queens that ever wore a crown, but her conduct towards her kinswoman Mary, from beginning to end, indicated a degree of envy and deceit totally unworthy of her general character. She adopted a mean and shuffling policy, recommending one match after another, but throwing in obstacles whenever any of them seemed likely to take place.

Meantime the views of Queen Mary turned towards a young nobleman of high birth, nearly connected both with her own family and that of Elizabeth. This was Henry Stewart, Lord Darnley, eldest son of the Earl of Lennox.

The young Lord Darnley's father being of high rank, Mary imagined that in marrying him she would gratify the wishes of the English Queen. Elizabeth seemed to receive the proposal favourably, and suffered the young man, and his father Lennox, to visit the court of Scotland, thinking that, in case the match should be likely to take place, she might easily break it off by recalling them as her subjects; a command which she supposed they would not dare to disobey, as enjoying all their lands and means of living in England.

Young Darnley was remarkably tall and handsome, perfect in all external and showy accomplishments, but unhappily destitute of sagacity, prudence, steadiness of character, and exhibiting only doubtful courage, though extremely violent in his passions. Had this young man possessed a very moderate portion of sense, or even of gratitude, we might have had a different story to tell of Mary's reign. Mary had the misfortune to look upon this young nobleman with partiality, and was the more willing to gratify her own inclinations in his favour, that she longed to put an end to the intrigues by which Queen Elizabeth had endeavoured to impose upon her, and prevent her marriage. Indeed, while the two Queens used towards each other the language of the most affectionate cordiality, there was betwixt them neither plain dealing nor upright meaning, but great dissimulation, envy, and fear.

Darnley, in the meantime, endeavouring to strengthen the interest which he had acquired in the Queen's affections, had recourse to the friendship of a man, of low rank, indeed, but who was understood to possess particular influence over the mind of Mary. This was an Italian, called David Rizzio, who had been promoted from being a menial in the Queen's family, to the confidential office of French Secretary. His talents for music gave him frequent admission to Mary's presence, as she delighted in that art; and his address and arts of insinuation gained him a considerable influence over her mind. It was almost necessary that the Queen should have near her person some confidential officer, skilled at once in languages and in business, through whom she might communicate with foreign states, and with her friends in France in particular. No such agent was likely to be found in Scotland, unless she had chosen a Catholic priest, which would have given more offence to her Protestant subjects than even the employment of a man like Rizzio. Still the elevation of this person, a stranger, a Catholic, and a man of mean origin, to the rank of a minister of the crown—and, yet more, the personal familiarity to which the Queen condescended to admit him, and the airs of importance which this low-born foreigner pretended to assume, became the subject of offence to the proud Scottish nobles, and of vulgar scandal among the common people.

Darnley, anxious to strengthen his interest with the Queen on every hand, formed an intimacy with Rizzio, who employed all the arts of flattery and observance to gain possession of his favour, and unquestionably was serviceable to him in advancing his suit. The Queen, in the meanwhile, exerted herself to remove the obstacles to her union with Darnley, and with such success, that, with the approbation of far the greater part of her subjects, they were married at Edinburgh on the 29th July 1565.

When Elizabeth had received news that this union was determined upon, she gave way to all the weakness of an envious woman, and remonstrated against the match, though, in fact, Mary could scarcely have made a choice less dangerous to England.

The Earl of Moray was by far the most able and powerful of those who were displeased by Mary's marriage. Darnley and he were personal enemies;

and besides, Moray was the principal of the Lords of the Congregation, who affected to see danger to the Protestant religion in Mary's choice of a husband.

After the marriage, Moray and his confederates actually took up arms. The Queen, in this emergency, assembled her subjects around her. They came in such numbers as shows her popularity. Darnley rode at their head in gilded armour accompanied by the Queen herself, having loaded pistols at her saddle-bow. Unable to stand their ground, Moray and his accomplices eluded the pursuit of the royal army, and made a sudden march on Edinburgh, where they hoped to find friends. But the citizens not adopting their cause, and the castle threatening to fire on them, the insurgents were compelled to retreat, until they finally disbanded their forces in despair, and the leaders fled into England. This insurrection was called the Runabout Raid.

Mary had thus overcome her refractory subjects, but she soon found that she had a more formidable enemy in the foolish and passionate husband whom she had chosen. This headstrong young man behaved to his wife with great disrespect, both as a woman and as a queen, and gave himself up to intoxication, and other disgraceful vices. Although already possessed of more power than fitted his capacity or age, for he was but nineteen, he was importunate in his demands for obtaining what was called in Scotland the Crown Matrimonial; that is, the full equality of royal right in the crown with his consort. Until he obtained this eminence he was not held to be King, though called so in courtesy. He was only the husband of the Queen.

This Crown Matrimonial had been bestowed on Mary's first husband, Francis, and Darnley was determined to be possessed of the same rank. But Mary, whose bounty had already far exceeded his deserts, as well as his gratitude, was resolved not to make this last concession.

The childish impatience of Darnley made him regard with mortal hatred whatever interfered with the instant execution of his wishes; and his animosity on this occasion turned against the Italian Secretary, once his friend, but whom he now esteemed his deadly foe, because he supposed that Rizzio encouraged the Queen in resisting his hasty ambition. His resentment against the unhappy stranger arose to such a height, that he threatened to poniard him with his own hand; and as Rizzio had many enemies, and no friends save his mistress, Darnley easily procured instruments, and those of no mean rank, to take the execution of his revenge on themselves.

The chief of Darnley's accomplices, on this unhappy occasion, was

James Douglas, Earl of Morton, uncle to the Earl of Angus (who chanced then to be a minor), and administrator, therefore, of all the power of the great house of Douglas. He was a nobleman of high military talent and great political wisdom; but although a pretender to sanctity of life, his actions show him to have been a wicked and unscrupulous man. Notwithstanding he was Chancellor of the kingdom, and therefore bound peculiarly to respect the laws, he did not hesitate to enter into Darnley's cruel and unlawful purpose. Lord Ruthven too, whose frame was exhausted by illness, nevertheless undertook to buckle on his armour for the enterprise; and they had no difficulty in finding other agents.

Those lords who engaged in the conspiracy stipulated, as the price of their assistance, that he should in turn aid them in obtaining pardon and restoration to favour for Moray and his accomplices in the Run-about Raid; and intimation was dispatched to these noblemen, apprising them of the whole undertaking, and desiring them to be at Edinburgh on the night appointed for doing the deed.

Queen Mary, like her father, James V, was fond of laying aside the state of a sovereign, and indulging in small private parties. On these occasions, she admitted her favourite domestics to her table, and Rizzio seems frequently to have had that honour. On the 9th of March 1566 six persons had partaken of supper in a small cabinet adjoining to the Queen's bedchamber, and having no entrance save through it. Rizzio was of the number. About seven in the evening, the gates of the palace were occupied by Morton, with a party of two hundred men; and a select band of the conspirators, headed by Darnley himself, came into the Queen's apartment by a secret staircase. Darnley first entered the cabinet, and stood for an instant in silence, gloomily eyeing his victim. Lord Ruthven followed in complete armour, looking pale and ghastly, as one scarcely recovered from long sickness. Others crowded in after them, till the little closet was full of armed men. While the Queen demanded the purpose of their coming, Rizzio, who saw that his life was aimed at, got behind her, and clasped the folds of her gown, that the respect due to her person might protect him. The assassins threw down the table, and seized on the unfortunate object of their vengeance, while Darnley himself took hold of the Queen, and forced Rizzio and her asunder. It was their intention, doubtless, to have dragged Rizzio out of Mary's presence, and to have killed him elsewhere; but their fierce impatience hurried them into instant murder. George Douglas, a natural brother of the Earl of Morton, set the example by snatching Darnley's dagger from his belt, and striking Rizzio with it. He received many other blows. They dragged him through the bedroom and antechamber, and dispatched him at the head of the staircase, with no less than fifty-six wounds.

The Queen continued to beg his life with prayers and tears; but when she learned he was dead, she dried her tears, "I will now," she said, "study revenge."

As fickle as he was vehement, and as timorous as he had shown himself cruel, Rizzio was no sooner slain, than Darnley became terrified at what had been done.

Finding her weak-minded husband in a state between remorse and fear, Mary prevailed on him to take part against the very persons whom he had instigated to the late atrocious proceeding. Darnley and Mary escaped together out of Holyrood House, and fled to Dunbar, where the Queen issued a proclamation which soon drew many faithful followers around her.

It was now the turn of the conspirators to tremble. That the Queen's conquest over them might be more certain, she pardoned the Earl of Moray, and those concerned in the Run-about Raid, and thus Moray, and others, were received into favour, while Morton, Ruthven, and his comrades fled in their turn to England. No Scottish subject, whatever his crime, could take refuge there without finding secret support, if not an open welcome. Such was Elizabeth's constant policy.

On the 19th of June 1566, Mary was delivered of a son, afterwards James VI.

After a splendid solemnity at christening the heir of Scotland, Queen Mary seems to have turned her mind towards settling the disorders of her nobility; and, sacrificing her own justifiable resentment, she yielded so far as to grant pardon to all those concerned in the murder of Rizzio. Two men of low rank, and no more, had been executed for that crime. Lord Ruthven, the principal actor, had died in England.

James Hepburn, Earl of Bothwell, a man in middle age, had for several years played a conspicuous part in these troubled times. He had sided with the Queen Regent against the Reformed party, and was in general supposed to be attached rather to the reigning Queen than to any of the factions who opposed her. He was head of the powerful family of Hepburn, and possessed great influence in East Lothian and Berwickshire, where excellent soldiers could always be obtained. In his morals Bothwell was wild and licentious, and irregular and daring in his ambition.

As this nobleman displayed great zeal in Mary's cause she was naturally led to advance him at Court, until many persons, and particularly the preachers of the Reformed religion, thought that she admitted to too great intimacy a man of so fierce and profligate a character.

In the meantime, the dissensions between Darnley and the Queen continued to increase. He pretended he would leave the kingdom, and by this and other capricious resolutions, hastily adopted and abandoned, he so far alienated the affections of the Queen, that many of the unscrupulous and plotting nobles, by whom she was surrounded, formed the idea that it would be very agreeable to Mary if she could be freed from her union with this unreasonable and ill-tempered young man.

The first proposal made to her was, that she should be separated from Darnley by a divorce, but she rejected it steadily. A conspiracy of a darker kind was then agitated, for the murder of the unhappy Darnley; and Bothwell seems to have entertained little doubt that Mary, thus rid of an unacceptable husband, would choose him for a successor. He spoke with the Earl of Morton on the subject of dispatching Darnley, and represented it as an enterprise which had the approbation of the Queen. Morton refused to stir in a matter of so great consequence, unless he received a mandate under the Queen's hand. Bothwell undertook to procure him such a warrant, but he never kept his word.

While these schemes were in agitation against his life, Darnley fell ill at Glasgow, and his indisposition proved to be the smallpox. The Queen sent her physician, and after an interval went herself to wait upon him, and an apparent reconciliation was effected between them. They came together to Edinburgh on the 31st of January 1567. The King was lodged in a religious house called the Kirk-of-Field, just outside the walls of the city. The Queen and the infant Prince were accommodated in the palace of Holyrood. The reason assigned for their living separate was the danger of the child catching the smallpox. But the Queen showed much attention to her husband, visiting him frequently; and they never seemed to have been on better terms than when the conspiracy against Darnley's life was on the eve of being executed. Meanwhile Darnley and his groom of the chamber were alone during the night time, and separated from any other persons, when measures were taken for his destruction in the following horrible manner:

On the evening of the 9th February, several persons, kinsmen, retainers, and servants of the Earl of Bothwell, came in secret to the Kirk-of-Field They had with them a great quantity of gunpowder; and by means of false keys they obtained entrance into the cellars of the building, where they disposed the powder in the vaults under Darnley's apartment, and especially beneath the spot where his bed was placed. About two hours after midnight upon the ensuing morning, Bothwell himself came disguised in a riding cloak, to see the execution of the cruel project. Two of his ruffians went in and took means of firing the powder, by lighting a piece of slow-burning match at one end, and placing the other amongst the gunpowder. They remained for some time watching the event, and Bothwell became so impatient, that it was with difficulty he was prevented from entering the house, to see whether the light had not been extinguished by some accident. One of his accomplices, by looking through a window, ascertained that it was still burning. The explosion presently took place, blew up the Kirk-of-Field, and alarmed the whole city. The body of Darnley was found in the adjoining orchard. The bed in which he lay had preserved him from all action of the fire, which occasioned a general belief that he and his chamber-groom, who was found in the same situation, had been strangled and removed before the house was blown up. But this was a mistake. It is clearly proved, by the evidence of those who were present at the event, that there were no means employed but gunpowder—a mode of destruction sufficiently powerful to have rendered any other unnecessary.

The horrible murder or the unhappy Darnley excited the greatest discontent in the city of Edinburgh, and through the whole kingdom. Bothwell was pointed out by the general voice as the author of the murder, and as she still continued to enjoy the favour of Mary, her reputation was not spared.

Lennox, father of the murdered Darnley had, as was his natural duty, accused Bothwell of the murder of his son. But he received little countenance in prosecuting the accused. Everything seemed to be done as hastily as if it were determined to defeat the operations of justice. At so short warning as fourteen days Lennox was summoned as nearest relation of the murdered man to appear as accuser and to support the charge he had made against Bothwell. The Earl of Lennox complained that the time allowed him to prepare the charge, and evidence necessary for convicting so powerful a criminal was greatly too short, but he could not get it extended.

It was a usual thing in Scotland for persons accused of crime to come to the bar of a court of justice attended by all their friends, retainers, and dependents, the number of whom was frequently so great, that the judges and accusers were overawed, and became afraid to proceed in the investigation; so that the purposes of justice were for the time frustrated. Bothwell, conscious of guilt, was desirous to use this means of protection to the utmost. He appeared in Edinburgh with full five thousand attendants. Two hundred chosen musketeers kept close by his side, and guarded the doors of the court as soon as the criminal had entered. In such circumstances, there could be no chance of a fair trial. Lennox did not appear, saving by one of his vassals, who protested against the proceedings of the day. No charge was made,—no proof of innocence, of course, was required,—and a jury, consisting of nobles and gentlemen of the first rank, acquitted Bothwell of a crime of which all the world believed him to be guilty.

The public mind remained dissatisfied with this mockery of justice; but Bothwell, without regarding the murmurs of the people, hurried forward to possess himself of the situation which he had made vacant by the murder of Darnley. He convened a number of the principal nobility, at a feast given in a tavern, and prevailed on them to sign a bond, in which they not only declared Bothwell altogether innocent of the King's death, but recommended him as the fittest person whom her Majesty could choose for a husband.

Moray, the most important person in Scotland, had kept aloof from all these proceedings, and, about three days before Bothwell's trial, he obtained leave of the Queen to travel to France.

The Earl of Bothwell, thus authorised by the apparent consent of the nobility, and, no doubt, thinking himself secure of the Queen's approbation, suddenly appeared at the bridge of Cramond, with a thousand horse, as Mary arrived there on her return from Stirling to Edinburgh. Bothwell took the Queen's horse by the bridle, and surrounding and disarming her attendants, he led her as if by an appearance of force, to the strong castle of Dunbar, of which he was governor. On this occasion Mary seems neither to have attempted to resist, nor to have expressed that feeling of anger and shame which would have been proper to her as a queen and as a woman. They remained at Dunbar ten days, after which they again appeared in Edinburgh, apparently reconciled; the Earl carefully leading the Queen's palfrey, and conducting her up to the castle.

While these strange proceedings took place, Bothwell had been enabled to procure a sentence of divorce against his wife, a sister of the Earl of Huntly. On the 12th of May the Queen made a public declaration, that she forgave Bothwell the late violence which he had committed, and that, although she was at first highly displeased with him, she was now resolved not only to grant him her pardon, but also to promote him to further honours. She was as good as her word, for she created him Duke of Orkney; and, on the 15th of the same month, did Mary, with unpardonable indiscretion, commit the great folly of marrying this ambitious and profligate man, stained as he was with the blood of her husband.

The Queen was not long in discovering that by this unhappy marriage she had gotten a more ruthless and wicked husband than she had in the flexible Darnley. Bothwell used her grossly ill, and being disappointed in his plans of getting the young Prince into his keeping, used such up-braiding language to Mary, that she prayed for a knife with which to stab herself, rather than endure his ill-treatment.

In the meantime the public discontent rose high, and Morton, Maitland, and others, who had been privy to the murder of Darnley, placed them-selves, notwithstanding, at the head of a numerous party of the nobility, who resolved to revenge his death, and remove Bothwell from his usurped power. They took arms hastily, and had nearly surprised the Queen and Bothwell, while feasting in the castle of the Lord Borthwick, from whence they fled to Dunbar, the Queen being concealed in the disguise of a page.

The confederated lords marched towards Dunbar, and the Queen and Bothwell, having assembled an army, advanced to the encounter, and met them on Carberry Hill, not far from the place where the battle of Pinkie was fought. This was on the 15th of June 1567. Mary would have acted more wisely in postponing the threatened action, for the Hamiltons, in great force, were on their way to join her. But she had been accustomed to gain advantages by rapid and ready movements, and was not at first sufficiently aware what an unfavourable impression existed against her even in her own army. Her army began to disband, and it became obvious that they would not fight in her cause, while they considered it as the same with that of Bothwell. She therefore recommended to him to fly from the field of action; and advice which he was not slow in following, riding to Dunbar as fast as he could, and from thence escaping by sea.

Mary surrendered herself, upon promise of respect and kind treatment, to the Laird of Grange, and was conducted by him to the headquarters of the confederate amry. When she arrived there, the lords received her with silent respect; but some of the common soldiers hooted at and insulted her, until Grange, drawing his sword, compelled them to be silent. The lords adopted the resolution of returning to the capital, and conveying Mary thither, surrounded by their troops.

As the unhappy Queen approached Edinburgh, led as it were in triumph by the victors, the most coarse and insulting behaviour was used towards her by the lower classes. There was a banner prepared for this insur-rection, displayng on the one side the portrait of Darnley, as he lay mur-dered under a tree in the fatal orchard, with these words embroidered, "Judge and defend my cause, O Lord!" and on the other side the little Prince on his knees, holding up his hands, as if praying to Heaven to punish his father's murderers. As the Queen rode through the streets, with her hair loose, her garments disordered, covered with dust and overpowered with grief, shame, and fatigue, this fatal flag was displayed before her eyes, while the voices of the rude multitude upbraided her with having been an accomplice in Darnley's murder. The better class of craftsmen and citizens were at length moved by her sorrows, and showed such a desire to take her part, that the lords determined to remove her from the city. Accordingly on the next evening, Mary, in disguised apparel, and escorted by a strong armed force, was conveyed from Holyrood to the castle of Lochleven, which stands on a little island, surrounded by a lake and was there detained a prisoner.

The insurgent lords now formed themselves into a Secret Council for managing the affairs of the nation. Their first attention was turned to securing Bothwell.

Kirkaldy of Grange followed Bothwell with two vessels, and had nearly surprised him in the harbour of Lerwick, the fugitive making his escape at one issue of the bay, while Grange entered at another, and Bothwell might even then have been captured, but that Grange's ship ran upon a rock, and was wrecked, though the crew escaped. Bothwell was only saved for a more melancholy fate. He took to piracy in the Northern Seas, in order to support himself and his sailors. He was in consequence assaulted and taken by some Danish ships of war. The Danes threw him into the dungeons of the castle of Malmay, where he died in captivity about the end of the year 1576.

Meantime, poor Mary reaped the full consequences of Bothwell's guilt, and of her own infatuated attachment to him. She was imprisoned in a rude and inconvenient tower, on a small islet, where there was scarce room to walk fifty yards; and not even the intercession of Queen Elizabeth, who seems for the time to have been alarmed at the successful insurrection of subjects against their sovereign, could procure any mitigation of her captivity. There was a proposal to proceed against the Queen as an accomplice in Darnley's murder, and to take her life under that pretence. But the Lords of the Secret Council resolved to adopt somewhat of a gentler course, by compelling Mary to surrender her crown to her son, then an infant, and to make the Earl of Moray Regent during the child's minority. Deeds to this purpose were drawn up, and sent to the castle of Lochleven, to be signed by the Queen. Lord Lindsay, the rudest and fiercest of the confederated lords, was deputed to enforce Mary's compliance with the commands of the Council. He behaved with such peremptory brutality, and was so unmanly as to pinch with his iron glove the arm of the poor Queen, to compel her to subscribe the deeds.

If Mary had any quarter to which, in her disastrous condition she might look for love and favour, it was to her brother Moray. She may have been criminal—she had certainly been grossly infatuated—yet she deserved her brother's kindness and compassion. She had loaded him with favours, and pardoned him considerable offences. But Moray was ambitious; and ambition breaks through the ties of blood, and forgets the obligations of gratitude. He visited his imprisoned sister and benefactress in Lochleven Castle, but it was not to bring her comfort; on the contrary, he pressed all her errors on her with such hard-hearted severity, that she burst into floods of tears, and abandoned herself to despair.

Moray accepted of the regency, and in doing so broke all remaining ties of tenderness betwixt himself and his sister. He was now at the head of the ruling faction, consisting of what were called the King's Lords; while such of the nobility as desired that Mary, being now freed from the society of Bothwell, should be placed at liberty, and restored to the administration of the kingdom, were termed the Queen's party.

Sir William Douglas, the Laird of Lochleven, owner of the castle where Mary was imprisoned, discharged with severe fidelity the task of Mary's jailer; but his youngest brother, George, became more sensible to the Queen's distress, and perhaps to her beauty, than to the interests of the Regent, or of his own family. A plot laid by him for the Queen's deliverance was discovered, and he was expelled from the island in consequence. But he kept up a correspondence with a kinsman, called Little Douglas, a boy of fifteen, who had remained in the castle. On Sunday, the 2nd May 1568, Little Douglas contrived to steal the keys of the castle while the family were at supper. He let Mary and her attendant out of the tower when all had gone to rest—locked the gates of the castle to prevent pursuit —placed the Queen and her waiting woman in a little skiff, and rowed them to the shore, throwing the keys of the castle into the lake in the course of their passage. Just when they were about to set out on this adventurous voyage, the youthful pilot had made a signal, by a light in a particular window visible at the upper end of the lake, to intimate that all was safe. Lord Seaton and a party of the Hamiltons were waiting at the landing-place. The Queen instantly mounted, and hurried off to Niddry Castle, in West Lothian; she proceeded next day to Hamilton. The news flew like lightning throughout the country, and spread enthusiasm everywhere. The people remembered Mary's gentleness, grace, and beauty—they remembered her misfortunes also—and if they reflected on her errors, thought they had been punished with sufficient severity. On Sunday, Mary was a sad and helpless captive in a lonely tower. On the Saturday following she was at the head of a powerful confederacy, by which nine earls, nine bishops, eighteen lords, and many gentlemen of high rank, engaged to defend her person and restore her power. But this gleam of success was only temporary.

It was the Queen's purpose to place her person in security in the castle of Dumbarton, and her army under the Earl of Argyle proposed to carry her thither in a species of triumph. The Regent was lying at Glasgow with much inferior forces.

On the 13th May 1568 Moray occupied the village of Langside, which lay full in the march of the Queen's army. The Hamiltons, and other gentlemen of Mary's troop, rushed forth with ill-considered valour to dispute the pass. They fought, however, with obstinacy, after the Scottish manner; that is, they pressed on each other front to front, each fixing his spear in his opponent's target, and then endeavouring to bear him down, as two bulls do when they encounter each other. Morton decided the battle by attacking the flank of the Hamiltons, while their column was closely engaged in the front. The measure was decisive, and the Queen's army was completely routed.

Queen Mary beheld this final and fatal defeat from a castle called Crookstane, about four miles from Paisley, where she and Darnley had spent some happy days after their marriage, and which, therefore, must have been the scene of bitter recollections. It was soon evident that there was no resource but in flight, and escorted by Lord Herries and a few faithful followers, she rode sixty miles before she stopped at the abbey of Dundrennan, in Galloway. From this place she had the means of retreating either to France or England, as she should ultimately determine. In France she was sure to have been well received; but England afforded a nearer, and, as she thought, an equally safe place of refuge.

Forgetting, therefore, the various causes of emulation which existed betwixt Elizabeth and herself, and remembering only the smooth and flattering words which she had received fom her sister sovereign, it did not occur to the Scottish Queen that she should incur any risk by throwing herself upon the mercy of the English sovereign. She therefore resolved to take refuge in Elizabeth's kingdom, in spite of the opposition of her wiser attendants. They kneeled and entreated in vain. She entered the fatal boat, crossed the Solway, and delivered herself up to a gentleman named Lowther, the English deputy-warden. Much surprised, doubtless, at the incident, he sent express to inform Queen Elizabeth; and receiving the Scottish Queen with as much respect as he had the means of showing, lodged her in Carlisle Castle.

Elizabeth, great as she was upon other occasions of her reign, acted on the present from mean and envious motives; the unfortunate Mary was surrounded by English guards; and, as Elizabeth reasonably doubted that if she were left upon the Border, the fugitive Queen might obtain aid from her adherents in Scotland, she was removed to Bolton Castle, in Yorkshire. But some pretext was wanting for a conduct so violent, so ungenerous, and so unjust, and Elizabeth contrived to find one.

The messengers of Queen Elizabeth informed Mary that their mistress regretted extremely that she could not at once admit her to her presence, nor give her the affectionate reception which she longed to afford her, until her visitor stood clear, in the eyes of the world, of the scandalous accusations of her Scottish subjects. Mary at once undertook to make her innocence evident to Elizabeth's satisfaction; and this the Queen of England pretended to consider as a call upon herself to act as umpire in the quarrel betwixt Mary and the party by which she had been deposed and exiled. It was in vain that Mary remonstrated, that, in agreeing to remove Elizabeth's scruples, she acted merely out of respect to her opinion, and a desire to conciliate her favour, but not with the purpose of constituting the English Queen her judge in a formal trial. Elizabeth was determined to keep the advantage which she had attained, and to act as if Mary had, of her full free will, rendered her rival the sole arbiter of her fate.

The Queen of England accordingly appointed Commissioners to hear the parties, and consider the evidence which was to be laid before them by both sides. The Regent Moray appeared in person before these Commissioners, in the odious character of the accuser of his sister, benefactress, and sovereign. Queen Mary also sent the most able of her adherents to plead the case on her side. The Commission met at York in October 1568. It was not without hesitation that Moray was induced to state his accusation: the odious charges of matrimonial infidelity and accession to the murder of her husband. Something like proof was wanted, and at length a box of letters and papers was produced, stated to have been taken from a servant of Bothwell. These letters, if genuine, certainly proved that Mary was a paramour of Bothwell while Darnley was yet alive and that she knew and approved of the murder of that ill-fated young man. But the letters were alleged by the Queen's Commissioners to be gross forgeries.

At the end of five months' investigation the Queen of England informed both parties that she had, on the one hand, seen nothing which induced her to doubt the worth and honour of the Earl of Moray, while, on the other hand, he had, in her opinion, proved nothing of the criminal charges which he had brought against his sovereign. She was therefore, she said, determined to leave the affairs of Scotland as she had found them.

To have treated both parties impartially, as her sentence seemed intended to imply her desire to do, the Queen ought to have restored Mary to liberty. But while Moray was sent down with the loan of a large sum of money, Mary was retained in that captivity which was only to end with her life.

WALES

THE LADY OF THE FOUNTAIN[1]

"The Mabinogion"

KING ARTHUR was at Caerlleon upon Usk; and one day he sat in his chamber; and with him were Owain the son of Urien, and Kynon the son of Clydno, and Kai the son of Kyner; and Gwenhwyvar and her hand-maidens at needlework by the window. And if it should be said that there was a porter at Arthur's palace, there was none. Glewlwyd Gavaelvawr was there, acting as porter, to welcome guests and strangers, and to receive them with honour, and to inform them of the manners and customs of the Court; and to direct those who came to the Hall or to the presence-chamber, and those who came to take up their lodging.

In the centre of the chamber King Arthur sat upon a seat of green rushes, over which was spread a covering of flame-coloured satin, and a cushion of red satin was under his elbow.

Then Arthur spoke, "If I thought you would not disparage me," said he, "I would sleep while I wait for my repast; and you can entertain one another with relating tales, and can obtain a flagon of mead and some meat from Kai." And the King went to sleep. And Kynon the son of Clydno asked Kai for that which Arthur had promised them. "I, too, will have the good tale which he promised to me," said Kai. "Nay," answered Kynon, "fairer will it be for thee to fulfill Arthur's behest, in the first place, and then we will tell thee the best tale that we know." So Kai went to the kitchen and to the mead-cellar, and returned bearing a flagon of mead and a golden goblet, and a handful of skewers, upon which were broiled collops of meat. Then they ate the collops and began to drink the mead. "Now," said Kai, "it is time for you to give me my story." "Kynon," said Owain, "do thou pay to Kai the tale that is his due." "Truly," said Kynon, "thou art older, and art a better teller of tales, and hast seen more marvellous things than I; do thou therefore pay Kai his tale." "Begin thyself," quoth Owain, "with the best that thou knowest." "I will do so," answered Kynon.

"I was the only son of my mother and father, and I was exceedingly aspiring, and my daring was very great. I thought there was no enterprise in the world too mighty for me, and after I had achieved all the adven-

[1] From Lady Charlotte Guest's translation of The Mabinogion.

tures that were in my own country, I equipped myself, and set forth to journey through deserts and distant regions. And at length it chanced that I came to the fairest valley in the world, wherein were trees of equal growth; and a river ran through the valley, and a path was by the side of the river. And I followed the path until mid-day, and continued my journey along the remainder of the valley until the evening; and at the extremity of a plain I came to a large and lustrous Castle, at the foot of which was a torrent. And I approached the Castle, and there I beheld two youths with yellow curling hair, each with a frontlet of gold upon his head, and clad in a garment of yellow satin, and they had gold clasps upon their insteps. In the hand of each of them was an ivory bow, strung with the sinews of the stag; and their arrows had shafts of the bone of the whale, and were winged with peacock's feathers; the shafts also had golden heads. And they had daggers with blades of gold, and with hilts of the bone of the whale. And they were shooting their daggers.

"And a little way from them I saw a man in the prime of life, with his beard newly shorn, clad in a robe and a mantle of yellow satin; and round the top of his mantle was a band of gold lace. On his feet were shoes of variegated leather, fastened by two bosses of gold. When I saw him, I went towards him and saluted him, and such was his courtesy that he no sooner received my greeting than he returned it. And he went with me towards the Castle. Now there were no dwellers in the Castle except those who were in one hall. And there I saw four-and-twenty damsels, embroidering satin at a window. And this I tell thee, Kai, that the least fair of them was fairer than the fairest maid thou hast ever beheld in the Island of Britain, and the least lovely of them was more lovely than Gwenhwyvar, the wife of Arthur, when she has appeared loveliest at the Offering, on the day of the Nativity, or at the feast of Easter. They rose up at my coming, and six of them took my horse, and divested me of my armour; and six others took my arms, and washed them in a vessel until they were perfectly bright. And the third six spread cloths upon the tables and prepared meat. And the fourth six took off my soiled garments, and placed others upon me; namely, an under-vest and a doublet of fine linen, and a robe, and a surcoat, and a mantle of yellow satin with a broad gold band upon the mantle. And they placed cushions both beneath and around me, with coverings of red linen; and I sat down. Now the six maidens who had taken my horse, unharnessed him, as well as if they had been the best squires in the Island of Britain. Then, behold, they brought bowls of silver wherein was water to wash, and towels of linen, some green and some white; and I washed. And in a little while the man sat down to the table. And I sat next to him, and below me sat all the maidens, except those who waited on us. And the table was of silver, and the cloths upon the table were of linen; and no vessel was served upon the table that was not either of gold or of silver, or of buffalo-horn. And our meat was brought ot us. And verily, Kai, I saw there every sort of meat and every sort of liquor that I have ever seen elsewhere; but the meat and the liquor were better served there than I have ever seen them in any other place.

"Until the repast was half over, neither the man nor any one of the damsels spoke a single word to me; but when the man perceived that it would be more agreeable to me to converse than to eat any more, he began to inquire of me who I was. I said I was glad to find that there was some one who would discourse with me, and that it was not considered so great a crime at that Court for people to hold converse together. 'Chieftain,' said the man, 'we would have talked to thee sooner, but we feared to disturb thee during thy repast; now, however, we will discourse.' Then I told the man who I was, and what was the cause of my journey; and said that I was seeking whether any one was superior to me, or whether I could gain the mastery over all. The man looked upon me, and he smiled and said, 'If I did not fear to distress thee too much, I would show thee that which thou seekest.' Upon this I became anxious and sorrowful, and when the man perceived it, he said, 'If thou wouldest rather that I should show thee thy disadvantage than thine advantage, I will do so. Sleep here to-night, and in the morning arise early, and take the road upwards through the valley until thou reachest the wood through which thou camest hither. A little way within the wood thou wilt meet with a road branching off to the right, by which thou must proceed, until thou comest to a large sheltered glade with a mound in the centre. And thou wilt see a black man of great stature on the top of the mound. He is not smaller in size than two of the men of this world. He has but one foot; and one eye in the middle of his forehead. And he has a club of iron, and it is certain that there are no two men in the world who would not find their burden in that club. And he is not a comely man, but on the contrary he is exceedingly ill-favoured; and he is the woodward of that wood. And thou wilt see a thousand wild animals grazing around him. Inquire of him the way out of the glade and he will reply to thee briefly, and will point out the road by which thou shalt find that which thou art in quest of.'

"And long seemed that night to me. And the next morning I arose and equipped myself, and mounted my horse, and proceeded straight through the valley to the wood; and I followed the cross-road which the man had pointed out to me, till at length I arrived at the glade. And there was I three times more astonished at the number of wild animals that I beheld, than the man had said I should be. And the black man was there, sitting upon the top of the mound. Huge of stature as the man had told me that he was, I found him to exceed by far the description he had given me of him. As for the iron club which the man had told me was a burden for two men, I am certain, Kai, that it would be a heavy weight for four warriors to lift; and this was in the black man's hand. And he only spoke to me in answer to my questions. Then I asked him what power he held over those animals. 'I will show thee, little man," said he. And he took his club in his hand, and with it he struck a stag a great blow so that he brayed vehemently, and at his braying the animals came together, as numerous as the stars in the sky, so that it was difficult for me to find room in the glade to stand among them. There were serpents, and dragons, and divers sorts of animals. And he looked at them, and bade them go and feed; and they bowed their heads, and did him homage as vassals to their lord.

"Then the black man said to me, 'Seest thou now, little man, what power I hold over these animals?' Then I inquired of him the way, and he became very rough in his manner to me; however, he asked me whither I would go? And when I told him who I was and what I sought, he directed me. 'Take,' said he, 'that path that leads towards the head of the glade, and ascend the wooded steep until thou comest to its summit; and there thou wilt find an open space like to a large valley, and in the midst of it a tall tree, whose branches are greener than the greenest pine-trees. Under this tree is a fountain, and by the side of the fountain a marble slab, and on the marble slab a silver bowl, attached by a chain of silver, so that it may not be carried away. Take the bowl and throw a bowlful of water upon the slab, and thou wilt hear a mightly peal of thunder, so that thou wilt think that heaven and earth are trembling with its fury. With the thunder there will come a shower so severe that it will be scarce possible for thee to endure it and live. And the shower will be of hailstones; and after the shower, the weather will become fair, but every leaf that was upon the tree will have been carried away by the shower. Then a flight of birds will come and alight upon the tree; and in thine own country thou didst never hear a strain so sweet as that which they will sing. And at the moment thou art most delighted with the song of the birds, thou wilt hear a murmuring and complaining coming towards thee along the valley. And thou wilt see a knight upon a coal-black horse, clothed in black velvet, and with a pennon of black linen upon his lance; and he will ride unto thee to encounter thee with the utmost speed. If thou fleest from him he will overtake thee, and if thou abidest there, as sure as thou art a mounted knight, he will leave thee on foot. And if thou dost not find trouble in that adventure, thou needest not seek it during the rest of thy life.'

"So I journeyed on, until I reached the summit of the steep, and there I found everything as the black man had described it to me. And I went up to the tree, and beneath it I saw the fountain, and by its side the marble slab, and the silver bowl fastened by the chain. Then I took the bowl, and cast a bowlful of water upon the slab; and thereupon, behold, the thunder came, much more violent than the black man had led me to expect; and after the thunder came the shower; and of a truth I tell thee, Kai, that there is neither man nor beast that can endure that shower and live. For not one of those hailstones would be stopped, either by the flesh or by the skin, until it had reached the bone. I turned my horse's flank towards the shower, and placed the beak of my shield over his head and neck, while I held the upper part of it over my own head. And thus I withstood the shower. When I looked on the tree there was not a single leaf upon it, and then the sky became clear, and with that, behold the birds lighted upon the tree, and sang. And truly Kai, I never heard any melody equal to that, either before or since. And when I was most charmed with listening to the birds, lo, a murmuring voice was heard through the valley, approaching me and saying, 'Oh, Knight, what has brought thee hither? What evil have I done to thee, that thou shouldst act towards me and my possessions as thou hast this day? Dost thou not know that the shower to-day has left in my dominions neither man nor beast alive that was exposed to it?' And thereupon, behold, a Knight on a black horse appeared, clothed in jet-black velvet, and with a tabard of black linen about him. And we charged each other, and, as the onset was furious, it was not long before I was overthrown. Then the Knight passed the shaft of his lance through the bridle rein of my horse, and rode off with the two horses, leaving me where I was. And he did not even bestow so much notice upon me as to imprison me, nor did he despoil me of my arms. So I returned along the road by which I had come. And when I reached the glade where the black man was, I confess to thee, Kai, it is a marvel that I did not melt down into a liquid pool, through the shame that I felt at the black man's derision. And that night I came to the same castle where I had spent the night preceding. And I was more agreeably entartained that night than I had been the night before; and I was better feasted, and I conversed freely with the inmates of the castle, and none of them alluded to my expedition to the fountain, neither did I mention it to any; and I remained there that night. When I arose on the morrow, I found, ready saddled, a dark bay palfrey, with nostrils as red as scarlet; and after putting on my armour, and leaving there my blessing, I returned to my own Court. And that horse I still possess, and he is in the stable younder. And I declare that I would not part with him for the best palfrey in the Island of Britain.

"Now of a truth, Kai, no man ever before confessed to an adventure so much to his own discredit, and verily it seems strange to me, that neither before nor since have I heard of any person besides myself who knew of this adventure, and that the subject of it should exist within King Arthur's dominions, without any other person lighting upon it."

"Now," quoth Owain, "would it not be well to go and endeavour to discover that place?"

"By the hand of my friend," said Kai, "often dost thou utter that with thy tongue which thou wouldst not make good with thy deeds."

"In very truth," said Gwenhwyvar, "it were better thou wert hanged, Kai, than to use such uncourteous speech towards a man like Owain."

"By the hand of my friend, good lady," said Kai, "thy praise of Owain is not greater than mine."

With that Arthur awoke, and asked if he had not been sleeping a little.

"Yes, Lord," answered Owain, "thou hast slept awhile."

"Is it time for us to go to meat?"

"It is, Lord," said Owain.

Then the horn for washing was sounded, and the King and all his household sat down to eat. And when the meal was ended, Owain withdrew to his lodging, and made ready his horse and his arms.

On the morrow, with the dawn of day, he put on his armour, and mounted his charger, and travelled through distant lands and over desert mountains. And at length he arrived at the valley which Kynon had described to him; and he was certain that it was the same that he sought. And journeying along the valley by the side of the river, he followed its course till he came to the plain and within sight to the Castle. When he approached the Castle, he saw the youths shooting their daggers in the place where Kynon had seen them, and the yellow man, to whom the Castle belonged, standing hard by. And no sooner had Owain saluted the yellow man than he was saluted by him in return.

And he went forward towards the Castle, and there he saw the chamber, and when he had entered the chamber he beheld the maidens working at satin embroidery, in chairs of gold. And their beauty and their comeliness seemed to Owain far greater than Kynon had represented to him. And they rose to wait upon Owain, as they had done to Kynon, and the meal which they set before him gave more satisfaction to Owain than it had done to Kynon.

About the middle of the repast, the yellow man asked Owain the object of his journey. And Owain made it known to him, and said, "I am in quest of the Knight who guards the fountain." Upon this the yellow man smiled, and said that he was as loth to point out that adventure to Owain as he had been to Kynon. However, he described the whole to Owain, and they retired to rest.

The next morning Owain found his horse made ready for him by the damsels, and he set forward and came to the glade where the black man was. And the stature of the black man seemed more wonderful to Owain than it had done to Kynon, and Owain asked of him his road, and he showed it to him. And Owain followed the road, as Kynon had done, till he came to the green tree; and he beheld the fountain, and the slab beside the fountain, with the bowl upon it. And Owain took the bowl, and threw a bowlful of water upon the slab. And, lo, the thunder was heard, and after the thunder came the shower, much more violent than Kynon had described, and after the shower the sky became bright. And when Owain looked at the tree, there was not one leaf upon it. And immediately the birds came, and settled upon the tree, and sang. And when their song was most pleasing to Owain, he beheld a Knight coming towards him through the valley, and he prepared to receive him; and encountered him violently. Having broken both their lances, they drew their swords, and fought blade to blade. Then Owain struck the Knight a blow through his helmet, head-piece and visor, and through the skin, and the flesh, and the bone, until it wounded the very brain. Then the black Knight felt that he had received a mortal wound, upon which he turned his horse's head, and fled. And Owain pursued him, and followed close upon him, although he was not near enough to strike him with his sword. Thereupon Owain descried a vast and resplendent Castle. And they came to the Castle gate. And the black Knight was allowed to enter, and the portcullis was let fall upon Owain; and it struck his horse behind the saddle, and cut him in two, and carried away the rowels of the spurs that were upon Owain's heels. And the portcullis descended to the floor. And the rowels of the spurs and part of the horse were without, and Owain with the other part of the horse remained between the two gates, and the inner gate was closed, so that Owain could not go thence; and Owain was in a perplexing situation. And while he was in this state, he could see through an aperture in the gate, a street facing him, with a row of houses on each side. And he beheld a maiden, with yellow curling hair, and a frontlet of gold upon her head; and she was clad in a dress of yellow satin, and on her feet were shoes of variegated leather. And she approached the gate, and desired that it should be opened. "Heaven knows, Lady," said Owain, "it is no more possible for me to open to thee from hence, than it is for thee to set me free." "Truly," said the damsel, "it is very sad that thou canst not be released, and every woman ought to succour thee, for I never saw one more faithful in the service of ladies than thou. As a friend thout art the most sincere, and as a lover the most devoted. Therefore," quoth she, "whatever is in my power to do for thy release, I will do it. Take this ring and put it on thy finger, with the stone inside thy hand; and close thy hand upon the stone. And as long as thou concealest it, it will conceal thee. When they have consulted together, they will come forth to fetch thee, in order to put thee to death; and they will be much grieved that they cannot find thee. And I will await thee on the horseblock yonder; thou wilt be able to see me, though I cannot see thee; tnerefore come and and place thy hand upon my shoulder, that I may know that thou art near me. And by the way that I go hence, do thou accompany me."

Then she went away from Owain, and he did all that the maiden had told him. And the people of the Castle came to seek Owain, to put him to death, and when they found nothing but the half of his horse, they were sorely grieved.

And Owain vanished from among them, and went to the maiden, and placed his hand upon her shoulder; whereupon she set off, and Owain followed her, until they came to the door of a large and beautiful chamber, and the maiden opened it, and they went in, and closed the door. And Owain looked around the chamber, and behold there was not even a single nail in it that was not painted with gorgeous colours; and there was not a single panel that had not sundry images in gold portrayed upon it.

The maiden kindled a fire, and took water in a silver bowl, and put a towel of white linen on her shoulder, and gave Owain water to wash. Then she placed before him a silver table, inlaid with gold; upon which was a cloth of yellow linen; and she brought him food. And of a truth, Owain had never seen any kind of meat that was not there in abundance, but it was better cooked there than he had ever found it in any other place. Nor did he ever see so excellent a display of meat and drink, as there. And there was not one vessel from which he was served, that was not of gold or of silver. And Owain ate and drank, until late in the afternoon, when lo, they heard a mighty clamour in the Castle; and Owain asked the maiden what that outcry was. "They are administering extreme unction," said she, "to the Nobleman who owns the Castle." And Owain went to sleep.

The couch which the maiden had prepared for him was meet for Arthur himself; it was of scarlet, and fur, and satin, and sendal, and fine linen. In the middle of the night they heard a woful outcry. "What outcry again is this?" said Owain. "The Nobleman who owned the Castle is now dead," said the maiden. And a little after daybreak, they heard an exceeding loud clamour and wailing. And Owain asked the maiden what was the cause of it. "They are bearing to the church the body of the Nobleman who owned the Castle."

And Owain rose up, and clothed himself, and opened a window of the chamber, and looked towards the Castle; and he could see neither the bounds, nor the extent of the hosts that filled the streets. And they were fully armed; and a vast number of women were with them, both on horseback and on foot; and all the ecclesiastics in the city, singing. And it seemed to Owain that the sky resounded with the vehemence of their cries, and with the noise of the trumpets, and with the singing of the ecclesiastics. In the midst of the throng, he beheld the bier, over which was a veil of white linen; and wax tapers were burning beside and around it, and none that supported the bier was lower in rank than a powerful Baron.

Never did Owain see an assemblage so gorgeous with satin, and silk, and sendal. And following the train, he beheld a lady with yellow hair falling over her shoulders, and stained with blood; and about her a dress of yellow satin, which was torn. Upon her feet were shoes of variegated leather. And it was a marvel that the ends of her fingers were not bruised, from the violence with which she smote her hands together. Truly she would have been the fairest lady Owain ever saw, had she been in her usual guise. And her cry was louder than the shout of the men, or the clamour of the trumpets. No sooner had he beheld the lady, than he became inflamed with her love, so that it took entire possession of him.

Then he inquired of the maiden who the lady was. "Heaven knows," replied the maiden, "she may be said to be the fairest, and the most chaste, and the most liberal, and the wisest, and the most noble of women. And she is my mistress; and she is called the Countess of the Fountain, the wife of him whom thou didst slay yesterday." "Verily," said Owain, "she is the woman that I love best." "Verily," said the maiden, "she shall also love thee not a little."

And with that the maid arose, and kindled a fire, and filled a pot with water, and placed it to warm; and she brought a towel of white linen, and placed it around Owain's neck; and she took a goblet of ivory, and a silver basin, and filled them with warm water, wherewith she washed Owain's head. Then she opened a wooden casket, and drew forth a razor, whose haft was of ivory, and upon which were two rivets of gold. And she sha-ved his beard, and she dried his head, and his throat, with the towel. Then she rose up from before Owain, and brought him to eat. And truly Owain had never so good a meal, nor was he ever so well served.

When he had finished his repast, the maiden arranged his couch. "Come here," said she, "and sleep, and I will go and woo for thee." And Owain went to sleep, and the maiden shut the door of the chamber after her, and went towards the Castle. When she came there, she found nothing but mourning, and sorrow; and the Countess in her chamber could not bear the sight of any one through grief. Luned came and saluted her, but the Countess answered her not. And the maiden bent down towards her, and said, "What aileth thee, that thou answerest no one to-day?" "Luned," said the Countess, "what change hath befallen thee, that thou hast not come to visit me in my grief? It was wrong in thee, and I having made thee rich; it was wrong in thee that thou didst not come to see me in my distress. That was wrong in thee." "Truly," said Luned, "I thought thy good sense was greater than I find it to be. Is it well for thee to mourn after that good man, or for anything else, that thou canst not have?" "I declare to heaven," said the Countess, "that in the whole world there is not a man equal to him." "Not so," said Luned, "for an ugly man would be as good as, or better than he." "I declare to heaven," said the Countess, "that were it not re-pugnant to me to cause to be put to death one whom I have brought up, I would have thee executed, for making such a comparison to me. As it is, I will banish thee." "I am glad," said Luned, "that thou hast no other cause to do so, than that I would have been of service to thee where thou didst not know what was to thine advantage. And henceforth evil betide whichever of us shall make the first advance towards reconciliation to the other; whether I should seek an invitation from thee, or thou of thine own accord shouldst send to invite me."

With that Luned went forth: and the Countess arose and followed her to the door of the chamber, and began coughing loudly. And when Luned looked back, the Countess beckoned to her; and she returned to the Countess. "In truth," said the Countess, "evil is thy disposition; but if thou knowest what is to my advantage, declare it to me." "I will do so," quoth she.

"Thou knowest that except by warfare and arms it is impossible for thee to preserve thy possessions; delay not, therefore, to seek some one who can defend them." "And how can I do that?" said the Countess. "I will tell thee," said Luned. "Unless thou canst defend the fountain, thou canst not maintain thy dominions; and no one can defend the fountain, except it

211

be a knight of Arthur's household; and I will go to Arthur's Court, and ill betide me, if I return thence without a warrior who can guard the fountain as well as, or even better than, he who defended it formerly." "That will be hard to perform," said the Countess. "Go, however, and make proof of that which thou hast promised."

Luned set out, under the pretence of going to Arthur's Court; but she went back to the chamber where she had left Owain; and she tarried there with him as long as it might have taken her to have travelled to the Court of King Arthur. And at the end of that time, she apparelled herself and went to visit the Countess. And the Countess was much rejoiced when she saw her, and inquired what news she brought from the Court. "I bring thee the best of news," said Luned, "for I have compassed the object of my mission. When wilt thou, that I should present to thee the chieftain who has come with me hither?" "Bring him here to visit me to-morrow, at mid-day," said the Countess, "and I will cause the town to be assembled by that time."

And Luned returned home. And the next day, at noon, Owain arrayed himself in a coat, and a surcoat, and a mantle of yellow satin, upon which was a broad band of gold lace; and on his feet were high shoes of variegated leather, which were fastened by golden clasps, in the form of lions. And they proceeded to the chamber of the Countess.

Right glad was the Countess of their coming, and she gazed steadfastly upon Owain, and said, "Luned, this knight has not the look of a traveller." "What harm is there in that, lady?" said Luned. "I am certain," said the Countess, "that no other man than this chased the soul from the body of my lord." "So much the better for thee, lady," said Luned, "for had he not been stronger than thy lord he could not have deprived him of life. There is no remedy for that which is past, be it as it may." "Go back to thine abode," said the Countess, "and I will take counsel."

The next day the Countess caused all her subjects to assemble, and showed them that her earldom was left defenceless, and that it could not be protected but with horse and arms, and military skill. "Therefore," said she, "this is what I offer for your choice: either let one of you take me, or give your consent for me to take a husband from elsewhere to defend my dominions."

So they came to the determination that it was better that she should have permission to marry some one from elsewhere; and, thereupon, she sent for the bishops and archbishops to celebrate her nuptials with Owain. And the men of the earldom did Owain homage.

And Owain defended the fountain with lance and sword. And this is the manner in which he defended it: Whensoever a knight came there he overthrew him, and sold him for his full worth, and what he thus gained he divided among his barons and his knights; and no man in the whole world could be more beloved than he was by his subjects. And it was thus for the space of three years.

It befell that as Gwalchmai went forth one day with King Arthur, he perceived him to be very sad and sorrowful. And Gwalchmai was much grieved to see Arthur in this state; and he questioned him, saying, "Oh, my lord! what has befallen thee?" "In sooth, Gwalchmai," said Arthur, "I am grieved concerning Owain, whom I have lost these three years, and I shall certainly die if the fourth year passes without my seeing him. Now I am sure, that it is through the tale which Kynon the son of Clydno related, that I have lost Owain." "There is no need for thee," said Gwalchmai, "to summon to arms thy whole dominions on this account, for thou thyself and the men of thy household will be able to avenge Owain, if he be slain; or to set him free, if he be in prison; and, if alive, to bring him back with thee." And it was settled according to what Gwalchmai had said.

Then Arthur and the men of his household prepared to go and seek Owain, and their number was three thousand, besides their attendants. And Kynon the son of Clydno acted as their guide. And Arthur came to the Castle where Kynon had been before, and when he came there the youths were shooting in the same place, and the yellow man was standing hard by. When the yellow man saw Arthur he greeted him, and invited him to the Castle; and Arthur accepted his invitation, and they entered the Castle together. And great as was the number of his retinue, their presence was scarcely observed in the Castle, so vast was its extent. And the maidens rose up to wait on them, and the service of the maidens appeared to them all to excel any attendance they had ever met with; and even the pages who had charge of the horses were no worse served, that night, than Arthur himself would have been in his own palace.

The next morning Arthur set out thence, with Kynon for his guide, and came to the place where the black man was. And the stature of the black man was more surprising to Arthur than it had been represented to him. And they came to the top of the wooded steep, and traversed the valley till they reached the green tree, where they saw the fountain, and the bowl, and she slab. And upon that, Kai came to Arthur and spoke to him. "My lord," said he, "I know the meaning of all this, and my request is, that thou wilt permit me to throw the water on the slab, and to receive the first adventure that may befall." And Arthur gave him leave.

Then Kai threw a bowlful of water upon the slab, and immediately there came the thunder, and after the thunder the shower. And such a thunderstorm they had never known before, and many of the attendants who were in Arthur's train were killed by the shower. After the shower had ceased the sky became clear; and on looking at the tree they beheld it completely leafless. Then the birds descended upon the tree, and the song of the birds was far sweeter than any strain they had ever heard before. Then they beheld a knight on a coal-black horse, clothed in black satin, coming rapidly towards them. And Kai met him and encountered him, and it was not long before Kai was overthrown. And the knight withdrew, and Arthur and his host encamped for the night.

And when they arose in the morning, they perceived the signal of combat upon the lance of the Knight. And Kai came to Arthur, and spoke to him: "My lord," said he, "though I was overthrown yesterday, if it seem good to thee, I would gladly meet the Knight again to-day." "Thou mayst do so," said Arthur. And Kai went towards the Knight. And on the spot he overthrew Kai, and struck nim with the head of his lance in the forehead, so that it broke his helmet and the head-piece, and pierced the skin and the flesh, the breadth of the spear-head, even to the bone. And Kai returned to his companions.

After this, all the household of Arthur went forth, one after the other, to combat the Knight, until there was not one that was not overthrown by him, except Arthur and Gwalchmai. And Arthur armed himself to encounter the Knight. "Oh, my lord," said Gwalchmai, "permit me to fight with him first." And Arthur permitted him. And he went forth to meet the Knight, having over himself and his horse a satin robe of honour which had been sent him by the daughter of the Earl of Rhangyw, and in this dress he was not known by any of the host. And they charged each other, and fought all that day until the evening, and neither of them was able to unhorse the other.

The next day they fought with strong lances, and neither of them could obtain the mastery.

And the third day they fought with exceeding strong lances. And they were incensed with rage, and fought furiously, even until noon. And they gave each other such a shock that the girths of their horses were broken, so that they fell over their horses' cruppers to the ground. And they rose up speedily, and drew their swords, and resumed the combat; and the multitude that witnessed their encounter felt assured that they had never before seen two men so valiant or so powerful. And had it been midnight, it would have been light from the fire that flashed from their weapons. And the Knight gave Gwalchmai a blow that turned his helmet from off his face, so that the Knight knew that it was Gwalchmai. Then Owain said, "My lord Gwalchmai, I did not know thee for my cousin, owing to the robe of honour that enveloped thee; take my sword and my arms." Said Gwalchmai, "Thou, Owain, art the victor; take thou my sword." And with that Arthur saw that they were conversing, and advanced towards them. "My lord Arthur," said Gwalchmai, "here is Owain who has vanquished me, and will not take my arms." "My lord," said Owain, "it is he that has vanquished me, and he will not take my sword." "Give me your swords," said Arthur, "and then neither of you has vanquished the other." Then Owain put his arms around Arthur's neck, and they embraced. And all the host hurried forward to see Owain, and to embrace him; and there was nigh being a loss of life, so great was the press.

And they retired that night, and the next day Arthur prepared to depart. "My lord," said Owain, "this is not well of thee; for I have been absent from thee these three years, and during all that time, up to this very day, I have been preparing a banquet for thee, knowing that thou wouldst come to seek me. Tarry with me, therefore, until thou and thy attendants have recovered the fatigues of the journey, and have been anointed."

And they all proceeded to the Castle of the Countess of the Fountain, and the banquet which had been three years preparing was consumed in three months. Never had they a more delicious or agreeable banquet. And Arthur prepared to depart. Then he sent an embassy to the Countess, to beseech her to permit Owain to go with him for the space of three months, that he might show him to the nobles and the fair dames of the Island of Britain. And the Countess gave her consent, although it was very painful to her. So Owain came with Arthur to the Island of Britain. And when he was once more amongst his kindred and friends, he remained three years, instead of three months, with them.

And as Owain one day sat at meat, in the city of Caerlleon upon Usk, behold a damsel entered upon a bay horse, with a curling mane and covered with foam, and the bridle and so much as was seen of the saddle were of gold. And the damsel was arrayed in a dress of yellow satin. And she came up to Owain, and took the ring from off his hand. "Thus," said she, "shall be treated the deceiver, the traitor, the faithless, the disgraced, and the beardless." And she turned her horse's head and departed.

Then his adventure came to Owain's remembrance, and he was sorrowful; and having finished eating he went to his own abode and made preparations that night. And the next day he arose but did not go to the

Court, but wandered to the distant parts of the earth and to uncultivated mountains. And he remained there until all his apparel was worn out, and his body was wasted away, and his hair was grown long. And he went about with the wild beasts and fed with them, until they became familiar with him; but at length he grew so weak that he could no longer bear them company. Then he descended from the mountains to the valley, and came to a park that was the fairest in the world, and belonged to a widowed Countess.

One day the Countess and her maidens went forth to walk by a lake, that was in the middle of the park. And they saw the form of a man. And they were terrified. Nevertheless they went near him, and touched him, and looked at him. And they saw that there was life in him, though he was exhausted by the heat of the sun. And the Countess returned to the Castle, and took a flask full of precious ointment, and gave it to one of her maidens. "Go with this," said she, "and take with thee yonder horse and clothing, and place them near the man we saw just now. And anoint him with this balsam, near his heart; and if there is life in him, he will arise through the efficacy of this balsam. Then watch what he will do."

And the maiden departed from her, and poured the whole of the balsam upon Owain, and left the horse and the garments hard by, and went a little way off, and hid herself to watch him. In a short time she saw him begin to move his arms; and he rose up, and looked at his person, and became ashamed of the unseemliness of his appearance. Then he perceived the horse and the garments that were near him. And he crept forward till he was able to draw the garments to him from off the saddle. And he clothed himself, and with difficulty mounted the horse. Then the damsel discovered herself to him, and saluted him. And he was rejoiced when he saw her, and inquired of her, what land and what territory that was. "Truly," said the maiden, "a widowed Countess owns yonder Castle; at the death of her husband, he left her two Earldoms, but at this day she has but this one dwelling that has not been wrested from her by a young Earl, who is her neighbour, because she refused to become his wife." "That is pity," said Owain. And he and the maiden proceeded to the Castle; and he alighted there, and the maiden conducted him to a pleasant chamber, and kindled a fire and left him.

And the maiden came to the Countess, and gave the flask into her hand. "Ha! maiden," said the Countess, "where is all the balsam?" "Have I not used it all?" said she. "Oh, maiden," said the Countess, "I cannot easily forgive thee this; it is sad for me to have wasted seven-score pounds' worth of precious ointment upon a stranger whom I know not. However, maiden, wait thou upon him, until he is quite recovered."

And the maiden did so, and furnished him with meat and drink, and fire, and lodging, and medicaments, until he was well again. And in three months he was restored to his former guise, and became even more comely than he had ever been before.

One day Owain heard a great tumult, and a sound of arms in the Castle, and he inquired of the maiden the cause thereof. "The Earl," said she, "whom I mentioned to thee, has come before the Castle, with a numerous army, to subdue the Countess." And Owain inquired of her whether the Countess had a horse and arms in her possession. "She has the best in the world," said the maiden. "Wilt thou go and request the loan of a horse and arms for me," said Owain, "that I may go and look at this army?" "I will, " said the maiden.

And she came to the Countess, and told her what Owain had said. And the Countess laughed. "Truly," said she, "I will even give him a horse and arms for ever; such a horse and such arms had he never yet, and I am glad that they should be taken by him to-day, lest my enemies should have them against my will to-morrow. Yet I know not what he would do with them."

The Countess bade them bring out a beautiful black steed, upon which was a beechen saddle, and a suit of armour, for man and horse. And Owain armed himself, and mounted the horse, and went forth, attended by two pages completely equipped, with horses and arms. And when they came near to the Earl's army, they could see neither its extent nor its extremity. And Owain asked the pages in which troop the Earl was. "In yonder troop," said they, "in which are four yellow standards. Two of them are before, and two behind him." "Now," said Owain, "do you return and await me near the portal of the Castle." So they returned, and Owain pressed forward until he met the Earl. And Owain drew him completely out of his saddle, and turned his horse's head towards the Castle, and though it was with difficulty, he brought the Earl to the portal, where the pages awaited him. And in they came. And Owain presented the Earl as a gift to the Countess. And said to her, "Behold a requital to thee for thy blessed balsam."

The army encamped around the Castle. And the Earl restored to the Countess the two Earldoms he had taken from her, as a ransom for his life; and for his freedom he gave her the half of his own dominions, and all his gold, and his silver, and his jewels, besides hostages.

And Owain took his departure. And the Countess and all her subjects besought him to remain, but Owain chose rather to wander through distant lands and deserts.

And as he journeyed, he heard a loud yelling in a wood. And it was repeated a second and a third time. And Owain went towards the spot, and beheld a huge craggy mound, in the middle of the wood; on the side of which was a grey rock. And there was a cleft in the rock, and a serpent was within the cleft. And near the rock stood a black lion, and every time the lion sought to go thence, the serpent darted towards him to attack him. And Owain unsheathed his sword, and drew near to the rock; and as the serpent sprang out, he struck him with his sword, and cut him in two. And he dried his sword, and went on his way, as before. But behold the lion followed him, and played about him, as though it had been a greyhound that he had reared.

They proceeded thus throughout the day, until the evening. And when it was time for Owain to take his rest, he dismounted, and turned his horse loose in a flat and wooded meadow. And he struck fire, and when the fire was kindled, the lion brought him fuel enough to last for three nights. And the lion disappeared. And presently the lion returned, bearing a fine large roebuck. And he threw it down before Owain, who went towards the fire with it.

And Owain took the roebuck, and skinned it, and placed collops of ist flesh upon skewers, around the fire. The rest of the buck he gave to the lion to devour. While he was doing this, he heard a deep sigh near him, and a second and a third. And Owain called out to know whether the sigh he heard proceeded from a mortal; and he received answer that it did. "Who art thou?" said Owain. "Truly," said the voice, "I am Luned, the hand-maiden of the Countess of the Fountain." "And what dost thou here?" said Owain. "I am imprisoned," said she, "on account of the knight who came from Arthur's Court, and married the Countess. And he stayed a short time with her, but he afterwards departed for the Court of Arthur, and has not returned since. And he was the friend I loved best in the world. And two of the pages in the Countess's chamber traduced him, and called him a deceiver. And I told them that they two were not a match for him alone. So they imprisoned me in the stone vault, and said that I should be put to death, unless he came himself to deliver me, by a certain day; and that is no further off than the day after to-morrow. And I have no one to send to seek him for me. And his name is Owain the son of Urien." "And art thou certain that if that knight knew all this, he would come to thy rescue?" "I am most certain of it," said she.

When the collops were cooked, Owain divided them into two parts, between himself and the maiden; and after they had eaten, they talked together, until the day dawned. And the next morning Owain inquired

of the damsel, if there was any place where he could get food and entertainment for that night. "There is, Lord," said she; "cross over yonder,
and go along the side of the river, and in a short time thou wilt see a great
Castle, in which are many towers, and the Earl who owns that Castle
is the most hospitable man in the world. There thou mayst spend the
night."

Never did sentinel keep stricter watch over his lord, than the lion that
night over Owain.

And Owain accoutred his horse, and passed across by the ford, and came
in sight of the Castle. And he entered it, and was honourably received.
And his horse was well cared for, and plenty of fodder was placed before
him. Then the lion went and lay down in the horse's manger; so that none
of the people of the Castle dared to approach him. The treatment which
Owain met with there was such as he had never known elsewhere, for
every one was as sorrowful as though death had been upon him. And they
went to meat; and the Earl sat upon one side of Owain, and on the other
side his only daughter. And Owain had never seen any more lovely than she.
Then the lion came and placed himself between Owain's feet, and he fed
him with every kind of food that he took himself. And he never saw anything equal to the sadness of the people.

In the middle of the repast the Earl began to bid Owain welcome.
"Then," said Owain, "behold, it is time for thee to be cheerful." "Heaven
knows," said the Earl, "that it is not thy coming that makes us sorrowful,
but we have cause enough for sadness and care." "What is that?" said
Owain. "I have two sons," replied the Earl, "and yesterday they went
to the mountains to hunt. Now there is on the mountain a monster who
kills men and devours them, and he seized my sons; and to-morrow is
the time he has fixed to be here, and he threatens that he will then slay
my sons before my eyes, unless I will deliver into his hands this my daughter.
He has the form of a man, but in stature he is no less than a giant."

"Truly," said Owain, "that is lamentable. And which wilt thou do?"
"Heaven knows," said the Earl, "it will be better that my sons should
be slain against my will, then that I should voluntarily give up my daughter
to him to ill-treat and destroy." Then they talked about other things,
and Owain stayed there that night.

The next morning they heard an exceeding great clamour, which was
caused by the coming of the giant with the two youths. And the Earl
was anxious both to protect his Castle and to release his two sons. Then
Owain put on his armour and went forth to encounter the giant, and the
lion followed him. And when the giant saw that Owain was armed, he

219

rushed towards him and attacked him. And the lion fought with the giant much more fiercely than Owain did. "Truly," said the giant, "I should find no difficulty in fighting with thee, were it not for the animal that is with thee." Upon that Owain took the lion back to the Castle and shut the gate upon him, and then he returned to fight the giant, as before. And the lion roared very loud, for he heard that it went hard with Owain. And he climbed up till he reached the top of the Earl's hall, and thence he got to the top of the Castle, and he sprang down from the walls and went and joined Owain. And the lion gave the giant a stroke with his paw, which tore him from his shoulder to his hip, and his heart was laid bare, and the giant fell down dead. Then Owain restored the two youths to their father.

The Earl besought Owain to remain with him, and he would not, but set forward towards the meadow where Luned was. And when he came there he saw a great fire kindled, and two youths with beautiful curling auburn hair were leading the maiden to cast her into the fire. And Owain asked them what charge they had against her. And they told him of the compact that was between them, as the maiden had done the night before. "And," said they, "Owain has failed her, therefore we are taking her to be burnt." "Truly," said Owain, "he is a good knight, and if he knew that the maiden was in such peril. I marvel that he came not to her rescue; but if you will accept me in his stead, I will do battle with you." "We will," said the youths, "by him who made us."

And they attacked Owain, and he was hard beset by them. And with that the lion came to Owain's assistance, and they two got the better of the young men. And they said to him, "Chieftain, it was not agreed that we should fight save with thyself alone, and it is harder for us to contend with yonder animal than with thee." And Owain put the lion in the place where the maiden had been imprisoned, and blocked up the door with stones, and he went to fight with the young men, as before. But Owain had not his usual strength, and the two youths pressed hard upon him. And the lion roared incessantly at seeing Owain in trouble; and he burst through the wall until he found a way out, and rushed upon the young men, and instantly slew them. So Luned was saved from being burned.

Then Owain returned with Luned to the dominions of the Countess of the Fountain. And when he went thence he took the Countess with him to Arthur's Court, and she was his wife as long as she lived.

And then he took the road that led to the Court of the savage black man, and Owain fought with him, and the lion did not quit Owain until he had vanquished him. And when he reached the Court of the savage black man he entered the hall, and beheld four-and-twenty ladies, the fairest that could be seen. And the garments which they had on were not worth four-and-twenty pence, and they were as sorrowful as death. And Owain asked them the cause of their sadness. And they said, "We are the daughters of Earls, and we all came here with our husbands, whom we dearly loved. And we were received with honour and rejoicing. And we were thrown into a state of stupor, and while we were thus, the demon who owns this Castle slew all our husbands, and took from us our horses, and our raiment, and our gold, and our silver; and the corpses of our husbands are still in this house, and many others with them. And this, Chieftain, is the cause of our grief, and we are sorry that thou art come hither, lest harm should befall thee."

And Owain was grieved when he heard this. And he went forth from the Castle, and he beheld a knight approaching him, who saluted him in a friendly and cheerful manner, as if he had been a brother. And this was the savage black man. "In very sooth," said Owain, "it is not to seek thy friendship that I am here." "In sooth," said he, "thou shalt find it then." And with that they charged each other, and fought furiously. And Owain overcame him, and bound his hands behind his back. Then the black savage besought Owain to spare his life, and spoke thus: "My lord Owain," said he, "it was foretold that thou shouldst come hither and vanquish me, and thou hast done so. I was a robber here, and my house was a house of spoil; but grant me my life, and I will become the keeper of an Hospice, and I will maintain this house as an Hospice for weak and for strong, as long as I live, for the good of thy soul." And Owain accepted this proposal of him, and remained there that night.

And the next day he took the four-and-twenty ladies, and their horses, and their raiment, and what they possessed of goods and jewels, and proceeded with them to Arthur's Court. And if Arthur was rejoiced when he saw him, after he had lost him the first time, his joy was now much greater. And of those ladies, such as wished to remain in Arthur's Court remained there, and such as wished to depart departed.

And thenceforward Owain dwelt at Arthur's Court greatly beloved, as the head of his household, until he went away with his followers; and those were the army of three hundred ravens which Kenverchyn had left him. And wherever Owain went with these he was victorious.

And this is the tale of THE LADY OF THE FOUNTAIN.

LOCHINVÁROVIČ[1]

Richard Hughes

I

FOR weeks, often, after autumn has definitely taken hold of the Balkan uplands, summer still lingers on the low shores of the Adriatic. Even Trieste still keeps a semblance of summer: though Trieste is now far too melancholy a town to be able to do much with it. Up is the Giulian Alps it is almost winter: on the bare limestone levels of the Karst a steady and biting wind makes a real hardship of sleeping in the open: but once one has dived over the almost precipitous ledge of the plateau that overhangs the city one is once more able to feel the hot dust of the roadway blowing up against one's hands, and to sit for hours on the Mole, staring at the wish-wash of the sea—or at the other people sitting there staring.

But that is, really, another story: it is not my present purpose to explain why I found myself in Trieste. This story is concerned with a rather remarkable love-affair: of which I would have known nothing if it had not happened that I was practically destitute at that time. I took a bed in a common lodging-house, in a row of other beds, and used to buy my food cheap in the market—it was cheap because it certainly would not have been saleable the next day; and go to bed, as late as possible, in my clothes.

The end of it all was that I started off on a long expedition with Mitar Lochinvárovič: but we neither of us emerged from it much richer. It was his idea, and quite a good one: he was distinctly clever, and as loyal a friend as one could hope for, and a very good shot with an automatic, which he much preferred to a knife: but the whole thing broke down because his health was giving way; as generally comes sooner rather than later to men who lead such a hard life as he had led. Indeed, I doubt whether he is still alive. He had long ceased to draw any satisfaction from smoking, and, when I gave him a cigarette, used to rip it up with his thumb-nail and eat the tobacco. He had suffered from chronic heartburn for years, he told me: and unless he had plenty to drink his hand shook so that he could hardly control it.

His bed was next to mine: On the other side of me was a young Sudanese negro who was always too drunk to be of much use for social purposes. Mitar kept a walking-stick of Napoleon's under his bed, wrapped up in newspaper: and he showed it me one morning, by way of fraternization.

---

[1] From *A Moment of Time*. Reprinted by permission of Messrs Chatto and Windus.

The Emperor had sent it as a present to some Montenegrin lady: Mitar had kept the letter which accompanied it too. He never told me how he came by them: nor how he came by the Great Seal of that once glorious rival to Venice, the Republic of Ragusa, which he carried in his waistcoat pocket. In another pocket of his waistcoat was some very old cheese, and some Greek and Roman coins. It is true that he had been a brigand when he was quite a lad, but I think he acquired these things later. Indeed, he did not make much out of brigandage, or he would not have become an ironmonger—which he did in desperation, he told me: despair of making a living by more normal means. But he presently gave up trade, and became a spy in the Turkish secret service. At last he was caught by the Greeks, court-martialled, and rather badly shot; so that he had a different scar to ache for every possible change of the weather. Indeed, for several years after his execution he was too crippled for a very active life. However, he managed to extract quite a creditable living from the white slave traffic which tided him over till the Great War came, when he obtained a responsible position in the administration of an American Relief Fund in the Balkans.

At the time I met him he had developed an excellent scheme for smuggling opium into the United States. It was very ingenious, because it was so contrived that there was no possible chance of getting imprisoned. The only difficulty lay in making the American buyer pay up. As a second string, he was blackmailing his brother officers of the Relief Fund, who were mostly very well off by now.

But, in spite of all these resources, he had got himself landed in Trieste in a destitute condition. We used to go and sup together at a little slum wine-shop where he was allowed credit: and sit there afterwards drinking the filthy ink they call *Vino Nero* in Trieste: or *šljivovica*, which is a spirit extracted from plums. Sometimes he would pull out the Great Seal, and expatiate on the glories of the dead Republic: or tell rather fabulous stories about King Dukljan the First—who was, he explained, the earliest king there ever was in the world, and seemed somehow mixed up with Deucalion: or vague and misty stories about being shot and knifed and strangled and raped; or of having one's eyes put out before one was crucified, which is the Macedonian custom. But one evening he explored in the lining of his coat and brought out a woman's photograph, which he handed to me to look at.

It was a bad photograph, but it was enough to convince me that I had never seen so beautiful a woman; and probably never would see.

Mitar took it from my hands and stared at it doggedly. Then he hiccoughed, sighed, and replaced it in his pocket.

II

Love at first sight is a strange and beautiful invention of the Deity. It is curiously discrete: that is to say, it bears little relation or resemblance to anything else in the Universe: a kind of hint that God is not reasonable by necessity but because He prefers to be: an everlasting reminder of the sort of Universe He could have created had He preferred to be absurd. Of course, looking at it after the event, one can shake one's head and point out this or that reason why it should have occurred, contributive causes as it were: but one can never say that, given such and such circumstances, it *will* occur. One might shake one's head and say that, given an almost Oriental upbringing—in other words, having never seen any man except her father and brothers at close quarters—Natya was bound to fall head over heels in love with the first man she should meet: provided, of course, that he was not her lawfully intended husband. And yet one could not be sure.... Or one might say that, given such a beautiful girl as Natya, and given romantic circumstances, given sufficient difficulty in attaining her, an adventurous and inflammable man like Mitar was bound to fall in love with her the moment he saw her. One might go further: one might argue that, though Mitar can never have been in his person particularly striking, yet the glory of a perfectly colourless American uniform (for it was during the Relief Fund phase) would single him out to her from among the bright-coloured costumes she was used to. One might say that, while in her case she had seen so few men that she might fall in love with anyone, he had seen so many women that he would be able to appreciate how far above other women she was: that while her eye would have the primitive keenness of its appetite completely unspoilt, his would have the added and truer keenness of the connoisseur: like the man who found the treasure in the field, and sold all that he had to buy it.

Those, at any rate, are the arguments one *might* set out, if one was told that Mitar went to Natya's home to borrow a wheelbarrow in the name of the United States of America, and that by some incredible happening he was met at the door by Natya herself, eye to eye.

Mitar borrowed the wheelbarrow: and then, with all the dignity of an American officer in his bearing, trundled it off down the little sandy road to his quarters in the village of Dobruca.

Of course, it was not very long before Natya's mother guessed there was something in the wind. Young girls do not, except on the stage, lean out of their windows night after night talking only to the moon. However fond they may be of their gardens, they do not pour into the dark bushes beneath quite such a flood of endearments as Natya, constant-voiced as the nightingale, used to shower down into the darkness from her little casement each night. And if it had not been that the moonlight lit up the whole white wall of the house, so that if the mother had herself leant from her window she would have been visible from below, she might have heard that these outpourings were no mere monologue. Constant as the nightingale-song from above, there came from the bushes below a murmur like the unstillable sea, a thrilling voice that rose to Naya's window more persistently, more intoxicatingly, more over-poweringy than all the musky perfumes of the garden. If her mother had dared to lan out, she might have seen a little silk kerchief flutter down into the darkness, which Mitar caught and folded neatly, and placed in his pocket-book together with the notes he kept against a rainy day of his brother-officers' embezzlements. And presently she might have seen a long ribband let down and then drawing up a small, heavy object tied to it—the Great Seal of the Republic of Ragusa, which Natya quickly hid between her two little breasts. Moreover, she could not fail to notice that Natya by day was changed: that when she should have been industriously embroidering shirts for her brothers, she used instead to lie on her back on her bed, staring vaguely at the ceiling and occasionally touching with the very tips of her fingers the little lump between her breasts.

No more could Major Thuddey fail to notice that Mitar was changed: then when he should have been standing in the hot sun distributing hand-knitted mittens to starving refugees, he would lie instead sound asleep in his bunk till nearly dusk.

You might have thought it was Major Thuddey's duty to reprimand Mitar—as it was certainly Natya's mother's duty to reprimand her daughter: but Major Thuddey was more than a little afraid of Mitar. Major Thuddey was an honest man: but he was also, in the American sense, an Idealist: the good name of his Relief Fund and of the United States was dear to him. He deprecated very much the way his subordinates had of selling to the refugees for their own pockets stores they were supposed to distribute free—but to bring dishonour on his country by exposing the practice was a crime to so good a patriot quite unthinkable. It was consequently a matter of considerable anxiety to him to notice that Mitar, whose Idealism he had no reason to respect and who was not an American Citizen, was scrupulously honest in all his dealings. He felt (and rightly) that the Good Name of America was somehow imperilled by this honesty: and though he had not the acumen to realize just how Mitar was investing his renunciation of his present chances for the support of his old age—though he did not suspect the existence of Mitar's little sheaf of notes, nor the use he intended to put them to—yet he could not but feel that the presence of a man as honest as himself but without his saving grace of Idealism was somehow dangerous; and, if Mitar lay abed and did nothing—well, all the better.

But Natya's mother had no such reason for silence: she took an early opportunity of coming into Natya's room, and sitting on Natya's bed and telling her in as calm a voice as possible that all was discovered: that the young man would certainly be shot at the first opportunity. By this means she hoped to terrify the child into a complete confession that would include the identity of her lover: for all was *not* discovered: the old lady had not the least idea who the nightly visitant was: and it is difficult to arrange for the unobtrusive assassination of a man you have not yet identified. The course of laying an ambush and shooting him under her daughter's window was to be avoided if possible, owing to the way tongues would certainly wag: a dead man at such a time and in such a place would quite belie the proverb, would tell a very obvious tale.

Now at the calm way her mother exploded her bomb Natya, who had all a child's belief in the intuitive omniscience of its mother, was nearly terrified out of her young life: and the Great Seal of Ragusa, that before had almost seemed to flutter like a live bird against her skin, suddenly seemed to crush through her flesh like a mill-stone. She was seized with a lively sense of the futility of ever attempting to hide anything from one's mother, who knows everything about one by light of nature. But fortunately this sad conviction did not prevent her lying to her mother with skill and coolness. Although having no hope whatever of success, she lied as a matter of principle. Her mother, who had started so calmly, not through calmness of nature, but because she had an unconscious appreciation of the value of crescendo when making a scene, gradually increased in fury and sound: and as her passion increased her discretion decreased: until Natya, while outwardly growing more and more stricken by her mother's wrath, inwardly became more and more elated: for she soon discovered that in the first place her mother did not know who her visitor was: and in the second that her father had not yet been told, but only was about to be. She resolved immediately that wild horses should not drag her lover's name from her; but at the same time she realized what a valuable weapon it was, in making terms for herself; by mildness, tempered by maidenly grief and pity—by abandonment of all defiance, and promising always to reveal the great secret in a day or two—she might get the game into her own hands: for as long as they thought they were likely to worm her lover's name out of her, so long would they be unable to take drastic measures on her own person.

Quite suddenly, the storm ceased: long before it had run its natural course. Possibly there was enough foundation for Natya's belief in her mother's intuition for the latter to have realized that her wrath was not having the effect it appeared to have, but that inwardly Natya was greatly cheered by it. So she too dissolved in tears, and kissed her daughter very lovingly, and told her in a sad, melancholy way what rosy hopes she had for her future. This was more than poor Natya had bargained for: she was still a child in many ways, and it was difficult to harden herself against the fountain-head of all the love she had ever known: far harder than to harden herself against the same person when regarded simply as the fountain-head of Authority. However, for the time being she succeeded; and her mother left her at last, bearing away no more information than she brought with her. Indeed, she had only shown her own hand, and consequently had little hope even of taking the young man in an ambush: for she was sensible enough to realize that if Natya were locked up in an iron box and she sat on the lid day and night, the girl would still find some means of conveying a warning to her lover. And so she left, somewhat downcast, but subconsciously determined, if need should arise, to worry herself on to a sick-bed. If her little Natya could stand against that, she reflected, she was not her little Natya.

She did not consider that little Natya was no longer wholly and only *her* little Natya.

As she expected, Natya immediately set about sending a message to her lover, warn him of the danger of coming to see her. "*Dear One*," she began to compose in her head, "*you must never try and see me again, or you will certainly be shot.*" In her heart of hearts she was singularly well pleased: this was a love-affair with a vengeance! And then her blood ran cold: suppose her hero laughed at warnings, and came, and was shot dead from a window as cats are shot when they yowl in the night? And then her blood ran colder: suppose he took her warning, and never did come to see her again? Both possibilities were equally unthinkable; *ergo*, she would not think of them. She went on composing her message in her head.

She had wholly overlooked till this moment one sovereign fact. Wild horses certainly could not drag his name from her, for she did not know it! Among all the hundred thousand things she had said to him, she had entirely forgotten to ask him who he was. And therefore she could not send him a message: for she could hardly write a letter to be pinned up in the American Mess, a sort of Battalion Orders:

"*Officers will cease to visit Natya Perunič by night, as arrangements have been*

227

made to assassinate them...."

So, though her brain went round in her head like a wheel, no way of identifying him could she contrive. Well, it could not be helped: he must come once more, and take his chance. After all, it was quite impossible that so glorious and wonderful a person as he was could be laid low by an ordinary bullet: love-stories simply do not end that way. And, at any rate, it removed the awful possibility of his *not* coming at all.

But Natya, with her mind full of these stupendous happenings and her heart bubbling over with its single stupendous emotion, little knew what a matter of touch-and-go it was whether she would ever see Mitar again. I have shown in an entirely convincing fashion how certain it was that these two should fall in love with each other. So convincing, indeed, were the arguments that Mitar never had the least doubt about it; it was, he realized, quite inevitable that he should fall in love with Natya: for he had a logical mind, as well as considerable experience of the subject, and always bowed to the dictates of his reason. Natya might fall in love without in the least knowing why: but for Mitar, who did know why and fully acquiesced in it, assurance was doubly sure. It was accordingly without the least hesitation that he flung himself into the affair, with absolute singleness of mind, absolute conviction of the stupendous nature of his own emotions. Each night, as he thrilled to the very core at the recital of his own devotion, it became more and more plain to him that he could not fail to be madly in love with this marvellous creature whose passion for him was so wonderful and so complete. So that when his Heart every now and then protested somewhat grumpily that it was not in love with her in the least, his Head told it quite flatly that it did not know what it was talking about: that it was in love with her without knowing it: that it *knew* it was in love with her and was simply being contrary: that outsiders see most of the game, and that it lay with Head, as an intelligent spectator, to decide whether Heart was in love, not with Heart itself at all: that presently Heart would be repenting its wilfulness in the flames of such a consuming passion as it had never felt before.

But still Heart protested, with all the obstinacy of which that organ is capable, that it was not in love with Natya Perunič.

Whereupon Head, realizing the futility of logical argument, tried to work upon Heart's feelings. It, Head, had done everything for Heart the latter could wish: had even sacrificed time that should have been given to the elaboration of that little note-book: had risked career, personal safety,—everything, in its readiness to follow the dictates of Heart: and now Heart repaid it by having no dictates at all!

But still Heart persisted that that was as it might be, but that it was not in love with Natya Perunič.

Very well then, said Head, your obstinacy has got us into the soup. For that we have between us worked the poor girl into a pretty state of passion there can be no doubt. An organ of your sensibility surely cannot propose that we should now desert her. All I ask of you is to suspend judgment. We owe it to her to go through with this business as we have begun: and I have no doubt whatever that the time will come when you will thank me, when you will be madly in love with her, and will be extremely grateful that I have refused to listen to you now.

That is as it may be, replied Heart: the future is not my province and you can act as you like: my only duty is to record the state of my feelings at the present moment, and the long and the short of it is, that I am not in love with Natya Perunič.

—It must not be supposed that this dialogue actually took place, or that Mitar argued it out clearly at all: it is simply an analysis for the reader's benefit of the generally uneasy state of mind in which he found himself; now deciding to carry her off to the other side of the world, now deciding never to go near her again; and absolutely refusing to admit to himself that he was not in love with Natya Perunič.

Moreover, it was only natural that to a man of his matured senses there should be something unsatisfactory in such love-making, with the two persons as securely separated by the barrier of ten vertical feet of air as they would have been by ten horizontal feet of adamant.

It was therefore, as I have said, touch-and-go whether Natya would ever see her ardent lover again: just as it was touch-and-go whether *he* would ever see the light of day again if she did. But it was inevitable that in a man of Mitar's type, as the reader will have guessed from the details of his past and future which I have given, that unselfishness should ultimately conquer: that the thought of leaving a girl so extremely lovely to pine for him unrequited would be ultimately put out of court. One must, on these occasions, occasionally sacrifice one's own feelings. Accordingly, before setting out he provided himself with a rope long enough and strong enough to overcome the ten-foot airy barrier he found so irksome; and resolved to see Natya Perunič once and for all.

The next night, then, found him once more at his place in the bushes, bubbling his devotions into the air like a garden fountain, where they met and mingled with the sighs and protestations of the maiden so far over his head; for just as he found it quite impossible to tell her (so unselfish he was) that all he said was said, so to speak, through his hat, so Natya, in *her* unselfishness, found it quite impossible to shatter his happiness (and interrupt the flow) by rude news of the imminent personal danger to which it exposed him.

Mitar, with the whole night before him and a nice sense of the pleasures of anticipation, was in no hurry to broach his project: and so an hour passed, and still the rope remained coiled under his coat.

But at length he resolved to act: and without for a moment interrupting the scintillation of his love-making, uncoiled it, ready to throw.

And now at last little Natya leant from the window as far as she could, hands outstretched to catch the line: and Mitar stood below, in act to throw.

A large and quite unprepossessing hand appeared in the moonlight over Natya's head, and twined itself very firmly in her hair. One tug, one scream—and where before her arms and cheek had gleamed in the moonlight, now nothing was visible except the spouts of two rifles, that poked out a few inches from the sill like the little lead cistern-overflow pipes in the wall of an English villa. Nor were they long in discharging their accumulation of wrath into the garden: and very near that cat came, who had so long yowled unmolested through the night, to a mortal soaking.

But Mitar was more adapted to making quick decisions, acting on the merits of the situation without undue delay, than are most officials in charge of the distribution of charitable funds. At the first gleam of those fingers in the moonlight, Mitar, all his eloquence checked, was crawling away on his stomach through the shrubbery, dragging his ridiculous ten-foot tail wriggling behind him.

III

After this incident it was only natural that Head should somewhat weaken in the opposition it raised to Heart. It is all very well to run risks when one is madly infatuated: but deliberately to get oneself shot in a shrubbery in the cause of Unselfishness that amounted to little more than a point of punctilio is altogether absurd: while the sole very moderate personal satisfaction with which Mitar had intended to reward himself could be purchased in any town of considerable size with perfect safety for about four *lire*. And it only shows the perverseness of Heart, that it, too, began to weaken in its opposition to Head: that after a week of enforced separation it was no longer at all so firm in its conviction that it was not in the least in love with Natya Perunič.

However, in this contest of adaptability to the opposite point of view, it was Head which ultimately carried the day, being even more ready to give up the whole affair then Heart was to continue it. It is highly probable that the two lovers would never have seen each other again if it had not been for Zdenka: who now enters the story in the *rôle* of Fairy Godmother, or *Diabolus ex machina*, whichever way you like to look at it. Zdenka was the assistant in the photographic studio which some enterprising person had established in Dobruca. It was only a small wooden shanty, but excellently equipped: being furnished with a red plush sofa, a plaster balustrade with no behind to it, a white calico screen, and a monochrome landscape background of Fifth Avenue.

There was, of course, no camera. On its first establishment it had actually done a little business with the American Relief-workers: but after they had been photographed in every possible position, and in every combination and permutation of grouping, business languished. Most of the villagers, after being photographed at one age in one position, made it last a lifetime. In consequence, the proprietor had been compelled to dismount his machine from its complicated stand, and now earned a precarious living by touring the country, photographing atrocities for sale to the propaganda departments of all the belligerent governments; and also by photographing politicians surrounded by thousands of their supporters, which they bought by the gross at little more than cost price to distribute among their opponents. Meanwhile Zdenka remained in charge of the studio: nominally, at any rate, to make appointments for the proprietor, if ever he should happen to pass that way.

It will therefore be seen that Zdenka, being a New Woman with a profession of her own, possessed a great deal more freedom of movement than a nicely brought up girl like Natya would ever be allowed. Hitherto, Natya had felt nothing but contempt for those hoydens who struggled in the outer darkness of life, instead of vegetating in the inner light of seclusion: her attitude towards Zdenka had been friendly, but decidedly superior; but now she found herself greatly envying that freedom which formerly had so shocked her. For it must not be imagined that having her hair nearly pulled out by the roots was the chief of the unpleasantnesses she had to endure during the next few days: and if her family failed to proceed to extreme measures, it was only for two reasons. In the first place, they had still failed to identify her lover, and still hoped to worm the secret out of her; in the second, it was less than a month now from the date of her wedding, and it is unbecoming in a bride to be black and blue.

Although this matter of her wedding certainly saved Natya from a good deal of physical discomfort, she nevertheless found herself anticipating it with more and more annoyance. Under ordinary circumstances it would have seemed to her quite in the course of nature that she should be married to a man she had never seen: but now she found herself regarding the prospect almost with aversion.

For the betrothal customs of Western and Eastern Europe, although they coincide in the main, have one important difference. It is a matter of philosophy, the opposition of the Idealistic and the Realistic. In Eastern Europe, when a girl is still a very small child, her parents choose for her a husband, and the betrothal is fixed: and this may be said for the plan, that if the girl has never seen her intended husband, at least her parents have. But in Western Europe, while she is still a child, or even before she is born, her parents choose for her an imaginary husband, and, in their minds, betroth her to him quite as irrevocably as do Balkan parents: an Idea, say, of a sober business man, handsome but steady, clever at his work but without any taint of Inquiry in his mind. So that in Western Europe, when the child-betrothal takes place, not only has the girl never seen her intended husband, but her parents have not either.

In Natya's case, it was a prominent director of the Eskomptne Banke at Zagreb to whom she was betrothed: a man of quite respectable means, and some intelligence, and a fair allowance of years, called Dr Pedar Srdič: and it was very wrong of Natya to repine against so excellent a husband.

Nevertheless, an almost unheard-of project began to suggest itself to her. She would run away with Mitar to America.

For several days after that disgraceful incident of course she was not allowed to see anyone at all: but it was not long before she obtained leave to see her friend Zdenka: and it was not long before Zdenka, having with difficulty identified him, began to pass on mysterious messages to Mitar. They proved very disturbing to his peace of mind: for he had hardly come to the decision never to see Natya again when those devoted little communications from her began to leak through, telling him how she languished, what she suffered for his sake: begging him to come and see her once again, if only *once*: messages which almost fired him to forget his new resolution. But each time when he almost decided to go, the memory of those two little overflow pipes projecting from the wall was too much for him: try as he would, he could not go. Meanwhile, he was quite sensible of a new danger: if he did not go, Zdenka might suspect him of being a coward, and a deceiver: and if she got angry with him, she might give away the whole affair to Natya's parents—which would be disastrous. In consequence, he took the most elaborate pains with his excuses, and made them so specious and convincing that for a time they failed to arouse the suspicions not only of the ingenuous Natya, but even of the more worldly-wise Zdenka.

It is improbable, however, that this could have lasted: the crisis would have been bound to be precipitated, were it not for a fortunate occurrence. A fortnight before her marriage, Natya got leave to go and be photographed. The proprietor was spending a few hours in Dobruca to collect some plates which Zdenka had developed: and an appointment was arranged. Zdenka hurried with the news to Mitar. So he was concealed in a cupboard, ready to step out the moment the proprietor left. Small wonder if Natya were even more nervous than girls usually are, when they pose for their photographs—knowing that Mitar was watching her through the keyhole of the tall cupboard in the corner. As a matter of fact, he was not: the cupboard was so tightly sealed that he put his nose, not his eye, to the only aperture.

But at last the sitting was over, and the proprietor bundled out of the studio, and Zdenka on guard at the door: and on the red plush sofa, witnessed only by the plaster balustrade that had no behind and the faint, fantastic shadow of Fifth Avenue, Mitar and Natya conducted their first proper love-making.

As soon as she was able sufficiently to collect her wits, Natya broke to Mitar the news that she intended to elope with him. He was to come once more with his rope to her window, but in perfect silence this time: she would climb down, and together they would fly to America.

When she first told him of her imminent marriage he was torn by conflicting emotions, unable to decide whether he was more desolated to lose her or more rejoiced at this ready-made solution of a position grown impossible: but when she suggested elopement, his mind was made up at once: duly and firmly married to Dr Srdič she must be! This did not, of course, prevent him welcoming the notion with every expression of joy: and by the time their short hour was up, he had promised to make all arrangements for flight and to call for Natya within the next three days.

Needless to say, he did not.

Now for the first time Zdenka began to reproach him. But there were so many difficulties, he urged; and plenty of time: Natya would not be married for a whole week: or later, for three days: at length, even:

"Why, she will not be married till to-morrow! What more suitable night than to-night to carry her off?"

Zdenka shook her head, unappeased. She had by now more than grave doubts of Mitar's intentions: she urged him at least to go and see the poor girl once more, eve if he could not save her from the imminent ceremony.

"Why, of course I shall," he answered. "I shall go to-night, with my rope, and have a car waiting... after to-night, you will never hear of either of us again!"

But Zdenka still shook her head: and Mitar, feeling himself to be quite unconvincing, went out and got very drunk indeed, in order to forget all about it.

IV

The wedding procession started out the next morning at six: and Natya, who had sat the whole night by her window in growing despair, looked the most pinched and peaked and hollow-eyed and unhappy young bride. Dr Srdič was second cousin to a bishop, and so it was towards the little cathedral city of Vojvdo that the wedding procession set out so early, laughing and chaffing, with the prospect of half a day's drive through the mountains ahead of them, and much merrymaking at the end of it, and a return in the evening. They passed up the street of Dobruca, the highly decorated little carts jingling as they went, the men calling and guffawing, the women singing and giggling, the bride quietly sobbing to herself. They passed right under Mitar's window: but he was far too sound alseep to be woken by so slight a disturbance. He slept on, the deep and innocent sleep of the intoxicated.

When he did wake, his head was awful. It was nine o'clock. The blinding sun shone straight in at his window. He sat up, clutching at his brows. (It is an unjust God who has decreed that man should purchase oblivion and irresponsibility at such a price.) His skull seemed to come to pieces in his hands, like a cup in the grasp of a housemaid. It was agony. It felt as if some one with a Victorian sense of humour had wittily attempted to saw his head in two while he slept: and, being surprised at the task, had left his saw wedged in the cleft.

Mitar pressed his hands to his eyeballs and staggered across the room, groping for his belt and boots. Then out into the blinding street and across to the *café*, where he sank into a little green chair, and ordered a whole bottle of šljivovica—by way of a hair of the dog that had bitten him.

Ten o'clock. Natya would have started four hours ago.

For a moment the pain lulled, and when it lulled he began to remember, which was highly annoying. He tackled the šljivovica seriously, determined that the return of the wedding party should find him as paralytically unconscious and incapable as had its departure.—But, after all, why should

234

he worry? Brazen little minx! It had all been on her side, she had entrapped him: he had never been in love with her in the least: and 'hadn't he nearly got himself, shot, just to gratify her whims? His hair bristled uncomfortably at the thought of her two fierce brothers, their incredibly long moustaches, those two little overflow pipes. *Question*: What right has a girl to fall in love with a man? *Answer*: None, if it is going to cause him danger and inconvenience.

That gave place to a more placid mood, in which he congratulated himself on the part he had played: management of a difficult situation which for skill, tact, and moral rectitude could hardly be excelled. He really came out of it all very well.

Gradually his headache softened under the bite of the spirit: and soon everything receded from him in a beatific way, just as the world of sense *ought* to recede from a spiritual man. He gradually melted into the Infinite—already his bodily senses were left behind, or at any rate all mixed up: so that the little green tables of the *café* only penetrated to him as a tinkling arpeggio to the blaring bass of the sunlight, the booming sky outside: while the rattle of a passing bullock-cart was translated into a series of vivid flashes of colour, and the discomfort of the rickety chair he sat on smelt bitter in his nostrils.

But something was pushing him, shoving up against him, prodding him in his Nirvana. That was monstrous! He pulled himself together, just enough to ascertain through which of his senses the attack was really directed. Finally, he traced it to his ears: yes, some one was shouting at him. And his bottle had been removed.

With great difficulty he focused his eyes on the scene around him: and at last discovered Zdenka, standing over him, covering him with abuse from head to foot.

But she did more than that. Seizing a carafe of iced water from a table near by, she poured half of it over his head: and then deliberately tipped the rest, lumps of ice and all, down the back of his neck, holding away the collar of his tunic with her hand.

The remedy was drastic, but it certainly made him better able to listen to what she had to say. He even succeeded in asking her what the devil she meant by it.

"You wicked liar, making poor little Natya fall in love with you! You, to promise to run away with her, and then to sit there drinking like an owl while the poor child is being married to old Srdič! You, to call yourself a brigand! You, to call yourself an officer! You, to call yourself a male man at all!"

235

"But, my dear little girl, what is all the fuss? You don't dare to suggest I'm a coward, that I'm not going to run away?"

"But, you great embroiderd he-liar, she's half-way to Vojvdo by now!"

"There's plenty of time, my child, plenty of time. She won't be married for a couple of hours yet. Must have a drink before starting!"

"But she's twenty miles ahead of you by now!"

"There's plenty of time!... Overtakings are in the Hands of God!"

He staggered out of his chair: he had caught sight of one of the Relief Fund Fords which Major Thuddey had left standing outside the mess with the engine running. As he climbed into the driver's seat he turned to repeat solemnly to the astonished Zdenka:

"*In the Hands of God...*"

Then he accidentally trod on the gear-pedal and began zig-zagging erratically up the street in low gear, like a lamed rocket, clinging sideways to the steering wheel.

What the ice down his back had begun, the fresh air continued. By the time he had destroyed a fruitstall, and left a mudguard as a sort of pious offering on the corner of the church, he was beginning to drive fairly creditably: at any rate, he sat facing in the right direction, and had succeeded in getting into top gear. Moreover, he had all the drunk man's feeling of confidence in his own skill: he felt that never had he driven so well before. He also had the drunk man's luck: for he drove as hard as he could pelt and miss destruction by inches, yet for the present at any rate, missed it.

Soon he was eating up the miles to Vojvdo: and all the fire in his blood was stirred at his romantic quest. *Natya! Natya!* Her name sang in his ears like a choir of birds. Her lovely face danced in front of him all up the road. Gone was his terror for her villainous brothers, her father, the whole pack of them! He would snatch her from them, carry off his beloved from the altar steps: true love and constancy, youth and the beautiful dreams of youth should conquer in the end, as they always conquered. His name would go down to posterity among the names of Great Lovers: his exploit would be celebrated in poems and plays, along with the heroic elopements of antiquity.

As, indeed, leaving out the little matter of his mental indecision, of which no one need ever know: leaving out the part played by Zdenka with the carafe of iced water, and the amount of stimulant he had consumed before starting on his heroic expedition, and various details of his private life (such as the little note-book), all of which a romantic writer with an eye to a good story would quite certainly suppress: taking the plain, staring facts of the story and asking no awkward questions about mental processes: employing, in short, an artist's undoubted Right of Selection—there was no reason whatever why it should not.

Who knows why Paris ran off with Helen, or what crossed Leander's mind as he swam the Hellespont? Who would be fool enough not to accept these stories at their face value, when their face value was so stirring? Then who would dare to suggest that Mitar, who had braved death to vist his Natya, and now charged recklessly across the mountains to snatch her from the altar steps, was not the most romantic lover of them all?

For it must not be imagined that there was anything comic in the turn affairs had taken. Mitar might be drunk, but he was not ignorant of the difficulty of his task: and being accustomed to danger, he had also a remarkable power of forcing his mind to sober itself when action was necessary. To carry Natya off from her own house would have been comparatively easy: to carry her off at the church door, when all the wedding guests would have rifles, and would certainly shoot him at sight if they had the least inkling that he was Natya's anonymous lover, was a very serious matter, requiring all the daring and all the coolness he could muster. That it was *l'amour propre* rather than *l'amour* which prompted the adventure did not affect its *dangerousness* a whit. Mitar was no romantic townling, battened on picture-plays and fiction magazines, he was a man who all his life had lived face to face with danger: and if that gave him the necessary practice and skill with which alone such an enterprise could be successfully carried out, it also meant that he knew very well how difficult it all was. As he drove his Ford for all it was worth in the direction of Vojvdo he knew, with a certainty no mere amateur adventurer could have had, how slender were the chances of his ever coming back alive.

And yet he was still so drunk that he could hardly cling to the wheel.

Poor Natya! She had almost given up hope. As the cathedral drew nearer, hope sank lower: she began to envisage the old bishop as if he were some kind of inexorable ogre. Presently the whole party stopped at a little wayside inn, for lunch: dived under the low, vine-covered door, and grouped themselves formally round the bare trestle tables. Natya tried to eat with the rest: but all the time her eye was fixed on the door, or on the window. She hardly heard what they said to her. *He cometh not!*

And yet, what would be the good? Could he venture right into the lion's den?

A long-drawn-out grinding squeak proclaimed that a car had pulled up outside: and presently the door was darkened by the figure of an American officer. Natya dropped her spoon, gazing a moment with popping eyes.

Then she recovered herself. No one had noticed. Mitar came in and sat down in a corner, and ordered food.

Natya could not bear to look at him. He had come! But why had he come? Was it to gaze his last at her? Or was it to carry her off? And why was he pretending to be drunk? Was that a piece of cunning on his part?

So the meal went on: the wedding party eating heartily, Natya eating nothing at all, Mitar eating as well as the state of his stomach would allow.

It was over. The wedding party adjourned to their carts. Mitar did not move: he sat there, as if there was no hurry: and never once looked at Natya.

So that *looking* could not be his purpose in coming.

It was not till they were mounting once more into their seats that they discovered how near an accident they must have been. The axle-pin had come out of the wheel of one of the carts, the wheel itself had been wrenched crooked by the strain. The whole party conferred over it a while, and came to the conclusion that nothing could be done: the vehicle must be left behind. But all the other carts were packed: what about its passengers?

They looked round, and there was the American officer's motor-car; and inside the inn the American officer was dawdling over his lunch.

The solution was obvious; so old Perunič, Natya's father, took the negotiations on his own shoulders. He wandered aimlessly back into the inn: began an aimless conversation with the innkeeper; aimlessly trod on Mitar's toe, and overwhelmed himself with apologies. From that to an equally aimless conversation with the stranger was a short step: and purely in order to make conversation, he recited the story of their mishap. Mitar, who knew perfectly well what was coming, was laconic, and no more helpful than necessary: and it must be confessed that though he expressed sympathy at the mishap, inwardly it caused him little surprise. ... So, when the moment was ripe, he suggested that, as he also was going to Vojvdo to buy eggs for the Relief Fund, could he give any of them a lift? Would the bride and her mother honour him?

The old man was grateful and astonished: such an idea would never have entered his head, but since the nobleman was so kind...

He went out to tell the others of his success: and Natya, with as little haste as she could contrive, began to climb down again from her seat. Meanwhile they were stripping the derelict vehicle of its decorations and draping the old Ford in proper bridal manner, to take its place in the procession: while Mitar stood in the door of the inn with a bored and superior, if still rather intoxicated, air.

All were ready to start: all but the bride's mother, who still sat in her cart. So they explained to her that she was to ride in the car. Now, whether her famous intuition had begun to work, or whether it was sheer fright, I do not know: but she flatly refused. She never had ridden in a car, and she never would ride in a car: they were inventions of the devil as well as being highly unsafe: and to be terrified out of her life on the day of her daughter's wedding was not at all her idea of pleasure. Why, she would hardly feel Natya was properly married if the girl rode to her wedding in such a thing! (As, indeed, was high probable.) In short, she refused outright: and there was nothing for it but for Natya to climb down yet again, and back into the cart: and instead of being able to carry off his lady, Mitar had to be content to take his place meekly in her wedding procession, with four of the bridegroom's caterwauling younger brothers in the car beside him. So do the plans, even of Heroic Lovers, gang all awry.

How often it is that our patron saint looks after us in a way that at first makes us livid with rage—only afterwards we realize his kindly offices, and are properly grateful! As they left the little inn, Mitar inwardly abused his patron by every name his spiritual tongue could curl round. But as they neared Vojvdo, sobriety gradually returned to him, and he was overcome with astonishment at the part he had set out to play. *He*, to run off with another man's affianced bride! And she a girl with whom he was not in love in the least! All because of the sharp tongue of a wretched photographer's assistant. He thanked his saint with proper fervour, as they entered the narrow streets of Vojvdo, for saving him from so monstrous and so extremely unsafe an act: and he deposited the wedding guests at the door of the cathedral with all unction, promising to call for them in a couple of hours, while he set off to the market to buy two gross of excusatory eggs.

If one were buying two gross of eggs for oneself in the market of Vojvdo, two hours would certainly not be enough for the necessary bargaining: but buying them with public money was a different matter, and in less than thirty minutes they were all stowed in the bedizened Ford, and Mitar found himself with nothing to do. For a moment he thought of going to the cathedral to see the wedding; but his innate tact revolted against this. Moreover, he reflected, the actual ceremony would be over by now. Then he thought longingly of the wedding feast: so longingly that he turned into a little Gostilna, determined to celebrate the occasion of Natya's wedding by himself, over a bottle or two of his favourite liqueur.

But as the flames of the habitual šljivovica mounted to his head, they wrought a decided change of mind. In the first place, it is well known that intoxication, like sleep, loosens the tongue of the subconscious: and deep in his subconscious, however positively Head and Heart might agree to the contrary, there lurked a certain regret for the lovely girl (call it love or not as you like, for the stirrings of the subconscious are used to hard names, by now). In the second place, a man may get drunk overnight and drunk again the morning after without much happening: but if he deliberately gets drunk the following afternoon as well, something is bound to give, somewhere: discretion and reason go completely by the board, and whether he wins the Victoria Cross, or finds himself sentenced to several years' hard labour, or matter for the sexton, will be purely a question of the circumstances in which he is situated.

All this Mitar should have known, and gone easy with the bottle: but he did not go easy, and that is how it came to pass that his ambition to become the subject of song and story was fulfilled. By the time he went to pick up the returning wedding guests they were fairly uproariously drunk: but *he* was drunk with a superlative drunkenness, as different from theirs as cheese from chalk: a cold, mad drunkenness, that left him fairly well able to walk and talk, but cut off all memory and all prescience as with a knife: he had no Past and no Future, only a vivid Present with which he grappled with the energy of a tiger. I have seen a man in this state make his teeth meet through another man's leg: I have myself walked round a high building on a lead gutter that sagged in festoons under my weight. But it is rare, this true Bacchic frenzy: and only those who have seen it can realize how far removed from the ordinary puerile bravado of intoxication it is.

But of all this Mitar, as is the way in such cases, gave no hint till the moment was ripe. They were on the homeward journey, the narrow road passing between the rock and a terrific precipice. Mitar had drawn a little ahead of the others with his four young men, and as he rounded a bend he suddenly drew up. Then he pulled out a couple of automatics, and covering his astonished passengers with one hand, trained the other on the bend behind him; determined to shoot, if necessary, the whole wedding party, thirty or forty of them.

As the first cart came in sight he fired. His aim, always good, was now deadly. Three men dropped. The horses were mad with confusion: other men sprang to their heads to force them back into cover. Mitar fired again. A rifle volley replied: but they aimed in order to miss their relatives in the back seat. And Mitar volleyed another three or four shots. Then silence: his clip was empty. He lifted his other gun, alternately firing and covering the terrified four, all the while feeling desperately in his pocket for a spare clip to charge his empty gun. He was not firing aimlessly, be it understood: Natya, her mother, and the other women were as safe as they had been

240

when in the cathedral itself: but one man after another dropped on the narrow road. Only Dr Srdič himself, lying flat on his stomach at his bride's feet, Mitar could not reach.

By the time he had fired his last shot, the two families of Perunič and Srdič were both reduced by about one half, but if anything the family of Perunič had suffered most. In order to redress the balance, Mitar loosened the brake, and deliberately drove his car with himself and his four passengers straight over the edge of the cliff.

But his patron saint, who had formerly saved him from indiscretion, now saved him in indiscretion. As the car heeled over sideways he was flung out, and somehow caught with both hands at a tamarisk bush some four feet below the edge. But the bestreamered car and the four young men and the two gross of eggs turned over and over on their eight-hundred-foot drop into the ravine beneath. As he hung there, Mitar bitterly regretted those eggs... But then, he reflected, one cannot make so grand an omelette without the breaking of eggs.

As the astonished wedding party craned their necks over the cliff, they were just in time to see the Ford, now grown minute and distant, come finally to rest. But they did not see a pair of hands twined firmly in a tamarisk bush a few feet below their noses.

Presently they went on their way—considerably chastened in their merrymaking, it is true; but it must not be imagined that the incident seemed to them unusual, or of quite so much importance, as it would to the guests at one of our Western weddings. Only Dr Srdič himself, who, from his many years as a Zagreb banker, had grown used to ways of comparative security, considered it a matter of great import. He had always wondered what to do with his four turbulent younger brothers.

V

It must be confessed against Natya's count, that she did not treat her husband with that politeness or consideration one civilized being owes to another, let alone a wedded wife to her husband. Once she had ensconced herself in her bedroom, she produced a small but very sharp stiletto of Sheffield steel, and told him she would kill him if he came in side the door. She was wild with grief and love at Mitar's heroic end, and determined to have her cry out in private, without the intrusion of a husband.

Pedar Srdič was not very much impressed by her stiletto, for there are more ways than one of disarming a woman: but his residence in Zagreb, and contact with that Western world whose outpost it was, had taught him that the marriage customs of his native country were more than a little barbarous: and though he had followed them in form (for he was a true conservative), he was quite ready, now that Natya and he were married, to give her time for them to get acquainted—even to go through an abridged form of courtship—in deference to Western opinion. He was quite prepared to let her have her own wilful way; say, for three days, by which time, if she did not surrender willingly, his conscience would no longer reproach him for taking his rights by force: one day for them to get to know each other, one for him to make love to her, and one for her to fall in love with him: it was a generous allowance.

Meanwhile Natya sat on her bed day and night, without food or sleep, nursing her little steel imp, with which she more than once decided to kill herself. Of this Srdič had no inkling: for it had not occurred to Natya's mother—let alone her husband, who, of course, had not been told—to connect the uncertain temper of the American officer in the Ford with Natya's secret love-affair. They all put it down to the natural vagaries of a man who had taken too much to drink, and thought no more about it.

Two days passed, and time brought no alleviation to Natya's sorrow. Two days, and still she loved Mitar, still mourned his death in the abysm of despair. Pedar's programme had to be abandoned, owing to her peevish conduct; for when he came to the door she used to go to the window and threaten to throw herself down into the stone courtyard below, if he so much as entered the room. Love-making, and even acquaintance, were thus indefinitely postponed: till presently Pedar lost his temper and told her that if she could not even treat him with common politeness she should get no more law, but be strapped to the bed.

Natya, being no more moved by his threats than his cajoleries, determined at last to make an end to herself: life without Mitar was unbearable, life with Pedar was unbearable, life must end. Perhaps she might be allowed to meet her lover in purgatory: indeed, her only dread was that so angelic a man could scarcely be kept there for more than a week or two at most: she shuddered to think of the æons she might have to spend there alone.

And so the story winds to a tragic close, for Mitar, that she believed dead, was alive and well: and even now making plans for her ultimate abduction.

There were many reasons why he had not acted at once on his return to Dobruca. In the first place, it took a couple of days' sleep to restore him to passable health. In the second, he had to explain to Major Thuddey the loss of the car and the eggs—but Major Thuddey was so used, by now, to fantastic explanations of the 'loss' of government property that it was not a very difficult matter. And in the third place, it took him a little while to make up his mind. But he soon realized that what he had begun he must finish: that the new respect with which Zdenka treated him would be forfeit if he confined his exploits to a mere meat omelette, and did not carry the girl off in the end at all.

So at last he started off for Srdič's country house, bowling along in yet another stolen Ford with a rope-ladder under the seat. His heart was as full of hope as Natya's of despair. But the scene, with its fitful, moon-splashed sky, was all set for tragedy: for the night she had finally chosen for suicide was the selfsame night he had fixed on for their elopement: and as her lover drove carelessly through the darkness, Natya lay on the great walnut bed for the last time in her life, dressed in her bridal gown, feeling with the point of her stiletto for the right spot between her ribs.

The sudden ping of a pebble on her window so startled her that she actually pricked herself... but it was too late. There came another ping. Hardly knowing what she was doing, she rose and opened the casement. Out of the darkness below floated the incredible voice of her beloved.

Her long hair rose away from her head like a mane: the little scratch on her breast smarted. Was it so simple then: was she already dead? Had he risen from the grave to summon her to join him there? Then the end of a rope-ladder floated up into sight, and mechanically she caught it. That reassured her. One does not need a ladder to descend into the grave.

Mitar and Natya were together at last; the last barrier down, driving away through the night, their happiness at last in their own hands: Natya full of love and trust in her hero, Mitar full of satisfaction in the accomplishment of his task, and a growing uneasiness as to what should be done with the girl now he had got her: for that they were irrevocably committed to each other he could not deny. Of one thing only he was absolutely certain: that he was not in the least in love with Natya Srdič.

Most assuredly the story was winding to a tragic close: gone was even that little thread of Sheffield steel by which it had so nearly been avoided.

Mitar drove straight to the house of a married sister of his, who lived some forty miles from Dobruca: and just had time to dump Natya at the door and drive like Hell back to his quarters, if he was to be in before it was light. But he knew very well that could be only a temporary expedient.

VI

When Natya's flight was discovered, Dr Srdič was annoyed almost beyond words. It was not merely the loss of his newly wed wife, for her beauty hardly compensated for her uncompromising temper. It was the social consequences which so exercised him.

Dr Srdič, as I have shown, was a man of humane and advanced views, caught in the toils of a conservative etiquette, against which he had not the courage to revolt. Now immemorial etiquette dictated that in a case like this the injured husband should telegraph for his wife's nearest male relations; and on their arrival should avenge the insult that had been offered him by shooting them dead. Etiquette was equally firm that the unhappy father and brother should accept the invitation as if they were ignorant of its import: and allow themselves to be shot with expressions of polite, if fictitious, surprise. Then, and not till then, the ball was open, and that mortal catch as-catch-can called a blood-feud would begin between the two families until one or other was exterminated.

Now, it may well be imagined that an enlightened and peaceable banker like Dr Srdič was much embarrassed at the demands made of him by this social code: little as he wished to shoot old Perunič and his sons, he had even less desire to expose himself to the subsequent bullets of their relations —especially since the loss of his four younger brothers, whose usefulness he now for the first time recognized. He spent several sleepless nights trying to think of a way out: but there was no way out: etiquette was inexorable. With a heavy heart, therefore, he sent the wire: and then sat down to clean an old rusty rifle that he had not handled since he was a boy.

If Dr Srdič was reluctant to send the wire, it was nothing to the despondency of the Perunič family on its receipt. If Dr Srdič had debated for three nights before sending it, they debated for six nights before replying.

But it is a sign of true breeding to know when to waive etiquette: and where the banker had failed, they succeeded. They found a way by which honour would be satisfied: and instead of accepting the invitation for himself and his sons, Old Perunič sent his wife and daughters-in-law.

At this no one was more overjoyed than Srdič himself: for he was under no obligation to shoot the women: instead, they were able to sit down quietly together and hold a family parliament.

It was Natya's mother who put two and two together, and confessed the story of Natya's clandestine visitor, and finally drew the thread through the irascible American officer (of whose miraculous escape they had just heard) to her ultimate disappearance.

It was now Srdič's plain duty to set off for Dobruca and shoot Mitar in the street.

But so far had he wandered from the paths of the strict morality of his fathers, that he was singularly loath even to do this. Degenerate times, indeed, when a husband could so shirk his responsibilities! The position, he explained, was extremely difficult. He had, what they of course had not, some knowledge of international affairs, and he assured the eager women that if he were to shoot, under whatever provocation, an American officer, and more especially an officer engaged in the charitable relief of their country, there would be, diplomatically speaking, the devil to pay. The Americans, he explained, are a people with a very weak moral sense, and, so far from recognizing the justice of his action, would be certain not only to hang him, but to visit their wrath on the entire countryside. Even if he himself escaped, the catholic outpouring of their wrath would only be all the fiercer: the whole nation would be made to suffer for it, if he allowed himself the luxury of following the dictates of his conscience.

Difficult as the women found it to realize that a Great People could be so unenlightened, so lost to all sense of moral fitness, they had to admit that in questions of the outside world they knew very much less than Pedar. They had to accept his judgment.

Then there was only one thing to be done. They must call in the bishop. He, the Bishop of Vojvdo, Srdič's cousin, who had officiated at the ceremony: it was for him to visit the American (for they were unaware how slender were Mitar's claims to that title) and to reason with him. It only shows how far gone they were in laxity, how quickly and harmfully the smallest breach of etiquette widens, that they should be so easily driven to have recourse to Reason.

All this time, of course, Mitar went about in a state of double uneasiness. He was extremely worried as to what was to be done with Natya: and he was not at all sure that he might not be shot at any hour of the day or night.

Then came the news that the bishop wished to see him, and, in some trepidation, he went. At first it seemed incredible that the enemy should have been reduced to so mild a form of retaliation as mere talk: but that this was the case the old man made clear.

"My son," he began, "you are in danger of Hell. You are living in adultery with another man's wife."

Mitar, with an air of great innocence, asked: "Whose?"

"With Natya, the wife of Dr Pedar Srdič."

Mitar's countenance expressed relief: it was untrue, he explained: Mme

245

Srdič was staying in the mountains with a married sister of his, and he had not himself been near the place.

The bishop had to admit that this was true, and that it was hardly the conduct of the usual adulterer.

"At any rate," he went on, "you are conniving at keeping a married woman forcibly from her husband."

"I am not," said Mitar, "for, as Srdič himself will tell you, she won't go within ten miles of him."

The old man was not used to being answered back. He decided to clinch the matter.

"Well, my son, whatever you are doing, you have got to stop it."

But Mitar was by no means cowed. He explained, gently and respectfully, that he had no intention of stopping it.

The old man was overcome by amazement.

"Then, what *do* you intend to do?"

That was the one question Mitar could not easily answer. But in a flash he made up his mind:

"I intend to marry her!"

"But"—the bishop gasped—"she is married already!"

"True," said Mitar gently, "she has been married according to the rites of the Church, but according to the Constitution of January last, it is only the civil ceremony which is valid in law: and the civil ceremony had not, in this case, yet taken place. *I* shall depart with her to Belgrade, and marry her in a registry office!"

The bishop shook with rage.

"But do you imagine that such a crime would be tolerated? Do you think, when the law was framed, it was ever thought such a situation would arise?—It was simply to ensure the proper registration of marriages, impossible otherwise in a State where there are so many religions —Why, it is an insult to Mother Church, a downright insult, sir!"

Mitar leant back, and his expression was certainly insulting.

"Yes," he said, "I am afraid it will be a little awkward for Mother Church. What will she do about it?"

"You would be excommunicated ... but the crime cannot be allowed to be committed!"

"I am not much worried by the prospect of excommunication, and I certainly intend to carry out my proposition as soon as I can get three days' leave. I repeat, what will Mother Church do about it?"

And then, before the bishop could reply, Mitar leant forward and continued:

"There is only *one* thing she can do, if the so-called insult is to be avoided: you must annul the former marriage! Find out that you made a mistake, that Natya was never properly married to Srdič at all! Then she and I can be married by Church and State both: and no insult, no awkward precedent, will have occurred."

Without a word the bishop rose and left the room. For nine sleepless nights he tried to discover a way out ... degenerate days, indeed, when morality, etiquette, even the Church, could be openly defied!

He found none. The only thing that he found was a flaw in the ceremony that he had himself conducted. He had to break it to Srdič that he and Natya had never been properly married at all.

At which the good banker heaved a sigh of relief: for now he was free of the whole affair—unless the pig-headed old Perunič should take it into his head to shoot him for living with his daughter when they were not properly married!

On the whole, it seemed best to avoid all complications by returning at once to Zagreb.

And so the last obstacle was down, and the romantic story of Natya and Mitar, which already had begun to circulate through the marketplaces in the mouth of ballad-singers and story-tellers, ended at the altar, to which Natya was led for the second time in a month. Compared with it, the stories of Paris and Helen or of Hero and Leander paled: it was told and sung with such a wealth of detail, such fervour, such gallantry, such romance, such bravery, such exaltation of the divine spirit of love, as never were heard in any story before: in short, it was told exactly as Natya herself believed it all to have happened: and as I should have believed it to have happened, if the story had been told me by Natya herself or even by some outsider—by anyone except Mitar Lochinvárovič himself, in the little Trieste wine-shop, when he was too drunk to remember to be discreet.

But the tragic ending? The shattering of all poor little Natya's dreams and illusions? The perpetual exasperation of Mitar, forced to pretend love in the glare of publicity to a woman for whom he did not care two pins? The horror of an innocent girl, when she discovered what manner of man he was?

I have said that the ways of love are inscrutable: that no man can prophesy them. Mitar, whose heart had remained hard when he had every reason to love Natya, was no sooner married to her, no sooner had every reason to hate and loathe her, then he saw her (as he put it) with clear eyes for the first time—in other words, fell as madly in love with her as she had with him. I cannot explain it, I can only state it. They had three children, to whom Mitar proved a devoted father: when he was forced for financial reasons to leave home, he carried the photograph taken of her on that memorable occasion in Zdenka's studio everywhere he went: and all the time he and I were together, he never failed to write to her at least once a day—this, after they had been married for over five years.

It only shows how important it is, once one has set one's hand to the plough, never to look back on any excuse whatever.

Ireland

THE WILD GOOSE[1]

George Moore

HE REMEMBERED a green undulating country out of which the trees seemed to emerge like vapours, and a line of pearl-coloured mountains showing above the horizon on fine days. And this was all. But this slight colour memory had followed him through all his wanderings. His parents had emigrated to Manchester when he was nine, and when he was sixteen he felt that he must escape from Manchester, form the overwhelming dreariness of the brick chimneys and their smoke cloud. He had joined a travelling circus on its way to the Continent and he crossed with it from New Haven to Dieppe in charge of the lions. The circus crossed in a great storm; Ned was not able to get about, the tossing of the vessel closed the ventilating slides, and when they arrived at Dieppe the finest lion was dead.

"Well, there are other things to do in life besides feeding lions," he said, and taking up his fiddle he became interested in it. He played it all the way across the Atlantic, and every one said there was no reason why he should not play in the opera house. But an interview with the music conductor dispelled illusions. Ned learnt from him that improvisations were not admissible in an opera house; and when the conductor told him what would be required of him he began to lose interest in his musical career. As he stood jingling his pence on the steps of the Opera House a man went by who had crossed with Ned, and the two getting into conversation, Ned was asked if he could draw a map according to scale. It would profit him nothing to say no; he remembered he had drawn maps in the school in Manchester. A bargain was struck! he was to get ten pounds for his map! He ordered a table; he pinned out the paper, and the map was finished in a fortnight. It was of a mining district, and having nothing to do when it was finished he thought he would like to see the mine; the owners encouraged him to go there, and he did some mining in the morning —in the evenings he played his fiddle. Eventually he became a journalist.

He wandered and wrote, and wandered again, until one day, finding

---

[1] From *The Untilled Field*. Reprinted by permission of the author, Messrs William Heinemann, Ltd., London, and Messrs Brentano's, New York.

himself in New York, he signed an agreement and edited a newspaper. But he soon wearied of expressing the same opinions, and as the newspaper could not change its opinions Ned volunteered to go to Cuba and write about the insurgents. And he wrote articles that inflamed the Americans against the Spaniards, and went over to the American lines to fight when the Americans declared war against Spain, and fought so well that he might have become a general if the war had lasted. But it was over, and, overpowered by an extraordinary dislike to New York, he felt he must travel. He wanted to see Europe again, and remembering the green plain of Meath, he said—"I'll go to Ireland."

His father and mother were dead, and without a thought of his relations, he read the legends of Meath on his way out; he often sat considering his adventures: the circus, the mining camp, his sympathy with the Cubans in their revolt against Spain, convinced him of his Gaelic inheritance and that something might be done with Ireland. England's power was great, but Spain's power had been great too, and when Spain thought herself most powerful the worm had begun. Everything has its day, and as England decayed, Ireland would revive. A good time might be on its way to Ireland; if so he would like to be there or thereabouts; for he always liked to be in the van of a good time.

He went straight to Tara, his mind bending rather to pagan than to Christian Ireland. Traces of Cormac's banqueting hall were pointed out to him, and he imagined what this great hall, built entirely of wood and hung about with skins, must have been. He was shown the Rath of Kings and the Rath of Grania. Her name brought to his mind her flight with Diarmuid and how when they had had to cross a stream and her legs were wetted, she had said to Diarmuid, who would not break his oath to Finn, "Diarmuid, you are a great warrior, but this water is braver than you!" "Perhaps this very stream!" he said, looking toward a stream that flowed from the well of Neamhtach or Pearly. But he was told it was this stream that had turned the first water mill in Ireland, and that Cormac had put up the mill to save a beautiful bondmaid from toiling at the quern.

The morning was spent in seeking the old sites, and in the afternoon he went to the inn and found a good number of villagers in the tap room. He learned from them that there were cromlechs and Druid altars within walking distance of Tara, and decided on a walking tour. He wandered through the beautiful country, interested in Ireland's slattern life, touched by the kindness and simplicity of the people. "Poor people," he thought, "how touching it is to find them learning their own language," and he began to think out a series of articles about Ireland.

"They talk of Cuchulain," he said, "but they prefer an Archbishop, and at every turn in their lives they are paying the priest. The title of my book shall be *A Western Thibet*, an excellent title for my book!" and leaning on a gate, and looking across a hay field he saw the ends of chapters.

Now that he had a book to write, his return to America was postponed; a postponement was to Ned an indefinite period, and he was glad he was not returning to America till the Spring, for he had found pleasant rooms in a farm house. He would make them his head-quarters; for it was only by living in a farmhouse he could learn the life of the people and its real mind. And he would have written his book just as he had planned it if he had not met Ellen Cronin.

She was the only daughter of a rich farmer in the neighbourhood. He had heard so much about her learning and her pretty face that he was disposed to dispute her good looks; but in spite of his landlady's praise he had liked her pretty oval face. "Her face is pretty when you look at it," he said to his landlady. But this admission did not satisfy her. "Well, enthusiasm is pleasant," he thought, and he listened to her rambling talk.

"She used to like to come to tea here, and after her tea she and my son James, who was the same age, used to make paper boats under the alder trees."

And the picture of making boats under alder trees pleased Ned's fancy, and he encouraged the landlady to tell him more about her. She told him that Ellen had not taken to study till she was twelve, and that it was the priest who had set her reading books and had taught her Latin.

Ned lay back in his chair smiling, listening to the landlady telling him about Ellen. She had chosen her own school. She had inquired into the matter, and had taken her father into her confidence one day by telling him of the advantages of this school. But this part of the story did not please Ned, and he said he did not like her a bit better for having chosen her own school. Nor did he like her better because her mistress had written to her father to say she had learned all that she could learn in Ireland. He liked her for her love of Ireland and her opposition to her father's ideas. Old Cronin thought Ireland a miserable country and England the finest in the world, whereas Ellen thought only of Irish things, and she had preferred the Dublin University to Oxford or Cambridge. He was told that her university career had been no less brilliant than her school career, and he raised his eyebrows when the landlady said that Miss Ellen used to have her professors staying at Mount Laurel, and that they used to talk Latin in the garden.

But she was long ago done with the professors, and Ned asked the landlady to tell him what change had come over the mind of this somewhat pedantic young woman. And he was told that Ellen had abandoned her studies and professors for politics and politicians, and that these were a great trial to her father, into whose house no Nationalist member of Parliament had ever put his foot before. "Now the very men that Mr Cronin used to speak of as men who were throwing stones at the police three years ago are dining with him to-day," and worse than her political opinions, according to Mr Cronin, was her resolution to speak the language of her own country. "When he had heard her talking it to a boy she had up from the contry to teach her, Mr Cronin stuck both his hands into his stubbly hair and rushed out of the house like a wild man."

It was pleasant to listen to the landlady's babble about the Cronins, for he was going to spend the evening with them; he had been introduced to her father, a tall, thin, taciturn man, who had somewhat gruffly, but not unkindly, asked him to come to spend the evening with them, saying that some friends were coming in, and there would be some music.

Ned's life had been lived in newspaper offices, in theatres, circuses, and camps. He knew very little of society—nothing at all of European society—and was curious to see what an Irish country house was like. The Cronins lived in a dim, red brick, eigthteenth-century house. It stood in the middle of a large park, and the park was surrounded by old grey walls and Ned liked to lean on these walls, for in places they had crumbled, and admire the bracken in the hollows and the wind-blown hawthorn trees growing on the other side of the long winding drive. He had long wished to walk in the park and now he was there. The hawthorns were in bloom and the cuckoo was calling. They sky was dark over head, but there was light above the trees, and long herds of cattle wandered and life seemed to Ned extraordinarily lovely and desirable at that moment. "I wonder what she is like, living in this beautiful place, walking among these mysterious hollows and these abundant hawthorn groves?"

The young lady had been pointed out to him as she went by, and he was impatient to be introduced to Ellen, but she was talking to some friends near the window, and she did not see him. He liked her white dress, there were pearls round her neck, and her red hair was pinned up with a tortoiseshell comb. She and her friends were looking over a photograph album, and Ned was left with Mr Cronin to talk to him as best he could; for it was difficult to talk to this hard, grizzled man, knowing nothing about the war in Cuba nor evincing any interest in America. When Ned asked him about Ireland he answered in short sentences, which brought the conversation to abrupt closes. America and Ireland having failed to draw him out, Ned began to talk of his landlady. But it was not until he related the conversation he had had with her that evening about Miss Cronin that the old farmer began to talk a little. Ned could see he was proud of his daughter; he regretted that she had not gone to Oxford, and said she would have carried all before her if she had gone there. Ned could see that what his landlady had told him was true—that old Cronin thought very little of Ireland. He hoped to get three minutes' conversation, at least, out of Girton, but the old farmer seemed to have said everything he had to say on the subject. The conversation failed again, and Ned was forced to speak to him of the interest that Miss Cronin took in the Irish language and her desire to speak it. At the mention of the Irish language, the old man grew gruffer, and remembering that the landlady had said that Miss Cronin was very religious, Ned spoke of the priests—there were two in the room—and he asked Mr Cronin which of them had encouraged Miss Cronin to learn Irish. He had never heard the language spoken, and would like to hear it.

"I believe, Mr Cronin, it was Father Egan who taught your daughter Latin?"

"It was so, " said Mr Cronin; "but he might have left the Irish alone, and politics, too. We keep them as fat as little bonhams, and they ought to be satisfied with that."

Ned did not know what were little bonhams, and pretended a great interest when he was told that bonham was the Irish for sucking pig, and glancing at the priests he noticed they were fat indeed, and he said, "There is nothing like faith for fattening. It it better than any oil cake."

Mr Cronin gave a grunt and Ned thought he was going to laugh at this sally, but he suddenly moved away and Ned wondered what had happened. It was Ellen who had cossed the room to speak to her father, and Ned could see that she had heard his remark, and he could see that the remark had angered her, that she thought it in bad taste. He prepared quickly a winning speech which would turn the edge of her indignation but before he had time to speak the expression of her face changed and a look of pleasure passed into it; he could see that the girl liked him, and he hastened to tell her that his landlady had told him about the paper boats and the alder trees. And Ellen began to speak about the landlady, saying she was a very good kind woman, and she wanted to know if Ned were comfortable at the farm house. But she seemed to have some difficulty in speaking, and then, as if moved by some outside influence, they walked across the room towards the window and sat under the shadow of the red damask curtains. A gentle breeze was blowing and the curtains filled with it and sank back with a mysterious rustle. And beyond them the garden lay dark and huddled in the shadows of great trees. He heard her say she was sorry that James, the landlady's son, had gone to America, and then they spoke of the forty thousand that were leaving Ireland every year. It was Ned who continued the conversation, but he could see that what he said hardly entered her ear at all. Yet she heard his voice in her heart, and he, too, heard her voice in his heart, and several times she felt she could not go on talking, and once she nearly lost consciousness and must have swayed a little, for he put out his hand to save her.

They went into the garden and walked in the dusk. He told her about the war in Cuba and about the impulse which had brought him back to Ireland, and his tale seemed to her the most momentous thing she had ever heard. She listened to his first impressions about Tara, and every moment it seemed to her that she was about to hear a great secret, a secret that had been troubling her a long while; every moment she expected to hear him speak it, and she almost cried when her father came to ask Ned if he would play for them.

Ellen was not a musician, and another woman would have to accompany him. How tall and thin he was and what manly hands! She could hardly look at his hands without shuddering, so beautiful were they when they played the violin; and that night music said something more to her than it had ever said before. She heard again the sounds of birds and insects, and she saw again the gloom of the trees, and she felt again and more intensely the overpowering ecstasy, and she yielded herself utterly and without knowing why. When he finished playing he came to her and sat by her, and everything she said fell from her lips involuntarily. She seemed to have lost herself utterly, she seemed to have become fluid, she yielded herself like a fluid; it was like dying: for she seemed to pass out of herself to become absorbed in the night. How the time passed she knew not, and when her guests came to bid her good-bye she hardly saw them, and listened to their leave-taking with a little odd smile on her lips, and when every one was gone she bade her father good-night absent-mindedly, fearing, however, that he would speak to her about Ned. But he only said good-night, and she went up the wide staircase conscious that the summer night was within the house and without it; that it lay upon the world, a burden sweet and still, like happiness upon the heart.

She opened her window, and sat there hoping that something would come out of the night and whisper in her ear the secret that tormented her. The stars knew! If she could only read them! She felt she was feeling a little more than she was capable of understanding. The ecstasy grew deeper, and she waited for the revelation. But none came and feeling a little ashamed she got up to close the window, and it was then that the revelation broke upon her. She had met the man who was to lead the Irish people! They wanted a new leader, a leader with a new idea; the new leader must come from the outside, and he had come to them from America, and her emotion was so great that she would have liked to have awakened her father. She would have liked to have gone into the country waking the people up in the cottages, telling them that the leader had come. She stood entranced, remembering all he had said to her. He had told her he had been moved to return to Ireland after the war in Cuba, and she had not understood. The word married passed through her mind before she could stay it. But she was necessary to this man, of this she was sure; the Voice had told her. She was feeling more than she could understand, and she lay down in her bed certain that she had accomplished the first stage of her journey.

Just then Ned was leaning on the garden gate. The summer night was sweet and still, and he wanted to think of this girl who had come so suddenly into his life. The idea of marriage flitted across his mind as it had flitted across hers, and he tried to remember the exact moment in Cuba when the wish to see Ireland had come into his mind. To believe in fate and predestination is an easy way out of life's labyrinth, and if one does not believe in something of the kind the figures will not come right. How did he know that he had not met this girl for some unknown purpose. He could see a great white star through a vista in the trees, and he said: "I believe that that star knows. Why will it not tell me?"

And then he walked into the woods, and out under the moon, between the little grey fields. Some sheep had come out on the road and were lying upon it. "I suppose it's all very natural," he said, "the circus aspiring to the academy and the academy spying the circus. Now, what am I going to do to-morrow? I suppose I must go to see her."

He had visited all the ruins and pondered by all the cromlechs and was a little weary of historic remains; the girl was too much in his mind to permit of his doing much writing. He might go to Dublin, where he had business, and in the morning he looked out the trains, but none seemed to suit his convenience, and at 5 o'clock he was at Laurel Hill listening to Ellen. She was anxious to talk to him about the political opportunity he could seize if he were so minded.

"Men have always believed in fate," Ned said, and, interrupting him suddenly, she asked him if he would come to see a pretty house in the neighbourhood—a house that would suit him perfectly, for he must have a house if he intended to go in for politics.

They came back in the dusk, talking of painting and papering and the laying out of the garden. Ellen was anxious that the garden should be nice, and he had been much interested in the old family furniture at Laurel Hill, not in the spindle-legged Sheraton sideboard, but in the big Victorian furniture which the Cronins thought ugly. He liked especially the black mahogany sideboards in the dining-room, and he was enthusiastic about the four-post bed that Mr Cronin had slept in for thirty years without ever thinking it was a beautiful thing. This massive furniture represented a life that Ned perceived for the first time, a sedate monotonous life; and he could see these people accomplishing the same tasks from daylight to dark; he admired the well-defined circle of their interests and the calm security with which they spoke of the same things every evening, deepening the tradition of their country and their own characters; and he conceived a sudden passion for tradition, and felt he would like to settle down in these grass lands in an eighteenth-century house, living always amid heavy mahogany furniture, sleeping every night in a mahogany four-post bed: and he could not help thinking that if he did not get the mahogany four-post bed with the carved top perhaps he would not care to marry Ellen at all.

The next time he saw her their talk turned upon the house she had found for him, and she said if he did not take it he would certainly go back to America in the spring. She forgot herself a little; her father had to check her, and Ned returned home sure in his mind that she would marry him—if he asked her. And the next day he chose a pair of trousers that he thought becoming—they were cut wide in the leg and narrow over the instep. He looked out for a cravat that she had not seen him wear, and he chose the largest, and he put on his braided coat. He could see that his moustache was not in keeping with his clothes: he had often intended to shave it, but to-day was not the day for shaving. She had liked his moustache and he thought it would be a pity she should not enjoy it, how ever reprehensible her taste for it might be. And he pondered his side whiskers, remembering they were in keeping with his costume (larger whiskers would be still more in keeping), and amused by his own fantastic notions, he thought he was beginning to look like the gentleman of seventy or eighty years ago that he had seen in varnished maplewood frames in the drawing-room at the Cronins'. His trousers were of a later period, but they were, nevertheless, contemporaneous with the period of mahogany sideboard, and that was what he liked best.

Suddenly he stopped, remembering that he had never wished to be married, because he never thought that he could love the same woman always, and now he asked himself if Ellen were an exception, and if he had been led back to Ireland to marry her. He had grown tired of women before, but it seemed to him that he never could grow tired of her. That remained to be seen, the one certain thing was that he was going to propose to her.

He was told she was in the garden, and he was glad to dispense with the servant's assistance: he would find his way there himself, and, after some searching, he found the wicket. The thing itself and its name pleased him. When he had a garden he would have a wicket. He had already begun to associate Ellen with her garden. She was never so much herself as when attending her flowers, and to please her he had affected an interest in them, but when he had said that the flowers were beautiful his eyes went to the garden walls and Ellen had seen that they interested him more than the flowers. He had said that the buttresses were of no use; they had been built because in those days people took a pleasure in making life seem permanent. The buttresses had enabled him to admire the roses planted between them, and he had grown enthusiastic; but she had laughed at his enthusiasm, seeing quite clearly that he admired the flowers because they enhanced the beauty of the walls.

At the end of the garden there was a view of the Dublin mountains, and the long walk that divided the garden had been designed in order to draw attention to them. The contrast between the wild mountain and the homely primness of the garden appealed to his sense of the picturesque; and even now though the fate of his life was to be decided in a few minutes he could not but stay to admire the mysterious crests and hollows. In this faint day the mountains seemed more like living things, more mysterious and moving, than he had ever seen them before, and he would have stood looking at them for a long while if he had not had to find Ellen. She was at the furthest end of the garden, where he had never been, beyond the rosery, beyond the grass plot, and she was walking up and down. She seemed to have a fishing net in her hand. But how could she be fishing in her garden? Ned did not know that there was a stream at the end of it; for the place had once belonged to monks, and they knew how to look after their bodily welfare and had turned the place into a trout preserve. But when Mr Cronin had bought the property the garden was waste and the stream overgrown with willow weed and meadow-sweet and every kind of brier. And it was Ellen who had discovered that the bottom ot the stream was flagged and she had five feet of mud taken out of it, and now the stream was as bright and clear as in the time of the monks, and as full

257

of trout. She had just caught two which lay on the grass panting, their speckled bellies heaving painfully.

"There is a great big trout here," Ellen said, "he must be a pound weight, and we tried to catch him all last season but he is very cunning, he dives and gets under the net."

"I think we shall be able to catch him," said Ned, "if he is in the stream and if I could get another net."

"The gardener will give you one."

And presently Ned came back with a net, and they beat up the stream from different ends, Ellen taking the side next the wall. There was a path nearly free from briers, and she held her light summer dress round her tightly. Ned thought he had never seen anyone so prettily dressed. She wore a striped muslin variegated with pink flowers; there were black bows in her hat and black ribbon was round the bottom of her dress; she looked very pretty against the old wall touched here and there with ivy. And the grace of her movement enchanted Ned when she leaned forward and prevented the trout from escaping up the stream. But Ned's side of the stream was overgrown with briers and he could not make his way through them. Once he very nearly slipped into the strem, and only saved himself by catching some prickly briers and Ellen had to come over to take the thorns out of his hand. Then they resumed their fishing, hunting the trout up and down the stream. But the trout had been hunted so often that he knew how to escape the nets, and dived at the right moment. At last wearied out he let Ned drive him against the bank. Ellen feared he would jump out of the net at the last moment, but he was tired and they landed him safely.

And proud of having caught him they sat down beside him on the grass and Ellen said that the gardener and the gardener's boy had tried to catch him many times; that whenever they had company to dinner her father said it was a pity they had not the big trout on the table.

The fishing had been great fun, principally on account of Ellen's figure which Ned admired greatly, and now he admired her profile—its gravity appealed to him—and her attitude full of meditation. He watched her touching the gasping trout with the point of her parasol. She had drawn one leg under her. Her eyes were small and grey and gem-like, and there was a sweet look of interrogation in them now and then.

"I like it, this lustreless day," said Ned, "and those swallows pursuing their food up and down the boding sky. It all seems like a fairy tale, this catching of the fish, you and I. The day so dim," he said, "so quiet and low, and the garden hushed. These things would be nothing to me were it not for you," and he put his hand upon her knee.

She withdrew her knee quickly and a moment after got up, and Ned got up and followed her across the grass plot and through the rosery; not a word was said, and she began to wonder he did not plead to be forgiven. She felt she should send him away, but she could not find words to tell him to go. His conduct was so unprecedented; no one had ever taken such a liberty before. It was shameful that she was not more angry, for she knew she was only trying to feel angry.

"But," he said, suddenly, as if he divined her throghts, "we've forgotten the fish; won't you come back and help me to carry them. I cannot carry three trout by myself."

She was about to answer severely but as she stood looking at him her thoughts yielded before an extraordinary feeling of delight; she tried in vain to collect her scattered mind—she wished to reproach him.

"Are you going to answer me, Ellen," and he took her hand.

"Ned, are you a Catholic?" she said, turning suddenly.

"I was born one, but I have thought little about religion. I have had other things to think about. What does it matter? Religion doesn't help us to love one another."

"I should like you better if you were a good Catholic."

"I wonder how that is?" he said, and he admired the round hand and its pretty articulations, and she closed her hand on his with a delicious movement.

"I could like you better, Ned, if you were a Catholic.... I think I could."

"What has my being a good Catholic got to do with your love of me?"

And he watched the small and somewhat severe profile looking across the old grey wall into the flat grey sky.

"I did not say I loved you," she said, almost angrily; "but if I did love you," she said, looking at him tenderly, "and you were religious, I should be loving something eternal. You don't understand what I mean? What I am saying to you must seem like nonsense."

"No, it doesn't, Ellen, only I am content with the reality. I can love you without wings."

He watched for the look of annoyance in her face that he knew his words would provoke, but her face was turned away.

"I like you, but I am afraid of you. It is a very strange feeling. You ran away with a circus and you let the lion die and you went to fight in Cuba. You have loved other women, and I have never loved anyone. I never cared for a man until I saw you, until I looked up from the album."

"I understand very well, Ellen; I knew something was going to happen to me in Ireland."

She turned; he was glad to see her full face again. Her eyes were fixed upon him, but she saw through him, and jealous of her thought he drew her towards him.

"Let us go into the arbour," he said. "I have never been into the arbour of clipped limes with you."

"Why do you want to go into the arbour?"

"I want to kiss you.... The gardener can see us now; a moment ago he was behind the Jerusalem artichokes."

"I hadn't noticed the gardener; I hadn't thought about him."

She had persuaded herself before she went into the arbour, and coming out of the arbour she said:

"I don't think father will raise any objection."

"But you will speak to him. Hello! we're forgetting the fish, and it was the fish that brought all this about. Was it to bring this about that they lived or to be eaten to-night at dinner?"

"Ned, you take a strange pleasure in making life seem wicked."

"I'm sorry I've been so unsuccessful, but will you ask your father to invite me, Ellen? and I'll try and make life seem nice—and the trout will try, too."

Ellen did not know whether she liked or disliked Ned's levity, but when she looked at him an overpowering emotion clouded her comprehension and she walked in silence, thinking of when he would kiss her again. At the end of the walk she stopped to bind up a carnation that had fallen from its stake.

"Father will be wondering what has become of us."

"I think," said Ned, and his own cowardice amused him, "I think you had better tell your father yourself. You will tell him much better than I."

"And what will you do?" she said, turning suddenly and looking at him with fervid eyes. "Will you wait here for me?"

"No, I will go home and do you come and fetch me—and don't forget to tell him I caught the trout and have earned an invitation to dinner."

His irresponsibility enchanted her in spite of herself—Ned had judged the situation rightly when he said: "It is the circus aspiring to the academy and the academy spying the circus." His epigram occurred to him as he walked home and it amused him, and he thought of how unexpected their lives would be, and he hummed beautiful music as he went along the roads, Schumann's *Lotus Flower* and *The Moonlight.* Then he recalled the beautiful duet, Siegmund's and Sieglinde's *May Time,* and turning from sublimity suddenly into triviality he chanted the somewhat common but expressive duet in *Mireille,* and the superficiality of its emotion pleased him at the moment and he hummed it until he arrived at the farm house.

Mrs Grattan could tell his coming from afar, for no one in the country whistled so beautifully as Mr Carmady, she said, "every note is clear and distinct; and it does not matter how many there are in the tune he will not let one escape him and there is always a pleasant look in his face when you open the door to him"; and she ran to the door.

"Mrs Grattan, won't you get me a cup of tea?" And then he felt he must talk to some one. "You needn't bring it upstairs, I will take it in the kitchen if you'll let me."

Mrs Grattan had a beautiful kitchen. It had an old dresser with a carved top and a grandfather's clock, and Ned liked to sit on the table and watch the stove. She poured him out a cup of tea and he drank it, swinging his legs all the time.

"Well, Mrs Grattan, I'll tell you some news—I think I am going to marry Miss Cronin."

"Well," said she, "it doesn't astonish me," but she nearly let the teapot drop. "From the first day you came here I always thought something was going to happen to you."

He had no sooner told her the news than he began to regret he had told her, and he said that Miss Cronin had gone to her father to ask his consent. Of course, if he did not give it, there would be no marriage.

"But he will give it. Miss Ellen does exactly as she likes with him, and it's a fine fortune you will be having with her."

"It isn't of that I am thinking," said Ned, "but of her red hair."

"And you wouldn't believe me when I said she was the prettiest girl in the country. Now you will see for yourself."

Ned hadn't finished his tea when there was a knock at the door.

"And how do you do, Miss Ellen?" said Mrs Grattan, and Ellen guessed from her manner that Ned had told her.

"Well, Mrs Grattan. I am glad that you are the first person to bear the news to. I have just asked my father's consent and he has given it. I am going to marry Mr Carmady."

Mrs Grattan was sorry there was no cake on the table, but there was some buttered toast in the oven; and Ellen reminded her of the paper boats and the alder trees, and they spoke for a long time about her son James and about people that Ned knew nothing of, until Ned began to feel bored and went to the window. Every now and again he heard a word referring to their marriage, and when the women had done their talk, Ellen said:

"Father says you are to come back to dinner."

"Mrs Grattan," said Ned, "we caught three trout this afternoon," and Ellen wondered why Ned should linger to explain how they had caught the big trout.

As they walked down the road Ellen said: "As our love began in a love of Ireland, we might go for a tour round Ireland and see the places that Ireland loves best."

She was eager for a change of scene, and as soon as the wedding was over they began their wanderings. The first place they visited was Tara, and, standing on the Mound of the Hostages, Ellen pointed out the Rath of Grania. All over Ireland there are Cromlechs, and the people point to those as the places where the lovers had rested in their flight. Grania became one of Ned's heroines, and he spoke so much of her that Ellen grew a little jealous. They talked of her under the ruins of Dun Angus and under the arches of Cormac's Chapel, the last and most beautiful piece of Irish architecture.

"We were getting on very well," Ned said, "until the English came. This was the last thing we did and after this no more."

On another occasion he ascribed the failure of the Irish in art and literature to the fact that they had always loved the next world, and that the beautiful world under their feet had been neglected or given over to priests. "I hope, Ned," said she, "that you will soon be at the head of affairs."

He took her hand and they wandered on amid the ruins, saying that as soon as their honeymoon was over they would be furnishing a pretty house as the foot of the Dublin mountains.

Her father had offered to make her an allowance, but she preferred a lump sum, and this lump sum of many thousands had been invested in foreign securities, for Ellen wished that Ned should be free to advocate whatever policy he judged best for Ireland.

"My dear, shall we buy this table?"

And while the price and the marquetry were discussed she remembered suddenly that a most experienced electioneering agent was coming to dinner.

"I wished you hadn't asked him" said Ned; "I looked forward to spending the evening with you," and he watched happiness flash into her eyes.

"There are plenty of evenings before us, and I hope you won't be tired of spending them with me."

He said he never wished for better company, and they strolled on through the show rooms.

Turning from some tapestried curtains, he told her he was weary of the life of the camp. One night in Cuba they had crossed a mountain by a bridle path. At the top of the mountain they had come to a ledge of rock three feet high and had to leap their horses one by one up this ledge, and the enemy might have attacked them at any moment. And this incident was typical of what his life had been for the last few years. It had been a skein of adventure, and now his wife was his adventure. Flowers stood in pretty vases on his table in the summer time and around the room were his books, and on the table his pens and paper. The dining-room was always a little surprise, so profusely was the table covered with silver. There were beautiful dinner and dessert services to look at; the servants were well trained, they moved about the table quickly—in a word his home was full of grace and beauty. Lately he had been a great deal from home and had come to look on Ellen as a delicious recompense for the fatigue of a week's electioneering in the West. The little train journey from Dublin was an extraordinary excitement, the passing of the stations one by one, the discovery of his wife on the platform, and walking home through the bright evening, telling how his speech had been received.

Ellen always took Ned round the garden before they went into dinner, and after dinner he went to the piano; he loved his music as she loved her garden. She would listen to him for a while, pleased to find that she liked music. But she would steal away to her garden in a little while and he would go on playing for a long while before he would notice her absence; then he would follow her.

"There were no late frosts this year and I have never seen so many caterpillars!" she said one evening when he joined her; "See they have eaten this flower nearly all away."

"How bright the moon is, we can find them by the light of the moon."

Ellen passed behind the hollyhocks and threw the snails to Ned, not liking to tread upon them herself; she was intent on freeing her flowers from gnawing insects and Ned tried to feel interested, but he liked the moonlight on the hills far better than the flowers. He could not remember which was Honesty and which was Rocket, thought the difference had been pointed out to him many times. He liked Larkspur and Canterbury bells, maybe it was their names that he liked, for he sometimes mistook one for the other just as Ellen mistook one sonata for another, yet she always liked the same sonatas.

"In another month the poppies will be over everything," she said, "and my pansies are beautiful—see these beautiful yellow pansies! But you're not looking at my garden."

They went towards their apple tree, and Ellen said it was the largest she had ever seen; its boughs were thickest over the seat, and shot straight out, making as it were a little roof. The moon was brilliant among the boughs that night, and they left their seat and passed out of the garden by the wicket, moved by a desire to see the long fields with the woods sloping down to the shore.

And they stood on the hillside, thinking that they had never seen the sea so beautiful before. On the other side was the dim hill, and the moon led them up the hillside, up the little path by a ruined church and over a stream that was difficult to cross, for the stepping-stones were placed crookedly. Ellen took Ned's hand and a little further on there were ash trees and not a wind in the boughs.

"How grey the moonlight is on the mountain," Ned said. They went through the furze where the cattle were lying, and the breath of the cattle was odorous in the night like the breath of the earth itself, and Ned said that the cattle were part of the earth. They sat on a druid stone and wondered how they could have lived if chance had not brought them together.

Now, the stone they were sitting upon was a druid stone, and it was from Ellen's lips that Ned heard how Brian had conquered the Danes, and how a century later a traitor had brought the English over; and she told the story of Ireland's betrayal with such fervour that Ned felt she was the support he had been looking for all his life; her self-restraint and her gravity were the supports his character required, and these being thrown into the scale life stood at equipoise. The women who had preceded Ellen were strange, fantastic women, counterparts of himself, but he had always aspired to a grave and well-mannered woman who was never ridiculous.

She protested, saying that she wished Ned to express his own ideas. He pleaded that he was learning Ireland from her lips and that his own ideas about Ireland were superficial and false. Every day he was catching up new ideas and every day he was shedding them. He must wait until he had re-knit himself firmly to the tradition, and in talking to her he felt that she was the tradition and was sure that he could do no better than accept her promptings, at least for the present.

"We shall always think the same. Do you not feel that?" and when they returned to the house he fetched a piece of paper and pencil and begged of her to dictate, and then begged of her to write what she would like him to say. He said that the sight of her handwriting helped him, and he thought his life would crumble to pieces if she were taken from him.

He told her that she had said he would be a success. He was a success! Success had begun to revolve about him, and he had begun to feel that he was the centre of things: Every one listened when he spoke; his opinion was sought out, and he could see the people looking towards him for guidance. It pleased Ellen that he should confide in her and his confidence seemed complete. We do not tell all because we do not know all and Ned was only half aware of the little dissatisfaction dormant in his heart. He knew that he had given himself as hostage—half of himself was in his wife's keeping—and he sometimes wondered if he would break out of her custody in spite of his vows.

He had told her that though he was no friend of the church, he was not its active enemy, and he believed he was speaking the truth. The fight for free will would have to be fought in Ireland some day, and this fight was the most vital; but he agreed with her that other fights would have to be fought and won before the great fight could be arranged for. The order of the present day was for lesser battles, and he promised again and again he would not raise the religious question, and every time he promised his wife his life seemed to vanish. The lesser battles were necessary, but it was the fight for free will that interested him. A politician is the man who does the day's work; he must not forget that; and he was a politician. So he agreed to go to America to speechify and to get money for the lesser battles. He was the man who could get the money—what better man could they send than an Irish-American? An American soldier and a journalist! These were the words that were on every one's lips, but after speaking them every one paused, for, nothwithstanding Ellen's care, Ned was suspected; the priests had begun to suspect him, but there were no grounds for opposing him.

He was despondent, but Ellen was enthusiastic. Her knowledge of Irish politics enabled her to see that his chance had come.

"If you succeed in America, you'll come back the first man in Ireland."

"Even so," said Ned, "it would be more natural for you to be sorry that I am going."

"I cannot be sorry and glad at the same time."

"You will be lonely."

"Very likely; but, Ned, I shall not be looking very well for the next two months."

"You mean on account of the baby. The next few months will be a trying time for you and I should be with you."

They continued to walk round and round their apple tree and Ellen did not answer for a long while.

"I want you to go to America, I don't care that you should see me losing my figure."

"We have spent many pleasant hours under this apple tree."

"Yes, it has been a dear tree," she said.

"And in about six years there will be one who will appreciate this tree as we have never appreciated it. I can see the little chap running after the apples."

"But, Ned, it may be a girl."

She said she would send a telegram and Ned shook the boughs, and their apple-gathering seemed portentous. The sound of apples falling in the dusk garden, and a new life coming into the world!

"Men have gathered apples and led their fruitful wives towards the house since the beginning of time." He said these words as he looked over the waste of water seeing Ireland melting away.

A new life was about to begin and he was glad of that. "For the next three months I shall be carried along on the tide of human affairs. In a week I shall be dining in a restaurant." He turned and entered into conversation with some people who interested him, and the day passed in conversation. "It is a curious change," he said, three weeks later, as he walked home from a restaurant; and he enjoyed the change so much that he wondered if his love for his wife would be the same when he returned. "Yes, that will be another change." He was carried like a piece of wreckage from hotel to hotel. "How different this life is from the life in Ireland," he said one night as he dressed to go to a meeting, and he began to wonder. And he had not been thinking five minutes when a knock came to the door, and he was handed a telegram containing two words: "A boy." He had always felt it was going to be a boy. "Though it does cost a shilling a word they might have let me know how she is," he thought. He lay back in his chair thinking of his wife — indulging in sensations of her beauty, seeing her gem-like eyes, her pretty oval face, and her red hair scattered about the pillow. At first he was not certain whether the baby was lying by the side of the mother, but now he saw it, and he thrilled with a sense of wonder. The commonest of all occurrences never ceases to be the most wonderful, and there lay his wife and child in the room he knew so well—the curtains with a fruit pattern upon them, the pale wall-paper with roses climbing up a trellis, and pretty blue ribbons intervening between each line of roses. The room was painted white, and he knew the odour of the room well, and the sensation of the carpet. He could see the twilight, and the bulky nurse passing to and fro; and his thoughts went back to his child, and he began to wonder if it were like him or like its mother. It was probably like both. His eyes went to the clock, and he thought of the meeting he was going to. The notes of his speech were upon the table, but he found great difficulty in rousing himself out of his chair; it was so pleasant to lie there, thinking of his wife, of his home, and of his child. But into this vague wandering sensation of happy and beautiful things there came a sudden vision and a thought. He saw his wife take the baby and put it to her breast and he could not bear to think that that beautiful breast, so dear to him, should suffer harm. He had often thought of Ellen as a beautiful marble—she was as full of exquisite lines as any marble—and only very rarely had he thought of her as a mother; the thought had never been entertained long, for it was never wholly sympathetic.

Now his thoughts quickened, and it seemed urgent that he must communicate at once with his wife. She must not suckle the baby! Only by telegram could he reach her soon enough, but it was not possible to telegraph such a thing. He must write, but the letter would take six days to reach her, and he stood thinking. The post was going out: if he wrote at once she would get this letter in a week. He was due at the meeting in about twenty minutes; the notes of his speech lay on the table, and he gathered them up and put them in his pocket, and drawing a sheet of paper towards him, he began a hurried letter. But as soon as he dipped his pen in the ink, he experienced great difficulty in expressing his feelings; they were intense enough, but they were vague, and he must find reasons. He must tell her that he loved her beauty, and that it must suffer no disfigurement from a baby's lips. No sooner did he put his feelings into words than they shocked him, and he knew how much more they would shock Ellen, and he wondered how he could think such things about his own child. The truth was, there was little time for thinking, and he had to tell Ellen what she must do. It so happened that he had heard only the other day that goat's milk was the exact equivalent to human, but it was often difficult to procure. "You will find no difficulty," he said, "at the foot of the Dublin mountains in procuring goat's milk." His thought rushed on, and he remembered the peasant women. One could easily be found who would put her baby on goat's milk and come and nurse his child for a few shillings—ten or fifteen shillings a week; Ellen's beauty was worth a great deal more. The hands of the clock went on, he had to close his letter and post it; and no sooner was it posted than he was beset by qualms of conscience. During the meeting he wondered what Ellen would think of his letter, and he feared it would shock her and trouble her; for, while considering the rights of the child, she would remember his admiration of her.

He passed the following days uneasily, and when the seventh day came he had no difficulty in imagining Ellen reading his letter, and the scene he imagined was very like what really happened. His letter troubled Ellen greatly. She had been thinking only of her baby, she had been suckling it for several days, and it had given her pleasure to suckle it. She had not thought of herself at all, and Ned's order that she should pass her child on to another, and consider her personal charm for him, troubled her even to tears; and when she told the nurse her husband's wishes the nurse was sorry that Mrs Carmady had been troubled, for she was still very weak. Now the child was crying; Ellen put it to her little cup-like breast, which was, nevertheless, full of milk, and it was for the nurse to tell her that a foster-mother could easily be found in the village, but this did not console her and she cried very bitterly. The doctor called. And did not think there was anything strange in Ned's letter. He approved of it! He said that Ellen was delicate and had nursed her baby long enough, and it appeared that he had been thinking of recommending a nurse to her, and he spoke of a peasant woman he had just seen. He spoke with so much assurance that Ellen was soothed, but he had not left her very long before she felt that medical opinion would not satisfy her, that she must have theological opinion as well, and she wrote a letter to Father Brennan asking him to come down to see her, mentioning that she had had a baby and could not go to see him. It would be a great relief to her to see him for a few minutes, and if he would come at once she would consider it a great favour. If it were possible for him to come down that very afternoon she would be deeply grateful. She wished to consult him, and on a matter on which she felt very deeply, and nothing, she said, but a priest's advice could allay her scruples.

The nurse gave her a sheet of paper and a pencil, and she scribbled a letter as best she could in her bed, and lay back fatigued. The nurse said she must not fret, that Father Brennan would be sure to come to her at once if he were at home, and Ellen knew that that was so; she felt that she was peevish, but she felt that Ned ought not to have written her that letter.

The hours that afternoon were very long and she restless and weary of them, and she asked the nurse many times to go to the window to see if Father Brennan were coming. At last he came, and she told him of the letter she had received, not wishing to show him the letter, for it was somewhat extravagant, and she did not like a priest to read Ned's praise of her body. She was anxious, however, to give him a true account of the letter, and would have talked a long while if the priest had not stopped her, saying the matter was one for the doctor to decide. The church had never expressed any views on the subject: whether a mother was justified in nursing her child or in passing it over to a foster-mother. It was entirely a question for the doctor, and if the doctor advised such a course she would be wrong not to follow it. Ellen felt that she had been misunderstood, and she tried to tell the priest that Ned's letter had been inspired by his admiration of her, and that this seemed to her selfish. She wondered how a father could consider a wife before the child, but when she said this she did not feel she was speaking quite sincerely, and this troubled her; she was on the verge of tears, and the nurse came in and said she had spoken enough that afternoon, and the priest bade her good-bye. The doctor came in soon after; there was some whispering, and Ellen knew that the woman he had brought with him was the foster-mother, and the baby was taken from her, and she saw it fix its gluttonous little lips on the foster-mother's breast.

Now that the priest had ordered her conscience, she got well rapidly, and it was a pleasure to her to prepare herself for her husband's admiration. The nurse thought he would perceive no difference in her, but when they put on her stays it was quite clear that she had grown stouter, and she cried out, "I'm quite a little mother!" But the nurse said her figure would come back all right. Ned's return had been delayed, and this she regarded as fortunate, for there was no doubt that in a month she would be able to meet him, slight and graceful as she had ever been.

As soon as she was able she went for long walks on the hills and every day she improved in health and in figure; and when she read Ned's letter saying he would be in Cork in a few days she felt certain he would see no change in her. She opened her dress and could discern no difference; perhaps a slight wave in the breast's line; she was not quite sure and she hoped Ned would not notice it. And she chose a white dress. Ned liked her in white, and she tied it with a blue sash; she put on a white hat trimmed with china roses, and the last look convinced her that she had never looked prettier.

"I never wore so becoming a hat," she said. She walked slowly so as not to be out of breath, and, swinging her white parasol over the tops of her tan boots, she stood at the end of the platform waiting for the train to come up.

"I had expected to see you pale," he said, "and perhaps a little stouter, but you are the same, the very same." And saying that he would be able to talk to her better if he were free from his bag, he gave it to a boy to carry. And they strolled down the warm dusty road.

They lived about a mile and a half from the station, and there were great trees and old crumbling walls, and, beyond the walls, water meadows, and it was pleasant to look over the walls and watch the cattle grazing peacefully. And to-day the fields were so pleasant that Ned and Ellen could hardly speak from the pleasure of looking at them.

"You've seen nothing more beautiful in America, have you, Ned?"

There was so much to say it was difficult to know where to begin, and it was delicious to be stopped by the scent of the honeysuckle. Ned gathered some blossoms to put into his wife's dress, but while admiring her dress and her hat and her pretty red hair he remembered the letter he had written to her in answer to her telegram.

"I've had many qualms about the letter I wrote you in answer to your telegram. After all a child's right upon the mother is the first right of all. I wrote the letter in a hurry, and hardly knew what I was saying."

"We got an excellent nurse, Ned, and the boy is doing very well."

"So you said in your letters. But after posting my letter I said to myself: if it causes me trouble, how much more will it cause her?"

"Your letter did trouble me, Ned. I was feeling very weak that morning and the baby was crying for me, for I had been nursing him for a week. I did not know what to do. I was torn both ways, so I sent up a note to Father Brennan asking him to come to see me, and he came down and told me that I was quite free to give my baby to a foster-mother."

"But what does Father Brennan know about it more than anyone of us?"

"The sanction of the Church, Ned——"

"The sanction of the Church! What childish nonsense is this?" he said. "The authority of a priest. So it was not for me, but because a priest——"

"But, Ned, there must be a code of morality, and these men devote their lives to thinking out one for us."

He could see that she was looking more charming than she had ever looked before, but her beauty could not crush the anger out of him; and she never seemed further from him, not even when the Atlantic divided them.

'Those men devote their lives to thinking out a code of morality for us! You submit your soul to their keeping. And what remains of you when you have given over your soul?"

"But, Ned, why this outbreak? You knew I was a Catholic when you married me."

"Yes,... of course, and I'm sorry, Ellen, for losing my temper. But it is only in Ireland that women submit themselves body and soul. It is extraordinary; it is beyond human reason."

They walked on in silence, and Ned tried to forget that his wife was a Catholic. Her religion did not prevent her from wearing a white dress and a hat with roses in it.

"Shall I go upstairs to see the baby, or will you bring him down?"

"I'll bring him down."

And it was a great lump of white flesh with blue eyes and a little red down on its head that she carried in her arms.

"And now, Ned, forget the priest and admire your boy."

"He seems a beautiful boy, so healthy and sleepy."

"I took him out of his bed but he never cries. Nurse said she never heard of a baby that did not cry. Do you know I'm sometimes tempted to pinch him to see if he can cry."

She sat absorbed looking at the baby; and she was so beautiful and so intensely real at that moment that Ned began to forget that she had given the child out to nurse because the priest had told her that she might do so without sin.

"I called him after you, Ned. It was Father Stafford who baptised him."

"So he has been baptised!"

"He was not three days old when he was baptised."

"Of course, he could not have gone to heaven if he had not been baptised."

"Ned, I don't think it kind of you to say these things to me. You never usedto say them."

"I am sorry, Ellen; I'll say no more, and I'm glad it wasF ather Stafford who baptised him. He is the most sensible priest we have. If all the clergy were like him I should find it easier to believe."

"But religion has nothing to do with the clergy. It is quite possible to think the clergy foolish and yet to believe that the religion is the true one."

"I like the clergy far better than their religion, and believe them to be worthy of a better one. I like Father Stafford, and you like having a priest to dinner. Let us ask him."

"I'm afraid, Ned, that Father Stafford is getting old. He rarely leaves the house now, and Father Maguire does all the work of the parish."

She liked clerical gossip, and she told him that the church was finished, and how Biddy heard the saints singing in the window made a fine tale.

"So now we have a local saint."

"Yes, and miracles!"

"But do you believe in miracles?"

"I don't know. I shouldn't like to say. One is not obliged to believe in them."

"I'm sure you would enjoy believing in Biddy."

"Oh, Ned, how aggressive you are, and the very day you come back."

But why hadn't she asked him about America and about his speeches?

271

He had looked forward to telling her about them. She seemed to care nothing about them; even when she spoke about them after dinner, he could see that she was not as much interested in politics as she used to be. However, she wore a white dress and black stockings; her red hair was charmingly pinned up with a tortoiseshell comb, and taking her upon his knee he thought it would be well to please himself with her as she was and forget what she was not.

Next morning when he picked up the newspaper and the daily instalment of a cardinal's tour through Ireland caught his eye, he remembered that Ellen had sent for a theologian.... His eyes went down the columns of the newspaper and he said, "All the old flummery. Ireland's fidelity to her religion, etc., her devotion to Rome, etc.,—to everything," he said, "except herself. Propagations of the faith, exhortations to do as our ancestors had done, to do everything except make life joyous and triumphant." Looking across the page his eye was caught by the headline, "Profession of Irish Nuns in France." Further on in large letters, "Killmessan Cathedral: Bazaar." And these items of news were followed by a letter from a Bishop. "What a lot of Bishops!" he said. He read of "worthy" parish priests, and a little further on of "brilliant" young clergymen, and at every meeting the chair was taken by the "worthy" or by the "good" parish priest.

"Well," he said, "if the newspaper reflects the mind of the people there is no hope."

And he heard daily of new churches and new convents and the acqustion of property by the clergy. He heard tales of esuriency and avarice, and the persecution of the dancing girl and the piper.

"The clergy," he said, "are swallowing up the country," and he looked for some means whereby he might save the Gael.

About this time an outcry was made against the ugliness of modern ecclesiastical architecture, and a number of enthusiasts were writing to the newspapers proposing a revival of Irish romanesque; they instanced Cormac's Chapel as the model that should be followed. Ned joined in the outcry that no more stained glass should be imported from Birmingham, and wrote to the newspapers many times that good sculpture and good painting and good glass were more likely to produce a religious fervour than bad. His purpose was to point a finger of scorn at the churches, and he hoped to plead a little later that there were too many churches, and that no more should be built until the population had begun to increase again. He looked forward to the time when he would be able to say right out that the Gael had spent enough of money on his soul, and should spend what remained to him on his body. He looked forward to the time when he should tell the Gael that his soul was his greatest expense, but the time was far off when he could speak plainly.

The clergy were prepared to admit that German glass was not necessary for their successful mediation, but they were stubborn when Ned asked them to agree that no more churches were neccessary. They were not moved by the argument that the population was declining and would not admit that there were too many churches or even that there were churches enough. The ecclesiastical mind is a subtle one and it knows that when men cease to build churches they cease to be religious. The instinct of the clergy was against Ned, but they had to make concessions, for the country was awakened to its danger, and Ned began to think that all its remaining energies were being concentrated in an effort of escape.

Long years ago in America he had watched a small snake trying to swallow a frog. The snake sucked down the frog, and the frog seemed to acquiesce until the half of his body was down the snake's gullet, and then the frog bestirred himself and succeeded in escaping. The snake rested awhile and the next day he renewed his attack. At last the day came when the weary frog delayed too long and Ned watched him disappear down the snake's gullet.

A good deal of Ireland was down the clerical throat and all would go down if Ireland did not bestir herself. Ireland was weakening daily and every part of her that disappeared made it more difficult for her to extricate herself. Ned remembered that life and death, sickness and health, success and failure are merely questions of balance. A nation is successful when its forces are at balance, and nations rise and fall because the centre of gravity shifts. A single Spaniard is as good as a single German, but the centre of gravity is in Spain no longer.

Ned did not look upon religion as an evil; he knew religion to be necessary; but it seemed to him that the balance had been tilted in Ireland.

He threw himself more and more into the education of the people, and politics became his chief interest. At last he had begun to live for his idea, and long absence from home and long drives on outside cars and evenings spent in inn parlours were accepted without murmuring; these discomforts were no longer perceived, whereas when he and Ellen used to sit over the fire composing speeches together, the thought of them filled him with despair. He used to complain that Ellen was always sending him away from home and to hard mutton chops and dirty bedrooms. He reminded her no more of these discomforts. He came back and spent a day or two with her, and went away again. She had begun no notice that he did not seem sorry to leave, but she did not reproach him, because he said he was

273

working for Ireland. He tried to think the explanation a sufficient one. Did he not love his home? His home was a delightful relaxation. The moment he crossed the threshold his ideas went behind him and in the hour before dinner he played with his child and talked to Ellen about the house and the garden and the things he thought she was most interested in. After dinner she read or sewed and he spent an hour at the piano, and then he took her on his knees.

And sometimes in the morning as he walked, with Ellen at his side, to catch the train, he wondered at his good fortune—the road was so pleasant, so wide and smooth and shaded, in fact just as he imagined the road should be, and Ellen was the very pleasantest companion a man could wish for. He looked on her, on his child and his house at the foot of the Dublin mountains, as a little work of art which he had planned out and the perfection of which entitled him to some credit. He compared himself to one who visits a larder, who has a little snack of something and then puts down the cover, saying, "Now that's all right, that's safe for another week."

Nevertheless he could see a little shadow gathering. His speeches were growing more explicit, and sooner or later his wife would begin to notice that he was attacking the clergy. Had she no suspicion? She was by nature so self-restrained that it was impossible to tell. He knew she read his speeches, and if she read them she must have noticed their anticlerical tone. Last Saturday he had spoken to her about politics, but she had allowed the conversation to drop, and that had puzzled him. He was not well reported. The most important parts of his speech were omitted and for these omissions he looked upon the reporters and the editors as his best friends. He had managed to steer his way very adroitly up to the present, but the day of reckoning could not much longer be postponed, and one day coming home from a great meeting he remembered that he had said more than he intended to say, though he had intended to say a good deal. This time the reporter could not save him, and when his wife would read the newspaper to-morrow an explanation could hardly be avoided.

He had thrown a book on the seat opposite, and he put it into his bag. Its Nihilism had frightened him at first but he had returned to the book again and again and every time the attraction had become stronger. The train passed the signal box, and Ned was thinking of the aphorisms— the new Gospel was written in aphorisms varying from three to twenty lines in length—and he thought of these as meat lozenges each containing enough nutriment to make a gallon of weak soup suitable for invalids, and of himself as a sort of illicit dispensary.

Ellen was not on the platform; something had delayed her, and he could see the road winding under trees, and presently he saw her white summer dress and her parasol aslant. There was no prettier, no more agreeable woman than Ellen in Ireland, and he thought it a great pity to have to worry her and himself with explanations about politics and about religion. To know how to sacrifice the moment is wisdom, and it would be better to sacrifice their walk than that she should read unprepared what he had said. But the evening would be lost! It would be lost in any case, for his thoughts would be running all the while on the morning paper.

And they walked on together, he a little more silent than usual, for he was thinking how he could introduce the subject on which he had decided to speak to her, and Ellen more talkative, for she was telling how the child had delayed her, and it was not until they reached the prettiest part of the road that she noticed that Ned was answering perfunctorily.

"What is the matter, dear? I hope you are not disappointed with the meeting?"

"No, the meeting was well enough. There were a great number of people present and my speech was well received."

"I am glad of that," she said, "but what is the matter, Ned?"

"Nothing. I was thinking about my speech. I hope it will not be mis-understood. People are so stupid, and some will understand it as an attack on the clergy, whereas it is nothing of the kind."

"Well," she said, "if it isn't it will be different from your other speeches."

"How is that?"

"All your speeches lately have been an attack upon the clergy direct or indirect. I daresay many did not understand them but anyone who knows your opinions can read between the lines."

"If you had read between the lines, Ellen, you would have seen that I have been trying to save the clergy from themselves. They are so con-vinced of their own importance that they forget that after all there must be a laity."

Ellen answered very quietly, and there was a sadness in her gravity which Ned had some difficulty in appreciating. He went on talking, telling her that some prelate had pointed out lately, and with approbation, that although the population had declined the clergy had been increasing steadily year after year.

"I am really," he said, "trying to save them from themselves. I am only pleading for the harmless and the necessary laity."

Ellen did not answer him for a long while.

"You see, Ned, I am hardly more to you now than any other woman. You come here occasionally to spend a day or two with me. Our married life has dwindled down to that. You play with the baby and you play with the piano, and you write your letters. I don't know what you are writing in them. You never speak to me of your ideas now, I know nothing of your politics."

"I haven't spoken about politics much lately, Ellen, because I thought you had lost interest in them."

"I have lost interest in nothing that concerns you. I have not spoken to you about politics because I know quite well that my ideas don't interest you any longer. You're absorbed in your own ideas, and we're divided. You sleep now in the spare room, so that you may have time to prepare your speeches."

"But I sometimes come to see you in your room, Ellen."

"Sometimes," she said, sadly, "but that is not my idea of marriage, nor is it the custom of the country, nor is it what the Church wishes."

"I think, Ellen, you are very unreasonable, and you are generally so reasonable."

"Well, don't let us argue any more," she said. "We shall never agree, I'm afraid."

Ned remembered that he once used to say to her, "Ellen, we are agreed in everything."

"If I had only known that it was going to turn out so disagreeable as this," Ned said to himself, "I should have held my tongue," and he was sorry for having displeased Ellen, so pretty did she look in her white dress and her hat trimmed with china roses; and though he did not care much for flowers he liked to see Ellen among her flowers; he liked to sit with her under the shady apple tree, and the hollyhocks were making a fine show up in the air.

"I think I like hollyhocks better than any flowers, and the sunflowers are coming out," he said.

He hesitated whether he should speak about the swallows, Ellen did not care for birds. The swallows rushed round the garden in groups of six and seven filling the air with piercing shrieks. He had never seen them so restless. He and Ellen walked across the sward to their seat and then Ellen asked him if he would like to see the child.

"I've kept him out of bed and though you might like to see him."

"Yes," he said, "go fetch the baby and I will shake the boughs, and it will amuse him to run after the apples."

"Differences of opinion arise," he said to himself, "for the mind changes and desire wanes, but the heart is always the same, and what an extraordinary bond the child is," he said, seeing Ellen leading the child across the sward. He forgot Ireland, forgot priests and forgot politics, forgot everything. He lifted his little son in his arms and shook the boughs and saw the child run after the falling apples, stumbling and falling but never hurting himself.

The quarrels of the day died down; the evening grew more beautiful under the boughs, and this intimate life round their apple tree was strangely intense, and it grew more and more intense as the light died. Every now and then the child came to show them an apple he had picked up, and Ned said: "He thinks he has found the largest apples that have ever been seen." The secret of their lives seemed to approach and at every moment they expected to hear it. The tired child came to his mother and asked to be taken on her lap. An apple fell with a thud, the stars came out, and Ned carried his son, now half asleep, into the house, and they undressed him together, having forgotten, seemingly, their differences of opinion.

But after dinner when they were alone in the drawing-room their relations grew strained again. Ned wanted to explain to Ellen that his movement was not anticlerical, but he could see she did not wish to hear. He watched her take up her work and wondered what he could say to persuade her, and after a little while he began to think of certain pieces of music. But to go to the piano would be like a hostile act. The truth was that he had looked forward to the evening he was going to spend with her, he had imagined an ideal evening with her and could not reconcile himself to the loss. "The hour we passed in the garden was extraordinarily intense," he said to himself, and he regretted ever having talked to her about anything except simple things. "It is unwise of a man to make a comrade of his wife.... Now I wonder if she would be angry with me if I went to the piano—if I were to play something very gently? Perhaps a book would seem less aggressive." He went into his study and fetched his book, and very soon forgot Ellen. But she had not forgotten him, and she raised her eyes to look at him from time to time, knowing quite well that he was reading the book out of which he drew the greater part of his doctrine that he had alluded to on his way home, and that he had called the Gospel of Life.

He turned the pages, and seeing that his love of her had been absorbed by the book, she stuck her needle in her work, folded it up, and put it into the work basket.

"I am going to bed, Ned." He looked up, and she saw he had returned from a world that was unknown to her, a world in which she had no part, and did not want to have a part, knowing it to be wicked.

"You have been reading all the evening. You prefer your book to me. Good night."

She had never spoken to him so rudely before. He wondered awhile and went to the piano. She had gone out of the room very rudely. Now he was free to do what he liked, and what he liked most was to play Bach. The sound of the piano would reach her bedroom! Well, if it did— he had not played Bach for four weeks and he wanted to play Bach. Yes, he was playing Bach to please himself. He knew the piano would annoy her. And he was right.

She had just lighted the candles on her dressing table, and she paused and listened. It annoyed her that he should go to the piano the moment she left him, and that he should play dry intellectual Bach, for he knew that Bach did not interest her. She was tempted to ring for her maid, and would have sent down word to Ned that she would be obliged if he would stop playing, had it not seemed undignified to do so.

As she undressed she lost control over herself, and lying in bed it seemed to her that Ned had hidden himself in a veil of kindness and good humour, and that the man she had married was a man without moral qualities, a man who would leave her without resentment, without disgust, who would say good-bye to her as to some brief habit. She could hear Bach's interminable twiddles, and this exasperated her nerves and she wept through many preludes and fugues. Later on she must have heard the fugues in a dream, for the door opened; it passed over the carpet softly; and she heard Ned saying that he hoped the piano had not kept her awake. She heard him lay the candle on the table and come over to her bedside, and, leaning over her, he begged of her to turn round and speak to him.

"My poor little woman, I hope I have not been cross with you this evening."

She turned away petulantly, but he took her hand and held it and whispered to her, and gradually tempted her out of her anger, and taking some of her red hair from the pillow he kissed it. She still kept her head turned from him, but she could not keep back her happiness; it followed her like fire, enfolding her, and at last, raising herself up in the bed, she said:

"Oh, Ned, do you still love me?"

When he came into her bed she slipped down so that she could lie upon his breast, and they fell asleep thinking of the early train he would have to catch in the morning.

He was going to Dublin, and the servant knocked at the door at seven o'clock; Ellen roused a little asking if he must go to Dublin. She would like him to stay with her. But he could not stay, and she felt she must give

him his breakfast. While tying her petticoats she went to the door of
Ned's dressing-room asking him questions, for she liked to' talk to him
while he was shaving. After breakfast they walked to the station together,
and she stood on the platform smiling and waving.

She turned home, her thoughts chattering like the sunshine among the
trees; she leaned over the low, crumbling walls and looked across the
water meadows. Two women were spending the morning under the
trees; they were sewing. A man was lying at length talking to them. This
group was part of external nature. The bewitching sunlight found a way
into her heart, and it seemed to her that she would never be unhappy
again.

Ned had told her that he was not going to say anything more about
the priests at this meeting. Ah, if she were only sure he would not attack
religion she would not mind him criticising the priests. They were not
above criticism; they courted criticism, approving of a certain amount
of lay criticism. But it was not the priests that Ned hated, it was religion;
and his hatred of religion had increased since he began to read those
books—she had seen him put one into his bag, and the rest of the set were
in his study. When she got home she paused a moment, and, without
knowing exactly why, she turned aside and did not go into his study.

But next day the clock in the drawing-room stopped and, wanting to
know the time, she went into the study and looked at the clock, trying to
keep her eyes from the book-case. But in spite of herself she looked. The
books were there: they had been thrust so far back that she could not
read the name of the writer. Well, it did not matter, she did not care to
know the name of the writer—Ned's room interested her more than the
books. There was his table covered with his papers; and the thought
passed through her mind that he might be writing the book he had promised her not to write. What he was writing was certainly for the printer—
he was writing only on one side of the paper—and one of these days what
he was writing would be printed.

The study was on the ground floor, its windows overlooking the garden,
and she glanced to see if the gardener were by, but her wish to avoid
observation reminded her that she was doing a dishonourable action, and,
standing with the papers in her hand, she hoped she would go out of the
study without reading them. She began to read.

The papers in her hand were his notes for the book he was writing,
and the title caught her eye, *A Western Thibet*. "So he is writing the book
he promised me not to write," she said. But she could feel no anger, so
conscious was she of her own shame. And she did not forget her shame

until she remembered that it was her money that was supporting the agitation. He had been spending a great deal of money lately—they were rich now; her father had died soon after their marriage and all his money had come to her, and Ned was spending it on an anti-religious agitation. She had let Ned do what he liked; she had not cared what happenned so long as she kept his love, and her moral responsibility became clearer and clearer. She must tell Ned that she could give him no more money unless he promised he would not say anything against the priests. He would make no such promise, and to speak about her money would exhibit her in a mean light, and she would lose all her influence. Now that they were reconciled she might win him back to religion; she had been thinking of this all yesterday. How could she tell him that she would take all her money away from him? Ned was the last person in the world who would be influenced by a threat.

And looking round the room she asked herself why she had ever come into it to commit a dishonourable act! and much trouble had come upon her. But two thousand a year of her money was being spent in robbing the people of Ireland of their religion! Maybe thousands of souls would be lost—and through her fault.

Ellen feared money as much as her father had loved it.

"Good Heavens," she murmured to herself, "what am I to do?" Confession... Father Brennan. She must consult him. The temptation to confide her secret became more decisive. Confession! She could ask the priest what she liked in confession, and without betraying Ned. And it was not ten o'clock yet. She would be in time for eleven o'clock Mass, Father Brennan would be hearing confession after Mass, and she could get to Dublin on her bicycle in an hour. In three quarters of an hour she was at the presbytery, and before the attendant could answer she caught sight of Father Brennan running down stairs.

"I only want to speak to you for a few minutes."

"I am just going into church."

"Can't I say a word to you before you go in."

And seeing how greatly agitated she was, he took her into the parlour, and she told him that though she trusted him implicitly she could not consult him on this particular question except in the confessional.

"I shall be hearing confessions after Mass."

If the priest told her she must withdraw her money from Ned, her marriage was a broken one. It was she who had brought Ned into politics; she had often spoken of her money in order to induce him to go into politics, and now it was her money that was forcing her to betray him. She had not thought of confession in her present difficult as a betrayal, but it was one, and a needless one; Father Brennan could only tell her to withdraw her money; yet she must consult the priest—nothing else would satisfy her. She lacked courage: his advice would give her courage. But when she had told Ned that she could give him no more money, she would have to tell him she was acting on the priest's advice, for she could not go on living with him and not tell him everything. A secret would poison her life, and she had no difficulty in imagining how she would remember it; she could see it stopping her suddenly as she crossed the room when she was thinking of something quite different. The hardest confession of all would be to tell Ned that she had consulted the priest, and she did not think he would ever love her again. But what matter, so long as she was not weak and contemptible in the eyes of God. That is what she had to think of. The love of one's husband is of this world and temporary, but the love of God is for all eternity. All things are in the will of God. It was God that had sent her·into Ned's room. She had been compelled, and now she was compelled again. It was God that had sent her to the priest; she was a mere puppet in the hands of God, and she prayed that she might be reconciled to His will, only daring to implore His mercy with one "Our Father" and one "Hail Mary." Further imploration would be out of place, she must not insist too much. God was all wisdom, and would know if the love of her husband might be spared to her, and she hoped she would be reconciled to His will if her child should be taken from her.

There were two penitents before her. One a woman, faded by toil and deformed by work. From the black dress, come down to her through a succession of owners and now as nondescript as herself, Ellen guessed the woman to be one of the humblest class of servants, one of those who get their living by going out to work by the day. She leaned over the bench, and Ellen could see she was praying all the while, and Ellen wondered how Ned could expect this poor woman, earning a humble wage in humble service, to cultivate what he called "the virtue of pride." Was it not absurd to expect this poor woman to go through life trying to make life "exuberant and triumphant"? and Ellen wished she could show Ned this poor woman waiting to go into the confessional. In the confessional she would find a refined and learned man to listen to her, and he would have patience with her. Where else would she find a patient listener? Where else would she find consolation? "The Gospel of Life," indeed! How many may listen to the gospel of life, and for how long may anyone listen? Sooner or later we are that poor woman waiting to go into the confession; she is the common humanity.

The other penitent was a girl about sixteen. Her hair was not yet pinned up, and her dress was girlish even for her age, and Ellen judged her to be one of the many girls who come up to Dublin from the suburbs to an employment in a shop or in a lawyer's office, and who spend a few pence in the middle of the day in tea rooms. The girl looked round the church so frequently that Ellen could not think of her as a willing penitent, but as one who had been sent to confession by her father and mother. At her age sensuality is omnipresent, and Ellen thought of the check confession is at such an age. If that girl overstepped the line she would have to confess everything, or face the frightful danger of a bad confession, and that is a danger that few Catholic girls are prepared to face.

The charwoman spent a long time in the confessional, and Ellen did not begrudge her the time she spent, for she came out like one greatly soothed, and Ellen remembered that Ned had once described the soothed look which she noticed on the poor woman's face as "a look of foolish ecstasy, wholly divorced from the intelligence." ·But what intellectual ecstasy did he expect from this poor woman drifting towards her natural harbour—the poor house?

It was extraordinary that a man so human as Ned was in many ways should become so inhuman the moment religion was mentioned, and she wondered if the sight of that poor woman leaving the confessional would allay his hatred of the sacrament. At that moment the young girl came out. She hurried away and Ellen went into the confessional to betray her husband.

She was going to betray Ned, but she was going to betray him under the seal of confession, and entertained no thought that the priest would avail himself of any technicality in her confession to betray her. She was, nevertheless, determined that her confession should be technically perfect. She went into the confessional to confess her sins, and one of the sins she was going to confess was her culpable negligence regarding the application of her money. There were other sins. She had examined her conscience, and had discovered many small ones. She had lost her temper last night, and her temper had prevented her from saying her prayers, her temper and her love of Ned; for it were certainly a sin to desire anything so fervidly that one cannot give to God the love, the prayers that belong to Him.

During Mass the life of her soul had seemed to her strange and complex, and she thought that her confession would be a long one; but on her knees before the priest her soul seemed to vanish, and all her interesting scruples and phases of thought dwindled to almost nothing—she could not put her soul into words. The priest waited, but the matter on which she had come to consult him had put everything else out of her head.

"I am not certain that what I am going to tell you is a sin, but I consider it as part of my confession," and she told him how she had given Ned her money and allowed him to apply it without inquiring into the application. "Since my child was born I have not taken the interest I used to take in politics. I don't think my husband is any longer interested in my ideas, and now he has told me that some kind of religious reformation is necessary in Ireland."

"When did he tell you that?"

"Yesterday—the day before. I went to the station to meet him and he told me as we walked home. For a long time I believed him: I don't mean that he told me falsehoods; he may have deceived himself. Anyhow he used to tell me that though his agitation might be described as anticlerical no one could call it anti-religious. But this morning something led me into his room and. I looked through his papers. I daresay I had no right to do so but I did."

"And you discovered from his papers that his agitation was directed against religion?"

Ellen nodded.

"I cannot think of anything more unfortunate," said the priest.

Father Brennan was a little fat man with small eyes and a punctilious deferential manner, and his voice was slightly falsetto.

"I cannot understand how your husband can be so unwise. I know very little of him, but I did not think he was capable of making so grave a mistake. The country is striving to unite itself, and we have been uniting, and now that we have a united Ireland, or very nearly, it appears that Mr Carmady has come from America to divide us again. What can he gain by these tactics? If he tells the clergy that the moment Home Rule is granted an anti-religious party will rise up and drive them out of the country, he will set them against Home Rule, and if the clergy are not in favour of Home Rule who, I would ask Mr Carmady, who will be in favour of it? And I will ask you, my dear child, to ask him—I suggest that you should ask him to what quarter he looks for support."

"Ned and I never talk politics; we used to, but that is a long time ago."

"He will only ruin himself. But I think you said you came to consult me about something."

"Yes. You see a very large part of my money is spent in politics and I am not certain that I should not withdraw my money. It is for that I have come to consult you."

Ellen had been addressing the little outline of the priest's profile, but when he heard the subject on which she had come to consult him he turned and she saw his large face, round and mottled. A little light gathered in his wise and kindly eyes, and Ellen guessed that he had begun to see his way out of the difficulty, and she was glad of it, for she reckoned her responsibility at a number of souls. The priest spoke very kindly, he seemed to understand how difficult it would be for her to tell her husband that she could not give him any more money unless he promised not to attack the clergy or religion, but she must do so. He pointed out that to attack one was to attack the other, for the greater mass of mankind understands religion only through the clergy.

"You must not only withdraw the money," he said, "but you must use your influence to dissuade him."

"I am afraid," said Ellen, "that when I tell him that I must withdraw my money, and that you have told me to do so——"

"You need not say that I told you to do so."

"I cannot keep anything back from my husband. I must tell him the whole truth," she said. "And when I tell him everything, I shall not only lose any influence that may remain, but I doubt very much if my husband will continue to live with me."

"But your marriage was a love marriage?"

"Yes, but that is a long time ago. It is four years ago."

"I don't think your husband will separate himself from you, but even so I think——"

"You will give me absolution?"

She said this a little defiantly, and the priest wondered, and she left the confessional perplexed and a little ashamed and very much terrified.

There was nothing for her to do in Dublin, she must go home and wait for her husband. He was not coming home until evening, and she rode home wondering how the day would pass, thinking the best time to tell him would be after dinner when he left the piano. If he were very angry with her she would go to her room. He would not go on living with her, she was sure of that, and her heart seemed to stand still when she entered the house and saw the study door open and Ned looking through the papers.

"I have come back to look for some papers," he said. "It is very annoying. I have lost half the day," and he went on looking among his papers and she could see that he suspected nothing. "Do you know when is the next train?"

She looked out the trains for him, and she could see that he suspected nothing, and after he had found the papers he wanted they went into the garden.

She talked of her flowers with the same interest as she had done many times before, and when he asked her to go for a walk with him on the hill she consented, although it was almost unbearable to walk with him for the last time through the places where they had walked so often, thinking that their lives would move on to the end unchanged; and they walked about the hill talking of Irish history, their eyes often resting on the slender outlines of Howth, until it was time for Ned to go to the station.

"I shall be back in time for dinner. You will wait dinner a little for me, I may have to come back by a later train."

And they walked down the hill together, Ned bidding her good-bye at the garden gate, saying she had walked enough that day, and she feeling the moment was at hand.

"But, Ned, why are you going to Dublin? You are only going to see people who are anti-Catholic, who hate our religion, who are prejudiced against it."

"But," he said, "why do you talk of these things. We have got on very much better since we have ceased to discuss politics together. We are agreed in everything else."

She did not answer for a long while and then she said:

"But I don't see how we are to avoid discussing them, for it is my money that supports the agitation."

"I never thought of that. So it is. Do you wish to withdraw it?"

"You are not angry with me, Ned? You won't think it mean of me to withdraw my money? You see I am wrecking your political career."

"Oh," he said. "I shall be able to get on without it. Now, good-bye."

"May I go to the station with you."

"If you like, only let us talk of something else. Every one's conscience is his own law and you must act accordingly."

She trotted by his side, and she begged of him not to laugh at her when he said that to be truly logical she would have to turn him out of the house, or at least to charge him for his board and lodging.

The intonation of his voice laid her heart waste; she felt she was done for, and she walked home repeating the words, "I am done for."

As she passed through her garden she saw that her flowers were dying for want of water, and she gave them a few cans of water; but she could not do much work, and though the cans were heavy, they were not as heavy as her heart. She sat down under the apple tree and remembered her life. Her best days were her school days. Then life was beginning.

Now it seemed to her nearly over, and she only five-and-twenty. She never could take the same interest in politics as she had once taken, nor in books. She felt that her intelligence had declined. She was cleverer as a girl than she was as a woman.

Ned was coming home for dinner, and some time that evening she would have to tell him that she had read his manuscript. She would have liked to meet him at the station, but thought it would be better not to go. The day wore away. Ned was in his best humour, and when she told him why she did not go to the station to meet him, he said it was foolish of her not to have come, for there was nothing he liked better than to stroll home with her in the evening, the road was so pleasant, etc.

She could see that he had not noticed her dress or what he was eating, and it was irritating to see him sitting there with his spoon full of soup telling her how the Irish people would have to reduce their expenditure and think a little less of priests—for a while, at least—unless they were minded to pass away, to become absorbed in America.

"I like Brennan," he said, throwing himself back in his chair. "He is a clever man. Brennan knows as well as I do there's too much money spent upon religion in Ireland. But, tell me, did he tell you explicitly that you should give me no more money?"

"Yes. But Ned——"

"No, no, I am not in the least angry," he said, "I shall always get money to carry on politics. But what a game it is! And I suppose, Ellen, you consult him on every detail of your life?"

Her admission that Father Brennan had taken down books and put on his spectacles delighted him.

"Taking down tomes!" he said. "Splendid! Some of these gentlemen would discuss theology with God. I can see Father Brennan getting up: 'Sire, my reason for entering the said sin as a venial sin, etc.'"

Very often during the evening the sewing dropped from her hands, and she sat thinking. Sooner or later she would have to tell Ned she had read his manuscript. He would not mind her reading his manuscript, and though he hated the idea that anyone should turn to a priest and ask him for his interpretation regarding right and wrong, he had not, on the whole, been as angry as she expected.

At last she got up. "I am going to bed, Ned."

"Isn't it very early?"

"There is no use my stopping here. You don't want to talk to me; you'll go on playing till midnight."

"Now, why this petulancy, Ellen? I think it shows a good deal of forgiveness for me to kiss you after the way you behaved."

She held a long string of grease in her fingers, and was melting it, and when she could no longer hold it in her fingers, she threw the end into the flame.

"I've forgiven you, Ellen.... You never tell me anything of your ideas now; we never talk to each other, and if this last relation is broken there will be nothing...will there?"

"I sought Father Brennan's advice under the seal of confession, that was all. You don't think that——"

"There are plenty of indirect ways in which he will be able to make use of the information he has got from you."

"You have not yet heard how it happened, and perhaps when you do you will think worse of me. I went into your room to see what books you were reading. There was no harm in looking at a book; but you had put the books so far into the book-case that I could not see the name of the author. I took up the manuscript from the table and glanced through it. I suppose I ought not to have done that: a manuscript is not the same as a book. And now good night."

He imagined her going slowly up the stairs and knew she would not expect him. Well, the sensual coil was broken, and if he did not follow her now she would understand that it was broken. He had wanted freedom this long while. They had come to the end of the second period, and there are three—a year of mystery and passion, and then some years of passion without mystery. The third period is one of resignation. The lives of the parents pass into the children, and the mated journey on, carrying their packs. Seldom, indeed, the man and the woman weary of the life of passion at the same time and turn instinctively into the way of resignation like animals. Sometimes it is the man who turns first, sometimes it is the woman. In this case it was the man. He had his work to do, and Ellen had her child to think of, and each must think of his and her task from henceforth. Their tasks were not the same. Each had a different task; she had thrown, or tried to throw, his pack from his shoulders. She had thwarted him, or tried to thwart him. He grew angry as he thought of what she had done. She had gone into his study and read his papers, and she had then betrayed him to a priest. He lay awake thinking how he had been deceived by Ellen; thinking that he had been mistaken; that her character was not the noble character he had imagined. But at the bottom of his heart he was true to the noble soul that religion could not extinguish nor even his neglect.

She said one day: "Is it because I read your manuscript and told the priest, that you would not come to my room, or is it because you are tired of me?"

"I cannot tell you; and, really, this conversation is very painful. I am engaged upon my work, and I have no thoughts for anything but it."

Another time when he came from the piano and sat opposite to her she raised her eyes from her sewing and sat looking at him, and then getting up suddenly she put her hands to her forehead and said to herself: "I will conquer this," and she went out of the room.

And from that day she did not trouble him with love. She obtained control over herself, and he remembered a mistress who had ceased to love him, and he had persecuted her for a long while with supplication. "She is at one with herself always," he said, and he tried to understand her. "She is one of those whose course through life is straight, and not zig-zag, as mine is." He liked to see her turn and look at the baby, and he said, "That love is the permanent and original element of things, it is the universal substance"; and he could trace Ellen's love of her child in her love of him; these loves were not two loves, but one love. And when walking one evening through the shadows, as they spoke about the destiny we can trace in our lives, about life and its loneliness, the conversation verged on the personal, and she said, with a little accent of regret, but not reproachfully:

"But, Ned, you could not live with anyone, at least not always. I think you would sooner not live with anyone."

He did not dare to contradict her; he knew that she had spoken the truth; and Ned was sorry he was giving pain to Ellen, for there was no one he would have liked to please better. He regretted that he was what he was, that his course was zig-zag. For a moment he regretted that such a fate should have befallen Ellen. "I am not the husband that would have suited her," he said.... And then, after a moment's reflection, "I was her instinct; another would not have satisfied her instinct; constancy is not everything. It's a pity I cannot love her always, for none is more worthy of being loved."

They became friends; he knew there was no danger of her betraying him again. Her responsibility ended with her money, and he told her how the agitation was progressing.

"Oh, Ned, if I were only sure that your agitation was not directed against religion I would follow you. But you will never believe in me."

"Yes, I believe in you. Come to Dublin with me; come to the meeting. I'd like you to hear my speech."

"I would like to hear you speak, Ned; but I don't think I can go to the

288

meeting."

They were on their way to the station, and they walked some time without speaking. Then, speaking suddenly and gravely as if prompted by some deep instinct, Ellen said:

"But if you fail, Ned, you will be an outcast in Ireland, and if that happens you will go away, and I shall never see you again."

He turned and stood looking at her. That he should fail and become an outcast were not at all unlikely. Her words seemed to him like a divination! But it is the unexpected that happens, she said to herself, and the train came up to the station, and he bade her good-bye, and settled himself down in a seat to consider his speech for the last time.

"I shall say everything I dare, the moment is ripe: and the threat to hold out is, that Ireland is becoming a Protestant country. And the argument to use is that the Catholics are leaving because there is no joy in Ireland."

He went through the different sections of his speech introducing the word joy: Is Ireland going to become joyous? She has dreamed long enough among dead bones and ancient formulae. The little stations went by and the train rolled into Harcourt Street. He called a car. He was speaking at the Rotunda.

He was speaking on the depopulation question, and he said that this question came before every other question. Ireland has now confronted with the possibility that in five-and-twenty years the last of Ireland would have disappeared in America. There were some who attributed the Irish emigration to economic causes: that was a simple and obvious explanation, one that could be understood by everybody; but these simple and obvious explanations are not often, if they are ever, the true ones. The first part of Ned's speech was taken up with the examination of the economic causes, and proving that these were not the origin of the evil. The country was joyless; man's life is joyless in Ireland. In every other country there were merry-makings. "You have only to go into the National Gallery," he said, "to see how much time the Dutch spent in merry-makings." All their pictures with the exception of Rembrandt's treated of joyful subjects, of peasants dancing under trees, peasants drinking and singing songs in taverns, and caressing servant girls. Some of their merry-makings were not of a very refined character, but the ordinary man is not refined and in the most refined men there is often admiration and desire for common pleasure. In the country districts Irish life is one of stagnant melancholy, the only aspiration that comes into their lives is a religious one. "Of course it will be said that the Irish are too poor to pay for pleasure, but they are not too poor to spend fifteen millions a year upon religion." He was the last man in the world who would say that religion was not necessary, but if he were right in saying that numbers were leaving Ireland because Ireland was joyless, he was right in saying that it was the duty of every Irishman to spend his money in making Ireland a joyful country. He was speaking now in the interests of religion. A country is antecedent to religion. To have religion you must first have a country, and if Ireland was not made joyful Ireland would become a Protestant country in about twenty-five years. In support of this contention he produced figures showing the rate at which the Catholics were emigrating. But not only were the Catholics emigrating— those who remained were becoming nuns and priests. As the lay population declined the clerics became more numerous. "Now," he said, "there must be a laity. It is a very commonplace thing to say, but this very commonplace truth is forgotten or ignored, and I come here to plead to-day for the harmless and necessary laity." He knew that these words would get a laugh, and that the laugh would get him at least two or three minutes grace, and these two or three minutes could not be better employed than with statistics, and he produced some astonishing figures. These figures were compiled, he said, by a prelate bearing an Irish name, but whose object in Ireland was to induce Irishmen and Irishwomen to leave Ireland. This would not be denied, though the pretext on which he wished Irish men and women to leave Ireland would be pleaded as justification. "But of this I shall speak," Ned said, "presently. I want you first to give your attention to the figures which this prelate produced, and with approbation. According to him there were ten convents and one hundred nuns in the beginning of the century, now there were twelve hundred convents and twenty thousand nuns. The prelate thinks that this is a matter for us to congratulate ourselves on. In view of our declining population I cannot agree, and I regret that prelates should make such thoughtless observation. Again I have to remind you of a fact that cannot be denied, but which is ignored, and it is that a celibate clergy cannot continue the population, and that if the population be not continued the tail of the race will disppear in America in about twenty-five years.... Not only does this prelate think that we should congratulate ourselves on the fact that while the lay population is decreasing the clerical population is increasing, but he thinks that Ireland should still furnish foreign missions. He came to Ireland to get recruits, to beseech Irishmen and Irishwomen to continue their noble work of the conversion of the world. No doubt the conversion of the world is a noble work. My point now is that Ireland has done her share in this noble work, and that Ireland can no longer spare one single lay Irishman or cleric or any Irishwoman. If the foreign mission is to be recruited it must be recruited at the expense of some other country."

Ned suggested Belgium as the best recruiting ground. But it was the prelate's own business to find recruits, it was only Ned's business to say that Ireland had done enough for the conversion of the world. And this prelate with the Irish name and cosmopolitan heart, who thought it an admirable thing that the clerical population should increase, while the lay population declined; who thought that with the declining population Ireland should still send out priests and nuns to convert the world—was no true Irishman. He cared not a jot what became of his country, so long as Ireland continued to furnish him with priests and nuns for the foreign mission. This prelate was willing to bleed Ireland to death to make a Roman holiday. Ireland did not matter to him, Ireland was a speck—Ned would like to have said, a chicken that the prelate would drop into the caldron which he was boiling for the cosmopolitan restaurant; but this would be an attack upon religion, it would be too direct to be easily understood by the audience, and as the words came to his lips he changed the phrase and said, "a pinch of snuff in the Roman snuff box." After this, Ned passed on to perhaps the most important part of his speech—to the acquisition of wealth by the clergy. He said that if the lay population had declined, and if the clerical population had increased, there was one thing that had increased with the clergy, and that was the wealth of the clergy. "I wish the cosmopolitan prelate had spoken upon this subject. I wonder if he inquired how much land has passed into the hands of the clergy in the last twenty years, and how many mortgages the religious hold upon land. I wonder if he inquired how many poultry farms the nuns and the friars are adding to their convents and their monasteries; and now they are starting new manufactories for weaving—the weaving industry is falling into their hands. And there are no lay teachers in Ireland, now all the teaching is done by clerics. The Church is very rich in Ireland. If Ireland is the poorest country in the world, the Irish Church is richer then any other. All the money in Ireland goes into religion. There is only one other trade that can compete with it. Heaven may be for the laity, but this world is certainly for the clergy."

More money was spent upon religion in Ireland than in any other country. Too much money was spent for the moment in building churches, and the great sums of money that were being spent on religion were not fairly divided. And passing rapidly on Ned very adroitly touched upon the relative positions of the bishops and the priests and the curates. He told harrowing stories of the destitution of the curates, and he managed so well that his audience had not time to stop him. Everything he thought that

291

they could not agree with he sandwiched between things that he knew they would agree with.

Father Murphy stood a little distance on his right, a thick-set man, and as the sentences fell from Ned's lips he could see that Father Murphy was preparing his answer, and he guessed what Father Murphy's answer would be like. He knew Father Murphy to be an adroit speaker, and the priest began in a low key as Ned had expected him to do. He began by deploring the evils of emigration, and Mr Carmady deserved their best thanks for attracting popular attention to this evil. They were indebted to him for having done this. Others had denounced the evil, but Mr Carmady's eloquence had enabled him to do so as well as, perhaps even better than, it had been done before. He complimented Mr Carmady on the picturesque manner in which he described the emptying of the country, but he could not agree with Mr Carmady regarding the causes that had brought about this lamentable desire to leave the fatherland. Mr Carmady's theory was that the emptying of Ireland was due to the fact that the Irish priests had succeeded in inducing men to refrain from the commission of sin. Mr Carmady did not reproach the priests with having failed; he reproached them with having succeeded. A strange complaint. The cause of the emigration, which we all agreed in deploring, was, according to Mr Carmady, the desire of a sinless people for sin. A strange accusation. The people, according to Mr Carmady, were leaving Ireland because they wished to indulge in indecent living. Mr Carmady did not use these words; the words he used were "The joy of life," but the meaning of the words were well known.

"No race," he said, "had perhaps ever been libelled as the Irish race had been, but of all the libels that had ever been levelled against it, no libel had ever equalled the libel which he had heard uttered to-day, that the Irish were leaving Ireland in search of sin.

"They had heard a great deal about the dancing girl, and according to Mr Carmady it would seem that a nation could save itself by jigging."

"He is speaking very well, from his point of view," said Ned to himself.

Father Murphy was a stout, bald-headed man with small pig-like eyes, and a piece seemed to have been taken from the top of his bony forehead. He was elegantly dressed in broad cloth and he wore a gold chain and he dangled his chain from time to time. He was clearly the well-fed, well-housed cleric who was making, in this world, an exellent living of his advocacy for the next, and Ned wondered how it was that the people did not perceive a discrepancy between Father Murphy's appearance and the theories he propounded. "The idealism of the Irish people," said the priest, "was inveterate," and he settled himself on his short legs and began his peroration.

Ned had begun to feel that he had failed, he began to think of his passage back to America. Father Murphy was followed by a young curate, and the curate began by saying that Mr Carmady would be able to defend his theories, and that he had no concern with Mr Carmady's theories, though, indeed, he did not hear Mr Carmady say anything which was contrary to the doctrine of our "holy religion." Father Murphy had understood Mr Carmady's speech in quite a different light, and it seemed to the curate that he, Father Murphy, had put a wrong interpretation upon it; at all events he had put one which the curate could not share. Mr Carmady had ventured, and, he thought, very properly, to call attention to the number of churches that were being built and the number of people who were daily entering the orders. He did not wish to criticise men and women who gave up their lives to God, but Mr Carmady was quite right when he said that without a laity there could be no country. In Ireland the clergy were apt to forget this simple fact that celibates do not continue the race. Mr Carmady had quoted from a book written by a priest in which the distinguished author had said he looked forward to the day when Ireland would be one vast monastery, and the curate agreed with Mr Carmady that no more foolish wish had ever found its way into a book. He agreed with Mr Carmady that a real vocation is a rare thing. No country had produced many painters or many sculptors or many poets, and a true religious vocation was equally rare. Mr Carmady had pointed out that although the population had diminished the nuns and priests had increased, and Father Murphy must hold that Ireland must become one vast monastery, and the laity ought to become extinct, or he must agree with Mr Carmady that there was a point when a too numerous clergy would overbalance the laity.

Altogether an unexpected and plucky little speech, and long before it closed Ned saw that Father Murphy's triumph was not complete. Father Murphy's face told the same tale.

The curate's argument was taken up by other curates, and Ned began to see he had the youth of the country on his side.

He was speaking at the end of the week at another great meeting, and received even better support at this meeting than he had done at the first, and he returned home wondering what his wife was thinking of his success. But what matter? Ireland was waking from her sleep.... The agitation was running from parish to parish, it seemed as if the impossible were going to happen, and that the Gael was going to be free.

The curates had grievances, and he applied himself to setting the inferior clergy against their superiors, and as the agitation developed he told the curates that they were no better than ecclesiastical serfs, that although the parish priests dozed in comfortable armchairs and drank champagne, the curates lived by the wayside and ate and drank very little and did all the work.

One day at Maynooth it was decided that curates had legitimate grievances, and that the people had grievances that were likewise legitimate. And at this great council it was decided that the heavy marriage fees and the baptismal fees demanded by the priests should be reduced. Concessions were accompanied by threats. Even so it required all the power of the Church to put down the agitation. Every one stood agape, saying the bishops must win in the end. An indiscretion on Ned's part gave them the victory. In a moment of excitement he was unwise enough to quote John Mitchel's words "that the Irish would be free long ago only for their damned souls." A priest wrote to the newspapers pointing out that after these words there could be no further doubt that it was the doctrine of the French Revolution that Mr Carmady was trying to force upon a Christian people. A bishop wrote saying that the words quoted were fit words for Anti-Christ. After that it was difficult for a priest to appear on the same platform, and the curates whose grievances had been redressed deserted, and the fight became an impossible one.

Very soon Ned's meetings were interrupted, disagreeable scenes began to happen, and his letters were not admitted to the newspapers. A great solitude formed about him.

"Well," he said one morning, "I suppose you have read the account in the paper of my ignominious escape. That is what they called it."

"The wheel," Ellen said, "is always going round. You may be at the bottom now, but the wheel is going round, only there is no use opposing the people in their traditions, in their instinct.... And whether the race is destined to disappear or to continue it's certain that the last Gael will die a Catholic."

"And the Red Indian will die with the scalp at his girdle."

"We won't talk about religion, we'll talk about things we are agreed upon. I have heard you say yourself that you would not go back to America again, that you never enjoyed life until you came here."

"That was because I met you, Ellen."

"I have heard you praise Ireland as being the most beautiful and sympathetic country in the world."

"It is true that I love these people, and I wish I could become one of them."

"You would become one of them and yet you would tear them to pieces because they are not what you want them to be."

Sometimes he thought he would like to write *A Western Thibet*, but he was more a man of action than of letters. His writings had been so long confined to newspaper articles that he could not see his way from chapter to chapter. He might have overcome the difficulty, but doubt began to poison his mind. "Every race," he said, "has its own special genius. The Germans have or have had music. The French or Italians have or have had painting and sculpture. The English have or have had poetry. The Irish had, and alas! they still have their special genius, religious vocation."

He used to go for long walks on the hills, and one day, lying in the furze amid the rough grass, his eyes following the course of the ships in the bay, he said: "Was it accident or my own fantastic temperament that brought me back from Cuba?" It seemed as if a net had been thrown over him and he had been drawn along like a fish in a net. "For some purpose," he said. "But for what purpose? I can perceive none, and yet I cannot believe that an accident brought me to Ireland and involved me in the destiny of Ireland for no purpose."

And he did not need to take the book from his pocket, he knew the passage well, and he repeated it word for word while he watched the ships in the bay.

"We were friends and we have become strangers one to the other. Ay, yes; but it is so, and we do not wish to hide our strangerhood, or to dissemble as if we were ashamed of it. We are two ships each with a goal and a way; and our ways may grow together again and we may make holiday as before. And how peacefully the good ships used to lie in the same harbour, under the same sun; it seemed as if they had reached their goal, and it seemed as if there was a goal. But soon the mighty sway of our tasks laid on us as from of old sundered and drove us into different seas and different zones; and it may be that we shall never meet again and it may be that we shall meet and not know each other, so deeply have the different seas and suns changed us. The law that is over us decreed that we must become strangers one to the other; and for this we must reverence each other the more, and for this the memory of our past friendship become more sacred. Perhaps there is a vast invisible curve and orbit and our different goals and ways are parcel of it, infinitesimal segments. Let us uplift ourselves to this thought! But our life is too short and our sight too feeble for us to be friends except in the sense of this sublime possibility.

So, let us believe in our stellar friendship though we must be enemies on earth."

"A deep and mysterious truth," he said, "I must go, I must go," he said to himself. "My Irish life is ended. There is a starry orbit and Ireland and I are parts of it, 'and we must believe in our stellar friendship though we are enemies upon earth.' "

He wandered about admiring the large windless evening and the bright bay. Great men had risen up in Ireland and had failed before him, and it were easy to account for their failure by saying they were not close enough to the tradition of their race, that they had just missed it, but some of the fault must be the fault of Ireland.... The anecdote varies, but substantially it is always the same story: The interests of Ireland sacrificed to the interests of Rome.

There came a whirring sound, and high overhead he saw three great birds flying through the still air, and he knew them to be wild geese flying south....

War had broken out in South Africa, Irishmen were going out to fight once again; they were going to fight the stranger abroad when they could fight him at home no longer. The birds died down on the horizon, and there was the sea before him, bright and beautiful, with ships passing into the glimmering dusk, and among the hills a little mist was gathering. He remembered the great pagans who had wandered over these hills before scapulars and rosaries were invented. His thoughts came in flashes, and his happiness grew intense. He had wanted to go and the bird had shown him where he might go. His instinct was to go, he was stifling in Ireland. He might never find the country he desired, but he must get out of Ireland, "a mean ineffectual atmosphere," he said, "of nuns and rosaries."

A mist was rising, and the lovely outlines of Howth reminded him of pagan Ireland; "they're like music," he said, and he thought of Usheen and his harp. "Will Usheen ever come again?" he said. "Better to die than to live here." The mist thickened—he could see Howth no longer. "The land is dolorous," he said, and as if in answer to his words the most dolorous melody he had ever heard came out of the mist. "The wailing of an abandoned race," he said. "This is the soul sickness from which we are fleeing." And he wandered about calling to the shepherd, and the shepherd answered, but the mist was so thick in the hollows that neither could find the other. After a little while the shepherd began to play his flute again; and Ned listened to it singing it after him, and he walked home quickly, and the moment he entered the drawing-room he said to Ellen, "Don't speak to me; I am going to write something down," and this is what she wrote:

"A mist came on suddenly, and I heard a shepherd playing this folk tune. Listen to it. Isn't it like the people? Isn't it like Ireland? Isn't it like everything that has happened? It is melancholy enough in this room, but no words can describe its melancholy on a flute played by a shepherd in the mist. It is the song of the exile; it is the cry of one driven out in the night—into a night of wind and rain. It is night, and the exile on the edge of the waste. It is like the wind sighing over bog water. It is a prophetic echo and final despair of a people who knew they were done for from the

beginning. A mere folk tune, mere nature, raw and unintellectual; and these raw folk tunes are all that we shall have done: and by these, and these alone, shall we be remembered."

"Ned," she said at last, "I think you had better go away. I can see you're wearing out your heart here."

"Why do you think I should go? What put that idea into your head?"

"I can see you are not happy."

"But you said that the wheel would turn, and that what was lowest would come to the top."

"Yes, Ned, but sometimes the wheel is a long time in turning, and maybe it would be better for you to go away for a while."

He told her that he had seen wild geese on the hill.

"And it was from you I heard about the wild geese. You told me the history of Ireland, sitting on a druid stone."

"You want to go, Ned? And the desire to go is as strong in you as in the wild geese."

"Maybe; but I shall come back, Ellen."

"Do you think you will, Ned? How can you if you go to fight for the Boers?"

"There's nothing for me to do here. I want new life. It was you who said that I should go."

"For five years you have been devoted to Ireland, and now you and Ireland are separated like two ships."

"Yes, like two ships. Ireland is still going Romeward, and Rome is not my way."

"You are the ship, Ned, and you came to harbour in Ireland. But you and I are like two ships that have lain side by side in the harbour, and now——"

"And now what, Ellen? Go on!"

"It seemed to me that we were like two ships."

"That is the very thing I was thinking on the hills. The comparison of two ships rose up in my mind on the hill, and then I remembered a passage." And when he had repeated it she said—

"So there is no hope for us on earth. We are but segments of a starry curve, and must be content with our stellar friendship. But, Ned, we shall never be enemies on earth. I am not your enemy, and never shall be. So we have nothing to think of now but our past friendship. The memory of our past—is all that remains? And it was for that you left America after the Cuban war? There is our child. You love the little boy, don't you, Ned?"

"Yes," he said, "I love the little boy.... But you'll bring him up a Catholic. You'll bring him up to love the things that I hate."

"Let there be no bitterness between us to-night, Ned dear. Let there be only love. If not love, affection at least. This is our last night."

"How is that?"

"Because, Ned, when one is so bent upon going as you are it is better he should go at once. I give you your freedom. You can go in the morning or when you please. But remember, Ned, that you can come back when you please, that I shall be always glad to see you."

They went upstairs and looked for some time on the child, who was sleeping. Ellen took him out of his bed, and she looked very pretty, Ned thought, holding the half-awakened child, and she kept the little quilt about him so that he might not catch cold.

He put his hands into his eyes and looked at his father, and then hid his face in his mother's neck, for the light blinded him and he wished to go to sleep.

"Let me put him back in his bed," Ned said, and he took his son and put him back, and he kissed him. As he did so he wondered how it was that he could feel so much affection for his son and at the same time desire to leave his home.

"Now, Ned, you must kiss me, and do not think I am angry with you for going. I know you are dull here, that you have got nothing further to do in Ireland, but it will be different when you come back."

"And is it possible that you aren't angry with me, Ellen, for going?"

"I am sorry you are going, Ned—in a way, but I should be more sorry to see you stay here and learn to hate me."

"You are very wise, Ellen. But why did you read that manuscript?"

"I suppose because God wished me to."

One thing Ireland had done for him, and for that he would be always grateful to Ireland—Ireland had revealed a noble woman to him; and distance would bring a closer and more intimate appreciation of her.

He left early next morning before she was awake in order to save her the pain of farewells, and all that day in Dublin he walked about, possessed by the great joyful yearning of the wild goose when it rises one bright morning from the warm marshes, scenting the harsh north through leagues of air, and goes away on steady wing-beats. But he did not feel he was a free soul until the outlines of Howth began to melt into the grey drift of evening. There was a little mist on the water, and he stood watching the waves tossing in the mist thinking that it were well that he had left home—if he had stayed he would have come to accept all the base moral coinage in circulation; and he stood watching the green waves tossing in the mist, at one moment ashamed of what he had done, at the next overjoyed that he had done it.

PROUD COSTELLO, MACDERMOT'S DAUGHTER, AND THE BITTER TONGUE[1]

W. B. Yeats

COSTELLO had come up from the fields and lay upon the ground before the door of his square tower, resting his head upon his hands and looking at the sunset, and considering the chances of the weather. Though the customs of Elizabeth and James, now going out of fashion in England, had begun to prevail among the gentry, he still wore the great cloak of the native Irish; and the untroubled confidence of his face and his big body had the pride and strength of a simpler age. His eyes wandered from the sunset to where the long white road lost itself over the south-western horizon and to a horseman who toiled slowly up the hill. A few more minutes and the horseman was near enough for his little shapeless body, his long Irish cloak, and the dilapidated bagpipes hanging from his shoulders, and the rough-haired garron under him, to be seen distinctly in the grey dusk. So soon as he had come within earshot, he began crying: "Is it sleeping you are, Tumaus Costello, when better men break their hearts on the great white road? Get up out of that, proud Tumaus, for I have news! Get up out of that, you great omadhaun! Shake yourself out of the earth, you great weed of a man!"

Costello had risen to his feet, and as the piper came up to him seized him by the neck of his jacket, lifted him out of his saddle and shook him.

"Let me alone, let me alone," said the other, but Costello still shook him.

"I have news from MacDermot's daughter Una." The great fingers were loosened, and the piper fell gasping.

"Why did you not tell me," said Costello, "that you came from her? You might have railed your fill."

"I have come from her, but I will not speak until I am paid for the shaking."

Costello fumbled at the bag in which he carried his money, and it was

---

[1] From *Early Poems and Stories*. Reprinted by permission of the author and Messrs Macmillan and Co., Ltd.

some time before it would open, for his hand trembled. "Here is all the money in my bag," he said, dropping some French and Spanish money into the hand of the piper, who bit the coins before he would answer.

"That is right, that is a fair price, but I will not speak till I have good protection, for if the MacDermots lay their hands upon me in any boreen after sundown, or in Cool-a-vin by day, I will be left to rot among the nettles of a ditch, or hung where they hung the horse-thieves last Beltaine four years." And while he spoke he tied the reins of his garron to a bar of rusty iron that was mortared into the wall.

"I will make you my piper and my body-servant," said Costello, "and no man dare lay hands upon a man or a dog if he belong to Tumaus Costello."

"And I will only tell my message," said the other, flinging the saddle on the ground, "with a noggin of whisky in my hand, for though I am ragged and empty, my old fathers were well clothed and full, until their house was burnt down and their cattle driven away seven centuries ago by the Dillons, whom I shall yet see on the hob of hell, and they screeching."

Costello led him up a narrow winding stone stair into a rush-strewn chamber, where were none of the comforts which had begun to grow common among the gentry, and pointed to a seat in the great chimney; and when the piper had sat down, filled up a horn noggin and set it on the floor beside him, and a jug beside that, and then turned towards him and said: "Will MacDermot's daughter come to me, Duallach, son of Daly?"

"MacDermot's daughter will not come to you, for her father has set women to watch her, but I am to tell you that this day week will be the eve of St John and the night of her betrothal to MacNamara of the Lake, and she wants you to be there that, when they tell her to drink to him she loves best, she may drink to you, Tumaus Costello, and let all know where her heart is; and I myself advise you to go with good men about you, for I have seen the horse-thieves with my own eyes." And then he held the now empty noggin towards Costello, and cried: "Fill my noggin again, for I wish the day had come when all the water in the world is to shrink into a periwinkle-shell, that I might drink nothing but whisky."

Finding that Costello made no reply, but sat in a dream, he burst out: "Fill my noggin, I tell you, for no Costello is so great in the world that he should not wait upon a Daly, even though the Daly travel the road with his pipes and the Costello have a bare hill, and empty house, a horse, and a handful of cows."

"Praise the Dalys if you will," said Costello as he filled the noggin, "for you have brought me a kind word from my love."

For the next few days Duallach went here and there trying to raise a bodyguard, and every man he met had some story of Costello: one told how he killed the wrestler when but a boy by so straining at the belt that went about them both that he broke the big wrestler's back; another how he dragged fierce horses through a ford for a wager; another how when grown to be a man he broke the steel horseshoe in Mayo; but none who would trust himself with a man so passionate and poor in a quarrel with careful and wealthy persons like MacDermot of the Sheep and MacNamara of the Lake.

Then Costello went out himself, and brought in a big half-witted fellow, a farm-labourer who worshipped him for his strength, a fat farmer whose forefathers had served his family, and a couple of lads who looked after his goats and cows; and marshalled them before the fire. They had brought with them their heavy sticks, and Costello gave them an old pistol apiece, and kept them all night drinking and shooting at a white turnip which he pinned against the wall with a skewer. Duallach sat on the bench in the chimney playing "The Green Bunch of Rushes," "The Unchion Stream," and "The Princes of Breffeny" on his old pipes, and abusing now the appearance of the shooters, now their clumsy shooting, and now Costello because he had no better servants. The labourer, the half-witted fellow, the farmer, and the lads were well accustomed to Duallach's abusiveness, but they wondered at the forbearance of Costello, who seldom came either to wake or wedding, and if he had would not have been patient with a scolding piper.

On the next evening they set out for Cool-a-vin, Costello riding a tolerable horse and carrying a sword, the others upon rough-haired ponies, and with their cudgels under their arms. As they rode over the bogs and in the boreens among the hills they could see fire answering fire from hill to hill, from horizon to horizon, and everywhere groups who danced in the red light of the turf. When they came to MacDermot's house they saw before the door an unusually large group of the very poor, dancing about a fire, in the midst of which was a blazing cartwheel, and from the door and through the loopholes on either side came the light of candles and the sound of many feet dancing a dance of Elizabeth and James.

They tied their horses to bushes, for the number so tied already showed that the stables were full, and shoved their way through a crowd of peasants who stood about the door, and went into the big hall where the dance was. The labourer, the half-witted fellow, the farmer, and the two lads mixed with a group of servants who were looking on from an alcove, and Duallach sat with the pipers on their bench, but Costello made his way through the dancers to where MacDermot stood pouring out whisky, MacNamara at his side.

"Tumaus Costello," said the old man, "you have done a good deed to forget what has been, and come to the betrothal of my daughter."

"I come," answered Costello, "because when in the time of Costello De Angalo my ancestors overcame your ancestors and afterwards made peace, a compact was made that a Costello might go with his body-servants and his piper to every feast given by a MacDermot for ever, and a MacDermot with his body-servants and his piper to every feast given by a Costello for ever."

"If you come with evil thought and armed men," said MacDermot flushing, "no matter how good you are with your weapons, it shall go badly with you, for some of my wife's clan have come out of Mayo, and my three brothers and their servants have come down from the Ox Mountains"; and while he spoke he kept his hand inside his coat as though upon the handle of a weapon.

"No," answered Costello, "I but come to dance a farewell dance with your daughter."

MacDermot drew his hand out of his coat and went over to a pale girl who was now standing but a little way off with her mild eyes fixed upon the ground.

"Costello has come to dance a farewell dance, for he knows that you will never see one another again."

As Costello led her among the dancers her gentle and humble eyes were fixed in love upon his pride and violence. They took their place in Pavane, that stately dance which, with the Saraband, the Gallead, and the Moris dances, had driven out, among all but the most Irish of the gentry, the quicker rhythms of the verse-interwoven, pantomimic dances of earlier days; and while they danced there came over them the weariness with the world, the melancholy, the pity one for the other, which is the exultation of love. And when a dance ended and the pipers laid down the pipes and lifted the noggins, they stood a little from the others waiting pensively and silently for the dance to begin again and the fire in their hearts to leap up and to wrap them anew; and so they danced Pavane and Saraband and Gallead and Morris the night long, and many stood still to watch them, and the peasants came about the door and peered in, as though they understood that they would gather their children's children about them long hence, and tell how they had seen Costello dance with MacDermot's daughter Una; and through all the dancing and piping MacNamara went hither and thither talking loudly and making foolish jokes that all might seem well, and old MacDermot grew redder and redder, waiting for the dawn.

At last he saw that the moment to end had come, and in a pause after a dance, cried out that his daughter would now drink the cup of betrothal; then Una came over to where he was, and the guests stood round in a half-circle, Costello close to the wall, and the piper, the labourer, the farmer, the half-witted man, and the two farm lads close behind him. The old man took out of a niche in the wall the silver cup from which her mother and her mother's mother had drunk the toasts of their betrothals, filled it with Spanish wine and handed the cup to his daughter with the customary words, "Drink to him whom you love the best."

She held the cup to her lips for a moment, and then said in a clear soft voice: "I drink to my true love, Tumaus Costello."

And then the cup rolled over and over on the ground, ringing like a bell, for the old man had struck her in the face and the cup had fallen, and there was a deep silence.

There were many of MacNamara's people among the servants now come out of the alcove, and one of them, a story-teller and poet, who had a plate and chair in MacNamara's kitchen, drew a French knife out of his girdle, but in a moment Costello had struck him to the ground. The click of steel had followed quickly, had not there come a muttering and shouting from the peasants about the door and from those crowding up behind them; for all knew that these were no children of Queen's Irish, but of the wild Irish about Lough Gara and Lough Cara, Kellys, Dockerys, Drurys, O'Regans, Mahons, and Lavins, who had left the right arms of their children unchristened that they might give the better blows, and were even said to have named the wolves godfathers to their children.

Costello's knuckles had grown white upon the handle of his sword, but now he drew his hand away, and followed by those who were with him, went towards the door, the dancers giving way before him, the most angrily and slowly, and with glances at the muttering and shouting peasants, but some gladly and quickly, because the glory of his fame was over him. He passed through the fierce and friendly peasant faces, and came where his horse and the ponies were tied to bushes; and mounted and made his bodyguard mount also and ride into the narrow boreen. When they had gone a little way, Duallach, who rode last, turned towards the house where a little group of Mac Dermots and MacNamaras stood next to a bigger group of countrymen, and cried: "MacDermot, you deserve to be as you are this hour, for your hand was always niggardly to piper and fiddler and to poor travelling people." He had not done before the three old MacDermots from the Ox Mountains had run towards their horses, and old MacDermot himself had caught the bridle of a pony belonging to the MacNamaras and was calling to the others to follow him; and many blows and many deaths had been had not the countrymen caught up still blazing sticks from the ashes of the fires and thrown them among the horses to that they broke away from those who held them and scattered through the fields, and before they could be gathered again Costello was far off.

For the next few weeks Costello had no lack of news of Una, for now a woman selling eggs, and now a man or a woman going to the Holy Well, would tell him how his love had fallen ill the day after St John's Eve and how she was a little better or a little worse.

At last a serving-man rode up to Costello, who was helping his two lads to reap a meadow, and gave him a letter, and rode away; and the letter contained these words in English: "Tumaus Costello, my daughter is very ill. She will die unless you come to her. I therefore command you come to her whose peace you stole by treachery."

Costello threw down his scythe, and sent one of the lads for Duallach, and himself saddled his horse and Duallach's pony.

When they came to MacDermot's house it was late afternoon, and Lough Gara lay down below them, blue, and deserted; and though they had seen, when at a distance, dark figures moving about the door, the house appeared not less deserted than the Lough. The door stood half open, and Costello knocked upon it again and again, but there was no answer.

"There is no one here," said Duallach, "for MacDermot is too proud to welcome Proud Costello," and he threw the door open, and they saw a ragged, dirty, very old woman, who sat upon the floor leaning against the wall. Costello knew that it was Bridget Delaney, a deaf and dumb beggar; and she, when she saw him, stood up and made a sign to him to follow, and led him and his companion up a stair and down a long corridor to a closed door. She pushed the door open and went a little way off and sat down as before; Duallach sat upon the ground also, but close to the door, and Costello went and gazed upon Una sleeping upon a bed. He sat upon a chair beside her and waited, and a long time passed and still she slept, and then Duallach motioned to him through the door to wake her, but he hushed his very breath, that she might sleep on. Presently he turned to Duallach and said: "It is not right that I stay here where there are none of her kindred, for the common people are always ready to blame the beautiful." And then they went down and stood at the door of the house and waited, but the evening wore on and no one came.

"It was a foolish man that called you Proud Costello," Duallach said at last; "had he seen you waiting and waiting where they left none but a beggar to welcome you, it is Humble Costello he would have called you."

Then Costello mounted and Duallach mounted, but when they had ridden a little way Costello tightened the reins and made his horse stand still. Many minutes passed, and then Duallach cried: "It is no wonder that you fear to offend MacDermot, for he has many brothers and friends, and though he is old, he is a strong and stirring man, and he is of the Queen's Irish, and the enemies of the Gael are upon his side."

And Costello answered flushing and looking towards the house: "I swear by the Mother of God that I will never return there again if they do not send after me before I pass the ford in the Brown River," and he rode on, but so very slowly that the sun went down and the bats began to fly over the bogs. When he came to the river he lingered awhile upon the edge, but presently rode out into the middle and stopped his horse in a shallow. Duallach, however, crossed over and waited on a further bank above a deeper place. After a good while Duallach cried out again, and this time very bitterly: "It was a fool who begot you and a fool who bore you, and they are fools who say you come of an old and noble stock, for you come of whey-faced beggars who travelled from door to door, bowing to serving-men."

With bent head, Costello rode through the river and stood beside him, and would have spoken had not hoofs clattered on the futher bank and a horseman splashed towards them. It was a serving-man of MacDermot's and he said, speaking breathlessly like one who had ridden hard: "Tumaus Costello, I come to bring you again to MacDermot's house. When you had gone, his daughter Una awoke and called your name, for you had been in her dreams. Bridget Delaney the Dummy saw her lips move, and came where we were hiding in the wood above the house and took MacDermot by the coat and brought him to his daughter. He saw the trouble upon her, and bid me ride his own horse to bring you the quicker."

Then Costello turned towards the piper Duallach Daly, and taking him about the waist lifted him out of the saddle and threw him against a big stone that was in the river, so that he fell lifeless into a deep place. Then plunging his spurs into the horse, he rode away furiously towards the north-west, along the edge of the river, and did not pause until he came to another and smoother ford, and saw the rising moon mirrored in the water. He paused for a moment irresolute, and then rode into the ford and on over the Ox Mountains, and down towards the sea; his eyes almost continually resting upon the moon. But now his horse, long dark with sweat and breathing hard, for he kept spurring it, fell heavily, throwing him on the roadside. He tried to make it stand up, and failing in this, went on alone towards the moonlight; and came to the sea and saw a schooner lying there at anchor. Now that he could go no further because of the sea, he found that he was very tired and the night very cold, and went into a shebeen close to the shore and threw himself down upon a bench. The room was full of Spanish and Irish sailors who had just smuggled a cargo of wine, and were waiting a favourable wind to set out again. A Spaniard offered him a drink in bad Gaelic. He drank it and began talking wildly and rapidly.

For some three weeks the wind blew inshore or with too great violence, and the sailors stayed drinking and talking and playing cards, and Costello stayed with them, sleeping upon a bench in the shebeen, and drinking and talking and playing more than any. He soon lost what little money he had, and then his long cloak and his spurs and even his boots. At last a gentle wind blew toward Spain, and the crew rowed out to their schooner, and in a little while the sails had dropped under the horizon. Then Costello turned homeward, his life gaping before him, and walked all day, coming in the early evening to the road that went from near Lough Gara to the southern edge of Lough Cay. Here he overtook a crowd of peasanst and farmers, who were walking very slowly after two priests and a group of well-dressed persons, certain of whom were carrying a coffin. He stopped an old man and asked whose burying it was and whose people they were, and the old man answered: "It is the burying of Una, MacDermot's daughter, and we are the MacNamaras and the MacDermots and their following, and you are Tumaus Costello who murdered her."

Costello went on towards the head of the procession, passing men who looked angrily at him, and only vaguely understood what he had heard. Presently he stopped and asked again whose burying it was, and a man answered: "We are carrying MacDermot's daughter Una, whom you murdered, to her burying upon Insula Trinitatis," and the man picked up a stone and threw it at Costello, striking him on the cheek and making the blood flow out over his face. Costello went on scarcely feeling the blow, and coming to those about the coffin, shouldered his way into the midst of them, and laying his hand upon the coffin, asked in a loud voice: "Who is in this coffin?"

The three old MacDermots from the Ox Mountains caught up stones and told those about them to do the same; and he was driven from the road, covered with wounds.

When the procession had passed on, Costello began to follow again, and saw from a distance the coffin laid upon a large boat, and those about it get into other boats, and the boats move slowly over the water to Insula Trinitatis; and after a time he saw the boats return and their passengers mingle with the crowd upon the bank, and all scatter by many roads and boreens. It seemed to him that Una was somewhere on the island smiling gently, and when all had gone he swam in the way the boats had been rowed and found the new-made grave beside the ruined Abbey, and threw himself upon it, calling to Una to come to him.

He lay there all that night and through the day after, from time to time calling her to come to him, but when the third night came he had forgotten that her body lay in the earth beneath, but only knew she was somewhere near and would not come to him.

Just before dawn, the hour when the peasants hear his ghostly voice crying out, he called loudly: "If you do not come to me, Una, I will go and never return," and before his voice had died away a cold and whirling wind had swept over the island and he saw women of the Sidhe rushing past; and then Una, but no longer smiling, for she passed him swiftly and angrily, and as she passed struck him upon the face, crying: "Then go and never return."

Costello got up from the grave, understanding nothing but that he had made his sweetheart angry and that she wished him to go, and wading out into the lake, began to swim. He swam on, but his limbs seemed too weary to keep him afloat, and when he had gone a little way he sank without a struggle.

The next day a fisherman found him among the reeds upon the lake shore, lying upon the white lake sand, and carried him to his own house. And the peasants lamented over him and sang the keen, and laid him in the Abbey on Insula Trinitatis with only the ruined altar between him and MacDermot's daughter, and planted above them two ash-trees that in after days wove their branches together and mingled their leaves.

THE FATE OF THE SONS OF USNA[1]

P. W. Joyce

Avenging and bright fall the swift sword of Erin
On him who the brave sons of Usna betrayed.

MOORE

CHAPTER I

THE FLIGHT TO ALBAN

CONCOBAR MACNESSA, king of Ulaid, ruled in Emain. And his chief story-teller, Felimid, made a feast for the king and for the knights of the Red Branch, who all came to partake of it in his house. While they were feasting right joyously, listening to the sweet music of the harps and the mellow voices of the bards, a messenger brought word that Felimid's wife had given birth to a little daughter, an infant of wondrous beauty. And when Caffa, the king's druid and seer, who was of the company, was ware of the birth of the child, he went forth to view the stars and the clouds, if he might thereby glean knowledge of what was in store for that little babe. And when he had returned to his place, he sat deep pondering for a time: and then standing up and obtaining silence, he said:—

"This child shall be called Deir-dre[2]; and fittingly is she so named: for much of woe will befall Ulaid and Erin in general on her account. There shall be jealousies, and strifes, and wars: evil deeds will be done: many heroes will be exiled: many will fall."

When the heroes heard this, they were sorely troubled, and some said that the child should be killed. But the king said:— "Not so, ye Knights of the Red Branch; it is not meet to commit a base deed in order to escape evil that may never come to pass. This little maid shall be reared out of the reach of mischief, and when she is old enough she shall be my wife: thus shall I be the better able to guard against those evils that Caffa forecasts for us."

And the Ultonians did not dare to gainsay the word of the king.

Then king Concobar caused the child to be placed in a strong fortress on a lonely spot nigh the palace, with no opening in front, but with door and windows looking out at the back on a lovely garden watered by

---

[1] From *Old Celtic Romances*. Reprinted by permission of The Talbot Press, Ltd., Dublin.
[2] "Deirdre" is said to mean "alarm."

a clear rippling stream: and house and garden were surrounded by a wall that no man could surmount. And those who were put in charge of her were, her tutor, and her nurse, and Concobar's poetess, whose name was Lavarcam: and save these three, none were permitted to see her. And so she grew up in this solitude, year by year, till she was of marriageable age, when she excelled all the maidens of her time for beauty.

One snowy day as she and Lavarcam looked forth from the window, they saw some blood on the snow, where her tutor had killed a calf for dinner; and a raven alighted and began to drink of it. 'I should like,' said Deirdre, "that he who is to be my husband should have these three colours: his hair as black as the raven: his cheeks red as the blood: his skin like the snow. And I saw such a youth in a dream last night; but I know not where he is, or whether he is living on the ridge of the world."

"Truly," said Lavarcam, ' the young hero that answers to thy words is not far from thee; for he is among Concobar's knights: namely, Naisi the son of Usna."

Now Naisi and his brothers, Ainnli and Ardan, the three sons of Usna, were the best beloved of all the Red Branch Knights, so gracious and gentle were they in time of peace, so skilful and swift-footed in the chase, so strong and valiant in battle.

And when Deirdre heard Lavarcam's words, she said:—"If it be as thou sayest, that this young knight is near us, I shall not be happy till I see him: and I beseech thee to bring him to speak to me."

"Alas, child," replied Lavarcam, "thou knowest not the peril of what thou askest me to do: for if thy tutor come to know of it, he will surely tell the king; and the king's anger none can bear."

Deirdre answered not: but she remained for many days sad and silent: and her eyes often filled with tears through memory of her dream: so that Lavarcam was grieved: and she pondered on the thing if it could be done, for she loved Deirdre very much, and had compassion on her. At last she contrived that these two should meet without the tutor's knowledge: and the end of the matter was that they loved each other: and Deirdre said she would never wed the king, but she would wed Naisi.

Knowing well the doom that awaited them when Concobar came to hear of this, Naisi and his young wife and his two brothers, with thrice fifty fighting men, thrice fifty women, thrice fifty attendants, and thrice fifty hounds, fled over sea to Alban. And the king of the western part of Alban received them kindly, and took them into military service. Here they remained for a space, gaining daily in favour: but they kept Deirdre apart, fearing evil if the king should see her.

And so matters went on till it chanced that the king's steward, coming one day by Naisi's house, saw the couple as they sat on their couch: and going directly to his master, he said:—

"O king, we have long sought in vain for a woman worthy to be thy wife, and now at last we have found her: for the woman, Deirdre, who is with Naisi, is worthy to be the wife of the king of the western world. And now I give thee this counsel:—Let Naisi be killed, and then take thou Deirdre for thy wife."

The king basely agreed to do so; and forthwith he laid a plot to slay the sons of Usna; which matter coming betimes to the ears of the brothers, they fled by night with all their people. And when they had got to a safe distance, they took up their abode in a wild place, where with much ado they obtained food by hunting and fishing. And the brothers built them three hunting booths in the forest, a little distance from that part of the seashore looking towards Erin: and the booth in which their food was prepared, in that they did not eat; and the one in which they ate, in that they did not sleep. And their people in like manner built themselves booths and huts, which gave them but scant shelter from wind and weather.

Now when it came to the ears of the Ultonians, that the sons of Usna and their people were in discomfort and danger, they were sorely grieved: but they kept their thoughts to themselves, for they dared not speak their mind to the king.

CHAPTER II

CONCOBAR'S GUILEFUL MESSAGE

At this same time a right joyous and very splendid feast was given by Concobar in Emain Macha to the nobles and the knights of his household. And the number of the kings's household that sat them down in the great hall of Emain on that occasion was five and three score above six hundred and one thousand. Then arose, in turn, their musicians to sound their melodious harpstrings, and their poets and their story-tellers to sing their sweet poetic strains, and to recount the deeds of the mighty heroes of the olden time. And the feasting and the enjoyment went on, and the entire assembly were gay and cheerful. At length Concobar arose from where he sat high up on his royal seat; whereupon the noise of mirth was instantly hushed. And he raised his kingly voice and said:—

"I desire to know from you, ye Nobles and Knights of the Red Branch, have you ever seen in any quarter of Erin a house better than this house of Emain, which is my mansion: and whether you see any want in it."

And they answered that they saw no better house, and that they knew of no want in it.

And the king said: "I know of a great want: namely, that we have not present among us the three noble sons of Usna. And why now should they be in banishment on account of any woman in the world?"

And the nobles replied:—"Truly it is a sad thing that the sons of Usna, our dear comrades, should be in exile and distress. They were a shield of defence to Ulaid: and now, O king, it will please us well that thou send for them and bring them back, lest they and their people perish by famine or fall by their enemies."

"Let them come," replied Concobar, "and make submission to me: and their homes, and their lands, and their places among the Knights of the Red Branch shall be restored to them."

Now Concobar was mightily enraged at the marriage and flight of Naisi and Deirdre, though he hid his mind from all men; and he spoke these words pretending forgiveness and friendship. But there was guile in his heart, and he planned to allure them back to Ulaid that he might kill them.

When the feast was ended, and the company had departed, the king called unto him Fergus mac Roy, and said:—"Go thou, Fergus, and bring back the sons of Usna and their people. I promise thee that I will receive them as friends should be received, and that what awaits them here is not enmity or injury, but welcome and friendship. Take my message of peace and good will, and give thyself as pledge and surety for their safety. But these two things I charge thee to do:—That the moment you land in Ulaid on your way back, you proceed straight to Barach's house which stands on the sea cliff high over the landing place fronting Alban: and that whether the time of your arrival be by day or by night, thou see that the sons of Usna tarry not, but let them come hither direct to Emain, that they may not eat food in Erin till they eat of mine."

And Fergus, suspecting no evil design, promised to do as the king directed: for he was glad to be sent on this errand, being a fast friend to the sons of Usna.

Fergus set out straightway, bringing with him only his two sons, Illan the Fair and Buinni the Red, and his shield-bearer to carry his shield. And as soon as he had departed, Concobar sent for Barach and said to him:

"Prepare a feast in thy house for Fergus: and when he visits thee returning with the sons of Usna, invite him to partake of it." And Barach there-

312

upon departed for his home to do the bidding of the king and prepare the feast.

Now those heroes of old, on the day they received knighthood, were wont to make certain pledges, which were to bind them for life, some binding themselves to one thing, some to another. And as they made the promises on the faith of their knighthood, with great vows, in presence of kings and nobles, they dared not violate them; no, not even if it was to save the lives of themselves and all their friends: for whosoever broke through his knighthood pledge was foully dishonoured for evermore. And one of Fergus's obligations was never to refuse an invitation to a banquet: a thing which was well known to King Concobar and to Barach.

As to Fergus mac Roy and his sons: they went on board their galley and put to sea, and made no delay till they reached the harbour nigh the campment of the sons of Usna. And coming ashore, Fergus gave the loud shout of a mighty man of chase. The sons of Usna were at that same hour in their booth; and Naisi and Deirdre were sitting with a polished chessboard between them playing a game.

And when they heard the shout, Naisi said:—"That is the call of a man from Erin."

"Not so," replied Deirdre, "it is the call of a man of Alban."

And after a little time when a second shout came, Naisi said:—"That of a certainty is the call of a man of Erin!"

But Deirdre again replied: "No, indeed: it concerns us not: let us play our game."

But when a third shout came sounding louder than those before, Naisi arose and said:—"Now I know the voice: that is the shout of Fergus!" And straightway he sent Ardan to the shore to meet him.

Now Deirdre knew the voice of Fergus from the first: but she kept her thoughts to herself: for her heart misgave her that the visit boded evil. And when she told Naisi that she knew the first shout, he said:— "Why, my queen, didst thou conceal it then?"

And she replied:—"Lo, I saw a vision in my sleep last night: three bird came to us from Emain Macha, with three drops of honey in their beaks, and they left us the honey and took away three drops of our blood."

"What dost thou read from that vision, O princess?" said Naisi.

"It denotes the message from Concobar to us," said Deirdre; "for sweet as honey is the message of peace from a false man, while he has thoughts of blood hidden deep in his heart."

When Ardan arrived at the shore, the sight of Fergus and his two sons was to him like rain on the parched grass; for it was long since he had seen any of his dear comrades from Erin. And he cried out as he came near, "An affectionate welcome to you, my dear companions": and he fell on Fergus's neck and kissed his cheeks, and did the like to his sons. Then he brought them to the hunting-booth; and Naisi, Ainnli, and Deirdre gave them a like kind welcome: after which they asked the news from Erin.

"The best news I have," said Fergus, "is that Concobar has sent me to you with kindly greetings, to bring you back to Emain and restore you to your lands and homes, and to your places in the Red Branch; and I am myself a pledge for your safety."

"It is not meet for them to go," said Deirdre: "for here they are under no man's rule; and their sway in Alban is even as great as the sway of Concobar in Erin."

But Fergus said: "One's mother country is better than all else, and gloomy is life when a man sees not his home each morning."

"Far dearer to me is Erin than Alban," said Naisi, "even though my sway should be greater here."

It was not with Deirdre's consent he spoke these words: and she still earnestly opposed their return to Erin.

But Fergus tried to re-assure her:—"If all the men of Erin were against you," said he, "it would avail nought once I have passed my word for your safety."

"We trust in thee," said Naisi, "and we will go with thee to Erin."

CHAPTER III

THE RETURN TO EMAIN

Going next morning on board their galleys, Fergus and his companions put out on the wide sea: and oar and wind bore them on swiftly till they landed on the shore of Erin near the house of Barach.

And Deirdre, seating herself on a cliff, looked sadly over the waters at the blue headlands of Alban: and she uttered this farewell:

I

"Dear to me is yon eastern land: Alban with its wonders. Beloved is Alban with its bright harbours and its pleasant hills of the green slopes. From that land I would never depart except to be with Naisi.

314

II

"Kil-Cuan, O Kil-Cuan, whither Ainnli was wont to resort: short seemed the time to me while I sojourned there with Naisi on the margins of its streams and waterfalls.

III

"Glen-Lee, O Glen-Lee, where I slept happy under soft coverlets: fish and fowl, and the flesh of red deer and badgers; these were our fare in Glen-Lee.

IV

"Glen-Masan, O Glen-Masan: tall its cresses of white stalks: often were we rocked to sleep in our curragh in the grassy harbour of Glen-Masan.

V

"Glen-Orchy, O Glen-Orchy: over thy straight glen rises the smooth ridge that oft echoed to the voices of our hounds. No man of the clan was more light-hearted than my Naisi when following the chase in Glen-Orchy.

VI

"Glen-Ettive, O Glen-Ettive: there it was that my first house was raised for me: lovely its woods in the smile of the early morn: the sun loves to shine on Glen-Ettive.

VII

"Glen-da-Roy, O Glen-da-Roy: the memory of its people is dear to me: sweet is the cuckoo's note from the bending bough on the peak over Glen-da-Roy.

VIII

"Dear to me is Dreenagh over the resounding shore: dear to me its

315

crystal waters over the speckled sand. From those sweet places I would never depart, but only to be with my beloved Naisi."

After this they entered the house of Barach; and when Barach had welcomed them, he said to Fergus: "Here I have a three-days' banquet ready for thee, and I invite thee to come and partake of it."

When Fergus heard this, his heart sank and his face waxed all over a crimson red: and he said fiercely to Barach:—"Thou hast done an evil thing to ask me to this banquet: for well thou knowest I cannot refuse thee. Thou knowest, too, that I am under solemn pledge to send the Sons of Usna this very hour to Emain: and if I remain feasting in thy house, how shall I see that my promise of safety is respected?"

But none the less did Barach persist; for he was one of the partners in Concobar's treacherous design.

Then Fergus turned to Naisi and said:—"I dare not violate my knighthood promise: what am I to do in this strait?" But Deirdre answered for her husband:—"The choice is before thee, Fergus; and it is more meet for thee to abandon thy feast than to abandon the sons of Usna, who have come over on thy pledge."

Then Fergus was in sore perplexity; and pondering a little he said:—"I will not forsake the sons of Usna: for I will send with them to Emain Macha my two sons, Illan the Fair and Buinni the Red, who will be their pledge instead of me."

But Naisi said: "We need not thy sons for guard or pledge: we have ever been accustomed to defend ourselves!" And he moved from the place in great wrath: and his two brothers, and Deirdre, and the two sons of Fergus followed him, with the rest of the clan; while Fergus remained behind silent and gloomy: for his heart misgave him that mischief was brewing for the sons of Usna.

Then Deirdre tried to persuade the sons of Usna to go to Rathlin, between Erin and Alban, and tarry there till Barach's feast was ended: but they did not consent to do so, for they deemed it would be a mark of cowardice: and they sped on by the shortest ways towards Emain Macha.

When now they had come to Fincarn of the Watch-tower on Slieve Fuad, Deirdre and her attendants stayed behind the others a little: and she fell asleep. And when Naisi missed her, he turned back and found her just awakening; and he said to her:—"Why didst thou tarry, my princess?"

And she answered:—"I fell asleep and had a dream. And this is what I saw in my dream:—Illan the Fair took your part: Buinni the Red did not: and I saw Illan without his head: but Buinni had neither wound nor hurt."

"Alas, O beauteous princess," said Naisi, "thou utterest nought but evil forebodings: but the king is true and will not break his plighted word."

So they fared on till they had come to the Ridge of the Willows, an hour's journey from the palace: and Deirdre, looking upwards in great fear, said to Naisi:—"O Naisi, see yonder cloud in the sky over Emain, a fearful chilling cloud of a blood-red tinge: a baleful red cloud that bodes disaster! Come ye now to Dundalgan and abide there with the mighty hero Cuculainn till Fergus returns from Barach's feast; for I fear Concobar's treachery."

But Naisi answered:—"We cannot follow thy advice, beloved Deirdre, for it would be a mark of fear: and we have no fear."

And as they came nigh the palace Deirdre said to them:—"I will now give you a sign if Concobar meditates good or evil. If you are brought into his own mansion where he sits surrounded by his nobles, to eat and drink with him, this is a token that he means no ill; for no man will injure a guest that has partaken of food at his table: but if you are sent to the house of the Red Branch, be sure he is bent on treachery."

When at last they arrived at the palace, they knocked loudly with the handwood: and the door-keeper swang the great door wide open. And when he had spoken with them, he went and told Concobar that the sons of Usna and Fergus's two sons had come, with their people.

And Concobar called to him his stewards and attendants and asked them:—"How is it in the house of the Red Branch as to food and drink?" And they replied that if the seven battalions of Ulaid were to come to it, they would find enough of all good things. "If that is so," said Concobar, "take the sons of Usna and their people to the Red Branch."

Even then Deirdre besought them not to enter the Red Branch: for she deemed now that of a certainty there was mischief afoot. But Illan the Fair said:—"Never did we show cowardice or unmanliness, and we shall not do so now." Then she was silent and went with them into the house.

And the company, when they had come in, sat them down so that they filled the great hall: and alluring viands and delicious drinks were set before them: and they ate and drank till they became satisfied and cheerful: all except Deirdre and the sons of Usna, who did not partake much of food or drink. And Naisi asked for the king's chessboard and chessmen; which were brought: and he and Deirdre began to play.

317

CHAPTER IV

TROUBLE LOOMING

Let us now speak of Concobar. As he sat among his nobles, the thought of Deirdre came into his mind, and he said:—"Who among you will go to the Red Branch and bring me tidings of Deirdre, whether her youthful shape and looks still live upon her: for if so there is not on the ridge of the world a woman more beautiful." And Lavarcam said she would go.

Now the sons of Usna were very dear to Lavarcam: and Naisi was dearer than the others. And rising up she went to the Red Branch, where she found Naisi and Deirdre with the chessboard between them, playing. And she saluted them affectionately: and she embraced Deirdre, and wept over her, and kissed her many times with the eagerness of her love: and she kissed the cheeks of Naisi and of his brothers.

And when her loving greeting was ended, she said:—" Beloved children, evil is the deed that is to be done this night in Emain: for the three torches of valour of the Gaels will be treacherously assailed, and Concobar is certainly resolved to put them to death. And now set your people on guard, and bolt and bar all doors, and close all windows; and be steadfast and valorous, and defend your dear charge manfully, if you may hold the assailants at bay till Fergus comes." And she departed weeping piteously.

And when Lavarcam had returned to Concobar he asked what tidings she brought. "Good tidings have I," said she: "for the three sons of Usna have come, the three valiant champions of Ulaid: and now that they are with thee, O king, thou wilt hold sway in Erin without dispute. And bad tidings I bring also: Deirdre indeed is not as she was, for her youthful form and the splendour of her countenance have fled from her."

And when Concobar heard this, his jealousy abated, and he joined in the feasting.

But again the thought of Deirdre came to him, and he asked:—"Who now will go for me to the Red Branch, and bring me further tidings of Deirdre and of the sons of Usna?" for he distrusted Lavarcam. But the Knights of the Red Branch had misgivings of some evil design, and all remained silent.

Then he called to him Trendorn, one of the lesser chiefs: and he said:—"Knowest thou, Trendorn, who slew thy father and thy three brothers in battle?" And Trendorn answered:—"Verily, it was Naisi, the son of Usna, that slew them." Then the king said:—"Go now to the Red Branch and bring me back tidings of Deirdre and of the sons of Usna."

Trendorn went right willingly. But when he found the doors and windows of the Red Branch shut up, he was seized with fear, and he said:—"It is not safe to approach the sons of Usna, for they are surely in wrathful mood: nevertheless I must needs bring back tidings to the king."

Whereupon, not daring to knock at the door, he climbed nimbly to a small window high up that had been unwittingly left open, through which he viewed the spacious banquet hall, and saw Naisi and Deirdre playing chess. Deirdre chanced to look up at that moment, and seeing the face of the spy with eyes intently gazing on her, she started with affright and grasped Naisi's arm, as he was making a move with the chessman. Naisi, following her gaze, and seeing the evil-looking face, flung the chessman with unerring aim, and broke the eye in Trendorn's head.

Trendorn dropped down in pain and rage; and going straight to Concobar, he said:—"I have tidings for thee, O king: the three sons of Usna are sitting in the banquet hall, stately and proud like kings: and Deirdre is seated beside Naisi; and verily for beauty and queenly grace her peer cannot be found."

When Concobar heard this, a flame of jealousy and fury blazed up in his heart, and he resolved that by no means should the sons of Usna escape the doom he planned for them.

CHAPTER V

THE ATTACK ON THE SONS OF USNA

Coming forth on the lawn of Emain, King Concobar now ordered a large body of hireling troops to beset the Red Branch: and he bade them force the doors and bring forth the sons of Usna. And they uttered three dreadful shouts of defiance, and assailed the house on every side; but the strong oak stood bravely, and they were not able to break through doors or walls. So they heaped up great piles of wood and brambles, and kindled them till the red flames blazed round the house.

Buinni the Red now stood up and said to the sons of Usna:—"To me be entrusted the task to repel this first assault: for I am your pledge in place of my father." And marshalling his men, and causing the great door to be thrown wide open, he sallied forth and scattered the assailants, and put out the fires: slaying thrice fifty hirelings in that onslaught.

But Buinni returned not to the Red Branch: for the king sent to him

319

with a secret offer of great favours and bribes: namely, his own royal friendship, and a fruitful tract of land; which Buinni took and basely abandoned the sons of Usna. But none the better luck came to him of it: for at that same hour a blight fell on the land, so that it became a moor, waste and profitless, which is at this day called Slieve Fuad.

When Illan the Fair became aware of his brother's treason, he was grieved to the heart, and he said:—"I am the second pledge in place of my father for the sons of Usna, and of a certainty I will not betray them: while this straight sword lives in my hand I will be faithful: and I will now repel this second attack." For at this time the king's hirelings were again thundering at the doors.

Forth he issued with his band: and he made three quick furious circuits round the Red Branch, scattering the troops as he went: after which he returned to the mansion and found Naisi and Deirdre still playing. But as the hireling hordes returned to the attack, he went forth a second time and fell on them, dealing death and havoc whithersoever he went.

Then, while the fight was still raging, Concobar called to him his son Ficra, and said to him:—"Thou and Illan the Fair were born on the same night: and as he has his father's arms, so thou take mine, namely, my shield which is called the Ocean, and my two spears which are called Dart and Slaughter, and my great sword, the Blue-green blade. And bear thyself manfully against him, and vanquish him, else none of my troops will survive."

Ficra did so and went against Illan the Fair; and they made a stout, warlike, red-wounding attack on each other, while the others looked on anxious: but none dared to interfere. And it came to pass that Illan prevailed, so that Ficra was fain to shelter himself behind his father's shield the Ocean, and he was like to be slain. Whereupon the shield moaned, and the Three Waves of Erin uttered their hollow melancholy roar.

The hero Conall Carnagh, sitting in his dun afar off, heard the moan of the shield and the roar of the Wave of Tuath: and springing up from where he sat, he said: "Verily, the king is in danger: I will go to his rescue."

He ran with the swiftness of the wind, and arrived on the Green of Emain, where the two young heroes were fighting. Thinking it was Concobar that crouched beneath the shield, he attacked Illan, not knowing him, and wounded him even unto death. And Illan looking up said, "Is it thou, Conall? Alas, dreadful is the deed thou hast done, not knowing me, and not knowing that I am fighting in defence of the sons of Usna, who are now in deadly peril from the treachery of Concobar."

And Conall, finding he had unwittingly wounded his dear young friend

Illan, turned in his grief and rage on the other, and swept off his head.
And he stalked fierce and silent out of the battlefield.

Illan, still faithful to his charge, called aloud to Naisi to defend himself
bravely: then putting forth his remaining strength, he flung his arms,
namely, his sword and his spears and his shield, into the Red Branch;
and falling prone on the green sward, the shades of death dimmed his
eyes, and his life departed.

And now when it was the dusk of evening, another great battalion of
the hirelings assailed the Red Branch, and kindled faggots around it: whereupon Ardan sallied out with his valorous band and scattered them, and
put out the fires, and held guard for the first third of the night. And during
the second third Ainnli kept them at bay.

Then Naisi took his turn, issuing forth, and fought with them till the
morning's dawn: and until the sands of the seashore, or the leaves of the
forest, or the dew-drops on the grass, or the stars of heaven are counted,
it will not be possible to number the hirelings that were slain in that fight
by Naisi and his band of heroes.

And as he was returning breathless from the rout, all grimy and terrible
with blood and sweat, he spied Lavarcam, as she stood watching the battle
anxiously; and he said:—"Go, Lavarcam, go and stand on the outer
rampart, and cast thine eyes eastwards, if perchance thou shouldst see
Fergus and his men coming."

For many of Naisi's brave followers had fallen in these encounters: and
he doubted that he and the others could sustain much longer the continual
assaults of superior numbers. And Lavarcam went, but returned downcast,
saying she saw nought eastwards, but the open plain with the peaceful
herds browsing over it.

Chapter VI

DEATH OF THE SONS OF USNA

Believing now that they could no longer defend the Red Branch, Naisi
took council with his brothers; and what they resolved on was this:
—To sally forth with all their men and fight their way to a place of safety.
Then making a close, firm fence of shields and spears round Deirdre,
they marched out in solid ranks and attacked the hireling battalions and
slew three hundred in that onslaught.

Concobar, seeing the rout of his men, and being now sure that it was not possible to subdue the sons of Usna in open fight, cast about if he might take them by falsehood and craft. And sending for Caffa, the druid, who loved them, he said:

"These sons of Usna are brave men, and it is our pleasure to receive them back into our service. Go now unto them, for thou art their loved friend; and say to them that if they lay down their arms and submit to me, I will restore them to favour and give them their places among the Red Branch Knights. And I pledge thee my kingly word and my troth as a true knight, that no harm shall befall them."

Caffa, by no means distrusting him, went to the sons of Usna, and told them all the king had said. And they, suspecting neither guile nor treachery, joyfully threw their swords and spears aside, and went towards the king to make submission. But now, while they stood defenceless, the king caused them to be seized and bound. Then, turning aside, he sought for some one to put them to death; but he found no man of the Ultonians willing to do so.

Among his followers was a foreigner named Maini of the Rough Hand, whose father and two brothers had fallen in battle by Naisi: and this man undertook to kill the sons of Usna.

When they were brought forth to their doom, Ardan said:—"I am the youngest: let me be slain first, that I may not see the death of my brothers." And Ainnli earnestly pleaded for the same thing for himself, saying that he was born before Ardan, and should die before him.

But Naisi said:—"Lo, I have a sword, the gift of Mannanan mac Lir, which leaves no remnant unfinished after a blow: let us be struck with it, all three together, and we shall die at the same moment."

This was agreed to: and the sword was brought forth, and they laid their heads close together, and Maini swept off all three with one blow of the mighty sword. And when it became known that the sons of Usna were dead, the men of Ulaid sent forth three great cries of grief and lamentation.

As for Deirdre, she cried aloud, and tore her golden hair, and became like one distracted. And after a time, when her calmness had a little returned, she uttered a lament:

I

"Three lions of the hill are dead, and I am left alone to weep for them. The generous princes who made the stranger welcome have been guilefully lured to their doom.

II

"The three strong hawks of Slieve Cullinn, a king's three sons, strong and gentle: willing obedience was yielded to them by heroes who had conquered many lands.

III

"Three generous heroes of the Red Branch, who loved to praise the valour of others: three props of the battalions of Quelna: their fall is the cause of bitter grief.

IV

"Ainnli and Ardan, haughty and fierce in battle, to me were ever loving and gentle: Naisi, Naisi, beloved spouse of my choice, thou canst not hear thy Deirdre lamenting thee.

V

"When they brought down the fleet red deer in the chase, when they speared the salmon skilfully in the clear water, joyful and proud were they if I looked on.

VI

"Often when my feeble feet grew weary wandering along the valleys, and climbing the hills to view the chase, often would they bear me home lightly on their linked shields and spears.

VII

"It was gladness of heart to be with the sons of Usna: long and weary is the day without their company: short will be my span of life since they have left me.

VIII

"Sorrow and tears have dimmed my eyes, looking at the grave of Naisi: a dark deadly sickness has seized my heart: I cannot, I cannot live after Naisi.

IX

"O thou who diggest the new grave, make it deep and wide: let it be a grave for four; for I will sleep for ever beside my beloved."

When she had spoken these words, she fell beside the body of Naisi and died immediately. And a great cairn of stones was piled over their grave, and their names were inscribed in Ogham, and their funeral rites were performed.

This is the sorrowful tale of The Fate of the Sons of Usna.

UNITED STATES

RAPPACCINI'S DAUGHTER[1]

[From the Writings of Aubépine]

Nathaniel Hawthorne

WE DO not remember to have seen any translated specimens of the productions of M. de l'Aubépine,—a fact the less to be wondered at, as his very name is unknown to many of his own countrymen as well as to the student of foreign literature. As a writer, he seems to occupy an unfortunate position between the Transcendentalists (who, under one name or another, have their share in all the current literature of the world) and the great body of pen-and-ink men who address the intellect and sympathies of the multitude. If not too refined, at all events too remote, too shadowy and unsubstantial in his modes of development, to suit the taste of the latter class, and yet too popular to satisfy the spritual or metaphysical requisitions of the former, he must necessarily find himself without an audience, except here and there an individual or possibly an isolated clique. His writings, to do them justice, are not altogether destitute of fancy and originality; they might have won him greater reputation but for an inveterate love of allegory, which is apt to invest his plots and characters with the aspect of scenery and people in the clouds and to steal away the human warmth out of his conceptions. His fictions are sometimes historical, sometimes of the present day, and sometimes, so far as can be discovered, have little or no reference either to time or space. In any case, he generally contents himself with a very slight embroidery of outward manners,—the faintest possible counterfeit of real life,—and endeavours to create an interest by some less obvious peculiarity of the subject. Occasionally a breath of Nature, a raindrop of pathos and tenderness, or a gleam of humour, will find its way into the midst of his fantastic imagery, and make us feel as if, after all, we were yet within the limits of our native earth. We will only add to this very cursory notice that M. de l'Aubépine's productions, if the reader chance to take them in precisely the proper point of view, may amuse a leisure hour as well as

---

[1] From *Mosses from an Old Manse*.

those of a brighter man; if otherwise, they can hardly fail to look excessively like nonsense.

Our author is voluminous; he continues to write and publish with as much praiseworthy and indefatigable prolixity as if his efforts were crowned with the brilliant success that so justly attends those of Eugene Sue. His first appearance was by a collection of stories in a long series of volumes entitled *Contes deux fois racontées*. The titles of some of his more recent works (we quote from memory) are as follows: *Le Voyage Céleste à Chemin de Fer*, 3 tom., 1838. *Le nouveau Père Adam et la nouvelle Mère Eve*, 2 tom., 1839. *Roderic; ou le Serpent à l'estomac*, 2 tom., 1840. *Le Culte du Feu*, a folio volume of ponderous research into the religion and ritual of the old Persian Ghebers, published in 1841. *La Soirée du Chateau en Espagne*, 1 tom. 8vo, 1842; and *L'Artiste du Beau; ou le Papillon Mécanique*, 5 tom. 4to, 1843. Our somewhat wearisome perusal of this startling catalogue of volumes has left behind it a certain personal affection and sympathy, though by no means admiration, for M. de l'Aubépine; and we would fain do the little in our power towards introducing him favourably to the American public. The ensuing tale is a translation of his *Beatrice; ou la Belle Empoisouneuse*, recently published in *La Revue Anti-Aristocratique*. This journal, edited by the Comte de Bearhaven, has for some years past led the defence of liberal principles and popular rights with a faithfulness and ability worthy of all praise.

A young man, named Giovanni Guasconti, came, very long ago, from the more southern region of Italy, to pursue his studies at the University of Padua. Giovanni, who had but a scanty supply of gold ducats in his pocket, took lodgings in a high and gloomy chamber of an old edifice which looked not unworthy to have been the palace of a Paduan noble, and which, in fact, exhibited over its entrance the armorial bearings of a family long since extinct. The young stranger, who was not unstudied in the great poem of his country, recollected that one of the ancestors of this family, and perhaps an occupant of this very mansion, had been pictured by Dante as a partaker of the immortal agonies of his Inferno. These reminiscences and associations, together with the tendency to heartbreak natural to a young man for the first time out of his native sphere, caused Giovanni to sigh heavily as he looked around the desolate and ill-furnished apartment.

"Holy Virgin, signor!" cried old Dame Lisabetta, who, won by the youth's remarkable beauty of person, was kindly endeavouring to give the chamber a habitable air, "what a sigh was that to come out of a young man's heart! Do you find this old mansion gloomy? For the love of Heaven, then, put your head out of the window, and you will see as bright sunshine as you have left in Naples."

Guasconti mechanically did as the old woman advised, but could not quite agree with her that the Paduan sunshine was as cheerful as that of Southern Italy. Such as it was, however, it fell upon a garden beneath the window and expended its fostering influences on a variety of plants, which seemed to have been cultivated with exceeding care.

"Does this garden belong to the house?" asked Giovanni.

"Heaven forbid, signor, unless it were fruitful of better potherbs than any that grow there now," answered old Lisabetta. "No; that garden is cultivated by the own hands of Signor Giacomo Rappaccini, the famous doctor, who, I warrant him, has been heard of as far as Naples. It is said that he distils these plants into medicines that are as potent as a charm. Oftentimes you may see the signor doctor at work, and perchance the signora, his daughter, too, gathering the strange flowers that grow in the garden."

The old woman had now done what she could for the aspect of the chamber; and, commending the young man to the protection of the saints, took her departure.

Giovanni still found no better occupation than to look down into the garden beneath his window. From its appearance, he judged it to be one of those botanic gardens which were of earlier date in Padua than else-where in Italy or in the world. Or, not improbably, it might once have been the pleasure-place of an opulent family; for there was the ruin of a marble fountain in the centre, sculptured with rare art, but so wofully shattered that it was impossible to trace the original design from the chaous of remaining fragments. The water, however, continued to gush and sparkle into the sunbeams as cheerfully as ever. A little gurgling sound ascended to the young man's window and made him feel as if the fountain were an immortal spirit, that sung its song unceasingly and without heeding the vicissitudes around it, while one century embodied it in marble and another scattered the perishable garniture on the soil. All about the pool into which the water subsided grew various plants, that seemed to require a plentiful supply of moisture for the nourishment of gigantic leaves, and, in some instances, flowers gorgeously magnificent. There was one shrub in particular, set in a marble vase in the midst of the pool, that bore a profusion of purple blossoms, each of which had the lustre and richness of a gem; and the whole together made a show so resplendent, that it seemed enough to illuminate the garden, even had there been no sunshine. Every portion of the soil was peopled with plants and herbs, which, if less beautiful, still bore tokens of assiduous care, as if all had their individual virtues, known to the scientific mind that fostered them. Some were placed in urns, rich with old carving, and others in common garden-pots; some crept serpent-like along the ground or climbed on high, using whatever means of ascent was offered them. One plant had wreathed itself round a statue of Vertumnus, which was thus quite veiled and shrouded in a drapery of hanging foliage, so happily arranged that it might have served a sculptor for a study.

While Giovanni stood at the window he heard a rustling behind a screen of leaves, and became aware that a person was at work in the garden. His figure soon emerged into view, and showed itself to be that of no common labourer, but a tall, emaciated, sallow, and sickly-looking man, dressed in a scholar's garb of black. He was beyond the middle term of life, with grey hair, a thin, grey beard, and a face singularly marked with intellect and cultivation, but which could never, even in his more youthful days, have expressed much warmth of heart.

Nothing could exceed the intentness with which this scientific gardener examined every shrub which grew in his path: it seemed as if he was looking into their inmost nature, making observations in regard to their creative essence, and discovering why one leaf grew in this shape and another in that, and wherefore such and such flowers differed among themselves in hue and perfume. Nevertheless, in spite of this deep intelligence on his part, there was no approach to intimacy between himself and these vege-table existences. On the contrary, he avoided their actual touch or the direct inhaling of their odours with a caution that impressed Giovanni most disagreeably; for the man's demeanour was that of one walking among malignant influences, such as savage beasts, or deadly snakes, or evil spirits, which should he allow them one moment of licence, would wreak upon him some terrible fatality. It was strangely frightful to the young man's imagination to see this air of insecurity in a person cultivating a garden, that most simple and innocent of human toils, and which had been alike the joy and labour of the unfallen parents of the race. Was this garden, then, the Eden of the present world? And this man, with such a perception of harm in what his own hands caused to grow,—was he the Adam?

The distrustful gardener, while plucking away the dead leaves or pruning the too luxuriant growth of the shrubs, defended his hands with a pair of thick gloves. Nor were these his only armour. When, in his walk through the garden, he came to the magnificent plant that hung its purple gems beside the marble fountain, he placed a kind of mask over his mouth and nostrils, as if all this beauty did but conceal a deadlier malice; but, finding his task still too dangerous, he drew back, removed the mask, and called loudly, but in the infirm voice of a person affected with inward disease,—

"Beatrice! Beatrice!"

"Here am I, my father. What would you?" cried a rich and youthful voice from the window of the opposite house,—a voice as rich as a tropical sunset, and which made Giovanni, though he knew not why, think of deep hues of purple or crimson and of perfumes heavily delectable. "Are you in the garden?"

"Yes, Beatrice," answered the gardener; "and I need your help."

Soon there emerged from under a sculptured portal the figure of a young girl, arrayed with as much richness of taste as the most splendid of the flowers, beautiful as the day, and with a bloom so deep and vivid that one shade more would have been too much. She looked redundant with life, health, and energy; all of which attributes were bound down and compressed, as it were, and girdled tensely, in their luxuriance, by her virgin zone. Yet Giovanni's fancy must have grown morbid while he looked down into the garden; for the impression which the fair stranger made upon him was as if here were another flower, the human sister of those vegetable ones, as beautiful as they, more beautiful than the richest of them, but still to be touched only with a glove, nor to be approached without a mask. As Beatrice came down the garden path, it was observable that she handled and inhaled the odour of several of the plants which her father had most sedulously avoided.

"Here, Beatrice," said the latter, "see how many needful offices require to be done to our chief treasure. Yet, shattered as I am, my life might pay the penalty of approaching it so closely as circumstances demand. Henceforth, I fear, this plant must be consigned to your sole charge."

"And gladly will I undertake it," cried again the rich tones of the young lady, as she bent towards the magnificent plant and opened her arms as if to embrace it. "Yes, my sister, my splendour, it shall be Beatrice's task to nurse and serve thee; and thou shalt reward her with thy kisses and perfumed breath, which to her is as the breath of life."

Then, with all the tenderness in her manner that was so strikingly expressed in her words, she busied herself with such attentions as the plant seemed to require; and Giovanni, at his lofty window, rubbed his eyes, and almost doubted whether it were a girl tending her favourite flower, or one sister performing the duties of affection to another. The scene soon terminated. Whether Dr Rappaccini had finished his labours in the garden, or that his watchful eye had caught the stranger's face, he now took his daughter's arm and retired. Night was already closing in; oppressive exhalations seemed to proceed from the plants and steal upward past the open window; and Giovanni, closing the lattice, went to his couch and dreamed of a rich flower and beautiful girl. Flower and maiden were different, and yet the same, and fraught with some strange peril in either shape.

But there is an influence in the light of morning that tends to rectify whatever errors of fancy, or even of judgement, we may have incurred during the sun's decline, or among the shadows of the night, or in the less wholesome glow of moonshine. Giovanni's first movement, on starting from sleep, was to throw open the window and gaze down into the garden which his dreams had made so fertile of mysteries. He was surprised, and a little ashamed, to find how real and matter-of-fact an affair it proved to be, in the first rays of the sun which gilded the dewdrops that hung upon leaf and blossom, and, while giving a brighter beauty to each rare flower, brought everything within the limits of ordinary experience. The young man rejoiced that, in the heart of the barren city, he had the privilege of overlooking this spot of lovely and luxuriant vegetation. It would serve, he said to himself, as a symbolic language to keep him in communion with nature. Neither the sickly and thought-worn Dr Giacomo Rappaccini, it is true, nor his brilliant daughter, were now visible; so that Giovanni could not determine how much of the singularity which he attributed to both was due to their own qualities and how much to his wonder-working fancy; but he was inclined to take a most rational view of the whole matter.

In the course of the day he paid his respects to Signor Pietro Baglioni, professor of medicine in the university, a physician of eminent repute, to whom Giovanni had brought a letter of introduction. The professor was an elderly personage, apparently of genial nature and habits that might almost be called jovial. He kept the young man to dinner, and made himself very agreeable by the freedom and liveliness of his conversation, especially when warmed by a flask or two or Tuscan wine. Giovanni, conceiving that men of science, inhabitants of the same city, must needs be on familiar terms with one another, took an opportunity to mention the name of Dr Rappaccini. But the professor did not respond with so much cordiality as he had anticipated.

"Ill would it become a teacher of the divine art of medicine," said Professor Pietro Baglioni, in answer to a question of Giovanni, "to withhold due and well-considered praise of a physician so eminently skilled as Rappaccini; but on the other hand, I should answer it but scantily to my conscience were I to permit a worthy youth like yourself, Signor Giovanni, the son of an ancient friend, to imbibe erroneous ideas respecting a man who might hereafter chance to hold your life and death in his hands. The truth is, our worshipful Dr Rappaccini has as much science as any member of the faculty—with perhaps one single exception—in Padua, or all Italy; but there are certain grave objections to his professional character."

"And what are they?" asked the young man.

"Has my friend Giovanni any disease of body or heart, that he is so inquisitive about physicians?" said the professor, with a smile. "But as for Rappaccini, it is said of him—and I, who know the man well, can answer for its truth—that he cares infinitely more for science than for mankind. His patients are interesting to him only as subjects for some new experiment. He would sacrifice human life, his own among the rest, or whatever else was dearest to him, for the sake of adding so much as a grain of mustard seed to the great heap of his accumulated knowledge."

"Methinks he is an awful man indeed"; remarked Guasconti, mentally recalling the cold and purely intellectual aspect of Rappaccini. "And yet, worshipful professor, is it not a noble spirit? Are there many men capable of so spiritual a love of science?"

"God forbid," answered the professor, somewhat testily; "at least, unless they take sounder views of the healing art than those adopted by Rappaccini. It is his theory that all medicinal virtues are comprised within those substances which we term vegetable poisons. These he cultivates with his own hands, and is said even to have produced new varieties of poison more horribly deleterious than nature, without the assistance of this learned person, would ever have plagued the world withal. That the signor doctor does less mischief than might be expected with such dangerous substances is undeniable. Now and then, it must be owned, he has effected, or seemed to effect, a marvellous cure; but, to tell you my private mind, Signor Giovanni, he should receive little credit for such instances of success,—they being probably the work of chance,—but should be held strictly accountable for his failures, which might justly be considered his own work."

The youth might have taken Baglioni's opinions with many grains of allowance had he known that there was a professional warfare of long continuance between him and Dr Rappaccini, in which the latter was generally thought to have gained the advantage. If the reader be inclined to judge for himself, we refer him to certain black-letter tracts on both sides, preserved in the medical department of the University of Padua.

"I know not, most learned professor," returned Giovanni, after musing on what had been said of Rappaccini's exclusive zeal for science,—"I know not how dearly this physician may love his art; but surely there is one object more dear to him. He has a daughter."

"Aha!" cried the professor, with a laugh. "So now our friend Giovanni's secret is out. You have heard of this daughter, whom all the young men in Padua are wild about, though not half a dozen have ever had the good hap to see her face. I know little of the Signora Beatrice save that Rappaccini is said to have instructed her deeply in his science, and that, young and beautiful as fame reports her, she is already qualified to fill a professor's chair. Perchance her father destines her for mine! Other absurd rumours there be, not worth talking about or listening to. So now, Signor Giovanni, drink off your glass of lachryma."

Guasconti returned to his lodgings somewhat heated with the wine he had quaffed, and which caused his brain to swim with strange fantasies in reference to Dr Rappaccini and the beautiful Beatrice. On his way, happening to pass by a florist's, he bought a fresh bouquet of flowers.

Ascending to his chamber, he seated himself near the window, but within the shadow thrown by the depth of the wall, so that he could look down into the garden with little risk of being discovered. All beneath his eye was a solitude. The strange plants were basking in the sunshine, and now and then nodding gently to one another, as if in acknowledgement of sympathy and kindred. In the midst, by the shattered fountain, grew the magnificent shrub, with its purple gems clustering all over it; they glowed in the air, and gleamed back again out of the depths of the pool, which thus seemed to overflow with coloured radiance from the rich reflection that was steeped in it. At first, as we have said, the garden was a solitude. Soon, however,—as Giovanni had half hoped, half feared, would be the case,—a figure appeared beneath the antique sculptured portal, and came down between the rows of plants, inhaling their various perfumes as if she were one of those beings of old classic fable that lived upon sweet odours. On again beholding Beatrice, the young man was even startled to perceive how much her beauty exceeded his recollection of it; so brilliant, so vivid, was its character, that she glowed amid the sunlight, and, as Giovanni whispered to himself, positively illuminated the more shadowy intervals of the garden path. Her face being now more revealed than on the former occasion, he was struck by its expression of simplicity and sweetness,—qualities that had not entered into his idea of her character, and which made him ask anew what manner of mortal she might be. Nor did he fail again to observe, or imagine, an analogy between the beautiful girl and the gorgeous shrub that hung its gem-like flowers over the fountain,—a resemblance which Beatrice seemed to have indulged a fantastic humour in heightening, both by the arrangement of her dress and the selection of its hues.

Approaching the shrub, she threw open her arms, as with a passionate ardour, and drew its branches into an intimate embrace,—so intimate that her features were hidden in its leafy bosom and her glistening ringlets all intermingled with the flowers.

"Give me thy breath, my sister," exclaimed Beatrice; "for I am faint with common air. And give me this flower of thine, which I separate with gentlest fingers from the stem and place it close beside my heart."

With these words the beautiful daughter of Rappaccini plucked one of the richest blossoms of the shrub, and was about to fasten it in her bossom. But now, unless Giovanni's draughts of wine had bewildered his senses, a singular incident occurred. A small orange-coloured reptile, of the lizard or chameleon species, chanced to be creeping along the path, just at the feet of Beatrice. It appeared to Giovanni,—but, at the distance from which he gazed, he could scarcely have seen anything so minute,—it appeared to him, however, that a drop or two of moisture from the broken stem of the flower descenced upon the lizard's head. For an instant the reptile contorted itself violently, and then lay motionless in the sunshine. Beatrice observed this remarkable phenomenon, and crossed herself, sadly, but without surprise; nor did she therefore hesitate to arrange the fatal flower in her bosom. There it blushed, and almost glimmered with the dazzling effect of a precious stone, adding to her dress and aspect the one appropriate charm which nothing else in the world could have supplied. But Giovanni, out of the shadow of his window, bent forward and shrank back, and murmured and trembled.

"Am I awake? Have I my senses?" said he to himself. "What is this being? Beautiful shall I call her, or inexpressibly terrible?"

Beatrice now strayed carelessly through the garden, approaching closer beneath Giovanni's window, so that he was compelled to thrust his head quite out of its concealment in order to gratify the intense and painful curiosity which she excited. At this moment there came a beautiful insect over the garden wall: it had, perhaps, wandered through the city, and found no flowers or verdure among those antique haunts of men until the heavy perfumes of Dr Rappaccini's shrubs had lured it from afar. Without alighting on the flowers, this winged brightness seemed to be attracted by Beatrice, and lingered in the air and fluttered about her head. Now, here it could not be but that Giovanni Guasconti's eyes deceived him. Be that as it might, he fancied that, while Beatrice was gazing at the insect with childish delight, it grew faint and fell at her feet; its bright wings shivered; it was dead,—from no cause that he could discern, unless it were the atmosphere of her breath. Again Beatrice crossed herself and sighed heavily as she bent over the dead insect.

An impulsive movement of Giovanni drew her eyes to the window. There she beheld the beautiful head of the young man—rather a Grecian than an Italian head, with fair, regular features, and a glistening of gold among his ringlets—gazing down upon her like a being that hovered in mid-air. Scarcely knowing what he did, Giovanni threw down the bouquet which he had hitherto held in his hand.

"Signora," said he, "they are pure and healthful flowers. Wear them for the sake of Giovanni Guasconti."

"Thanks, signor," replied Beatrice, with her rich voice, that came forth as it were like a rush of music, and with a mirthful expression half childish and half woman-like. "I accept your gift, and would fain recompense it with this precious purple flower; but, if I toss it into the air, it will not reach you. So Signor Guasconti must even content himself with my thanks."

She lifted the bouquet from the ground, and then, as if inwardly ashamed at having stepped aside from her maidenly reserve to respond to a stranger's greeting, passed swiftly homeward through the garden. But, few as the moments were, it seemed to Giovanni, when she was on the point of vanishing beneath the sculptured portal, that his beautiful bouquet was already beginning to wither in her grasp. It was an idle throught; there could be no possibility of distingushing a faded flower from a fresh one at so great a distance.

For many days after this incident the young man avoided the window that looked into Dr Rappaccini's garden, as if something ugly and monstrous would have blasted his eyesight had he been betrayed into a glance. He felt conscious of having put himself, to a certain extent, within the influence of an unintelligible power by the communication which he had opened with Beatrice. The wisest course would have been, if his heart were in any real danger, to quit his lodgings and Padua itself at once; the next wiser, to have accustomed himself, as far as possible, to the familiar and daylight view of Beatrice,—thus bringing her rigidly and systematically within the limits of ordinary experience. Least of all, while avoiding her sight, ought Giovanni to have remained so near this extraordinary being that the proximity and possibility even of intercourse should give a kind of substance and reality to the wild vagaries which his imagination ran riot continually in producing. Guasconti had not a deep heart,—or, at all events, its depths were not sounded now; but he had a quick fancy, and an ardent Southern temperament, which rose every instant to a higher fever pitch. Whether or no Beatrice possessed those terrible attributes, that fatal breath, the affinity with those so beautiful and deadly flowers, which were indicated by what Giovanni had witnessed, she had at least instilled a fierce and subtle poison into his system. It was not love, although her rich beauty was a madness to him; nor horror, even while he fancied her spirit to be imbued with the same baneful essence that seemed to pervade her physical frame; but a wild offspring of both love and horror that had each parent in it, and burned like one and shivered like the other. Giovanni knew not what to dread; still less did he know what to hope; yet hope and dread kept a continual warfare in his breast, alternately vanquishing one another and starting up afresh to renew the contest. Blessed are all simple emotions, be they dark or bright! It is the lurid intermixture of the two that produces the illuminating blaze of the infernal regions.

Sometimes he endeavoured to assuage the fever of his spirit by a rapid walk throught the streets of Padua or beyond its gates: his footsteps kept time with the throbbings of his brain, so that the walk was apt to accelerate itself to a race. One day he found himself arrested; his arm was seized by a portly personage, who had turned back on recognizing the young man and expended much breath in overtaking him.

"Signor Giovanni! Stay, my young friend!" cried he. "Have you forgotten me? That might well be the case if I were as much altered as yourself."

It was Baglioni, whom Giovanni had avoided ever since their first meeting, from a doubt that the professor's sagacity would look too deeply into his secrets. Endeavouring to recover himself, he stared forth wildly from his inner world into the outer one and spoke like a man in a dream.

"Yes; I am Giovanni Guasconti. You are Professor Pietro Baglioni. Now let me pass!"

"Not yet, not yet, Signor Giovanni Guasconti," said the professor, smiling, but at the same time scrutinizing the youth with an earnest glance. "What! did I grow up side by side with your father? and shall his son pass me like a stranger in these old streets of Padua? Stand still, Signor Giovanni; for we must have a word or two before we part."

"Speedily, then, most worshipful professor, speedily," said Giovanni, with feverish impatience. "Does not your worship see that I am in haste?"

Now, while he was speaking there came a man in black along the street, stooping and moving feebly, like a person in inferior health. His face was all overspread with a most sickly and sallow hue, but yet so pervaded with an expression of piercing and active intellect that an observer might easily have overlooked the merely physical attributes and have seen only this wonderful energy. As he passed, this person exchanged a cold and distant salution with Baglioni, but fixed his eyes upon Giovanni with an intentness that seemed to bring out whatever was within him worthy of notice. Nevertheless, there was a peculiar quietness in the look, as if taking merely a speculative, not a human, interest in the young man.

"It is Dr Rappaccini!" whispered the professor when the stranger had passed. "Has he ever seen your face before?"

"Not that I know," answered Giovanni, starting at the name.

"He *has* seen you! he must have seen you!" said Baglioni, hastily. "For some purpose or other, this man of science is making a study of you. I know that look of his! It is the same that coldly illuminates his face as he bends over a bird, a mouse, or a butterfly; which, in pursuance of some experiment, he has killed by the perfume of a flower; a look as deep as nature itself, but without nature's warmth of love. Signor Giovanni, I will stake my life upon it, you are the subject of one of Rappaccini's experiments!"

"Will you make a fool of me?" cried Giovanni, passionately. "*That* signor professor, were an untoward experiment."

"Patience! patience!" replied the imperturbable professor. "I tell thee, my poor Giovanni, that Rappaccini has a scientific interest in thee. Thou hast fallen into fearful hands! And the Signora Beatrice,—what part does she act in this mystery?"

But Guasconti, finding Baglioni's pertinacity intolerable, here broke away, and was gone before the professor could again seize his arm. He looked after the young man intently and shook his head.

"This must not be," said Baglioni to himself. "The youth is the son of my old friend, and shall not come to any harm from which the arcana of medical science can perserve him. Besides, it is too insufferable an impertinence in Rappaccini thus to snatch the lad out of my own hands, as I may say, and make use of him for his infernal experiments. This daughter of his! It shall be looked to. Perchance, most learned Rappaccini, I may foil you where you little dream of it!"

Meanwhile Giovanni had pursued a circuitous route, and at length found himself at the door of his lodgings. As he crossed the threshold he was met by old Lisabetta, who smirked and smiled, and was evidently desirous to attract his attention; vainly, however, as the ebullition of his feelings had momentarily subsided into a cold and dull vacuity. He turned his eyes full upon the withered face that was puckering itself into a smile, but seemed to behold it not. The old dame, therefore, laid her grasp upon his cloak.

336

"Signor! signor!" whispered she, still with a smile over the whole breadth of her visage, so that it looked not unlike a grotesque carving in wood, darkened by centuries. "Listen, signor! There is a private entrance into the garden!"

"What do you say?" exclaimed Giovanni, turning quickly about, as if an inanimate thing should start into feverish life. "A private entrance into Dr Rappaccini's garden?"

"Hush! hush! not so loud!' 'whispered Lisabetta, putting her hand over his mouth. "Yes; into the worshipful doctor's garden, where you may see all his fine shrubbery. Many a young man in Padua would give gold to be admitted among those flowers."

Giovanni put a piece of gold into her hand.

"Show me the way," said he.

A surmise, probably excited by his conversation with Baglioni, crossed his mind, that this interpostition of old Lisabetta might perchance be connected with the intrigue, whatever were its nature, in which the professor seemed to suppose that Dr Rappaccini was involving him. But such a suspicion, though it disturbed Giovanni, was inadequate to restrain him. The instant that he was aware of the possibility of approaching Beatrice, it seemed an absolute necessity of his existence to do so. It mattered not whether she were angel or demon; he was irrevocably within her sphere, and must obey the law that whirled him onward, in everlessening circles, towards a result which he did not attempt to foreshadow; and yet, strange to say, there came across him a a sudden doubt whether this intense interest on his part was not delusory; whether it were really of so deep and positive a nature as to justify him in now thrusting himself into a incalculable position; whether it were not merely the fantasy of a young man's brain, only slightly or not at all connected with his heart.

He paused, hesitated, turned half about, but again went on. His withered guide led him along several obscure passages, and finally undid a door, through which, as it was opened, there came the sight and sound of rustling leaves, with the broken sunshine glimmering among them. Giovanni stepped forth, and, forcing himself through the entanglement of a shrub that wreathed its tendrils over the hidden entrance, stood beneath his own window in the open area of Dr Rappaccini's garden.

How often is it the case that, when impossibilities have come to pass, and dreams have condensed their misty substance into tangible realities, we find ourselves calm, and even coldly self-possessed, amid circumstances which it would have been a delirium of joy or agony to anticipate! Fate delights to thwart us thus. Passion will choose his own time to rush upon the scene, and lingers sluggishly behind when an appropriate adjustment of events would seem to summon his appearance. So was it now with Giovanni. Day after day his pulses had throbbed with feverish blood at the improbable idea of an interview with Beatrice, and of standing with her, face to face, in this very garden, basking in the Oriental sunshine of her beauty, and snatching from her full gaze the mystery which he deemed the riddle of his own existence. But now there was a singular and untimely equanimity within his breast. He threw a glance around the garden to discover if Beatrice or her father were present, and, perceiving that he was alone, began a critical observation of the plants.

The aspect of one and all of them dissatisfied him; their gorgeousness seemed fierce, passionate, and even unnatural. There was hardly an individual shrub which a wanderer, straying by himself through a forest, would not have been startled to find growing wild, as if an unearthly face had glared at him out of the thicket. Several also would have shocked a delicate instinct by an appearance of artificialness indicating that there had been such commixture, and, as it were, adultery of various vegetable species, that the production was no longer of God's making, but the monstrous offspring of man's depraved fancy, glowing with only an evil mockery of beauty. They were probably the result of experiment, which in one or two cases had succeeded in mingling plants individually lovely into a compound possessing the questionable and ominous character that distinguished the whole growth of the garden. In fine, Giovanni recognized but two or three plants in the collection, and those of a kind that he well knew to be poisonous. While busy with these contemplations he heard the rustling of a silken garment, and, turning, beheld Beatrice emerging from beneath the sculptured portal.

Giovanni had not considered with himself what should be his deportment; whether he should apologize for his intrusion into the garden, or assume that he was there with the privity at least, if not by the desire, of Dr Rappaccini or his daugher; Beatrice's manner placed him at his ease, though leaving him still in doubt by what agency he had gained admittance. She came lightly along the path, and met him near the broken fountain. There was surprise in her face, but brightened by a simple and kind expression of pleasure.

"You are a connoisseur in flowers, signor," said Beatrice, with a smile, alluding to the bouquet which he had flung her from the window. "It is no marvel, therefore, if the sight of my father's rare collection has tempted you to take a nearer view. If he were here he could tell you many strange and interesting facts as to the nature and habits of these shrubs; for he

338

has spent a lifetime in such studies, and this garden is his world."

"And yourself, lady," observed Giovanni, "if fame says true, you likewise are deeply skilled in the virtues indicated by these rich blossoms and these spicy perfumes. Would you deign to be my instructress, I should prove an apter scholar than if taught by Signor Rappaccini himself."

"Are there such idle rumours?" asked Beatrice, with the music of a pleasant laugh. "Do people say that I am skilled in my father's science of plants? What a jest is there! No; though I have grown up among these flowers, I know no more of them than their hues and perfume; and sometimes methinks I would fain rid myself of even that small knowledge. There are many flowers here, and those not the least brilliant, that shock and offend me when they meet my eye. But pray, signor, do not believe these stories about my science. Believe nothing of me save what you see with your own eyes."

"And must I believe all that I have seen with my own eyes?" asked Giovanni, pointedly, while the recollection of former scenes made him shrink. "No, signora; you demand too little of me. Bid me believe nothing save what comes from your own lips."

It would appear that Beatrice understood him. There came a deep flush to her cheek; but she looked full into Giovanni's eyes, and responded to his gaze of uneasy suspicion with a queen-like haughtiness.

"I do so bid you, signor," she replied. "Forget whatever you may have fancied in regard to me. If true to the outward senses, still it may be false in its essence; but the words of Beatrice Rappaccini's lips are true from the depths of the heart outward. Those you may believe."

A fervour glowed in her whole aspect, and beamed upon Giovanni's consciousness like the light of truth itself; but while she spoke there was a fragrance in the atmosphere around her, rich and delightful, though evanescent, yet which the young man, from an indefinable reluctance, scarcely dared to draw into his lungs. It might be the odour of the flowers. Could it be Beatrice's breath which thus embalmed her words with a strange richness, as if by steeping them in her heart? A faintness passed like a shadow over Giovanni and flitted away; he seemed to gaze through the beautiful girl's eyes into her transparent soul, and felt no more doubt or fear.

The tinge of passion that had coloured Beatrice's manner vanished; she became gay, and appeared to derive a pure delight from her communion with the youth not unlike what the maiden of a lonely island might have felt conversing with a voyager from the civilized world. Evidently her experience of life had been confined within the limits of that garden. She talked now about matters as simple as the daylight or summer clouds, and now asked questions in reference to the city, or Giovanni's distant home, his friends, his mother, and his sisters,—questions indicating such seclusion, and such lack of familiarity with modes, and forms, that Giovanni responded as if to an infant. Her spirit gushed out before him like a fresh rill that was just catching its first glimpse of the sunlight and wondering at the reflections of earth and sky which were flung into its bosom. There came thoughts, too, from a deep source, and fantasies of a gemlike brilliancy, as if diamonds and rubies sparkled upward among the bubbles of the fountain. Ever and anon there gleamed across the young man's mind a sense of wonder that he should be walking side by side with the being who had so wrought upon his imagination, whom he had idealized in such hues of terror, in whom he had positively witnessed such manifestations of dreadful attributes,—that he should be conversing with Beatrice like a brother, and should find her so human and so maidenlike. But such reflections were only momentary; the effect of her character was too real not to make itself familiar at once.

In this free intercourse they had strayed through the garden, and now, after many turns among its avenues, were come to the shattered fountain, beside which grew the magnificent shrub, with its treasury of glowing blossoms. A fragrance was diffused from it which Giovanni recognized as identical with that which he had attributed to Beatrice's breath, but incomparably more powerful. As her eyes fell upon it, Giovanni beheld her press her hand to her bosom as if her heart were throbbing suddenly and painfully.

"For the first time in my life," murmured she, addressing the shrub, "I had forgotten thee."

"I remember, signora," said Giovanni, "that you once promised to reward me with one of these living gems for the bouquet which I had the happy boldness to fling to your feet. Permit me now to pluck it as a memorial of this interview."

He made a step towards the shrub with extended hand; but Beatrice darted forward, uttering a shriek that went through his heart like a dagger. She caught his hand and drew it back with the whole force of her slender figure. Giovanni felt her touch thrilling through his fibres.

"Touch it not!" exclaimed she, in a voice of agony. "Not for thy life! It is fatal!"

Then, hiding her face, she fled from him and vanished beneath the sculptured portal. As Giovanni followed her with his eyes, he beheld the emaciated figure and pale intelligence of Dr Rappaccini, who had been watching the scene, he knew not how long, within the shadow of the entrance.

No sooner was Guasconti alone in his chamber than the image of Beatrice came back to his passionate musings, invested with all the witchery that had been gathering around it ever since his first glimpse of her, and now likewise imbued with a tender warmth of girlish womanhood. She was human; her nature was endowed with all gentle and feminine qualities; she was worthiest to be worshipped; she was capable, surely, on her part, of the height and heroism of love. Those tokens which he had hitherto considered as proofs of a frightful peculiarity in her physical and moral system were now either forgotten or by the subtle sophistry of passion transmitted into a golden crown of enchantment, rendering Beatrice the more admirable by so much as she was the more unique. Whatever had looked ugly was now beautiful; or, if incapable of such a change, it stole away and hid itself among those shapeless half-ideas which throng the dim region beyond the daylight of our perfect consciousness. Thus did he spend the night, nor fell asleep until the dawn had begun to awake the slumbering flowers in Dr Rappaccini's garden, whither Giovanni's dreams doubtless led him. Up rose the sun in his due season, and, flinging his beams upon the young man's eyelids, awoke him to a sense of pain. When thoroughly aroused, he became sensible of a burning and tingling agony in his hand,—in his right hand,—the very hand which Beatrice had grasped in her own when he was on the point of plucking one of the gem-like flowers. On the back of that hand there was now a purple print like that of four small fingers, and the likeness of a slender thumb upon his wrist.

Oh, how stubbornly does love,—or even that cunning semblance of love which flourishes in the imagination, but strikes no depth of root into the heart,—how stubbornly does it hold its faith until the moment comes when it is doomed to vanish into thin mist! Giovanni wrapped a handkerchief about his hand and wondered what evil thing had stung him, and soon forgot his pain in a reverie of Beatrice.

After the first interview, a second was in the inevitable course of what we call fate. A third; a fourth; and a meeting with Beatrice in the garden was no longer an incident in Giovanni's daily life, but the whole space in which he might be said to live; or the anticipation and memory of that ecstatic hour made up the remainder. Nor was it otherwise with the daughter of Rappaccini. She watched for the youth's appearance and flew to his side with confidence as unreserved as if they had been playmates from early infancy,—as if they were such playmates still. If, by any unwonted chance, he failed to come at the appointed moment, she stood beneath the window and sent up the rich sweetness of her tones to float around him in his chamber and echo and reverberate throughout his heart: "Giovanni!

Giovanni! Why tarriest thou? Come down!" And down he hastened into that Eden of poisonous flowers.

But, with all this intimate familiarity, there was still a reserve in Beatrice's demeanour, so rigidly and invariably sustained, that the idea of infringing it scarcely occurred to his imagination. By all appreciable signs, they loved; they had looked love with eyes that conveyed the holy secret from the depths of one soul into the depths of the other, as if it were too sacred to be whispered by the way; they had even spoken love in those gushes of passion when their spirits darted forth in articulated breath like tongues of long-hidden flame; and yet there had been no seal of lips, no clasp of hands, nor any slightest caress such as love claims and hallows. He had never touched one of the gleaming ringlets of her hair; her garment—so marked was the physical barrier between them—had never been waved against him by a breeze. On the few occasions when Giovanni had seemed tempted to overstep the limit, Beatrice grew so sad, so stern, and withal wore such a look of desolate separation, shuddering at itself, that not a spoken word was requisite to repel him. At such times he was startled at the horrible suspicions that rose, monster-like, out of the caverns of his heart and stared him in the face; his love grew thin and faint as the morning mist; his doubts alone had substance. But, when Beatrice's face brightened again after the momentary shadow, she was transformed at once from the mysterious, questionable being whom he had watched with so much awe and horror; she was now the beautiful and unsophisticated girl whom he felt that his spirit knew with a certainty beyond all other knowledge.

A considerable time had now passed since Giovanni's last meeting with Baglioni. One morning, however, he was disagreeably surprised by a visit from the professor, whom he had scarcely thought of for whole weeks, and would willingly have forgotten still longer. Given up as he had long been to a pervading excitement, he could tolerate no companions except upon condition of their perfect sympathy with his present state of feeling. Such sympathy was not to be expected from Professor Baglioni.

The visitor chatted carelessly for a few moments about the gossip of the city and the university, and then took up another topic.

"I have been reading an old classic author lately, "said he, "and met with a story that strangely interested me. Possibly you may remember it. It is of an Indian prince, who sent a beautiful woman as a present to Alexander the Great. She was as lovely as the dawn and gorgeous as the sunset; but what especially distinguished her was a certain rich perfume in her breath,—richer than a garden of Persian roses. Alexander, as was natural to a youthful conqueror, fell in love at first sight with this magnificent stranger; but a certain sage physician, happening to be present, discovered a terrible secret in regard to her."

"And what was that?" asked Giovanni, turning his eyes downward, to avoid those of the professor.

"That this lovely woman," continued Baglioni, with emphasis, "had been nourished with poisons from her birth upward, until her whole nature was so imbued with them that she herslf had become the deadliest poison in existence. Poison was her element of life. With that rich perfume of her breath she blasted the very air. Her love would have been poison,—her embrace death. Is not this a marvellous tale?"

"A childish fable," answered Giovanni, nervously starting from his chair. "I marvel how your worship finds time to read such nonsense among your graver studies."

"By the by," said the professor, looking uneasily about him, "what singular fragrance is this in your apartment? Is it the perfume of your gloves? It is faint, but delicious; and yet, after all, by no means agreeable. Were I to breathe it long, methinks it would make me ill. It is like the breath of a flower; but I see no flowers in the chamber."

"Nor are there any," replied Giovanni, who had turned pale as the professor spoke; "nor, I think, is there any fragrance, except in your worship's imagination. Odours, being a sort of element combined of the sensual and the spiritual, are apt to deceive us in this manner. The recollection of a perfume, the bare idea of it, may easily be mistaken for a present reality."

"Ay; but my sober imagination does not often play such tricks," said Baglioni; "and, were I to fancy any kind of odour, it would be that of some vile apothecary drug, wherewith my fingers are likely enough to be imbued. Our worshipful friend Rappaccini, as I have heard, tinctures his medicaments with odours richer than those of Araby. Doubtless, likewise, the fair and learned Signora Beatrice would minister to her patients with draughts as sweet as a maiden's breath; but woe to him that sips them!"

Giovanni's face evinced many contending emotions. The tone in which the professor alluded to the pure and lovely daughter of Rappaccini was a torture to his soul; and yet the intimation of a view of her character, opposite to his own, gave instantaneous distinctness to a thousand dim suspicions, which now grinned at him like so many demons. But he strove hard to quell them and to respond to Baglioni with a true lover's perfect faith.

"Signor professor," said he, "you were my father's friend; perchance, too, it is your purpose to act a friendly part towards his son. I would fain feel nothing towards you save respect and deference; but I pray you to observe, signor, that there is one subject on which we must not speak. You know not the Signora Beatrice. You cannot, therefore, estimate the wrong—the blasphemy, I may even say—that is offered to her character by a light or injurious word."

"Giovanni! my poor Giovanni!" answered the professor, with a calm expression of pity, "I know this wretched girl far better than yourself. You shall hear the truth in respect to the poisoner Rappaccini and his poisonous daughter; yes, poisonous as she is beautiful. Listen; for, even should you do violence to my grey hairs, it shall not silence me. That old fable of the Indian woman has become a truth by the deep and deadly science of Rappaccini and in the person of the lovely Beatrice."

Giovanni groaned and hid his face.

"Her father," continued Baglioni, "was not restrained by natural affection from offering up his child in this horrible manner as the victim of his insane zeal for science; for, let us do him justice, he is as true a man of science as ever distilled his own heart in an alembic. What, then, will be your fate? Beyond a doubt you are selected as the material of some new experiment. Perhaps the result is to be death; perhaps a fate more awful still. Rappaccini, with what he calls the interest of science before his eyes, will hesitate at nothing."

"It is a dream," muttered Giovanni to himself; "surely it is a dream."

"But," resumed the professor, "be of good cheer, son of my fiend. It is not yet too late for the rescue. Possibly we may even succeed in bringing back this miserable child within the limits of ordinary nature, from which her father's madness has estranged her. Behold this little silver vase! It was wrought by the hands of the renowned Benvenuto Cellini, and is well worthy to be a love-gift to the fairest dame in Italy. But its contents are invaluable. One little sip of this antidote would have rendered the most virulent poisons of the Borgias innocuous. Doubt not that it will be as efficacious against those of Rappaccini. Bestow the vase, and the precious liquid within it, on your Beatrice, and hopefully await the result."

Baglioni laid a small, exquisitely wrought silver vial on the table and withdrew, leaving what he had said to produce its effect upon the young man's mind.

"We will thwart Rappaccini yet," thought he, chuckling to himself as he descended the stairs; "but, let us confess the truth of him, he is a wonderful man,—a wonderful man indeed; a vile empiric, however, in his practice, and therefore not to be tolerated by those who respect the good old rules of the medical profession."

Throughout Giovanni's whole acquaintance with Beatrice, he had occasionally, as we have said, been haunted by dark surmises as to her character; yet so thoroughly had she made herself felt by him as a simple, natural, most affectionate, and guileless creature, that the image now held up by Professor Baglioni looked as strange and incredible as if it were not in accordance with his own original conception. True, there were ugly recollections connected with his first glimpses of the beautiful girl; he could not quite forget the bouquet that withered in her grasp, and the insect that perished amid the sunny air, by no ostensible agency save the fragrance of her breath. These incidents, however, dissolving in the pure light of her character, had no longer the efficacy of facts, but were acknowledged as mistaken fantasies, by whatever testimony of the senses they might appear to be substantiated. There is something truer and more real than what we can see with the eyes and touch with the finger. On such better evidence had Giovanni founded his confidence in Beatrice, though rather by the necessary force of her high attributes than by any deep and generous faith on his part. But now his spirit was incapable of sustaining itself at the height to which the early enthusiasm of passion had exalted it; he fell down, grovelling among earthly doubts, and defiled therewith the pure whiteness of Beatrice's image. Not that he gave her up; he did but distrust. He resolved to institute some decisive test that should satisfy him, once for all, whether there were those dreadful peculiarities in her physical nature which could not be supposed to exist without some corresponding monstrosity of soul. His eyes, gazing down afar, might have deceived him as to the lizard, the insect, and the flowers; but if he could witness, at the distance of a few paces, the sudden blight of one fresh and healthful flower in Beatrice's hand, there would be room for no further question. With this idea he hastened to the florist's and purchased a bouquet that was still gemmed with the morning dewdrops.

It was now the customary hour of his daily interview with Beatrice. Before descending into the garden, Giovanni failed not to look at his figure in the mirror,—a vanity to be expected in a beautiful young man, yet, as displaying itself at that troubled and feverish moment, the token of a certain shallowness of feeling and insincerity of character. He did gaze, however, and said to himself that his features had never before possessed so rich a grace, nor his eyes such vivacity, nor his cheeks so warm a hue of superabundant life.

"At least," thought he, "her poison has not yet insinuated itself into my system. I am no flower to perish in her grasp."

With that thought he turned his eyes on the bouquet, which he had never once laid aside from his hand. A thrill of indefinable horror shot through his frame on perceiving that these dewy flowers were already beginning to droop; they wore the aspect of things that had been fresh and lovely yesterday. Giovanni grew white as marble, and stood motionless before the mirror, staring at his own reflection there as at the likeness of something frightful. He remembered Baglioni's remark about the fragrance that seemed to pervade the chamber. It must have been the poison in his breath! Then he shuddered,—shuddered at himself. Recovering from his stupor, he began to watch with curious eye a spider that was busily at work hanging its web from the antique cornice of the apartment, crossing and recrossing the artful system of interwoven lines,—as vigorous and active a spider as ever dangled from an old ceiling. Giovanni bent towards the inscet, and emitted a deep, long breath. The spider suddenly ceased its toil; the web vibrated with a tremor originating in the body of the small artisan. Again Giovanni sent forth a breath, deeper, longer and imbued with a venomous feeling out of his heart: he knew not whether he were wicked, or only desperate. The spider made a convulsive grip with his limbs and hung dead across the window.

"Accursed! accursed!" muttered Giovanni, addressing himself. "Hast thou grown so poisonous that this deadly insect perishes by thy breath?"

At that moment a rich, sweet voice came floating up from the garden.

"Giovanni! Giovanni! It is past the hour! Why tarriest thou? Come down!"

"Yes," muttered Giovanni again. "She is the only being whom my breath may not slay! Would that it might!"

He rushed down, and in an instant was standing before the bright and loving eyes of Beatrice. A moment ago his wrath and despair had been so fierce that he could have desired nothing so much as to wither her by a glance; but with her actual presence there came influences which had too real an existence to be at once shaken off; recollections of the delicate and benign power of her feminine nature, which had so often enveloped him in a religious calm; recollections of many a holy and passionate outgush of her heart, when the pure fountain had been unsealed from its depths and made visible in its transparency to his mental eye; recollections which, had Giovanni known how to estimate them, would have assured him that all this ugly mastery was but an earthly illusion, and that, whatever mist of evil might seem to have gathered over her, the real Beatrice was a heavenly angel. Incapable as he was of such high faith, still her presence had not utterly lost its magic. Giovanni's rage was quelled into an aspect of sullen insensibility. Beatrice, with a quick spiritual sense, immediately felt that there was a gulf of blackness between them which neither he nor she could pass. They walked on together, sad and silent. and came thus to the marble fountain and to its pool of water on the ground, in the midst of which grew the shrub that bore gem-like blossoms. Giovanni was affrighted at the eager enjoyment—the appetite, as it were— with which he found himself inhaling the fragrance of the flowers.

"Beatrice," asked he, abruptly, "whence came this shrub?"

"My father created it," answered she, with simplicity.

"Created it! created it!" repeated Giovanni. "What mean you, Beatrice?"

"He is a man fearfully acquainted with the secrets of nature," replied Beatrice; "and, at the hour when I first drew breath, this plant sprang from the soil, the offspring of his science, of his intellect, while I was but his earthly child. Approach it not!" continued she, observing with terror that Giovanni was drawing nearer to the shrub. "It has qualities that you little dream of. But I, dearest Giovanni,—I grew up and blossomed with the plant and was nourished with its breath. It was my sister, and I loved it with a human affection, for, alas!—hast thou not suspected it?—there was an awful doom."

Here Giovanni frowned so darkly upon her that Beatrice paused and trembled. But her faith in his tenderness reassured her, and made her blush that she had doubted for an instant.

"There was an awful doom," she continued, "the effect of my father's fatal love of science, which estranged me from all society of my kind. Until Heaven sent thee, dearest Giovanni, oh, how lonely was thy poor Beatrice!"

"Was it a hard doom?" asked Giovanni, fixing his eyes upon her.

"Only of late have I known how hard it was," answered she, tenderly. "Oh yes; but my heart was torpid, and therefore quiet."

Giovanni's rage broke forth from his sullen gloom like a lightning flash out of a dark cloud.

"Accursed one!" cried he, with venomous scorn and anger. "And, finding thy solitude wearisome, thou hast severed me likewise from all the warmth of life and enticed me into thy region of unspeakable horror!"

"Giovanni!" exclaimed Beatrice, turning her large bright eyes upon his face. The force of his words had not found its way into her mind; she was merely thunderstruck.

"Yes, poisonous thing!" repeated Giovanni, beside himself with passion. "Thou hast done it! Thou hast blasted me! Thou hast filled my veins with poison! Thou hast made me as hateful, as ugly, as loathsome and deadly a creature as thyself,—a world's wonder of hideous monstrosity! Now, if our breath be happily as fatal to ourselves as to all others, let us join our lips in one kiss of unutterable hatred, and so die!"

"What has befallen me?" murmured Beatrice, with a low moan out of her heart. "Holy Virgin, pity me, a poor heart-broken child!"

"Thou,—dost thou pray?" cried Giovanni, still with the same fiendish scorn. "Thy very prayers, as they come from thy lips, taint the atmosphere with death. Yes, yes; let us pray! Let us to church and dip our fingers in the holy water at the portal! They that come after us will perish as by a pestilence! Let us sign crosses in the air! It will be scattering curses abroad in the likeness of holy symbols!"

"Giovanni," said Beatrice, calmly, for her grief was beyond passion, "why dost thou join thyself with me thus in those terrible words? I, it is true, am the horrible thing thou namest me. But thou,—what hast thou to do, save with one other shudder at my hideous misery to go forth out of the garden and mingle with thy race, and forget that there ever crawled on earth such a monster as poor Beatrice?"

"Dost thou pretend ignorance?" asked Giovanni, scowling upon her. "Behold! this power have I gained from the pure daughter of Rappaccini."

There was a swarm of summer insects flitting through the air in search of the food promised by the flower-odours of the fatal garden. They circled round Giovanni's head, and were evidently attracted towards him by the same influence which had drawn them for an instant within the sphere of several of the shrubs. He sent forth a breath among them, and smiled bitterly at Beatrice as at least a score of the insects fell dead upon the ground.

"I see it! I see it!" shrieked Beatrice. "It is my father's fatal science! No, no, Giovanni; it was not I! Never! never! I dreamed only to love thee and be with thee a little time, and so to let thee pass away, leaving but thine image in mine heart; for, Giovanni, believe it, though my body be nourished with poison, my spirit is God's creature, and craves love as its daily food. But my father,—he has united us in this fearful sympathy. Yes; spurn me, tread upon me, kill me! Oh, what is death after such words as thine? But it was not I. Not for a world of bliss would I have done it."

Giovanni's passion had exhausted itself in its outburst from his lips. There now came across him a sense, mournful, and not without tenderness, of the intimate and peculiar relationship between Beatrice and himself. They stood, as it were, in an utter solitude, which would be made none the less solitary by the densest throng of human life. Ought not, then, the desert of humanity around them to press this insulated pair closer together? If they should be cruel to one another, who was there to be kind to them? Besides, thought Giovanni, might there not still be a hope of his returning within the limits of ordinary nature, and leading Beatrice, the redeemed Beatrice, by the hand? O weak and selfish and unworthy spirit, that could dream of an earthly union and earthly happiness as possible, after such deep love had been so bitterly wronged as was Beatrice's love by Giovanni's blighting words! No, no; there could be no such hope. She must pass heavily, with that broken heart, across the borders of Time; she must bathe her hurts in some fount of paradise, and forget her grief in the light of immortality, and *there* be well.

But Giovanni did not know it.

"Dear Beatrice," said he, approaching her, while she shrank away as always at his approach, but now with a different impulse—"dearest Beatrice, our fate is not yet so desperate. Behold! there is a medicine, potent, as a wise physician has assured me, and almost divine in its efficacy. It is composed of ingredients the most opposite to those by which thy awful father has brought this calamity upon thee and me. It is distilled of blessed herbs. Shall we not quaff it together, and thus be purified from evil?"

"Give it me!" said Beatrice, extending her hand to receive the little silver vial which Giovanni took from his bosom. She added, with a peculiar emphasis, "I will drink; but do thou await the result."

She put Baglioni's antidote to her lips; and, at the same moment, the figure of Rappaccini emerged from the portal and came slowly towards the marble fountain. As he drew near, the pale man of science seemed to gaze with a triumphant expression at the beautiful youth and maiden, as might an artist who should spend his life in achieving a picture or a group of statuary and finally be satisfied with his success. He paused; his bent form grew erect with conscious power; he spread out his hands over them in the attitude of a father imploring a blessing upon his children; but those were the same hands that had thrown poison into the stream of their lives. Giovanni trembled. Beatrice shuddered nervously, and pressed her hand upon her heart.

"My daughter," said Rappaccini, "thou art no longer lonely in the world. Pluck one of those precious gems from thy sister shrub and bid thy bridegroom wear it in his bosom. It will not harm him now. My science and the sympathy between thee and him have so wrought within his system that he now stands apart from common men, as thou dost, daughter of my pride and triumph, from ordinary women. Pass on, then, through the world, most dear to one another and dreadful to all besides!"

"My father," said Beatrice, feebly,—and still as she spoke she kept her hand upon her heart,—"wherefore didst thou inflict this miserable doom upon thy child?"

"Miserable!" exclaimed Rappaccini. "What mean you, foolish girl? Dost thou deem it misery to be endowed with marvellous gifts against which no power nor strength could avail an enemy,—misery, to be able to quell the mightiest with a breath,—misery, to be as terrible as thou art beautiful? Wouldst thou, then, have preferred the condition of a weak woman, exposed to all evil and capable of none?"

"I would fain have been loved, not feared," murmured Beatrice, sinking down upon the ground. "But now it matters not. I am going, father, where the evil which thout hast striven to mingle with my being will pass away like a dream,—like the fragrance of these poisonous flowers, which will no longer taint my breath among the flowers of Eden. Farewell, Giovanni! Thy words of hatred are like lead within my heart; but they, too, will fall away as I ascend. Oh, was there not, from the first, more poison in thy nature then in mine?"

To Beatrice,—so radically had her earthly part been wrought upon by Rappaccini's skill,—as poison had been life, so the powerful antidote was death; and thus the poor victim of man's ingenuity and of thwarted nature, and of the fatality that attends all such efforts of perverted wisdom, perished there, at the feet of her father and Giovanni. Just at that moment Professor Pietro Baglioni looked forth from the window, and called loudly, in a tone of triumph mixed with horror, to the thunderstricken man of science,—

"Rappaccini! Rappaccini! and is *this* the upshot of your experiment?"

ELEONORA[1]

Edgar Allan Poe

Sub conservatione formae specificae salva anima.
RAYMOND LULLY

I AM come of a race noted for vigour of fancy and ardour of passion. Men have called me mad; but the question is not yet settled, whether madness is or is not the loftiest intelligence—whether much that is glorious—whether all that is profound—does not spring from disease of

---

[1] From *Essays and Stories.*

thought—from *moods* of mind exalted at the expense of the general intellect. They who dream by day are cognizant of many things which
escape those who dream only by night. In their grey visions they obtain
glimpses of eternity, and thrill, in awaking, to find that they have been
upon the verge of the great secret. In snatches, they learn something of
the wisdom which is of good, and more of the mere knowledge which is
of evil. They penetrate, however rudderless or compassless, into the vast
ocean of the "light ineffable" and again, like the adventurers of the Nubian
geographer, "*aggressi sunt mare tenebrarum, quid in eo esset exploraturi.*"

We will say, then, that I am mad. I grant, at least, that there are two
distinct conditions of my mental existence—the condition of a lucid reason,
not to be disputed, and belonging to the memory of events forming the
first epoch of my life—and a condition of shadow and doubt, appertaining
to the present, and to the recollection of what constitutes the second great
era of my being. Therefore, what I shall tell of the earlier period, believe;
and to what I may relate of the later time, give only such credit as may
seem due; or doubt it altogether; or, if doubt it ye cannot, then play unto
its riddle the Œdipus.

She whom I loved in youth, and of whom I now pen calmly and distinctly
these remembrances, was the sole daughter of the only sister of my mother
long departed. Eleonora was the name of my cousin. We had always dwelled
together, beneath a tropical sun, in the Valley of the Many-Coloured Grass.
No unguided footstep ever came upon that vale; for it lay far away up
among a range of giant hills that hung beetling around about it, shutting
out the sunlight from its sweetest recesses. No path was trodden in its
vicinity; and, to reach our happy home, there was need of putting back,
with force, the foliage of many thousands of forest trees, and of crushing
to death the glories of many millions of fragrant flowers. Thus it was that
we lived all alone, knowing nothing of the world without the valley—I,
and my cousin, and her mother.

From the dim regions beyond the mountains at the upper end of our
encircled domain, there crept out a narrow and deep river, brighter than
all save the eyes of Eleonora; and, winding stealthily about in mazy courses,
it passed away, at length, through a shadowy gorge, among hills still
dimmer then those whence it had issued. We called it the "River of Silence";
for there seemed to be a hushing influence in its flow. No murmur arose
from its bed, and so gently it wandered along, that the pearly pebbles upon
which we loved to gaze, far down within its bosom, stirred not at all,
but lay in a motionless content, each in its old own station, shining on
gloriously for ever.

The margin of the river, and of the many dazzling rivulets that glided, through devious ways, into its channel, a well as the spaces that extended from the margins away down into the depths of the streams until they reached the bed of pebbles at the bottom,—these spots, not less than the whole surface of the valley, from the river to the mountains that girdled it in, were carpeted all by a soft green grass, thick, short, perfectly even, and vanilla-perfumed, but so besprinkled throughout with the yellow buttercup, the white daisy, the purple violet, and the ruby-red asphodel, that its exceeding beauty spoke to our heart, in loud tones, of the love and of the glory of God.

And, here and there, in groves about this grass, like wildernesses of dreams, sprang up fantastic trees, whose tall slender stem stood not upright, but slanted gracefuly towards the light that peered at noonday into the centre of the valley. Their bark was speckled with the vivid alternate splendour of ebony and silver, and was smoother than all save the cheeks of Eleonora; so that but for the brilliant green of the huge leaves that spread from their summits in long tremulous lines, dallying with the zephyrs, one might have fancied them giant serpents of Syria doing homage to their sovereign the Sun.

Hand in hand about this valley, for fifteen years, roamed I with Eleonora before Love entered within our hearts. It was one evening at the close of the third lustrum of her life, and of the fourth of my own, that we sat, locked in each other's embrace, beneath the serpent-like trees, and looked down within the waters of the River of Silence at our images therein. We spoke no words during the rest of that sweet day; and our words even upon the morrow were tremulous and few. We had drawn the god Eros from that wave, and now we felt that he had enkindled within us the fiery souls of our forefathers. The passions which had for centuries distinguished our race, came thronging with the fancies for which they had been equally noted, and together breathed a delirious bliss over the Valley of the Many-Coloured Grass. A change fell upon all things. Strange brilliant flowers, star-shaped, burst out upon the trees where no flowers had been known before. The tints of the green carpet deepened; and when, one by one, the white daisies shrank away, there sprang up, in place of them, ten by ten of the rubby-red asphodel. And life arose in our paths; for the tall flamingo, hitherto unseen, with all gay glowing birds, flaunted his scarlet plumage before us. The golden and silver fish haunted the river, out of the bosom of which issued, little by little, a murmur that swelled, at length, into a lulling melody more divine than that of the harp of Æolus—sweeter than all save the voice of Eleonora. And now, too, a voluminous cloud, which we had long watched in the regions of Hesper, floated out thence, all gorgeous in crimson and gold, and settling in peace above us, sank, day by day, lower and lower, until its edges rested upon the tops of the mountains, turning all their dimness into magnificence, and shutting us up, as if for ever, within a magic prison-house of grandeur and of glory.

The loveliness of Eleonora was that of the Seraphim; but she was a maiden artless and innocent as the brief life she had led among the flowers. No guile disguised the fervour of love which animated her heart, and she examined with me its inmost recesses as we walked together in the Valley of the Many-Coloured Grass, and discoursed of the mighty changes which had lately taken place therein.

At length, having spoken one day, in tears, of the last sad change which must befall Humanity, she thenceforward dwelt only upon this one sorrowful theme, interweaving it into all our converse, as, in the songs of the bard of Schiraz, the same images are found occurring, again and again, in every impressive variation of phrase.

She had seen that the finger of Death was upon her bosom—that, like the ephemeron, she had been made perfect in loveliness only to die; but the terrors of the grave, to her, lay solely in a consideration which she revealed to me, one evening at twilight, by the banks of the River of Silence. She grieved to think that, having entombed her in the Valley of the Many-Coloured Grass, I would quit for ever its happy recesses, transferring the love which now was so passionately her own to some maiden of the outer and every-day world. And, then and there, I threw myself hurriedly at the feet of Eleonora, and offered up a vow, to herself and to Heaven, that I would never bind myself in marriage to any daughter of Earth—that I would in no manner prove recreant to her dear memory, or to the memory of the devout affection with which she had blessed me. And I called the Mighty Ruler of the Universe to witness the pious solemnity of my vow. And the curse which I invoked of *Him* and of her, a saint in Helusion, should I prove traitorous to that promise, involved a penalty the exceeding great horror of which will not permit me to make record of it here. And the bright eyes of Eleonora grew brighter at my words; and she sighed as if a deadly burthen had been taken from her breast; and she trembled and very bitterly wept; but she made acceptance of the vow (for what was she but a child?), and it made easy to her the bed of her death. And she said to me, not many days afterwards, tranquilly dying, that, because of what I had done for the comfort of her spirit, she would watch over me in that spirit when departed, and, if so it were permitted her, return to me visibly in the watches of the night; but, if this thing were, indeed, beyond the power of the souls in Paradise, that she would, at least, give me frequent indications of her presence; sighing upon me in the evening winds, or filling the air which I breathed with perfume from the censers of the angels. And, with these words upon her lips, she yielded up her innocent life, putting an end to the first epoch of my own.

Thus far I have faithfully said. But as I pass the barrier in Time's path formed by the death of my beloved, and proceed with the second era of my existence, I feel that a shadow gathers over my brain, and I mistrust the perfect sanity of the record. But let me on. Years dragged themselves along heavily, and still I dwelled within the Valley of the Many-Coloured Grass; but a second change had come upon all things. The star-shaped flowers shrank into the stems of the trees, and appeared no more. The tints of the green carpet faded, and one by one, the ruby-red asphodels withered away; and there sprang up, in place of them, ten by ten, dark eye-like violets that writhed uneasily and were ever encumbered with dew. And Life departed from our paths; for the tall flamingo flaunted no longer his scarlet plumage before us, but flew sadly from the vale into the hills, with all the gay glowing birds that had arrived in his company, And the golden and silver fish swam down through the gorge at the lower end of our domain and bedecked the sweet river never again. And the lulling melody that had been softer than the wind-harp of Æolus and more divine than all save the voice of Eleonora, it died little by little away, in murmurs growing lower and lower, until the stream returned, at length, utterly, into the solemnity of its original silence. And then, lastly, the voluminous cloud uprose, and, abandoning the tops of the mountains to the dimness of old, fell back into the regions of Hesper, and took away all its manifold golden and gorgeous glories from the Valley of the Many-Coloured Grass.

Yet the promises of Eleonora were not forgotten; for I heard the sounds of the swinging of the censers of the angels; and streams of a holy perfume floated ever and ever about the valley; and at lone hours, when my heart beat heavily, the winds that bathed my brow came unto me laden with soft sighs; and indistinct murmurs filled often the night air; and once—oh, but once only! I was awakened from a slumber like the slumber of death by the pressing of spiritual lips upon my own.

But the void within my heart refused, even thus, to be filled. I longed for the love which had before filled it to overflowing. At length the valley *pained* me through its memories of Eleonora, and I left it for ever for the vanities and the turbulent triumphs of the world.

I found myself within a strange city, where all things might have served to blot from recollection the sweet dreams I had dreamed so long in the Valley of the Many-Coloured Grass. The pomps and pageantries of a stately court, and the mad clangour of arms, and the radiant loveliness of woman, bewildered and intoxicated my brain. But as yet my soul had proved true to its vows, and the indications of the presence of Eleonora were still given me in the silent hours of the night. Suddenly, these manifestations ceased; and the world grew dark before mine eyes; and I stood aghast at the burning thoughts which possessed—at the terrible temptations which beset me; for there came from some far, far distant and unknown land, into the gay court of the king I served, a maiden whose beauty my whole recreant heart yielded at once—at whose footstool I bowed down without a struggle, in the most ardent, in the most abject worship of love. What indeed was my passion for the young girl of the valley in comparison with the fervour, and the delirium, and the spiritlifting ecstasy of adoration with which I poured out my whole soul in tears at the feet of the ethereal Ermengarde? Oh bright was the seraph Ermengarde! and in that knowledge I had room for none other. Oh divine was the angel Ermengarde! and as I looked down into the depths of her memorial eyes I thought only of them —and of *her*.

I wedded; nor dreaded the curse I had invoked; and its bitterness was not visited upon me. And once—but once again in the silence of the night, there came through my lattice the soft sighs which had forsaken me; and they modelled themselves into familiar and sweet voice, saying:

"Sleep in peace!—for the Spirit of Love reigneth and ruleth, and, in taking to thy passionate heart her who is Ermengarde, thou art absolved, for reasons which shall be made known to thee in Heaven, of the vows unto Eleonora."

MIGGLES[1]

Francis Bret Harte

WE WERE eight, including the driver. We had not spoken during the passage of the last six miles, since the jolting of the heavy vehicle over the roughening road had spoiled the Judge's last poetical quotation. The tall man beside the Judge was asleep, his arm passed through the swaying strap

---

[1] From *Choice Tales*.

and his head resting upon it—altogether a limp, helpless-looking object, as if he had hanged himself and been cut down too late. The French lady on the back seat was asleep, too, yet in a half-conscious propriety of attitude, shown even in the disposition of the handkerchief which she held to her forehead, and which partially veiled her face. The lady from Virginia City, travelling with her husband, had long since lost all individuality in a wild confusion of ribbons, veils, furs, and shawls. There was no sound but the rattling of wheels and the dash of rain upon the roof. Suddenly the stage stopped, and we became dimly aware of voices. The driver was evidently in the midst of an exciting colloquy with some one in the road—a colloquy of which such fragments as "bridge gone," "twenty feet of water," "can't pass," were occasionally distinguishable above the storm. Then came a lull, and a mysterious voice from the road shouted the parting adjuration,—

"Try Miggles's."

We caught a glimpse of our leaders as the vehicle slowly turned, of a horseman vanishing through the rain, and we were evidently on our way to Miggles's.

Who and where was Miggles? The Judge, our authority, did not remember the name, and he knew the country thoroughly. The Washoe traveller thought Miggles must keep a hotel. We only knew that we were stopped by high water in front and rear, and that Miggles was our rock of refuge. A ten minutes' splashing through a tangled by-road, scarcely wide enough for the stage, and we drew up before a barred and boarded gate in a wide stone wall or fence about eight feet high. Evidently Miggles's, and evidently Miggles did not keep a hotel.

The driver got down and tried the gate. It was securely locked.

"Miggles! O Miggles!"

No answer.

"Migg-ells! You Miggles!" continued the driver, with rising wrath.

"Migglesy!" joined in the expressman, persuasively. "O Miggy! Mig!"

But no reply came from the apparently insensate Miggles. The Judge, who had finally got the window down, put his head out and propounded a series of questions, which if answered categorically would have undoubtedly elucidated the whole mystery, but which the driver evaded by replying that "if we didn't want to sit in the coach all night, we had better rise up and sing out for Miggles."

So we rose up and called on Miggles in chorus; then separately. And when we had finished, a Hibernian fellow-passenger from the roof called for "Maygells!" whereat we all laughed. While we were laughing, the driver cried "Shoo!"

356

We listened. To our infinite amazement the chorus of "Miggles" was repeated from the other side of the wall, even to the final and supplemental "Maygells."

"Extraordinary echo," said the Judge.

"Extraordinary d——d skunk!" roared the driver, contemptuously. "Come out of that, Miggles, and show yourself! Be a man, Miggles! Don't hide in the dark; I wouldn't if I were you, Miggles," continued Yuba Bill, now dancing about in an excess of fury.

"Miggles!" continued the voice, "O Miggles!"

"My good man! Mr Myghail!" said the Judge, softening the asperities of the name as much as possible. "Consider the inhospitality of refusing shelter from the inclemency of the weather to helpless females. Really, my dear sir——" But a succession of "Miggles," ending in a burst of laughter, drowned his voice.

Yuba Bill hesitated no longer. Taking a heavy stone from the road, he battered down the gate, and with the expressman entered the enclosure. We followed. Nobody was to be seen. In the gathering darkness all that we could distinguish was that we were in a garden—from the rose-bushes that scattered over us a minute spray from their dripping leaves—and before a long, rambling wooden building.

"Do you know this Miggles?" asked the Judge of Yuba Bill.

"No, nor don't want to," said Bill, shortly, who felt the Pioneer Stage Company insulted in his person by the contumacious Miggles.

"But, my dear sir," expostulated the Judge, as he thought of the barred gate.

"Lookee here," said Yuba Bill, with fine irony, "hadn't you better go back and sit in the coach till yer introduced? I'm going in," and he pushed open the door of the building.

A long room lighted only by the embers of a fire that was dying on the large hearth at its further extremity. The walls curiously papered, and the flickering firelight bringing out its grotesque pattern; somebody sitting in a large armchair by the fireplace. All this we saw as we crowded together into the room, after the driver and expressman.

"Hello, be you Miggles?" said Yuba Bill to the solitary occupant.

The figure neither spoke nor stirred. Yuba Bill walked wrathfully toward it, and turned the eye of his coach-lantern upon its face. It was a man's face, prematurely old and wrinkled, with very large eyes, in which there was that expression of perfectly gratuitous solemnity which I had sometimes seen in an owl's. The large eyes wandered from Bill's face to the lantern, and finally fixed their gaze on that luminous object, without further recognition.

Bill restrained himself with an effort.

"Miggles! Be you deaf? You ain't dumb anyhow, you know"; and Yuba Bill shook the insensate figure by the shoulder.

To our great dismay, as Bill removed his hand, the venerable stranger apparently collapsed,—sinking into half his size and an undistinguishable heap of clothing.

"Well, dern my skin," said Bill, looking appealingly at us, and hopelessly retiring from the contest.

The Judge now stepped forward, and we lifted the mysterious invertebrate back into his original position. Bill was dismissed with the lantern to reconnoitre outside, for it was evident that from the helplessness of this solitary man there must be attendants near at hand, and we all drew around the fire. The Judge, who had regained his authority, and had never lost his conversational amiability,—standing before us with his back to the hearth,—charged us, as an imaginary jury, as follows:

"It is evident that either our distinguished friend here has reached that condition described by Shakespeare as 'the sere and yellow leaf,' or has suffered some premature abatement of his mental and physical faculties. Whether he is really the Miggles——"

Here he was interrupted by "Miggles! O Miggles! Migglesy! Mig!" and, in fact, the whole chorus of Miggles in very much the same key as it had once before been delivered unto us.

We gazed at each other for a moment in some alarm. The Judge, in particular, vacated his position quickly, as the voice seemed to come directly over his shoulder. The cause, however, was soon discovered in a large magpie who was perched upon a shelf over the fireplace, and who immediately relapsed into a sepulchral silence, which contrasted singularly with his previous volubility. It was, undoubtedly, his voice which we had heard in the road, and our friend in the chair was not responsible for the discourtesy. Yuba Bill, who re-entered the room after an unsuccessful search, was loath to accept the explanation, and still eyed the helpless sitter with suspicion. He had found a shed in which he had put up his horses, but he came back dripping and sceptical. "Thar ain't nobody but him within ten mile of the shanty, and that 'ar d——d old skeesicks knows it."

But the faith of the majority proved to be securely based. Bill had scarcely ceased growling before we heard a quick step upon the porch, the trailing of a wet skirt, the door was flung open and with a flash of white teeth a sparkle of dark eyes, and an utter absence of ceremony or diffidence, a young woman entered, shut the door, and, panting, leaned back against it.

"Oh, if you please, I'm Miggles!"

And this was Miggles! this bright-eyed, full-throated young woman, whose wet gown of coarse blue stuff could not hide the beauty of the feminine curves to which it clung; from the chestnut crown of whose head, topped by a man's oil-skin sou'wester, to the little feet and ankles, hidden somewhere in the recesses of her boys' brogans, all was grace;— this was Miggles, laughing at us, too, in the most airy, frank, off-hand manner imaginable.

"You see, boys," said she, quite out of breath, and holding one little hand against her side, quite unheeding the speechless discomfiture of our party, or the complete demoralization of Yuba Bill, whose features had relaxed into an expression of gratuitous and imbecile cheerfulness,—"you see, boys, I was mor'n two miles away when you passed down the road. I thought you might pull up here, and so I ran the whole way, knowing nobody was home but Jim,—and—and—I'm out of breath—and—that lets me out."

And here Miggles caught her dripping oil-skin hat from her head, with a mischievous swirl that scattered a shower of rain-drops over us; attempted to put back her hair; dropped two hair-pins in the attempt; laughed and sat down beside Yuba Bill, with her hands crossed lightly on her lap.

The Judge recovered himself first, and essayed an extravagant compliment.

"I'll trouble you for that thar har-pin," said Miggles, gravely. Half a dozen hands were eagerly stretched forward; the missing hair-pin was restored to its fair owner; and Miggles, crossing the room, looked keenly in the face of the invalid. The solemn eyes looked back at hers with an expression we had never seen before. Life and intelligence seemed to struggle back into the rugged face. Miggles laughed again,—it was a singularly eloquent laugh,—and turned her black eyes and white teeth once more towards us.

"This afflicted person is——" hesitated the Judge.

"Jim," said Miggles.

"Your father?"

"No."

"Brother?"

"No."

"Husband?"

Miggles darted a quick, half-defiant glance at the two lady passengers who I had noticed did not participate in the general masculine admiration of Miggles, and said, gravely, "No; it's Jim."

There was an awkward pause. The lady passengers moved closer to each other; the Washoe husband looked abstractedly at the fire; and the tall man apparently turned his eyes inward for self-support at this emergency. But Miggles's laugh, which was very infectious, broke the silence. "Come," she said briskly, "you must be hungry. Who'll bear a hand to help me get tea?"

She had no lack of volunteers. In a few moments Yuba Bill was engaged like Caliban in bearing logs for this Miranda; the expressman was grinding coffee on the verandah; to myself the arduous duty of slicing bacon was assigned; and the Judge lent each man his goodhumoured and voluble counsel. And when Miggles, assisted by the Judge and our Hibernian "deck passenger," set the table with all the available crockery, we had become quite joyous, in spite of the rain that beat against windows, the wind that whirled down the chimney, the two ladies who whispered together in the corner, or the magpie who uttered a satirical and croaking commenatary on their conversation from his perch above. In the now bright, blazing fire we could see that the walls were papered with illustrated journals, arranged with feminine taste and discrimination. The furniture was extemporized, and adapted from candleboxes and packing-cases, and covered with gay calico, or the skin of some animal. The arm-chair of the helpless Jim was an ingenous variation of a flour-barrel. There was neatness, and even a taste for the picturesque, to be seen in the few details of the long low room.

The meal was a culinary success. But more, it was a social triumph,—chiefly, I think, owing to the rare tact of Miggles in guiding the conversation, asking all the questions herself, yet bearing throughout a frankness that rejected the idea of any concealment on her own part, so that we talked of ourselves, of our prospects, of the journey, of the weather, of each other,—of everything but our host and hostess. It must be confessed that Miggles's conversation was never elegant, rarely grammatical, and that at times she employed expletives, the use of which had generally been yielded to our sex. But they were delivered with such a lighting up of teeth and eyes, and were usually followed by a laugh—a laugh peculiar to Miggles—so frank and honest that it seemed to clear the moral atmosphere.

Once, during the meal, we heard a noise like the rubbing of a heavy body against the outer walls of the house. This was shortly followed by a scratching and sniffling at the door. "That's Joaquin," said Miggles, in reply to our questioning glances; "would you like to see him?" Before we could answer she had opened the door, and disclosed a half-grown grizzly, who instantly raised himself on his haunches, with his forepaws hanging down in the popular attitude of mendicancy, and looked admiringly at Miggles, with a very singular resemblance in his manner to Yuba Bill. "That's my watch-dog," said Miggles, in explanation. "Oh, he don't bite," she added, as the two lady passengers fluttered into a corner. "Does he, old Toppy?" (the latter remark being addressed directly to the sagacious Joaquin). "I tell you what, boys," continued Miggles, after she had fed and closed the door on *Ursa Minor*, "you were in big luck that Joaquin wasn't hanging round when you dropped in to-night." "Where was he?" asked the Judge. "With me," said Miggles. "Lord love you; he trots round with me nights like as if he was a man."

We were silent for a few moments, and listened to the wind. Perhaps we all had the same picture before us,—of Miggles walking through the rainy woods, with her savage guardian at her side. The Judge, I remember, said something about Una and her lion; but Miggles received it as she did other compliments, with quiet gravity. Whether she was altogether unconscious of the admiration she excited,—she could hardly have been oblivious of Yuby Bill's adoration,—I know not; but her very frankness suggested a perfect sexual equality that was cruelly humiliating to the younger members of our party.

The incident of the bear did not add anything in Miggles's favour to the opinions of those of her own sex who were present. In fact, the repast over, a chillness radiated from the two lady passengers that no pine-boughs brought in by Yuba Bill and cast as a sacrifice upon the hearth could wholly overcome. Miggles felt it; and, suddenly declaring that it was time to "turn in," offered to show the ladies to their bed in an adjoining room. "You, boys, will have to camp out here by the fire as well as you can," she added, "for thar ain't but the one room."

Our sex—by which, my dear sir, I allude of course to the stronger portion of humanity—has been generally relieved from the imputation of curiosity, or a fondness for gossip. Yet I am constrained to say, that hardly had the door closed on Miggles than we crowded together, whispering, snickering, smiling, and exchanging suspicions, surmises, and a thousand speculations in regard to our pretty hostess and her singular companion. I fear that we even hustled that imbecile paralytic, who sat like a voiceless Memnon in our midst, gazing with the serene indifference of the Past in his passionless eyes upon our wordy counsels. In the midst of an exciting discussion, the door opened again, and Miggles re-entered.

But not, apparently, the same Miggles who a few hours before had flashed upon us. Her eyes were downcast, and as she hesitated for a moment on the threshold, with a blanket on her arm, she seemed to have left behind her the frank fearlessness which had charmed us a moment before. Coming into the room, she drew a low stool beside the paralytic's chair, sat down, drew the blanket over her shoulders, and saying, "If it's all the same to you, boys, as we're rather crowded, I'll stop here to-night," took the invalid's withered hand in her own, and turned her eyes upon the dying fire. An instinctive feeling that this was only premonitory to more confidential relations, and perhaps some shame at our previous curiosity, kept us silent. The rain still beat upon the roof, wandering gusts of wind stirred the embers into momentary brightness, until, in a lull of the elements, Miggles suddenly lifted up her head, and, throwing her hair over her shoulder, turned her face upon the group and asked,—

"Is there any of you that knows me?"

There was no reply.

"Think again! I lived at Marysville in '53. Everybody knew me there, and everybody had the right to know me. I kept the Polka Saloon until I came to live with Jim. That's six years ago. Perhaps I've changed some."

The absence of recognition may have disconcerted her. She turned her head to the fire again, and it was some seconds before she again spoke, and then more rapidly,—

"Well, you see, I thought some of you must have known me. There's no great harm done, anyway. What I was going to say was this: Jim here"—she took his hand in both of hers as she spoke—"used to know me, if you didn't, and spent a heap of money upon me. I reckon he spent all he had. And one day—it's six years ago this winter—Jim came into my back room, sat down on my sofy, like as you see him in that chair, and never moved again without help. He was struck all of a heap, and never seemed to know what ailed him. The doctors came and said as how it was caused all along of his way of life,—for Jim was mighty free and wild like,—and that he would never get better, and couldn't last long anyway. They advised me to send him to Frisco to the hospital, for he was no good to any one and would be a baby all his life. Perhaps it was something in Jim's eye, perhaps it was that I never had a baby, but I said 'No.' I was rich then, for I was popular with everybody,—gentlemen like yourself, sir, came to see me,—and I sold out my business and bought this yer place, because it was sort of out of the way of travel, you see, and I brought my baby here."

With a woman's intuitive tact and poetry, she had, as she spoke, slowly shifted her position so as to bring the mute figure of the ruined man between her and her audience, hiding in the shadow behind it, as if she offered it as a tacit apology for her actions. Silent and expressionless, it yet spoke for her; helpless, crushed, and smitten with the Divine thunderbolt, it still stretched an invisible arm around her.

Hidden in the darkness, but still holding his hand, she went on,—

"It was a long time before I could get the hang of things about yer, for I was used to company and excitement. I couldn't get any women to help me, and a man I dursent trust; but what with the Indians hereabout, who'd do odd jobs for me, and having everything sent from the North Fork, Jim and I managed to worry through. The Doctor would run up from Sacramento once in a while. He'd ask to see 'Miggles's baby,' as he called Jim, and when he'd go away, he'd say, 'Miggles, you're a trump,— God bless you!' and it didn't seem so lonely after that. But the last time he was here he said, as he opened the door to go,'Do you know, Miggles, your baby will grow up to be a man yet and an honour to his mother; but not here, Miggles, not here!' And I thought he went away sad—and— and"—and here Miggles's voice and head were somehow both lost completely in the shadow.

"The folks about here are very kind," said Miggles, after a pause, coming a little into the light again. "The men from the Fork used to hang around here, until they found they wasn't wanted, and the women are kind—and don't call. I was pretty lonely until I picked up Joaquin in the woods yonder one day, when he wasn't so high, and taught him to beg for his dinner; and then thar's Polly—that's the magpie—she knows no end of tricks, and makes it quite sociable of evenings with her talk, and so I don't feel like as I was the only living being about the ranch. And Jim here," said Miggles with her old laugh again, and coming out quite into the firelight, "Jim— why, boys, you would admire to see how much he knows for a man like him. Sometimes I bring him flowers, and he looks at 'em just as natural as if he knew 'em; and times, when we're sitting alone, I read him those things on the wall. Why Lord!" said Miggles, with her frank laugh, "I've read him that whole side of the house this winter. There never was such a man for reading as Jim."

"Why," asked the Judge, "do you not marry this man to whom you have devoted your youthful life?"

"Well, you see," said Miggles, "it would be playing it rather low down on Jim, to take advantage of his being so helpless. And then, too, if we were man and wife, now, we'd both know that I was *bound* to do what I do now of my own accord."

"But you are young yet and attractive———"

"It's getting late," said Miggles, gravely, "and you'd better all turn in. Good night, boys"; and, throwing the blanket over her head, Miggles laid herself down beside Jim's chair, her head pillowed on the low stool that held his feet, and spoke no more. The fire slowly faded from the hearth; we each sought our blankets in silence; and presently there was no sound in the long room but the pattering of the rain upon the roof, and the heavy breathing of the sleepers.

It was nearly morning when I awoke from a troubled dream. The storm had passed, the stars were shining, and through the shutterless window the full moon, lifting itself over the solemn pines without, looked into the room. It touched the lonely figure in the chair with an infinite compassion, and seemed to baptize with a shining flood the lowly head of the woman whose hair, as in the sweet old story, bathed the feet of him she loved. It even lent a kindly poetry to the rugged outline of Yuba Bill, half reclining on his elbow between them and his passengers, with savagely patient eyes keeping watch and ward. And then I fell asleep and only woke at broad day, with Yuba Bill standing over me, and "All aboard" ringing in my ears.

Coffee was waiting for us on the table, but Miggles was gone. We wandered about the house and lingered long after the horses were harnessed, but she did not return. It was evident that she wished to avoid a formal leave-taking, and had so left us to depart as we had come. After we had helped the ladies into the coach, we returned to the house and solemnly shook hands with the paralytic Jim, as solemnly settling him back into position after each hand-shake. Then we looked for the last time around the long low room, at the stool where Miggles had sat, and slowly took our seats in the waiting coach. The whip cracked, and we were off!

But as we reached the high road, Bill's dexterous hand laid the six horses back on their haunches, and the stage stopped with a jerk. For there, on a little eminence beside the road, stood Miggles, her hair flying, her eyes sparkling, her white handkerchief waving, and her white teeth flashing a last "good-bye." We waved our hats in return. And then Yuba Bill, as if fearful of further fascination, madly lashed his horses forward, and we sank back in our seats. We exchanged not a word until we reached the North Fork and the stage drew up at the Independence House. Then, the Judge leading, we walked into the bar-room and took our places gravely at the bar.

"Are your glasses charged, gentlemen?" said the Judge, solemnly taking off his white hat.

They were.

"Well, then, here's to *Miggles*, God bless her!"

Perhaps He had. Who knows?

"A DEATH IN THE DESERT" [1]

Willa Cather

EVERETT HILGARDE was conscious that the man in the seat across the aisle was looking at him intently. He was a large, florid man, wore a conspicuous diamond solitaire upon his third finger, and Everett judged him to be a travelling salesman of some sort. He had the air of an adaptable fellow who had been about the world and who could keep cool and clean under almost any circumstances.

The "High Line Flyer," as this train was derisively called among railroad men, was jerking along through the hot afternoon over the monotonous country between Holdredge and Cheyenne. Besides the blond man and himself the only occupants of the car were two dusty, bedraggled-looking girls who had been to the Exposition at Chicago, and who were earnestly discussing the cost of their first trip out of Colorado. The four uncomfortable passengers were covered with a sediment of fine, yellow dust which clung to their hair and eyebrows like gold powder. It blew up in clouds from the bleak, lifeless country through which they passed, until they were one colour with the sage-brush and sand-hills. The grey and yellow desert was varied only by occasional ruins of deserted towns, and the little red boxes of station-houses, where the spindling trees and sickly vines in the blue-grass yards made little green reserves fenced off in that confusing wilderness of sand.

As the slanting rays of the sun beat in stronger and stronger through the car-windows, the blond gentleman asked the ladies' permission to remove his coat, and sat in his lavender striped shirt-sleeves, with a black silk handkerchief tucked about his collar. He had seemed interested in Everett since they had boarded the train at Holdredge; kept glancing at him curiously and then looking reflectively out of the window, as though he were trying to recall something. But wherever Everett went,

---

[1] From *Youth and the Bright Medusa*. Reprinted by permission of Messrs Alfred A. Knopf, Inc.

some one was almost sure to look at him with that curious interest, and it had ceased to embarrass or annoy him. Presently the stranger, seeming satisfied with his observation, leaned bock in his seat, half closed his eyes, and began softly to whistle the Spring Song from *Proserpine*, the cantata that a dozen years before had made its young composer famous in a night. Everett had heard that air on guitars in Old Mexico, on mandolins at college glees, on cottage organs in New England hamlets, and only two weeks ago he had heard it played on sleigh-bells at a variety theatre in Denver. There was literally no way of escaping his brother's precocity. Adriance could live on the other side of the Atlantic, where his youthful indiscretions were forgotten in his mature achievements, but his brother had never been able to outrun *Proserpine*,—and here he found it again, in the Colorado sand-hills. Not that Everett was exactly ashamed of *Proserpine;* only a man of genius could have written it, but it was the sort of thing that a man of genius outgrows as soon as he can.

Everett unbent a trifle, and smiled at his neighbour across the aisle. Immediately the large man rose and coming over dropped into the seat facing Hilgarde, extending his card.

"Dusty ride, isn't it? I don't mind it myself; I'm used to it. Born and bred in de briar patch, like Br'er Rabbit. I've been trying to place you for a long time; I think I must have met you before."

"Thank you," said Everett, taking the card; "my name is Hilgarde. You've probably met my brother, Adriance; people often mistake me for him."

The travelling-man brought his hand down upon his knee with such vehemence that the solitaire blazed.

"So I was right after all, and if you're not Adriance Hilgarde you're his double. I thought I couldn't be mistaken. Seen him? Well, I guess! I never missed one of his recitals at the Auditorium, and he played the piano score of *Proserpine* through to us once at the Chicago Press Club. I used to be on the *Commercial* there before I began to travel for the publishing department of the concern. So you're Hilgarde's brother, and here I've run into you at the jumping-off place. Sounds like a newspaper yarn, doesn't it?"

The travelling-man laughed and offering Everett a cigar plied him with questions on the only subject that people ever seemed to care to talk to him about. At length the salesman and the two girls alighted at a Colorado way station, and Everett went on to Cheyenne alone.

The train pulled into Cheyenne at nine o'clock, late by a matter of four hours or so; but no one seemed particularly concerned at its tardiness except the station agent, who grumbled at being kept in the office over

366

time on a summer night. When Everett alighted from the train he walked
down the platform and stopped at the track crossing, uncertain as to what
direction he should take to reach a hotel. A phaeton stood near the crossing
and a woman held the reins. She was dressed in white, and her figure was
clearly silhouetted against the cushions, though it was too dark to see her
face. Everett had scarcely noticed her, when the switch-engine came puffing
up from the opposite direction, and the head-light threw a strong glare
of light on his face. The woman in the phaeton uttered a low cry and dropped the reins. Everett started forward and caught the horse's head, but
the animal only lifted its ears and whisked its tail in impatient surprise.
The woman sat perfectly still, her head sunk between her shoulders and
her handkerchief pressed to her face. Another woman came out of the
depot and hurried toward the phaeton, crying, "Katharine, dear, what is
the matter?"

Everett hesitated a moment in painful embarrassment, then lifted his
hat and passed on. He was accustomed to sudden recognitions in the most
impossible places, especially from women.

While he was breakfasting the next morning, the head waiter leaned
over his chair to murmur that there was a gentleman waiting to see him
in the parlour. Everett finished his coffee, and went in the direction indicated, where he found his visitor restlessly pacing the floor. His whole
manner betrayed a high degree of agitation, though his physique was
not that of a man whose nerves lie near the surface. He was something
below medium height, square-shouldered, and solidly built. His thick,
closely cut hair was beginning to show grey about the ears, and his bronzed
face was heavily lined. His square brown hands were locked behind him,
and he held his shoulders like a man conscious of responsibilities, yet, as he
turned to greet Everett, there was an incongruous diffidence in his address.

"Good morning, Mr Hilgarde," he said, extending his hand; "I found
your name on the hotel register. My name is Gaylord. I'm afraid my sister
startled you at the station last night, and I've come around to explain."

"Ah! the young lady in the phaeton? I'm sure I didn't know whether
I had anything to do with her alarm or not. If I did, it is I who owe an
apology."

The man coloured a little under the dark brown of his face.

"Oh, it's nothing you could help, sir, I fully understand that. You see,
my sister used to be a pupil of your brother's, and it seems you favour
him; when the switch-engine threw a light on your face, it startled her."

Everett wheeled about in his chair. "Oh! *Katharine* Gaylord! Is it possible! Why, I used to know her when I was a boy. What on earth——"

"Is she doing here?" Gaylord grimly filled out the pause. "You've got at the heart of the matter. You know my sister had been in bad health for a long time?"

"No. The last I knew of her she was singing in London. My brother and I correspond infrequently, and seldom get beyond family matters. I am deeply sorry to hear this."

The lines in Charley Gaylord's brow relaxed a little.

"What I'm trying to say, Mr Hilgarde, it that she wants to see you. She's set on it. We live several miles out of town, but my rig's below, and I can take you out any time you can go."

"At once, then. I'll get my hat and be with you in a moment."

When he came downstairs Everett found a cart at the door, and Charley Gaylord drew a long sigh of relief as he gathered up the reins and settled back into his own element.

"I think I'd better tell you something about my sister before you see her, and I don't know just where to begin. She travelled in Europe with your brother and his wife, and sang at a lot of his concerts; but I don't know just how much you know about her."'

"Very little, except that my brother always thought her the most gifted of his pupils. When I knew her she was very young and very beautiful, and quite turned my head for a while."

Everett saw that Gaylord's mind was entirely taken up by his grief. "That's the whole thing," he went on, flecking his horses with the whip.

"She was a great woman, as you say, and she didn't come of a great family. She had to fight her own way from the first. She got to Chicago, and then to New York, and then to Europe, and got a taste for it all; and now she's dying here like a rat in a hole, out of her own world, and she can't fall back into ours. We've grown apart, some way—miles and miles apart—and I'm afraid she's fearfully unhappy."

"It's a tragic story you're telling me, Gaylord," said Everett. They were well out into the country now, spinning along over the dusty plains of red grass, with the ragged blue outline of the mountains before them.

"Tragic!" cried Gaylord, starting up in his seat, "my God, nobody will ever know how tragic! It's a tragedy I live with and eat with and sleep with, until I've lost my grip on everything. You see she had made a good bit of money, but she spent it all going to health resorts. It's her lungs. I've got money enough to send her anywhere, but the doctors all say it's no use. She hasn't the ghost of a chance. It's just getting through the days now. I had no notion she was half so bad before she came to me. She just wrote that she was run down. Now that she's here, I think she'd be happier anywhere under the sun, but she won't leave. She says it's easier to let go of life here. There was a time when I was a brakeman with a run out of Bird City, Iowa, and she was a little thing I could carry on my shoulder, when I could get her everything on earth she wanted, and she hadn't a wish my $80 a month didn't cover; and now, when I've got a little property together, I can't buy her a night's sleep!"

Everett saw that, whatever Charley Gaylord's present status in the world might be, he had brought the brakeman's heart up the ladder with him.

The reins slackened in Gaylord's hand as they drew up before a showily painted house with many gables and a round tower. "Here we are," he said, turning to Everett, "and I guess we understand each other."

They were met at the door by a thin, colourless woman, whom Gaylord introduced as "My sister, Maggie." She asked her brother to show Mr Hilgarde into the music-room where Katharine would join him.

When Everett intered the music-room he gave a little start of surprise, feeling that he had stepped from the glaring Wyoming sunlight into some New York studio that he had always known. He looked incredulously out of the window at the grey plain that ended in the great upheaval of the Rockies.

The haunting air of familiarity perplexed him. Suddenly his eye fell upon a large photograph of his brother above the piano. Then it all became clear enough: this was veritably his brother's room. If it were not an exact copy of one of the many studios that Adriance had fitted up in various parts of the world, wearying of them and leaving almost before the renovator's varnish had dried, it was at least in the same tone. In every detail Adriance's taste was so manifest that the room seemed to exhale his personality.

Among the photographs on the wall there was one of Katharine Gaylord, taken in the days when Everett had known her, and when the flash of her eye or the flutter of her skirt was enough to set his boyish heart in a tumult. Even now, he stood before the portrait with a certain degree of embarrassment. It was the face of a woman already old in her first youth, a trifle hard, and it told of what her brother had called her fight. The *camaraderie* of her frank, confident eyes was qualified by the deep lines about her mouth and the curve of the lips, which was both sad and cynical. Certainly she had more good-will than confidence toward the world. The chief charm of the woman, as Everett had known her, lay in her superb figure and in her eyes, which possessed a warm, life-giving quality like the sunlight; eyes which glowed with a perpetual *salutat* to the world.

Everett was still standing before the picture, his hands behind him and his head inclined, when he heard the door open. A tall woman advanced toward him, holding out her hand. As she started to speak she coughed slightly, then, laughing, said in a low, rich voice, a trifle husky: "You see I make the traditional Camille entrance. How good of you to come, Mr Hilgarde."

Everett was acutely conscious that while addressing him she was not looking at him at all, and, as he assured her of his pleasure in coming, he was glad to have an opportunity to collect himself. He had not reckoned upon the ravages of a long illness. The long, loose folds of her white gown had been especially designed to conceal the sharp outlines of her body, but the stamp of her disease was there; simple and ugly and obtrusive, a pitiless fact that could not be disguised or evaded. The splendid shoulders were stooped, there was a swaying unevenness in her gait, her arms seemed disproportionately long, and her hands were transparently white, and cold to the touch. The changes in her face were less obvious; the proud carriage of the head, the warm, clear eyes, even the delicate flush of colour in her cheeks, all defiantly remained, though they were all in a lower key—older, sadder, softer.

She sat down upon the divan and began nervously to arrange the pillows. "Of course I'm ill, and I look it, but you must be quite frank and sensible about that and get used to it at once, for we've no time to lose. And if I'm a trifle irritable you won't mind?—for I'm more than usually nervous."

"Don't bother with me this morning, if you are tired," urged Everett. "I can come quite as well to-morrow."

"Gracious, no!" she protested, with a flash of that quick, keen humour that he remembered as a part of her. "It's solitude that I'm tired to death of—solitude and the wrong kind of people. You see, the minister called on me this morning. He happened to be riding by on his bicycle and felt it his duty to stop. The funniest feature of his conversation is that he is always excusing my own profession to me. But how we are losing time! Do tell me about New York; Charley says you're just on from there. How does it look and taste and smell just now? I think a whiff of the Jersey ferry would be as flagons of cod-liver oil to me. Are the trees still green in Madison Square, or have they grown brown and dusty? Does the chaste Diana still keep her vows through all the exasperating changes of weather? Who has your brother's old studio now, and what misguided aspirants practise their scales in the rookeries about Carnegie Hall? What do people go to see at the theatres, and what do they eat and drink in the world nowadays? Oh, let me die in Harlem!" she was interrupted by a violent attack of coughing, and Everett, embarrassed by her discomfort, plunged into gossip about the professional people he had met in town during the summer, and the musical outlook for the winter. He was diagramming with his pencil some new mechanical device to be used at the Metropolitan in the production of the *Rheingold*, when he became conscious that she was looking at him intently, and that he was talking to the four walls.

Katharine was lying back among the pillows, watching him through half-closed eyes, as a painter looks at a picture. He finished his explanation vaguely enough and put the pencil back in his pocket. As he did so, she said, quietly: "How wonderfully like Adriance you are!"

He laughed, looking up at her with a touch of pride in his eyes that made them seem quiet boyish. "Yes, isn't it absurd? It's almost as awkward as looking like Napoleon——But, after all, there are some advantages. It has made some of his friends like me, and I hope it will make you."

Katharine gave him a quick, meaning glance from under her lashes. "Oh, it did that long ago. What a haughty, reserved youth you were then, and how you used to stare at people, and then blush and look cross. Do you remember that night you took me home from a rehearsal, and scarcely spoke a word to me?"

"It was the silence of admiration," protested Everett, "very crude and boyish, but certainly sincere. Perhaps you suspected something of the sort?"

"I believe I suspected a pose; the one that boys often affect with singers. But it rather surprised me in you, for you must have seen a good deal of your brother's pupils." Everett shook his head. "I saw my brother's pupils come and go. Sometimes I was called on to play accompaniments, or to fill out a vacancy at a rehearsal, or to order a carriage for an infuriated soprano who had thrown up her part. But they never spent any time on me, unless it was to notice the resemblance you speak of."

"Yes," observed Katharine, thoughtfully, "I noticed it then, too; but it has grown as you have grown older. That is rather strange, when you have lived such different lives. It's not merely and ordinary family likeness of features, you know, but the suggestion of the other man's personality in your face—like an air transposed to another key. But I'm not attempting to define it; it's beyond me; something altogether unusual and a trifle— well, uncanny," she finished, laughing.

Everett sat looking out under the red window-blind which was raised just a little. As it swung back and forth in the wind it revealed the glaring panorama of the desert—a blinding stretch of yellow, flat as the sea in dead calm, splotched here and there with deep purple shadows; and, beyond, the ragged blue outline of the mountains and the peaks of snow, white as the white clouds. "I remember, when I was a child I used to be very sensitive about it. I don't think it exactly displeased me, or that I would have had it otherwise, but it seemed like a birthmark, or something not to be lightly spoken of. It came into even my relations with my mother. Ad went abroad to study when he was very young, and mother was all broken up over it. She did her whole duty by each of us, but it was generally understood among us that she'd have made burnt offerings of us all for him any day. I was a little fellow then, and when she sat alone on the porch on summer evenings, she used sometimes to call me to her and turn my face up in the light that streamed out through the shutters and kiss me, and then I always knew she was thinking of Adriance."

"Poor little chap," said Katharine, in her husky voice. "How fond people have always been of Adriance! Tell me the latest news of him. I haven't heard, except through the press, for a year or more. He was in Algiers then, in the valley of the Chelif, riding horseback, and he had quite made up his mind to adopt the Mahometan faith and become an Arab. How many countries and faiths has he adopted, I wonder?"

"Oh, that's Adriance," chuckled Everett. "He is himself barely long enough to write cheques and be measured for his clothes. I didn't hear from him while he was an Arab; I missed that."

"He was writing an Algerian *suite* for the piano then; it must be in the publisher's hands by this time. I have been too ill to answer his letter, and have lost touch with him."

Everett drew an envelope from his pocket. "This came a month ago. Read it at your leisure."

"Thanks. I shall keep it as a hostage. Now I want you to play for me. Whatever you like; but if there is anything new in the world, in mercy let me hear it."

He sat down at the piano, and Katharine sat near him, absorbed in his remarkable physical likeness to his brother, and trying to discover in just what it consisted. He was of a larger build than Adriance, and much heavier. His face was of the same oval mould, but it was grey, and darkened about the mouth by continual shaving. His eyes were of the same inconstant April colour, but they were reflective and rather dull; while Adriance's were always points of high light, and always meaning another thing than the thing they meant yesterday. It was hard to see why this earnest man should so continually suggest that lyric, youthful face, as gay as his was grave. For Adriance, though he was ten years the elder, and though his hair was streaked with silver, had the face of a boy of twenty, so mobile that it told his thoughts before he could put them into words. A contralto, famous for the extravagance of her vocal methods and of her affections, once said that the shepherd-boys who sang in the Vale of Tempe must certainly have looked like young Hilgarde.

Everett sat smoking on the veranda of the Inter-Ocean House that night, the victim of mournful recollections. His infatuation for Katharine Gaylord, visionary as it was, had been the most serious of his boyish love-affairs. The fact that it was all so done and dead and far behind him, and that the woman had lived her life out since then, gave him an oppressive sense of age and loss.

He remembered how bitter and morose he had grown during his stay at his brother's studio when Katharine Gaylord was working there, and how he had wounded Adriance on the night of his last concert in New York. He had sat there in the box—while his brother and Katharine were called back again and again, and the flowers went up over the footlights until they were stacked half as high as the piano—brooding in his sullen boy's heart upon the pride those two felt in each other's work—spurring each other to their best and beautifully contending in song. The footlights had seemed a hard, glittering line drawn sharply between their life and his. He walked back to his hotel alone, and sat in his window staring out on Madison Square until long after midnight, resolved to beat no more at doors that he could never enter.

Everett's week in Cheyenne stretched to three, and he saw no prospect of release except through the thing he dreaded. The bright, windy days of the Wyoming autumn passed swiftly. Letters and telegrams came urging him to hasten his trip to the coast, but he resolutely postponed his business engagements. The mornings he spent on one of Charley Gaylord's ponies, or fishing in the mountains. In the afternoon he was usually at his post of duty. Destiny, he reflected, seems to have very positive notions about the sort of parts we are fitted to play. The scene changes and the compensation varies, but in the end we usually find that we have played the same class of business from first to last. Everett had been a stop-gap all his life. He remembered going through a looking-glass labyrinth when he was a boy, and trying gallery after gallery, only at every turn to bump his nose against his own face—which, indeed, was not his own, but his brother's. No matter what his mission, east or west, by land or sea, he was sure to find himself employed in his brother's business, one of the tributary lives which helped to swell the shining current of Adriance Hilgarde's. It was not the first time that his duty had been to comfort, as best he could, one of the broken things his brother's imperious speed had cast aside and forgotten. He made no attempt to analyse the situation or to state it in exact terms; but he accepted it as a commission from his brother to help this woman to die. Day by day he felt her need for him grow more acute and positive; and day by day he felt that in his peculiar relation to her, his own individuality played a smaller part. His power to minister to her comfort lay solely in his link with his brother's life. He knew that she sat by him always watching for some trick of gesture, some familiar play of expression, some illusion of light and shadow, in which he should seem wholly Adriance. He knew that she lived upon this, and that in the exhaustion which followed this turmoil of her dying senses, she slept deep and sweet, and dreamed of youth and art and days in a certain old Florentine garden, and not of bitterness and death.

A few days after his first meeting with Katharine Gaylord, he had cabled his brother to write her. He merely said that she was mortally ill; he could depend on Adriance to say the right thing—that was a part of his gift. Adriance always said not only the right thing, but the opportune, graceful, exquisite thing. He caught the lyric essence of the moment, the poetic suggestion of every situation. Moreover, he usually did the right thing—except when he did very cruel things—bent upon making people happy when their existence touched his, just as he insisted that his material environment should be bautiful; lavishing upon those near him all the warmth and radiance of his rich nature, all the homage of the poet and troubadour, and, when they were no longer near, forgetting—for that also was a part of Adriance's gift.

Three weeks after Everett had sent his cable, when he made his daily call at the gaily painted ranch-house, he found Katharine laughing like a girl. "Have you ever thought," she said, as he entered the music-room, "how much these séances of ours are like Heine's *Florentine Nights*, except that I don't give you an opportunity to monopolize the conversation?" She held his hand longer than usual as she greeted him. "You are the kindest man living, the kindest," she added, softly.

Everett's grey face coloured faintly as he drew his hand away, for he felt that this time she was looking at him, and not at a whimsical caricature of his brother.

She drew a letter with a foreign postmark from between the leaves of a book and held it out, smiling. "You got him to write it. Don't say you didn't, for it came direct, you see, and the last address I gave him was a place in Florida. This deed shall be remembered of you when I am with the just in Paradise. But one thing you did not ask him to do, for you

374

didn't know about it. He has sent me his latest work, the new sonata, and you are to play it for me directly. But first for the letter; I think you would better read it aloud to me."

Everett sat down in a low chair facing the window-seat in which she reclined with a barricade of pillows behind her. He opened the letter, his lashes half-veiling his kind eyes, and saw to his satisfaction that it was a long one; wonderfully tactful and tender, even for Adriance, who was tender with his valet and his stable-boy, with his old gondolier and the beggar-women who prayed to the saints for him.

The letter was from Granada, written in the Alhambra, as he sat by the fountain of the Patio di Lindaraxa. The air was heavy with the warm fragrance of the South and full of the sound of splashing, running water, as it had been in a certain old garden in Florence, long ago. The sky was one great turquoise, heated until it glowed. The wonderful Moorish arches threw graceful blue shadows all about him. He had sketched an outline of them on the margin of his note-paper. The letter was full of confidences about his work, and delicate allusions to their old happy days of study and comradeship.

As Everett folded it he felt that Adriance had divined the thing needed and had risen to it in his own wonderful way. The letter was consistently egotistical, and seemed to him even a trifle patronizing, yet it was just what she had wanted. A strong realization of his brother's charm and intensity and power came over him; he felt the breath of that whirlwind of flame in which Adriance passed, consuming all in his path, and himself even more resolutely than he consumed others. Then he looked down at this white, burnt-out brand that lay before him.

"Like him, isn't it?" she said, quietly. "I think I can scarcely answer his letter, but when you see him next you can do that for me. I want you to tell him many things for me, yet they can all be summed up in this: I want him to grow wholly into his best and greatest self, even at the cost of what is half his charm to you and me. Do you understand me?"

"I know perfectly well what you mean," answered Everett, thoughtfully. "And yet it's difficult to prescribe for those fellows; so little makes, so little mars."

Katharine raised herself upon her elbow, and her face flushed with feverish earnestness. "Ah, but it is the waste of himself that I mean; his lashing himself out on stupid and uncomprehending people until they take him at their own estimate."

"Come, come," expostulated Everett, now alarmed at her excitement. "Where is the new sonata? Let him speak for himself."

He sat down at the piano and began playing the first movement, which was indeed the voice of Adriance, his proper speech. The sonata was the most ambitious work he had done up to that time, and marked the transition from his early lyric vein to a deeper and nobler style. Everett played intelligently and with that sympathetic comprehension which seems peculiar to a certain lovable class of men who never accomplish anything in particular. When he had finished he turned to Katharine.

"How he has grown!" she cried. "What the three last years have done for him! He used to write only the tragedies of passion; but this is the tragedy of effort and failure, the thing Keats called Hell. This is my tragedy, as I lie here, listening to the feet of the runners as they pass me—ah, God! the swift feet of the runners!"

She turned her face away and covered it with her hands. Everett crossed over to her and knelt beside her. In all the days he had known he she had never before, beyond an occasional ironical jest, given voice to the bitterness of her own defeat. Her courage had become a point of pride with him.

"Don't do it" he gasped. "I can't stand it I really can't, I feel it too much."

When she turned her face back to him there was a ghost of the old brave, cynical smile on it, more bitter than the tears she could not shed. "No, I won't; I will save that for the night, when I have no better company. Run over that theme at the beginning again, will you? It was running in his head when we were in Venice years ago, and he used to drum it on his glass at the dinner-table. He had just begun to work it out when the late autumn came on, and he decided to go to Florence for the winter. He lost touch with his idea, I suppose, during his illness. Do you remember those frightful days? All the people who have loved him are not strong enough to save him from himself! When I got word from Florence that he had been ill, I was singing at Monte Carlo. His wife was hurrying to him from Paris, but I reached him first. I arrived at dusk, in a terrific storm. They had taken an old palace there for the winter, and I found him in the library—a long, dark room full of old Latin books and heavy furniture and bronzes. He was sitting by a wood fire at one end of the room, looking, oh, so worn and pale!—as he always does when he is ill, you know. Ah, it is so good that you *do* know! Even his red smoking-jacket lent no colour to his face. His first words were not to tell me how ill he had been, but that that morning he had been well enough to put the last strokes to the score of his *Souvenirs d'Automne*, and he was as I most like to remember him; calm and happy, and tired with that heavenly tiredness that comes after a good work done at last. Outside, the rain poured down in torrents, and the

wind moaned and sobbed in the garden and about the walls of that desolated old palace. How that night comes back to me! There were no lights
in the room, only the wood fire. It glowed on the black walls and floor
like the reflection of purgatorial flame. Beyond us it scarcely penetrated
the gloom at all. Adriance sat staring at the fire with the weariness of
all his life in his eyes, and of all the other lives that must aspire and suffer
to make up one such life as his. Somehow the wind with all its world-pain
had got into the room, and the cold rain was in our eyes, and the wave
came up in both of us at once—that awful vague, universal pain, that cold
fear of life and death and God and hope—and we were like two clinging
together on a spar in mid-ocean after the shipwreck of everything. Then
we heard the front door open with a great gust of wind that shook even
the walls, and the servants came running with lights, announcing that
Madame had returned, *'and in the book we read no more that night'*."

She gave the old line with a certain bitter humour, and with the hard,
bright smile in which of old she had wrapped her weakness as in a glittering garment. That ironical smile, worn through so many years, had
gradually changed the lines of her face, and when she looked in the mirror
she saw not herself, but the scathing critic, the amused observer and
satirist of herself.

Everett dropped his head upon his hand. "How much you have cared!"
he said.

"Ah, yes, I cared," she replied, closing her eyes. "You can't imagine
what a comfort it is to have you know how I cared, what a relief it is to
be able to tell it to some one."

Everett continued to look helplessly at the floor. "I was not sure how
much you wanted me to know," he said.

"Oh, I intended you should know from the first time I looked into your
face, when you came that day with Charley. You are so like him, that it is
almost like telling him himself. At least, I feel now that he will know some
day, and then I will be quite sacred from his compassion."

"And has he never known at all?" asked Everett, in a thick voice.

"Oh! never at all in the way that you mean. Of course, he is accustomed
to looking into the eyes of women and finding love there; when he doesn't
find it there he thinks he must have been guilty of some discourtesy. He,
has a genuine fondness for every woman who is not stupid or gloomy, or
old or preternaturally ugly. I shared with the rest; shared the smiles and the
gallantries and the droll little sermons. It was quite like a Sunday-school
picnic; we wore our best clothes and a smile and took our turns. It was his
kindness that was hardest."

"Don't; you'll make me hate him," groaned Everett.

Katharine laughed and began to play nervously with her fan. "It wasn't in the slightest degree his fault; that is the most grotesque part of it. Why, it had really begun before I ever met him. I fought my way to him, and I drank my doom greedily enough."

Everett rose and stood hesitating. "I think I must go, You ought to be quiet, and I don't think I can hear any more just now."

She put out her hand and took his playfully. "You've put in three weeks at this sort of thing, haven't you? Well, it ought to square accounts for a much worse life than yours will ever be."

He knelt beside her, saying, brokenly: "I stayed because I wanted to be with you, that's all. I have never cared about other women since I knew you in New York when I was a lad. You are a part of my destiny, and I could not leave you if I would."

She put her hands on his shoulders and shook her head. "No, no; don't tell me that. I have seen enough tragedy. It was only a boy's fancy, and your divine pity and my utter pitiableness have recalled it for a moment. One does not love the dying, dear friend, Now go, and you will come again to-morrow, as long as there are to-morrows." She took his hand with a smile that was both courage and despair, and full of infinite loyalty and tenderness, as she said softly:

"For ever and for ever, farewell, Cassius;
If we do meet again, why, we shall smile;
If not, why then, this parting was well made."

The courage in her eyes was like the clear light of a star to him as he went out.

On the night of Adriance Hilgarde's opening concert in Paris, Everett sat by the bed in the ranch-house in Wyoming, watching over the last battle that we have with the flesh before we are done with it and free of it for ever. At times it seemed that the serene soul of her must have left already and found some refuge from the storm, and only the tenacious animal life were left to do battle with death. She laboured under a delusion at once pitiful and merciful, thinking that she was in the Pullman on her way to New York, going back to her life and her work. When she roused from her stupor, it was only to ask the porter to waken her half an hour out of Jersey City, or to remonstrate about the delays and the roughness of the road. At midnight Everett and the nurse were left alone with her. Poor Charley Gaylord had lain down on a couch outside the door. Everett sat looking at the sputtering night-lamp until it made his eyes ache. His head dropped forward, and he sank into heavy, distressful slumber. He was dreaming of Adriance's concert in Paris, and of Adriance, the troubadour. He heard the applause and he saw the flowers going up over the footlights until they were stacked half as high as the piano, and the petals fell and scattered, making crimson splotches on the floor. Down this crimson pathway came Adriance with his youthful step, leading his singer by the hand; a dark woman this time, with Spanish eyes.

The nurse touched him on the shoulder, he started and awoke. She screened the lamp with her hand. Everett saw that Katharine was awake and conscious, and struggling a little. He lifted her gently on his arm and began to fan her. She looked into his face with eyes that seemed never to have wept or doubted. "Ah, dear Adriance, dear, dear!" she whispered.

Everett went to call her brother, but when they came back the madness of art was over for Katharine.

Two days later Everett was pacing the station siding, waiting for the west-bound train. Charley Gaylord walked beside him, but the two men had nothing to say to each other. Everett's bags were piled on the truck, and his step was hurried and his eyes were full of impatience, as he gazed again and again up the track, watching for the train. Gaylord's impatience was not less than his own; these two, who had grown so close, had now become painful and impossible to each other, and longed for the wrench of farewell.

As the train pulled in, Everett wrung Gaylord's hand among the crowd of alighting passengers. The people of a German opera company, *en route* for the coast, rushed by them in frantic haste to snatch their breakfast during the stop. Everett herad an exclamation, and a stout woman rushed up to him, glowing with joyful surprise, and caught his coat-sleeve with her tightly gloved hands.

"*Her Gott*, Adriance, *lieber Freund*," she cried.

Everett lifted his hat, blushing. "Pardon me, madame, I see that you have mistaken me for Adriance Hilgarde. I am his brother." Turning from the crestfallen singer he hurried into the car.

FRANCE

BEAUTY AND THE BEAST[1]

A VERY wealthy merchant was left, at his wife's death, with a family of three sons and three daughters.

As he was a highly intelligent man, he determined to give his children the best education that money could procure for them, and he spared no expense to engage the very best masters to teach them.

The three daughters were exeedingly handsome both in face and person, but the youngest was especially admired for the sweetness of her countenance. When she was only a very little girl everyone called her the beauty of the family, and as she grew up the name was still used, and all friends addressed her as "My Beauty," to the disgust of her elder sisters, who were jealous of her.

Beauty was not only prettier than her sisters but she had a very much finer character, being good-tempered, gentle-mannered, obliging, and considerate.

The sisters, on the contrary, were haughty and purse-proud. They liked to imagine themselves great ladies, and they despised the daughters of the other merchants, refusing to visit them or to receive their visits. They spent all their time driving in the park or going to balls and theatres, and they amused themselves by making game of their younger sister because she spent her leisure painting, studying her music, or reading the works of the best authors.

As everyone knew of their great wealth, these young ladies had many suitors from among the families of the other rich merchants but when these gentlemen asked them in marriage, the two sisters replied contemptuously that no one less than a duke, or at the very least an earl, need take the trouble to propose to them. When any gentleman proposed marriage to Beauty, she thanked him politely for the honour he did her, but told him she was too young to marry, and wished to stay at home to cheer her father for some years yet.

Quite suddenly the merchant lost the whole of his great fortune, and all he had left was a few acres of land with a small cottage on it, quite far away in the country.

[1] From *Favourite French Fairy Tales*. Reprinted by permission of Messrs George G. Harrap and Co., Ltd.

Almost broken-hearted, he called his children together and told them of the calamity, and that they must prepare to leave town and accompany him to the cottage, where, by industry and hard work, they would be able to live plainly, like the peasants, and pay their way honestly.

The two elder daughters laughed scornfully at the idea of living in such a place, and replied that they had lovers enough desirous of marrying them for their beauty, even if they had not a penny. They were woefully disappointed, however, for these very lovers refused to look at them now that they were poor. As they had always been so disdainful in their treatment of their neighbours, no one was sorry for them.

"They do not deserve to be pitied. It is a good thing to know their pride is humbled," was all one heard, but with regard to the youngest sister it was quite different, and on all sides one heard:

"Oh! how sorry we are for poor Beauty—she was always so gentle and kind, and she was so polite when she spoke to us!"

There were even several gentlemen who came, now when she had not a farthing, to ask if she would marry them; but while she thanked them from her heart, she told them that she could not leave her father in his misfortune, but would go with him to the country, where she would grudge no trouble to try to make him comfortable, and to help him all she could in his work.

Poor Beauty had certainly been grieved by the loss of their wealth—it could not have been otherwise; but when she felt inclined to cry over it, she said to herself:

"Why should I cry? An ocean of tears would not mend matters. I must try and be happy without riches, like the people I see round about me."

When they were settled in their country cottage, the merchant and his three sons set to work to dig and cultivate their land. Beauty rose at four o'clock every morning and busied herself cleaning the house and preparing and cooking food for the family.

At first she found it all very difficult, but it gradually became easier, and at the end of a few months she did not think it a trouble at all. Also, she was very much stronger—air and exercise had given her perfect health, so that she became more beautiful than ever. When she had finished her household tasks she read, played on the harpsichord, or sang to herself while spinning.

Her two sisters, on the contrary, were bored to death with their surroundings. They did not get out of bed till ten o'clock, and spent their time wandering aimlessly about, talking to each other about their former grandeur, and regretting their fine clothes and gay companions. They twitted their sister with being mean and poor-spirited because she was contented in her poverty. Their father did not think as they did. He knew that Beauty was better fitted than they were to shine in a high position. He greatly admired the character of his youngest daughter, and especially her gentle patience with her sisters, who not only left all the housework for her to do, but constantly insulted her while she was doing it.

When the family had lived about a year at the cottage, the merchant got a letter informing him that a ship in which he had valuable cargo had just arrived safely in port. The two elder girls nearly lost their heads with joy at the news, thinking that now they would be able to leave the cottage where time had hung so heavy on their hands, and when their father was ready to start upon the journey which he must make to town, they gave him a list of the dresses, mantles, and hats that he was to bring them. Beauty asked for nothing, thinking to herself that the price of the cargo would hardly pay for all the things her sisters had asked.

"Do you not want me to bring you anything?" said her father.

"Oh! thank you!" said Beauty. "I should be so glad to have a rose, if you can get one, for there are none in our little garden."

It was not really that Beauty wanted a rose so much, but she did not want to look superior to her sisters for fear of hurting their feelings, and she knew a rose would not cost much.

The good father set off with hope in his heart, but when he arrived in town someone brought a lawsuit against him, and though he won his case, it took all the money he had received to pay the lawyers, so that after all his trouble he had to return home as poor as when he went away, and very much sadder. But he comforted himself with the thought that he would soon be among his own family again, and urged his horse on as quickly at it could go.

When he was only thirty miles from home it began to snow heavily, so that he could only see a few yards before him. The road lay through a large forest, with many paths branching in different directions. He took a wrong turning and soon found himself completely lost. The wind had risen to a furious gale, and he was twice blown off his horse. Then darkness came down, and the thought of spending the night in the forest, with the wolves already howling in the distance, filled him with dismay. Also he was stiff with cold and very hungry. Leading his tired horse he almost groped his way, but he felt safer on foot, as the swaying branches were too high to hurt him. All of a sudden he saw a distant light and going in its direction soon found himself in a long avenue, at the end of which were many lights. Thanking God for such a deliverance, he mounted his horse. The intelligent animal also saw the lights and needed no urging to gallop toward them. They came from the windows of a great castle, but though it was illuminated as if for a feast, there was no sign or sound of life anywhere around it.

From the court they could see the open door of a great stable, toward which the horse turned of its own accord, and, finding both corn and hay there, the tired, hungry animal attacked them without hesitation and made a good meal.

The merchant tied him up for the night and turned toward the house, but no one was to be seen. He entered the open door and found himself in a great dining-hall, with a good fire blazing on the hearth, and a fine dinner already on the table, but with only one cover laid. As he was wet to the skin, he stood up before the fire, saying to himself:

"Both master and servants will pardon me, under the circumstances, and no doubt they will soon be here."

He waited long, but no one came, and when the clock struck eleven o'clock he could resist no longer, for he was faint with hunger, so he took some chicken from a dish and ate it greedily, but trembling with fear of the consequences. As no one came, he filled a glass of wine for himself and drank it off, then another, and another. His courage returned, he went from the dining-hall, through one splendid apartment after another, all magnificently furnished, and soon found himself in a beautiful bedroom, evidently prepared for a guest, and as it was past midnight, and he was greatly fatigued, he made up his mind to lock the door of the room and go to bed.

He did not wake till ten o'clock next morning, and the first thing his eye fell on was a fine new suit of clothes laid where his wet, muddy garments had been the night before.

"Surely," said he to himself, "this palace must belong to some good fairy, who has taken pity on me in my misery."

He rose and looked out of the window. The snow was all gone, and under a bright sun lawns of velvety grass, avenues of shady trees, and arbours of roses, with fountains and flowers, enchanted the eye.

He dressed and went down to the great hall where he had supped the previous night, and there, on a small table, was a cup of delicious chocolate and some crisp toast.

"Thank you, my lady fairy," said he, "for having had the goodness to think of my breakfast."

When he had taken his chocolate, the good man went out to the stable for his horse, and, as he passed under a bower of roses, Beauty's request

383

came to his mind, so he broke off a branch which had several roses on it. As he did so, a sudden fearful sound arose, and, looking round, he saw coming toward him a beast so horrible in appearance that he almost fainted.

"Monster of ingratitude!" said the Beast in a terrible voice. "I saved your life by receiving you into my castle, and, for my thanks, you rob me of my roses, which I love above all else in the world! Your life is the price you must pay for such a deed. I give you one quarter of an hour to prepare for your death!"

The merchant, clasping his hands, threw himself on his knees before the monster and cried:

"Pardon me, my lord, I did not dream of offending you. I was only gathering a rose for one of my daughters who had asked me to take her one."

"I am not called 'my lord,' but 'the Beast,' " replied the odious creature. "I hate compliments, and only wish people to say what they really think, so you need not try to make me change my mind by your flatteries.

"You say, however, that you have daughters, so if one of them will come, of her own free will, to die in your stead, I am willing to pardon you—no arguing!—I have told you my will—off with you! And if none of your daughters will die for you, give me your oath that you will return yourself three months from this day."

The good man had no intention of letting any one of his daughters sacrifice herself for him, but he saw the opportunity of seeing his family once more, and of bidding them farewell, so he promised, and the Beast told him he was free to go at any hour that suited him, adding:

"I do not wish you, however, to leave my house empty-handed. Go back to the room you slept in. There you will see a large empty chest. You may fill it with whatever you see around you, and I shall see that it is taken to your cottage." Then the Beast disappeared.

The merchant consoled himself a little by thinking that, if he had to die, he would now be able to provide his children with something to help them to live, so he returned to the bedroom. Looking around him, he discovered quite a heap of gold coins lying on the floor. With these he quickly filled the chest and locked it; then, taking his horse from the stable, he remounted, and left the palace with a very heavy heart.

The horse, of its own accord, took the shortest way to the cottage, where they arrived in a few hours.

On his arrival the family crowded round him, kissing him and welcoming him home, but instead of returning their caresses he burst into tears.

He held the rose branch in his hand, and when he could speak he turned to his daughter, and gave it to her, saying:

"My Beauty, take the roses—they are going to cost your unfortunate father very dear!"

Then he told his family the dire strait in which he found himself.

On hearing his story, the two elder daughters uttered piercing shrieks, and heaped insults and bad names on poor Beauty, who did not shed a tear.

"Only think what the pride of that small creature has brought about!" said they. "Why could she not ask for useful garments, like us? But no! the young lady wished to distinguish herself. Look, she does not even cry for causing the death of her father!"

"That would be a useless thing to do," said Beauty. "Why should I weep for my father's death? He shall not die! Since the monster is willing to accept one of his daughters in his place, I shall give myself up to it, and shall be proud if by the sacrifice of my life I can save that of my dear father."

"No! my dear sister," cried the three brothers, with one voice. "We shall go and find this monster, and we shall kill him or perish ourselves."

"Do not indulge in such hopes," said the merchant. "The power of this Beast is so great that I have no hope of anyone being able to kill him. I am charmed with the kind heart of my Beauty, but I cannot let her risk her life. I am old, and, at best could only live a few years longer. I have nothing to regret but leaving you alone, my dear children."

"I assure you, dearest Father," said Beauty, "that you shall not go to the Beast's palace without me. You could not possibly hinder me from following you. Although I am young, life has no great attractions for me, and I prefer being devoured by the monster to dying of grief for the loss of my father."

It was useless to try to dissuade her. Beauty was quite determined to go with her father when the time chould come for him to return to the palace, and the jealous sisters could hardly hide their pleasure at her decision.

The merchant was so grieved at the thought of perhaps losing his favourite daughter that he quite forgot to speak of the chest of gold coins which the Beast had promised to send, but on going to bed he found it there at his bedside.

He made up his mind not to tell his two elder daughters about it, as he felt sure they would want to go back to their extravagant life in town, and he had determined to spend what of his life might still be before him in the country. He however, confided the secret to Beauty, who at once remembered to tell him that during his absence two gentlemen who had made their acquaintance had fallen in love with her sisters, and, in the goodness of her heart, she advised her father to use a great part of the money in getting them married and comfortably provided for. The sweet-tempered girl cherished no resentment against them for their daily unkindness to her. She wanted to see them happy.

When the sisters saw Beauty ready to start with her father, at the date fixed, they rubbed their eyelids with an onion to make them look as if they were weeping; but the brothers, as well as their father, wept in earnest, not knowing what might happen. Beauty alone did not cry, for she did not wish to add to their grief.

They set off on horseback, Beauty riding on a pillion behind her father. The horse took the road to the palace without being guided, and they arrived in the evening, finding the whole place brilliantly lighted as before. They alighted at the entrance. The horse went to the stable, while the father and daughter entered the dining-hall, where they found a magnificently spread table, with covers for two. The merchant was too sad to care to eat, but Beauty made a great effort not to seem afraid, and sitting down, began to help him to the different dishes which he preferred. While they were eating, Beauty remarked to herself:

"The Beast must wish to fatten me before eating me, as he has provided such a feast."

Just when they had finished their supper they heard a strange noise and the merchant, feeling sure it was the Beast, bade his daughter adieu, weeping bitterly.

Beauty could not help shuddering when she saw the horrible face of the frightful creature, but she made a brave effort to overcome her fear, and when the monster asked her if it was really of her own free will that she had come, although she was trembling from head to foot she answered, "Yes."

"You are a good girl, and I am much obliged to you," said the Beast; then he turned to the father and said:

"Good man, leave this palace to-morrow morning, and do not take it into your head to return.

"Good night, my Beauty."

"Good night, Beast," the maiden replied, and the Beast withdrew.

"Oh, my child," said the merchant, embracing his daughter, "I am half dead already with horror. Hear me! Let me stay."

"No, dear Father," said she firmly; "you will go home to-morrow, and you will leave me to the care of kind Providence, who will perhaps take pity on me."

They parted to go to their bedrooms; neither of them expected to sleep that night, but their heads were no sooner on their pillows than they fell into a deep slumber.

During her sleep, Beauty dreamt she saw a lady, who said to her:

"Beauty, I am charmed with your tenderness of heart. Your kind action in giving your life to save your father's will not go unrewarded."

In the morning Beauty told the dream to her father, and it comforted him a little, but it did not keep him from crying aloud in his distress when the moment came for parting with his beloved daughter.

When he was out of sight, Beauty could not help throwing herself on a couch and sobbing as if her heart would break. This relieved her feelings, and, being of a brave nature, she sat up, commended herself to the care of God, and though she quite expected to be eaten by the Beast that evening, she resolved not to waste the few last hours of her life by meeting her trouble half-way.

She therefore took a walk through the lovely grounds, and then began to explore the interior of the castle. She could not help admiring the magnificent decorations and priceless tapestries, as well as the costly furniture.

She came to a door on which was written:

Beauty's Boudoir

Extremely surprised, she quickly opened the door, and was dazzled by the brilliance of her surroundings—every comfort and luxury she could desire was there.

One of the first things that caught her eye was an exquisite bookcase, filled with handsome editions of her favourite books, and near it was a harpsichord with an abundance of music.

"The Beast does not want me to weary," said she in a low voice; then she thought to herself, "If I had only one day to live, he would surely not have provided so much for my entertainment." This thought gave her courage. She opened the bookcase, and took out a volume with a very long title in gold letters; it was this:

Desire. Command.

You are Lady and Mistress here.

"Alas!" thought she, with a sigh, "I desire nothing but to see my poor father, and to know what he is doing just now."

She laid down the book without speaking a word. Judge then of her surprise when, in a great mirror on the opposite wall, she saw the cottage where her father was just arriving, broken down with grief. Her sisters came out to meet him, pretending to be sorry, but, in spite of their false grimaces, joy was visible in the eyes to see him returning without her. Then it all disappeared, and, standing there, she could not help thinking how considerate and kind the Beast seemed to have been in trying to make her happy, and in her heart she felt she need not be so much afraid of him.

At noon an excellent dinner was on the table, and while she was eating she listened to a fine band playing lovely music, but no one was visible.

In the evening, as she sat down to supper, she heard the peculiar noise made by the Beast, and she could not help trembling violently when he appeared.

"Beauty," said the monster, "are you willing to let me look at you while you sup?"

"You are master here," said Beauty, in a tremulous voice.

"No!" replied the Beast, "you alone are mistress here. You have only to bid me go away if my presence annoys you and I shall go at once. Tell me frankly—do you not think me extremely ugly?"

"I do indeed," said Beauty, "for I cannot tell an untruth, but I think you are very kind."

"You are right," said the monster, "but besides being ugly, I am very stupid. I know quite well that I am only a fool."

"No one is really stupid who thinks he is not clever. No fool ever considers himself one."

"Enjoy your supper, then, Beauty," said the monster, "and try not to feel weary in your own house, for all you see is yours, and it would grieve me much to see you unhappy."

"You are very kind," said Beauty, "and your goodness of heart gives me great pleasure. Indeed, when I think how good you are, I do not seem to see you so ugly."

"Oh! for that part," said the Beast, "my heart is tender enough, but it does not hinder me from being a monster."

"There are many men far worse monsters then you are," said Beauty, "and I prefer you with the face you have to many men I have met, who, behind a handsome face, hide a false bad heart."

"If I had wit enough I should pay you a great compliment to thank you for the pleasure your words give me," said the Beast, "but, being so stupid, all I can say is that I am greatly obliged to you."

Beauty took a hearty supper, and quite forgot her fear of the Beast, but

she was again in an agony of terror when he suddenly said to her:
"Beauty, will you be my wife?"

It was some time before she could find words to reply, but at last she answered simply:

"No, Beast."

At this the poor monster heaved a dreadful sigh, which seemed more like a shriek, and the whole palace shook with the sound. Beauty thought her last hour had come. The Beast, however, only said gently: "Good night, then, Beauty," and went slowly to the door, turning his head from time to time to look wistfully at her as he went.

Left alone, Beauty felt a great wave of pity rising within her.

"What a pity it is that he is so ugly!" said she. "He is so very good and kind!"

Three months passed thus in the palace, without any special event. Every evening Beauty received a visit from the Beast, who did his best to entertain her during supper with his simple talk, which never lacked good sense, but which was far from being what is called, in society, brilliant conversation. Every day Beauty noticed some new token of the goodness which lay below the repulsive outward appearance of the monster. She was becoming accustomed to his ugliness, and instead of dreading his visits she often found herself looking at her watch as nine o'clock drew near, for that was the hour when he made his appearance. There was only one thing which really distressed her. It was that the monster, before leaving her, never failed to ask her if she would become his wife, and never seemed less pained at her refusal.

One evening, Beauty said to him:

"Beast, you grieve me greatly. I only wish I could bring myself to marry you, but I am too sincere to pretend to you that I can ever do so. I shall always be your friend—will you not try to be contented with that?"

"I suppose I must," said the Beast. "I can judge justly, and I know how horribly ugly I am, only I love you greatly. I ought to be very thankful that you are willing to remain here to keep me company. Promise me, I entreat you, that you will never leave me."

Beauty blushed deeply at these words. That afternoon she had seen in her mirror that her father was very ill from his grief at losing her, and she wished greatly to visit him, and reassure him.

"I could readily promise," said she, "never to leave you altogether, but I wish so much to see my father again that I shall die of grief if I may not do so."

"I would rather die myself than grieve you," said the monster. "I shall send you home to your father, you will stay there, and your poor Beast will die of grief."

"Oh, no!" said Beauty, weeping. "I love you too much to wish to cause your death. I promise you to return in eight days. You have enabled me to see that my sisters are both married, and that my brothers have joined the army. My father is quite alone. Let me stay with him for a week, I beg of you."

"You shall be there to-morrow morning," said the Beast, "but do remember your promise. When you are ready to return, you have only to lay your ring on the table when you go to bed. Good-bye, Beauty."

The Beast sighed, in his usual fearful way, when he said these words, and Beauty went to bed, much grieved at having hurt him. She awoke next morning in her father's house. She rang a bell which was on the table by the side of her bed, and it was answered by the servant-maid, who gave a great cry of astonishment when she saw her. The father went quickly upstairs to know what had happened, and was beside himself with joy when he saw his dear daughter. He clasped her in his arms and they embraced each other long and tenderly.

When she got up to dress, Beauty remembered that she had no clothes to put on, but the maid told her that she had just found a chest in the next room, and on opening it she saw it was filled with magnificent robes of costly materials, trimmed with gold lace and embroidered with jewels, and Beauty felt most grateful to the kind Beast for his attentions. She chose the plainest of these beautiful dressses; then she asked the maid to lock the chest, as she wished to give the others to her sister, but she had hardly said the words when the chest disappeared. Her father said it looked as if the Beast only intended the dresses for herself, and at these words the chest was again in its place.

While Beauty was dressing, word of her arrival was sent to her sisters, who appeared soon after with their husbands. Both of them were miserably unhappy. One had married a man who was exceedingly handsome, but who was so vain that he thought of nothing but his own good looks, and took no notice whatever of his wife. The other had married a man who was extraordinarily clever, but the only use he made of his brains was to utter sarcastic remarks to everyone, and particularly to his wife.

These sisters were very envious when they saw Beauty looking prettier than ever and dressed like a princess. In vain she kissed and fondled them; they could not hide their jealousy, which increased as they saw how happy she was. They both went into the garden to vent their spite, and to complain to each other.

"Why," said they, "is that creature so much happier than we? Are we not as deserving of happiness as she is?"

"Sister," said the eldest, "I have an idea; let us persuade her to overstay her time. Her stupid Beast will be enraged with her for not keeping her word, and probably he will devour her."

"What a clever plan!" said the other. "We must pretend to be very fond of her and make a great fuss about her."

With this wicked thought in their minds they went back into the cottage and were so very loving in their speech and manner that poor Beauty almost wept for joy. At the end of the eight days, they made such a show of grief, tearing their hair and wringing their hands, that Beauty consented to stay another week, not without being very sorry for the disappointment she was causing her poor Beast, whom she had grown so fond of, and whom she was longing to see again. On the tenth night of her visit, she dreamt she was in the palace garden, where she saw the Beast lying prone upon the grass, dying, and reproaching her for her ingratitude. She awoke with a start; then she began to weep.

"How wicked I am!" she said to herself. "How could I grieve the poor Beast who has been so good to me? Is it his fault that he is ugly and not clever? He is good, and that is worth more than cleverness or good looks. Why could I not marry him? I should have been much happier with him than my sisters are with their husbands. It is neither the good looks nor the cleverness of her husband that can make a woman happy; it is kindness of heart, uprightness, and readiness to oblige, and my poor Beast has all these good qualities. I may not be in love with him, but my heart is full of heart, uprightness, and readiness to oblige, and my poor Beast has all these good quallities. I may not be in love with him, but my heart is full of respect, friendship, and gratitude whenever I think of him. Come! I must not make him unhappy. I should reproach myself all my life if I did."

Beauty got up, put her ring on the table, and went back to bed. She quickly fell asleep, and when she awoke next morning she was pleased to find herself back in the palace of the Beast. She dressed herself magnificently to give him pleasure, and found the day pass all too slowly, waiting for nine o'clock. At last the hour struck, but the Beast did not make his appearance.

Beauty was greatly alarmed, fearing lest she had caused his death. She ran from room to room, calling him loudly but she got no answer. She was almost in despair when she suddenly remembered her dream. Quick as thought, she turned and ran toward the garden. There, on the very spot she had seen in her sleep, lay her poor Beast, prone on the grass near the brook, quite unconscious and apparently dead. In an agony of grief she threw herself down over his body, without any sense of horror; then, finding that his heart was still beating, she brought water from the stream and bathed his temples. This revived him a little, and at length he opened his eyes.

After a little, the Beast found strength to speak.

"You forgot your promise," said he, gazing at Beauty. "My grief at losing you was so great that I determined to starve myself to death, but I shall die happy now that I have had the great pleasure of seeing you again."

"No, my dear Beast, you shall not die," cried Beauty. "You must live to become my husband. From this moment I am yours. I imagined I had no stronger feeling for you then friendship, but now I know that I cannot live without you."

Just as Beauty finished this speech, the whole palace was brilliantly illuminated, while fireworks and music showed that some great event was being celebrated. Beauty looked up for a moment, but immediately turned again toward her dear Beast, for whose life she trembled. But where was he? What did it all mean? At her feet knelt a young Prince, handsome as Adonis, who was gratefully thanking her for having broken the spell of his enchantment. Although this Prince well deserved her attention, she quickly asked him:

"Where is my Beast?"

"You see him at your feet," was the reply. "A wicked fairy had condemned me to remain in that dreadful form till a beautiful young lady should, of her own free will, consent to marry me, and I was strictly forbidden to show my intelligence. You alone of all those I have met were touched by my kindness of disposition in spite of my forbidding appearance, and in offering you my crown and my heart I do not pretend to be able to repay all I owe to you."

Beauty held out her hand to the Prince, in a dream of delighted surprise. He rose and clasped her hand in his, and they walked together to the palace. On entering the great hall, Beauty was overjoyed to see her dear father and all the family there. The beautiful lady whom she had seen in her dream had transported them there from the cottage.

This lady, who was a great fairy, now came forward.

"Beauty," said she, "come and receive the reward of your wise choice. You preferred high character to mere beauty, or even cleverness; you deserve to find all these united in one person. You are going to be a great queen. I hope that the throne will not alter your character."

"As for you, ladies," said the fairy to the sisters, "I know the malice which fills your hearts. You shall become statues, but you shall retain your reason inside the stone which imprisons you. You shall be placed one on each side of the door of your sister's palace, where your only punishment will be seeing your sister's happiness. When you recognize your faults and repent of them, you will be restored to your human forms, but I fear you are likely to remain statues. One may correct oneself of pride, bad temper, greed, or sloth, but to change an evil, envious heart is little short of a miracle."

Then, with one touch of her wand, she transported the whole company to the kingdom of the Prince, whose subjects received him with joy. Beauty and he were married with great pomp the festivities lasting many days. The union was a very happy one, and at the end of a long life their love for each other was still undiminished.

CARMEN[1]

Prosper Mérimée

CHAPTER I

I HAVE always suspected geographers of not knowing what they were talking about when they place the battle-field of Munda in the country of the Bastuli-Pœni, near the modern Monda, some leagues to the north of Marbella. According to my own interpretation of the text of the anonymous author of *Bellum Hispaniensis*, and after some information collected in the excellent library of the Duke of Osuena, I considered it necessary to seek in the environs of Montilla for the memorable spot where for the last time Cæser played double or quits against the champions of the Republic. Finding myself in Andalusia about the beginning of the autumn of 1830, I made a rather lengthened excursion with a view to clear up the doubts which still remained in my mind on this question. A pamphlet which I shall shortly publish will, I trust, leave no uncertainty in the minds of all honest archæologists. Pending the time when my dissertation shall resolve once for all this geographical problem which keeps all scientific Europe in suspense, I wish to relate a little story, which will in no degree prejudice the interesting question of the site of Munda.

I had engaged a guide and two horses at Cordova, and set out with

---

[1] Translated by H. Morley.

Cæsar's *Commentaries* and a few shirts as my only baggage. One day, while wandering in the elevated part of the pain of Cachena, tired out, dying of thirst, broiled by a vertical sun. I was just consigning Cæsar and the sons of Pompey to the devil, when I perceived at some distance from the path which I was following a little green space dotted with rushes and reeds. These announced the vicinity of a spring. In fact, as I approached I perceived that the seeming greensward was a marsh in which a streamlet, emerging, as it seemed, from a narrow gorge between two lofty buttresses of the Sierra di Calva, lost itself. I concluded that if I ascended a little farther I should find clearer and fresher water, and fewer leeches and frogs, with perhaps a little shade between the boulders. At the entrance of the gorge my horse neighed, and another horse, which I could not see, immediately replied.

I had scarcely advanced a hundred paces when the gorge suddenly opened out and displayed to my view a kind of natural amphitheatre, entirely shaded by the lofty cliffs which enclosed it. It was impossible to meet with any spot which promised a traveller a more agreeable resting-place. At the base of the perpendicular cliffs the stream rushed out and fell bubbling into a little basin lined with sand white as snow. Five or six beautiful and verdant oaks, always sheltered from the wind here, and watered by the stream, rose beside its source, and covered it with their leafy shade; lastly, around the basin grew a rich fine grass which offered a better bed than one could find in any inn for ten leagues round.

But the honour of discovering this charming retreat did not rest with me. A man was already reposing there, and was no doubt asleep when I penetrated thither. Awakened by the neighing of the horses, he arose and approached his steed, which had taken advantage of his master's sleeping to make a good meal of the luxuriant grass around him. His owner was a young fellow of medium height, but of robust build, and with a gloomy and proud look on his face. His complexion, which may have been good, had by exposure become even darker than his hair. In one hand he grasped the halter of his steed, and in the other he held a brass blunderbuss. I must confess that at first the sight of the blunderbuss and the fierce aspect of the man surprised me; but I no longer believed in brigands, having only heard of them, but never having met any of them. Besides, I had seen so many honest farmers armed to the teeth to proceed to market, that the mere sight of fire-arms was not sufficient evidence upon which to base the dishonesty of the unknown. And then I thought, what would he want with my shirts and my volume of Elzevir *Commentaries?*

So I saluted the man of the blunderbuss with an easy bow, and inquired with a smile whether I had disturbed him from his siesta. Without answering, he measured me with his eyes from head to foot; then, as if satisfied with his scrutiny, he paid the same attention to my guide, who was approaching. I perceived the latter turn pale, and pull up with every symptom of terror. An unlucky meeting, I thought; but prudence immediately counselled me not to display any uneasiness. I dismounted, told the guide to unbridle the horses and kneeling down beside the spring, I plunged my head and hands into it; then lying flat on the ground like the wicked soldiers of Gideon, I took a deep draught.

Nevertheless, I managed to keep an eye on the guide and the unknown. The former approached with manifest hesitation; the latter did not appear to harbour any evil intentions against us, for he had released his horse again, and his blunderbuss, which he had at first grasped horizontally and held, 'ready,' was now held muzzle downwards.

Not thinking it worth while to be offended at the slight value put upon me, I lay down upon the grass, and in an easy manner asked the man with the blunderbuss whether he had a tinder-box about him. At the same time I took out my cigar-case. The unknown, still in silence, fumbled in his pocket for the box, and taking it out hastened to strike a light for me. He was evidently getting sociable, for he came and sat down opposite me, but without putting aside his weapon. My cigar alight, I selected the best of those remaining in my case, and inquired whether he would smoke.

"Yes, sir," he replied. These were the first words he had uttered, and I remarked that he did not pronounce tha S's in the Andalusian manner, from which circumstance I concluded that he was a traveller like myself, less the archæological inspiration.

"You will find this pretty good," I said, as I handed him a genuine regalia Habaña.

He bowed slightly, lighted his cigar from mine, thanked me with another bow, and began to smoke with every appearance of intense satisfaction.

"Ah!" he exclaimed as he permitted the smoke to escape slowly from his mouth and nostrils, "what a time it is since I have smoked!"

In Spain a cigar offered and accepted establishes friendly relations, as in the East the partaking of bread and salt ensures hospitality. My companion proved himself more communicative then I had hoped. However, although he declared himself a native of the province of Montilla, he appeared to be very slightly acquainted with the district. He did not know the name of the charming valley in which we were resting. He could not name any village in the neighbourhood; and at length, in reply to my question as to whether he had not noticed in the environs some ruined walls and carved stones, he confessed that he never paid any attention to such things. On the other hand, he showed himself a connoisseur in horse-flesh. He criticized my steed—which was not difficult; then he told me the pedigree of his own, which came from the famous Cordova stud: a noble animal indeed, and so insensible to fatigue that, as his master, said, he had on one occasion made ninety miles in the day at speed. In the midst of this tirade the unknown suddenly checked himself, as if surprised and sorry that he had said so much.

"It was when I was in a great hurry to reach Cordova," he continued with some embarrassment. "I had to prosecute a lawsuit"

As he was speaking he looked at my guide, Antonio, who lowered his eyes.

The shade and the spring charmed me so that I recollected some slices of an excellent ham which my friends in Montilla had put in my guide's haversack. I made him fetch them, and invited the stranger to join me in my impromptu picnic. If he had not smoked for a long while, it seemed to me that he must have fasted for forty-eight hours at least. He ate like a famished wolf. I thought my appearance had been quite providential for the poor devil. My guide, however, ate little, drank less, and spoke not at all, although at the beginning of our journey he had been a tremendous chatterer. The presence of our guest seemed to be a restraint upon him, and a kind of mutual distrust kept them apart; the cause of this I could not determine.

The last morsels of bread and ham had been eaten; we had each smoked a second cigar; I ordered the guide to bridle the horses, and I was about to take leave of my new acquaintance, when he asked me where I intended to pass the night.

Before I could attend to a sign from my guide, I had replied that I was making for the Venta del Cuervo.

"A bad lodging for such a person as you, sir. I am going thither, and if you will permit me to accompany you we will go together."

"Very willingly," I replied as I mounted my horse. My guide, who was holding the stirrup, made me another sign. I replied to it by shrugging my shoulders, as if to assure him that I was quite easy in my mind; and then we started.

The mysterious signs of Antonio, his uneasiness, the few words that escaped the unknown, particularly the account of the thirty-league ride and the by no means plausible explanation which he had offered, had already formed my opinion concerning my travelling companion. I had no doubt whatever that I had to do with a *contrabandista*, perhaps with a brigand. What matter? I knew enough of the Spanish character to be certain that I had nothing to fear from a man who had eaten and smoked with me. His very presence was a protection against all untoward adventures. Moreover, I was rather glad to know what a brigand was like. One does not meet them every day, and there is a certain charm in finding oneself in company with a dangerous person, particularly when one finds him gentle and subdued.

I hoped to lead the unknown to confide in me by degrees, and notwithstanding the winks of my guide, I led the conversation to the bandits. Of course I spoke of them with all respect. There was at that time a famous bandit in Andalusia named José-Maria, whose exploits were in everyone's mouth. "Suppose I am in the company of José-Maria!" I said to myself. I told all the anecdotes of this hero that I knew—all those in his praise, of course, and I loudly expressed my admiration of his bravery and generosity.

"José-Maria is only a scamp," replied the stranger coldly.

"Is he doing himself justice, or is it only modesty on his part?" I asked myself; for, after considering my companion carefully, I began to apply to him the description of José-Maria which I had read posted up on the gates of many towns of Andalusia. Yes, it is he, certainly. Fair hair, blue eyes, large mouth, good teeth, small hand, a fine shirt, a velvet vest with silver buttons, gaiters of white skin, a bay horse. No doubt about it. But let us respect his *incognito!*

We arrived at the venta. It was just what he had described it—that is to say, one of the most miserable inns I had ever seen. One large room served for kitchen, parlour, and bedroom. A fire was burning on a flat stone in the middle of the room, and the smoke went out through a hole in the roof, or rather it stopped there, and hung in a cloud some feet above the ground. Beside the wall, on the floor, were extended five or six horse-cloths, which were the beds for travellers. About twenty paces from the house—or rather from the single room which I have described—was a kind of shed, which did duty for a stable. In this delightful dwelling there were for the time being no inhabitants except an old woman and a little girl of ten or twelve years old, both as black as soot, and in rags.

"Here," though I, "are all that remain of the population of the ancient Munda Bætica. O Cæsar, O Sextus Pompey, how astonished you would be if you were to return to this mundane sphere!"

When she perceived my companion the old woman uttered an exclamation of surprise. "Ah! Señor Don José!" she cried.

Don José frowned and raised his hand with a gesture of command which made the old woman pause. I turned to my guide, and with a sign imperceptible to José made Antonio understand that I needed no information respecting the man with whom I had to pass the night. The supper was better then I had anticipated. They served up upon a small table about a foot high an old cock fricasseed with rice and pimentos, then pimentos in oil, and lastly, *gaspacho*, a kind of pimento salad. Three such highly seasoned dishes obliged us often to have recourse to the flask of Montilla, which we found delicious.

Having supped, and perceiving a mandolin hanging against the wall— there are mandolins everywhere in Spain—I asked the little girl who waited on us if she knew how to play it.

"No," she replied; "but Don José plays it very well."

Will you be so good as to sing something?" I said to him, "I passionately love your national music."

"I can refuse nothing to so polite a gentleman who gives me such excellent cigars," replied Don José good-humouredly, and being handed the mandolin, he sang to his own accompaniment. His voice was harsh, but rather agreeable; the air was sad and wild; as for the words, I did not understand one of them.

"If I am not mistaken," I said, "that is not a Spanish air which you have just sung. It strikes me as resembling the *zorzicos* which I have heard in the 'Provinces,' and the words seem to be in the Basque tongue."

"Yes," replied José with a sombre air. He placed the mandolin on the ground, and sat contemplating the dying embers with a singularly sad expression. Illumined by the lamp placed on the little table, his face, at once noble and ferocious, recalled Milton's Satan. Like him, perhaps, my companion was thinking of a heaven he had quitted—of the exile to which his sin had condemned him. I endeavoured to engage him in conversation, but he did not reply, so absorbed was he in his sad reflections.

By this time the old woman had retired to rest in a corner of the room behind a primitive screen formed of a rug suspended from a cord. The little girl had followed her into this retreat reserved for the fair sex. Then my guide, rising, invited me to follow him up to the stable, but at this José, as if waking up with a start, demanded in a rough tone whither he was going.

"To the stable," replied the guide.

"What for? The horses have plenty to eat. Lie down here; the gentleman will permit it."

"I am afraid the Señor's horse may be ill, I want the Señor to see it; perhaps he will know what to do."

398

It was evident that Antonio wished to speak to me in private, but I did not care to arouse Don José's suspicions, and in the circumstances it appeared to me that the best line to take would be to display the greatest confidence. So I informed Antonio that I knew nothing about horses, and that I was very sleepy. Don José followed the man to the stable, and soon returned alone. He told me that the horse had nothing the matter with him, but that the guide valued the steed so highly that he was rubbing him with his vest to make him perspire, and intended to continue this occupation during the night. However, I was soon extended beneath the rugs, carefully wrapped in my cloak so as to avoid contact with them. After begging pardon for the liberty which he was taking in lying close to me, Don José lay down before the door, first having renewed the priming of his blunderbuss, which he took care to place beneath the haversack which served him for a pillow. Five minutes after we had wished each other good night we were both buried in profound slumber.

I had believed that I was sufficiently tired to sleep in such a place as that, but after an hour a very disagreeable itching aroused me from my first nap. As soon as I understood the nature of the disturbing cause I rose, firmly convinced that it would be better to past the night in the open air than under such an inhospitable roof. I gained the door on tiptoe, and stepping over Don José who was sleeping the sleep of the just, I managed to quit the house without arousing him. Near the door was a large wooden bench; on this I lay down and settled myself for the night as well as I could. I was about to shut my eyes for the second time, when I fancied I perceived the shadows of a man and a horse passing in front of me and not making the slightest noise. I jumped up, and thought I recognized Antonio. Surprised to see him out of the stable at such an hour I advanced to meet him. He stopped when he perceived me approaching.

"Where is he?" asked Antonio in a low voice.

"In the venta; he is asleep; he has no fear of fleas. Why have you brought the horse out?"

Then I remarked that Antonio—so as not to make any noise in quitting the shed, had carefully enveloped the horse's feet in the fragments of an old cloth.

"Speak lower, in the name of God," he said. "You do not know who that man is. He is José Navarro, the most famous bandit in Andalusia. I have been making signs to you all day which you would not understand."

"Bandit or not, what does it matter to me?" I replied. "He has not robbed us, and I will wager that he has no intention to do so."

"All very well, but there is a price of two hundred ducats on his head. I know where there is a detachment of lancers about a league and a half distant; and before daybreak I will bring some stout fellows here. I would have taken his horse, but he is so vicious that no one save Navarro can go near him."

"What the devil are you about?" I said. "What harm has the poor man done to you that you should betray him? Besides, are you certain that he *is* the brigand you say he is?"

"Perfectly certain. Just now he followed me into the stable and said, 'You seem to know me. If you tell this good gentleman who I am, I will wring your neck!' Remain with him, sir, you have nothing to fear. So long as you are there he will have no suspicions."

While we were speaking we had got some distance from the venta, and no one in it would hear the sound of the horse's hoofs. In the twinkling of an eye Antonio took off the wrapping and prepared to mount. I endeavoured to detain him by prayers, and even by threats.

"I am a poor devil, sir," he replied, "and I cannot afford to lose two hundred ducats; particularly when I can also rid the country of such vermin as is yonder. But take care! If Navarro wakes he will rush for his blunderbuss, so mind yourself. I have gone too far to retreat. You can suit yourself."

The scoundrel was already in the saddle. He spurred his horse, and was soon hidden from my view in the darkness.

I was very much annoyed with my guide, and not a little uneasy. After a moment's reflection I made up my mind what course to pursue, and re-entered the venta. Don José was still asleep, repairing, no doubt, the fatigues and watches of many days preceding. I was obliged to shake him roughly before I could arouse him. Never shall I forget his fierce look and the action with which he sought to grasp his blunderbuss which I had removed as a matter of precaution.

"Sir," said I, "I ask your pardon for disturbing you, but I have a simple question to ask. Would you be pleased to see half a dozen lancers come here?"

He leaped to his feet, and in a terrible tone, said, "Who has told you that?"

"No matter whence comes the advice so that it is good."

"Your guide has betrayed me, but he shall answer for it. Where is he?"

"I do not know. In the stable I think—but someone has told me——"

"Who told you? The old woman, perhaps?"

"Someone whom I do not know. Without more words, have you— yes or no—any reasons which render it advisable for you to avoid the soldiers? If you have, do not lose time—if not, then good night; and I beg your pardon for awakening you."

"Ah, your guide—your guide! I suspected him at first; but his account will be settled! Adieu, sir; God reward you for the service I owe you. I am not so bad as you believe me to be; yes, there is still in me something which deserves the sympathy of a brave man. Adieu, sir, I have only one regret, and that is my inability to pay my debt to you."

"For the service which I render you, Don José, promise me to suspect no one—do not think of vengeance. Hold—here are some cigars for you. *Bon voyage!"*—and I extended my hand to him.

He shook mine without replying; seized his blunderbuss and his sack, and after saying a few words to the old woman in a slang I did not understand, he hurried to the shed. A few minutes afterwards I heard him gallop away into the open country.

As for me, I retired to my bench but I could not sleep. I interrogated myself as to whether I had any right to save a robber—perhaps a murderer—from the gallows, and that only because I had eaten with him some ham and rice. Had I not betrayed my guide, who was upholding the laws? had I not exposed myself to the revenge of a villain? But the duties of hospitality? "A prejudice of savagery," I said to myself; "I shall have to be responsible for all the crimes that the bandit hereafter may commit." However, *is* it a prejudice—this instinct of conscience which defies all reasoning? Perhaps in the delicate situation in which I was placed, I might be able to escape without remorse? I was balanced in the greatest uncertainty respecting the morality of my action when I saw half a dozen horse-soldiers returning with Antonio, who kept prudently in the rear. I met them half way, and informed them that the bandit had escaped two hours previously. The old woman, when questioned by the corporal, replied that she knew Navarro, but that, living alone, she did not dare to risk her life by denouncing him. She added that he was always in the habit of departing in the middle of the night when he came to her house. As for me, I was compelled to proceed a distance of some leagues to show my passport, and sign a declaration before the alcalde, after which I was permitted to resume my archæological researches. Antonio nursed a grudge against me—for he suspected that it was I who had prevented him from gaining the reward of two hundred ducats. Nevertheless we parted good friends at Cordova, where I presented him with a gratuity as large as the condition of my finances permitted me to give.

Chapter II

I spent some days in Cordova. I had been told of a certain manuscript in the Dominican library in which I expected to find some interesting information concerning the ancient Munda. Being very well received by the good monks I passed the days in their monastery; and in the evenings I walked about the town. At Cordova at sunset there are always a number of idlers about the quay which borders the right bank of the Guadalquiver. There one breathes the odours of a tannery which still preserves the old reputation of the country for the preparation of leather; but on the other hand one enjoys a sight which is well worth seeing. Some minutes before the Angelus is rung a number of women assemble on the bank of the river at the end of the quay. which is raised considerably. Not a man dares to mingle with this troop. Immediately the Angelus sounds night is supposed to have set in. At the last stroke of the bell all the women undress and plunge into the water. Then arise cries, laughter, and an infernal din. From the top or the quay the men contemplate the bathers, staring at them with open eyes, but seeing little. Nevertheless these white and undefined forms, which are perceptible in the deep azure waters of the river, cause poetic minds to conceive, and with a little imagination it is not difficult to represent to oneself Diana and her nymphs in the bath, without fear of sharing the fate of Actæon. I was informed that on one occasion some scapegraces, by bribing the bell-ringer of the cathedral, induced him to ring the Angelus twenty minutes in advance of the usual hour. Although it was broad daylight, the nymphs of the Guadalquiver did not hesitate, and trusting more to the Angelus than the sun, they made innocence their bathing-dress—which is always of the simplest fashion. I was not there. In my time the bell-ringer was incorruptible, the twilight not very clear, and only a cat would have been able to distinguish the oldest orange-seller from the prettiest *grisette* in Cardova.

One evening at the hour when there is nothing to be seen, I was smoking, leaning upon the parapet of the quay, when a woman ascended the steps which led down to the river, and seated herself close to me. She had in her hair a large bunch of jessamine, which emitted a strong perfume. She was simply, perhaps poorly, clad, in black, as most of the girls are in the evening. The fashionable ladies only wear black in the morning; in the evening they dress *à la Francesca*. As she approached me the bather let fall on her shoulders the mantilla with which she had covered her head, and in the starlight I could perceive that she was pretty, young, well made, and that she had very large eyes. I quickly threw away my cigar. She at once appreciated this attention—a politeness entirely French—and hastened to inform me that she liked the smell of tobacco-smoke very much, and that even she herself smoked when she could get very mild cigarettes. Fortunately I had some such in my case, and hastened to offer them to her. She condescended to take one, and lighted it at the burning end of a cork which a child brought us for a halfpenny. Smoking together we conversed so long—the pretty bather and I—that we found ourselves alone upon the quay. I did not consider that there was anything indiscreet in suggesting that we should go and have some ices at a *neveria*.[1] After some modest hesitation she consented, but before deciding she wished to know what time it was. I made my repeater strike the hour, and this astonished her very much. "What inventions they have in your country! What countryman are you?"

"A Frenchman, and your humble servant, mademoiselle, or madame. You are probably of Cordova?"

"No."

"You are at least Andalusian? I fancy I can detect so much in your soft accent."

"If you remark people's accents so closely you ought to be able to divine who I am."

"I believe you are of the Holy Land—a few steps from Paradise."

I had learnt this metaphor, which refers to Andalusia, from my friend Francisco Sevilla, the well-known *picador*.

"Bah!—Paradise! People here say it is not for such as we."

"Then you must be Moorish, or——" I stopped, not liking to say "a Jewess."

"Go along! go along! You see quite well that I am a gipsy. Do you wish me to tell you *la baji* (good-fortune)? Have you ever heard of *La Carmencita*? I am she!"

I was such an infidel at that time—it is fifteen years ago, remember! —that I did not recoil with horror at finding myself in company with a sorceress. "All right," I said to myself. "Last week I supped with a bandit —a highway robber; to-day I am eating ices with a handmaiden of the devil! When travelling it is as well to see everything!" I had besides another reason for cultivating her acquaintance. When I quitted the University I confess to my shame that I had lost some time in studying the occult sciences, and many times I had attempted to summon up the spirits of darkness. Although long before cured of my passion for such researches,

---

[1] A café furnished with an ice-house, or rather with a depot of snow.

I nevertheless still retained a certain curiousity regarding all superstitions, and it was interesting to me to ascertain to what pitch the arts of magic had attained among the gipsies.

As we chatted we had entered the *neveria*, and seated ourselves at a small table lighted by a wax candle placed within a glass shade. I had then plenty of opportunity to observe the *gitana*, while respectable people eating their ices were astounded to see me in such society.

I very much doubt whether Mademoiselle Carmen was of the true blood—at any rate, she was the prettiest of all the women of her race whom I ever met. To be beautiful, a woman, say the Spaniards, must unite in herself thirty points; or, if you please, you may define her by ten adjectives, each applicable to three parts of her person. For instance, she should have three black points—the eyes, the eyelids, and the eyebrows; three delicate, fine—the fingers the lips, and the hair, etc. See Brantôme for the others. My Bohemian could not pretend to the necessary perfection. Her skin, though quite smooth, approached somewhat to the coppery tinge. Her eyes were obliquely set, but large and full; her lips rather thick, but well cut, and permitted the teeth—white as blachend almonds—to be seen. Her hair was perhaps a trifle coarse, but had a blue sheen running through it, like that one sees in a raven's wings, and was long and luxuriant. Not to weary you with a detailed description, I will merely say that with each fault she united a good point, which came out perhaps more by virtue of the contrast. She was of a strange and savage beauty—a face which at first surprised you, but it was one you could never forget. Her eyes especially had an expression at once voluptuous and fierce, which I have never since noticed in any human eyes. "Eye of gipsy, eye of wolf" is a Spanish saying which denotes quick observation. If you have not time to go to the Zoological Gardens to study the expression of the wolf's eyes, look at your cat when he is watching a sparrow!

One felt that it would be ridiculous to have one's fortune told in a *café*, so I begged the pretty sorceress to permit me to accompany her home. She agreed without difficulty, but again she was anxious to know how time sped, and begged me to strike my repeater once more.

"Is it *really* gold?" she asked, as she gazed at the watch attentively.

When we resumed our way it was dark night, the majority of the shops were shut, and the streets were almost deserted. We passed the bridge over the Guadalquiver, and at the end of the suburb we reached a house with nothing of the palatial about it. A child opened the door to us. The gipsy said something to her in a language unknown to me, which I have since discovered was the Romany, or *chepé-calli*, the idiom of the *gitanos*. The child immediately disappeared, leaving us in a room of considerable dimensions, furnished with a small table, two stools, and a chest. I must not forget a jar of water, a pile of oranges, and a hank of onions.

As soon as we were alone the gipsy took from the chest a pack of cards, which appeared to have seen much service, a loadstone, a dried chameleon, and some other objects necessary for the practice of her art. Then she bade me cross my left hand with a piece of silver, and the magic ceremonies began. It is useless to repeat her predictions, but by her manner of operating it was evident that she was a practised sorceress.

Unfortunately it was not long ere we were disturbed. The door was suddenly and violently thrown open; a man wrapped up to the eyes in a brown cloak entered the room, and apostrophized the gipsy in a by no means gentle fashion. I did not understand what he was saying, but the tone of his voice indicated that he was in a very bad temper. The *gitana* exhibited neither surprise nor anger at his appearance, but she hastened to meet him, and with extraordinary volubility addressed some words to him in the mysterious language which she had already made use of in my presence. The word *payllo*, frequently repeated, was the only one I understood. I was aware that by this term the gipsies designate any stranger. Supposing that it referred to me, I anticipated a rather delicate explanation; already I had grasped one of the legs of the stool, and was communing with myself as to the precise moment when I should hurl it at the head of the intruder, when the latter, pushing the girl rudely aside, advanced toward me, and then recoiling exclaimed:

"Ah, sir, it is *you* then!"

I looked at him in my turn, and recognized my acquaintance Don José. At that moment a feeling of regret that I had not let him be hanged came over me.

"Ah, it is you, my brave fellow!" I exclaimed, laughing with as little bitterness as I could manage. "You have interrupted mademoiselle and me at the very moment when she was revealing to me some very interesting things."

"Always the same—this shall finish it!" he muttered between his teeth, and darting a furious look at her.

The gipsy nevertheless continued to address him in her language. She got more excited by degrees. Her eyes flashed, became suffused with blood, and terrible in their aspect; her features contracted; she stamped her foot; it seemed to me that she was inciting him to do something which he had some hesitation in doing. What it was I understood only too well when I saw her pass and repass her little hand rapidly across her neck. I was constrained to believe that it was a question of cutting somebody's throat, and I had some suspicion that this throat was my own!

To all this torrent of eloquence Don José only replied sharply in a few words. Then the gipsy darted at him a glance of profound contempt, and seating herself *à la turque* in a corner of the room, she selected an orange from the heap, peeled it, and began to eat it.

Don José took me by the arm, opened the door, and led me into the street. We proceeded about two hundred paces in silence. Then extending his hand he said, "Keep straight on and you will come to the bridge!"

He immediately turned his back upon me, and hurried away. I reached my inn feeling somewhat sheepish and in a bad temper. The worst of it was that when I undressed, I perceived my watch was missing!

Several considerations prevented me from seeking to recover it in the morning, or to solicit the aid of the law in seeking it. I finished my work on the manuscript in the convent, and started for Seville. After several months' wandering in Andalusia I returned to Madrid, and I was obliged to pass Cordova. I had no intention of making a long stay there, for I had taken a dislike to this fine city and its bathers. However, there were some friends to be visited, some commissions to be executed, which would detain me in the ancient capital of the Mussulman princes for three or four days.

As soon as I made my appearance at the convent of the Dominicans one of the fathers, who had always displayed the keenest interest in my researches concerning the site of Munda, welcomed me with open arms.

"God be praised," he said. "Welcome indeed, my dear friend. We believed you dead, and I myself have said *paters* and *aves*—which I do not regret—for the repose of your soul! So you have not been assassinated; we knew you had been robbed!"

"How so?" I inquired in surprise.

"Well, you remember you used to strike that beautiful watch of yours when we wanted to know the time in the library. It has been found, and will be returned to you——"

"That is to say," interrupted I, somewhat put out of countenance, "supposing I have lost it."

"The scoundrel is in custody," continued the friar; "and as we knew he was the kind of fellow to shoot a man in order to take a *piécette*, we were all terribly afraid he had killed you. I will go with you to the *corré-gidor*, and we will recover your beautiful watch. And then don't say that justice is not done in Spain!"

"I confess," I replied, "that I would rather lose my watch than be instrumental in hanging a poor devil, particularly because—because——"

"Oh, do not be in the least alarmed; he is well certified to, and they cannot hang him twice. When I say hang him, I mean garrotte him. This robber of yours is a *hidalgo*, and so he will be garrotted the day after to-morrow without fail.[1] You perceive that a robbery more or less can make no difference in his case. I would to Heaven it were only robbery, but he has committed many murders, each one more horrible than that which preceded it."

"What is his name?"

"He is known in this country as José Navarro, but he has another Basque name which neither you nor I shall ever succeed in pronouncing. He is a man to see, and you who love to study the curious characteristics of the country ought not to neglect the opportunity of learning how in Spain these scoundrels are sent out of the world. He is in the chapel, and Fra Martinez will conduct you thither."

My friend the Dominican insisted so strongly upon my seeing the apparatus for the *petit pendement pien choli*, that I was unable to resist him. I went to see the prisoner, furnished with a bundle of cigars, which I trusted would atone for my intrusion.

They admitted me to see Don José just as he was finishing a meal. He bowed coldly to me and thanked me politely for the cigars which I had brought him. After counting them he selected a few and returned the remainder, observing that he should not want any more than those he then had!

I inquired whether by money or some little influence I could not in some measure ameliorate his condition. At first he shrugged his shoulders, smiling sadly; but after a while changing his mind he begged that I would cause a mass to be said for his soul.

"Would you," he added, timidly, "would you have another said for a woman who injured you?"

"Assuredly," I replied, "but I do not think that any woman has injured me in this country."

He took my hand and shook it gravely. After a momentary silence, he resumed:

"Dare I venture to ask you a favour? When you return to your own land perhaps you will pass through Navarre, at least you will pass by Vittoria, which is not very far from it."

"Yes," I replied, "I shall certainly pass by Vittoria, but it is not unlikely

---

[1] In 1830 the nobility still enjoyed this privilege. In the present day, under constitutional government, the common criminals have gained the right to be garrotted.

that I shall turn aside to Pampeluna and on your account I will willingly make the *détour*."

"Well, if you go to Pampeluna you will find more than one object of interest to detain you. It is a beautiful city. I will give you this medal (he showed me a silver medal which he wore round his neck), you will wrap it in paper"—he paused for an instant to master his emotion— "and you will send it or it to be sent to a good woman, whose address I will give you. You will say that I am dead, but do not tell her in what manner I died."

I promised to carry out his wishes. I saw him again on the following morning, and I passed a portion of the day with him. It was from his own lips that I learned the sad story which follows:

Chapter III

I was born, said he, at Elizondo, in the valley of Batzan. My name is Don José Lizarabengoa, and you know Spain well enough, sir, to understand that I am of the Basque country, and of ancient Christian lineage. If I take the title of Don it is because I have a right to it, and if I were at Elizondo I would show you my genealogy on parchment. I was destined for the Church, and compelled to study for it; but I did not profit by it. I was too fond of playing tennis and that was the ruin of me. When we Navarros play tennis we forget all else. One day when I had won a match a youth of Alava picked a quarrel with me. We fought with *maquilas*,[1] and still I had the advantage, but I was obliged to fly the country. I fell in with some dragoons and enlisted in the Almanza regiment of cavalry. People from our parts soon pick up the trade of a soldier. I quickly became a corporal, and was in a fair way to become quartermaster when to my misfortune I was put on guard at the tobacco manufactory of Seville. If you have ever been to Seville you have noticed that great building outside the ramparts near the Guadalquiver. It seems as if I can still see the door and the guard-house beside it. When they are off duty the Spaniards play cards or sleep, but I, a free Navarro, was always accustomed to employ myself. I made a chain of brass wire to sustain my priming-needle. One day my comrades exclaimed, "The clock is striking, the girls are going to work!" You know there are about four hundred or five hundred women employed in the cigar-making. They roll the cigars in the large room into which no man is permitted to enter without permission from the municipal

---

[1] Iron-shod sticks.

magistrate, because the girls work in undress, the young ones particularly, when the weather is warm. When the young women return to work after dinner, many young fellows go to see them pass, and there are some of all sorts. There are few of these ladies who would refuse a silk mantilla, and the inexperienced ones at this fishing have only to stoop to catch a fish. While the other men were looking on I remained on my bench near the door. I was young then and home-sick, and did not believe that there were anywhere pretty girls without blue skirts and plaits of hair falling over their shoulders. Besides, these Andalusians frightened me; I had not yet grown accustomed to their manners. They were always full of raillery, never serious or speaking a sensible word. I was working away at my chain when I heard some townspeople say, "Look at the *gitanella!*" I looked up and saw her. It was on a Friday, and I shall never forget it. I saw that Carmen, whom you know of, at whose house I found you some months ago.

She wore a red skirt, very short, which exposed to view her white silk stockings, with many a hole in them, and tiny shoes of morocco leather, tied with scarlet ribbons. She had thrown back her mantilla so as to display her shoulders, and an immense bunch of acacia blossom, which was stuck in her chemise. She also carried a flower in her mouth, and she walked with a movement of a thoroughbred filly from the Cordova stud. In my country a woman in such a costume would have made people cross themselves. At Seville every one paid some gay compliments to the girl on her appearance. She replied to them all, looking sideways as she went along, with her hand on her hip, as bold as the true gipsy she was. At first she did not take my fancy, and I continued my occupation, but she—after the nature of women and cats, which will not come when they are called and which come when they are not called—stopped in front of me and said, in the Andalusian form:

"*Conpadre*, will you give me your chain to hang the key of my strong box on?"

"It is to hang my priming-needle on," I replied.

"Your priming-needle! Ah, the señor makes laces, then; he requires needles."

Everyone began to laugh at me. I felt myself growing red, and could make no reply.

"Well, my love," she continued, "make me seven ells of black lace for a mantilla, thou primer of my soul."

Then, taking the flower from between her lips, she flipped it at me with a mouvment of her thumb, and struck me between the eyes. Sir, I felt as if I had received a bullet in the forehead. I did not know what to do with myself; I stood as stiff a board. When she had entered the factory I perceived the flower, which had fallen at my feet. I do not know what possessed me, but I picked it up when my comrades were not looking, and put it carefully in my vest. That was the first act of folly.

Two or three hours after, while I was still thinking of the incident, a porter arrived at the guard-house, out of breath and greatly discomposed. He told us that a woman had been assassinated in the great room of the factory, and that it was necessary to have the guard in. The sergeant ordered me to take two men and go and see what was the matter. I took the men and went up. Picture to yourself, sir, the sight that met my view when I entered—about three hundred women *en chemise*, or with as little as possible on them—screaming, crying, gesticulating, and making such a row that you couldn't have heard thunder. At one side a female was sprawling on the floor drenched in blood, with a cross—an X—cut on her face with a knife. Opposite the wounded woman, who was being tended by the best of the females, I perceived Carmen, restrained by five or six of her associates. The wounded woman kept crying out that she was dying and wanted a priest. Carmen said nothing; she clenched her teeth, and rolled her eyes like a chameleon.

"What is all this about?" I inquired. I had considerable difficulty in ascertaining what had passed, for all the women talked at once.

It would appear that the injured woman had boasted of having sufficient money in her pocket to buy a donkey at the market of Tirona.

"Shup up!" exclaimed Carmen, who had a tongue of her own, "why you haven't enough to purchase a brush."

The other, stung by the reproach, perhaps because she felt there were some suspicions concerning the article, replied that she did not know anything about brushes, not having the honour to be a gipsy or a daughter of Satan, but that Mademoiselle Carmencita would soon make the donkey's acquaintance when the *corrégidor* led it out for a walk with two lacqueys behind to beat the flie off.

"Well, then, for my part," replied Carmen, "I will make places for the flies to settle on your cheeks, for I will make a draught-board of them."

On that, criss-cross, she began, with the knife she used for cutting the cigars, to slash a St Andrew's cross on the woman's face.

The case was perfectly clear. I seized Carmen by the arm.

"Sister," I said politely, "you must come with me."

She darted a look of recognition at me, but she said resignedly:

"Let us go then. Where is my mantilla?"

She put it over her head in such a fashion as only to permit her fine eyes to be seen, and followed my two men as quiet as a lamb. When we reached the guard-house the quartermaster said the case was a serious one, and that he must send the culprit to prison. I was told off to conduct her. I placed her between two dragoons, and I marched behind as a corporal should do. We started for the city. At first the gipsy maintained a strict silence, but in Serpent Street—you know it, it well deserves its name with all its windings—in Serpent Street she began her manœuvres by letting her mantilla fall upon her shoulders so as to enable me to see her winning face, and, turning towards me as far as she could, she said:

"My officer, whither are you taking me?"

"To prison, my poor child," I replied, as gently as I could—just as a true soldier ought to talk to his prisoner, particularly when the prisoner is a woman.

"Alas! what will become of me! Señor officer, have pity on me! You are so young, so kind." Then, in a lower tone, she continued, "Let me escape. I will give you a piece of *bar lachi*, which will make you beloved by all the women."

(The *bar lachi*, sir, is a loadstone, with which the gipsies say one may work charms when one knows how to make use of it. Give a woman a pinch of it, grated, in a glass of water, and she will not be able to resist you.)

I replied, as seriously as I could:

"We are not here to talk nonsense, we must proceed to the prison; such is the order, and there is no help for it."

We Basque people have a dialect which the Spaniards can readily recognize, but there is scarcely one of them who can even say *vai jaoni* (yes, sir). Carmen, then, had no difficulty in discovering that I came from the Provinces. You know, sir, that the gipsies, having no definite country of their own, are always wandering hither and thither, speaking all languages, and the majority of them are as much at home in Portugal as in France, or in the Provinces, or Catalonia; even amongst the Moors and the English they can make themselves understood. Carmen, then, knew the Basque dialect pretty well.

"*Laguna ene bihotsarena*, friend of my soul," she said suddenly. "Are you from the country?"

(Our language, sir, is so beautiful that when we hear it spoken in a strange place it thrills us. I wish I had a confessor from the Provinces, he muttered. Then, after a pause, he resumed:)

"I am from Elizondo," I replied in Basque, very much moved at hearing my native tongue.

"And I am from Etchalar," she said. (That is a district some four hours' journey from us.) "I was brought to Seville by the gipsies. I have been working in the factory so as to make money sufficient to take me back to Navarre again to my dear mother, whose only support I am, and the little *barretcea* (garden), with its twenty cider apple-trees. Ah, if I were only there again, near the white mountains! They have insulted me because I do not belong to this country of pick-pockets, merchants of rotten oranges; and these low women are all against me because I declared that all their 'jacks' of Seville, with their knives, would not frighten one fellow from our part of the country, with only his blue *beret* and his *maquila*."

She was lying, sir; she has always lied. Indeed I doubt whether in all her life that girl ever spoke a word of truth. But when she spoke I believed her. She was stronger than I. She talked broken Basque, and I believed she came from Navarre. Her eyes, mouth, and complexion stamped her a gipsy. I was befooled—mad—and no longer paid attention to anything. I thought that if the two Spaniards with me had said anything in disparagement of the country I would have slashed them across the face just as she had treated her comrade. In fact I was like a man intoxicated. I began to talk nonsense, and was ready to commit any folly.

"If I were to give you a push, countryman, and you were to fall down, I should have only those two Castilian conscripts to detain me," she said.

Faith, I quite forgot my orders, and I replied: "Well, my friend, my countrywoman, try it; and may Our Lady of the Mountain aid you." At that moment we were passing by one of those narrow alleys of which there are so many in Seville. Suddenly Carmen turned round and gave me a blow with her clenched hand on the chest. I fell head over heels purposely. With one bound she jumped over me and ran away, exhibiting a pair of legs such as—well: they talk of "Basque legs"—hers outshone them all. They were as quick as they were well turned! I got up immediately, but I managed to get my lance barwise across the alley, so my companions were prevented from starting in pursuit for a while. Then I set off running myself and my men after me, but there was no chance of our overtaking her, accoutred as we were with our spurs, our sabres, and lances! In less time than I take to tell you the incident, the prisoner had disappeared. Besides, all the gossips of the quarter assisted her flight and laughed at us, putting us also on the wrong scent. After much marching and counter-marching it became necessary for us to return to the guard-house without the receipt from the governor of the prison!

My men, to escape punishment, said that Carmen and I had conversed in the Basque dialect, and that it did not seem quite natural, to tell the truth, that a blow from such a little girl would knock over a man of my weight. All this looked very suspicious for me—rather too clear, in fact. When I went downstairs again I was degraded and sent to prison for a month. This was my first punishment since I had enlisted. Farewell then to the quartermaster's stripes of which I had already made sure.

My first days in prison passed very sadly. When I became a soldier I had pictured to myself that I should at least reach the grade of officer. Longa, Mina, my compatriots, are even "captains-general"; Chapalangarra, who is a negro and a refugee like Mina in your country, Chapalangarra was a colonel, and I have played tennis twenty times with his brother, who was a poor devil, like myself. Then, I said to myself, "All that time you served without punishment is now so much time lost. You have a black mark against you; to reinstate yourself in the opinion of your superiors you will have to work ten times harder than when you were a conscript. And for what have I been punished? For a chit of a gipsy who laughs at me, and who at this moment is at large in some corner of the town. Nevertheless I could not help thinking of her. Will you believe it, sir, those stockings full of holes, which she so liberally displayed when she made her escape, were always before my eyes. I looked out between the bars of my prison window, and among all the women who passed in the street I did not see one who was worth that little devil. And then, in spite of myself, I would clasp the flower which she had thrown at me, and which, dried though it was, still preserved its perfume. If there are witches this girl was one of them.

One day the gaoler entered and gave me a loaf of Alcala bread.

"Look here," he said, "see what your cousin has sent you."

I took the bread—very much surprised for I had no cousin in Seville. It is a mistake perhaps, I thought, as I looked at the loaf, but it was so appetizing—it felt so fresh and good, that without troubling myself to find out whence it had come, or for whom it was intended, I determined to eat it. As I was cutting it my knife struck against something hard. I looked carefully and found a small English file, which had been slipped into the oven before the bread was baked. There was also in the loaf a piece of gold (two piastres). There was no longer room for doubt. The present came from Carmen. Liberty is everything with people of her race, and they would set fire to a town to avoid a day in prison. Besides, the girl was shrewd, and with that loaf had befooled the gaolers. In an hour the thickest bar could be cut with the little file, and with the asistance of the two piastre piece I could exchange my uniform for a civilian dress at the next clothes-shop. You can imagine that a man who had many times gone bird's-nesting for young eaglets over our cliffs would not be much put out to descend into the street from a window less than thirty feet from the ground. But I did not want to escape. I still preserved my honour as a soldier, and desertion seemed to me a great crime. But I was touched by this token of remembrance. When one is in prison one loves to think that one has a friend outside who is interested in one. The gold piece rather offended me. I would have liked very much to have sent it back, but where could I find my creditor? That did not appear a very easy task.

After having been degraded I did not think I had anything more to suffer, but there was a humiliation in store for me. That was when, on my release from prison, I was sent to duty and put on sentry, like a common soldier. You can scarcely imagine what a sensitive man feels on such an occasion as this. I believe I would rather have been shot. Then, at least, one marches alone in front of the platoon; one feels of importance, everyone is looking at you.

I was posted as sentry at the door of the colonel's house. He was a young man, rich, a "good fellow," who lived to amuse himself. All the young officers came thither and many citizens, women, and actresses—so it was said. For my own part, I felt as if everyone in the city had agreed to meet there to stare at me. The colonel's carriage arrived, with his valet on the box. Whom did I see descend from it? *La Gitanilla!* She was dressed up and bedizened, all gold and ribbons. A spangled dress, blue spangled shoes; flowers and trimmings all over her. She had a Basque tambourine in her hand. With her were two other gipsy women, one young and the other old. There is always an old woman to lead them. Then an old man with a guitar, also a gipsy, to play and make them dance. You know that people often amuse themselves by inviting gipsies to their parties and making them dance the *romalis*, their characteristic dance; and often for other purposes.

Carmen recognized me, and we exchanged glances. I don't know why, but at that moment I wished myself a hundred feet underground.

"*Agur laguna* (good day, comrade). My officer, you are mounting guard like a raw recruit."

And ere I could find words to reply, she had entered the house.

All the guests were assembled in the *patio*, and notwithstanding the crowd I could see through the railings almost all that was passing I could hear the castanets, the tambourine, the laughter and applause; sometimes I could perceive *her* head when she sprang up with her tambourine. Then I heard the officers address to her remarks which made the blood mount to my face, but what she said in reply I do not know. On that day, I think

I began to love her in earnest, for three or four times came into my head the notion to rush into the *patio* and stab those coxcombs who were flirting with her. My purgatory lasted a good hour; then the gipsies came out, and the carriage rolled up to fetch them. Carmen, in passing, looked at me with those eyes of hers—you know them—and said to me, in a low voice:

"Countryman, when one likes good fritters one goes to Triana, to Pastia's."

Lightly as a kid she sprang into the carriage, the coachman whipped his mules, and the joyous band drove off; I knew not whither.

You will guess that when I came off duty I went to Triana; but first I got shaved and brushed up, as if for a parade. She was at Lillas Pastia's. He was an old fruit-seller, a gipsy, as swarthy as a Moor, at whose establishment many of the townspeople came to eat fried fish, more particularly, I believe, since Carmen had taken up her quarters there.

"Lillas," she said, when she caught sight of me, "I will do nothing more to-day. To-morrow it will be day again.[1] Come along, *pays*; let us have a stroll together."

She threw her mantilla over her face, and we were in the street before I knew where I was going.

"Señorita," I said, "I believe I have to thank you for a present that you sent me when I was in prison. I have eaten the bread; the file served to sharpen my lance- point, and I keep it in remembrance of you; but the money, here it is."

"Why, he has kept the money!" she exclaimed, with a burst of laughter "Well, so much the better, for at present I am not well in funds. But what matter? A wondering dog will not die of hunger.[2] Come along, let us eat it all; you shall treat me."

We had taken the road to Seville. At the entrance of Serpent Street she purchased a dozen oranges, which she made me carry in my pocket handkerchief. A little farther on she purchased some bread, sausage, and a bottle of Manzanilla. At length she entered a confectioner's shop. There she threw upon the counter the piece of gold which I had returned to her and another which she had in her own pocket, with some silver. At last she asked me for all I had too. I had only some small change, which I handed to her, feeling very much ashamed that I had no more. I believe she would have carried off all the stock if she could. She chose the best and the dearest articles—*yemas* (yokes of eggs, sugared), *turm* (a kind of

---

[1] "*Mànana sera otro dia.*"—Spanish proverb.
[2] *Chuèuel sos pirela cocal terela.* "A wandering dog finds a bone."—Bohemian proverb.

nougat), crystallized fruits—so long as the money lasted. I had to carry all these in paper bags. Perhaps you know Candilejo Street, where is a head of Don Pedro the Juscticiary.

It ought to have "given me pause." We halted before an old house in this street. She entered the walk and rapped at the ground-floor. A gipsy, a true servant of Satan, opened the door to us. Carmen said something to her in Romany. The old woman grumbled at first, but to appease her Carmen gave her two oranges and a handful of *bonbons*; she also permitted her to taste the wine. Then she put her cloak on her, and led her to the door, which she secured with a bar of wood. As soon as we were alone Carmen began to dance as if she were possessed, singing, "You are my *rom* and I am your *romi*."[1]

I was standing in the middle of the room burthened with all the packages, not knowing where to put them. She threw them all upon the floor and clasping me round the neck, exclaimed "I pay my debts; I pay my debts—it is the law of the Cales."[2]

Ah, sir—that day! that day! when I recall it I forget *to-morrow!*

(The brigand was silent for a while, then after he had relighted his cigar he continued:)

We remained together the whole of the day, eating, drinking, and—and all the rest of it. When she had devoured the sweets, like a child of six years old, she thrust her hands into the old woman's water-jar. "Now to make a *sorbet*," she said. She broke the *yemas* by dashing them against the wall—"so that the flies may leave us in peace," she remarked. There was no trick or folly that she did not perpetrate. I expressed a wish to see her dance, but where could we find castanets? She without hesitation took the old woman's only plate, smashed it in pieces, and then she danced the *romalis*, clattering the pieces of the plate as if they had been castanets of ebony or ivory. One would never feel bored with a girl like her—I can answer for that! Evening closed in, and I could hear the drums beating the "retreat."

"I must return to barracks," I said, "for roll-call."

"To barracks!" she echoed in a contemptuous tone. "So you are a negro-slave and permit yourself to be driven with the whip! You are a regular canary in appearance and disposition.[3] Go along with you! You have a chicken's heart!"

I stayed, resigned in advance to the police-cell. In the morning it was

---

[1] *Rom*—husband; *Romi*—wife.
[2] Dark people—a name the gipsies give themselves.
[3] The Spanish dragoons wear yellow uniforms.

she who first spoke of our separation.

"Listen to me, Joseita," she said, "I have paid you—haven't I? According-ing to our law I owed you nothing, since you are a *payllo*; but you are a good fellow, and you have pleased me. We are quits! Good -day."

I asked when I should see her again.

"When you are a little less stupid," she replied, laughing. Then in a more serious tone she continued, "Do you know, my friend, that I believe I love you a little bit? But that cannot last. Dog and wolf cannot keep house together long. Perhaps if you were to subscribe to the Egyptian law I should love to be your *romi*. But this is all nonsense—that cannot be. Take my word for, it, you have had the best of the bargain. You have forgthered with the devil; yes—with the devil! He is not always black, and he has not twisted your neck. I am dressed in wool, but I am not a sheep.[1] Go and put a taper before your *majari*.[2] She has well deserved it. Come; good-bye once again. Think no more of Carmencita or she may make you marry a widow with wooden legs."

As she ceased speaking she unfastened the bar which closed the door; and once in the street she wrapped herself in her mantilla, and showed me her heels.

She had said what was true. I would have been wise to have thought no more about her, but after that day in Candilejo Street I could not think of anything else. I walked about all day long in the hope of meeting her again. I inquired about her from the old woman and from the seller of fried fish. Both declared she had gone to Laloro,[4] as they call Portugal. Probably it was in accordance with Carmen's instructions that they said so, but it was not long before I discovered that they were lying. Some weeks after my long day in Candilejo Street I was put on sentry at one of the city gates. Some little distance from this gate a breach had been made in the wall whereat people used to walk during the day, and where a sentry was posted at night to guard against smugglers. During the day I perceived Lillas Pastia lingering around the guardhouse chatting with my comrades, all of whom were acquainted with him, his fish, and his fritters which were better still. He approached me and inquired whether I had had any news of Carmen.

"No," I replied.

"Well then, you soon will, comrade."

He was right. At night I was posted at the breach in the wall. As soon

---

[1] "*Medicas viardà de jorpoy bis ne sini braco.*"—Gipsy Proverb.
[2] The Virgin Mary.
[3] The gallows—widow of the last man hanged.
[4] The red land.

as the corporal had disappeared I perceived a woman approaching my post. My heart told me it was Carmen; nevertheless I said, "Be off, you cannot pass here!"

"Come, don't be obstreperous," she replied, as she made herself known to me.

"What! are *you* there, Carmen?"

"Yes, I, countryman; let us have a little conversation together. Do you want to earn a duoro? Some people with packs are coming this way— let them pass."

"No," I replied, "I must oppose their passage. Such are my orders."

"Orders, orders! You did not think of them in Candilejo Street."

"Ah!" I replied, quite upset by the very remembrance, "that was worth the danger of forgetting my duty: but I do not want any money from smugglers."

"Let me see, then. If you do not want any money from smugglers what do you say to going to dine at old Dorothea's house again?"

"No," I replied, half suffocated by the effort I was making, "I cannot."

"Very well; if you are so hard to move I know to whom to apply. I will make your officer the offer to go to Dorothea's house. He seems to be a good fellow, and he will put on guard a lad who will not see more than is necessary. Good-bye, canary. I shall laugh when the order is issued for your hanging!"

I was weak enough to call her back, and I promised to permit all the gipsies to pass, if it must be so, provided I obtained the recompense I wished for. She swore to meet me on the following day, and ran off to apprise her friends who were close by. There were five of them, one being Pastia, and all heavily laden with English goods. Carmen kept watch. She agreed to give the alarm with her castanets whenever she should perceive the rounds, but she had no need to do so. The smugglers very quickly accomplished their business.

Next day I went to Candilejo Street. Carmen was waiting for me, but in a by no means good humour.

"I do not care for people who require to be begged of," she said. "You rendered me a great service the first time without any idea that you would gain anything by it. To-day you are bartering with me. I do not know why I have come, for I don't care for you any longer. So go away; there is a duoro for your trouble!"

I was within an ace of throwing the money at her head, and was obliged to excercise a violent control over myself to avoid striking her. After we had argued for an hour I went away in a furious rage. I wandered for a long time about the city, hither and thither, like a man demented. At length I entered a church, and seating my self in the darkest corner I could find I gave way to tears. Suddenly I heard a voice say:

"A dragoon's tears! I should like to make a philtre of them!"

I looked up. There was Carmen standing before me!

"Well, countryman, are you still wishing for me? I really think I must love you still, for since you left me I have not known what to do with myself. There now, you see I am the supplicant, and want you to come to Candilejo Street."

We made it up then; but Carmen's humour was as variable as our climate. The storm is most likely to break when the sun is shining most brilliantly. She had promised to meet me once again at Dorothea's house and she did not come, and Dorothea told me, in the calmest manner, that Carmen had gone to Laloro "on Egyptian affairs!"

Guided by experience, I sought for Carmen in every place where I fancied she might be found, and I passed up and down Candilejo Street twenty times a day. One evening I was at Dorothea's house, for I had almost tamed the old woman by means of repeated glases of *anisette*, when Carmen entered, followed by a young man, a lieutenant in my regiment.

"Get away at once," she said to me in the Basque tongue. I remained stupefied, rage boiling in my heart.

"What is that fellow doing here?" said the lieutenant. "Be off; get out of this!"

I could not move. I felt as if I had quite lost the use of my limbs. The officer seeing that I did not budge, and that I had not even removed my cap, took me by the collar and shook me violently. I do not know what I said. He drew his sword and I drew mine. The old woman seized my arm, and the lieutenant gave me a cut in the forehead, the scar of which remains to this day. I stepped back and with a shove sent old Dorothea sprawling on the floor. Then, as the lieutenant followed me up, I gave him my point, and he spitted himself on my sword. Then Carmen extinguished the lamp and bade Dorothea fly. As for myself, I rushed into the street and ran I knew not whither. It seemed to me that some one was following me. When I came to myself I found Carmen beside me. She had not left me.

"You great stupid canary," she said, "you are only good at committing follies. You see I was right when I told you I would only bring trouble upon you. Well there is a remedy for every ill when one has a 'Fleming of Rome'[1] for his friend. You must begin by tying this handkerchief over your head, and giving me your sword belt. Wait for me in this alley, I will be back again in two minutes."

She disappeared and quickly returned, carrying a striped cloak for me; how she obtained it I can't tell. She made me doff my uniform, and put the cloak on over my shirt. Thus accoutred, with the handkerchief bound over the cut on my head, I had something of the appearance of a peasant of Valencia, of whom many come to Seville to sell their *chufas*—orangeade. Then she took me to a house, which bore a striking resemblance to Dorothea's, at the end of a narrow court. She and another gipsy woman washed me, doctored me better than the surgeon-major would have done, and gave me something—I know not what—to drink. At length they laid me on a mattress and I fell fast asleep.

The women probably had put some soprific in my drink, for I did not awake until very late next day. I had a fearful headache, and was rather feverish. It was some time before I could recall the incidents of the terrible drama in which I had taken part on the pravious day.

After having dressed my wound, Carmen and her friend both crouched down beside my mattress, and exchanged a few words in *chepé-calli*, which seemed to be a medical consultation. They both assured me that I would be cured before long; but meanwhile it was absolutely necessary to leave Seville, and as quickly as possible, for if I were arrested I would be shot, to a certainty.

"My boy," said Carmen, "you must do something; now that the king will give you neither rice nor salt cod,[2] you must find some means of existence. You are too stupid to rob *à pastesas*;[3] but you are lithe and strong. If you have courage enough, go to the coast and be a contrabandist. Have I not promised to get you hanged? That is better than being shot. Besides, if you know how to look after yourself, your may live like a prince so long as the *minons*[4] and the coast-guard do not catch you."

It was in this way that that devil of a girl indicated to me the new career for which she destined me—and to tell the truth, it was the only one which lay open to me, now that I had rendered myself liable to the punishment of death. Need I confess to you, sir, that she brought me to the decision without much trouble! It seemed to me that we shoudl be thrown into closer contact by this existence so full of risks, and so unlawful. Thenceforth, I believed

---

[1] *Flamenco de Roma*—a slang term for gipsies. *Roma* in this sense does not refer to the Eternal City, but to the Romi (or married people), as the Bohemians call them. The first seen in Spain came probably from the Netherlands—hence the name Fleming.
[2] The ordinary rations of a Spanish soldier.
[3] *Ustilar d pastesas* to rob skilfully, without violence.
[4] A species of free-corps.

myself sure of her affection. I had often heard of the contrabandists who traversed Andalusia well-mounted, blunderbuss in hand, and with their mistresses seated behind them. I already pictured myself trotting over hills and vales with this handsome gipsy behind me. When I mentioned this to her, she laughed until she was obliged to hold her sides, and told me there was nothing so pleasant as a night passed in the camp when each *rom* retired with his *romi* beneath the shelter of the little tent formed of three hoops with a blanket thrown over them.

"If I keep with you in the mountains, I shall always be sure of you," I said. "There will there be no lieutenants to share with me."

"Ah, you are jealous," she replied; "so much the worse for you. How can you be such a fool! Don't you see that I love you, since I have never asked you for any money?"

When she talked in this fasion I felt inclined to strangle her.

To cut the story short, sir, Carmen procured me a civilian dress, in which I escaped from Seville unrecognized. I proceeded to Jerez with a letter from Pastia to a seller of *anisette*, at whose house the smugglers used to assemble. I was presented to these men, whose chief, named Dancaire, received me into the company. We proceeded to Gaucin, where I again found Carmen, who had appointed to meet me there. In the expedition, she acted as spy for us, and no one could have been a better one. She had returned from Gibraltar, and had arranged with the captain of a vessel concerning the disembarkation of the English merchandise which we expected to arrive at the coast. We went to await its arrival near Estepona; then we hid a portion of it in the mountains, and laden with the remainder proceeded to Ronda, whither Carmen had preceded us. Then she once more gave us the hint when to enter the town. This first expedition, and some others, were fortunate. The life of a smuggler pleased me more then that of a soldier. I made Carmen presents. I had money and a mistress. I suffered scarcely any remorse, for as the gipsies say—an itching of pleasure is no itch at all.[1] We were well received everywhere; my associates treated me well, and even evinced some consideration for me. This was because I had killed a man, and among them there was no one who had not a similar exploit to boast of. But what influenced me more than all else in my new life was the frequent presence of Carmen. She displayed more friendship for me than formerly—nevertheless, before her comrades she did not pretend that she was my mistress, and had even made me swear with all kinds of

---

[1] *Sarapia sat pesquital ne punzava.*

oaths not to say a word to them on the subject. I was so utterly weak before this creature that I obeyed all her caprices. Besides, this was the first occasion on which she had displayed any of the reserve of an "honest woman," and I was foolish enough to believe that she had abandoned all her former practices.

Our troop, which was composed of eight or ten men only, assembled together in important junctures, but were usually scattered in pairs or threes in the towns and villages. Each one of us assumed a calling or trade; one was a tinker, another a horse dealer. I was a pedlar; but I very seldom showed myself in large towns, because of that little affair in Seville. One day, or rather one night, our rendezvous was below Vega. Dancaire and I found ourselves there before the others. He seemed in excellent spirits.

"We shall soon have another comrade," he said. "Carmen has executed one of her best moves. She has managed the escape of her *rom* from the *presidio* at Tarifa."

I was just beginning to understand the gipsy dialect, which nearly all my associates made use of, and the word *rom* gave me a chill.

"What, her husband! Is she married?" I asked.

"Yes," replied the captain, "to Garcia, the one-eyed, a gipsy as 'deep' as she is. The poor fellow was in penal servitude. Carmen got round the surgeon so cleverly that she obtained her *rom's* liberty. Ah! that girl is worth her weight in gold. It is two years since she first began to plan his escape. Nothing had succeeded until the officer was changed. With the latter it seems she quickly found the means to make herself understood."

You can imagine how I listened to this news. I soon met Garcia the one-eyed; he was one of the most repulsive villains whom Bohemia ever reared, a dark skin and a still blacker soul. He was the most unmitigated ruffian that I ever met in my life. Carmen came with him, and when she called her *rom* in my presence you should have seen the 'eyes' she made to me, and the grimaces at him when his back was turned. I was very angry, and would not speak to her all the evening. In the morning we had made up our bales and were already on our way when we perceived that a dozen horsemen were after us. The Andalusian boasters, who always talk in the most bloodthirsty manner, cut a pitiful figure at once. There was a general stampede. Dancaire, Garcia, a fine young fellow from Edja, called Remendado, and Carmen did not lose their presence of mind. The others abandoned the mules and threw themselves into the ravines, where the dragoons could not follow them. We could not save out mules and we hastened to loose the most valuable portion of our booty and to take it on our shoulders. We then endeavoured to escape over the rocks, and by the steepest and roughest slopes. We cast our bales before us, and followed them as best we could, sliding down on our heels, all this time the enemy was firing at us. It was the first time that I had heard the whistling of bullets, and it did not make me feel quite at ease. When one has a wife in prospect there is no merit in risking death. We all escaped except poor Remendado, who got a bullet in his loins. I threw away my pack and endeavoured to assist him.

"Fool!" exclaimed Garcia, "what have we to do with that carrion? Pick up your load, and don't lose the cotton stockings."

"Let him go," said Carmen to me.

Fatigue obliged me to lay the lad for a moment beneath the shelter of a rock. Garcia advanced and discharged his blunderbuss at his head.

"He will be a clever fellow who will recognize him now," he remarked, as he gazed at the features which a dozen bullets had shattered.

Such, sir, was the kind of life I had embraced. In the evening we found ourselves in a thicket, worn out with fatigue, having nothing to eat, and ruined by the loss of our mules. What did that infernal Garcia do? He took a pack of cards from his pocket and began to play with Dancaire by the light of the fire which had been kindled. Meanwhile I lay down and was watching the stars, thinking of Remendado and wishing I were in his place. Carmen was crouched near me, and from time to time she rattled her castanets and hummed a tune. Then, approaching me, as if with the intention of whispering to me, she kissed me, almost against my will, two or three times.

"You are the devil," I said to her.

"Yes," she answered.

After some hours' rest she departed for Gaucin, and next morning a little goatherd brought us some bread. We remained all day in the same place, and at night we moved towards Gaucin. We waited for news of Carmen: none came. At daybreak we perceived a muleteer who was guiding a well-dressed woman holding a parasol, and accompanied by a little girl, who seemed to be her servant. Garcia said to us:

"There are two mules and two women which St Nicholas has sent us. I would rather have had four mules. Never mind. This is my business."

He seized his blunderbuss and descended towards the path; hiding in the brushwood. Dancaire and I followed him at a little distance. When we were within range, we showed ourselves, and called to the muleteer to halt. The woman instead of being frightened—and our dress was sufficient for that—burst out laughing.

423

"Ah, the *lillipendi,* they take me for an *erani!*" [1] It was Carmen, but so well disguised, that I would not have recognized her, had she spoken in any other language.

She sprang from the mule and spoke for a while in a low tone with Garcia and Dancaire. Then she said to me:

"Canary, we shall meet again before you are hanged. I am going to Gibraltar on 'affairs of Egypt.' You will soon hear me talked about."

We parted after she had indicated to us a place where we could find shelter for some days. This girl was the saving of our troop. We soon received some money which she sent, and a hint, which was worth more to us, namely, that two British noblemen were about to proceed from Gibraltar to Granada by such a route. A word to the wise! They had plenty of money. Garcia wanted to kill them, but Dancaire and I were opposed to such a measure. We could relieve them of their money, their watches, and their shirts, of which last articles we had great need.

Sir, one may become a rogue without thinking about it. A pretty girl causes you to lose your head; you fight for her: a misfortune happens, it becomes necessary to dwell amid the mountains, and from a smuggler you become a robber before you are aware of the change. We concluded that it would not be well for us to remain in the environs of Gibraltar after that little business with the Englishmen, and we concealed ourselves in the Sierra de Ronda. You have mentioned José-Maria; well, it was there that I made his acquaintance. He brought his mistress with him on these expeditions. She was a pretty girl, well behaved and modest, with good manners, never uttering an unbecoming word, and of a devoted-ness——! By way of compensation, he treated her very badly. He was always running after other girls; he bullied her; then sometimes he took it into his head to be jealous. Once he struck her with his knife. Well, she only loved him the more for that. That is the way women, particularly Andalusians, are constituted! She was quite proud of the scar on her arm, and exhibited it as one of the most beautiful things in the world. And then José-Maria was the very worst comrade you could possibly meet. On one expedition which we undertook he managed so well, that all the profit fell to him, and all the blows fell on us. But I must resume my story. As we heard nothing more of Carmen, Dancaire said:

"One of us must proceed to Gibraltar to get news of her; he ought to have prepared something. I would go willingly, but I am too well known there."

---

[1] Ah, the fools! do they take me for a lady?

The one-eyed fellow said:

"So am I. I have played too many tricks upon the lobsters,[1] and as I have only one eye, it is not easy to escape detection."

"Then I must go," I said in my turn, delighted at the very idea of seeing Carmen again. "Let us see; what must be done?"

The others replied:

"You can go to St Roque whichever way you please, and when you have got to Gibraltar, ask where a person named Rollona, a seller of chocolate, lives; when you have found her out, you will find out what has happened yonder."

It was arranged that we three should start for the Sierra de Gaucin; that I should leave my companions there, and proceed to Gibraltar as a fruit merchant. At Ronda one of our fraternity procured me a passport; at Gaucin I was given a donkey; I loaded him with oranges and melons, and went on my way. When I reached Gibraltar I found that Rollona was well known, but that she had either died or had been sent to the galleys, and in my opinion her absence explained how our means of correspondence with Carmen had failed. I put my donkey up in a stable, and with oranges wandered about the town as if to sell them; but, in fact, to endeavour to find some face I knew. There are plenty of vagrants in "Gib," people from all parts of the globe, and it is like the Tower of Babel, for one cannot go ten paces along a street without hearing as many different languages. I met many gipsies, but I scarcely dared to trust them. I recognized them and they recognized me. We ascertained that we were of the same class. After two days spent in useless search, I learned nothing concerning either Rollona or Carmen, and was considering whether I should not return to my comrades after making some purchases, when as I was walking down a street at sunset, I heard a woman's voice from a window say," "Here, you orange-seller!" I looked up, and on a balcony I perceived Carmen, leaning over the rail beside an officer in scarlet, with gold epaulets, curled hair, and the appearance generally of a grandee. As for her, she was dressed spendidly: a shawl over her shoulders, a gold comb in her hair, attired in silk, and as cunning as ever—just the same, laughing immoderately. The Englishman, in barbarous Spanish, hailed me and bade me come up, as madame wanted some oranges and Carmen said to me in Basque, "Come up, and be astonished at nothing." Nothing could astonish me where she was concerned. I cannot tell whether I was the more glad or disappointed to see her again. A tall, powdered servant let me in, and ushered me into

---

[1] A term applied to the English, because of the colour of their uniforms.

a splendid apartment. Carmen at once addressed me in Basque.

"Mind, you do not understand a word of Spanish; and you do not know me."

Then, turning to the Englishman, she said, "I told you all along he was a Basque—you will hear a curious dialect. What a silly look he has, hasn't he? You would take him for a cat surprised in the larder!"

"And you," I replied in my own tongue, "have the air of a brazenfaced husy, and I am greatly disposed to scar your face before your lover."

"My lover!" she exclaimed. "So you have found out that all by yourself. And you are jealous of that fool? Why, you are a greater simpleton than you were before our evenings in Candilejo Street. Don't you see—fool that you are—that I am engaged upon affairs of Egypt, and in the most brilliant fashion? This house is mine; the lobster's guineas will be mine. I shall lead him by the nose, and bring him whence he shall never escape."

"And as for me," I replied, "if you conduct the affairs of Egypt any more in this manner, I will do something which will effectually prevent your beginning again."

"Ah, indeed! Are you my *rom* that you give me orders? The One-Eyed is satisfied. What have you seen here? Ought not you to be content to be the only one who can call himself my *minchorro?*" [1]

"What does he say," asked the Englishman.

"He says that he is thirsty, and could manage a good drink," replied Carmen. Then she fell back upon a sofa, screaming with laughter at the translation.

Sir, when that girl laughed there was no use in trying to talk sense. Every one laughed with her. The great Englishman laughed also, like the idiot he was, and bade his people bring me something to drink.

While I was drinking, Carmen said:

"Do you see that ring on his finger? If you like, I will give it to you."

But I answered:

"I would give a finger to have my lord on the mountain, each of us with a *maquila* in our hands."

"*Maquila?* What does he mean?" asked the Englishman.

"*Maquila!*" cried Carmen, still laughing. "*Maquila* is an orange. Is it not a queer term for an orange? He says he would like to make you eat an orange."

"Yes?" replied the Englishman. "Very well, bring more *maquilas* tomorrow."

---

[1] Lover—or rather, 'fancy-man.'

As we were conversing, the servant announced dinner. Then the Englishman offered his arm to Carmen—as if she could not go in by herself, and threw me a pistole. Carmen, laughing all the time, said to me:

"My boy, I cannot invite you to dinner; but to-morrow, as soon as you hear the drums beating for parade, come here with your oranges. You will find a room better furnished then that in Candilejo Street, and you will see that I am always your Carmencita; and then we can chat over Egyptian affairs."

I made no reply, and was in the street when the Englishman called out, "Bring the *maquilas* to-morrow." Then I heard Carmen's laughter once more.

I went away, not knowing whither, or what I was doing. I scarcely slept and the morning found me so incensed against the traitress that I resolved to quit Gibraltar without seeing her again. But at the first roll of the drums all my fortitude deserted me. I took my straw basket of oranges and hurried to Carmen. Her window-shutters had been pulled apart a little, and I saw her great eyes watching me. The powdered servant let me in. Carmen sent him on an errand, and as soon as we were alone she burst into one of her peals of crocodile laughter and threw herself on my neck. I had never seen her so lovely. Dressed like a bride, perfumed, surrounded with costly furniture and silken hangings ——Ah! and I like the robber that I was!

"*Minchorro*," said Carmen, "I have a great mind to smash everything here, to set fire to the house and be off to the Sierra!"

Then her caresses, and her laughter! She danced and tore her dress; never did ape perform more gambols, make more grimaces, or play more tricks. When she had regained her composure she said:

"Listen; it is a question of Egypt. I want him to take me to Ronda, where I have a sister—a nun. (More laughter.) We will pass by a place which I will tell you of. You can fall upon him and rob him. The better way will be to murder him; but," she added, with a diabolical smile which she displayed at certain times, and no one would ever be inclined to imitate it—"do you know what you must do? Let the One-Eyed appear first. Keep a little in the rear yourself. The Lobster is brave and skilful; he has good pistols. Do you understand?"

She interrupted herself with another peal of laughter, which made me shiver.

"No," I replied, "I detest Garcia, but he is my comrade. One day perhaps I will relieve you of him, but we will settle our accounts after the fashion of our country. I am only an Egyptian by chance, and in certain ways I shall always remain a pure *Navarro*, as the proverb says" (*Navarro fino*).

She replied, "You are a fool—an idiot—a regular *payllo*. You are like the dwarf who believed himself big because he could spit a long distance.[1] You do not love me—go along with you!"

When she said "Go along!" I could not go. I promised to leave, to return with my comrades and lie in wait fot the Englishman. On her side she promised to be indisposed until the time came for leaving Gibraltar for Ronda. I remained two days longer at Gibraltar. She had the audacity to come in disguise to see me at my inn. I quitted the town, for I also had my own project. I returned to our rendezvous, knowing the place and the hour at which the Englishman and Carmen would pass by. I found Dancaire and Garcia awaiting me. We passed the night in a wood by a fire of pine-cones, which burned splendidly. I proposed to Garcia to have a game of cards. He agreed. At the second game I declared he was cheating. He laughed. I threw the cards in his face. He went for his blunderbuss, but I put my foot upon it and said:

"They tell me you can brandish a knife with any Jack of Malaga. Will you try a bout with me?"

Dancaire wanted to separate us. I had given Garcia a few blows with my fist. Rage had made him courageous. He had drawn his knife and I mine. We told Dancaire to stand aside and see fair play. He saw that it was no use attempting to stop us and he stood back. Garcia was already crouching like a cat about to spring upon a mouse. He held his hat in his left hand, as a guard, his knife advanced in his right. That is the Andalusian method. I stood like the Navarros, right in front of him, the left arm raised, the left leg advanced, the knife held down by the right thigh. I felt stronger than a giant. He threw himself upon me like a flash. I turned on my left foot and he found nothing before him; but I caught him in the throat and the knife entered so far that my hand came chock under his chin. I drew back. the blade so forcibly that it broke. All was over! The blade was expelled from the wound in a rush of blood as big as my arm. He fell on his face like a log.

"What have you done?" said Dancaire.

"Listen," I said. "We could not have lived together. I love Carmen and I want to be the only one! Besides, Garcia was a brute, and I remember how he served poor Remendado. We are only two now, but we are good fellows. Look here; will you have me for a comrade—for life or death?"

Dancaire held out his hand. He was a man fifty years old.

"To the devil with your love affairs," he exclaimed. "If you had asked

---

[1] *"Or esorjie de or narsichisle sin chismar lachinguel."*—Gipsy proverb.

for Carmen he would have sold her to you for a piastre. We are only two now—what shall we do to-morrow?"

"Let me manage it," I replied. "Now I can snap my fingers at the whole world!"

We buried Garcia and pitched our camp two hundred paces farther on. Next day Carmen and her Englishman passed with two muleteers and a servant. I said to Dancaire:

"I will account for the Englishman. You can frighten the others; they are not armed."

The Englishman was a brave fellow. If Carmen had not jogged his arm he would have shot me. To be brief, I reconquered Carmen that day, and my first words were to tell her that she was a widow. When she understood how it came to pass, she said:

"You will always be a *lillipendi*. Garcia ought to have killed you. Your Navarre guard is all nonsense, and he has conquered better men than you. His time had come no doubt! Yours will come too!"

"And yours," I replied, "if you are not a true *romi* to me!"

"Well and good!" she replied. "I have seen in the coffee-grounds many a time that our destinies lie together. But he who sows reaps!" And she rattled her castanets as she was in the habit of doing when she wished to get rid of any unpleasant thoughts.

One is apt to forget others when speaking of oneself; all these details bore you no doubt, but I shall soon finish now. The life we lead will last long enough! Dancaire and I associated ourselves with some comrades more trustworthy than the former; we practised smuggling, and sometimes it must be confessed we stopped people on the highways, but only as a last resource and when he had no other means of livelihood. Besides, we never ill-treated travellers and we confined ourselves strictly to taking their money.

For many months I was happy with Carmen; she continued to be useful to us in our operations and gave us notice of the good things we could "bring off." She stayed sometimes at Malaga, sometimes at Cordova, sometimes at Granada; but at a word from me she would leave any place and come to meet me in an isolated inn, or even in the camp. Once only, it was at Malaga, did she give me any uneasiness. I knew that she had thrown a glamour over a very rich merchant, with whom probably she proposed to repeat the little arrangement carried out at Gibraltar. Notwithstanding all Dancaire could say to me I went after her and got to Malaga in full daylight. I looked for Carmen, and brought her away immediately. We had some sharp words.

"Do you know," she said, "that since you have really become my *rom*, I care less for you than when you were only my lover. I don't want to be worried and ordered about; what I wish is to be free and to do as I please. Take care—do not push me too far. If you trouble me too much I will find some fellow who will serve you as you served Garcia."

Dancaire reconciled us, but we said things to each other which rankled in our hearts and we were not on such good terms as formerly. A short time afterwards evil befell us. The troops surprised us. Dancaire was killed with two others of our band; two more were made prisoners. I was badly wounded, and without the aid of my trusty horse would have been left in the hands of the soldiers. Worn out by fatigue, with a bullet in my body, I hid myself with only one companion in the forest. I fainted when I dismounted, and thought I was going to die like a wounded hare in the brushwood. My comrade carried me to a grotto which we knew and then went to seek Carmen. She was at Granada and she came back at once. For fifteen days she never quitted me for a moment. She did not close her eyes; she nursed me with a skill and attention which no woman ever before displayed for a man she loved best. As soon as I could stand up again she carried me off to Granada in secrecy. The gipsies everywhere found us safe lodging and I passed more than six weeks in a house two doors from the official who was searching for me. More than once from behind a shutter I saw him pass by. At length my health was restored, but I had thought a great deal while on my bed of sickness and I made up my mind to amend my life. I spoke to Carmen about leaving Spain and endeavouring to live honestly in America. She laughed at me.

"We are not fitted for cabbage growing," she replied; "our destiny is to live at the expense of the *payllos*. Look here, I have just arranged a little business with Nathan ben-Joseph, of Gibraltar. He has a cargo of cotton stuffs which only want your assistance in passing through. He knows you are alive still. He reckons upon you. What shall we say to our correspondents in Gibraltar if you break your word to them?"

I permitted myself to be persuaded and resumed my villainous career.

While I was in hiding at Granada there was a bullfight there to which Carmen went. When she came back she spoke of a very adroit *picador* named Lucas. She knew the name of his horse and how much his embroidered vest had cost. Inanito, the comrade who had remained with me, said some days afterwards that he had seen Carmen and Lucas at the house of a tradesman of Zacatin. That alarmed me. I asked Carmen how and why she had made the acquaintance of the *picador*.

"He is a man," she said, "with whom we can do some business. The river that makes a noise has either water or pebbles.[1] He has won 1,200 reals at the bull-ring. One of two things must happen—we must have this money—or, as he is a good rider and a brave fellow, we must enrol him in our band. So-and-so are dead; you must replace them. Take him with you."

"I don't want either his money or himself," I replied, "and I forbid you to speak to him."

"Take care," she replied. "When people defy me to do a thing it is very soon done."

Fortunately the *picador* left for Malaga, and I set about smuggling in the Jew's cottons. I had a great deal to do in this expedition, and so had Carmen. I forgot Lucas; perhaps she also forgot him, for the time at any rate. It was about that time, sir, that I met with you first, near Montilla, then afterwards at Cordova. I will not say anything about our last interview. You perhaps know more about it than I. Carmen robbed you of your watch; she also wanted your money, and particularly the ring you wear on your finger, which she said is a magic ring, which she was very anxious to possess. We had a violent quarrel; I struck her. She turned pale and cried. This was the first time I had ever seen her weep, and her tears had a great effect upon me. I begged her pardon, but she sulked all day; and when I departed for Montilla she did not want to kiss me. I was heavy-hearted when, three days afterwards, she came to see me, as gay as a lark. All was forgotten, and we passed two days in lover-like fashion. As we were again about to part she said:

"There is a *festa* at Cordova; I am going to see it. Then I shall find out who has money, and will tell you."

I let her go. When alone I thought of the *festa*, and this change of humour in Carmen. She must have avenged herself already, I thought, since she had yielded first. A peasant told me that there was a bull-fight in Cordova. How my blood boiled, and, like a fool, I went there. He pointed out Lucas to me, and, in a seat near the barrier, I recognized Carmen. I had only to look at her for a moment to be fully assured of the fact I had suspected. Lucas played the bull "with a light heart," as I had anticipated. He snatched the cockade from the animal and carried it to Carmen, who placed it in her hair immediately. The bull tried to avenge me! Lucas was overthrown with his horse, and the bull fell upon both of them. I looked at Carmen; she was no longer in her place. It was quite impossible for me to get out, and I was compelled to wait until the courses were run. Then I went to the house

---

[1] *Len sos sunsi abela Pani o rebiendani terela.*—Gipsy proverb.

that you know of, and there I remained quite quiet all the evening and a part of the night. Towards two o'clock in the morning Carmen returned, and was somewhat astonished to see me.

"Come with me," I said.

"Very well," she replied, "let us go."

I went to fetch my horse, and I put her *en croupe*. We rode all the remainder of the night without saying a single word to each other. We halted at daybreak at a solitary inn near a small hermitage. Then I said to Carmen:

"Listen! I forget everything; I will speak of nothing that has pased. Only swear to me that you will follow me to America, and that you will remain quietly there."

"No," she replied in a sulky tone, "I won't go to America. I like being here best."

"Because you are near Lucas," I said, "but do not imagine, even if he recover, that he will ever make old bones. Yet after all, why should I trouble about him? I am tired of killing all your lovers; it is *you* whom I shall kill."

She gazed at me steadily with her wild eyes, and said:

"I have always imagined that you would kill me. The first time I saw you I met a priest at the door of my house, and did you see nothing to-night as we quitted Cordova? A hare crossed the road between your horse's feet. It is written!"

"Carmencita?" I asked, "is it true that you no longer love me?"

She made no reply; she was seated cross-legged on a mat, tracing patterns with her finger on the floor.

"Let us change our mode of life, Carmen," I pleaded. "Let us go and live in some place where we shall never be separated. You know that we have a hundred and twenty onzas buried beneath a tree not far from here. Besides, we still have money in ben-Joseph's hands."

She smiled and replied:

"I first, you afterwards. I knew that it would come to this."

"Reflect," I continued. "I have lost all patience with you; I am at the end of my tether! Make up your mind, and I will make up mine."

I left her and walked towards the hermitage. I found the hermit at prayer. I waited until his devotions were concluded. I wanted to pray too, but I could not. When he rose I went up to him.

"Father," I said, "will you pray for one who is in great danger?"

"I pray for all the afflicted, my son."

"Can you pray for a soul that is about to appear before its Creator?"

"Yes," he replied, looking at me fixedly, and as there was something strange in my manner he wanted to make me speak out.

"It seems to me that I have seen you before," he remarked.

I put a piastre on the bench. "When will you say mass?" I asked.

"In half an hour. The son of the inn-keeper, yonder, comes to serve it. Tell me, young man, have not you something on your conscience which is tormenting you? Will you hearken to the counsel of a Christian?"

I felt ready to cry. I said I would return, and then I got away. I lay down on the grass till I heard the bell. Then I rose and went near, but remained outside the chapel. When mass was said I returned to the inn. I almost hoped that Carmen had run away; she might have taken my horse and escaped. But I found her. She would never have it said that she was afraid of me. During my absence she had unpicked the hem of her dress, and taken out the lead. She was then sitting at the table, gazing into a bowl of water at the lead which had sunk to the bottom, and which she continued to throw in. She was so immersed in her occupation that she did not at first perceive me. Then she took a piece of the lead and turned it in all directions, with a sad expression in her face; sometimes she hummed one of the mystic songs in which gipsies invoke Marie Padilla, the mistress of Don Pedro, who was, they say, the Bari Crallisa, or great Queen of the Gipsies.

"Carmen," I said, "will you come with me?"

She rose; threw away her bowl, and put on her mantilla as if ready to go. They brought me my horse; she mounted behind me, and we departed.

"So, my Carmen," I said, after a while, "you really wish to follow me, is it not so?"

"I will follow you to death, yes; but I will not live with you any longer!"

We were in a solitary gorge; I pulled up.

"It is here?" she said, as she sprang to the ground. She took off her mantilla, threw it at her feet and stood motionless, her hand upon her hip, looking straight at me.

"You are going to kill me, I see that quite well," she said. "It is fated; but you will never make me yield."

"I implore you, be reasonable," I said. "Listen to me; all the past is forgotten. Nevertheless, you know it, it is I who have lost myself; it was for your sake that I became a brigand and a murderer! Carmen, my Carmen, let me save you, and myself with you!"

"José," she replied, "you ask me to do what is impossible. I no longer love you; you love me still, and for that reason you want to kill me. I could very easily lie to you, but do not care to take the trouble. All is over between us. As my *rom* you have the right to kill your *romi*, but Carmen will always be free. Calli she was born, and Calli she will die!"

"So you love Lucas?" I said.

"Yes, I have loved him, like you, for a while; perhaps less than you. At present, I love no one, and I hate myself for having loved you."

I threw myself at her feet; I took her hands in mine; I bedewed them with tears; I recalled to her mind all the happy times we had had together. I offered to remain a brigand all my life to please her. I did everything, sir, everything. I offered her all, provided that she would still love me. But she said:

"It is impossible to love you any longer, and I do not want to live with you!"

Fury took possession of me—I drew my knife; I wished she had displayed some fear and pleaded for mercy, but the woman was a demon.

"For the last time," I exclaimed, "will you remain with me?"

"No, no, no!" she replied, stamping her foot. Then she drew from her finger a ring that I had given her, and threw it among the bushes.

I stabbed her twice. It was Garcia's knife, which I had appropriated after breaking my own. She fell at the second thrust without a cry. I can still fancy I see her splendid black eyes regarding me steadily; then they became troubled, and closed. I remained insensible beside the body for a good hour. Then I remembered that Carmen had often said that she would like to be buried in a wood. I excavated a grave with my knife, and placed her in it. For a long time I searched for the ring, and at length found it. I placed it in the grave with her and also a small cross. Perhaps I was wrong! Then I mounted my horse, galloped to Cordova, and at the first guard-house I made myself known. I said I had killed Carmen, but did not wish to divulge where I had buried her. The hermit is a holy man. He has prayed for her. He has said a mass for her soul. Poor girl! It is the Calli who are to blame for having made her what she was.

THE CHAIRMENDER[1]

Guy de Maupassant

IT WAS the opening of the shooting-season at the house of the Marquis de Bertrans. Dinner was over; eleven sportsmen, eight ladies, all of them

---

[1] Translated by Mariette Léon. Reprinted by permission of Messrs George G. Harrap and Co., Ltd.

still youthful, and the doctor of the district were seated round the great lighted table, decorated with fruit and flowers. They began to talk of love, and a great discussion ensued, that ever-recurring discussion as to whether true love is possible once only or many times.

Examples were quoted of people who had only had one love affair; other examples were given of persons who had loved often and passionately. The men, in general, held that passion, like disease, can attack the same person many times, attack fatally even should he meet with some obstacle.

Althought this aspect of the subject was incontestable, the women, whose opinions rested on poetry rather than on observation, affirmed that love, true love, the great love, could descend but once upon an individual, that such love was like a thunderbolt, and that a heart once touched by it remained ever after so emptied, ravaged, seared, that no other powerful feeling, not even a dream, could be born again within it.

The Marquis, having loved often, keenly combated this belief. "I assure you that one can love many times, with all one's heart and with all one's soul. You tell me of people who have killed themselves for love, as proof of the impossibility of a second passion. I answer that had they not committed the blunder of suicide, which took from them all chance of relapse, they would have recovered; they would have begun again and again till their natural death. Lovers are like drunkards: those who have drunk drink again; those who have loved will love again; it is a matter of temperament."

They chose as arbiter the doctor, an old Parisian practitioner retired to the country, and begged him to give his opinion; but actually he had none. "As the Marquis says, it is an affair of temperament. As for me, I have known of a passion that lasted for fifty-five years, without a day of respite, and which ended only with death."

The Marchioness clapped her hands. "How beautiful, and what a dream to be loved thus! What happiness to live for fifty-five years wrapped round by such deep and ardent affection! How happy and how full of joy in life must the man thus adored have been!"

The doctor smiled. "Indeed, madame, you are not mistaken about one point: that the beloved object was a man. You know him; it was M. Chouquet, the chemist of the town. As for the woman, you know her too. She was the old chairmender who used to come to the castle every year; but I will explain myself more clearly."

The enthusiasm of the women had subsided. Their disgusted faces said, "Faugh!" As though it were not meet that love should visit any but refined and distinguished people, alone worthy of the interest of the well-bred!

The doctor continued: "Three months ago I was called to the deathbed of this old woman; she had arrived, the evening before, in the cart which was her house, drawn by the wretched back horse which you have seen, and accompanied by two great black dogs, her friends and guardians. The parish priest was already there; she appointed us her legal executors, and, in order to reveal to us the significance of her last wishes, she told us her life-story. I know of nothing more strange or more touching. Her father was a chairmender, and her mother also; she had never lived in a house built on solid ground. As a small child she had wandered about in rags, verminous and filthy.

"They stayed on the outskirts of villages. By the hedge-sides they would unharness the cart while the horse grazed and the dog slept, his nose on his paws; and the little one would play about on the grass while the father and mother, under the shade of the elms, by the roadside, would repair all the old seats of the hamlet. There was little conversation in this itinerant dwelling. After the few necessary words to settle who should make the round of the housed crying out the well-known 'Chairs to mend,' they would begin to plait the straw, sitting opposite each other or side by side; when the child strayed too far, or tried to make friends with some village urchin, the angry voice of her father would recall her: "Will you come back, you rascal!'

"They were the only words of affection that she heard. When she grew older she was sent to collect the damaged chair-bottoms; then she would scrape acquaintance here and there with village boys, but now it was the parents of her new friends who roughly recalled their offspring: 'Will you come here, scamps! Just let me catch you talking to ragamuffins!'

"Often the little boys would throw stones at her. The coppers given her by ladies she hoarded with care.

"Passing one day through this part of the world when she was eleven years old, she came across the little Chouquet boy, behind the cemetery, crying because a comrade had stolen two sous from him. These tears on the part of a gentleman's child, one of those whom in her foolish little waif's mind she had imagined to be always contented and happy, overwhelmed her; she drew near, and when she learnt the cause of his trouble she poured into his hand all her savings—seven sous-which he naturally took, drying his tears. Then, wild with delight, she was emboldened to kiss him. Being absorbed in the contemplation of his money, he made no resistance, and she, finding herself neither rebuffed nor beaten, began again, clasp-him in her arms, kissing him heartily, and then running away.

"What process went on in the mind of the waif? Had she taken a fancy to this youngster because she had sacrificed to him her vagrant's fortune, or because she had given him her first loving kiss? The mystery is the same whether with children or grown-ups.

"For months she dreamed of this corner of the cemetery and of this boy. On the chance of seeing him again, she stole from her parents, scraping up a sou here and a sou there, on the chairmending or on the provisions she went to buy. On her return she had two francs in her pocket, but she could only catch a glimpse of the little chemist, looking very clean, behind the windows of his father's shop, between a crimson bow, and a tapeworm specimen. Charmed, excited, enraptured by the splendour of the coloured water and the glittering glass, she loved him all the more dearly.

"She treasured the unfading memory of him in her heart, and when she met him again, the year after, playing marbles with his comrades behind the school, she threw herself upon him, kissing him so vehemently that he began to howl with fear. Then to pacify him she gave him her money—three francs twenty centimes—a real fortune, which he looked at with wide- open eyes. He took it and allowed her to caress him as much as she liked.

"For four years longer she poured into his hands all her savings, which he pocketed conscientiously in exchange for so many kisses. Once it was thirty sous, once two francs, once twelve sous (she wept for sorrow, dismay, and humiliation, but it had been a bad year), and the last time it was five francs, a great round coin which made him laugh ith delight.

"He had become her only interest; and he awaited her return with a certain amount of impatience, running to meet her when whe saw her, making the little girl's heart beat with joy.

"Then he disappeared; they had sent him to school, as she discovered by adroit questionings. Then with much manœuvring she tried to change her parents' route, making them pass here at holiday times; she succeeded, but only after a year of stratagem.

"Two years had thus passed since she had seen him, and he was so changed, so tall, handsome, and imposing in his tunic with gilt buttons, that she could scarcely recognize him. He pretended not to see her, and proudly passed her by. For two days she wept, and after that continued to suffer without respite.

"Every year she returned, passing him without daring even to greet him, while he did not deign even to glance at her.

"She loved him to distraction.

" 'Doctor,' she said to me, 'I had no eyes for any other man; in fact, no others existed for me.'

"Her parents died, and she carried on their trade, but she had two dogs instead of one, two terrifying dogs that no one would have dared to confront.

"One day she was returning to the village where her affections lay when she saw a young woman coming out of the Chouquets' shop, arm in arm with her beloved; it was his wife: they were married!

"That very evening she threw herself into the pond in the town-hall square.

"A belated drunkard pulled her out and carried her to the chemist's shop. Chouquet's son came downstairs in his dressing-gown to attend to her and, without appearing to recognize her, took her clothes off, rubbed her, and then said in a hard voice: 'You are mad! You must not play the fool like this.' That was sufficient to cure her. He had spoken to her! It made her happy for a long time. He would accept no remuneration for curing her, thought she eagerly offered to pay.

"Thus her life passed. She mended chairs, dreaming of Chouquet. Every year she had a sight of him through his windows; she took to buying small supplies of remedies from him; in this way she could get near him, talk to him, and give him more money.

"As I said at first, she died this spring.

"After telling me all this sad story, she begged me to hand over to him whom she had loved so patiently all the savings of a lifetime, for she had worked solely for him, she said, even going short of food in order to lay by, and to make sure that he should think of her, once at least, when she was dead. So she gave me two thousand, three hundred, and twenty-seven francs. I left the twenty-seven francs with the priest for the funeral and took the rest away, after she had breathed her last.

"The following day I went to the Chouquets'; they were finishing luncheon, sitting opposite each other, fat, red, consequential, and content, and redolent of the products of the chemist's shop.

"They made me sit down and offered me a 'Kirsch,' which I accepted. Then I began my discourse in a voice charged with emotion, fully expecting that they would weep.

"As soon as he understood that he had been loved by this vagabond, this chairmender, this scum of the high-roads, Chouquet bristled with indignation, as though she had stolen from him his reputation, the esteem of respectable people, his personal honour, something delicate and more precious than life itself. His wife, as exasperated as he was, could only repeat over and over again: 'That beggar-woman! that beggar-woman!' He had got up and was striding rapidly up and down behind the table, his skull-cap askew over his ear. He stammered out: 'Can you understand it, doctor? It's one of those horrible things that happen to men! What can one do? Oh, had I only known it while she was alive, I would have had her arrested by the police and flung into prison, and she should never have come out again, I'll answer for that.' I was astounded at the result of my well-meant action. I had no idea what to do, nor what to say, but I had to fulfil my mission, so I went on: 'She bade me give you her whole savings, which amount to two thousand, three hundred francs. As what I have told you seems very distasteful to you, perhaps the best thing to do would be to give the money to the poor.' The man and woman looked at me, transfixed with amazement. I drew the money out of my pocket, a wretched collection of coins of every country and of every mint, gold and coppers mixed. Then I asked: 'What is your decision?'

"Madame Chouquet spoke first. 'Well, as it was this woman's last wish... I suppose we can hardly refuse.' The husband somewhat shame-facedly replied: 'We could always buy something for the children with it.' I answered drily: 'As you wish!' He rejoined: 'Oh, well, let's have it, as she asked you to do this; we can always find some means of employing it for some good work.'

"I handed over the money, bowed, and went away. The next morning Chouquet came to find me and said brusquely: 'That—that woman has left her cart here.... What shall you do with the cart?'

" 'Nothing! Take it if you wish.'

" 'Good! That's just what I want. I shall make a shed for my kitchen-garden with it.'

"He was going off when I called him back. 'She left her old horse and her two dogs as well. Do you want them too?'

"He paused, astonished. 'Oh, no, of course not. What should I do with them? Make what use you like of them!' And he laughed. Then he put out his hand, which I shook.

"After all, it is not possible for the doctor and the chemist of the same district to be enemies.

"I kept the dogs for myself, and the priest, who has a large yard, took the horse. Chouquet uses the cart as a shed, and he has bought five railway bonds with the money.

"That is the only case of deep love that I have met in my life."

The doctor was silent.

Then the Marquise, with tears in her eyes, sighed. "Undoubtedly," she said, "women are the only ones who know how to love!"

GERMANY

UNDINE

La Motte Fouqué

CHAPTER I

ON A beautiful evening, many hundred years ago, a worthy old fisherman sat mending his nets. The spot where he dwelt was exceedingly picturesque. The green turf on which he had built his cottage ran far out into a great lake; and this slip of verdure appeared to stretch into it as much through love of its clear water as the lake, moved by a like impulse, strove to fold the meadow, with its waving grass and flowers, and the cooling shade of the trees, in its embrace of love. They seemed to be drawn toward each other, and the one to be visiting the other as a guest.

With respect to human beings, indeed, in this pleasant spot, excepting the fisherman and his family, there were few, or rather none, to be met with. For as in the background of the scene, toward the west and northwest, lay a forest of extraordinary wildness, which, owing to its sunless gloom and almost impassable recesses, as well as to fear of the strange creatures and visionary illusions to be encountered in it, most people avoided entering, unless in cases of extreme necessity. The pious old fisherman, however, many times passed through it without harm, when he carried the fine fish which he caught by his beautiful strip of land to a great city lying only a short distance beyond the forest.

Now the reason he was able to go through this wood with so much ease may have been chiefly this, because he entertained scarcely any thoughts but such as were of a religious nature; and besides, every time he crossed the evil-reported shades, he used to sing some holy song with a clear voice and from a sincere heart.

Well, while he sat by his nets this evening, neither fearing nor devising evil, a sudden terror seized him, as he heard a rushing in the darkness of the wood, that resembled the trampling of a mounted steed, and the noise continued every instant drawing nearer and nearer to his little territory.

What he had fancied, when abroad in many a stormy night, respecting the mysteries of the forest, now flashed through his mind in a moment, especially the figure of a man of gigantic stature and snow-white appear-

440

ance, who kept nodding his head in a portentous manner. And when he raised his eyes towards the wood, the form came before him in perfect distinctness, as he saw the nodding man burst forth from the mazy web-work of leaves and branches. But he immediately felt emboldened, when he reflected that nothing to give him alarm had ever befallen him even in the forest; and moreover, that on this open neck of land the evil spirit, it was likely, would be still less daring in the exercise of his power. At the same time he prayed aloud with the most earnest sincerity of devotion, repeating a passage of the Bible. This inspired him with fresh courage, and soon perceiving the illusion, and the strange mistake into which his imagination had betrayed him, he could with difficulty refrain from laughing. The white nodding figure he had seen became transformed, in the twinkling of an eye, to what in reality it was, a small brook, long and familiarly known to him whick ran foaming from the forest, and discharged itself int the lake.

But what had caused the startling sound was a knight arrayed in sumptuous apparel, who from under the shadows of the trees came riding toward the cottage. His doublet was violet embroidered with gold, and his scarlet cloak hung gracefully over it; on his cap of burnished gold waved red and violet-coloured plumes; and in his golden shoulder-belt flashed a sword, richly ornamented and extremely beautiful. The white barb that bore the knight was more slenderly built than war-horses usually are, and he touched the turf with a step so light and elastic that the green and flowery carpet seemed hardly to receive the slightest injury from his tread. The old fisherman, notwithstanding, did not feel perfectly secure in his mind, although he was forced to believe that no evil could be feared from an appearance so pleasing, and therefore, as good manners dictated, he took off his hat on the knight's coming near, and quietly remained by the side of his nets.

When the stranger stopped, and asked whether he with his horse could have shelter and entertainment there for the night, the fisherman returned answer: "As to your horse, fair sir, I have no better stable for him than this shady meadow, and no better provender than the grass that is growing here. But with respect to yourself, you shall be welcome to our humble cottage, and to the best supper and lodging we are able to give you."

The knight was well contented with this reception; and alighting from his horse, which his host assisted him to relieve from saddle and bridle, he let him hasten away to the fresh, pasture, and thus spoke: "Even had I found you less hospitable and kindly disposed, my worthy old friend, you would still, I suspect, hardly have got rid of me to-day; for here, I perceive, a broad lake lies before us, and as to riding back into that wood of wonders, with the shades of evening deepening around me, may Heaven in its grace preserve me from the thought."

"Pray, not a word of the wood, or of returning into it!" said the fisherman, and took his guest into the cottage.

There beside the hearth, from which a frugal fire was diffusing its light through the clean twilight room, sat the fisherman's aged wife in a great chair. At the entrance of their noble guest, she rose and gave him a courteous welcome, but sat down again in her seat of honour, not making the slightest offer of it to the stranger. Upon this the fisherman said with a smile:

"You must not be offended with her, young gentleman, because she has not given up to you the best chair in the house; it is a custom among poor people to look upon this as the privilege of the aged."

"Why, husband!" cried the old lady, with a quiet smile, "where can your wits be wandering? Our guest, to say the least of him, must belong to a Christian; country; and how is it possible, then, that so well-bred a young man as he appears to be could dream of driving old people from their chairs? Take a seat, my young master," continued she, turning to the knight; "there is still quite a snug little chair on the other side of the room there, only be careful not to shove it about too roughly, for one of its legs, I fear, is none of the firmest."

The knight brought up the seat as carefully as she could desire, sat down upon it good-humouredly, and it seemed to him almost as if he must be somehow related to this little household, and have just returned home from abroad.

These three worthy people now began to converse in the most friendly and familiar manner. In relation to the forest, indeed, concerning which the knight occasionally made some inquiries, the old man chose to know and say but little; he was of opinion that slightly touching upon it, at this hour of twilight, was most suitable and safe; but of the cares and comforts of their home, and their business abroad, the aged couple spoke more freely and listened also with eager curiosity as the knight recounted to them his travels, and how he had a castle near one of the sources of the Danube, and that his name was Sir Huldbrand of Ringstetten.

Already had the stranger, while they were in the midst of their talk, heard at times a splash against the little low window, as if someone were dashing water against it. The old man, every time he heard the noise, knit his brows with vexation; but at last, when the whole sweep of a shower came pouring like a torrent against the panes, and bubbling through the decayed frame into the room, he started up indignant, rushed to the window, and cried with a threatening voice—

"Undine! will you never leave off these fooleries?—not even to-day, when we have a stranger-knight with us in the cottage?"

All without now became still, only a low laugh was just audible, and the fisherman said, as he came back to his seat, "You will have the goodness, my honoured guest, to pardon this freak, and it may be a multitude more; but she has no thought of evil, or of any harm. This mischievous Undine, to confess the truth, is our adopted daughter, and she stoutly refuses to give over this frolicsome childishness of hers, although she has already entered her eighteenth year. But in spite of this, as I said before, she is at heart one of the very best children in the world."

"*You* may say so," broke in the old lady, shaking her head; "you can give a better account of her than I can. When you return home from fishing, or from selling your fish in the city, you may think her frolics very delighful. But to have her dancing about you the whole day long, and never from morning to night to hear her speak one word of sense; and then as she grows older, instead of having any help from her in the family, to find her a continual cause of anxiety, lest her wild humours should completely ruin us, that is quite another thing, and enough at last to weary out the patience even of a saint."

"Well, well," replied the master of the house, with a smile, "you have your trials with Undine, and I have mine with the lake. The lake often beats down my dams, and breaks the meshes of my nets, but for all that I have a strong affection for it, and so have you, in spite of you mighty crosses and vexations, for our graceful little child. Is it not true?"

"One cannot be very angry with her," answered the old lady, as she gave her husband an approving smile.

That instant the door flew open, and a fair girl, of wondrous beauty, sprang laughing in, and said. "You have only been making a mock of me, father; for where now is the guest you mentioned?"

The same moment, however, she perceived the knight also, and continued standing before the young man in fixed astonishment. Huldbrand was charmed with her graceful figure, and viewed her lovely features with the more intense interest, as he imagined it was only her surprise that allowed him the opportunity, and that she would soon turn away from his gaze with increased bashfulness. But the event was the very reverse of what he expected; for, after looking at him for a long while, she became more confident, moved nearer, knelt down before him, and while she played with a gold medal which he wore attached to a rich chain on his breast, exclaimed,

"Why, you beautiful, you kind, guest! how have you reached our poor cottage at last? Have you been obliged for years and years to wander about the world before you could catch one glimpse of our nook? Do you come out of that wild forest, my beautiful knight?"

The old woman was so prompt in her reproof, as to allow him no time answer. She commanded the maiden to rise, show better manners, and go to her work. But Undine, without making any reply, drew a little footstool near Huldbrand's chair, sat down upon it with her netting, and said in a gentle tone—

"I will work here."

The old man did as parents are apt to do with children to whom they have been over-indulgent. He affected to observe nothing of Undine's strange behaviour, and was beginning to talk about something else. But this the maiden did not permit him to do. She broke in upon him, "I have asked our kind guest from whence he has come among us, and he has not yet answered me."

"I come out of the forest, you lovely little vision," Huldbrand returned; and she spoke again:

"You must also tell me how you came to enter that forest, so feared and shunned, and the marvellous adventures you met with in it; for there is no escaping without something of this kind."

Huldbrand felt a slight shudder on remembering what he had witnessed, and looked involuntarily toward the window, for it seemed to him that one of the strange shapes which had come upon him in the forest must be there grinning in through the glass; but he discerned nothing except the deep darkness of night, which had now enveloped the whole prospect. Upon this he became more collected, and was just on the point of beginning his account, when the old man thus interrupted him:

"Not so, sir knight; this is by no means a fit hour for such relation."

But Undine, in a state of high excitement, sprang up from her little stool and cried, placing herself directly before the fisherman: "He shall not tell his story, father? he shall not? But it is my will:—he shall!—stop him who may!"

Thus speaking, she stamped her little foot vehemently on the floor, but all with an air of such comic and good-humoured simplicity, that Huldbrand now found it quite as hard to withdraw his gaze from her wild emotion, as he had before from her gentleness and beauty. The old man, on the contrary, burst out in unrestrained displeasure. He severely reproved Undine for her disobedience and her unbecoming carriage toward the stranger, and his good old wife joined him in harping on the same string.

By these rebukes Undine was only excited the more.

"If you want to quarrel with me," she cried, "and will not let me hear what I so much desire, then sleep alone in your smoky old hut!" And swift as an arrow she shot from the door, and vanished amid the darkness of the night.

Huldbrand and the fisherman sprang from their seats, and were rushing to stop the angry girl; but before they could reach the cottage door, she had disappeared in the stormy darkness without, and no sound, not so much even as that of her light footstep, betrayed the course she had taken. Huldbrand threw a glance of inquiry toward his host; it almost seemed to him as if the whole of the sweet apparition, which had so suddenly plunged again amid the night, were no other than a continuation of the wonderful forms that had just played their mad pranks with him in the forest. But the old man muttered between his teeth, "

"This is not the first time she has treated us in this manner. Now must our hearts be filled with anxiety, and our eyes find no sleep the whole night; for who can assure us, in spite of her past escapes, that she will not sometime or other come to harm, if she thus continue out in the dark and alone until daylight?"

"Then pray, for God's sake, father, let us follow her," cried Huldbrand anxiously.

"Wherefore should we?" replied the old man. "It would be a sin were I to suffer you, all alone, to search after the foolish girl amid the lonesomeness of night; and my old limbs would fail to carry me to this wild rover, even if I knew to what place she has betaken herself."

"Still we ought at least to call after her, and beg her to return," said Huldbrand; and he began to call in tones of earnest entreaty, "Undine! Undine! come back, come back!"

The old man shook his head, and said, "All your shouting, however loud and long, will be of no avail; you know not as yet, sir knight, how self-willed the little thing is." But still, even hoping against hope, he could not himself cease calling out every minute, amid the gloom of night, "Undine! ah, dear Undine! I beseech you, pray come back—only this once."

It turned out, however, exactly as the fisherman had said. No Undine could they hear or see; and as the old man would on no account consent that Huldbrand should go in quest of the fugitive, they were both obliged at last to return into the cottage. There they found the fire on the hearth almost gone out, and the mistress of the house, who took Undine's flight and danger far less to heart than her husband, had already gone to rest. The old man blew up the coals, put on dry wood, and by the firelight hunted for a flask of wine, which he brought and set between himself and his guest.

"You, sir knight, as well as I," said he, "are anxious on the silly girl's account; and it would be better, I think, to spend part of the night in chatting and drinking, than keep turning and turning on our rush-mats, and trying in vain to sleep. What is your opinion?"

Huldbrand was well pleased with the plan; the fisherman pressed him to take the empty seat of honour, its worthy occupant having now left it for her couch; and they relished their beverage and enjoyed their chat as two such good men and true ever ought to do. To be sure, whenever the slightest thing moved before the windows, or at times when even nothing was moving, one of them would look up and exclaim, "Here she comes!" Then would they continue silent a few moments, and afterward, when nothing appeared, would shake their heads, breathe out a sigh and go on with their talk.

But as neither could think of anything but Undine the best plan they could devise was, that the old fisherman should relate, and the knight should hear, in what manner Undine had come to the cottage. So the fisherman began as follows:

"It is now about fifteen years since I one day crossed the wild forest with fish for the city market. My wife had remained at home as she was wont to do; and at this time for a reason of more than common interest, for although we were beginning to feel the advances of age, God had bestowed upon us an infant of wonderful beauty. It was a little girl; and we already began to ask ourselves the question, whether we ought not, for the advantage of the new-comer, to quit our solitude, and, the better to bring up this precious gift of Heaven, to remove to some more inhabited place. Poor people, to be sure, cannot in these cases do all you may think they ought, sir knight; but we must all do what we can.

"Well, I went on my way, and this affair would keep running in my head. This slip of land was most dear to me, and I trembled when, amidst the bustle and broils of the city, I thought to myself, 'In a scene of tumult like this, or at least in one not much more quiet, I must soon take up my abode.' But I did not for this murmur against our good God; on the contrary, I paised Him in silence for the new-born babe. I should also speak an untruth, were I to say that anything befell me, either on my passage through the forest to the city, or on my returning homeward, that gave me more alarm than usual, as at that time I had never seen any appearance there which could terrify or annoy me. The Lord was ever with me in those awful shades."

Thus speaking he took his cap reverently from his bald head, and continuead to sit for a considerable time in devout thought. He then covered himself again, and went on with his relation.

"On this side the forest, alas! it was on this side, that woe burst upon me. My wife came wildly to meet me, clad in mourning apparel, and her eyes streaming with tears. 'Gracious God!' I cried, 'where's our child? Speak!'

" 'With Him on whom you have called, dear husband,' she answered, and we now entered the cottage together, weeping in silence. I looked for the little corpse, almost fearing to find what I was seeking; and then it was I first learnt how all had happened.

"My wife had taken the little one in her arms, and walked out to the shore of the lake. She there sat down by its very brink; and while she was playing with the infant, as free from all fear as she was full of delight, it bent forward on a sudden, as if seeing something very beautiful in the water. My wife saw her laugh, the dear angel, and try to catch the image in her tiny hands; but in a moment—with a motion swifter than sight—she sprang from her mother's arms, and sank in the lake, the watery glass into which she had been gazing. I searched for our lost darling again and again; but it was all in vain; I could nowhere find the least trace of her.

"The same evening we childless parents were sitting together by our cottage hearth. We had no desire to talk, even if our tears would have permitted us. As we thus sat in mournful stillness, gazing into the fire, all at once we heard something without,—a slight rustling at the door. The door flew open, and we saw a little girl, three or four years old, and more beautiful than I can say, standing on the threshold, richly dressed, and smiling upon us. We were struck dumb with astonishment, and I knew not for a time whether the tiny form were a real human being, or a mere mockery of enchantment. But I soon perceived water dropping from her golden hair and rich garments, and that the pretty child had been lying in the water, and stood in immediate need of our help.

" 'Wife,' said I, 'no one has been able to save our child for us; but let us do for others what would have made us so blessed could anyone have done it for us.'

"We undressed the little thing, put her to bed, and gave her something to drink: at all this she spoke not a word, but only turned her eyes upon useyes blue and bright as sea or sky—and continued looking at us with a smile.

"Next morning we had no reason to fear that she had received any other harm than her wetting, and I now asked her about her parents, and how she could have come to us. But the account she gave was both confused and incredible. She must surely have been born far from here, not only because I have been unable for these fifteen years to learn anything of her birth, but because she then said, and at times continues to say, many things of so very singular a nature, that we neither of us know, after all, whether she may not have dropped among us from the moon; for her talk runs upon golden castles, crystal domes, and Heaven knows what extravagances beside. What, however, she related with most distinctness was this: that while she was once taking a sail with her mother on the great lake, she fell out of the boat into the water; and that when she first recovered her senses, she was here under our trees, where the gay scenes of the shore filled her with delight.

"We now had another care weighing upon our minds, and one that caused us no small perplexity and uneasiness. We of course very soon determined to keep and bring up the child we had found, in place of our own darling that had been drowned; but who could tell us whether she had been baptised or not? She herself could give us no light on the subject. When we asked her the question, she commonly made answer, that she well knew she was created for God's praise and glory, and that she was willing to let us to with her all that might promote His glory and praise.

"My wife and I reasoned in this way: 'If she has not been baptised, there can be no use in putting off the ceremony; and if she has been, it still is better to have too much of a good thing than too little.'

"Taking this view of our difficulty, we now endeavoured to hit upon a good name for the child, since, while she remained without one, we were often at a loss in our familiar talk, to know what to call her. We at length agreed that Dorothea would be most suitable for her, as I had somewhere heard it said that this name signified a *gift of God*, and surely she had been sent to us by Providence as a gift, to comfort us in our misery. She, on the contrary, would not so much as hear Dorothea mentioned; she insisted, that as she had been named Undine by her parents, Undine she ought still to be called. It now occurred to me that this was a heathenish name, to be found in no calendar, and I resolved to ask the advice of a priest in the city. He would not listen to the name of Undine; and yielding to my urgent request, he came with me through the enchanted forest in order to perform the rite of baptism here in my cottage.

"The little maid stood before us so prettily adorned, and with such an air of gracefulness, that the heart of the priest softened at once in her presence; and she coaxed him so sweetly, and jested with him so merrily, that he at last remembered nothing of his many objections to the name of Undine.

"Thus, then, was she baptised Undine; and during the holy ceremony she behaved with great propriety and gentleness, wild and wayward as at other times she invariably was; for in this my wife was quite right, when she mentioned the anxiety the child has occasioned us. If I should relate to you——"

At this moment the knight interrupted the fisherman, to direct his attention to a deep sound as of a rushing flood, which had caught his ear during the talk of the old man. And now the waters came pouring on with redoubled fury before the cottage-windows. Both sprang to the door. There they saw, by the light of the now risen moon, the brook which issued from the wood rushing wildly over its banks, and whirling onward with it both stones and branches of trees in its rapid course. The storm, as if awakened by the uproar burst forth from the clouds, whose immense masses of vapour coursed over the moon with the swiftness of thought; the lake roared beneath the wind that swept the foam from its waves; while the trees of this narrow peninsula groaned from root to topmost branch as they bowed and swung above the torrent.

"Undine! in God's name, Undine!" cried the two men in an agony. No answer was returned. And now, regardless of everything else, they hurried from the cottage, one in this direction, the other in that, searching and calling.

CHAPTER II

The longer Huldbrand sought Undine beneath the shades of night, and failed to find her, the more anxious and confused he became. The impression that she was a mere phantom of the forest gained a new ascendency over him; indeed, amid the howling of the waves and the tempest, the crashing of the trees, and the entire change of the once so peaceful and beautiful scene, he was tempted to view the whole peninsula, together with the cottage and its inhabitants, as little more than some mockery of his senses. But still he heard afar off the fisherman's anxious and incessant shouting, "Undine!" and also his aged wife, who was praying and singing psalms.

At length, when he drew near to the brook, which had overflowed its banks, he perceived by the moonlight, that it had taken its wild course directly in front of the haunted forest, so as to change the peninsula into an island.

"Merciful God!" he breathed to himself, "if Undine has ventured a step within that fearful wood, what will become of her? Perhaps it was all owing to her sportive a wayward spirit, because I would give her no account of my adventures there. And now the stream is rolling between us, she may be weeping alone on the other side in the midst of spectral horrors!"

A shuddering groan escaped him; and clambering over some stones and trunks of overthrown pines, in order to step into the impetuous current, he resolved either by wading or swimming, to seek the wanderer on the further shore. He felt, it is true, all the dread and shrinking awe creeping over him which he had already suffered by daylight among the now tossing and roaring branches of the forest. More than all, a tall man in white, whom he knew but too well, met his view, as he stood grinning and nodding on the grass beyond the water. But even monstrous forms like this only impelled him to cross over toward them, when the thought rushed upon him that Undine might be there alone and in the agony of death.

He had already grasped a strong branch of a pine, and stood supporting himself upon it in the whirling current, against which he could with difficulty keep himself erect; but he advanced deeper in with a courageous spirit. That instant a gentle voice of warning cried near him, "Do not venture, do not venture!—that OLD MAN, the STREAM, is too full of tricks to be trusted!" He knew the soft tones of the voice; and while he stood as it were entranced beneath the shadows which had now duskily veiled the moon, his head swam with the swell and rolling of the waves as he saw them momentarily rising above his knee. Still he disdained the thought of giving up his purpose.

"If you are not really there, if you are merely gambolling round me like a mist, may I, too, bid farewell to life, and become a shadow like you, dear, dear Undine!" Thus calling aloud, he again moved deeper into the stream. "Look round you—ah, pray look round you, beautiful young stranger! why rush on death so madly?" cried the voice a second time close by him; and looking on one side he perceived, by the light of the moon, again cloudless, a little island formed by the flood; and crouching upon its flowery turf, beneath the branches of embowering trees, he saw the smiling and lovely Undine.

O how much more gladly than before the young man now plied his sturdy staff! A few steps, and he had crossed the flood that was rushing between himself and the maiden; and he stood near her on the little spot of greensward in security protected by the old trees. Undine half rose, and she threw her arms around his neck to draw him gently down upon the soft seat by her side.

"Here you shall tell me your story, my beautiful friend," she breathed in a low whisper; "here the cross old people cannot disturb us; and, besides, our roof of leaves here will make quite as good a shelter as their poor cottage."

"It is heaven itself," cried Huldbrand; and folding her in his arms, he kissed the lovely girl with fervour.

The old fisherman, meantime, had come to the margin of the stream, and he shouted across, "Why, how is this, sir knight! I received you with the welcome which one true-hearted man gives to another; and now you sit there caressing my foster-child in secret, while you suffer me in my anxiety to wander through the night in quest of her."

"Not till this moment did I find her myself, old father," cried the knight cross the water.

"So much the better," said the fisherman; "but now make haste, and bring her over to me upon firm ground."

To this, however, Undine would by no means consent. She declared that she would rather enter the wild forest itself with the beautiful stranger, than return to the cottage where she was so thwarted in her wishes, and from which the knight would soon or late go away. Then, throwing her arms round Huldbrand, she sung the following verse with the warbling sweetness of a bird:

> "A rill would leave its misty vale,
>   And fortunes wild explore;
> Weary at length it reached the main,
>   And sought its vale no more."

The old fisherman wept bitterly at her song, but his emotion seemed to awaken little or no sympathy in her. She kissed and caressed her new friend, who at last said to her: "Undine, if the distress of the old man does not touch your heart, it cannot but move mine. We ought to return to him."

She opened her large blue eyes upon him in amazement, and spoke at last with a slow and doubtful accent, "If you think so, it is well; all is right to me which you think right. But the old man over there must first give me his promise that he will allow you, without objection, to relate what you saw in the wood, and—well, other things will settle themselves."

451

"Come—only come!" cried the fisherman to her, unable to utter another word. At the same time he stretched his arms wide over the current towards her, and to give her assurance that he would do what she required, nodded his head. This motion caused his white hair to fall strangely over his face, and Huldbrand could not but remember the nodding white man of the forest. Without allowing anything, however, to produce in him the least confusion, the young knight took the beautiful girl in his arms, and bore her across the narrow channel which the stream had torn away between her little island and the solid shore. The old man fell upon Undine's neck, and found it impossible either to express his joy or to kiss her enough even the ancient dame came up and embraced the recovered girl most cordially. Every word of censure was carefully avoided; the more so, indeed, as even Undine, forgetting her waywardness, almost overwhelmed her foster-parents with caresses and the prattle of tenderness.

When at length the excess of their joy at recovering their child had subsided, morning had already dawned, shining upon the waters of the lake; the tempest had become hushed, the small birds sang merrily on the moist branches.

As Undine now insisted upon hearing the recital of the knight's promised adventures, the aged couple readily agreed to her wish. Breakfast was brought out beneath the trees which stood behind the cottage toward the lake on the north, and they sat down to it with contented hearts; Undine at the knight's feet on the grass. These arrangements being made, Huldbrand began his story in the following manner:—

"It is now about eight days since I rode into the free imperial city which lies yonder on the farther side of the forest. Soon after my arrival a splendid tournament and running at the ring took place there, and I spared neither my horse nor my lance in the encounter.

"Once, while I was pausing at the lists to rest from the brisk exercise, and was handing back my helmet to one of my attendants, a female figure of extraordinary beauty caught my attention, as, most magnificently attired, she stood looking on at one of the balconies. I learned, on making inquiry of a person near me, that the name of the young lady was Bertalda, and that she was a foster-daughter of one of the powerful dukes of this country. She too, I observed, was gazing at me, and the consequences were such as we young knights are wont to experience; whatever success in riding I might have had before, I was now favoured with still better fortune. That evening I was Bertalda's partner in the dance, and I enjoyed the same distinction during the remainder of the festival."

A sharp pain in his left hand, as it hung carelessly beside him, here interrupted Huldbrand's relation, and drew his eye to the part affected. Undine had fastened her pearly teeth, and not without some keenness too, upon one of his fingers, appearing at the same time very gloomy and displeased. On a sudden, however, she looked up in his eyes with an expression of tender melancholy, and whispered almost inaudibly,—

"It is all your own fault."

She then covered her face; and the knight, strangely embarrassed and thoughtful, went on with his story.

"This lady, Bertalda, of whom I spoke, is of a proud and wayward spirit. The second day I saw her she pleased me by no means so much as she had the first, and the third day still less. But I continued about her because she showed me more favour than she did any other knight, and it so happened that I playfully asked her to give me one of her gloves. 'When you have entered the haunted forest all alone,' said she; 'when you have explored its wonders, and brought me a full account of them, the glove is yours.' As to getting her glove it was of no importance to me whatever, but the word had been spoken, and no honourable knight would permit himself to be urged to such a proof of valour a second time."

"I thought," said Undine, interrupting him, "that she loved you."

"It did appear so," replied Huldbrand.

"Well!" exclaimed the maiden, laughing, "this is beyond belief; she must be very stupid. To drive from her one who was dear to her! And worse than all, into that ill-omened wood! The wood and its mysteries, for all I should have cared, might have waited long enough."

"Yesterday morning, then," pursued the knight, smiling kindly upon Undine, "I set out from the city, my enterprise before me. The early light lay rich upon the verdant turf. It shone so rosy on the slender boles of the trees, and there was so merry a whispering among the leaves, that in my heart I could not but laugh at people who feared meeting anything to terrify them in a spot so delicious. 'I shall soon pass through the forest, and as speedily return,' I said to myself, in the overflow of joyous feeling, and ere I was well aware, I had entered deep among the green shades, while of the plain that lay behind me I was no longer able to catch a glimpse.

"Then the conviction for the first time impressed me, that in a forest of so great extent I might very easily become bewildered, and that this, perhaps, might be the only danger which was likely to threaten those who explored its recesses. So I made a halt, and turned myself in the direction of the sun, which had meantime risen somewhat higher, and while I was looking up to observe it, I saw something black among the boughs of a lofty oak. My first thought was, 'It is a bear!' and I grasped my weapon. The object then accosted me from above in a human voice, but in a tone most harsh and hideous: 'If I, overhead here, do not gnaw off these dry branches, Sir Noodle, what shall we have to roast you with when midnight comes?' And with that it grinned, and made such a rattling with the branches that my courser became mad with affright, and rushed furiously forward with me before I had time to see distinctly what sort of a devil's beast it was."

"You must not speak so," said the old fisherman, crossing himself. His wife did the same, without saying a word, and Undine, while her eye sparkled with delight, looked at the knight and said, "The best of the story is, however, that as yet they have not roasted you! Go on, now, you beautiful knight."

The knight then went on with his adventures. "My horse was so wild, that he well-nigh rushed with me against limbs and trunks of trees. He was dripping with sweat through terror, heat, and the violent straining of his muscles. Still he refused to slacken his career. At last, altogether beyond my control, he took his course directly up a stony steep, when suddenly a tall white man flashed before me, and threw himself athwart the way my mad steed was taking. At this apparition he shuddered with new affright, and stopped trembling. I took this chance of recovering my command of him, and now for the first time perceived that my deliverer, so far from being a white *man*, was only a brook of silver brightness, foaming near me in its descent from the hill, while it crossed and arrested my horse's course with its rush of waters."

"Thanks, thanks, dear brook!" cried Undine, clapping her little hands. But the old man shook his head, and looked down in deep thought.

"Hardly had I well settled myself in my saddle, and got the reins in my grasp again," Huldbrand pursued, "when a wizard-like dwarf of a man was already standing at my side, diminutive and ugly beyond conception, his complexion of a brownish yellow, and his nose scarcely smaller than the rest of him together. The fellow's mouth was slit almost from ear to ear, and he showed his teeth with a grinning smile of idiot courtesy, while he overwhelmed me with bows and scrapes innumerable. The farce now becoming excessively irksome, I thanked him in the fewest words I could well use, turned about my still trembling charger, and purposed either to seek another adventure or should I meet with none, to take my way back to the city; for the sun, during my wild chase, had passed the meridian, and was now hastening toward the west. But this villain of a dwarf sprang at the same instant, and, with a turn as rapid as lightning, stood before my horse again. 'Clear the way there!' I cried fiercely; 'that beast is wild, and will make nothing of running over you.'

454

" 'Ay, ay,' cried the imp with a snarl, and snorting out a laugh still more frightfully idiotic; 'pay me, first pay what you owe me. I stopped your fine little nag for you; without my help, both you and he would be now sprawling below there in that stony ravine. Hu! from what a horrible plunge I've saved you!'

" 'Well, don't make any more faces,' said I, 'but take your money and be off, though every word you say is false. It was the brook there, you miserable thing, and not you that saved me,' and at the same time I dropped a piece of gold into his wizard cap, which he had taken from his head while he was begging before me.

"I then trotted off and left him, but he screamed after me; and on a sudden, with inconceivable quickness, he was close by my side. I started my horse into a gallop. He galloped on with me, though it seemed with great difficulty, and with a strange movement, half ludicrous and half horrible, forcing at the same time every limb and feature into distortion, he held up the gold piece and screamed at every leap, 'Counterfeit! false! false coin! counterfeit!' and such was the strange sound that issued from his hollow breast, you would have supposed that at every scream he must have tumbled upon the ground dead. All this while his disgusting red tongue hung lolling from his mouth.

"I stopped bewildered, and asked, 'What do you mean by this screaming? Take another piece of gold, take two, but leave me.'

"He then began again his hideous salutations of courtesy, and snarled out as before, 'Not gold, it shall not be gold, my young gentleman. I have too much of that trash already, as I will show you in no time.'

"At that moment, and thought itself could not have been more instantaneous, I seemed to have acquired new powers of sight. I could see through the solid green plain, as if it were green glass, and the smooth surface of the earth were round as a globe, and within it I saw crowds of goblins, who were pursuing their pastime and making themselves merry with silver and gold. They were tumbling and rolling about, heads up and heads down; they pelted one another in sport with the precious metals, and with irritating malice blew gold-dust in one another's eyes. My odious companion ordered the others to reach him up a vast quantity of gold; this he showed to me with a laugh, and then flung it again ringing and chinking down the measureless abyss.

"After this contemptuous disregard of gold, he held up the piece I had given him, showing it to his brother goblins below, and they laughed immoderately at a coin so worthless, and hissed me. At last, raising their fingers all smutched with ore, the pointed them at me in scorn; and wilder and wilder, and thicker and thicker, and madder and madder, the crowd were clambering up to where I sat gazing at these wonder. Then terror seized me, as it had before seized my horse. I drove my spurs into his sides, and how far he rushed with me through the forest, during this second of my wild heats, it is impossible to say.

"At last, when I had now come to a dead halt again, the cool of evening was around me. I caught the gleam of a white footpath through the branches of the trees; and presuming it would lead me out of the forest toward the city, I was desirous of working my way into it. But a face, perfectly white and indistinct, with features ever changing, kept thrusting itself out and peering at me between the leaves. I tried to avoid it, but where-ever I went, there too appeared the unearthly face. I was maddened with rage at this interruption, and determined to drive my steed at the appearance full tilt, when such a cloud of white foam came rushing upon me and my horse, that we were almost blinded and glad to turn about and escape. Thus from step to step it forced us on, and ever aside from the footpath, leaving us for the most part only one direction open. When we advanced in this it, kept following close behind us, yet did not occasion the smallest harm or inconvenience.

"When at times I looked about me at the form, I perceived that the white face, which had splashed upon us its shower of foam, was resting on a body equally white, and of more then gigantic size. Many a time, too, I received the impression that the whole appearance was nothing more than a wandering stream or torrent; but respecting this I could never attain to any certainty. We both of us, horse and rider, became weary as we shaped our course according to the movements of the white man, who continued nodding his head at us, as if he would say, 'Quite right!' And thus, at length, we came out here, at the edge of the wood, where I saw the fresh turf, the waters of the lake, and your little cottage, and where the tall white man disappeared."

'Well, Heaven be praised that he is gone!" cried the old fisherman; and he now began to talk of how his guest could most conveniently return to his friends in the city. Upon this, Undine began laughing to herself, but so very low that the sound was hardly perceivable. Huldbrand observing it, said, "I thought you were glad to see me here; why, then, do you now appear so happy when our talk turns upon my going away?"

"Because you cannot go away," answered Undine. "Pray make a single attempt; try with a boat, with your horse, or alone, as you please, to cross that forest stream which has burst its bounds; or rather, make no trial at all for you would be dashed to pieces by the stones and trunks of trees which you see driven on with such violence. And as to the lake I know that well; even my father dares not venture out with his boat far enough to help you."

Huldbrand rose smiling in order to look about and observe whether the state of things were such as Undine had represented it to be. The old man accompanied him, and them maiden went merrily dancing beside them. They found all in fact, just as Undine has said, and that the knight, whether willing or not willing, must submit to remaining on the island, so lately a peninsula, until the flood should subside.

When the three were now returning to the cottage after their ramble, the knight whispered in the ear of the little maiden, "Well, dear Undine, are you angry at my remaining?"

"Ah," she pettishly replied, "do not speak to me! If I had not bitten you, who knows what fine things you would have put into your story about Bertalda?"

Chapter III

. It may have happened to thee, my dear reader, after being much driven to and fro in the world, to reach at length a spot where all was well with thee. The love of home and of its peaceful joys, innate to all, again sprang up in thy heart; thout thoughtest that thy home was decked with all the flowers of childhood, and of that purest, deepest love which had grown upon the graves of the beloved, and that here it was good to live and to build houses. Even if thou didst err, and hast had bitterly to mourn thy error, it is nothing to my purpose, and thou thyself wilt not like to dwell on the sad recollection. But recall those unspeakably sweet feelings, that angelic greeting of peace, and thou wilt be able to understand what was the happiness of the knight Huldbrand during his abode on that narrow slip of land.

He frequently observed, with heartfelt satisfaction, that the forest-stream continued every day to swell and roll on with a more impetuous sweep; and this forced him to prolong his stay on the island. Part of the day he wandered about with an old cross-bow, which he found in a corner of the cottage, and had repaired in order to shoot the water-fowl that flew over; and all that he was lucky enough to hit he brought home for a good roast in the kitchen. When he came in with his booty, Undine seldom failed to greet him with a scolding, because he had cruelly deprived the happy joyous little creatures of life as they were sporting above in the blue ocean of the air; nay more, she often wept bitterly when she viewed the water-fowl dead in his hand. But at other times, when he returned without having shot any, she gave him a scolding equally serious, since, owing to his carelessness and want of skill, they must now put up with a dinner of fish. Her playful taunts ever touched his heart with delight; the more so, as she generally strove to make up for her pretended ill-humour with endearing caresses.

The old people saw with pleasure this familiarity of Undine and Huld-brand; they looked upon them as betrothed, or even as married, and living with them in their old age on their island, now torn off from the mainland. The loneliness of his situation strongly impressed also the young Huldbrand with the feeling that he was already Undine's bridegroom. It seemed to him as if, beyond those encompassing floods, there were no other world in existence, or at any rate as if he could never cross them, and again associate with the world of other men; and when at times his grazing steed raised his head and neighed to him, seemingly inquiring after his knightly achievements and reminding him of them, or when his coat-of-arms sternly shone upon him from the embroidery of his saddle and the caparisons of his horse, or when his sword happened to fall from the nail on which it was hanging in the cottage, and flashed on his eye as it slipped from the scabbard in its fall, he quieted the doubts of his mind by saying to himself, "Undine cannot be a fisherman's daughter. She is, in all probability, a native of some remote region, and a member of some illustrious family."

There was one thing, indeed, to which he had a strong aversion: this was to hear the old dame reproving Undine. The wild girl, it is true, commonly laughed at the reproof, making no attempts to conceal the extravagance of her mirth; but it appeared to him like touching his own honour; and still he found it impossible to blame the aged wife of the fisherman, since Undine always deserved at least ten times as many reproofs as she received; so he continued to feel in his heart an affectionate tenderness for the ancient mistress for the house, and his whole life flowed on in the calm stream of contentment.

There came, however, an interruption at last. The fisherman and the knight had been accustomed at dinner, and also in the evening when the wind roared without, as it rarely failed to do towards night, to enjoy together a flask of wine. But now their whole stock, which the fisherman had from time to time brought with him from the city, was at last exhausted, and they were both quite out of humour at the circumstance. That day Undine laughed at them excessively, but they were not disposed to join in her jests with the same gaiety as usual. Toward evening she went out of the cottage, to escape, as she said, the sight of two such long and tiresome faces.

While it was yet twilight, some appearances of a tempest seemed to be again mustering in the sky, and the waves already heaved and roared aroud them: the knight and the fisherman sprang to the door in terror, to bring home the maiden, remembering the anguish of that night when Huldbrand had first entered the cottage. But Undine met them at the same moment, clapping her little hands in high glee.

"What will you give me," she cried, "to provide you with wine? or rather, you need not give me anything," she continued; "for I am already satisfied, if you look more cheerful, and are in better spirits, than throughout this last most wearisome day. Only come with me; the forest stream has driven ashore a cask; and I will be condemned to sleep through a whole week, if it is not a wine-cask."

The men followed her, and actually found, in a bushy cove of the shore, a cask, which inspired them with as much joy as if they were sure it contained the generous old wine for which they were thirsting. They first of all, and with as much expedition as possible, rolled it toward the cottage; for heavy clouds were again rising in the west, and they could discern the waves of the lake in the fading light lifting their white foaming heads, as if looking out for the rain, which threatened every instant to pour upon them. Undine helped the men as much as she was able; and as the shower, with a roar of wind, came suddenly sweeping on in rapid pursuit, she raised her finger with a merry menace toward the dark mass of clouds, and cried:

"You cloud, you cloud, have a care! beware how you wet us; we are some way from shelter yet."

The old man reproved her for this sally, as a sinful presumption; but she laughed to herself softly, and no mischief came from her wild behaviour. Nay more, what was beyond their expectation, they reached their comfortable hearth unwet, with their prize secured; but the cask had hardly been broached, and proved to contain wine of a remarkably fine flavour, when the rain first poured down unrestrained from the black cloud, the tempest raved through the tops of the trese, and swept far over the billows of the deep.

Having immediately filled several bottles from the cask, which promised them a supply for a long time, they drew round the glowing hearth; and, comfortably secured from the tempest, they sat tasting the flavour of their wine and bandying jests.

But the old fisherman suddenly became extremely grave, and said;

"Ah, great God! here we sit, rejoicing over this rich gift, while he to whom it first belonged, and from whom it was wrested by the fury of the stream, must there also, it is more than probable, have lost his life."

"No such thing," said Undine, smiling, as she filled the knight's cup to the brim.

But he exclaimed: "By my unsullied honour, old father, if I knew where to find and rescue him, no fear of exposure to the night, nor any peril, should deter me from making the attempt. At least, I can promise you that if I again reach an inhabited country, I will find out the owner of this wine or his heirs, and make double and triple reimbursement."

The old man was gratified with this assurance; he gave the knight a nod of approbation, and now drained his cup with an easier conscience and more relish.

Undine, however, said to Huldbrand: "As to the repayment and your gold, you may do whatever you like. But what you said about your venturing out, and searching, and exposing yourself to danger, appears to me far from wise. I should cry my very eyes out, should you perish in such a wild attempt; and is it not true that you would prefer staying here with me and the good wine?"

"Most assuredly," answered Huldbrand, smiling.

"Then, you see," replied Undine, "you spoke unwisely. For charity begins at home; and why need we trouble ourselves about our neighbours?"

The mistress of the house turned away from her, sighing and shaking her head; while the fisherman forgot his wonted indulgence toward the graceful maiden, and thus rebuked her:

"That sounds exactly as if you had been brought up by heathens and Turks;" and he finished his reproof by adding, "May God forgive both me and you—unfeeling child!"

"Well, say what you will, that is what *I* think and feel" replied Undine, "whoever brought me up; and all your talking cannot help it."

"Silence!" exclaimed the fisherman, in a voice of stern rebuke; and she, who with all her wild spirit was extremely alive to fear, shrank from him, moved close up to Huldbrand, trembling, and said very softly:

"Are you also angry, dear friend?"

The knight pressed her soft hand, and tenderly stroked her locks. He was unable to utter a word, for his vexation, arising from the old man's severity towards Undine, closed his lips; and thus the two couples sat opposite to each other, at once heated with anger and in embarrasssed silence.

In the midst of this stillness a low knocking at the door startled them all; for there are times when a slight circumstance, coming unexpectedly upon us, startles us like something supernatural. But there was the further source of alarm, that the enchanted forest lay so near them, and that their place of abode seemed at present inaccessible to any human being. While they were looking upon one another in doubt, the knocking was again heard, accompanied with a deep groan. The knight sprang to seize his sword. But the old man said, in a low whisper:

"If it be what I fear it is, no weapon of yours can protect us."

Undine in the meanwhile went to the door, and cried with the firm voice of fearless displeasure: "Spirits of the earth! if mischief be your aim, Kühleborn shall teach you better manners."

The terror of the rest was increased by this wild speech; they looked fearfully upon the girl, and Huldbrand was just recovering presence of mind enough to ask what she meant, when a voice reached them from without:

"I am no spirit of the earth, though a spirit still in its earthly body. You that are within the cottage there, if you fear God and would afford me assistance, open your door to me."

By the time these words were spoken, Undine had already opened it; and the lamp throwing a strong light upon the stormy night, they perceived an aged priest without, who stepped back in terror, when his eye fell on the unexpected sight of a little damsel of such exquisite beauty. Well might he think there must be magic in the wind and witchcraft at work, when a form of such surpassing loveliness appeared at the door of so humble a dwelling. So he lifted up his voice in prayer:

"Let all good spirits praise the Lord God!"

"I am no spectre," said Undine, with a smile. "Do I look so very frightful? And you see that I do not shrink from holy words. I too have knowledge of God, and understand the duty of praising Him; every one, to be sure, has his own way of doing this, for so He has created us. Come in, father; you will find none but worthy people here."

The holy man came bowing in, and cast round a glance of scrutiny, wearing at the same time a very placid and venerable air. But water was dropping from every fold of his dark garments, from his long white beard and the white locks of his hair. The fisherman and the knight took him to another apartment, and furnished him with a change of raiment, while they gave his own clothes to the women to dry. The aged stranger thanked them in a manner the most humble and courteous; but on the knight's offering him his splendid cloak to wrap round him, he could not be persuaded to take it, but chose instead an old grey coat that belonged to the fisherman.

They then returned to the common apartment. The mistress of the house immediately offered her great chair to the priest, and continued urging it upon him till she saw him fairly in possession of it. "You are old and exhausted," said she, "and are, moreover, a man of God."

Undine shoved under the stranger's feet her little stool, on which at all other times she used to sit near to Huldbrand, and showed herself most gentle and amiable towards the old man. Huldbrand whispered some raillery in her ear, but she replied, gravely:

"He is a minister of that Being who created us all; and holy things are not to be treated with lightness."

The knight and the fisherman now refreshed the priest with food and wine; and when he had somewhat recovered his strength and spirits, he began to relate how he had the day before set out from his cloister, which was situated far off beyond the great lake, in order to visit the bishop, and acquaint him with the distress into which the cloister and its tributary villages had fallen, owing to the extraordinary floods. After a long and wearisome wandering, on account of the rise of the waters, he had been this day compelled toward evening to procure the aid of a couple of boatmen, and cross over an arm of the lake which had burst its usual boundary.

"But hardly," continued he, "had our small ferry-boat touched the waves, when that furious tempest burst forth which is still raging over our heads. It seemed as if the billows had been waiting our approach only to rush on us with a madness the more wild. The oars were wrested from the grasp of my men in an instant; and shivered by the resistless force, they drove farther and farther out before us upon the waves. Unable to direct our course, we yielded to the blind power of nature, and seemed to fly over the surges toward your distant shore, which we already saw looming through the mist and foam of the deep. Then it was at last that our boat turned short from its couse, and rocked with a motion that became more and more wild and dizzy: I know not whether it was overset, or the violence of the motion threw me overboard. In my agony and struggle at the thought of a near and terrible death, the waves bore me onward, till I was cast ashore here beneath the trees of your island."

"Yes, an island!" cried the fisherman; "a short time ago it was only a point of land. But now, since the forest-stream and lake have become all but mad, it appears to be entirely changed."

"I observed something of it," replied the priest, "as I stole along the shore in the obscurity; and hearing nothing around me but a sort of wild uproar, I perceived at last that the noise came from a point exactly where a beaten footpath disappeared. I now caught the light in your cottage, and ventured hither, where I cannot sufficiently thank my heavenly Father that, after preserving me from the waters, He has also conducted me to such pious people as you are, and the more so, as it is difficult to say whether I shall ever behold any other persons in this world except you four."

"What mean you be those words?" asked the fisherman.

"Can you tell me, then how long this commotion of the elements will last?" replied the priest. "I am old; the stream of my life may easily sink into the ground and vanish before the overflowing of that forest stream shall subside. And, indeed, it is not impossible that more and more of the foaming waters may rush in between you and yonder forest, until you are so far removed from the rest of the world, that your small fishing-canoe may be incapable of passing over, and the inhabitants of the continent entirely forget you in your old age amid the dissipation and diversions of life."

At this melancholy foreboding the old lady shrank back with a feeling of alarm, crossed herself, and cried, "God forbid!"

But the fisherman looked upon her with a smile, and said, "What a strange being is man! Suppose the worst to happen; our state would not be different; at any rate, your own would not, dear wife, from what it is at present. For have you, these many years, been farther from home than the border of the forest? And have you seen a single human being beside Undine and myself? It is now only a short time since the coming of the knight and the priest. They will remain with us even if we do become a forgotten island; so after all, you will be a gainer."

"I know not," replied the ancient dame; "it is a dismal thought. when brought fairly home to the mind, that we are for ever separated from mankind, even though in fact we never do know nor see them"

"Then *you* will remain with us—then you will remain with us!" whispered Undine, in a voice scarcely audible and half singing, while she nestled closer to Huldbrand's side. But he was immersed in the deep and strange musings of his own mind. The region, on the farther side of the forest-river, seemed, since the last words of the priest, to have been withdrawing farther and farther, in dim perspective, from his view; and the blooming island on which he lived grew green and smiled more freshly in his fancy. His bride glowed like the fairest rose, not of this obscure nook only, but even of the whole wide world; and the priest was now present.

Added to which, the mistress of the family was directing an angry glance at Undine, because, even in the presence of the priest, she leant so fondly on the knight; and it seemed as if she was on the point of breaking out in harsh reproof. Then burst forth from the mouth of Huldbrand, as he turned to the priest, "Father, you here see before you an affianced pair; and if this maiden and these good old people have no objection, you shall unite us this very evening."

The aged couple were both exceedingly surprised. They had often, it is true, thought of this, but as yet they had never mentioned it; and now when the knight spoke, it came upon them like something wholly new and unexpected. Undine became suddenly grave, and looked down thoughtfully, while the priest made inquiries respecting the circumstances of their acquaintance, and asked the old people whether they gave their consent to the union. After a great number of questions and answers, the affair was arranged to the satisfaction of all; and the mistress of the house went to prepare the bridal apartment for the young couple, and also, with a view to grace the nuptial solemnity, to seek for two consecrated tapers, which she had for a long time kept by her, for this occasion.

The knight in the meanwile busied himself about his golden chain, for the purpose of disengaging two of its links, that he might make an exchange of rings with his bride. But when she saw his object, she started from her trance of musing, and exclaimed—

"Not so! my parents by no means sent me into the world so perfectly destitute; on the contrary they foresaw, even at that early period, that such a night as this would come."

Thus speaking she went out of the room, and a moment after returned with two costly rings, of which she gave one to her bridegroom, and kept the other for herself. The old fisherman was beyond measure astonished at this; and his wife, who was just re-entering the room, was even more surprised than he, that neither of them had ever seen these jewels in the child's possession.

"My parents," said Undine, "sewed these trinkets to that beautiful raiment which I wore the very day I came to you. They also charged me on no account whatever to mention them to anyone before my wedding evening. At the time of my coming, therefore, I took them off in secret, and have kept them concealed to the present hour."

The priest now cut short all further questioning and wondering, while he lighted the consecrated tapers, placed them on a table, and ordered the bridal pair to stand opposite to him. He then pronounced the few solemn words of the ceremony, and made them one. The elder couple gave the younger their blessing; and the bride, gently trembling and thoughtful, leaned upon the knight.

The priest then spoke out: "You are strange people, after all; for why did you tell me that you were the only inhabitants of the island? so far is this from being true, I have seen, the whole time I was performing the ceremony, a tall stately man, in a white mantle, standing opposite to me, looking in at the window. He must be still waiting before the door, if peradventure you would invite him to come in."

"God forbid!" cried the old lady, shrinking back; the fisherman shook his head, without opening his lips; and Huldbrand sprang to the window. It seemed to *him* that he could still discern a white streak, which soon disappeared in the gloom. He convinced the priest that he must have been mistaken in his impression; and they all sat down together round a bright and comfortable hearth.

CHAPTER IV

Before the nuptial ceremony, and during its performance, Undine had shown a modest gentleness and maidenly reserve; but it now seemed as if all the wayward freaks that effervesced within her burst forth with an extravagence only the more bold and unrestrained. She teased her bridegroom, her foster-parents, and even the priest, whom she had just now revered so highly, with all sorts of childish tricks; but when the ancient dame was about to reprove her too frolicsome spirit, the knight, in a few words, imposed silence upon her by speaking of Undine as his wife.

The knight was himself, indeed, just as little pleased with Undine's childish behaviour as the rest; but all his looks and half-reproachful words were to no purpose. It is true, whenever the bride observed the dissatisfaction of her husband—and this occasionally happened—she became more quiet, placed herself beside him, stroked his face with caressing fondness, whispered something smilingly in his ear, and in this manner smoothed the wrinkles that were gathering on his brow. But the moment after, some wild whim would make her resume her antic movements: and all went worse than before.

The priest then spoke in a kind although serious tone: "My fair young maiden, surely no one can look on you without pleasure; but remember betimes so to attune your soul that it may produce a harmony ever in accordance with the soul of your wedded bridegroom."

"SOUL!" cried Undine, with a laugh. "What you say has a remarkably pretty sound; and for most people, too, it may be a very instructive and profitable caution. But when a person has no soul at all, how, I pray you, can such attuning be then possible? And this, in truth, is just my condition."

The priest was much hurt, but continued silent in holy displeasure, and turned away his face from the maiden in sorrow. She, however, went up to him with the most winning sweethess and said:

"Nay, I entreat you, first listen to me, before you are angry with me; for your anger is painful to me, and you ought not to give pain to a creature that has not hurt you. Only have patience with me, and I will explain to you every word of what I meant."

It was evident that she had come to say something important; when she suddenly faltered as if seized with inward shuddering, and burst into a passion of tears. They were none of them able to understand the intenseness of her feelings; and with mingled emotions of fear and anxiety, they gazed on her in silence. Then wiping away her tears, and looking earnestly at the priest, she at last said:

"There must be something lovely, but at the same time something most awful, about a soul. In the name of God, holy man, were it not better that we never shared a gift so mysterious?"

Again she paused, and restrained her tears, as if waiting for an answer. All in the cottage had risen from their seats, and stepped back from her with horror. She, however, seemed to have eyes for no one but the holy man: an awful curiosity was painted on her features, which appeared terrible to the others.

"Heavily must the soul weigh down its possessor," she pursued, when no one returned her any answer—"very heavily! for already its approaching image overshadows me with anguish and mourning. And, alas, I have till now been so merry and light-hearted!" and she burst into another flood of tears, and covered her face with her veil.

The priest, going up to her with a solemn look, now addressed himself to her, and conjured her, by the name of God most holy, if any spirit of evil possessed her, to remove the light covering from her face. But she sank before him on her knees, and repeated after him every sacred expression he uttered, giving praise to God, and protesting "that she wished well to the whole world."

The priest then spoke to the knight: "Sir bridegroom, I leave you alone with her whom I have united to you in marriage. So far as I can discover, there is nothing of evil in her, but assuredly much that is wonderful. What I recommend to you is—prudence, love, and fidelity."

Thus speaking, he left the apartment; and the fisherman, with his wife, followed him, crossing themselves.

Undine had sunk upon her knees. She uncovered her face, and exclaimed, while she looked feafully round upon Huldbrand, "Alas! you will now refuse to look upon me as your own; and still I have done nothing evil, poor unhappy child that I am!" She spoke these words with a look so infinitely sweet and touching, that her bridegroom forgot both the confession that had shocked, and the mystery that had perplexed him; and hastening to her, he raised her in his arms. She smiled through her tears; and that smile was like the morning light playing upon a small stream. "You cannot desert me!" she whispered, confidingly, and stroked the knight's cheeks with her little soft hands. He turned away from the frightful thoughts that still lurked in the recesses of his soul, and were persuading him that he had been married to a fairy, or some spiteful and mischievous being of the spirit-world. Only the single question, and that almost unawares, escaped from his lips:

"Dearest Undine, tell me this one thing: what was it you meant by 'spirits of earth' and 'Kühleborn,' when the priest stood knocking at the door?"

"Tales! mere tales of children!" answered Undine, laughing, now quite restored to her wonted gaiety. "I first frightened you with them, and you frightened me. This is the end of the story, and of our nuptial evening."

"Nay, not so," replied the enamoured knight, extinguishing the tapers, and a thousand times kissing his beautiful and beloved bride; while, lighted by the moon that shone brightly through the windows, he bore her into their bridal apartment.

The fresh light of morning woke the young married pair: but Huldbrand lay lost in silent reflection. Whenever, during the night he had fallen asleep, strange and horrible dreams of spectres had disturbed him; and these shapes, grinning at him by stealth, strove to disguise themselves as beautiful females; and from beautiful females they all at once assumed the appearance of dragons. And when he started up, aroused by the intrusion of these hideous forms, the moonlight shone pale and cold before the windows without. He looked affrighted at Undine, in whose arms he had fallen asleep: and she was reposing in unaltered beauty and sweetness beside him. Then pressing her rosy lips with a light kiss, he again fell into a slumber, only to be awakened by new terrors.

When fully awake, he had thought over this connection. He reproached himself for any doubt that could lead him into error in regard to his lovely wife. He also confessed to her his injustice; but she only gave him her fair hand, sighed deeply, and remained silent. Yet a glance of fervent tenderness, an expression of the soul beaming in her eyes, such as he had never witnessed there before, left him in undoubted assurance that Undine bore him no ill-will.

He then rose joyfully, and leaving her, went to the common apartment, where the inmates of the house had already met. The three were sitting round the hearth with an air of anxiety about them, as if they feared trusting themselves to raise their voice above a low, apprehensive undertone. The priest appeared to be praying in his inmost apirit, with a view to avert some fatal calamity. But when they observed the young husband come forth so cheerful, they dispelled the cloud that remained upon their brows: the old fisherman even began to laugh with the knight till his aged wife herself could not help smiling with great good-humour.

Undine had in the meantime got ready, and now entered the room; all rose to meet her, but remained fixed in perfect admiration—she was so changed, and yet the same. The priest, with paternal affection beaming from his countenance, first went up to her; and as he raised his hand to pronounce a blessing, the beautiful bride sank on her knees before him with religious awe; she begged his pardon in terms both respectful and submissive for any foolish things ahe might have uttered the evening before, and entreated him with emotion to pray for the welfare of her soul. She then rose, kissed her foster-parents, and after thanking them for all the kindness they had shown her, said:

"Oh, I now feel in my inmost heart how much, how infinitely much, you have done for me, you dear, dear friends of my childhood!"

At first she was wholly unable to tear herself away from their affectionate caresses; but the moment she saw the good old mother busy in getting breakfst, she went to the hearth, applied herself to cooking the food and putting it on the table, and would not suffer her to take the least share in the work.

She continued in this frame of spirit the whole day: calm, kind, attentive —half matronly, and half girlish. The three who had been longest acquainted with her expected every instant to see her capricious spirit break out in some whimsical change or sportive vagary. But their fears were quite unnecessary. Undine continued as mild and gentle as an angel. The priest found it all but impossible ro remove his eyes from her; and he often said to the bridegroom:

"The bounty of Heaven, sir, through me its unworthy instrument, entrusted to you yesterday an invaluable treasure; cherish it as you ought, and it will promote your temporal and eternal welfare."

Toward evening Undine was hanging upon the knight's arm with lowly tenderness, while she drew him gently out before the door, where the setting sun shone richly over the fresh grass, and upon the high, slender boles of the trees. Her emotion was visible: the dew of sadness and love swam in her eyes, while a tender and fearful secret seemed to hover upon her lips, but was only made known by hardly-breathed sighs. She led her husband farther and farther onward without speaking. When he asked her questions, she replied only with looks, in which, it is true, there appeared to be no immediate answer to his inquiries, but a whole heaven of love and timid devotion. Thus they reached the margin of the swollen forest-stream, and the knight was astonished to see it gliding away with so gentle a murmuring of its waves, that no vestige of its former swell and wildness was now discernible.

"By morning it will be wholly drained off," said the beautiful wife, almost weeping, "and you will then be able to travel, without anything to hinder you, whithersoever you will."

"Not without you, dear Undine," replied the knight, laughing; "think, only, were I disposed to leave you, both the chuch and the spiritual powers, the emperor and the laws of the ralm, would require the fugitive to be seized and restored to you."

"All this depends on you—all depends on you," whispered his little companion, half weeping and half smiling. "But I still feel sure that you will not leave me; I love you too deeply to fear that misery. Now bear me over to that little island which lies before us. There shall the decision be made. I could easily, indeed, glide through that mere rippling of the water without your aid, but it is so sweet to lie in your yrms; and should you determine to put me away, I shall have rested in them once more,... for the last time."

Huldbrand was so full of strange anxiety and emotion that he knew not what answer to make her. He took her in his arms and carried her over, now first realising the fact that this was the same little island from which he had borne her back to the old fisherman, the first night of his arrival. On the father side, he placed her upon the soft grass, and was throwing himself lovingly near his beautiful burden; but she said to him, "Not here, but opposite me. I shall read my doom in your eyes, even before your lips pronounce it: now listen attentively to what I shall relate to you." And she began:

"You must know, my own love, that there are beings in the elements which bear the strongest resemblance to the human race, and which, at the same time, but seldom become visible to you, The wonderful salamanders sparkle and sport amid the flames; deep in the earth the mcagre and malicious gnomes pursue their revels; the forest-spirits belong to the air, and wander in the woods; while in the seas, rivers, and streams live the widespread race of water-spirits. These last, beneath resounding domes of crystal, through which the sky can shine with its sun and stars, inhabit a region of light and beauty; lofty coral-trees glow with blue and crimson fruits in their gardens; they walk over the pure sand of the sea, among exquisitely variegated shells, and amid whatever of beauty the old world possessed, such as the present is no more worthy to enjoy—creations which the floods covered with their secret veils of silver; and now these noble monuments sparkle below, stately and solemn, and bedewed by the water, which loves them, and calls forth from their crevices delicate moss-flowers and enwreathing tufts of sedge.

"Now the nation that dwell there are very fair and lovely to behold, for the most part more beautiful than human beings. Many a fisherman has been so fortunate as to catch a view of a delicate maiden of the waters, while she was floating and singing upon the deep. He would then spread far the fame of her beauty; and to such wonderful females men are wont to give the name of Undines. But what need of saying more?—You, my dear husband, now actually behold an Undine before you."

The knight would have persuaded himself that his lovely wife was under the influence of one of her odd whims, and that she was ony amusing herself and him with her extravagant inventions. He wished it might be so. But with whatever emphasis he said this to himself, he still could not credit the hope for a moment: a strange shivering shot through his soul; unable to utter a word, he gazed upon the sweet speaker with a fixed eye. She shook her head in distress, sighed from her full heart, and then proceeded in the following manner:—

"We should be far superior to you, who are another race of the human family,—for we also call ourselves human beings, as we resemble them in form and features—had we not one evil peculiar to ourselves. Both we and the beings I have mentioned as inhabiting the other elements vanish into air at death and go out of existence, spirit and body, so that no vestige of us remains; and when you hereafter awake to a purer state of being, we shall remain where sand, and sparks, and wind, and waves remain. Thus we have no souls, the element moves us, and, again, is obedient to our will, while we live though it scatters us like dust when we die; and as we have nothing to trouble us, we are as merry as nightingales, little gold-fishers, and other pretty children of nature.

"But all beings aspire to rise in the scale of existence higher than they are. It was therefore the wish of my father, who is a powerful water-prince in the Mediterranean Sea, that his only daughter should become possessed of a soul, although she should have to endure many of the sufferings of those who share that gift.

"Now the race to which I belong have no other means of obtaining a soul than by forming with an individual of your own the most intimate union of love. I am now possessed of a soul, and my soul thanks you my best beloved, and never shall cease to thank you, if you do not render my whole future life miserable. For what will become of me, if you avoid and reject me? Still, I would not keep you as my own by artifice. And should you decide to cast me off, then do it now, and return alone to the shore. I will plunge into this brook, where my uncle will receive me; my uncle, who here in the forest, far removed from his other friends, passes his strange and solitary existence. But he is powerful, as well as revered and beloved by many great rivers; and as he brought me hither to the fisherman a light-hearted and and laughing child, he will take me home to my parents a woman, gifted with a soul, with power to love and to suffer."

She was about to add something more, when Huldbrand, with the most heartfelt tenderness and love clasped her in his arms, and again bore her back to the shore. There, amid tears and kisses, he first swore never to forsake his affectionate wife, and esteemed himself even more happy than Pygmalion, for whom Venus gave life to his beautiful statue, and thus changed it into a beloved wife. Supported by his arm, and in the confidence of affection, Undine returned to the cottage; and now she first realised with her whole heart how little cause she had for regretting what she had left—the crystal palaces of her mysterious father.

CHAPTER V

Next morning, when Huldbrand awoke from slumber, and perceived that his beautiful wife was not by his side, he began to give way again to his wild imaginations,—that his marriage, and even the lovely Undine herself, were only shadows without substance—only mere illusions of enchantment. But she entered the door at the same moment, kissed him, seated herself on the bed by his side, and said:

"I have been out somewhat early this morning, to see whether my uncle keeps his word. He has already restored the waters of the flood to his own calm channel, and he now flows through the forest a rivulet as before, in a lonely and dreamlike current. His friends, too, both of the water and the air, have resumed their usual peaceful tenor; all will

471

again proceed with order and tranquillity; and you can travel homeward, without fear of the flood, whenever you choose."

It seemed to the mind of Huldbrand that he must be in some waking dream, so little was he able to understand the nature of his wife's strange relative. Notwithstanding this, he made no remark upon what she had told him, and her surpassing loveliness soon lulled every misgiving and discomfort to rest.

Some time afterward, while he was standing with her before the door, and surveying the verdant point of land, with its boundary of bright waters, such a feeling of bliss came over him in this cradle of his love, that he exclaimed:

"Shall we, then, so early as to-day, begin our journey? Why should we? It is probable that abroad in the world we shall find no days more delightful than those we have spent in this green isle so secret and so secure. Let us yet see the sun go down here two or three times more."

"Just as my lord wills," replied Undine meekly. "Only we must remember, that my foster-parents will, at all events, see me depart with pain; and should they now, for the first time, discover the true soul in me, and how fervently I can now love and honour them, their feeble eyes would surely become blind with weeping. As yet they consider my present quietness and gentleness as of no better promise than they were formerly— like the calm of lake just while the air remains tranquil—and they will learn soon to cherish a little tree or flower as they have cherished me. Let me not, then, make known to them this newly bestowed, this loving heart, at the very moment they must lose if for this world; and how could I conceal what I have gained, if we continued longer together?"

Huldbrand yielded to her representation, and went to the aged couple to confer with them respecting his journey, on which he proposed to set out that very hour. The priest offered himself as a companion to the young married pair; and, after taking a short farewell, he held the bridle, while the knight lifted his beautiful wife upon his horse; and with rapid step they crossed the dry channel with her toward the forest. Undine wept in silent but intense emotion; the old people, as she moved away, were more clamorous in the expression of their grief. They appeared to feel, at the moment of separation, all that they were losing in their affectionate foster-daughter.

The three travellers had reached the thickest shades of the forest without interchanging a word. It must have been a fair sight, in that hall of leafy verdure, to see this lovely woman's form sitting on the noble and richly-ornamented steed, on her right hand the venerable priest in the white garb of his order, on her left the blooming young knight, clad in splendid raiment of scarlet, gold, and violet, girt with a sword that flashed in the sun, and attentively walking beside her. Huldbrand had no eyes but for his wife; Undine, who had dried her tears of tenderness, had no eyes but for him; and they soon entered into the still and voiceless converse of looks and gestures, from which, after some time, they were awaken ed by the low discourse which the priest was holding with a fourth traveller, who had meanwhile joined them unobserved.

He wore a white gown, resembling in form the dress of the priest's order, except that his hood hung very low over his face, and that the whole drapery floated in such wide folds around him as obliged him every moment to gather it up and throw it over his arm, or by some management of this sort to get it out of his way, and still it did not seem in the least to impede his movements. When the young couple became aware of his presence, he was saying:

"And so, venerable sir, many as have been the years I have dwelt here in this forest, I have never received the name of hermit in your sense of the word. For, as I said before, I know nothing of penance and I think, too, that I have no particular need of it. Do you ask me why I am so attached to the forest? It is because its scenery is so peculiarly picturesque, and affords me so much pastime when, in my floating white garments, I pass through its world of leaves and dusky shadows; —and when a sweet sunbeam glances down upon me at times unexpectedly."

"You are a very singular man," replied the priest, "and I should like to have a more intimate acquaintance with you."

"And who, then, may you be yourself, to pass from one thing to another?" inquired the stranger.

"I am called Father Heilmann," answered the holy man; "and I am from the cloister of Our Lady of the Salutation, beyond the lake."

"Well, well," replied the stranger, "my name is Kühleborn; and were I a stickler for the nice distinctions of rank, I might, with equal propriety, require you to give me the title of noble lord of Kühleborn, or free lord of Kühleborn; for I am as free as the birds in the forest, and, it may be, a trifle more so. For example, I now have something to tell that young lady there." And before they were aware of his purpose, he was on the other side of the priest, close to Undine, and stretching himself high into the air, in order to whisper something in her ear. But she shrank from him in terror, and exclaimed:

"I have nothing more to do with you."

"Ho, ho," cried the stranger, with a laugh, "you have made a grand marriage indeed, since you no longer know your own relations! Have you no recollection, then, of your uncle Kühleborn, who so faithfully bore you on his back to this region?"

"However that may be," replied Undine, "I entreat you never to appear in my presence again. I am now afraid of you; and will not my husband fear and forsake me, if he sees me associate with such strange company and kindred?"

"You must not forget, my little niece," said Kühleborn, "that I am with you here as a guide; otherwise those madcap spirits of the earth, the gnomes that haunt this forest, would play you some of their mischievous pranks. Let me therefore still accompany you in peace. Even the old priest there had a better recollection of me then you appear to have; for he just now assured me that I seemed to be very familiar to him, and that I must have been with him in the ferry-boat, out of which he tumbled into the waves. He certainly did see me there; for I was no other than the waterspout that tore him out of it, and kept him from sinking while I safely wafted him ashore to your wedding."

Undine and the knight turned their eyes upon Father Heilmann; but he appeared to be moving forward, just as if he were dreaming or walking in his sleep, and no longer to be conscious of a word that was spoken. Undine than said to Kühleborn: "I already see yonder the end of the forest. We have no further need of your assistance, and nothing now gives us alarm but yourself. I therefore beseech you, by our mutual love and goodwill, to vanish, and allow us to proceed in peace."

Kühleborn seemed to become angry at this: he darted a frightful look at Undine, and grinned fiercely upon her. She shrieked aloud, and called her husband to protect her. The knight sprang round the horse as quick as lightning, and, brandishing his sword, struck at Kühleborn's head. But, instead of severing it from his body, the sword merely flashed through a torrent, which rushed foaming near them form a lofty cliff; and with a splash, which much resembled in sound a burst of laughter, the stream all at once poured upon them, and gave them a thorough wetting. The priest, as if suddenly awaking from a trance, coolly observed: "This is what I have been some time expecting, because the brook has descended from the steep so close beside us—though at first sight, indeed, it appeared to resemble a man, and to possess the power of speech."

As the waterfall came rushing from its crag, it distinctly uttered these words in Huldbrand's ear: "Rash knight! valiant knight! I am not angry with you; I have no quarrel with you; only continue to defend your lovely little wife with the same spirit, you bold knight! you valiant champion!"

After advancing a few steps father, the travellers came out upon open ground. The imperial city lay bright before them; and the evening sun, which gilded its towers with gold, kindly dried their garments that had been so completely drenched.

The sudden disappearance of the young knight, Huldbrand of Ringstetten, had occasioned much remark in the imperial city, and no small concern amongst those who, as well on account of his expertness in tourney and dance as of his mild and amiable manners, had become attached to him. His attendants were unwilling to quit the place without their master, although not a soul of them had been courageous enough to follow him into the fearful recesses of the forest. They remained, therefore, at the hostelry, idly hoping, as men are wont to do, and keeping the fate of their lost lord fresh in remembrance by their lamentations.

Now when the violent storms and floods had been observed immediately after his departure, the destruction of the handsome stranger became all but certain; even Bertalda had openly discovered her sorrow, and detested herself for having been the cause of his taking that fatal excursion into the forest. Her foster-parents, the duke and duchess, had meanwhile come to take her away; but Bertalda persuaded them to remain with her until some certain news of Huldbrand should be obtained, whether he were living or dead. She endeavoured also to prevail upon several young knights, who were assiduous in courting her favour, to go in quest of the noble adventurer in the forest. But she refused to pledge her hand as the reward of the enterprise, because she still cherished, it might be, a hope of its being claimed by the returning knight; and no one would consent, for a glove, a riband, or even a kiss, to expose his life to bring back so very dangerous a rival.

When Huldbrand now made his sudden and unexpected appearance, his attendants, the inhabitants of the city. and almost every one, rejoiced. This was not the case with Bertalda; for although it might be quite a welcome event to others that he brought with him a wife of such exquisite loveliness, and Father Heilmann as a witness of their marriage, Bertalda could not but view the affair with grief and vexation. She had, in truth, become attached to the young knight with her whole soul; and her mourning for his absence, or supposed death, had shown this more than she could now have wished.

But notwithstanding all this, she conducted herself like a wise maiden in circumstances of such delicacy and lived on the most friendly terms with Undine whom the whole city looked upon as a princess that Huldbrand had rescued in the forest from some evil enchantment. When ever anyone questioned either herself or her husband relative to surmises of this nature they had wisdom enough to remain silent, or wit enough to evade the inquiries. The lips of Father Heilmann had been sealed in regard to idle gossip of every kind; and besides, on Huldbrand's arrival, he had immediately returned to his cloister: so that people were obliged to rest contented with their own wild conjectures; and even Bertalda herself ascertained nothing more of the truth than others.

For the rest, Undine daily felt more love for the fair maiden. "We must have been before acquainted with each other," she often used say to her, "or else there must be some mysterious connection between us, for it is incredible that anyone so perfectly without cause—I mean, without some deep and secret cause—should be so fondly attached to another as I have been to you from the first moment of our meeting."

And even Bertalda could not deny that she felt a confiding impulse, an attraction of tenderness, toward Undine, much as she deemed this fortunate rival the cause of her bitterest disappointment. Under the influence of this mutual regard, they found means to persuade, the one her foster-parents, and the other her husband, to defer, the day of separation to a period more and more remote; nay, more, they had already begun to talk of a plan for Bertalda's accompanying Undine to Castle Ringstetten, near one of the sources of the Danube.

Once on a fine evening they happened to be talking over their scheme just at they passed the high trees that bordered the public walk. The young married pair, though it was somewhat late, had called upon Bertalda to invite her to share their enjoyment; and all three proceeded familiarly up and down beneath the dark blue heaven, not seldom interrupted in their converse by the admiration which they could not but bestow upon the wonderful rush and shooting upward of its water. All was sweet and soothing to their minds. Among the shadows of the trees stole in glimmerings of light from the adjacent houses. A low murmur as of children at play, and of other persons who were enjoying their walk, floated around them—they were so alone, and yet sharing so much of social happiness in the bright and stirring world, that whatever had appeared rough by day, now became smooth of its own accord. And the three friends could no longer see the slightest cause for hesitation in regard to Bertalda's taking the journey.

At that instant, while they were just fixing the day of their departure, a tall man approached them from the middle of the square, bowed respectfully to the company, and spoke something in the young bride's ear. Though displeased with the interruption and its cause, she walked aside a few steps with the stranger; and both began to whisper, as it seemed, in a foreign tongue. Huldbrand thought he recognised the strange man of the forest, and he gazed upon him so fixedly, that he neither heard nor answered the astonished inquiries of Bertalda. All at once Undine clapped her hands with delight, and turned back from the stranger, laughing: he, frequently shaking his head, retired with a hasty step and discontented air, and descended into the fountain. Huldbrand now felt perfectly certain that his conjecture was correct. But Bertalda asked:

"What, then, dear Undine, did the master of the fountain wish to say to you?"

Undine laughed within herself, and made answer: "The day after to-morrow, my dear child, when the anniversary of your name-day returns, you shall be informed." And this was all she could be prevailed upon to disclose. She merely asked Bertalda to dinner on the appointed day, and requested her to invite her foster-parents; and soon afterward they separated.

"Kühleborn?" said Huldbrand to his lovely wife, with an inward shudder when they had taken leave of Bertalda, and were now going home through the darkening streets.

"Yes, it was he," answered Undine; "and he would have wearied me with his foolish warnings. But, in the midst, quite contrary to his intentions, he delighted me with a most welcome piece of news. If you, my dear lord and husband, wish me to acquaint you with it now, you need only command me, and I will freely and from my heart tell you all without reserve. But would you confer upon your Undine a very, very great pleasure, wait till the day after to-morrow, and then you too shall have your share of the surprise."

The knight was quite willing to gratify his wife in what she had asked so sweetly. And even as she was falling asleep, she murmured to herself, with a smile: "How she will rejoice and be astonished at what her master of the fountain had told me!—dear, dear Bertalda!"

Chapter VI

The company were sitting at dinner. Bertalda, adorned with jewels and flowers without number, the presents of her foster parents and friends, and looking like some goddess of spring, sat beside Undine and Huldbrand at the head of the table. When the sumptuous repast was ended, and the dessert was placed before them, permission was given that the doors should be left open: this was in accordance with the good old custom in Germany, that the common people might see and rejoice in the festivity of their superiors. Among these spectators the servants carried round cake and wine.

Huldbrand and Bertalda waited with secret impatience for the promised explanation, and hardly moved their eyes from Undine. But she still continued silent, and merely smiled to herself with secret and heartfelt satisfaction. All who were made acquainted with the promise she had given could perceive that she was every moment on the point of revealing a happy secret; and yet, as children sometimes delay tasting their choicest dainties, she still withheld the communication. Bertalda and Huldbrand shared the same delightful feeling, while in anxious hope they were expecting the unknown disclosure which they were to receive from the lips of their friend.

At this moment several of the company pressed Undine to sing. This she seemed pleased at; and ordering her lute to be brought, she sang the following words:

> "Morning so bright,
> Wild flowers so gay,
> Where high grass so dewy
> Crowns the wavy lake's border.

> "On the meadow's verdant bosom
> What glimmers there so white?
> Have wreaths of snowy blossoms,
> Soft-floating, fallen from heaven?

> "Ah, see! a tender infant!—
> It plays with flowers, unwitting;
> It strives to grasp morn's golden beams.
> O where, sweet stranger, where's your home?
> Afar from unknown shores
> The waves have wafted hither
> This helpless little one.

> "Nay, clasp not, tender darling,
> With tiny hand the flowers!
> No hand returns the pressure,
> The flowers are strange and mute.

> "They clothe themselves in beauty,
> They breathe a rich perfume:
> But cannot fold around you

478

A mother's loving arms;—
Far, far away that mother's fond embrace.

"Life's early dawn just opening faint,
Your eye yet beaming Heaven's own smile,
So soon your tenderest guardians gone;
Severe, poor child, your fate,—
All, all to you unknown.

"A noble duke has crossed the mead,
And near you checked his steed's career:
Wonder and pity touch his heart;
With knowledge high, and manners pure,
He rears you,—makes his castle home your own.

"How great, how infinite your gain!
Of all the land you bloom the loveliest;
Yet, ah! the priceless blessing,
The bliss of parents' fondness,
You left on strands unknown!"

Undine let fall her lute with a melancholy smile. The eyes of Bertalda's noble foster-parents were filled with tears.

"Ah yes, it was so—such *was* the morning on which I found you, poor orphan!" cried the duke, with deep emotion; "the beautiful singer is certainly right: still

'The priceless blessing,
The bliss of parents' fondness,'

it was beyond our power to give you."

"But we must hear, also, what happened to the poor parents," said Undine, as she struck the chords, and sung:—

"Through her chambers roams the mother
Searching, searching everywhere;
Seeks, and knows not what with yearning,
Childless house still finding there.

"Childless house!—O sound of anguish!
She alone the anguish knows,
There by day who led her dear one,
There who rocked its night-repose.

"Beechen buds again are swelling,
  Sunshine warms again the shore;
Ah, fond mother, cease your searching!
  Comes the loved and lost no more.

"Then when airs of eve are fresh'ning,
  Home the father wends his way,
While with smiles his woe he's veiling,
  Gushing tears his heart betray.

"Well he knows, within his dwelling,
  Still as death he'll find the gloom,
Only hear the mother moaning.—
  No sweet babe to *smile* him home."

"O, tell me, in the name of Heaven tell me, Undine, where are my parents?" cried the weeping Bertalda. "You certainly know; you must have discovered them, you wonderful being; for otherwise you would never have thus torn my heart. Can they be already here? May I believe it possible?" Her eye glanced repidly over the brilliant company, and rested upon a lady of high rank who was sitting next to her foster-father.

Then, bending her head, Undine beckoned toward the door, while her eyes overflowed with the sweetest emotion. "Where, then, are the poor parents waiting?" she asked; and the old fisherman, hesitating, advanced with his wife from the crowd of spectators. They looked inquiringly, now at Undine, and now at the beautiful lady who was said to be their daughter.

"It is she! It is she there before you"; exclaimed the restorer of their child, her voice half choked with rapture. And both the aged parents embraced their recovered daughter, weeping aloud and praising God.

But, terrified and indignant, Bertalda tore herself from their arms. Such a discovery was too much for her proud spirit to bear, especially at the moment when she had doubtless expected to see her former splendour increased, and when hope was picturing to her nothing less brilliant than a royal canopy and a crown. It seemed to her as if her rival had contrived all this on purpose to humble her before Hulbrand and the whole world. She reproached Undine; she reviled the old people; and even such offensive words as "deceiver, bribed and perjured impostors," burst from her lips.

The aged wife of the fisherman then said to herself, in a low voice: "Ah, my God, she has become wicked! and yet I feel in my heart that she is my child."

The old fisherman had meanwhile folded his hands, and offered up a silent prayer that she might *not* be his daughter.

Undine, faint and pale as death, turned from the parents to Bertalda, from Bertalda to the parents. She was suddenly cast down from all that heaven of happiness in which she had been dreaming, and plunged into an agony of terror and disappointment, which she had never known even in dreams.

"Have you, then, a soul? Have you indeed a soul, Bertalda?" she cried again and again to her angry friend, as if with vehement effort she would rouse her from a sudden delirium or some distracting dream of night, and restore her to recollection.

But when Bertalda became every moment only more and more enraged—when the disappointed parents began to weep aloud—and the company, with much warmth of dispute, were espousing opposite sides —she begged, with such earnestness and dignity, for the liberty of speaking in this her husband's hall, that all around her were in an instant hushed to silence. She then advanced to the upper end of the table, where, both humbled and haughty, Bertalda had seated herself, and, while every eye was fastened upon her, spoke in the following manner:

"My friends, you appear dissatisfied and disturbed; and you are interrupting, with your strife, a festivity I had hoped would bring joy to you and to me. Ah! I knew nothing of your heartless ways of thinking; and never shall I understand them. I am not to blame for the mischief this disclosure has done. Believe me, little as you may imagine this to be the case, it is wholly owing to yourselves. One word more, therefore, is all I have to add; but this is one that must be spoken:—I have uttered nothing but truth. Of the certainty of the fact, I give you the strongest assurance. No other proof can I or will I produce, but this I will affirm in the presence of God. The person who gave me this information was the very same who decoyed the infant Bertalda into the water, and who, after thus taking her from her parents, placed her on the green grass of the meadow, where he knew the duke was to pass."

"She is an enchantress!" cried Bertalda; "a witch, that has intercourse with evil spirits. She acknowledges it herself."

"Never! I deny it!" replied Undine, while a whole heaven of innocence and truth beamed from her eyes. "I am no witch; look upon me, and say if I am."

"Then she utters both falsehood and folly," cried Bertalda; "and she is unable to prove that I am the child of these low people. My noble parents, I entreat you to take me from this company, and out of this city, where they do nothing but shame me."

But the aged duke, a man of honourable feeling, remained unmoved; and his wife remarked: "We must thoroughly examine into this matter. God forbid that we should move a step from this hall before we do so."

Then the aged wife of the fisherman drew near, made a low obeisance to the duchess, and said: "Noble and pious lady, you have opened my heart. Permit me to tell you, that if this evil-disposed maiden is my daughter, she has a mark like a violet between her shoulders, and another of the same kind on the instep of her left foot. If she will only consent to go out of the hall with me——"

"I will not consent to uncover myself before the peasant woman," interrupted Bertalda, haughtily turning her back upon her.

"But before me you certainly will," replied the duchess, gravely. "You will follow me into that room, maiden; and the old woman shall go with us."

The three disappeared, and the rest continued where they were, in breathless expectation. In a few minutes the females returned—Bertalda pale as death; and the duchess said: "Justice must be done; I therefore declare that our lady hostess has spoken exact truth. Bertalda is the fisherman's daughter; no further proof is required; and this is all of which on the present occasion, you need to be informed."

The princely pair went out with their adopted daughter; the fisherman, at a sign from the duke, dollowed them with his wife. The other guests retired in silence, or suppressing their murmurs; while Undine sank weeping into the arms of Huldbrand.

The lord of Ringstetten would certainly have been more gratified, had the events of this day been different; but even such as they now were, he could by no means look upon them as unwelcome, since his lovely wife had shown herself so full of goodness, sweetness, and kindliness.

"If I have given her a soul," he could not help saying to himself, "I have assuredly given her a better one than my own"; and now he only thought of soothing and comforting his weeping wife, and of removing her even so early as the morrow from a place which, after this cross accident, could not fail to be distasteful to her. Yet it is certain that the opinion of the public concerning her was not changed. As something extraordinary had long before been expected of her, the mysterious discovery of Bertalda's parentage had occasioned little or no surprise; and every one who became acquainted with Bertalda's story, and with the violence of her behaviour on that occasion, was only disgusted and set against her. Of this state of things, however, the knight and his lady were as yet ignorant; besides, whether the public condemned Bertalda or herself, the one view of the affair would have been as distressing to Undine as the other; and thus they came to the conclusion that the wisest course they could take, was to leave behind them the walls of the old city with all the speed in their power.

With the earliest beams of morning, a brilliant carriage for Undine drove up to the door of the inn; the horses of Huldbrand and his attendants stood near, stamping the pavement, impatient to proceed. The knight was leading his beautiful wife from the door, when a fisher-girl came up and met them in the way.

"We have no need of your fish," said Huldbrand, accosting her; "we are this moment setting out on a journey."

Upon this the fisher-girl began to weep bitterly; and then it was that the young couple first perceived it was Bertalda. They immediately returned with her to their apartment, when she informed them that, owing to her unfeeling and violent conduct of the preceding day, the duke and duchess had been so displeased with her, as entirely to withdraw from her their protection, thought not before giving her a generous portion. The fisherman, too, had received a handsome gift, and had, the evening before, set out with his wife for his peninsula.

"I would have gone with them," she pursued, "but the old fisherman, who is said to be my father——"

"He is, in truth, your father, Bertalda," said Undine, interrupting her. "See, the stranger whom you took for the master of the water-works gave me all the particulars. He wished to dissuade me from taking you with me to Castle Ringstetten, and therefore disclosed to me the whole mystery."

"Well then," continued Bertalda, "my father—if it must needs be so—my father said: 'I will not take you with me until you are changed. If you will venture to come to us alone through the ill-omened forest, that shall be a proof of your having some regard for us. But come not to me as a lady; come merely as a fisher-girl.' I do as he bade me, for since I am abandoned by all the world, I will live and die in solitude, a poor fisher-girl, with parents equally poor. The forest, indeed, appears very terrible to me. Horrible spectres make it their haunt, and I am so fearful. But how can I help it? I have only come here at this early hour to beg the noble lady of Ringstetten to pardon my unbecoming behaviour of yesterday. Sweet lady, I have the fullest persuasion that you meant to do me a kindness, but you were not aware how severely you would wound me; and then, in my agony and surprise, so many rash and frantic expressions burst from my lips. Forgive me, ah, forgive me! I am in truth so unhappy already. Only consider what I was but yesterday morning, what I was even at the beginning of your yesterday's festival, and what I am to-day!"

483

Her words, now became inarticulate, lost in a passionate flow of tears, while Undine, bitterly weeping with her, fell upon her neck. So powerful was her emotion, that it was a long time before she could utter a word. At length she said:

"You shall still go with us to Ringstetten; all shall remain just as we lately arranged it; but say 'thou' to me again, and do not call me 'noble lady' any more. Consider, we were changed for each other when we were children; even then we were united by a like fate, and we will strengthen this union with such close affection as no human power shall dissolve. Only first of all you must go with us to Ringstetten. How we shall share all things as sister, we can talk of after we arrive."

Bertalda looked up to Huldbrand with timid inquiry. He pitied her in her affliction, took her hand, and begged her tenderly to entrust herself to him and his wife.

"We will send a message to your parents," continued he, "giving them the reason why you have not come";—and he would have added more about his worthy friends of the peninsula, when, perceiving that Bertalda shrank in distress at the mention of them, he refrained. He took her under the arm, lifted her first into the carriage, then Undine, and was soon riding blithely beside them; so persevering was he, too, in urging forward their driver, that in a short time they had left behind them the limits of the city, and a crowd of painful recollections; and now the ladies could take delight in the beautiful country which their progress was continually presenting.

After a journey of some days, they arrived, on a fine evening, at Castle Ringstetten. The young knight being much engaged with the overseers and menials of his establishment, Undine and Bertalda were left alone. They took a walk upon the high rampart of the fortress, and were charmed with the delightful landscape which the fertile Suabia spread around them. While they were viewing the scene, a tall man drew near, who greeted them with respectful civility, and who seemed to Bertalda much to resemble the director of the city fountain. Still less was the resemblance to be mistaken, when Undine, indignant at his intrusion, waved him off with an air of menace; while he, shaking his head, retreated with rapid strides, as he had formerly done, then glided among the trees of a neighbouring grove and disappeared.

"Do not be terrified, Bertalda," said Undine; "the hateful master of the fountain shall do you no harm this time." And then she related to her the particulars of her history, and who she was herself—how Bertalda had been taken away from the people of the peninsula, and Undine left in her place. This relation at first filled the young maiden with amazement and alarm; she imagined her friend must be seized with a sudden madness. But, from the consistency of her story, she became more and more convinced that all was true, it so well agreed with former occurrences, and still more convinced from that inward feeling with which truth never fails to make itself known to us. She could not but view it as an extraordinary circumstance that she was herself now living, as it were, in the midst of one of those wild tales which she had formerly heard related. She gazed upon Undine with reverence, but could not keep from a shuddering feeling which seemed to come between her and her friend; and she could not but wonder when the knight, at their evening repast, showed himself so kind and full of love towards a being who appeared to her, after the discoveries just made, more to resemble a phantom of the spirit-world than one of the human race.

CHAPTER VII

The writer of this tale, both because it moves his own heart and he wishes it to move that of others, asks a favour of you, dear reader. Forgive him if he passes over a considerable space of time in a few words, and only tells you generally what therein happened. He knows well that it might be unfolded skilfully, and step by step, how Huldbrand's heart began to turn from Undine and towards Bertalda—how Bertalda met the young knight with ardent love, and how they both looked upon the poor wife as a mysterious being, more to be dreaded than pitied—how Undine wept, and her tears stung the conscience of her husband, without recalling his former love; so that though at times he showed kindness to her, a cold shudder soon forced him to turn from her to his fellow-mortal Bertalda; —all this, the writer knows, might have been drawn out fully, and perhaps it ought to have been. But it would have made him too sad; for he has witnessed such things, and shrinks from recalling even their shadow. Thou knowest, probably, the like feeling, dear reader; for it is the lot of mortal man. Happy art thou if thou hast received the injury, not inflicted it; for in this case it is more blessed to receive than to give. Then only a soft sorrow at such a recollection passes through they heart, and perhaps a quiet tear trickles down thy cheek over the faded flowers in which thou once so heartily rejoiced. This is enough: we will not pierce our hearts with a thousand separate stings, but only bear in mind that all happened as I just now said.

Poor Undine was greatly troubled; and the other two were very far from being happy. Bertalda in particular, whenever she was in the slightest degree opposed in her wishes, attributed the cause to the jealousy and oppression of the injured wife. She was therefore daily in the habit of showing a haughty and imperious demeanour, to which Undine yielded with a sad submission; and which was generally encouraged strongly by the now blinded Huldbrand.

What disturbed the inmates of the castle still more, was the endless variety of wonderful apparitions which assailed Huldbrand and Bertalda in the vaulted passages of the building, and of which nothing had ever been heard before within the memory of man. The tall white man, in whom Huldbrand but too plainly recognised Undine's uncle Kühleborn, and Bertalda the spectral master of the water-works, often passed before them with threatening aspect and gestures; more especially, however, before Bertalda, so that, through terror, she had several times already fallen sick, and had, in consequence, frequently thought of quitting the castle. Yet partly because Huldbrand was but too dear to her, and she trusted to her innocence, since no words of love had passed between them, and partly also because she knew not whither to direct her steps, she lingered where she was.

The old fisherman, on receiving the message from the lord of Ringstetten that Bertalda was his guest, returned answer in some lines almost too illegible to be deciphered, but still the best his advanced life and long disuse of writing permitted him to form.

"I have now become," he wrote, "a poor old widower, for my beloved and faithful wife is dead. But lonely as I now sit in my cottage, I prefer Bertalda's remaining where she is, to her living with me. Only let her do nothing to hurt my dear Undine, else she will have my curse."

The last words of this letter, Bertalda flung to the winds; but the permission to remain from home, which her father had granted her, she remembered and clung to—just as we are all of us wont to do in similar circumstances.

One day, a few moments after Huldbrand had ridden out, Undine called together the domestics of the family, and ordered them to bring a large stone, and carefully to cover with it a mangificent fountain, that was situated in the middle of the castle court. The servants objected that it would oblige them to bring water from the valley below. Undine smiled sadly.

"I am sorry, my friends," replied she, "to increase your labour; I would rather bring up the water-vessels myself: but this fountain must indeed be closed. Believe me when I say that it must be done, and that only by doing it we can avoid a greater evil."

The domestics were all rejoiced to gratify their gentle mistress; and making no further inquiry, they seized the enormous stone. While the were raising it in their hands, and were now on the point of adjusting it over the fountain, Bertalda came running to the place, and cried, with an air of command, that they must stop; that the water she used, so improving to her complexion, was brought from this fountain, and that she would by no means allow it to be closed.

This time, however, Undine, while she showed her usual gentleness, showed more than her usual resolution: she said it belonged to her, as mistress of the house, to direct the household according to her best judgement; and that she was accountable in this to no one but her lord and husband.

"See, O pray see," exlaimed the dissatisfied and indignant Bertalda, "how the beautiful water is curling and curving, winding and waving there, as if disturbed at being shut out from the bright sunshine, and from the cheerful view of the human countenance, for whose mirror it was created."

In truth the water of the fountain was agitated, and foaming, and hissing in a surprising manner; it seemed as if there were something within possessing life and will, that was struggling to free itself from confinement. But Undine only the more earnestly urged the accomplishment of her commands. This earnestness was scarcely required. The servants of the castle were as happy in obeying their gentle lady, as in opposing the haughty spirit of Bertalda; and however the latter might scold and threaten, still the stone was in a few minutes lying firm over the opening of the fountain. Undine leaned thoughtfully over it, and wrote with her beautiful fingers on the flat surface. She must, however, have had something very sharp and corrosive in her hand, for when she retired, and the domestics went up to examine the stone, they discovered various strange characters upon it, which none of them had seen there before.

When the knight returned home, toward evening, Bertalda received him with tears, and complaints of Undine's conduct. He cast a severe glance or reproach at his poor wife, and she looked down in distress; yet she said, very calmly:

"My lord and husband, you never reprove even a bond-slave before you hear his defence; how much less, then, your wedded wife!"

"Speak, what moved you to this singular conduct?" said the knight, with a gloomy countenance.

"I could wish to tell you when we are entirely alone," said Undine, with a sigh.

"You can tell me equally well in the presence of Bertalda," he replied.

"Yes, if you command me," said Undine; "but do not command me—pray, pray do not!"

She looked so humble, affectionate, and obedient, that the heart of the knight was touched and softened, as if it felt the influence of a ray from better times. He kindly took her arm within his, and led her to his apartment, where she spoke as follows:

"You already know something, my beloved lord, of Kühleborn, my evil-disposed uncle, and have often felt displeasure at meeting him in the passages of this castle. Several times has he terrified Bertalda even to swooning. He does this because he possesses no soul, being a mere elemental mirror of the outward world, while of the world within he can give no reflection. Then, too, he sometimes observes that you are displeased with me, that in my childish weakness I weep at this, and that Bertalda, it may be, laughs at the same moment. Hence it is that he imagines all is wrong with us, and in various ways mixes with our circle unbidden. What do I gain by reproving him, by showing displeasure, and sending him away? He does not believe a word I say. His poor nature has no idea that the joys and sorrows of love have so sweet a resemblance, and are so intimately connected that no power on earth is able to separate them. A smile shines in the midst of tears, and a smile calls forth tears from their dwelling-place."

She looked up at Huldbrand, smiling and weeping, and he again felt within his heart all the magic of his former love. She percived it, and pressed him more tenderly to her, while with tears of joy she went on thus:

"When the disturber of our peace would not be dismissed with words, I was obliged to shut the door upon him; and the only entrance by which he has access to us is that fountain. His connection with the other water-spirits here in this region is cut off by the valleys that border upon us; and his kingdom first commences farther off on the Danube, in whose tributary streams some of his good friends have their abode. For this reason I caused the stone to be placed over the opening of the fountain, and inscribed characters upon it, which baffle all the efforts of my suspicious uncle; so that he now has no power of intruding either upon you, or me, or Bertalda. Human beings, it is true, notwithstanding the characters I have inscribed there, are able to raise the stone without any extraordinary trouble; there is nothing to prevent them. If you choose, therefore, remove it, according to Bertalda's desire; but she assuredly knows not what she asks. The rude Kühleborn looks with peculiar ill-will upon her; and should those things come to pass that he has predicted to me, and which may happen without your meaning any evil, ah! dearest, even you yourself would be exposed to peril."

Huldbrand felt the generosity of his gentle wife in the depth of his heart, since she had been so active in confining her formidable defender, and even at the very moment she' was reproached for it by Bertalda. He pressed her in his arms with the tenderest affection and said, with emotion: "The stone shall remain unmoved; all remains, and ever shall remain, just as you choose to have it, my sweetest Undine!"

At these long-withheld expressions of tenderness, she returned his caresses with lowly delight, and at length said: "My dearest husband, since you are so kind and indulgent to-day, may I venture to ask a favour of you? See now, it is with you as with summer. Even amid its highest splendour, summer puts on the flaming and thundering crown of glorious tempests, in which it strongly resembles a king and god on earth. You, too, are sometimes terrible in your rebukes; your eyes flash lighning, while thunder resounds in your voice; and although this may be quite becoming to you, I in my folly cannot but sometimes weep at it. But never, I entreat you, behave thus toward me on a river, or even when we are near any water. For if you should, my relations would acquire a right over me. They would inexorably tear me from you in their fury, because they would conceive that one of their race was injured; and I should be compelled, as long as I lived, to dwell below in the crystal palaces, and never dare ascend to you again; or should *they send* me up to you!—O God! that would be far worse still. No, no, my beloved husband; let it not come to that, if your poor Undine is dear to you."

He solemnly promised to do as she desired, and, inexpressibly happy and full of affection, the married pair returned from the apartment. At this very moment, Bertalda came with some work-people whom she had meanwhile ordered to attend her, and said with a fretful air, which she had assumed of late:

"Well, now the secret consultation is at an end, the stone may be removed. Go out, workmen, and see to it."

The knight, however, highly resenting her impertinence, said, in brief and very decisive terms: "The stone remains where it is!" He reproved Bertalda also for the vehemence that she had shown towards his wife. Whereupon the workmen, smiling with secret satisfaction, withdrew; while Bertalda, pale with rage, hurried away to her room.

When the hour of supper came, Bertalda was waited for in vain. They sent for her; but the domestic found her apartments empty, and brought back with him only a sealed letter, addressed to the knight. He opened it in alarm, and read:

"I feel with shame that I am only the daughter of a poor fisherman. That I for one moment forgot this, I will make expiation in the miserable hut of my parents. Farewell to you and your beautiful wife!"

Undine was troubled at heart. With eagerness she entreated Huldbrand to hasten after their friend, who had flown, and bring her back with him. Alas! she had no occasion to urge him. His passion for Bertalda again burst forth with vehemence. He hurried round the castle, inquiring whether any one had seen which way the fair fugitive had gone. He could gain no information; and was already in the court on his horse, determining to take at a venture the road by which he had conducted Bertalda to the castle, when there appeared a page, who assured him that he had met the lady on the path to the Black Valley. Swift as an arrow, the knight sprang through the gate in the direction pointed out, without hearing Undine's voice of agony, as she cried after him from the window:

"To the Black Valley? Oh, not there! Huldbrand, not there! Or if you will go, for Heaven's sake take me with you!"

But when she perceived that all her calling was of no avail, she ordered her white palfrey to be instantly saddled, and followed the knight, without permitting a single servant to accompany her.

The Black Valley lies secluded far among the mountains. What its present name may be I am unable to say. At the time of which I am speaking, the country-people gave it this appellation from the deep obscurity produced by the shadows of lofty trees, more especially by a crowded growth of firs that covered this region of moorland. Even the brook, which bubbled between the rocks, assumed the same dark hue, and showed nothing of that cheerful aspect which streams are wont to wear that have the blue sky immediately over them.

It was now the dusk of evening; and between the heights it had become extremely wild and gloomy. The knight, in great anxiety, skirted the border of the brook. He was at one time fearful that, by delay, he should allow the fugitive to advance too far before him; and then again, in his too eager rapidity, he was afraid he might somewhere overlook and pass by her, should she be desirous of concealing herself from his search. He had in the mean time penetrated pretty far into the valley, and might hope soon to overtake the maiden, provided he were pursuing the right track. The fear, indeed, that he might not as yet have gained it, made his heart beat with more and more of anxiety. In the stormy night which was now approaching, and which always fell more fearfully over this valley, where would the delicate Bertalda shelter herself, should he fail to find her? At last, while these thoughts were darting across his mind, he saw something white glimmer through the branches on the ascent of the mountain. He thought he recognised Bertalda's robe; and he directed his course toward it. But his horse refused to go forward; he reared with a fury so uncontrollable, and his master was so unwilling to lose a moment, that (especially as he saw the thickets were altogether impassable on horseback) he dismounted, and having fastened his snorting steed to an elm, worked his way with caution through the matted underwood. The branches, moistened by the cold drops of the evening dew, struck against his forehead and cheeks; distant thunder muttered from the further side of the mountains; and everything put on so strange an appearance, that he began to feel a dread of the white figure, which now lay at a short distance from him upon the ground. Still, he could see distinctly that it was a female, either asleep or in a swoon, and dressed in long white garments such as Bertaldda had worn the past day. Approaching quite near to her, he made a rustling with the brances and a ringing with his sword; but she did not move.

"Bertalda!" he cried, at first low, then louder and louder; yet she heard him not. At last, when he uttered the dear name with an energy yet more powerful, a hollow echo from the mountain-summits around the valley returned the deadened sound, "Bertalda!" Still the sleeper continued insensible. He stooped down; but the duskiness of the valley, and the obscurity of twilight would not allow him to distinguish her features. While, with painful uncertainty, he was bending over her, a flash of lightning suddenly shot across the valley. By this stream of light he saw a frightfully distorted visage close to his own, and a hoarse voice reached his ear:

"You enamoured swain, give me a kiss!" Huldbrand sprang upon his feet with a cry of horror; and the hideous figure rose with him.

"Go home!" it cried, with a deep murmur: "the fiends are abroad. Go home! or I have you!" And it stretched toward him its long white arms.

"Malicious Kühleborn!" exclaimed the knight, with restored energy; "if Kühleborn you are, what business have you here?—what's your will, you goblin? There, take your kiss!" And in fury he struck his sword at the form. But it vanished like vapour; and a rush of water, which wetted him through and through, left him in no doubt with what foe he had been engaged.

491

"He wishes to frighten me back from my pursuit of Bertalda," said he to himself. "He imagines that I shall be terrified at his senseless tricks, and resign the poor distressed maiden to his power, so that he can wreak his vengeance upon her at will. But that he shall not, weak spirit of the flood! What the heart of man can do, when it exerts the full force of its will and of its noblest powers, the poor goblin cannot fathom."

He felt the truth of his words, and that they had inspired his heart with fresh courage. Fortune, too, appeared to favour him; for, before reaching his fastened steed, he distinctly heard the voice of Bertalda, weeping not far before him, amid the roar of the thunder and the tempest, which every moment increased. He flew swiftly toward the sound, and found the trembling maiden, just as she was attempting to climb the steep, hoping to escape from the dreadful darkness of this valley. He drew near her with expressions of love; and bold and proud as her resolution had so lately been, she now felt nothing but joy that the man whom she so passionately loved should rescue her from this frightful solitude, and thus call her back to the joyful life in the castle. She followed almost unresisting, but so spent with fatigue, that the knight was glad to bring her to his horse, which he now hastily unfastened from the elm, in order to lift the fair wanderer upon him, and then to lead him carefully by the reins through the uncertain shades of the valley.

But, owing to the wild apparition of Kühleborn, the horse had become wholly unmanageable. Rearing and wildly snorting as he was, the knight must have used uncommon effort to mount the beast himself; to place the trembling Bertalda upon him was impossible. They were compelled, therefore, to return home on foot. While with one hand the knight drew the steed after him by the bridle, he supported the tottering Bertalda with the other. She exerted all the strength in her power in order to escape speedily from this vale of terrors. But weariness weighed her down like lead; and all her limbs trembled, partly in consequence of what she had suffered from the extreme terror which Kühleborn had already caused her, and partly from her present fear at the roar of the tempest and thunder amid the mountain-forest.

At last she slid from the arm of the knight; and sinking upon the moss, she said: "Only let me lie here, my noble lord. I suffer the punishment due to my folly; and I must perish here through faintness and dismay."

"Never, gentle lady, will I leave you," cried Huldbrand, vainly trying to restrain the furious animal he was leading, for the horse was all in a foam, and began to chafe more ungovernably than before, till the knight was glad to keep him at such a distance from the exhausted maiden as to save her from a new alarm. But hardly had he withdrawn five steps with the frantic steed when she began to call after him in the most sorrowful accents, fearful that he would actually leave her in this horrible wilderness. He was at a loss what course to take. He would gladly have given the enraged beast his liberty; he would have let him rush away amid the night and exhaust his fury, had he not feared that in this narrow defile his iron-shod hoofs might come thundering over the very spot where Bertalda lay.

In this extreme peril and embarrassment he heard with delight the rumbling wheels of a wagon as it came slowly descending the stony way behind them. He called out for help; answer was returned in the deep voice of a man, bidding them have patience, but promising assistance; and two grey horses soon after shone through the bushes, and near them their driver in the white frock of a carter; and next appeared a great sheet of white linen, with which the goods he seemed to be conveying were covered. The greys, in obedience to a shout from their master, stood still. He came up to the knight, and aided him in checking the fury of the foaming charger.

"I know well enough," said he, "what is the matter with the brute. The first time I travelled this way my horses were just as wilful and headstrong as yours. The reason is, there is a water-spirit haunts this valley—and a wicked wight they say he is—who takes delight in mischief and witcheries of this sort. But I have learned a charm; and if you will let me whisper it in your horse's ear, he will stand just as quiet as my silver greys there."

"Try your luck, then, and help us as quickly as possible!" said the impatient knight.

Upon this the wagoner drew down the head of the rearing courser close to his own, and spoke some words in his ear. The animal instantly stood still and subdued; only his quick panting and smoking sweat showed his recent violence.

Huldbrand had little time to inquire by what means this had been effected. He agreed with the man that he should take Bertalda in his wagon where, as he said, a quantity of soft cotton was stowed, and he might in this way convey her to Castle Ringstetten, the knight could accompany them on horseback. But the horse appeared to be too much exhausted to carry his master so far. Seeing this, the man advised him to mount the wagon with Bertalda. The horse could be attached to it behind.

"It is down hill," said he, "and the load for my greys will therefore be light."

The knight accepted his offer, and entered the wagon with Bertalda. The horse followed patiently after, while the wagoner, sturdy and attentive, walked beside them.

Amid the silence and deepening obscurity of the night, the tempest sounding more and more remote, in the comfortable feeling of their security, a confidential conversation arose between Huldbrand and Bertalda. He reproached her in the most flattering words for her resentful flight. She excused herself with humility and feeling; and from every tone of her voice it shone out, like a lamp guiding to the beloved through night and darkness, that Huldbrant was still dear to her. The knight felt the *sense* of her words rather than heard the words themselves, and answered simply to this sense.

Then the wagoner suddenly shouted, with a startling voice: "Up, my greys, up with your feet! Hey, now together!—show your spirit!—remember who you are!"

The knight bent over the side of the wagon, and saw that the horses had stepped into the midst of a foaming stream, and were, indeed, almost swimming, while the wheels of the wagon were rushing round and flashing like mill-wheels; and the wagoner had got on before, to avoid the swell of the flood.

"What sort of a road is this? It leads into the middle of the stream!" cried Huldbrand to his guide.

"Not at all, sir," returned he, with a laugh; "it is just the contrary. The stream is running in the middle of our road. Only look about you, and see how all is overflowed!"

The whole valley, in fact, was in commotion, at the waters, suddenly raised and visibly rising, swept over it.

"It is Kühleborn, that evil water-spirit, who wished to drown us!" exclaimed the knight. "Have you no charm of protection against him, friend?"

"I have one," answered the wagoner; "but I cannot and must not make use of it before you know who I am."

"Is this a time for riddles?" cried the knight. "The flood is every moment rising higher; and what does it concern *me* to know who *you* are?"

"But mayhap it does concern you, though," said the guide; "for *I* am Kühleborn."

Thus speaking, he thrust his head into the wagon, and laughed with a distorted visage. But the wagon remained a wagon no longer; the grey horses were horses no longer; all was transformed to foam—all sank into the waters that rushed and hissed around them; while the wagoner himself, rising in the form of a gigantic wave, dragged the vainly struggling courser under the waters, then rose again huge as a liquid tower, swept over the heads of the floating pair, and was on the point of burying them irrecoverably beneath it. Then the soft voice of Undine was heard through the uproar; the moon emerged from the clouds; and by its light Undine was seen on the heights above the valley. She rebuked, she threatened the floods below her. The menacing and towerlike billow vanished, muttering and murmuring; the waters gently flowed away under the beams of the moon; while Undine, like a hovering white dove, flew down from the hill, raised the knight and Bertalda, and bore them to a green spot, where, by her earnest efforts, she soon restored them and dispelled their terrors. She then assisted Bertalda to mount the white palfrey on which she had herself been borne to the valley; and thus all three returned homeward to Castle Ringstetten.

Chapter VIII

After this last adventure they lived at the castle undisturbed and in peaceful enjoyment. The knight was more and more impressed with the heavenly goodness of his wife, which she had so nobly shown by her instant pursuit and by the rescue she had effected in the Black Valley, where the power of Kühleborn again commenced. Undine herself enjoyed that peace and security which never fails the soul as long as it knows distinctly that it is on the right path; and besides, in the newly-awakened love and regard of her husband, a thousand gleams of hope and joy shone upon her.

Bertalda, on the other hand, showed herself grateful, humble, and timid, without taking to herself any merit for so doing. Whenever Huldbrand or Undine began to explain to her their reason for covering the fountain, or their adventures in the Black Valley, she would earnestly entreat them to spare her the recital, for the recollection of the fountain occasioned her too much shame, and that of the Black Valley too much terror. She learnt nothing more about either of them; and what would she have gained from more knowledge? Peace and joy had visibly taken up their abode at Castle Ringstetten. They enjoyed their present blessings in perfect security, and now imagined that life could produce nothing but pleasant flowers and fruits.

In this happiness winter came and passed away; and spring, with its foliage of tender green, and its heaven of softest blue, succeeded, to gladden the hearts of the three inmates of the castle. The season was in harmony with their minds, and their minds imparted their own hues to the season. What wonder, then, that its storks and swallows inspired them also with a disposition to travel? On a bright morning, while they were wandering down to one of the sources of the Danube, Huldbrand spoke of the magnificence of this noble stream, how it continued swelling as it flowed through countries enriched by its waters, with what splendour Vienna rose and sparkled on its banks, and how it grew lovelier and more imposing throughout its progress.

"It must be glorious to trace its course down to Vienna!" Bertalda exclaimed, with warmth; but immediately resuming the humble and modest demeanour she had recently shown, she paused and blushed in silence.

This much moved Undine; and with the liveliest wish to gratify her friend, she said, "What hinders our taking this little voyage?"

Bertalda leapt up with delight, and the two friends at the same moment began painting this enchanting voyage on the Danube in the most brilliant colours. Huldbrand, too, agreed to the project with pleasure; only he once whispered, with something of alarm, in Undine's ear—

"But at that distance Kühleborn becomes possessed of his power again!"

"Let him come, let him come" she answered with a laugh; "I shall be there, and he dares do none of his mischief in my presence."

Thus was the last impediment removed. They prepared for the expedition, and soon set out upon it with lively spirits and the brightest hopes.

But be not surprised, O man, if events almost always happen very differently from what you expect. That malicious power which lies in ambush for our destruction delight to lull its chosen victim asleep with sweet songs and golden delusions; while, on the other hand, the messenger of Heaven often strikes sharply at our door, to alarm and awaken us.

During the first days of their passage down the Danube they were unusually happy. The farther they advanced upon the waters of this proud river, the views became more and more fair But amid scenes otherwise most delicious, and from which they had promised themselves the purest delight, the subborn Kühleborn, dropping all disguise, began to show his power of annoying them. He had no other means of doing this, indeed, than by tricks—for Undine often rebuked the swelling waves or the contrary winds, and then the insolence of the enemy was instantly humbled and subdued; but his attacks were renewed, and Undine's reproofs again became necessary, so that the pleasure of the fellow travellers was completely destroyed. The boatmen, too, were continually whispering to one another in dismay and eyeing their three superiors with distrust, while even the servants began more and more to form dismal surmises, and to watch their master and mistress with looks of suspicion.

Huldbrand often said in his own mind, "This comes when like marries not like—when a man forms an unnatural union with a sea-maiden." Excusing himself, as we all love to do, he would add: "I did not, in fact, know that she *was* a maid of the sea. It is my misfortune that my steps are haunted and disturbed by the wild humours of her kindred, but it is not my crime."

By reflections like these, he felt himself in some measure strengthened; but, on the other hand, he felt the more ill-humour, almost dislike, towards Undine. He would look angrily at her, and the unhappy wife but too well understood his meaning. One day, grieved by this unkindness, as well as exhausted by her unremitted exertions to frustrate the artifices of Kühleborn, she toward evening fell into a deep slumber, rocked and soothed by the gentle motion of the bark. But hardly had she closed her eyes, when every person in the boat, in whatever direction he might look, saw the head of a man, frightful beyond imagination: each head rose out of the waves, not like that of a person swimming, but quite perpendicular, as if firmly fastened to the watery mirror, and yet moving on with the bark. Every one wished to show to his companion what terrified himself, and each perceived the same expression of horror on the face of the other, only hands and eyes were directed to a different quarter, as if to a point where the monster, half laughing and half threatening, rose opposite to each.

When, however, they wished to make one another understand the sight, and all cried out, "Look there!" "No, there!" the frightful heads all became visible to each, and the whole river around the boat swarmed with the most horrible faces. All raised a scream of terror at the sight, and Undine started from sleep. As she opened her eyes, the deformed visages disappeared. But Huldbrand was made furious by so many hideous visions. He would have burst out in wild imprecations, had not Undine with the meekest looks and gentlest tone of voice said—

"For God's sake, my husband, do not express displeasure against me here—we are on the water."

The knight was silent, and sat down absorbed in deep thought. Undine whispered in his ear, "Would it not be better, my love, to give up this foolish voyage, and return to Castle Ringstetten in peace?"

But Huldbrand murmured wrathfully: "So I must become a prisoner in my own castle, and not be allowed to breathe a moment but while the fountain is covered? Would to Heaven that your cursed kindred——"

Then Undine pressed her fair hand on his lips caressingly. He said no more; but in silence pondered on all that Undine had before said.

497

Bertalda, meanwhile, had given herself up to a crowd of thronging thoughts. Of Undine's origin she knew a good deal, but not the whole; and the terrible Kühleborn especially remained to her an awful, an impenetrable mystery—never, indeed, had she once heard his name. Musing upon these wondrous things, she unclasped, without being fully conscious of what she was doing, a golden necklace, which Huldbrand, on one of the preceding days of their passage, had bought for her of a travelling trader; and she was now letting it float in sport just over the surface of the stream, while in her dreamy mood she injoyed the bright reflection it threw on the water, so clear beneath the glow of evening. That instant a huge hand flashed suddenly up from the Danube, seized the necklace in its grasp, and vanished with it beneath the flood. Bertalda shrieked aloud, and a scornful laugh came pealing up from the depth of the river.

The knight could now restrain his wrath no longer. He started up, poured forth a torrent of reproaches, heaped curses upon all who interfered with his friends and troubled his life, and dared them all, waterspirits or mermaids, to come within the sweep of his sword.

Bertalda, meantime, wept for the loss of the ornament so very dear to her heart, and her tears were to Huldbrand as oil poured upon the flame of his fury; while Undine held her hand over the side of the boat, dipping it in the waves, softly murmuring to herself, and only at times interrupting her strange mysterious whisper to entreat her husband—

"Do not reprove me here, beloved; blame all others as you will, but not me. You know why!" And in truth, though he was trembling with excess of passion, he kept himself from any word directly against her.

She then brought up in her wet hand, which she had been holding under the waves, a coral necklace, of such exquisite beauty, such sparkling brilliancy, as dazzled the eyes of all who beheld it. "Take this," said she, holding it out kindly to Bertalda, "I have ordered it to be brought to make some amends for your loss; so do not grieve any more, poor child."

But the knight rushed between them, and snatching the beautiful ornament out of Undine's hand, hurled it back into the flood; and, mad with rage, exclaimed: "So, then, you have still a connection with them! In the name of all witches go and remain among them with your presents, you sorceress, and leave us human beings in peace!"

With fixed but streaming eyes, poor Undine gazed on him, her hand still stretched out, just as when she had so lovingly offered her brilliant gift to Bertalda. She then began to weep more and more, as if her heart would break, like an innocent tender child, cruelly aggrieved. At last, wearied out, she said: "Farewell, dearest, farewell. They shall do you no harm; only remain true, that I may have power to keep them from you. But I must go hence! go hence even in this early youth! Oh, woe, woe! what have you done! Oh, woe, woe!"

And she vanished over the side of the boat. Whether she plunged into the stream, or whether, like water melting into water, she flowed away with it, they knew not—her disappearance was like both and neither. But she was lost in the Danube, instantly and completely; only little waves were yet whispering and sobbing around the boat, and they could almost be heard to say, "Oh, woe, woe! Ah, remain true! Oh, woe!"

But Huldbrand, in a passion of burning tears, threw himself upon the deck of the bark; and a deep swoon soon wrapped the wretched man in a blessed forgetfulness of misery.

Shall we call it a good or an evil thing, that our mourning has no long duration? I mean that deep mourning which comes from the very well-springs of our being, which so becomes one with the lost objects of our love that we hardly realise their loss, while our grief devotes itself religiously to the honouring of their image until we reach that bourne which they have already reached!

Truly all good men observe in a degree this religious devotion; but yet it soon ceases to be that first deep grief. Other and new images throng in, until, to our sorrow, we experience the vanity of all earthly things. Therefore I must say: Alas, that our mourning should be of such short duration!

The lord of Ringstetten experienced this; but whether for his good, we shall discover in the sequel of this history. At first he could do nothing but weep—weep as bitterly as the poor gentle Undine had wept when he snatched out of her hand that brilliant ornament, with which she so kindly wished to make amends for Bertalda's loss. And then he stretched his hand out, as she had done, and wept again like her, with renewed violence. He cherished a secret hope, that even the springs of life would at last become exhausted by weeping. And has not the like thought passed through the minds of many of us with a painful pleasure in times of sore affliction? Bertalda wept with him; and they lived together a long while at the castle of Ringstetten in undisturbed quiet, honouring the memory of Undine, and having almost wholly forgotten their former attachment. And therefore the good Undine, about this time, often visited Huldbrand's dreams: she soothed him with soft and affectionate caresses, and then went away again, weeping in silence; so that when he awoke, he sometimes knew not how his cheeks came to be so wet—whether it was caused by *her* tears, or only by his own.

But as time advanced, these visions became less frequent, and the sorrow of the knight less keen; still he might never, perhaps, have entertained any other wish than thus quietly to think of Undine, and to speak of her, had not the old fisherman arrived unexpectedly at the castle, and earnestly insisted on Bertalda's returning with him as his child. He had received information of Undine's disappearance; and he was not willing to allow Bertalda to continue longer at the castle with the widowed knight. "For," said he, "whether my daughter loves me or not is at present what I care not to know; but her good name is at stake: and where that is the case, nothing else may be thought of."

This resolution of the old fisherman, and the fearful solitude that, on Bertalda's departure, threatened to oppress the knight in every hall and passage of the deserted castle, brought to light what had disappeared in his sorrow for Undine,—I mean, his attachment to the fair Bertalda; and this he made known to her father.

The fisherman had many objections to make to the proposed marriage. The old man had loved Undine with exceeding tenderness, and it was doubtful to his mind that the mere disappearance of his beloved child could be properly viewed as her death. But were it even granted that her corpse were lying stiff and cold at the bottom of the Danube, or swept away by the current to the ocean, still Bertalda had had some share in her death; and it was unfitting for her to step into the place of the poor injured wife. The fisherman, however, haf felt a strong regard also for the knight: this and the entreaties of his daughter, who had become much more gentle and respectful, as well as her tears for Undine, all exerted their influence; and he must at last have been forced to give up his opposition, for he remained at the castle without objection, and a messenger was sent off express to Father Heilmann, who in former and happier days had united Undine and Huldbrand, requesting him to come and perform the ceremony at the knight's second marriage.

Hardly had the holy man read through the letter from the lord of Ringstetten, ere he set out upon the journey, and made much greater dispatch on his way to the castle than the messenger from it had made in reaching him. Whenever his breath failed him in his rapid progress, or his old limbs ached with fatigue, he would say to himself:

"Perhaps I shall be able to prevent a sin; then sink not, withered body, before I arrive at the end of my journey!" And with renewed vigour he pressed forward, hurrying on without rest or repose, until, later one evening, he entered the shady courtyard of the castle of Ringstetten.

The betrothed were sitting side by side under the trees, and the aged fisherman in a thoughtful mood sat near them. The moment they saw

Father Heilmann, they rose with a spring of joy, and pressed round him with eager welcome. But he in a few words, asked the bridegroom to return with him into the castle; and when Huldbrand stood mute with surprise, and delayed complying with his earnest request, the pious priest said to him—

"I do not know why I should want to speak to you in private; what I have to say as much concerns Bertalda and the fisherman as yourself; and what we must at some time hear, it is best to hear as soon as possible. Are you, then, so very certain, Knight Huldbrand, that your first wife is actually dead? I can hardly think it. I will say nothing, indeed, of the mysterious state in which she may be now existing; I know nothing of it with certainty. But that she was a most devoted and faithful wife is beyond all dispute. And for fourteen night past, she has appeared to me in a dream, standing at my bedside wringing her tender hands in anguish, and sighing out, 'Ah, prevent him, dear father! I am still living! Ah, save his life! Ah, save his soul!'

"I did not understand what this vision of the night could mean, then came your messenger; and I have now hastened hither, not to unite, but, as I hope, to separate what ought not to be joined together. Leave her, Huldbrand! leave him, Bertalda! He still belongs to another; and do you not see on his pale cheek his grief for his lost wife? That is not the look of a bridegroom; and the spirit says to me, that 'if you do not leave him you will never be happy!'"

The three felt in their inmost hearts that Father Heilmann spoke the truth; but they would not believe it. Even the old fisherman was so infatuated, that he thought it could not be otherwise than as they had latterly settled amongst themselves. They all, therefore, with a determined and gloomy eageness, struggled against the representations and warnings of the priest, until, shaking his head and oppressed with sorrow, he finally quitted the castle, not choosing to accept their offered shelter even for a single night, or indeed so much as to taste a morsel of the refreshment they brought him. Huldbrand persuaded himself, however, that the priest was a mere visionary; and sent at daybreak to a monk of the nearest monastery, who without scruple, promised to perform the ceremony in a few days.

CHAPTER IX

It was between night and dawn of day that Huldbrand was lying on his couch, half waking and half sleeping. Whenever he attempted to compose himself to sleep, a terror came upon him and scared him, as if his slumbers were haunted with spectres. But he made an effort to rouse himself fully. He felt fanned as by the wings of a swan, and lulled as by the murmuring of waters, till in sweet confusion of the senses he sank back into his state of half-consciousness.

At last, however, he must have fallen perfectly asleep; for he seemed to be lifted up by wings of the swans, and to be wafted far away over land and sea, while their music swelled on his ear most sweetly. "The music of the swan! the song of the swan!" he could not but repeat to himself every moment; "is it not a sure foreboding of death?" Probably, however, it had yet another meaning. All at once he seemed to be hovering over the Mediterranean Sea. A swan sang melodiously in his ear, that this *was* the Mediterranean Sea. And while he was looking down upon the waves, they became transparent as crystal, so that he could see through them to the very bottom.

At this a thrill of delight shot through him, for her could see Undine where she was sitting beneath the clear crystal dome. It is true she was weeping very bitterly, and looked much sadder than in those happy days when they lived together at the castle of Ringstetten, both on their arrival and afterward, just before the set out upon their fatal passage down the Danube. The knight could not help thinking upon all this with deep emotion, but it did not appear that Undine was aware of his presence.

Kühleborn had meanwhile approached her, and was about to reprove her for weeping, when she drew herself up, and looked upon him with an air so majestic and commanding, that he almost shrank back.

"Although I now dwell here beneath the waters," said she, "yet I have brought my soul with me. And therefore I may weep, little as you can know what such tears are. They are blessed, as everything is blessed to one gifted with a true soul."

He shook his head incredulously; and after some thought, replied, "And yet, niece, you are subject to our laws, as a being of the same nature with ourselves; and should *he* prove unfaithful to you and marry again, you are obliged to take away his life."

"He remains a widower to this very hour," replied Undine; "and I am still dear to his sorrowful heart."

"He is, however, betrothed," said Kühleborn, with a laugh of scorn;

"and let only a few days wear away, and then comes the priest with his nuptial blessing; and then you must go up to the death of the husband with two wives."

"I have not the power," returned Undine, with a smile. "I have sealed up the foutain securely against myself and all of my race."

"Still, should he leave his castle," said Kühleborn, "or should he once allow the fountain to be uncovered, what then? for he thinks little enough of these things."

"For that very reason," said Undine, still smiling amid her tears, "for that very reason he is at this moment hovering in spirit over the Mediterranean Sea, and dreaming of the warning which our discourse gives him. I thoughtfully planned all this."

That instant, Kühleborn, inflamed with rage, looked up at the knight, wrathfully threatened him, stamped on the ground, and then shot like an arrow beneath the waves. He seemed to swell in his fury to the size of a whale. Again the swans began to sing, to wave their wings and fly; the knight seemed to soar away over mountains and streams, and at last to alight at Castle Ringstetten, and to awake on his couch.

Upon his couch he actually did awake; and his attendant entering at the same moment, informed him that Father Heilmann was still lingering in the neighbourhood; that he had the evening before met with him in the forest, where he was sheltering himself under a hut, which he had formed by interweaving the branches of trees, and covering them with moss and fine brushwood; and that to the question, "What he was doing there, since he would not give the marriage-blessing?" his answer was—

"There are many other blessings than those given at marriages; and through I did not come to officiate at the wedding, I may still officiate at a very different solemnity. All things have their seasons; we must be ready for them all. Besides, marrying and mourning are by no means so very unlike; as every one not wilfully blinded must know full well."

The knight made many bewildered reflections on these words and on his dream. But it is very difficult to give up a thing which we have once looked upon as certain; so all continued as had been arranged previously.

Should I relate to you how passed the marriage-feast at Castle Ringstetten, it would be as if you saw a heap of bright and pleasant things, but all overspread with a black mourning crape, through whose darkening veil their brilliancy would appear but a mockery of the nothingness of all earthly joys.

It was not that any spectral delusion disturbed the scene of festivity; for the castle, as we well know, had been secured against the mischief of water-spirits. But the knight, the fisherman, and all the guests were unable to banish the feeling that the chief personage of the feast was still wanting, and that this chief personage could be no other than the gentle and beloved Undine.

Whenever a door was heard to open, all eyes were involuntarily turned in that direction; and if it was nothing but the steward with new dishes, or the cup-bearer with a supply of wine of higher flavour than the last, they again looked down in sadness and disappointment, while the flashes of wit and merriment which had been passing at times from one to another, were extinguished by tears of mournful remembrance.

The bride was the least thoughtful of the company, and therefore the most happy; but even to her it sometimes seemed strange that she should be sitting at the head of the table, wearing a green wreath and gold embroidered robe, while Undine was lying a corpse, stiff and cold at the bottom of the Danube, or carried out by the current into the ocean. For ever since her father had suggested something of this sort, his words were continually sounding in her ear; and this day in particular, they would neither fade from her memory, nor yield to other thoughts.

Evening had scarcely arrived, when the company returned to their homes; not dismissed by the impatience of the bridegroom, as wedding parties are sometimes broken up but constrained solely by heavy sadness and forebodings of evil. Bertalda retired with her maidens, and the knight with his attendants, to undress; but there was no gay laughing company of bridesmaids and bridesmen at this mournful festival.

Bertalda wished to awake to more cheerful thoughts; she ordered her maidens to spread before her a brilliant set of jewels, a present from Huldbrand, together with rich apparel and veils, that she might select from among them the brightest and most beautiful for her dress in the morning. The attendants rejoiced at this opportunity of pouring forth good wishes and promises of happiness to their young mistress, and failed not to extol the beauty of the bride with the most glowing eloquence. This went on for a long time, until Bertalda at last looking in a mirror, said with a sigh—

"Ah, but do you not see plainly how freckled I am growing? Look here on the side of my neck."

They looked at the place and found the freckles, indeed as their fair mistress had said; but they called them mere beauty-spots, the faintest touches of the sun, such as would only heighten the whiteness of her delicate complexion. Bertalda shook her head, and still viewed them as a blemish.

"And I could remove them," she said at last, sighing. "But the castle-fountain is covered, from which I formerly used to have that precious

504

water, so purifying to the skin. Oh, had I this evening only a single flask of it!"

"Is that all?" cried an alert waiting-maid, laughing as she glided out of the apartment.

"She will not be so foolish," said Bertalda, well-pleased and surprised, "as to cause the stone cover of the fountain to be taken off this very evening?" That instant they heard the tread of men already passing along the court-yard, and could see from the window where the officious maiden was leading them directly up to the fountain, and that they carried levers and other instruments on their shoulders.

"It is certainly my will," said Bertalda with a smile, "if it does not take them too long." And pleased with the thought, that a word from her was now sufficient to accomplish what had formerly been refused with a painful reproof, she looked down upon their operations in the bright moonlit castle-court.

The men raised the enormour stone with an effort; some one of the number indeed would occasionally sigh, when he recollected they were destroying the work of their former beloved mistress. Their labour, however, was much lighter than they had expected. It seemed as if some power from within the founain itself aided them in raising the stone.

"It appears," said the workmen to one another in astonishment, "ás if the confined water had become a springing fountain." And the stone rose more and more, and almost, without the assistance of the work-people, rolled slowly down upon the pavement with a hollow sound. But an appearance from the opening of the fountain filled them with awe, as it rose like a white column of water, at first they imagined it really to be a fountain, until they perceived the rising form to be a pale female, veiled in white. She wept bitterly, raised her hands above her head, wringing them sadly and with slow and solemn step she moved toward the castle. The servants shrank back, and fled from the spring, while the bride, pale and motionless with horror, stood with her maidens at the window. When the figure had now come close beneath their room, it looked up to them sobbing, and Bertalda thought she recognised through the veil the pale feautres of Undine. But the mourning form passed on sad, reluctant, and lingering, as if going to the place of execution. Bertalda screamed to her maids to call the knight; not one of them dared to stir from her place; and even the bride herself became again mute, as if trembling at the sound of her own voice.

While they continued standing at the window motionless as statues, the mysterious wanderer had entered the castle, ascended the well-known stairs, and traversed the well-known halls, in silent tears. Alas, how different had she once passed through these rooms!

The knight had in the meantime dismissed his attendants. Half-undressed and in deep dejection, he was standing before a large mirror, a wax taper burned dimly beside him. At this moment some one tapped at his door very, very softly. Undine had formerly tapped in this way, when she was playing some of her endearing wiles.

"It is all an illusion!" said he to himself. "I must to my nuptial bed."

"You must indeed, but to a cold one!" he heard a voice, choked with sobs, repeat from without; then he saw in the mirror, that the door of his room was slowly, slowly opened, and the white figure entered, and gently closed it behind her.

"They have opened the spring," said she in a low tone; "and now I am here, and you must die."

He felt, in his failing breath, that this must indeed be; but covering his eyes with his hands, he cried: "Do not in my death-hour, do not make me mad with terror. If that veil conceals hideous features, do not lift it! Take my life, but let me not see you."

"Alas!" replied the pale figure, "will you not then look upon me once more? I am as fair now as when you wooed me on the island!"

"Oh, if it indeed were, so," sighed Huldbrand, "and that I might die by a kiss from you!"

"Most willingly, my own love," said she. She threw back her veil; heavenly fair shone forth her pure countenance. Trembling with love and the awe of approaching death, the knight leant towards her. She kissed him with a holy kiss; but she relaxed not her hold, pressing him more closely in her arms, and weeping as if she would weep away her soul. Tears rushed into the knight's eyes, while a thrill both of bliss and agony shot through his heart, until he at last expired, sinking softly back from her fair arms upon the pillow of his couch a corpse.

"I have wept him to death!" said she to some domestics, who met her in the ante-chamber; and passing through the terrified group, she went slowly out, and disappeared in the fountain.

CHAPTER X

Father Heilmann had returned to the castle as soon as the death of the lord of Ringstetten was made known in the neighbourhood; and he arrived at the very hour when the monk who had married the unfortunate couple was hurrying from the door, overcome with dismay and horror.

When Father Heilmann was informed of this, he replied, "It is all well; and now come the duties of my office, in which I have no need of an assistant."

He then began to console the bride, now a widow, though with little benefit to her worldly and thoughtless spirit.

The old fisherman, on the other hand, though severely afflicted, was far more resigned to the fate of his son-in-law and daughter; and while Bertalda could not refrain from accusing Undine as a murderess and sorceress, the old man calmly said, "After all, it could not happen otherwise. I see nothing in it but the judgment of God; and no one's heart was more pierced by the death of Huldbrand than she who was obliged to work it, the poor forsaken Undine!"

He then assisted in arranging the funeral solemnities as suited the rank of the deceased. The knight was to be interred in a village church-yard, in whose consecrated ground were the graves of his ancestors; a place which they, as well as himself, had endowed with rich privileges and gifts. His shield and helmet lay upon his coffin, ready to be lowered with it into the grave, for Lord Huldbrand of Ringstetten had died the last of his race. The mourners began their sorrowful march, chanting their melancholy songs beneath the calm unclouded heaven; Father Heilmann preceded the procession, bearing a high crucifix, while the inconsolable Bertalda followed, supported by her aged father.

Then they suddenly saw in the midst of the mourning females in the widow's train, a snow-white figure closely veiled, and wringing its hands in the wild vehemence of sorrow. Those next to whom it moved, seized with a secret dread, started back or on one side; and owing to their movements, the others, next to whom the white stranger now came, were terrified still more, so as to produce confusion in the funeral train. Some of the military escort ventured to address the figure, and attempt to remove it from the procession, but it seemed to vanish from under their hands, and yet was immediately seen advancing again, with slow and solemn step, among the followers of the body. At last, in consequence of the shrinking away of the attendants, it came close behind Bertalda. It now moved so slowly, that the widow was not aware of its presence, and it walked meekly and humbly behind her undisturbed.

This continued until they came to the churchyard, where the procession formed a circle round the open grave. Then it was that Bertalda perceived her unbidden companion, and, half in anger and half in terror, she com-

manded her to depart from the knight's place of final rest. But the veiled
female, shaking her head with a gentle denial, raised her hands towards
Bertalda in lowly supplication, by which she was greatly moved, and
could not but remember with tears how Undine had shown such sweetness of spirit on the Danube when she held out to her the coral necklace.

Father Heilmann now motioned with his hand, and gave order for all
to observe perfect stillness, that they might breathe a prayer of silent
devotion over the body, upon which earth had already been thrown. Bertalda knelt without speaking; and all knelt, even the grave-diggers, who
had now finished their work. But when they arose, the white stranger
had disappeared. On the spot where she had knelt, a little spring, of silver
brightness, was gushing out from the green turf, and it kept swelling
and flowing onward with a low murmur, till it almost encircled the mound
of the knight's grave; it then continued its course, and emptied itself
into a calm lake, which lay by the side of the consecrated ground. Even
to this day, the inhabitants of the village point out the spring; and hold fast
the belief that it is the poor deserted Undine, who in this manner still
fondly encircles her beloved in her arms.

LUKARDIS[1]

Jacob Wassermann

IN THE course of the long drawn out revolution which afflicted the
Russian Empire in the last decade but one, a brawl took place in the streets
of Moscow. The immediate cause of this brawl was the exile to Siberia
of thirty-five students of both sexes, who had been celebrating with excessive exuberance the jubilee of a professor whom they revered and who
was the object of police suspicion. A contributing cause was the fact that
the preparations for this celebration had been made in a series of secret
meetings. Certain of the most highly respected families of Moscow were
affected by this harsh measure, and the sorrow and indignation of so many
hitherto peaceful citizens created an atmosphere more fraught with danger
than if it had resulted merely from the instigation of political agitators.

Among the students deported with such cruel haste was a girl named
Anna Pavlovna Nadinsky. She had a brother living in Moscow, Eugene—

[1] From *Worlds' Ends*. Translated by Louis Galantière. Reprinted by permission of
Messrs George Allen und Unwin, Ltd., and Messrs Horace Liveright, Inc.

or, as the Russians say, Evgen Pavlovitch—who was an officer in a regiment of dragoons. Eugene was a proud, handsome young man, twenty-three years old, and apparently assured of a brilliant future. He was excedingly fond of his sister, who had been his close friend and confidante throughout his life. Seeing her now lost to herself and to the world, a prey to the want and humiliation which the years in Siberia would bring, his sorrow was so great, his sense of justice was so deeply outraged, that the very foundations of his existence crumbled, and he determined to protest against the institution in whose services he had, until now, been so eager. What followed seemed to happen of its own accord, and astonished him as much as anybody else. A few days after the arbitrary action of the police, his regiment was ordered out to quell a revolt in the streets. Of a sudden he left the column at the head of which he was riding, jumped down from his horse, and ran towards a barricade which had been hastily erected out of paving-blocks, wheelbarrows, baskets, and articles of furniture. As he ran, he gestured frantically to its defenders in a way they could not misunderstand, particularly since desertions from the army to their ranks, even in the midst of battle, were not uncommon. But scarcely had Nadinsky reached the top of the barricade from whose shelter he hoped to fight against the real enemies of his country, when he was struck by two bullets from the guns trained on him by his dragoons. Hands stretched towards him, eyes filled with enthusiasm welcomed him; he seemed to hear a chant of thanksgiving which stilled his last doubts. Even his name was called aloud, as if some of these revolutionists knew him. Despite his weakness, the joy in their voices seemed to him sufficient reward. He turned, drew his revolver, fired upon the assailants, his former comrades, then plunged forward on his face, the fingers of one hand caught in a cane chair wedged into the barricade.

He was seized immediately by two young men who bore his unconscious form away and laid him on the stone stoop of a house near by. Hastily, they ripped open his coat and shirt, bound up his wound, which was bleeding freely, and looked about in search of help. A pedlar's cart stood at the curb. Its owner had vanished, and its lean little horse seemed frozen in the shafts. Quickly they laid the officer on a bed of vegetables and greens and covered him with leaves. One of them returned to the barricade while the other led the cart down the street, through numerous alleys, and finally into an open square where stood the University hospital. He went on into the courtyard and called an 'interne,' who gave orders at once to place Nadinsky in one of the wards. His wound was severe. One of the bullets had merely grazed his throat, but the other was lodged in his lung and had to be removed by an operation. On the third day, Nadinsky awoke out of a feverish unconsciousness. It was some time before he knew he was and what had befallen him.

Meanwhile, all Moscow had been talking of the young officer's desertion, and the police, through one of its numerous spies, had discovered his hiding-place. An Ispravnik turned up at the hospital to arrest the fatally wounded man. Although the critical condition of the patient was clear even to the policeman's eye, he flourished his written order and insisted upon taking Nadinsky away. An 'interne' was still arguing with him when the surgeon stepped forward, glanced at Nadinsky's apathetic countenance, was touched by his youth, and said: "If he is removed now he will die within fifteen minutes. The police will do better to wait." The Ispravnik stood irresolute. He was still a novice and not yet hardened. Moreover, in the maze of his multiple orders and commissions, he had lost his head. He thought a while, and then declared himself willing to leave the officer in the hospital until his strength had returned in sufficient measure to permit of removal.

Thus, a few days were gained by Nadinsky. During these days the surgeon's sympathy for him grew greater, and he made efforts to interest others in the fate of his patient. Friends appeared who were willing to help him escape. One morning he was taken into a private room. In the evening, a young man arrived with an orderly's uniform in which Nadinsky was to be conveyed to Sokolnikin, a park in the environs of Moscow. In his wakened condition, there was still a life and death chance of saving him. Nadinsky agreed to accompany the young man, for to remain meant the certainty either of death or of life imprisonment in remotest Siberia. In the dead of night, amid snow and ice (for it was the middle of March), he was taken to Sokolnikin, where he lived in the villa of a scientist who was presumed to be above suspicion by the police. But twenty-four hours had scarcely passed when messengers appeared from the city who, after strolling casually and unconcernedly about, entered the villa and announced that the police were again on Nadinsky's track and were planning to swoop down and arrest him the following night. No choice remained, therefore, but to seek another refuge. This scientist, who was of German birth, had living with him his sister, Anastasia Karlovna, a woman whose courage was as great as her kindly spirit. She had been living in Moscow for more then forty years, enjoyed a great many influental and benevolent friends in high position, and was, besides, greatly loved by many of the common folk. It was she who kept house for her brother, nursed the young officer, tended him, and arranged cleverly to conceal his presence in the villa. Her first concern was to procure for Nadinsky a new disguise. Having attired him as a labourer, she conveyed him, with the aid of a total stranger who had offered his services, to the house of a wood-turner in the suburbs. He was able to remain there only the night, for by mornight the wood-turner had become fearful for himself and his family, and refused to harbour the fugitive any longer. Nadinsky was dragged in this way for five days from one house to another, to a coachman's, a widow's, a gardener's, and finally to a laboratory worker's. Each time, at the end of a few hours these people realized to whom they were giving asylum. Fear of the police outweighed considerations of pity and hardened them against the eloquence of Anastasia, whose zeal never flagged. She spent her nights with Nadinsky, for he was not in a condition to be left by himself. He had to be washed, dressed, and have his bandages changed twice a day; the irregularity and excitation of his mode of living prevented his wound from healing rapidly. And now that the laboratory worker, who had been plied with gold and eloquence, refused any longer to shelter Nadinsky, Anastasia Karlovna feared that there was nothing more to be done. Those friends who had stood by her until now could do no more; the police were on their track and every fresh step led in the direction of their ruin. Anastasia herself felt that she was being spied upon and was menaced. She tried for the last time, by prayer and entreaty, to soften the laboratory worker: would he not practise Christian indulgence for only one night more? The life of her brother—for so she represented Nadinsky—was at stake. But her words served only to increase the man's distrust of the business, and she secured merely a respite of three hours. If, at the end of that period, Nadinsky had not been removed from the house, the man would go to the police.

It was now three o'clock in the afternoon. By six, therefore, Anastasia would have to find another hiding-place for her ward. She drifted for a time through the streets, stopping first before one house and then another, but turning back each time at the door in fear of an unfavourable response, or even of betrayal. At last, in her distress, she fell back upon the idea of taking Nadinsky to one of those assignation houses in which rooms are let out to lovers. In such a place only could she introduce a man who carried no passport. Given two days of rest and care, he would pull through, the doctor had told her that morning. Thereafter, he could get to the frontier by himself.

But to carry out this plan she would need an accomplice, a creature who could make the love-affair seem plausible, who was strong, discreet, and intelligent. She thought of all the young women she knew, but none of them seemed suited to such an undertaking. Anastasia had no friends among the revolutionists; moreover, it would be folly to confide in a person who might be under police surveillance. Nor was it possible to consider a woman of the lower class, or any woman to whom one might offer money; it had to be a lady or a girl of good family.

The exertion of the past few days had wearied her. Rather more to be seated somewhere than for refreshment, she went into a little pastry shop and stepped into a twilit back room. Two women sat at a small table, drinking chocolate. Anastasia took a seat absent-mindedly, but she saw presently that the elder of the two women was looking in her direction and greeting her with a friendly nod. She recognized the woman as Anna Ivanovna Schmoll, the deaf-mute wife of a retired general. With her was her daughter Lukardis, a nineteen-year-old girl of unusual beauty. Scarcely had Anastasia glanced at Lukardis when she said to herself: there is the only girl who can to it. Years before she had been a frequent guest at the Schmolls', when Lukardis Nikolaievna was a little girl. She had often played and chatted with the child and remembered her well. She remembered that, already at the age of thirteen, this child had impressed her as do only those people who possess a peculiar quality, a peculiar strength. What sort of quality or strength that was, she had never been able to fathom, much as she had reflected upon it. The mother, Anna Ivanovna, was a rather simple-minded person, pious, apathetic, harmless, unconscious in a vague way of her infirmity.

Anastasia took a seat at their table and, having inquired by look and gesture about the health of the general's wife, began to speak to Lukardis Nikolaievna in a low tone. The general's wife looked inquiringly at Anastasia's lips, but, unable to follow the conversation, she lowered her eyes modestly and refrained from interrupting their speech by any sign of curiosity. Anastasia was conscious of the boldness of her design. and anxious about it. She had no time to lose. It was essential that she speak briefly. In a few sentences she had to tell her story, make an extraordinary demand, arouse Lukardis's innermost sympathies, and at the same time move with care and cunning, for one word, one awkward gesture, could frustrate the whole plan. Lukardis knew nothing of revolutionary trigues. She suspected much, but she had no information about these matters. She lived in a sphere of gentle dreaming, with the dolls of her past and the jewel-cases of her present, with echoes of the comical gallantries of married men and the careful protestations of scented, unmarried men. Yet, there was something in her of the young animal in the forest that listens to the sound of the distant hunt, the tremendous commotion of pain and blood and death. She was ready for action, but unaware of her expectancy. There were moments when she was seized by a vehement unrest, an unreasoning desire, an impulse to escape from the realm of hypocritical calm in which her life was taking shape. But she was afraid of the world, of people; she trembled at each strange hand that was stretched forth to her. It seemed to her that everything that lay outside her home, even outside her room, was troubled, soiled. She never overheard people in conversation in the street without a shudder; never opened a newspaper without the sense that, side by side with all that was savage and mysterious to her in the outer world, there was something unclean, something that would soil her. Even the books she read, a snatch of verse, a street song, a jest, awakened in her this terrible, unconquerable impression.

Motionless, she listened while Anastasia spoke. There was no lure for her in the story; she felt no girlish impurity or lust for excitement. All that she could read in the stern features of Anastasia Karlovna was a call to duty. She had no decision to make. What there was for her to do was immediately and unalterably clear to her.

Lukardis had been engaged these six weeks past to a Petersburg nobleman, a privy councillor named Alexander Mikhailovitch Kussin. Her parents and their friends felt that as the wife of this rich nobleman and enviable future lay before her; and indeed she herself was happy about it. If anything could make her hesitate, it was the thought of him to whom she felt herself bound by a sisterly affection. But when Anastasia, who divined her preoccupation, suggested that she might be tranquil on this point, she wrinkled her forehead and replied that she did not need this assurance. Her fiancé, she said, would never dream for a moment that she might do anything evil or ugly.

"I take it, then, that you have made up your mind to do it," said Anastasia in a low voice, her gray eyes fixed on the girl.

"I have made up my mind to do it," Lukardis answered in an equally low tone without raising her eyes. "But there is one difficulty——."

"Can there still be a difficulty when one has made up one's mind?" Anastasia interrupted sharply, with a note of fanaticism in her voice.

"But how am I to explain my remaining away from home for two days and nights?" asked Lukardis, crossing the fingers of her white hands.

Anastasia stared, gloomily pondering, at a plate of cakes.

Lukardis went on in a whisper. "The only thing possible is to disappear quietly, to leave a letter for mother ——."

"Yes, yes. A few lines. Anything. And beg them to keep it secret. Say you will explain everything on your return. But you too must be silent,

Lukardis Nikolaievna," she added almost menacingly. "You must be as silent as though it had never happened."

Lukardis merely nodded. Her eyes were now wide open and gazing straight in front of her. Anastasia explained down to the last detail how she was to dress and act. After telling her where to come and at what time, she added to their serious conversation—which despite its gravity had lasted but a quarter of an hour—a few jesting remarks, in order that Lukardis might smile and divert any suspicion which might have arisen in the mind of her mother. Then she arose with a lighter heart and went her way.

She returned to Nadinsky and told him what she had planned. He lay on a sofa in the wretched room of the laboratory worker, and pressed her hand. "My life," he said, "is no longer worth such great effort, Anastasia Karlovna. It is a lost life." She retorted that she had hoped for livelier thanks than were contained in these spiritless phrases, and set about changing his dressing. Nadinsky sighed. "What is the use?" he said in a tired voice. "Everything about me is changed, eye, hand, and emotions. I seem to be surrounded by ghosts. I do not seem to mind being cut off from the world. I can see my mother on our estate. As yet, she suspects nothing. I see her opening a locket and looking at a picture in it. It is a picture of me. She does not know that she will never see me again, she has no idea of that, and yet she sheds tears on the locket. But I have no feelings whatever. The world is to me unreal, because I can no longer love anything."

To Anastasia, these words were the ravings of a feverish mind. She shook her head indignantly. After a while, when it had grown dark, a carriage drove up before the door. Anastasia had bought some handsome clothes for Nadinsky, had helped him with his toilette, and now she looked at him critically before once more escorting him downstairs. In the carriage sat Lukardis Nikolaievna Schmoll, heavily veiled. Anastasia handed her a package of gauze bandages, and said to Nadinsky that she would be waiting for him on the second morning thereafter at a certain hour and at a particular place in the railway station. Meanwhile, she added, she would set about procuring him a passport to foreign countries. She gave an address to the coachman, waved her hand in farewell, and the carriage drove off.

Lukardis and Nadinsky sat in silence. Their situation was too unreal, too threatening, too fateful for embarrassment. When the occasional street lamps lit up the interior of the carriage, Lukardis saw that Nadinsky's eyes were closed and his face was pallid. He had given her his hand on

514

first sitting down beside her; that was all. She discovered that his proximity was not frightening her and that silence was easy.

The house to which they drove stood in a remote street. Nadinsky had to summon all his strength to get out of the carriage. He offered Lukardis his arm, but it was rather she who supported him than he her. He asked for two rooms, and was received with great assiduity. Dragging himself with an effort up the stairs, he strove to preserve the air of a man of the world engaged in a passing adventure. In accordance with the custom of the house, a servent was placed at their especial disposal. This person, suffocating in silver-embroidered livery, had malicious pop eyes, wore an unvaryingly insipid smile on his thick lips, and was obsequious in his humility. Lukardis felt her heart contract at his glance. He set the table and stood listening in a doglike manner while Nadinsky, exhausted and indifferent, ordered the dinner, the wines, the champagne. His appraising glance seemed to insist that they be really what they pretended to be. Lukardis was rouged and wore a low cut gown. It was difficult for her to be anything else than herself. She was forced to put off the childlike innocence which shone ordinarily in her face and put on an air of frivolity. She had to chatter, coquette, laugh, throw her arms about Nadinsky, and sit from time to time on his knees. She had to sketch passionate, wanton, seductive gestures. All those things that she had never noticed, never wished to see, never thought about save with horror, known only through careless words and pictures, the things from which she had hitherto averted her mind and her eye, she had now to do in order to deceive this man who came in with plates, bowls, glasses, and bottles, who chilled the champagne, served the food, and then, silently, smilingly spying from under lowered eyelids, awaited further orders. She had to fit herself into the voluptuous lights, the multicoloured cushions, the mirrored walls, for this house with its sham and glitter put her mind in a tumult. Nor was that all. She had to act so as to arouse no doubt about the reality and naturalness of her behaviour. Everything had to be done casually, cunningly, and transparently, with no overt shudder or haste. She had to eat what was set before her, to drink the wines placed before her, and not only the wine in her glass but, when the waiter was out, in Nadinsky's, too, for he might neither drink nor leave his glass filled. She was entirely unaccustomed to drinking, and it filled her with fright and depression to have to continue in this rôle which she played instinctively and out of a spirit of self-scrifice. Whenever the waiter left the room she got up. The terrific tension that strained the muscles of her face gave way to an expression of bewilderment and even of frightened recollection, for it seemed to her that many years had elapsed since she had driven away from the home of her parents. Nadinsky gazed at her in pain and astonishment, sought her as behind a mask, pitied her dumbly, accused himself in a gesture,—and then, with an effort, brought back the studied smile to his lips and continued his acting when the fellow returned.

After the table had been cleared away, a maid came in, wearing a little white cap. She was young, but she appeared old. Her face had grown gray from this life in lamplight and in badly aired rooms. She brought water, tended the fire, asked if there was anything else she could do. Her voice was sweet, but her features were stony with hatred of the upper world, hatred of those who came to this house to indulge themselves in contemptible, quickly snatched pleasures. Lukardis's knees trembled whenever her glance fell on the maid. She was ashamed of her feet, her hands, her neck, and her shoulders. At last this trial too ended, and she was able to lock the door. They were alone. A clock in a tower somewhere struck ten, its tones vibrating through the apartment. Nadinsky went into the adjoining room where stood a double bed over which was stretched a blue satin counterpane. Bereft of strength, he fell upon the bed, and it was only after he had rested thus a quarter of an hour that Lukardis could help him undress. The cover drawn half way up, he lay there with his chest bare. This is a human thing, said Lukardis to herself. Suddenly the tears started in her eyes and she thought with a kind of fright of the red-cheeked face of Alexander Mikhailovitch, her fiancé. She bathed Nadinsky's wound and bound it. As in a dream one sees perfumes, so Nadinsky saw her delicate hand. He was incapable of thanking her. He was afraid to catch her eye, afraid that a glance of gratitude might offend her. He wished that she might be able to look upon him as nothing but a body, a thing devoid of feature and of feeling. And while Lukardis, half shocked and half in pity, was thinking—a human being! he, half blissful and half in fear for her, thought—an unearthly being!

He fell asleep. Lukardis sat motionless in an armchair. She had brought a book in her little bag, but she knew she would be unable to read. She tried to think of her mother, her father, her friends, the last ball, of the opera she had last heard, but she could think of nothing. Everything faded out, everything eluded her. She heard Nadinsky's deep breathing, saw his pale, fine face, wearied by pain,—but he too, he whom she was to tend and guard, seemed out of reach of her thoughts. It was as if miles separated her chair from his bed. She heard tittering on the stairs and shuffling steps in the hall. Voices, women's voices and men's voices, pierced in muffled tones through the walls, from above and from below. Glasses clinked. Then came the sound of a waltz played on a piano with, doubtless, one string missing, for at a certain point there was a hole in the melody, like a gap between two teeth in a smiling mouth. Shrieks arose. The piano was silent. Beyond the wall to the left arose a creaking, and then a sighing note at the sound of which Lukardis's blood curdled in her veins. The smell of perfumes came in from the locked rooms; garments rustled; doors banged open and shut. Every sound called up a picture from which she could not turn away. She trembled, yet, trembling, she had to look. She had never imagined that the world was like this, that this was life. Encounters in the darkness, strange hands clasping one another, forms reeling against suddenly illuminated mirrors, consent given in shameless words, the unknown unveiled, the crypt of mystery emptied, the consecrated soiled, the secret treasures of the imagination cheapened. She covered her face with her hands; the blood rushed to her rouged cheeks and her heart filled with horror.

Nadinsky opened his eyes and moaned. She walked the many miles to his bedside and held forth a glass of water. His forehead was hot. She put a damp cloth over it. At that moment he awoke and began to speak. He spoke in broken sentences of the hospital, the surgeon, Anastasia Karlovna. Whenever he paused, Lukardis interjected a timid word. He said: "To-morrow I shall be strong enough to leave here!" to which she replied: "That is impossible. You are still feverish. Besides, Anastasia Karlovna is not expecting you until the morning after, early, at seven o'clock." These softly spoken words seemed suddenly to show him her soul, her hitherto unclouded youth, her strong clean instincts; but he could not see that she had not stopped trembling. Once more the piano was being played, but this time by a different hand, a rough, riotous, drunken hand. Throughout the performance Nadinsky and Lukardis gazed in torment into each other's eyes. It was past midnight. Out of the silence that fell came a hollow knocking at the street door. Nadinsky half raised himself. His fingers stiffened and his face was full of dark expectancy. Lukardis stood up and listened breathlessly. It was long before the door was opened. Steps sounded on the stair. They gazed in fear at the latched door, waited for the knock that was to decide their terrible fate. Voices reached them from the hall in a hurried exchange of words. Then all grew calm again and their pulses commenced once more to beat regularly. In these three or four minutes they felt themselves strangely united, their strength and their fear were directed against a common enemy. It was as if they had been lifted into the air by a hurricane, propelled against one another breast to breast, and had thrown their arms about each other in order to help avert the crash that threatened. Lukardis forgot herself; Nadinsky forgot himself. He felt only the intensity of her fear, the forfeiture of her happiness, the shame and the misery of her. She, for her part, was thinking courageously of his fate, realizing now for the first time why his life hung in the balance.

Meanwhile sleep had once more overcome the feverish man. But he could not sleep soundly while the glaring electric lights shone upon him. He said nothing about his desire for darkness, out of consideration for Lukardis, but she saw the nervous flicker of his eyelids and guessed what the matter was. She lighted a candle in the adjoining room and switched off the lights. She too was weary. The late hour was like a paralysing poison, and she sought a place to lie down. There was no bed in this room, merely a sofa, whose plush covering filled her with repugnance. She was repelled also by the chairs and the carpet. She rolled back the carpet from the threshold of Nadinsky's room, spread her fur coat on the floor, and lay down. The candle still glowed, but it seemed to bring nearer to her each sound in the house that had until now been vague—a call, a laugh, a single word. And she heard also the beating of the snow on the window-pane; its mildly crackling noise quieted her. She heard the breathing of Nadinsky, and was reminded of her responsibility. Each breath chained her more closely to his destiny. The things that had once been significant became meaningless to her; what she had done, wanted, and been in the course of her life now seemed childish and frivolous. She gazed back longingly, as from the deck of a ship, to the home that faded into the distance. She was asleep, and yet not asleep. Nadinsky had spoken words of comfort and encouragement to her—that was a dream; his throat had rattled feverishly— that was a fact. In dream she bent over him, nursed him; in fact she was chained to the floor, listening to the Bacchic cry of a woman. In the gray light of dawn she saw a rat running across the carpet. It seemed to her fantastically large, and moved, she thought, like a ghost. She rose to her knees and sought the sky in the parting of the curtains, but all that she could see was a vague blot of gray and below it a window out of which peered an angular face. There was a second of crushing helplessness, and then she crept, nay fled, to Nadinsky's bed. His right arm was hanging limp. Beads of perspiration stood on his forehead. He looked frighteningly strange. A painful sense of hatred flared up in her. Yet there was no longer anybody in the world at whom she could look in this fashion. She had much to demand of him, everything, in fact; except for him, her world was but this house.

They had said nothing on their arrival about how long they wished to remain in these rooms. It was customary to let them only for the night.

Anastasia's plan had been that they should lock themselves in until noon, and then declare their wish to spend a second night in the house. A gold-piece to the waiter and another to the chambermaid would suffice for this. But fresh water was needed for Nadinsky's wound; his condition demanded nourishment. If they arose early, how were they to justify staying all day? Nadinsky, who had been lying open-eyed and silent, was the first to broach this subject. He asked her to hand him his coat, drew out his wallet, and gave it to her. Two gold-pieces, he thought, would not be enough; fifty roubles would be better. Lukardis remarked that such extravagance would create suspicion and induce the proprietor to spy upon them. She held the note between trembling fingers. Never had money seemed to her at once so real and so incomprehensible. They were behaving with outward coolness, but their voices seemed smothered. Lukardis said something about the nastiness in the waiter's face, which induced Nadinsky to retort, more spitefully than he intended, that she had certainly led a life excessively sheltered in cotton-wool, since none of these people who lived in dirt and squalor could please. her. He was revolting against the yoke of gratitude which she had laid upon him, and at the same time, trying to draw her out of herself and let light and darkness play about her features. But she gazed sadly at the floor. She granted his point, and thus disarmed him. Her gentleness touched him, but also it goaded him into further cruelty. He protested against the idea that chance alone was responsible for making her his companion during these twenty-eight hours; she seemed to him herself guilty of the humiliation she was suffering, and he was angry with her because of that. He thought of her as having worn, before she met him, only robes of purest white, as having spoken, with those beautiful lips, only meaningless words, the dregs of her pampered class. It was only now, beside her, that he became a true revolutionist. His flight and concealment seemed to him now ignominious, and he imagined that very likely they lowered him in Lukardis's eyes. And therefore he declared suddenly his determination to get up and leave the house. He was trying to show her that it meant nothing to him, indeed, it was his duty, to share the lot of so many of the condemned, who had accomplished more and dared more then he. Once across the frontier, to whom could he be of use? Not to the Russian people, not to his friends, not to his unfortunate sister!

Lukardis begged him to control himself and tried vainly to reason with him, though she had only a child's reasons to present. Then, seeing that he remained obdurate, she assumed a tone of command and the air of a young queen. Of a sudden she was silent. She had heard steps. She raised her finger and pressed it to her lips. Some one stood listening at the door. Her proud glance became a plea for protection, and Nadinsky hung his head. Then Lukardis accepted the inevitable. She tiptoed to the door, unbolted it, hurried back to the bed, and slipped quickly in beside Nadinsky. Pulling the covers up under her chin, she reached for the electric bell-cord and rang. They lay breathless until a knock came. It was the maid. She stood in the doorway with an air of Nornlike gloom and took Nadinsky's order to bring fresh water and call the waiter so that breakfast might be ordered. Back she came with two jugs of water, followed by the waiter. His watchful eye took in the first room and as much of the next as it could see, and to Lukardis it appeared as if he were seeking the clothes she wore as she lay in bed, a circumstance she thought proper to arouse his suspicion. She shut her eyes, for the sight of this man was horrible to her. Nadinsky held out the fifty-rouble note. "Twenty for the maid and thirty for you," he said in a tone of studied indifference. "We shall stay until to-morrow morning, if it can be arranged." The waiter bowed nearly to the ground. He had not looked for so generous a tip. The maid, who was feeding the fire, came over and tried to kiss his hand, but Nadinsky warded her off. "If it please the lady and gentleman, and there is nothing against it," said the waiter with a catlike gesture and a wink. Nadinsky ordered breakfast, and at the end of a quarter of an hour the tea and things were brought in. Meanwhile, Lukardis lay on coals of fire. Her whole body was penetrated with something for which she found no name, a feeling composed of grief and fear, that clouded her face with a deathly pallor. Nadinsky lay motionless, sharing her sensation. He understood her agony and averted his eyes from her. The waiter had set the table, bowed again to the ground, and left. When the maid had gone, Lukardis threw back the cover and rose as if fleeing from flames. She bolted the door and opened a window. Her hair had come unbound, and she let it hang freely, for it covered her bare shoulders. An hour earlier she would have resented appearing thus before Nadinsky, but since she had lain beside him, uncovered despite all covering, immeasurably his, her blood now revolted at the notion of his mercy. It was no longer improper that her hair hang loose about her shoulders.

When the room was filled with fresh air, she shut the window and said to Nadinsky that it was time to change the dressing. Silently, he uncovered the sheet. Even to Lukardis's untrained eyes it was clear that the wound was healing rapidly and that Nadinsky's fever had passed. She was already more adroit then yesterday in the dressing and the binding of the wound. When she had finished she offered him bread and milk. He asked to have a little tea in his milk, and she gave it him. She herself swallowed something in great haste, as if she begrudged her body its hunger. The house was strangely silent. In the street, wagons rolled and children shouted. Nadinsky fell asleep, and Lukardis went into the other room. She pulled off her slippers in order to make no noise, and walked back and forth for hours, holding the strands of her hair in both hands. From time to time she would stand still and muse. Then she would stare at the pictures on the wall without really seeing them. One represented a Leda, holding the swan between her knees. By the door hung another: a German student with a rucksack on his back, flourishing his cap in the direction of a girl with two long braids, looking out of a window. The two rooms were reflected on both sides in the mirrors with the effect of an endless succession of rooms, all of them peopled by the fat, ugly nakedness of Leda, the sentimental student, the bed in which Nadinsky lay asleep, and the portrait of Czar Nicholas that hung above it. Endless, multiple reflections, far into the dim, dim distance. Often, too, she would stand at the window and look at the vehicles and the children, at the snow on the ledges and the faces seen faintly behind window-panes, and it would seem to her that all this, too, was endlessly repeated in the faint distance. Where had the world vanished to? Where was everything she had loved, embraced with harmless affection? Where was she herself, Lukardis, who had spent her life in the elegant boudoir of a general's daughter? Where was Alexander Mikhailovitch, ever ruddy and ever smiling? And where was brilliant Moscow with the tempting displays of its shops, the friendly acquaintances who turned up on every hand, the distinguished young officers and the gay women? Where had the world vanished to? She could see only the man who lay before her in the many mirrors of the many rooms; she could see only his wound on his white skin, his wound that was like a flitting flame which she, with an enchantment put upon her, was forced to follow.

The chimes struck twelve, and it was a long time thereafter, how long she could not judge, before Nadinsky awoke. He sat up, and she came forward with some hesitation. More determinedly than she had expected, he said that she must leave this same evening. He felt strong enough now to stay alone and would intimate to the waiter that she would be back later in the night. And in the night, nobody would bother to think about it again. Lukardis shook her head and said that it was as much for her own sake as for his that she preferred to stay. The scar had only just begun to form, and the wound would need to be dressed at least twice again before he could stir. If she left and he met with an accident, she would never forgive herself. Nadinsky gazed searchingly into her face; then he stretched

521

forth his arm in such fashion that she held out her hand to him. At that moment they both grew frightened .It was like some blissful but disastrous transformation which each underwent in the eyes of the other. Then Lukardis stepped with beating heart before one of the mirrors and pinned up her hair. Her fingers shook. If at this moment he had ordered her to leave, she would probably have gone without protest. But instead he began to lament that he had not died an honourable death in battle; what was he to do in foreign lands, eternally wandering, gnawed by grief and by the ever-present thought of his tortured comrades, worried by the business of earning a bare living? For he was not rich. He had many debts. His mother's estate belonged to his creditors, really. Discouraged by so much discouragement, Lukardis stood still before the mirror and examined her tired face. He went on. He reviled his deed: he had not known what he was taking upon himself; it had been the result of impulse, not of decision; heroes did not act this way, did not deliver themselves up to chance, in order to be crushed. And here was she who had fled with him to this sewer: had she acted with a clear sense of what she was doing, or had she not, in reality, allowed herself to be swept away by sentiment, by pity, by the temptation of the unusual, the seduction of an enthusiastic friend? Had she not been uprooted and shaken, robbed of all her strength by Medusa-like visions? "So are we all," he cried, throwing himself back upon his pillows; "all of us, delivered up, cast down, beggars of fantasy, sacrifices to the moment, deceived by our actions!"

Lukardis moved over and sat on the edge of his bed. Quietly and firmly, she looked into his face. Her eyes gave the lie to his words; there was a soulful harmony in the expression of her features. It was as though, in the simple silence or bewilderment, a godlike nature had come to the aid of its heart. A beam of happiness sped across Nadinsky's brow. His sceptical spirit bowed in shame before the confidence and serenity of this girl, who was able to take him out of himself, out of this house. Night fell. They sat in silence amid the darkness. When it came time to continue the comedy demanded by their situation, Lukardis switched on the light, drew the curtains together, and went out of the room in order that Nadinsky might dress. He called to her after a moment to help him on with his coat. Dinner was served as on the previous evening by the liveried waiter, with even more humility, with a smile even more insipid and any eye even more alert behind his evil grimaces, than before. They sat at table mirthlessly and avoided one another's glance. Only their hands moved,—mute obedient spirits, passing to and fro, pretending a casual innocuousness under the eyes of the spy. This evening Lukardis was playing her part badly. He laughter was artificial, her frivolity was even less convincing. Nadinsky came to her rescue by whispering, when they were alone, that they should pretend to quarrel. He invented the name of a Countess Shuilov and insisted that the collar of pearls she had worn at Princess Karamsin's last reception was false. Lukardis contradicted him. He persisted peevishly in his opinion, and with such success that a crimson glow overspread Lukardis's cheeks. She was astounded at this hypocrisy within hypocrisy and suddenly was afraid of Nadinsky. The waiter came and went, poured champagne, with a look in his face that seemed to implore them to be friends, as if he were afraid of anything else than dove-like cooing. Finally Nadinsky got up ill humouredly and ordered the waiter to clear out. He was amazed by Lukardis's pleading glance. Acting as though he regretted his impetuosity, he stepped towards her with outstretched hands. The waiter grinned with joy. Lukardis too stood up. She let her head fall on his shoulder, but only in order to whisper to him not to forget that the carriage must be ordered for the next morning.

All at once a piercing shriek resounded through the house, followed by a second and then a third cry. Lukardis clasped her hands in fright while Nadinsky looked uneasily in the direction of the door. The waiter stood with a metal tray in the open doorway. A half naked woman ran by. "Shut the door," breathed Lukardis faintly. A shot sounded and the ghastly howl of a man filled the air. Nadinsky pushed the servant out and slammed the door. In a few minutes all was quiet; then steps ran to and fro, voices murmured, a tone of command arose from below and was answered by a wail of lament from above. This was followed by sobs so heartrending that Lukardis ran, wringing her hands, to the sofa, and flung herself face downward upon it. A lively tumult arose in the street, in the midst of which the voice of a policeman was clearly audible. Heavy feet through the hall indicated that some one was being carried out. The waiter came in with a look of contrition in his face and said: "I beg your Excellency to be without anxiety; I beg the lady to calm herself. It is nothing. An insignificant accident has occurred. Your Excellency will not be disturbed again." With this he vanished.

Nadinsky went over to Lukardis and sat down beside her, stroking her hair with a trembling hand. She shrank from his touch and moved her head away. He withdrew his hand, weary of life. A storm rattled at the windows. As if in defiance, the piano sounded again; some one was playing the same waltz, the same gap-toothed melody. Was it only one day, one day and one night, since they had last heard that air? Had not years elapsed? years filled with images and moods, joy and pain, splendour and wretchedness, expectancy and disappointment, greed and deprivation, dream and death? And was this already the end? Was not another night imminent? An endless, mysterious night? To Nadinsky it seemed that in the moment when he had climbed the barricade and been shot, he had stepped into another existence, conditioned by hitherto unknown laws and demands; and that his earlier existence with all that it comported had been shed like a cloak; that on coming into this house he had taken upon himself his destined life, divorced from past and future, devoid of bridges leading either backward or forward.

Oppressed and nerve-racked, he fell upon his bed. Lukardis came in. A lamp burned in the sitting-room, but in this room there was no light. The rooms repeated themselves in the mirrors, gray and vague. Lukardis found that one jug of water was still full, and again she dressed Nadinsky's wound. In drawing the fresh bandage from her bag, she pulled out a book, and when Nadinsky had been bandaged he asked if she would read to him. The book was a volume of Lermontov's poems. Lukardis, in her chair, had read only for a few minutes when her arms fell to her sides, her head sank, and sleep overcame her. Thus without resistance or transition do children fall asleep. Nadinsky was careful not to stir. His eyes clung to her face, and it seemed to him that his own face must follow the change of expression to which her features were being subjected. A sense of ineffable peace entered his soul. He stretched his legs and breathed deeply, as in a garden. Her lips were moving. She was whispering, smilling gently. Her hands opened and the book fell from her lap. She started, opened her eyes, glanced in horror at the dim room, and slept on. Sleep mastered her completely and her body lost its equilibrium so that she would have fallen to the floor had not Nadinsky caught her in his arms. He laid her across his bed, her feet on the chair. Her head rested on his knees, her arms were crossed above it, and her breast rose and fell in a powerful rhythm. Gradually Nadinsky commenced to feel her weight; the blood ceased to circulate in his thighs, and it was hard for him to remain motionless. He let himself fall back on his pillows, slipped his hands under the covers and under the girl's back, and tried thus to hold up the unconscious body. In this way the burden fell in rotation on the arms, the thighs, and the knees. A glow of happiness went through him. He felt that he was repaying her care and trouble, and also he was happy because she was so close to him, so utterly under his protection. His eyes dwelt long on the sleeping girl while his mind was filled with a rapturous gratitude. Her life, her slumber, the lines of her relaxed and unconscious form, each of which seemed a sort of spiritual barrier against the chaos of the world, filled him with a sense of limitless bliss and poured new strength into his heart.

She had been asleep for hours when she was awakened by the drums of a military patrol marching through the street. Ndinsky was pulling himself up to a sitting posture when he saw that her eyes were full of dull astonishment. They seemed to be trying to glow serenely, and then to be covered by a veil of shame. Lukardis uttered a little cry, and sprang up. Her face was suffused with blood. She pressed her hands to her breast and looked mutely ahead; and although Nadinsky spoke to her, she continued to appear embarrassed. He made an effort to speak casually, inquiring about the weather and the hour. She answered absentmindedly, her face revealing alternately shyness and fright, and gratitude and secret questioning. For the last time she washed and bound Nadinsky's wound, maintaining, meanwhile, her composure with difficulty. The world outside seemed to her like the open jaws of a savage beast. It was a quarter to six. They had to make themselves ready. Nadinsky was growing more and more calm; he was very pale, when, having dressed, he went into the other room where Lukardis stood. They sat opposite each othe at the table. Lukardis was wearing her hat and fur coat; her handbag lay at her feet. Thus they waited in silence and with averted eyes for the time of their deliverance.

The clatter of wheels sounded finally in the street, and in a moment there was a knock on their door. The waiter came in wearing not his livery but a greasy bathrobe. His hair hung in oily strands over his forehead and his face was sullen and evil. He presented the bill, which Nadinsky paid, including at the same time the coachman's fee. They went downstairs. Two pails filled with sweepings stood at the foot of the stairs, and in the entrance lay a black dog. The dog followed them, sniffing, to the carriage. Not a soul was to be seen in the streets as they drove the long way to the station.

In one of the waiting-rooms stood Anastasia Karlovna, beside a pillar. She greeted them and asked about Nadinsky's condition. Then she handed him a passport and a filled travelling bag, they hurried out to the platform, and Nadinsky took his place in the train. After a moment he came back, walked over to Lukardis, and stretched forth his hand. An unaccountable lack of muscular response prevented Lukardis's lifting her head and turning her face towards him. He took both her hands in his, and the four hands lay together like the links of a chain. So they remained for a moment and seemed to themselves figures in a dream. Anastasia Karlovna gestured warningly. With a dragging step, Nadinsky turned back to the car and climbed in, placing himself at the window where, in the black frame and the gray of the fog, his face was a chalk-white blot. The whistle blew, and the train rolled slowly out of the station.

When Lukardis reached home she found her mother dissolved in tears. The poor woman had not dared tell her husband of Lukardis's letter, and had been at great pains to keep her disappearance from his knowledge. A strange argument ensued between daughter and mother, a scene in which the deaf and dumb mother gesticulated in her most excited and imploring manner while the girl merely shook her head and told nothing. Bit by bit the general's wife grew uneasy about Lukardis, and this uneasiness grew into dismay when the girl refused to see her fiancé, who had turned up for a few days in Moscow. Even her fater's anger could not move her. She spoke no word, but looked calmly at the ground. The engagement was broken; and even more deliberately than before, Lukardis persisted in avoiding other people—friends, strangers, parents, sisters. She retired deep within herself, became a different person. The doctors having counselled travel, her mother took her first to Paris and then by the sea in Brittany. One night the general's wife came upon her daughter unexpectedly as she lay out on the flasgtone terrace of her room. Hands folded behind her head, the girl was gazing with wide-open indescribably brilliant eyes, upward at the starry heavens. In her face was an expression of infinite loneliness.

Nadinsky had vanished. Several people insisted that he was living on a farm in western Canada, but Lukardis never heard his name spoken, nor heard he ever hers.

AUSTRIA

REDEGONDA'S DIARY[1]

Arthur Schnitzler

YESTERDAY night, as I was sitting for a while on a bench in the park on my way home, I suddenly saw a man of whose presence I had been quite unaware leaning back in the opposite corner. As there is no lack of empty benches at this late hour, the appearance of this nocturnal neighbour struck me as rather suspicious; and I was just about to make a move when the stranger, who was wearing a long grey overcoat and yellow gloves, raised his hat, addressed me by name, and wished me good evening. And I recognised him with a feeling of agreeable surprise. It was Dr Gottfried Wehwald, a well-mannered young gentleman, with, indeed, a certain distinction of demeanour, which seemed to be, to him at least, a source of perpetual silent satisfaction. About four years before he had been transferred from the offices of the Vienna municipality to a small country town in Lower Austria, but emerged from time to time among his friends at the *café*, where he was always greeted with that restrained warmth that seemed appropriate to his elegant reserve. So I thought it better, although I had not seen him since Christmas, to display no sort of surprise at the time and place of our meeting: I returned his greeting politely but with an air of indifference, and prepared to start a conversation as between men men of the world who must not show the slightest surprise if they happened to run across each other in Australia, when, with an impatient wave of the hand, he remarked shortly:

"I beg your pardon, my dear fellow, but my time is limited, and I have come here specially to tell you a rather singular story, provided, of course, that you are willing to hear it."

I was rather taken aback by this address; however, I said I was quite ready to listen, but I could not help expressing my surprise that Dr Wehwald had not come to see me at the *café* how he had succeeded in finding me at night here in the park; and why I should be selected for the honour of listening to his story.

"The answer to the first two questions," he replied, with unusual

[1] From *Little Novels*. Translated by Eric Sutton. Reprinted by permission of the author, Messrs Constable and Co., and Messrs Simon and Schuster.

sharpness, "will appear in the course of my narration. My choice fell on you, my dear fellow" (as he continued to address me), "because I knew you were something of an author, and I thought I might rely on my strange but rather unconventional communication being tolerably reproduced and published."

I made some deprecatory remark, whereupon Dr Wehwald, with a singular twitch of the nostrils, began without further preamble:

"The heroine of my story is called Redegonda. She was the wife of a cavalry Captain, Baron T., of the X Dragoons, then quartered in our little town of Z." (He actually used these letters, although not only the name of the little town, but for reasons that will soon appear, both the captain's name and the number of the Dragoon regiment could be no secret to me.) "Redegonda," proceeded Dr Wehwald, "was a woman of extraordinary beauty, and I fell in love with her, as the phrase goes, at first sight. Unfortunately, I had no opportunity of making her personal acquaintance, as the officers scarcely mixed at all with the civil population and extended this exclusiveness, in a manner that was almost offensive, to those who, like myself, were members of the administrative services. So I only saw Redegonda from afar, alone or by her husband's side, and often in the company of other officers and officers' wives, walking through the streets: many a time I caught sight of her at a window of her house on the Central Square, or saw her in the evening driving in a jolting carriage to the little theatre, when I had the satisfaction of looking up from the pit to her box, which was much frequented by young officers in the intervals. Sometimes it seemed as though she condescended to notice me. But her glance flashed on me for so brief an instant and then passed that I could draw no conclusions from it.

"I had already given up the hope of ever being able to lay my homage at her feet when one marvellous autumn morning she came upon me quite unexpectedly in the small park-like wood that stretches from the eastern gate of the town far into the country. With an imperceptible smile she passed me by—perhaps, in fact, she did not notice me—and had soon disappeared behind the yellowing foliage. I had let her pass without even considering whether I could have greeted her or addressed so much as a word to her; and now that she had disappeared from my ken I did not think of regretting that I had not tried, since I could hardly have expected any success. But then something singular happened. I felt myself suddenly impelled to imagine what would have been the result if I had found the courage to go up and speak to her. And, in my fancy, I saw Redegonda, so far from repulsing me, not trying to conceal her satisfaction at my boldness, and in the course of a lively conversation freely lamenting the emptiness of her existence and the inferiority of her society, and expressing her pleasure at having found in me an understanding and sympathetic soul. And so encouraging was the look she gave me at parting that on the evening of the same day—all this, including the parting glance, existing only in my imagination—when I saw her again in her box, I felt just as though a precious secret made an invisible bond between us. You will not be surprised, my dear fellow, that I, who had received so extraordinary a proof of the power of my imagination, was careful we should soon meet again in the same way, and upon each occasion the intercourse should grow more friendly, more confidential, and more ardent, until one lovely day, under the now leafless branches, the adored one sank into my longing arms. Then I gave rein to my delicious frenzy and it was not long before Redegonda visited me in my small lodging at the far end of the town, and I knew such intoxicating bliss the like of which paltry reality had never brought to me. We did not lack dangers, either, to season our adventure. It happened once in the course of the winter that the Captain galloped past us as we were driving, covered with furs, along a country road into the night: and already there arose in my mind a foreboding of what was soon to come upon us with the full weight of destiny. In early spring it was reported in the town that the Dragoon regiment, to which Redegonda's husband belonged, was to be transferred to Galicia. My—nay, our—despair was boundless. Nothing that could enter lovers' minds in such extremity, nothing was left unsaid: we would fly together, die together, or sadly acquiesce in the inevitable. However, the last evening came without our having made a definite resolution. I was expecting Redegonda in my flower-decked room. So as to be prepared for all emergencies my trunk was packed, my revolver loaded, and my farewell letters written. That, my dear fellow, is actual fact. For so entirely had I been mastered by my madness that I not merely thought that, on this, the last evening before the regiment went off, my mistress would be able to come, but I actually expected her. I could not, as of old, summon up her shadow picture, dream the heavenly creature into my arms; no, I felt as though something unaccountable, perhaps frightful, was holding her at home. A hundred times I went to the door, listened down the stairs, looked out of the window, strained my eyes to see Redegonda approaching along the street. Yes, in my impatience, I was on the point of rushing forth to find Redegonda, clasp her to me, and, with the right of the lover and his beloved, claim her from her husband— until at last, stricken as though by fever, I sank down upon my divan. Then suddenly—it was near midnight—the bell rang outside. For the ring at the bell, you must understand, was no longer imagination. It rang a second and third time, and its tinkle, shrill and not to be denied, awoke me to the full consciousness of reality. But at the same moment, as I recognised that until this evening my adventure had been but a strange succession of dreams, I felt a rash hope awake within me—a hope that Redegonda, gripped in her very soul by the power of my longing, had been drawn and driven to my house, and now stood outside upon my threshold, and that in another minute I should hold her very self in my arms. In this delicious expectation I went to the door and opened it. But it was not Redegonda that stood before me, it was Redegonda's husband: he himself, as real and as living as you who sit at the other end of this bench, and he stared into my face.

"There was, of course, nothing for me to do but to let him come into my room, where I invited him to sit down. But he remained standing, and, with an expression of indescribable contempt on his lips, he said:

" 'You are expecting Redegonda. Unfortunately she is prevented from coming. She is, in fact, dead.' 'Dead!' I repeated, and the world stood still. Unmoved, the Captain continued: 'An hour ago I found her sitting at her writing-table, with this small book in front of her, which, to avoid any possibility of misunderstanding, I have brought with me. She probably died of fright when I came so unexpectedly into the room. These lines here are the last she wrote. Look!'

"He handed me a small open book, bound in violet leather, and I read the following words:

" 'Now I am leaving my home for ever; my lover waits for me.'

"I merely nodded slowly, as if in confirmation.

" 'You will have guessed,' continued the Captain, 'that what you have in your hand is Redegonda's diary. Perhaps you will have the goodness to look through it, so as to make any attempt at denial useless.' I looked it through—no, I read it. I read it for nearly an hour, while the Captain sat motionless on the divan; I read the whole history of our love—that sweet and marvellous tale in all its details: the autumn morning when I first spoke to Redegonda in the wood; our first kiss; our walks; our trips into the country; our hours of bliss in my flower-decked room; our plans for death and flight; our happiness and our despair. All was there, set down in those pages, all that had never happened to me in reality, and yet exactly as it had happened in my imagination. And I did not find that at all so inexplicable as you, my dear fellow, seem clearly to find it at this moment. For it came over me that Redegonda had loved me as I had loved her, and that she had thus acquired the mysterious power of realising

530

in her own imagination the adventures that took place in mine. And since she, being a woman, was nearer than I to the springs of life, where desire and fulfilment are one, she was probably profoundly convinced that she had really felt and done all that was set down in her little violet book. But there was yet another thing that I thought possible: that the whole diary was nothing more nor less than a deliberate revenge upon me, a revenge for my irresolution in not letting my, and her, dreams become a reality; yes, that her sudden death was the work of her own will, and that it had been her intention in this way to get the treacherous diary into her deceived husband's hands. But I had no time to dwell upon these problems; for the Captain there could be only one—the natural—explanation, and I placed myself at his disposal in the words appropriate to such occasions."

"Without attempting..."

"To deny anything?" interrupted Dr Wehwald sharply. "Oh, even if such an attempt had had the slightest prospect of success, it would have seemed to me deplorable. For I felt myself entirely responsible for all the consequences of an adventure that I had wanted to experience, though I had been too cowardly to try. 'I am anxious,' said the Captain, 'to dispose of our business before Redegonda's death is known. It is now one in the morning; our witnesses can meet at three, and by five o'clock the affair should be over.' I again nodded as a sign of understanding. The Captain departed with a cold salutation. I put my papers in order, went out of the house, fetched two acquaintances of mine from the office out of their beds—one was a Count—told them no more than was necessary to get them to despatch the affair as quickly as possible, and then walked up and down the Central Square, opposite the darkened windows behind which I knew Redegonda's body was lying, and I had the clear conviction that the fulfilment of my destiny was upon me. At five in the morning, in the little wood, quite near the place where I could have spoken to Redegonda the first time, the Captain and I faced each other, pistol in hand."

"And you killed him?"

"No. My bullet grazed his temple. But he shot me through the heart. I fell dead on the spot, as the phrase goes."

"What!" I gasped, turning a perplexed glance on my singular neighbour. But there was no one. Dr Wehwald was no longer sitting in the corner of the bench. Indeed, I have reasons for thinking that he had never sat there. On the other hand I at once remembered that in the *café* yesterday evening there had been much talk of a duel in which our friend, Dr Weh-

531

wald, had been shot by a cavalry Captain of the name of Teuerheim. The circumstance that Frau Redegonda, on the very same day, had vanished into space with a young Lieutenant of the regiment, roused the company, out of their serious mood, to a sort of melancholic amusement, and they were all inclined to suspect that Dr Wehwald, whom we had all known as the paragon of correctness, discretion, and refinement, had—quite in his own style—half willingly and half against his will, paid for another's happiness with his own death.

As regards the appearance of Dr Wehwald on the park bench, it would certainly have considerably gained in impressiveness and singularity if it had been forthcoming before the chivalrous end of the Original. And I will not deny that it did occur to me to heighten the effect of my narrative by this quite trifling alteration. But after brief reflection I shrank before the possibility of the charge that the description of such a mystery provided fresh evidence for spiritualism and other dangerous matters, and I foresaw enquiries as to whether the story was true or fictitious and whether I believed such happenings were possible or not—and I should have had before me the painful alternative of figuring, in accordance with my answer, as an occultist or a fraud. Finally, therefore, I thought it better to set down the history of my nocturnal encounter exactly as it happened, fully realising the danger that many people will, even so, doubt its truth—in that widespread mistrust which authors, though with less reason than most other people, always seem to provoke.

SWITZERLAND

DOROTHEA'S ROSE-BASKET[1]

Gottfried Keller

But so to lose oneself is rather to find oneself.
FRAN. LUDOV. BLOSIUS, *Spiritual Instrucion*, ch. xii.

ON THE southern shores of the Euxine Sea, not far from the mouth of the river Halys, a Roman country house lay in the light of the most brilliant spring morning. A north-east wind bore a refreshing coolness from the waters of the sea through the gardens, and the heathens and the secret Christians revelled in it like the leaves which quivered on the trees.

In a bower near the sea, apart from the rest of the world, stood a young couple, a handsome young man facing a most tender girl. She was holding up for the admiration of the youth a big, finely chased cup of translucent red stone; the morning sun shone gloriously through the cup, and its ruddy glow on the girl's face concealed her own blushes.

She was Dorothea, a patrician's daughter, who was being ardently wooed by Fabricius, the Governor of the province of Cappadocia. But, as he was a bigoted persecutor of the Christians, while Dorothea's parents felt drawn towards the new faith and were doing their utmost to adopt it completely, they resisted as best they could the importunities of the mighty inquisitor. Not that they desired to drag their children into spiritual conflicts and use their hearts as the price of their faith—they were much too noble and large-minded for that—but they thought that a religious persecutor was hardly the man to satisfy the needs of the heart.

Dorothea herself had no need of such considerations, for she possessed another safeguard against the Governor's suit, namely, her attachment to his scribe Theophilus, who was at that very moment standing beside her and looking strangely into the cup.

Theophilus was a man of Hellenic extraction, cultured of mind and noble of stature, who had, by his own efforts, risen above adverse circumstances, and was held in high esteem. But the trials of his youth had implanted a certain distrust and reserve in his character, and while he was satisfied with what he owed to nobody but himself, he did not find it easy

---

[1] From *The People of Seldwyla*, translated by M. D. Hottinger. Reprinted by permission of Messrs J. M. Dent and Sons, Ltd.

to believe that anyone could be attached to him of their own free will. The sight of the youthful Dorothea was life itself to him, but the mere fact that the most distinguished man in Cappadocia was paying court to her prevented him from having any hope for himself, and for nothing in the world would he have wished to cut a ridiculous figure beside that gentleman.

Nevertheless, Dorothea was trying to lead her wishes to a happy issue, and, for the present, to ensure his presence near her as often as possible. And as he always maintained his calm indifference, her passion grew. She took to clumsy little stratagems, and tried to move him by jealousy, pretending to take a great deal of notice of Fabricius and to treat him more kindly. But poor Theophilus did not understand tricks of that kind, and if he had, he would have been too proud to show his jealousy. Nevertheless, he gradually grew troubled and perplexed, and betrayed himself from time to time, but only to remaster himself at once and withdraw behind his reserve, and the sensitive, loving girl saw nothing for it but to precipitate matters a little and draw the net tighter at the right moment.

He was staying in the Pontine district on state business, and Dorothea, knowing this, had accompanied her parents from Cæsarea to spend the early spring days there. And this morning she had, with much pains, thought out a clever way of enticing him into the bower, half as if by chance, half as if with kind intentions, so that both his good luck and the kindness showed him might make him more cheerful and confiding, as indeed they did.

She was just showing him the vase, which a kindly uncle had sent from Trebisond for her birthday. Her face was glowing with joy to be alone with her loved one beside her, and to have something beautiful to show him, and he too was glad. The sun at last rose within him, he could not keep a trustful smile from his lips and his eyes shone.

But the ancients have forgotten to give a name to the envious god who, standing beside the lovely Eros, casts a veil over the eyes of lovers at the fateful moment when happiness stands nearest, and twists their words in their mouths.

When she laid the cup confidingly in his hands and he asked who had given it to her, her joyous excitement betrayed her into answering mischievously with the name of Fabricius, for she felt sure that he could not miss the joke. As she was incapable of giving her happy, excited smile that trace of mockery for the absent Fabricius which would have made her fun obvious, Theophilus was convinced that her charming, spontaneous joy was only for the gift and the giver, and that he had fallen into a cruel trap by stepping into a circle which was closed and strange to him. Speechless with mortification, he dropped his eyes and let the shining vase fall to the ground, where it broke in pieces. In her first dismay, Dorothea quite forgot her joke, and even Theophilus too, a little, and bent down sadly to pick up the pieces, crying "How clumsy!" without looking at him, and so she did not notice the change in his face and had no inkling of the misunderstanding.

When she rose again and, recovering herself, turned to him, Theophilus had already proudly mastered himself. He looked at her with sombre indifference, asked her pardon in almost mocking tones, promising full reparation for the shattered vase, bowed to her and left the garden.

Pale and sad, she looked after his slim figure as he drew his white toga firmly round him, while his black curly head drooped to one side as if his thoughts were already busy far away from her.

The waves of the silver sea lapped softly and slowly against the marble steps on the shore, all else was still, far and wide, and Dorothea was at the end of her little wiles.

Weeping, she gathered up the fragments of the cup and carried them to her room to hide them there.

They did not see each other again for months. Theophilus went straight back to the capital, and when Dorothea returned too in the autumn, he carefully avoided a meeting, for the mere possibility of seeing her again made him anxious and restless, and so the whole story was at an end for the time being.

So now it came about quite naturally that Dorothea sought comfort in her parents' new creed, and as soon as they noticed this, they did not hesitate to encourage their child and to lead her for good and all into their new ways of faith and expression.

Meanwhile, Dorothea's pretended kindness had had its unlucky effect on the Governor, and Fabricius redoubled the vehemence of his wooing, imagining he was justified in doing so. He was all the more aghast when Dorothea would scarcely look at him, and he seemed to have become more repugnant to her than her own unhappiness. But he did not withdraw; on the contrary, he increased his importunities by beginning to take her to task for her new faith and to assail her conscience, mingling flattery with ill-concealed menaces. Yet Dorothea confessed her faith openly and fearlessly and turned form him as from an incorporeal shadow which passes unseen before the eyes.

Theophilus heard of all this, and of the unhappy life his beloved was leading. He was most surprised by the news that she would simply have nothing to do with the Proconsul. Although his religious attitude was antique or indifferent, yet the maiden's new faith caused him no difficulty, and, full of sympathy, he began to approach her again in order that he might better see and hear how things were going. But wherever she was and whatever she was doing, she could speak of nothing save, in the most tender and longing expressions, of a Heavenly Bridegroom she had found, who was waiting for her in immortal beauty to take her to His shining breast, to place in her hand the roses of eternal life, and so on.

He simply could not understand this manner of speech at all. It vexed and hurt him and filled his heart with strange aching jealousy against the unknown god who was thus perverting the mind of a frail woman, for he could only interpret Dorothea's way of speaking in her lonely, excited state in the old mythological fashion. But while it did not wound his pride to be jealous of an immortal, his sympathy grew dumb for a woman who boasted of her union with the gods. And yet it was her fruitless love for him which put those expressions into her mouth, just as he himself had never lost the sting of passion in his heart.

So things went on awhile, when Fabricius suddenly brought matters to a head. Under the pretext of renewed imperial orders for the persecution of the Christians, he had Dorothea and her parents cast into prison. But the daughter he ordered to be put alone into a dungeon and searchingly examined in her faith. He himself approached curiously and heard how, with a loud voice, she confessed Christ alone the only Lord of the world and her sole Betrothed. Then a furious jealousy took possession of the Governor. He resolved to destroy her, commanded that she should be tortured, and, if she stood firm, put to death. She was laid on an iron grill which was heated in such a way from beneath that the heat increased but slowly. But how it hurt the tender body! From time to time she uttered stifled screams, her limbs, bound to the grill, quivered, and tears flowed from her eayes. Meanwhile Theophilus, who generally refrained from taking any part in such persecutions, had heard what was going on and hurried to the spot, uneasy and afraid. Forgetting his own safety, he pushed his way through the gaping crowd, and when he heard Dorothea herself softly moaning, he snatched a sword from a soldier and with one bound was standing by her bed of martyrdom.

"Does it hurt, Dorothea?" he said, with a painful smile, and set about cutting her bonds. But she answered, as if all her pain had left her, and a great joy was in her, 'How should it hurt, Theophilus? These are the roses of my beloved Bridegroom on which I lie. For see, to-day is my wedding-day."

A sweet, mischievous humour seemed to play about her lips, and her eyes as she looked at him were filled with rapture. An unearthly light seemed to transfigure her and her couch and a solemn stillness spread over all. Theophilus let his sword fall, threw it away and retired, again humiliated and ashamed as on that morning in the garden by the sea.

Then the fire blazed up anew. Dorothea sighed and prayed for death, and it was granted to her. She was led out to the place of execution to be beheaded.

She moved forward with a light step, followed by the heedless, shouting mob. She saw Theophilus standing by the way, his eyes fixed on her. Their eyes met, Dorothea stood still a moment and said, "O Theophilus, could you but know how sweet and glorious are the rose-gardens of my Lord, to which I am going, and how sweet are the apples which grow there, you would come with me!"

Then Theophilus answered with a bitter smile, "I'll tell you what, Dorothea. Send me a few of your roses and apples once you are there, that I may try them!"

Then she nodded kindly to him and went her way.

Theophilus stood looking after her until the cloud of dust, gilded by the evening sun, which accompanied the procession, had disappeared in the distance and all was still. Then, with veiled head, he went to his house, and climbed with faltering steps to the roof, whence he could see the Argeus mountains, on one of whose foothills the place of execution lay. He could quite well see a dark swarm of people there and stretched out his arms in longing towards it. Then it seemed to him that he saw the flash of the falling axe in the glow of the setting sun, and fell himself to the ground. And indeed, Dorothea's head had fallen at that instant.

But he had not long lain there motionless when a bright light illumined the dusk, passed dazzling under Theophilus's hands, on which his face lay, and poured into his eyes like liquid gold. And at that moment a sweet perfume filled the air. As if inspired with strange new life, the young man arose. A lovely boy stood before him with golden curls, clad in a starry robe, with shining bare feet, and carrying in his shining hands a little basket. The little basket was full of roses such as no mortal eye had ever seen, and on the roses lay three apples of Paradise. With an infinitely warm-hearted and candid childish smile, and yet not without a certain pretty mischief, the child said, "This comes from Dorothea," gave him the basket and said, "Have you really got it fast?" and vanished.

And Theophilus in fact was holding the little basket in his hands, for it had not vanished. In each apple there was the mark of two little teeth, as was the custom among lovers of old times. He ate them slowly, with the flaming starry sky above him. Violent longing streamed through him like sweet fire, and, pressing the basket to his breast and veiling it with his mantle, he hurried down from the roof, through the streets and into the Governor's palace. The Governor was at table, trying to benumb with Colchian wine the wild rage which filled him.

With shining eyes, Theophilus came before him, and without uncovering his basket, cried in the face of the whole house, "I confess the faith of Dorothea, whom you have slain. It is the only true faith!"

"Then follow the witch," answered the Governor, who, racked with sudden anger and burning jealousy, sprang up and ordered his scribe to be beheaded within the hour.

So, that very day, Theophilus was eternally united to Dorothea. She received him with the calm gaze of the blessed. Like two doves, parted by a storm, who have found each other again, and at first circle widely round their home, the united pair hovered hand in hand, swiftly, swiftly and without a pause, round the uttermost circles of Heaven, untrammelled by earthly weight and yet themselves. Then in sport they parted, and were lost in infinite distance, though each knew where the other was and what the other thought, and together with the other embraced all creatures and all life in sweet love. Then they sought each other again with growing longing which knew no pain and no impatience. They found each other again, and floated away together, or rested in contemplation of each other and gazed near and far into the infinite world. But once, in sweetest oblivion, they came too near the crystal house of the Holy Trinity and went in. There they lost consciousness, for, like twins in their mother's womb, they fell asleep and are probably sleeping still, unless in the meantime they have been able to find their way out again.

SPAIN

THE SPANISH-ENGLISH LADY[1]

Miguel de Cervantes

AMONGST the spoils which the English carried away from the city of Cadiz,[2] Clotaldo, an English gentleman, captain of a squadron of ships, brought to London a girl of the age of seven years, little more or less; and this, contrary to the will and knowledge of the Earl of Essex,[3] who with great diligence caused search to be made for the child, that she might be returned back to her parents. For they had complained unto him of the wanting of their daughter, humbly beseeching him that since his Excellency was pleased to content himself with their goods, and had left their persons free, that they only might not be so miserable and unhappy; and that seeing they were now left poor, they might not be robbed of their daughter, who was the joy of their hearts, the light of their eyes, and the fairest and most beautiful creature that was in all the city. The Earl caused proclamation to be made throughout all the whole fleet, that upon pain of death he whosoever had the child should restore her back to her parents. But no penalties nor fears of punishment could move Clotaldo to obey the Earl's command; for he kept her very secret and close in his own ship, standing wonderfully affectioned, though very Christianly, to the incomparable beauty of Isabella (for so was the child called).

In conclusion, her parents remained without her very sad and disconsolate, and Clotaldo beyond measure exceeding glad and joyful. He arrived in London, and delivered up this fair maid as a most rich spoil to his wife; but as good luck would have it, all they of Clotaldo's house were Catholics in heart, though in public they made show to follow the religion of their Queen.

Clotaldo had a son named Ricaredo,[4] about some twelve years of age, taught by his parents to love and fear God, and to be acquainted with all the truths of the Catholic faith. Catalina,[5] the wife of Clotaldo, a noble Christian, and prudent lady, bare such great love and affection to Isabella

---

[1] Translated by James Mabbe.
[2] June, 1596.
[3] Cervantes has *Leste* (Leicester).
[4] Richard.
[5] Katherine.

that as if she had been her own daughter she bred, cherished, and instructed her; and the child had such good natural abilities that she did easily apprehend and learn whatsoever they taught her. With time, and the kind usage she received, she went forgetting those cockerings of her true parents, but not so much that she did cease to think on them and to sigh often for them; and although she went learning the English tongue, yet did she not lose her Spanish, for Clotaldo took care to bring Spaniards secretly to his house to talk and converse with her; and so, without forgetting her own natural language, she spake English as well as if she had been born in London.

After that they had taught her all manner of needlework which a well-bred damsel could or ought to learn, they taught her to read and to write more than indifferently well. But that wherein she did excel was in playing upon all those instruments of music which might with most decency become a woman, accompanying the same with such a voice, which Heaven had bestowed on her in so rare and singular a kind, that when she chanted she enchanted all that heard her.

All these her acquired graces, besides those that were natural unto her, went by little and little kindling the coals of love in Ricaredo's heart; to whom, as to her master's son, she wished all good and happiness, and carried herself towards him with all fair respects.

At first love led him on with only a kind of liking and complacency in beholding the unmatchable beauty of Isabella, and in considering her infinite virtues and graces, and loving her as if she had been his sister, his desires not going beyond their honest and virtuous bounds. But whenas Isabella began to grow towards woman (for then when Ricaredo burned in the flames of love she was twelve years of age) that his former goodwill and that complacency and liking was turned into most fervent desires of enjoying and possessing her; not that he did aspire thereunto by any other means than by those of being her husband, since that from the incomparable virtue of Isabella (for so did they call her) no other thing could be hoped for, neither would he himself, though he could, have expected that favour from her, because his noble condition and the high esteem wherein he held Isabella would not give the least way or consent that any the least evil thought should take any rooting in his soul.

A thousand times did he determine with himself to manifest the love he bare her to his parents, and again as oft did he not approve this his determination, because he knew that they had dedicated him for to be the husband of a very rich and principal gentlewoman, a Scottish damsel, who was likewise, like them, in secret a Catholic Christian; and it was clear and apparent, as he conceived and said with himself, that they would not be willing to give unto a slave (if this name may be given to Isabella) that which they had treated and in a manner concluded on to give to a gentle-woman; and therefore being much perplexed and pensive, not knowing what course to take for to attain to the end of his good desire, he passed such a kind of life as had almost brought him to the point of losing it. But it seeming unto him to be great cowardice and faint-heartedness to suffer himself to die without seeking out some kind of remedy for his grief, he did hearten and encourage himself to open his mind and declare his intent to Isabella.

All they of the house were very sad and heavy and much troubled by reason of Ricaredo's sickness, for he was well beloved of them all; but his father and mother were exceeding sorrowful, as well for that they had no other child as also for that his great virtue, valour, and understanding did deserve it. The physicians did not hit right upon his disease, neither durst he, neither would he, discover it unto them.

In the end, being fully resolved to break through these difficulties which he imagined with himself, one day amongst the rest that Isabella came in to serve and attend him, seeing her all alone, with a low voice and a troubled tongue he spake unto her after this manner:

"Fair Isabella, thy much worth, thy great virtue, and exceeding beauty, not to be equalled by any, have brought me to that extremity wherein you see me; and therefore if you will that I should leave my life in the hands of the greatest extremity that may be imagined, let thy good desire be answerable unto mine, which is no other than to receive thee for my spouse. But this must be carried closely, and kept hid from my parents, of whom I am afraid (who because they know not that which I know, thy great deservingness) that they will deny me that good which doth so much concern me. If thou wilt give me they word to be mine, I shall forthwith pass mine as a true Christian to be thine. And put case that I should never come to enjoy thee, as I will not till that I have the Church's benediction and my parents' goodwill, yet, with this my imagining that thou wilt be assuredly mine, it will be sufficient to recover me my health and to make me live merrily and contented till that happy and desired time shall come."

Whilst that Ricaredo discoursed thus with her, Isabella stood hearkening unto him with downcast eyes, showing in that her modest and sober look that her honesty did equal her beauty, and her circumspection her great discretion. And seeing that Ricaredo had made an end of speaking and was silent, this honest, fair, and discreet damsel made him this answer:

"Since that the rigour or clemency of Heaven (for I know not to which of these extremes I may attribute it) would, Señor Ricaredo, quit me of my parents and give me unto yours, thankfully acknowledging the infinite favours they have done me, I resolved with myself that my will should never be any other than theirs; and therefore, without it, the inestimable grace and favour which you are willing to do me I should not hold it a happiness but a misery, not a good but a bad fortune. But if, they being made acquainted therewith, I might be so happy as to deserve you, from this day forward I offer unto you that will and consent which they shall give me. And in the meanwhile if this shall be deferred or not effected at all, let your desires entertain themselves with this, that mine shall be eternal and pure in wishing you all that good which Heaven can give you."

Here did Isabella put a period to her honest and discreet words, and there began Ricaredo's recovery. And now began to be revived those hopes of his parents which in this his sickness were almost quite dead.

These two modest lovers, with a great deal of courtesy and kindness, took leave each of other; he with tears in his eyes, she with admiration in her soul to see that Ricaredo should render up his love to hers. And being raised from his bed, to his parents' seeming, by miracle, he would not now any longer conceal his thoughts, and therefore one day he manifested them to his mother, telling her in the end of his discourse that if they did not marry him to Isabella, that to deny him her and give him his death it was one and the same thing. With such words and with such endearings Ricaredo did extol to the heavens the virtues of Isabella, that it seemed to his mother that Isabella had not wrought upon her son to win him to be her husband. She did put her son in good hope so to dispose his father that he might like as well thereof as she did; and it so fell out, that repeating to her husband word by word what her son had said unto her, he was easily moved to give way to that which his son so earnestly desired, framing excuses to hinder that marriage which was in a manner agreed upon for the Scottish damsel.

When this was in agitation Isabella was fourteen years of age and Ricaredo twenty, but in these their so green and flourishing years their great discretion and known prudence made them older.

There were but four days wanting to come, which being accomplished, Ricaredo's parents were willing that their son should enter into the state of matrimony, holding themselves both wise and happy in having chosen their prisoner to be their daughter, esteeming more the dowry of her virtues than the great store of wealth that was offered with the Scottish damsel.

The wedding-clothes were already made, their kinsfolk and friends invited thereunto; and there was no other thing wanting save making the Queen acquainted with the marriage, because without her goodwill

542

and consent, amongst those of noble blood not any marriage is effected; but they doubted not of her good leave and licence, and therefore had so long deferred the craving of it.

I say, then, that all things standing in this estate, when there wanted but four days till that of the wedding, one evening gave disturbance to all this their joy. A servant of the Queen's came and brought a mesage to Clotaldo, with express command from her Majesty that the next morning he should bring to her presence his Spanish prisoner that he brought from Cadiz.

Clotaldo returned answer that her Majesty's pleasure should most willingly be obeyed. The gentleman went his way, leaving the hearts of all the whole house full of passion, perturbations, and fears.

"Ay me," said the lady Catalina, "if it be come to the Queen's knowledge that I have bred up this child in the Catholic religion, and shall from thence infer that all we of this family are Catholics! Besides, if the Queen shall ask her what she hath learned in eight years since that she was our prisoner, what can the poor harmless soul answer which shall not, notwithstanding all her discretion, condemn us?"

Which Isabella hearing, spake thus unto her:

"Let not, dear lady, this fear give you any trouble at all; for my trust is in God that He will put words into my mouth at that instant, out of His divine mercy towards me, that shall not only not condemn you, but shall much redound to your good."

Ricaredo was much startled therewith, as divining thereby some ill success. Clotaldo sought out means that might give some courage to his great fear, but found none save in the great confidence which he had in God and in the wisdom of Isabella; and he earnestly entreated her that by all the ways she possibly could devise she should excuse her condemning of them to be Catholics; for though in spirit they were ready to receive martyrdom, yet notwithstanding the flesh was weak, and was loath to drink of that bitter cup.

Not once, but often, Isabella assured them that they were secure, and that, because of her, that thing should not come to pass which they feared and suspected; for albeit she then knew not what answer to make to those interrogatories and questions which in such a case as this might be put unto her, yet had she such a lively and assured hope that she should answer thereunto in such sort (as she had at other times told them) that her answers should rather do them good than hurt.

They discoursed that night on many things, especially on this particular, that if the Queen had known that they were Catholics she would not have sent them so mild a message; whence they might infer that she was only desirous to see Isabella, whose unequalled beauty and ability had come to her ears, and to those of the Court, as it did to all those of the city. But because they had not before this presented her unto her Majesty, they found themselves faulty, of which fault they thought good to excuse themselves by saying that from that very instant that she came into his power he had made choice of her, and as it were marked her out for to be the wife of his son Ricaredo. But in this, too, they likewise found themselves faulty for having made such a match without her Majesty's leave and licence; howbeit this fault did not seem unto them worthy of any great punishment. With this they comforted themselves, and agreed amongst themselves, by a joint consent, that Isabella should not go meanly clad to Court, but like a bride, since that she was the spouse of his son Ricaredo.

Being thus resolved, the next day they apparelled Isabella after the Spanish fashion, in a gown of green satin cut upon cloth of gold, embroidered with esses of pearls, wearing a great chain of most rich orient pearls about her neck, having a hatband of diamonds, and a fan in her hand, after the manner of your Spanish ladies. The hairs of her head, which were full and long, and of a bright pleasing colour, sown and interwoven with diamonds and pearls, did serve her instead of a coif. With this most rich dressing, and lively disposition and admirable beauty, she showed herself that day in London, riding in a fair caroche, carrying along with her, taken by so beautiful a sight, the souls and eyes of as many as looked on her. There were with her in the same caroche Clotaldo and his wife and Ricaredo, and on horseback many noble gentlemen of their kindred and alliance. All this honour Clotaldo was willing to do his prisoner for to oblige the Queen to use her as the spouse of his son.

Being come now to the Court, and brought into the chamber of presence where the Queen was, Isabella entered thereinto, presenting there the fairest show which can fall within the compass of imagination. The room was large and spacious, and the train that came with her had not gone above two steps forward but they stood still, and Isabella, alone by herself, advanced herself towards the state where the Queen sat; and being thus alone, she seemed to appear just like that star or exhalation which by the region of fire is wont to move itself in a clear and quiet night, or like unto a ray or beam of the sun which at the opening of the day discovers itself between two mountains. All this did she seem to be, or rather like a comet which did prognosticate the inflaming and setting on fire of many of those souls that were present, which love had thoroughly heated if not burned with the rays of those resplendent suns of beautiful Isabella; who, full of humility and courtesy, made her approaches by degrees, addressing herself to kneel down before the Queen, and then, after a short pausing, said thus unto her:

"May it please your most excellent Majesty so far forth to honour this your servant that she may kiss your royal hand; so shall I ever hereafter hold myself to be a lady, since that I have been so happy as to come to see your greatness."

The Queen continued looking upon her a good while without speaking one word, it seeming unto her, as she afterwards told a great lady of her bedchamber, that she had a starry heaven before her, whose stars were those many pearls and diamonds which Isabella bare about her. Her fair face and eyes were the sun and moon; and take all together in the whole piece, she was a new wonder of beauty. The ladies that attended about the Queen's person wished that they had been all eyes, that there might not remain anything in or about Isabella which they might not behold and view a full. Some commended the quickness of her eyes, some the colour of her face and pureness of complexion, some the properness of her body, and some the sweetness of her speech; and some likewise, who out of mere envy said:

"The Spaniard is a very handsome woman, but her habit and dressing seemeth very strange and out of fashion."

After some little suspense, the Queen causing Isabella to rise up, she said unto her:

"Speak, pretty maid, unto me in Spanish; for I understand it well, and shall take much pleasure therein."[1]

And turning herself towards Clotaldo, she said unto him:

"Clotaldo, you have done Us wrong in keeping this treasure so long concealed from Us; but it is such and so rich that it hath moved you to covetousness. You are bound to restore it unto Us, for by right it is Ours, and properly belongeth unto Us."

"Madam," answered Clotaldo, "It is true which your Majesty saith. I confess my fault, if it be a fault to have kept this treasure, that it might be preserved in that perfection as was fitting to appear in your Majesty's presence. And now that it is here before your eye, I thought to have much improved it by craving your Majesty's leave that Isabella might be the spouse of my son Ricaredo, and to give your most excellent Majesty in these two all that I am able to give you."

---

[1] The editors of the *Obras completas* of Cervantes, vol. ii (1923), point out that in 1564 the Spanish ambassador in London, Guzman de Silva, wrote to Philip II that Queen Elizabeth had addressed him in Italian (not Spanish), and continued the conversation in Latin, "which she spoke with elegance and facility." Later on in this story she makes use of an interpreter.

"Her very name gives Us very good content," replied the Queen; "there could nothing have been more wanting save the name of Isabella the Spaniard to take off something from that perfection which is in her. But how is it, Clotaldo, that without Our leave you have promised her to your son?"

"It is true, madam," answered Clotaldo, "I have made him a promise of her, but it was upon the confidence that the many and noble services which myself and my ancestors have done this crown might obtain of your Majesty other more difficult favours than this of your leave, and the rather for that my son is not yet espoused unto her."

"Neither shall he," said the Queen, "marry Isabella till he by himself and in his own person shall deserve her. Our meaning is, that I will not that either your own or your ancestors' services shall any whit benefit him in this particular, but that he in his own person shall dispose himself to serve me, and to merit for himself, and by his own prowess, this sweet pledge, whom We esteem and reckon of as if she were Our own daughter."

Isabella had scarce heard this last word delivered when, humbling herself again on her knees before the Queen, she spake unto her in the Spanish tongue, to this effect:

"Disgraces, which bring such graces with them, most noble Queen, are rather to be accounted happiness than misfortunes; and since that your Majesty hath been pleased to grace me with the name of daughter upon so good a pledge, what ill can I fear, or what good may I not hope for?"

Lo, what Isabella uttered came from her so gracefully and so wittingly that the Queen stood extremely affected towards her, and commanded that she should remain at Court in her service, and recommended her to a great lady, the chiefest amongst those of her bedchamber, that she might train her up according to the Court fashion.

Ricaredo, who saw that his life was taken away in taking away Isabella, was ready almost to have lost his wits; and therefore, though overtaken with a tumbling and sudden passion of heart, he went and fell upon his knees before the Queen, and said unto her: "That I may serve your Majesty, I need not to be incited thereunto by any other rewards than by those which my forefathers and ancestors have gotten by serving their kings; but since that it is your Majesty's pleasure that I should serve you with good desires and pretensions, I would gladly know in what kind and in what employment I may manifest that I comply with that obligation which I owe unto your Majesty, and put myself to that which you shall impose upon me."

"I have two ships royal," answered the Queen, "ready to put forth to sea, whereof I have made General the Baron of Lansac;[1] of one of these I make you Captain, for the blood from whence you come, doth assure me that it will supply the defect of your years. And consider well the favour which We do you, since that therein I give you occasion that, corresponding with that which you are, and doing things answerable to the race from whence you come, by serving your Queen you may show the worth of your noble disposition and of your person, and you shall receive thereby the greatest reward which in your opinion you can wish or desire. I myself will be Isabella's guard, though she give Us manifest tokens that her own honesty will be her safest and surest protection. God bless you in your voyage; and since that you go hence deeply, as I imagine, in love, I promise great matters unto myself of your noble exploits. Happy shall be that king that goes to war who shall have in his army ten thousand soldiers that are in love, for they will live in hope that the reward of their victories shall be the enjoying of their best beloved. Rise up, Ricaredo, and bethink yourself if you will or have anything to say to Isabella, for to-morrow you must be gone."

Ricaredo kissed the Queen's hand, humbly thanking her, and highly esteeming the favour which she did him, and presently went from her to Isabella, and would fain have spoken unto her, but could not, for love and grief had knit such a knot in his throat, and so tied his tongue, that had his life lain upon it he could not utter one word. But the water stood in his eyes, and were so brimful that they ran over and silently trickled down his cheeks, which he thought to dissemble and smother them all that he possibly could. Yet notwithstanding could he not hide them from the eyes of the Queen, and therefore she said unto him:

"Think it no shame, Ricaredo, to weep, neither value yourself the less for having given at this your farewell such tender demonstrations of your heart; for it is one thing to fight with your enemies, and another thing to take your leave of her you love. Isabella, embrace Ricaredo, and give him your benediction, for his excessive sorrow and loathness to leave you doth very well deserve it."

Isabella, who stood amazed and astonished to see Ricaredo's tenderheartedness and how truly he did grieve, and all for her sake, whom she loved as her husband, did not understand what the Queen had commanded her; but began to shed tears, without thinking what she did, and stood so still, and without any motion, that it seemed not to be a living soul but a statue of alabaster that wept.

---

[1] The first edition prints 'Lansae'.

The affections of these two true and tender lovers made the standers-by to melt likewise into tears. And so Ricaredo, without speaking a word to Isabella, or Isabella to him, they turned each from other; and Clotaldo and they that came with him, doing reverence to the Queen, went out of the presence full of compassion, discontent, and tears.

Isabella now remained like a poor orphan coming from the burial of her father and mother, and as full now of fear as before of grief, lest that her new lady to whom she was recommended would make her to change those manners and customs wherein she had been formerly bred up.

In conclusion, there she remained; and within two days after, Ricaredo hoisted sail and put forth to sea, beaten amongst many others with this thought, that he must do some notable piece of service that might entitle him to be the deserver of Isabella.

But in conclusion he besought Heaven to be propitious unto him that such occasions might be offered unto him wherein by showing himself valiant he might comply with the duty of a Christian, leaving the Queen satisfied and Isabella deserved.

Six days these two ships sailed with a prosperous wind, shaping their course for the Terceira Islands[1] —a place where never are wanting either ships of Portugal, from the East Indies, or some that come thither from the West Indies. And at six days' end there arose such a cross-wind full in the teeth of them, and continued so long and so strong, that without suffering them to reach the islands, they were enforced to make for Spain; near unto whose coast, at the mouth of the Strait of Gibraltar, they descried three ships, the one a very tall and goodly ship, and the other two much less.

Ricaredo's ship made up to that which was admiral, for to know of his General whether or no he would set upon those three ships which they had descried; but before that he came up unto them he might discern that upon the top of the mainmast there was hung out a black streamer, and coming a little nearer, he might hear fifes and trumpets sounding faintly and hoarsely; clear and apparent signs that the General was dead, or some other principal person of the ship. At last, coming within hearing, that they might speak one to another, which they had not done since their first putting forth, they might hear them from out the admiral call out aloud unto them to have the Vice-Admiral Ricaredo to come aboard their ship, because the General the night before died of an apoplexy.

All upon this news were very sad save Ricaredo, who was inwardly glad,

---

[1] The Azores.

not for the loss of his General, but to see that he was left at liberty, and might freely command both ships; for so was it ordered by the Queen, that the General miscarrying, Ricaredo should succeed in his room; who presently went aboard the admiral, where he found some that mourned for their dead General, and others that rejoiced with him that was now living. In a word, both the one and the other presently yielded him obedience, and with short ceremonies cried him up for their general, two of those three ships which they had discovered not giving leave for greater; for going aloof from the great ship, they made up to the two. They straight knew them to be galleys, and Turkish galleys, by the half-moons which they bare in their flags, which gave Ricaredo great contentment, it seeming unto him that that prize, if Heaven should grant it him, would be of great benefit, without having given offence to any Catholic.

The Turkish galleys came to know the English ships, who did not carry the arms of England in their flags, but of Spain, for to deceive those that should chance to descry them, and might take them to be ships of piracy. The Turks thought they had been ships that had come from the Indies, and that they would quickly yield and be taken; whereupon they came encroaching by little and little upon them, thinking presently to board them. And Ricaredo suffered them to come nearer and nearer unto him, till he had them in command of his ordnance, and then let fly at them, and giving them a broadside, discharged so luckily, that he put five balls into one of the galleys with such fury, that one half of it lay all open and naked. She heeled over forthwith and began to sink, without any possibility of righting herself. The other galley seeing its fellow's ill success, threw out a tow rope in all haste, and strove to bring her under the side of the great ship; but Ricaredo, who had ships that were light laden, and were quick and nimble, and such excellent sailers that they would turn and wind and come off and on as if they had been plied with oars, commanded them to charge the ordnance anew, chasing them even to the ship, showering upon them a world of shot. They of the opened galley, as soon as they came to the ship, forsook their galley, and with all possible haste endeavoured to get into the ship. This being perceived by Ricaredo, and that the sound galley employed itself in relieving the other, he sets upon her with both his ships; and without giving her leave to tack about, or to make any use of her oars, he did put her to that strait, that the Turks likewise that were in her were forced to flee for refuge to the ship, not with any hope to defend themselves therein, or to stand it out in fight, but for to escape for the present with their lives. The Christians wherewith those galleys were manned, tearing out the rings and breaking their chains, intermingled with the Turks, sought to recover their ship; and as they were clambering up by the side of her, with musket shot from the ships they went shooting at them as at a mark. But Ricaredo gave order that they should shoot only at the Turks, and spare the Christians. Thus were all the Turks almost slain; and they who entered the ship with the Christians, for they were mingled one amongst another, making use of their weapons, were cut in pieces; for the force of the valiant when they begin to fall must yield to the weakness of those that are rising. And therefore the Christians, taking heart, laid about them with such courage and mettle that they did wonders for the working of their liberty, thinking all this while that those English ships were Spanish.

In conclusion, the Christians having killed nearly all the Turks, some Spaniards put themselves on board the large ship, and called out aloud unto those whom they supposed to be Spaniards that they would come aboard them, and enjoy the reward of their victory. Ricaredo asked them in Spanish what ship that was. They told him that she was come from the Portuguese East Indies laden with spices and as many pearls and diamonds as were worth a million, and that by a storm they were driven upon that coast, all rent and torn, and without any ordnance, for the foulness of the weather and high working of the sea enforced them to throw it overboard; that their men were most of them sick, and almost dead of thirst and hunger; and that those two galleys, which were belonging to the pirate Arnaut Mamí,[1] had taken her but the day before, without making any defence at all; and that, as it was told them, because they were not able to carry so great a quantity of riches in those two small vessels, they towed her along, with purpose to put her into the river of Larache, which was near thereunto.

Ricaredo returned them answer that if they conceived that those his two ships were Spanish they were deceived, for they were nothing less but ships belonging to the Queen of England; which news gave those that heard it occasion of fear and sorrow, imagining, and not without reason, that they were fallen out of one net into another. But Ricaredo told them that they should receive no harm, and that they should rest assured of their liberty, on condition that they should not put themselves upon their defence.

"Nor is it possible for us," replied they, "so to do; for, as we formerly told you, this ship hath no ordnance, nor we any offensive arms. And therefore we must of force, whether we will or no, have recourse to the gentle and noble disposition of your General, and the liberality and courtesy

---

[1] The pirate who captured Cervantes in 1575.

which he shall use towards us; since that it is meet and just that he who hath freed us from the insufferable captivity of the Turks should reap the reward and benefit thereof, and shall be made famous of all those to whose ears the news shall come of this memorable victory and of his kind usage towards them."

These words of the Spaniard did not sound ill in Ricaredo's ears, and therefore calling those of his ship to a council, he demanded of them how he might send all the Christians to Spain, without putting themselves in danger of any sinister result, if being so many as they were they should take courage unto them for to rise up against them. Some were of opinion that he should pass them one by one to his own ship, and clapping them under hatches, kill them man after man; and so they might easily and without any noise kill them all, and carry the great ship along with them to London without any further fear or care-taking.

But to this Ricaredo thus replied:

"Since that God hath done us this so great a favour in giving us such great riches, I will not requite Him with a cruel and unthankful mind; nor is it meet that that which I may remedy by industry I should remedy by the sword. And therefore I, for my part, am of opinion that no Catholic Christian should die the death; not because I wish them so well, but because I wish well to myself, and would that this day's noble action, neither to me nor to you, should mingle the name of valiant with the surname of cruel, for cruelty did never sort well with valour. That which is to be done is this: that all the ordnance of one of these our ships be put into the great Portugal ship, without leaving the ship any arms, or any other thing, save sufficient victual, and so manning that ship with our men, we will carry it home, and the Spaniards go in the other to Spain."

None durst contradict that which Ricaredo had propounded, and some held him to be valiant, magnanimous, and of good understanding and judgement, and others in their hearts to be more Catholic than he ought to have been.

Ricaredo then having resolved on this course, he put fifty musketeers into the Portugal ship all ready fitted and furnished, their pieces charged with shot, and their matches burning in their cocks. He found in the ship well near three hundred persons, with those that had escaped out of the galleys. He presently called for their cocket, or bill of lading, and the same person who at first spake to him from the deck made him answer that the Turkish pirate had already taken their cocket from them, and that it was drowned with him. He did instantly put his pulley in order, and bringing his lesser vessel and lashing it close to the side of the great ship, with wonderful celerity and with the help of strong ropes they hoisted all their ordnance with their carriages out of the lesser into the greater ship.

This being done, he forthwith made a short speech to the Christians. He commanded them to go into the ship that was now disencumbered, where they should find good store of victual for more than a month, and more mouths than they had. And as they went embarking themselves, he gave to every one of them four Spanish pistolets, which he caused to be brought from his own ship, for to relieve in part their necessity when they came on land; which was so near that from thence they might ken the high mountains of Abyla and Calpe.[1] All of them gave him infinite thanks for the favour he had done them; and the last that went to embark himself was he who had been the mouth of the rest, who said unto Ricaredo:

"Most valiant sir, I should hold it a happiness for me, that you would rather carry me along with you to London than send me into Spain; for albeit that it be my country, and that it is not above six days since I left it, yet shall I not find anything therein which will not minister occasions unto me of reviving my former sorrows and solitudes. I would have you to know, noble sir, that in the loss of Cadiz, which is now some fifteen years since, I lost a daughter, which some of the English carried away into their own country; and with her I lost the comfort of my old age, and the light of mine eyes, which since they might not see her have never seen that thing which could be pleasing unto them. The great discontentment wherein her loss left me, together with that of my wealth, which likewise was taken from me, brought me to that low ebb that I neither would nor could any more exercise the trade of merchandise, whose great dealings in that kind made me in the opinion of the world held to be the richest merchant in all that city. And indeed so I was, for besides my credit, which would pass for many hundred thousands of crowns, the wealth that I had within the doors of mine own house was more than fifty thousand ducats, all which I lost; yet had I lost nothing so as I had not lost my daughter. After this general misfortune, and so particularly mine, necessity, the more to vex me, set upon me, never ceasing to give me over till such a time as not being able any longer to resist her, my wife and I (which is that sorrowful woman that sits there) resolved to go for the Indies, the common refuge of poor gentlemen. And having embarked ourselves but six days since in a ship of advice, we had no sooner put out of Cadiz but that those two vessels of the pirates took our ship, and we became their slaves; whereupon our misery was renewed, and our misfortune confirmed; and it had been

---

[1] Jebel Mùsa, in Africa (to the west of Ceuta), and Gibraltar—the "Pillars of Hercules."

greater had not the pirates taken that ship of Portugal, who entertained
them so long, till that succeeded which you have seen."

Ricaredo then asked him what was his daughter's name? He answered,
Isabella.

With this Ricaredo was confirmed in that which before he suspected,
which was that he who recounted this unto him was his beloved Isabella's
father; and without giving him any tidings of her, he told him that very
willingly he would carry him and his wife to London, where happily
they might hear some news of that which they so much desired. He made
them presently go aboard his own ship, leaving mariners and soldiers
sufficient in that of Portugal.

That night they hoisted sail and set themselves to get off from the coast
of Spain; and for that in the ship wherein were the freed captives there
were likewise twenty Turks, whom Ricaredo had also set at liberty, for
to show that more out of his own noble disposition and generous mind
he had dealt so graciously with them, than enforced by that love which
he bare to the Christians, he entreated the Spaniards at their parting that
upon the first occasion that should offer itself they should set the Turks
at liberty, wherein they should show themselves thankful unto him.

The wind, which gave good tokens of being large and prosperous,
began to be very much calmer, which calm did stir up a great tempest
of fear in the mariners and soldiers, who blamed Ricaredo and his bounty,
not sticking to tell him that they whom he had freed might give advice
of these happenings in Spain, and that if happily they should have their
galleons lying there in the haven, they might put forth to sea in search
of them, and so put them to a narrow strait and in danger of losing, together
with their lives, all that treasure which they had got.

Ricaredo knew very well that they had reason on their side, but over-
coming all of them with good words, he made them quiet; but that which
did most quiet them was the wind, which returned again to refresh itself
in such sort, that having as fair a gale as could blow in the sky, they clapped
on all their sails, and without having need to strike any one of them, or
but in the least manner to restrain them, within nine days they came within
sight of London; and when they were returned home thus victorious, there
were thirty wanting of those that went that voyage.

Ricaredo would not enter the river with tokens of joy, by reason of the
death of his General, and therefore mixed his joyful with sorrowful signs,
one while the trumpets sounding loud and shrill, and another while low
and hoarse; one while the drums did beat lively and the fifes go merrily
and another while dead and softly, answering each other with mournful

and lamentable notes. On one of the cages of the ship hung the contrary way a flag embroidered with half-moons, and on another a long streamer of black taffeta, whose points did touch the water.

In conclusion, with these and the like contrary extremes, they entered the London river with their own ship, because the other drew so much water that the river could not bear her, and therefore lay at anchor in the sea.

These such contrary signs and tokens held a world of people in suspense, who beheld them from each side of the shore. They knew very well by some arms and coats in their colours that that lesser ship was the admiral wherein the Lord of Lansac went; but they could not guess how that other ship should come to be changed for that great vast ship which lay at sea. But they were quickly put out of this doubt by Ricaredo's leaping out of his boat on shore in rich and resplendent arms like a soldier; who afoot, without staying for any other company, attended only with the innumerable vulgar that followed him, he went directly to the Court, where the Queen being in a gallery, stood expecting the news should be brought her of her ships.

There was, besides, many other ladies with the Queen, Isabella, apparelled after the English fashion, though with a little touch of the Spanish. Before that Ricaredo came, there came another, who told the Queen that Ricaredo was come. Isabella hearing the name of Ricaredo, began to change colour, and seemed to be somewhat troubled, and in that very instant did fear and hope both the evil and good success of his coming.

Ricaredo was tall of stature, a gentleman, and well proportioned, and for that he came armed, with his gorget, corselet, and pouldrons all Milan work, richly gilded and engraven, it became him extremely well, and did please the eyes of the beholders. He had no casque on his head, but a broad-brimmed hat of a lion colour, with a great large feather, diversified with a few different colours, a broad short sword by his side, a very rich girdle and hangers, and his breeches somewhat large and full, like unto those of the Swizzers.

Being thus accoutred, what with the goodliness of his presence and stateliness of his gait, some were so taken therewith that they compared him to Mars, the god of war; and others, taken with the beauty of his countenance, compared him to Venus, who for to put a jest upon Mars had put this disguise upon him. In conclusion, he came before the Queen, and humbling himself on his knee he said unto her:

"Most renowned and redoubted Sovereign, in the strength of your good fortune, and in the consecution of my desire, after that our General, the

Lord of Lansac, was dead of an apoplexy, I succeeding in his place, thanks be rendered therefor to your Majesty, I lighted by chance on two Turkish galleys, which went towing away that great ship which I have now brought home, and lies not far off, safe in the road. I did set upon them; your soldiers fought, as they always use to do, very manfully. We sunk both the Turkish vessels, and in one of ours I gave, in your Majesty's royal name, liberty to the Christians which escaped out of the hands of the Turks. Only I brought along with me one man and a woman, both Spaniards, who out of their own liking and election were wonderfully desirous to come with me into our Island, that they might see the greatness of your Majesty's person and Court. That ship which is now yours is a Portugal, one of those great carracks which come from the East Indies, the which by a storm came to fall into the power of the Turks, who with little trouble, or, to say better, none at all, made her to yield herself unto them; and as I am informed by some of those Portugals that came in her, she is worth above a million in gold and spice, and other rich merchandise of pearls and diamonds which are in her. Whereof nothing hath hitherto been touched, neither did the Turks come to finger anything therein, because Heaven hath dedicated it wholly unto you, and I have commanded it to be kept and reserved whole and entire for your Majesty. With one jewel only that your Majesty shall be pleased to bestow upon me, I shall remain indebted for ten such other ships. That jewel your Majesty hath already promised me, which is my good Isabella. With her I shall rest rich and rewarded, not only for this service that I have done your Majesty, but for many others which I mean to do, for to pay some part of that great if not infinite worth which in this jewel your Majesty offereth me."

"Arise, Ricaredo," replied the Queen, "and believe me, that if I should upon a price give you Isabella according to that value I esteem her at, you would never be able to pay it, neither with that which you have brought home in this ship nor with all that treasure which remaineth in the Indies. Well, I will give her you, because I made you a promise of her, and because she is worthy of you, and you of her; your valour only doth deserve her. And if you have kept those jewels of the ship for me, I have likewise kept this your jewel for you; and albeit it may seem unto you that I have not done any great matter for you in returning you that which is your own, yet I know that I do you an especial favour therein, for those pledges that are bought by our desires, and have their estimation and value in the soul of the buyer, they are worth a world, there being no price that can countervail it. Isabella is yours, there she is; and when you will yourself, you may take possession of her, and I believe with her good liking and content, for she is discreet, and knows well how to weigh the friendship which you do her, for I will not style it by the name of favour but friendship; for I will take that name only upon me of doing favours. Go, and take your ease, and come and wait upon Us to-morrow, and then will I more particularly hear you relate unto Us what you did in this voyage, and how valiantly you behaved yourself; and bring those two with you who you say were so willing to come and see Us, that We may thank them for their love."

Ricaredo thanked her Majesty for the many favours she had done him, and then the Queen presently left the gallery and retired herself. And the ladies came round about Ricaredo, and one of them, which held great love and friendship with Isabella, called the lady Tansi, accounted the discreetest, the wittiest, and pleasantest amongst them, said unto Ricaredo:

"What means this, Ricaredo? what arms are these? Did you happily imagine that you came to fight with your enemies? Believe me, we all here are your friends, unless it be Isabella, who for that she is a Spaniard is bound not to bear you any goodwill."

"Sure, my lady Tansi, she bears me some; for since that she hath me in her remembrance," said Ricaredo, "I know that her goodwill is towards me; for the foulness of being unthankful cannot have the least footing in her so great worth, understanding, and incomparable beauty."

Whereunto Isabella replied:

"Señor Ricaredo, since that I am to be yours, it is in your power to take all satisfaction whatsoever you will of me, that I may make you some small requital of those undeserved praises which you have given me, and of those further favours which you intend to do me."

These and other the like honest discoursings Ricaredo passed with Isabella and with the rest of the ladies, amongst which there was a pretty little damsel, young both in growth and years, who did nothing but gaze upon Ricaredo all the while he was there. She lifted up his bases[1] to see if he had anything under them; she tampered with his sword, and in a childish simplicity would make his glittering armour her looking-glass, coming very near, thinking to see her face in them. And when she went away from him, turning herself to the ladies, she said, "Now, ladies, I assure you I imagine that war is a most beautiful thing, since that even amongst women armed men look lovely."

"And how can they otherwise choose?" replied the lady Tansi; "if not, look upon Ricaredo, who looks like the sun come down from heaven on earth, and in that habit goes walking up and down amongst us."

---

[1] *Escarcelas*, "pieces of armour which fell from the waist to the thigh" (Dict. of the Royal Spanish Academy, 1925).

They all of them laughed at the little maid's simplicity, and no less at the ridiculous rodomontado of the lady Tansi; and some murmurers were not wanting who held it an impertinency that Ricaredo should come armed to Court. Though other some sought as much to excuse him, saying that as a soldier he might do it for to show his bravery and gallantry.

Ricaredo was by his parents, friends, kinsfolk, and acquaintance received with lively expressions of singular love and affection; and that night there were made general bonfires throughout London, and other public tokens of their joy. The father and mother of Isabella were already in Clotaldo's house, whom Ricaredo had acquainted who they were, but entreated his parents that they might not have any the least notice given them of Isabella till that he himself should give it them; the like advice was given to all the servants of the house.

That very night, accompanied with many boats, barges, and barks, and with no fewer eyes to look on them, the great ship began to discharge her lading, which in eight days could not be disburdened of her pepper, and other rich merchandise which she had in her bulk. The next day after Ricaredo went to Court, carrying with him the father and mother of Isabella, both of them being newly clad after the fashion of London, telling them that the Queen desired to see them.

They came all of them where the Queen was sitting amidst her ladies expecting Ricaredo, whom she was willing to grace and favour by placing Isabella next to her, having on the same attire and dressing which she wore when she came first to the Court, appearing therein no less beautiful now than she did then. The parents of Isabella were stricken with admiration and wonder to see so much greatness and bravery met together. They settled their eyes on Isabella, but did not know her, though their hearts, presagers of that good which was so near them, began to leap in their bosoms; not out of any sudden passion that might cause sorrow or grief in them, but out of I know not what pleasure and contentment, which they could not hit upon to understand aright.

The Queen would not suffer Ricaredo to continue kneeling before her, but made him rise, and willed him to sit down in a velvet chair, which was by her appointment set there for that purpose—an unusual favour, considering the stately condition of the Queen. And one whispered in another's ear, "Ricaredo sits not on the chair which was brought him, but on the pepper which he brought in.' Another says unto him that stood by him, "Now is that old proverb verified, *Dadivas quebrantan penas*—that 'gifts will break through stone walls'; for those that Ricaredo hath given her Majesty hath softened and mollified our Queen's hard heart." Another tells his next fellow, "Now that he is well seated, more hands than two must go to it to heave him out."

In conclusion, from that grace and honour which the Queen was pleased to do Ricaredo, envy took occasion to grow in many of those courtiers' breasts, who were eyewitnesses of this her Majesty's extraordinary favour extended towards him; for there is not that favour which a prince confers on his favourite which is not a spear that pierceth the heart of the envious.

The Queen was desirous to know from Ricaredo, point by point, how that fight passed with the Turkish pirates' galleys; he recounted it anew, attributing the victory to God and the valour of his soldiers, endearing the services of them all jointly, and particularizing the valiant acts of some of them who had put themselves most forward, and done her Majesty very notable service; whereby he obliged the Queen to do all of them favours, and in particular those particular persons.

And when he began to speak of the liberty which in her Majesty's name he had given the Turks and Christians, he said unto her:

"That woman and that man who stand there" (pointing to Isabella's parents) "are they whom yesterday I told your Majesty, who out of the great desire which they had to see your greatness and magnificence did so earnestly entreat me that I would bring them along with me. They are of Cadiz, and by that which they have told me, and by that likewise which I have seen and observed in them, I know that they are of especial rank and worth."

The Queen commanded them that they should draw near unto her. Isabella lifted up her eyes that she might see these who said they were Spaniards, and more particularly of Cadiz, out of a desire that she had to learn if happily they knew her parents. And just as Isabella lifted up her eyes, her mother fixed hers upon her, and stood still a while, that she might view and behold her the more attentively; and on the other side there began to be awakened in Isabella's memory some certain confused notions which gave her to understand that heretofore she had seen that woman which stood before her. Her father was in the like confusion, without daring to determine to give credit to that truth which his eyes represented unto him.

Ricaredo was very attentive to see and observe the affections and motions of these three doubtful and perplexed souls, which were so confounded an amazed between the yea and nay of knowing each other. The Queen took notice of both their suspense, as also of Isabella's distraction, by her interwhile sweatings, by her changing colour, and by her lifting up her hand to order and compose her hair.

558

Isabella thus troubled, not knowing well what to think of it, did earnestly wish that she would speak whom she imagined might be her mother, for peradventure her ears would put her out of that doubt whereinto her eyes had put her. The Queen willed Isabella that she should speak Spanish to that woman and that man, and they should tell her what was the cause that moved them not to accept and enjoy that their liberty which Ricaredo had given them, being that liberty is a thing above all other the dearest and best beloved, not only of reasonable creatures, but of those that want it.

All this Isabella demanded of her mother, who, without returning her any one word, suddenly and half stumbling for haste, came unto Isabella, and without regarding respect, fear, or the courtiers looking on her, with her hand she lifted up Isabella's right ear, and having there discovered a black mole, which mark confirmed her suspicion, and plainly perceiving that it was her daughter Isabella, she could no longer contain herself, but embracing her, cried out aloud, saying, "O daughter of my heart! O dear pledge of my soul!" and not being able to utter a word more, her speech failing, she fainted and fell into a swoon in Isabella's arms.

Her father, no less tender than prudent, gave manifest signs how sensible he was of all this, but with no other words than a silent shedding of tears, which softly trickling down bedewed both his cheeks and beard. Isabella laid her face to that of her mother, and turning her eyes towards her father, in such a kind of manner looked on him that thereby she gave him to understand the pleasure and contentment her soul took in seeing them there.

The Queen wondering at this so rare and strange an accident, said to Ricaredo:

"I conceive, Ricaredo, that this interview was thus preordered in your discretion; but I must tell you I know not whether you did well in so doing, for we see by experience that a sudden joy as soon kills as a sudden sorrow."

And having said this, she turned herself to Isabella, and took her apart from her mother, who having a little water sprinkled in her face, came again to herself, and calling her wits a little better about her, humbling herself on her knees before the Queen, she said unto her:

'I beseech your Majesty to pardon my boldness, for it is no marvel that I should forget myself and lose my senses with the overmuch joy I have received in the finding out this my beloved pledge."

The Queen made answer that she had a great deal of reason on her side, making use of an interpreter that she might the better understand her.

Isabella came in this manner, as I told you before, to the knowledge of her parents, and her parents of her; whom the Queen commanded to reside in the Court, to the end that they might with the better leisure both see and talk with their daughter, and rejoice and make merry with her. Wherewith Ricaredo was wonderfully well pleased, and craved anew of the Queen that she would be pleased to make good her promise by bestowing Isabella upon him, in case he did deserve her; and if not, he humbly besought her Majesty that she would be pleased presently to put him upon some other employment that might make himself worthy of obtaining that which he so earnestly desired.

The Queen understood very well that Ricaredo rested well satisfied of himself and of his great valour, insomuch that there needed not any new proofs for to qualify him; and therefore told him that four days from that present being fully ended, she would deliver Isabella unto him, doing both of them all the grace and honour she possibly could. Upon this answer Ricaredo took his leave, being the most joyful and most contented man in the world, transported with that near hope which he now had of having Isabella in his power without any fear of losing her, which is the last and utmost desire of lovers.

Time ran, but not with that light and nimble foot as he wished; for they who live by the hope of promise to come do evermore imagine that time doth not fly with wings swift enough, but that he hath lead tied to his heels, and treads the steps of slothfulness itself.

Well, at last come that desired day, not wherein Ricaredo thought to put an end to his desires, but to find in Isabella new graces which might move him to love her the more, if more he could, than he did already. But in that short time whenas he thought the ship of his good fortune sailed with a prosperous wind towards the desired port, a contrary chance and cross accident raised up in this calm sea such a tempestuous storm that he feared a thousand times to see it sunk.

The case, then, is this. The chief bedchamber lady to the Queen, to whose charge Isabella was committed, had a son of the age of twenty two years, called the Earl of Arnesto. The greatness of his estate, the nobleness of his blood, and the great favour which his mother held with the Queen, made him not only do those things which did not become him, and to break out into excesses, but also made him arrogant, proud, haughty, and confident of himself.

This Arnesto, then, was enamoured of Isabella, and so inflamedly that his very soul did burn in the sparkling light of Isabella's eyes; and albeit in that time that Ricaredo was absent he had by some signs discovered his desires, yet was he never admitted by Isabella, or received any the least encouragement. And howbeit that repugnancy and disdains in love's infancy are wont to make lovers to desist from their enterprise, yet in Arnesto the many and known disdains which Isabella showed him wrought the clean contrary, for he was set on fire with his own jealousies, and burned with desire to attempt her honesty.

And for that he saw that Ricaredo in the Queen's opinion had deserved Isabella, and that within so little a while she was to be given unto him for wife, he was ready to run into despair, and to offer violence to himself. But before that he would go about to use so infamous and cowardly a remedy, he spake with his mother, entreating her that she would speak unto the Queen to give him Isabella to be his wife, which if she did not bring to pass, that he would then have her to know, and assuredly believe, that death stood knocking at the doors of his life.

The mother wondered to hear such words fall from her son, and for that she knew the roughness of his harsh nature and headstrong condition, and the fastness wherewith these desires did cleave unto his soul, she was afraid that this his love would end in some sinister event and unhappy issue. Yet notwithstanding, as a mother (to whom it is natural to desire and procure the good of her children), she promised to prefer his pretension to the Queen; though not with any hope to obtain such an impossibility of her as the breaking of her princely word, but that she might not omit to try in so desperate a case the utmost remedy.

And Isabella being that morning apparelled, by order from the Queen, so richly that my pen dares not presume to deliver the manner thereof unto you, and the Queen herself having put a chain of pearl about her neck, the best that was brought home by Ricaredo in the ship, valued at twenty thousand ducats, and a diamond ring on her finger worth six thousand or thereabouts, and the ladies being assembled and met together for to celebrate the approaching feast of this glorious wedding, came in the chief bedchamber woman to the Queen, and besought her on her knees that she would be pleased to suspend Isabella's espousals two days more; for with this favour only which her Majesty should do her she should hold herself well satisfied and recompensed for all whatsoever she deserved or hoped for her service.

The Queen would first know of her why she did so earnestly desire this suspension, which went so directly against her word which she had given to Ricaredo. But that lady would not render her the reason until that she had granted her request, and that then she would make it known unto her. The Queen longed to know the cause of that her demand. And therefore, after that the lady had obtained that which she much desired, she recounted

561

to her Majesty the love that her son bare to Isabella, and how that she feared that if she were not given him to wife he would either grow desperate to his utter undoing, or do some scandalous act or other. And that whereas she had craved those two days of delaying the business, it was only to this end and purpose, that her Majesty might have time to think upon some course, which might in her Majesty's wisdom be most fit and convenient for her son's good.

The Queen made answer that if she had not passed unto her her royal word she would easily have found a way to get out of that labyrinth, but that she would neither break her promise with her nor yet defraud Ricaredo of his hopes for all the interest of the world.

This answer the lady of the bedchamber gave her son, who flying instantly from his mother, frying in the flames of love and jealousy, armed himself at all points, and being mounted upon a fair and strong-limbed horse, presented himself before the house of Clotaldo, and with a loud voice requested that Ricaredo would come to the window that he might speak a word with him. He at that instant was all in his gallantry, like a bridegroom, and was even upon the point of going to Court with such company as such a solemnity required. But having heard a loud call, and being told who he was that called unto him, and in what kind of fashion he came, being somewhat troubled with it, he came to the window; whom as soon as Arnesto saw, he said unto him:

"Ricaredo, hearken well unto that which I shall now tell thee. My mistress the Queen commanded thee to go forth in her service, and to do such noble exploits as should make thee worthy of deserving the not-to-be-paralleled, incomparable Isabella. Thou didst go, and returnedst with thy ships laden with gold, wherewith thou thinkst that thou hast bought and deserved Isabella. And albeit the Queen my mistress hath promised her unto thee, it was as being persuaded that there was not any one in Court that hath done her better service, not any that with better title may deserve Isabella, and herein it may very well be that she was deceived. And therefore leaning to this opinion, which I hold for an approved truth, I tell thee that thou hast neither done such things as may make thee to deserve Isabella, neither canst thou do any which may be able to raise thee to so great a height of happiness. And therefore in regard that thou nor dost nor canst deserve her, if thou shalt avouch the contrary, I challenge thee the field, and defy thee to the death."

And here the Earl ended his speech, and Ricaredo made answer thereunto after this manner:

"This challenge, my lord, doth in no manner of wise concern me, for

I confess that I not only do not deserve Isabella, but that there is not that man now living in the world that doth deserve her. So that I confessing that to be true which you say, this your challenge no way toucheth me; yet notwithstanding I accept of it for that your insolence and indiscretion which you have shown in this your challenging of me."

And with this he withdrew himself from the window, and called in all haste for his arms. This unexpected cross accident much troubled his parents, and all those that were come to Clotaldo's house to accompany Ricaredo to the Court.

Amongst those many that had seen the Earl Arnesto armed, and had heard the challenge he had made, there were not some wanting who acquainted the Queen therewith, who commanded the captain of her guard that he should go presently and apprehend the Earl. The captain made such good haste that he came just in the very nick whenas Ricaredo was going out of his house, armed with those arms wherein he disembarked, being mounted on a goodly horse.

When the Earl saw the captain of the guard, he forthwith imagined the cause of his coming, and determined (if possibly he could avoid it) not to be apprehended; and speaking aloud to Ricaredo, said:

"Thou now seest, Ricaredo, the impediment which hinders us from deciding this quarrel. If, notwithstanding this interruption, thou shalt have a mind to chastise me, thou wilt seek after me, and I shall have the like mind to chastise thee, and seek likewise after thee; and since two that seek after each other are easily found, let the execution of our desires surcease for the present."

"Content," replied Ricaredo.

By this time the captain was come in with all the guard, and told the Earl that he must yield himself his prisoner, for in her Majesty's name he was to apprehend him. The Earl yielded himself unto him, and told the captain that he submitted himself to her Majesty's command, but with this condition, that he should not carry him to any other place save the Queen's presence.

The captain remained therewith satisfied, and carrying him in the midst of the guard, brought him to Court before the Queen, who had already been informed by his mother of the great love which her son bare to Isabella, and with tears besought her Majesty that she would pardon the Earl, who being a young man, and deeply in love, was liable to far greater errors. Arnesto was brought before the Queen, who, without entertaining any speech with him, commanded his sword to be taken from him, and afterwards sent him to prison.

All these things tormented the heart of Isabella, as likewise of her parents, who so suddenly saw the sea of their quietness troubled.

The lady of the bedchamber, Arnesto's mother advised the Queen that for to remove that mischief betwixt her house and that of Ricaredo, the cause thereof might be taken away (which was Isabella, by sending her into Spain) and so those effects would cease which now were to be feared. She added to these reasons the assertion that Isabella was a Catholic, and so Christian a one that none of her persuasions (which had been many) had been able to bend her in any way from her Catholic intent.

Whereunto the Queen answered, that for the sending of her into Spain she should treat no more on that point, because her fair presence and her many graces and virtues gave her great content, and that doubtless, if not that very day, the next following without all fail she would marry her to Ricaredo, according to the promise she had made him.

With this resolution of the Queen's, Arnesto's mother was so disheartened and discomforted that she replied not so much as one word. And approving that for good which she had already forecast in her mind: that there was no other way, no other means in the world, for the mollifying of that rigorous condition of her son, nor for the reducing of Ricaredo to terms of peace, save by taking away Isabella; she determined to put in practice one of the greatest cruelties that could ever enter into the thought of any noble woman, and especially so principal a one as she was. And this her determination was, to make away with Isabella by poison. And because it is commonly the condition of women to be speedy and resolute in what they go about, that very evening she gave Isabella poison in a certain conserve, forcing her in a manner to take it, telling her that it was excellent good against those passions of the heart wherewith she seemed to be troubled.

Having satisfied her importunity, within a little while after that Isabella had taken it, her tongue and her throat began to swell, and her lips to grow black, her voice hoarse, her eyes troubled, and her stomach and bowels tormented with gripings: all manifest signs and tokens that she was poisoned.

The ladies came to the Queen, acquainting her Majesty how it was with her, and certifying her how that the lady of her bedchamber who had the charge of Isabella had done her this ill office. There needed not much pressing to induce the Queen to believe that it was true, and therefore went presently to see Isabella, who was almost breathing her last.

The Queen commanded her physicians should be sent for in all haste, and in the meanwhile, before they came, she caused a quantity of the powder of unicorn's horn to be given her, and some other preservatives against poison, which great princes use always to have ready at hand upon the like cases of necessity.[1] The physicians came and applied their best remedies, and besought the Queen that she would be pleased to cause that lady of her bedchamber to make known unto them what kind of poison that was which she had given her, for it was not to be doubted that any other person but herself had poisoned her. She did discover what she had given her, and having notice of it, the physicians applied so many and such effectual remedies, that by them and God's helping hand Isabella remained with life, or at least in good hope of having it.

The Queen commanded her bedchamber woman to be apprehended, and to be locked up in a strait and narrow lodging in her Court, with intention to punish her according to the nature and quality of this her foul offence, although that she sought to excuse herself by saying that in killing Isabella she did sacrifice to heaven above by ridding the earth of a Catholic, and together with her, removing the occasion of her son's further quarrels.

This sad news being brought to Ricaredo made him almost out of his wits; such were the things he did, and such were the complaints he made.

In conclusion, Isabella did not lose her life; yet the poison had gotten that power over her that she lost the hair of her head and of her eyebrows, her face was strangely puffed up, the grain of her skin spoiled, her complexion marred, her whole body mightily swollen, and her eyes distilling watery humours. In a word, she was grown so foul and ill favoured, that she who till then seemed to be a miracle of beauty did now seem to be a monster of ugliness; and they who knew her before held it the greater misfortune of the two that she remained in this evil plight than if she had died of the poison. Notwithstanding all this, Ricaredo sued anew unto the Queen for her, and besought her Majesty that she would give him leave to carry her home to his house, because the love which he bare her passed from his body to his soul; yet comforted himself with this, that though Isabella had lost her beauty, yet could she not lose her infinite virtues.

"Thou sayest true," replied the Queen; "go, take her home with thee, Ricaredo, and make account that thou carriest with thee a most rich jewel in a coarse case. I would have given her as fair to thee as thou deliveredst her unto me; but since this is not possible, forgive me that fault; happily

---

[1] This is one of those fantastic notions which delighted Cervantes through their sheer improbability. Yet unicorn's horn was seriously regarded as an antidote to poison, even in the time of Sir Thomas Browne, who in his *Vulgar Errors*, point out that all the specimens of 'unicorn's horn' known to him had come from different species of animals.

the chastisement which I shall give to the committers of thi sfoul offence shall in part satisfy thy desire of revenge."

Many things did Ricaredo say unto the Queen, seeking to excuse the lady of her bedchamber, beseeching her Majesty to pardon her, since that the reasons she alleged in her excuse were sufficient for to move her to forgive her greater excesses than these.

In conclusion, Isabella and her parents were delivered unto him, and Ricaredo carried them home, I mean to his father's house. To those rich pearls and that diamond the Queen added other jewels and other changes of raiment, which were such and so costly that they discovered the great love which she bare to Isabella, who remained for the space of two months without being able to be reduced to her former beauty. But the time being past, her skin began to peel and fall away, and a fair and smooth grain of skin to disclose itself.

In this interim, Ricaredo's parents presuming that it was not possible that Isabella should become the same woman which heretofore she was, resolved to send for that Scottish damsel with whom, before that ever they treated with Isabella, Ricaredo (by agreement) was to marry; and all this they did without his knowledge, not doubting but that the present beauty of this new bride would blot out of his son's remembrance that of Isabella, which was now past; whom either they purposed to send into Spain, together with her father and mother, giving them such store of wealth and riches as should fully recompense their former received losses.

There passed not above a month and a half whenas, without Ricaredo's privity, the new spouse entered within his father's doors, accompanied as befitted her station, and so fair and beautiful a creature, that next to Isabella, when she was in her prime, there was not the like unto her in all London. Ricaredo was mightily startled with the sudden and unexpected sight of the damsel, and feared lest the suddenness of her coming would put Isabella into some passion, and make an end of her life; and therefore, for to remove this fear, he went to the bed's side where Isabella lay, and finding her only accompanied with her father and mother, before them he spake unto her after this manner:

"Isabella of my soul, my parents out of the great love which they bear unto me, being not as yet well informed of that exceeding love which I still bear unto thee, have brought a damsel into this house, with whom they have treated and concluded to marry me, before that I should know the worth that is in thee, or that thou shouldst recover thy lost health. And this they have done, as I verily believe, with intention that the great beauty of this damsel should blot thine out of my soul, which is therein so deeply

566

engraven. I, Isabella, from the very instant that I loved thee, it was with another kind of love than that which hath its aim and end in satisfying the sensual appetite. For albeit that thy corporal beauty did captivate my senses, yet thy infinite virtues were they which imprisoned my soul; so that if being fair I did love thee, being now foul I adore thee. And for the further confirming of this truth give me this hand"; and she giving him her right hand, and he holding it fast in his, prosecuted his speech, saying, "By that faith which my Christian parents taught me, and by that true God who heareth what we say, I promise thee, my dear Isabella, the one half of my heart. I vow myself thy husband, and am so even from this very hour, if thou wilt raise me to that height of happiness to be thine."

Isabella remained in some suspense upon these words of Ricaredo, and her parents amazed and astonished. She knew not what to say, nor do any other thing save her often kissing of Ricaredo's hand, and telling him with a voice intermingled with tears that she accepted him for hers, and rendered herself to be his servant. Ricaredo kissed that her foul face, which when it was fair he durst never presume to touch. Isabella's parents with tender and many tears solemnized this nuptial feast. Ricaredo told them that he would put off his marrying with the Scottish damsel which was now in the house, in such manner as he would hereafter give them to understand. And in case that his parents should send all three of them into Spain, that they should not decline it, but by all means get them gone; and that they should look for him within two years, either in Cadiz or Seville; assuring them on the word of a gentleman that ere that time were expired he would not fail to be with them, if Heaven should so long lend him life; and that if the time prefixed should be preterlapsed they should then rest assured that some great impediment, or death, which was the more certain, had crossed his intended journey.

Isabella made him answer that she would not stay only two years for him but all those of his life, till that she were truly certified that he had left this life, and that in that instant that this should come to her knowledge the same likewise would be her death.

With these kind words fresh tears fell from them all. And Ricaredo went and told his parents that he would by no means be married, nor give his hand to the Scottish damsel to be his spouse, till he had quieted his mind by a year's travel. He knew well how to express himself, and gave them such good reasons for it, as likewise to the parents that came with Clisterna (for that was the damsel's name), that being, as they were, all Catholics, they did easily give credit unto them; and Clisterna was contented to remain in her father-in-law's house till Ricaredo should return, who craved a year's time.

This being thus concluded and agreed upon, Clotaldo told Ricaredo how that he was resolved to send Isabella and her parents to Spain, if the Queen would give him leave so to do. "For," said he, "peradventure the air of her own country will hasten and facilitate her health," which she now began to recover.

Ricaredo, that he might not give any the least inkling of his designs, answered (though but coldly) his father, that he should do that which seemed best in his own eyes; only he besought him that he would not take aught of those riches from Isabella which the Queen had bestowed on her. Clotaldo promised he would not; and that very day he went to crave license of the Queen, as well for the marrying of his son to Clisterna as for the sending of Isabella with her father and mother into Spain.

The Queen was well contented with both his requests, and approved Clotaldo's determination. And that very day, without calling her bed-chamber woman in question, she dismissed her of her service, and condemned her (besides the loss of her place) in ten thousand crowns to Isabella. And the Earl Arnesto, for his challenging of Ricaredo, she banished him for six years. Four days were scarce spent and gone but that Arnesto was upon the point to go to comply with his banishment, and the money had been paid.

The Queen commanded a rich merchant to come unto her that dwelt in London, and was a Frenchman who had very good correspondence in France, Italy, and Spain; to whom she delivered ten thousand crowns, and required of him bills of exchange for the returning of them to Isabella's father in Seville or in any other part of Spain. The merchant discounting his interest and profit, told the Queen that he would make certain and sure payment of them in Seville, by bills of exchange upon another French merchant, his correspondent, in this manner and form, viz., that he would write to Paris, to the end that the bills might be made there by another correspondent of his, because they would accept and allow of those that came from France, but not from England, by reason of the prohibition of commerce betwixt those two kingdoms, and that a letter of advice from him should serve the turn, by a privy mark that passed between them two; and that without any more ado the merchant of Seville should give him the moneys, who should be advised thereof from Paris.

In fine, the Queen took such good security of the merchant that she made no doubt of the true payment of it. And not contenting herself with this, she sent for the master of a Flemish ship that lay in the river, and was to put forth the day following for France, to take a certificate thereof in some port, that he might be the better able to pass into Spain under the title of coming from France, and not from England; whom she earnestly entreated to carry with him in his ship Isabella and her parents, and that he should use them well and kindly, and land them in Spain at the very first place he should come at on that coast.

The master, who desired to give the Queen contentment, told her that he would do it, and that he would land them either in Lisbon, Cadiz, or Seville. Having taken sufficient security of the merchant, and assurance from the master, the Queen, by way of message, sent unto Clotaldo that he should not take anything of that away from Isabella which she had given her, as well in jewels as in clothes.

The next day came Isabella with her father and mother to take their leave of the Queen, who received them with a great deal of love. The Queen gave them the merchant's letter and many other gifts, as well in money as other curious dainties for their voyage. And Isabella with such courtship thanked her Majesty, that she left the Queen anew obliged unto her for to continue her favours still towards her. She took her leave likewise of the ladies, who now that she was grown disfigured would not that she should have left them, seeing themselves free from that envy which they bare unto her beauty, and would have been very well content to enjoy her gifts of wit and discretion. The Queen embraced all three of them, and recommending them to their good fortune and to the master of the ship, and desiring Isabella to advertise her of her safe arrival in Spain, and from time to time of her welfare, by the way of the French merchant, she took her leave of Isabella and her parents, who that very evening embarked themselves, not without the tears of Clotaldo and his wife, and of all those of the house, of whom she was extremely beloved.

At this their taking of their leaves Ricaredo was not present, who that he might not make show of his tender-heartedness and manifest his sorrow, procured some of his friends to go abroad that day a-hunting with him. The gifts which the lady Catalina gave Isabella for her voyage were many, her embracings infinite, her tears in abundance, her entreatings that she would write often unto her without number. And the thanks rendered by Isabella and her parents were answerable thereunto, so that though weeping they left each other well satisfied.

That night the ship hoisted sail, and having with a prosperous gale of wind touched upon the coast of France, and there taking in such provisions as were necessary for their voyage into Spain, within thirty days after they entered the bar of Cadiz, where Isabella and her parents disembarked themselves. And being known by all those of the city, they received them with expressions of much content. They received a thousand congratulations of the finding out of Isabella, and of the liberty which they had gotten, being first captured by the Moors and afterwards by the English, having been made acquainted with all the passages of that business by those captives whom the liberality of Ricaredo had set free.

Now, Isabella in the meanwhile began to give great hopes of returning to recover her former beauty. They remained but a little more than a month in Cadiz, refreshing themselves of their weariness in their voyage, and then they went to Seville for to see whether the payment would prove good of the ten thousand crowns which were to be put to the account of the French merchant who had undertaken for to see it disbursed. Two days after their arrival at Seville they inquired after him, and found him, and gave him the French merchant's letter; he did acknowledge the bill, but told them that until he had received letters from Paris and a letter of advice he could not let them have the money, but yet that he looked every moment to be advertised thereof.

Isabella's parents had hired a very fair house, right over against Santa Paula,[1] by reason that there was a nun in that nunnery a near kinswoman of theirs, who had the rarest and sweetest voice in all Spain, as well that they might be near unto her as also for that Isabella had told Ricaredo that if he should come to seek her he should find her in Seville, and that her cousin the nun of Santa Paula would direct him to her house, and that for to know where to find her he needed not to give himself any further trouble than to inquire after that nun which had the best voice in the nunnery, because this token could not easily be forgotten.

It was forty days before letters of advice came from Paris, and within two days after they were come the French merchant delivered the ten thousand crowns to Isabella, and she them to her parents; and with them and some other which they had got together by selling some of those many of Isabella's jewels, her father began again to follow his trade of merchandise, not without the admiration of those who knew his great losses.

In conclusion, within a few months he went repaying his lost credit, and Isabella's beauty returned to its former perfection; insomuch that when any speech was had of fair women all of them gave the laurel to the English Spaniard, who was as well known by this name as she was for her beauty throughout the whole city.

---

[1] The house still stands. It has been pointed out a coincidence that a lady bearing the name of Cervantes became a nun in the convent in 1577, while another entry contains the name of Cifuentes, mentioned at the end of the story.

By means of the French merchant of Seville Isabella and her parents writ letters to the Queen of England of their safe arrival in Spain, with such acknowledgements and submissions at her Majesty's feet as the many favours from her received did require. They likewise writ to Clotaldo and to his lady Catalina—Isabella styling them her father and mother and her father and mother them their lords. From the Queen they received no answer, but from Clotaldo and his wife they did; whom in their letters gave them the felicitation of their safe arrival, certifying them besides how that their son Ricaredo the next day after that they had hoisted sail was gone for France, and from thence to pass to some other parts of Christendom, whither it was fitting for him to go for the settling and securing of his conscience. Adding to these other discourses and compliments of much love and affection, besides many other fair and friendly offers. To which letters of theirs they made answer with another, no less courteous and loving than thankful.

Isabella presently imagined that Ricaredo's leaving his country was to come to seek her out in Spain, and feeding herself with this hope she began to lead the most contented life in the world, and studied to live in such sort that when Ricaredo should come to Seville he might sooner hear the good report that went of her virtues than come to the knowledge of her house. Seldom or never did she go out of doors unless it were to the nunnery; she reaped no benefit by any other jubilees save those which she gained by the convent. From her house and from her oratory she visited in her meditations on the Fridays in Lent, and on the seven days of Whitsun week, the most holy stations of the Cross. She never visited the river, nor walked to the Triana;[1] she never went to see the common pastimes in the Field of Tablada, nor to see the Gate of Xeres, nor to go, if it were a fair day, to the feast of Saint Sebastian, celebrated by so many people as can hardly be reduced to any number. In short, she did not witness any public rejoicing or other festival in Seville: but spent all her whole time in retirement, in prayers, and good desires, still looking for the coming of her Ricaredo.

This her great retirement did set on fire and inflame the desires not only of those young gallants of that street where she dwelt but of all those that had but once had a sight of her. Hence they made nightmusic at her window, and by day careers with their jennets. And from this her not suffering herself to be seen, and from others much desiring to see her, increased their seeking out of cunning bawds which were mistresses in

---

[1] The suburb of Seville across the river.

their art, and promised to show themselves no less in soliciting Isabella; and there were not some wanting who endeavoured to bring this their wicked purpose to pass by witchcraft, charms, sorcery, and the like lewd courses. But against all these Isabella was like a rock in the midst of the sea, against which the waves and the winds dash and beat but do not move it.

A year and a half was now past when the approaching hope of those two years promised by Ricaredo began with more earnestness than hitherto it had done to vex and grieve the heart of Isabella; and whiles she was now and then thinking with herself that her husband was come, and that she had him before her eyes, and asked him what was the cause that hindered his coming and had kept him so long from her. And while again she imagined the just excuses that Ricaredo made her for his long absence, and how willingly she did believe and receive them, and how lovingly she embraced him in her arms and hugged him in her bosom as being the half part of her own soul. Then, even then when she was thinking on these love fancies, a letter came to her hands from the lady Catalina, bearing date from London some fifty days since. It was written in the English tongue, but she reading it in Spanish saw that it spake thus:

Daughter of my soul, thou knowest very well Guillarte, Ricaredo's page; he went along with him in this his journey. And by a former of mine unto you I advertised you that Ricaredo made for France the second day after your departure, and from thence was to travel farther. Now this his servant Guillarte, at the end of sixteen months, in all which time we had no news of our son, came home to us yesterday, and brought us these sad tidings that the Earl Arnesto had by treachery killed Ricaredo in France.

Now then, daughter, consider in what case his father, myself, and his spouse are in with this heavy news; being such, I say, that they have not left us any hope of putting this our misfortune in doubt. That which Clotaldo and myself entreat of you again and again is that you will truly and earnestly remember Ricaredo, who well deserveth this good office from you, considering how dearly he loved you, as you yourself best know.

You shall likewise beg of God that He will give us patience and bring us to a good death; to whom we likewise will make the same request, and humbly beseech Him that He will give unto you and your parents many long and happy years of life.

By the letter, hand, and seal there was not any the least doubt left to Isabella for not giving credit to the death of her husband. She knew very well his page Guillarte, and knew that he was true and trusty, and that in his own nature he hated a lie, and that he had no reason in the world for to feign that his death, and as little his mother lady Catalina, being that it imported nothing to send her such sorrowful news. In conclusion, no discourse that she could make with herself, nothing that she could imagine, could put it out of her thought that this unfortunate news was not true.

Having ended the reading of her letter without shedding a tear and without showing any signs of sorrow, with a composed countenance and with to appearance a quieted and contented mind, she arose from the parlour where she sat, and kneeling down devoutly, she made a solemn vow to be a nun, since that she might lawfully do it being now a widow.

Her parents dissembled their grief and covered that sorrow with the cloak of discretion which this sad news had caused in them, that they might be the better able to comfort Isabella in this bitterness of her soul; who being now as it were fully satisfied of her sorrow, moderating it with the resolution which she had put on, she fell to comforting of her parents, to whom she discovered her intent. But they did advise her that she should not put it in execution until that those two years were overpast which Ricaredo had set down for the term of his coming; for thereupon much depended the confirming of the truth of Ricaredo's death, and she might then with the more safety and security change this her estate.

Isabella followed their counsel, and the six months and a half which remained for the accomplishing of the two years she spent them in the exercises of a religious damsel, and for the better preparing and fitting of herself for her entering into the nunnery, having made choice of that of Santa Paula, where her cousin was.

The term of the two years was expired, and the day was come wherein she was to take upon her the habit; the news whereof was spread throughout the whole city amongst those who knew her by sight and by those that knew her only by report. Now the convent stood not far off from Isabella's house, and her father inviting his friends, and they others, Isabella had one of the noblest and most honourable trains to accompany her thither as in the like occasions was never seen in Seville.

There accompanied her the Asistente, the Dean of the Church, and the Vicar-General of the Archbishop, and all the ladies and gentlemen of title and quality that were in the city, so great was the desire that all of them had to see that sun of Isabella's beauty which had so many months been eclipsed. And because it is the custom and fashion of those damsels which go to take the habit to be as gallant and as bravely adorned as possibly they can devise, who as one that ever after from that instant takes her leave and farewell of all bravery and wholly discards it, Isabella was willing, that she might not break so ancient a custom, to trick and set forth herself in the best and most curious manner that possibly she could invent. And therefore she did put on that gown and kirtle and those rich dressings which she had on when she went to see the Queen of England, and we have heretofore told you how rich, how sightly, and how magnificent it was. There came forth to public view those orient pearls and that glittering diamond, with the carcanet, chain, and girdle, which likewise were of great value.

With this adornment and her own good looks, that gave occasion to all to praise God in her, Isabella went out of her house on foot, for her being so near unto the convent excused coaches and caroches. The concourse of the people was so great that it repented them that they had not taken coach, for they would not give them way to get to the nunnery. Some blessed her parents, others Heaven that had enriched her with so much beauty; some did stand on tiptoe for to see her, others having seen her once, ran to get afore that they might see her again.

But he that showed himself most solicitous in this kind, and so much that many took notice of him for it, was a man clad in one of those habits which they wear who return home redeemed from their captivity with a mark of the Trinity on their breasts, in token that they have been liberated by the charity of their redeemers. This captive, then, at that very time that Isabella had set one foot within the porch of the convent, whither were come forth to receive her, as the use is amongst them, the Prioress and the nuns, with a loud voice he cried out, "Stay, Isabella, stay! for whilst that I shall be alive thou canst not enter into any religious order."

At the hearing of these words Isabella and her parents looked back, and saw that, cleaving out his way through the thickest of the throng, that captive came making towards them, whose blue round bonnet being fallen off which he wore on his head, he discovered a confused and entangled skein of golden-wired hairs, curling themselves into rings, and a face intermixed with crimson and snow, so pure red and white was his complexion, all of them assured signs and tokens inducing all of them to take and hold him to be a stranger.

In effect, one while falling through too much haste, and then getting him up quickly again, he came at last where Isabella was, and taking her by the hand said unto her, "Knowest thou me, Isabella? Look well upon me; behold that I am Ricaredo thy husband."

"Yes, I know thee," replied Isabella, "if thou art not a phantasma, that is come to disturb my repose."

Her parents drew nearer and nearer unto him, and did view and eye him very narrowly, and in conclusion came certainly to know that this captive was Ricaredo; who with tears in his eyes, falling down on his knees before Isabella besought her that the strangeness of that habit wherein she now saw him might not be a bar to her better knowledge of him, nor that this his mean and baser fortune should be a hindrance to the making good of that word and faithful promise which they had given and plighted each to other.

Isabella, maugre the impression which Ricaredo's mother's letter had made in her memory, sending her the news of his death, chose rather to give more credit to her eyes and the truth which she had present before her, than to trouble herself to make a further needless inquiry. And therefore, kindly embracing the captive, she said unto him:

"You doubtless, sir, are the only man who can hinder my determination; since that you are truly my husband, you can be no less than the better half of my soul. I have thee imprinted in my memory, and have laid thee up in my heart. The news of your death, which my lady and your mother wrote to me, if it did not take away my life, made me choose the life of religion, which at this moment I sought to enter, to live in it. But since God by so just an impediment shows that He desires otherwise, neither can we hinder it nor does it become me that on my part His will should be hindered. Come therefore, sir, unto my father's house, which is yours, and there I will deliver up unto you the possession of my person, on the terms which our holy Catholic faith demands."

All these words the standers-by heard, together with the Asistente, the Dean, and the Archbishop's Vicar-General of Seville; at the hearing whereof they were all of them stricken with admiration, and stood a while as men astonished; and were desirous that it might presently be told them what history this, and what stranger that was, and of what marriage they treated. Whereunto Isabella's father made answer, saying that that history required another place and some time for to tell it; and therefore besought them, since that they were so willing to know it, that they would be pleased to return back with him to his house, seeing that it was so near, and that there it should be recounted unto them, and in such a manner that with the truth thereof they should remain satisfied, and at the strangeness of that sequel amazed.

This was no sooner said but that one of those there present spake aloud, saying, "Gentlemen, this young man is a great English pirate, for I know him well enough; and this is he who, some two years since and somewhat more, took from the pirates of Algiers that ship of Portugal which came from the Indies. Ye need not doubt that this is the man, for I confidently tell you that I know him; for he gave me my liberty and money to bring me home to Spain, and did not only free me, but three hundred captive more, furnishing them with victuals and moneys." With these words the vulgar were in an uproar, and the desire afresh revived which all of them had to know and see such intricate things as these to be fully cleared.

In fine, the gentlemen of more especial rank and quality, with the Asistente and those two principal Churchmen, returned back to accompany Isabella to her house, leaving the nuns sorrowful and weeping that they had lost so fair a sister and companion as Isabella; who being come home, and having brought the gentlemen into a spacious large hall, entreated them to sit down. And albeit Ricaredo was willing enough to take upon him the relating of this desired history, yet notwithstanding it seemed good unto him rather to trust Isabella's tongue and discretion with it than his own, who did not very perfectly speak the language of Spain. All that were present were in a still silence, and having their ears and souls ready prepared to hear what Isabella would say, she began to recount the story, which I reduce briefly to this: that she delivered all that unto them which happened from the day that Clotaldo by stealth carried her away from Cadiz till her return thither again; not omitting the battle which Ricaredo fought with the Turks, and the liberality and bounty which he had used towards the Christians, and the faith which both of them had plighted each to other to be man and wife; the promise of two years, the news which she had received of his death, and that so certain to her seeming that it put her into that course which they had so lately seen of professing herself a nun. She did endear the Queen of England's bounty towards her, and the Christianity of Ricaredo and his parents; and ended her speech with desiring Ricaredo that he would relate what had befallen him from the time that he left London until this very present, wherein they saw him clad in the habit of a captive and with a badge in his breast, betokening that he was redeemed by way of alms.

"It is true as you say," replied Ricaredo, "and in a few short words I will sum up unto you my many and great troubles. After that I went out of London for to excuse the marriage which I could not make with Clisterna (that Scottish Catholic damsel with whom Isabella told you my parents would have me to marry,) taking Guillarte along with me (that page who as my mother's letters made mention, brought the news to London of my death), crossing France, I came to Rome, where my soul was cheered and my faith fortified. I kissed the feet of the chief Pontiff, I confessed my sins to the Grand Penitentiary; he absolved me of them, and handed me the necessary credentials which should give testimony of my confession and penitence, and of the submission I had made to our universal mother, the Church. This done, I visited the places, as holy as they are numerous, that there are in that holy city; and of those two thousand crowns which I had in gold, I delivered a thousand and six hundred to a banker, who gave me a bill to receive so much in this city, upon one Roqui, a Florentine; and with those four hundred which remained with me, with intention to come for Spain, I made for Genoa; whence I had notice given me that there were two galleys of that signory to go for Spain.

"I came with Guillarte my servant to a certain town called Aquapendente, which as you come from Rome to Florence is the last which the Pope holds; and in an *osteria* or inn where I alighted I found the Earl Arnesto, my mortal enemy, who with four servants went disguised, and went, as I conceive, more from curiosity than from being a Catholic, to Rome. I did verily believe that he had not known me; I shut myself up in my lodging with my servant, and there kept myself close, and with a great deal of care and vigilance, and with a determination and purpose at the shutting-in of night to get me gone, and to change that my lodging for a safer. But I did not do it, because the great carelessness which I observed in the Earl and his followers did assure me that he did not know me. I supped in my lodging; I made fast the door, stood upon my guard with my sword in my hand; I recommended myself to God, and would not that night go to bed. Myself and my servant lay down on a bench to take a little rest and sleep, and myself was half fallen asleep.

"But a little after midnight they awakened me with purpose to make me sleep an eternal sleep. Four pistols, as I afterwards understood, the Earl and his servants discharged against me, leaving me for dead; and having their horses already in a readiness, they presently put foot in stirrup and went away, bidding the host of the inn that he would see me fairly buried, for that I was a man of principal note and quality. My servant, as mine host afterwards told me, awakened with the noise, out of very fear leapt down from a window that looked out into a base-court, crying out, 'O miserable and unfortunate that I am! they have slain my lord and master!' and having said this he hied him out of the inn, and that with such fear and haste that he did not so much as look back or make any stay till he came to London, so that it was he who brought the news of my death.

"They of the inn got up, found me shot athwart my body with four bullets and wounded with many other lesser shot, but all of them lighting on such parts that there was not one mortal wound amongst them all. I begged for confession and all the sacraments, like a Catholic Christian. They gave me them, and cured me, but it was two months and longer before I was able to travel.

"At the end whereof I came to Genoa, where I found no other passage save in two small boats[1] which myself and two other principal Spaniards hired, the one to go before as a vessel of advice for discovery, and the other we went in ourselves.

"With this security we embarked ourselves; sailing along the shore with intention not to go out to sea. But coming over against that place which they call Las Tres Marias, or The Three Marys,[2] which is on the coast of France, and our first boat going forward to see if she could discover anything, in an unlucky hour there came forth two Turkish galleys that lay lurking there in a little creek of the sea, and the one of them putting herself forth to the sea and the other keeping close by the land, when we meant to run ashore, we were prevented in our course, and taken by the Turks. We went on board, and they stripped us of all that we had even to our naked skins. They rifled the boats of all that they had, and suffered them to run ashore, without offering to sink them, saying that they would serve another time to bring them another *galima* (for by this name they call those spoils and booties which they take from the Christians).

"Ye may very well believe me if I tell you that I felt in my soul the soreness of my captivity, and above all the loss of those certificates and provisions I received at Rome, which I brought along with me, lapped up in a little box of tin, as likewise my bill of exchange for a thousand and six hundred crowns. But, as good luck would have it, they lighted into the hands of a Christian captive, a Spaniard, who kept them safe; for if they had once come to the Turks' fingering, I should at least have given for my ransom as much as my bill made mention of.

"They brought me to Algiers, where I found the Fathers of the Order of the Blessed Trinity treating of the redeeming of Christian captives. I spake with them; I told them who I was; and moved out of charity, though I was a stranger unto them, they redeemed me in this form and manner following. They gave for me three hundred ducats, one hundred to be laid down presently, and the other two at the next return of the ship that should come to redeem the father of that society, who remained in Algiers, engaged in four thousand ducats more than those that he brought with him; for to such great pity and compassion extendeth the charity of these men, that they give their own for other folk's liberty, and remain themselves captives for to free others from captivity. And for an addition of

---

[1] *Falugas*, feluccas.

[2] Probably Les Saintes Maries, a little walled town at the mouth of the Rhone, 25 miles S. of Arles. Here is said to have taken place the piratical attack in which Cervantes and his brother were captured by the Turks, in 1575.

this happiness of my liberty, I found my lost box, with my certificates and my bill also of exchange. I showed it to that holy father who had ransomed me, and I offered him five hundred ducats more than my ransom came to, towards the payment of his engagement.

"It was almost a year ere the ship of alms returned, and that which in the interim happened unto me, if I should go about to recount it now unto you, it would be another new history. Only I will tell you that I was known of one of the twenty Turks whom I had set at liberty with the rest of the Christians before mentioned. But he was so thankful and so honest a man that he would not discover me. For had the Turks known that I was the man that sunk their two galleys, and took out of their hands that great ship of India, they would either have presented me to the Great Turk, or have taken away my life; and to have presented me to the Great Turk had been the loss of my liberty during life.

"In conclusion, the father that did ransom me came to Spain with me, together with other fifty redeemed captives. In Valencia we made a general procession,[1] and from thence every one went his own way which he liked best, with these ensigns and tokens of their liberty which are these poor kind of habits. This day I came to this city, with so great and earnest a desire to see my espoused Isabella, that without any other thing detaining me, I inquired for this convent, where I was to have notice given me of my spouse. That which herein hath befallen me ye have already seen; that which remaineth to be seen are these certificates in order that my story may be known to be true, for it has in it as much of miracle as of truth."

And with that he took out from a tin box the certificates of which he spoke, and put them into the Dean's hand, who perused them together with the Asistente, who did not find anything in them that might make doubt of the truth of that which Ricaredo had delivered unto them; and for further confirmation thereof, Heaven had so ordained it that the Florentine merchant was present at all this upon whom the bill was for the payment of sixteen hundred ducats. He entreated that they would let him see the bill; and they showing it him, he presently acknowledged and accepted it, for it was many months since that he had ordered for it. All this was but to add admiration to admiration, and amazement to amazement.

The Asistente embraced Ricaredo, and Isabella's parents, and herself; all of them in very courteous language offering them their service. The like did the two clergymen, and entreated Isabella that she would set

---

[1] To the Cathedral, to give thanks for their release.

down this story in writing, that the Archbishop might read it, which she promised she would.

The great silence, which all those standing by had preserved in listening to this strange tale, was broken in giving thanks to God for His marvellous works; and the people from the highest to the lowest giving congratulation to Isabella, Ricaredo, and their parents, they took their leaves. And they on the other side besought the Asistente that he would honour their wedding with his presence, which some eight days hence they did purpose to celebrate. The Asistente was very well pleased with the motion; and within eight days after, accompanied with all the highest and principal persons of the city, he waited on them to church.

By these turnings and windings, and by these circumstances, Isabella's parents recovered their daughter, and were restored to their former wealth; and she, assisted by her many virtues, in despite of so many inconveniencies, lighted on a husband of such especial rank and quality as Ricaredo; in whose company, it is said, she still liveth in that house which they rented right over against Santa Paula, which since they bought of the heirs of a gentleman of Burgos, called Hernando de Cifuentes.

This tale may teach us what great power virtue and beauty have, since that both of them together, and each of them by themselves, are of force to make even their enemies in love with them, as likewise how that Heaven knows from the greatest adversities and afflictions to draw the greatest benefits and comforts.

GEORGIA

ELGUJA[1]

A ROMANCE OF THE CAUCASIAN MOUNTAINS

Alexander Kazbek

IN THE pass of Darial where now the fine high road runs and twists like a serpent between black rocks, there was in former times only a narrow track along which caravans of horses could barely travel. This track went from the north of the Caucasus into Georgia, it traversed the narrow gorge of Lars, but when it reached the rocks of Darial the rock was pierced, the road went through a tunnel, and at the entrance of the tunnel stood a guard of villagers and protected Georgia from uninvited guests.

One cold night, when the mist was thick and the place even darker than usual on that account, at the mouth of the tunnel several guards had lighted a fire and sat round it. They were cooking roast steaks of mountain goat and waiting for supper. Just then the sound of horses' feet was heard. The guards seized their guns and in a moment hid themselves behind rocks on each side of the road. This took place so quickly and quietly that no one could have noticed them and the unsuspicious traveller must easily fall into their hands... A few moments passed, and then a horseman appeared and rode boldly up. The silent guards, who until now were resting their guns on the rocks and were motionless as statues, at once leaped up and surrounded the horseman.

"Who art thou?" asked one of the guards.

"I am Makhametha, an Osset, *seni tsirime*,"[2] answered the horseman.

"Whence dost thou come, and whither art thou bound?"

"To Chophicashvili's... I am his guest."

"Eh? What hast thou there rolled up in thy *nabadi* [felt cloak]?" asked the guard, noticing something tied up on the saddle.

"A girl. I am taking her to him."

"Where hast thou been hunting? Where?" asked the guard, and smiled.

---

[1] Translated by Sir Oliver Wardrop.

[2] *I.e. sheni dchirime*, meaning "thy plague on me," an expletive used to express intense devotion to a person, but never to be employed in addressing a woman.

"I stole her in Circassia," said the Osset, lying as usual....

"May God's wrath come upon thee!" muttered the guard.

"I swear by thy sun [*i.e.*, life] that she is from Circassia."

"Enough! I know... don't I know thee? Thou hast bought her from Sulonanthi (an Osset chief) and now thou sayest thou hast stolen her in Circassia."

"No, by my sun!"

"Enough! Enough!" roughly interrupted the guard, and turning to his comrades he said: "Could he go to Circassia?"

"He is not an Osset, *sheni dchirime*," said another guard. "How could he go to Circassia?"

"What are the Ossets?... They are cats and nothing else."

"Elguja!" cried that guard who had first spoken with Makhametha, and who was in command.

"What dost thou want?"

"Go, go with him, take him to the Chophicashvili's and if he has lied kill him like a dog and throw away his carcase."

"Very well!"

"If he tries to run away on the road, don't give him the chance."

"Very well!" was the answer, as before.

Elguja was a young man of twenty-two, of fine figure and commanding presence, the bravest man in the country, an excellent shot; besides this he was a good-hearted youth, as for the most part were the men of that region.

Elguja took his gun on his shoulder and cried to Makhametha: "Go!" Makhametha went on in front, Elguja carefully following him in order fulfil literally his chief's command. At that time God forbid that Makhametha should in the least degree swerve from the road. Elguja would have killed him like a dog and thrown him over the cliff. So they went silently, without uttering a word. Makhametha was convinced that the eye of his guard keenly watched him, and the guard was sure that if Makhametha dared to do anything he could not go far without being laid low by a bullet; if for any cause he missed and Makhametha tried to escape then it would be easy for Elguja to get in front of him, because he was on foot and the path was four times shorter for him than for a mounted man. They arrived at the village of Stephan-tsminda and went straight to the door of Gagi Chophicashvili, where Elguja went in front and cried aloud:

"Gagi! Hey Gagi-i-i! Gagi!"

At this word a gun appeared on the verandah, which was protected by a wall, and a voice was heard:

"Who is there? Who is calling?"

"'Tis I! Elguja!"

"What is the matter at this time of night?"

"I have brought a cat," said Elguja, and looked at the Osset.

"Is he alone?"

"No!... He has a girl with him."

Gagi quietly turned, roused his men, who at his call armed themselves with their guns, and came out. This was at the time when Georgia had come under the protection of Russia; it was a time of disorder and constant warfare between those who were satisfied to accept the new rule and those who were not, so nobody went about unarmed.

"Onise, go out, see!... Take the guest into the parlour, hand over the prisoner to the women, let them see that she does not escape." Onise went to fulfil the command, but Gagi stopped him, muttered something, and said aloud:

"Wait, I myself will go."

Gagi immediately recognized Makhametha, with whom more than once he had dealings of this kind, therefore they saluted each other, shook hands and began to speak in a friendly manner. Makhametha acknowledged that the girl was a Circassian, and that a Kisthian had brought her for sale into Ossetia, where Makhametha had met him and had bought her for Gagi. He then praised the girl, saying that she was as straight as an arrow and her lips were like a newly opened rose. Gagi removed the girl's hood, came close to her face and with the eye of a buyer began his examination.

"Yes, she is pretty!" he remarked, and turning to Elguja he continued: "But thou art tired, put the woman into this bed and sleep outside her door... Do not forget to bar the door."

Elguja took the girl away and Gagi led Makhametha into the parlour, where he wished to do honour to his dear guest, in order that he should put a lower price on the woman. Elguja took the girl to her bedroom, he lighted a pine-torch and as soon as he looked at the girl he was struck motionless. Before his eyes appeared a beautiful, attractive girl of fifteen or sixteen who unexpectedly made his heart palpitate and in his veins the blood boiled. What was he doing? Where was he?—He forgot completely. He was mastered by his desire alone thus to gaze constantly at the beauty of the girl, and enjoy that feeling which, for the first time, awoke in his heart. The girl stood pale and sad, with downcast eyes, abstracted in some deep thought. Elguja was grieved at her condition. He wished to speak some comforting word, but he did not know the language, and it would have been difficult for him to speak even if he had known it. There are sometimes occasions in a man's life when he feels, suffers, wishes to say something, but the tongue will not obey, and words cannot be found. In such a state was Elguja. At last, somehow, he came to himself, he stuck the torch in the wall, pointed to the bedclothes and signed to her to make the bed. He stayed a short time, gazed, and turned away. When he came to the door he turned again and saw that the girl's eyes were fixed upon him, and looked in such a way as if they sympathized with the motion of Elguja's heart and thanked him... Elguja could bear it no longer; he leaped forward and pressed the girl to his breast; she, frightened and agitated by some hitherto unknown feeling, was submissive, and closely clasped him to her bosom. At that moment desire, fear, love were expressed; a struggle took place between the feelings aroused, but neither of them could have said what was happening, what they were doing, or why they did thus and not otherwise. God knows this blissful moment would have lasted a long time and it would have carried them too far unless their self-forgetfulness had been interrupted by a noise which was heard at the door of the parlour. Elguja gave her a last fond embrace and ardently kissed her, and then went out intoxicated, mad, and with a beating heart lay down outside the door. Gagi went out to the front of the house and ordered his men to treat the guest well.

When the master of the house had sent the men about their business he went to the bedroom where the prisoner was shut up. Makhametha had claimed such beauty for the girl and had drawn such a picture of her graceful carriage, her lips, her eyes, her hair, that Gagi was quite captivated, and a thousand shameful thoughts dominated his lustful heart... Gagi could not wait till dawn, and wished that very night to enjoy the beauty of the Circassian. He came to the place where Elguja was lying, stood there for some time and listened. Elguja snored, though he was not asleep. This encouraged Gagi; he quietly stepped over Elguja, opened the door, and went into the bedroom. As the door was shut, Elguja leaped to his feet, and with furious eyes looked through the window. The girl, when she saw a strange man enter, pressed trembling against the wall. As soon as Gagi saw her, he was at once seized by a brutal passion, and with bloodshot eyes he went towards her. The girl was terrified, screamed and pressed still more closely to the wall. Elguja's eyes shot fire, his heart rose within him, he seized his dagger with a quivering hand and looked fierce. In another moment he could bear it no longer, and rushed into the room like a madman.

"Who is there? What cry was that?" said he, as if he had been roused by the woman's cry.

Gagi shivered, and inwardly cursed Elguja a thousand times for coming in uninvited at such a time; shame, however, prevented him from saying anything but: "Nobody! It is I. I came to see if the door was shut, and came in..." and then he bethought himself: If not to-day, then to-morrow thou shalt be mine. He turned to Elguja: "Now let us go. Lock the door; that will be enough."

Day dawned and the rays of the sun put a golden crown on the brow of Mount Kazbek. The sleeping village woke, people began to move about, and Gagi's household rose too. The women found out that a Circassian prisoner had been brought in; they began to whisper to one another about her and were anxious to see her, to find out who she was and all about her. At last a man came in, brought a key and gave it to the women.

"Gagi says there is a woman in that room, and you are to bring her out," said the man.

"Who is she? Is she really a Circassian? How old is she? Is she pretty?" shouted the women, pressing round the servant.

"How do I know? I have not seen her... Gagi said you were to look after her carefully."

"Where is Gagi?" asked somebody.

"A man came for him and he left before dawn for the land of the Khevsurs."

"But why did he go?"

"Enough! Go and look after the girl, she must be hungry," interrupted the man. "Get along with you, Jajala! Take the key and bring her out."

Jajala was the youngest woman in the house, and so she was ordered about by everybody and had to obey everybody; even if it had not been so she would have gone gladly to release the prisoner, would have waited upon her and tried with all her might to comfort her, for Jajala's mother had been just such a prisoner and she remembered her mother's stories about the condition of prisoners and their feelings. She knew a little Circassian which her mother had taught her.

On the entrance of Jajala the prisoner trembled and leaped to her feet. Jajala came up, made her sit down, and sympathetically said in Circassian: "Sit down, sit down. Thou must be tired." The Circassian was surprised to hear her native tongue, and gladly said: "So they speak Circassian here?"

"Why not? Yes, yes, they do. Don't be afraid, the people here are just the same as in Circassia."

"And they won't torture and kill me?"

"Surely thou dost not think we are heathens. Do not fear."

"A man frightened me so much last night... He had such a look, such

585

eyes, that I almost fainted. If that young man had not come in I should certainly have been killed."

Jajala understood that the man who had startled her was Gagi, but who the youth was she could not imagine. "Art thou a Circassian?" asked Jajala. "I am." "My mother was a Circassian too." "Indeed?" "Yes... She also was carried off. What is thy name?" "Mzagho" (*i.e.* Moonbeam). "Art thou not hungry?" "No." "Let us go and eat something or thou wilt faint." "Whither shall we go?" "To our women."

They left the room and went away together to the women's quarters, where the women surrounded the Circassian as soon as she entered, and inspected her from head to foot as if they had never seen a human being before. At last they all settled down quietly to their work and Jajala was left to look after Mzagho. Mzagho was astonished that she did not see anywhere the young man who had pleased her so much, and who had so unexpectedly kindled the fire of love in her heart. Perhaps Elguja's love had departed as swiftly as it came. She wished to talk to somebody about this, but she dared not trust anybody... But where is that hideous monster with the bloodshot eyes? thought she, though she was glad he did not appear.

Hardly had Gagi and Elguja left the room when a horseman rode up to Gagi's house, quickly dismounted, went up to the master of the house and told him that the Mthiuleth-Gudamakhrelians had revolted and surrounded the Russians in a thicket in Mthiulethi, whither they summoned him to come at once as leader of the men of his valley. There the Mthiulians had assembled under Prince Alexander to check the Russians. Gagi left that night, taking Elguja with him. This was why Elguja had not the chance of looking again at his incomparable Circassian who had set his blood rushing along like a mountain stream. On the road, Elguja thought of his lovely Mzagho, and in his heart heaped curses on the mountaineers for rising at such an inopportune moment. Elguja went along the road, but his heart stayed behind. The girl so completely possessed his mind that he sought a thousand pretexts for going back... At last he resolved that he was behaving like a woman at a time when his fellow-countrymen were on the point of making an effort to free themselves from the common enemy; it would be the behaviour of an old woman to go home to woo his love. He thought it shameful for a brave youth at such a time to stand back from his fellows and hide himself in a house... I am a man, a hat (and not a veil) covers me. I shall go and show my bravery, get glory, do service to my people, and when we return in peace then I shall ask Gagi for the girl and he will give her to me.

Elguja's hope was not realized. Instead of a cruel battle taking place, a neighbouring chieftain soon pacified the people by bribes, and Gagi and Elguja had to go home again. At this time the Russian army in Georgia was reinforced, strong positions were taken up, villages were occupied and fortified, so that any movement on the part of the mountaineers became impossible. Gagi saw his position and, realizing where his advantage lay, went over to the Russians, who made him an officer.

All this happened do quickly, and in Georgia there was then such an agitation and things were in such a state that all forgot their personal affairs and duties. Of course, Gagi was no exception, and he forgot or postponed his brutal instincts with regard to his prisoner. For this reason, Elguja had plenty of opportunity to woo Mzagho, and he took advantage of it as far as his ignorance of the language allowed. Jajala acted as interpreter between the lovers and thus she and Mzagho became so friendly that they hid nothing from each other, and of course they had no secrets from Elguja. The lovers decided that Elguja should demand Mzagho and pay Gagi whatever he asked, and if he would not agree Elguja would carry her off. Thus passed days, weeks, and still the matter was not concluded, on account of the absence of Gagi, to whom several soldiers had been entrusted, and who had been sent to chastise various guilty districts of mountaineers, so could not come home, and Elguja could not speak to him.

One moonlight evening, when the whole valley was out at haymaking, Gagi's mowers lighted a fire, put a sheep in the pot and prepared supper. The men and women sat round, and as they waited for the meal their usually merry faces had an extraordinary appearance of sadness. All these people were still ignorant of the fate which awaited them, and with trembling looked to the future, in which they saw, rightly or wrongly, oppression and mastery from another people, another race. The spread of this idea was aided by the appearance of officials, wild and brutal in manner. Among the haymakers was the new prisoner. She had retired to one side, and with sad eyes looked towards the mountain covered with eternal snows on which the moonbeams fell and made a picture quite as beautiful as at morning. The people went to supper and called Mzagho. As soon as the portions were served out, a haymaker came with a scythe on his shoulder and cried: "God prosper you!" "God give you long life!" was the reply, and they invited him to supper. "Come here, come here!" and they made room for Elguja. Generally on the mountain in such cases people are not shy of one another, one labourer goes to another to pass the time and share a meal. Elguja was well acquainted with Gagi's haymakers, since he belonged to the same village, and while he was on guard often went to Gagi's house.

After supper, when all had lain down and were sound asleep, Elguja slipped noiselessly over to that side where Mzagho was lying. On Elguja's approach, Mzagho started up, but as soon as she saw him, she was quiet. Elguja made a sign for her to follow him, and quietly, like thieves, they moved towards the forest, which began quite near there. Silent, holding their breath, they went like lifeless spectres till they entered the wood, but when the thick foliage concealed them, and no eye could see them, Elguja suddenly turned to the girl, seized her in his strong arms, pressed her to his heart and began to kiss her... By this time Mzagho had learned a few words of Georgian, and they were thus able, without interpreter, to tell each other the feelings of their hearts. After the first caresses, Elguja, with a groan, sadly told Mzagho that he had sent a man to Gagi to demand her, but Gagi refused, and there was nothing left for it but to carry her off. Finally, he added:

"What dost thou say?... Will thou go with me or not?"

"I have wholly given myself up to thee. Take me with thee whither thou wilt..."

"I shall have to take thee to the land of the Tushes."

"Whithersoever thou wilt!"

"But if thou becomest tired of it, what then?"

"The love of our women is hard to win, but he whom they love is their lord... Tell me what thou wouldst have me do."

To these words Elguja replied with a passionate kiss:

"I have prepared everything. In the wood here I have horses and weapons hidden. We cannot go by the Gudamaqari valley, for the roads are closed, and it is a narrow valley. We must go by Mthiulethi."

"Thou knowest best."

"So we shall not delay, my sun?"

"Thou knowest."

"Art thou not afraid?"

"With thee?..." She replied in such a tone that Elguja was ashamed of having asked her.

On these words, Elguja three times gave a long, low whistle. A short time passed, and before them suddenly appeared a young man fully armed.

"Is it thou, Givargi [George]?"

"Yes! it is I."

"Where hast thou put the arms?"

"Here they are," answered the new arrival, and handed over the weapons.

"And the horses?"

"The horses are here," said George, and pointed into the forest.

"Go and bring them."

George went for the horses, while Elguja quietly and resolutely armed himself. It was clear that he had made up his mind not to let anybody take his Mzagho easily, and any who stopped him on the road would pay dearly for their boldness. George came with the horses and they mounted. When everything was ready for the start, Elguja turned to George:

"George!"

"What is thy will?"

"I am starting on a dangerous and bad road, go back now!"

"What is that thou art saying?" said George with astonishment.

"Who knows what may happen! Why shouldst thou risk thy head?"

"Did I become thy blood-brother for this, that I should hear such things?" said George, with a pained expression. "Enough, let us go, do not waste time!"

"So thou wilt go too?"

"I go. Where thou diest, there must I die too."

"Thou knowest best," was the reply, and George took off his hat: "Great God of the peak, angel of the Persians, help Thou us, grant that we may take with us Thy blessing!" uttered Elguja. "O God, demand retribution from a traitorous comrade wherever he may be," added George. "Amen," said both together. For a few moments longer they stood bareheaded, silently they prayed to the icons and angels of the place, and there was something grand in this prayer, a certain menace, a certain hope and comfort. At last they both put on their caps. "Go on in front," cried Elguja. George struck his horse with his whip, Mzagho followed him, and last of all came Elguja.

Our travellers went along quietly and carefully, guided by George. They went undisturbed through the village of Cobi, where there was most to be feared, and safely reached the mountains they had to cross. They went towards the thickets of Mthiulethi, which they wished to enter by night, because there the dense woods began in which they would be able to hide. So thought our travellers, and therefore from moment to moment the gazed at the sky, where the stars would show them the hour. "Go on, George, hasten!" Elguja said frequently to his guide. "Dawn has already come, and we shall not reach the valley of Kaishaur by nightfall." "God is merciful!" George would say, striking with his whip his trusty horse, which went along with that peculiar jogtrot which the mountaineers call the "wolf's pace." In this way they soon got over the ground.

Dawn broke, light spread over the earth and showed the travellers a lovely slope. Here nature changed altogether and became more beautifully rich and varied. The bush-covered plains were encircled by wooded hills, the trees of which had here and there been felled by the Mthiulians; they had made clearings and had there erected their tower-like abodes. The pleasant, refreshing zephyr which blows unceasingly round those spots cooled the brow and roused new life in the wearied minds of the travellers. The limpid streams murmured and tenderly caressed the ear. The little birds awoke and twittered forth the praise of nature's power. Everything was so ordered that a man would wish to dismount there to roast his meat and for a short time enjoy the scene. Such was the influence the place had, not only on men but on beasts, whom it attracted by its luscious, rich, green grass adorned by a thousand flowers and scents. Elguja gazed on this picture and his heart began to beat quickly... He longed for the happiness of enjoying in freedom the beauty of such scenes.

While Elguja was thinking thus, and completely absorbed in his dream, George suddenly stopped his horse.

"What is the matter?" enquired Elguja.

"See! some horsemen have appeared down there on the slope... Let us turn the horses' heads into these bushes before it is too light."

"So be it!" briefly answered Elguja, and began to look at the place where George had pointed out the horsemen.

They turned aside the horses and entered among the bushes, in which they would be sufficiently hidden from the eye of man. There they dismounted and spread out a cloak on which they laid Mzagho. George led the horses a little way off, tied them and left them to feed; he himself got ready his gun, changed the tinder in the flintlock and lay down on his side carelessly, as if he were at home. Elguja went quietly to the edge of the road and took up a position in the bushes by the roadside, whence he could look out and, unseen by all, could see and hear everything.

The horsemen, numbering twenty-five, gradually approached the spot, and came along in such order as if they were prepared to fight. First came the guide, then the others in fours. When they were near the place into which Elguja and his companions had ridden, the guide of the unknown travellers suddenly stopped his horse and began to examine the ground. The others came up and asked why he had stopped. The leading man replied:

"There are marks of horses' feet, and I do not know whither they go."

"What should horses do here?" said a grey-haired man who was chief of the band, and in whose glittering epaulettes one might recognize Gagi. He stopped his horse, leaned over its side, and began to look for the tracks with puckered brows; for some time he moved his head backwards and forwards, taking care that his own horse should not obliterate the marks.

"There are three of them. The tracks are clear. The horses needed shoeing," he muttered disjointedly, as if speaking to himself. On looking at the dew on the ground it was easy to see the footprints of unshod horses, which had left what is called by the mountaineers a "frog's mark," a sign that a horse is unshod. •

"These could not have been good men," cried out Gagi, raising his head.

"If they were good men, why should they leave the road?"

"Is there no footpath then?" said Gagi, turning to the Mthiulian who accompanied him.

"No! (May thy sufferings fall on me!) No! How should there be a path? There is no village anywhere there," was the answer.

"If there is no village, what are these things here?" enquired Gagi, and pointed with his hand towards the mountain, where here and there on the sides the houses of the Mthiulians could be seen.

"There are villages, but there is no way to them (May thy sufferings fall on me!). There lies between such a ravine (I swear it by the lion St George!) that no bird could fly over it."

"Then they must be in this thicket."

"Then I don't know why the devil they went there. Over by that mountain there is a ravine, and there there is a rock that no man could bear even to look at."

They were deep in this conversation, when from above, on the slope, there appeared a horseman who galloped as fast as he could. He paid no heed to the steeps nor the holes nor the ravines, where one false step of his horse would have meant ruin. It was evident that he was on some important errand. The band saw the horseman and turned their attention to him.

Elguja, who had been looking anxiously at the new arrivals, cast a glance at the new horseman, and felt in his heart a presentiment of evil.

"This must be one of our pursuers."

Elguja knew very well that if Gagi learnt of the abduction of the girl, and that they were there, then the matter would not end without bloodshed, the stubborn Gagi would not for anything endure such a disgrace and dishonour as that a girl should be carried off from his house. Elguja did not trouble about this, he knew that he could bravely meet the attack, but, besides this, there was one there whose one breath was dearer to him than life. And this tortured him and burned his heart. This was why he thought so bitterly, and the sweat of grief flowed, while if he had been alone it would not have cost him much thought, and he would have shown those impertinent fellows who had stopped to examine the tracks how handy hs was with his gun. Elguja was angry that Gagi had stopped there and begun to look at the tracks where they turned aside and left the road to him. In such a case in the mountains even his bitterest enemy would have left him alone and not followed him. While Elguja was thinking this, the horseman approached Gagi and his companions; they knew this horseman very well.

"What news is there, Martia?" cried Gagi from a distance.

"What news indeed? Elguja has carried off the girl. He has disgraced the house. He has insulted the chief of our people."

"Phew! Did Elguja dare to do this? Elguja?"

"Elguja! Who else would have dared to do it? Are you not men? How did you let him carry off the girl? You cowards! You old women, you... instead of hats you should wear *chikilas* [*i.e. lechakis* the long white veils worn by women over their hair]. Pooh! you have no honour!"

"He carried her off by night, like a thief, or we should have behaved like sons of our fathers."

Then Gagi thought, like a man of experience, that those horse tracks doubtless had something to do with Elguja, and he made up his mind to find those horses, and seize their riders.

Elguja distinctly heard the conversation of Gagi and Martia, and went towards George to let him know that they were discovered and that Gagi meant to seize them. The comrades then left their horses, took the girl's hand and fled to seek a strong place where they could hide the girl without fear, and then... let these people know with what sort of fellows they had to deal, and that it was not easy to capture two mountaineers.

As we said before, this plain on one side is edged by a steep, precipitous rock, over which a bird might fly, but certainly no man could scale it. On the other side was a great ravine. Just at the higher end of the rock, and near the ravine, they found exactly the sort of place they were looking for. A few steps from the rock, as if prepared on purpose, was a hillock, which overlooked the plain and commanded it all round. At the beginning of this hillock there rose teeth-like rocks, and in the middle was a hollow in which twenty or thirty men might freely find shelter. As soon as they saw this place they gladly hastened to it.

"God and St George are with us!" cried Elguja.

"Let us go up there and we'll lead them a pretty dance," replied George.

Mzagho until now had been pale, silent, and trembling. At these last words, hope returned and she said: "If we go up there have we no cause for fear?"

"God is merciful!" was Elguja's reply.

"What do they want with us?" said Mzagho so sadly that any heart would have been moved.

"What indeed do they want?" asked George.

"What they want is that we should kill them like dogs and cast them as carrion to the birds of prey."

"Then there will be a battle, and you must kill each other. O God! O God!" said the girl mournfully.

"Do not be afraid, when they find the horses the greedy eyes of Gagi will be satisfied, but if, nevertheless, they are not hindered and come here, I swear by St George, we shall make them pay dearly for their greed."

"We shall make it so hot for them, by the grace of the Angel of the Peak and of the Persians, that each of them will curse his fate."

During this conversation they had reached the top of the hillock where they took up as strong a position as was possible for two men. They showed Mzagho a place where no bullet could reach her, and told her not to move from there. Finally, they stretched out their cloaks and threw on them their powder-horns and shot-pouches and changed the tinder in their flint-locks. At last, when they had finished their preparations, Elguja cried out: "Now let our visitors come! They are good guests, but, by God's help, we shall show ourselves good hosts! Is it not so?"—"Aye! Aye! We shall give them a good reception!" was the answer.

Recent events made Gagi bethink himself. Just when he thought he had raised himself by his duplicity and found honour and power, an when he had taken the oath to the mighty Russian Emperor and entered his service as an officer, that fellow Elguja had stood in his way, dishonoured his name, carried off the girl and made him the laughing stock of the countryside. Thus thought and judged Gagi, and he could not see how he was to get the better of Elguja and pay him out for the dishonour he had brought on him. If this had been in the old days, Gagi, on an occasion like this would have assembled the whole tribe, he would have chosen umpires and the decision of the tribe would have been obeyed; but those times were past... The tribe had lost its power, it had become impossible to fulfil the wish of the people, and the care for their fate had fallen into the hands of one man. Gagi had become one of those who had this power, and therefore Elguja's boldness must be dearly paid for; he must mete out an examplary punishment and torture him as much as possible. Gagi thought about this for some time, and could not make up his mind. At last his wrinkled brow relaxed and a sinister smile flitted across his face. He raised his head and cried with a cruel voice:

"Martia!"

"Here am I!" replied the Mthiulian, and came out in front of him.

"Go down below and tell the Russian commander that a certain rebel came to my house now when I was away on the service of His Majesty the Emperor, stole in, and carried off a woman."

"Very well, it is well!"

"Say that he did this because I am in the Russian service. Tell him that we have checked these traitors here, and that he should send me troops to help me to capture them."

"Troops?" asked Martia in surprise.

"Well! Traitors to His Majesty the Emperor should be taken by Russian troops."

"Why do we want troops? Are not we enough?" angrily replied Martia, who looked upon Gagi's words as humiliating. "Give the word, and (by the lion St George) we will bring down the wrath of God on them whithersoever they flee."

"No, the Russians will torture them more," said Gagi cruelly, and then, as if to himself, he added: "Death alone is not enough!"

"They are thine enemies, and thou shouldst take their blood, what have others to do with it?"

"Because they should be tortured as a warning to others," replied Gagi, knitting his brow.

Martia hung his head and fell into a reverie; it was clear that he would be in no hurry to carry out Gagi's orders.

"Get thee gone, what art thou waiting for?"

"By St George," began Martia, taking off his cap and speaking in an entreating voice, "let us not deliver them into the hands of the Russians; what is the good of torturing them? They are enemies, let us kill them and throw them away; what else do we want? If they fall into the hands of the Russians, they will torture them as the Jews tortured Christ (May the sun-faced Thamara bless me!)."

"They will torture? What else do I want?" cried Gagi, and a flash of brutal desire blazed from his eyes.

"Do not this (May they sufferings fall on me!). Do it not. They will write songs about us among our people, by St George! and we shall be put to shame. We cannot dare to have so many people to take three, 'Sdeath, no! Command me and I will go out alone, sword against sword."

Martia was ashamed at such cowardice; he would not admit that enemies should be handed over to torture, and in his opinion every man who fell into the hands of the Russians must be tortured. Martia was not to blame

594

for having this opinion of the newcomers, since he had been a witness of the shameful acts perpetrated by their representatives. For example, he had been present at the death of two Mthiulians who had been beaten to death by Cossacks when the road was being made, merely because one of the Cossacks' horses had stumbled. In winter when it snowed the workmen on the road were not allowed to seek shelter; an avalanche came down and buried three men; women were harnessed in sledges and beaten and forced to drag burdens. Martia had seen many things of this kind, and therefore he thought like the rest of his fellow-countrymen. Thus, though Elguja's act was in his opinion so blameworthy that he deserved punishment and his blood should be shed, yet he considered that it would be shameful to subject him to torture and degradation. Gagi's opinion of the Russians did not differ from Martia's, and for this very reason he wished to deliver Elguja into their hands.

"Away, away! What art thou looking at?" cried Gagi angrily.

"I am going, I am going!" answered Martia sadly, and the turned his horse's head.

When he was out on the road, Gagi again addressed him: "Is there a strong place anywhere near here?"

"Of course there is," replied Martia, and pointed towards the hillock where Elguja and his companions were waiting. "There is such a strong place that if a man had powder and lead he need not trouble about anything for a whole year."

"It is well, now thou canst go, and try to be as quick as possible."

"Very well, I shall hurry." He turned his horse and disappeared. On his face could be seen sadness and an active mind; at last he looked back to Gagi, shook his whip and cried: "Thou wouldst not listen to me, now wait for me, ruffian." In that place was a bend in the road, so that Martia could not be seen by Gagi and his band. Martia looked back once again, threw himself from the saddle at full gallop, and swiftly disappeared in the bushes, like a stone from a sling. He ran with all his might towards the hillock on which was Elguja; at intervals he uttered words giving vent to his agitated feelings. "Death is not enough, thou sinner? Their blood was not sufficient for thee. Thou wouldst have them tortured? We shall see. Very well! I'll go there. Either I die with them or I shall help them somehow." With these words and threats, Martia hurried to join Elguja and pay out Gagi for his dishonourable, humiliating wish.

Meanwhile Gagi was not idle. He came to the conclusion that the troops would come up to him at midday, but before they came he wished to examine and reconnoitre thoroughly the place where were hidden those

595

for whom he had resolved to make the day a bitter one. Gagi gave orders that his men should scatter, that they should go into the bushes and carefully reconnoitre the enemy. If they met them anywhere let them try to take them alive and not dare to use their arms unless it was absolutely necessary. So the men crossed themselves, commended themselves to their patron saints, dispersed, and entered the wood. Every one felt that Gagi's orders were difficult to carry out, and that armed men ready for anything would not easily give in. They went carefully, they looked in almost every bush, and were in that state of agitation which men generally feel when they go into action. After going a little way they found three saddled horses which were peacefully munching the grass. Gagi followed his men, and when he noticed any suspicious place he turned aside. Thus, silently, frowning, they went into those places, while Martia had reached the hillock where Elguja was. George was the first to see him, and by his dress knew him to be a Mthiulian.

"Elguja, come, here is a Mthiulian running hither, and I do not know who he is."

"Where is he?" Elguja looked round. "It is indeed a Mthiulian."

"Hast thou any friends among the Mthiulians?" asked George.

"No."

"Then who can it be? Does he come as a friend or foe?"

"How do I know? We shall soon find out," said Elguja, and took aim with his gun. "Stand, or by the favour of God I'll make thee cold."

Martia stopped and called out in a friendly way.

"Who art thou, and what dost thou want?" asked Elguja.

"I am Martia, a Mthiulian. I am anxious to swear brotherhood with thee."

Elguja and George were astonished at the wish of the unknown Mthiulian.

"Martia," replied Elguja, after thinking a little, "if thou art lying go back, it is true thou art a brave fellow, but we are not inferior to thee, do not make us bring trouble on thee to no purpose."

"St George be your surety! May he who is a traitor to you marry his mother! [This is the most fearful of Georgian oaths.]"

On these words Elguja turned to George and said:

"I shall keep the sight of my gun fixed on Martia, go down and swear brotherhood, maybe, like us, he is in trouble, and in such a position one man more is worth a whole troop."

George silently took his gun and went down from the hillock. He hurried towards Martia and stopped a little way from him.

"Peace be to thy path! St George give thee peace."

"Let us disarm and swear brotherhood."

"So be it!"

Both put off their weapons, laid them on the ground, and approached each other—they took bullets and exchanged them. After this they embraced each other and kissed three times. Then they swore one to the other that until they drew their last breath they would not be false to each other. They took up their weapons again, and went to Elguja, who, in his turn, swore brotherhood with the Mthiulian. Martia told of Gagi's conduct, his request, and how since Martia could not agree to execute such a dishonourable order, he had come hither either to help them or die with them.

During this conversation, Gagi was approaching the hillock with his men, who had decided that Elguja must be there, since they could not find him in the woody plains. Gagi stood in front and shouted: "Elguja! We know thou art hiding there. Look out! We want to say a couple of words to thee." To this there was no reply, and Gagi went on: "Coward, coward! If thou fearest the sight of me so much why didst thou steal the girl? Look out for a moment if thou art not a woman." At these words Elguja lost his temper; he stood upright on the rock: "What! am I a coward? Thou knowest what sort of a coward I am, but in God's name, Gagi, do not spill thine own blood. Leave the road clear for us. I took the girl away from thee and I am ready to pay for her according to the custom of the tribe. Only let me alone."—"God bring confusion on thee and on thy tribe! Come out at once and bring that shameless girl with thee. If not, I swear I shall make this a black day for thee!"—"Gagi, Gagi do not curse the tribe! It is not right, and it is not fitting that a man should curse a woman. Silence! or by God, blood will be shed."

At this threat, Gagi became enraged and forgot his former plan. "Just look at that dog!" he burst out furiously. "Fire at him, men!" On these words smoke rose and the sound of firing was heard. Bullets whistled round the spot where Elguja was standing, but he succeeded in sheltering himself behind the rocks, and cried out: "So, Gagi? Thou wilt not go away? We shall see what happens. Whatever blood is spilt here thy soul will have to answer for."

Three shots were heard, and three of Gagi's band fell to the ground, and blood spurted from their wounds. Firing began on both sides, and several of Gagi's men were killed. It was so dangerous for them that they sought cover, they scattered and hid themselves behind rocks and heaps of stones. Of course Gagi himself sought out a safe place, and with threats and curses awaited the arrival of the soldiers. He had not lost hope, and however long such a state of affairs might last Elguja must fall into his hands in the end, for Gagi would not leave the spot and thus blocked the road. The firing did not cease, though the bullets were wasted and did not fulfil their purpose. Such was the state of affairs when Gagi, whose excitement increased every moment, cried out in a sad voice: "Why have they not come? It is past midday. What has become of Martia?"

The cause of Gagi's excitement was that he could neither catch nor kill Elguja and his companions. He saw from the lie of the land that such a small company as he had could not block the road all round, and they might easily creep out at night and escape for ever from his hands. In proportion as Gagi suffered, those on the hillock were comforted and hoped that in the darkness of night the road would be open to them, and they would be able to escape peacefully from those who thirsted for their blood. "Now we can rest, by St George! They will not dare to move."—"I do not think that Gagi will rest thus. What does it matter to him if others are killed for his sake? He is in hiding himself and he is letting us kill the others," added George.—"No, now the people are quiet, and nobody trusts Gagi. When the people were excited then he was dangerous, but now we have nothing to fear." As he spoke thus he was reassured, and as a proof of this he unslung his gun and laid it on his cloak.

Evening approached while the three friends were still engaged in this conversation; Elguja suddenly crept out from his place, quietly seized his gun, and lay down under cover on the hillock. "What does thou see?" quietly asked George, as if afraid of being overheard.—"Look there," said he, and pointed with his finger towards the edge of the rock. George and Martia looked and were struck dumb with astonishment; down on the edge of the rock, where the plain ended, Gagi was riding down with some horsemen.—"Is not that dog Gagi? Where the deuce is he going?" While they were talking Elguja was aiming at Gagi.—"But how do I know where he is going? By God! Wherever he is going peace will not go with him." At these words he fired. Gagi's horse reared, turned towards the rock, stumbled, and rider and steed together fell over the precipice. This was so unexpected and happened so quickly that Gagi's companions could not help him, and when they looked over the rock they saw in the ravine the mangled bodies of man and horse. Gagi had grown tired of waiting for the troops and the Russian commander, and had gone to look for them himself. He knew, it is true, that he would not capture Elguja there, but, instead, he could block the roads down below, and kill the dogs who had resisted him and caused such damage. This was why we saw Gagi on the edge of that rock from which he made such an unlucky descent.

Gagi's companions dismounted and talked among themselves, and finally decided that they would go and tell the Russian commander of the misfortune that had happened, since they could not do anything for Gagi. Those above saw Gagi's fall with joy.—"St George give power to thine arm!" cried Martia, taking off his cap.—"Ah!" said George, "that dog is dead!"—Elguja laid down his gun, crossed himself, and with a sad voice said: "Why did he make us kill him? Why! God knows that I would not willingly raise my hand against a brother!"—"He was no blood-brother but a traitor," said Martia frowning. "He cheated his brethren and his tribe."—"He was a dog, and died like a dog. God did not even think him worth a bullet. He has died unshriven."[1]

By that time night had fallen. Elguja went for Mzagho, whom he had to prepare and to inform her that the chief of her enemies was no longer in existence, and that nobody could separate them now. Mzagho who from the morning sat pale in the place appointed for her, with wildly beating heart awaited the end of the affair. At that time she had forgotten everything and cared for nothing but the safety of her friends. She was afraid that some audacious bullet might strike one of those who so bravely defended her freedom. She was ready to go down to her friends, and together with them share their good or bad fortune. But the submissive character which had become habitual to her among the Circassians did not permit her to transgress Elguja's command. So she sat quietly in the place where she had been put, though this was almost as painful to her as death. There she prayed and entreated God, trembling at every shot, fearing, with unspeakable torment of heart. She came out of her hiding place and looked at her friends. As soon as she saw them safe and sound her joy knew no bounds. She then went back to her place, fell on her knees and with flowing tears gave thanks to God. She prayed and gave thanks to God, but this was wonderful, that in her prayer there was no wish for the death of the aggressors though she desired the safety of her protectors; she asked that all should end in peace, that nobody should be killed, and with loving heart she desired for all happiness, joy, and peace.

Mzagho was in this state when she saw Elguja coming towards her, and when she caught sight of him she joyfully rushed to him and, blushing from excess of emotion, hung round his neck.—"Is it finished, have they gone? Won't the fight be continued? O God I thank Thee that Thou hast kept him safe."—"Mzagho, my sun!" said Elguja with feeling, "do not be afraid."—"Have they gone? Have they left us?"—"Yes, yes! they

---

[1] The same word is used of an unwounded corpse and an unshriven one.

have left us."—"Then let us go too. What are we doing here?"—"Let us go, my heart."—At that moment Martia and George came, called on the name of God, and slowly came down from the hillock. Assured that nobody was looking, they carefully crept among the bushes where they suspected Gagi's men of being. They safely descended the slope of Kveshethi and went on.

A little below Kveshethi there is a church which is called Naghvaravi (*i.e.* the place of the rivulet). At that time this was a wooded place, and there many outlawed mountaineers hid themselves and escaped from the lawless persecution of those times. Our travellers directed their steps thither, for day was approaching, and they must travel at night, journeying by day being still dangerous. When the wayfarers had established themselves, George and Martia took their guns and went to keep guard, while Elguja and Mzagho remained in the enclosure of the churchyard. The moon rose over the mountains, and tenderly spread its rays over the scene.—"Will they not come here?" asked Mzagho of Elguja.—"No, no! Do not fear."—"But I think they will not let us alone even here."—"If they do not let us alone, they will gain no more than they got at the other place."—"Oh God! Why will they not let us alone? What do they want of us? What?" said the girl sadly.—"They want this, my all! That thou art too beautiful!" said Elguja with passion, and pressed her to his heart.— "But, by God's mercy," continued he, "even if the whole world becomes mine enemy I will not give thee up to anybody."—Mzagho bent her head at these words, a fire of joy burned in her face, and thought her lips trembled she could not say a word, and what could she say at such a moment? These were such moments when one can only feel, and one look, one single sigh, says more than a whole year of talking, causes more emotion. They felt perfect happiness, something of the highest gladness, and unconsciously yielded themselves slaves to that feeling. Elguja quietly bent his head and approached the girl's excited face; he was almost delirious with joy. In another moment, unexpectedly, unthinking, their lips united, and both fell into a state of forgetfulness....

They were in this state of bliss when the sound of a gun roused the lovers. Then other guns were heard, and there came a cry from the side where Martia and George were watching. Elguja started up and rushed thither, and his eyes saw a horrible picture forming a great contrast with his feelings of a few minutes ago. Martia and George were surrounded by soldiers. These two devoted friends bravely held their own. Several men who were left from Gagi's band had remained near the hill to look after Elguja and his companions; they had seen the fugitives, followed silently and discovered their hiding place. They told the Russian commander, who gave strict orders, and took with him a whole company. These were the soldiers who, like flies, were surrounding Martia and George. Elguja, with naked sword, leaped forward and rushed to his comrades. A Russian blocked his way and pointed his lance at him. Elguja thrust aside the lance with his hand and avoided the blow, and so swiftly and strongly struck off the wretched man's head that it and the body fell in different directions. After some fighting, Elguja joined his comrades, though this union did not help them. In the place where they stood the people at once thickened, and, as in a scrimmage at the game of ball, closed round the spot where the struggle was going on. When the people opened out, the maimed and wounded victims were seen on the ground. Among them were to be recognized Elguja and his two comrades, pitilessly riddled by lances. Elguja rolled on his back, his mouth wide open, and from his breast the blood gurgled in several places. A soldier went to him, and again thrust his lance through him several times....

Of course they seized Mzagho....

POLAND

THE LOVE STORY OF ZYGMUNT II AUGUST OF POLAND AND BARBARA RADZIWILL

Monica Gardner

IN 1547 a Polish prince, Zygmunt August, who later ascended the throne of Poland as Zygmunt II August, was residing in the royal palace at Vilno, governing Lithuania for his father, Zygmunt I, king of Poland. He was then twenty-seven years of age. At the age of twenty-five he had lost his wife. Her death was no great grief to him, and his compulsory mourning irked him. He therefore satisfied his taste for pleasure by indulging in private amusements in the society of gay companions of his own age. On one occasion, as the talk turned on beautiful women, one of the youths present praised the beauty of his kinswoman, a young widow, Barbara Radziwill. Zygmunt determined to see this lady with his own eyes. In the company of some noble youths of the Court, he went out to the manor beyond the gates of Vilno, where she was living with her mother and brothers. He found a beautiful woman, with regular features, a complexion of alabaster and exquisite dark eyes; with gentle, tranquil manners. Enraptured, the prince visited her again and again. Their love was kept as far as possible a secret. The prince built a bridge between the .palace and the manor, so that he could meet the lady in the seclusion of her garden. The garden was laid out by an Italian architect. Framed by limes and firs, it lay behind cherry and apple orchards, and was fragrant with sweet smelling flowering shrubs. Here in the evening the prince and Barbara walked, murmuring together in the Italian language, at that time beloved of lovers in Poland.

Months passed by, and the secret began to leak out. Rumours of it reached the king and queen in Cracow, then the capital of Poland; and the queen—Bona Sforza—wrote in a fury to her son, bidding him break off the affair. The mother and brothers of Barbara held a family council, after which they requested Zygmunt for the sake of Barbara's honour and that of the family to cease his visits. The prince gave the brothers his word that he would not again cross the threshold of the Radziwill house; and with deep obeisances they retired. For long Zygmunt did not see his love, while the brothers kept watch at the gate of the garden to assure themselves that he did not come. On a serene night in late September,

1547, Zygmunt took two of his old friends—who were also confidants of the Radziwills, and leaving them in the garden of the manor, he went to Barbara's rooms. While he and she were exchanging lovers' vows, her two brothers entered.

"Gracious king," said they—he had been crowned king at the age of ten years during his father's reign—"thou didst promise not to enter our sister's house. Then why hast thou come here?"

"Who knows," the prince replied haughtily, "but that my presence here to-day may bring you lasting glory and honour?"

"God grant it," was their answer. Going to the door, they summoned a priest who was in readiness outside, and in the presence of the family Zygmunt and Barbara were married. The marriage was kept a secret. It was in fact a transgression against the law of the realm, that forbade the Polish monarchs to marry without the Senate's permission. Barbara therefore remained in her house, and Zygmunt continued to visit her as of old. After some weeks the prince prepared to journey to Cracow, to lay the matter of his marriage before the king and queen and the Seym (Diet). On account of the certain anger of his parents and of his nation when the secret should be disclosed, Zygmunt to ensure Barbara's safety hid her in a fortified and secluded castle, a few hours' journey from Vilno, on a hill in the midst of a plain, the horizon of which was shut in by the dense Lithuanian forests. There she soon fell sick with weeping for her lover and husband. She sought to cheer her dreary solitude by pious exercises. She doffed her costly garments, and lived a life of conventual observance. Two or three hours before daybreak she rose and went to the church; and each day she distributed alms to the poor with her own hands. Her husband often wrote to her; and by a confidential courier of his she sent a letter to him shortly after his departure, which runs thus:

"I wish your royal Majesty and my lord long good health of God to the eternal consolation of her who is the humblest servant of your royal Majesty." With the letter she sent the prince a ring "which I humbly beg His royal Majesty kindly and graciously to deign to accept, and carrying it on his person to deign to keep me and my service in his gracious memory and favour." She signed the letter as the prince's "humblest servant and eternal slave," but on the outer cover she styled herself Queen.

At first Zygmunt dared not confess his act to the king and queen, and began by taking two senators into his confidence. Thorough the winter Barbara, guarded night and day, sat at her window watching the frozen plain for any sign of her absent husband. Stories were carried to her that the prince's love for her had grown cold and that his heart had turned elsewhere, but Zygmunt's letters bade her know that these were lies, and at last he returned to Vilno, having gained nothing more by his journey than a few supporters of his marriage. The Lithuanian magnates, jealous of the distinction conferred upon the already powerful Radziwill family by the marriage, met Zygmunt at Vilno, and requested him to give up Barbara. In revenge for his refusal, they showered calumnies against Barbara in private and in public, while the prince sent her messages assuring her of his unbroken faith, and exhorting her to patience. Only a few miles divided them, and yet they could not meet. Then there came a day when Zygmunt sent a courier to Barbara's brother, bidding him bring his sister in secret that night to her manor in Vilno, emphatically repeating that whatever happened she must be in Vilno before the morrow. The reason of this was that the old king was dead, and Zygmunt intended to proclaim Barbara as his wife at the royal castle.

Crowds of nobles had come into Vilno to pay their allegiance to the new king. He summoned all the lords and officials in Vilno to a great council in the castle. As they sat deliberating, a great stir was heard in the antechamber. With a joyful countenance, Zygmunt rose, saying: "To-day I am about to disclose to you what righteous and weighty reasons have compelled me hitherto to hide. Barbara Radziwill is my wife, given to me in marriage by Christian rites in the presence of her kinsfolk. You know that no power in the world can break a like bond, lawfully contracted between Christians." He went to the door of the hall, opened it, and revealed Barbara, in royal robes, with her brothers and a retinue of lords and ladies. The king gave her his hand, and led her to the royal apartments; and a festive banquet closed the day.

But in ten days' time the king had once more to leave her, being bound to return to Cracow. On this occasion his love letters, always full of tender solicitude for her comfort, had to deal with the petty jealousies and heart burnings of an ambitious woman raised suddenly to the highest rank in the realm, who took it ill that the obeisances of the ladies of the court were not as low as she deemed they should be. At last—almost a year after the marriage—the king was able to summon her to his side, and she set out for Cracow. In the towns through which she passed she was received as queen: and at Radom the king rode out to meet her in regal state.

But the storm was now breaking upon the heads of the royal lovers. After three weeks spent in each other's company, the king had to account for his marriage to an infuriated Seym, and Barbara was left, in no small apprehension, to await the issue at Radom. For two months the battle raged, letters passing all the time between the constant lovers. It seemed as if it were to be a question of the king choosing between his crown or his wife. His one answer to the storm that raged about his head was that he would keep faith with his wedded wife. Finally after a protracted struggle the king rose in front of the assembled Seym, and spoke thus:

"What has been done may not be undone. It does not beseem your lordships to ask me to break faith with my wife. Rather you should ask me to keep faith with every man. I have sworn to my wife, and I will not abandon her so long as the Lord God shall keep me in this world. My troth to her is dearer to me than all the kingdoms of the world." Deeply moved, he left the hall. There was now talk of deposing him. The king gave secret orders that Barbara should be brought to Cracow: and, accompanied by those lords who adhered to his cause, he went forth to meet her, and, amidst the pealing of bells, led her to the apartments in the royal castle of the Vavel, which were reserved for the queens of Poland. Opposition was thus proved to be useless. One by one the most violent opponents of the marriage paid their public homage to the king's wife, and all passed over to his side.

But the happiness of the royal couple was shortlived. Barbara withdrew from the turmoil of the court. All that she lived for was the company of the king, and she grudged every moment of his absence on State affairs. At the same time she had a passionate longing to be crowned queen of Poland. Her desire was gratified: the crown was solemnly placed on her brow in the Vavel cathedral. But, returning from the ceremony, she replied in answer to the congratulations of her attendants: "Our heavenly Lord is about to call me to another crown. Pray to Him for me that He may change this earthly sceptre for a heavenly palm, and may comfort my sweet husband's grief." She lived six months longer. Only her husband never lost hope; and it was with her hand held in his that she died. Rumour went round that Queen Bona had poisoned her, but this story has been disproved. At her request her body was taken back to be buried in her native Lithuania; and as the funeral procession wended its way through town and countryside the broken-hearted husband never left the coffin, riding close to its side. Although compelled for reasons of State to marry again, Zygmunt August remained devoted for ever to Barbara's memory. and wore mourning for her till the day of his death, twenty-one years later.

RUSSIA

FIRST LOVE[1]

Ivan Turgenev

THE party had long ago broken up. The clock struck half-past twelve. There was left in the room only the master of the house and Sergei Nikolaevitch and Vladimir Petrovitch.

The master of the house rang and ordered the remains of the supper to be cleared away. "And so it's settled," he observed, sitting back farther in his easy-chair and lighting a cigar; "each of us is to tell the story of his first love. It's your turn, Sergei Nikolaevitch."

Sergei Nikolaevitch, a round little man with a plump, light-complexioned face, gazed first at the master of the house, then raised his eyes to the ceiling. "I had no first love," he said at last; "I began with the second."

"How was that?"

"It's very simple. I was eighteen when I had my first flirtation with a charming young lady, but I courted her just as though it were nothing new to me; just as I courted others later on. To speak accurately, the first and last time I was in love was with my nurse when I was six years old; but that's in the remote past. The details of our relations have slipped out of my memory, and even if I remembered them, whom could they interest?"

"Then how's it to be?" began the master of the house. "There was nothing much of interest about my first love either; I never fell in love with any one till I met Anna Nikolaevna, now my wife,—and everything went as smoothly as possible with us; our parents arranged the match, we were very soon in love with each other, and got married without loss of time. My story can be told in a couple of words. I must confess, gentlemen, in bringing up the subject of first love, I reckoned upon you, I won't say old, but no longer young, bachelors. Can't you enliven us with something, Vladimir Petrovitch?"

"My first love, certainly, was not quite an ordinary one," responded, with some reluctance, Vladimir Petrovitch, a man of forty, with black hair turning grey.

---

[1] From *The Torrents of Spring*. Translated by Constance Garnett. Reprinted by permission of Messrs William Heinemann, Ltd.

"Ah!" said the master of the house and Sergei Nikolaevitch with one voice: "So much the better.... Tell us about it."

"If you wish it... or no; I won't tell the story; I'm no hand at telling a story; I make it dry and brief, or spun out and affected. If you'll allow me, I'll write out all I remember and read it you."

His friends at first would not agree, but Vladimir Petrovitch insisted on his own way. A fortnight later they were together again, and Vladimir Petrovitch kept his word.

His manuscript contained the following story:

I

I was sixteen then. It happened in the summer of 1833.

I lived in Moscow with my parents. They had taken a country-house for the summer near the Kalouga gate, facing the Neskutchny gardens. I was preparing for the university, but did not work much and was in no hurry.

No one interfered with my freedom. I did what I liked, especially after parting with my last tutor, a Frenchman who had never been able to get used to the idea that he had fallen "like a bomb" (*comme une bombe*) into Russia, and would lie sluggishly in bed with an expression of exasperation on his face for days together. My father treated me with careless kindness; my mother scarcely noticed me, though she had no children except me; other cares completely absorbed her. My father, a man still young and very handsome, had married her from mercenary considerations; she was ten years older than he. My mother led a melancholy life; she was for ever agitated, jealous, and angry, but not in my father's presence; she was very much afraid of him, and he was severe, cold, and distant in his behaviour.... I have never seen a man more elaborately serene, self-confident, and commanding.

I shall never forget the first weeks I spent at the country house. The weather was magnificent; we left town on the 9th of May, on St Nicholas's day. I used to walk about in our garden, in the Neskutchny gardens, and beyond the town gates; I would take some book with me—Keidanov's Course, for instance—but I rarely looked into it, and more often than anything declaimed verses aloud; I knew a great deal of poetry by heart; my blood was in a ferment and my heart ached—so sweetly and absurdly; I was all hope and anticipation, was a little frightened of something, and full of wonder at everything, and was on the tiptoe of expectation; my imagination played continually, fluttering rapidly about the same fancies, like martins about a bell-tower at dawn; I dreamed, was sad, even wept;

but through the tears and through the sadness, inspired by a musical verse, or the beauty of evening, shot up like grass in spring the delicious sense of youth and effervescent life.

I had a horse to ride; I used to saddle it myself and set off alone for long rides, break into a rapid gallop and fancy myself a knight at a tournament. How gaily the wind whistled in my ears! or turning my face towards the sky, I would absorb its shining radiance and blue into my soul, that opened wide to welcome it.

I remember that at that time the image of woman, the vision of love, scarcely ever arose in definite shape in my brain; but in all I thought, in all I felt, lay hidden a half-conscious, shamefaced presentiment of something new, unutterably sweet, feminine....

This presentiment, this expectation, permeated my whole being; I breathed in it, it coursed through my veins with every drop of blood... it was destined to be soon fulfilled.

The place, where we settled for the summer, consisted of a wooden manor-house with columns and two small lodges; in the lodge on the left there was a tiny factory for the manufacture of cheap wall-papers.... I had more than once strolled that way to look at about a dozen thin and dishevelled boys with greasy smocks and worn faces, who were perpetually jumping on to wooden levers, that pressed down the square blocks of the press, and so by the weight of their feeble bodies struck off the variegated pattens of the wall-papers. The lodge on the right stood empty, and was to let. One day—three weeks after the 9th of May—the blinds in the windows of this lodge were drawn up, women's faces appeared at them—some family had installed themselves in it. I remember the same day at dinner, my mother inquired of the butler who were our new neighbours, and hearing the name of the Princess Zasyekin, first observed with some respect, "Ah! a princess!"... and then added, "A poor one, I suppose?"

"They arrived in three hired flies," the butler remarked deferentially, as he handed a dish: "they don't keep their own carriage, and the furniture's of the poorest."

"Ah," replied my mother, "so much the better."

My father gave her a chilly glance; she was silent.

Certainly the Princess Zasyekin could not be a rich woman; the lodge she had taken was so dilapidated and small and low-pitched that people, even moderately well-off in the world, would hardly have consented to occupy it. At the time, however, all this went in at one ear and out at the other. The princely title had very little effect on me; I had just been reading Schiller's *Robbers*.

II

I was in the habit of wandering about our garden every evening on the look-out for rooks. I had long cherished a hatred for those wary, sly, and rapacious birds. On the day of which I have been speaking, I went as usual into the garden, and after patrolling all the walks without success (the rooks knew me, and merely cawed spasmodically at a distance), I chanced to go close to the low fence which separated our domain from the narrow strip of garden stretching beyond the lodge to the right, and belonging to it. I was walking along, my eyes on the ground. Suddenly I heard a voice; I looked across the fence, and was thunderstruck.... I was confronted with a curious spectacle.

A few paces from me on the grass between the green raspberry bushes stood a tall slender girl in a striped pink dress, with a white kerchief on her head; four young men were close round her, and she was slapping them by turns on the forehead with those small grey flowers, the name of which I don't know, though they are well known to children; the flowers form little bags, and burst open with a pop when you strike them against anything hard. The young men presented their foreheads so eagerly, and in the gestures of the girl (I saw her in profile), there was something so fascinating, imperious, caressing, mocking, and charming, that I almost cried out with admiration and delight, and would, I thought, have given everything in the world on the spot only to have had those exquisite fingers strike me on the forehead. My gun slipped on to the grass, I forgot everything, I devoured with my eyes the graceful shape and neck and lovely arms and the slightly disordered fair hair under the white kerchief, and the half-closed clever eye, and the eyelashes and the soft cheek beneath them....

"Young man, hey, young man," said a voice suddenly near me: "is it quite permissible to stare so at unknown young ladies?"

I started, I was struck dumb.... Near me, the other side of the fence, stood a man with close-cropped black hair, looking ironically at me. At the same instant the girl too turned towards me.... I caught sight of big grey eyes in a bright mobile face, and the whole face suddenly quivered and laughed, there was a flash of white teeth, a droll lifting of the eyebrows. ... I crimsoned, picked up my gun from the ground, and pursued by a musical but not ill-natured laugh, fled to my own room, flung myself on the bed, and hid my face in my hands. My heart was fairly leaping: I was greatly ashamed and overjoyed; I felt an excitement I had never known before.

After a rest, I brushed my hair, washed, and went downstairs to tea. The image of the young girl floated before me, my heart was no longer leaping, but was full of a sort of sweet oppression.

"What's the matter?" my father asked me all at once: "have you killed a rook?"

I was on the point of telling him all about it, but I checked myself, and merely smiled to myself. As I was going to bed, I rotated—I don't know why—three times on one leg, pomaded my hair, got into bed, and slept like a top all night. Before morning I woke up for an instant, raised my head, looked round me in ecstasy, and fell asleep again.

III

"How can I make their acquaintance?" was my first thought when I waked in the morning. I went out in the garden before morning tea, but I did not go too near the fence, and saw no one. After drinking tea, I walked several times up and down the street before the house, and looked into the windows from a distance.... I fancied her face at a curtain, and I hurried away in alarm.

"I must make her acquaintance, though," I thought, pacing distractedly about the sandy plain that stretches before Neskutchny park... "but how, that is the question." I recalled the minutest details of our meeting yesterday; I had for some reason or other a particularly vivid recollection of how she had laughed at me.... But while I racked my brains, and made various plans, fate had already provided for me.

In my absence my mother had received from her new neighbour a letter on grey paper, sealed with brown wax, such as is only used in notices from the post-office or on the corks of bottles of cheap wine. In this letter, which was written in illiterate language and in a slovenly hand, the princess begged my mother to use her powerful influence in her behalf; my mother, in the words of the princess, was very intimate with persons of high position, upon whom her fortunes and her children's fortunes depended, as she had some very important business in hand. "I address myself to you," she wrote, "as one gentlewoman to another gentlewoman, and for that reason am glad to avail myself of the opportunity." Concluding, she begged my mother's permission to call upon her. I found my mother in an unpleasant state of indecision; my father was not at home, and she had no one of whom to ask advice. Not to answer a gentlewoman, and a princess into the bargain, was impossible. But my mother was in a difficulty as to how to answer her. To write a note in French struck her as unsuitable, and Russian spelling was not a strong point with my mother herself, and she was aware of it, and did not care to expose herself. She was overjoyed when I made my appearance, and at once told me to go round to the princess's, and to explain to her by word of mouth that my mother would always be glad to do her excellency any service within her powers, and begged her to come to see her at one o'clock. This unexpectedly rapid fulfilment of my secret desires both delighted and appalled me. I made no sign, however, of the perturbation which came over me, and as a preliminary step went to my own room to put on a new necktie and tail coat; at home I still wore short jackets and lay-down collars, much as I abominated them.

IV

In the narrow and untidy passage of the lodge, which I entered with an involuntary tremor in all my limbs, I was met by an old grey-headed servant with a dark copper-coloured face, surly little pig's eyes, and such deep furrows on his forehead and temples as I had never beheld in my life. He was carrying a plate containing the spine of a herring that had been gnawed at; and shutting the door that led into the room with his foot, he jerked out, "What do you want?"

"Is the Princess Zasyekin at home?" I inquired.

"Vonifaty!" a jarring female voice screamed from within.

The man without a word turned his back on me, exhibiting as he did so the extremely threadbare hindpart of his livery with a solitary reddish heraldic button on it; he put the plate down on the floor, and went away.

"Did you go to the police station?" the same female voice called again. The man muttered something in reply. "Eh.... Has some one come?" I heard again.... "The young gentleman from next door. Ask him in, then."

"Will you step into the drawing-room?" said the servant, making his appearance once more, and picking up the plate from the floor. I mastered my emotions, and went into the drawing-room.

I found myself in a small and not over clean apartment, containing some poor furniture that looked as if it had been hurriedly set down where it stood. At the window in an easy-chair with a broken arm was sitting a woman of fifty, bareheaded and ugly, in an old green dress, and a striped worsted wrap about her neck. Her small black eyes fixed me like pins.

I went up to her and bowed.

"I have the honour of addressing the Princess Zasyekin?"

"I am the Princess Zasyekin; and you are the son of Mr V.?"

"Yes. I have come to you with a message from my mother."

"Sit down, please. Vonifaty, where are my keys, have you seen them?"
I communicated to Madame Zasyekin my mother's reply to her note.
She heard me out, drumming with her fat red fingers on the windowpane,
and when I had finished, she stared at me once more.

"Very good; I'll be sure to come," she observed at last. "But how young
you are! How old are you, may I ask?"

"Sixteen," I replied, with an involuntary stammer.

The princess drew out of her pocket some greasy papers covered with
writing, raised them right up to her nose, and began looking through them.

"A good age," she ejaculated suddenly, turning round restlessly on her
chair. "And do you, pray, make yourself at home. I don't stand on ceremony."

"No, indeed," I thought, scanning her unprepossessing person with a
disgust I could not restrain.

At that instant another door flew open quickly, and in the doorway
stood the girl I had seen the previous evening in the garden. She lifted
her hand, and a mocking smile gleamed in her face.

"Here is my daughter," observed the princess, indicating her with her
elbow. "Zinotchka, the son of our neighbour, Mr V. What is your name,
allow me to ask?"

"Vladimir," I answered, getting up, and stuttering in my excitement.

"And your father's name?"

"Petrovitch."

"Ah! I used to know a commissioner of police whose name was Vladimir
Petrovitch too. Vonifaty! don't look for my keys; the keys are in my
pocket."

The young girl was still looking at me with the same smile, faintly
fluttering her eyelids, and putting her head a little on one side.

"I have seen Monsieur Voldemar before," she began. (The silvery note
of her voice ran through me with a sort of sweet shiver.) "You will let
me call you so?"

"Oh, please," I faltered.

"Where was that?" asked the princess.

The young princess did not answer her mother.

"Have you anything to do just now?" she said, not taking her eyes off
me.

"Oh, no."

"Would you like to help me wind some wool? Come in here, to me."
She nodded to me and went out of the drawing-room. I followed her.
In the room we went into, the furniture was a little better, and was

arranged with more taste. Though, indeed, at the moment, I was scarcely capable of noticing anything; I moved as in a dream and felt all through my being a sort of intense blissfulness that verged on imbecility.

The young princess sat down, took out a skein of red wool and, motioning me to a seat opposite her, carefully untied the skein and laid it across my hands. All this she did in silence with a sort of droll deliberation and with the same bright sly smile on her slightly parted lips. She began to wind the wool on a bent card, and all at once she dazzled me with a glance so brilliant and rapid, that I could not help dropping my eyes. When her eyes, which were generally half closed, opened to their full extent, her face was completely transfigured; it was as though it were flooded with light.

"What did you think of me yesterday, M'sieu Voldemar?" she asked after a brief pause. "You thought ill of me, I expect?"

"I... princess... I thought nothing... how can I?..." I answered in confusion.

"Listen," she rejoined. "You don't know me yet: I'm a very strange person; I like always to be told the truth. You, I have just heard, are sixteen, and I am twenty-one: you see I'm a great deal older than you, and so you ought always to tell me the truth... and to do what I tell you," she added. "Look at me: why don't you look at me?"

I was still more abashed; however, I raised my eyes to her. She smiled, not her former smile, but a smile of approbation. "Look at me," she said, dropping her voice caressingly: "I don't dislike that... I like your face; I have a presentiment we shall be friends. But do you like me?" she added slyly.

"Princess..." I was beginning.

"In the first place, you must call me Zinaïda Alexandrovna, and in the second place it's a bad habit for children"—(she corrected herself) "for young people—not to say straight out what they feel. That's all very well for grown-up people. You like me, don't you?"

Though I was greatly delighted that she talked so freely to me, still I was a little hurt. I wanted to show her that she had not a mere boy to deal with, and assuming as easy and serious an air as I could, I observed, "Certainly. I like you very much, Zinaïda Alexandrovna; I have no wish to conceal it."

She shook her head very deliberately. "Have you a tutor?" she asked suddenly.

"No; I've not had a tutor for a long, long while."

I told a lie; it was not a month since I had parted with my Frenchman.

"Oh! I see then—you are quite grown-up."

She tapped me lightly on the fingers. "Hold your hands straight!" And she applied herself busily to winding the ball.

I seized the opportunity when she was looking down and fell to watching her, at first stealthily, then more and more boldly. Her face struck me as even more charming than on the previous evening; everything in it was so delicate, clever, and sweet. She was sitting with her back to a window covered with a white blind, the sunshine, streaming in through the blind, shed a soft light over her fluffy golden curls, her innocent neck, her sloping shoulders, and tender untroubled bosom. I gazed at her, and how dear and near she was already to me! It seemed to me I had known her a long while and had never known anything nor lived at all till I met her.... She was wearing a dark and rather shabby dress and an apron; I would gladly, I felt, have kissed every fold of that dress and apron. The tips of her little shoes peeped out from under her skirt; I could have bowed down in adoration to those shoes.... "And here I am sitting before her," I thought; "I have made acquaintance with her... what happiness, my God!" I could hardly keep from jumping up from my chair in ecstasy, but I only swung my legs a little, like a small child who has been given sweetmeats.

I was as happy as a fish in water, and I could have stayed in that room for ever, have never left that place.

Her eyelids were slowly lifted, and once more her clear eyes shone kindly upon me, and again she smiled.

"How you look at me!" she said slowly, and she held up a threatening finger.

I blushed... "She understands it all, she sees all," flashed through my mind. "And how could she fail to understand and see it all?"

All at once there was a sound in the next room—the clink of a sabre.

"Zina!" screamed the princess in the drawing-room, "Byelovzorov has brought you a kitten."

"A kitten!" cried Zinaïda, and getting up from her chair impetuously, she flung the ball of worsted on my knees and ran away.

I too got up and, laying the skein and the ball of wool on the window-sill, I went into the drawing-room and stood still, hesitating. In the middle of the room, a tabby kitten was lying with outstretched paws; Zinaïda was on her knees before it, cautiously lifting up its little face. Near the old princess, and filling up almost the whole space between the two windows, was a flaxen curly-headed young man, a hussar, with a rosy face and prominent eyes.

"What a funny little thing!" Zinaïda was saying; "and its eyes are not grey, but green, and what long ears! Thank you, Viktor Yegoritch! you are very kind."

The hussar, in whom I recognised one of the young men I had seen the evening before, smiled and bowed with a clink of his spurs and a jingle of the chain of his sabre.

"You were pleased to say yesterday that you wished to possess a tabby kitten with long ears... so I obtained it. Your word is law." And he bowed again.

The kitten gave a feeble mew and began sniffing the ground.

"It's hungry!" cried Zinaïda. "Vonifaty, Sonia! bring some milk."

A maid, in an old yellow gown with a faded kerchief at her neck, came in with a saucer of milk and set it before the kitten. The kitten started, blinked, and began lapping.

"What a pink little tongue it has!" remarked Zinaïda, putting her head almost on the ground and peeping at it sideways under its very nose.

The kitten having had enough began to purr and move its paws affectedly. Zinaïda got up, and turning to the maid said carelessly, "Take it away."

"For the kitten—your little hand," said the hussar, with a simper and a shrug of his strongly-built frame, which was tightly buttoned up in a new uniform.

"Both," replied Zinaïda, and she held out her hands to him. While he was kissing them, she looked at me over his shoulder.

I stood stockstill in the same place and did not know whether to laugh, to say something, or to be silent. Suddenly through the open door into the passage I caught sight of our footman, Fyodor. He was making signs to me. Mechanically I went out to him.

"What do you want?" I asked.

"Your mamma has sent for you," he said in a whisper. "She is angry that you have not come back with the answer."

"Why, have I been here long?"

"Over an hour."

"Over an hour!" I repeated unconsciously, and going back to the drawing-room I began to make bows and scrape with my heels.

"Where are you off to?" the young princess asked, glancing at me from behind the hussar.

"I must go home. So I am to say," I added, addressing the old lady, "that you will come to us about two."

"Do you say so, my good sir."

The princess hurriedly pulled out her snuffbox and took snuff so loudly that I positively jumped. "Do you say so," she repeated, blinking tearfully and sneezing.

I bowed once more, turned, and went out of the room with that sensation of awkwardness in my spine which a very young man feels when he knows he is being looked at from behind.

"Mind you come and see us again, M'sieu Voldemar," Zinaïda called, and she laughed again.

"Why is it she's always laughing?" I thought, as I went back home escorted by Fyodor, who said nothing to me, but walked behind me with an air of disapprobation. My mother scolded me and wondered what ever I could have been doing so long at the princess's. I made her no reply and went off to my own room. I felt suddenly very sad.... I tried hard not to cry.... I was jealous of the hussar.

<h2 style="text-align:center">V</h2>

The princess called on my mother as she had promised and made a disagreeable impression on her. I was not present at their interview, but at table my mother told my father that this Princess Zasyekin struck her as a *femme très vulgaire*, that she had quite worn her out begging her to interest Prince Sergei in their behalf, that she seemed to have no end of lawsuits and affairs on hand—*de vilaines affaires d'argent*—and must be a very troublesome and litigious person. My mother added, however, that she had asked her and her daughter to dinner the next day (hearing the word 'daughter' I buried my nose in my plate), for after all she was a neighbour and a person of title. Upon this my father informed my mother that he remembered now who this lady was; that he had in his youth known the deceased Prince Zasyekin, a very well-bred, but frivolous and absurd person; that he had been nicknamed in society "*le Parisien*," from having lived a long while in Paris; that he had been very rich, but had gambled away all his property; and for some unknown reason, probably for money, though indeed he might have chosen better, if so, my father added with a cold smile, he had married the daughter of an agent, and after his marriage had entered upon speculations and ruined himself utterly.

"If only she doesn't try to borrow money," observed my mother.

"That's exceedingly possible," my father responded tranquilly. "Does she speak French?"

"Very badly."

"H'm. It's of no consequence anyway. I think you said you had asked the daughter too; some one was telling me she was a very charming and cultivated girl."

"Ah! Then she can't take after her mother."

"Nor her father either," rejoined my father. "He was cultivated indeed, but a fool."

My mother sighed and sank into thought. My father said no more. I felt very uncomfortable during this conversation.

After dinner I went into the garden, but without my gun. I swore to myself that I would not go near the Zasyekins' garden, but an irresistible force drew me thither, and not in vain. I had hardly reached the fence when I caught sight of Zinaïda. This time she was alone. She held a book in her hands, and was coming slowly along the path. She did not notice me.

I almost let her pass by; but all at once I changed my mind and coughed.

She turned round, but did not stop, pushed back with one hand the broad blue ribbon of her round straw hat, looked at me, smiled slowly, and again bent her eyes on the book.

I took off my cap, and after hesitating a moment, walked away with a heavy heart. *"Que suis-je pour elle?"* I thought (God knows why) in French.

Familiar footsteps sounded behind me; I looked round, my father came up to me with his light, rapid walk.

"Is that the young princess?" he asked me.

"Yes."

"Why, do you know her?"

"I saw her this morning at the princess's."

My father stopped, and, turning sharply on his heel, went back. When he was on a level with Zinaïda, he made her a courteous bow. She, too, bowed to him, with some astonishment on her face, and dropped her book. I saw how she looked after him. My father was always irreproachably dressed, simply and in a style of his own; but his figure had never struck me as more graceful, never had his grey hat sat more becomingly on his curls, which were scarcely perceptibly thinner than they had once been.

I bent my steps toward Zinaïda, but she did not even glance at me; she picked up her book again and went away.

VI

The whole evening and the following day I spent in a sort of dejected apathy. I remember I tried to work and took up Keidanov, but the boldly printed lines and pages of the famous text-book passed before my eyes in vain. I read ten times over the words: "Julius Caesar was distinguished by warlike courage." I did not understand anything and threw the book aside. Before dinner-time I pomaded myself once more, and once more put on my tail-coat and necktie.

"What's that for?" my mother demanded. "You're not a student yet, and God knows whether you'll get through the examination. And you've not long had a new jacket! You can't throw it away!"

"There will be visitors," I murmured almost in despair.

"What nonsense! fine visitors indeed!"

I had to submit. I changed my tail-coat for my jacket, but I did not take off the necktie. The princess and her daughter made their appearance half an hour before dinner-time; the old lady had put on, in addition to the green dress with which I was already acquainted, a yellow shawl, and an old-fashioned cap adorned with flame-coloured ribbons. She began talking at once about her money difficulties, sighing, complaining of her poverty, and imploring assistance, but she made herself at home; she took snuff as noisily, and fidgeted and lolled about in her chair as freely as ever. It never seemed to have struck her that she was a princess. Zinaïda on the other hand was rigid, almost haughty in her demeanour, every inch a princess. There was a cold immobility and dignity in her face. I should not have recognised it; I should not have known her smiles, her glances, though I thought her exquisite in this new aspect too. She wore a light barége dress with pale blue flowers on it; her hair fell in long curls down her cheek in the English fashion; this style went well with the cold expression of her face. My father sat beside her during dinner, and entertained his neighbour with the finished and serene courtesy peculiar to him. He glanced at her from time to time, and she glanced at him, but so strangely, almost with hostility. Their conversation was carried on in French; I was surprised, I remember, at the purity of Zinaïda's accent. The princess, while we were at table, as before made no ceremony; she ate a great deal, and praised the dishes. My mother was obviously bored by her, and answered her with a sort of weary indifference; my father faintly frowned now and then. My mother did not like Zinaïda either. "A conceited minx," she said next day. "And fancy, what she has to be conceited about, *avec sa mine de grisette!*"

"It's clear you have never seen any grisettes," my father observed to her.

"Thank God, I haven't!"

"Thank God, to be sure... only how can you form an opinion of them, then?"

To me Zinaïda had paid no attention whatever. Soon after dinner the princess got up to go.

"I shall rely on your kind offices. Maria Nikolaevna and Piotr Vassilitch," she said in a doleful sing-song to my mother and father. "I've no help for it! There were days, but they are over. Here I am, an excellency, and a poor honour it is with nothing to eat!"

My father made her a respectful bow and escorted her to the door of the hall. I was standing there in my short jacket, staring at the floor, like a man under sentence of death. Zinaïda's treatment of me had crushed me utterly. What was my astonishment, when, as she passed me, she whispered quickly with her former kind expression in her eyes: "Come to see us at eight, do you hear, be sure...." I simply threw up my hands, but already she was gone, flinging a white scarf over her head.

VII

At eight o'clock precisely, in my tail-coat and with my hair brushed up into a tuft on my head, I entered the passage of the lodge, where the princess lived. The old servant looked crossly at me and got up unwillingly from his bench. There was a sound of merry voices in the drawing-room. I opened the door and fell back in amazement. In the middle of the room was the young princess, standing on a chair, holding a man's hat in front of her; round the chair crowded some half a dozen men. They were trying to put their hands into the hat, while she held it above their heads, shaking it violently. On seeing me, she cried, "Stay, stay, another guest, he must have a ticket too," and leaping lightly down from the chair she took me by the cuff of my coat. "Come along," she said, "why are you standing still? *Messieurs*, let me make you acquainted: this is M'sieu Voldemar, the son of our neighbour. And this," she went on, addressing me, and indicating her guests in turn, "Count Malevsky, Doctor Lushin, Meidanov the poet, the retired captain Nirmatsky, and Byelovzorov the hussar, whom you've seen already. I hope you will be good friends."

I was so confused that I did not even bow to any one; in Doctor Lushin I recognised the dark man who had so mercilessly put me to shame in the garden; the others were unknown to me.

"Count!" continued Zinaïda, "write M'sieu Voldemar a ticket."

"That's not fair," was objected in a slight Polish accent by the count, a very handsome and fashionably dressed brunette, with expressive brown eyes, a thin little white nose, and delicate little moustaches over a tiny mouth. "This gentleman has not been playing forfeits with us."

"It's unfair," repeated in chorus Byelovzorov and the gentleman described as a retired captain, a man of forty, pock-marked to a hideous degree, curly-headed as a negro, round-shouldered, bandy-legged, and dressed in a military coat without epaulets, worn unbuttoned.

"Write him a ticket I tell you," repeated the young princess. "What's this mutiny; M'sieu Voldemar is with us for the first time, and there are no rules for him yet. It's no use grumbling—write it, I wish it."

The count shrugged his shoulders but bowed submissively, took the pen in his white, ring-bedecked fingers, tore off a scrap of paper and wrote on it.

"At least let us explain to Mr Voldemar what we are about," Lushin began in a sarcastic voice, "or else he will be quite lost. Do you see, young man, we are playing forfeits? the princess has to pay a forfeit, and the one who draws the lucky lot is to have the privilege of kissing her hand. Do you understand what I've told you?"

I simply stared at him, and continued to stand still in bewilderment, while the young princess jumped up on the chair again, and again began waving the hat. They all stretched up to her, and I went after the rest.

"Meidanov," said the princess to a tall young man with a thin face, little dim-sighted eyes, and exceedingly long black hair, "you as a poet ought to be magnanimous, and give up your number to M'sieu Voldemar so that he may have two chances instead of one."

But Meidanov shook his head in refusal, and tossed his hair. After all the others I put my hand into the hat, and unfolded my lot.... Heavens! what was my condition when I saw on it the word, Kiss!

"Kiss!" I could not help crying aloud.

"Bravo! he has won it," the princess said quickly. "How glad I am!" She came down from the chair and gave me such a bright sweet look, that my heart bounded. "Are you glad?" she asked me.

"Me?"... I faltered.

"Sell me your lot," Byelovzorov growled suddenly just in my ear. "I'll give you a hundred roubles."

I answered the hussar with such an indignant look, that Zinaïda clapped her hands, while Lushin cried, "He's a fine fellow!"

"But, as master of the ceremonies," he went on, "it's my duty to see that all the rules are kept. M'sieu Voldemar, go down on one knee. That is our regulation."

Zinaïda stood in front of me, her head a little on one side as though to get a better look at me; she held out her hand to me with dignity. A mist passed before my eyes; I meant to drop on one knee, sank on both, and pressed my lips to Zinaïda's fingers so awkwardly that I scratched myself a little with the tip of her nail.

"Well done!" cried Lushin, and helped me to get up.

The game of forfeits went on. Zinaïda sat me down beside her. She invented all sorts of extraordinary forfeits! She had among other things to represent a 'statue,' and she chose as a pedestal the hideous Nirmatsky, told him to bow down in an arch, and bend his head down on his breast. The laughter never paused for an instant. For me, a boy constantly brought up in the seclusion of a dignified manor-house, all this noise and uproar, this unceremonious, almost riotous gaiety, these relations with unknown persons, were simply intoxicating. My head went round, as though from wine. I began laughing and talking louder than the others, so much so that the old princess, who was sitting in the next room with some sort of clerk from the Tversky gate, invited by her for consultation on business, positively came in to look at me. But I felt so happy that I did not mind anything, I didn't care a straw for any one's jeers, or dubious looks. Zinaïda continued to show me a preference, and kept me at her side. In one forfeit, I had to sit by her, both hidden under one silk handkerchief: I was to tell her *my secret*. I remember our two heads being all at once in a warm, half-transparent, fragrant darkness, the soft, close brightness of her eyes in the dark, and the burning breath from her parted lips, and the gleam of her teeth and the ends of her hair tickling me and setting me on fire. I was silent. She smiled slyly and mysteriously, and at last whispered to me, "Well, what is it?" but I merely blushed and laughed, and turned away, catching my breath. We got tired of forfeits—we began to play a game with a string. My God! what were my transports when, for not paying attention, I got a sharp and vigorous slap on my fingers from her, and how I tried afterwards to pretend that I was absent-minded, and she teased me, and would not touch the hands I held out to her! What didn't we do that evening! We played the piano, and sang and danced and acted a gypsy encampment. Nirmatsky was dressed up as a bear, and made to drink salt water. Count Malevsky showed us several sorts of card tricks, and finished, after shuffling the cards, by dealing himself all the trumps at whist, on which Lushin "had the honour of congratulating him." Meidanov recited portions from his poem "The Manslayer" (romanticism was at its height at this period), which he intended to bring out in a black cover with the title in blood-red letters; they stole the clerk's cap off his knee, and made him dance a Cossack dance by way of ransom for it; they dressed up old Vonifaty in a woman's cap, and the young princess put on a man's hat.... I could not enumerate all we did. Only Byelovzorov kept more and more in the background, scowling and angry.... Sometimes his eyes looked bloodshot, he flushed all over, and it seemed every minute as though he would rush out upon us all and scatter us like shavings in all directions; but the young princess would glance at him, and shake her finger at him, and he would retire into his corner again.

We were quite worn out at last. Even the old princess, though she was ready for anything, as she expressed it, and no noise wearied her, felt tired at last, and longed for peace and quiet. At twelve o'clock at night, supper was served, consisting of a piece of stale dry cheese, and some cold turnovers of minced ham, which seemed to me more delicious than any pastry I had ever tasted; there was only one bottle of wine, and that was a strange one; a dark-coloured bottle with a wide neck, and the wine in it was of a pink hue; no one drank it, however. Tired out and faint with happiness, I left the lodge; at parting Zinaïda pressed my hand warmly, and again smiled mysteriously.

The night air was heavy and damp in my heated face; a storm seemed to be gathering; black stormclouds grew and crept across the sky, their smoky outlines visibly changing. A gust of wind shivered restlessly in the dark trees, and somewhere, far away on the horizon, muffled thunder angrily muttered as it were to itself.

I made my way up to my room by the back stairs. My old man-nurse was asleep on the floor, and I had to step over him; he waked up, saw me, and told me that my mother had again been very angry with me, and had wished to send after me again, but that my father had prevented her. (I had never gone to bed without saying good-night to my mother, and asking her blessing. There was no help for it now!)

I told my man that I would undress and go to bed by myself, and I put out the candle. But I did not undress, and did not go to bed.

I sat down on a chair, and sat a long while, as though spell-bound. What I was feeling was so new and so sweet.... I sat still, hardly looking round and not moving, drew slow breaths, and only from time to time laughed silently at some recollection, or turned cold within at the thought that I was in love, that this was she, that this was love. Zinaïda's face floated slowly before me in the darkness—floated, and did not float away; her lips still wore the same enigmatic smile, her eyes watched me, a little from one side, with a questioning, dreamy, tender look... as at the instant of parting from her. At last I got up, walked on tiptoe to my bed, and without undressing, laid my head carefully on the pillow, as though I were afraid by an abrupt movement to disturb what filled my soul.... I lay down, but did not even close my eyes. Soon I noticed that faint glimmers of light of some sort were thrown continually into the room.... I sat up and looked at the window. The window-frame could be clearly distinguished from the mysteriously and dimly-lighted panes. It is a storm, I thought; and a storm it really was, but it was raging so very far away that the thunder could not be heard; only blurred, long, as it were branching, gleams of lightning flashed continually over the sky; it was not flashing, though, so much as quivering and twitching like the wing of a dying bird. I got up, went to the window, and stood there till morning.... The lightning never ceased for an instant; it was what is called among the peasants a *sparrow night*. I gazed at the dumb sandy plain, at the dark mass of the Neskutchny gardens, at the yellowish facades of the distant buildings, which seemed to quiver too at each faint flash.... I gazed, and could not turn away; these silent lightning flashes, these gleams seemed in response to the secret silent fires which were aglow within me. Morning began to dawn; the sky was flushed in patches of crimson. As the sun came nearer, the lightning grew gradually paler, and ceased; the quivering gleams were fewer and fewer, and vanished at last, drowned in the sobering positive light of the coming day....

And my lightning flashes vanished too. I felt great weariness and peace... but Zinaïda's image still floated triumphant over my soul. But it too, this image, seemed more tranquil: like a swan rising out of the reeds of a bog, it stood out from the other unbeautiful figures surrounding it, and as I fell asleep, I flung myself before it in farewell, trusting adoration....

Oh, sweet emotions, gentle harmony, goodness and peace of the softened heart, melting bliss of the first raptures of love, where are they, where are they?

VIII

The next morning, when I came down to tea, my mother scolded me— less severely, however, than I had expected—and made me tell her how I had spent the previous evening. I answered her in few words, omitting many details, and trying to give the most innocent air to every-thing.

"Anyway, they're people who're not *comme il faut*," my mother com-mented, "and you've no business to be hanging about there, instead of preparing yourself for the examination, and doing your work."

As I was well aware that my mother's anxiety about my studies was confined to these few words, I did not feel it necessary to make any rejoinder; but after morning tea was over, my father took me by the arm, and turning into the garden with me, forced me to tell him all I had seen at the Zasyekins'.

A curious influence my father had over me, and curious were the relations existing between us. He took hardly any interest in my education, but he never hurt my feelings; he respected my freedom, he treated me—if I may so express it—with courtesy, ... only he never let me by really close to him. I loved him, I admired him, he was my ideal of a man—and Heavens! how passionately devoted I should have been to him, if I had not been continually conscious of his holding me off! But when he liked, he could almost instantaneously, by a single word, a single gesture, call forth an unbounded confidence in him. My soul expanded, I chattered away to him, as to a wise friend, a kindly teacher... then he as suddenly got rid of me, and again he was keeping me off, gently and affectionately, but still he kept me off.

Sometimes he was in high spirits, and then he was ready to romp and frolic with me, like a boy (he was fond of vigorous physical exercise of every sort); once—it never happened a second time!—he caressed me with such tenderness that I almost shed tears.... But high spirits and tenderness alike vanished completely, and what had passed between us, gave me nothing to build on for the future—it was as though I had dreamed it all. Sometimes I would scrutinise his clever handsome bright face... my heart would throb, and my whole being yearn to him... he would seem to feel what was going on within me, would give me a passing pat on the cheek, and go away, or take up some work, or suddenly freeze all over as only he knew how to freeze, and I shrank into myself at once, and turned cold too. His rare fits of friendliness to me were never called forth by my silent, but intelligible entreaties: they always occurred unexpectedly. Thinking over my father's character later, I have come to the conclusion that he had no thoughts to spare for me and for family life; his heart was in other things, and found complete satisfaction elsewhere. "Take for yourself what you can, and don't be ruled by others; to belong to oneself—the whole savour of life lies in that," he said to me one day. Another time, I, as a young democrat, fell to airing my views on liberty (he was 'kind,' as I used to call it, that day; and at such times I could talk to him as I liked). "Liberty," he repeated; "and do you know what can give a man liberty?"

"What?"

"Will, his own will, and it gives power, which is better than liberty. Know how to will, and you will be free, and will lead."

My father, before all, and above all, desired to live, and lived.... Perhaps he had a presentiment that he would not have long to enjoy the 'savour' of life; he died at forty-two.

I described my evening at the Zasyekins' minutely to my father. Half attentively, half carelessly, he listened to me, sitting on a garden seat, drawing in the sand with his cane. Now and then he laughed, shot bright, droll glances at me, and spurred me on with short questions and assents. At first I could not bring myself even to utter the name of Zinaïda, but I could not restrain myself long, and began singing her praises. My father still laughed; then he grew thoughtful, stretched, and got up.

I remembered that as he came out of the house he had ordered his horse to be saddled. He was a splendid horseman, and, long before Rarey, had the secret of breaking in the most vicious horses.

"Shall I come with you, father?" I asked.

"No," he answered, and his face resumed its ordinary expression of friendly indifference. "Go alone, if you like; and tell the coachman I'm not going."

He turned his back on me and walked rapidly away. I looked after him; he disappeared through the gates. I saw his hat moving along beside the fence; he went into the Zasyekins'.

He stayed there not more than an hour, but then departed at once for the town, and did not return home till evening.

After dinner I went myself to the Zasyekins'. In the drawing-room I found only the old princess. On seeing me she scratched her head under her cap with a knitting-needle, and suddenly asked me, could I copy a petition for her.

"With pleasure," I replied, sitting down on the edge of a chair.

"Only mind and make the letters bigger," observed the princess, handing me a dirty sheet of paper; "and couldn't you do it to-day, my good sir?"

"Certainly, I will copy it to-day."

The door of the next room was just opened, and in the crack I saw the face of Zinaïda, pale and pensive, her hair flung carelessly back; she stared at me with big chilly eyes, and softly closed the door.

"Zina, Zina!" called the old lady. Zinaïda made no response. I took home the old lady's petition and spent the whole evening over it.

IX

My 'passion' dated from that day. I felt at that time, I recollect, something like what a man must feel on entering the service: I had ceased now to be simply a young boy; I was in love. I have said that my passion dated from that day; I might have added that my sufferings too dated from the same day. Away from Zinaïda I pined; nothing was to my mind; everything went wrong with me; I spent whole days thinking intensely about her... I pined when away,... but in her presence I was no better off. I was jealous; I was conscious of my insignificance; I was stupidly sulky or stupidly abject, and, all the same, an invincible force drew me to her, and I could not help a shudder of delight whenever I stepped through the doorway of her room. Zinaïda guessed at once that I was in love with her, and indeed I never even thought of concealing it. She amused herself with my passion, made a fool of me, petted and tormented me. There is a sweetness in being the sole source, the autocratic and irresponsible cause of the greatest joy and profoundest pain to another, and I was like wax in Zinaïda's hands; though, indeed, I was not the only one in love with her. All the men who visited the house were crazy over her, and she kept them all in leading-strings at her feet. It amused her to arouse their hopes and then their fears, to turn them round her finger (she used to call it knocking their heads together), while they never dreamed of offering resistance and eagerly submitted to her. About her whole being, so full of life and beauty, there was a peculiarly bewitching mixutre of slyness and carelessness, of artificiality and simplicity, of composure and frolicsomeness; about everything she did or said, about every action of hers, there clung a delicate, fine charm, in which an individual power was manifest at work. And her face was ever changing, working too; it expressed, almost at the same time, irony, dreaminess, and passion. Various emotions, delicate and quick-changing as the shadows of clouds on a sunny day of wind, chased one another continually over her lips and eyes.

Each of her adorers was necessary to her. Byelovzorov, whom she sometimes called "my wild beast," and sometimes simply "mine," would gladly have flung himself into the fire for her sake. With little confidence in his intellectual abilities and other qualities, he was for ever offering her marriage, hinting that the others were merely hanging about with no serious intention. Meidanov responded to the poetic fibres of her nature; a man of rather cold temperament, like almost all writers, he forced himself to convince her, and perhaps himself, that he adored her, sang her praises in endless verses, and read them to her with a peculiar enthusiasm, at once affected and sincere. She sympathised with him, and at the same time jeered at him a little; she had no great faith in him, and after listening to his outpourings, she would make him read Pushkin, as she said, to clear the air. Lushin, the ironical doctor, so cynical in words, knew her better than any of them, and loved her more than all, though he abused her to her face and behind her back. She could not help respecting him, but made him smart for it, and at times, with a peculiar, malignant pleasure, made him feel that he too was at her mercy. "I'm a flirt, I'm heartless, I'm an actress in my instincts," she said to him one day in my presence; "well and good! Give me your hand then; I'll stick this pin in it, you'll be ashamed of this young man's seeing it, it will hurt you, but you'll laugh for all that, you truthful person." Lushin crimsoned, turned away, bit his lips, but ended by submitting his hand. She pricked it, and he did in fact begin to laugh,... and she laughed, thrusting the pin in pretty deeply, and peeping into his eyes, which he vainly strove to keep in other directions....

I understood least of all the relations existing between Zinaïda and Count Malevsky. He was handsome, clever, and adroit, but something equivocal, something false in him was apparent even to me, a boy of sixteen, and I marvelled that Zinaïda did not notice it. But possibly she did notice this element of falsity really and was not repelled by it. Her irregular education, strange acquaintances and habits, the constant presence of her mother, the poverty and disorder in their house, everything, from the very liberty the young girl enjoyed, with the consciousness of her superiority to the people around her, had developed in her a sort of half-contemptuous carelessness and lack of fastidiousness. At any time anything might happen; Vonifaty might announce that there was no sugar, or some revolting scandal would come to her ears, or her guests would fall to quarrelling among themselves—she would only shake her curls, and say, "What does it matter?" and care little enough about it.

But my blood, anyway, was sometimes on fire with indignation when Malevsky approached her, with a sly, fox-like action, leaned gracefully on the back of her chair, and began whispering in her ear with a self-satisfied and ingratiating little smile, while she folded her arms across her bosom, looked intently at him and smiled too, and shook her head.

"What induces you to receive Count Malevsky?" I asked her one day.

"He has such pretty moustaches," she answered. "But that's rather beyond you."

"You needn't think I care for him," she said to me another time. "No; I can't care for people I have to look down upon. I must have some one who can master me.... But, merciful heavens, I hope I may never come across any one like that! I don't want to be caught in any one's claws, not for anything."

"You'll never be in love, then?"

"And you? Don't I love you?" she said, and she flicked me on the nose with the tip of her glove.

Yes, Zinaïda amused herself hugely at my expense. For three weeks I saw her every day, and what didn't she do with me! She rarely came to see us, and I was not sorry for it; in our house she was transformed into a young lady, a young princess, and I was a little overawed by her. I was afraid of betraying myself before my mother; she had taken a great dislike to Zinaïda, and kept a hostile eye upon us. My father I was not so much afraid of; he seemed not to notice me. He talked little to her, but always with special cleverness and significance. I gave up working and reading; I even gave up walking about the neighbourhood and riding my horse. Like a beetle tied by the leg, I moved continually round and round my beloved little lodge. I would gladly have stopped there altogether, it seemed... but that was impossible. My mother scolded me, and sometimes Zinaïda herself drove me away. Then I used to shut myself up in my room, or go down to the very end of the garden, and climbing into what was left of a tall stone greenhouse, now in ruins, sit for hours with my legs hanging over the wall that looked on to the road, gazing and gazing and seeing nothing. White butterflies flitted lazily by me, over the dusty nettles; a saucy sparrow settled not far off on the half crumbling red brickwork and twittered irritably, incessantly twisting and turning and preening his tail-feathers; the still mistrustful rooks cawed now and then, sitting high, high up on the bare top of a birch-tree; the sun and wind played softly on its pliant branches; the tinkle of the bells of the Don monastery floated across to me from time to time, peaceful and dreary; while I sat, gazed, listened, and was filled full of a nameless sensation in which all was contained: sadness and joy and the foretaste of the future, and the desire and dread of life. But at that time I understood nothing of it, and could have given a name to nothing of all that was passing at random within me, or should have called it all by one name—the name of Zinaïda.

Zinaïda continued to play cat and mouse with me. She flirted with me, and I was all agitation and rapture; then she would suddenly thrust me away, and I dared not go near her—dared not look at her.

I remember she was very cold to me for several days together; I was completely crushed, and creeping timidly to their lodge, tried to keep close to the old princess, regardless of the circumstance that she was particularly scolding and grumbling just at that time; her financial affairs had been going badly, and she had already had two 'explanations' with the police officials.

One day I was walking in the garden beside the familiar fence, and I caught sight of Zinaïda; leaning on both arms, she was sitting on the grass, not stirring a muscle. I was about to make off cautiously, but she suddenly raised her head and beckoned me imperiously. My heart failed me; I did not understand her at first. She repeated her signal. I promptly jumped over the fence and ran joyfully up to her, but she brought me to a halt with a look, and motioned me to the path two paces from her. In confusion, not knowing what to do, I fell on my knees at the edge of the path. She was so pale, such bitter suffering, such intense weariness, was expressed in every feature of her face, that it sent a pang to my heart, and I muttered unconsciously, "What is the matter?"

Zinaïda stretched out her head, picked a blade of grass, bit it and flung it away from her.

"You love me very much?" she asked at last. "Yes."

I made no answer—indeed, what need was there to answer?

"Yes," she repeated, looking at me as before. "That's so. The same eyes,"—she went on; sank into thought, and hid her face in her hands. "Everything's grown so loathsome to me," she whispered, "I would have gone to the other end of the world first—I can't bear it, I can't get over it.... And what is there before me!... Ah, I am wretched.... My God, how wretched I am!"

"What for?" I asked timidly.

Zinaïda made no answer, she simply shrugged her shoulders. I remained kneeling, gazing at her with intense sadness. Every word she had uttered simply cut me to the heart. At that instant I felt I would gladly have given my live, if only she should not grieve. I gazed at her—and though I could not understand why she was wretched, I vividly pictured to myself, how in a fit of insupportable anguish, she had suddenly come out into the garden, and sunk to the earth, as though mown down by a scythe. It was all bright and green about her; the wind was whispering in the leaves of the trees, and swinging now and then a long branch of a raspberry bush over Zinaïda's head. There was a sound of the cooing of doves, and the bees hummed, flying low over the scanty grass. Overhead the sun was radiantly blue—while I was so sorrowful....

"Read me some poetry," said Zinaïda in an undertone, and she propped herself on her elbow; "I like your reading poetry. You read it in sing-song, but that's no matter, that comes of being young. Read me 'On the Hills of Georgia.' Only sit down first."

I sat down and read 'On the Hills of Georgia.'

"'That the heart cannot choose but love,'" repeated Zinaïda. "That's where poetry's so fine; it tells us what is not, and what's not only better

629

than what is, but much more like the truth, 'cannot choose but love,'— it might want not to, but it can't help it." She was silent again, then all at once she started and got up. "Come along. Meidanov's indoors with mamma, he brought me his poem, but I deserted him. His feelings are hurt too now... I can't help it! you'll understand it all some day... only don't be angry with me!"

Zinaïda hurriedly pressed my hand and ran on ahead. We went back into the lodge. Meidanov set to reading us his "Manslayer," which had just appeared in print, but I did not hear him. He screamed and drawled his four-foot iambic lines, the alternating rhythms jingled like little bells, noisy and meaningless, while I still watched Zinaïda and tried to take in the import of her last words.

> "Perchance some unknown rival
> Has surprised and mastered thee?"

Meidanov bawled suddenly through his nose—and my eyes and Zinaïda's met. She looked down and faintly blushed. I saw her blush, and grew cold with terror. I had been jealous before, but only at that instant the idea of her being in love flashed upon my mind. "Good God! she is in love!"

X

My real torments began from that instant. I racked my brains, changed my mind, and changed it back again, and kept an unremitting, though, as far as possible, secret watch on Zinaïda. A change had come over her, that was obvious. She began going walks alone—and long walks. Sometimes she would not see visitors; she would sit for hours together in her room. This had never been a habit of hers till now. I suddenly became—or fancied I had become—extraordinarily penetrating.

"Isn't it he? or isn't it he?" I asked myself, passing in inward agitation from one of her admirers to another. Count Malevsky secretly struck me as more to be feared than the others, though, for Zinaïda's sake, I was ashamed to confess it to myself.

My watchfulness did not see beyond the end of my nose, and its secrecy probably deceived no one; any way, Doctor Lushin soon saw through me. But he, too, had changed of late; he had grown thin, he laughed as often, but his laugh seemed more hollow, more spiteful, shorter, an involuntary nervous irritability took the place of his former light irony and assumed cynicism.

"Why are you incessantly hanging about here, young man?" he said to me one day, when we were left alone together in the Zasyekins' drawing-room. (The young princess had not come home from a walk, and the shrill voice of the old princess could be heard within; she was scolding the maid.) "You ought to be studying, working—while you're young—and what are you doing?"

"You can't tell whether I work at home," I retorted with some haughtiness, but also with some hesitation.

"A great deal of work you do! that's not what you're thinking about! Well, I won't find fault with that... at your age that's in the natural order of things. But you've been awfully unlucky in your choice. Don't you see what this house is?"

"I don't understand you," I observed.

"You don't understand? so much the worse for you. I regard it as a duty to warn you. Old bachelors, like me, can come here, what harm can it do us! we're tough, nothing can hurt us, what harm can it do us; but your skin's tender yet—this air is bad for you—believe me, you may get harm from it."

"How so?"

"Why, are you well now? Are you in a normal condition? Is what you're feeling—beneficial to you—good for you?"

"Why, what am I feeling?" I said, while in my heart I knew the doctor was right.

"Ah, young man, young man," the doctor went on with an intonation that suggested that something highly insulting to me was contained in these two words, "what's the use of your prevaricating, when, thank God, what's in your heart is in your face, so far? But there, what's the use of talking? I shouldn't come here myself, if... (the doctor compressed his lips)... if I weren't such a queer fellow. Only this is what surprises me; how it is, you, with your intelligence, don't see what is going on around you?"

"And what is going on?" I put in, all on the alert.

The doctor looked at me with a sort of ironical compassion.

"Nice of me!" he said as though to himself, "as if he need know anything of it. In fact, I tell you again," he added, raising his voice, "the atmosphere here is not fit for you. You like being here, but what of that! It's nice and sweet-smelling in a greenhouse—but there's no living in it. Yes! do as I tell you, and go back to your Keidanov."

The old princess came in, and began complaining to the doctor of her toothache. Then Zinaïda appeared.

"Come," said the old princess, "you must scold her, doctor. She's drinking iced water all day long; is that good for her, pray, with her delicate chest?"

"Why do you do that?" asked Lushin.

"Why, what effect could it have?"

"What effect? You might get a chill and die."

"Truly? Do you mean it? Very well—so much the better."

"A fine idea!" muttered the doctor. The old princess had gone out.

"Yes, a fine idea," repeated Zinaïda. "Is life such a festive affair? Just look about you.... Is it nice, eh? Or do you imagine I don't understand it, and don't feel it? It gives me pleasure—drinking iced water; and can you seriously assure me that such a life is worth too much to be risked for an instant's pleasure—happiness I won't even talk about."

"Oh, very well," remarked Lushin, "caprice and irresponsibility.... Those two words sum you up; your whole nature's contained in those two words."

Zinaïda laughed nervously.

"You're late for the post, my dear doctor. You don't keep a good look-out; you're behind the times. Put on your spectacles. I'm in no capricious humour now. To make fools of you, to make a fool of myself... much fun there is in that!—and as for irresponsibility... M'sieu Voldemar," Zinaïda added suddenly, stamping, "don't make such a melancholy face. I can't endure people to pity me." She went quickly out of the room.

"It's bad for you, very bad for you, this atmosphere, young man," Lushin said to me once more.

XI

On the evening of the same day the usual guests were assembled at the Zasyekins'. I was among them.

The conversation turned on Meidanov's poem. Zinaïda expressed genuine admiration of it. "But do you know what?" she said to him. "If I were a poet, I would choose quite different subjects. Perhaps it's all nonsense, but strange ideas sometimes come into my head, especially when I'm not asleep in the early morning, when the sky begins to turn rosy and grey both at once. I would, for instance... You won't laugh at me?"

"No, no!" we all cried, with one voice.

"I would describe," she went on, folding her arms across her bosom and looking away, "a whole company of young girls at night in a greet boat, on a silent river. The moon is shining, and they are all in white, and wearing garlands of white flowers, and singing, you know, something in the nature of a hymn."

"I see—I see; go on," Meidanov commented with dreamy significance.

"All of a sudden, loud clamour, laughter, torches, tambourines on the bank.... It's a troop of Bacchantes dancing with songs and cries. It's your business to make a picture of it, Mr Poet;... only I should like the torches to be red and to smoke a great deal, and the Bacchantes' eyes to gleam under their wreaths, and the wreaths to be dusky. Don't forget the tiger-skins, too, and goblets and gold—lots of gold...."

"Where ought the gold to be?" asked Meidanov, tossing back his sleek hair and distending his nostrils.

"Where? on their shoulders and arms and legs—everywhere. They say in ancient times women wore gold rings on their ankles. The Bacchantes call the girls in the boat to them. The girls have ceased singing their hymn—they cannot go on with it, but they do not stir, the river carries them to the bank. And suddenly one of them slowly rises.... This you must describe nicely: how she slowly gets up in the moonlight, and how her companions are afraid.... She steps over the edge of the boat, the Bacchantes surround her, whirl her away into night and darkness.... Here put in smoke in clouds and everything in confusion. There is nothing but the sound of their shrill cry, and her wreath left lying on the bank."

Zinaïda ceased. ("Oh! she is in love!" I thought again.)

"And is that all?" asked Meidanov.

"That's all."

"That can't be the subject of a whole poem," he observed pompously, "but I will make use of your idea for a lyrical fragment."

"In the romantic style?" queried Malevsky.

"Of course, in the romantic style—Byronic."

"Well, to my mind, Hugo beats Byron," the young count observed negligently; "he's more interesting."

"Hugo is a writer of the first class," replied Meidanov; "and my friend, Tonkosheev, in his Spanish romance, *El Trovador*..."

"Ah! is that the book with the question-marks turned upside down?" Zinaïda interrupted.

"Yes. That's the custom with the Spanish. I was about to observe that Tonkosheev..."

"Come! you're going to argue about classicism and romanticism again," Zinaïda interrupted him a second time. "We'd much better play…"

"Forfeits?" put in Lushin.

"No, forfeits are a bore; at comparisons." (This game Zinaïda had invented herself. Some object was mentioned, every one tried to compare it with something, and the one who chose the best comparison got a prize.)

She went up to the window. The sun was just setting; high up in the sky were large red clouds.

"What are those clouds like?" questioned Zinaïda; and without waiting for our answer, she said, "I think they are like the purple sails on the golden ship of Cleopatra, when she sailed to meet Antony. Do you remember, Meidanov, you were telling me about it not long ago?"

All of us, like Polonius in *Hamlet*, opined that the clouds recalled nothing so much as those sails, and that not one of us could discover a better comparison.

"And how old was Antony then?" inquired Zinaïda.

"A young man, no doubt," observed Malevsky.

"Yes, a young man," Meidanov chimed in in confirmation.

"Excuse me," cried Lushin, "he was over forty."

"Over forty," repeated Zinaïda, giving him a rapid glance….

I soon went home. "She is in love," my lips unconsciously repeated…. "But with whom?"

XII

The days passed by. Zinaïda became stranger and stranger, and more and more incomprehensible. One day I went over to her, and saw her sitting in a basket-chair, her head pressed to the sharp edge of the table. She drew herself up… her whole face was wet with tears.

"Ah, you!" she said with a cruel smile. "Come here."

I went up to her. She put her hand on my head, and suddenly catching hold of my hair began pulling it.

"It hurts me," I said at last.

"Ah! does it? And do you suppose nothing hurts me?" she replied.

"Ai!" she cried suddenly, seeing she had pulled a little tuft of hair out. "What have I done? Poor M'sieu Voldemar!"

She carefully smoothed the hair she had torn out, stroked it round her finger, and twisted it into a ring.

"I shall put your hair in a locket and wear it round my neck," she said, while the tears still glittered in her eyes. "That will be some small consolation to you, perhaps... and now good-bye."

I went home, and found an unpleasant state of things there. My mother was having a scene with my father; she was reproaching him with something, while he, as his habit was, maintained a polite and chilly silence, and soon left her. I could not hear what my mother was talking of, and indeed I had no thought to spare for the subject; I only remember that when the interview was over, she sent for me to her room, and referred with great displeasure to the frequent visits I paid the princess, who was, in her words, *une femme capable de tout*. I kissed her hand (this was what I always did when I wanted to cut short a conversation) and went off to my room. Zinaïda's tears had completely overwhelmed me; I positively did not know what to think, and was ready to cry myself; I was a child after all, in spite of my sixteen years. I had now given up thinking about Malevsky, though Byelovzorov looked more and more threatening every day, and glared at the wily count like a wolf at a sheep; but I thought of nothing and of no one. I was lost in imaginings, and was always seeking seclusion and solitude. I was particularly fond of the ruined greenhouse. I would climb up on the high wall, and perch myself, and sit there, such an unhappy, lonely, and melancholy youth, that I felt sorry for myself—and how consolatory were those mournful sensations, how I revelled in them!...

One day I was sitting on the wall looking into the distance and listening to the ringing of the bells.... Suddenly something floated up to me—not a breath of wind and not a shiver, but as it were a whiff of frangrance—as it were, a sense of some one's being near.... I looked down. Below, on the path, in a light greyish gown, with a pink parasol on her shoulder, was Zinaïda, hurrying along. She caught sight of me, stopped, and pushing back the brim of her straw hat, she raised her velvety eyes to me.

"What are you doing up there at such a height?" she asked me with a rather queer smile. "Come," she went on, "you always declare you love me; jump down into the road to me if you really do love me."

Zinaïda had hardly uttered those words when I flew down, just as though some one had given me a violent push from behind. The wall was about fourteen feet high. I reached the ground on my feet, but the shock was so great that I could not keep my footing; I fell down, and for an instant fainted away. When I came to myself again, without opening my eyes, I felt Zinaïda beside me. "My dear boy," she was saying, bending over me, and there was a note of alarmed tenderness in her voice, "how could you do it, dear; how could you obey?... You know I love you.... Get up."

Her bosom was heaving close to me, her hands were caressing my head, and suddenly—what were my emotions at that moment—her soft, fresh lips began covering my face with kisses... they touched my lips.... But then Zinaïda probably guessed by the expression of my face that I had regained consciousness, though I still kept my eyes closed, and rising rapidly to her feet, she said: "Come, get up, naughty boy, silly, why are you lying in the dust?" I got up. "Give me my parasol," said Zinaïda, "I threw it down somewhere, and don't stare at me like that... what ridiculous nonsense! you're not hurt, are you? stung by the nettles, I daresay? Don't stare at me, I tell you.... But he doesn't understand, he doesn't answer," she added, as though to herself.... "Go home, M'sieu Voldemar, brush yourself, and don't dare to follow me, or I shall be angry, and never again..."

She did not finish her sentence, but walked rapidly away, while I sat down by the side of the road... my legs would not support me. The nettles had stung my hands, my back ached, and my head was giddy; but the feeling of rapture I experienced then has never come a second time in my life. It turned to a sweet ache in all my limbs and found expression at last in joyful hops and skips and shouts. Yes, I was still a child.

XIII

I was so proud and light-hearted all that day, I so vividly retained on my face the feeling of Zinaïda's kisses, with such a shudder of delight I recalled every word she had uttered, I so hugged my unexpected happiness that I felt positively afraid, positively unwilling to see her, who had given rise to these new sensations. It seemed to me that now I could ask nothing more of fate, that now I ought to "go, and draw a deep last sigh and die." But, next day, when I went into the lodge, I felt great embarrassment, which I tried to conceal under a show of modest confidence, befitting a man who wishes to make it apparent that he knows how to keep a secret. Zinaïda received me very simply, without any emotion, she simply shook her finger at me and asked me, whether I wasn't black and blue? All my modest confidence and air of mystery vanished instantaneously and with them my embarrassment. Of course, I had not expected anything particular, but Zinaïda's composure was like a bucket of cold water thrown over me. I realised that in her eyes I was a child, and was extremely miserable! Zinaïda walked up and down the room, giving me a quick smile, whenever she caught my eye, but her thoughts were far away, I saw that clearly.... "Shall I begin about what happened yesterday myself," I pondered; "ask her, where she was hurrying off so fast, so as to find out once for all"... but with a gesture of despair, I merely went and sat down in a corner.

Byelovzorov came in; I felt relieved to see him.

"I've not been able to find you a quiet horse," he said in a sulky voice; "Freitag warrants one, but I don't feel any confidence in it, I'm afraid."

"What are you afraid of?" said Zinaïda; "allow me to inquire."

"What am I afraid of? Why, you don't know how to ride. Lord save us, what might happen! What whim is this has come over you all of a sudden?"

"Come, that's my business, Sir Wild Beast. In that case I will ask Piotr Vassilievitch."...(My father's name was Piotr Vassilievitch.) I was surprised at her mentioning his name so lightly and freely, as though she were confident of his readiness to do her a service.)

"Oh, indeed," retorted Byelovzorov, "you mean to go out riding with him then?"

"With him or with some one else is nothing to do with you. Only not with you, anyway."

"Not with me," repeated Byelovzorov. "As you wish. Well, I shall find you a horse."

"Yes, only mind now, don't send some old cow. I warn you I want to gallop."

"Gallop away by all means... with whom is it, with Malevsky, you are going to ride?"

"And why not with him, Mr Pugnacity? Come, be quiet," she added, "and don't glare. I'll take you too. You know that to my mind now Malevsky's—ugh!" She shook her head.

"You say that to console me," growled Byelovzorov.

Zinaïda half closed her eyes. "Does that console you? O... O... O... Mr Pugnacity!" she said at last, as though she could find no other word. "And you, M'sieu Voldemar, would you come with us?"

"I don't care to... in a large party," I muttered, not raising my eyes.

"You prefer a *tête-à-tête?*... Well, freedom to the free, and heaven to saints," she commented with a sigh. "Go along, Byelovzorov, and bestir yourself. I must have a horse for to-morrow."

"Oh, and where's the money to come from?" put in the old princess. Zinaïda scowled.

"I won't ask you for it; Byelovzorov will trust me."

"He'll trust you, will he?"... grumbled the old princess, and all of a sudden she screeched at the top of her voice, "Duniashka!"

"Maman, I have given you a bell to ring," observed Zinaïda.

"Duniashka!" repeated the old lady.

Byelovzorov took leave; I went away with him. Zinaïda did not try to detain me.

XIV

The next day I got up early, cut myself a stick, and set off beyond the town-gates. I thought I would walk off my sorrow. It was a lovely day, bright and not too hot, a fresh sportive breeze roved over the earth with temperate rustle and frolic, setting all things a-flutter and harassing nothing. I wandered a long while over hills and through woods; I had not felt happy, I had left home with the intention of giving myself up to melancholy, but youth, the exquisite weather, the fresh air, the pleasure of rapid motion, the sweetness of repose, lying on the thick grass in a solitary nook, gained the upper hand; the memory of those never-to-be-forgotten words, those kisses, forced itself once more upon my soul. It was sweet to me to think that Zinaïda could not, anyway, fail to do justice to my courage, my heroism.... "Others may seem better to her than I," I mused, "let them! But others only say what they would do, while I have done it. And what more would I not do for her?" My fancy set to work. I began picturing to myself how I would save her from the hands of enemies; how, covered with blood I would tear her by force from prison, and expire at her feet. I remembered a picture hanging in our drawing-room—Malek-Adel bearing away Matilda—but at that point my attention was absorbed by the appearance of a speckled woodpecker who climbed busily up the slender stem of a birch-tree and peeped out uneasily from behind it, first to the right, then to the left, like a musician behind the bass-viol.

Then I sang "Not the white snows," and passed from that to a song well known at that period: "I await thee, when the wanton zephyr," then I began reading aloud Yermak's address to the stars from Homyakov's tragedy. I made an attempt to compose something myself in a sentimental vein, and invented the line which was to conclude each verse: "O Zinaïda, Zinaïda!" but could get no further with it. Meanwhile it was getting on towards dinner-time. I went down into the valley; a narrow sandy path winding through it led to the town. I walked along this path.... The dull thud of horses' hoofs resounded behind me. I looked round instinctively, stood still and took off my cap. I saw my father and Zinaïda. They were riding side by side. My father was saying something to her, bending right over to her, his hand propped on the horse's neck, he was smiling. Zinaïda listened to him in silence, her eyes severely cast down, and her lips tightly pressed together. At first I saw them only; but a few instants later, Byelovzorov came into sight round a bend in the glade, he was wearing a hussar's uniform with a pelisse, and riding a foaming black horse. The gallant horse tossed its head, snorted and pranced from side to side, his rider was at once holding him in and spurring him on. I stood aside. My father gathered up the reins, moved away from Zinaïda, she slowly raised her eyes to him, and both galloped off.... Byelovzorov flew after them, his sabre clattering behind him. "He's as red as a crab," I reflected, "while she... why's she so pale? out riding the whole morning, and pale?"

I redoubled my pace, and got home just at dinner-time. My father was already sitting by my mother's chair, dressed for dinner, washed and fresh; he was reading an article from the *Journal des Débats* in his smooth musical voice; but my mother heard him without attention, and when she saw me, asked where I had been to all day long, and added that she didn't like this gadding about God knows where, and God knows in what company. "But I have been walking alone," I was on the point of replying, but I looked at my father, and for some reason or other held my peace.

XV

For the next five or six days I hardly saw Zinaïda; she said she was ill, which did not, however, prevent the usual visitors from calling at the lodge to pay—as they expressed it, their duty—all, that is, except Meidanov, who promptly grew dejected and sulky when he had not an opportunity of being enthusiastic. Byelovzorov sat sullen and red-faced in a corner, buttoned up to the throat; on the refined face of Malevsky there flicked continually an evil smile; he had really fallen into disfavour with Zinaïda, and waited with special assiduity on the old princess, and even went with her in a hired coach to call on the Governor-General. This expedition turned out unsuccessful, however, and even led to an unpleasant experience for Malevsky; he was reminded of some scandal to do with certain officers of the engineers, and was forced in his explanations to plead his youth and inexperience at the time. Lushin came twice a day, but did not stay long; I was rather afraid of him after our last unreserved conversation, and at the same time felt a genuine attraction to him. He went a walk with me one day in the Neskutchny gardens, was very good-natured and nice, told me the names and properties of various plants and flowers, and suddenly, *à propos* of nothing at all, cried, hitting himself on his forehead, "And I, poor fool, thought her a flirt! it's clear self-sacrifice is sweet for some people!"

"What do you mean by that?" I inquired.

"I don't mean to tell you anything," Lushin replied abruptly.

Zinaïda avoided me; my presence—I could not help noticing it—affected her disagreeably. She involuntarily turned away from me... involuntarily; that was what was so bitter, that was what crushed me! But there was no help for it, and I tried not to cross her path, and only to watch her from a distance, in which I was not always successful. As before, something incomprehensible was happening to her; her face was different, she was different altogether. I was specially struck by the change that had taken place in her one warm still evening. I was sitting on a low garden bench under a spreading elderbush; I was fond of that nook; I could see from there the window of Zinaïda's room. I sat there; over my head a little bird was busily hopping about in the darkness of the leaves; a grey cat, stretching herself at full length, crept warily about the garden, and the first beetles were heavily droning in the air, which was still clear, though it was not light. I sat and gazed at the window, and waited to see if it would open; it did open, and Zinaïda appeared at it. She had on a white dress, and she herself, her face, shoulders, and arms, were pale to whiteness. She stayed a long while without moving, and looked out straight before her from under her knitted brows. I had never known such a look on her. Then she clasped her hands tightly, raised them to her lips, to her forehead, and suddenly pulling her fingers apart, she pushed back her hair behind her ears, tossed it, and with a sort of determination nodded her head, and slammed-to the window.

Three days later she met me in the garden. I was turning away, but she stopped me of herself.

"Give me your arm," she said to me with her old affectionateness, "it's a long while since we have had a talk together."

I stole a look at her; her eyes were full of a soft light, and her face seemed as it were smiling through a mist.

"Are you still not well?" I asked her.

"No, that's all over now," she answered, and she picked a small red rose. "I am a little tired, but that too will pass off."

"And will you be as you used to be again?" I asked.

Zinaïda put the rose up to her face, and I fancied the reflection of its bright petals had fallen on her cheeks. "Why, am I changed?" she questioned me.

"Yes, you are changed," I answered in a low voice.

"I have been cold to you, I know," began Zinaïda, "but you mustn't pay attention to that... I couldn't help it.... Come, why talk about it!"

"You don't want me to love you, that's what it is!" I cried gloomily, in an involuntary outburst.

"No, love me, but not as you did."

"How then?"

"Let us be friends—come now!" Zinaïda gave me the rose to smell. "Listen, you know I'm much older than you—I might be your aunt, really; well, not your aunt, but an older sister. And you..."

"You think me a child," I interrupted.

"Well, yes, a child, but a dear, good clever one, whom I love very much. Do you know what? From this day forth I confer on you the rank of page to me; and don't you forget that pages have to keep close to their ladies. Here is the token of your new dignity," she added, sticking the rose in the buttonhole of my jacket, "the token of my favour."

"I once received other favours from you," I muttered.

"Ah!" commented Zinaïda, and she gave me a sidelong look. "What a memory he has! Well? I'm quite ready now..." And stooping to me, she imprinted on my forehead a pure, tranquil kiss.

I only looked at her, while she turned away, and saying, "Follow me, my page," went into the lodge. I followed her—all in amazement. "Can this gentle, reasonable girl," I thought, "be the Zinaïda I used to know?" I fancied her very walk was quieter, her whole figure statelier and more graceful...

And, mercy! with what fresh force love burned within me!

XVI

After dinner the usual party assembled again at the lodge, and the young princess came out to them. All were there in full force, just as on that first evening which I never forgot; even Nirmatsky had limped to see her; Meidanov came this time earliest of all, he brought some new verses. The games of forfeits began again, but without the strange pranks, the practical jokes and noise—the gipsy element had vanished. Zinaïda gave a different tone to the proceedings. I sat beside her by virtue of my office as page. Among other things, she proposed that any one who had to pay a forfeit should tell his dream; but this was not successful. The dreams were either uninteresting (Byelovzorov had dreamed that he fed his mare on carp, and that she had a wooden head), or unnatural and invented. Meidanov regaled us with a regular romance; there were sepulchres in it, and angels with lyres, and talking flowers and music wafted from afar. Zinaïda did not let him finish. "If we are to have compositions," she said, "let every one tell something made up, and no pretence about it." The first who had to speak was again Byelovzorov.

The young hussar was confused. "I can't make up anything!" he cried.

"What nonsense!" said Zinaïda. "Well, imagine, for instance, you are married, and tell us how you would treat your wife. Would you lock her up?"

"Yes, I should lock her up."

"And would you stay with her yourself?"

"Yes, I should certainly stay with her myself."

"Very good. Well, but if she got sick of that, and she deceived you?"

"I should kill her."

"And if she ran away?"

"I should catch her up and kill her all the same."

"Oh. And suppose now I were your wife, what would you do then?"

Byelovzorov was silent a minute. "I should kill myself...."

Zinaïda laughed. "I see yours is not a long story."

The next forfeit was Zinaïda's. She looked at the ceiling and considered. "Well, listen," she began at last, "what I have thought of.... Picture to yourselves a magnificent palace, a summer night, and a marvellous ball. This ball is given by a young queen. Everywhere gold and marble, crystal, silk, lights, diamonds, flowers, fragrant scents, every caprice of luxury."

"You love luxury?" Lushin interposed.

"Luxury is beautiful," she retorted; "I love everything beautiful."

"More than what is noble?" he asked.

"That's something clever, I don't understand it. Don't interrupt me. So the ball is magnificent. There are crowds of guests, all of them are young, handsome, and brave, all are frantically in love with the queen."

"Are there no women among the guests?" queried Malevsky.

"No—or wait a minute—yes, there are some."

"Are they all ugly?"

"No, charming. But the men are all in love with the queen. She is tall and graceful; she has a little gold diadem on her black hair."

I looked at Zinaïda, and at that instant she seemed to me so much above all of us, there was such bright intelligence, and such power about her unruffled brows, that I thought: "You are that queen!"

"They all throng about her," Zinaïda went on, "and all lavish the most flattering speeches upon her."

"And she likes flattery?" Lushin queried.

"What an intolerable person! he keeps interrupting... who doesn't like flattery?"

"One more last question," observed Malevsky, "has the queen a husband?"

"I hadn't thought about that. No, why should she have a husband?"

"To be sure," assented Malevsky, "why should she have a husband?"

"*Silence!*" cried Meidanov in French, which he spoke very badly.

"*Merci!*" Zinaïda said to him. "And so the queen hears their speeches, and hears the music, but does not look at one of the guests. Six windows are open from top to bottom, from floor to ceiling, and beyond them is a dark sky with big stars, a dark garden with big trees. The queen gazes out into the garden. Out there among the trees is a fountain; it is white in the darkness, and rises up tall, tall as an apparition. The queen hears, through the talk and the music, the soft splash of its waters. She gazes and thinks: you are all, gentlemen, noble, clever, and rich, you crowd round me, you treasure every word I utter, you are all ready to die at my feet, I hold you in my power... but out there, by the fountain, by that splashing water, stands and waits he whom I love, who holds me in his power. He has neither rich raiment nor precious stones, no one knows him, but he awaits me, and is certain I shall come—and I shall come—and there is no power that could stop me when I want to go out to him, and to stay with him, and be lost with him out there in the darkness of the garden, under the whispering of the trees, and the splash of the fountain...." Zinaïda ceased.

"Is that a made-up story?" Malevsky inquired slyly. Zinaïda did not look at him.

"And what should we have done, gentlemen?" Lushin began suddenly, "if we had been among the guests, and had known of the lucky fellow at the fountain?"

"Stop a minute, stop a minute," interposed Zinaïda, "I will tell you myself what each of you would have done. You, Byelovzorov, would have challenged him to a duel; you, Meidanov, would have written an epigram on him.... No, though, you can't write epigrams, you would have made up a long poem on him in the style of Barbier, and would have inserted your production in the *Telegraph*. You, Nirmatsky, would have borrowed... no, you would have lent him money at high interest; you, doctor,..." she stopped. "There, I really don't know what you would have done...."

"In the capacity of court physician," answered Lushin, "I would have advised the queen not to give balls when she was not in the humour for entertaining her guests...."

"Perhaps you would have been right. And you, Count?..."

"And I?" repeated Malevsky with his evil smile....

"You would offer him a poisoned sweetmeat."

Malevsky's face changed slightly, and assumed for an instant a Jewish expression, but he laughed directly.

"And as for you, Voldemar,..." Zinaïda went on, "but that's enough, though; let us play another game."

"M'sieu Voldemar, as the queen's page, would have held up her train when she ran into the garden," Malevsky remarked malignantly.

I was crimson with anger, but Zinaïda hurriedly laid a hand on my shoulder, and getting up, said in a rather shaky voice: "I have never given your excellency the right to be rude, and therefore I will ask you to leave us." She pointed to the door.

"Upon my word, princess," muttered Malevsky, and he turned quite pale.

"The princess is right," cried Byelovzorov, and he too rose.

"Good God, I'd not the least idea," Malevsky went on, "in my words there was nothing, I think, that could... I had no notion of offending you.... Forgive me."

Zinaïda looked him up and down coldly, and coldly smiled. "Stay, then, certainly," she pronounced with a careless gesture of her arm. "M'sieu Voldemar and I were needlessly incensed. It is your pleasure to sting... may it do you good."

"Forgive me," Malevsky repeated once more; while I, my thoughts dwelling on Zinaïda's gesture, said to myself again that no real queen could with greater dignity have shown a presumptuous subject to the door.

The game of forfeits went on for a short time after this little scene; every one felt rather ill at ease, not so much on account of this scene, as from another, not quite definite, but oppressive feeling. No one spoke of it, but every one was conscious of it in himself and in his neighbour. Meidanov read us his verses; and Malevsky praised them with exaggerated warmth. "He wants to show how good he is now," Lushin whispered to me. We soon broke up. A mood of reverie seemed to have come upon Zinaïda; the old princess sent word that she had a headache; Nirmatsky began to complain of his rheumatism....

I could not for a long while get to sleep. I had been impressed by Zinaïda's story. "Can there have been a hint in it?" I asked myself: "and at whom and at what was she hinting? And if there really is anything to hint at...

how is one to make up one's mind? No, no, it can't be," I whispered, turning over from one hot cheek on to the other.... But I remembered the expression of Zinaïda's face during her story.... I remembered the exclamation that had broken from Lushin in the Neskutchny gardens, the sudden change in her behaviour to me, and I was lost in conjectures. "Who is he?" These three words seemed to stand before my eyes traced upon the darkness; a lowering malignant cloud seemed hanging over me, and I felt its oppressiveness, and waited for it to break. I had grown used to many things of late; I had learned much from what I had seen at the Zasyekins; their disorderly ways, tallow candle-ends, broken knives and forks, grumpy Vonifaty, and shabby maid-servants, the manners of the old princess—all their strange mode of life no longer struck me.... But what I was dimly discerning now in Zinaïda, I could never get used to.... "An adventuress!" my mother had said of her one day. An adventuress— she, my idol, my divinity? This word stabbed me, I tried to get away from it into my pillow, I was indignant—and at the same time what would I not have agreed to, what would I not have given only to be that lucky fellow at the fountain!... My blood was on fire and boiling within me. "The garden... the fountain," I mused.... "I will go into the garden." I dressed quickly and slipped out of the house. The night was dark, the trees scarcely whispered, a soft chill air breathed down from the sky, a smell of fennel trailed across from the kitchen garden. I went through all the walks; the light sound of my own footsteps at once confused and emboldened me; I stood still, waited, and heard my heart beating fast and loudly. At last I went up to the fence and leaned against the thin bar. Suddenly, or was it my fancy, a woman's figure flashed by, a few paces from me... I strained my eyes eagerly into the darkness, I held my breath. What was that? Did I hear steps, or was it my heart beating again? "Who is here?" I faltered, hardly audibly. What was that again, a smothered laugh... or a rustling in the leaves... or a sigh just at my ear? I felt afraid... "Who is here?" I repeated still more softly.

The air blew in a gust for an instant; a streak of fire flashed across the sky; it was a star falling. "Zinaïda?" I wanted to call, but the word died away on my lips. And all at once everything became profoundly still around, as is often the case in the middle of the night.... Even the grasshoppers ceased their churr in the trees—only a window rattled somewhere. I stood and stood, and then went back to my room, to my chilled bed. I felt a strange sensation; as though I had gone to a tryst, and had been left lonely, and had passed close by another's happiness.

XVII

The following day I only had a passing glimpse of Zinaïda: she was driving somewhere with the old princess in a cab. But I saw Lushin, who, however, barely vouchsafed me a greeting, and Malevsky. The young count grinned, and began affably talking to me. Of all those who visited at the lodge, he alone had succeeded in forcing his way into our house, and had favourably impressed my mother. My father did not take to him, and treated him with a civility almost insulting.

"Ah, *monsieur le page*," began Malevsky, "delighted to meet you. What is your lovely queen doing?"

His fresh handsome face was so detestable to me at that moment, and he looked at me with such contemptuous amusement that I did not answer him at all.

"Are you still angry?" he went on. "You've no reason to be. It wasn't I who called you a page, you know, and pages attend queens especially. But allow me to remark that you perform your duties very badly."

"How so?"

"Pages ought to be inseparable from their mistresses; pages ought to know everything they do, they ought, indeed, to watch over them," he added, lowering his voice, "day and night."

"What do you mean?"

"What do I mean? I express myself pretty clearly, I fancy. Day and night. By day it's not so much matter; it's light, and people are about in the daytime; but by night, then look out for misfortune. I advise you not to sleep at nights and to watch, watch with all your energies. You remember in the garden, by night, at the fountain, that's where there's need to look out. You will thank me."

Malevsky laughed and turned his back on me. He, most likely, attached no great importance to what he had said to me, he had a reputation for mystifying, and was noted for his power of taking people in at masquerades, which was greatly augmented by the almost unconscious falsity in which his whole nature was steeped.... He only wanted to tease me; but every word he uttered was a poison that ran through my veins. The blood rushed to my head. "Ah! so that's it!" I said to myself; "good! So there was reason for me to feel drawn into the garden! That shan't be so!" I cried aloud, and struck myself on the chest with my fist, though precisely what should not be so I could not have said. "Whether Malevsky himself goes into the garden," I thought (he was bragging, perhaps; he has insolence enough for that), "or some one else (the fence of our garden was very low, and there was no difficulty in getting over it), anyway, if any one falls into my hands, it will be the worse for him! I don't advise any one to meet me! I will prove to all the world and to her, the traitress (I actually used the word 'traitress') that I can be revenged!"

I returned to my own room, took out of the writing-table an English knife I had recently bought, felt its sharp edge, and knitting my brows with an air of cold and concentrated determination, thrust it into my pocket, as though doing such deeds was nothing out of the way for me, and not the first time. My heart heaved angrily, and felt heavy as a stone. All day long I kept a scowling brow and lips tightly compressed, and was continually walking up and down, clutching, with my hand in my pocket, the knife, which was warm from my grasp, while I prepared myself beforehand for something terrible. These new unknown sensations so occupied and even delighted me, that I hardly thought of Zinaïda herself. I was continually haunted by Aleko, the young gipsy— "Where art thou going, young handsome man? Lie there," and then, "thou art all besprent with blood.... Oh, what hast thou done?... Naught!" With what a cruel smile I repeated that "Naught!" My father was not at home; but my mother, who had for some time past been in an almost continual state of dumb exasperation, noticed my gloomy and heroic aspect, and said to me at supper, "Why are you sulking like a mouse in a meal-tub?" I merely smiled condescendingly in reply, and thought, "If only they knew!" It struck eleven; I went to my room, but did not undress; I waited for midnight; at last it struck. "The time has come!" I muttered between my teeth; and buttoning myself up to the throat, and even pulling my sleeves up, I went into the garden.

I had already fixed on the spot from which to keep watch. At the end of the garden, at the point where the fence, separating our domain from the Zasyekins', joined the common wall, grew a pine-tree, standing alone. Standing under its low thick branches, I could see well, as far as the darkness of the night permitted, what took place around. Close by, ran a winding patch which had always seemed mysterious to me; it coiled like a snake under the fence, which at that point bore traces of having been climbed over, and led to a round arbour formed of thick acacias. I made my way to the pine-tree, leaned my back against its trunk, and began my watch.

The night was as still as the night before, but there were fewer clouds in the sky, and the outlines of bushes, even of tall flowers, could be more distinctly seen. The first moments of expectation were oppressive, almost terrible. I had made up my mind to everything. I only debated how to act;

whether to thunder, "Where goest thou? Stand! show thyself—or death!" or simply to strike.... Every sound, every whisper and rustle, seemed to me portentous and extraordinary.... I prepared myself.... I bent forward. ... But half-an-hour passed, an hour passed; my blood had grown quieter, colder; the consciousness that I was doing all this for nothing, that I was even a little absurd, that Malevsky had been making fun of me, began to steal over me. I left my ambush, and walked all about the garden. As if to taunt me, there was not the smallest sound to be heard anywhere; everything was at rest. Even our dog was asleep, curled up into a ball at the gate. I climbed up into the ruins of the greenhouse, saw the open country far away before me, recalled my meeting with Zinaïda, and fell to dreaming....

I started.... I fancied I heard the creak of a door opening, then the faint crack of a broken twig. In two bounds I got down from the ruin, and stood still, all aghast. Rapid, light, but cautious footsteps sounded distinctly in the garden. They were approaching me. "Here he is... here he is, at last!" flashed through my heart. With spasmodic haste, I pulled the knife out of my pocket; with spasmodic haste, I opened it. Flashes of red were whirling before my eyes; my hair stood up on my head in my fear and fury.... The steps were coming straight towards me; I bent—I craned forward to meet him.... A man came into view.... My God! it was my father!

I recognised him at once, though he was all muffled up in a dark cloak, and his hat was pulled down over his face. On tip-toe he walked by. He did not notice me, though nothing concealed me; but I was so huddled up and shrunk together that I fancy I was almost on the level of the ground. The jealous Othello, ready for murder, was suddenly transformed into a school-boy.... I was so taken aback by my father's unexpected appearance that for the first moment I did not notice where he had come from or in what direction he disappeared. I only drew myself up, and thought, "Why is it my father is walking about in the garden at night?" when everything was still again. In my horror I had dropped my knife in the grass, but I did not even attempt to look for it; I was very much ashamed of myself. I was completely sobered at once. On my way to the house, however, I went up to my seat under the elder-tree, and looked up at Zinaïda's window. The small slightly-convex panes of the window shone dimly blue in the faint light thrown on them by the night sky. All at once—their colour began to change.... Behind them—I saw this, saw it distinctly—softly and cautiously a white blind was let down, let down right to the window-frame, and so stayed.

"What is that for?" I said aloud almost involuntarily when I found myself once more in my room. "A dream, a chance, or..." The suppositions which suddenly rushed into my head were so new and strange that I did not dare to entertain them.

XVIII

I got up in the morning with a headache. My emotion of the previous day had vanished. It was replaced by a dreary sense of blankness and a sort of sadness I had not known till then, as though something had died in me.

"Why is it you're looking like a rabbit with half its brain removed?" said Lushin on meeting me. At lunch I stole a look first at my father, then at my mother: he was composed, as usual; she was, as usual, secretly irritated. I waited to see whether my father would make some friendly remarks to me, as he sometimes did.... But he did not even bestow his everyday cold greeting upon me. "Shall I tell Zinaïda all?" I wondered.... "It's all the same, anyway; all is at an end between us." I went to see her, but told her nothing, and, indeed, I could not even have managed to get a talk with her if I had wanted to. The old princess's son, a cadet of twelve years old, had come from Petersburg for his holidays; Zinaïda at once handed her brother over to me. "Here," she said, "my dear Volodya,"—it was the first time she had used this pet-name to me—"is a companion for you. His name is Volodya, too. Please, like him; he is still shy, but he has a good heart. Show him Neskutchny gardens, go walks with him, take him under your protection. You'll do that, won't you? you're so good, too!" She laid both her hands affectionately on my shoulders, and I was utterly bewildered. The presence of this boy transformed me, too, into a boy. I looked in silence at the cadet, who stared as silently at me. Zinaïda laughed, and pushed us towards each other. "Embrace each other, children!" We embraced each other. "Would you like me to show you the garden?" I inquired of the cadet. "If you please," he replied, in the regular cadet's hoarse voice Zinaïda laughed again.... I had time to notice that she had never had such an exquisite colour in her face before. I set off with the cadet. There was an old-fashioned swing in our garden. I sat him down on the narrow plank seat, and began swinging him. He sat rigid in his new little uniform of stout cloth, with its broad gold braiding, and kept tight hold of the cords. "You'd better unbutton your collar," I said to him. "It's all right; we're used to it," he said, and cleared his throat. He was like his sister. The eyes especially recalled her. I liked being nice to him; and at the same time an aching sadness was gnawing at my heart. "Now I certainly am a child," I thought; "but yesterday...." I remembered where I had dropped my knife the night before, and looked for it. The cadet asked me for it, picked a thick stalk of wild parsley, cut a pipe out of it, and began whistling. Othello whistled too.

But in the evening how he wept, this Othello, in Zinaïda's arms, when, seeking him out in a corner of the garden, she asked him why he was so depressed. My tears flowed with such violence that she was frightened. "What is wrong with you? What is it, Volodya?" she repeated; and seeing I made no answer, and did not cease weeping, she was about to kiss my wet cheek. But I turned away from her, and whispered through my sobs, "I know all. Why did you play with me?... What need had you of my love?"

"I am to blame, Volodya..." said Zinaïda. "I am very much to blame..." she added, wringing her hands. "How much there is bad and black and sinful in me!... But I am not playing with you now. I love you; you don't even suspect why and how.... But what is it you know?"

What could I say to her? She stood facing me, and looked at me; and I belonged to her altogether from head to foot directly she looked at me.... A quarter of an hour later I was running races with the cadet and Zinaïda. I was not crying, I was laughing, though my swollen eyelids dropped a tear or two as I laughed. I had Zinaïda's ribbon round my neck for a cravat, and I shouted with delight whenever I succeeded in catching her round the waist. She did just as she liked with me.

XIX

I should be in a great difficulty, if I were forced to describe exactly what passed within me in the course of the week after my unsuccesful midnight expedition. It was a strange feverish time, a sort of chaos, in which the most violently opposed feelings, thoughts, suspicions, hopes, joys, and sufferings, whirled together in a kind of hurricane. I was afraid to look into myself, if a boy of sixteen ever can look into himself; I was afraid to take stock of anything; I simply hastened to live through every day till evening; and at night I slept... the light-heartedness of childhood came to my aid. I did not want to know whether I was loved, and I did not want to acknowledge to myself that I was not loved; my father I avoided— but Zinaïda I could not avoid.... I burnt as in a fire in her presence... but what did I care to know what the fire was in which I burned and melted—it was enough that it was sweet to burn and melt. I gave myself up to all my passing sensations, and cheated myself, turning away from memories, and shutting my eyes to what I foreboded before me.... This weakness would not most likely have lasted long in any case... a thunderbolt cut it all short in a moment, and flung me into a new track altogether.

Coming in one day to dinner from a rather long walk, I learnt with amazement that I was to dine alone, that my father had gone away and my mother was unwell, did not want any dinner, and had shut herself up in her bedroom. From the faces of the footmen, I surmised that something extraordinary had taken place.... I did not dare to cross-examine them, but I had a friend in the young waiter Philip, who was passionately fond of poetry, and a performer on the guitar. I addressed myself to him. From him I learned that a terrible scene had taken place between my father and mother (and every word had been overheard in the maids' room; much of it had been in French, but Masha the lady's-maid had lived five years' with a dressmaker from Paris, and she understood it all); that my mother had reproached my father with infidelity, with an intimacy with the young lady next door, that my father at first had defended himself, but afterwards had lost his temper, and he too had said something cruel, "reflecting on her age," which had made my mother cry; that my mother too had alluded to some loan which it seemed had been made to the old princess, and had spoken very ill of her and of the young lady too, and that then my father had threatened her. "And all the mischief," continued Philip, "came from an anonymous letter; and who wrote it, no one knows, or else there'd have been no reason whatever for the matter to have come out at all."

"But was there really any ground," I brought out with difficulty, while my hands and feet went cold, and a sort of shudder ran through my inmost being.

Philip winked meaningly. "There was. There's no hiding those things; for all that your father was careful this time—but there, you see, he'd, for instance, to hire a carriage or something... no getting on without servants, either."

I dismissed Philip, and fell on to my bed. I did not sob, I did not give myself up to despair; I did not ask myself when and how this had happened; I did not wonder how it was I had not guessed it before, long ago; I did not even upbraid my father.... What I had learnt was more than I could take in; this sudden revelation stunned me.... All was at an end. All the fair blossoms of my heart were roughly plucked at once, and lay about me, flung on the ground, and trampled underfoot.

651

XX

My mother next day announced her intention of returning to the town. In the morning my father had gone into her bedroom, and stayed there a long while alone with her. No one had overheard what he said to her; but my mother wept no more; she regained her composure, and asked for food, but did not make her appearance nor change her plans. I remember I wandered about the whole day, but did not go into the garden, and never once glanced at the lodge, and in the evening I was the spectator of an amazing occurrence: my father conducted Count Malevsky by the arm through the dining-room into the hall, and, in the presence of a footman, said icily to him: "A few days ago your excellency was shown the door in our house; and now I am not going to enter into any kind of explanation with you, but I have the honour to announce to you that if you ever visit me again, I shall throw you out of window. I don't like your handwriting." The count bowed, bit his lips, shrank away, and vanished.

Preparations were beginning for our removal to town, to Arbaty Street, where we had a house. My father himself probably no longer cared to remain at the country-house; but clearly he had succeeded in persuading my mother not to make a public scandal. Everything was done quietly, without hurry; my mother even sent her compliments to the old princess, and expressed her regret that she was prevented by indisposition from seeing her again before her departure. I wandered about like one possessed, and only longed for one thing, for it all to be over as soon as possible. One thought I could not get out of my head: how could she, a young girl, and a princess too, after all, bring herself to such a step, knowing that my father was not a free man, and having an opportunity of marrying, for instance, Byelovzorov? What did she hope for? How was it she was not afraid of ruining her whole future? Yes, I thought, this is love, this is passion, this is devotion... and Lushin's words came back to me: to sacrifice oneself for some people is sweet. I chanced somehow to catch sight of something white in one of the windows of the lodge.... "Can it be Zinaïda's face?" I thought... yes, it really was her face. I could not restrain myself. I could not part from her without saying a last good-bye to her. I seized a favourable instant, and went into the lodge.

In the drawing-room the old princess met me with her usual slovenly and careless greetings.

"How's this, my good man, your folks are off in such a hurry?" she observed, thrusting snuff into her nose. I looked at her, and a load was taken off my heart. The word "loan," dropped by Philip, had been torturing me. She had no suspicion... at least I thought so then. Zinaïda came in from the next room, pale, and dressed in black, with her hair hanging loose; she took me by the hand without a word, and drew me away with her.

"I heard your voice," she began, "and came out at once. Is it so easy for you to leave us, bad boy?"

"I have come to say good-bye to you, princess," I answered, "probably for ever. You have heard, perhaps, we are going away."

Zinaïda looked intently at me.

"Yes, I have heard. Thanks for coming. I was beginning to think I should not see you again. Don't remember evil against me. I have sometimes tormented you, but all the same I am not what you imagine me."

She turned away, and leaned against the window.

"Really, I am not like that. I know you have a bad opinion of me."

"I?"

"Yes, you... you."

"I?" I repeated mournfully, and my heart throbbed as of old under the influence of her overpowering, indescribable fascination. "I? Believe me, Zinaïda Alexandrovna, whatever you did, however you tormented me, I should love and adore you to the end of my days."

She turned with a rapid motion to me, and flinging wide her arms, embraced my head, and gave me a warm and passionate kiss. God knows whom that long farewell kiss was seeking, but I eagerly tasted its sweetness. I knew that it would never be repeated. "Good-bye, good-bye," I kept saying...

She tore herself away, and went out. And I went away. I cannot describe the emotion with which I went away. I should not wish it ever to come again; but I should think myself unfortunate had I never experienced such an emotion.

We went back to town. I did not quickly shake off the past; I did not quickly get to work. My wound slowly began to heal; but I had no ill-feeling against my father. On the contrary he had, as it were, gained in my eyes... let psychologists explain the contradiction as best they can. One day I was walking along a boulevard, and to my indescribable delight, I came across Lushin. I liked him for his straightforward and unaffected character, and besides he was dear to me for the sake of the memories he aroused in me. I rushed up to him. "Aha!" he said, knitting his brows, "so it's you, young man. Let me have a look at you. You're still as yellow as ever, but yet there's not the same nonsense in your eyes. You look like a man, not a lap-dog. That's good. Well, what are you doing? working?"

I gave a sigh. I did not like to tell a lie, while I was ashamed to tell the truth.

"Well, never mind," Lushin went on, "don't be shy. The great thing is to lead a normal life, and not be the slave of your passions. What do you get if not? Wherever you are carried by the tide—it's all a bad lookout; a man must stand on his own feet, if he can get nothing but a rock to stand on. Here, I've got a cough... and Byelovzorov—have you heard anything of him?"

"No. What is it?"

"He's lost, and no news of him; they say he's gone away to the Caucasus. A lesson to you, young man. And it's all from not knowing how to part in time, to break out of the net. You seem to have got off very well. Mind you don't fall into the same snare again. Good-bye."

"I shan't," I thought.... "I shan't see her again." But I was destined to see Zinaïda once more.

XX

My father used every day to ride out on horseback. He had a splendid English mare, a chestnut piebald, with a long slender neck and long legs, an inexhaustible and vicious beast. Her name was Electric. No one could ride her except my father. One day he came up to me in a good humour, a frame of mind in which I had not seen him for a long while; he was getting ready for his ride, and had already put on his spurs. I began entreating him to take me with him.

"We'd much better have a game of leapfrog," my father replied. "You'll never keep up with me on your cob."

"Yes, I will; I'll put on spurs too."

"All right, come along then."

We set off. I had a shaggy black horse, strong, and fairly spirited. It is true it had to gallop its utmost, when Electric went at full trot, still I was not left behind. I have never seen any one ride like my father; he had such a fine carelessly easy seat, that it seemed that the horse under him was conscious of it, and proud of its rider. We rode through all the boulevards, reached the "Maidens' Field," jumped several fences (at first I had been afraid to take a leap, but my father had a contempt for cowards, and I soon ceased to feel fear), twice crossed the river Moskva, and I was under the impression that we were on our way home, especially as my father of his own accord observed that my horse was tired, when suddenly he turned off away from me at the Crimean ford, and galloped along the river-bank. I rode after him. When he had reached a high stack of old timber, he slid quickly off Electric, told me to dismount, and giving me his horse's bridle, told me to wait for him there at the timber-stack, and, turning off into a small street, disappeared. I began walking up and down the river-bank, leading the horses, and scolding Electric, who kept pulling, shaking her head, snorting and neighing as she went; and when I stood still, never failed to paw the ground, and whining, bite my cob on the neck; in fact she conducted herself altogether like a spoilt thorough-bred. My father did not come back. A disagreeable damp mist rose from the river; a fine rain began softly blowing up, and spotting with tiny dark flecks the stupid grey timber-stack, which I kept passing and repassing, and was deadly sick of by now. I was terribly bored, and still my father did not come. A sort of sentry-man, a Fin, grey all over like the timber, and with a huge old fashioned shako, like a pot, on his head, and with a halberd (and how ever came a sentry, if you think of it, on the banks of the Moskva!) drew near, and turning his wrinkled face, like an old woman's, towards me, he observed, "What are you doing here with the horses, young master? Let me hold them."

I made him no reply. He asked me for tobacco. To get rid of him (I was in a fret of impatience, too), I took a few steps in the direction in which my father had disappeared, then walked along the little street to the end, turned the corner, and stood still. In the street, forty paces from me, at the open window of a little wooden house, stood my father, his back turned to me; he was leaning forward over the window-sill, and in the house, half hidden by a curtain, sat a woman in a dark dress talking to my father; this woman was Zinaïda.

I was petrified. This, I confess, I had never expected. My first impulse was to run away. "My father will look round," I thought, "and I am lost..." but a strange feeling—a feeling stronger than curiosity, stronger than jealousy, stronger even than fear—held me there. I began to watch; I strained my ears to listen. It seemed as though my father were insisting on something. Zinaïda would not consent. I seem to see her face now—mournful, serious, lovely, and with an inexpressible impress of devotion, grief, love, and a sort of despair—I can find no other word for it. She uttered monosyllables, not raising her eyes, simply smiling—submissively, but without yielding. By that smile alone, I should have known my Zinaïda of old days. My father shrugged his shoulders, and straightened his hat on his head, which was always a sign of impatience with him.... Then I caught the words: *"Vous devez vous séparer de cette..."* Zinaïda sat up, and stretched out her arm.... Suddenly, before my very eyes, the impossible happened. My father suddenly lifted the whip, with which he had been switching the dust off his coat, and I heard a sharp blow on that arm, bare to the elbow. I could scarcely restrain myself from crying out; while Zinaïda shuddered, looked without a word at my father, and slowly raising her arm to her lips, kissed the streak of red upon it. My father flung away the whip, and running quickly up the steps, dashed into the house.... Zinaïda turned round, and with outstretched arms and downcast head, she too moved away from the window.

My heart sinking with panic, with a sort of awe-struck horror, I rushed back, and running down the lane, almost letting go my hold of Electric, went back to the bank of the river. I could not think clearly of anything. I knew that my cold and reserved father was sometimes seized by fits of fury; and all the same, I could never comprehend what I had just seen.... But I felt at the time that, however long I lived, I could never forget the gesture, the glance, the smile, of Zinaïda; that her image, this image so suddenly presented to me, was imprinted for ever on my memory. I stared vacantly at the river, and never noticed that my tears were streaming. "She is beaten," I was thinking,... "beaten... beaten...."

"Hullo! what are you doing? Give me the mare!" I heard my father's voice saying behind me.

Mechanically I gave him the bridle. He leaped on to Electric... the mare, chill with standing, reared on her haunches, and leaped ten feet away... but my father soon subdued her; he drove the spurs into her sides, and gave her a blow on the neck with his fist.... "Ah, I've no whip," he muttered.

I remembered the swish and fall of the whip, heard so short a time before, and shuddered.

"Where did you put it?" I asked my father, after a brief pause.

My father made no answer, and galloped on ahead. I overtook him. I felt that I must see his face.

"Were you bored waiting for me?" he muttered through his teeth.

"A little. Where did you drop your whip?" I asked again.

My father glanced quickly at me. "I didn't drop it," he replied; "I threw it away." He sank into thought, and dropped his head... and then, for the first, and almost for the last time, I saw how much tenderness and pity his stern features were capable of expressing.

He galloped on again, and this time I could not overtake him; I got home a quarter of an hour after him.

"That's love," I said to myself again, as I sat at night before my writing-table, on which books and papers had begun to make their appearance;

656

"that's passion!... To think of not revolting, of bearing a blow from any one whatever... even the dearest hand! But it seems one can, if one loves.... While I... I imagined..."

I had grown much older during the last month; and my love, with all its transports and sufferings, struck me myself as something small and childish and pitiful beside this other unimagined something, which I could hardly fully grasp, and which frightened me like an unknown, beautiful, but menacing face, which one strives in vain to make out clearly in the half-darkness....

A strange and fearful dream came to me that same night. I dreamed I went into a low dark room.... My father was standing with a whip in his hand, stamping with anger; in the corner crouched Zinaïda, and not on her arm, but on her forehead, was a stripe of red... while behind them both towered Byelovzorov, covered with blood; he opened his white lips, and wrathfully threatened my father.

Two months later, I entered the university; and within six months my father died of a stroke in Petersburg, where he had just moved with my mother and me. A few days before his death he received a letter from Moscow which threw him into a violent agitation.... He went to my mother to beg some favour of her: and, I was told, he positively shed tears—he, my father! On the very morning of the day when he was stricken down, he had begun a letter to me in French. "My son," he wrote to me, "fear the love of woman; fear that bliss, that poison...." After his death, my mother sent a considerable sum of money to Moscow.

XXII

Four years passed. I had just left the university, and did not know exactly what to do with myself, at what door to knock; I was hanging about for a time with nothing to do. One fine evening I met Meidanov at the theatre. He had got married, and had entered the civil service; but I found no change in him. He fell into ecstasies in just the same superfluous way, and just as suddenly grew depressed again.

"You know," he told me among other things, "Madame Dolsky's here."

"What Madame Dolsky?"

"Can you have forgotten her?—the young Princess Zasyekin whom we were all in love with, and you too. Do you remember at the countryhouse near Neskutchny gardens?"

"She married a Dolsky?"

"Yes."

"And is she here, in the theatre?"

"No: but she's in Petersburg. She came here a few days ago. She's going abroad."

"What sort of fellow is her husband?" I asked.

"A splendid fellow, with property. He's a colleague of mine in Moscow. You can well understand—after the scandal... you must know all about it..." (Meïdanov smiled significantly) "it was no easy task for her to make a good marriage; there were consequences... but with her cleverness, everything is possible. Go and see her; she'll be delighted to see you. She's prettier than ever."

Meïdanov gave me Zinaïda's address. She was staying at the Hotel Demut. Old memories were astir within me.... I determined next day to go to see my former 'flame.' But some business happened to turn up; a week passed, and then another, and when at last I went to the Hotel Demut and asked for Madame Dolsky, I learnt that four days before, she had died, almost suddenly, in childbirth.

I felt a sort of stab at my heart. The thought that I might have seen her, and had not seen her, and should never see her—that bitter thought stung me with all the force of overwhelming reproach. "She is dead!" I repeated, staring stupidly at the hall-porter. I slowly made my way back to the street, and walked on without knowing myself where I was going. All the past swam up and rose at once before me. So this was the solution, this was the goal to which that young, ardent, brilliant life had striven, all haste and agitation! I mused on this; I fancied those dear features, those eyes, those curls—in the narrow box, in the damp underground darkness—lying here, not far from me—while I was still alive, and, maybe, a few paces from my father.... I thought all this; I strained my imagination, and yet all the while the lines:

> "From lips indifferent of her death I heard,
> Indifferently I listened to it, too,"

were echoing in my heart. O youth, youth! little dost thou care for anything; thou art master, as it were, of all the treasures of the universe—even sorrow gives thee pleasure, even grief thou canst turn to thy profit; thou art self-confident and insolent; thou sayest, "I alone am living—look you!"—but thy days fly by all the while, and vanish without trace or reckoning; and everything in thee vanishes, like wax in the sun, like snow.... And, perhaps, the whole secret of thy charm lies, not in being able to do anything, but in being able to think thou wilt do anything; lies just in thy throwing to the winds, forces which thou couldst not make other use of; in each of us gravely regarding himself as a prodigal, gravely supposing that he is justified in saying, "Oh, what might I not have done if I had not wasted my time!"

I, now... what did I hope for, what did I expect, what rich future did I foresee, when the phantom of my first love, rising up for an instant, barely called forth one sigh, one mournful sentiment?

And what has come to pass of all I hoped for? And now, when the shades of evening begin to steal over my life, what have I left fresher, more precious, than the memories of the storm—so soon over—of early morning, of spring?

But I do myself injustice. Even then, in those light-hearted young days, I was not deaf to the voice of sorrow, when it called upon me, to the solemn strains floating to me from beyond the tomb. I remember, a few days after I heard of Zinaïda's death, I was present, through a peculiar, irresistible impulse, at the death of a poor old woman who lived in the same house as we. Covered with rags, lying on hard boards, with a sack under her head, she died hardly and painfully. Her whole life had been passed in the bitter struggle with daily want; she had known no joy, had not tasted the honey of happiness. One would have thought, surely she would rejoice at death, at her deliverance, her rest. But yet, as long as her decrepit body held out, as long as her breast still heaved in agony under the icy hand weighing upon it, until her last forces left her, the old woman crossed herself, and kept whispering, "Lord, forgive my sins"; and only with the last spark of consciousness, vanished from her eyes the look of fear, of horror of the end. And I remember that then, by the death-bed of that poor old woman, I felt aghast for Zinaïda, and longed to pray for her, for my father—and for myself.

THE ETERNAL HUSBAND[1]

Fyodor Dostojevsky

CHAPTER I

Velchaninov

THE summer had come and, contrary to expectations, Velchaninov remained in Petersburg. The trip he had planned to the south of Russia had fallen through, and the end of his case was not in sight. This case—a lawsuit concerning an estate—had taken a very unfortunate turn. Three months earlier it had appeared to be quite straightforward, almost impossible to contest; but suddenly everything was changed. "And, in fact, everything has changed for the worse!" Velchaninov began frequently and resentfully repeating that phrase to himself. He was employing an adroit, expensive, and distinguished lawyer, and was not sparing money; but through impatience and lack of confidence he had been tempted to meddle in the case himself too. He read documents and wrote statements which the lawyer rejected point-blank, ran from one court to another, collected evidence, and probably hindered everything; the lawyer complained, at any rate, and tried to pack him off to a summer villa. But Velchaninov could not even make up his mind to go away. The dust, the stifling heat, the white nights of Petersburg that always fret the nerves were what he was enjoying in town. His flat was near the Grand Theatre; he had only recently taken it, and it, too, was a failure. "Everything is a failure!" he thought. His nervousness increased every day; but he had for a long time past been subject to nervousness and hypochondria.

He was a man whose life had been full and varied, he was by no means young, thirty-eight or even thirty-nine, and his "old age," as he expressed it himself, had come upon him "quite unexpectedly"; but he realized himself that he had grown older less by the number than by the quality, so to say, of his years, and that if he had begun to be aware of waning powers, the change was rather from within than from without. In appearance he was still strong and hearty. He was a tall, sturdily-built fellow, with thick flaxen hair without a sign of greyness and a long fair beard almost half-way down his chest; at first sight he seemed somewhat slack

---

[1] From *The Eternal Husband and Other Stories*. Translated by Constance Garnett. Reprinted by permission of Messrs William Heinemann, Ltd.

and clumsy, but if you looked more attentively, you would detect at once that he was a man of excellent breeding, who had at some time received the education of an aristocrat. Velchaninov's manners were still free, assured and even gracious, in spite of his acquired grumpiness and slackness. And he was still, even now, full of the most unhesitating, the most snobbishly insolent self-confidence, the depth of which he did not himself suspect, although he was a man not merely intelligent, but even sometimes sensible, almost cultured, and unmistakably gifted. His open and ruddy face had been in old days marked by a feminine softness of complexion which attracted the notice of women; and even now some people, looking at him, would say: "What a picture of health! What a complexion!" And yet this picture of health was cruelly subject to nervous depression. His eyes were large and blue, ten years earlier they had possessed great fascination; they were so bright, so gay, so careless that they could not but attract every one who came in contact with him. Now that he was verging on the forties, the brightness and good-humour were almost extinguished. Those eyes, which were already surrounded by tiny wrinkles, had begun to betray the cynicism of a worn-out man of doubtful morals, a duplicity, an ever-increasing irony and another shade of feeling, which was new: a shade of sadness and of pain—a sort of absent-minded sadness as though about nothing in particular and yet acute. This sadness was especially marked when he was alone. And, strange to say, this man who had been only a couple of years before fond of noisy gaiety, careless and good-humoured, who had been so capital a teller of funny stories, liked nothing now so well as being absolutely alone. He purposely gave up a great number of acquaintances whom he need not have given up even now, in spite of his financial difficulties. It is true that his vanity counted for something in this. With his vanity and mistrustfulness he could not have endured the society of his old acquaintances. But, by degrees, in solitude, even his vanity began to change its character. It grew no less, quite the contrary, indeed; but it began to develop into a special sort of vanity which was new in him; it began at times to suffer from different causes—from unexpected causes which would have formerly been quite inconceivable, from causes of a "higher order" than ever before—"if one may use such an expression, if there really are higher or lower causes.... This he added on his own account.

Yes, he had even come to that; he was worrying about some sort of *higher* ideas of which he would never have thought twice in earlier days. In his own mind and in his conscience he called "higher" all "ideas" at which (he found to his surprise) he could not laugh in his heart—there had never been such hitherto—in his secret heart only, of course; oh, in company it was a different matter! He knew very well, indeed, that—if only the occasion were to arise—he would the very next day, in spite of all the mysterious and reverent resolutions of his conscience, with perfect composure disavow all these "higher ideas" and be the first to turn them into ridicule, without, of course, admitting anything. And this was really the case, in spite of a certain and, indeed, considerable independence of thought, which he had of late gained at the expense of the "lower ideas" that had mastered him till then. And how often, when he got up in the morning, he began to be ashamed of the thoughts and feelings he had passed through during a sleepless night! And he had suffered continually of late from sleeplessness. He had noticed for some time past that he had become excessively sensitive about everything, trifles as well as matters of importance, and so he made up his mind to trust his feelings as little as possible. But he could not overlook some facts, the reality of which he was forced to admit. Of late his thoughts and sensations were sometimes at night completely transformed, and for the most part utterly unlike those which came to him in the early part of the day. This struck him— and he even consulted a distinguished doctor who was, however, an acquaintance; he spoke to him about it jocosely, of course. The answer he received was that the transformation of ideas and sensations, and even the possession of two distinct sets of thoughts and sensations was a universal fact among persons "who think and feel," that the convictions of a whole lifetime were sometimes transformed under the melancholy influences of night and sleeplessness; without rhyme or reason most momentous decisions were taken; but all this, of course, was only true up to a certain point—and, in fact, if the subject were too conscious of the double nature of his feelings, so that it began to be a source of suffering to him, it was certainly a symptom of approaching illness; and then steps must be taken at once. The best thing of all was to make a radical change in the mode of life, to alter one's diet, or even to travel. Relaxing medicine was beneficial, of course.

Velchaninov did not care to hear more; but to his mind it was conclusively shown to be illness.

"And so all this is only illness, all these 'higher ideas' are mere illness and nothing more!" he sometimes exclaimed to himself resentfully. He was very loth to admit this.

Soon, however, what had happened exclusively in the hours of the night began to be repeated in the morning, only with more bitterness than at night, with anger instead of remorse, with irony instead of emotion. What really happened was that certain incidents in his past, even in his distant past, began suddenly, and God knows why, to come more and more frequently back to his mind, but they came back in quite a peculiar way. Velchaninov had, for instance, complained for a long time past of loss of memory: he would forget the faces of acquaintances, who were offended by his cutting them when they met; he sometimes completely forgot a book he had read months before, and yet in spite of this loss of memory, evident every day (and a source of great uneasiness to him), everything concerning the remote past, things that had been quite forgotten for ten or fifteen years, would sometimes come suddenly into his mind now with such amazing exactitude of details and impressions that he felt as though he were living through them again. Some of the facts he remembered had been so completely forgotten that it seemed to him a miracle that they could be recalled. But this was not all, and, indeed, what man of wide experience has not some memory of a peculiar sort? But the point was that all that was recalled came back now with a quite fresh, surprising and, till then, inconceivable point of view, and seemed as though some one were leading up to it on purpose. Why did some things he remembered strike him now as positive crimes? And it was not a question of the judgments of his mind only: he would have put little faith in his gloomy, solitary, and sick mind; but it reached the point of curses and almost of tears, of inward tears. Why, two years before, he would not have believed it if he had been told that he would ever shed tears! At first, however, what he remembered was rather of a mortifying than of a sentimental character: he recalled certain failures and humiliations in society; he remembered, for instance, how he had been slandered by an intriguing fellow, and in consequence refused admittance to a certain house; how, for instance, and not so long ago, he had been publicly and unmistakably insulted, and had not challenged the offender to a duel; how in a circle of very pretty women he had been made the subject of an extremely witty epigram and had found no suitable answer. He even recollected one or two unpaid debts—trifling ones, it is true, but debts of honour—owing to people whom he had given up visiting and even spoke ill of. He was also worried (but only in his worst moments) by the thought of the two fortunes, both considerable ones, which he had squandered in the stupidest way possible. But soon he began to remember things of a "higher order."

Suddenly, for instance, apropos of nothing, he remembered the forgotten, utterly forgotten, figure of a harmless, grey-headed, and absurd old clerk, whom he had once, long, long ago, and with absolute impunity, insulted in public simply to gratify his own conceit, simply for the sake of an amusing and successful jest, which was repeated and increased his prestige. The incident had been so completely forgotten that he could not even recall the old man's surname, though all the surroundings of the incident rose before his mind with incredible clearness. He distinctly remembered that the old man was defending his daughter, who was unmarried, though no longer quite young, and had become the subject of gossip in the town. The old man had begun to answer angrily, but he suddenly burst out crying before the whole company, which made some sensation. They had ended by making him drunk with champagne as a joke and getting a hearty laugh out of it. And now when, apropos of nothing, Velchaninov remembered how the poor old man had sobbed and hidden his face in his hands like a child, it suddenly seemed to him as though he had never forgotten it. And, strange to say, it had all seemed to him very amusing at the time, especially some of the details, such as the way he had covered his face with his hands; but now it was quite the contrary.

Later, he recalled how, simply as a joke, he had slandered the very pretty wife of a schoolmaster, and how the slander had reached the husband's ears. Velchaninov had left the town soon after and never knew what the final consequences of his slander had been, but now he began to imagine how all might have ended—and there is no knowing to what lengths his imagination might not have gone, if this memory had not suddenly been succeeded by a much more recent reminiscence of a young girl of the working-class, to whom he had not even felt attracted, and of whom, it must be admitted, he was actually ashamed. Yet, though he could not have said what had induced him, he had got her into trouble and had simply abandoned her and his child without even saying goodbye (it was true, he had no time to spare), when he left Petersburg. He had tried to find that girl for a whole year afterwards, but he had not succeeded in tracing her. He had, it seemed, hundreds of such reminiscences—and each one of them seemed to bring dozens of others in its train. By degrees his vanity, too, began to suffer.

We have said already that his vanity had degenerated into something peculiar. That was true. At moments (rare moments, however), he even forgot himself to such a degree that he ceased to be ashamed of not keeping his own carriage, that he trudged on foot from one court to another, that he began to be somewhat negligent in his dress. And if some one of his own acquaintance had scanned him with a sarcastic stare in the street or had simply refused to recognize him, he might really have had pride enough to pass him by without a frown. His indifference would have been

664

genuine, not assumed for effect. Of course, this was only at times: these were only the moments of forgetfulness and nervous irritation, yet his vanity had by degrees grown less concerned with the subjects that had once affected it, and was becoming concentrated on one question, which haunted him continually.

"Why, one would think," he began reflecting satirically sometimes (and he almost always began by being satirical when he thought about himself), "why, one would think some one up aloft were anxious for the reformation of my morals, and were sending me these cursed reminiscences and 'tears of repentance!' So be it, but it's all useless! It is all shooting with blank cartridge! As though I did not know for certain, more certainly than certainty, that in spite of these fits of tearful remorse and self-reproach, I haven't a grain of independence for all my foolish middle age! Why, if the same temptation were to turn up to-morrow, if circumstances, for instance, were to make it to my interest to spread a rumour that the schoolmaster's wife had taken presents from me, I should certainly spread it, I shouldn't hesitate—and it would be even worse, more loathsome than the first time, just because it would be the second time and not the first time. Yes, if I were insulted again this minute by that little prince whose leg I shot off eleven years ago, though he was the only son of his mother, I should challenge him at once and condemn him to crutches again. So they are no better than blank cartridges, and there's no sense in them! And what's the good of remembering the past when I've not the slightest power of escaping from myself?"

And though the adventure with the schoolmaster's wife was not repeated, though he did not condemn any one else to crutches, the very idea that it inevitably would be the same, if the same circumstances arose, almost killed him... at times. One cannot, in reality, suffer from memories all the time; one can rest and enjoy oneself in the intervals.

So, indeed, Velchaninov did: he was ready to enjoy himself in the intervals; yet his sojourn in Petersburg grew more and more unpleasant as time went on. July was approaching. Intermittently he had flashes of determination to give up everything, the lawsuit and all, and to go away somewhere without looking back, to go suddenly, on the spur of the moment, to the Crimea, for instance. But, as a rule, an hour later he had scorned the idea and had laughed at it: "These hateful thoughts won't stop short at sending me to the south, if once they've begun and if I've any sense of decency, and so it's useless to run away from them, and, indeed, there's no reason to."

"And what's the object of running away?" he went on brooding in his despondency; "it's so dusty here, so stifling, everything in the house is so messy. In those law-courts where I hang about among those busy people, there is such a scurrying to and fro like mice, such a mass of sordid cares! All the people left in town, all the faces that flit by from morning till night so naïvely and openly betray their self-love, their guileless insolence, the cowardice of their little souls, the chicken-heartedness of their little natures—why, it's a paradise for a melancholy man, seriously speaking! Everything is open, everything is clear, no one thinks it necessary to hide anything as they do among our gentry in our summer villas or at watering-places abroad—and so it's more deserving of respect, if only for its openness and simplicity!... I won't go away! I'll stay here if I burst!"

CHAPTER II

The Gentleman with Crape on His Hat

It was the third of July. The heat and stuffiness were insufferable. The day had been a very busy one for Velchaninov; he had had to spend the whole morning in walking and driving from place to place, and he had before him the prospect of an unavoidable visit that evening to a gentleman—a lawyer and a civil councillor—whom he hoped to catch unawares at his villa out of town. At six o'clock Velchaninov went at last into a restaurant (the fare was not beyond criticism, though the cooking was French), on the Nevsky Prospect, near the Police Bridge. He sat down at the little table in his usual corner and asked for the dinner of the day.

He used to eat the dinner that was provided for a rouble and paid extra for the wine, and he regarded this as a sacrifice to the unsettled state of his finances and an act of prudence on his part. Though he wondered how he could possibly eat such stuff, he nevertheless used to devour it to the last crumb—and every time with as much appetite as though he had not eaten for three days before. "There's something morbid about it," he would mutter to himself sometimes, noticing his appetite. But on this occasion he took his seat at his little table in a very bad humour, tossed his hat down angrily, put his elbows on the table, and sank into thought.

Though he could be so polite and, on occasion, so loftily imperturbable, he would probably now, if some one dining near him had been noisy, or the boy waiting on him had failed to understand at the first word, have been as blustering as a *junker* and would perhaps have made a scene.

The soup was put before him. He took up the ladle, but before he had time to help himself, he dropped it, and almost jumped up from the table. A surprising idea suddenly dawned upon him: at that instant—and God knows by what process—he suddenly realized the cause of his depression, of the special extra depression which had tormented him of late for several days together, had for some unknown reason fastened upon him and for some unknown cause refused to be shaken off; now he suddenly saw it all and it was as plain as a pikestaff.

"It's all that hat," he muttered as though inspired. "It's nothing but that cursed bowler hat with that beastly mourning crape that is the cause of it all!"

He began pondering—and the more he pondered the more morose he grew, and the more extraordinary "the whole adventure" seemed to him.

"But... it is not an adventure, though," he protested, distrustful of himself. "As though there were anything in the least like an adventure about it!"

All that had happened was this. Nearly a fortnight before (he did not really remember, but he fancied it was a fortnight), he had first met somewhere in the street, near the corner of Podyatchesky Street and Myestchansky Street, a gentleman with crape on his hat. The gentleman was like any one else, there was nothing peculiar about him, he passed quickly, but he stared somewhat too fixedly at Velchaninov, and for some reason at once attracted his attention in a marked degree. His countenance struck Velchaninov as familiar. He had certainly at some time met it somewhere. "But I must have seen thousands of faces in my life, I can't remember them all!"

Before he had gone twenty paces further he seemed to have forgotten the encounter, in spite of the impression made at first. But the impression persisted the whole day—and it was somewhat singular, it took the form of a peculiar undefined annoyance. Now, a fortnight later, he remembered all that distinctly; he remembered, too, what he had failed to grasp at the time—that is, what his annoyance was due to; and he had so utterly failed to grasp it that he had not even connected his ill-humour all that evening with the meeting that morning.

But the gentleman had lost no time in recalling himself to Velchaninov's mind, and next day had come across the latter in the Nevsky Prospect again, and again stared at him rather strangely. Velchaninov dismissed him with a curse and immediately afterwards wondered why he cursed. It is true that there are faces that at once arouse an undefined and aimless aversion.

"Yes, I certainly have met him somewhere," he muttered thoughtfully, an hour after the meeting. And he remained in a very bad humour the whole evening afterwards; he even had a bad dream at night, and yet it never entered his head that the whole cause of this new fit of despondency was nothing but that gentleman in mourning, although he did not once think of him that evening! He had even been wrathful at the moment that such a "wretched object" could occupy his attention as long as it did and would certainly have thought it degrading to ascribe his agitation to him, if it had ever occurred to his mind to do so. Two days later they met again in a crowd coming off one of the Nevsky steamers. On this third occasion Velchaninov was ready to swear that the gentleman with the crape on his hat recognized him and made a dash for him, but was borne away in the crush; he fancied he had even had the "effrontery" to hold out his hand to him; perhaps he had even cried out and shouted his name. That, however, Velchaninov had not heard distinctly, but... "Who is the low fellow, though, and why does he not come up to me, if he really does know me, and if he is so anxious to?" he thought angrily, as he got into a cab and drove towards Smolny monastery. Half-an-hour later he was noisily arguing with his lawyer, but in the evening and the night he was suffering again from the most abominable and most fantastic attack of acute depression. "Am I in for a bilious attack?" he wondered uneasily, looking at himself in the looking-glass.

This was the third meeting. Afterwards, for five days in succession, he met "no one," and not a sign was seen of the low fellow. And yet the gentleman with the crape on his hat was continually in his mind. With some surprise Velchaninov caught himself wondering: "What's the matter with me—am I sick on his account, or what? H'm!... and he must have a lot to do in Petersburg, too—and for whom is he wearing crape? He evidently recognized me, but I don't recognize him. And why do these people put on crape? It's out of keeping with him somehow.... I fancy if I look at him closer, I shall recognize him...."

And something seemed faintly stirring in his memory, like some familiar but momentarily forgotten word, which one tries with all one's might to recall; one knows it very well and knows that one knows it; one knows exactly what it means, one is close upon it and yet it refuses to be remembered, in spite of one's efforts.

"It was.... It was long ago... and it was somewhere.... There was... there was... but, damn the fellow, whatever there was or wasn't...." he cried angrily all at once; "it is not worth while to demean and degrade myself over that wretched fellow...."

He grew horribly angry, but in the evening, when he suddenly remembered that he had been angry that morning, and "horribly" angry, it was extremely disagreeable to him; he felt as though some one had caught him in something shameful. He was bewildered and surprised.

"Then there must be reasons for my being so angry... apropos of nothing... at a mere reminiscence...." He left the thought unfinished.

And next day he felt angrier than ever, but this time he fancied he had grounds for it, and that he was quite right in feeling so; "it was unheard-of insolence," he thought. What had happened was the fourth meeting. The gentleman with crape on his hat had suddenly made his appearance again, as though he had sprung out of the earth. Velchaninov had just caught in the street the indispensable civil councillor before mentioned, of whom he was still in pursuit, meaning to pounce on him unawares at his summer villa, for the gentleman, whom Velchaninov scarcely knew, though it was so necessary to see him about his business, on that occasion as on this eluded him, and was evidently keeping out of sight and extremely reluctant to meet him. Delighted at coming across him at last, Velchaninov walked hurriedly beside him, glancing into his face and straining every effort to bring the wily old fellow to the discussion of a certain subject, in which the latter might be indiscreet enough to let slip the facts of which he had so long been on the track; but the crafty old man had his own views, and kept putting him off with laughter or silence—and it was just at this extremely absorbing moment that Velchaninov descried on the opposite pavement the gentleman with crape on his hat. He was standing, staring at them both—he was watching them, that was evident, and seemed to be jeering at them.

"Damnation!" cried Velchaninov in a fury, as he left the civil councillor at his destination and ascribed his failure with him to the sudden appearance of that "impudent fellow." "Damnation! is he spying on me? He's evidently following me. Hired by some one, perhaps, and... and... and, by Jove! he was jeering at me! By Jove! I'll thrash him.... I'm sorry I've no stick with me! I'll buy a stick! I won't let it pass. Who is he? I insist on knowing who he is."

It was three days after this fourth meeting that Velchaninov was at his restaurant, as we have described him, agitated in earnest and even somewhat overwhelmed. He could not help being conscious of it himself, in spite of his pride. He was forced at last, putting all the circumstances together, to suspect that all his depression, all this *peculiar* despondency and the agitation that had persisted for the last fortnight was caused by no other than this gentleman in mourning, "nonentity as he was."

"I may be a hypochondriac," thought Velchaninov, "and so I am ready to make a mountain out of a mole-hill, but does it make it any the better for me that all this is *perhaps* only fancy! Why, if every rogue like that is going to be able to upset one in this way, why... it's... why...."

Certainly in the meeting of that day (the fifth), which had so agitated Velchaninov, the mountain had proved to be little more than a mole-hill: the gentleman had as before darted by him, but this time without scrutinizing Velchaninov, and without, as before, betraying that he recognized him; on the contrary, he dropped his eyes and seemed to be very anxious to escape being noticed. Velchaninov turned round and shouted at the top of his voice—

"Hi! you with the crape on your hat! Hiding now! Stop: who are you?"

The question (and his shouting altogether) was very irrational, but Velchaninov only realized that after he had uttered it. The gentleman turned round at the shout, stood still for a minute disconcerted, smiled, seemed on the point of doing or saying something, was obviously for a minute in a state of the utmost indecision, then he suddenly turned and rushed away without looking back. Velchaninov looked after him with astonishment.

"And what if it's a case of my forcing myself on him, not his forcing himself on me?" he thought. "And that's all it amounts to?"

When he had finished dinner he made haste to set off to the summer villa to see the civil councillor. He did not find him; he was informed that "his honour had not returned that day, and probably would not come back till three or four o'clock in the morning, as he was staying in town to a birthday party." This was so mortifying that, in his first fury, Velchaninov decided himself to go to the birthday party, and even set off to do so; but reflecting on the road that it was a long way to go he dismissed the cab and trudged home on foot to his flat near the Grand Theatre. He felt that he wanted exercise. He must, at all costs, overcome his usual sleeplessness, and sleep sound that night, to soothe his excited nerves; and in order to sleep he must anyway be tired. And, as it was a long walk, it was half-past ten before he reached home, and he certainly was very tired.

Though he so criticized the flat that he had taken the previous March, and abused it so malignantly, excusing himself to himself on the plea that he was only "camping there temporarily," and stranded in Petersburg through that "damned lawsuit"—the flat was by no means so bad and so unsuitable as he made out. The approach was certainly rather dark and "grubby" under the gateway, but the flat itself, on the second storey, consisted of two big, lofty and bright rooms, separated from one another by a dark entry, and looking one into the street, the other into the courtyard.

Adjoining the room the windows of which looked into the courtyard was a small study, which had been designed for a bedroom; but Velchaninov kept it littered with books and papers; he slept in one of the larger rooms, the one that looked into the street. He had a bed made up on the sofa. The furniture was quite decent, though second-hand, and he had besides a few articles of value—the relics of his former prosperity: bronze and china, and big, genuine Bokhara rugs; even two good pictures had been preserved; but everything had been unmistakably untidy and even dusty and nothing had been put in its place ever since his servant, Pelagea, had gone home to Novgorod for a holiday and left him alone. The oddity of having a solitary female servant for a bachelor and man of the world who was still anxious to keep up the style of a gentleman almost made Velchaninov blush, though he was very well satisfied with his Pelagea. The girl had come to him when he was taking the flat in the spring, from a family of his acquaintance who were going abroad, and she had put the flat to rights. But when she went away he could not bring himself to engage another woman; to engage a manservant was not worth while for a short time; besides, he did not like menservants. And so it was arranged that the sister of the porter's wife should come in every morning to clear up and that Velchaninov should leave the key at the porter's lodge when he went out. She did absolutely nothing, merely pocketed her wages; and he suspected her of pilfering. Yet he dismissed everything with a shrug and was positively glad that he was left quite alone in the flat. But there are limits to everything; and at some jaundiced moments the "filth" was absolutely insufferable to his nerves, and he almost always went into his rooms with a feeling of repugnance on returning home.

But this time he barely gave himself time to undress; flinging himself on the bed, he irritably resolved to think of nothing, but to go to sleep "this minute," whatever might happen; and, strange to say, he did fall asleep as soon as his head touched the pillow; such a thing had not happened to him for almost a month.

He slept for nearly three hours, but his sleep was uneasy, and he had strange dreams such as one has in fever. He dreamed of some crime which he had committed and concealed and of which he was accused by people who kept coming up to him. An immense crowd collected, but more people still came, so that the door was not shut but remained open. But his whole interest was centred on a strange person, once an intimate friend of his, who was dead, but now somehow suddenly came to see him. What made it most worrying was that Velchaninov did not know the man, had forgotten his name and could not recall it. All he knew was that he had once liked him very much. All the other people who had come up seemed expecting from this man a final word that would decide Velchaninov's guilt or innocence, and all were waiting impatiently. But he sat at the table without moving, was mute and would not speak. The noise did not cease for a moment, the general irritation grew more intense, and suddenly in a fury Velchaninov struck the man for refusing to speak, and felt a strange enjoyment in doing it. His heart thrilled with horror and misery at what he had done, but there was enjoyment in that thrill. Utterly exasperated, he struck him a second time and a third, and, drunk with rage and terror, which reached the pitch of madness, but in which there was an intense enjoyment, he lost count of his blows, and went on beating him without stopping. He wented to demolish *it* all, all. Suddenly something happened: they all shrieked horribly and turned round to the door, as though expecting something, and at that instant there came the sound of a ring at the bell, repeated three times, with violence enough to pull the bell off. Velchaninov woke up and was wide awake in an instant. He leapt headlong out of bed and rushed to the door; he was absolutely convinced that the ring at the bell was not a dream and that some one really had rung at his bell that moment. "It would be too unnatural for such a distinct, such a real, palpable ring to be only a dream!"

But to his surprise the ring at the bell turned out to be a dream, too. He opened the door, went out on the landing, even peeped down the stairs—there was absolutely no one there. The bell hung motionless. Surprised, but relieved, he went back into his room. When he had lighted a candle he remembered that he had left the door closed but not locked or bolted. He had sometimes in the past forgotten when he came home to lock the door for the night, not thinking it of much importance.

Pelagea had often given him a talking-to about it. He went back into the passage, shut the door, opened it once more and looked out on the landing, but only fastened the door on the inside with the hook, without taking the trouble to turn the key. The clock struck half-past two; so he must have slept three hours.

His dream had so disturbed him that he did not want to go to bed again at once, and made up his mind to walk up and down his room for half-an-hour or—"Time enough to smoke a cigar"—he thought. Hastily dressing, he went to the window and lifted the thick stuff curtain and the white blind behind it. It was already daylight in the street. The light summer nights of Petersburg always worked on his nerves and of late had intensified his insomnia, so that it was expressly on this account that he had, a fortnight previously, put up thick stuff curtains which completely excluded the light when they were fully drawn. Letting in the daylight and forgetting the lighted candle on the table, he fell to pacing up and down the room, still oppressed by a sort of sick and heavy feeling. The impression of the dream was still upon him. A real feeling of distress that he should have been capable of raising his hand against that man and beating him still persisted.

"That man doesn't exist, and never has existed; it's all a dream. Why am I worrying about it?"

He began thinking with exasperation, as though all his troubles were concentrated on this, that he was certainly beginning to be ill—"a sick man."

It was always painful to him to think that he was getting old and growing feebler, and in his bad moments he exaggerated his age and failing powers on purpose to irritate himself.

"Old age," he muttered; "I'm getting quite old, I'm losing my memory, I see apparitions, I dream dreams, bells ring.... Damn it all, I know from experience, that such dreams are always a sign of fever with me.... I am convinced that all this business with the crape gentleman is a dream too. I was certainly right yesterday: it's I, I, who am pestering him, not he me. I've woven a romance about him, and I am hiding under the table in my fright at it. And why do I call him a low fellow? He may be a very decent person. His face is not attractive, certainly, though there is nothing particularly ugly about it; he's dressed like any one else. Only in his eyes there's something.... Here I'm at it again! I'm thinking about him again!! What the devil does the look in his eyes matter to me? Can't I get on without that...."

Among the thoughts that kept starting up in his mind, one rankled painfully: he felt suddenly convinced that this gentleman with the crape on his hat had once been an acquaintance on friendly terms with him, and now sneered at him when he met him because he knew some great secret about him in the past and saw him now in such a humiliating position. He went mechanically to the window, meaning to open it and get a breath of the night air, and—and he suddenly shuddered all over: it seemed to him that something incredible and unheard of was suddenly happening before his eyes.

He had not yet opened the window but he made haste to slip behind the corner of the window and hide himself: on the deserted pavement opposite he had suddenly seen directly facing the house the man with the crape on his hat. The gentleman was standing on the pavement looking towards his windows, but evidently not noticing him, stared inquisitively at the house as though considering something. He seemed to be deliberating

673

and unable to decide: he lifted his hand and seemed to put his finger to his forehead. At last he made up his mind: took a cursory glance round, and began stealthily on tiptoe crossing the street. Yes: he had gone in at the gateway by the little gate (which sometimes in summer was left unbolted till three o'clock).

"He's coming to me," flashed on Velchaninov's mind, and, also on tiptoe, he ran headlong to the door and stood before it silent and numb with suspense, softly laying his trembling right hand on the hook of the door he had just fastened, listening intently for the sound of footsteps on the stairs.

His heart beat so violently that he was afraid he might not hear the stranger come up on tiptoe. He did not understand what it meant, but he felt it all with tenfold intensity. His dream seemed to have melted into reality. Velchaninov was by temperament bold. He sometimes liked to display fearlessness in the face of danger even if he were only admiring himself with no one else to look at him. But now there was something else as well. The man who had so lately been given up to hypochondria and nervous depression was completely transformed; he was not the same man. A nervous, noiseless laugh broke from him. From behind the closed door he divined every movement of the stranger.

"Ah! now he's coming in, he has come in, he's looking about him; he's listening downstairs; he's holding his breath, stealing up... ah! He has taken hold of the handle, he's pulling it, trying it! He reckoned on its not being locked! So he knows I sometimes forget to lock it! He's pulling at the handle again; why, does he imagine that the hook will come out? It's a pity to part! Isn't it a pity to let him go like this?"

And indeed everything must have happened just as he pictured it; some one really was standing on the other side of the door, and was softly and noiselessly trying the lock, and was pulling at the handle and—"Of course, had his object in doing so." But by now Velchaninov had resolved to settle the question, and with a sort of glee got ready for the moment. He had an irresistible longing to unfasten the hook, suddenly to fling open the door, and to confront the "bugbear" face to face. "What may you be doing here, pray, honoured sir?"

And so he did: seizing the moment, he suddenly lifted the hook, pushed the door and—almost fell over the gentleman with crape on his hat.

CHAPTER III

Pavel Pavlovitch Trusotsky

The latter stood speechless, rooted to the spot. They stood facing one another in the doorway, and stared fixedly into each other's faces. Some moments passed and suddenly—Velchaninov recognized his visitor!

At the same time the visitor evidently realized that Velchaninov recognized him fully. There was a gleam in his eye that betrayed it. In one instant his whole face melted into a sugary smile.

"I have the pleasure, I believe, of addressing Alexey Ivanovitch?" he almost chanted in a voice of deep feeling, ludicrously incongruous with the circumstances.

"Surely you are not Pavel Pavlovitch Trusotsky?" Velchaninov brought out with an air of perplexity.

"We were acquainted nine years ago at T——, and if you will allow me to remind you—we were intimately acquainted."

"Yes... to be sure, but now it's three o'clock, and for the last ten minutes you've been trying whether my door was locked or not."

"Three o'clock!" cried the visitor, taking out his watch and seeming positively grieved and surprised; "why, so it is. Three! I beg your pardon, Alexey Ivanovitch, I ought to have considered before coming up: I'm quite ashamed. I'll come again and explain, in a day or two, but now...."

"No! If there's to be an explanation will you kindly give it me this minute!" Velchaninov caught him up. "Please walk inside, into this room—no doubt you intended to come into the room yourself, and have not turned up in the middle of the night simply to try the lock."

He was excited and at the same time disconcerted, and felt that he could not grasp the position. He was even somewhat ashamed—there proved to be neither mystery nor danger. The whole phantasmagoria had proved to be nothing; all that had turned up was the foolish figure of some Pavel Pavlovitch. And yet he did not believe that it was all so simple; he had a vague presentiment and dread of something. Making his visitor sit down in an armchair, he seated himself impatiently on his bed, not a yard away, bent forward with his hands on his knees and waited irritably for him to speak. He scanned him greedily and remembered him. But, strange to say, the man was silent, quite silent, and seemed not to realize that he was "in duty bound" to speak at once; on the contrary, he, too, gazed at Velchaninov with a look of expectation. It was possible that he was simply timid, feeling at first a certaip awkwardness like a mouse in a trap; but Velchaninov flew into a rage.

"What do you mean by it!" he cried; "you are not a phantom or a dream, I suppose! You've not come to play at being dead, surely? Explain yourself, my good man!"

The visitor fidgeted, smiled, and began warily—

"So far as I see, what strikes you most of all is my coming at such an hour and under such peculiar circumstances.... So that, remembering all the past, and how we parted—it's really strange to me now.... Though, indeed, I had no intention of calling, and it has only happened by accident...."

"How by accident? Why, I saw you through the window run across the street on tiptoe!"

"Ah, you saw me! So perhaps you know more about it all than I do! But I'm only irritating you... You see, I arrived here three weeks ago on business of my own.... I am Pavel Pavlovitch Trusotsky, you know; you recognized me yourself. I am here to try to get transferred to another province, and to a post in another department considerably superior.... But all that's neither here nor there, though... The point is, if you must know, that I have been hanging about here for the last three weeks, and I seem to be spinning out my business on purpose—that is, the business of my transfer—and really, if it comes off I do believe I shan't notice that it has come off and shall stay on in your Petersburg, feeling as I do now. I hang about as though I had lost sight of my object and, as it were, pleased to have lost sight of it—feeling as I do!..."

"Feeling how?" Velchaninov asked, frowning.

The visitor raised his eyes to him, lifted his hat and pointed to the crape on it.

"Why, look; that's how I'm feeling."

Velchaninov gazed blankly first at the crape and then at the countenance of his visitor. Suddenly the colour rushed into his cheeks and he grew terribly agitated.

"Surely not Natalya Vassilyevna?"

"Yes! Natalya Vassilyevna! Last March... consumption, and almost suddenly, after two or three months' illness! And I am left—as you see!'

As he said this the visitor, in deep emotion, put out his hands on each side, the hat with the crape on it flapping in his left one, while he made a low bow that displayed his bald head for ten seconds at least.

His air and his gesture seemed to revive Velchaninov; an ironical and even provocative smile hovered on his lips—but only for a moment: the news of the death of this lady (whom he had known so long ago and had long ago succeeded in forgetting) gave him a shock which was a complete surprise to him.

"Is it possible?"—he muttered the first words that came to his tongue; "and why didn't you come straight and tell me?"

"I thank you for your sympathy. I see it and appreciate it, in spite of..."

"In spite of?"

"In spite of so many years of separation, you have just shown such sympathy for my sorrow and even for me that I am, of course, sensible of gratitude. That was all I wanted to express. It's not that I had doubts of my friends: I can find here the truest friends at once—Stepan Mihalovitch Bagautov, for instance. But you know, Alexey Ivanovitch, our acquaintance with you—friendship rather, as I gratefully recall it—was over nine years ago, you never came back to us; there was no interchange of letters...."

The visitor chanted his phrases as though to music, but all the while that he was holding forth he looked at the floor, though, no doubt, all the time he saw everything. But Velchaninov had by now regained his composure.

With a very strange impression, which grew stronger and stronger, he listened to Pavel Pavlovitch and watched him, and when the latter suddenly paused, the most incongruous and surprising ideas rushed in a sudden flash into his mind.

"But how was it I didn't recognize you till now?" he cried, growing more animated. "Why, we've stumbled across each other five times in the street!"

"Yes; I remember that, too; you were constantly crossing my path—twice, or perhaps three times. ..."

"That is, you were constantly coming upon me, not I upon you?"

Velchaninov stood up and suddenly, quite unexpectedly, he began laughing. Pavel Pavlovitch paused, looked at him attentively, but at once continued—

"And as for your not recognizing me, you might well have forgotten me, and, besides, I've had smallpox and it has left some traces on my face."

"Smallpox? To be sure, he has had smallpox! However did you——"

"Manage that? Anything may happen. One never can tell, Alexey Ivanovitch; one does have such misfortunes."

"Only it's awfully funny all the same. But continue, continue, my dear friend!"

"Though I met you, too——"

"Stay! Why did you say 'manage that' just now? I meant to use a much more polite expression. But go on, go on!"

For some reason he felt more and more good-humoured. The feeling of shock was completely effaced by other emotions. He walked up and down the room with rapid steps.

"Even though I met you, and though when I set out for Petersburg I intended to seek you out, yet now, I repeat, I have been feeling so broken in spirit ... and mentally shattered ever since March..."

"Oh, yes! shattered since March. ... Stop a minute. Don't you smoke?"

"As you know, in old days when Natalya Vassilyevna was living I. ..."

"To be sure, to be sure; and since March?"

"Just a cigarette, perhaps."

"Here is a cigarette. Light it—and go on! Go on, it's awfully——"

And, lighting a cigar, Velchaninov quickly settled himself on the bed again.

Pavel Pavlovitch paused.

"But how excited you are yourself. Are you quite in good health?"

"Oh, damn my health!" Velchaninov was suddenly exasperated. "Continue!"

The visitor, for his part, looking at his companion's agitation, seemed better pleased and grew more self-confident.

"But what is there to continue?" he began again. "Imagine, Alexey Ivanovitch, in the first place, a man destroyed—that is, not simply destroyed, but fundamentally, so to say; a man whose existence is transformed after twenty years of married life, wandering about the streets with no consistent object, as though in a wilderness, almost in a state of oblivion, and finding a certain fascination in that oblivion. It is natural that sometimes, when I meet an acquaintance, even a real friend, I purposely go out of my way to avoid approaching him, at such a moment of oblivion, I mean. And at another moment one remembers everything so, and so longs to see any one who has witnessed that recent past, gone now never to return, and has taken part in it, and one's heart beats so violently that one is ready to risk throwing oneself upon a friend by night as well as by day, even though one might have to wake him up at four o'clock in the morning on purpose.... I have made a mistake about the time only, not about our friendship; for this moment more than makes up for it. And as for the time, I really thought it was only twelve, feeling as I do. One drinks the cup of one's sorrow till one is drunk with it. And it's not sorrow, indeed, but the novelty of my state that crushes me. ..."

"How strangely you express yourself?" Velchaninov observed gloomily, becoming extremely grave again.

"Yes, I do express myself strangely..."

"And you're... not joking?"

"Joking!" exclaimed Pavel Pavlovitch in pained surprise, "and at the moment when I am announcing the sad..."

"Ach, don't speak of that, I entreat you!"

Velchaninov got up and began pacing the room again.

So passed five minutes. The visitor seemed about to get up too, but Velchaninov shouted: "Sit still, sit still!" and Pavel Pavlovitch obediently sank back into his armchair at once.

"But, how you have changed though," Velchaninov began again, suddenly stopping before him as though all at once struck by the thought. "You're dreadfully changed! Extraordinarily! Quite a different person."

"That's not strange: nine years."

"No, no, no, it's not a question of years! It's incredible how you've changed in appearance; you've become a different man!"

"That, too, may well be, in nine years."

"Or is it since March!"

"He—he!" Pavel Pavlovitch sniggered slily. "That's a funny idea of yours. ... But if I may venture—what is the change exactly?"

"You ask what! The Pavel Pavlovitch I used to know was such a solid, decorous person, that Pavel Pavlovitch was such a clever chap, and now —this Pavel Pavlovitch is a regular *vaurien!*"

He was at that stage of irritability in which even reserved people say more than they ought.

"*Vaurien!* you think so? And not a clever chap now—not clever?" Pavel Pavlovitch chuckled with relish.

"Clever chap be damned! now I daresay you really are too clever."

"I'm insolent, but this low fellow's more so and ... and what is his object?" Velchaninov was thinking all the while.

"Ach, dearest, most precious friend!" cried the visitor suddenly, growing extremely agitated and turning round in his chair. "What are we saying? We are not in the world now, we're not in the society of the great and the worldly! We're two old friends, very old friends! And we've come together in the fullest sincerity to recall to one another the priceless bond of friendship of which the dear departed was the precious link!"

And he was so carried away by the ecstasy of his feeling that he bowed his head as before, hiding his face in his hat. Velchaninov watched him with aversion and uneasiness.

"What if he's simply a buffoon," flashed through his mind; "but n-no, n-no! I don't think he's drunk—he may be drunk, though: his face is red. Even if he were drunk—it comes to the same thing. What's he driving at? What does the low fellow want?"

"Do you remember, do you remember," cried Pavel Pavlovitch, removing the hat a little and seeming more and more carried away by his reminiscences, "do you remember our expeditions into the country, our evenings and little parties with dancing and innocent games at the house of his Excellency, our most hospitable Semyon Semyonovitch? And how we used to read together, the three of us, in the evening! And our first acquaintance with you, when you called on me that morning to make inquiries about your business, and even began to speak rather warmly, and suddenly Natalya Vassilyevna came in, and within ten minutes you had become a real friend of the family and so you were for a whole year, exactly as in Turgenev's play, *A Provincial Lady.*"

Velchaninov paced slowly up and down, looked at the floor, listened with impatience and repulsion, but—listened intently.

"The thought of *A Provincial Lady* never entered my head," he interrupted, somewhat confused, "and you never used to talk in such a shrill voice and such ... unnatural language. What is that for?"

"I certainly used to be more silent—that is, I was more reserved," Pavel Pavlovitch interposed hurriedly. "You remember how she used to talk, how wittily. ... And in regard to *A Provincial Lady* and Stupendyev particularly, you are quite right, for I remember it was we ourselves, the precious departed and I, used to speak of that at quiet moments after you'd gone away—comparing our first meeting with that drama, for there really was a resemblance. About Stupendyev especially."

"What Stupendyev? Damn him!" cried Velchaninov, and he actually stamped, utterly disconcerted at the mention of "Stupendyev," owing to a disturbing recollection that was evoked by the name.

"Stupendyev is a character, a character in a play, the husband in *A Provincial Lady*," Pavel Pavlovitch piped in a voice of honeyed sweetness; "but it belonged to a different series of our precious and happy memories, when after your departure Stepan Mihalovitch Bagautov bestowed his friendship on us, exactly as you did, for five whole years."

"Bagautov? What do you mean? What Bagautov?" Velchaninov stood still as though petrified.

"Bagautov, Stepan Mihalovitch, who bestowed his friendship on us, a year after you and ... and exactly as you did."

"Good heavens, yes! I know that!" cried Velchaninov, recovering himself at last. "Bagautov! Why, of course, he had a berth in your town. ..."

"He had, he had! At the Governor's! From Petersburg. A very elegant young man, belonging to the best society!" Pavel Pavlovitch exclaimed in a positive ecstasy.

"Yes, yes, yes! What was I thinking of? Why, he, too——"

"He too, he too," Pavel Pavlovitch repeated in the same ecstasy, catching up the word his companion had incautiously dropped. "He too! Well, we acted *A Provincial Lady* at his Excellency's, our most hospitable Semyon Semyonovitch's private theatre—Stepan Mihalovitch was the 'count,' I was the 'husband,' and the dear departed was 'The Provincial Lady'—only they took away the 'husband's' part from me, Natalya Vassilyevna insisted on it, so that I did not act the 'husband' because I was not fitted for the part. ..."

"How the devil could you be Stupendyev? you're pre-eminently Pavel Pavlovitch Trusotsky and not Stupendyev," said Velchaninov, speaking with coarse rudeness and almost trembling with irritation. "Only, excuse me; Bagautov's in Petersburg, I saw him myself in the spring! Why don't you go and see him too?"

"I have been every blessed day, for the last fortnight. I'm not admitted! He's ill, he can't see me! and, only fancy, I've found out from firsthand sources that he really is very dangerously ill! The friend of six years. Ach, Alexey Ivanovitch, I tell you and I repeat it, that sometimes one's feelings are such that one longs to sink into the earth; yes, really; at another moment one feels as though one could embrace any one of those who have been, so to say, witnesses and participators of the past and simply that one may weep, absolutely for nothing else but that one may weep. ..."

"Well, anyway, I've had enough of you for to-day, haven't I?" Velchaninov brought out abruptly.

"More than enough, more!" Pavel Pavlovitch got up from his seat at once. "It's four o'clock and, what's worse, I have so selfishly upset you. ..."

"Listen, I will be sure to come and see you myself, and then, I hope ... Tell me straight out, tell me frankly, you are not drunk to-day?"

"Drunk! Not a bit of it. ..."

"Hadn't you been drinking, just before you came, or earlier?"

"Do you know, Alexey Ivanovitch, you're in a regular fever."

"I'll come and see you to-morrow morning before one o'clock."

"And I've been noticing for a long time that you seem, as it were, delirious," Pavel Pavlovitch interrupted with zest, still harping on the same subject. "I feel conscience-stricken, really, that by my awkwardness ... but I'm going, I'm going! And you lie down and get some sleep!"

"Why, you haven't told me where you're living?" Velchaninov called hastily after him.

"Didn't I tell you? At the Pokrovsky Hotel."

"What Pokrovsky Hotel?"

"Why, close to the Pokrovsky Church, close by, in the side street. I've forgotten the name of the street and I've forgotten the number, only it's close by the Pokrovsky Church."

"I shall find it!"

"You'll be very welcome."

He was by now on his way downstairs.

"Stay," Velchaninov shouted after him again; "you are not going to give me the slip?"

"How do you mean, give you the slip?" cried Pavel Pavlovitch, staring at him open-eyed and turning round to smile on the third step.

Instead of answering, Velchaninov shut the door with a loud slam, carefully locked it and fastened the hook. Returning to the room, he spat as though he had been in contact with something unclean.

After standing for some five minutes in the middle of the room, he flung himself on the bed without undressing and in one minute fell asleep. The forgotten candle burnt itself out on the table.

CHAPTER IV

The Wife, the Husband, and the Lover

He slept very soundly and woke up at half-past nine; he remembered everything instantly, sat down on his bed and began at once thinking of "that woman's death." The shock of the sudden news of that death the night before had left a certain agitation and even pain. That pain and agitation had only for a time been smothered by a strange idea while Pavel Pavlovitch was with him.

But now, on waking up, all that had happened nine years before rose before his mind with extraordinary vividness.

This woman, this Natalya Vassilyevna, the wife of "that Trusotsky," he had once loved, and he had been her lover for the whole year that he had spent at T——, ostensibly on business of his own (that, too, was a lawsuit over a disputed inheritance), although his presence had not really been necessary for so long. The real cause of his remaining was this intrigue. The *liaison* and his love had such complete possession of him that it was as though he were in bondage to Natalya Vassilyevna, and he would probably have been ready on the spot to do anything, however monstrous and senseless, to satisfy that woman's slightest caprice.

He had never felt anything of the sort before. At the end of the year, when separation was inevitable, although it was expected to be only a brief one, Velchaninov was in such despair, as the fatal time drew near, that he proposed to Natalya Vassilyevna that she should elope with him, that he should carry her off from her husband, that they should throw up everything and that she should come abroad with him for ever. Nothing but the gibes and firm determination of the lady (who had, probably from boredom, or to amuse herself, quite approved of the project at first) could have dissuaded him and forced him to go alone. And actually, before two months had passed, he was asking himself in Petersburg the question which had always remained unanswered. Had he really loved that woman or had it been nothing but an "infatuation"? And it was not levity or the influence of some new passion that had given rise to this question: for those first two months in Petersburg he had been plunged in a sort of stupefaction and had scarcely noticed any woman, although he had at once mixed with his former acquaintances again and had seen a hundred women. At the same time he knew that if he were transported that moment to T—— he would promptly fall under the yoke of that woman's fascination again, in spite of any questions. Even five years later his conviction was unchanged. But five years later he used to admit this to himself with indignation and he even thought of "that woman" herself with hatred. He was ashamed of that year at T——; he could not even understand how such a "stupid" passion could have been possible for him, Velchaninov. All his memories of that passion had become absurd to him; and he blushed to the point of tears and was tormented by conscience-pricks at the thought of it. It is true that a few years later he had become somewhat calmer; he tried to forget it all—and almost succeeded. And now, all at once, nine years afterwards, all this had so suddenly and strangely risen up before him again, after hearing that night of the death of Natalya Vassilyevna.

Now, sitting on his bed, with confused thoughts crowding in disorder on his mind, he felt and realized clearly one thing only—that in spite of the "shock" he had felt at the news, he was nevertheless quite undisturbed by the fact of her death. "Can it be that I have no feeling for her?" he asked himself. It is true that he had now no feeling of hatred for her, and that he could criticize her more impartially, more fairly. In the course of those nine years of separation he had long since formulated the view that Natalya Vassilyevna belonged to the class of absolutely ordinary provincial ladies moving in good provincial society "and, who knows? perhaps she really was such, perhaps it was only I who idealized her so fantastically." He had always suspected, however, that there might be an error in that view; and he felt it even now. And, indeed, the facts were opposed to it; this Bagautov, too, had for several years been connected with her and apparently he, too, had been "under the yoke of her fascination." Bagautov certainly was a young man belonging to the best Petersburg society and, as he was a most "empty-headed fellow," he could only have had a successful career in Petersburg (Velchaninov used to say of him). Yet he had neglected Petersburg—that is, sacrificed his most important interests—and remained for five years in T—— solely on account of that woman! Yes, and he had finally returned to Petersburg, perhaps only because he, too, had been cast off like "an old, worn-out shoe." So there must have been in that woman something exceptional—a power of attracting, of enslaving, of dominating.

And yet one would have thought that she had not the gifts with which to attract and to enslave. She was not exactly pretty; perhaps she was actually plain. She was twenty-eight when Velchaninov first knew her. Though not altogether beautiful, her face was sometimes charmingly animated, but her eyes were not pretty: there was something like an excess of determination in them. She was very thin. On the intellectual side she had not been well educated; her keen intelligence was unmistakable, though she was one-sided in her ideas. Her manners were those of a provincial lady and at the same time, it is true, she had a great deal of tact; she had artistic taste, but showed it principally in knowing how to dress. In character she was resolute and domineering; she could never make up her mind to compromise in anything: it was all, or nothing. In difficult positions her firmness and stoicism were amazing. She was capable of generosity and at the same time would be utterly unjust. To argue with that lady was impossible: "twice two makes four" meant nothing to her. She never thought herself wrong or to blame in anything. Her continual deception of her husband and the perfidies beyond number which she practised upon him did not weigh on her in the least. But, to quote Velchaninov's own comparison, she was like the "Madonna of the Flagellants," who believes implicitly herself that she is the mother of God—so Natalya Vassilyevna believed implicitly in everything she did. She was faithful to her lover, but only as long as he did not bore her. She was fond of tormenting her lover, but she liked making up for it too. She was of a passionate, cruel, and sensual type. She hated depravity and condemned it with exaggerated severity and—was herself depraved. No sort of fact could have made her recognize her own depravity. "Most likely she *genuinely* does not know it," Velchaninov thought about her even before he left T——. (We may remark, by the way, that he was the accomplice of her depravity.) "She is one of those women who are born to be unfaithful wives. Such women never become old maids; it's a law of their nature to be married to that end. The husband is the first lover but never till after the wedding. No one gets married more adroitly and easily than this type of woman. For her first infidelity the husband is always to blame. And it is all accompanied by the most perfect sincerity: to the end they feel themselves absolutely right and, of course, entirely innocent."

Velchaninov was convinced that there really was such a type of woman; but, on the other hand, he was also convinced that there was a type of husband corresponding to that woman, whose sole vocation was to correspond with that feminine type. To his mind, the essence of such a husband lay in his being, so to say, "the eternal husband," or rather in being, all his life, a husband and nothing more. "Such a man is born and grows up only to be a husband, and, having married, is promptly transformed into a supplement of his wife, even when he happens to have unmistakable character of his own. The chief sign of such a husband is a certain decoration. He can no more escape wearing horns than the sun can help shining; he is not only unaware of the fact, but is bound by the very laws of his nature to be unaware of it." Velchaninov firmly believed in the existence of these two types and in Pavel Pavlovitch Trusotsky's being a perfect representative of one of them. The Pavel Pavlovitch of the previous night was, of course, very different from the Pavel Pavlovitch he had known at T——. He found him incredibly changed, but Velchaninov knew that he was bound to have changed and that all that was perfectly natural; Trusotsky could only as long as his wife was alive have remained all that he used to be, but, as it was, he was only a fraction of a whole, suddenly cut off and set free, that is something wonderful and unique.

As for the Pavel Pavlovitch of the past at T——, this is how Velchaninov remembered him and recalled him now.

"Of course, at T——, Pavel Pavlovitch had been simply a husband," and nothing more. If he were, for instance, an official in the service as well, it was solely because such a position was one of the obligations of his married life; he was in the service for the sake of his wife and her social position in T——, though he was in himself zealous in his duties. He was thirty-five then and was possessed of some little fortune. He showed no special ability in his department and showed no special lack of it either. He used to mix with all the best people in the province and was said to be on an excellent footing with them. Natalya Vassilyevna was deeply respected in T——; she did not, however, greatly appreciate that, accepting it as simply her due, but in her own house she was superb at entertaining guests, and Pavel Pavlovitch had been so well trained by her that he was able to behave with dignity even when entertaining the highest magnates of the province. Perhaps (it seemed to Velchaninov) he had intelligence too, but as Natalya Vassilyevna did not like her spouse to talk too much, his intelligence was not very noticeable. Perhaps he had many natural good qualities, as well as bad ones. But his good qualities were kept under a shade, as it were, and his evil propensities were almost completely stifled. Velchaninov remembered, for instance, that Pavel Pavlovitch sometimes betrayed a disposition to laugh at his neighbours, but this was sternly forbidden him. He was fond, too, at times of telling anecdotes; but a watch was kept on that weakness too: and he was only allowed to tell such as were brief and of little importance. He had a weakness for a festive glass outside the house and was even capable of drinking too much with a friend; but this failing had been severely nipped in the bud. And it is noteworthy that no outside observer would have said that Pavel Pavlovitch was a henpecked husband; Natalya Vassilyevna seemed an absolutely obedient wife, and most likely believed herself to be one. It was possible that Pavel Pavlovitch loved Natalya Vassilyevna passionately; but no one noticed it, and, indeed, it was impossible to notice it, and this reserve was probably due to her domestic discipline. Several times during his life at T—— Velchaninov had asked himself whether the husband had any suspicion at all of his wife's intrigue. Several times he questioned Natalya Vassilyevna seriously about it, and always received the answer, uttered with a certain annoyance, that her husband knew nothing and never could know anything about it and that "it was no concern of his." Another characteristic of hers was that she never laughed at Pavel Pavlovitch and did not consider him absurd or very plain and would, indeed, have taken his part very warmly if any one had dared to show him incivility. Having no children, she was naturally bound to become a society woman, but her home life, too, was essential to her. Social pleasures never had complete sway of her, and at home she was very fond of needlework and looking after the house. Pavel Pavlovitch had recalled, that night, the evenings they had spent in reading; it happened that sometimes Velchaninov read aloud and sometimes Pavel

686

Pavlovitch: to Velchaninov's surprise he read aloud excellently. Meanwhile, Natalya Vassilyevna did sewing as she listened, always calmly and serenely. They read a novel of Dickens, something from a Russian magazine, sometimes even something "serious." Natalya Vassilyevna highly appreciated Velchaninov's culture, but appreciated it in silence, as something final and established, of which there was no need to talk. Altogether, her attitude to everything intellectual and literary was rather one of indifference, as to something irrelevant though perhaps useful. Pavel Pavlovitch sometimes showed considerable warmth on the subject.

The *liaison* at T—— was broken suddenly when on Velchaninov's side it had reached its zenith—that is, almost the point of madness. In reality he was abruptly dismissed, though it was all so arranged that he went away without grasping that he had been cast off "like a worthless old shoe."

Six weeks before his departure, a young artillery officer who had just finished at the training college arrived in T—— and took to visiting the Trusotsky's. Instead of three, they were now a party of four. Natalya Vassilyevna welcomed the boy graciously but treated him as a boy. No suspicion crossed Velchaninov's mind and indeed he had no thought to spare for it, for he had just been told that separation was inevitable. One of the hundreds of reasons urged by Natalya Vassilyevna for his leaving her as soon as possible was that she believed herself to be with child: and therefore, naturally, he must disappear at once for three or four months at least, so that it would not be so easy for her husband to feel any doubt if there were any kind of gossip afterwards. It was rather a far-fetched argument. After a stormy proposition on the part of Velchaninov that she should fly with him to Paris or America, he departed alone to Petersburg, "only for a brief moment, of course," that is, for no more than three months, or nothing would have induced him to go, in spite of any reason or argument. Exactly two months later he received in Petersburg a letter from Natalya Vassilyevna asking him never to return, as she already loved another; she informed him that she had been mistaken about her condition. This information was superfluous. It was all clear to him now: he remembered the young officer. With that it was all over for good. He chanced to hear afterwards, some years later, that Bagautov had appeared on the scene and spent five whole years there. He explained the disproportionate duration of that affair partly by the fact that Natalya Vassilyevna, by now, was a good deal older, and so more constant in her attachments.

He remained sitting on his bed for nearly an hour; at last he roused himself, rang for Mavra to bring his coffee, drank it hastily, and at eleven o'clock set out to look for the Pokrovsky Hotel. In going there he had a special idea which had only come to him in the morning. He felt somewhat ashamed of his behaviour to Pavel Pavlovitch the night before and now he wanted to efface the impression.

The whole fantastic business with the door handle, the night before, he now put down to chance, to the tipsy condition of Pavel Pavlovitch, and perhaps to something else, but he did not really know, exactly, why he was going now to form new relations with the former husband, when everything had so naturally and of its own accord ended between them. Something attracted him. He had received a peculiar impression and he was attracted in consequence of it.

CHAPTER V

Liza

Pavel Pavlovitch had no idea of "giving him the slip," and goodness knows why Velchaninov had asked him the question the night before; he was, indeed, at a loss to explain it himself. At his first inquiry at a little shop near the Pokrovsky Church, he was directed to the hotel in the side street a couple of paces away. At the hotel, it was explained that M. Trusotsky was staying in the lodge close by in the courtyard, in furnished rooms at Marya Sysoevna's. Going up the narrow, wet, and very dirty stone stairs, to the second storey, where these rooms were, he suddenly heard the sound of crying. It seemed like the crying of a child of seven or eight; the sound was distressing; he heard smothered sobs which would break out and with them the stamping of feet and shouts of fury, which were smothered, too, in a hoarse falsetto voice, evidently that of a grown-up man. This man seemed to be trying to suppress the child and to be very anxious that her crying should not be heard, but was making more noise than she was. The shouts sounded pitiless, and the child seemed to be begging forgiveness. In a small passage at the top, with doors on both sides of it, Velchaninov met a tall, stout, slovenly-looking peasant woman of forty and asked for Pavel Pavlovitch. She pointed towards the door from which the sounds were coming. There was a look of some indignation on the fat, purple face of this woman.

"You see how he amuses himself!" she said gruffly and went downstairs.

Velchaninov was just about to knock at the door, but on second thoughts he walked straight in. In a small room, roughly though amply furnished with common painted furniture, stood Pavel Pavlovitch without his coat and waistcoat. With a flushed and exasperated face he was trying, by means of shouts, gesticulations, and even (Velchaninov fancied) kicks, to silence a little girl of eight, shabbily dressed in a short, black, woollen frock. She seemed to be actually in hysterics, she gasped hysterically and held out her hands to Pavel Pavlovitch as though she wanted to clutch at him, to hug him, to beseech and implore him about something. In one instant the whole scene was transformed: seeing the visitor, the child cried out and dashed away into a tiny room adjoining, and Pavel Pavlovitch, for a moment disconcerted, instantly melted into smiles, exactly as he had done the night before, when Velchaninov flung open the door upon him on the stairs.

"Alexey Ivanovitch!" he cried, in genuine surprise. "I could never have expected... but come in, come in! Here, on the sofa, or here in the armchair, while I..."

And he rushed to put on his coat, forgetting to put on his waistcoat.

"Stay as you are, don't stand on ceremony."

Velchaninov sat down in the chair.

"No, allow me to stand on ceremony; here, now I am more respectable. But why are you sitting in the corner? Sit here in the armchair, by the table. ... Well, I didn't expect you, I didn't expect you!"

He, too, sat down on the edge of a rush-bottomed chair, not beside his "unexpected" visitor, but setting his chair at an angle so as to sit more nearly facing him.

"Why didn't you expect me? Why, I told you last night that I would come at this time."

"I thought you wouldn't come; and when I reflected on all that happened yesterday, on waking this morning, I despaired of ever seeing you again."

Meanwhile Velchaninov was looking about him. The room was in disorder, the bed was not made, clothes were lying about, on the table were glasses with dregs of coffee in them, crumbs and a bottle of champagne, half full, with the cork out and a glass beside it. He stole a glance towards the next room, but there all was quiet; the child was in hiding and perfectly still.

"Surely you are not drinking that now," said Velchaninov, indicating the champagne.

"The remains..." said Pavel Pavlovitch in confusion.

"Well, you have changed!"

"It's a bad habit, come upon me all at once; yes, really, since that date. I'm not lying! I can't restrain myself. Don't be uneasy, Alexey Ivanovitch. I'm not drunk now, and I'm not going to play the fool now as I did at your flat yesterday; but I'm telling the truth, it's all since then! And if any one had told me six months ago that I should break down like this, if I'd been shown myself in the looking-glass—I shouldn't have believed it."

"You were drunk last night, then?"

"I was," Pavel Pavlovitch admitted in a low voice, looking down in embarrassment. "And you see I wasn't exactly drunk then, but I had been a little before. I want to explain, because I'm always worse a little while after. If I get ever so little tipsy, it is followed by a sort of violence and foolishness, and I feel my grief more intensely too. It's because of my grief, perhaps, I drink. Then I'm capable of playing all sorts of pranks and I push myself forward quite stupidly and insult people for nothing. I must have presented myself very strangely to you yesterday?"

"Do you mean to say you don't remember?"

"Not remember! I remember it all..."

"You see, Pavel Pavlovitch, that's just what I thought," Velchaninov said in a conciliatory voice. "What's more, I was myself rather irritable with you last night and... too impatient, readily admit it. I don't feel quite well at times, and then your unexpected arrival last night..."

"Yes, at night!" Pavel Pavlovitch shook his head, as though surprised and disapproving. "And what possessed me! Nothing would have induced me to come in to you if you had not opened the door yourself; I should have gone away from the door. I came to you a week ago, Alexey Ivanovitch, and you were not at home, but perhaps I should never have come again. I have some pride, too, Alexey Ivanovitch, although I do recognize the position I am in. We met in the street, too, and I kept thinking: 'Why, he must recognize me and yet he turns away; nine years are no joke,' and I couldn't make up my mind to come. And last night I had wandered from the Petersburg Side and I forgot the time. It all came from that" (he pointed to the bottle), "and from my feelings. It was stupid! Very! And if it had been any one but you—for you've come to see me even after what happened yesterday, for the sake of old times—I should have given up all hope of renewing our acquaintance!"

Velchaninov listened attentively. The man seemed to him to be speaking sincerely and even with a certain dignity; and yet he did not believe one word he had heard since he came into the room.

"Tell me, Pavel Pavlovitch, you are not alone here, then? Whose little girl is that I found with you just now?"

Pavel Pavlovitch was positively amazed and raised his eyebrows, but he looked frankly and pleasantly at Velchaninov.

"Whose little girl? Why, it's Liza!" he said, with an affable smile.

"What Liza?" muttered Velchaninov, with a sort of inward tremor. The shock was too sudden. When he came in and saw Liza, just before, he was surprised, but had absolutely no presentiment of the truth, and thought nothing particular about her.

"Yes, our Liza, our daughter Liza!" Pavel Pavlovitch smiled.

"Your daughter? Do you mean that you and Natalya ... Natalya Vassilyevna had children?" Velchaninov asked timidly and mistrustfully, in a very low voice.

"Why, of course! But there, upon my word, how should you have heard of it? What am I thinking about! It was after you went away, God blessed us with her!"

Pavel Pavlovitch positively jumped up from his chair in some agitation, though it seemed agreeable too.

"I heard nothing about it," said Velchaninov, and he turned pale.

"To be sure, to be sure; from whom could you have heard it?" said Pavel Pavlovitch, in a voice weak with emotion. "My poor wife and I had lost all hope, as no doubt you remember, and suddenly God sent us this blessing, and what it meant to me—He only knows! Just a year after you went away, I believe. No, not a year, not nearly a year. Wait a bit; why, you left us, if my memory does not deceive me, in October or November, I believe."

"I left T—— at the beginning of September, the twelfth of September; I remember it very well."

"In September, was it? H'm!... what was I thinking about?" cried Pavel Pavlovitch, much surprised. "Well, if that's so, let me see: you went away on the twelfth of September, and Liza was born on the eighth of May, so—September—October—November—December—January—February—March—April—a little over eight months! And if you only knew how my poor wife..."

"Show me... call her..." Velchaninov faltered in a breaking voice.

"Certainly!" said Pavel Pavlovitch fussily, at once breaking off what he was saying, as though it were of no consequence. "Directly, directly, I'll introduce her!"

And he went hurriedly into the other room to Liza.

Fully three or perhaps four minutes passed; there was a hurried, rapid whispering in the room, and he just caught the sound of Liza's voice. "She's begging not to be brought in," thought Velchaninov. At last they

691

came out.

"You see, she's all confusion," said Pavel Pavlovitch; "she's so shy, and so proud... the image of my poor wife!"

Liza came in, looking down and no longer tearful; her father was holding her hand. She was a tall, slim, very pretty little girl. She raised her big blue eyes to glance with curiosity at the visitor, looked at him sullenly, and dropped them again at once. Her eyes were full of that gravity one sees in children, when they are left alone with a stranger and, retreating into a corner, look out solemnly and mistrustfully at the unfamiliar visitor; but she had, perhaps, some other thought, by no means childish, in her mind—so Velchaninov fancied.

Her father led her straight up to him.

"This is an uncle mother used to know long ago; he was our friend. Don't be shy, hold out your hand."

The child bent forward a little, and timidly held out her hand.

"Natalya Vassilyevna would not have her trained to curtsey, but taught her to make a little bow, and hold out her hand in the English fashion," he added by way of explanation to Velchaninov, watching him intently.

Velchaninov knew that he was being watched, but had quite ceased to trouble himself to conceal his emotion; he sat perfectly still in his chair, held Liza's hand in his and gazed at the child. But Liza was in great anxiety about something, and, forgetting her hand in the visitor's hand, she kept her eyes fixed on her father. She listened apprehensively to all that he said. Velchaninov recognized those big blue eyes at once, but what struck him most of all was the wonderful soft whiteness of her face and the colour of her hair; these characteristics were so marked and so significant. Her features and the lines of the lips reminded him vividly of Natalya Vassilyevna. Meanwhile, Pavel Pavlovitch had for some time been telling him something, speaking, it seemed, with very great warmth and feeling, but Velchaninov did not hear him. He only caught the last sentence—

"... so that you can't imagine our joy at this gift from the Lord, Alexey Ivanovitch! She became everything to me as soon as she came to us, so that I used to think that even if my tranquil happiness should, by God's will, be at an end, Liza would always be left me; that I reckoned upon for certain!"

"And Natalya Vassilyevna?" Velchaninov queried.

"Natalya Vassilyevna?" said Pavel Pavlovitch affectedly. "You know her way, you remember that she never cared to say a great deal, but the way she said good-bye to her on her deathbed... everything came out then! I said just now 'on her deathbed,' but yet only a day before her death she was upset and angry, said that they were trying to cure her with drugs, that there was nothing wrong with her but an ordinary fever, and that neither of our doctors understood it, and that as soon as Koch came back (do you remember our old friend the army doctor?) she would be up again in a fortnight! But there! five hours before her decease she remembered that in three weeks' time we must visit her aunt, Liza's godmother, on her name-day..."

Velchaninov suddenly got up from his chair, still holding the child's hand. Among other things it struck him that there was something reproachful in the intense look the child kept fixed upon her father.

"She's not ill?" he asked hurriedly and somewhat strangely.

"I don't think so, but... our circumstances are here so..." said Pavel Pavlovitch, with mournful solicitude. "She's a strange child and nervous at all times; after her mother's death she was ill for a fortnight, hysterical. Why, what a weeping and wailing we had just before you came in... do you hear, Liza, do you hear? And what was it all about? All because I go out and leave her; she says it shows I don't love her any more as I used to when mother was alive—that's her complaint against me. And a child like that who ought to be playing with her toys, instead of fretting over a fantastic notion like that. Though here she has no one to play with."

"Why, how... you're surely not alone here?"

"Quite alone; the servant only comes in once a day."

"And you go out and leave her like this alone?"

"What else could I do? And when I went out yesterday I locked her in, into that little room there, that's what the tears have been about to-day. But what else could I do? Judge for yourself: the day before yesterday she went down when I was out, and a boy threw a stone at her in the yard and hit her on the head. Or else she begins crying and runs around to all the lodgers in the yard, asking where I've gone. And that's not nice, you know. And I'm a nice one, too; I go out for an hour and come back next morning; that's what happened yesterday. It was a nice thing, too, that while I was away the landlady let her out, sent for a locksmith to break the lock—such a disgrace—I literally feel myself a monster. All mental aberration, all mental aberration. ..."

"Father!" the child said timidly and uneasily.

"There you are, at it again! You're at the same thing again. What did I tell you just now?"

"I won't, I won't!" Liza repeated in terror, hurriedly clasping her hands before him.

"You can't go on like this in these surroundings," Velchaninov said impatiently, in a voice of authority. "Why, you... why, you're a man of property; how is it you're living like this—in this lodge and in such surroundings?"

"In the lodge? But, you see, we may be going away in a week's time, and we've wasted a great deal of money already, even though I have property. ..."

"Come, that's enough, that's enough." Velchaninov cut him short with increasing impatience, as it were expressing plainly: "There's no need to talk. I know all that you have to say, and I know with what feelings you are speaking."

"Listen, I'll make a suggestion. You said just now that you'll be staying a week, maybe possibly even a fortnight. I know a household here, that is, a family where I'm quite at home—have known them twenty years. The father, Alexandr Pavlovitch Pogoryeltsev, is a Privy Councillor; he might be of use to you in your business. They are at their summer villa now. They've got a splendid villa. Klavdia Petrovna is like a sister to me or a mother. They have eight children. Let me take Liza to them at once... that we may lose no time. They will be delighted to take her in for the whole time you are here, and will treat her like their own child, their own child!"

He was terribly impatient and did not disguise it.

"That's scarcely possible," said Pavel Pavlovitch, with a grimace, looking, so Velchaninov fancied, slily in his face.

"Why, why impossible?"

"Why, how can I let the child go so suddenly—with such a real friend as you, of course—I don't mean, but into a house of strangers, and of such high rank, where I don't know how she'd be received either?"

"But I've told you that I'm like one of the family!" cried Velchaninov, almost wrathfully. "Klavdia Petrovna will be delighted to take her at a wor—from me—as though it were my child. Damn it all! Why, you know yourself that you only say all this for the sake of saying something ... there's nothing to discuss!"

He positively stamped his foot.

"I only mean, won't it seem strange? I should have to go and see her once or twice anyway, or she would be left without a father! He—he! ... and in such a grand household."

"But it's the simplest household, not 'grand' at all!" shouted Velchaninov. "I tell you there are a lot of children. She'll revive there, that's the whole object. ... And I'll introduce you myself to-morrow, if you like. And of course you would have to go to thank them; we'll drive over every day, if you like."

"It's all so——"

"Nonsense! And, what's more, you know that yourself! Listen. Come to me this evening, and stay the night, perhaps, and we'll set off early in the morning so as to get there at twelve."

"My benefactor! And even to stay the night with you..." Pavel Pavlovitch agreed suddenly in a tone of fervent feeling. "You are doing me a charity literally. ... Where is their villa?"

"Their villa is in Lyesnoe."

"Only, I say, what about her dress? For, you know, in such a distinguished household and in their summer villa, too, you know yourself... a father's heart..."

"What about her dress? She's in mourning. She couldn't be dressed differently, could she? It's the most suitable one could possibly imagine! The only thing is she ought to have clean linen... a clean tucker..."

Her tucker and what showed of her underlinen were, in fact, very dirty.

"She must change her things at once," said Pavel Pavlovitch fussily, "and we'll get together the rest of what she needs in the way of underclothes; Marya Sysoevna has got them in the wash."

"Then you should tell them to fetch a carriage," Velchaninov interposed; "and make haste if you can."

But a difficulty presented itself: Liza resolutely opposed it; she had been listening all the time in terror, and, if Velchaninov had had time to look at her attentively while he was persuading Pavel Pavlovitch, he would have seen a look of utter despair upon her little face.

"I am not going," she said firmly, in a low voice.

"There, there! You see, she's her mother over again."

"I'm not my mother over again, I'm not my mother over again!" cried Liza in despair, wringing her little hands, and as it were trying to defend herself before her father from the awful reproach of being like her mother. "Father, father, if you leave me..."

She suddenly turned on Velchaninov, who was in dismay.

"If you take me I'll..."

But before she had time to say more, Pavel Pavlovitch clutched her by the arm and with undisguised exasperation dragged her almost by the collar into the little room. Whispering followed for some minutes; there was the sound of suppressed crying. Velchaninov was on the point of going in himself, but Pavel Pavlovitch came out and with a wry smile announced that she was coming directly. Velchaninov tried not to look at him and kept his eyes turned away.

Marya Sysoevna appeared. She was the same peasant woman that he had met just before in the passage; she began packing the linen she had brought with her in a pretty little bag belonging to Liza.

"Are you taking the little girl away then, sir?" she asked, addressing Velchaninov. "Have you a family, then? It's a good deed, sir: she's a quiet child; you are taking her from a perfect Bedlam."

"Come, come, Marya Sysoevna!" muttered Pavel Pavlovitch.

"Marya Sysoevna, indeed! That's my name, right enough. It is a Bedlam here, isn't it? Is it the proper thing for a child that can understand to see such disgraceful goings on? They've fetched you a carriage, sir— to Lyesnoe, is it?"

"Yes, yes."

"Well, it's a blessing you came!"

Liza came out pale and, looking down, took her bag. Not one glance in Velchaninov's direction; she restrained herself and did not, as before, rush to embrace her father, even at parting; evidently she was unwilling to look at him either. Her father kissed her decorously on the head and patted it; her lips twitched as he did so and her little chin quivered, but still she did not raise her eyes to her father. Pavel Pavlovitch looked pale, and his hands were trembling—Velchaninov noticed that distinctly, though he was doing his utmost not to look at him. The one thing he longed for was to get away as quickly as possible.

"After all, it's not my fault," he thought. "It was bound to be so."

They went downstairs; there Marya Sysoevna kissed Liza good-bye, and only when she was sitting on the carriage Liza lifted her eyes to her father, flung up her hands and screamed; another minute and she would have flung herself out of the carriage to him, but the horses had started.

CHAPTER VI

A New Fancy of An Idle Man

"Are you feeling ill?" asked Velchaninov in alarm. "I will tell them to stop, I'll tell them to bring water. ..."

She turned her eyes upon him and looked at him passionately, reproachfully.

"Where are you taking me?" she asked sharply and abruptly.

"It's a very nice family, Liza. They're in a delightful summer villa now; there are a lot of children; they'll love you; they are kind. Don't be angry with me, Liza; I only wish for your good."

How strange it would have seemed to all who knew him if any one could have seen him at that moment.

"How—how—how... how horrid you are!" said Liza, choking with stifled tears, glaring at him with her beautiful eyes full of anger.

"Liza, I..."

"You are wicked, wicked, wicked, wicked!"

She wrung her hands. Velchaninov was completely at a loss.

"Liza, darling, if you knew how despairing you make me!"

"Is it true that he will come to-morrow? Is it true?" she asked peremptorily.

"Yes, yes, I'll bring him myself; I'll take him with me and bring him."

"He'll deceive me," she whispered, looking down.

"Doesn't he love you, Liza?"

"He doesn't love me."

"Does he ill-treat you? Does he?"

Liza looked at him gloomily and was mute. She turned away from him again and sat with her eyes obstinately cast down. He began trying to coax her; he talked to her warmly, he was in a perfect fever. Liza listened with mistrust and hostility, but she did listen. Her attention delighted him extremely; he even began explaining to her what was meant by a man's drinking. He told her that he loved her himself and would look after her father. Liza lifted her eyes at last and looked at him intently. He began telling her how he used to know her mother and he saw that what he told her interested her. Little by little she began answering his questions, though cautiously and in monosyllables. She still stubbornly refused to answer his leading questions; she remained obstinately silent about everything to do with her relations with her father in the past. As he talked to her, Velchaninov took her hand in his as before and held it; she did not pull it away. The child was not silent all the time, however; she let out in her confused answers that she loved her father more than her mother, because he had always been fonder of her, and her mother had not cared so much for her, but that when her mother was dying she had kissed her and cried a great deal when every one had gone out of the room and they were left alone ... and that now she loved her more than any one, more than any one, more than any one in the world, and every night she loved her more than any one. But the child was certainly proud. Realizing that she had spoken too freely, she suddenly shrank into herself again and glanced with positive hatred at Velchaninov, who had led her into saying so much. Towards the end of the journey her hysterical agitation almost passed off, but she sank into brooding and had the look of a wild creature, sullen and gloomily, resolutely stubborn. The fact that she was being taken to a strange family, in which she had never been before, seemed for the time being not to trouble her much. What tormented her was something else.

Velchaninov saw that; he guessed that she was ashamed before *him*, that she was ashamed of her father's having so easily let her go with him, of his having, as it were, flung her into his keeping.

"She is ill," he thought, "perhaps very ill; she's been worried to death. ... Oh, the drunken, abject beast! I understand him now!"

He urged on the driver; he rested his hopes on the country, the fresh air, the garden, the children, and the new, unfamiliar life, and then, later on ... But of what would come afterwards he had no doubts at all; of the future he had the fullest, brightest hopes. One thing only he knew for certain: that he had never before felt what he was experiencing now and that it would never leave him all his life.

"Here was an object, here was life!" he thought triumphantly.

A great many thoughts flashed upon his mind, but he did not dwell upon them and obstinately put away details; so long as he avoided details it all seemed clear and unassailable. His plan of action was self-evident.

"It will be possible to work upon that wretch," he mused, "by our united forces, and he will leave Liza in Petersburg at the Pogoryeltsevs', though at first only temporarily, for a certain time, and will go away alone, and Liza will be left to me; that's the whole thing. What more do I want? And ... of course, he wants that himself; or else why does he torment her?"

At last they arrived. The Pogoryeltsevs' country home really was a charming place; they were met first of all by a noisy crowd of children, flocking out into the porch. Velchaninov had not been there for a long time, and the children were in a frenzy of delight; they were fond of him. The elder ones shouted to him at once, before he got out of the carriage—

"And how about the case, how is your case getting on?"

The cry was caught up even by the smallest, and they shrieked it mirthfully in imitation of their elders. They used to tease him about the lawsuit. But, seeing Liza, they surrounded her at once and began scrutinizing her with intent, dumb, childish curiosity. Klavdia Petrovna came out, followed by her husband. She and her husband, too, began with a laughing question about the lawsuit.

Klavdia Petrovna was a lady about thirty-seven, a plump and still good-looking brunette, with a fresh, rosy face. Her husband was fifty-five, a shrewd and clever man, but above everything good-natured. Their house was in the fullest sense of the word "a home" to Velchaninov, as he had said himself. But underlying this was the special circumstance that, twenty years before, Klavdia Petrovna had been on the point of marrying Velchaninov, then a student, hardly more than a boy. It was a case of first love, ardent, ridiculous, and splendid. It had ended, however, in her marrying Pogoryeltsev. Five years later they had met again, and it had all ended in a quiet, serene friendship. A certain warmth, a peculiar glow suffusing their relations, had remained for ever. All was pure and irreproachable in Velchaninov's memories of this friendship, and it was the dearer to him for being perhaps the solitary case in which this was so. Here in this family he was simple, unaffected, and kind; he used to fondle the children, he admitted all his failings, confessed his shortcomings, and never gave himself airs. He swore more than once to the Pogoryeltsevs that he should before long give up the world, come and live with them, and never leave them again. In his heart he thought of this project seriously.

He told them all that was necessary about Liza in some detail; but a mere request from him was enough, without any special explanations. Klavdia Petrovna kissed the "orphan" and promised for her part to do everything. The children took possession of Liza and carried her off to play in the garden.

After half-an-hour of lively conversation Velchaninov got up and began saying good-bye. He was so impatient that every one noticed it. They were all astonished; he had not been to see them for three weeks and now he was going in half-an-hour. He laughed and pledged himself to come next day. They remarked that he seemed to be in a state of great excitement; he suddenly took Klavdia Petrovna's hand and, on the pretext of having forgotten to tell her something important, drew her aside into another room.

"Do you remember what I told you—you alone—what even your husband does not know—of my year at T——?"

"I remember perfectly; you often talked of it."

"It was not talking, it was a confession, to you alone, to you alone! I never told you the surname of that woman; she was the wife of this man Trusotsky. She is dead, and Liza is her daughter—my daughter!"

"Is it certain? You are not mistaken?" Klavdia Petrovna asked with some excitement.

"It's perfectly certain, perfectly certain; I am not mistaken!" Velchaninov pronounced ecstatically.

And as briefly as he could, in haste and great excitement, he told her everything. Klavdia Petrovna already knew the whole story, but not the lady's name.

Velchaninov had always been so alarmed at the very idea that any one who knew him might ever meet Madame Trusotsky and think that *he* could *so* have loved that woman, that he had not till that day dared to reveal "that woman's" name even to Klavdia Petrovna, his one friend.

"And the father knows nothing?" asked Klavdia Petrovna, when she had heard his story.

"Y-yes, he does know. ... It worries me that I've not got to the bottom of it yet!" Velchaninov went on eagerly. "He knows, he knows; I noticed it to-day and yesterday. But I must know how much he knows. That's why I'm in a hurry now. He is coming to me this evening. I can't imagine, though, how he can have found out—found out *everything*, I mean. He knows about Bagautov, there's no doubt of that. But about me? You know how clever women are in reassuring their husbands in such cases! If an angel came down from heaven—the husband would not believe him, but he would believe his wife! Don't shake your head and don't blame me; I blame myself and have blamed myself, for the whole affair, long ago, long ago! ... You see, I was so certain he knew when I was there this morning that I compromised myself before him. Would you believe it, I felt so wretched and ashamed at having met him so rudely yesterday (I will tell you all about it fully afterwards). He came to me yesterday from an irresistible, malicious desire to let me know that he knew of the wrong done him, and knew who had done it; that was the whole reason of his stupid visit when he was drunk. But that was so natural on his part! He simply came to work off his resentment! I was altogether too hasty with him this morning and yesterday! Careless—stupid! I betrayed myself to him. Why did he turn up at a moment when I was upset? I tell you he's even been tormenting Liza, tormenting the child, and probably that, too, was to work off his resentment—to vent his malice if only on the child! Yes, he is spiteful—insignificant as he is, yet he is spiteful; very much so, indeed. In himself he is no more than a buffoon, though, God knows, in old days he seemed to be a very decent fellow within his limits—it's so natural that he should be going to the dogs! One must look at it from a Christian point of view! And you know, my dear, my best of friends, I want to be utterly different to him; I want to be kind to him. That would be really a 'good deed' on my part. For, you know, after all, I have wronged him! Listen, you know there's something else I must tell you. On one occasion in T—— I was in want of four thousand roubles, and he lent me the money on the spot, with no security, and showed genuine pleasure at being of use to me; and, do you know, I took it then, I took it from his hands. I borrowed money from him, do you understand, as a friend!"

"Only be more careful," Klavdia Petrovna anxiously observed, in response to all this. "And what a state of ecstasy you're in; I feel uneasy about you! Of course, Liza will be like a child of my own now. But there's so much, so much still to be settled! The great thing is that you must be more circumspect; you absolutely must be more circumspect when you are happy or so ecstatic; you're too generous when you are happy," she added, with a smile.

They all came out to see Velchaninov off. The children, who had been playing with Liza in the garden, brought her with them. They seemed to look at her with more amazement now than at first. Liza was overcome with shyness when, at parting, Velchaninov kissed her before them all, and warmly repeated his promise to come next day with her father. To the last minute she was silent and did not look at him, but then suddenly she clutched at his arm and drew him aside, fixing an imploring look on him; she wanted to tell him something. He promptly took her away into another room.

"What is it, Liza?" he asked her tenderly and reassuringly; but she, still looking about her apprehensively, drew him into the furthest corner; she wanted to be hidden from them all.

"What is it, Liza? What's the matter?"

She was dumb, she could not bring herself to speak; she gazed fixedly with her blue eyes into his face, and every feature of her little face expressed nothing but frantic terror.

"He'll ... hang himself!" she whispered, as though in delirium.

"Who will hang himself?" asked Velchaninov in dismay.

"He, he! He tried to hang himself with a cord in the night!" the child said breathlessly. "I saw him! He tried to hang himself with a cord, he told me so, he told me so! He meant to before, he always meant to ... I saw him in the night. ..."

"Impossible," whispered Velchaninov in amazement.

She suddenly fell to kissing his hands; she cried, almost choking with sobs, begged and besought him, but he could making nothing of her hysterical whisperings. And the tortured face of that terror-stricken child who looked to him as her last hope remained printed on his memory for ever, haunting him awake and visiting his dreams.

"And can she, can she really love him so much?" he thought, jealously and enviously, as with feverish impatience he returned to town. "She had told him herself that morning that she loved her mother more ...

701

perhaps she hated him and did not love him at all! ... And what did that mean: he will hang himself? What did she mean by that? would the fool hang himself? ... He must find out, he must certainly find out! He must get to the bottom of it as soon as possible—once and for all."

Chapter VII

The Husband and the Lover Kiss Each Other

He was in terrible haste "to find out."

"This morning I was so overwhelmed. This morning I hadn't the time to realize the position," he thought, recalling his first sight of Liza, "but now I must find out." To find out more quickly he was on the point of telling the driver to take him to Trusotsky's lodging, but on second thoughts decided: "No, better let him come to me, and meanwhile I'll make haste and get this accursed legal business off my hands."

He set to work feverishly; but this time he was conscious himself that he was very absent-minded and that he was hardly capable that day of attending to business. At five o'clock, when he went out to dinner, he was struck for the first time by an absurd idea: that perhaps he really was only hindering the progress of his case, by meddling in the lawsuit himself, fussing about in the law courts and hunting up his lawyer, who was already beginning to hide from him. He laughed gaily at his supposition. "If this idea had occurred to me yesterday, I should have been dreadfully distressed," he added, even more gaily. In spite of his gaiety, he grew more and more preoccupied and more and more impatient. He fell to musing at last; and though his restless thought clutched at one thing after another, he could arrive at nothing that would satisfy him.

"I must have that man!" he decided finally. "I must solve the riddle of that man, and then make up my mind. It's—a duel!"

Returning home at seven o'clock, he did not find Pavel Pavlovitch and was extremely surprised, then extremely wrathful, and later still extremely depressed; finally he began to be actually frightened.

"God knows, God knows how it will end!" he repeated, as he walked about the room or stretched himself on the sofa, continually looking at his watch. At last, about nine o'clock, Pavel Pavlovitch appeared. "If the fellow were trying to dupe me, he couldn't have caught me at a more favourable time—I feel so unhinged at this moment," he thought, his confidence completely restored and his spirits rising again.

To his brisk and cheerful inquiry why he was so late coming, Pavel Pavlovitch gave a wry smile, seated himself with a free and easy air, very different from his manner the night before, and carelessly threw his hat with the crape on it on another chair close by. Velchaninov at once noticed this free and easy manner and made a note of it.

Calmly, without wasting words, with none of the excitement he had shown in the morning, he told him, as though giving a report, how he had taken Liza, how kindly she had been received, how good it would be for her, and little by little, as though forgetting Liza, he imperceptibly turned the conversation entirely on the Pogoryeltsevs—what charming people they were, how long he had known them, what a splendid and influential man Pogoryeltsev was, and so on. Pavel Pavlovitch listened inattentively and from time to time glanced up from under his brows at the speaker with an ill humoured and crafty sneer.

"You're an impulsive person," he muttered, with a particularly disagreeable smile.

"You're rather ill-humoured to-day, though," Velchaninov observed with vexation.

"And why shouldn't I be ill-humoured, like every one else!" Pavel Pavlovitch cried out suddenly, just as though he had only been waiting for that to bounce out.

"You're at liberty to please yourself," laughed Velchaninov. "I wondered if anything had happened to you."

"So it has!" the other exclaimed, as though boasting that something had happened.

"What is it?"

Pavel Pavlovitch delayed answering for a little.

"Why, our Stepan Mihalovitch has played me a trick ... Bagautov, that elegant young Petersburg gentleman of the best society."

"Was he not at home again?"

"No, this time he was at home. For the first time I was admitted, and I gazed upon his face ... only he was dead!"

"Wha—at! Bagautov is dead?" Velchaninov was awfully surprised, though there was no apparent reason for his being so surprised.

"Yes. For six years our true and constant friend! Only yesterday, almost at midday, he died, and I knew nothing of it! I was going maybe that very minute to inquire after his health. To-morrow there will be the service and the funeral, he's already in his coffin. The coffin is lined with crimson-coloured velvet trimmed with gold ... he died of brain fever. I was admitted—I was admitted to gaze upon his face! I told them at the door

703

that I was an intimate friend, that was why I was admitted. What's one to think of the way he's treated me now, my true and constant friend for six long years—I ask you that? Perhaps it was only on his account I came to Petersburg!"

"But what are you angry with him for?" laughed Velchaninov. "Why, he did not die on purpose!"

"But I speak with my heart full of regret; he was a precious friend; this was what he meant to me."

And all at once, quite unexpectedly, Pavel Pavlovitch put up his two fingers like two horns on his bald forehead and went off into a low, prolonged chuckle. He sat like that, chuckling, for a full half-minute, staring into Velchaninov's face in a frenzy of malignant insolence. The latter was petrified as though at the sight of some ghost. But his stupefaction lasted but one brief instant; a sarcastic and insolently composed smile came slowly upon his lips.

"What's the meaning of that?" he asked, carelessly drawling the words.

"The meaning of it is—horns!" Pavel Pavlovitch rapped out, taking away his fingers from his forehead at last.

"That is ... your horns?"

"My own, generously bestowed!" Pavel Pavlovitch said with a very nasty grimace. Both were silent.

"You're a plucky fellow, I must say!" Velchaninov pronounced.

"Because I showed you my decorations? Do you know, Alexey Ivanovitch, you'd better offer me something! You know I entertained you every blessed day for a whole year at T—— Send for just one bottle, my throat is dry."

"With pleasure; you should have said so before. What will you have?"

"Why *you?* Say *we;* we'll drink together, won't we?" said Pavel Pavlovitch, gazing into his face with a challenging, but at the same time strangely uneasy look.

"Champagne?"

"What else? It's not the time for vodka yet. ..."

Velchaninov got up deliberately, rang for Mavra, and gave instructions.

"To the joy of our delightful meeting after nine years' absence," said Pavel Pavlovitch, with a quite superfluous and inappropriate snigger. "Now you, and you only, are the one friend left me! Stepan Mihalovitch Bagautov is no more! As the poet says—

"Great Patroclus is no more,
Vile Thersites still lives on"

And at the word "Thersites" he poked himself in the chest.

"You'd better hurry up and speak out, you swine; I don't like hints," Velchaninov thought to himself. His anger was rising and for a long time he had hardly been able to restrain himself.

"Tell me," he said in a tone of vexation, "since you accuse Stepan Mihalovitch" (he could not call him simply Bagautov now), "I should have thought you would have been glad that the man who has wronged you is dead; why are you angry about it?"

"Glad? Why glad?"

"I imagine those must be your feelings."

"He—he! You are quite mistaken about my feelings on that subject; as some wise man has said, 'A dead enemy is good, but a living one is better,' he—he!"

"But you saw him living every day for five years, I believe; you had time to get tired of the sight of him," Velchaninov observed, with spiteful impertinence.

"But you don't suppose I knew then ... you don't suppose I knew?" Pavel Pavlovitch blurted out suddenly, just as though he had bounced out from behind a corner again, and as though he were delighted to be asked a question he had long been waiting for.

"What do you take me for, then, Alexey Ivanovitch?"

And there was a gleam in his face of something quite new and unexpected, which seemed to transform his countenance, till then full of spite and abjectly grimacing.

"Is it possible you didn't know, then!" said Velchaninov, disconcerted and completely taken by surprise.

"Is it possible I knew? Is it possible I knew? Oh, you race of Jupiters! For you a man's no more than a dog, and you judge all according to your own petty nature. I tell you that! You can swallow that!" And he banged frantically on the table with his fist, but was at once dismayed at the bang and began to look apprehensive.

Velchaninov assumed an air of dignity.

"Listen, Pavel Pavlovitch. It's absolutely nothing to me, as you can see for yourself, whether you knew, or whether you didn't. If you didn't know, it's to your credit in any case, though ... I can't understand, however, why you've chosen to make this confidence to me?"...

"I didn't mean you ... don't be angry. I didn't mean you ..." muttered Pavel Pavlovitch, looking down.

Mavra came in with the champagne.

"Here it is!" cried Pavel Pavlovitch, evidently relieved at her entrance.

"Glasses, my good girl, glasses; splendid! We ask for nothing more, my dear. And uncorked already! Honour and glory to you, charming creature! Come, you can go!"

And with renewed courage he looked impudently at Velchaninov again.

"Confess," he chuckled suddenly, "that all this is very interesting and by no means 'absolutely nothing to you,' as you were pleased to declare; so much so that you would be disappointed if I were to get up this minute and go away without explaining myself."

"I really shouldn't be disappointed."

"Oh, that's a lie!" was what Pavel Pavlovitch's smile expressed.

"Well, let's come to business!" And he filled his glass.

"Let's drink," he pronounced, taking up the glass, "to the health of our friend departed in God, Stepan Mihalovitch."

He raised his glass, and drank it.

"I'm not going to drink such a health," said Velchaninov, putting down his glass.

"Why not? It's a pleasant toast."

"I say, weren't you drunk when you came in just now?"

"I had had a little. But why?"

"Nothing particular, but I thought last night, and this morning still more, that you were genuinely grieved at the loss of Natalya Vassilyevna."

"And who told you that I'm not genuinely grieved at the loss of her now?" Pavel Pavlovitch bounced out again, exactly as though he were worked by springs.

"And I didn't mean that; but you must admit that you may be mistaken about Stepan Mihalovitch, and it is—a grave matter."

Pavel Pavlovitch smiled craftily and winked.

"And wouldn't you like to know how I found out about Stepan Mihalovitch?"

Velchaninov flushed.

"I tell you again that it's nothing to me." "Hadn't I better chuck him out this minute, bottle and all?" he thought furiously, and he flushed a deep crimson.

"That's all right!" said Pavel Pavlovitch, as though trying to encourage him, and he poured himself out another glass.

"I will explain at once how I found out all about it, and so gratify your ardent desire ... for you are an ardent man, Alexey Ivanovitch, a terribly ardent man! He—he! Only give me a cigarette, for ever since March...!"

"Here's a cigarette for you."

"I have gone to the dogs since March, Alexey Ivanovitch, and I'll tell you how it's all happened—listen. Consumption, as you know yourself, my best of friends," he grew more and more familiat, "is a curious disease. Consumptives have scarcely a suspicion they may be dying tomorrow and then all in a minute they're dead. I tell you that only five hours before Natalya Vassilyevna was planning a visit a fortnight later to her aunt, thirty miles away. You are aware, too, probably, of the practice, or rather bad habit—common in many ladies and very likely in their admirers as well—of preserving all sorts of rubbish in the way of love-letters. ... It would be much safer to put them in the stove, wouldn't it? No, every scrap of paper is carefully stored away in a box or a *nécessaire*; even docketed in years, and in months, and in series. Whether it's a comfort to them—I don't know; but, no doubt, it's for the sake of agreeable memories. Since only five hours before her end she was arranging to go to visit her aunt, Natalya Vassilyevna naturally had no thought of death to the very last hour. She was still expecting Koch. So it happened that Natalya Vassilyevna died, and an ebony box inlaid with mother-of-pearl and silver was left standing on her bureau. And it was a charming box, with a lock and key, an heirloom that had come to her from her grandmother. In that box everything lay revealed, absolutely everything; all, without exception, with the year and the day, everything for the last twenty years. And as Stepan Mihalovitch had a distinct literary bent (he actually sent a passionate love story to a journal), his contributions ran into the hundreds—to be sure they were spread out over five years. Some specimens had been annotated in Natalya Vassilyevna's own handwriting. A pleasant surprise for a husband. What do you think of it?"

Velchaninov reflected hurriedly and felt sure that he had never sent Natalya Vassilyevna a single letter, not a note of any kind. Though he had written twice from Petersburg, his letters, in accordance with a compact between them, had been addressed to the husband as well as the wife. To Natalya Vassilyevna's last letter, in which he had decreed his banishment, he had never answered.

When he had ended his story, Pavel Pavlovitch paused for a full minute with an importunate and expectant smile.

"Why do you give me no answer to my little question?" he brought out at last, with evident anxiety.

"What little question?"

"Why, the pleasant surprise for a husband on opening that box."

"Oh! what is it to do with me!" exclaimed Velchaninov, with a gesture of disgust, and he got up and walked about the room.

"And I bet you're thinking now, you're a swine to have shown me your shame. He—he! You're a very fastidious man ... you are."

"I think nothing about it. On the contrary, you are so much exasperated by the death of the man who wronged you and you've drunk so much wine, too. I see nothing extraordinary in all this; I quite understand why you wanted Bagautov alive, and I am ready to respect your annoyance: but——"

"And what did I want Bagautov for, do you suppose?"

"That's your affair."

"I bet that you were thinking of a duel!"

"Damn it all!" cried Velchaninov, growing more and more unable to control himself. "I imagine that a decent man ... in such cases does not stoop to ridiculous babble, to stupid antics, to ludicrous complaints, and disgusting insinuations, by which he only degrades himself more, but acts openly, directly, straightforwardly—like a decent man?"

"He—he! but perhaps I'm not a decent man!"

"That's your affair again ... but in that case, what the devil did you want Bagautov alive for?"

"Why, if only to see a friend. We'd have had a bottle and drunk together."

"He wouldn't have drunk with you."

"Why not? *Noblesse oblige!* Here, you're drinking with me; in what way is he better than you?"

"I haven't drunk with you."

"Why such pride all of a sudden?"

Velchaninov suddenly broke into a nervous and irritable laugh.

"Damnation! Why, you are really a 'predatory type'! I thought you were only 'the eternal husband,' and nothing more!"

"What do you mean by 'the eternal husband,' what's that?" Pavel Pavlovitch suddenly pricked up his ears.

"Oh, it's one type of husband ... it would be a long story. You'd better clear out, it's time you were gone; I'm sick of you."

"And predatory? You said 'predatory'!"

"I said you were a 'predatory type'; I said it ironically."

"What do you mean by a 'predatory type'? Tell me, please, Alexey Ivanovitch, for God's sake, or for Christ's sake!"

"Come, that's enough, that's enough!" cried Velchaninov, suddenly growing horribly angry. "It's time you were off. Get along."

"No, it's not enough!" Pavel Pavlovitch flared up; "even though you are sick of me it's not enough, for we must drink together and clink glasses! Let us drink together, and then I'll go, but as it is it's not enough!"

708

"Pavel Pavlovitch! Will you go to the devil to-day or will you not?"

"I can go to the devil, but first we'll drink! You said that you would not drink *with me*; but I *want* you to drink with me!"

There was no grimacing, no sniggering about him now. He seemed all at once entirely transformed, and to have become in his whole tone and appearance so completely the opposite of the Pavel Pavlovitch of the moment before, that Velchaninov was quite taken aback.

"Do let us drink, Alexey Ivanovitch! Don't refuse me," Pavel Pavlovitch persisted, gripping his hand tightly and looking strangely into his eyes.

Clearly there was more at stake than merely drinking.

"Yes, if you like," muttered Velchaninov; "but how can we? ... There's nothing left but the dregs. ..."

"There are just two glasses left, it's thick, but we'll drink it and clink glasses! Here, take your glass."

They clinked their glasses and emptied them.

"Since that's so—since that's so ... Ach!"

Pavel Pavlovitch clutched his forehead in his hand and remained for some moments in that position. Velchaninov had a feeling every moment that he would speak out and utter the very *final* word. But Pavel Pavlovitch uttered nothing; he simply gazed at him and smiled again the same sly, knowing smile.

"What do you want of me, you drunken fellow! You're playing the fool with me!" Velchaninov shouted furiously, stamping.

"Don't shout, don't shout; what is there to shout for?" cried Pavel Pavlovitch, gesticulating hurriedly. "I'm not playing the fool, I'm not playing the fool! Do you know what you are to me now?"

And he suddenly seized his hand and kissed it. Velchaninov was utterly taken aback.

"That's what you mean to me now! And now—and now I'll go to the devil as soon as you please!"

"Wait a minute, stay!" cried Velchaninov, recovering himself. "I forgot to tell you. ..."

Pavel Pavlovitch turned back from the door.

"You see," muttered Velchaninov, very quickly, flushing crimson and looking away, "you must be at the Pogoryeltsevs' to-morrow ... to make their acquaintance and thank them; you must ..."

"Certainly, I must. I understand that, of course!" Pavel Pavlovitch acquiesced with the utmost readiness, waving his hand quickly as though to protest that there was no need to remind him.

"And besides, Liza is very anxious to see you. I promised her——"

"Liza!" Pavel Pavlovitch turned back. "Liza? Do you know what Liza has meant to me and means? Has meant and still means!" he cried all at once, almost frantically. "But ... But of that later, all that can be later. ... But now it's not enough that we've drunk together, Alexey Ivanovitch, I must have something else to be satisfied. ..."

He laid his hat on a chair and gazed at him, gasping for breath a little as he had done just before.

"Kiss me, Alexey Ivanovitch!" he suggested suddenly.

"You're drunk!" Velchaninov declared, stepping back.

"Yes, but kiss me all the same, Alexey Ivanovitch. Oh, kiss me! Why, I kissed your hand just now."

For some minutes Velchaninov was silent, as though stunned by a blow on the head. But suddenly he bent down to Pavel Pavlovitch, whose face was on a level with his shoulder, and kissed him on the lips, which smelt very strongly of spirits. He was not, however, perfectly certain that he had kissed him.

"Well, now, now. ..." Pavel Pavlovitch cried again in a drunken frenzy, his drunken eyes flashing; "now I'll tell you; I thought then, What if he too? What if that one, I thought; what if he too ... whom can I trust after that!"

Pavel Pavlovitch suddenly burst into tears.

"So you understand, you're the one friend left me now!"

And he ran with his hat out of the room. Velchaninov again stood still for some minutes in the same place, just as he had done after Pavel Pavlovitch's first visit.

"Ah! a drunken fool and nothing more!" He waved his hand, dismissing the subject.

"Absolutely nothing more," he repeated energetically as he undressed and got into bed.

Chapter VIII

Liza Ill

Next morning Velchaninov walked about his room expecting Pavel Pavlovitch, who had promised to arrive in good time to go to the Pogoryeltsevs. As he smoked and sipped his coffee he was conscious at every moment that he was like a man who, on waking up in the morning cannot forget for one instant that he has received a slap in the face overnight. "H'm! ... he quite understands the position and will take his revenge on me through Liza!" he thought with horror.

The charming figure of the poor child rose mournfully before him for a moment. His heart beat faster at the thought that he would soon, within two hours, see *his* Liza again. "Ah! it's no use talking about it!" he decided hotly—"It's my whole life and my whole object now! what do slaps in the face or memories of the past matter? What has my life been till now? Muddle and sadness ... but now—it's all different, everything's changed!"

But in spite of his enthusiasm, he grew more and more doubtful.

"He is tormenting me by means of Liza—that's clear! And he is tormenting Liza too. It's in that way he will devour me utterly in revenge for everything. H'm! ... Of course, I can't allow him to go on as he did yesterday"—he flushed crimson all at once—"and ... here it's twelve o'clock, though, he doesn't come."

He waited a long time, till half-past twelve, and his depression grew more and more acute. Pavel Pavlovitch did not appear. At last the thought that had long been stirring in his mind, that Pavel Pavlovitch had not come on purpose, simply in order to get up another scene like that of the night before, put the finishing touch to his irritation. "He knows that I depend on him, and what a state Liza will be in now. And how can I appear before her without him?"

At last he could stand it no longer, and at one o'clock he rushed off to the Pokrovsky Hotel alone. At the lodging he was told that Pavel Pavlovitch had not slept at home, but had only turned up at nine o'clock in the morning, had stayed no more than a quarter of an hour, and then gone out again. Velchaninov stood at the door of Pavel Pavlovitch's room, listening to what the servant said, and mechanically turned the handle of the locked door and pulled it backwards and forwards. Realizing what he was doing, he uttered a curse and asked the servant to take him to Marya Sysoevna. But the landlady, hearing he was there, came out readily.

She was a good-natured woman. "A woman with generous feelings," as Velchaninov said of her when he was reporting his conversation afterwards to Klavdia Petrovna. Inquiring briefly about his journey with the child the day before, Marya Sysoevna launched out into accounts of Pavel Pavlovitch's doings. In her words: "If it had not been for the child, she would have sent him about his business long ago. He was turned out of the hotel because of his disorderly behaviour. Wasn't it wicked to bring home a wench with him when there was a child here old enough to understand? He was shouting: 'She will be your mother, if I choose!' And, would you believe it? what that street wench did, she even spat in

711

his face. 'You're not my daughter, but he's a ——!' she cried.

"Really!" Velchaninov was horrified.

"I heard it myself. Though the man was drunk till he was almost senseless, yet it was very wrong before the child; though she is but young, she broods over everything in her mind! The child cries. I can see she is worried to death. And the other day there was a terrible thing done in our building: a clerk, so folks say, took a room in the hotel overnight, and in the morning hanged himself. They say he had squandered all his money. People flocked to see. Pavel Pavlovitch was not at home, and the child was running about with no one to look after her; I looked, and there she was in the passage among the people, and peeping in behind the others: she was looking so strangely at the body. I brought her away as quickly as I could. And what do you think—she was all of a tremble, she looked quite black in the face, and as soon as I brought her in she flopped on the floor in a faint. She struggled and writhed, and it was all I could do to bring her round. It was a fit, and she's been poorly ever since that hour. He heard of it, came home, and pinched her all over—for he's not one for beating, he's more given to pinching her, and afterwards, when he came home after having a drop, he'd frighten her: 'I'll hang myself too,' he'd say; 'you'll make me hang myself; on this blind-cord here,' he'd say; and he'd make a noose before her eyes. And she'd be beside herself—she'd scream and throw her little arms round him: 'I won't!' she'd cry, 'I never will again.' It was pitiful."

Though Velchaninov had expected something strange, this story amazed him so much that he could not believe it.

Marya Sysoevna told him a great deal more; on one occasion, for instance, had it not been for Marya Sysoevna Liza might have thrown herself out of the window.

Velchaninov went out of the house reeling as though he were drunk.

"I'll knock him on the head like a dog!" was the thought that floated before his mind. And for a long time he kept repeating it to himself.

He took a cab and drove to the Pogoryeltsevs. On the way the carriage was obliged to stop at the cross roads, near the bridge on the canal, over which a long funeral procession was passing. And on both sides of the bridge there were several carriages waiting in a block; people on foot were stopped too. It was a grand funeral and there was a very long string of carriages following it, and lo and behold! in the windows of one of these carriages Velchaninov caught a passing glimpse of the face of Pavel Pavlovitch. He would not have believed his eyes if Pavel Pavlovitch had not thrust his head out and nodded to him with a smile. Evidently he was delighted at recognizing Velchaninov; he even began beckoning to him from the carriage. Velchaninov jumped out of his cab and, in spite of the crush, in spite of the police, and in spite of the fact that Pavel Pavlovitch's carriage was driving on to the bridge, he ran right up to the window. Pavel Pavlovitch was alone.

"What's the matter with you?" cried Velchaninov; "why didn't you come? How is it you are here?"

"I'm repaying a debt. Don't shout, don't shout, I am repaying a debt," sniggered Pavel Pavlovitch, screwing up his eyes jocosely. "I'm following the mortal remains of my faithful friend, Stepan Mihalovitch."

"That's all nonsense, you drunken, senseless man," Velchaninov shouted louder than ever, though he was taken aback for an instant. "Get out this minute and come into the cab with me."

"I can't, it's a duty. ..."

"I'll drag you out!" Velchaninov yelled.

"And I'll scream! I'll scream!" said Pavel Pavlovitch, sniggering as jocosely as before, as though it were a game, though he did huddle into the furthest corner of the carriage. ...

"Look out, look out! you'll be run over!" shouted a policeman.

At the further end of the bridge a carriage cutting across the procession did, in fact, cause a commotion. Velchaninov was forced to skip back; the stream of carriages and the crowd of people immediately carried him further away. With a curse he made his way back to the cab.

"No matter, I couldn't have taken a fellow like that with me at any rate!" he thought, with a feeling of bewildered anxiety that persisted.

When he told Klavdia Petrovna Marya Sysoevna's story and described the strange meeting in the funeral procession, she grew very thoughtful.

"I feel afraid for you," she said. "You ought to break off all relations with him, and the sooner the better."

"He's a drunken fool and nothing more!" Velchaninov cried passionately; "as though I could be afraid of him! And how can I break off relations with him when there's Liza to be considered. Think of Liza!"

Liza meanwhile was lying ill; she had begun to be feverish the evening before and they were expecting a celebrated doctor, for whom they had sent an express messenger to the town in the morning. This completed Velchaninov's distress.

Klavdia Petrovna took him to the invalid.

"I watched her very carefully yesterday," she observed, stopping outside Liza's room. "She's a proud and reserved child; she is ashamed that she

713

is here, and that her father has cast her off; that's the whole cause of her illness, to my thinking."

"How cast her off? Why do you say he's cast her off?"

"The very fact that he let her come here, among complete strangers and with a man ... who's almost a stranger, too, or on such terms ..."

"But it was I took her, I took her by force; I don't perceive——"

"Oh, my God, and even Liza, a child, perceives it! It's my belief that he simply won't come at all."

Liza was not astonished when she saw Velchaninov alone; she only smiled mournfully and turned her feverishly hot little head to the wall. She made no response to Velchaninov's timid efforts to comfort her and his fervent promises to bring her father next day without fail. On coming away from her, he suddenly burst into tears.

It was evening before the doctor came. After examining the patient, he alarmed them all from the first word, by observing that they had done wrong not to have sent for him before. When it was explained to him that the child had been taken ill only the evening before, he was at first incredulous.

"It all depends how things go on to-night," he said in conclusion. After giving various instructions, he went away, promising to come again next day as early as possible. Velchaninov would have insisted on staying the night, but Klavdia Petrovna begged him once more "to try and bring that monster."

"Try once more," Velchaninov retorted in a frenzy. "Why, this time I'll tie him hand and foot and carry him here in my arms!" The idea of tying Pavel Pavlovitch hand and foot and carrying him there took possession of him and made him violently impatient to carry it out. "I don't feel in the least guilty towards him now, not in the least!" he said to Klavdia Petrovna, as he said good-bye. "I take back all the abject, snivelling things I said here yesterday," he added indignantly.

Liza was lying with her eyes shut, apparently asleep; she seemed to be better. When Velchaninov cautiously bent over her head, to say good-bye and to kiss, if only the edge of her garment, she suddenly opened her eyes, as though she had been expecting him, and whispered to him—

"Take me away!"

It was a gentle, pitiful prayer, without a shade in it of the irritability of the previous day, but at the same time he could hear in it the conviction that he would not do what she asked. Velchaninov, in complete despair, began trying to persuade her that this was impossible.

In silence she closed her eyes and did not utter another word, as though she did not see or hear him.

On getting into Petersburg he told the driver to take him straight to Pokrovsky Hotel. It was ten o'clock; Pavel Pavlovitch was not in his lodging. Velchaninov spent a full half-hour in waiting for him and walking up and down the passage in sickening suspense. Marya Sysoevna assured him at last that Pavel Pavlovitch would not be back till early next morning. "Then I will come early in the morning," Velchaninov decided, and, beside himself, he set off for home.

But what was his astonishment when, at the door of his flat, he learned from Mavra that his yesterday's visitor had been waiting for him since ten o'clock.

"And has been pleased to drink tea here, and has sent out for wine again, and has given me a blue note to get it."

CHAPTER IX

An Apparition

Pavel Pavlovitch had made himself exceedingly comfortable. He was stting in the same chair as the day before, smoking a cigarette, and had just poured himself out the fourth and last glass from a bottle of wine. The teapot and an unfinished glass of tea was standing on a table close by. His flushed face was beaming with bliss. He had even taken off his coat, as it was warm, and was sitting in his waistcoat.

"Excuse me, most faithful of friends!" he cried, seeing Velchaninov and jumping up to put on his coat. "I took it off for the greater enjoyment of the moment..."

Velchaninov went up to him menacingly.

"Are you not quite drunk yet? Is it still possible to talk to you?"

Pavel Pavlovitch was a little fluttered.

"No, not quite. ... I've been commemorating the deceased, but—not quite——"

"Will you understand me too?"

"That's what I've come for, to understand you."

"Well, then; I begin by telling you straight out that you are a worthless scoundrel!" cried Velchaninov.

"If you begin like that, how will you end?" Pavel Pavlovitch protested,

715

evidently cowed, but Velchaninov went on shouting without heeding him.

"Your daughter is dying, she is ill; have you abandoned her or not?"

"Can she really be dying?"

"She is ill, ill, exceedingly, dangerously ill!"

"Possibly some little fit ..."

"Don't talk nonsense! She is ex—ceed—ing—ly, dangerously ill! You ought to have gone if only to ..."

"To express my gratitude, my gratitude for their hospitality! I quite understand that! Alexey Ivanovitch, my precious, perfect friend"—he suddenly clutched Velchaninov's hand in both of his, and with drunken sentimentality, almost with tears, as though imploring forgiveness, he kept crying out: "Alexey Ivanovitch, don't shout, don't shout! Whether I die or fall drunk into the Neva—what does it matter in the real significance of things? We have plenty of time to go to Mr Pogoryeltsev ..."

Velchaninov pulled himself together and restrained himself a little.

"You're drunk, and so I don't understand the sense of what you are saying," he observed sternly. "I am always ready to have things out with you, shall be glad to, in fact, as soon as possible. ... I've come indeed. ... But first of all I warn you that I shall take steps: you must stay the night here! To-morrow morning I'll take you and we'll go together. I won't let you go," he yelled again. "I'll tie you up and carry you there in my arms! ... Would you like this sofa?" he said breathlessly, pointing to a wide, soft sofa, which stood opposite the one against the other wall, where he used to sleep himself.

"By all means, I can sleep anywhere ..."

"Not anywhere, but on that sofa! Here, take your sheets, your quilt, your pillow." All these Velchaninov took out of the cupboard and hurriedly flung them to Pavel Pavlovitch, who held out his arms submissively. "Make the bed at once, make it at once!"

Pavel Pavlovitch, loaded with his burden, stood in the middle of the room as though hesitating, with a broad drunken grin on his drunken face. But at a second menacing shout from Velchaninov he suddenly began bustling about at full speed; he pushed back the table and began, sighing and groaning, to unfold the sheets and make the bed. Velchaninov went to assist him; he was, to some extent, appeased by the alarm and submissiveness of his visitor.

"Finish your glass and go to bed," he ordered him again; he felt as though he could not help giving orders. "You sent for that wine yourself, didn't you?"

"Yes. ... I knew you wouldn't send for any more, Alexey Ivanovitch."

"It was well you knew it, and there is something more you must know too. I tell you once more I've taken measures, I won't put up with any more of your antics, I won't put up with your drunken kisses as I did yesterday."

"I understand myself, Alexey Ivanovitch, that that was only possible once," sniggered Pavel Pavlovitch.

Hearing his answer, Velchaninov, who had been striding up and down the room, stopped almost solemnly before Pavel Pavlovitch.

"Pavel Pavlovitch, tell me frankly! You're a sensible man, I've recognized that again, but I assure you, you are on the wrong tack! Speak straightforwardly, act straightforwardly and I give you my word of honour I will answer any question you like."

Pavel Pavlovitch grinned his broad grin again, which was enough in itself to drive Velchaninov to fury.

"Stop!" Velchaninov shouted again. "Don't sham, I see through you! I repeat: I give you my word of honour, that I am ready to answer *anything* and you shall receive every satisfaction possible, that is every sort, even the impossible! Oh, how I wish you could understand me! ..."

"Since you are so good"—Pavel Pavlovitch moved cautiously towards him—"I was much interested in what you said last night about a 'predatory type'! ..."

Velchaninov, with a curse, fell to pacing about the room more rapidly than ever.

"No, Alexey Ivanovitch, don't curse, because I'm so much interested, and have come on purpose to make sure. ... I'm not very ready with my tongue, but you must forgive me. You know of that 'predatory type,' and of that 'peaceable type' I read in a magazine, in the literary criticism. I remembered it this morning ... only I had forgotten it, and to tell the truth I did not understand it at the time. This is what I wanted you to explain; the deceased, Stepan Mihalovitch Bagautov—was he 'predatory' or 'peaceable'? How do you classify him?"

Velchaninov still remained silent, and did not cease his pacing up and down.

"The predatory type," he began, stopping suddenly in exasperation, "is the man who would sooner have put poison in Bagautov's glass when drinking champagne with him in honour of their delightful meeting, as you drank with me yesterday, than have followed his coffin to the cemetery as you have to-day, the devil only knows from what secret, underground, loathsome impulse and distorted feeling that only degrades you! Yes, degrades you!"

717

"It's true that I shouldn't have gone," Pavel Pavlovitch assented; "but you do pitch into me ..."

"It's not the man," Velchaninov, getting hotter, went on shouting, without heeding him; "it's not the man who poses to himself as goodness knows what, who reckons up his score of right and wrong, goes over and over his grievance as though it were a lesson, frets, goes in for all sorts of antics and apishness, hangs on people's necks—and most likely he has been spending all his time at it too! Is it true that you tried to hang yourself—is it?"

"When I was drunk, I did talk wildly—I don't remember. It isn't quite seemly, Alexey Ivanovitch, to put poison in wine. Apart from the fact that I am a civil servant of good repute, you know I have money of my own, and, what's more, I may want to get married again."

"Besides, you'll be sent to the gallows."

"To be sure, that unpleasantness also, though nowadays they admit many extenuating circumstances in the law courts. I'll tell you a killing little anecdote, Alexey Ivanovitch. I thought of it this morning in the carriage. I wanted to tell you of it then. You said just now 'hangs on people's necks.' You remember, perhaps, Semyon Petrovitch Livtsov, he used to come and see us when you were in T——; well, his younger brother, who was also a young Petersburg swell, was in attendance on the governor at V—, and he, too, was distinguished for various qualities. He had a quarrel with Golubenko, a colonel, in the presence of ladies and the lady of his heart, and considered himself insulted, but he swallowed the affront and concealed it; and, meanwhile, Golubenko cut him out with the lady of his heart and made her an offer. And what do you think? This Livtsov formed a genuine friendship with Golubenko, he quite made it up with him, and, what's more—insisted on being his best man, he held the wedding crown, and when they came from under the wedding crown, he went up to kiss and congratulate Golubenko; and in the presence of the governor and all the honourable company, with his swallow-tail coat, and his hair in curl, he sticks the bridegroom in the stomach with a knife—so that he rolled over! His own best man! What a disgrace! And, what's more, when he'd stabbed him like that, he rushed about crying: 'Ach! what have I done! Oh, what is it I've done!' with floods of tears, trembling all over, flinging himself on people's necks, even ladies. 'Ah, what have I done!' he kept saying. 'What have I done now!' He—he—he! he was killing. Though one feels sorry for Golubenko, perhaps, but after all he recovered."

"I don't see why you told me the story," observed Velchaninov, frowning sternly.

"Why, all because he stuck the knife in him, you know," Pavel Pavlovitch tittered; "you can see he was not the type, but a snivelling fellow, since he forgot all good manners in his horror and flung himself on the ladies' necks in the presence of the governor—but you see he stabbed him, he got his own back! That was all I meant."

"Go to hell!" Velchaninov yelled suddenly, in a voice not his own, as though something had exploded in him. "Go to hell with your underground vileness; you are nothing but underground vileness. You thought you'd scare me—you base man, torturing a child; you scoundrel, you scoundrel, you scoundrel!" he shouted, beside himself, gasping for breath at every word.

A complete revulsion came over Pavel Pavlovitch which actually seemed to sober him; his lips quivered.

"It is you, Alexey Ivanovitch, call me a scoundrel, *you* call *me?*"
But Velchaninov had already realized what he had done.

"I am ready to apologize," he answered, after a pause of gloomy hesitation; "but only if you will act straightforwardly at once yourself."

"In your place I would apologize without any ifs, Alexey Ivanovitch."

"Very good, so be it," said Velchaninov, after another slight pause. "I apologize to you; but you'll admit yourself, Pavel Pavlovitch, that, after all this, I need not consider that I owe you anything. I'm speaking with reference to the *whole* matter and not only to the present incident."

"That's all right, why consider?" Pavel Pavlovitch sniggered, though he kept his eyes on the ground.

"So much the better, then, so much the better! Finish your wine and go to bed, for I won't let you go, anyway ..."

"Oh, the wine ..." Pavel Pavlovitch seemed, as it were, a little disconcerted. He went to the table, however, and finished the last glass of wine he had poured out so long before.

Perhaps he had drunk a great deal before, for his hand trembled and he spilt part of the wine on the floor, and on his shirt and waistcoat. He finished it all, however, as though he could not bear to leave a drop, and respectfully replacing the empty glass on the table, he went submissively to his bed to undress.

"But wouldn't it be better for me not to stay the night!" he brought out for some reason, though he had taken off one boot and was holding it in his hand.

"No, it wouldn't," Velchaninov answered wrathfully, still pacing up and down the room without looking at him.

Pavel Pavlovitch undressed and got into bed. A quarter of an hour later Velchaninov went to bed too, and put out the candle.

He fell asleep uneasily. The new element that had turned up unexpectedly and complicated the whole business more than ever worried him now, and at the same time he felt that he was for some reason ashamed of his uneasiness. He was just dozing off, but he was waked up all at once by a rustling sound. He looked round at once toward Pavel Pavlovitch's bed. The room was dark (the curtains were drawn), but Velchaninov fancied that Pavel Pavlovitch was not lying down, but was sitting on the bed.

"What's the matter?" Velchaninov called to him.

"A ghost," Pavel Pavlovitch said, scarcely audibly, after a brief pause.

"What do you mean, what sort of ghost?"

"There in that room, I seem to see a ghost in the doorway."

"Whose ghost?" Velchaninov asked again, after a pause.

"Natalya Vassilyevna's."

Velchaninov stood up on the rug, and looked across the passage, into the other room, the door of which always stood open. There were only blinds, instead of curtains on the window, and so it was much lighter there.

"There's nothing in that room and you are drunk. Go to bed!" said Velchaninov. He got into bed and wrapped himself in the quilt.

Pavel Pavlovitch got into bed, too, without uttering a word.

"And have you ever seen ghosts before," Velchaninov asked suddenly, ten minutes afterwards.

Pavel Pavlovitch, too, was silent for a while.

"I thought I saw one once," he responded faintly.

Silence followed again.

Velchaninov could not have said for certain whether he had been asleep or not, but about an hour had passed—when he suddenly turned round again: whether he was roused again by a rustle—he was not sure, but felt as though in the pitch dark something white was standing over him, not quite close, but in the middle of the room. He sat up in bed and for a full minute gazed into the darkness.

"Is that you, Pavel Pavlovitch?" he said, in a failing voice.

His own voice ringing out suddenly in the stillness and the dark seemed to him somehow strange.

No answer followed, but there could be no doubt that some one was standing there.

"Is that you ... Pavel Pavlovitch?" he repeated, more loudly—so loudly, in fact, that if Pavel Pavlovitch had been quietly asleep in his bed he would certainly have waked up and answered.

But again no answer came, yet he fancied that the white, hardly distinguishable figure moved nearer to him. Then something strange followed: something seemed to explode within him, exactly as it had that evening, and he shouted at the top of his voice, in a most hideous, frantic voice, gasping for breath at each word:

"If you ... drunken fool ... dare to imagine ... that you can ... frighten me, I'll turn over to the wall, I'll put the bedclothes over my head, and won't turn round again all night ... to show you how much I care ... if you were to stand there till morning ... like a fool ... and I spit upon you ..."

And he spat furiously in the direction, as he supposed, of Pavel Pavlovitch, turned over to the wall, drew the bedclothes over his head as he had said and grew numb in that position, not stirring a muscle. A deathlike silence followed. Whether the phantom was moving nearer or standing still he could not tell, but his heart was beating, beatingy beating violently, Fully five minutes passed, and suddenly, two steps from him, he heard the meek and plaintive voice of Pavel Pavlovitch.

"I got up, Alexey Ivanovitch, to look for the ..." (and he mentioned a quite indispensable domestic article). "I didn't find one there. ... I meant to look quietly under your bed."

"Why didn't you speak when I shouted?" Velchaninov asked in a breaking voice, after an interval of half a minute.

"I was frightened, you shouted so. ... I was frightened."

"There in the corner on the left, in the little cupboard. Light the candle ..."

"I can do without the candle," Pavel Pavlovitch brought out meekly, making for the corner. "Forgive me, Alexey Ivanovitch, for disturbing you so. ... I was so bewildered ..."

But Velchaninov made no reply. He still lay with his face to the wall, and lay so all night, without once turning over. Whether it was that he wanted to do as he had said and so show his contempt,—he did not know himself what he was feeling; his nervous irritability passed at last almost into delirium, and it was a long time before he went to sleep. Waking next morning between nine and ten, he jumped up and sat up in bed, as though some one had given him a shove,—but Pavel Pavlovitch was not in the room—the unmade bed stood there empty; he had crept away at dawn.

"I knew it would be so," cried Velchaninov, slapping himself on the forehead.

CHAPTER X

In the Cemetery

The doctor's fears turned out to be justified; Liza was suddenly worse —worse than Velchaninov and Klavdia Petrovna had imagined possible the evening before. Velchaninov found the invalid conscious in the morning, though she was in a high fever; afterwards he declared that she had smiled and even held out her feverish little hand to him. Whether this was really so, or whether he had imagined it, in an unconscious effort to comfort himself, he had no time to make sure; by nightfall the sick child was unconscious, and she remained so till the end. Ten days after her coming to the Pogoryeltsevs' she died.

It was a sorrowful time for Velchaninov; the Pogoryeltsevs were very anxious about him. He spent those bitter days for the most part with them. During the last days of Liza's illness he would sit for whole hours together in a corner apparently thinking of nothing; Klavdia Petrovna attempted to distract his mind, but he made little response, and seemed to find it a burden even to talk to her. Klavdia Petrovna had not expected that "all this would have such an effect upon him." The children succeeded best in rousing him; in their company he sometimes even laughed, but almost every hour he would get up from his chair and go on tiptoe to look at the invalid. He sometimes fancied that she recognized him. He had no hope of her recovery, nor had any one, but he could not tear himself away from the room in which she lay dying, and usually sat in the next room.

On two occasions in the course of those days, however, he showed great activity: he roused himself and rushed off to Petersburg to the doctors, called on all the most distinguished of them, and arranged for a consultation. The second and last consultation took place the evening before Liza's death. Three days before that Klavdia Petrovna urged upon Velchaninov the necessity of seeking out M. Trusotsky: pointing out that "if the worst happened, the funeral would be impossible without him." Velchaninov mumbled in reply that he would write to him. Pogoryeltsev thereupon declared that he would undertake to find him through the police. Velchaninov did finally write a note of two lines and took it to the Pokrovsky Hotel. Pavel Pavlovitch, as usual, was not at home, and he left the letter for him with Marya Sysoevna.

At last Liza died, on a beautiful summer evening at sunset, and only then Velchaninov seemed to wake up. When they dressed the dead child in a white frock that belonged to one of Klavdia Petrovna's daughters and was kept for festivals, and laid her on the table in the drawing-room with flowers in her folded hands, he went up to Klavdia Petrovna with glittering eyes, and told her that he would bring the "murderer" at once. Refusing to listen to their advice to put off going till next day, he set off for Petersburg at once.

He knew where to find Pavel Pavlovitch; he had not only been to fetch the doctors when he went to Petersburg before. He had sometimes fancied during those days that if he brought her father to Liza, and she heard his voice, she might come to herself; so he had fallen to hunting for him like one possessed. Pavel Pavlovitch was in the same lodging as before, but it was useless for him to inquire there: "he hasn't slept here for the last three nights or been near the place," Marya Sysoevna reported; "and if he does come he's bound to be drunk, and before he's been here an hour he's off again; he's going to rack and ruin." The waiter at the Pokrovsky Hotel told Velchaninov, among other things, that Pavel Pavlovitch used to visit some young women in Voznesensky Prospect. Velchaninov promptly looked up these young women. When he had treated them and made them presents these persons readily remembered their visitor, chiefly from the crape on his hat, after which, of course, they abused him roundly for not having been to see them again. One of them, Katya, undertook "to find Pavel Pavlovitch any time, because nowadays he was always with Mashka Prostakov, and he had no end of money, and she ought to have been Mashka Prohvostov (*i.e.* scoundrelly) instead of Prostakov (*i.e.* simple), and she'd been in hospital, and if she (the speaker) liked she could pack the wench off to Siberia—she had only to say the word." Katya did not, however, look up Pavel Pavlovitch on that occasion, but she promised faithfully to do so another time. It was on her help that Velchaninov was reckoning now.

On reaching Petersburg at ten o'clock, he went at once to ask for her, paid the keeper to let her go, and set off to search with her. He did not know himself what he was going to do with Pavel Pavlovitch: whether he would kill him, or whether he was looking for him simply to tell him of his daughter's death and the necessity of his presence at the funeral. At first they were unsuccessful. It turned out that this Mashka had had a fight with Pavel Pavlovitch two days before, and that a cashier "had broken his head with a stool." In fact, for a long time the search was in vain, and it was only at two o'clock in the afternoon that Velchaninov, coming out of an 'establishment,' to which he had been sent as a likely place, unexpectedly hit up against him.

Pavel Pavlovitch, hopelessly drunk, was being conducted to this 'establishment' by two ladies; one of whom was holding his arm and supporting him. They were followed by a tall, sturdy fellow, who was shouting at the top of his voice and threatening Pavel Pavlovitch with all sorts of horrors. He bawled among other things "that Pavel Pavlovitch was exploiting him and poisoning his existence." There seemed to have been some dispute about money; the women were much frightened and flustered. Seeing Velchaninov, Pavel Pavlovitch rushed to him with outstretched hands and screamed as though he were being murdered:

"Brother, defend me!"

At sight of Velchaninov's athletic figure the bully promptly disappeared; Pavel Pavlovitch in triumph shook his fist after him with a yell of victory; at that point Velchaninov seized him by the shoulder in a fury, and, without knowing why he did it, shook him until his teeth chattered. Pavel Pavlovitch instantly ceased yelling and stared at his tormentor in stupid, drunken terror. Probably not knowing what to do with him next, Velchaninov folded him up and sat him on the curbstone.

"Liza is dead!" he said to him.

Pavel Pavlovitch, still staring at Velchaninov, sat on the curbstone supported by one of the ladies. He understood at last, and his face suddenly looked pinched.

"Dead ..." he whispered strangely. Whether his face wore his loathsome, drunken grin, or whether it was contorted by some feeling, Velchaninov could not distinguish, but a moment later Pavel Pavlovitch, with an effort, lifted his trembling hand to make the sign of the cross; his trembling hand dropped again without completing it. A little while after he slowly got up from the curbstone, clutched at his lady, and leaning upon her, went on his way, as though oblivious,—as though Velchanionov had not been present. But the latter seized him by the shoulder again.

"Do you understand, you drunken monster, that without you she can't be buried?" he shouted breathlessly.

Pavel Pavlovitch turned his head towards him.

"The artillery ... the lieutenant ... do you remember him?" he stammered.

"Wha—at!" yelled Velchaninov, with a sickening pang.

"There's her father for you! Find him—for the burial."

"You're lying," Velchaninov yelled like one distraught. "You say that from spite. ... I knew you were preparing that for me."

Beside himself, he raised his terrible fist to strike Pavel Pavlovitch. In another minute he might have killed him at one blow; the ladies squealed and were beating a retreat, but Pavel Pavlovitch did not turn a hair. His face was contorted by a frenzy of ferocious hatred.

"Do you know," he said, much more steadily, almost as though he were sober, "our Russian ... ? (and he uttered an absolutely unprintable term of abuse) Well, you go to it, then!"

Then with a violent effort he tore himself out of Velchaninov's hands, stumbled, and almost fell down. The ladies caught him and this time ran away, squealing and almost dragging Pavel Pavlovitch after them. Velchaninov did not follow them.

On the afternoon of the next day a very presentable-looking middle-aged government clerk in uniform arrived at the Pogoryeltsevs' villa and politely handed Klavdia Petrovna an envelope addressed to her by Pavel Pavlovitch Trusotsky. In it was a letter enclosing three hundred roubles and the legal papers necessary for the burial. Pavel Pavlovitch wrote briefly, respectfully, and most properly. He warmly thanked her excellency for the kind sympathy she had shown for the little motherless girl, for which God alone could repay her. He wrote vaguely that extreme ill-health would prevent him from coming to arrange the funeral of his beloved and unhappy daughter, and he could only appeal to the angelic kindness of her excellency's heart. The three hundred roubles were, as he explained later in the letter, to pay for the funeral, and the expenses caused by the child's illness. If any of this money were left over he must humbly and respectfully beg that it might be spent on "a perpetual mass for the rest of the soul of the departed." The clerk who brought the letter could add nothing in explanation; it appeared, indeed, from what he said that it was only at Pavel Pavlovitch's earnest entreaty that he had undertaken to deliver the letter to her excellency. Pogoryeltsev was almost offended at the expression "the expenses caused by the child's illness," and after setting aside fifty roubles for the funeral—since it was impossible to prevent the father from paying for his child's burial—he proposed to send the remaining two hundred and fifty roubles back to M. Trusotsky at once. Klavdia Petrovna finally decided not to send back the two hundred and fifty roubles, but only a receipt from the cemetery church for that sum in payment for a perpetual mass for the repose of the soul of the deceased maiden Elizaveta. This receipt was afterwards given to Velchaninov to be dispatched to Pavel Pavlovitch. Velchaninov posted it to his lodging.

After the funeral he left the villa. For a whole fortnight he wandered about the town aimless and alone, so lost in thought that he stumbled against people in the street. Sometimes he would lie stretched out on his sofa for days together, forgetting the commonest things of everyday life. Several times the Pogoryeltsevs went to ask him to go to them; he promised to go, but immediately forgot. Klavdia Petrovna even went herself to see him, but did not find him at home. The same thing happened to his lawyer; the lawyer had, indeed, something to tell him: his lawsuit had been very adroitly settled and his opponents had come to an amicable arrangement, agreeing to accept an insignificant fraction of the disputed inheritance. All that remained was to obtain Velchaninov's own consent. When at last he did find him at home, the lawyer was surprised at the apathy and indifference with which Velchaninov, once such a troublesome client, listened to his explanation.

The very hottest days of July had come, but Velchaninov was oblivious of time. His grief ached in his heart like a growing abscess, and he was distinctly conscious of it and every moment with agonizing acuteness. His chief suffering was the thought that, before Liza had had time to know him, she had died, not understanding with what anguish he loved her! The object in life of which he had had such a joyful glimpse had suddenly vanished into everlasting darkness. That object—he thought of it every moment now—was that Liza should be conscious of his love every day, every hour, all her life. "No one has a higher object and no one could have," he thought sometimes, with gloomy fervour. "If there are other objects none can be holier than that!" "By my love for Liza," he mused, "all my old putrid and useless life would be purified and expiated; to make up for my own idle, vicious, and wasted life I would cherish and bring up that pure and exquisite creature, and for her sake everything would be forgiven me and I could forgive myself everything."

All these *conscious* thoughts always rose before his mind, together with the vivid, ever-present, and ever-poignant memory of the dead child. He re-created for himself her little pale face, remembered every expression on it: he thought of her in the coffin decked with flowers, and as she had lain unconscious in fever, with fixed and open eyes. He suddenly remembered that when she was lying on the table he had noticed one of her fingers, which had somehow turned black during her illness; this had struck him so much at the time, and he had felt so sorry for that poor little finger, that for the first time he thought of seeking out Pavel Pavlovitch and killing him; until that time he had been "as though insensible." Was it wounded pride that had tortured her wounded heart, or was it those three months of suffering at the hands of her father, whose love had suddenly changed to hatred, who had insulted her with shameful words, laughing at her terror, and had abandoned her at last to strangers. All this he dwelt upon incessantly in a thousand variations. "Do you know what Liza has been to me?"—he suddenly recalled the drunkard's exclamation and felt that that exclamation was sincere, not a pose, and that there was love in it.

"How could that monster be so cruel to a child whom he had loved so much, and is it credible?" But every time he made haste to dismiss that question and, as it were, brush it aside; there was something awful in that question, something he could not bear and could not solve.

One day, scarcely conscious where he was going, he wandered into the cemetery where Liza was buried and found her little grave. He had not been to the cemetery since the funeral; he had always fancied it would be too great an agony, and had been afraid to go. But, strange to say, when he had found her little grave and kissed it, his heart felt easier. It was a fine evening, the sun was setting; all round the graves the lush green grass was growing; the bees were humming in a wild rose close by; the flowers and wreaths left by the children and Klavdia Petrovna on Liza's grave were lying there with the petals half dropping. There was a gleam of something like hope in his heart after many days.

"How serene!" he thought, feeling the stillness of the cemetery, and looking at the clear, peaceful sky.

A rush of pure, calm faith flooded his soul.

"Liza has sent me this, it's Liza speaking to me," he thought.

It was quite dark when he left the cemetery and went home. Not far from the cemetery gates, in a low-pitched wooden house on the road, there was some sort of eating-house or tavern; through the windows he could see people sitting at the tables. It suddenly seemed to him that one of them close to the window was Pavel Pavlovitch, and that he saw him, too, and was staring at him inquisitively. He walked on, and soon heard some one pursuing him; Pavel Pavlovitch was, in fact, running after him; probably he had been attracted and encouraged by Velchaninov's conciliatory expression as he watched him from the window. On overtaking him he smiled timidly, but it was not his old drunken smile; he was actually not drunk.

"Good evening," he said.

"Good evening," answered Velchaninov.

CHAPTER XI

Pavel Pavlovitch Means to Marry

As he responded with this "good-evening," he was surprised at himself. It struck him as extremely strange that he met this man now without a trace of anger, and that in his feeling for him at that moment there was something quite different, and actually, indeed, a sort of impulse towards something new.

"What an agreeable evening," observed Pavel Pavlovitch, looking into his face.

"You've not gone away yet," Velchaninov observed, not by way of a question, but simply making that reflection aloud as he walked on.

"Things have dragged on, but—I've obtained a post with an increase of salary. I shall be going away the day after to-morrow for certain."

"You've got a post?" he said this time, asking a question.

"Why shouldn't I?" Pavel Pavlovitch screwed up his face.

"Oh, I only asked ..." Velchaninov said, disclaiming the insinuation, and, with a frown, he looked askance at Pavel Pavlovitch.

To his surprise, the attire, the hat with the crape band, and the whole appearance of M. Trusotsky were incomparably more presentable than they had been a fortnight before.

"What was he sitting in that tavern for?" he kept wondering.

"I was intending, Alexey Ivanovitch, to communicate with you on a subject for rejoicing," Pavel Pavlovitch began again.

"Rejoicing?"

"I'm going to get married."

"What?"

"After sorrow comes rejoicing, so it is always in life; I should be so gratified, Alexey Ivanovitch, if ... but—I don't know, perhaps you're in a hurry now, for you appear to be ..."

"Yes, I am in a hurry ... and I'm unwell too."

He felt a sudden and intense desire to get rid of him; his readiness for some new feeling had vanished in a flash.

"I should have liked ..."

Pavel Pavlovitch did not say what he would have liked; Velchaninov was silent.

"In that case it must be later on, if only we meet again. ..."

"Yes, yes, later on," Velchaninov muttered rapidly, without stopping or looking at him.

They were both silent again for a minute; Pavel Pavlovitch went on walking beside him.

"In that case, good-bye till we meet again," Pavel Pavlovitch brought out at last.

"Good-bye; I hope ..."

Velchaninov returned home thoroughly upset again. Contact with "that man" was too much for him. As he got into bed he asked himself again: "Why was he at the cemetery?"

Next morning he made up his mind to go to the Pogoryeltsevs. He made up his mind to go reluctantly; sympathy from any one, even from the Pogoryeltsevs, was too irksome for him now. But they were so anxious about him that he felt absolutely obliged to go. He suddenly had a foreboding that he would feel horribly ashamed at their first meeting again.

Should he go or not, he thought, as he made haste to finish his breakfast; when, to his intense amazement, Pavel Pavlovitch walked in.

In spite of their meeting the day before Velchaninov could never have conceived that the man would come to see him again, and was so taken aback that he stared at him and did not know what to say. But Pavel Pavlovitch was equal to the occasion. He greeted him, and sat down on the very same chair on which he had sat on his last visit. Velchaninov had a sudden and peculiarly vivid memory of that visit, and gazed uneasily and with repulsion at his visitor.

"You're surprised?" began Pavel Pavlovitch, interpreting Velchaninov's expression.

He seemed altogether much more free and easy than on the previous day, and at the same time it could be detected that he was more nervous than he had been then. His appearance was particularly curious. M. Trusotsky was not only presentably but quite foppishly dressed—in a light summer jacket, light-coloured trousers of a smart, close-fitting cut, a light waistcoat; gloves, a gold lorgnette, which he had suddenly adopted for some reason. His linen was irreproachable; he even smelt of scent. About his whole get-up there was something ridiculous, and at the same time strangely and unpleasantly suggestive.

"Of course, Alexey Ivanovitch," he went on, wriggling, "I'm surprising you by coming, and I'm sensible of it. But there is always, so I imagine, preserved between people, and to my mind there should be preserved, something higher, shouldn't there? Higher, I mean, than all the conditions and even unpleasantnesses that may come to pass. ... Shouldn't there?"

"Pavel Pavlovitch, say what you have to say quickly, and without ceremony," said Velchaninov, frowning.

"In a couple of words," Pavel Pavlovitch began hastily, "I'm going to get married and I am just setting off to see my future bride. They are in a summer villa too. I should like to have the great honour to make bold to introduce you to the family, and have come to ask an unusual favour" (Pavel Pavlovitch bent his head humbly), "to beg you to accompany me. ..."

"Accompany you, where?" Velchaninov stared with open eyes.

"To them, that is, to their villa. Forgive me, I am talking as though in a fever, and perhaps I've not been clear; but I'm so afraid of your declining."

And he looked plaintively at Velchaninov.

"Do you want me to go with you now to see your future bride?" Velchaninov repeated, scrutinizing him rapidly, unable to believe his eyes or ears.

"Yes," said Pavel Pavlovitch, extremely abashed. "Don't be angry, Alexey Ivanovitch. It's not impudence; I only beg you most humbly as a great favour. I had dreamed that you might not like, that being so, to refuse. ..."

"To begin with, it's utterly out of the question." Velchaninov turned round uneasily.

"It is merely an intense desire on my part and nothing more," Pavel Pavlovitch went on, imploring him. "I will not conceal, either, that there are reasons for it, but I should have preferred not to have revealed them till later, and for the present to confine myself to the very earnest request. ..."

And he positively got up from his seat to show his deference.

"But in any case it is quite impossible, you must admit that yourself. ..." Velchaninov, too, stood up.

"It is quite possible, Alexey Ivanovitch. I was proposing to present you as a friend; and besides, you are an acquaintance of theirs already; you see, it's to Zahlebinin's, to his villa. The civil councillor, Zahlebinin."

"What?" cried Velchaninov.

It was the civil councillor for whom he had been constantly looking for a month before, and had never found at home. He had, as it turned out, being acting in the interests of the other side.

"Yes, yes; yes, yes," said Pavel Pavlovitch, smiling and seeming to be greatly encouraged by Velchaninov's great astonishment; "the very man, you remember, whom you were walking beside, and talking to, while I stood opposite watching you; I was waiting to go up to him when you had finished. Twenty years ago we were in the same office, and that day, when I meant to go up to him after you had finished, I had no idea of the sort. It occurred to me suddenly, only a week ago."

"But, upon my word, they are quite a decent family," said Velchaninov, in naïve surprise.

"Well, what then, if they are?" Pavel Pavlovitch grimaced.

"No, of course, I didn't mean ... only as far as I've observed when I was there ..."

"They remember, they remember your being there," Pavel Pavlovitch put in joyfully; "only you couldn't have seen the family then; but he remembers you and has a great esteem for you. We talked of you with great respect."

"But when you've only been a widower three months?"

"But you see the wedding will not be at once; the wedding will be in nine or ten months, so that the year of mourning will be over. I assure you that everything is all right. To begin with, Fedosey Petrovitch has known me from a boy; he knew my late wife, he knows my style of living, and what people think of me, and what's more, I have property, and I'm receiving a post with increase of salary—so all that has weight."

"Why, is it his daughter?"

"I will tell you all about it." Pavel Pavlovitch wriggled ingratiatingly. "Allow me to light a cigarette. And you'll see her yourself to-day too. To begin with, such capable men as Fedosey Petrovitch are sometimes very highly thought of here in Petersburg, if they succeed in attracting notice. But you know, apart from his salary and the additional and supplementary fees, bonuses, hotel expenses, and moneys given in relief, he has nothing— that is, nothing substantial that could be called a capital. They are comfortably off, but there is no possibility of saving where there's a family. Only imagine: Fedosey Petrovitch has eight girls, and only one son, still a child. If he were to die to-morrow there would be nothing left but a niggardly pension. And eight girls! just imagine—only imagine—what it must run into simply for their shoes! Of these eight girls five are grown up, the eldest is four-and-twenty (a most charming young lady, as you will see) and the sixth, a girl of fifteen, is still at the high school. Of course, husbands must be found for the five elder ones, and that ought to be done in good time, as far as possible, so their father ought to bring them out, and what do you suppose that will cost? And then I turn up, the first suitor they have had in the house, and one they know all about, that I really have property, I mean. Well, that's all."

Pavel Pavlovitch explained with fervour.

"You're engaged to the eldest?"

"N—no, I ... no, not to the eldest; you see, I'm proposing for the sixth, the one who is still at the high school."

"What?" said Velchaninov, with an involuntary smile. "Why, you say she's only fifteen!"

"Fifteen now; but in nine months she'll be sixteen, she'll be sixteen and three months, so what of it? But as it would be improper at present, there will be no open engagement but only an understanding with the parents. ... I assure you that everything is all right!"

"Then it's not settled yet?"

"Yes, it is settled, it's all settled. I assure you, all is as it should be."

"And does she know?"

"Well, it's only in appearance, for the sake of propriety, that they are not telling her; of course she knows." Pavel Pavlovitch screwed up his eyes insinuatingly. "Well, do you congratulate me, Alexey Ivanovitch?" Pavel Pavlovitch concluded very timidly.

"But what should I go there for? However," he added hurriedly, "since I'm not going in any case, don't trouble to find a reason."

"Alexey Ivanovitch ..."

"But do you expect me to get in beside you and drive off there with you. Think of it!"

The feeling of disgust and aversion came back after the momentary distraction of Pavel Pavlovitch's chatter about his future bride. In another minute he would have turned him out. He even felt angry with himself for some reason.

"Do, Alexey Ivanovitch, do, and you won't regret it!" Pavel Pavlovitch implored him in a voice fraught with feeling. "No, no, no!"—he waved his hands, catching an impatient and determined gesture from Velchaninov. "Alexey Ivanovitch, Alexey Ivanovitch, wait a bit before you decide! I see that you have perhaps misunderstood me. Of course, I know only too well that you cannot be to me, nor I to you ... that we're not comrades; I am not so absurd as not to understand that. And that the favour I'm asking of you will not pledge you to anything in the future. And, indeed, I'm going away after to-morrow altogether, absolutely; just as though nothing had happened. Let this day be a solitary exception. I have come to you resting my hopes on the generosity of the special feelings of your heart, Alexey Ivanovitch—those feelings which might of late have been awakened. ... I think I'm speaking clearly, am I not?"

Pavel Pavlovitch's agitation reached an extreme point. Velchaninov looked at him strangely.

"You ask for some service from me?" he questioned, hesitatingly, "and are very insistent about it. That strikes me as suspicious; I should like to know more about it."

"The only service is that you should come with me. And afterwards, on our way back, I will unfold all to you as though at confession. Alexey Ivanovitch, believe me!"

But Velchaninov still refused, and the more stubbornly because he was conscious of an oppressive and malignant impulse. This evil impulse had been faintly stirring within him from the very beginning, ever since Pavel Pavlovitch had talked of his future bride: whether it was simply curiosity, or some other quite obscure prompting, he felt tempted to consent. And the more he felt tempted, the more he resisted. He sat with his elbow on one hand, and hesitated.

Pavel Pavlovitch beside him kept coaxing and persuading.

"Very good, I'll come," he consented all at once, uneasily and almost apprehensively, getting up from his seat.

Pavel Pavlovitch was extremely delighted.

"But, Alexey Ivanovitch, you must change your clothes now," Pavel Pavlovitch cajoled him, hanging gleefully about him; "put on your best suit."

"And why must he meddle in this, too, strange fellow?" Velchaninov thought to himself.

"This is not the only service I'm expecting of you, Alexey Ivanovitch. Since you have given your consent, please be my adviser."

"In what, for example?"

"The great question, for instance, of crape. Which would be more proper, to remove the crape, or keep it on?"

"As you prefer."

"No, I want you to decide; what would you do yourself in my place, that is, if you had crape on your hat? My own idea is that if I retain it, it points to the constancy of my feelings, and so is a flattering recommendation."

"Take it off, of course."

"Do you really think it's a matter of course?" Pavel Pavlovitch hesitated. "No, I think I had better keep it. ...."

"As you like."

"He doesn't trust me, that's a good thing," thought Velchaninov.

They went out; Pavel Pavlovitch gazed with satisfaction at Velchaninov's smartened appearance; his countenance seemed to betray an even greater degree of deference and of dignity! Velchaninov wondered at him and even more at himself. A very good carriage stood waiting for them at the gate.

"So you had a carriage all ready too? So you felt sure I should come?"

"I engaged the carriage for myself, but I did feel confident that you would consent to accompany me," Pavel Pavlovitch replied, with the air of a perfectly happy man.

"Ah, Pavel Pavlovitch," Velchaninov said, laughing as it were irritably when they were in the carriage and had set off; "weren't you too sure of me?"

"But it's not for you, Alexey Ivanovitch, it's not for you to tell me that

I'm a fool for it," Pavel Pavlovitch responded, in a voice full of feeling.

"And Liza," thought Velchaninov, and at once hastened to dismiss the thought of her as though afraid of sacrilege. And it suddenly seemed to him that he was so petty, so insignificant at that moment; it struck him that the thought that had tempted him was a thought so small and nasty ... and he longed again, at all costs, to fling it all up, and to get out of the carriage at once, even if he had to thrash Pavel Pavlovitch. But the latter began talking and the temptation mastered his heart again.

"Alexey Ivanovitch, do you know anything about jewels?"

"What sort of jewels?"

"Diamonds."

"Yes."

"I should like to take a little present. Advise me, should I or not?"

"I think you shouldn't."

"But I feel I should so like to," returned Pavel Pavlovitch, "only, what am I to buy? A whole set, that is, a brooch, earrings, bracelets, or simply one article?"

"How much do you want to spend?"

"About four hundred or five hundred roubles."

"Ough!"

"Is it too much, or what?" asked Pavel Pavlovitch in a flutter.

"Buy a single bracelet for a hundred roubles."

Pavel Pavlovitch was positively mortified; he was so eager to spend more and buy a "whole set" of jewels. He persisted. They drove to a shop. It ended, however, in his only buying a bracelet, and not the one that he wanted to, but the one that Velchaninov fixed upon. Pavel Pavlovitch wanted to take both. When the jeweller, who had asked a hundred and seventy-five roubles for the bracelet, consented to take a hundred and fifty for it, Pavel Pavlovitch was positively vexed; he would have paid two hundred if that sum had been asked, he was so eager to spend more.

"It doesn't matter, does it, my being in a hurry with presents?" he gushed blissfully, when they had set off again. "They're not grand people, they are very simple. The innocent creatures are fond of little presents," he said, with a sly and good-humoured grin. "You smiled just now, Alexey Ivanovitch, when you heard she was fifteen; but that's just what bowled me over; that she was still going to school with the satchel on her arm full of copy-books and pens, he—he! That satchel fascinated me! It's innocence that charms me, Alexey Ivanovitch; it's not so much beauty of face, it's that. She giggles in the corner with her school friend, and how she laughs, my goodness! And what at? It's all because the kitten jumped

off the chest of drawers on to the bed and was curled up like a little ball. ...
And then there's that scent of fresh apples! Shall I take off the crape?"

"As you please."

"I will take it off."

He took off his hat, tore off the crape and flung it in the road. Velchaninov saw that his face was beaming with the brightest hopes, as he replaced his hat upon his bald head.

"Can it be that he is really like this?" he thought, feeling genuinely angry; "can it be there isn't some trick in his inviting me? Can he be really reckoning on my generosity?" he went on, almost offended at the last supposition. "What is he—a buffoon, a fool, or the 'eternal husband' —but it's impossible!"

Chapter XII

At the Zahlebinins'

The Zahlebinins were really a "very decent family," as Velchaninov had expressed it, and Zahlebinin himself had an assured position in a government office and was well thought of by his superiors. All that Pavel Pavlovitch had said about their income was true too: "They live very comfortably, but if he dies there'll be nothing left."

Old Zahlebinin gave Velchaninov a warm and affable welcome, and his former "foe" seemed quite like a friend.

"I congratulate you, it was better so," he began at the first word, with a pleasant and dignified air. "I was in favour of settling it out of court myself and Pyotr Karlovitch (Velchaninov's lawyer) is priceless in such cases. Well, you get sixty thousand without any bother, without delay and dispute! And the case might have dragged on for three years!"

Velchaninov was at once presented to Madame Zahlebinin, an elderly lady of redundant figure, with a very simple and tired-looking face. The young ladies, too, began to sail in one after the other or in couples. But a very great many young ladies made their appearance; by degrees they gathered to the number of ten or twelve—Velchaninov lost count of them; some came in, others went out. But among them several were girl friends from the neighbouring villas. The Zahlebinins' villa, a large wooden house, built in quaint and whimsical style, with parts added at different periods, had the advantage of a big garden; but three or four other villas looked into the garden on different sides, and it was common property, an arrangement which naturally led to friendly relations among the girls

735

of the different households. From the first words of conversation Velchaninov observed that he was expected, and that his arrival in the character of a friend of Pavel Pavlovitch, anxious to make their acquaintance, was hailed almost triumphantly.

His keen and experienced eye quickly detected something special; from the over-cordial welcome of the parents, from a certain peculiar look about the girls and their get-up (though, indeed, it was a holiday), from all that, the suspicion dawned upon him that Pavel Pavlovitch had been scheming and, very possibly, without, of course, saying it in so many words, had been suggesting a conception of him as a bachelor of property and of the "best society," who was suffering from ennui and very, very likely to make up his mind to "change his state and settle down," especially as he had just come into a fortune. The manner and the appearance of the eldest Mademoiselle Zahlebinin, Katerina Fedosyevna, the one who was twenty-four and who had been described by Pavel Pavlovitch as a charming person, struck him as being in keeping with that idea. She was distinguished from her sisters by her dress and the original way in which her luxuriant hair was done. He sisters and the other girls all looked as though they were firmly convinced that Velchaninov was making their acquaintance "on Katya's account" and had come "to have a look at her." Their glances and even some words, dropped in the course of the day, confirmed him in this surmise. Katerina Fedosyevna was a tall blonde of generous proportions, with an exceedingly sweet face, of a gentle, unenterprising, even torpid character. "Strange that a girl like that should still be on hand," Velchaninov could not help thinking, watching her with pleasure. "Of course, she has no dowry and she'll soon grow too fat, but meantime lots of men would admire her. ..." All the other sisters, too, were nice-looking, and among their friends there were several amusing and even pretty faces. It began to divert him; he had come, moreover, with special ideas.

Nadyezhda Fedosyevna, the sixth, the schoolgirl and Pavel Pavlovitch's bride-elect, did not appear till later. Velchaninov awaited her coming with an impatience which surprised him and made him laugh at himself. At last she made her entrance, and not without effect, accompanied by a lively, keen-witted girl friend, a brunette with a comical face whose name was Marie Nikititchna, and of whom, as was at once apparent, Pavel Pavlovitch stood in great dread. This Marie Nikititchna, a girl of twenty-three, with a mocking tongue and really clever, was a nursery governess in a friend's family. She had long been accepted by the Zahlebinins as one of themselves and was thought a great deal of by the girls. It was evident that Nadya found her indispensable now. Velchaninov discerned at once that all the girls were antagonistic to Pavel Pavlovitch, even the friends, and two minutes after Nadya's arrival he had made up his mind that she *detested* him. He observed, too, that Pavel Pavlovitch either failed to notice this or refused to.

Nadya was unquestionably the handsomest of the lot—a little brunette with a wild, untamed look and the boldness of a nihilist; a roguish imp with blazing eyes, with a charming but often malicious smile, with wonderful lips and teeth, slender and graceful, her face still childlike but glowing with the dawn of thought. Her age was evident in every step she took, in every word she uttered. It appeared afterwards that Pavel Pavlovitch did see her for the first time with an American leather satchel on her arm, but this time she had not got it.

The presentation of the bracelet was a complete failure, and, indeed, made an unpleasant impression. As soon as Pavel Pavlovitch saw his "future bride" come into the room he went up to her with a smirk. He presented it as a "testimonial to the agreeable gratification he had experienced on his previous visit on the occasion of the charming song sung by Nadyezhda Fedosyevna at the piano. ..." He stammered, could not finish, and stood helpless, holding out the case with the bracelet and thrusting it into the hand of Nadyezhda Fedosyevna, who did not want to take it, and, crimson with shame and anger, drew back her hands. She turned rudely to her mother, whose face betrayed embarrassement, and said aloud:

"I don't want to take it, maman!"

"Take it and say thank you," said her father, with calm severity: but he, too, was displeased. "Unnecessary, quite unnecessary!" he muttered reprovingly to Pavel Pavlovitch.

Nadya, seeing there was no help for it, took the case and, dropping her eyes, curtsied, as tiny children curtsy—that is, suddenly bobbed down, and popped up again as though on springs. One of her sisters went up to look at it and Nadya handed her the case unopened, showing, for her part, that she did not care to look at it. The bracelet was taken out and passed from one to the other; but they all looked at it in silence, and some even sarcastically. Only the mother murmured that the bracelet was very charming. Pavel Pavlovitch was ready to sink into the earth.

Velchaninov came to the rescue.

He began talking, loudly and eagerly, about the first thing that occurred to him, and before five minutes were over he had gained the attention of every one in the drawing-room. He was a brilliant master of the art of small talk—that is, the art of seeming perfectly frank and at the same time appearing to consider his listeners as frank as himself. He could, with perfect naturalness, appear when necessary to be the most light-hearted and happy of men. He was very clever, too, in slipping in a witty remark, a gibe, a gay insinuation or amusing pun, always as it were accidentally and as though unconscious of doing it—though the epigram or pun and the whole conversation, perhaps, had been prepared and rehearsed long, long before and even used on more than one previous occasion. But at the present moment nature and art were at one, he felt that he was in the mood and that something was drawing him on; he felt the most absolute confidence in himself and knew that in a few minutes all these eyes would be turned upon him, all these people would be listening only to him, talking to no one but him, and laughing only at what he said. And, in fact, the laughter soon came, by degrees the others joined in the conversation—and he was exceedingly clever in making other people talk—three or four voices could be heard at once. The bored and weary face of Madame Zahlebinin was lighted up almost with joy; it was the same with Katerina Fedosyevna, who gazed and listened as though enchanted. Nadya watched him keenly from under her brows; it was evident that she was prejudiced against him. This spurred him on the more. The "mischievous" Marie Nikititchna succeeded in getting in rather a good thrust at him; she asserted quite fictitiously that Pavel Pavlovitch had introduced him as the friend of his boyhood, so putting with obvious intent at least seven years on to his age. But even the malicious Marie Nikititchna liked him. Pavel Pavlovitch was completely nonplussed. He had, of course, some idea of his friend's abilities and at first was delighted at his success; he tittered himself and joined in the conversation; but by degrees he seemed to sink into thoughtfulness, and finally into positive dejection, which was clearly apparent in his troubled countenance.

"Well, you're a visitor who doesn't need entertaining," old Zahlebinin commented gaily, as he got up to go upstairs to his own room, where, in spite of the holiday, he had some business papers awaiting his revision; "and, only fancy, I thought of you as the most gloomy, hypochondriacal of young men. What mistakes one makes!"

They had a piano; Velchaninov asked who played, and suddenly turned to Nadya:

"I believe you sing?"

"Who told you?" Nadya snapped out.

"Pavel Pavlovitch told me just now."

"It's not true. I only sing for fun. I've no voice."

"And I've no voice either, but I sing."

"Then you'll sing to us? Well, then, I'll sing to you," said Nadya, her eyes gleaming; "only not now, but after dinner. I can't endure music," she added. "I'm sick of the piano: they're all singing and playing from morning to night here—Katya's the only one worth hearing."

Velchaninov at once took this up, and it appeared that Katerina Fedosyevna was the only one who played the piano seriously. He at once begged her to play. Every one was evidently pleased at his addressing Katya, and the mamma positively flushed crimson with gratification. Katerina Fedosyevna got up, smiling, and went to the piano, and suddenly, to her own surprise, she flushed crimson and was horribly abashed that she, such a big girl, four-and-twenty and so stout, should be blushing like a child—and all this was written clearly on her face as she sat down to play. She played something from Haydn and played it carefully though without expression, but she was shy. When she had finished Velchaninov began warmly praising to her, not her playing but Haydn, and especially the little thing which she had played, and she was evidently so pleased and listened so gratefully and happily to his praises, not of herself but of Haydn, that he could not help looking at her with more friendliness and and attention: "Ah, but you are a dear!" was reflected in the gleam of his eye—and every one seemed instantly to understand that look, especially Katerine Fedosyevna herself.

"You have a delightful garden," he said, suddenly addressing the company and looking towards the glass door that led on to the balcony. "What do you say to our all going into the garden?"

"Let us, let us!" they shrieked joyfully, as though he had guessed the general wish.

They walked in the garden till dinner-time. Madame Zahlebinin, though she had been longing to have a nap, could not resist going out with them, but wisely sat down to rest on the verandah, where she at once began to doze. In the garden Velchaninov and the girls got on to still more friendly terms. He noticed that several very young men from the villas joined them; one was a student and another simply a high school boy. They promptly made a dash each for *his* girl, and it was evident that they had come on their account; the third, a very morose and dishevelled-looking youth of twenty, in huge blue spectacles, began, with a frown, whispering hurriedly with Marie Nikititchna and Nadya. He scanned Velchaninov sternly, and seemed to consider it incumbent upon himself to treat him with extraordinary contempt. Some of the girls suggested that they should play games. To Velchaninov's question, what games they played, they said all sorts of games, and catch-catch, but in the evening they would play proverbs—that is, all would sit down and one would go out, the others choose a proverb—for instance: "More haste, less speed," and when the one outside is called in, each in turn has to say one sentence to him. One, for instance, must say a sentence in which there is the word "more," the second, one in which there is the word "haste," and so on. And from their sentences he must guess the proverb.

"That must be very amusing," said Velchaninov.

"Oh, no, it's awfully boring," cried two or three voices at once.

"Or else we play at acting," Nadya observed, suddenly addressing him. "Do you see that thick tree, round which there's a seat: behind that tree is behind the scenes, and there the actors sit, say a king, a queen, a princess, a young man—just as any one likes; each one enters when he chooses and says anything that comes into his head, and that's the game."

"But that's delightful!" Velchaninov repeated again.

"Oh, no, it's awfully dull! At first it did turn out amusing, but lately it's always been senseless, for no one knows how to end it; perhaps with you, though, it will be more interesting. We did think you were a friend of Pavel Pavlovitch's, though, but it seems he was only bragging. I'm very glad you have come ... for one thing. ..."

She looked very earnestly and impressively at Velchaninov and at once walked away to Marie Nikititchna.

"We're going to play proverbs this evening," one of the girl friends whom Velchaninov had scarcely noticed before, and with whom he had not exchanged a word, whispered to him confidentially. "They're all going to make fun of Pavel Pavlovitch, and you will too, of course."

"Ah, how nice it is that you've come, we were all so dull," observed another girl in a friendly way. She was a red-haired girl with freckles, and a face absurdly flushed from walking and the heat. Goodness knows where she had sprung from; Velchaninov had not noticed her till then.

Pavel Pavlovitch's uneasiness grew more and more marked. In the garden Velchaninov made great friends with Nadya. She no longer looked at him from under her brows as she had at first; she seemed to have laid aside her critical attitude towards him, and laughed, skipped about, shrieked, and twice even seized him by the hand; she was extremely happy, she continued to take not the slightest notice of Pavel Pavlovitch, and behaved as though she were not aware of his existence. Velchaninov felt certain that there was an actual plot against Pavel Pavlovitch; Nadya and the crowd of girls drew Velchaninov aside, while some of the other girl friends lured Pavel Pavlovitch on various pretexts in another direction; but the latter broke away from them, and ran full speed straight to them—that is, to Velchaninov and Nadya, and suddenly thrust his bald head in between them with uneasy curiosity. He hardly attempted to restrain himself; the *naïveté* of his gestures and actions were sometimes amazing. He could not resist trying once more to turn Velchaninov's attention to Katerina Fedosyevna; it was clear to her now that he had not come on her account, but was much more interested in Nadya; but her expression was just as sweet and good-humoured as ever. She seemed to be happy simply at being beside them and listening to what their new visitor was saying; she, poor thing, could never keep up her share in a conversation cleverly.

"What a darling your sister Katerina Fedosyevna is?" Velchaninov said aside to Nadya.

"Katya! No one could have a kinder heart than she has. She's an angel to all of us. I adore her," the girl responded enthusiastically.

At last dinner came at five o'clock; and it was evident that the dinner, too, was not an ordinary meal, but had been prepared expressly for visitors. There were two or three very elaborate dishes, which evidently were not part of their ordinary fare, one of them so strange that no one could find a name for it. In addition to the everyday wine there was a bottle of Tokay, obviously for the benefit of the visitors; at the end of dinner champagne was brought in for some reason. Old Zahlebinin took an extra glass, became extraordinarily good-humoured and ready to laugh at anything Velchaninov said.

In the end Pavel Pavlovitch could not restrain himself. Carried away by the spirit of rivalry he suddenly attempted to make a pun too; at the end of the table, where he was sitting by Madame Zahlebinin, there was a sudden roar of loud laughter from the delighted girls.

"Papa, papa! Pavel Pavlovitch has made a pun too," the fourth and fifth Zahlebinin girls shouted in unison. "He says we're 'damsels who dazzle all. ...'"

"Ah, so he's punning too! well, what was his pun?" the old man responded sedately, turning patronizingly to Pavel Pavlovitch and smiling in readiness for the expected pun.

"Why, he says we're 'damsels who dazzle all.'"

"Y-yes, well, and what then?" The old man did not understand and smiled more good-humouredly in expectation.

"Oh, papa, how tiresome you are; you don't understand. Why, 'damsels' and then 'dazzle'; 'damsel' is like 'dazzle,' 'damsels who dazzle all. ...'"

"A-a-ah," the old man drawled in a puzzled voice. "H'm, well, he'll make a better one next time!"

And the old man laughed good-humouredly.

"Pavel Pavlovitch, you can't have all the perfections at once," Marie Nikititchna jerked aloud. "Oh, my goodness! he's got a bone in his throat," she exclaimed, jumping up from her chair.

There was a positive hubbub, but that was just what Marie Nikititchna wanted. Pavel Pavlovitch had simply choked over the wine which he was sipping to cover his confusion, but Marie Nikititchna vowed and declared that it was a "fish bone," that she had seen it herself and that people sometimes died of it.

"Slap him on the nape of the neck," some one shouted.

"Yes, really that's the best thing to do!" the old man approved aloud.

Eager volunteers were already at him; Marie Nikititchna and the red-haired girl (who had also been invited to dinner), and, finally, the mamma herself, greatly alarmed; every one wanted to slap Pavel Pavlovitch on the back. Jumping up from the table, Pavel Pavlovitch wriggled away and was for a full minute asseverating that he had swallowed his wine too quickly and that the cough would soon be over, while the others realized that it was all a trick of Marie Nikititchna's.

"But, really, you tease ...!" Madame Zahlebinin tried to say sternly to Marie Nikititchna: but she broke down and laughed as she very rarely did, and that made quite a sensation of a sort.

After dinner they all went out on the verandah to drink coffee.

"And what lovely days we're having!" said the old man, looking with pleasure into the garden, and serenely admiring the beauties of nature. "If only we could have some rain. Enjoy yourselves and God bless you! And you enjoy yourself too," he added, patting Pavel Pavlovitch on the shoulder as he went out.

When they had all gone out into the garden again, Pavel Pavlovitch suddenly ran up to Velchaninov and pulled him by the sleeve.

"Just one minute," he whispered impatiently.

They turned into a lonely side path.

"No, in this case, excuse me, no, I won't give up ..." he stuttered in a furious whisper, clutching Velchaninov's arm.

"What? what?" Velchaninov asked, opening his eyes in amazement.

Pavel Pavlovitch stared at him mutely, his lips moved, and he smiled furiously.

"Where are you going? Where are you? Everything's ready," they heard the ringing, impatient voices of the girls.

Velchaninov shrugged his shoulders and returned to the rest of the party.

Pavel Pavlovitch, too, ran after him.

"I'll bet he asked you for a handkerchief," said Marie Nikititchna; "he forgot one last time too."

"He'll always forget it!" the fifth Zahlebinin girl put in.

"He's forgotten his handkerchief, Pavel Pavlovitch has forgotten his handkerchief, mamma, Pavel Pavlovitch has forgotten his pocket-handkerchief, mamma, Pavel Pavlovitch has a cold in his head again!" cried voices.

"Then why doesn't he say so! You do stand on ceremony, Pavel Pavlovitch!" Madame Zahlebinin drawled in a sing-song voice. "It's dangerous to trifle with a cold; I'll send you a handkerchief directly. And why has he always got a cold in his head?" she added, as she moved away, glad of an excuse for returning home.

"I have two pocket-handkerchiefs and I haven't a cold in my head!" Pavel Pavlovitch called after her, but the lady apparently did not grasp what he said, and a minute later, when Pavel Pavlovitch was ambling after the others, keeping near Velchaninov and Nadya, a breathless maidservant overtook him and brought him a handkerchief.

"Proverbs, a game of proverbs," the girls shouted on all sides, as though they expected something wonderful from "a game of proverbs."

They fixed on a place and sat down on a seat; it fell to Marie Nikititchna's lot to guess; they insisted that she should go as far away as possible and not listen; in her absence they chose a proverb and distributed the words. Marie Nikititchna returned and guessed the proverb at once. The proverb was: "It's no use meeting troubles half-way."

Marie Nikititchna was followed by the young man with dishevelled hair and blue spectacles. They insisted on even greater precautions with him—he had to stand in the arbour and keep his face to the fence. The gloomy young man did what was required of him contemptuously, and seemed to feel morally degraded by it. When he was called he could guess nothing, he went the round of all of them and listened to what they said twice over, spent a long time in gloomy meditation, but nothing came of it. They put him to shame. The proverb was: "To pray to God and serve the Tsar ne'er fail of their reward."

"And the proverb's disgusting!" the exasperated young man exclaimed indignantly, as he retreated to his place.

"Oh, how dull it is!" cried voices.

Velchaninov went out; he was hidden even further off; he, too, failed to guess.

"Oh, how dull it is!" more voices cried.

"Well, now, I'll go out," said Nadya.

"No, no, let Pavel Pavlovitch go out now, it's Pavel Pavlovitch's turn," they all shouted, growing more animated.

Pavel Pavlovitch was led away, right up to the fence in the very corner, and made to stand facing it, and that he might not look round, the red-haired girl was sent to keep watch on him. Pavel Pavlovitch, who had regained his confidence and almost his cheerfulness, was determined to do his duty properly and stood stock-still, gazing at the fence and not daring to turn round. The red-haired girl stood on guard twenty paces behind him nearer to the party in the arbour, and she exchanged signals with the girls in some excitement; it was evident that all were expecting something with trepidation; something was on foot. Suddenly the red-haired girl waved her arms as a signal to the arbour. Instantly they all jumped up and ran off at breakneck speed.

"Run, you run, too," a dozen voices whispered to Velchaninov, almost with horror at his not running.

"What's the matter? what has happened?" he asked, hurrying after them.

"Hush, don't shout! Let him stand there staring at the fence while we all run away. See, Nastya is running."

The red-haired girl (Nastya) was running at breakneck speed, waving her hands as though something extraordinary had happened. They all ran at last to the other side of the pond, the very opposite corner of the garden. When Velchaninov had got there he saw that Katerina Fedosyevna was hotly disputing with the others, especially with Nadya and Marie Niki-titchna.

"Katya, darling, don't be angry!" said Nadya, kissing her.

"Very well, I won't tell mamma, but I shall go away myself, for it's very horrid. What must he be feeling at the fence there, poor man."

She went away—from pity, but all the others were merciless and as, ruthless as before. They all insisted sternly that when Pavel Pavlovitch came back, Velchaninov should take no notice of him, as though nothing had happened.

"And let us all play catch-catch!" cried the red-headed girl ecstatically.

It was at least a quarter of an hour before Pavel Pavlovitch rejoined the party. For two-thirds of that time he had certainly been standing at the fence. The game was in full swing, and was a great success—everybody was shouting and merry. Frantic with rage, Pavel Pavlovitch went straight up to Velchaninov and pulled at his sleeve again.

"Just half a minute!"

"Good gracious, what does he want with his half minutes!"

"He's borrowing a handkerchief again," was shouted after him once more.

"Well, this time it was you; now it's all your doing. ..."

Pavel Pavlovitch's teeth chattered as he said this.

Velchaninov interrupted him, and mildly advised him to be livelier, or they would go on teasing him. "They tease you because you are cross, when all the rest are enjoying themselves." To his surprise, these words of advice made a great impression on Pavel Pavlovitch; he subsided at once—so much so, in fact, that he went back to the party with a penitent air and submissively took his place in the game; after which they left him alone and treated him like the rest—and before half an hour had passed he had almost regained his spirits. In all the games when he had to choose a partner he picked out by preference the red-haired traitress, or one of the Zahlebinin sisters. But to his still greater surprise Velchaninov noticed that Pavel Pavlovitch did not dare try to speak to Nadya, although he continually hovered about her. At any rate he accepted his position, as an object of scorn and neglect to her, as though it were a fitting and natural thing. But towards the end they played a prank upon him again.

The game was "hide-and-seek." The one who hid, however, was allowed to run anywhere in the part of the garden allotted him. Pavel Pavlovitch, who had succeeded in concealing himself completely in some thick bushes, conceived the idea of running out and making a bolt for the house. He was seen and shouts were raised; he crept hurriedly upstairs to the first floor, knowing of a place behind a chest of drawers, where he could hide. But the red-haired girl flew up after him, crept on tiptoe to the door and turned the key on him. All left off playing and ran just as they had done before to the other side of the pond, at the further end of the garden. Ten minutes later, Pavel Pavlovitch, becoming aware that no one was looking for him, peeped out of the window. There was no one to be seen. He did not dare to call out for fear of waking the parents; the maids had been sternly forbidden to answer Pavel Pavlovitch's call or go to him. Katerina Fedosyevna might have unlocked him, but, returning to her room and sitting down to dream a little, she had unexpectedly fallen asleep too. And so he stayed there about an hour. At last the girls came, as it were by chance, in twos or threes.

"Pavel Pavlovitch, why don't you come out to us? Oh, it has been fun! We've been playing at acting. Alexey Ivanovitch has been acting 'a young man.' "

"Pavel Pavlovitch, why don't you come, we want to admire you!" others observed as they passed.

"Admire what now?" they suddenly heard the voice of Madame Zahle-binin, who had only just woken up and made up her mind to come out into the garden and watch the "children's" games while waiting for tea.

"But here's Pavel Pavlovitch," they told her, pointing to the window where Pavel Pavlovitch's face, pale with anger, looked out with a wry smile.

"It's an odd fancy for a man to sit alone, when you're all enjoying your-selves!" said the mamma, shaking her head.

Meanwhile, Nadya had deigned to give Velchaninov an explanation of her words that she "was glad he had come for one reason."

The explanation took place in a secluded avenue. Marie Nikititchna purposely summoned Velchaninov, who was taking part in some game and was horribly bored, and left him alone in the avenue with Nadya.

"I am absolutely convinced," she said boldly, in a rapid patter, "that you are not such a great friend of Pavel Pavlovitch's as he boasted you were. I am reckoning on you as the one person who can do me a very great service." She took the case out of her pocket. "I humbly beg you to give this back to him at once, as I shall never speak to him again in my life. You can say so from me, and tell him not to dare to force his com-pany and his presents on me. I'll let him know the rest through other people. Will you be so kind as to do what I want?"

"Oh, for mercy's sake, spare me!" Velchaninov almost cried out, wav-ing his hand.

"What? spare you?" Nadya was extraordinarily surprised at his refusal, and she gazed at him round-eyed.

The tone she had assumed for the occasion broke down immediately, and she was almost in tears.

Velchaninov laughed.

"I don't mean that. ... I should be very glad ... but I have my own account to settle with him ..."

"I knew that you were not his friend and that he was telling lies!" Nadya interrupted quickly and passionately. "I'll never marry him, I tell you! Never! I can't understand how he could presume. ... Only you must give him back his disgusting present or else what shall I do? I particularly, particularly want him to have it back to-day, the same day, so that his hopes may be crushed, and if he sneaks about it to papa he shall see what he gets by it."

And from behind the bushes there suddenly emerged the young man in the blue spectacles.

"It's your duty to return the bracelet," he blurted out furiously, pouncing on Velchaninov. "If only from respect for the rights of women, that is—if you are capable of rising to the full significance of the question."

But before he had time to finish Nadya tugged at his sleeve with all her might, and drew him away from Velchaninov.

"My goodness, how silly you are, Predposylov!" she cried. "Go away, go away, go away, and don't dare to listen; I told you to stand a long way off ... !" She stamped her little foot at him, and when he had crept back into the bushes she still walked up and down across the path, with her eyes flashing and her arms folded before her, as though she were beside herself with anger.

"You wouldn't believe how silly they are!" She stopped suddenly before Velchaninov. "It amuses you, but think what it means to me."

"That's not *he*, it's not *he*, is it?" laughed Velchaninov.

"Of course it isn't, and how could you imagine it!" cried Nadya, smiling and blushing. "That's only his friend. But I can't understand the friends he chooses; they all say that he's a 'future leader,' but I don't understand it. ... Alexey Ivanovitch, I've no one I can appeal to; I ask you for the last time, will you give it back?"

"Oh, very well, I will; give it me."

"Ah, you are kind, you are good!" she cried, delighted, handing him the case. "I'll sing to you the whole evening for that, for I sing beautifully, do you know. I told you a fib when I said I didn't like music. Oh, you must come again—once at any rate; how glad I should be. I would tell you everything, everything, everything, and a great deal more besides, because you're so kind—as kind, as kind, as—as Katya!"

And when they went in to tea she did sing him two songs, in an utterly untrained and hardly mature, but pleasant and powerful voice. When they came in from the garden Pavel Pavlovitch was stolidly sitting with the parents at the tea-table, on which the big family samovar was already boiling, surrounded by cups of Sèvres china. He was probably discussing very grave matters with the old people, as two days later he was going away for nine whole months. He did not glance at the party as they came in from the garden, and particularly avoided looking at Velchaninov. It was evident, too, that he had not been sneaking and that all was serene so far.

But when Nadya began singing he put himself forward at once. Nadya purposely ignored one direct question he addressed her, but this did not disconcert Pavel Pavlovitch, or make him hesitate. He stood behind her chair and his whole manner showed that this was his place and he was not going to give it up to any one.

"Alexey Ivanovitch sings, mamma; Alexey Ivanovitch wants to sing, mamma!" almost all the girls shouted at once, crowding round the piano at which Velchaninov confidently installed himself, intending to play his own accompaniment. The old people came in, and with them Katerina Fedosyevna, who had been sitting with them, pouring out the tea.

Velchaninov chose a song of Glinka's, now familiar to almost every one—

"In the glad hour when from thy lips
Come murmurs tender as a dove's."

He sang it, addressing himself entirely to Nadya, who was standing at his elbow nearer to him than any one. His voice had passed its prime, but what was left of it showed that it had once been a fine one. Velchaninov had, twenty years before, when he was a student, the luck to hear that song for the first time sung by Glinka himself, at the house of a friend of the composer's. It was at a literary and artistic bachelor gathering, and Glinka, growing expansive, played and sang his own favourite compositions, among them this song. He, too, had little voice left then, but Velchaninov remembered the great impression made by that song. A drawing-room singer, however skilful, would never have produced such an effect. In that song the intensity of passion rises, mounting higher and higher at every line, at every word; and, from this very intensity, the least trace of falsity, of exaggeration or unreality, such as passes muster so easily at an opera, would distort and destroy the whole value of it. To sing that slight but exceptional song it was essential to have truth, essential to have real inspiration, real passion, or a complete poetical comprehension of it. Otherwise the song would not only be a failure but might even appear unseemly and almost shameless: without them it would be impossible to express such intensity of passion without arousing repulsion, but truth and simplicity saved it. Velchaninov remembered that he had made a success with this song on some occasion. He had almost reproduced Glinka's manner of singing, but now, from the first note, from the first line, there was a gleam of inspiration in his singing which quivered in his voice.

At every word the torrent of feeling was more fervent and more boldly displayed; in the last lines the cry of passion is heard, and when, with blazing eyes, Velchaninov addressed the last words of the song to Nadya—

"Grown bolder, in thine eyes I gaze;
Draw close my lips, can hear no more,

I long to kiss thee, kiss thee, kiss thee!
I long to kiss thee, kiss thee, kiss thee!"

she trembled almost with alarm, and even stepped back; the colour rushed into her cheeks, and at the same time Velchaninov seemed to catch a glimpse of something responsive in her abashed and almost dismayed little face. The faces of all the audience betrayed their enchantment and also their amazement: all seemed to feel that it was disgraceful and impossible to sing like that, and yet at the same time all their faces were flushed and all their eyes glowed and seemed to be expecting something more. Among those faces Velchaninov had a vision especially of the face of Katerina Fedosyevna, which looked almost beautiful.

"What a song," old Zahlebinin muttered, a little flabbergasted; "but ... isn't it too strong? charming, but strong. ..."

"Yes ..." Madame Zahlebinin chimed in, but Pavel Pavlovitch would not let her go on; he dashed forward suddenly like one possessed, so far forgetting himself as to seize Nadya by the arm and pull her away from Velchaninov; he skipped up to him, gazed at him with a desperate face and quivering lips that moved without uttering a sound.

"Half a minute," he uttered faintly at last.

Velchaninov saw that in another minute the man might be guilty of something ten times as absurd; he made haste to take his arm and, regardless of the general amazement, drew him out into the verandah, and even took some steps into the garden with him, where it was now almost dark.

"Do you understand that you must go away with me, this minute!" said Pavel Pavlovitch.

"No, I don't understand. ..."

"Do you remember," Pavel Pavlovitch went on, in his frenzied whisper, "do you remember that you insisted that I should tell you everything, *everything* openly, 'the very last word ...' do you remember? Well, the time has come to say that word ... let us go!"

Velchaninov thought a minute, looked at Pavel Pavlovitch, and agreed to go.

The sudden announcement of their departure upset the parents, and made all the girls horribly indignant.

"At least have another cup of tea," said Madame Zahlebinin plaintively.

"Come, what's upset you?" old Zahlebinin said in a tone of severity and displeasure, addressing Pavel Pavlovitch, who stood simpering and silent.

"Pavel Pavlovitch, why are you taking Alexey Ivanovitch away?" the girls began plaintively, looking at him with exasperation.

Nadya gazed at him so wrathfully that he positively squirmed, but he did not give way.

"You see, Pavel Pavlovitch has reminded me—many thanks to him for it—of a very important engagement which I might have missed," Velchaninov said, smiling, as he shook hands with Zahlebinin, and bowed to the mamma and the girls, especially distinguishing Katerina Fedosyevna in a manner apparent to all.

"We are very grateful for your visit and shall always be glad to see you," Zahlebinin said ponderously, in conclusion.

"Ah, we shall be so delighted ..." the mamma chimed in with feeling.

"Come again, Alexey Ivanovitch, come again!" numerous voices were heard calling from the verandah, when he had already got into the carriage with Pavel Pavlovitch; there was perhaps one voice that called more softly than the others, "Come again, dear, dear Alexey Ivanovitch."

"That's the red-haired girl," thought Velchaninov.

CHAPTER XIII

On Whose Side Most?

He might think about the red-haired girl, and yet his soul was in agonies of vexation and remorse. And, indeed, during the whole of that day, which seemed on the surface so amusingly spent, a feeling of acute depression had scarcely left him. Before singing the song he did not know how to get away from it; perhaps that was why he had sung it with such fervour.

"And I could demean myself like that ... tear myself away from everything," he began reproaching himself, but he hurriedly cut short his thoughts. Indeed, it seemed to him humiliating to lament; it was a great deal more pleasant to be angry with some one.

"Fool!" he whispered wrathfully, with a side glance at the silent figure of Pavel Pavlovitch sitting beside him in the carriage.

Pavel Pavlovitch remained obstinately silent, perhaps concentrated on preparing what he had got to say. With an impatient gesture he sometimes took off his hat and wiped his brow with his handkerchief.

"Perspiring!" Velchaninov thought spitefully.

On one occasion only Pavel Pavlovitch addressed a question to the coachman. "Is there going to be a storm?" he asked.

"Storm, indeed! Not a doubt of it; it's been brewing up all day."

750

The sky was indeed growing dark and there were flashes of lightning in the distance.

They reached the town about half-past ten.

"I am coming in with you, of course," Pavel Pavlovitch warned him, not far from the house.

"I understand, but I must tell you that I feel seriously unwell."

"I won't stay, I won't stay long."

When they went in at the gate, Pavel Pavlovitch ran in at the porter's lodge to find Mavra.

"What were you running off there for?" Velchaninov said sternly, as the latter overtook him and they went into the room.

"Oh ... nothing ... the driver ..."

"I won't have you drink!"

No answer followed. Velchaninov lighted the candle, and Pavel Pavlovitch at once sat down on the chair. Velchaninov remained standing before him, with a frown on his face.

"I, too, promised to say my 'last' word," he began, with an inward, still suppressed irritation. "Here it is—that word: I consider on my conscience that everything between us is over, so that, in fact, there is nothing for us to talk about—do you hear?—nothing; and so wouldn't it be better for you to go away at once, and I'll close the door after you?"

"Let us settle our account, Alexey Ivanovitch," said Pavel Pavlovitch, looking in his face, however, with peculiar mildness.

"Set-tle our ac-count!" repeated Velchaninov, greatly surprised. "That's a strange thing to say! Settle what account? Bah! Isn't that perhaps that 'last word' you promised ... to reveal to me?"

"It is."

"We've no account to settle; we settled our account long ago!" Velchaninov pronounced proudly.

"Can you really think so?" Pavel Pavlovitch brought out in a voice full of feeling, clasping his hands strangely and holding them before his breast.

Velchaninov made him no answer, but continued pacing up and down the room. "Liza! Liza!" he was moaning in his heart.

"What did you want to settle, though?" he asked him, frowning, after a rather prolonged silence.

Pavel Pavlovitch had been following him about the room with his eyes all this time, still holding his hands clasped before him.

"Don't go there again," he almost whispered in a voice of entreaty, and he suddenly got up from his chair.

751

"What! So that's all you are thinking about?" Velchaninov laughed spitefully. "You've surprised me all day, though!" he was beginning malignantly, but suddenly his whole face changed. "Listen," he said mournfully, with deep and sincere feeling; "I consider that I have never lowered myself as I have to-day—to begin with, by consenting to go with you, and then—by what happened there. ... It was so paltry, so pitiful. ... I've defiled and debased myself by mixing myself up in it ... and forgetting ... But there!" he cried hastily. "Listen, you attacked me to-day in an unguarded moment when I was nervous and ill ... but there's no need to justify myself! I'm not going there again, and I assure you I take no interest in them whatever," he concluded resolutely.

"Really, really?" cried Pavel Pavlovitch, not disguising his relief and excitement.

Velchaninov looked at him contemptuously, and began pacing up and down the room again.

"You seem to have made up your mind to be happy?" he could not refrain from observing.

"Yes," Pavel Pavlovitch repeated naïvely, in a low voice.

"What is it to me," Velchaninov reflected, "that he's a buffoon and only spiteful through stupidity? I can't help hating him, though he isn't worth it!"

"I am 'the eternal husband'!" said Pavel Pavlovitch, with an abjectly submissive smile at his own expense. "I heard that expression from you, Alexey Ivanovitch, long ago, when you were staying with us in those days. I remember a great many of your sayings in that year. Last time, when you said here, 'the eternal husband,' I reflected."

Mavra came in with a bottle of champagne and two glasses.

"Forgive me, Alexey Ivanovitch; you know that I can't get on without it! Don't think it's impudence; look upon me as an outsider not on your level."

"Yes ..." Velchaninov muttered with repugnance, "but I assure you I feel unwell. ..."

"Directly ... directly ... in one minute," said Pavel Pavlovitch fussily; "just one little glass because my throat ..."

He greedily tossed off a glassful at a gulp and sat down, looking almost tenderly at Velchaninov.

Mavra went out.

"How beastly!" Velchaninov murmured.

"It's only those girl friends," Pavel Pavlovitch said confidently, all of a sudden completely revived.

"What? Ah, yes, you are still at that ..."

"It's only those girl friends! And then she's so young; we have our little airs and graces! They're charming, in fact. But then—then, you know, I shall be her slave; when she's treated with deference, when she sees something of society ... she'll be transformed."

"I shall have to give him back that bracelet, though," thought Velchaninov, scowling, as he felt the case in his pocket.

"You say that I'm resolved to be happy? I must get married, Alexey Ivanovitch," Pavel Pavlovitch went on confidentially and almost touchingly, "or what will become of me? You see for yourself!" He pointed to the bottle. "And that's only one-hundredth of my vices. I can't get on at all without marriage and—without new faith; I shall have faith and shall rise up again."

"But why on earth do you tell me this?" Velchaninov asked, almost bursting with laughter. It all struck him as wild. "But tell me," he cried, "what was your object in dragging me out there? What did you want me there for?"

"As a test ..." Pavel Pavlovitch seemed suddenly embarrassed.

"A test of what?"

"The effect. ... You see, Alexey Ivanovitch, it's only a week altogether ... I've been looking around there" (Pavel Pavlovitch grew more and more confused). "Yesterday I met you and thought: 'I've never yet seen her in outside, so to say, society, that is, in men's, except my own. ...' A stupid idea; I feel that myself now; unnecessary. I expected too much ... it's my horrible character. ..."

He suddenly raised his head and flushed crimson.

"Can he be telling the whole truth?" Velchaninov was petrified with surprise.

"Well, and what then?" he asked.

Pavel Pavlovitch gave a sugary and, as it were, crafty smile.

"It's only charming childishness! It's all those girl friends! Only forgive me for my stupid behaviour before you to-day, Alexey Ivanovitch; I never will again; and indeed it will never happen again."

"And I shan't be there again," said Velchaninov, with a smile.

"That's partly what I mean."

Velchaninov felt a little piqued.

"But I'm not the only man in the world, you know," he observed irritably.

Pavel Pavlovitch flushed again.

"It's sad for me to hear that, Alexey Ivanovitch, and, believe me, I've such a respect for Nadyezhda Fedosyevna ..."

"Excuse me, excuse me, I didn't mean anything; it only seems a little strange to me that you have such an exaggerated idea of my attractions ... and ... such genuine confidence in me."

"I had such confidence just because it was after all ... that happened in the past."

"Then if so, you look upon me even now as a most honourable man?" said Velchaninov, suddenly halting.

At another time he would have been horrified at the *naïveté* of his own question.

"I always thought you so," said Pavel Pavlovitch, dropping his eyes.

"Why, of course. ... I didn't mean that; that is, not in that sense. I only meant to say that, in spite of any ... preconceptions ..."

"Yes, in spite of preconceptions."

"When you came to Petersburg?" Velchaninov could not resist asking, though he felt how utterly monstrous was his curiosity.

"When I came to Petersburg, too, I looked upon you as the most honourable of men. I always respected you, Alexey Ivanovitch."

Pavel Pavlovitch raised his eyes and looked candidly, without a trace of embarrassment, at his opponent. Velchaninov was suddenly panic-stricken; he was not at all anxious that anything should happen, or that anything should overstep a certain line, especially as he had provoked it.

"I loved you, Alexey Ivanovitch," Pavel Pavlovitch articulated, as though he had suddenly made up his mind to speak, "and all that year at T—— I loved you. You did not notice it," he went on, in a voice that quivered, to Velchaninov's positive horror; "I was too insignificant, compared with you, to let you see it. And there was no need, indeed, perhaps. And I've thought of you all these nine years, because there has never been another year in my life like that one" (Pavel Pavlovitch's eyes began to glisten). "I remembered many of your phrases and sayings, your thoughts. I always thought of you as a man with a passion for every noble feeling, a man of education, of the highest education and of ideas: 'Great ideas spring not so much from noble intelligence as from noble feeling.' You said that yourself; perhaps you've forgotten it, but I remembered it. I always looked on you, therefore, as a man of noble feeling ... and therefore believed in you—in spite of anything ..."

His chin suddenly began quivering. Velchaninov was in absolute terror; this unexpected tone must be cut short at all costs.

"That's enough, Pavel Pavlovitch, please," he muttered, flushing and irritably impatient. "And why," he screamed suddenly, "why do you fasten upon a man when he is nervous and ill, when he is almost delirious, and drag him into this darkness ... when it's ... when it's—nothing but delusion, mirage, and falsity, and shameful, and unnatural, and—exaggerated—and that's what's worst, that's what's most shameful—that it is so exaggerated! And it's all nonsense; we are both vicious, underground, loathsome people. ... And if you like I'll prove that you don't like me at all, but hate me with all your might, and that you're lying, though you don't know it; you insisted on taking me there, not with the absurd object of testing your future bride (what an idea!); you saw me yesterday and felt *vindictive*, and took me there to show me and say to me, 'See what a prize! She will be mine; do your worst now!' You challenged me, perhaps you didn't know it yourself; that's how it was, for that's what you were feeling ... and without hating me you couldn't have challenged me like that; and so you hate me!"

He rushed about the room as he shouted this. What harassed and mortified him most of all was the humiliating consciousness that he was demeaning himself so far to Pavel Pavlovitch.

"I wanted to be reconciled with you, Alexey Ivanovitch!" the other articulated suddenly, in a rapid whisper, and his chin began twitching again.

Velchaninov was overcome by furious rage, as though no one had ever insulted him so much.

"I tell you again," he yelled, "that you're fastening upon a man who's nervous and ill ... that you're fastening upon him to extort something monstrous from him in delirium! We ... we are men of different worlds, understand that, and ... and ... between us lies a grave!" he added in a furious whisper, and suddenly realized what he had done. ...

"And how do you know"—Pavel Pavlovitch's face was suddenly pale and distorted—"how do you know what that little grave here means ... for me!" he cried, stepping up to Velchaninov with a ridiculous but horrible gesture, pressing his fist against his heart. "I know that little grave here, and we both stand at the side of that little grave, but on my side there is more than on yours, more ..." he whispered as though in delirium, still thumping at his heart with his fist, "more, more, more ..."

Suddenly an extraordinarily loud ring at the door brought both of them to their senses. The bell rang so violently that it seemed as though some one had vowed to break it at the first pull.

"People don't ring like that to see me," said Velchaninov in perplexity.

"Nor to see me either," Pavel Pavlovitch whispered timidly, recovering himself too, and at once turning into the old Pavel Pavlovitch again.

Velchaninov scowled and went to open the door.

"M. Velchaninov, if I'm not mistaken?" they heard in a ringing, youthful, and exceptionally self-confident voice in the passage.

"What is it?"

"I have trustworthy information," continued the ringing voice, "that a certain Trusotsky is with you at this moment. I must see him instantly."

It would certainly have pleased Velchaninov at that moment to have given the self-confident young gentleman a vigorous kick and to have sent him flying out on the stairs; but he thought a moment, moved aside and let him in.

"Here is M. Trusotsky; come in. ..."

CHAPTER XIV

Sashenka and Nadenka

There walked into the room a very young man, of about nineteen, perhaps even less—to judge from the youthfulness of his handsome, self-confident, upturned face. He was fairly well dressed, or at any rate his clothes looked well on him; in height he was a little above the average; the black hair that hung in thick locks about his head, and the big, bold, dark eyes were particularly conspicuous in his face. Except that his nose was rather broad and turned up, he was a handsome fellow. He walked in solemnly.

"I believe I have the opportunity of conversing with M. Trusotsky," he pronounced in a measured tone, emphasizing with peculiar relish the word "opportunity"—giving him to understand thereby that he did not consider it either an "honour" or a "pleasure" to converse with M. Trusotsky.

Velchaninov began to grasp the position; something seemed to be dawning on Pavel Pavlovitch too. There was a look of uneasiness in his face; but he stood his ground.

"Not having the honour of your acquaintance," he answered majestically, "I imagine that you cannot have business of any sort with me."

"You had better hear me first and then give your opinion," the young man admonished him self-confidently, and, taking out a tortoiseshell lorgnette hanging on a cord, he examined through it the bottle of champagne standing on the table. When he had calmly completed his scrutiny of the bottle, he folded up the lorgnette and turned to Pavel Pavlovitch again.

"Alexandr Lobov."

"What do you mean by Alexandr Lobov?"

"That's me. Haven't you heard of me?"

"No."

"How should you, though? I've come on important business that chiefly concerns you. Allow me to sit down; I'm tired."

"Sit down," Velchaninov urged him; but the young man succeeded in sitting down before being invited to do so.

In spite of the increasing pain in his chest Velchaninov was interested in this impudent youth. In his pretty, childlike, and rosy face, he fancied a remote resemblance to Nadya.

"You sit down too," the lad suggested to Pavel Pavlovitch, motioning him with a careless nod of the head to a seat opposite.

"Don't trouble; I'll stand."

"You'll be tired. You needn't go away, M. Velchaninov, if you like to stay."

"I've nowhere to go; I'm at home."

"As you please. I must confess I should prefer you to be present while I have an explanation with this gentleman. Nadyezhda Fedosyevna gave me rather a flattering account of you."

"Bah! When had she time to do that?"

"Why, just now after you left; I've just come from there, too. I've something to tell you, M. Trusotsky." He turned round to Pavel Pavlovitch, who was standing. "We—that is, Nadyezhda Fedosyevna and I," he went on, letting his words drop one by one as he lolled carelessly in the armchair; "we've cared for each other for ever so long, and have given each other our promise. You are in our way now; I've come to suggest that you should clear out. Will it suit you to act on my suggestion?"

Pavel Pavlovitch positively reeled; he turned pale, but a diabolical smile came on to his lips at once.

"No, it won't suit me at all," he rapped out laconically.

"You don't say so!" The young man turned round in the armchair and crossed one leg over the other.

"I don't know who it is I'm speaking to," added Pavel Pavlovitch. "I believe, indeed, that there's no object in continuing our conversation."

Uttering this, he too thought fit to sit down.

"I told you you would be tired," the youth observed casually. "I told you just now that my name is Alexandr Lobov, and that Nadyezhda and I are pledged to one another; consequently you can't say, as you did just now, that you don't know who it is you have to deal with; you can't imagine, either, that I have nothing more to say to you; putting myself aside, it concerns Nadyezhda Fedosyevna, whom you persist in pestering so insolently. And that alone is sufficient reason for an explanation."

All this he let drop, word by word, through his closed lips, with the air of a coxcomb who did not deign to articulate his words; he even drew out his lorgnette again and turned it upon something while he was talking.

"Excuse me, young man!" Pavel Pavlovitch exclaimed irritably; but the young man instantly snubbed him.

"At any other time I should certainly forbid your calling me 'young man,' but now you will admit that my youth is my chief advantage over you, and that you would have been jolly glad, this morning, for instance, when you presented your bracelet, to be a tiny bit younger."

"Ah, you sprat!" murmured Velchaninov.

"In any case, sir," Pavel Pavlovitch corrected himself with dignity, "I do not consider the reasons you have advanced—most unseemly and dubious reasons—sufficient to continue discussing them. I see that this is all a foolish and childish business. To-morrow I'll make inquiries of my highly respected friend, Fedosey Semyonovitch; and now I beg you to retire."

"Do you see the sort of man he is?" the youth cried at once, unable to sustain his previous tone, and turning hotly to Velchaninov. "It's not enough for him that they've put out their tongues at him to-day and kicked him out—he'll go to-morrow to tell tales of us to the old man! Won't you prove by that, you obstinate man, that you want to take the girl by force, that you want to buy her of people in their dotage who in our barbarous state of society retain authority over her? I should have thought it would have been enough for you that she's shown you how she despises you; why, she gave you back your indecent present to-day, your bracelet. What more do you want?"

"No one has returned me a bracelet, and it's utterly out of the question!" Pavel Pavlovitch said, startled.

"Out of the question? Do you mean to say M. Velchaninov has not given it you?"

"Damnation take you!" thought Velchaninov. "Nadyezhda Fedosyevna did commission me," he said, frowning, "to give you this case, Pavel Pavlovitch. I refused to take it, but she begged me ... here it is ... I'm annoyed. ..."

He took out the case and, much embarrassed, laid it before Pavel Pavlovitch, who was struck dumb.

"Why didn't you give it to him before?" said the young gentleman, addressing Velchaninov severely.

"As you see, I hadn't managed to do so yet," the latter replied, frowning. "That's queer."

"Wha-a-at?"

"You must admit it's queer, anyway. Though I am ready to allow there may be a misunderstanding."

Velchaninov felt a great inclination to get up at once and pull the saucy urchin's ears, but he could not refrain from bursting out laughing in his face; the boy promptly laughed too. It was very different with Pavel Pavlovitch; if Velchaninov could have observed the terrible look he turned upon him when Velchaninov was laughing at Lobov, he would have realized that at that instant the man was passing through a momentous crisis. ... But though Velchaninov did not see that glance, he felt that he must stand by Pavel Pavlovitch.

"Listen, M. Lobov," he began in a friendly tone; "without entering into discussion of other reasons upon which I don't care to touch, I would only point out to you that, in paying his addresses to Nadyezhda Fedosyevna, Pavel Pavlovitch can in any case boast of certain qualifications: in the first place, the fact that everything about him is known to that estimable family; in the second place, his excellent and highly respectable position; finally, his fortune, and consequently he must naturally be surprised at the sight of a rival like you—a man, perhaps, of great merit, but so exceedingly young that he can hardly take you for a serious suitor ... and so he is justified in asking you to retire."

"What do you mean by 'exceedingly young'? I was nineteen last month. By law I could have been married long ago. That's all I can say."

"But what father could bring himself to give you his daughter now— even if you were to be a millionaire in the future or some benefactor of mankind? At nineteen a man cannot even answer for himself, and you are ready to take the responsibility of another person's future, that is, the future of another child like yourself! Why, do you think it's quite honourable? I have ventured to speak frankly to you because you appealed to me just now as an intermediary between you and Pavel Pavlovitch."

"Ah, to be sure, his name's Pavel Pavlovitch!" observed the boy; "how is it I kept fancying that he was Vassily Petrovitch? Well," he went on, addressing Velchaninov, "you haven't surprised me in the least; I knew you were all like that! It's odd, though, that they talked of you as a man rather new in a way. But that's all nonsense, though; far from there being anything dishonourable on my part, as you so freely expressed it, it's the very opposite, as I hope to make you see: to begin with, we've pledged our word to each other, and, what's more, I've promised her, before two witnesses, that if she ever falls in love with some one else, or simply regrets having married me and wants to separate, I will at once give her a formal declaration of my infidelity—and so will support her petition for divorce. What's more, in case I should later on go back upon my word and refuse to give her that declaration, I will give her as security on our wedding-day an I O U for a hundred thousand roubles, so that if I should be perverse about the declaration she can at once change my I O U and me into the bargain! In that way everything will be secured and I shouldn't be risking anybody's future. That's the first point."

"I bet that fellow—What's-his-name?—Predposylov invented that for you!" cried Velchaninov.

"He, he, he!" chuckled Pavel Pavlovitch viciously.

"What's that gentleman sniggering about? You guessed right, it was Predposylov's idea; and you must admit it was a shrewd one. The absurd law is completely paralysed by it. Of course, I intend to love her for ever, and she laughs tremendously; at the same time it's ingenious, and you must admit that it's honourable, and that it's not every man who would consent to do it."

"To my thinking, so far from being honourable, it's positively disgusting." The young man shrugged his shoulders.

"Again you don't surprise me," he observed, after a brief silence. "I have given up being surprised at that sort of thing long ago. Predposylov would tell you flatly that your lack of comprehension of the most natural things is due to the corruption of your most ordinary feelings and ideas by a long life spent idly and absurdly. But possibly we don't understand one another; they spoke well of you anyway ... you're fifty, I suppose, aren't you?"

"Kindly keep to the point."

"Excuse my indiscretion and don't be annoyed; I didn't mean anything. I will continue: I'm by no means a future millionaire, as you expressed it (and what an idea!); I have nothing but what I stand up in, but I have complete confidence in my future. I shan't be a hero or a benefactor of mankind either, but I shall keep myself and my wife. Of course, I've nothing now; I was brought up in their house, you see, from childhood. ..."

"How was that?"

"Well, you see, I'm the son of a distant relation of Zahlebinin's wife, and when all my people died and left me at eight years old, the old man took me in and afterwards sent me to the high school. He's really a good-natured man, if you care to know. ..."

"I know that."

"Yes; a bit antiquated in his ideas, but kind-hearted. It's a long time now, of course, since I was under his guardianship; I want to earn my own living, and to owe no one anything."

"How long have you been independent?" Velchaninov inquired.

"Why, four months."

"Oh, well, one can understand it then: you've been friends from childhood! Well, have you a situation, then?"

"Yes, a private situation, in a notary's office, for twenty-five roubles a month. Of course, only for the time, but when I made my offer I hadn't even that. I was serving on the railway then for ten roubles a month, but only for the time."

"Do you mean to say you've made an offer of marriage?"

"Yes, a formal offer, and ever so long ago—over three weeks."

"Well, and what happened?"

"The old man laughed awfully at first, and then was awfully angry, and locked her upstairs. But Nadya held out heroically. But that was all because he was a bit crusty with me before, for throwing up the berth in his department which he had got me into four months ago, before I went to the railway. He's a capital old chap, I tell you again, simple and jolly at home, but you can't fancy what he's like as soon as he's in his office! He's like a Jove enthroned! I naturally let him know that I was not attracted by his manners there, but the chief trouble was through the head clerk's assistant: that gentleman took it into his head that I had been 'rude' to him, and all that I said to him was that he was undeveloped. I threw them all up, and now I'm at a notary's."

"And did you get much in the department?"

"Oh, I was not on the regular staff! The old man used to give me an allowance too; I tell you he's a good sort, but we shan't give in, all the same. Of course, twenty-five roubles is not enough to support a wife, but I hope soon to have a share in the management of Count Zavileysky's neglected estates, and then to rise to three thousand straight off, or else I shall become a lawyer. People are always going to law nowadays. ... Bah! What a clap of thunder! There'll be a storm; it's a good thing I managed to get here before it; I came on foot, I ran almost all the way."

"But, excuse me, if so, when did you manage to talk things over with Nadyezhda Fedosyevna, especially if they refuse you admittance?"

"Why, one can talk over the fence! Did you notice that red-haired girl?" he laughed. "She's very active on our side, and Marie Nikititchna too; ah, she's a serpent, that Marie Nikititchna! ... Why do you wince? Are you afraid of the thunder?"

761

"No, I'm unwell, very unwell. ..."

Velchaninov, in positive agony from the pain in his chest, got up and tried to walk about the room.

"Oh, then, of course, I'm in your way. ... Don't be uneasy, I'm just going!"

And the youth jumped up from his seat.

"You're not in the way; it's no matter," said Velchaninov courteously.

"How can it be no matter? 'When Kobylnikov had a stomach-ache' ... do you remember in Shtchedrin? Are you fond of Shtchedrin?"

"Yes."

"So am I. Well, Vassily ... oh, hang it, Pavel Pavlovitch, let's finish!" He turned, almost laughing, to Pavel Pavlovitch. "I will once more for your comprehension formulate the question: do you consent to make a formal withdrawal of all pretensions in regard to Nadyezhda Fedosyevna to the old people to-morrow, in my presence?"

"I certainly do not." Pavel Pavlovitch, too, got up from his seat with an impatient and exasperated air. "And I beg you once more to spare me ... for all this is childish and silly."

"You had better look out." The youth held up a warning finger with a supercilious smile. "Don't make a mistake in your calculations! Do you know what such a mistake leads to? I warn you that in nine months' time, when you have had all your expense and trouble, and you come back here, you'll be forced to give up Nadyezhda Fedosyevna, or if you don't give her up it will be the worse for you; that's what will be the end of it! I must warn you that you're like the dog in the manger—excuse me, it's only a comparison—getting nothing yourself and preventing others. From motives of humanity I tell you again: reflect upon it, force yourself for once in your life to reflect rationally."

"I beg you to spare me your sermonizing!" cried Pavel Pavlovitch furiously; "and as for your nasty insinuations, I shall take measures to-morrow, severe measures!"

"Nasty insinuations? What do you mean by that? You're nasty yourself, if that's what you've got in your head. However, I agree to wait till to-morrow, but if ... Ah, thunder again! Good-bye; very glad to make your acquaintance"—he nodded to Velchaninov and ran off, apparently in haste to get back before the storm and not to get caught in the rain.

CHAPTER XV

The Account Is Settled

"You see? You see?" Pavel Pavlovitch skipped up to Velchaninov as soon as the youth had departed.

"Yes; you've no luck!" said Velchaninov carelessly.

He would not have said those words had he not been tortured and exasperated by the pain in his chest, which was growing more and more acute.

"It was because you felt for me, you didn't give me back the bracelet, wasn't it?"

"I hadn't time ..."

"You felt for me from your heart, like a true friend?"

"Oh yes, I felt for you," said Velchaninov, in exasperation.

He told him briefly, however, how the bracelet had been returned to him, and how Nadyezhda Fedosyevna had almost forced him to assist in returning it. ...

"You understand that nothing else would have induced me to take it; I've had unpleasantness enough apart from that!"

"You were fascinated and took it?" sniggered Pavel Pavlovitch.

"That's stupid on your part; however, I must excuse you. You saw for yourself just now that I'm not the leading person, that there are others in this affair."

"At the same time you were fascinated."

Pavel Pavlovitch sat down and filled up his glass.

"Do you imagine I'd give way to that wretched boy? I'll make mincemeat of him, so there! I'll go over to-morrow and polish him off. We'll smoke out that spirit from the nursery."

He emptied his glass almost at a gulp and filled it again; he began, in fact, to behave in an unusually free and easy way.

"Ah, Nadenka and Sashenka, the sweet little darlings, he—he—he!"

He was beside himself with anger. There came another louder clap of thunder, followed by a blinding flash of lightning, and the rain began streaming in bucketfuls. Pavel Pavlovitch got up and closed the open window.

"He asked you whether you were afraid of the thunder, he—he. Velchaninov afraid of thunder! Kobylnikov—what was it—Kobylnikov ... and what about being fifty too—eh? Do you remember?" Pavel Pavlovitch sneered diabolically.

"You've established yourself here, it seems!" observed Velchaninov, hardly able to articulate the words for the pain in his chest. "I'll lie down, you can do what you like."

"Why, you couldn't turn a dog out in weather like this!" Pavel Pavlovitch retorted in an aggrieved tone, seeming almost pleased, however, at having an excuse for feeling aggrieved.

"All right, sit down, drink ... stay the night, if you like!" muttered Velchaninov. He stretched himself on the sofa and uttered a faint groan.

"Stay the night? And you won't be afraid?"

"What of?" said Velchaninov, suddenly raising his head.

"Oh, nothing. Last time you were so frightened, or was it my fancy ..."

"You're stupid!" Velchaninov could not help saying. He turned his head to the wall angrily.

"All right," responded Pavel Pavlovitch.

The sick man fell asleep suddenly, a minute after lying down. The unnatural strain upon him that day in the shattered state of his health had brought on a sudden crisis, and he was as weak as a child. But the pain asserted itself again and got the upper hand of sleep and weariness; an hour later he woke up and painfully got up from the sofa. The storm had subsided; the room was full of tobacco smoke, on the table stood an empty bottle, and Pavel Pavlovitch was asleep on another sofa. He was lying on his back, with his head on the sofa cushion, fully dressed and with his boots on. His lorgnette had slipped out of his pocket and was hanging down almost to the floor. His hat was lying on the ground beside it. Velchaninov looked at him morosely and did not attempt to wake him. Writhing with pain and pacing about the room, for he could no longer bear to lie down, he moaned and brooded over his agonies.

He was afraid of that pain in his chest, and not without reason. He had been liable to these attacks for a very long time, but they had only occurred at intervals of a year or two. He knew that they came from the liver. At first a dull, not acute, but irritating feeling of oppression was, as it were, concentrated at some point in the chest, under the shoulderblade or higher up. Continually increasing, sometimes for ten hours at a stretch, the pain at last would reach such a pitch, the oppression would become so insupportable, that the sufferer began to have visions of dying. On his last attack, a year before, he was, when the pain ceased after ten hours of suffering, so weak that he could scarcely move his hands as he lay in bed, and the doctor had allowed him to take nothing for the whole day but a few teaspoonfuls of weak tea and of bread soaked in broth, like a tiny baby. The attacks were brought on by different things, but never occurred except when his nerves were out of order. It was strange, too, how the attack passed off; sometimes it was possible to arrest it at the very beginning, during the first half-hour, by simple compresses, and it would pass away completely at once; sometimes, as on his last attack, nothing was of any use, and the pain only subsided after numerous and continually recurring paroxysms of vomiting. The doctor confessed afterwards that he believed it to be a case of poisoning. It was a long time to wait till morning, and he didn't want to send for the doctor at night; besides, he didn't like doctors. At last he could not control himself and began moaning aloud. His groans waked Pavel Pavlovitch; he sat up on the sofa, and for some time listened with alarm and bewilderment, watching Velchaninov, who was almost running backwards and forwards through the two rooms. The bottle of champagne had had a great effect upon him, evidently more than usual, and it was some time before he could collect himself. At last he grasped the position and rushed to Velchaninov, who mumbled something in reply to him.

"It's the liver, I know it!" cried Pavel Pavlovitch, becoming extremely animated all at once. "Pyotr Kuzmitch Polosuhin used to suffer just the same from liver. You ought to have compresses. Pyotr Kuzmitch always had compresses. ... One may die of it! Shall I run for Mavra?"

"No need, no need!" Velchaninov waved him off irritably. "I want nothing."

But Pavel Pavlovitch, goodness knows why, seemed beside himself, as though it were a question of saving his own son. Without heeding Velchaninov's protests, he insisted on the necessity of compresses and also of two or three cups of weak tea to be drunk on the spot, "and not simply hot, but boiling!" He ran to Mavra, without waiting for permission, with her laid a fire in the kitchen, which always stood empty, and blew up the samovar; at the same time he succeeded in getting the sick man to bed, took off his clothes, wrapped him up in a quilt, and within twenty minutes had prepared tea and compresses.

"This is a hot plate, scalding hot!" he said, almost ecstatically, applying the heated plate, wrapped up in a napkin, on Velchaninov's aching chest. "There are no other compresses, and plates, I swear on my honour, will be even better: they were laid on Pyotr Kuzmitch, I saw it with my own eyes, and did it with my own hands. One may die of it, you know. Drink your tea, swallow it; never mind about scalding yourself; life is too precious ... for one to be squeamish."

He quite flustered Mavra, who was half asleep; the plates were changed every three or four minutes. After the third plate and the second cup of tea, swallowed at a gulp, Velchaninov felt a sudden relief.

"If once they've shifted the pain, thank God, it's a good sign!" cried Pavel Pavlovitch, and he ran joyfully to fetch a fresh plate and a fresh cup of tea.

"If only we can ease the pain. If only we can keep it under!" he kept repeating.

Half an hour later the pain was much less, but the sick man was so exhausted that in spite of Pavel Pavlovitch's entreaties he refused to "put up with just one more nice little plate." He was so weak that everything was dark before his eyes.

"Sleep, sleep," he repeated in a faint voice.

"To be sure," Pavel Pavlovitch assented.

"You'll stay the night.... What time is it?"

"It's nearly two o'clock, it's a quarter to."

"You'll stay the night."

"I will, I will."

A minute later the sick man called Pavel Pavlovitch again.

"You, you," he muttered, when the latter had run up and was bending over him; "you are better than I am! I understand it all, all. ... Thank you."

"Sleep, sleep," whispered Pavel Pavlovitch, and he hastened on tiptoe to his sofa.

As he fell asleep the invalid heard Pavel Pavlovitch noiselessly making up a bed for himself and taking off his clothes. Finally, putting out the candle, and almost holding his breath for fear of waking the patient, he stretched himself on his sofa.

There is no doubt that Velchaninov did sleep and that he fell asleep very soon after the candle was put out; he remembered this clearly afterwards. But all the time he was asleep, up to the very moment that he woke up, he dreamed that he was not asleep, and that in spite of his exhaustion he could not get to sleep. At last he began to dream that he was in a sort of waking delirium, and that he could not drive away the phantoms that crowded about him, although he was fully conscious that it was only delirium and not reality. The phantoms were all familiar figures; his room seemed to be full of people; and the door into the passage stood open; people were coming in in crowds and thronging the stairs. At the table, which was set in the middle of the room, there was sitting one man—exactly as in the similar dream he had had a month before. Just as in that dream, this man sat with his elbows on the table and would not speak; but this time he was wearing a round hat with crape on it. "What! could it have been Pavel Pavlovitch that time too?" Velchaninov thought, but, glancing at the face of the silent man, he convinced himself that it was some one quite different. "Why has he got crape on," Velchaninov wondered. The noise, the talking and the shouting of the people crowding round the table, was awful. These people seemed to be even more intensely exasperated against Velchaninov than in the previous dream; they shook their fists at him, and shouted something to him with all their might, but what it was exactly he could not make out. "But it's delirium, of course, I know it's delirium!" he thought; "I know I couldn't get to sleep and that I've got up now, because it made me too wretched to go on lying down. ..." But the shouts, the people, their gestures were so lifelike, so real, that sometimes he was seized by doubt: "Can this be really delirium? Good Heavens! What do these people want of me? But ... If it were not an hallucination, would it be possible that such a clamour should not have waked Pavel Pavlovitch all this time? There he is asleep on the sofa!" At last something suddenly happened again, just as in that other dream; all of them made a rush for the stairs and they were closely packed in the doorway, for there was another crowd forcing its way into the room. These people were bringing something in with them, something big and heavy; he could hear how heavily the steps of those carrying it sounded on the stairs and how hurriedly their panting voices called to one another. All the people in the room shouted: "They're bringing it, they're bringing it"—all eyes were flashing and fixed on Velchaninov; all of them pointed towards the stairs, menacing and triumphant. Feeling no further doubt that it was reality and not hallucination, he stood on tiptoe so as to peep over the people's heads and find out as soon as possible what they were bringing up the stairs. His heart was beating, beating, beating, and suddenly, exactly as in that first dream, he heard three violent rings at the bell. And again it was so distinct, so real, so unmistakable a ring at the bell, that it could not be only a dream. ...

But he did not rush to the door as he had done on awakening then. What idea guided his first movement and whether he had any idea at the moment it is impossible to say, but some one seemed to prompt him what he must do: he leaped out of bed and, with his hands stretched out before him as though to defend himself and ward off an attack, rushed straight towards the place where Pavel Pavlovitch was asleep. His hands instantly came into contact with other hands, stretched out above him, and he clutched them tight; so, some one already stood bending over him. The curtains were drawn, but it was not quite dark, for a faint light came from the other room where there were no such curtains. Suddenly, with an acute pain, something cut the palm and fingers of his left hand, and he instantly realized that he had clutched the blade of a knife or razor and was grasping it tight in his hand. ... And at the same moment something fell heavily on the floor with a thud.

Velchaninov was perhaps three times as strong as Pavel Pavlovitch, yet the struggle between them lasted a long while, fully three minutes. He soon got him down on the floor and bent his arms back behind him, but for some reason he felt he must tie his hands behind him. Holding the murderer with his wounded left hand, he began with his right fumbling for the cord of the window curtain and for a long time could not find it, but at last got hold of it and tore it from the window. He wondered himself afterwards at the immense effort required to do this. During those three minutes neither of them uttered a word; nothing was audible but their heavy breathing and the muffled sounds of their struggling. Having at last twisted Pavel Pavlovitch's arms behind him and tied them together, Velchaninov left him on the floor, got up, drew the curtain from the window and pulled up the blind. It was already light in the deserted street. Opening the window, he stood for some moments drawing in deep breaths of fresh air. It was a little past four. Shutting the window, he went hurriedly to the cupboard, took out a clean towel and bound it tightly round his left hand to stop the bleeding. At his feet an open razor was lying on the carpet; he picked it up, shut it, put it in the razor-case, which had been left forgotten since the morning on the little table beside Pavel Pavlovitch's sofa, and locked it up in his bureau. And, only when he had done all that, he went up to Pavel Pavlovitch and began to examine him.

Meantime, the latter had with an effort got up from the floor, and seated himself in an armchair. He had nothing on but his shirt, not even his boots. The back and the sleeves of his shirt were soaked with blood; but the blood was not his own, it came from Velchaninov's wounded hand. Of course it was Pavel Pavlovitch, but any one meeting him by chance might almost have failed to recognize him at the minute, so changed was his whole appearance. He was sitting awkwardly upright in the armchair, owing to his hands being tied behind his back, his face looked distorted, exhausted and greenish, and he quivered all over from time to time. He looked at Velchaninov fixedly, but with lustreless, unseeing eyes. All at once he smiled vacantly, and, nodding towards a bottle of water that stood on the table, he said in a meek half-whisper—

"Water, I should like some water."

Velchaninov filled a glass and began holding it for him to drink. Pavel

Pavlovitch bent down greedily to the water; after three gulps he raised his head and looked intently into the face of Velchaninov, who was standing beside him with the glass in his hand, but without uttering a word he fell to drinking again. When he had finished he sighed deeply. Velchaninov took his pillow, seized his outer garments and went into the other room, locking Pavel Pavlovitch into the first room.

The pain had passed off completely, but he was conscious of extreme weakness again after the momentary effort in which he had displayed an unaccountable strength. He tried to reflect upon what had happened, but his thoughts were hardly coherent, the shock had been too great. Sometimes there was a dimness before his eyes lasting for ten minutes or so, then he would start, wake up, recollect everything, remember his smarting hand bound up in a bloodstained towel, and would fall to thinking greedily, feverishly. He came to one distinct conclusion—that is, that Pavel Pavlovitch certainly had meant to cut his throat, but that perhaps only a quarter of an hour before he had not known that he would do it. The razor-case had perhaps merely caught his eye the evening before, and, without arousing any thought of it at the time, had remained in his memory. (The razors were always locked up in the bureau, and only the morning before Velchaninov had taken them out to shave round his moustache and whiskers, as he sometimes did.)

"If he had long been intending to murder me he would have got a knife or pistol ready; he would not have reckoned on my razor, which he had never seen till yesterday evening," was one reflection he made among others.

It struck six o'clock at last; Velchaninov roused himself, dressed, and went in to Pavel Pavlovitch. Opening the door, he could not understand why he had locked Pavel Pavlovitch in, instead of turning him out of the house. To his surprise, the criminal was fully dressed; most likely he had found some way of untying his hands. He was sitting in the armchair, but got up at once when Velchaninov went in. His hat was already in his hand. His uneasy eyes seemed in haste to say—

"Don't begin talking; it's no use beginning; there's no need to talk."

"Go," said Velchaninov. "Take your bracelet," he added, calling after him.

Pavel Pavlovitch turned back from the door, took the case with the bracelet from the table, put it in his pocket and went out on the stairs. Velchaninov stood at the door to lock it behind him. Their eyes met for the last time; Pavel Pavlovitch stopped suddenly, for five seconds the two looked into each other's eyes—as though hesitating; finally Velchaninov waved his hand faintly.

"Well, go!" he said in a low voice, and locked the door.

Chapter XVI

Analysis

A feeling of immense, extraordinary relief took possession of him; something was over, was settled; an awful weight of depression had vanished and was dissipated for ever. So it seemed to him. It had lasted for five weeks. He raised his hand, looked at the towel soaked with blood and muttered to himself: "Yes, now everything is absolutely at an end!" And all that morning, for the first time in three weeks, he scarcely thought of Liza—as though that blood from his cut fingers could "settle his account" even with that misery.

He recognized clearly that he had escaped a terrible danger. "These people," he thought, "just these people who don't know a minute beforehand whether they'll murder a man or not—as soon as they take a knife in their trembling hands and feel the hot spurt of blood on their fingers don't stick at cutting your throat, but cut off your head, 'clean off,' as convicts express it. That is so."

He could not remain at home and went out into the street, feeling convinced that he must do something, or something would happen to him at once; he walked about the streets and waited. He had an intense longing to meet some one, to talk to some one, even to a stranger, and it was only that which led him at last to think of a doctor and of the necessity of binding up his hand properly. The doctor, an old acquaintance of his, examined the wound, and inquired with interest how it could have happened. Velchaninov laughed and was on the point of telling him all about it, but restrained himself. The doctor was obliged to feel his pulse and, hearing of his attack the night before, persuaded him to take some soothing medicine he had at hand. He was reassuring about the cuts: "They could have no particularly disagreeable results." Velchaninov laughed and began to assure him that they had already had the most agreeable results. An almost irresistible desire to tell the whole story came over him twice again during that day, on one occasion to a total stranger with whom he entered into conversation at a tea-shop. He had never been able to endure entering into conversation with strangers in public places before.

He went into a shop to buy a newspaper; he went to his tailor's and ordered a suit. The idea of visiting the Pogoryeltsevs was still distasteful to him, and he did not think of them, and indeed he could not have gone to their villa: he kept expecting something here in the town. He dined with enjoyment, he talked to the waiter and to his fellow-diners, and drank half a bottle of wine. The possibility of the return of his illness of the day before did not occur to him; he was convinced that the illness had passed off completely at the moment when, after falling asleep so exhausted, he had, an hour and a half later, sprung out of bed and thrown his assailant on the floor with such strength. Towards evening he began to feel giddy, and at moments was overcome by something like the delirium he had had in his sleep. It was dusk when he returned home, and he was almost afraid of his room when he went into it. It seemed dreadful and uncanny in his flat. He walked up and down it several times, and even went into his kitchen, where he had scarcely ever been before. "Here they were heating plates yesterday," he thought. He locked the door securely and lighted the candles earlier than usual. As he locked the door he remembered, half an hour before, passing the porter's lodge, he had called Mavra and asked her whether Pavel Pavlovitch had come in his absence, as though he could possibly have come.

After locking himself in carefully, he opened the bureau, took out the razor-case and opened the razor to look at it again. On the white bone handle there were still faint traces of blood. He put the razor back in the case and locked it up in the bureau again. He felt sleepy; he felt that he must go to bed at once—or "he would not be fit for to-morrow." He pictured the next day for some reason as a momentous and "decisive" day.

But the same thoughts that had haunted him all day in the street kept incessantly and persistently crowding and jostling in his sick brain, and he kept thinking, thinking, thinking, and for a long time could not get to sleep......

"If it is settled that he tried to murder me *accidentally*," he went on pondering, "had the idea ever entered his head before, if only as a dream in a vindictive moment?"

He decided that qrestion strangely—that "Pavel Pavlovitch did want to kill him, but the thought of the murder had never entered his head." In short: "Pavel Pavlovitch wanted to kill him, but didn't know he wanted to kill him. It's senseless, but that's the truth," thought Velchaninov. "It was not to get a post and it was not on Bagautov's account he came here, though he did try to get a post here, and did run to see Bagautov and was furious when he died; he thought no more of him than a chip. He came here on my account and he came here with Liza..."

"And did I expect that he ... would murder me?" He decided that he did, that he had expected it from the moment when he saw him in the carriage following Bagautov's funeral. "I began, as it were, to expect something ... but, of course, not that; but, of course, not that he would murder me! ..."

"And can it be that all that was true?" he exclaimed again, suddenly raising his head from the pillow and opening his eyes. "All that that ... madman told me yesterday about his love for me, when his chin quivered and he thumped himself on the breast with his fist?"

"It was the absolute truth," he decided, still pondering and analysing, "that Quasimodo from T—— was quite sufficiently stupid and noble to fall in love with the lover of his wife, about whom he noticed nothing suspicious in twenty years! He had been thinking of me with respect, cherishing my memory and brooding over my 'utterances' for nine years. Good Heavens! and I had no notion of it! He could not have been lying yesterday! But did he love me yesterday when he declared his feeling and said 'Let us settle our account?' Yes, it was from hatred that he loved me; that's the strongest of all loves ..."

"Of course it may have happened, of course it must have happened that I made a tremendous impression on him at T——. Tremendous and 'gratifying' is just what it was, and it's just with a Schiller like that, in the outer form of a Quasimodo, that such a thing could happen! He magnified me a hundredfold because I impressed him too much in his philosophic solitude. ... It would be interesting to know by what I impressed him? Perhaps by my clean gloves and my knowing how to put them on. Quasimodos are fond of all that is æsthetic. Ough! aren't they fond of it! A glove is often quite enough for a noble heart, and especially one of these 'eternal husbands.' The rest they supply themselves a thousand times, and are ready to fight for you, to satisfy your slightest wish. What an opinion he had of my powers of fascination! Perhaps it was just my powers of fascination that made the most impression on him. And his cry then, 'If that one, too ... whom can one trust!' After that cry one may well become a wild beast! ...

"H'm! He comes here 'to embrace me and weep,' as he expressed it in the most abject way—that is, he came here to murder me and thought he came 'to embrace me and to weep.' ... He brought Liza too. But, who knows? if I had wept with him, perhaps, really, he would have forgiven me, for he had a terrible longing to forgive me! ... At the first shock all that was changed into drunken antics and caricature, and into loathsome, womanish whining over his wrongs. (Those horns! those horns he made on his forehead!) He came drunk on purpose to speak out, though he was playing the fool; if he had not been drunk, even he could not have done it. ... And how he liked playing the fool, didn't he like it! Ough! wasn't he pleased, too, when he made me kiss him! Only he didn't know then whether he would end by embracing me or murdering me. Of course, it's turned out that the best thing was to do both. A most natural solution! Yes, indeed, nature dislikes monstrosities and destroys them with natural solutions. The most monstrous monster is the monster with noble feelings; I know that by personal experience, Pavel Pavlovitch! Nature is not a tender mother, but a stepmother to the monster. Nature gives birth to the deformed, but instead of pitying him she punishes him, and with good reason. Even decent people have to pay for embraces and tears of for-giveness, nowadays, to say nothing of men like you and me, Pavel Pav-lovitch!

"Yes, he was stupid enough to take me to see his future bride. Good Heavens! His future bride! Only a Quasimodo like that could have con-ceived the notion of 'rising again to a new life' by means of the innocence of Mademoiselle Zahlebinin! But it was not your fault, Pavel Pavlovitch, it was not your fault: you're a monster, so everything about you is bound to be monstrous, your dreams and your hopes. But, though he was a monster, he had doubts of his dream, and that was why he needed the high sanction of Velchaninov whom he so revered. He wanted Velchaninov to approve, he wanted him to reassure him that the dream was not a dream, but something real. He took me there from a devout respect for me and faith in the nobility of my feelings, believing, perhaps, that there, under a bush, we should embrace and shed tears near all that youthful innocence. Yes! That 'eternal husband' was obliged, sooner or later, to punish himself for everything, and to punish himself he snatched up the razor—by accident, it is true, still he did snatch it up! 'And yet he stuck him with a knife, and yet he ended by stabbing him in the presence of the Governor.' And, by the way, had he any idea of that sort in his mind when he told me that anecdote about the best man? And was there really anything that night when he got out of bed and stood in the middle of the room? H'm! ... No, he stood there then *as a joke*. He got up for other reasons, and when he saw that I was frightened of him he did not answer me for ten minutes because he was very much pleased that I was frightened of him. ... It was at that moment, perhaps, when he stood there in the dark, that some idea of this sort first dawned upon him. ...

"Yet if I had not forgotten that razor on the table yesterday—maybe nothing would have happened. Is that so? Is that so? To be sure he had been avoiding me before—why, he had not been to see me for a fortnight;

he had been hiding from me to *spare* me! Of course, he picked out Bagautov first, not me! Why, he rushed to heat plates for me in the night, thinking to create a diversion—from the knife to pity and tenderness! ... He wanted to save himself and me, too—with his hot plates! ..."

And for a long time the sick brain of this "man of the world" went on working in this way, going round and round in a circle, till he grew calmer. He woke up next morning with the same headache, but with a quite *new* and quite unexpected terror in his heart. ...

This new terror came from the positive conviction, which suddenly grew strong within him that he, Velchaninov (a man of the world) would end it all that day by going of his own free will to Pavel Pavlovitch. Why? What for? He had no idea and, with repugnance, refused to know; all that he knew was that, for some reason, he would go to him.

This madness, however—he could give it no other name—did, as it developed, take a rational form and fasten upon a fairly legitimate pretext: he had even, the day before, been haunted by the idea that Pavel Pavlovitch would go back to his lodging and hang himself, like the clerk about whom Marya Sysoevna had told him. This notion of the day before had passed by degrees into an unreasoning but persistent conviction. "Why should the fool hang himself?" he kept protesting to himself every half-minute. He remembered Liza's words ... "Yet in his place, perhaps, I should hang myself" ... he reflected once.

It ended by his turning towards Pavel Pavlovitch instead of going to dinner. "I shall simply inquire of Marya Sysoevna," he decided. But before he had come out into the street he stopped short in the gateway: "Can it be, can it be?" he cried, turning crimson with shame. "Can it be that I'm crawling there, to 'embrace and shed tears'? That senseless abjectness was all that was needed to complete the ignominy!"

But from that "senseless abjectness" he was saved by the providence that watches over all decent and well-bred people. He had no sooner stepped into the street when he stumbled upon Alexandr Lobov. The young man was in breathless haste and excitement.

"I was coming to see you! What do you think of our friend, Pavel Pavlovitch, now?"

"He's hanged himself!" Velchaninov muttered wildly.

"Who's hanged himself? What for?" cried Lobov, with wide-open eyes.

"Never mind ... I didn't mean anything; go on."

"Foo! damn it all! what funny ideas you have, though. He's not hanged himself at all (why should he hang himself?). On the contrary—he's gone away. I've only just put him into the train and seen him off. Foo! how he drinks, I tell you! We drank three bottles, Predposylov with us—but how he drinks, how he drinks! He was singing songs in the train. He remembered you, blew kisses, sent you his greetings. But he is a scoundrel, don't you think so?"

The young man certainly was a little tipsy; his flushed face, his shining eyes and faltering tongue betrayed it unmistakably.

Velchaninov laughed loudly.

"So in the end they finished up with Brüderschaft! Ha-ha! They embraced and shed tears! Ah, you Schilleresque poets!"

"Don't call me names, please. Do you know he's given it all up over *there?* He was there yesterday, and he's been there to-day. He sneaked horribly. They locked Nadya up—she's sitting in a room upstairs. There were tears and lamentations, but we stood firm! But how he does drink, I say, doesn't he drink! And, I say, isn't he *mauvais ton*, at least not *mauvais ton* exactly, what shall I call it? ... He kept talking of you, but there's no comparison between you! You're a gentleman anyway, and really did move in decent society at one time and have only been forced to come down now through poverty or something. ... Goodness knows what, I couldn't quite understand him."

"Ah, so he spoke to you of me in those terms?"

"He did, he did; don't be angry. To be a good citizen is better than being in aristocratic society. I say that because in Russia, nowadays, one doesn't know whom to respect. You'll agree that it's a serious malady of the age, when people don't know whom to respect, isn't it?"

"It is, it is; what did he say?"

"He? Who? Ah, to be sure! Why did he keep saying 'Velchaninov fifty, but a rake,' why *but* a rake and not *and* a rake; he laughed and repeated it a thousand times over. He got into the train, sang a song and burst out crying—it was simply revolting, pitiful, in fact—from drunkenness. Oh! I don't like fools! He fell to throwing money to the beggars for the peace of the soul of Lizaveta—his wife, is that?"

"His daughter."

"What's the matter with your hand?"

"I cut it."

"Never mind, it will get better. Damn him, you know, it's a good thing he's gone, but I bet anything that he'll get married directly he arrives—he will—won't he?"

"Why, but you want to get married, too, don't you?"

"Me? That's a different matter. What a man you are, really! If you are fifty, he must be sixty: you must look at it logically, my dear sir! And

775

do you know I used, long ago, to be a pure Slavophil by conviction, but now we look for dawn from the West. ... But, good-bye; I'm glad I met you without going in; I won't come in, don't ask me, I've no time to spare!..."

And he was just running off.

"Oh, by the way," he cried, turning back; "why, he sent me to you with a letter! Here is the letter. Why didn't you come to see him off?"

Velchaninov returned home and opened the envelope addressed to him. There was not one line from Pavel Pavlovitch in it, but there was a different letter. Velchaninov recognized the handwriting. It was an old letter, written on paper yellow with age, with ink that had changed colour. It had been written to him ten years before, two months after he had left T—— and returned to Petersburg. But the letter had never reached him; he had received a different one instead of it; this was clear from the contents of this old yellow letter. In this letter Natalya Vassilyevna took leave of him for ever, and confessed that she loved some one else, just as in the letter he had actually received; but she also did not conceal from him that she was going to have a child. On the contrary, to comfort him, she held out hopes that she might find a possibility of handing over the future child to him, declared henceforth that they had other duties—in short, there was little logic, but the object was clear: that he should no longer trouble her with his love. She even sanctioned his coming to T—— in a year's time to have a look at the child. God knows why she changed her mind and sent the other letter instead.

Velchaninov was pale as he read it, but he pictured to himself Pavel Pavlovitch finding that letter and reading it for the first time, before the opened ebony box inlaid with mother-of-pearl which was an heirloom in the family.

"He, too, must have turned pale as a corpse," he thought, catching a glimpse of his own face in the looking-glass. "He must have read it and closed his eyes, and opened them again hoping that the letter would have changed into plain white paper. ... Most likely he had done that a second time and a third! ..."

Chapter XVII

The Eternal Husband

Almost exactly two years had passed since the incidents we have described. We meet Velchaninov again on a beautiful summer day, in the train on one of our newly opened railways. He was going to Odessa for his own pleasure, to see one of his friends, and also with a view to something else of an agreeable nature. He hoped through that friend to arrange a meeting with an extremely interesting woman whose acquaintance he had long been eager to make. Without going into details we will confine ourselves to observing that he had become entirely transformed, or rather reformed, during those two years. Of his old hypochondria scarcely a trace remained. Of the various "reminiscences" and anxiety—the result of illness which had beset him two years before in Petersburg at the time of his unsuccessful lawsuit, nothing remained but a certain secret shame at the consciousness of his faintheartedness. What partly made up for it was the conviction that it would never happen again, and that no one would ever know of it. It was true that at that time he had given up all society, had even begun to be slovenly in his dress, had crept away out of sight of every one—and that, of course, must have been noticed by all. But he so readily acknowledged his transgressions, and at the same time with such a self-confident air of new life and vigour, that "every one" immediately forgave his momentary falling away; in fact, those whom he had given up greeting were the first to recognize him and hold out their hands, and without any tiresome questions—just as though he had been absent on his own personal affairs, which were no business of theirs, and had only just come back from a distance. The cause of all these salutary changes for the better was, of course, the winning of his lawsuit. Velchaninov gained in all sixty thousand roubles—no great sum, of course, but of extreme importance to him; to begin with, he felt himself on firm ground again, and so he felt satisfied at heart; he knew for certain now that he would not, "like a fool," squander this money, as he had squandered his first two fortunes, and that he had enough for his whole life. "However the social edifice may totter, whatever trumpet call they're sounding," he thought sometimes, as he watched and heard all the marvellous and incredible things that were being done around him and all over Russia; "whatever shape people and ideas may take I shall always have just such a delicate, dainty dinner as I am sitting down to now, and so I'm ready to face anything." This voluptuous, comfortable thought by degrees gained complete possession of him and produced a transformation in his physical, to say nothing of his moral, nature. He looked quite a different man from the "sluggard" whom we have described two years before and to whom such unseemly incidents had befallen—he looked cheerful, serene, and dignified. Even the ill-humoured wrinkles that had begun to appear under his eyes and on his forehead had almost been smoothed away; the very tint of his face had changed, his skin was whiter and ruddier.

At the moment he was sitting comfortably in a first-class carriage and a charming idea was suggesting itself to his mind. The next station was a junction and there was a new branch line going off to the right. He asked himself, "How would it be to give up the direct way for the moment and turn off to the right? There, only two stations away, he could visit another lady of his acquaintance who had only just returned from abroad, and was now living in a provincial isolation, very tedious for her, but favourable for him; and so it would be possible to spend his time no less agreeably than at Odessa, especially as he would not miss his visit there either." But he was still hesitating and could not quite make up his mind; he was waiting for something to decide him. Meanwhile, the station was approaching and that something was not far off.

At this station the train stopped forty minutes, and the passengers had the chance of having dinner. At the entrance to the dining-room for the passengers of the first and second class there was, as there usually is, a crowd of impatient and hurried people, and as is also usual, perhaps, a scandalous scene took place. A lady from a second-class carriage, who was remarkably pretty but somewhat too gorgeously dressed for travelling, was dragging after her an Uhlan, a very young and handsome officer, who was trying to tear himself out of her hands. The youthful officer was extremely drunk, and the lady, to all appearance some elder relative, would not let him go, probably apprehending that he would make a dash for the refreshment bar. Meanwhile, in the crush, the Uhlan was jostled by a young merchant who was also disgracefully intoxicated. He had been hanging about the station for the last two days, drinking and scattering his money among the companions who surrounded him, without succeeding in getting into the train to continue his journey. A scuffle followed; the officer shouted; the merchant swore; the lady was in despair, and, trying to draw the Uhlan away from the conflict, kept exclaiming in an imploring voice, "Mitenka! Mitenka!" This seemed to strike the young merchant as too scandalous; every one laughed, indeed, but the merchant was more offended than ever at the outrage, as he conceived it, on propriety.

"Oh, I say: Mitenka!" he pronounced reproachfully, mimicking the shrill voice of the lady. "And not ashamed before folks!"

He went staggering up to the lady, who had rushed to the first chair and succeeded in making the Uhlan sit down beside her, stared at them both contemptuously and drawled in a sing-song voice—

"You're a trollop, you are, dragging your tail in the dirt!"

The lady uttered a shriek and looked about her piteously for some means of escape. She was both ashamed and frightened, and, to put the finishing touch, the officer sprang up from the chair and, with a yell, made a dash at the merchant, but, slipping, fell back into the chair with a flop. The laughter grew louder around them, and no one dreamed of helping her; but Velchaninov came to the rescue; he seized the merchant by the collar and, turning him round, thrust him five paces away from the frightened lady. And with that the scene ended; the merchant was overwhelmed by the shock and by Velchaninov's impressive figure; his companions led him away. The dignified countenance of the elegantly dressed gentleman produced a strong effect on the jeering crowd: the laughter subsided. The lady flushed and, almost in tears, was overflowing with expressions of gratitude. The Uhlan mumbled; "Fanks, fanks!" and made as though to hold out his hand to Velchaninov, but instead of doing so suddenly took it into his head to recline at full length with his feet on the chairs.

"Mitenka!" the lady moaned reproachfully, clasping her hands in horror.

Velchaninov was pleased with the adventure and with the whole situation. The lady attracted him; she was evidently a wealthy provincial, gorgeously but tastelessly dressed, and with rather ridiculous manners— in fact, she combined all the characteristics that guarantee success to a Petersburg gallant with designs on the fair sex. A conversation sprang up; the lady bitterly complained of her husband, who "had disappeared as soon as he had got out of the carriage and so was the cause of it all, for whenever he is wanted he runs off somewhere."

"Naturally," the Uhlan muttered.

"Ah, Mitenka!" She clasped her hands again.

"Well, the husband will catch it," thought Velchaninov.

"What is his name? I will go and look for him," he suggested.

"Pal Palitch," responded the Uhlan.

"Your husband's name is Pavel Pavlovitch?" Velchaninov asked, with curiosity, and suddenly a familiar bald head was thrust between him and the lady. In a flash he had a vision of the Zahlebinins' garden, the innocent games and a tiresome bald head being incessantly thrust between him and Nadyezhda Fedosyevna.

"Here you are at last!" cried his wife hysterically.

It was Pavel Pavlovitch himself; he gazed in wonder and alarm at Velchaninov, as panic-stricken at the sight of him as though he had been a ghost. His stupefaction was such that he evidently could not for some minutes take in what his offended spouse was explaining in a rapid and irritable flow of words. At last, with a start, he grasped all the horror of his position: his own guilt, and Mitenka's behaviour, "and that this monsieur" (this was how the lady for some reason described Velchaninov) "has been a saviour and guardian angel to us, while you—you are always out of the way when you are wanted ..."

Velchaninov suddenly burst out laughing.

"Why, we are friends, we've been friends since childhood!" he exclaimed to the astonished lady. Putting his right arm with patronizing familiarity round the shoulders of Pavel Pavlovitch, who smiled a pale smile, "Hasn't he talked to you of Velchaninov?"

"No, he never has," the lady responded, somewhat disconcerted.

"You might introduce me to your wife, you faithless friend!"

"Lipotchka ... it really is M. Velchaninov," Pavel Pavlovitch was beginning, but he broke off abashed.

His wife turned crimson and flashed an angry look at him, probably for the "Lipotchka."

"And, only fancy, he never let me know he was married, and never invited me to the wedding, but you, Olimpiada ..."

"Semyonovna," Pavel Pavlovitch prompted.

"Semyonovna," the Uhlan, who had dropped asleep, echoed suddenly.

"You must forgive him, Olimpiada Semyonovna, for my sake, in honour of our meeting ... he's a good husband."

And Velchaninov gave Pavel Pavlovitch a friendly slap on the shoulder.

"I was ... I was only away for a minute, my love," Pavel Pavlovitch was beginning to say.

"And left your wife to be insulted," Lipotchka put in at once. "When you're wanted there's no finding you, when you're not wanted you're always at hand ..."

"Where you're not wanted, where you're not wanted ... where you're not wanted ..." the Uhlan chimed in.

Lipotchka was almost breathless with excitement; she knew it was not seemly before Velchaninov, and flushed but could not restrain herself.

"Where you shouldn't be you are too attentive, too attentive!" she burst out.

"Under the bed ... he looks for a lover under the bed—where he shouldn't ... where he shouldn't ..." muttered Mitenka, suddenly growing extremely excited.

But there was no doing anything with Mitenka by now. It all ended pleasantly, however, and they got upon quite friendly terms. Pavel Pavlovitch was sent to fetch coffee and soup. Olimpiada Semyonovna explained to Velchaninov that they were on their way from O——, where her husband had a post in the service, to spend two months at their country place, that it was not far off, only thirty miles from that station, that they had a lovely house and garden there, that they always had the house full of visitors, that they had neighbours too, and if Alexey Ivanovitch would be so good as to come and stay with them "in their rustic solitude" she would welcome him "as their guardian angel," for she could not recall without horror what would have happened, if ... and so on, and so on—in fact, he was "her guardian angel ..."

"And saviour, and saviour," the Uhlan insisted, with heat.

Velchaninov thanked her politely, and replied that he was always at her service, that he was an absolutely idle man with no duties of any sort, and that Olimpiada Semyonovna's invitation was most flattering. He followed this at once with sprightly conversation, successfully introducing two or three compliments. Lipotchka blushed with pleasure, and as soon as Pavel Pavlovitch returned she told him enthusiastically that Alexey Ivanovitch had been so kind as to accept her invitation to spend a whole month with them in the country, and had promised to come in a week. Pavel Pavlovitch smiled in mute despair. Olimpiada Semyonovna shrugged her shoulders at him, and turned her eyes up to the ceiling. At last they got up: again a gush of gratitude, again the "guardian angel," again "Mitenka," and Pavel Pavlovitch at last escorted his wife and the Uhlan to their compartment. Velchaninov lighted a cigar and began pacing to and fro on the balcony in front of the station; he knew that Pavel Pavlovitch would run out again at once to talk to him till the bell rang. And so it happened. Pavel Pavlovitch promptly appeared before him with an uneasy expression in his face and whole figure. Velchaninov laughed, took him by the elbow in a friendly way, led him to the nearest bench, sat down himself, and made him sit down beside him. He remained silent; he wanted Pavel Pavlovitch to be the first to speak.

"So you are coming to us?" faltered the latter, going straight to the point.

"I knew that would be it! You haven't changed in the least!" laughed Velchaninov. "Why, do you mean to say"—he slapped him again on the shoulder—"do you mean to say you could seriously imagine for a moment that I could actually come and stay with you, and for a whole month too—ha—ha?"

Pavel Pavlovitch was all of a twitter.

"So you—are not coming!" he cried, not in the least disguising his relief.

"I'm not coming, I'm not coming!" Velchaninov laughed complacently.

He could not have said himself, however, why he felt so particularly amused, but he was more and more amused as time went on.

"Do you really ... do you really mean it?"

And saying this, Pavel Pavlovitch actually jumped up from his seat in a flutter of suspense.

"Yes, I've told you already that I'm not coming, you queer fellow."

"If that's so, what am I to say to Olimpiada Semyonovna a week hence, when she will be expecting you and you don't come?"

"What a difficulty! Tell her I've broken my leg or something of that sort."

"She won't believe it," Pavel Pavlovitch drawled plaintively.

"And you'll catch it?" Velchaninov went on laughing. "But I observe, my poor friend, that you tremble before your delightful wife—don't you?"

Pavel Pavlovitch tried to smile, but it did not come off. That Velchaninov had refused to visit them was a good thing, of course, but that he should be over-familiar to him about his wife was disagreeable. Pavel Pavlovitch winced; Velchaninov noticed it. Meanwhile the second bell rang; they heard a shrill voice from the train anxiously calling Pavel Pavlovitch. The latter moved, fidgeted in his chair, but did not rise at the first summons, evidently expecting something more from Velchaninov, no doubt another assurance that he would not come and stay with them.

"What was your wife's maiden name?" Velchaninov inquired, as though unaware of Pavel Pavlovitch's anxiety.

"She is our priest's daughter," replied the latter in uneasy trepidation, listening and looking towards the train.

"Ah, I understand, you married her for her beauty."

Pavel Pavlovitch winced again.

"And who's this Mitenka with you?"

"Oh, he's a distant relation of ours—that is, of mine; the son of my deceased cousin. His name's Golubtchikov, he was degraded for disorderly behaviour in the army, but now he has been promoted again and we have been getting his equipment. ... He's an unfortunate young man ..."

"To be sure, the regular thing; the party's complete," thought Velchaninov.

"Pavel Pavlovitch!" the call came again from the train, and by now with a marked tone of irritation in the voice.

"Pal Palitch!" they heard in another thick voice.

Pavel Pavlovitch fidgeted and moved restlessly again, but Velchaninov took him by the elbow and detained him.

"How would you like me to go this minute and tell your wife how you tried to cut my throat?"

"What, what!" Pavel Pavlovitch was terribly alarmed. "God forbid!"

"Pavel Pavlovitch! Pavel Pavlovitch!" voices were heard calling again.

"Well, be off now!" said Velchaninov, letting him go at last, and still laughing genially.

"So you won't come?" Pavel Pavlovitch whispered for the last time, almost in despair, and even put his hands before him with the palms together in his old style.

"Why, I swear I won't come! Run, there'll be trouble, you know."

And with a flourish he held out his hand to him—and was startled at the result: Pavel Pavlovitch did not take his hand, he even drew his own hand back.

The third bell rang.

In one instant something strange happened to both of them: both seemed transformed. Something, as it were, quivered and burst out in Velchaninov, who had been laughing only just before. He clutched Pavel Pavlovitch by the shoulder and held him in a tight and furious grip.

"If I—*I* hold out this hand to you," showing the palm of his left hand, where a big scar from the cut was still distinct, "you certainly might take it!" he whispered, with pale and trembling lips.

Pavel Pavlovitch, too, turned pale, and his lips trembled too; a convulsive quiver ran over his face.

"And Liza?" he murmured in a rapid whisper, and suddenly his lips, his cheeks, and his chin began to twitch and tears gushed from his eyes.

Velchaninov stood before him stupefied.

"Pavel Pavlovitch! Pavel Pavlovitch!" they heard a scream from the train as though some one were being murdered—and suddenly the whistle sounded.

Pavel Pavlovitch roused himself, flung up his hands and ran full speed to the train; the train was already in motion, but he managed to hang on somehow, and went flying to his compartment. Velchaninov remained at the station and only in the evening set off on his original route in another train. He did not turn off to the right to see his fair friend—he felt too much out of humour. And how he regretted it afterwards.

AN ARTIST'S STORY[1]

Anton Tchehov

I

IT WAS six or seven years ago when I was living in one of the districts of the province of T——, on the estate of a young landowner called Byelokurov, who used to get up very early, wear a peasant tunic, drink beer in the evenings, and continually complain to me that he never met with sympathy from anyone. He lived in the lodge in the garden, and I in the old seigniorial house, in a big room with columns, where there was no furniture except a wide sofa on which I used to sleep, and a table on which I used to lay out patience. There was always, even in still weather, a droning noise in the old Amos stoves, and in thunderstorms the whole house shook and seemed to be cracking into pieces; and it was rather terrifying, especially at night, when all the ten big windows were suddenly lit up by lightning.

Condemned by destiny to perpetual idleness, I did absolutely nothing. For hours together I gazed out of the window at the sky, at the birds, at the avenue, read everything that was brought me by post, slept. Sometimes I went out of the house and wandered about till late in the evening.

One day as I was returning home, I accidentally strayed into a place I did not know. The sun was already sinking, and the shades of evening lay across the flowering rye. Two rows of old, closely planted, very tall fir-trees stood like two dense walls forming a picturesque, gloomy avenue. I easily climbed over the fence and walked along the avenue, slipping over the fir-needles which lay two inches deep on the ground. It was still and dark, and only here and there on the high tree-tops the vivid golden light quivered and made rainbows in the spiders' webs. There was a strong, almost stifling smell of resin. Then I turned into a long avenue of limes. Here, too, all was desolation and age; last year's leaves rustled mournfully under my feet and in the twilight shadows lurked between the trees. From the old orchard on the right came the faint, reluctant note of the golden oriole, who must have been old too. But at last the limes ended. I walked by an old white house of two storeys with a terrace, and there suddenly opened before me a view of a courtyard, a large pond with a bathing-

---

[1] From *The Darling and Other Stories*, translated by Constance Garnett. Reprinted by permission of Messrs Chatto and Windus.

house, a group of green willows, and a village on the further bank, with a high, narrow belfry on which there glittered a cross reflecting the setting sun.

For a moment it breathed upon me the fascination of something near and very familiar, as though I had seen that landscape at some time in my childhood.

At the white stone gates which led from the yard to the fields, old-fashioned solid gates with lions on them, were standing two girls. One of them, the elder, a slim, pale, very handsome girl with a perfect hay-stack of chestnut hair and a little obstinate mouth, had a severe expression and scarcely took notice of me, while the other, who was still very young, not more than seventeen or eighteen, and was also slim and pale, with a large mouth and large eyes, looked at me with astonishment as I passed by, said something in English, and was overcome with embarrassment. And it seemed to me that these two charming faces, too, had long been familiar to me. And I returned home feeling as though I had had a delightful dream.

One morning soon afterwards, as Byelokurov and I were walking near the house, a carriage drove unexpectedly into the yard, rustling over the grass, and in it was sitting one of those girls. It was the elder one. She had come to ask for subscriptions for some villagers whose cottages had been burnt down. Speaking with great earnestness and precision, and not looking at us, she told us how many houses in the village of Siyanovo had been burnt, how many men, women, and children were left homeless, and what steps were proposed, to begin with, by the Relief Committee, of which she was now a member. After handing us the subscription list for our signatures, she put it away and immediately began to take leave of us.

"You have quite forgotten us, Pyotr Petrovitch," she said to Byelokurov as she shook hands with him. "Do come, and if Monsieur N. (she mentioned my name) cares to make the acquaintance of admirers of his work, and will come and see us, mother and I will be delighted."

I bowed.

When she had gone Pyotr Petrovitch began to tell me about her. The girl was, he said, of good family, and her name was Lidia Voltchaninov, and the estate on which she lived with her mother and sister, like the village on the other side of the pond, was called Shelkovka. Her father had once held an important position in Moscow, and had died with the rank of a privy councillor. Although they had ample means, the Voltchaninovs lived on their estate summer and winter without going away.

Lidia was a teacher in the Zemstvo school in her own village, and received a salary of twenty-five roubles a month. She spent nothing on herself but her salary, and was proud of earning her own living.

"An interesting family," said Byelokurov. "Let us go over one day. They will be delighted to see you."

One afternoon on a holiday we thought of the Voltchaninovs, and went to Shelkovka to see them. They—the mother and two daughters—were at home. The mother, Ekaterina Pavlovna, who at one time had been handsome, but now, asthmatic, depressed, vague, and over-feeble for her years, tried to entertain me with conversation about painting. Having heard from her daughter that I might come to Shelkovka, she had hurriedly recalled two or three of my landscapes which she had seen in exhibitions in Moscow, and now asked what I meant to express by them. Lidia, or as they all called her, Lida, talked more to Byelokurov than to me. Earnest and unsmiling, she asked him why he was not on the Zemstvo, and why he had not attended any of its meetings.

"It's not right, Pyotr Petrovitch," she said reproachfully. "It's not right. It's too bad."

"That's true, Lida—that's true," the mother assented. "It isn't right."

"Our whole district is in the hands of Balagin," Lida went on, addressing me. "He is the chairman of the Zemstvo Board, and he has distributed all the posts in the district among his nephews and sons-in-law; and he does as he likes. He ought to be opposed. The young men ought to make a strong party, but you see what the young men among us are like. It's a shame, Pyotr Petrovitch!"

The younger sister, Genya, was silent while they were talking of the Zemstvo. She took no part in serious conversation. She was not looked upon as quite grown up by her family, and like a child, was always called by the nickname of Misuce, because that was what she had called her English governess when she was a child. She was all the time looking at me with curiosity, and when I glanced at the photographs in the album, she explained to me: "That's uncle ... that's godfather," moving her finger across the photograph. As she did so she touched me with her shoulder like a child, and I had a close view of her delicate, undeveloped chest, her slender shoulders, her plait, and her thin little body tightly drawn in by her sash.

We played croquet and lawn tennis, we walked about the garden, drank tea, and then sat a long time over supper. After the huge empty room with columns, I felt, as it were, at home in this small snug house where there were no oleographs on the walls and where the servants were spoken to with civility. And everything seemed to me young and pure, thanks to the presence of Lida and Misuce, and there was an atmosphere of refinement over everything. At supper Lida talked to Byelokurov again of the Zemstvo, of Balagin, and of school libraries. She was an energetic, genuine girl, with convictions, and it was interesting to listen to her, though she talked a great deal and in a loud voice—perhaps because she was accustomed to talking at school. On the other hand, Pyotr Petrovitch, who had retained from his student days the habit of turning every conversation into an argument, was tedious, flat, longwinded, and unmistakably anxious to appear clever and advanced. Gesticulating, he upset a sauce-boat with his sleeve, making a huge pool on the tablecloth, but no one except me appeared to notice it.

It was dark and still as we went home.

"Good breeding is shown, not by not upsetting the sauce, but by not noticing it when somebody else does," said Byelokurov, with a sigh. "Yes, a splendid, intellectual family! I've dropped out of all decent society; it's dreadful how I've dropped out of it! It's all through work, work, work!"

He talked of how hard one had to work if one wanted to be a model farmer. And I thought what a heavy, sluggish fellow he was! Whenever he talked of anything serious he articulated "Er-er" with intense effort, and worked just as he talked—slowly, always late and behindhand. I had little faith in his business capacity if only from the fact that when I gave him letters to post he carried them about in his pocket for weeks together.

"The hardest thing of all," he muttered as he walked beside me—"the hardest thing of all is that, work as one may, one meets with no sympathy from anyone. No sympathy!"

II

I took to going to see the Voltchaninovs. As a rule I sat on the lower step of the terrace; I was fretted by dissatisfaction with myself; I was sorry at the thought of my life passing so rapidly and uninterestingly, and felt as though I would like to tear out of my breast the heart which had grown so heavy. And meanwhile I heard talk on the terrace, the rustling of dresses, the pages of a book being turned. I soon grew accustomed to. the idea that during the day Lida received patients, gave out books, and often went into the village with a parasol and no hat, and in the evening talked aloud of the Zemstvo and schools. This slim, handsome, invariably austere girl, with her small well-cut mouth, always said dryly when the conversation turned on serious subjects:

"That's of no interest to you."

She did not like me. She disliked me because I was a landscape painter and did not in my pictures portray the privations of the peasants, and that, as she fancied, I was indifferent to what she put such faith in. I remember when I was travelling on the banks of Lake Baikal, I met a Buriat girl on horseback, wearing a shirt and trousers of blue Chinese canvas; I asked her if she would sell me her pipe. While we talked she looked contemptuously at my European face and hat, and in a moment she was bored with talking to me; she shouted to her horse and galloped on. And in just the same way Lida despised me as an alien. She never outwardly expressed her dislike for me, but I felt it, and sitting on the lower step of the terrace, I felt irritated, and said that doctoring peasants when one was not a doctor was deceiving them, and that it was easy to be benevolent when one had six thousand acres.

Meanwhile her sister Misuce had no cares, and spent her life in complete idleness just as I did. When she got up in the morning she immediately took up a book and sat down to read on the terrace in a deep armchair, with her feet hardly touching the ground, or hid herself with her book in the lime avenue, or walked out into the fields. She spent the whole day reading, poring greedily over her book, and only from the tired, dazed look in her eyes and the extreme paleness of her face one could divine how this continual reading exhausted her brain. When I arrived she would flush a little, leave her book, and looking into my face with her big eyes, would tell me eagerly of anything that had happened—for instance, that the chimney had been on fire in the servants' hall, or that one of the men had caught a huge fish in the pond. On ordinary days she usually went about in a light blouse and a dark blue skirt. We went for walks together, picked cherries for making jam, went out in the boat. When she jumped up to reach a cherry or sculled in the boat, her thin, weak arms showed through her transparent sleeves. Or I painted a sketch, and she stood beside me watching rapturously.

One Sunday at the end of July I came to the Voltchaninovs about nine o'clock in the morning. I walked about the park, keeping a good distance from the house, looking for white mushrooms, of which there was a great number that summer, and noting their position so as to come and pick them afterwards with Genya. There was a warm breeze. I saw Genya and her mother both in light holiday dresses coming home from church, Genya holding her hat in the wind. Afterwards I heard them having tea on the terrace.

For a careless person like me, trying to find justification for my perpetual idleness, these holiday mornings in our country-houses in the summer have always had a particular charm. When the green garden, still wet with dew, is all sparkling in the sun and looks radiant with happiness, when there is a scent of mignonette and oleander near the house, when the young people have just come back from church and are having breakfast in the garden, all so charmingly dressed and gay, and one knows that all these healthy, well-fed, handsome people are going to do nothing the whole long day, one wishes that all life were like that. Now, too, I had the same thought, and walked about the garden prepared to walk about like that, aimless and unoccupied, the whole day, the whole summer.

Genya came out with a basket; she had a look in her face as though she knew she would find me in the garden, or had a presentiment of it. We gathered mushrooms and talked, and when she asked a question she walked a little ahead so as to see my face.

"A miracle happened in the village yesterday," she said. "The lame woman Pelagea has been ill the whole year. No doctors or medicines did her any good; but yesterday an old woman came and whispered something over her, and her illness passed away."

"That's nothing much," I said. "You mustn't look for miracles only among sick people and old women. Isn't health a miracle? And life itself? Whatever is beyond understanding is a miracle."

"And aren't you afraid of what is beyond understanding?"

"No. Phenomena I don't understand I face boldly, and am not overwhelmed by them. I am above them. Man ought to recognize himself as superior to lions, tigers, stars, superior to everything in nature, even what seems miraculous and is beyond his understanding, or else he is not a man, but a mouse afraid of everything."

Genya believed that as an artist I knew a very great deal, and could guess correctly what I did not know. She longed for me to initiate her into the domain of the Eternal and the Beautiful—into that higher world in which, as she imagined, I was quite at home. And she talked to me of God, of the eternal life, of the miraculous. And I, who could never admit that my self and my imagination would be lost for ever after death, answered: "Yes, men are immortal"; "Yes, there is eternal life in store for us." And she listened, believed, and did not ask for proofs.

As we were going home she stopped suddenly and said:

"Our Lida is a remarkable person—isn't she? I love her very dearly, and would be ready to give my life for her any minute. But tell me"— Genya touched my sleeve with her finger—"tell me, why do you always argue with her? Why are you irritated?"

"Because she is wrong."

Genya shook her head and tears came into her eyes.

"How incomprehensible that is!" she said.

At that minute Lida had just returned from somewhere, and standing with a whip in her hand, a slim, beautiful figure in the sunlight, at the steps, she was giving some orders to one of the men. Talking loudly, she hurriedly received two or three sick villagers; then with a busy and anxious face she walked about the rooms, opening one cupboard after another, and went upstairs. It was a long time before they could find her and call her to dinner, and she came in when we had finished our soup. All these tiny details I remember with tenderness, and that whole day I remember vividly, though nothing special happened. After dinner Genya lay in a long armchair reading, while I sat upon the bottom step of the terrace. We were silent. The whole sky was overcast with clouds, and it began to spot with fine rain. It was hot; the wind had dropped, and it seemed as though the day would never end. Ekaterina Pavlovna came out on the terrace, looking drowsy and carrying a fan.

"Oh, mother," said Genya, kissing her hand, "it's not good for you to sleep in the day."

They adored each other. When one went into the garden, the other would stand on the terrace, and, looking towards the trees, call "Aa-oo, Genya!" or "Mother, where are you?" They always said their prayers together, and had the same faith; and they understood each other perfectly even when they did not speak. And their attitude to people was the same. Ekaterina Pavlovna, too, grew quickly used to me and fond of me, and when I did not come for two or three days, sent to ask if I were well. She, too, gazed at my sketches with enthusiasm, and with the same openness and readiness to chatter as Misuce, she told me what had happened, and confided to me her domestic secrets.

She had a perfect reverence for her elder daughter. Lida did not care for endearments, she talked only of serious matters; she lived her life apart, and to her mother and sister was as sacred and enigmatic a person as the admiral, always sitting in his cabin, is to the sailors.

"Our Lida is a remarkable person," the mother would often say. "Isn't she?"

Now, too, while it was drizzling with rain, we talked of Lida.

"She is a remarkable girl," said her mother, and added in an undertone, like a conspirator, looking about her timidly: "You wouldn't easily find another like her; only, do you know, I am beginning to be a little uneasy. The school, the dispensary, books—all that's very good, but why go to extremes? She is three-and-twenty, you know; it's time for her to think seriously of herself. With her books and her dispensary she will find life has slipped by without having noticed it. ... She must be married."

Genya, pale from reading, with her hair disarranged, raised her head and said as it were to herself, looking at her mother:

"Mother, everything is in God's hands."

And again she buried herself in her book.

Byelokurov came in his tunic and embroidered shirt. We played croquet and tennis, then when it got dark, sat a long time over supper and talked again about schools, and about Balagin, who had the whole district under his thumb. As I went away from the Voltchaninovs that evening, I carried away the impression of a long, long idle day, with a melancholy consciousness that everything ends in this world, however long it may be.

Genya saw us out to the gate, and perhaps because she had been with me all day, from morning till night, I felt dull without her, and that all that charming family were near and dear to me, and for the first time that summer I had a yearning to paint.

"Tell me, why do you lead such a dreary, colourless life?" I asked Byelokurov as I went home. "My life is dreary, difficult, and monotonous because I am an artist, a strange person. From my earliest days I've been wrung by envy, self-dissatisfaction, distrust in my work. I'm always poor, I'm a wanderer, but you—you're a healthy, normal man, a landowner, and a gentleman. Why do you live in such an uninteresting way? Why do you get so little out of life? Why haven't you, for instance, fallen in love with Lida or Genya?"

"You forget that I love another woman," answered Byelokurov.

He was referring to Liubov Ivanovna, the lady who shared the lodge with him. Every day I saw this lady, very plump, rotund, and dignified, not unlike a fat goose, walking about the garden, in the Russian national dress and beads, always carrying a parasol; and the servant was continually calling her in to dinner or to tea. Three years before she had taken one of the lodges for a summer holiday, and had settled down at Byelokurov's apparently for ever. She was ten years older than he was, and kept a sharp hand over him, so much so that he had to ask her permission when he went out of the house. She often sobbed in a deep masculine note, and then I used to send word to her that if she did not leave off, I should give up my rooms there; and she left off.

When we got home Byelokurov sat down on the sofa and frowned thoughtfully, and I began walking up and down the room, conscious of

a soft emotion as though I were in love. I wanted to talk about the Voltchaninovs.

"Lida could only fall in love with a member of the Zemstvo, as devoted
to schools and hospitals as she is," I said. "Oh, for the sake of a girl like
that one might not only go into the Zemstvo, but even wear out iron
shoes, like the girl in the fairy tale. And Misuce? What a sweet creature
she is, that Misuce!"

Byelokurov, drawing out "Er—er," began a long-winded disquisition
on the malady of the age—pessimism. He talked confidently, in a tone that
suggested that I was opposing him. Hundreds of miles of desolate, monotonous, burnt-up steppe cannot induce such deep depression as one man
when he sits and talks, and one does not know when he will go.

"It's not a question of pessimism or optimism," I said irritably; "it's
simply that ninety-nine people out of a hundred have no sense."

Byelokurov took this as aimed at himself, was offended, and went away.

III

"The prince is staying at Malozyomovo, and he asks to be remembered
to you," said Lida to her mother. She had just come in, and was taking
off her gloves. "He gave me a great deal of interesting news. ... He promised
to raise the question of a medical relief centre at Malozyomovo again at
the provincial assembly, but he says there is very little hope of it." And
turning to me, she said: "Excuse me, I always forget that this cannot be
interesting to you."

I felt irritated.

"Why not interesting to me?" I said, shrugging my shoulders. "You
do not care to know my opinion, but I assure you the question has great
interest for me."

"Yes?"

"Yes. In my opinion a medical relief centre at Malozyomovo is quite
unnecessary."

My irritation infected her; she looked at me, screwing up her eyes, and
asked:

"What is necessary? Landscapes?"

"Landscapes are not, either. Nothing is."

She finished taking off her gloves, and opened the newspaper, which
had just been brought from the post. A minute later she said quietly,
evidently restraining herself:

"Last week Anna died in childbirth, and if there had been a medical relief centre near, she would have lived. And I think even landscape painters ought to have some opinions on the subject."

"I have a very definite opinion on that subject, I assure you," I answered; and she screened herself with the newspaper, as though unwilling to listen to me. "To my mind, all these schools, dispensaries, libraries, medical relief centres, under present conditions, only serve to aggravate the bondage of the people. The peasants are fettered by a great chain, and you do, not break the chain, but only add fresh links to it—that's my view of it."

She raised her eyes to me and smiled ironically, and I went on trying to formulate my leading idea.

"What matters is not that Anna died in childbirth, but that all these Annas, Mavras, Pelageas, toil from early morning till dark, fall ill from working beyond their strength, all their lives tremble for their sick and hungry children, all their lives are being doctored, and in dread of death and disease, fade and grow old early, and die in filth and stench. Their children begin the same story over again as soon as they grow up, and so it goes on for hundreds of years and milliards of men live worse than beasts—in continual terror, for a mere crust of bread. The whole horror of their position lies in their never having time to think of their souls, of their image and semblance. Cold, hunger, animal terror, a burden of toil, like avalanches of snow, block for them every way to spiritual activity— that is, to what distinguishes man from the brutes and what is the only thing which makes life worth living. You go to their help with hospitals and schools, but you don't free them from their fetters by that; on the contrary, you bind them in closer bonds, as, by introducing new prejudices, you increase the number of their wants, to say nothing of the fact that they've got to pay the Zemstvo for blisters and books, and so toil harder than ever."

"I am not going to argue with you," said Lida, putting down the paper. "I've heard all that before. I will only say one thing: one cannot sit with one's hands in one's lap. It's true that we are not saving humanity, and perhaps we make a great many mistakes; but we do what we can, and we are right. The highest and holiest task for a civilized being is to serve his neighbours, and we try to serve them as best we can. You don't like it, but one can't please every one."

"That's true, Lida," said her mother—"that's true."

In Lida's presence she was always a little timid, and looked at her nervously as she talked, afraid of saying something superfluous or inopportune. And she never contradicted her, but always assented: "That's true, Lida— that's true."

"Teaching the peasants to read and write, books of wretched precepts and rhymes, and medical relief centres, cannot diminish either ignorance or the death-rate, just as the light from your windows cannot light up this huge garden," said I. "You give nothing. By meddling in these people's lives you only create new wants in them, and new demands on their labour."

"Ach! Good heavens! But one must do something!" said Lida with vexation, and from her tone one could see that she thought my arguments worthless and despised them.

"The people must be freed from hard physical labour," said I. "We must lighten their yoke, let them have time to breathe, that they may not spend all their lives at the stove, at the wash-tub, and in the fields, but may also have time to think of their souls, of God—may have time to develop their spiritual capacities. The highest vocation of man is spiritual activity—the perpetual search for truth and the meaning of life. Make coarse animal labour unnecessary for them, let them feel themselves free and then you will see what a mockery these dispensaries and books are. Once a man recognizes his true vocation, he can only be satisfied by religion, science, and art, and not by these trifles."

"Free them from labour?" laughed Lida. "But is that possible?"

"Yes. Take upon yourself a share of their labour. If all of us, townspeople and country people, all without exception, would agree to divide between us the labour which mankind spends on the satisfaction of their physical needs, each of us would perhaps need to work only for two or three hours a day. Imagine that we all, rich and poor, work only for three hours a day, and the rest of our time is free. Imagine further that in order to depend even less upon our bodies and to labour less, we invent machines to replace our work, we try to cut down our needs to the minimum. We would harden ourselves and our children that they should not be afraid of hunger and cold, and that we shouldn't be continually trembling for their health like Anna, Mavra, and Pelagea. Imagine that we don't doctor ourselves, don't keep dispensaries, tobacco factories, distilleries—what a lot of free time would be left us after all! All of us together would devote our leisure to science and art. Just as the peasants sometimes work, the whole community together mending the roads, so all of us, as a community, would search for truth and the meaning of life, and I am convinced that the truth would be discovered very quickly; man would escape from this continual, agonizing, oppressive dread of death, and even from death itself."

"You contradict yourself, though," said Lida. "You talk about science, and are yourself opposed to elementary education."

"Elementary education when a man has nothing to read but the signs on public-houses and sometimes books which he cannot understand—such education has existed among us since the times of Rurik; Gogol's Petrushka has been reading for ever so long, yet as the village was in the days of Rurik so it has remained. What is needed is not elementary education, but freedom for a wide development of spiritual capacities. What are wanted are not schools, but universities."

"You are opposed to medicine, too."

"Yes. It would be necessary only for the study of diseases as natural phenomena, and not for the cure of them. If one must cure, it should not be diseases, but the causes of them. Remove the principal cause—physical labour, and then there will be no disease. I don't believe in a science that cures disease," I went on excitedly. "When science and art are real, they aim not at temporary, private ends, but at eternal and universal—they seek for truth and the meaning of life, they seek for God, for the soul, and when they are tied down to the needs and evils of the day, to dispensaries and libraries, they only complicate and hamper life. We have plenty of doctors, chemists, lawyers; plenty of people can read and write, but we are quite without biologists, mathematicians, philosophers, poets. The whole of our intelligence, the whole of our spiritual energy, is spent on satisfying temporary, passing needs. Scientific men, writers, artists, are hard at work; thanks to them, the conveniences of life are multiplied from day to day. Our physical demands increase, yet truth is still a long way off, and man still remains the most rapacious and dirty animal; everything is tending to the degeneration of the majority of mankind, and the loss for ever of all fitness for life. In such conditions an artist's work has no meaning, and the more talented he is, the stranger and the more unintelligible is his position, as when one looks into it, it is evident that he is working for the amusement of a rapacious and unclean animal, and is supporting the existing order. And I don't care to work and I won't work. ... Nothing is any use; let the earth sink to perdition!"

"Misuce, go out of the room!" said Lida to her sister, apparently thinking my words pernicious to the young girl.

Genya looked mournfully at her mother and sister, and went out of the room.

"These are the charming things people say when they want to justify their indifference," said Lida. "It is easier to disapprove of schools and hospitals, than to teach or heal."

"That's true, Lida—that's true," the mother assented.

"You threaten to give up working," said Lida. "You evidently set a high value on your work. Let us give up arguing; we shall never agree, since I put the most imperfect dispensary or library of which you have just spoken so contemptuously on a higher level than any landscape." And turning at once to her mother, she began speaking in quite a different tone: "The prince is very much changed, and much thinner than when he was with us last. He is being sent to Vichy."

She told her mother about the prince in order to avoid talking to me. Her face glowed and to hide her feeling she bent low over the table as though she were short-sighted, and made a show of reading the newspaper. My presence was disagreeable to her. I said good-bye and went home.

IV

It was quite still out of doors; the village on the further side of the pond was already asleep; there was not a light to be seen, and only the stars were faintly reflected in the pond. At the gate with the lions on it Genya was standing motionless, waiting to escort me.

"Every one is asleep in the village," I said to her, trying to make out her face in the darkness, and I saw her mournful dark eyes fixed upon me. "The publican and the horse-stealers are asleep, while we, well-bred people, argue and irritate each other."

It was a melancholy August night—melancholy because there was already a feeling of autumn; the moon was rising behind a purple cloud, and it shed a faint light upon the road and on the dark fields of winter corn by the sides. From time to time a star fell. Genya walked beside me along the road, and tried not to look at the sky, that she might not see the falling stars, which for some reason frightened her.

"I believe you are right," she said, shivering with the damp night air. "If people, all together, could devote themselves to spiritual ends, they would soon know everything."

"Of course. We are higher beings, and if we were really to recognize the whole force of human genius and lived only for higher ends, we should in the end become like gods. But that will never be—mankind will degenerate till no traces of genius remain."

When the gates were out of sight, Genya stopped and shook hands with me.

"Good night," she said, shivering; she had nothing but her blouse over her shoulders and was shrinking with cold. "Come to-morrow."

I felt wretched at the thought of being left alone, irritated and dissatisfied with myself and other people; and I, too, tried not to look at the falling stars.

"Stay another minute," I said to her, "I entreat you."

I loved Genya. I must have loved her because she met me when I came and saw me off when I went away; because she looked at me tenderly and enthusiastically.. How touchingly beautiful were her pale face, slender neck, slender arms, her weakness, her idleness, her reading. And intelligence? I suspected in her intelligence above the average. I was fascinated by the breadth of her views, perhaps because they were different from those of the stern, handsome Lida, who disliked me. Genya liked me, because I was an artist. I had conquered her heart by my talent, and had a passionate desire to paint for her sake alone; and I dreamed of her as of my little queen who with me would possess those trees, those fields, the mists, the dawn, the exquisite and beautiful scenery in the midst of which I had felt myself hopelessly solitary and useless.

"Stay another minute," I begged her. "I beseech you."

I took off my overcoat and put it over her chilly shoulders; afraid of looking ugly and absurd in a man's overcoat, she laughed, threw it off, and at that instant I put my arms round her and covered her face, shoulders, and hands with kisses.

"Till to-morrow," she whispered, and softly as though afraid of breaking upon the silence of the night, she embraced me. "We have no secrets from one another. I must tell my mother and my sister at once. ... It's so dreadful! Mother is all right; mother likes you—but Lida!"

She ran to the gates.

"Good-bye!" she called.

And then for two minutes I heard her running. I did not want to go home, and I had nothing to go for. I stood still for a little time hesitating, and made my way slowly back, to look once more at the house in which she lived, the sweet, simple old house, which seemed to be watching me from the windows of its upper storey, and understanding all about it. I walked by the terrace, sat on the seat by the tennis ground, in the dark under the old elm-tree, and looked from there at the house. In the windows of the top storey where Misuce slept there appeared a bright light, which changed to a soft green—they had covered the lamp with the shade. Shadows began to move. ... I was full of tenderness, peace, and satisfaction with myself—satisfaction at having been able to be carried away by my feelings and having fallen in love, and at the same time I felt uncomfortable at the thought that only a few steps away from me, in one of the rooms of that house there was Lida, who disliked and perhaps hated me. I went on sitting there wondering whether Genya would come out; I listened and fancied I heard voices talking upstairs.

About an hour passed. The green light went out, and the shadows were no longer visible. The moon was standing high above the house, and lighting up the sleeping garden and the paths; the dahlias and the roses in front of the house could be seen distinctly, and looked all the same colour. It began to grow very cold. I went out of the garden, picked up my coat on the road, and slowly sauntered home.

When next day after dinner I went to the Voltchaninovs, the glass door into the garden was wide open. I sat down on the terrace, expecting Genya every minute, to appear from behind the flower-beds on the lawn, or from one of the avenues, or that I should hear her voice from the house. Then I walked into the drawing-room, the dining-room. There was not a soul to be seen. From the dining-room I walked along the long corridor to the hall and back. In this corridor there were several doors, and through one of them I heard the voice of Lida:

"'God ... sent ... a crow,'" she said in a loud, emphatic voice, probably dictating—"'God sent a crow a piece of cheese. ... A crow. ... A piece of cheese. ...' Who's there?" she called suddenly, hearing my steps.

"It's I."

"Ah! Excuse me, I cannot come out to you this minute; I'm giving Dasha her lesson."

"Is Ekaterina Pavlovna in the garden?"

"No, she went away with my sister this morning to our aunt in the province of Penza. And in the winter they will probably go abroad," she added after a pause. "'God sent ... the crow ... a piece ... of cheese. ...' Have you written it?"

I went into the hall, and stared vacantly at the pond and the village, and the sound reached me of "A piece of cheese. ... God sent the crow a piece of cheese."

And I went back by the way I had come here for the first time—first from the yard into the garden past the house, then into the avenue of lime-trees. ... At this point I was overtaken by a small boy who gave me a note:

"I told my sister everything and she insists on my parting with you," I read. "I could not wound her by disobeying. God will give you happiness. Forgive me. If only you knew how bitterly my mother and I are crying!"

Then there was the dark fir avenue, the broken-down fence.... On the field where then the rye was in flower and the corncrakes were calling, now there were cows and hobbled horses. On the slopes there were bright green patches of winter corn. A sober workaday feeling came over me and I felt ashamed of all I had said at the Voltchaninovs', and felt bored with life as I had been before. When I got home, I packed and set off that evening for Petersburg.

．　．　．　．　．

I never saw the Voltchaninovs again. Not long ago, on my way to the Crimea, I met Byelokurov in the train. As before he was wearing a jerkin and an embroidered shirt, and when I asked how he was, he replied that, God be praised, he was well. We began talking. He had sold his old estate and bought another smaller one, in the name of Liubov Ivanovna. He could tell me little about the Voltchaninovs. Lida, he said, was still living in Shelkovka and teaching in the school; she had by degrees succeeded in gathering round her a circle of people sympathetic to her who made a strong party, and at the last election had turned out Balagin, who had till then had the whole district under his thumb. About Genya he only told me that she did not live at home, and that he did not know where she was.

I am beginning to forget the old house, and only sometimes when I am painting or reading I suddenly, apropos of nothing, remember the green light in the window, the sound of my footsteps as I walked home through the fields in the night, with my heart full of love, rubbing my hands in the cold. And still more rarely, at moments when I am sad and depressed by loneliness, I have dim memories, and little by little I begin to feel that she is thinking of me, too—that she is waiting for me, and that we shall meet....

Misuce, where are you?

NORWAY

HOPE IS GREEN[1]
Alexander L. Kielland

"YOU are kicking up the dust!" called out Hans.

Ole did not hear.

"He's getting as deaf as Auntie Maren," thought Hans. "You are kicking up the dust, Ole," he shouted louder.

"Oh, I'm sorry," said Ole, lifting his feet high at every step. Not for the world would he vex his brother; he had enough on his conscience already.

For was he not, at that very moment, thinking of her whom he knew his brother loved, and was it not sinful that he could not crush a passion unfair to his own brother, and utterly hopeless besides.

Ole blamed himself severely; and, keeping to the other side of the road, in order not to kick up the dust, he tried with all his might and main to think of the most indifferent things. But however far away he compelled his thoughts to begin, back they came by the queerest ways to the forbidden point, only to start fluttering again, like a moth round a candle.

The brothers, staying for the holidays with their uncle, the rector, were on their way to the judge's mansion near by, where there was to be a dance for the young people. A great many students were staying in the neighbourhood, and these dances went like an epidemic from one house to another.

So Hans was just in his element; he danced, he sang, he cracked jokes from morning till night, and if his tone had been somewhat sharp when he accused Ole of kicking up the dust, it was really because he felt vexed that he could not stir his brother up to the same high flow of spirits.

We know already what was the matter with Ole. But even under normal conditions he was more quiet and reticent than his brother. He danced "like a nutcracker"—Hans said—he could not sing at all (Hans even said that he had a monotonous and disagreeable voice when he spoke); he was a little absent-minded as well, and very timid with girls.

When they came near the judge's mansion, they heard a carriage behind them.

'It's the Doctor's," said Hans, and struck an attitude to greet it; the beloved one was the Doctor's daughter.

---

[1] From *Collected Works* of Alexander L. Kielland. Translated by Lady Wardrop. Reprinted by permission of Gyldendal Norsk Forlag, Oslo.

"Oh—how charming she is—in pink," said Hans.

Ole saw at once that the beloved one was dressed in green; but he dared not say a word, lest he should betray himself by his voice; his heart was in his mouth.

The carriage passed by at full speed; the young people waved to each other, and the old Doctor shouted, "See you later!"

"By Jove, it was the green one," said Hans; he had scarcely had time to move his fervent glances from the pale pink to the pale green; "but wasn't she lovely, Ole?"

"Well," said Ole with an effort.

"You are a slug!" Hans exclaimed indignantly, "but even if you are devoid of all sense of feminine beauty, I think you might take more interest in—in—your brother's intended——"

If you only knew how much interest I do take, thought the guilty Ole, lowering his eyes.

As a result of this delightful meeting, however, Hans was in a blissful ecstasy of love and happiness; he swung his stick, snapped his fingers, and sang at the top of his voice. And while thinking of her in the pale green frock—this drapery, fresh as the spring and light as a butterfly, as he styled it—there flashed upon his mind an old ditty, which he sang with great gusto.

> Oh hope, forever green—tumti-tumti-tum-tumti-tumti-tum.
> Fair hast thou ever been—tumti-tumti-tum-tumti-tumti-tum.

He thought that this verse suited the situation so perfectly, that he sang it over and over again, now in the waltz rhythm of the old tune, now as a march, now as a serenade—now in loud, joyous notes, now half whispering, as if betraying his love and his hope to the moon and the silent woods.

Ole felt quite sick. However much he admired his brother's singing, he grew so utterly bored by this green hope and the interminable "tumti-tumti-tums" that it was a relief to him when at last they arrived at the judge's mansion.

The afternoon passed in the way usual on such occasions; the young people enjoyed themselves thoroughly, for most of them were in love, and those who were not, enjoyed themselves even more in watching those who were.

They were playing at throwing hoops in the garden. Hans ran nimbly about and played ever so many pranks, muddling the game and showing his beloved all sorts of attentions.

Ole stuck to his post and did his job gravely; he caught the hoop and sent it off with unerring aim. Ole might have enjoyed himself, too, if only his conscience had not reproached him so bitterly for his sinful love of his brother's "intended."

As the evening was getting chilly, the party moved into the big hall, and dancing began.

Ole never danced much, and to-day he was not in the mood for it at all. He spent his time watching Hans who was fluttering about the "intended" the whole evening; Ole felt sick at heart, seeing the green girl whirling along in his brother's arms, and it seemed to him that they danced every dance together.

At last the time came to break up. Most of the elderly people had already left in their carriages, the young people having arranged to see each other home in the lovely moonlight.

But when the last gallop was finished, the hostess would not hear of letting the girls, who were very hot, go out immediately into the cold air. So she prescribed half-an-hour's cooling down, and, to make it pass in the most agreeable way, she asked Hans to sing them a song.

He was ready at once; he was not one of those silly people who have to be pressed: he knew what he could do.

But there was this about Hans's singing, or rather, about people's attitude to it, that opinions were more than usually divided. By three persons his singing was regarded as something of unique beauty. These persons were, first of all, Ole, then Auntie Maren, and finally, Hans himself. Then there were a great many who found his singing "rather nice"—"he always made something of it." Lastly, however, there were some malicious people who said that he could neither sing, nor play.

It was on this last point, the accompaniment, that Ole always felt a secret grudge against his brother—the only thing that marred his admiration for him.

He knew how much toil it had cost Hans to learn, and his sisters to teach him these accompaniments, particularly the three minor chords with which he usually finished up, and which he practised whenever he was going to a party.

So when he saw his brother at the piano, letting his fingers run lightly and casually over the keys, looking up at the ceiling, murmuring, "Well, in what key would that be, now!"—as if he were searching for the right one, Ole shuddered inwardly. For he knew that Hans was only capable of three accompaniments, one in the minor, and two in the major.

But as the singer rose from the piano, letting these three well practised

chords sound so casual, so spontaneous, as if it were something that just happened to come into his head and his fingers at the moment, Ole shook his head, saying to himself, "This is not quite fair of Hans."

In the meantime his brother was singing freely on from his rich repertoire; Schubert and Kierulf were his favourites; and so he gave "*Du bist die Ruh*," "Beloved, I'm tied," "*Ich grolle nicht*," "*Die alten, bösen Lieder*," etc., etc., all with the same supreme composure and this light, half playful accompaniment. The only thing that worried him a little, was the fatal point "*Ich legt' auch meine Liebe und meinen Schmerz hinein*"; still, he did make something of it.

Then Ole, who knew the exact limits of his brother's skill at the piano, suddenly noticed that he had left the beaten tracks and was beginning to experiment on the keyboard; and to his horror he realized that Hans was trying to get that wretched "Oh Hope, forever green." But luckily he did not find it, and so he confined himself to humming the tune half aloud, carelessly striking the three famous minor chords.

"I think we are cool by now," the green girl exclaimed hurriedly.

There was general laughter at her eagerness to get away, and she was actually blushing as she said good-night.

Ole, standing near the hostess, also took his leave. Hans, on the contrary, was kept back by the judge who wished to know under what masters he had studied music; and this took some time.

And thus it happened that Ole and the green girl came together into the hall, where the young people were crowding round the pegs, partly to find their own things, and partly to knock down other people's.

"It's no good pushing," said the green girl.

Now Ole's throat played him a spiteful trick, so that he only managed to make some silly noise. They were standing close together, as the hall was very crowded, and Ole would gladly have given one of his fingers to be able to say something nice to her, or even something sensible; but he simply could not.

"I don't think you have enjoyed yourself to-night," she said kindly.

Ole thought of the miserable part he had been playing the whole evening; his lack of geniality made him so depressed; and so he answered (the most stupid thing possible, he thought as soon as the words were uttered), "It is such a pity that I cannot sing."

"A family failing, I suppose," said the green girl with a quick glance.

"Oh, no," said Ole quite upset, "as you know, my brother is a very fine singer."

"Do you think so?" she said drily.

This was the most extraordinary thing that had ever happened to Ole, that there could be more than one opinion about his brother's singing, and that she, his "intended," did not seem to be among his admirers!— and yet, this was not altogether disagreeable to hear.

Another pause, which Ole in vain tried to break.

"Don't you like dancing?" she asked.

"Not with everybody," he blurted out.

She laughed, "Well, men can choose."

Now Ole began losing his feet. He felt like some one, lost in his own thoughts, walking through the streets on a winter's night, and suddenly finding himself on slippery ice. There was nothing for it but to keep his feet and trust to luck, and with the courage of despair he said, "If I knew —or ventured to hope that one of the girls—no, that the girl that I want to dance with—hm, that she would dance with me, then—then——" he did not get any further, and after some more "thens" he stopped short.

"Perhaps you might ask," said the green girl.

Her bracelet had come loose, and it had such a difficult snap, that to close it she had to bend low over it and press till she got quite red in the face.

"Would you, for instance, dance with me?" Ole's head began to whirl.

"Well, why not," she answered. She stood pressing the point of her shoe into a crack in the floor.

"On Friday there's going to be a party at the rectory—would you let me have a dance then?"

"With pleasure; what dance do you want?" she said, trying to speak in a natural voice.

"A Française?"—because they last a long time, thought Ole.

"I'm not engaged for the second Française," she answered.

"And a Gallop?"

"Yes—thank you; the first Gallop," she said a little hesitatingly.

"And a Polka?"

"Oh no, no more!" cried the green girl, looking at Ole with alarm.

At this moment Hans came dashing out at full speed: "What luck that I found you!—but in what company!"

Saying this he made off with her in his charming way, to find her things and join the others.

"A Française and a Gallop; but no more—well, well—well, well," Ole repeated to himself. He stood as if glued to the spot. At last he saw that he was alone. Hastily he seized a cap, slipped out by the back door, tiptoed through the garden, and with great difficulty climbed the fence not far from the gate which stood ajar.

He took the first footpath through the field, fixing his eyes on the chimneys of the rectory. He had a vague impression of being wet up to the knees in the high grass; but what he did not notice was that the judge's old uniform cap, which in his haste he had managed to grab, was slipping about on his head, until it came to rest when the large peak glided down over on his ear.

"A Française and a Gallop—but no more—well, well—well, well."

It was rather late when Hans came up to the rectory. He had seen the Doctor's girls home, and now he was summing up the day.

"She's rather shy; but I like that."

As he turned off from the road by the rectory garden, he said, "She's damned shy, rather more than I like!"

But as he crossed the yard, he swore that there was nothing in the world he hated more than pert and capricious girls.

The secret reason for this was that he was not at all satisfied with the result of the day. Not for a moment did he doubt that he was loved; but just because of this, he found her cold reserve doubly irritating. Never had she thrown the hoop to him, never had she chosen him for a single ladies' dance, and on the way home she had spoken to anybody but him. Next time, however, he would take a different line, and she was going to be sorry some day!

In the house he went about quietly so as not to make his uncle hear how late he was. To reach his and his brother's bedroom, he had to cross a big garret. Here there was a window, used by the young people as a door through which they could reach a sort of balcony, formed by the roof of the front door entrance.

Hans noticed that this window was open; and out there on the balcony he saw in the clear moonlight the figure of his brother.

Ole still wore the white gloves he had worn at the dance. He had grasped the railing with both hands and was looking the moon full in the face.

Hans could not for the life of him understand why his brother was out there at this time of night; and still less could he make out why Ole had put a flowerpot on his head.

"He's drunk," thought Hans, tiptoeing up to him.

Then he heard his brother murmur something about a Française and a Gallop; and then he began moving his hands in a strange way.

Hans got the impression that he was trying to snap his fingers; and now Ole said, slowly and distinctly in his monotonous and disagreeable voice, "Oh Hope forever green—tumti-tumti-tum." Of course he could not sing, poor fellow.

HOLLAND

SAÏDYAH AND ADINDA[1]

'Multatuli'

SAÏDYAH'S father had a buffalo with which he worked his field. After this buffalo had been taken from him by the District-Head of Parang Koodyang, he was full of sadness, and never spoke a word for many days. For ploughing-time was drawing near, and it was to be feared that if the rice-field was not prepared early, seeding-time also would pass by, and in the end there would be no paddy to cut and store in the shed of the house.

I must here remark, for readers who know Java but do not know Bantam, that in this residency personal landownership exists, which is not the case elsewhere. Saïdyah's father then was greatly distressed. He feared that his wife would lack rice, and also Saïdyah, who was still a child, and the younger brothers and sisters of Saïdyah.

Also the District-Head would doubtless cite him before the Assistant-Resident if he were behindhand in paying his land-rent, for there is a penalty for this.

Then Saïdyah's father took a dagger which was an heirloom from *his* father. The dagger was not very beautiful, but there were silver bands round the sheath, and also on the point of the sheath a small silver plate. He sold this dagger to a Chinaman who lived in the chief township, and came home with twenty-four guilders, which is two pounds of English money, for which sum he bought another buffalo.

Saïdyah, who was then about seven years old, soon contracted a friendship with the new buffalo. Not inadvisedly do I say 'friendship,' for it is indeed touching to see how the Javanese buffalo becomes attached to the little boy that watches and takes care of him. The strong animal willingly bows his heavy head to right or left or downward, according to the finger-pressure of the child that he knows, that he understands, that he has grown up with.

And such friendship little Saïdyah rapidly inspired in the new guest, whilst the encouragement of Saïdyah's child-voice seemed to give greater strength even to the powerful shoulders of the strong animal, when it

---

[1] From *Max Havelaar*. Translated by W. Siebenhaar. Reprinted by permission of Messrs Alfred A. Knopf, Inc.

tore up the heavy clay of the soil and marked its passage in deep, sharp furrows. The buffalo turned round docilely when he reached the end of the paddock, and lost not an inch-breadth of the ground in his backward course ploughing the new furrow, which ever lay alongside the old one as though the rice-field were a garden-plot raked by a giant.

Next to this field lay those of Adinda's father, the father of the child that was to marry Saïdyah. And when Adinda's little brothers came to the border that lay between, at exactly the same moment as Saïdyah was also there with his plough, they called out to each other merrily, and in friendly rivalry praised the strength and obedience of their respective buffaloes. But I believe that of Saïdyah was the best, perhaps because he knew better than the others how to speak to it, for buffaloes are very sensitive to a friendly way of speaking.

Saïdyah was nine, and Adinda already six, before this buffalo was taken from Saïdyah's father by the Disrict-Chief of Parang Koodyang.

Saïdyah' father, who was very poor, now sold to a Chinaman two silver curtain-clasps, heirlooms from the parents of his wife, for eighteen guilders. And for this money he bought a new buffalo.

But Saïdyah was heavy-hearted, for he knew from Adinda's little brothers that the last buffalo had been driven to the head-centre, and he had asked his father whether he had not seen the animal when he was there to sell the curtain-clasps. To which question Saïdyah's father had not wished to reply. Therefore he feared that his buffalo had been killed, as was the case with the other buffaloes which the District-Chief took from the people.

And Saïdyah cried much when he thought of the poor buffalo with which for two years he had been so closely associated. And for a long time he could not eat, for his throat tightened when he tried to swallow.

One must remember that Saïdyah was a child.

The new buffalo got to know Saïdyah, and very soon won in the affection of the child the place of its predecessor... too soon, really. For, alas, the impressions of our heart, impressions as in wax, are so easily smoothed out, to make room for other writing! However, though the new buffalo was not so strong as the former one... though the old yoke was too wide for its shoulders... yet the poor animal was as docile as its predecessor which had been killed, and if Saïdyah could no longer boast of the strength of his buffalo when meeting Adinda's little brothers on the boundary-line, he maintained that no other exceeded his in obedience; and if the furrow did not run as straight as before, or if lumps of earth were passed unbroken, he gladly remedied this deficiency with his spade as far as he could. Besides, no buffalo had a hair-twist like his. The priest himself had said that there was luck in the course of the hairy vertebræ at the back of the shoulders.

One day, in the field, Saïdyah called out in vain to his buffalo to speed up more. The animal stopped dead. Saïdyah, annoyed at an obstinacy so great and especially so unaccustomed, could not refrain from uttering an insult. He exclaimed a. s. Anyone that has been in Java will understand me, and those who do not understand can only gain by my sparing them the explanation of a coarse expression.

Saïdyah, however, meant nothing evil. He only said it because he had so often heard it from others when they were dissatisfied with their buffaloes. But he need not have said it, for it was of no avail; his buffalo took not another step forward. He shook his head as if to throw off the yoke... one saw the breath coming from his nostrils... he stood panting, he trembled, he quivered... there was fear in his blue eye, and his upper lip was drawn back until the gums lay bare...

"Run, run!" suddenly cried Adinda's brothers. "Saïdyah, run! there is a tiger."

And all undid the ploughing-yokes from their buffaloes, throwing themselves on the broad backs, and galloping away through rice-fields, across dykes, through mud, through scrub and bush and prairie-grass, by fields and roads. And when they rode panting and sweating into the village of Badoor, Saïdyah was not with them.

For when he, having freed his buffalo from the yoke, had mounted, like the others, to flee as they, an unexpected bound of the animal had made him lose his balance and thrown him to the ground. The tiger was very near....

Saïdyah's buffalo, driven forward by its own speed, rushed a few leaps past the spot where his little master awaited death. But only through its own speed, and not through its own will, had it gone past Saïdyah. For scarcely had it overcome the force that controls all matter, when it turned back, planted its clumsy body on its clumsy feet above the child like a roof, and turned its horned head to the tiger. The brute sprang... but it sprang for the last time. The buffalo caught it on his horns and only lost some flesh that the tiger tore out at the neck. The assailant lay on the ground with ripped-up belly... Saïdyah was saved. It was quite true that there had been luck in the hair-twist of that buffalo!

When this buffalo had been taken from Saïdyah's father and killed...
I have told you, reader, that my story is monotonous.
...when this buffalo was killed, Saïdyah was twelve years old, and

Adinda wove shawls and painted them with a pointed headpiece. She had already *thoughts* to work into the course of her paint-shuttle, and she painted sadness on the texture of her fabric, for she had seen Saïdyah very sad.

And Saïdyah's father also was deeply grived, but his mother most of all. For it was she who had healed the wound in the neck of the faithful animal that had brought home her child unhurt, when, after hearing the news told by Adinda's little brothers, she had thought that Saïdyah had been carried off by the tiger. So often had she looked at that wound, thinking how deep the claw that entered so far into the tough thews of the buffalo would have been driven into the soft body of her child; and every time after she had laid fresh healing herbs on the wound, she had caressed the buffalo, and spoken some kindly words to it, so that the good and faithful animal might know how grateful a mother is! She now hoped with all her heart that the buffalo might have understood her, for then it would also have known the meaning of her tears when it was taken away to be killed, and it would have known that it was not Saïdyah's mother who had ordered it to be killed.

Some time after this, Saïdyah's father fled the country. For he greatly feared the punishment if he were not able to pay his land-rent, and he had no more heirlooms to buy a new buffalo with, as his parents had always lived in Parang Koodyang, and had therefore left him but little. And also the parents of his wife had always lived in the same district. After the loss of his last buffalo he had still kept going a few years by working with hired plough-beasts. But that is a very thankless form of labour, and especially galling to one who has been in possession of his own buffaloes. Saïdyah's mother had died of grief; and then his father, in a despondent moment, ran away from Lebak and from Bantam, to look for work about Buitenzorg. He was flogged with the rattan cane for having left Lebak without a pass, and taken back by the police to Badoor. There he was thrown into the gaol because they took him to be mad, which would not have been altogether inexplicable, and because they feared that in a moment of half-madness he might run amuck or be guilty of some other misdeed. But he was not long in prison, for shortly after he died.

I do not know what became of the little brothers and sisters of Saïdyah. The little house where they had lived at Badoor was empty for awhile, and ere long it fell to pieces, as it was only built of bamboo and covered with palm-leaf. A little dust and dirt covered the spot where there had been much suffering. There are many such spots in Lebak.

Saïdyah was already fifteen when his father left Buitenzorg. He did not accompany him thither, because he carried greater projects in his mind. He had been told that in Batavia there were so many gentlemen who drove in bendies, a kind of tilbury, that he might find a place there as a bendie-boy, for which some one is usually chosen who is still young and not full-grown, so that he may not upset the balance of the two-wheeler by bearing with too much weight on the back. There was, he had been assured, with good conduct, much to be earned in such service. Perhaps in this manner he might even, within three years' time save enough money to buy two buffaloes. This prospect lured him. With proud step, as one who has big business in mind, he entered Adinda's house after his father's departure, and informed her of his plan.

"Just think," he said, "when I return we shall be old enough to get married, and we shall have two buffaloes!"

"Very well, Saïdyah! I shall be glad to be married to you when you return. I shall spin, and weave shawls and skirts, and paint, and be very industrious all the time."

"Oh, I believe you, Adinda! But... if I should find you married?"

"Saïdyah, you know very well that I shall marry no one. My father promised me to your father."

"And you yourseef?"

"I shall marry you, rest assured!"

"When I come back, I shall call from afar ...."

"Who will be able to hear that, when we are pounding rice in the village?"

"That is true. But, Adinda.... Oh, yes, this is better: wait for me near the diati-wood, under the ketapan-tree, where you gave me the melatti-flower."

"But, Saïdyah, how shall I know when I am to go and wait for you near the ketapan?"

Saïdyah thought a moment and said: "Count the moons. I shall stay away thrice twelve moons... the present moon does not count. See, Adinda, cut a notch in your rice-block every new moon. When you shall have cut three times twelve notches, then the next following day I shall arrive under the ketapan. Promise that you will be there!"

"Yes, Saïdyah, I shall be under the ketapan near the diati-wood when you return."

Saïdyah then tore a strip from his blue head-kerchief, which was very much worn, and he gave the little piece of linen to Adinda, that she might keep it as a pledge. And so he left her and Badoor.

810

He walked on for many days. He passed Rangkas-Betoong, that was not yet the chief centre of Lebak, and Waroong-Goonoong where the Assistant-Resident then lived, and the next day he saw Pandyglang, that lies there as in a garden. Yet another day and he arrived at Serang, and stood amazed at the splendour of so large a place with many houses, built of stone and roofed with red tiles, Saïdyah had never seen anything like it. He stayed there one day because he was tired, but at night in the coolness he went on, and came to Tangerang the following day, before the shadow had descended to his lips, although he wore the large straw hat which his father had left behind for him.

At Tangerang he bathed in the river near the ferry, and then rested in the house of an acquaintance of his father's, who showed him how to plait straw hats, such as those that came from Manilla. He stayed there one day to learn this, for he thought it might afterwards enable him to earn money, in case he should not succeed in Batavia. The following day, towards nightfall, as it grew cool, he thanked his host very much, and travelled on. As soon as it was quite dark, so that no one should see it, he took out the leaf in which he kept the melatti Adinda had given him under the ketapan-tree. For he had become heavy-hearted at the thought that he would not see her for so long a time. The first day, and also the second, he had felt less deeply how very much he was alone, for his soul had been wholly preoccupied with the great idea of earning money to buy two buffaloes with, as his father had never had more than one, and his thoughts had been too strongly concentrated on the return-meeting with Adinda, leaving no room for very great sadness about their parting. He had bidden her farewell with over-exalted hopes, and his thoughts had connected that farewell with the ultimate reunion under the ketapan. For so great a part the prospect of that reunion played in his heart that, passing the tree on leaving Badoor, he felt almost joyful, as though they were already over, the six-and-thirty moons which divided him from that moment. It had seemed to him as if he had only to turn round as though returning from the voyage, to see Adinda waiting for him under the tree.

But the further he went away from Badoor, and the more he felt the terrible length of only one day, the more he began to think the thirty-six moons that lay before him a time of endless duration. There was something in his soul that made him stride along less quickly. He felt sadness in his knees, and though it was no despondency that overcame him, still it was melancholy, which is not far removed from despondency. He thought of turning back, but what would Adinda say to so little courage?

So he went on, although less rapidly than the first day. He held the melatti in his hand, and often pressed it against his breast. In these three days he had grown much older, and could not now understand how formerly he had been so calm, when yet Adinda was so close to him, and he could see her every time, and as long as he liked! For *now* he would not be calm if he could expect that presently she would stand before him. And also he did not understand how it was that after their parting he had not turned back once more to look at her just once again. Also he remembered how quite recently he had quarrelled with her about the cord she had spun for the kite of her little brothers, and which had broken because, so he held, there was a flaw in her weft, and this had lost them a bet with the children of Tjipooroot. "How had it been possible," he thought, "to get angry with Adinda about this! For even if she *had* spun a flaw into the cord, and if the bet between Badoor and Tjipooroot had been lost through *this*, and not through the glass splinter so naughtily and dexterously thrown by little Djameen, who was hidden behind the hedge, should I even then have been right in behaving so harshly to her, and calling her unseemly names? How will it be if I die in Batavia without having asked her forgiveness for such great rudeness? Will it not be as though I were an evil person who flings bad names at a girl? And if people hear that I died in a strange land, will not every one in Badoor say: 'It is a good thing that Saïdyah died, for he opened a wide mouth at Adinda'?"

So then his thoughts took a course which differed widely from the previous exaltation, and involuntarily they expressed themselves first in half-words scarce audible, but soon in a monologue, and at last in the sorrowful chant of which I here give the translation. At first it had been my intention to write it in metre and rhyme, but like Havelaar I judge it more fitting to omit that corset.

"I know not where I shall die.
I saw the great sea on the South Coast when I was there with my father to make salt;
If I die on the sea, and my body is thrown into the deep water, sharks will come.
They will swim round me, and ask 'Which of us shall devour the dead body that sinks yonder through the water?'
I shall not hear.

"I know not where I shall die.
I have seen the burning house of Pa-ansoo, that he himself had set afire because

he was half-mad.

If I die in a burning house, the flaming timbers will fall on my body,

And outside the house there will be the hue and cry of people who throw water to quench the fire.

I shall not hear.

"I know not where I shall die.

I hav seen little Si-oonah fall from the klappa-tree when he plucked a klappa for his mother.

If I fall from a klappa-tree, I shall lie dead at it foot in the brushwood, like Si-oonah.

My mother will not weep for me, for she is dead. But others will cry with harsh-sounding voice, 'Lo, there lies Saidyah!'

I shall not hear.

"I know not where I shall die.

I have seen the dead body of Pa-lisoo, who had passed away in old age, for his hair was white.

If I die in old age, with white hair, the weeping-women will stand round my body.

And loudly they will lament as the mourners around Pa-lisoo's body, and the grandchildren also will cry with loud voices.

I shall not hear.

"I know not where I shall die.

I have seen many at Badoor who died. They were wrapped in a white garment and buried in the ground.

If I die at Badoor, and they bury me outside the village, eastward against the hill, where the grass is high,

Then will Adinda's footfall pass, and the hem of her garment will gently brush the grass in passing ...

And I shall hear."

Saïdyah arrived in Batavia. He asked a gentleman to take him into his service, which this gentleman did immediately, as he did not understand Saïdyah. For in Batavia people like to have servants who have not yet learnt Malay, and who are therefore not yet so corrupted as others who have been longer in touch with European civilization. Saïdyah soon learned Malay, but he behaved in an exemplary manner, for he thought ever of the new buffaloes that he wished to buy, and of Adinda. He grew tall and strong, because he ate every day, which was not always possible at Badoor. He was liked in the stables and would certainly not have been rejected if he had asked for the coachman's daughter in marriage. His master also liked Saïdyah so much that he soon raised him to the position of house-servant. His wages were increased, and he was continually given presents, for the people were particularly well satisfied with his services. The mistress had read the novels of Sue, whose brief renown was so sensational, and she always thought of Prince Djalma when she saw Saïdyah. The young ladies also understood better than before how it was that the Javanese artist, Radhen Saleh, had created such an impression in Paris.

But they thought Saïdyah ungrateful when, after nearly three years' service, he gave notice and asked for a certificate of good conduct. This, however, could not be refused, and Saïdyah set out for his native village with a happy heart.

He passed Pesing, where at one time Havelaar dwelt, long ago. But this Saïdyah did not know. And even if he had known, he carried in his soul other things altogether, that entirely occupied him. He counted the treasures that he brought home with him. In a bamboo roll he had his pass and the certificate of good conduct. In a small cylindrical case attached to a leather strap, something heavy seemed constantly to be tapping against his shoulder, but he liked to feel this... I should think so! In it were thirty Spanish dollars, enough to buy three buffaloes with. What would Adinda say! And this was not all. On his back one saw the silver-mounted sheath of a dagger which he wore in his belt. The hilt was no doubt of finely chiselled *kamooning*,[1] for he had wrapped it most carefully in a silk kerchief. And he had still more treasures. In the knot of the cloth round his loins he kept a stomacher of broad silver links with a golden fastening. It is true, the stomacher was short, but she was so slender... Adinda!

And attached to a cord round his neck, beneath his singlet, he carried a little silk bag containing some dried melatti.

Was it to be wondered that he did not delay at Tangerang longer than was necessary to visit the friend of his father who matted such dainty straw hats? Was it to be wondered that he had little to say to the girls he met on the road, who asked him "Whither and whence?" which is the greeting in these parts? Was it to be wondered that he no longer thought Serang so important looking, he who had come to know Batavia? That he no longer hid in the hedge as he had done three years before, when the Resident drove past, he that had seen the much greater lord

---

[1] A costly Javanese wood.

who lives at Buitenzorg, and who is the grandfather[1] of the prince of Solo? Was it to be wondered that he paid little attention to the stories of people who walked with him part of the way and told him all the news of Bantan Kedool? That he scarce listened when he was told that the coffee-culture, after much unrewarded labour, had been entirely abandoned? That the District-Chief of Parang Koodyang had been sentenced, for robbery on the public road, to fourteen days' detention in the house of his father-in-law? That the head-centre had been removed to Rangkas-Betoong? That a new Assistant-Resident had arrived because the previous one had died a few months since? And how this new official had spoken at the first meeting of the sebah? How for some time now no one had been punished on any charge, and how it was hoped among the population that all that had been stolen would be returned or made good?

No, before his soul's eye there were sweeter visions. He looked in the clouds for the ketapan-tree, as he was still too far to find it at Badoor. He grasped at the surrounding air, as though he would embrace the form that would be waiting for him under that tree. He pictured to himself Adinda's face, her head, her shoulder... he saw the heavy hair-tress, so shining black, caught in its own loop, hanging down on her neck... he saw her large eyes, lustrous in dark reflection... the nostrils she so proudly drew up as a child, when he—how was it possible!—teased her, and the corner of her lips wherein she kept a smile. He saw her breast, that would now be swelling under the shawl... he saw how the garment which she herself had woven narrowly enclosed her hips, and, following the thigh in its curve, fell along the knee in beautiful waving lines on to the small foot.

No, he heard but little of what people told him. He heard very different notes. He heard how Adinda would say: "Be welcome, Saïdyah! I have thought of you while spinning and weaving, and while pounding the rice in the block that carries three times twelve notches made by my hand. Here I am under the ketapan, the first day of the new moon. Be welcome, Saïdyah, I will be your wife!"

That was the music which sounded in his ear, and prevented him from listening to all the news people told him on the way.

At last he saw the ketapan. Or rather he saw a dark space which covered many stars before his eyes. That must be the diati-wood, near the tree where he was to see Adinda again, next day at sunrise. He searched in the dark, and felt the stems of many trees. Soon he found a well-known

---

[1] A naïve native conception.

unevenness on the south side of a tree, and laid his finger in a nick which Si-Panteh had cut in it with his hatchet, in order to exorcize the evil spirit who was the cause of the tooth-ache of Si-Panteh's mother, shortly before the birth of his little brother. This was the ketapan he sought.

Yes, this indeed was the spot where for the first time he had seen Adinda with other eyes than the rest of his playfellows, because there for the first time she had refused to take part in a game that, after all, she had played with all the children, boys and girls, only a little while before. There she had given him the melatti.

He sat down at the foot of the tree, and looked up at the stars. And when one of them set, he took it as a greeting on his return to Badoor. And he wondered whether Adinda would now be asleep. And whether she had correctly marked the moons in her rice-block. It would grieve him so very much if she had missed one, as though it were not enough ... six-and-thirty! And whether she had painted pretty shawls and skirts. And also he asked himself with some curiosity who might now be living in his father's house. And his youth came back to him, and his mother, and how the buffalo had saved him from the tiger, and he could not help musing on what might have become of Adinda if that buffalo had been less faithful.

He particularly watched the setting of the stars in the west, and with every star that vanished over the horizon he calculated how the sun was again a little nearer to its rising in the East, and how much nearer he himself was to the meeting with Adinda.

For she was sure to come at the first gleam, nay, she would already be there at the glimmer of early dawn. ... Ah! why had she not already come the day before?

It made him sad that she had not anticipated it, the glorious moment which for three years had shone before him with indescribable radiance. And unjust as he was in the selfishness of his love, it seemed to him that Adinda should have been there, waiting for *him*, who now complained— before the time already!—that he had to wait for *her*.

But he complained without cause. For still the sun had not yet risen, still the eye of day had not cast its first glance on the plain. Certainly, the stars were paling above, ashamed that soon there would be an end to their reign ... and strange colours floated across the summits of the mountains, which appeared darker as they were outlined more sharply on a lighter background ... and here and there through the clouds in the East sped something flaming—arrows of gold and fire shot hither and thither, parallel with the skyline—but anon they vanished and seemed to fall behind the impenetrable curtain that ever still hid the day from Saïdyah's eyes.

Yet gradually lighter and lighter it grew around him. He already saw the landscape, and already he distinguished the comb of the klappa-wood in which Badoor lies hidden. ... There slept Adinda.

No, she slept no longer! How could she sleep? Did she not know that Saïdyah would be waiting for her? Oh, surely, she had not slept all night! Doubtless the night-watcher had knocked at her door to ask why the lamp continued to burn in her little dwelling, and with a sweet laugh she had told him that a promise kept her awake to finish weaving the skirt she was working at, and that had to be ready for the first day of the new moon.

Or she had passed the night in darkness, sitting on her rice-block, and counting with eager finger, to see that for sure thirty-six deep notches were carved on it side by side. And she had amused herself with artful pretence of fright, imagining that perhaps she miscounted, and that perhaps one of them was still wanting, so that again, and still again, and every time she might delight in the glorious certainty that without a shadow of doubt three times twelve moons had passed by since Saïdyah saw her for the last time.

She also, seeing it already grow so light, would strain her eyes with vain endeavour to bend her glances beyond the horizon, that they might meet the sun, the laggard sun, that tarried ... tarried ...

Then came a line of bluish red, that fixed itself upon the clouds, and their rims grew light and glowing, and the lightning flashed, and again fiery arrows shot through the expanse, but this time they did not fall, they settled firmly on the dark background, and communicated their glow in ever larger and larger circles, and met crossing, swinging, winding, staying, and they united into fire sheaves, and flashed in golden gleams on a sky of nacre, and there were red, and blue, and yellow, and silver, and purple, and azure in it all ... O, God! that was the dawn; that was the coming of Adinda!

Saïdyah had not learnt to pray, and it would have been a pity to teach him, for holier prayer and thanksgiving more fervent than was found in the speechless ecstasy of his soul would be impossible to express in human language.

He wished not to go to Badoor. The actual meeting with Adinda in itself appeared to him less glorious than the certainty that presently he *would* meet her again. He sat down at the foot of the ketapan, and let his eyes stray about the landscape. Nature smiled on him and seemed to bid him welcome as a mother her returned child. And just as such a one depicts her joy by a deliberate remembrance of past sorrow in showing what she had preserved as a keepsake during absence, thus also Saïdyah derived pleasure from seeing again so many spots that had witnessed his short life. But however much his eyes or his thoughts might wander around, every time his glance and his longing returned to the path that leads from Badoor to the ketapan. All that his senses became aware of bore the name Adinda. He saw the precipice on the left, where the earth is so yellow, and where once a young buffalo sank into the depth; there the villagers had come together to remove the animal—for it is no small matter to lose a young buffalo—and they had let each other down by strong rattan cords. Adinda's father had been bravest ... Oh, how she had clapped her hands, Adinda!

And yonder, on the other side, where the small clump of coco-palms waves above the huts of the village, somewhere there Si-oonah had fallen out of a tree and died. How his mother had cried: "Because Si-oonah was still so small," she wailed ... as though she would have been less grived if Si-oonah had been bigger! But it is true that he *was* small, for he was smaller and weaker even than Adinda.

No one came along the little road that led from Badoor to the tree. Presently she would come: Oh, certainly ... it was still so early!

Saïdyah saw a badying[1] hopping to and fro with sportive nimbleness about the stem of a klappa-tree. The little creature—the vexation of the owner of the tree, yet so charming in its appearance and movements—clambered up and down indefatigably. Saïdyah saw it and forced himself to keep looking at it, because this gave some rest to his thoughts after the strenuous labour they had been engaged in since sunrise ... rest from the exhausting strain of waiting. Anon his impressions took the form of words, and he sang what was passing in his soul. I would sooner *read* his song to you in Malay, this Italian of the East, but here is the translation:

> "See how the badying seeks food for his sustenance
> In the klappa-tree. He climbs, descends, he frolics to right and left,
> He goes round the tree, leaps, falls, rises and falls again:
> He has no wings, and yet is swift as a bird.
>
> "Happiness to you, my badying, happiness and hail!
> Doubtless you will find the food you seek...
> But I sit lonely near the diati-wood,
> Waiting for the food of my heart.

---

[1] Squirrel.

818

"Long has the belly of my badying been filled...
Long has he returned to the comfort of his nest...
But ever my soul
And my heart are bitter with sadness...Adinda!"

Still there was no one on the path that leads from Badoor to the ketapan.

Saïdyah's glance fell on a butterfly that seemed to rejoice because it was growing warm.

"See how the butterfly flutters hither and thither.
His tiny wings shine like a many-tinted flower.
His little heart loves the blossom of the kenari:
He surely seeks his sweet-scented lover!

"Happiness to you, my butterfly, happiness and hail!
Doubtless you will find what you seek...
But I sit lonely near the diati-wood,
Waiting for the love of my heart.

"Long has the butterfly kissed
The kenari-blossom he so much loves...
But ever my soul
And my heart are bitter with sadness...Adinda!"

And there was no one on the path that led from Badoor to the tree. The sun was already rising high ... there was already heat in the air.

"See, how the sun glitters yonder: high,
High above the waringi-hill!
Too warm she feels, and wishes to sink down
To sleep in the sea as in the arms of a husband.

"Happiness to you, O sun, all hail and happiness!
What you seek you will surely find...
But I sit lonely near the diati-wood,
Waiting that my heart may find rest.

"Long will the sun have gone down,
And be asleep in the sea, while all is dark...
And still my soul
And my heart will be bitter with sadness...Adinda!"

Still there was no one on the road that leads from Badoor to the ketapan.

> "When butterflies no longer flutter round,
> When stars no more shall glitter,
> When the melatti is no longer sweet-scented,
> When there are no more sad hearts;
> Nor wild beasts in the forest...
> When the sun shall turn on her path,
> And the moon forget East and West...
> If then Adinda has still not come,
> Then an angel with bright glowing wings
> Shall come to the earth to find him that stayed behind.
> Then shall my body lie under the ketapan...
> My soul is bitter with sadness .... Adinda"!

Still there was no one on the road that leads from Badoor to the ketapan.

> "Then shall my body be seen by the angel.
> He will show it to his brothers with his finger:
>
> " 'See, a man has died and been forgotten!
> His rigid mouth kisses a melatti-flower.
> Come, let us lift him up and take him to heaven,
> Who waited for Adinda until he died!
> *He* surely ought not to be left behind,
> Whose heart had the strength to love so deeply!'
>
> "Then once more my rigid mouth will open
> To call Adinda, whom my heart loves...
> Once more I shall kiss the melatti
> Given to me by her   Adinda...Adinda:"

And ever still there was no one on the path that led from Badoor to the tree.

Oh, no doubt she had fallen asleep towards dawn, tired of keeping awake through the night, of keeping awake through the length of several nights! No doubt she had not slept for weeks: that was it!

Should he arise and go to Badoor? No! Could he let it appear as though he had a doubt of her coming?

Suppose he called the man yonder who was driving his buffalo to the field? But that man was too far. And besides, Saïdyah wished not to speak *about* Adinda, not to ask *after* Adinda ... he wished to *meet her alone, her first!* Oh, doubtless, doubtless she would soon come now!

He would wait, wait...

But if she were ill, or ... dead?

Like a wounded deer Saïdyah flew up the path that leads from the ketapan to the village where Adinda lived. He saw nothing and heard nothing, and yet he might have heard something, for there were people standing in the road at the entrance to the village, who called: "Saïdyah! Saïdyah!"

But ... was it his haste, his passion, which made him unable to find Adinda's house? Already he had rushed on to the end of the road where the village stops, and like a madman he returned, and beat his forehead because he had been able to pass her house without seeing it. But again he was at the entrance—and, my God, was it a dream? again he had not found Adinda's house! Once more he flew back, and all at once he stood still, grasped his head with both his hands, as if to press out of it the madness that came over him, and called loudly: "Drunk, I am drunk!"

And the women of Badoor came out of their houses, and with pity saw poor Saïdyah standing there, for they recognized him, and understood that he was looking for Adinda's house, and they knew that there was no house of Adinda in the village of Badoor.

For when the District-Chief of Parang Koodyang had taken the buffalo of Adinda's father ...

I have told you, reader, that my story is monotonous.

... then Adinda's mother had died with fretting. And her baby sister had died because she had not mother to suckle her. And Adinda's father feared the punishment if he did not pay his land-rent. ...

I know it, I know it, my story is monotonous!

... Adinda's father had gone away from the country, and had taken Adinda with him, and her brothers. But he had heard that Saïdyah's father had been punished at Buitenzorg with rattan-strokes, because he had left Badoor without a pass. And therefore Adinda's father had not gone to Buitenzorg, nor to Krawang, nor to the Preanger, nor to the Batavian out-districts ... he had gone to Tjilang-Kahan, the district of Lebak which borders on the sea. There he had hidden in the woods and awaited the arrival of Pa-Ento, Pa-Lontah, Si-Oonah, Pa-Ansioo, Abdool-Isma, and yet a few others who had been robbed of their buffaloes by the District-Chief of Parang Koodyang, and who all feared the punishment if they did not pay their land-rent. There, during the night, they had seized a fishing-prao, and had put out to sea. They had steered a westerly course, keeping the land to the right of them as far as Java-Point. Thence they had steered northwards until they saw before them Tanah-itam, that the European sailors call Prince's Island. They had sailed round the eastern coast of that island, and then they had made for Kaiser's Bay, taking their bearings by the high point in the Lampongs. This at any rate was the route that people in Lebak whispered into each other's ears whenever there was talk of official buffalo-theft and unpaid land-rent.

But Saïdyah, half dazed, did not clearly understand what they told him. He even did not quite grasp the tidings of his father's death. There was a dinning in his ears as though some one was beating a gong in his head. He felt the blood forced with jerks through the veins at his temples, that threatened to burst under the pressure of so severe an expansion. He did not speak, and stared around with a vacant look without seeing what was near and about him, and at last he burst into ghastly laughter.

An old woman took him along to her little house, and looked after the poor crazy one. Soon he no longer laughed so horribly, but yet he did not speak. Only during the night those who shared the hut with him were startled awake by his voice, when he sang in a toneless manner—"I know not where I shall die." Some of the inhabitants of Badoor put money together to pay for a sacrifice to the alligators of the Tjioodyoong for the recovery of Saïdyah, who was looked upon as demented.

But demented he was not.

For one night when the moon shone brightly, he rose from his stretcher, and stole softly out of the house, and searched for the place where Adinda had lived. It was not easy to find, as so many houses had fallen into ruins. But he seemed to recognize the place from the width of the angle which some of the lines of light between the trees formed in meeting his eye, as the sailor takes his bearings from certain beacons or from prominent mountain-heights.

Yes, it must be there ... there it was that Adinda had lived!

Stumbling over half-decayed bamboos and fragments of the fallen roof, he cleared for himself a way to the sanctuary he sought. And indeed, he still found portions of the upright fence next to which Adinda's stretcher had stood, and stuck in this fence there was still the bamboo pin on which she had hung her garment when she lay down to sleep. ...

But the stretcher had fallen in like the house, and was almost decayed to dust. He picked up a handful of it, pressed it to his open lips, and breathed very deeply. ...

Next day he asked the old woman who had looked after him where the rice-block was that had stood on the ground of Adinda's house. The woman was rejoiced to hear him speak, and went all over the village to find that block. When she was able to tell Saïdyah who was the new owner, he followed her silently, and, taken to the rice-block, he counted on it thirty-two carved notches. ...

Then he gave the old woman as many Spanish dollars as would pay for a buffalo, and left Badoor. At Tjilang-kahan, he bought a fisherman's prao, and with it, after a few days' sailing, reached the Lampongs, where the rebels resisted the Dutch Government.

He joined a band of Bantammers, not so much for the purpose of fighting as for that of finding Adinda. For he was of a gentle nature, and more susceptible to sorrow than to bitterness.

One day when the rebels had been again defeated, he wandered about in a village that had just been taken by the Dutch army, and that therefore was in flames. Saïdyah knew that the band which had there been annihilated had consisted largely of Bantammers. Like a ghost he roamed about in the huts that were not yet entirely destroyed by the fire, and found the dead body of Adinda's father with a klewang-bayonet wound in the breast. Next to him Saïdyah saw the three murdered brothers of Adinda, youths, almost children yet, and a little farther the body of Adinda, naked, horribly mutilated. ...

A narrow strip of blue linen had entered into the gaping breast-wound that appeared to have ended a prolonged struggle. ...

Then Saïdyah ran towards some Dutch soldiers who with levelled muskets drove the last surviving rebels into the fire of the burning houses. He threw himself on the broad-sword bayonets, pressed forward with all his might, and with a final effort pushed back the soldiers until the bayonets pierced him to the hilts.

And shortly after there was great jubilation in Batavia on account of the latest victory which again had added so many laurels to those already won by the Dutch-Indian army. And the Governor-General wrote to the Motherland that peace had been restored in the Lampongs. And the King of the Netherlands, advised by his Ministers, again rewarded so much heroism with many orders of knighthood.

ITALY

DANTE AND BEATRICE[1]

Dante Alighieri

IN THAT part of the book of my memory before the which is little that can be read, there is a rubric, saying, *Incipit Vita Nova*.[2] Under such rubric I find written many things; and among them the words which I purpose to copy into this little book; if not all of them, at the least their substance.

Nine times already since my birth had the heaven of light returned to the self-same point almost, as concerns its own revolution, when first the glorious Lady of my mind was made manifest to mine eyes; even she who was called Beatrice by many who knew not wherefore. She had already been in this life for so long as that, within her time, the starry heaven had moved towards the Eastern quarter one of the twelve parts of a degree; so that she appeared to me at the beginning of her ninth year almost and I saw her almost at the end of my ninth year. Her dress, on that day, was of a most noble colour, a subdued and goodly crimson, girdled and adorned in such sort as best suited with her very tender age. At that moment, I say most truly that the spirit of life, which hath its dwelling in the secretest chamber of the heart, began to tremble so violently that the least pulses of my body shook therewith; and in trembling it said these words: *Ecce deus fortior me, qui veniens dominabitur mihi.*[3] At that moment the animate spirit, which dwelleth in the lofty chamber whither all the senses carry their perceptions, was filled with wonder, and speaking more especially unto the spirits of the eyes, said these words: *Apparuit iam beatitudo vestra.*[4] At that moment the natural spirit, which dwelleth there where our nourishment is administered, began to weep, and in weeping said these words: *Heu miser! quia frequenter impeditus ero deinceps.*[5]

I say that, from that time forward, Love quite governed my soul; which was immediately espoused to him, and with so safe and undisputed a lordship (by virtue of strong imagination) that I had nothing left for it but to do all his bidding continually. He oftentimes commanded me to seek if I might see this youngest of the Angels: wherefore I in my

---

[1] From *La Vita Nuova*. Translated by Dante Gabriel Rossetti.
[2] Here beginneth the new life.
[3] "Here is a deity stronger than I; who, coming, shall rule over me."
[4] "Your beatitude hath now been made manifest unto you."
[5] "Woe is me! for that often I shall be disturbed from this time forth!"

boyhood often went in search of her, and found her so noble and praiseworthy that certainly of her might have been said those words of the
poet Homer, "She seemed not to be the daughter of a mortal man, but
of God." And albeit her image, that was with me always, was an exultation of Love to subdue me, it was yet of so perfect a quality that it never
allowed me to be overruled by Love without the faithful counsel of reason,
whensoever such counsel was useful to be heard. But seeing that were
I to dwell overmuch on the passions and doings of such early youth,
my words might be counted something fabulous, I will therefore put
them aside; and passing many things that may be conceived by the pattern of these, I will come to such as are writ in my memory with a better
distinctness.

After the lapse of so many days that nine years exactly were completed
since the above-written appearance of this most gracious being, on the
last of those days it happened that the same wonderful lady appeared to
me dressed all in pure white, between two gentle ladies elder than she.
And passing through a street, she turned her eyes thither where I stood
sorely abashed: and by her unspeakable courtesy, which is now guerdoned
in the Great Cycle, she saluted me with so virtuous a bearing that I seemed
then and there to behold the very limits of blessedness. The hour of her
most sweet salutation was exactly the ninth of that day; and because
it was the first time that any words from her reached mine ears, I came
into such sweetness that I parted thence as one intoxicated. And betaking
me to the loneliness of mine own room, I fell to thinking of this most
courteous lady, thinking of whom I was overtaken by a pleasant slumber,
wherein a marvellous vision was presented for me: for there appeared
to me in my room a mist of the colour of fire, within the which I discerned
the figure of a lord of terrible aspect to such as should gaze upon him,
but who seemed therewithal to rejoice inwardly that it was a marvel to see.
Speaking he said many things, among the which I could understand but
few; and of these, this: *Ego dominus tuus.*[1] In his arms it seemed to me that
a person was sleeping, covered only with a bloodcoloured cloth; upon
whom looking very attentively, I knew that it was the lady of the salutation
who had deigned the day before to salute me. And he who held her held
also in his hand a thing that was burning in flames; and he said to me,
Vide cor tuum.[2] But when he had remained with me a little while, I thought
that he set himself to awaken her that slept; after the which he made her

---

[1] "I am thy master."
[2] "Behold thy heart."

to eat that thing which flamed in his hand; and she ate as one fearing. Then, having waited again a space, all his joy was turned into most bitter weeping; and as he wept he gathered the lady into his arms, and it seemed to me that he went with her up towards heaven: whereby such a great anguish came upon me that my light slumber could not endure through it, but was suddenly broken. And immediately having considered, I knew that the hour wherein this vision had been made manifest to me was the fourth hour (which is to say, the first of the nine last hours) of the night.

From that night forth, the natural functions of my body began to be vexed and impeded, for I was given up wholly to thinking of this most gracious creature: whereby in short space I became so weak and so reduced that it was irksome to many of my friends to look upon me; while others, being moved by spite, went about to discover what it was my wish should be concealed. Wherefore I (perceiving the drift of their unkindly questions), by Love's will, who directed me according to the counsels of reason, told them how it was Love himself who had thus dealt with me: and I said so, because the thing was so plainly to be discerned in my countenance that there was no longer any means of concealing it. But when they went on to ask, "And by whose help hath Love done this?" I looked in their faces smiling, and spake no word in return.

Now it fell on a day, that this most gracious creature was sitting where words were to be heard of the Queen of Glory; and I was in a place whence mine eyes could behold their beatitude: and betwixt her and me, in a direct line, there sat another lady of a pleasant favour; who looked round at me many times, marvelling at my continued gaze which seemed to have *her* for its object. And many perceived that she thus looked; so that departing thence, I heard it whispered after me, "Look you to what a pass *such a lady* hath brought him"; and in saying this they named her who had been midway between the most gentle Beatrice and mine eyes. Therefore I was reassured, and knew that for that day my secret had not become manifest. Then immediately it came into my mind that I might make use of this lady as a screen to the truth: and so well did I play my part that the most of those who had hitherto watched and wondered at me, now imagined they had found me out. By her means I kept my secret concealed till some years were gone over; and for my better security, I even made divers rhymes in her honour. Moreover, about the same time while this lady was a screen for so much love on my part, I took the resolution to set down the name of this most gracious creature accompanied with many other women's names, and especially with hers whom I spake of. And to this end I put together the names of sixty of the most beautiful ladies in that city where God had placed mine own lady; and these names I introduced in an epistle in the form of a *sirvent*, which it is not my intention to transcribe here. Neither should I have said anything of this matter, did I not wish to take note of a certain strange thing, to wit: that having written the list, I found my lady's name would not stand otherwise than ninth in order among the names of these ladies.

Now it so chanced with her by whose means I had thus long time concealed my desire, that it behoved her to leave the city I speak of, and to journey afar: wherefore I, being sorely perplexed at the loss of so excellent a defence, had more trouble than even I could before have supposed. And thinking that if I spoke not somewhat mournfully of her departure, my former counterfeiting would be the more quickly perceived, I determined that I would make a grievous sonnet thereof.

A certain while after the departure of that lady, it pleased the Master of the Angels to call into His glory a damsel, young and of a gentle presence, who had been very lovely in the city I speak of: and I saw her body lying without its soul among many ladies, who held a pitiful weeping. Whereupon, remembering that I had seen her in the company of excellent Beatrice, I could not hinder myself from a few tears.

Some days after the death of this lady, I had occasion to leave the city I speak of, and to go thitherwards where she abode who had formerly been my protection; albeit the end of my journey reached not altogether so far. And notwithstanding that I was visibly in the company of many, the journey was so irksome that I had scarcely sighing enough to ease my heart's heaviness; seeing that as I went, I left my beatitude behind me. Wherefore it came to pass that he who ruled me by virtue of my most gentle lady was made visible to my mind, in the light habit of a traveller, coarsely fashioned. He appeared to me troubled, and looked always on the ground; saving only that sometimes his eyes were turned towards a river which was clear and rapid, and which flowed along the path I was taking. And then I thought that Love called me and said to me these words: "I come from that lady who was so long thy surety; for the matter of whose return, I know that it may not be. Wherefore I have taken that heart which I made thee leave with her, and do bear it unto another lady, who, as she was, shall be thy surety"; (and when he named her I knew her well.) "And of these words I have spoken if thou shouldst speak any again, let it be in such sort as that none shall perceive thereby that thy love was feigned for her, which thou must now feign for another." And when he had spoken thus, all my imagining was gone suddenly, for it seemed to me that Love became a part of myself:

so that, changed as it were in mine aspect, I rode on full of thought the whole of that day, and with heavy sighing.

On my return, I set myself to seek out that lady whom my master had named to me while I journeyed sighing. And because I would be brief, I will now narrate that in a short while I made her my surety, in such sort that the matter was spoken of by many in terms scarcely courteous; through the which I had oftenwhiles many troublesome hours. And by this it happened (to wit: by this false and evil rumour which seemed to misfame me of vice) that she who was the destroyer of all evil and the queen of all good, coming where I was, denied me her most sweet salutation, in the which alone was my blessedness.

And here it is fitting for me to depart a little from this present matter, that it may be rightly understood of what surpassing virtue her salutation was to me. To the which end I say that when she appeared in any place, it seemed to me, by the hope of her excellent salutation, that there was no man mine enemy any longer; and such warmth of charity came upon me that most certainly in that moment I would have pardoned whosoever had done me an injury; and if one should then have questioned me concerning any matter, I could only have said unto him "Love," with a countenance clothed in humbleness. And what time she made ready to salute me, the spirit of Love, destroying all other perceptions, thrust forth the feeble spirits of my eyes, saying, "Do homage unto your mistress," and putting itself in their place to obey: so that he who would, might then have beheld Love, beholding the lids of my eyes shake. And when this most gentle lady gave her salutation, Love, so far from being a medium beclouding mine intolerable beatitude, then bred in me such an overpowering sweetness that my body, being all subjected thereto, remained many times helpless and passive. Whereby it is made manifest that in her salutation alone was there any beatitude for me, which then very often went beyond my endurance.

And now, resuming my discourse, I will go on to relate that when, for the first time, this beatitude was denied me, I became possessed with such grief that, parting myself from others, I went into a lonely place to bathe the ground with most bitter tears: and when, by this heat of weeping, I was somewhat relieved, I betook myself to my chamber, where I could lament unheard. And there, having prayed to the Lady of all Mercies, and having said also, "O Love, aid thou thy servant," I went suddenly asleep, like a beaten sobbing child. And in my sleep, towards the middle of it, I seemed to see in the room, seated at my side, a youth in very white raiment, who kept his eyes fixed on me in deep thought.

And when he had gazed some time, I thought that he sighed and called to me in these words: *"Fili mi, tempus est ut praetermittantur simulata nostra.*[1]*"* And thereupon I seemed to know him; for the voice was the same wherewith he had spoken at other times in my sleep. Then looking at him, I perceived that he was weeping piteously, and that he seemed to be waiting for me to speak. Wherefore, taking heart, I began thus: "Why weepest thou, Master of all honour?" And he made answer to me: *"Ego tanquam centrum circuli, cui simili modo se habent circumferentiae partes: tu autem non sic."*[2] And thinking upon his words, they seemed to me obscure; so that again compelling myself unto speech, I asked of him: "What thing is this, Master, that thou hast spoken thus darkly?" To which he made answer in the vulgar tongue: "Demand no more than may be useful to thee." Whereupon I began to discourse with him concerning her salutation which she had denied me; and when I had questioned him of the cause, he said these words: "Our Beatrice hath heard from certain persons, that the lady whom I named to thee while thou journeyedst full of sighs is sorely disquieted by thy solicitations: and therefore this most gracious creature, who is the enemy of all disquiet, being fearful of such disquiet, refused to salute thee. For the which reason (albeit, in very sooth, thy secret must needs have become known to her by familiar observation) it is my will that thou compose certain things in rhyme, in the which thou shalt set forth how strong a mastership I have obtained over thee, through her; and how thou wast hers even from thy childhood. Also do thou call upon him that knoweth these things to bear witness to them, bidding him to speak with her thereof; the which I, who am he, will do willingly. And thus she shall be made to know thy desire; knowing which, she shall know likewise that they were deceived who spake of thee to her. And so write these things, that they shall seem rather to be spoken by a third person; and not directly by thee to her, which is scarce fitting. After the which, send them, not without me, where she may chance to hear them; but have them fitted with a pleasant music, into the which I will pass

---

[1] "My son, it is time for us to lay aside our counterfeiting."

[2] "I am as the centre of a circle, to the which all parts of thy cirumference bear an equal relation: but with thee it is not thus." This phrase seems to have remained as obscure to commentators as Dante found it at the moment. No one, as far as I know, has even fairly tried to find a meaning for it. To me the following appears a not unlikely one. Love is weeping on Dante's account, and not on his own. He says, "I am the centre of a circle (*Amor che muove il sole e l' altre stelle*); therefore all lovable objects whether in heaven or earth, or any part of the circle's circumference, are equally near to me. Not so thou, who wilt one day lose Beatrice when she goes to heaven." The phrase would thus contain an intimation of the death of Beatrice, accounting for Dante being next told not to enquire the meaning of the speech —"Demand no more than may be useful to thee."

whensoever it needeth." With this speech he was away, and my sleep was broken up.

After this vision I have recorded, and having written those words which Love had dictated to me, I began to be harassed with many and divers thoughts, by each of which I was sorely tempted; and in especial, there were four among them that left me no rest. The first was this: "Certainly the lordship of Love is good; seeing that it diverts the mind from all mean things." The second was this: "Certainly the lordship of Love is evil; seeing that the more homage his servants pay to him, the more grievous and painful are the torments wherewith he torments them." The third was this: "The name of Love is so sweet in the hearing that it would not seem possible for its effects to be other than sweet; seeing that the name must needs be like unto the thing named: as it is written: '*Nomina sunt consequentia rerum.*' "[1] And the fourth was this: "The lady whom Love hath chosen out to govern thee is not as other ladies, whose hearts are easily moved."

And by each one of these thoughts I was so sorely assailed that I was like unto him who doubteth which path to take, and wishing to go, goeth not. And if I bethought myself to seek out some point at the which all these paths might be found to meet, I discerned but one way, and that irked me; to wit, to call upon Pity, and to commend myself unto her.

After this battling with many thoughts, it chanced on a day that my most gracious lady was with a gathering of ladies in a certain place; to the which I was conducted by a friend of mine; he thinking to do me a great pleasure by showing me the beauty of so many women. Then I, hardly knowing whereunto he conducted me, but trusting in him (who yet was leading his friend to the last verge of life), made question: "To what end are we come among these ladies?" and he answered: "To the end that they may be worthily served." And they were assembled around a gentlewoman who was given in marriage on that day; the custom of the city being that these should bear her company when she sat down for the first time at table in the house of her husband. Therefore I, as was my friend's pleasure, resolved to stay with him and do honour to those ladies.

But as soon as I had thus resolved, I began to feel a faintness and a throbbing at my left side, which soon took possession of my whole body. Whereupon I remember that I covertly leaned my back unto a painting that ran round the walls of that house; and being fearful lest my trembling should be discerned of them, I lifted mine eyes to look on those ladies,

---

[1] 'Names are the consequents of things.'

and then first perceived among they the excellent Beatrice. And when I perceived her, all my senses were overpowered by the great lordship that Love obtained, finding himself so near unto that most gracious being, until nothing but the spirits of sight remained to me; and even these remained driven out of their own instruments, because Love entered in that honoured place of theirs, that so he might the better behold her. And although I was other than at first, I grieved for the spirits so expelled, which kept up a sore lament, saying: "If he had not in this wise thrust us forth, we also should behold the marvel of this lady." By this, many of her friends, having discerned my confusion, began to wonder; and together with herself, kept whispering of me and mocking me. Whereupon my friend, who knew not what to conceive, took me by the hands, and drawing me forth from among them, required to know what ailed me. Then, having first held me at quiet for a space until my perceptions were come back to me, I made answer to my friend: "Of a surety I have now set my feet on that point of life, beyond the which he must not pass who would return."

Afterwards, leaving him, I went back to the room where I had wept before; and again weeping and ashamed, said: "If this lady but knew of my condition, I do not think that she would thus mock at me; nay, I am sure that she must needs feel some pity."

A while after this strange disfigurement, I became possessed with a strong conception which left me but very seldom, and then to return quickly. And it was this: "Seeing that thou comest into such scorn by the companionship of this lady, wherefore seekest thou to behold her? If she should ask thee this thing, what answer couldst thou make unto her? yea, even though thou wert master of all thy faculties, and in no way hindered from answering." Unto the which, another very humble thought said in reply: "If I were master of all my faculties, and in no way hindered from answering, I would tell her that no sooner do I image to myself her marvellous beauty than I am possessed with the desire to behold her, the which is of so great strength that it kills and destroys in my memory all those things which might oppose it; and it is therefore that the great anguish I have endured thereby is yet not enough to restrain me from seeking to behold her."

Through the sore change in mine aspect, the secret of my heart was now understood of many. Which thing being thus, there came a day when certain ladies to whom it was well known (they having been with me at divers times in my trouble) were met together for the pleasure of gentle company. And as I was going that way by chance (but I think rather by the will of fortune), I heard one of them call unto me, and she that called was a lady of very sweet speech. And when I had come close up with them, and perceived that they had not among them mine excellent lady, I was reassured; and saluted them, asking of their pleasure. The ladies were many; divers of whom were laughing one to another, while divers gazed at me as though I should speak anon. But when I still spake not, one of them, who before had been talking with another, addressed me by my name, saying, "To what end lovest thou this lady, seeing that thou canst not support her presence? Now tell us this thing, that we may know it: for certainly the end of such a love must be worthy of knowledge." And when she had spoken these words, not she only, but all they that were with her, began to observe me, waiting for my reply. Whereupon I said thus unto them:—"Ladies, the end and aim of my Love was but the salutation of that lady of whom I conceive that ye are speaking; wherein alone I found that beatitude which is the goal of desire. And now that it hath pleased her to deny me this, Love, my Master, of his great goodness, hath placed all my beatitude there where my hope will not fail me." Then those ladies began to talk closely together; and as I have seen snow fall among the rain, so was their talk mingled with sighs. But after a little, that lady who had been the first to address me, addressed me again in these words: "We pray thee that thou wilt tell us wherein abideth this thy beatitude." And answering, I said but thus much: "In those words that do praise my lady." To the which she rejoined: "If thy speech were true, those words that thou didst write concerning thy condition would have been written with another intent."

Then I, being almost put to shame because of her answer, went out from among them; and as I walked, I said within myself: "Seeing that there is so much beatitude in those words which do praise my lady, wherefore hath my speech of her been different?" And then I resolved that thenceforward I would choose for the theme of my writings only the praise of this most gracious being. But when I had thought exceedingly, it seemed to me that I had taken to myself a theme which was much too lofty, so that I dared not begin; and I remained during several days in the desire of speaking, and the fear of beginning.

Not many days after this (it being the will of the most High God, who also from Himself put not away death), the father of wonderful Beatrice, going out of this life, passed certainly into glory. Thereby it happened, as of very sooth it might not be otherwise, that this lady was made full of the bitterness of grief: seeing that such a parting is very grievous unto those friends who are left, and that no other friendship is like to that between a good parent and a good child; and furthermore considering that this lady was good in the supreme degree, and her father (as by many it hath been truly averred) of exceeding goodness. And because it is the usage of that city that men meet with men in such a grief, and women with women, certain ladies of her companionship gathered themselves unto Beatrice, where she kept alone in her weeping: and as they passed in and out, I could hear them speak concerning her, how she wept. At length two of them went by me, who said: "Certainly she grieveth in such sort that one might die for pity, beholding her." Then, feeling the tears upon my face, I put up my hands to hide them: and had it not been that I hoped to hear more concerning her (seeing that where I sat, her friends passed continually in and out), I should assuredly have gone thence to be alone, when I felt the tears come. But as I still sat in that place, certain ladies again passed near me, who were saying among themselves: "Which of us shall be joyful any more, who have listened to this lady in her piteous sorrow?" And there were others who said as they went by me: "He that sitteth here could not weep more if he had beheld her as we have beheld her"; and again: "He is so altered that he seemeth not as himself." And still as the ladies passed to and fro, I could hear them speak after this fashion of her and of me.

A few days after this, my body became afflicted with a painful infirmity, whereby I suffered bitter anguish for many days, which at last brought me unto such weakness that I could no longer move. And I remember that on the ninth day, being overcome with intolerable pain, a thought came into my mind concerning my lady: but when it had a little nourished this thought, my mind returned to its brooding over mine enfeebled body. And then perceiving how frail a thing life is, even though health keep with it, the matter seemed to me so pitiful that I could not choose but weep; and weeping I said within myself: "Certainly it must some time come to pass that the very gentle Beatrice will die." Then, feeling bewildered, I closed mine eyes; and my brain began to be in travail as the brain of one frantic, and to have such imaginations as here follow.

And at the first, it seemed to me that I saw certain faces of women with their hair loosened, which called out to me, "Thou shalt surely die"; after the which, other terrible and unknown appearances said unto me, "Thou art dead." At length, as my phantasy held on in its wanderings, I came to be I knew not where, and to behold a throng of dishevelled ladies wonderfully sad, who kept going hither and thither weeping. Then the sun went out, so that the stars showed themselves, and they were of such a colour that I knew they must be weeping: and it seemed to me that the birds fell dead out of the sky, and that there were great earthquakes. With that, while I wondered in my trance, and was filled with a grievous fear, I conceived that a certain friend came unto me and said: "Hast thou not heard? She that was thine excellent lady hath been taken out of life." Then I began to weep very piteously; and not only in mine imagination, but with mine eyes, which were wet with tears. And I seemed to look towards Heaven, and to behold a multitude of angels who were returning upwards, having before them an exceedingly white cloud: and these angels were singing together gloriously, and the words of their song were these: "*Osanna in excelsis*"; and there was no more that I heard. Then my heart that was so full of love said unto me: "It is true that our lady lieth dead"; and it seemed to me that I went to look upon the body wherein that blessed and most noble spirit had had its abiding-place. And so strong was this idle imagining, that it made me to behold my lady in death, whose head certain ladies seemed to be covering with a white veil; and who was so humble of her aspect that it was as though she had said, "I have attained to look on the beginning of peace." And therewithal I came unto such humility by the sight of her, that I cried out upon Death, saying: "Now come unto me, and be not bitter against me any longer: surely, there where thou hast been, thou hast learned gentleness. Wherefore come now unto me who do greatly desire thee: seest thou not that I wear thy colour already?" And when I had seen all those offices performed that are fitting to be done unto the dead, it seemed to me that I went back unto mine own chamber, and looked up towards Heaven. And so strong was my phantasy that I wept again in very truth, and said with my true voice: "O excellent soul! how blessed is he that now looketh upon thee!"

And as I said these words, with a painful anguish of sobbing and another prayer unto Death, a young and gentle lady, who had been standing beside me where I lay, conceiving that I wept and cried out because of the pain of mine infirmity, was taken with trembling and began to shed tears. Whereby other ladies, who were about the room, becoming aware of my discomfort by reason of the moan that she made (who indeed was of my very near kindred), led her away from where I was, and then set themselves to awaken me, thinking that I dreamed, and saying: "Sleep no longer, and be not disquieted."

Then, by their words, this strong imagination was brought suddenly to an end, at the moment that I was about to say, "O Beatrice! peace be with thee." And already I had said, "O Beatrice!" when being aroused, I opened mine eyes, and knew that it had been a deception. But albeit I had indeed uttered her name, yet my voice was so broken with sobs, that it was not understood by these ladies; so that in spite of the sore shame that I felt, I turned towards them by Love's counselling. And when they beheld me, they began to say, "He seemeth as one dead," and to whisper among themselves, "Let us strive if we may not comfort him." Whereupon they spake to me many soothing words, and questioned me moreover touching the cause of my fear. Then I, being somewhat reassured, and having perceived that it was a mere phantasy, said unto them, "This thing it was that made me afeard"; and told them of all that I had seen, from the beginning even unto the end, but without once speaking the name of my lady.

After this empty imagining, it happened on a day, as I sat thoughtful, that I was taken with such a strong trembling at the heart, that it could not have been otherwise in the presence of my lady. Whereupon I perceived that there was an appearance of Love beside me, and I seemed to see him coming from my lady; and he said, not aloud but within my heart: "Now take heed that thou bless the day when I entered into thee; for it is fitting that thou shouldst do so." And with that my heart was so full of gladness, that I could hardly believe it to be of very truth mine own heart and not another.

A short while after these words which my heart spoke to me with the tongue of Love, I saw coming towards me a certain lady who was very famous for her beauty, and of whom that friend whom I have already called the first among my friends had long been enamoured. This lady's right name was Joan; but because of her comeliness (or at least it was so imagined) she was called of many *Primavera* (Spring), and went by that name among them. Then looking again, I perceived that the most noble Beatrice followed after her. And when both these ladies had passed by me, it seemed to me that Love spake again in my heart, saying: "She that came first was called Spring, only because of that which was to happen on this day. And it was I myself who caused that name to be given her; seeing that as the Spring cometh first in the year, so should she come first on this day,[1] when Beatrice was to show herself after the vision of her servant. And even if thou go about to consider her right name, it is also as one should say, 'She shall come first': inasmuch as her name, Joan, is taken from that John who went before the True Light, saying: '*Ego vox clamantis in deserto; Parate viam Domini.*'"[2] And also it seemed to me that he added other words, to wit: "He who should inquire delicately touching this

---

[1] There is a play in the original upon the words *Primavera* (Spring) and *prima verrà* (she shall come first), to which I have given as near an equivalent as I could.

[2] "I am the voice of one crying in the wilderness: 'Prepare ye the way of the Lord.'"

matter, could not but call Beatrice by mine own name, which is to say, Love; beholding her so like unto me."

This excellent lady of whom I spake in what hath gone before, came at last into such favour with all men, that when she passed anywhere folk ran to behold her; which thing was a deep joy to me: and when she drew near unto any, so much truth and simpleness entered into his heart, that he dared neither to lift his eyes nor to return her salutation: and unto this, many who have felt it can bear witness. She went along crowned and clothed with humility, showing no whit of pride in all that she heard and saw: and when she had gone by, it was said of many, "This is not a woman, but one of the beautiful angels of Heaven"; and there were some that said: "This is surely a miracle; blessed be the Lord, who hath power to work thus marvellously." I say, of very sooth, that she showed herself so gentle and so full of all perfection, that she bred in those who looked upon her a soothing quiet beyond any speech; neither could any look upon her without sighing immediately. These things, and things yet more wonderful, were brought to pass through her miraculous virtue.

Thereafter on a day, I began to consider that which I had said of my lady: and becoming aware that I had not spoken of her immediate effect on me at that especial time, it seemed to me that I had spoken defectively. Whereupon I resolved to write somewhat of the manner wherein I was then subject to her influence, and of what her influence then was. And conceiving that I should not be able to say these things in the small compass of a sonnet, I began therefore a poem with this beginning:

> Love hath so long possessed me for his own
>   And made his lordship so familiar
> That he, who at first irked me, is now grown
>   Unto my heart as its best secrets are.
>   And thus, when he in such sore wise doth mar
> My life that all its strength seems gone from it,
> Mine inmost being then feels throughly quit
>   Of anguish, and all evil keeps afar.
> Love also gathers to such power in me
>   That my sighs speak, each one a grievous thing,
>   Always soliciting
> My lady's salutation piteously.
> Whenever she beholds me, it is so,
> Who is more sweet than any words can show.

I was still occupied with this poem (having composed thereof only the above written stanza), when the Lord God of justice called my most gracious lady unto Himself, that she might be glorious under the banner of that blessed Queen Mary, whose name had always a deep reverence in the words of holy Beatrice.

On that day which fulfilled the year since my lady had been made of the citizens of eternal life, remembering me of her as I sat alone, I betook myself to draw the resemblance of an angel upon certain tablets. And while I did thus, chancing to turn my head, I perceived that some were standing beside me to whom I should have given courteous welcome, and that they were observing what I did: also I learned afterwards that they had been there a while before I perceived them. Perceiving whom, I arose for salutation, and said: "Another was with me."

Afterwards, when they had left me, I set myself again to mine occupation, to wit, to the drawing figures of angels.

Then, having sat for some space sorely in thought because of the time that was now past, I was so filled with dolorous imaginings that it became outwardly manifest in mine altered countenance. Whereupon, feeling this and being in dread lest any should have seen me, I lifted mine eyes to look; and then perceived a young and very beautiful lady, who was gazing upon me from a window with a gaze full of pity so that the very sum of pity appeared gathered together in her. And seeing that unhappy persons, when they beget compassion in others, are then most moved unto weeping, as though they also felt pity for themselves, it came to pass that mine eyes began to be inclined unto tears. Wherefore, becoming fearful lest I should make manifest mine abject condition, I rose up, and went where I could not be seen of that lady.

It happened after this that whensoever I was seen of this lady, she became pale and of a piteous countenance, as though it had been with love; whereby she remembered me many times of my own most noble lady, who was wont to be of a like paleness. And I know that often, when I could not weep nor in any way give ease unto mine anguish, I went to look upon this lady, who seemed to bring the tears into my eyes by the mere sight of her.

At length, by the constant sight of this lady, mine eyes began to be gladdened overmuch with her company; through which thing many times I had much unrest, and rebuked myself as a base person: also, many times I cursed the unsteadfastness of mine eyes, and said to them inwardly: "Was not your grievous condition of weeping wont one while to make others weep? And will ye now forget this thing because a lady looketh upon you? who so looketh merely in compassion of the grief ye then showed for your own blessed lady. But whatso ye can, that do ye, accursed eyes! many a time will I make you remember it! for never, till death dry you up, should ye make an end of your weeping." And when I had spoken thus unto mine eyes, I was taken again with extreme and grievous sighing.

The sight of this lady brought me into so unwonted a condition that I often thought of her as of one too dear unto me; and I began to consider her thus: "This lady is young, beautiful, gentle, and wise: perchance it was Love himself who set her in my path, that so my life might find peace." And there were times when I thought yet more fondly, until my heart consented unto its reasoning. But when it had so consented, my thought would often turn round upon me, as moved by reason, and cause me to say within myself: "What hope is this which would console me after so base a fashion, and which hath taken the place of all other imagining?" Also there was another voice within me, that said: "And wilt thou, having suffered so much tribulation through Love, not escape while yet thou mayst from so much bitterness? Thou must surely know that this thought carries with it the desire of Love, and drew its life from the gentle eyes of that lady who vouchsafed thee so much pity."

But against this adversary of reason, there rose up in me on a certain day, about the ninth hour, a strong visible phantasy, wherein I seemed to behold the most gracious Beatrice, habited in that crimson raiment which she had worn when I had first beheld her; also she appeared to me of the same tender age as then. Whereupon I fell into a deep thought of her: and my memory ran back, according to the order of time, unto all those matters in the which she had borne a part; and my heart began painfully to repent of the desire by which it had so basely let itself be possessed during so many days, contrary to the constancy of reason.

And then, this evil desire being quite gone from me, all my thoughts turned again unto their excellent Beatrice. And I say most truly that from that hour I thought constantly of her with the whole humbled and ashamed heart; the which became often manifest in sighs, that had among them the name of that most gracious creature, and how she departed from us. Also it would come to pass very often, through the bitter anguish of some one thought, that I forgot both it, and myself, and where I was. By this increase of sighs, my weeping, which before had been somewhat lessened, increased in like manner; so that mine eyes seemed to long only for tears and to cherish them, and came at last to be circled about with red as though they had suffered martyrdom: neither were they able to look again upon the beauty of any face that might again bring them to shame and evil:

from which things it will appear that they were fitly guerdoned for their unsteadfastness.

After this, it was given unto me to behold a very wonderful vision:[1] wherein I saw things which determined me that I would say nothing further of this most blessed one, until such time as I could discourse more worthily concerning her. And to this end I labour all I can: as she well knoweth. Wherefore if it be His pleasure through whom is the life of all things, that my life continue with me a few years, it is my hope that I shall yet write concerning her what hath not before been written of any woman. After the which, may it seem good unto Him who is the Master of Grace, that my spirit should go hence to behold the glory of its lady: to wit, of that blessed Beatrice who now gazeth continually on His countenance *qui est per omnia saecula benedictus*.[2] *Laus Deo*.

---

[1] The Vision of Hell, Purgatory, and Paradise, which furnished the triple argument of the *Divina Commedia*. The Latin words ending the *Vita Nuova* are almost identical with those at the close of the letter in which Dante, on concluding the *Paradise*, and accomplishing the hope here expressed, dedicates his great work to Can Grande della Scala.

[2] "Who is blessed throughout all ages."

CHINA

THE TWO BRIDES[1]

P'u Sung-ling

NOW Chi-shêng, or Wang Sun, was one of the cleverest young fellows in the district; and his father and mother, who had foreseen his ability from the time when, as a baby in long clothes, he distinguished them from other people, loved him very dearly. He grew up into a handsome lad; at eight or nine he could compose elegantly, and by fourteen he had already entered his name as a candidate for the first degree, after which his marriage became a question for consideration. Now his father's younger sister, Erh-niang, had married a gentleman named Chêng Tzu-ch'iao, and they had a daughter called Kuei-hsiu, who was extremely pretty, and with whom Chi-shêng fell deeply in love, being soon unable either to eat or to sleep. His parents became extremely uneasy about him, and inquired what it was ailed him; and when he told them, they at once sent off a match-maker to Mr Chêng. The latter, however, was rather a stickler for the proprieties, and replied that the near relationship precluded him from accepting the offer. Thereupon Chi-shêng became dangerously ill, and his mother, not knowing what to do, secretly tried to persuade Erh-niang to let her daughter come over to their house; but Mr Chêng heard of it, and was so angry that Chi-shêng's father and mother gave up all hope of arranging the match.

At that time there was a gentleman named Chang living near by, who had five daughters, all very pretty, but the youngest, called Wu-k'o, was singularly beautiful, far surpassing her four sisters. She was not betrothed to anyone, when one day, as she was on her way to worship at the family tombs, she chanced to see Chi-shêng, and at her return home spoke about him to her mother. Her mother guessed what her meaning was and arranged with a match-maker, named Mrs Yü, to call upon Chi-shêng's parents. This she did precisely at the time when Chi-shêng was so ill, and forthwith told his mother that her son's complaint was one she, Mrs Yü, was quite competent to cure; going on to tell her about Miss Wu-k'o and the proposed marriage, at which the good lady was delighted, and sent her in to talk about it to Chi-shêng himself. "Alas!" cried he, when he had

[1] From *Strange Stories from a Chinese Studio*. Translated by Herbert A. Giles. Reprinted by permission of Messrs Kelly and Walsh, Ltd.

heard Mrs Yü's story, "you are bringing me the wrong medicine for my complaint." "All depends upon the efficacy of the medicine," replied Mrs Yü; "if the medicine is good, it matters not what is the name of the doctor who administers the draught; while to set your heart on a particular person, and to lie there and die because that person doesn't come, is surely foolish in the extreme." "Ah," rejoined Chi-shêng, "there's no medicine under heaven that will do me any good." Mrs Yü told him his experience was limited, and proceeded to expatiate by speaking and gesticulating on the beauty and liveliness of Wu-k'o. But all Chi-shêng said was that she was not what he wanted, and, turning round his face to the wall, would listen to no more about her. So Mrs Yü was obliged to go away, and Chi-shêng became worse and worse every day, until suddenly one of the maids came in and informed him that the young lady herself was at the door. Immediately he jumped up and ran out, and lo! there stood before him a beautiful girl, whom, however, he soon discovered not to be Kuei-hsiu. She wore a light yellow robe with a fine silk jacket and an embroidered petticoat, from beneath which her two little feet peeped out; and altogether she more resembled a fairy than anything else. Chi-shêng inquired her name; to which she replied that it was Wu-k'o, adding that she couldn't understand his devoted attachment to Kuei-hsiu, as if there was nobody else in the world. Chi-shêng apologised, saying that he had never before seen anyone so beautiful as Kuei-hsiu, but that he was now aware of his mistake. He then swore everlasting fidelity to her, and was just grasping her hand when he awoke and found his mother rubbing him. It was a dream, but so accurately defined in all its details that he began to think if Wu-k'o was really such as he had seen her, there would be no further need to try for his impracticable cousin. So he communicated his dream to his mother; and she, only too delighted to notice this change of feeling, offered to go to Wu-k'o's house herself, but Chi-shêng would not hear of this, and arranged with an old woman who knew the family to find some pretext for going there, and to report to him what Wu-k'o was like. When she arrived Wu-k'o was ill in bed, and lay with her head propped up by pillows, looking very pretty indeed. The old woman approached the couch and asked what was the matter; to which Wu-k'o made no reply, her fingers fidgetting all the time with her waistband. "She's been behaving badly to her father and mother," cried the latter, who was in the room; "there's many a one has offered to marry her, but she says she'll have none but Chi-shêng; and then when I scold her a bit, she takes on and won't touch her food for days." "Madam," said the old woman, "if you could get that young man for your daughter they would make a truly pretty pair;

and as for him, if he could only see Miss Wu-k'o, I'm afraid it would be too much for him. What do you think of my going there and getting them to make proposals?" "No, thank you," replied Wu-k'o; "I would rather not risk his refusal"; upon which the old woman declared she would succeed, and hurried off to tell Chi-shêng, who was delighted to find from her report that Wu-k'o was exactly as he had seen her in his dream, though he didn't trust implicitly in all the old woman said. By-and-by, when he began to get a little better, he consulted with the old woman as to how he could see Wu-k'o with his own eyes; and, after some little difficulty, it was arranged that Chi-shêng should hide himself in a room from which he would be able to see her as she crossed the yard supported by a maid, which she did every day at a certain hour. This Chi-shêng proceeded to do, and in a little while out she came, accompanied by the old woman as well, who instantly drew her attention either to the clouds or the trees, in order that she should walk more leisurely. Thus Chi-shêng had a good look at her, and saw that she was truly the young lady of his dream. He could hardly contain himself for joy; and when the old woman arrived and asked if she would do instead of Kuei-hsiu, he thanked her very warmly and returned to his own home. There he told his father and mother, who sent off a match-maker to arrange the preliminaries; but the latter came back and told them that Wu-k'o was already betrothed. This was a terrible blow for Chi-shêng, who was soon as ill as ever, and offered no reply to his father and mother when they charged him with having made a mistake. For several months he ate nothing but a bowl of rice-gruel a day, and he became as emaciated as a fowl, when all of a sudden the old woman walked in and asked him what was the matter. "Foolish boy," said she, when he had told her all; "before you wouldn't have her, and do you imagine she is bound to have you now? But I'll see if I can help you; for were she the Emperor's own daughter, I should still find some way of getting her." Chi-shêng asked what he should do, and she then told him to send a servant with a letter next day to Wu-k'o's house, to which his father at first objected for fear of another repulse; but the old woman assured him that Wu-k'o's parents had since repented, besides which no written contract had as yet been made; "and you know the proverb," added she, "that those who are first at the fire will get their dinner first." So Chi-shêng's father agreed, and two servants were accordingly sent, their mission proving a complete success. Chi-shêng now rapidly recovered his health, and thought no more of Kuei-hsiu, who, when she heard of the intended match, became in her turn very seriously ill, to the great anger of her father, who said she might die for all he cared, but to the great sorrow of her mother, who was extremely fond of her daughter. The latter even went so far as to propose to Mr Chêng that Kuei-hsiu should go as second wife, at which he was so enraged that he declared he would wash his hands of the girl altogether. The mother then found out when Chi-shêng's wedding was to take place, and, borrowing a chair and attendants from her brother under pretence of going to visit him, put Kuei-hsiu inside and sent her off to her uncle's house. As she arrived at the door, the servants spread a carpet for her to walk on, and the band struck up the wedding march. Chi-shêng went out to see what it was all about, and there met a young lady in a bridal veil, from whom he would have escaped had not her servants surrounded them, and, before he knew what he was doing, he was making her the usual salutation of a bridegroom. They then went in together, and, to his further astonishment, he found that the young lady was Kuei-hsiu; and, being now unable to go and meet Wu-k'o, a message was sent to her father, telling him what had occurred. He, too, got into a great rage, and vowed he would break off the match; but Wu-k'o herself said she would go all the same, her rival having only got the start of her in point of time. And go she did; and the two wives, instead of quarrelling, as was expected, lived very happily together like sisters, and wore each other's clothes and shoes without distinction, Kuei-hsiu taking the place of an elder sister as being somewhat older than Wu-k'o. One day, after these events, Chi-shêng asked Wu-k'o why she had refused his offer; to which she replied that it was merely to pay him out for having previously refused her father's proposal. "Before you had seen me, your head was full of Kueihsiu; but after you had seen me, your thoughts were somewhat divided; and I wanted to know how I compared with her, and whether you would fall ill on my account as you had on hers, that we mightn't quarrel about our looks." "It was a cruel revenge," said Chi-shêng; "but how should I ever have got a sight of you if it had not been for the old woman?" "What had she to do with it?" replied Wu-k'o; "I knew you were behind the door all the time. When I was ill I dreamt that I went to your house and saw you, but I looked upon it only as a dream until I heard that you had dreamt that I had actually been there, and then I knew that my spirit must have been with you."

JAPAN

OF A DANCING-GIRL[1]

Lafcadio Hearn

I

IT WAS formerly, and indeed still is, a custom with young Japanese artists to travel on foot through various parts of the empire, in order to see and sketch the most celebrated scenery as well as to study famous art objects preserved in Buddhist temples, many of which occupy sites of extraordinary picturesqueness. It is to such wanderings, chiefly, that we owe the existence of those beautiful books of landscape views and life studies which are now so curious and rare, and which teach better than aught else that only the Japanese can paint Japanese scenery. After you have become acquainted with their methods of interpreting their own nature, foreign attempts in the same line will seem to you strangely flat and soulless. The foreign artist will give you realistic reflections of what he sees; but he will give you nothing more. The Japanese artist gives you that which he feels,—the mood of a season, the precise sensation of an hour and place; his work is qualified by a power of suggestiveness rarely found in the art of the West. The Occidental painter renders minute detail; he satisfies the imagination he evokes. But his Oriental brother either suppresses or idealises detail,—steeps his distances in mist, bands his landscapes with cloud, makes of his experience a memory in which only the strange and the beautiful survive, with their sensations. He surpasses imagination, excites it, leaves it hungry with the hunger of charm perceived in glimpses only. Nevertheless, in such glimpses he is able to convey the feeling of a time, the character of a place, after a fashion that seems magical. He is a painter of recollections and of sensations rather than of clear-cut realities; and in this lies the secret of his amazing power,—a power not to be appreciated by those who have never witnessed the scenes of his inspiration. He is above all things impersonal. His human figures are devoid of all individuality; yet they have inimitable merit as types embodying the characteristics of a class: the childish curiosity of the peasant, the shyness of the maiden, the fascination of the jorō, the self-consciousness of the

[1] From *Glimpses from Unfamiliar Japan*. Reprinted by permission of Messrs Jonathan Cape, Ltd., and the Houghton Mifflin Company.

samurai, the funny, placid prettiness of the child, the resigned gentleness of age. Travel and observation were the influences which developed this art; it was never a growth of studios.

A great many years ago, a young art student was travelling on foot from Kyōto to Yedo, over the mountains. The roads then were few and bad, and travel was so difficult compared to what it is now that a proverb was current, *Kawai ko wa tabi wo sasé* (A pet child should be made to travel). But the land was what it is to-day. There were the same forests of cedar and of pine, the same groves of bamboo, the same peaked villages with roofs of thatch, the same terraced rice-fields dotted with the great yellow straw hats of peasants bending in the slime. From the wayside, the same statues of Jizō smiled upon the same pilgrim figures passing to the same temples; and then, as now, of summer days, one might see naked brown children laughing in all the shallow rivers, and all the rivers laughing to the sun.

The young art student, however, was no *kawai ko*: he had already travelled a great deal, was inured to hard fare and rough lodging, and accustomed to make the best of every situation. But upon this journey he found himself, one evening after sunset, in a region where it seemed possible to obtain neither fare nor lodging of any sort,—out of sight of cultivated land. While attempting a short cut over a range to reach some village, he had lost his way.

There was no moon, and pine shadows made blackness all around him. The district into which he had wandered seemed utterly wild; there were no sounds but the humming of the wind in the pine-needles, and an infinite tinkling of bell-insects. He stumbled on, hoping to gain some river bank, which he could follow to a settlement. At last a stream abruptly crossed his way; but it proved to be a swift torrent pouring into a gorge between precipices. Obliged to retrace his steps, he revolved to climb to the nearest summit, whence he might be able to discern some sign of human life; but on reaching it he could see about him only a heaping of hills.

He had almost resigned himself to passing a night under the stars, when he perceived, at some distance down the farther slope of the hill he had ascended, a single thin yellow ray of light, evidently issuing from some dwelling. He made his way towards it, and soon discerned a small cottage, apparently a peasant's home. The light he had seen still streamed from it, through a chink in the closed storm-doors. He hastened forward, and knocked at the entrance.

845

II

Not until he had knocked and called several times did he hear any stir within; then a woman's voice asked what was wanted. The voice was remarkably sweet, and the speech of the unseen questioner surprised him, for she spoke in the cultivated idiom of the capital. He responded that he was a student, who had lost his way in the mountains; that he wished, if possible, to obtain food and lodging for the night; and that if this could not be given, he would feel very grateful for information how to reach the nearest village,—adding that he had means enough to pay for the services of a guide. The voice, in return, asked several other questions, indicating extreme surprise that anyone could have reached the dwelling from the direction he had taken. But his answers evidently allayed suspicion, for the inmate exclaimed: "I will come in a moment. It would be difficult for you to reach any village to-night; and the path is dangerous."

After a brief delay the storm-doors were pushed open, and a woman appeared with a paper lantern, which she so held as to illuminate the stranger's face, while her own remained in shadow. She scrutinised him in silence, then said briefly, "Wait; I will bring water." She fetched a wash-basin, set it upon the doorstep, and offered the guest a towel. He removed his sandals, washed from his feet the dust of travel, and was shown into a neat room which appeared to occupy the whole interior, except a small boarded space at the rear, used as a kitchen. A cotton zabuton was laid for him to kneel upon, and a brazier set before him.

It was only then that he had a good opportunity of observing his hostess, and he was startled by the delicacy and beauty of her features. She might have been three or four years older than he, but was still in the bloom of youth. Certainly she was not a peasant girl. In the same singularly sweet voice he said to him: "I am now alone, and I never receive guests here. But I am sure it would be dangerous for you to travel farther to-night. There are some peasants in the neighbourhood, but you cannot find your way to them in the dark without a guide. So I can let you stay here until morning. You will not be comfortable, but I can give you a bed. And I suppose you are hungry. There is only some shōjin-ryōri,[1]—not at all good, but you are welcome to it."

The traveller was quite hungry, and only too glad of the offer. The young woman kindled a little fire, prepared a few dishes in silence,—

---

[1] Buddhist food, containing no animal substance. Some kinds of shōjin-ryōri are quite appetising

stewed leaves of na, some aburagé, some kampyō, and a bowl of coarse rice,—and quickly set the meal before him, apologising for its quality. But during his repast she spoke scarcely at all, and her reserved manner embarrassed him. As she answered the few questions he ventured upon merely by a bow or by a solitary word, he soon refrained from attempting to press the conversation.

Meanwhile, he had observed that the small house was spotlessly clean, and the utensils in which his food was served were immaculate. The few cheap objects in the apartment were pretty. The fusuma of the oshire and zendana[1] were of white paper only, but had been decorated with large Chinese characters exquisitely written, characters suggesting, according to the law of such decoration, the favourite themes of the poet and artist: Spring Flowers, Mountain and Sea, Summer Rain, Sky and Stars, Autumn Moon, River Water, Autumn Breeze. At one side of the apartment stood a kind of low altar, supporting a butsudan, whose tiny lacquered doors, left open, showed a mortuary tablet within, before which a lamp was burning between offerings of wild flowers. And above this household shrine hung a picture of more than common merit, representing the Goddess of Mercy, wearing the moon for her aureole.

As the student ended his little meal the young woman observed: "I cannot offer you a good bed, and there is only a paper mosquito-curtain. The bed and the curtain are mine, but to-night I have many things to do, and shall have no time to sleep: therefore I beg you will try to rest, though I am not able to make you comfortable."

He then understood that she was, for some strange reason, entirely alone, and was voluntarily giving up her only bed to him upon a kindly pretext. He protested honestly against such an excess of hospitality, and assured her that he could sleep quite anywhere on the floor, and did not care about the mosquitoes. But she replied, in the tone of an elder sister, that he must obey her wishes. She really had something to do, and she desired to be left by herself as soon as possible; therefore, understanding him to be a gentleman, she expected he would suffer her to arrange matters in her own way. To this he could offer no objection, as there was but one room. She spread the mattress on the floor, fetched a wooden pillow, suspended her paper mosquito-curtain, unfolded a large screen on the side of the bed toward the butsudan, and then bade him good night in a manner that assured him she wished him to retire at once; which he did, not without

---

[1] The terms *oshire* and *zendana* might by partly rendered by 'wardrobe' and 'cupboard.' The *fusuma* are sliding screens serving as doors.

III

some reluctance at the thought of all the trouble he had unintentionally caused her.

Unwilling as the young traveller felt to accept a kindness involving the sacrifice of another's repose, he found the bed more than comfortable. He was very tired, and had scarcely laid his head upon the wooden pillow before he forgot everything in sleep.

Yet only a little while seemed to have passed when he was awakened by a singular sound. It was certainly the sound of feet, but not of feet walking softly. It seemed rather the sound of feet in rapid motion, as of excitement. Then it occurred to him that robbers might have entered the house. As for himself, he had little to fear because he had little to lose. His anxiety was chiefly for the kind person who had granted his hospitality. Into each side of the paper mosquito-curtain a small square of brown netting had been fitted, like a little window, and through one of these he tried to look; but the high screen stood between him and whatever was going on. He thought of calling, but this impulse was checked by the reflection that in case of real danger it would be both useless and imprudent to announce his presence before understanding the situation. The sounds which had made him uneasy continued, and were more and more mysterious. He resolved to prepare for the worst, and to risk his life, if necessary, in order to defend his young hostess. Hastily girding up his robes, he slipped noiselessly from under the paper curtain, crept to the edge of the screen, and peeped. What he saw astonished him extremely.

Before her illuminated butsudan the young woman, magnificently attired, was dancing all alone. Her costume he recognised as that of a shirabyōshi, though much richer than any he had ever seen worn by a professional dancer. Marvellously enhanced by it, her beauty, in that lonely time and place, appeared almost supernatural; but what seemed to him even more wonderful was her dancing. For an instant he felt the tingling of a weird doubt. The superstitions of peasants, the legends of Fox-women, flashed before his imagination; but the sight of the Buddhist shrine, of the sacred picture, dissipated the fancy, and shamed him for the folly of it. At the same time he became conscious that he was watching something she had not wished him to see, and that it was his duty, as her guest, to return at once behind the screen; but the spectacle fascinated him. He felt, with not less pleasure than amazement, that he was looking upon the most accomplished dancer he had ever seen; and the more he watched, the more the witchery of her grace grew upon him. Suddenly she paused, panting, unfastened her girdle, turned in the act of doffing her upper robe, and started violently as her eyes encountered his own.

He tried at once to excuse himself to her. He said he had been suddenly awakened by the sound of quick feet, which had caused him some uneasiness, chiefly for her sake, because of the lateness of the hour and the lonesomeness of the place. Then he confessed his surprise at what he had seen, and spoke of the manner in which it had attracted him. "I beg you," continued, "to forgive my curiosity, for I cannot help wondering who you are, and how you could have become so marvellous a dancer. All the dancers of Saikyō I have seen, yet I have never seen among the most celebrated of them a girl who could dance like you; and once I had begun to watch you, I could not take away my eyes."

At first she seemed angry, but before he had ceased to speak her expression changed. She smiled, and seated herself before him. "No, I am not angry with you," she said. "I am only sorry that you should have watched me, for I am sure you must have thought me mad when you saw me dancing that way, all by myself; and now I must tell you the meaning of what you have seen."

So she related her story. Her name he remembered to have heard as a boy,—her professional name, the name of the most famous of shirabyōshi, the darling of the capital, who, in the zenith of her fame and beauty, had suddenly vanished from public life, none knew whither or why. She had fled from wealth and fortune with a youth who loved her. He was poor, but between them they possessed enough means to live simply and happily in the country. They built a little house in the mountains, and there for a number of years they existed only for each other. He adored her. One of his greatest pleasures was to see her dance. Each evening he would play some favourite melody, and she would dance for him. But one long cold winter he fell sick, and, in spite of her tender nursing, died. Since then she had lived alone with the memory of him, performing all those small rites of love and homage with which the dead are honoured. Daily before his tablet she placed the customary offerings, and nightly danced to please him, as of old. And this was the explanation of what the young traveller had seen. It was indeed rude, she continued, to have awakened her tired guest; but she had waited until she thought him soundly sleeping, and then she had tried to dance very, very lightly. So she hoped he would pardon her for having unintentionally disturbed him.

When she had told him all, she made ready a little tea, which they drank together; then she entreated him so plaintively to please her by trying to sleep again that he found himself obliged to go back, with many sincere apologies, under the paper mosquito-curtain.

He slept well and long; the sun was high before he woke. On rising, he found prepared for him a meal as simple as that of the evening before, and he felt hungry. Nevertheless he ate sparingly, fearing the young woman might have stinted herself in thus providing for him; and then he made ready to depart. But when he wanted to pay her for what he had received, and for all the trouble he had given her, she refused to take anything from him, saying: "What I had to give was not worth money, and what I did was done for kindness alone. So I pray you will try to forget the discomfort you suffered here, and will remember only the good-will of one who had nothing to offer."

He still endeavoured to induce her to accept something; but at last, finding that his insistence only gave her pain, he took leave of her with such words as he could find to express his gratitude, and not without a secret regret, for her beauty and her gentleness had charmed him more than he would have liked to acknowledge to any but herself. She indicated to him the path to follow, and watched him descend the mountain until he had passed from sight. An hour later he found himself upon a highway with which he was familiar. Then a sudden remorse touched him: he had forgotten to tell her his name: For an instant he hesitated; then said to himself, "What matters it? I shall be always poor." And he went on.

IV

Many years passed by, and many fashions with them; and the painter became old. But ere becoming old he had become famous. Princes, charmed by the wonder of his work, had vied with one another in giving him patronage; so that he grew rich, and possessed a beautiful dwelling of his own in the City of the Emperors. Young artists from many provinces were his pupils, and lived with him, serving him in all things while receiving his instruction; and his name was known throughout the land.

Now, there came one day to his house an old woman who asked to speak with him. The servants, seeing that she was meanly dressed and of miserable appearance, took her to be some common beggar, and questioned her roughly. But when she answered: "I can tell to no one except your master why I have come," they believed her mad, and deceived her, saying: "He is not now in Saikyō, nor do we know how soon he will return."

But the old woman came again and again,—day after day, and week after week,—each time being told something that was not true: "to-day he is ill," or, "To-day he is very busy," or, "To-day he had much company, and therefore cannot see you." Nevertheless she continued to come always at the same hour each day, and always carrying a bundle wrapped in a ragged covering; and the servants at last thought it were best to speak to their master about her, so they said to him: "There is a very old woman, whom we take to be a beggar, at our lord's gate. More than fifty times she has come, asking to see our lord, and refusing to tell us why,—saying that she can tell her wishes only to our lord. And we have tried to discourage her, as she seemed to be mad; but she always comes. Therefore we have presumed to mention the matter to our lord, in order that we may learn what is to be done hereafter."

Then the Master answered sharply: "Why did none of you tell me of this before?" and went out himself to the gate, and spoke very kindly to the woman, remembering how he also had been poor. And he asked her if she desired alms of him.

But she answered that she had no need of money or of food, and only desired that he would paint for her a picture. He wondered at her wish, and bade her enter his house. So she entered into the vestibule, and, kneeling there, began to untie the knots of the bundle she had brought with her. When she had unwrapped it, the painter perceived curious rich quaint garments of silk broidered with designs in gold, yet much frayed and discoloured by wear and time,—the wreck of a wonderful costume of other days, the attire of a shirabyōshi.

While the old woman unfolded the garments one by one, and tried to smoothe them with her trembling fingers, a memory stirred in the Master's brain, thrilled dimly there a little space, then suddenly lighted up. In that soft shock of recollection, he saw again the lonely mountain dwelling in which he had received unremunerated hospitality,—the tiny room prepared for his rest, the paper mosquito-curtain, the faintly burning lamp before the Buddhist shrine, the strange beauty of one dancing there alone in the dead of the night. Then, to the astonishment of the aged visitor, he, the favoured of princes, bowed low before her, and said: "Pardon my rudeness in having forgotten your face for a moment; but it is more than forty years since we last saw each other. Now I remember you well. You received me once at your house. You gave me the only bed you had. I saw you dance, and you told me all your story. You had been a shirabyōshi, and I have not forgotten your name."

He uttered it. She, astonished and confused, could not at first reply to him, for she was old and had suffered much, and her memory had begun to fail. But he spoke more and more kindly to her, and reminded her of many things which she had told him, and described to her the house in which she had lived alone, so that at last she also remembered; and she answered with tears of pleasure: "Surely the Divine One who looketh down above the sound of prayer has guided me. But when my unworthy home was honoured by the visit of the august Master, I was not as I now am. And it seems to me like a miracle of our Lord Buddha that the Master should remember me."

Then she related the rest of her simple story. In the course of years, she had become, through poverty, obliged to part with her little house; and in her old age she had returned alone to the great city, in which her name had long been forgotten. It had caused her much pain to lose her home; but it grieved her still more that, in becoming weak and old, she could no longer dance each evening before the butsudan, to please the spirit of the dead whom she had loved. Therefore she wanted to have a picture of herself painted, in the costume and the attitude of the dance, that she might suspend it before the butsudan. For this she had prayed earnestly to Kwannon. And she had sought out the Master because of his fame as a painter, since she desired, for the sake of the dead, no common work, but a picture painted with great skill; and she had brought her dancing-attire, hoping that the Master might be willing to paint her therein.

He listened to all with a kindly smile, and answered her: "It will be only a pleasure for me to paint the picture which you want. This day I have something to finish which cannot be delayed. But if you will come here to-morrow, I will paint you exactly as you wish, and as well as I am able."

But she said: "I have not yet told the Master the thing which most troubles me. And it is this,—that I can offer in return for so great favour nothing except these dancer's clothes; and they are of no value in themselves, though they were costly once. Still, I hoped the Master might be willing to take them, seeing they have become curious; for there are no more shirabyōshi, and the maiko of these times wear no such robes."

"Of that matter," the good painter exclaimed, "you must not think at all! No; I am glad to have this present chance of paying a small part of my old debt to you. So to-morrow I will paint you just as you wish."

She prostrated herself thrice before him, uttering thanks, and then said, "Let my lord pardon, though I have yet something more to say. For I do not wish that he should paint me as I now am, but only as I used to be when I was young, as my lord knew me."

He said: "I remember well. You were very beautiful."

Her wrinkled features lighted up with pleasure, as she bowed her thanks to him for those words. And she exclaimed: "Then indeed all that I hoped and prayed for may be done! Since he thus remembers my poor youth, I beseech my lord to paint me, not as I now am, but as he saw me when I was not old and, as it has pleased him generously to say, not uncomely. O Master, make me young again! Make me seem beautiful that I may seem beautiful to the soul of him for whose sake I, the unworthy, beseech this! He will see the Master's work: he will forgive me that I can no longer dance."

Once more the Master bade her have no anxiety, and said: "Come to-morrow, and I will paint you. I will make a picture of you just as you were when I saw you, a young and beautiful shirabyōshi, and I will paint it as carefully and as skilfully as if I were painting the picture of the richest person in the land. Never doubt, but come."

V

So the aged dancer came at the appointed hour; and upon soft white silk the artist painted a picture of her. Yet not a picture of her as she seemed to the Master's pupils, but the memory of her as she had been in the days of her youth, bright-eyed as a bird, lithe as a bamboo, dazzling as a tennin[1] in her raiment of silk and gold. Under the magic of the Master's brush, the vanished grace returned, the faded beauty bloomed again. When the kakemono had been finished, and stamped with his seal, he mounted it richly upon silken cloth, and fixed to it rollers of cedar with ivory weights, and a silken cord by which to hang it; and placed it in a little box ot white wood, and so gave it to the shirabyōshi. And he would also have presented her with a gift of money. But though he pressed her earnestly, he could not persuade her to accept his help. "Nay," she made answer, with tears, "indeed I need nothing. The picture only I desired. For that I prayed; and now my prayer has been answered, and I know that I never can wish for anything more in this life, and that if I come to die thus desiring nothing, to enter upon the way of Buddha will not be difficult. One thought alone causes me sorrow,—that I have nothing to offer to the Master but this dancer's apparel, which is indeed of little worth, though I beseech him to accept it; and I will pray each day that his future life may be a life of happiness, because of the wondrous kindness which he has done me."

"Nay," protested the painter, smiling, "what is it that I have done? Truly nothing. As for the dancer's garments, I will accept them, it that

---

[1] *Tennin*, a "Sky-Maiden," a Buddhist angel.

can make you more happy. They will bring back pleasant memories of the night I passed in your home, when you gave up all your comforts for my unworthy sake, and yet would not suffer me to pay for that which I used; and for that kindness I hold myself to be still in your debt. But now tell me where you live, so that I may see the picture in its place." For he had resolved within himself to place her beyond the reach of want.

But she excused herself with humble words, and would not tell him, saying that her dwelling place was too mean to be looked upon by such as he; and then, with many prostrations, she thanked him again and again, and went away with her treasure, weeping for joy.

Then the Master called to one of his pupils: "Go quickly after that woman, but so that she does not know herself followed, and bring me word where she lives." So the young man followed her, unperceived.

He remained long away, and when he returned he laughed in a manner of one obliged to say something which is not pleasant to hear, and he said: "That woman, O Master, I followed out of the city to the dry bed of the river, near to the place where criminals are executed. There I saw a hut such as an Eta might dwell in, and that is where she lives. A forsaken and filthy place, O Master!"

"Nevertheless," the painter replied, "to-morrow you will take me to that forsaken and filthy place. What time I live she shall not suffer for food or clothing or comfort."

And as all wondered, he told them the story of the shirabyōshi, after which it did not seem to them that his words were strange.

VI

On the morning of the day following, an hour after sunrise, the Master and his pupil took their way to the dry bed of the river, beyond the verge of the city, to the place of outcasts.

The entrance of the little dwelling they found closed by a single shutter, upon which the Master tapped many times without evoking a response. Then, finding the shutter unfastened from within, he pushed it slightly aside, and called through the aperture. None replied, and he decided to enter. Simultaneously, with extraordinary vividness, there thrilled back to him the sensation of the very instant when, as a tired lad, he stood pleading for admission to the lonesome little cottage among the hills.

Entering alone softly, he perceived that the woman was lying there, wrapped in a single thin and tattered futon, seemingly asleep. On a rude shelf he recognised the butsudan of forty years before, with its tablet, and now, as then, a tiny lamp was burning in front of the kaimyō. The kakemono of the Goddess of Mercy with her lunar aureole was gone, but on the wall facing the shrine he beheld his own dainty gift suspended, and an ofuda beneath it,—an ofuda of Hitokoto-Kwannon,[1]—that Kwannon unto whom it is unlawful to pray more than once, as she answers but a single prayer. There was little else in the desolate dwelling; only the garments of a female pilgrim, and a mendicant's staff and bowl.

But the Master did not pause to look at these things, for he desired to awaken and to gladden the sleeper, and he called her name cheerily twice and thrice.

Then suddenly he saw that she was dead, and he wondered while he gazed upon her face, for it seemed less old. A vague sweetness, like a ghost of youth, had returned to it; the lines of sorrow had been softened, the wrinkles strangely smoothed, by the touch of a phantom Master mightier than he.

---

[1] Her shrine is at Nara—not far from the temple of the giant Buddha.

INDIA

SĀVITRĪ[1]

The Sister Nivedita and Amanda K. Coomaraswamy

THERE was a king named Lord-of-Horses; he was virtuous, generous, brave, and well-beloved. It grieved him much that he had no child. Therefore he observed hard vows and followed the rule of hermits. For eighteen years he made daily offerings to Fire, recited *mantras* in praise of Sāvitrī, and ate a frugal meal at the sixth hour. Then at last Sāvitrī was pleased and revealed herself to him in visible form within the sacrificial fire. "I am well pleased," she said, "with thy asceticism, thy wellkept vows, thy veneration. Ask, great king, whatever boon thou wilt." "Goddess," said the king, "may sons be born to me worthy of my race, for the Brāhmans tell me much merit lies in children. If thou art pleased with me, I ask this boon." Sāvitrī replied: "O, king, knowing thy wish, I have spoken already with Brahmā that thou shouldst have sons. Through his favour there shall be born to thee a glorious daughter. Thou shouldst not answer again; this is the grandsire's gift, who is well pleased with thy devotion." The king bowed down and prayed. "So be it," he said, and Sāvitrī vanished. It was not long before his queen bore him a shining girl with lotus eyes. Forasmuch as she was the gift of the goddess Sāvitrī, the wife of Brahmā, she was named Sāvitrī with all due ceremony, and she grew in grace and loveliness like unto Shrī herself. Like a golden image the people thought her, saying: "A goddess has come amongst us." But none dared wed that lady of the lotus eyes, for the radiant splendour and the ardent spirit that were in her daunted every suitor.

One holiday, after her service of the gods, she came before her father with an offering of flowers. She touched his feet, and stood at his side with folded hands. Then the king was sad, seeing his daughter of marriageable age and yet unwooed. He said to her: "My daughter, the time for thy bestowal has come; yet none seek thee. Do thou, therefore, choose for thyself a husband who shall be thy equal. Choose whom thou wilt; I shall reflect and give thee unto him, for a father that giveth not his daughter is disgraced. Act thou therefore so that we may not meet with the censure of the gods."

---

[1] From *Myths of the Hindus and Buddhists*. Reprinted by permission of Messrs George G. Harrap and Co., Ltd.

Then Sāvitrī meekly bowed to her father's feet and went forth with her attendants. Mounting a royal car she visited the forest hermitages of the sages. Worshipping the feet of those several saints, she roamed through all the forests till she found her lord.

One day when her father sat in open court, conversing with the counsellors, Sāvitrī returned, and, seeing her father seated beside the rishi Nārada, bowed to his feet and greeted him. Then Nārada said: "Why dost thou delay to wed thy girl, who is of marriageable age?" The king replied: "It was for this that she went forth, and even now she returns. Hear whom she has chosen for her husband." So saying, he turned to Sāvitrī, commanding her to relate all that had befallen her.

Standing with folded hands before the king and sage, she answered: "There was a virtuous king of the Shālwas, Dyumatsena by name. He grew blind; then an ancient foe wrested the kingdom from his hands, and he, with his wife and little child, went forth into the woods, where he practised the austerities appropriate to the hermit life. The child, his son, grew up in that forest hermitage. He is worthy to be my husband; him have I accepted in my heart as lord."

Then Nārada exclaimed: "Greatly amiss has Sāvitrī done in taking for her lord this boy, whose name is Satyavān; albeit I know him well, and he excels in all good qualities. Even as a child he took delight in horses and would model them in clay or draw their pictures; wherefore he has been named Horse-painter."

The king asked: "Has this Prince Satyavān intelligence, forgiveness, courage, energy?" Nārada replied: "In energy he is like the sun, in wisdom like Brihaspati, brave like the king of gods, forgiving as the earth herself. Eke he is liberal, truthful, and fair to look upon?" Then the king inquired again: "Tell me now what are his faults." Nārada answered: "He hath one defect that overwhelms all his virtues, and that fault is irremediable. It is fated that he will die within a year."

Then the king addressed his daughter: "Do thou, O Sāvitrī, fair girl, choose for thyself another lord; for thou hast heard the words of Nārada." But Sāvitrī answered: "The die can fall but once; a daughter can only once be given away; once only may it be said: 'I give away!' Forsooth, be life short or long, be he virtuous or vicious, I have chosen my husband once for all. I shall not choose twice. A thing is first thought of in the heart, then it is spoken, then it is done; my mind is witness thereof." Then Nārada said to the king: "Thy daughter's heart is unwavering; she may not be turned from the right way. Moreover, none excelleth Satyavān in virtue; the marriage has my approval." The king, with folded hands, answered again: "Whatsoever thou dost command is to be done." Nārada said again: "May peace attend the gift of Sāvitrī. I shall now go on my ways; be it well with all"; and therewith he ascended again to Heaven.

On an auspicious day King Lord-of-Horses with Sāvitrī fared to the hermitage of Dyumatsena. Entering on foot, he found the royal sage seated in contemplation beneath a noble tree; him the king reverenced duly, with presents meet for holy men, and announced the purpose of his visit. Dyumatsena answered: "But how may thy daughter, delicately nurtured, lead this hard forest life with us, practising austerity and following the rule of hermits?" The king replied: "Thou shouldst not speak such words to us; for my daughter knoweth like myself, that happiness and sorrow come and go, and neither endures. Thou shouldst not disregard my offer." It was arranged accordingly, and in the presence of the twice-born sages of the forest hermitages Sāvitrī was given to Satyavān. When her father had departed she laid aside her jewels and garbed herself in bark and brown. She delighted all by her gentleness and self-denial, her generosity and sweet speech. But the words of Nārada were ever present in her mind.

At length the hour appointed for the death of Satyavān approached; when he had but four days more to live Sāvitrī fasted day and night, observing the penance of "Three Nights." By the third day Sāvitrī was faint and weak, and she spent the last unhappy night in miserable reflections on her husband's coming death. In the morning she fulfilled the usual rites, and came to stand before the Brāhmans and her husband's father and mother, and they for her helping prayed that she might never be a widow.

Satyavān went out into the woods with axe in hand, suspecting nothing, to bring home wood for the sacrificial fire. Sāvitrī prayed to go with him, and he consented, if his parents also permitted it. She prayed them sweetly to allow it, saying that she could not bear to stay behind and that she desired exceedingly to see the blossoming trees. Dyumatsena gave her leave, saying: "Since Sāvitrī was given by her father to be my daughter-in-law I cannot remember that she has asked for anything at all. Now, therefore, let her prayer be granted. But do not," he added, "hinder Satyavān's sacred labour."

So Sāvitrī departed with her lord, seeming to smile, but heavy-hearted; for, remembering Nārada's words, she pictured him already dead. With half her heart she mourned, expectant of his end; with half she answered him with smiles, as they passed beside the sacred streams and goodly trees. Presently he fell to work, and as he hewed at the branches of a mighty tree he grew sick and faint, and came to his wife complaining that his head was racked with darting pains and that he would sleep awhile. Sāvitrī sat on the ground and laid his head upon her lap; that was the appointed time of Satyavān's death. Immediately Sāvitrī beheld a shining ruddy deity, dark and red of eye and terrible to look upon; he bore a noose in his hand. He stood and gazed at Satyavān. Then Sāvitrī rose and asked him humbly who he might be and what he sought to do. "I am Yama, Lord of Death," he answered, "and I have come for Satyavān, whose appointed span of life is ended." So saying, Yama drew forth the soul from Satyavān's body, bound in the noose, and altogether helpless; therewith he departed toward the south, leaving the body cold and lifeless.

Sāvitrī followed close; but Yama said: "Desist, O Sāvitrī. Return, perform thy husband's funeral rites. Thou mayst come no farther." But she answered: "Whither my lord is brought or goeth of his own will I shall follow; this is the lasting law. The way is open to me because of my obedience and virtue. Lo, the wise have said that friendship is sevenpaced. Relying on friendship thus contracted, I shall say thee somewhat more. Thou dost order me to follow another rule than that of wife; thou wouldst make of me a widow, following not the domestic rule. But the four rules are for those who have not attained their purpose, true religious merit. It is otherwise with me; for I have reached the truth by fulfilment of the duty of a wife alone. It needs not to make of me a widow." Yama replied: "Thou sayest well, and well thou pleasest me. Ask now a boon, whatsoever thou wilt, except thy husband's life." She prayed that Dyumatsena should regain his sight and health, and Yama granted it. Still Sāvitrī would not return, saying that she would still follow her lord, and, besides, that friendship with the virtuous must ever bear good fruit. Yama admitted the truth of this, and granted her another boon; she asked that her father should regain his kingdom. Yama gave his promise that it should be accomplished, and commanded Sāvitrī to return. Still she refused, and spoke of the duty of the great and good to protect and aid all those who seek their help. Yama then granted her a third boon, that her father should have a hundred sons. Still Sāvitrī persisted. "Thou art called the Lord of Justice," she said, "and men ever trust the righteous; for it is goodness of heart alone that inspireth the confidence of every creature." When Yama granted another boon, save and except the life of Satyavān, Sāvitrī prayed for a hundred sons born of herself and Satyavān. Yama replied: "Thou shalt, O Lady, obtain a hundred sons, renowned and mighty, giving thee great delight. But thou hast come too far; now I pray thee to return." But she again praised the righteous. "It is the righteous," she said, "who support the earth by their austere life; they protect all." Again Yama was propitiated by Sāvitrī's edifying words, and he granted another boon. But now Sāvitrī answered: "O giver of honour, what thou hast already granted cannot come to pass without union with my husband; therefore I ask his life together with other boons. Without him I am but dead, without him I do not even desire happiness. Thou hast given a hundred sons, and yet dost take away my lord, without whom I may not live. I ask his life, that thy words may be accomplished."

Then Yama yielded and gave back Satyavān, promising him prosperity and a life of four centuries, and decendants who should all be kings. Granting all that Sāvitrī asked, the lord of the ancestors went his way. Then Sāvitrī returned to Satyavān's body, and she lifted his head upon her lap; behold, he came to life, like one returning home from sojourn in a strange land. "I have slept overlong," he said; "why didst thou not awake me? Where is that dark being who would have carried me away?" Sāvitrī answered; "Thou hast slept long. Yama has gone his way. Thou art recovered; rise, if thou canst, for night is falling."

Then those two returned, walking through heavy night along the forest paths.

Meanwhile Dyumatsena and his wife and all the sages remained in grief. Yet the Brāhmans were of good hope, for they deemed that Sāvitrī's virtue must avail even against fate, and they gave words of comfort to the king. Moreover, Dyumatsena suddenly regained his sight, and all took this for an omen of good fortune, betokening the safety of Satyavān. Then Sāvitrī and Satyavān returned through the dark night, and found the Brāhmans and the king seated beside the fire. Warm was their welcome and keen the questioning; then Sāvitrī related all that had befallen, and all saluted her; then, forasmuch as it was late, all went to their own abodes.

Next day at dawn there came ambassadors from Shālwa to say that the usurper had been slain, and the people invited Dyumatsena to return and be again their king. So he returned to Shālwa and lived long; and he had a hundred sons. Sāvitrī and Satyavān had also the hundred sons bestowed by Yama. Thus did Sāvitrī by her goodness alone raise from a poor estate to the highest fortune herself, her parents, and her lord, and all those descended from them.

BIBLICAL LITERATURE

ISAAC AND REBEKAH[1]

AND Abraham was old, and well stricken in age: and the Lord had blessed Abraham in all things. And Abraham said unto his eldest servant of his house, that ruled over all that he had, Put, I pray thee, thy hand under my thigh: And I will make thee swear by the Lord, the God of heaven, and the God of the earth, that thou shalt not take a wife unto my son of the daughters of the Canaanites, among whom I dwell: But thou shalt go unto my country, and to my kindred, and take a wife unto my son Isaac. And the servant said unto him, Peradventure the woman will not be willing to follow me unto this land: must I needs bring thy son again unto the land from whence thou camest? And Abraham said unto him, beware thou that thou bring not my son thither again. The Lord God of heaven which took me from my father's house, and from the land of my kindred, and which spake unto me, and that sware unto me, saying, Unto thy seed will I give this land; he shall send his angel before thee, and thou shalt take a wife unto my son from thence. And if the woman will not be willing to follow thee, then thou shalt be clear from this my oath: only bring not my son thither again. And the servant put his hand under the thigh of Abraham his master, and sware to him concerning that matter.

And the servant took ten camels of the camels of his master, and departed; for all the goods of his master were in his hand: and he arose, and went to Mesopotamia, unto the city of Nahor. And he made his camels to kneel down without the city by a well of water at the time of the evening, even the time that women go out to draw water. And he said, O Lord God of my master Abraham, I pray thee, send me good speed this day, and shew kindness unto my master Abraham. Behold, I stand here by the well of water; and the daughters of the men of the city come out to draw water: And let it come to pass, that the damsel to whom I shall say, Let down thy pitcher, I pray thee, that I may drink; and she shall say, Drink, and I will give thy camels drink also: let the same be she that thou hast appointed for thy servant Isaac; and thereby shall I know that thou hast shewed kindness unto my master.

And it came to pass, before he had done speaking, that, behold, Rebekah came out, who was born to Bethuel, son of Milcah, the wife of Nahor, Abraham's brother, with her pitcher upon her shoulder. And the damsel

---

[1] From the Book of Genesis (Authorized Version).

was very fair to look upon, a virgin, neither had any man known her: and she went down to the well, and filled her pitcher, and came up. And the servant ran to meet her, and said, Let me, I pray thee, drink a little water of thy pitcher. And she said, Drink, my lord: and she hasted, and let down her pitcher upon her hand, and gave him drink. And when she had done giving him drink, she said, I will draw water for thy camels also, until they have done drinking. And she hasted, and emptied her pitcher into the trough, and ran again unto the well to draw water, and drew for all his camels. And the man wondering at her held his peace, to wit whether the Lord had made his journey prosperous or not. And it came to pass, as the camels had done drinking, that the man took a golden earring of half a shekel weight, and two bracelets for her hands of ten shekels weight of gold; And said, Whose daughter art thou? tell me, I pray thee: is there room in thy father's house for us to lodge in? And she said unto him, I am the daughter of Bethuel the son of Milcah, which she bare unto Nahor. She said moreover unto him, We have both straw and provender enough, and room to lodge in. And the man bowed down his head, and worshipped the Lord. And he said Blessed be the Lord God of my master Abraham, who hath not left destitute my master of his mercy and his truth: I being in the way, the Lord led me to the house of my master's brethren. And the damsel ran, and told them of her mother's house these things.

And Rebekah had a brother, and his name was Laban: and Laban ran out unto the man, unto the well. And it came to pass, when he saw the earring and bracelets upon his sister's hands, and when he heard the words of Rebekah his sister, saying, Thus spake the man unto me; that he came unto the man; and, behold, he stood by the camels at the well. And he said, Come in, thou blessed of the Lord; wherefore standest thou without? for I have prepared the house, and room for the camels.

And the man came into the house: and he ungirded his camels, and gave straw and provender for the camels, and water to wash his feet, and the men's feet that were with him. And there was set meat before him to eat; but he said, I will not eat, until I have told mine errand. And he said, Speak on.

And he said, I am Abraham's servant. And the Lord hath blessed my master greatly; and he is become great: and he hath given him flocks, and herds, and silver, and gold, and menservants, and maidservants, and camels, and asses. And Sarah my master's wife bare a son to my master when she was old: and unto him hath he given all that he hath. And my master made me sware, saying, Thou shalt not take a wife to my son of the daughters of the Canaanites, in whose land I dwell: But thou shalt go into my father's house, and to my kindred, and take a wife unto my son. And I said unto my master, Peradventure the woman will not follow me. And he said unto me, The Lord, before whom I walk, will send his angel with thee, and prosper thy way; and thou shalt take a wife for my son of my kindred, and of my father's house: Then shalt thou be clear from this my oath, when thou comest to my kindred, and if they give not thee one, thou shalt be clear from my oath. And I came this day unto the well, and said, O Lord God of my master Abraham, if now thou do prosper my way which I go: Behold, I stand by the well of water; and it shall come to pass, that when the virgin cometh forth to draw water, and I say to her, Give me, I pray thee, a little water of thy pitcher to drink; And she say to me, Both drink thou, and I will also draw for thy camels: let the same be the woman whom the Lord hath appointed out for my master's son. And before I had done speaking in mine heart, behold, Rebekah came forth with her pitcher on her shoulder; and she went down unto the well, and drew water: and I said unto her, Let me drink, I pray thee. And she made haste, and let down her pitcher from her shoulder, and said, Drink, and I will give thy camels drink also: so I drank, and she made the camels drink also. And I asked her, and said, Whose daughter art thou? And she said, The daughter of Bethuel, Nahor's son, whom Milcah bare unto him: and I put the earring upon her face, and the bracelets upon her hands. And I bowed down my head, and worshipped the Lord, and blessed the Lord God of my master Abraham, which had led me in the right way to take my master's brother's daughter unto his son. And now if ye will deal kindly and truly with my master, tell me: and if not, tell me; that I may turn to the right hand, or to the left.

Then Laban and Bethuel answered and said, The thing proceedeth from the Lord; we cannot speak unto thee bad or good. Behold, Rebekah is before thee, take her, and go, and let her be thy master's son's wife, as the Lord hath spoken. And it came to pass, that, when Abraham's servant heard their words, he worshipped the Lord, bowing himself to the earth. And the servant brought forth jewels of silver, and jewels of gold, and raiment, and gave them to Rebekah: he gave also to her brother and to her mother precious things.

And they did eat and drink, he and the men that were with him, and tarried all night; and they rose up in the morning, and he said, Send me away unto my master. And her brother and her mother said, Let the damsel abide with us a few days, at the least ten; after that she shall go. And he said unto them, Hinder me not, seeing the Lord hath prospered my way; send me away that I may go to my master. And they said, We will call the damsel, and enquire at her mouth. And they called Rebekah, and said unto her, Wilt thou go with this man. And she said, I will go. And they sent away Rebekah their sister, and her nurse, and Abraham's servant, and his men. And they blessed Rebekah, and said unto her, Thou art our sister, be thou the mother of thousands of millions, and let thy seed possess the gate of those which hate them.

And Rebekah arose, and her damsels, and they rode upon the camels, and followed the man: and the servant took Rebekah, and went his way. And Isaac came from the way of the well Lahai-roi; for he dwelt in the south country. And Isaac went out to meditate in the field at the eventide: and he lifted up his eyes, and saw, and, behold, the camels were coming. And Rebekah lifted up her eyes, and when she saw Isaac, she lighted off the camel. For she had said unto the servant, What man is this that walketh in the field to meet us. And the servant had said, It is my master: therefore she took a veail and covered herself. And the servant told Isaac all things that he had done. And Isaac brought her into his mother Sarah's tent, and took Rebekah, and she became his wife; and he loved her.

THE TRAGEDY OF SAMSON[1]

AND Samson went down to Timnath, and saw a woman in Timnath of the daughters of the Philistines. And he came up, and told his father and his mother, and said, I have seen a woman in Timnath of the daughters of the Philistines: now therefore get her for me to wife. Then his father and his mother said unto him, Is there never a woman among the daughters of thy brethren or among all my people, that thou goest to take a wife of the uncircumcised Philistines? And Samson said unto his father, Get her for me; for she pleaseth me well. But his father and his mother knew not that it was of the Lord, that he sought an occasion against the Philistines: for at that time the Philistines had dominion over Israel.

Then went Samson down, and his father and his mother, to Timnath, and came to the vineyards of Timnath: and, behold, a young lion roared against him. And the Spirit of the Lord came mightily upon him, and he rent him as he would have rent a kid, and he had nothing in his hand: but he told not his father or his mother what he had done. And he went down, and talked with the woman; and she pleased Samson well. And after a time he returned to take her, and he turned aside to see the carcase of the

---

[1] From the Book of Judges (Authorized Version).

lion, and, behold, there was a swarm of bees and honey in the carcase of the lion. And he took thereof in his hands, and went on eating, and came to his father and mother, and he gave them, and they did eat: but he told not them that he had taken the honey out of the carcase of the lion.

So his father went down unto the woman: and Samson made there a feast; for so used the young men to do. And it came to pass, when they saw him, that they brought thirty companions to be with him.

And Samson said unto them, I will now put forth a riddle unto you: if ye can certainly declare it me within the seven days of the feast, and find it out, then I will give you thirty sheets and thirty change of garments: But if ye cannot declare it me, then shall ye give me thirty sheets and thirty change of garments. And they said unto him, Put forth thy riddle, that we may hear it.

And he said unto them Out of the eater came forth meat, and out of the strong came forth sweetness. And they could not in three days expound the riddle. And it came to pass on the seventh day, that they said unto Samson's wife, Entice thy husband, that he may declare unto us the riddle, lest we burn thee and thy father's house with fire: have ye called us to take that we have? is it not so? And Samson's wife wept before him, and said, Thou dost hate me, and lovest me not: thou hast put forth a riddle unto the children of my people, and hast not told it me. And he said unto her, Behold, I have not told it my father nor my mother, and shall I tell it thee? And she wept before him the seven days, while their feast lasted; and it came to pass on the seventh day, that he told her, because she lay sore upon him: and she told the riddle to the children of her people.

And the men of the city said unto him on the seventh day before the sun went down, What is sweeter than honey? and what is stronger than a lion? And he said unto them, If ye had not plowed with my heifer, ye had not found out my riddle.

And the Spirit of the Lord came upon him, and he went down to Ashkelon, and slew thirty men of them, and took their spoil, and gave change of garments unto them which expounded the riddle. And his anger was kindled, and he went up to his father's house. But Samson's wife was given to his companion, whom he had used as his friend.

But it came to pass within a while after, in the time of wheat harvest, that Samson visited his wife with a kid; and he said, I will go in to my wife into the chamber. But her father would not suffer him to go in. And her father said, I verily thought that thou hadst utterly hated her; therefore I gave her to thy companion: is not her younger sister fairer than she? take her, I pray thee, instead of her.

And Samson said concerning them, Now shall I be more blameless than the Philistines, though I do them a displeasure. And Samson went and caught three hundred foxes, and took firebrands, and turned tail to tail, and put a firebrand in the midst between two tails. And when he had set the brands on fire, he let them go into the standing corn of the Philistines, and burnt up both the shocks, and also the standing corn, with the vineyards and olives.

Then the Philistines said, Who hath done this? And they answered, Samson, the son in law of the Timnite, because he had taken his wife, and given her to his companion. And the Philistines came up, and burnt her and her father with fire.

And Samson said unto them, Though ye have done this, yet will I be avenged of you, and after that I will cease. And he smote them hip and thigh with a great slaughter: and he went down and dwelt in the top of the rock Etam.

Then the Philistines went up, and pitched in Judah, and spread themselves in Lehi. And the men of Judah said, Why are ye come up against us? And they answered, To bind Samson are we come up, to do to him as he hath done to us. Then three thousand men of Judah went to the top of the rock Etam, and said to Samson, Knowest thou not that the Philistines are rulers over us? what is this that thou hast done unto us? And he said unto them, As they did unto me, so have I done unto them.

And they said unto him, We are come down to bind thee, that we may deliver thee into the hand of the Philistines. And Samson said unto them, Swear unto me, that ye will not fall upon me yourselves. And they spake unto him, saying, No; but we will bind thee fast, and deliver thee into their hand: but surely we will not kill thee. And they bound him with two new cords, and brought him up from the rock.

And when he came unto Lehi, the Philistines shouted against him: and the Spirit of the Lord came mightily upon him, and the cords that were upon his arms became as flax that was burnt with fire, and his bands loosed from off his hands. And he found a new jawbone of an ass, and put forth his hand, and took it, and slew a thousand men therewith. And Samson said, With the jawbone of an ass, heaps upon heaps, with the jaw of an ass have I slain a thousand men. And it came to pass, when he had made an end of speaking, that he cast away the jawbone out of his hand, and called that place Ramath-lehi.

And he was sore athirst, and called on the Lord, and said, Thou hast given this great deliverance into the hand of thy servant: and now shall I die for thirst, and fall into the hands of the uncircumcised? But God clave an hollow place that was in the jaw, and there came water thereout; and when he had drunk his spirit came again, and he revived: wherefore he called the name thereof En-hakkore, which is in Lehi unto this day.

And he judged Israel in the days of the Philistines twenty years.

Then went Samson to Gaza, and saw there an harlot, and went in unto her. And it was told the Gazites, saying, Samson is come hither. And they compassed him in, and laid wait for him all night in the city, and were quiet all the night, saying, In the morning, when it is day, we shall kill him. And Samson lay till midnight, and arose at midnight, and took the doors of the gate of the city, and the two posts, and went away with them, bar and all, and put them upon his shoulders, and carried them up to the top of an hill that is before Hebron.

And it came to pass afterward, that he loved a woman in the valley of Sorek, whose name was Delilah. And the lords of the Philistines came up unto her, and said unto her, Entice him, and see wherein his great strength lieth, and by what means we may prevail against him, that we may bind him to afflict him: and we will give thee every one of us eleven hundred pieces of silver.

And Delilah said to Samson, Tell me, I pray thee, wherein thy strength lieth, and wherewith thou mightest be bound to afflict thee. And Samson said unto her, If they bind me with seven green withs that were never dried, then shall I be weak, and be as another man. Then the lords of the Philistines brought up to her seven green withs which had not been dried, and she bound him with them.

Now there were men lying in wait, abiding with her in the chamber. And she said unto him, The Philistines be upon thee Samson. And he brake the withs, as a thread of tow is broken when it toucheth the fire. So his strength was not known. And Delilah said unto Samson, Behold, thou hast mocked me, and told me lies: now tell me, I pray thee, wherewith thou mightest be bound. And he said unto her, If they bind me fast with new ropes that never were occupied, then shall I be weak, and be as another man.

Delilah therefore took new ropes, and bound him therewith, and said unto him, The Philistines be upon thee, Samson. And there were liers in wait abiding in the chamber. And he brake them from off his arms like a thread. And Delilah said unto Samson, Hitherto thou hast mocked me, and told me lies; tell me wherewith thou mightest be bound. And he said unto her, If thou weavest the seven locks of my head with the web. And she fastened it with the pin and said unto him, The Philistines be upon thee, Samson, and he awaked out of his sleep, and went away with the pin of the beam, and with the web.

And she said unto him, How canst thou say, I love thee, when thine heart is not with me? thou hast mocked me wherein thy great strength lieth. And it came to pass, when she pressed him daily with her words, and urged him, so that his soul was vexed unto death; That he told her all his heart, and said unto her, There hath not come a razor upon mine head; for I have been a Nazarite unto God from my mother's womb: if I be shaven, then my strength will go from me, and I shall become weak, and be like any other man.

And when Delilah saw that he had told her all his heart, she sent and called for the lords of the Philistines, saying, Come up this once, for he hath shewed me all his heart. Then the lords of the Philistines came up unto her, and brought money in their hand. And she made him sleep upon her knees; and she called for a man, and she caused him to shave off the seven locks of his head; and she began to afflict him, and his strength went from him. And she said, The Philistines be upon thee, Samson. And he awoke out of his sleep, and said, I will go out as at other times before, and shake myself. And he wist not that the Lord was departed from him.

But the Philistines took him, and put out his eyes, and brought him down to Gaza, and bound him with fetters of brass; and he did grind in the prison house. Howbeit the hair of his head began to grow again after he was shaven. Then the lords of the Philistines gathered them together for to offer a great sacrifice unto Dagon their god, and to rejoice; for they said, Our god hath delivered Samson our enemy into our hand. And when the people saw him, they praised their god: for they said, Our god hath delivered into our hands our enemy, and the destroyer of our country, which slew many of us. And it came to pass, when their hearts were merry, that they said, Call for Samson, that he may make us sport. And they called for Samson out of the prison house; and he made them sport; and they sat him between the pillars. And Samson said unto the lad that held him by the hand, Suffer me that I may feel the pillars whereupon the house standeth, that I may lean upon them.

Now the house was full of men and women; and all the lords of the Philistines were there; and there were upon the roof about three thousand men and women, that beheld while Samson made sport. And Samson called unto the Lord, and said, O Lord God, remember me, I pray thee, and strengthen me, I pray thee, only this once, O God, that I may be at once avenged of the Philistines for my two eyes. And Samson took hold of the two middle pillars upon which the house stood, and on which it was borne up, of the one with his right hand, and of the other with his left. And

Samson said, Let me die with the Philistines. And he bowed himself with all his might; and the house fell upon the lords and upon all the people that were therein. So the dead which he slew at his death were more that they which he slew in his life. Then his brethren and all the house of his father came down, and took him, and brought him up, and buried him between Zorah and Eshtaol in the burying place of Manoah his father. And he judged Israel twenty years.

ANCIENT GREECE

HECTOR AND ANDROMACHÉ[1]

Homer

HECTOR came into the city by the Scæan gates, and as he went wives and mothers crowded about him, asking how it had fared with their husbands and sons. But he said nought, save to bid them pray; and indeed there was sore news for many, if he had told that which he knew. Then he came to the palace of King Priam, and there he saw Hecuba, his mother, and with her Laodicé, fairest of her daughters. She caught him by the hand and said:

"Why hast thou come from the battle, my son? Do the Greeks press thee hard, and art thou minded to pray to Father Zeus from the citadel? Let me bring thee honey-sweet wine that thou mayest pour out before him, aye, and that thou mayest drink thyself, and gladden thy heart."

But Hector said: "Give me not wine, my mother, lest thou weaken my knees and make me forget my courage. Nor must I pour out an offering with Zeus thus, with unwashed hands. But do thou gather the mothers of Troy together, and go to the temple of Athené and take a robe, the one that is the most precious and beautiful in thy stores, and lay it on the knees of the goddess, and pray her to keep this dreadful Diomed from the walls of Troy; and forget not to vow therewith twelve heifers as a sacrifice. As for me, I will go and seek Paris, if perchance he will come with me to the war. Would that the earth might open and swallow him up, for of a truth he is a curse to King Priam and to Troy."

Then went Queen Hecuba into her house, and gave command to her maids that they should assemble the aged women of the city. Afterwards she went to her store-chamber, where lay the well-wrought robes, work of Sidonian women, which Paris himself brought from Sidon, when he sailed upon the broad sea, bringing home with him high-born Helen. The fairest robe of all did the Queen take. Bright as a star it was, and it lay the undermost of all.

And when she and the aged women that were with her came to the temple of Athené that was in the citadel, Theano, Antenor's wife, whom the Trojans had made priestess of Athené, opened the doors to them.

---

[1] From A. J. Church's *Story of the Iliad*. Reprinted by permission of Messrs Seeley, Service and Co., Ltd.

They lifted their hands, and cried aloud, and Theano laid the garment on the knees of the goddess, and spake, saying:

"Lady Athené, that keepest the city, break now the spear of Diomed, and let him fall upon his face before the Scæan gates. So will we sacrifice to thee twelve heifers that have not felt the goad, if only thou wilt have pity upon our town, and on the wives and little ones of the men of Troy."

So prayed Theano, but Athené heeded not her words.

Meanwhile Hector went to the house of Paris, where it stood on the citadel, near to his own dwelling and the dwelling of Priam. He found him busy with his arms, and the fair Helen sat near him and gave their tasks to her maidens.

When Hector saw his brother, he spake to him bitter words, taunting him, as if it were by reason of his anger that he stood aloof from the battle. "Verily thou doest not well to be angry. The people perish about the walls, and the war burns hot round the city; and all for thy sake. Rouse thee, lest it be consumed."

And Paris answered: "Brother, thou hast spoken well. It was not in wrath that I sat here. I was vexed at my sore defeat. But now my wife has urged me to join the battle; and truly it is well, for victory comes now to one and now to another. Wait thou, then, till I put on my arms, or, if thou wouldst depart, I will overtake thee."

Then spake Helen with soothing words: "O my brother, would that I had perished on the day when my mother bare me! But if this might not be, would that the gods had made me the wife of one who feared the blame of his fellow-men; but this man hath no understanding, no, nor ever will have. Surely, he shall eat of the fruit of his ill-doing. But come in, sit thee down in this chair, for my heart is weary because of my sin and of the sin of my husband. Verily Zeus hath ordained for us an evil fate, so that our story shall be sung in days that are yet to come."

But Hector said: "Ask me not to rest, for I am eager to help the men of Troy, for verily their need is sore. But do thou urge thy husband that he overtake me while I am yet within the city, for now I go to my home that I may see my wife and my little son, because I know not whether I shall return to them again."

So Hector departed and went to his own home, seeking his wife Andromaché, but found her not, for she was on a tower of the wall with her child and her child's nurse, weeping sore for fear. And Hector spake to the maids:

"Tell me, whither went the white-armed Andromaché; to see some sister-in-law, or to the temple of Athené with the mothers of Troy?"

"Nay," said an aged woman, keeper of the house. "She went to one of the towers of the wall, for she had heard that the Greeks were pressing our people hard. She hasted like as she were mad, and the nurse carried the child."

So Hector ran through the city to the Scæan gates, and there Andromaché spied him, and hasted to meet him—Andromaché, daughter of King Eetion, of Thebé-under-Placus. And with her was the nurse, bearing the young child on her bosom—Hector's only child, beautiful, headed as a star. His father called him Scamandrius, after the river, but the sons of Troy called him Astyanax, the "City-King," because it was his father who saved the city. Silently he smiled when he saw the child, but Andromaché clasped his hand and wept, and said:

"O Hector, thy courage will bring thee to death. Thou hast no pity on thy wife and child, but sparest not thyself, and all the Greeks will rush on thee and slay thee. It were better for me, losing thee, to die; for I have no comfort but thee. My father is dead, for Achilles slew him in Thebé—slew him but spoiled him not, so much he reverenced him. With his arms he burnt him, and the mountain-nypmhs planted poplars about his grave. Seven brethren I had, and they all fell in one day by the hand of the great Achilles. And my mother, she is dead, for when she had been ransomed, Artemis smote her with an arrow in her father's house. But thou art father to me, and mother, and brother, and husband also. Have pity, then, and stay here upon the wall, lest thou leave me a widow and thy child an orphan. And set the people here in array by this fig tree, where the city is easiest to be taken; for there come the bravest of the Greeks, Ajax the Greater, and Ajax the Less, and Idomeneus, and the two sons of Atreus, and the son of Tydeus."

But Hector said: "Nay, let these things be my care. I would not that any son or daughter of Troy should see me skulking from the war. And my own heart loathes the thought, and bids me fight in the front. Well I know, indeed, that Priam, and the people of Priam, and holy Troy, will perish. Yet it is not for Troy, or for the people, or even for my father or my mother that I care so much, as for thee in the day when some Greek shall carry thee away captive, and thou shalt ply the loom or carry the pitcher in the land of Greece. And some one shall say when he sees thee, 'This was Hector's wife, who was the bravest of the sons of Troy.' May the earth cover me before that day!"

Then Hector stretched out his arms to his child. But the child drew back into the bosom of his nurse, with a loud cry, fearing the shining bronze and the horse-hair plume which nodded awfully from his helmet top. Then father and mother laughed aloud. And Hector took the helmet from his head, and laid it on the ground, and caught his child in his hands, and kissed him and dandled him, praying aloud to Father Zeus and all the gods.

"Grant, Father Zeus and all ye gods, that this child may be as I am, great among the sons of Troy; and may they say some day, when they see him carrying home the bloody spoils from the war, 'A better man than his father, this,' and his mother shall be glad at heart."

Then he gave the child to his mother, and she clasped him to her breast, and smiled a tearful smile. And her husband's heart was moved; and he stroked her with his hand, and spake:

"Be not troubled over much. No man shall slay me against the ordering of fate; but as for fate, that, methinks, no man may escape, be he coward or brave. But go, ply thy tasks, the shuttle and the loom, and give their tasks to thy maidens, and let men take thought for the battle."

Then Hector took up his helmet from the ground, and Andromaché went her way to her home, oft turning back her eyes. And when she was come, she and all her maidens wailed for the living Hector as though he were dead, for she thought that she should never see him any more returning safe from the battle.

And as Hector went his way, Paris came running, clad in shining arms, like to some proud steed which has been fed high in his stall, and now scours the plain with head aloft and mane streaming over his shoulders. And he spake to Hector:

"I have kept thee, I fear, when thou wast in haste, nor came at thy bidding."

But Hector answered: "No man can blame thy courage, only thou wilfully heldest back from the battle. Therefore do the sons of Troy speak shame of thee. But now let us go to the war."

So they went together out of the gates, and fell upon the hosts of the Greeks and slew many chiefs of fame, and Glaucus the Lycian went with them.

[But the great Achilles met Hector and drove in his spear where by the collar-bone the neck joins the shoulder, so that Hector fell in the dust].

Then Achilles cried aloud: "Hector, thou thoughtest in the day when thou didst spoil Patroclus of his arms that thou wouldst be safe from vengeance, taking, forsooth, no account of me. And lo! thou art fallen before me, and now the dogs and vultures shall devour thee, but to him all the Greeks shall give due burial."

But Hector, growing faint, spake to him: "Nay, great Achilles, by thy life, and by thy knees, and by thy parents dear, I pray thee, let not the dogs of the Greeks devour me. Take rather the ransom, gold and bronze, that my father and mother shall pay thee, and let the sons and daughters of Troy give me burial rites."

But Achilles scowled at him, and cried: "Dog, seek not to entreat me! I could mince that flesh of thine and devour it raw, such grief hast thou wrought me. Surely the dogs shall devour thee, nor shall any man hinder. No ransom, though it were ten times told, should buy thee back; no, not though Priam should offer thy weight in gold."

Then Hector, who was now at the point to die, spake to him: "I know thee well, what manner of man thou art, that the heart in thy breast is iron only. Only beware lest some vengeance from the gods come upon thee in the day when Paris and Apollo shall slay thee, for all thy valour, by the Scæan gates."

So speaking, he died. But Achilles said, "Die, hound; but my fate I meet when Zeus and the other gods decree."

Then he drew his spear out of the corpse, and stripped off the arms; and all the Greeks came about the dead man, marvelling at his stature and beauty, and no man came but wounded the dead corpse. And one would say to another, "Surely this Hector is less dreadful now than in the day when he would burn our ships with fire."

Then Achilles devised a ruthless thing in his heart. He pierced the ankle-bones of Hector, and so bound the body with thongs of ox-hide to the chariot, letting the head drag behind, the head that once was so fair, and now was so disfigured in the dust. So he dragged Hector to the ships. And Priam saw him from the walls, and scarce could his sons keep him back, but that he should go forth and beg the body of his dear son from him who had slain him. And Hecuba, his mother, also bewailed him, but Andromaché knew not as yet of what had befallen. For she sat in her dwelling, wearing a great purple mantle broidered with flowers. And she bade her maidens make ready a bath for Hector, when he should come back from the battle, nor knew that he should never need it more. But the voice of wailing from the town came to her, and she rose up hastily in great fear, and dropped the shuttle from her hand, and called to her maidens:

"Come with me, ye maidens, that I may see what has befallen, for I heard the voice of Queen Hecuba, and I fear me much that some evil has come to the children of Priam. For it may be that Achilles has run between Hector and the city, and is pursuing him to the plain, for never will Hector abide with the army, but will fight in the front, so bold is he."

Then she hastened through the city like as she were mad. And when she came to the wall, she stood and looked; and lo! the horses of Achilles were dragging Hector to the ships. Then did darkness come on her, and she fell back fainting, and from her fair head dropped the net and the wreath and the diadem which golden Aphrodité gave her on the day when Hector of the waving plume took her from the house of Eëtion to be his wife.

THE FAITHFUL WIFE OF SUSA[1]

Xenophon

CYRUS called to his side Araspas the Mede, who had been his comrade in boyhood. It was he to whom Cyrus gave the Median cloak he was wearing when he went back to Persia from his grandfather's court. Now he summoned him, and asked him to take care of the tent and the lady from Susa. She was the wife of Abradatas, a Susian, and when the Assyrian camp was captured it happened that her husband was away. And now Cyrus asked Araspas to guard the captive lady until her husband could take her back himself. To that Araspas replied, "Have you seen the lady whom you bid me guard?"

"No, indeed," said Cyrus, "certainly I have not."

"But I have," rejoined the other, "I saw her when we chose her for you. When we came into the tent, we did not make her out at first, for she was seated on the ground with all her maidens round her, and she was clad in the same attire as her slaves, but when we looked at them all to discover the mistress, we soon saw that one outshone the others, although she was veiled and kept her eyes on the ground. And when we bade her rise, all her women rose with her, and then we saw that she was marked out from them all by her height, and her noble bearing, and her grace, and the beauty that shone through her mean apparel. And, under her veil, we could see the big tear-drops trickling down her garments to her feet. At that sight the eldest of us said, 'Take comfort, lady, we know that your husband was beautiful and brave, but we have chosen you a man to-day who is no whit inferior to him in face or form or mind or power; Cyrus, we believe, is more to be admired than any soul on earth, and you shall be his from this day forward.' But when the lady heard that, she rent the veil that covered

---

[1] From the translation of the *Cyropaedia* by H. G. Dakyns, revised by F. M. Stawell, in the Everyman's Library. Reprinted by permission of Messrs. J. M. Dent and Sons, Ltd.

her head and gave a pitiful cry, while her maidens lifted up their voice and wept with their mistress. And thus we could see her face, and her neck, and her arms, and I tell you, Cyrus," he added, "I myself, and all who looked on her, felt that there never was, and never had been, in broad Asia a mortal woman half so fair as she. Nay, but you must see her for yourself."

"Say, rather, I must not," answered Cyrus, "if she be such as you describe."

"And why not?" asked the young man.

"Because," said he, "if the mere report of her beauty could persuade me to go and gaze on her to-day, when I have not a moment to spare, I fear she would win me back again and perhaps I should neglect all I have to do, and sit and gaze at her for ever."

At that the young man laughed outright and said:

"So you think, Cyrus, that the beauty of any human creature can compel a man to do wrong against his will? Take my own case," he added, "I have seen this lady myself, and passing fair I found her, and yet here I stand before you, and am still your trooper and can still perform my duty."

"I do not deny it," said Cyrus; "probably you came away in time. Love takes a little while to seize and carry off nis victim. You yourself, my friend, if you will follow my advice, will not let your own eyes linger there too long; burning fuel will only burn those who touch it, but beauty can fire the beholder from afar, until he is all aflame with love."

"Oh, fear me not, Cyrus," answered he; "if I looked till the end of time I could not be made to do what ill befits a man."

"A fair answer," said Cyrus. "Guard her then, as I bid you, and be careful of her. This lady may be of service to us all one day."

With these words they parted. But afterwards, after the young man saw from day to day how marvellously fair the woman was, and how noble and gracious in herself, after he took care of her, and fancied that she was not insensible to what he did, after she set herself, through her attendants to care for his wants and see that all things were ready for him when he came in, and that he should lack for nothing if ever he were sick, after all this, love entered his heart and took possession...

Cyrus decided to send a spy into Lydia to ascertain the movements of the king, and he thought that the right man for this purpose was Araspas, the officer in charge of the fair lady from Susa. Matters had gone ill with Araspas: he had fallen passionately in love with his prisoner, and been led to entreat her to be his paramour. She had refused, faithful to her husband who was far away, for she loved him dearly, but she forbore to accuse Araspas to Cyrus, being unwilling to set friend at strife with friend. But when at length Araspas, thinking it would help him in his desires, began to threaten her, saying that if she would not yield he would have his will of her by force, then in her dread of violence she could keep the matter hid no longer, and she sent her eunuch to Cyrus with orders to tell him everything. And when Cyrus heard it he smiled over the man who had boasted that he was superior to love, and sent Artabazus back with the eunuch to tell Araspas that he must use no violence against such a woman, but if he could persuade her, he might do so. But Artabazus, when he saw Araspas, rebuked him sternly, saying that the woman was a sacred trust, and his conduct disgraceful, impious, and wicked, till Araspas burst into tears of misery and shame, and was half dead at thought of what Cyrus would do. Learning this, Cyrus sent for him, saw him alone, and said to him face to face:

"Araspas, I know that you are afraid of me and in an agony of shame. Be comforted; we are told that the gods themselves are made subject to desire, and I could tell you what love has forced some men to undergo, men who seemed most lofty and most wise. Did I not pass sentence on myself, when I confessed I was too weak to consort with loveliness and remain unmoved? Indeed it is I who am most to blame in the matter, for I shut you up myself with this irresistible power."

But Araspas broke in on his words:

"Ah, Cyrus, you are ever the same, gentle and compassionate to human weaknesses. But all the rest of the world has no pity on me; they drown me in wretchedness. As soon as the tattlers got wind of my misfortune, all my enemies exulted, and my friends came to me, advising me to make away with myself for fear of you, because my iniquity was so great."

Then Cyrus said, "Now listen: this opinion about you may be the means by which you can do me a great kindness and your comrades a great service." "Oh, that it were possible," said Araspas, "for me ever to be of service to you!" "Well," said the other, "if you went to the enemy, feigoning that you had fled from me, I think they would believe you." "I am sure they would," said Araspas, "I know even my own friends would think that of course I ran away." "Then you will come back to us," Cyrus went on, "with full information about the enemy's affairs; for, if I am right in my expectation, they will trust you and let you see all their plans, so that you need miss nothing of what we wish to know." "I will be off this moment," said Araspas; "it will be my best credential to have it thought I was just in time to escape punishment from you."

"Then you can really bring yourself to leave the beautiful Pantheia?"

"Yes, Cyrus," he answered, "I can; for I see now that we have two souls.

When the beautiful soul prevails, all fair things are wrought, and when the evil soul has the mastery, she lays her hand to shame and wickedness. But to-day my good soul conquers, because she has you to help her."

Thereupon Araspas took his leave, called together his trustiest attendants, said what he thought necessary for the occasion, and departed.

Now Pantheia, when she heard that Araspas had fled, sent a messenger to Cyrus, saying:

"Grieve not, Cyrus, that Araspas has gone to join the foe: I will bring you a far trustier friend than he, if you will let me send for my husband, and I know he will bring with him all the power that he has. It is true that the old king was my husband's friend, but he who reigns now tried to tear us two asunder, and my husband knows him for a tyrant and a miscreant, and would gladly be quit of him and take service with such a man as you."

When Cyrus heard that, he bade Pantheia send word to her husband, and she did so. Now when Abradatas saw the tokens from his wife, and learnt how matters stood, he was full of joy, and set out for Cyrus' camp immediately, with a thousand horsemen in his train. And when he came to the Persian outposts he sent to Cyrus saying who he was, and Cyrus gave orders that he should be taken to Pantheia forthwith. So husband and wife met again after hope had well-nigh vanished, and were in each other's arms once more. And then Pantheia spoke of Cyrus, his nobleness, his honour, and the compassion he had shown her, and Abradatas cried:

"Tell me, tell me, how can I repay him all I owe him in your name and mine!" And she answered:

"So deal with him, my husband, as he has dealt with you."

Thus Abradatas went to Cyrus, and took him by the hand, and said:

"Cyrus, in return for the kindness you have shown us, I can say no more than this: I give myself to you, I will be your friend, your servant, and your ally: whatever you desire, I will help you to win, your fellow-worker always, so far as in me lies."

Then Cyrus answered:

"And I will take your gift: but for the moment you must leave me, and sup with your wife: another day you will let me play the host, and give you lodging with your friends and mine."

Meanwhile Cyrus continued his preparations for the war on a magnificent scale, like one who meant to accomplish no small achievement.

As soon as the victims were favourable, he set out with his force....

But Abradatas, the lord of Susa, cried:

"Cyrus, let me, I pray you, volunteer for the post in front."

And Cyrus, struck with admiration for the man, took him by the hand and turning to the Persians in command of the other centuries said: "Perhaps, gentlemen, you will allow this?"

But they answered that it was hard to resign the post of honour, and so they all drew lots, and the lot fell on Abradatas.

But early on the morrow Cyrus offered sacrifice, and mean while the rest of the army took their breakfast, and after the libation they armed themselves, a great and goodly company in bright tunics and splendid breastplates and shining helmets. All the horses had frontlets and chest plates, the chargers had armour on their shoulders, and the chariot-horses on their flanks; so that the whole army flashed with bronze, and shone like a flower with scarlet. whe eight-horse chariot of Abradatas was a marvel of beauty and richness; and just as he was about to put on the linen corslet of his native land, Pantheia came, bringing him a golden breastplate and a helmet of gold, and armlets and broad bracelets for his wrists, and a full flowing purple tunic, and a hyacinth-coloured helmet-plume. All these she had made for him in secret, taking the measure of his armour without his knowlege. And when he saw them, he gazed in wonder and said:

"Dear wife, and did you destroy your own jewels to make this armour for me?"

But she said, "No, my lord, at least not the richest of them all, for you shall be my loveliest jewel, when others see you as I see you now."

As she spoke, she put the armour on him, but then, though she tried to hide it, the tears rolled down her cheeks.

And truly, when Abradatas was arrayed in the new panoply, he, who had been fair enough to look upon before, was now a sight of splendour, noble and beautiful and free, as indeed his nature was. He took the reins from the charioteer, and was about to set foot on the car, when Pantheia bade the bystanders withdraw, and said to thim. "My own lord, little need to tell you what you know already, yet this l say, if any woman loved her husband more than her own soul, I am of her company. Why should I try to speak? Our lives say more than any words of mine. And yet, feeling for you what you know, I swear to you by the love between us that I would rather go down to the grave beside you after a hero's death than live on with you in shame. I have thought you worthy of the highest, and believed myself worthy to follow you. And I bear in mind the great gratitude we owe to Cyrus, who, when I was his captive, chosen for his spoil, was too high-minded to treat me as a slave, or dishonour me as a free woman; he took me and saved me for you, as though I had been his brother's wife. And when Araspas, my warder, turned from him, I promised, if he would let me send for you, I would bring him a friend in the other's place, far nobler and more faithful."

And as Pantheia spoke, Abradatas listened with rapture to her words, and when she ended, he laid his hand upon her head, and looking up to heaven he prayed aloud:

"O most mighty Zeus, make me worthy to be Pantheia's husband, and the friend of Cyrus who showed us honour!"

Then he opened the driver's seat and mounted the car, and the driver shut the door, and Pantheia could not take him in her arms again, so she bent and kissed the chariot-box. Then the car rolled forward and she followed unseen till Abradatas turned and saw her and cried, "Be strong, Pantheia, be of a good heart! Farewell, and hie thee home!"

Thereupon her chamberlains and her maidens took her and brought her back to her own carriage, and laid her down and drew the awning. But no man, of all who were there that day, splendid as Abradatas was in his chariot, had eyes to look on him until Pantheia had gone.

The next day Cyrus called some of his squires and said:

"Tell me, have any of you seen Abradatas? I wonder that he who used to come to me so often is nowhere to be found."

Then one of the squires made answer, "My lord, he is dead: he fell in the battle, charging straight into the Egyptian ranks: the rest, all but his own companions, swerved before their close array. And now," he added, "we hear that his wife has found his body and laid it in her own car, and has brought it here to the banks of the Pactolus. Her chamberlains and her attendants are digging a grave for the dead man upon a hill, and she, they say, has put her fairest raiment on him and her jewels, and she is seated on the ground with his head upon her knees."

Then Cyrus smote his hand upon his thigh and leapt up and sprang to horse, galloping to the place of sorrow, with a thousand troopers at his back. He bade Gadatas and Gobryas take what jewels they could find to honour the dear friend and brave warrior who had fallen, and follow with all speed: and he bade the keepers of the herds, the cattle, and the horses drive up their flocks wherever they heard he was, that he might sacrifice on the grave.

But when he saw Pantheia seated on the ground and the dead man lying there, the tears ran down his cheeks and he cried:

"O noble and loyal spirit, have you gone from us?"

Then he took the dead man by the hand, but the hand came away with his own: it had been hacked by an Egyptian blade. And when he saw that, his sorrow grew, and Pantheia sobbed aloud and took the hand from

Cyrus and kissed it and laid it in its place, as best she could, and said:

"It is all like that, Cyrus. But why should you see it?" And presently she said, "All this, I know, he suffered for my sake, and for yours too, Cyrus, perhaps as much. I was a fool: I urged him so to bear himself as became a faithful friend of yours, and he, I know, he never thought once of his own safety, but only of what he might do to show his gratitude. Now he has fallen, without a stain upon his valour: and I, who urged him, I live on to sit beside his grave."

And Cyrus wept silently for a while, and then he said:

"Lady, his end was the noblest and the fairest that could be: he died in the hour of victory. Take these gifts that I have brought and adorn him".

For now Gobryas and Gadatas appeared with store of jewels and rich apparel. "He shall not lack for honour," Cyrus said; "many hands will raise his monument: it shall be a royal one; and we will offer such sacrifice as befits a hero. And you, lady," he added, "you shall not be left desolate. I reverence your chastity and your nobleness, and I will give you a guardian to lead you whithersoever you choose, if you will but tell me to whom you wish to go."

And Pantheia answered:

"Be at rest, Cyrus, I will not hide from you to whom I long to go."

Therewith Cyrus took his leave of her and went, pitying from his heart the woman who had lost so brave a husband, and the dead man in his grave, taken from so sweet a wife, never to see her more. Then Pantheia bade her chamberlains stand aside "until," she said, "I have wept over him as I would." But she made her nurse stay with her and she said:

"Nurse, when I am dead, cover us with the same cloak." And the nurse entreated and besought her, but she could not move her, and when she saw that she did but vex her mistress, she sat down and wept in silence. Then Pantheia took the scimitar, that had been ready for her so long, and drew it across her throat, and dropped her head upon her husband's breast and died. And the nurse cried bitterly, but she covered the two with one cloak as her mistress had bidden her.

And when Cyrus heard what Pantheia had done he rushed out in horror to see if he could save her. And when the three chamberlains saw what had happened they drew their own scimitars and killed themselves, there where she had bidden them stand. And when Cyrus came to that place of sorrow, he looked with wonder and reverence on the woman, and wept for her and went his way and saw that all due honour was paid to those who lay there dead, and a mighty sepulchre was raised above them, mightier, men say, than had been seen in all the world before.

ANCIENT ROME
DIDO AND ÆNEAS[1]

Virgil

BUT the Queen, long ere now pierced sore with passion, feeds the wound with her life-blood, and wastes in a hidden fire. Again and again the valiance of Æneas and his line's renown flood back upon her spirit; look and accent cling fast in her bosom, and the pain allows not her limbs rest or calm. The morrow's dawn bore the torch of Phoebus across the earth, and had rolled away the dewy darkness from the sky, when, scarce herself, she thus addresses the sister of her heart:

"Anna, my sister, such dreams of terror thrill me through! What guest unknown is this who has entered our dwelling? How high his mien! how great in heart as in arms! I believe it well, with no vain assurance, his blood is divine. Fear proves the vulgar spirit. Alas, by what destinies is he driven! of what wars fought out he told! Were my mind not planted, fixed and immoveable, to ally myself to none in wedlock since my first love of old played me false in death; were I not sick to the heart of bridal torch and chamber, to this temptation alone I might haply yield. Anna, I will confess it; since Sychaeus mine husband met his piteous doom, and our household was shattered by a brother's murder, he only has touched mine heart and shaken my soul from its balance. I know the prints of the ancient flame. But rather, I pray, may earth first yawn deep for me, or the Lord omnipotent hurl me with his thunderbolt into gloom, the pallid gloom and profound night of Erebus, ere I soil thee, mine honour, or undo thy laws. He took my love away who made me one with him at first; he shall keep it with him, and guard it in the tomb." She spoke, and filled her bosom with welling tears.

Anna replies: "O dearer than the daylight to thy sister, wilt thou waste, sad and alone, all thy length of youth, and know not the sweetness of motherhood, nor love's bounty? Deemest thou the ashes care for that, or the ghost within the tomb? Be it so: in days gone by no wooers bent thy sorrow, not in Libya, not ere then in Tyre; Iarbas was slighted, and other princes nurtured by the triumphal land of Africa; wilt thou contend even with a love to thy liking? nor does it cross thy mind whose

---

[1] From *The Æneid of Virgil*. Translated by J. W. Mackail. Reprinted by permission of the translator and Messrs Macmillan and Co., Ltd.

are these fields about thy dwelling? On this side are the Gaetulian towns, a race unconouerable in war; the reinless Numidian riders and the Syrtis hem the in; on this lies a thirsty tract of desert, swept by the raiders of Barca. Why speak of the war gathering from Tyre, and thy brother's menaces? ... Under gods' control to my thinking, and with Juno's favour, has the Ilian fleet held on hither before the gale. What a city wilt thou discern here, O sister! what a realm will rise on such a union! the arms of Troy ranged with ours, what glory will exalt the Punic state! Do thou only, asking divine favour with peace-offerings, be bounteous in welcome and multiply reasons for delay, while the storm rages out at sea and Orion is rainy, and his ships are shattered and the sky unvoyageable." With these words she fired her spirit with resolved love, put hope in her wavering soul, and undid her shame.

First they visit the shrines, and desire grace from altar to altar; they sacrifice sheep fitly chosen to Ceres the Lawgiver, to Phoebus and lord Lyaeus, to Juno before all, guardian of the marriage bond. Dido herself, excellent in beauty, holds the cup in her hand, and pours libation between the horns of a milk-white cow, or moves in state to the rich altars before the gods' presences, day by day renewing her gifts, and plunges her gaze into the breasts of cattle laid open to take counsel from the throbbing entrails. Ah, witless souls of soothsayers! how may vows or shrines help her madness? All the while the subtle flame consumes her inly, and deep in her breast the wound is silent and alive. Stung to misery, Dido wanders in frenzy all down the city, even as an arrow-stricken deer, whom, far and heedless amid the Cretan woodland, a shepherd archer has pierced and left the flying steel in her unaware; she ranged in flight the Dictaean forest lawns; fast in her side clings the deadly reed. Now she leads Æneas with her through the town, and displays her Sidonian treasure and ordered city; she essays to speak, and breaks off half-way in utterance. Now, as day wanes, she seeks the repeated banquet, and again in her madness pleads to hear the agonies of Ilium, and again hangs on the teller's lips. Thereafter, when all are gone their ways, and the dim moon in turn quenches her light, and the setting stars counsel to sleep, alone in the empty house she mourns, and flings herself on the couch he left: distant she hears and sees him in the distance; or enthralled by some look of his father, she holds Ascanius on her lap, if so she may steal her love unuttered. No more do the unfinished towers rise, no more do the people exercise in arms, nor work for safety in war on harbour or bastion; the works hang broken off, vast looming walls and engines towering into the sky.

So soon as she perceives her thus fast in the toils, and madly careless of

her name, Jove's beloved wife, daughter of Saturn, accosts Venus thus:
"Noble indeed is the fame and splendid the spoils you win, thou and
that boy of thine, and mighty the renown of your deity, if two gods have
vanquished one woman by treachery. Nor am I so blind to thy terror of
our town, thine old jealousy of the high house of Carthage. But what shall
be the end? or why all this contest now? Nay, rather let us work an enduring
peace and a bridal compact. Thou hast what all thy soul desired: Dido is
on fire with love, and has caught the madness through and through. Then
rule we this people jointly in equal lordship; allow her to be a Phrygian
husband's slave, and to lay her Tyrians for dowry in thine hand."

To her—for she knew the dissembled purpose in her words, to turn the
kingdom of Italy away to the coasts of Libya—Venus thus began in answer:
"Who so mad as to reject these terms, or choose rather to try the fortune
of war with thee? if only when done, as thou sayest, fortune follow. But
I move uncertain of Jove's ordinance, whether he will that Tyrians and
wanderers from Troy be one city, or approve the mingling of peoples or
the treaty of union. Thou art his wife, and thy prayers may put his mind
to proof. Go on; I will follow."

Then Queen Juno thus rejoined: "That task shall be mine. Now, by what
means the present need may be fulfilled, attend and I will explain in brief.
Æneas and lovelorn Dido are to go hunting together in the woodland
when to-morrow's rising sun goes forth and his rays unveil the world.
On them, while the beaters run up and down, and encircle the lawns with
toils, will I pour down a blackening rain-cloud mingled with hail, and
wake all the sky with thunder. Their company will scatter for shelter in
the dim darkness; Dido and the Trojan captain will take covert in the
same cavern. I will be there, and if thy goodwill is assured me, I will unite
them in wedlock, and make her wholly his; here shall Hymen be present."
The Cytherean gave ready assent to her request, and laughed at the guileful
device.

Meanwhile Dawn has arisen forth of ocean. A chosen company issue
from the gates while the morning star is high; they pour forth with meshed
nets, toils, broad-headed hunting spears, Massylian horsemen and hounds
of scent. At her doorway the Punic princes await their queen, who yet
lingers in her chamber, and her horse stands, splendid in gold and purple
with clattering feet and jaws champing on the foamy bit. At last she comes
forth amid a great thronging train, girt in a Sidonian mantle, broidered
with needlework; her quiver is of gold, her tresses gathered into gold,
a golden buckle clasps up her crimson gown. Therewithal the Phrygian
train advances with joyous Iülus. Himself first and fairest of all Æneas

joins her company and mingles his train with hers: even as Apollo, when he leaves wintry Lycia and the streams of Zanthus to visit his mother's Delos, and renews the dance, while Cretans and Dryopes and painted Agathyrsians mingle clamorous about his altars: himself he treads the Cynthian ridges, and plaits his flowing hair with soft heavy sprays and entwines it with gold; the arrows rattle on his shoulder: as lightly as he went Æneas; such glow of beauty is on his princely face. When they are come to the mountain heights and pathless coverts, lo, wild goats driven from the cliff-tops run down the ridge; in another quarter stags speed over the open plain and gather their flying column in a cloud of dust as they leave the hills. But the boy Ascanius is in the valleys, exultant on his fiery horse, and gallops past one and another, praying that among the unwarlike herds a foaming boar may issue or a tawny lion descend the hill.

Meanwhile the sky begins to thicken and roar aloud. A rain-cloud comes down mingled with hail; the Tyrian train and the men of Troy, and Venus' Dardanian grandchild, scatter in fear and seek shelter far over the fields. Streams pour from the hills. Dido and the Trojan captain take covert in the same cavern. Primeval Earth and Juno the bridesmaid give the sign; fires flash out high in air, witnessing the union, and Nymphs cry aloud on the mountain-top. That day opened the gate of death and the springs of ill. For now Dido recks not of eye or tongue, nor sets her heart on love in secret: she calls it marriage, and with this word shrouds her blame.

Straightway Rumour runs through the great cities of Libya,—Rumour, than whom none other is more swift to mischief; she thrives on restlessness and gains strength by going: at first small and timorous; soon she lifts herself on high and paces the ground with head hidden among the clouds. Her, as they tell, Mother Earth, when stung by wrath against the gods, bore last sister to Cœus and Enceladus, fleet-footed and swift of wing, ominous, awful, vast; for every feather on her body is a waking eye beneath, wonderful to tell, and a tongue, and as many loud lips and straining ears. By night she flits between sky and land, shrilling through the dusk, and droops not her lids in sweet slumber; in daylight she sits on guard upon tall towers or the ridge of the house-roof, and makes great cities afraid; obstinate in perverseness and forgery no less than messenger of truth. She then exultingly filled the countries with manifold talk, and blazoned alike what was done and undone: one Æneas is come, born of Trojan blood; on him beautiful Dido thinks no shame to fling herself; now they pass the long wintertide together in revelry, regardless of their realms and enthralled by dishonouring passion. This the pestilent goddess spreads abroad in the mouths of men, and bends her course right on to King

Iarbas, and with her words fires his spirit and swells his wrath.

He, the seed of Ammon by a ravished Garamantian Nymph, had built to Jove in his wide realms an hundred great temples, an hundred altars, and consecrated the wakeful fire that keeps watch by night before the gods perpetually, where the soil is fat with blood of beasts and the courts blossom with pied garlands. And he, distraught at heart and on fire at the bitter tidings, before his altars, amid the divine presences, often, it is said, bowed in prayer to Jove with uplifted hands:

"Jupiter omnipotent, to whom from the broidered cushions of their banqueting halls the Maurusian people now pour offering of the winevat, lookest thou on this? or do we shudder vainly when our father hurls the thunder-bolt, and do blind fires in the clouds and idle rumblings appal our soul? The woman wanderer who in our coasts planted a small town on purchased ground, to whom we gave fields by the shore and laws of settlement, has spurned our alliance and taken Æneas for lord of her realm. And now that Paris, with his effeminate crew, his chin and oozy hair swathed in the turban of Mæonia, takes and keeps her; since to thy temples we bear oblation, and hallow an empty name."

In such words he pleaded, clasping the altars; the Lord omnipotent heard, and cast his eye on the royal city and the lovers forgetful of their fairer fame. Then he addresses this charge to Mercury:

"Up and away, O son! call the breezes and slide down them on thy wings: accost the Dardanian captain who now loiters in Tyrian Carthage and casts not a look on the cities destined for him; carry down my words through the fleet air. Not such an one did his mother most beautiful vouch him to us, nor for this twice rescue him from Grecian arms; but he was to rule an Italy teeming with empire and loud with war, to transmit the line of Teucer's royal blood, and lay all the world beneath his law. If such glories kindle him in nowise, and he take no trouble for his own honour, does a father grudge his Ascanius the towers of Rome? with what device or in what hope loiters he among a hostile race, and casts not a glance on his Ausonian children and the fields of Lavinium? Let him set sail: this is the sum: thereof be thou our messenger."

He ended: the other made ready to obey his father's high command. And first he laces to his feet the shoes of gold that bear him winging high over seas or land as fleet as the blast; then takes the rod wherewith he calls wan souls forth of Orcus, or sends them again to the sad depth of hell, gives sleep and takes it away and unseals dead eyes; in whose strength he courses the winds and swims through the tossing clouds. And now in flight he descries the peak and steep sides of toiling Atlas, whose crest sustains the sky; Atlas, whose pine-clad head is girt always with black clouds and beaten by wind and rain; snow is shed over his shoulders for covering; rivers tumble over his aged chin; and his rough beard is stiff with ice. Here the Cyllenian, poised evenly on his wings, first checked his flight; hence he shot himself sheer to the water. Like a bird that flies low, skirting the sea about the craggy shores of its fishery, even thus the brood of Cyllene left his mother's father, and flew, cutting the winds between sky and land, toward the sandy Libyan shore. So soon as his winged feet touched at the hut-villages, he espied Æneas founding towers and ordering new dwellings; his sword twinkled with yellow jasper, and a cloak hung from his shoulders ablaze with Tyrian sea-purple, a gift that Dido had made costly and shot the warp with threads of gold. Straightway he breaks in: "Layest thou now the foundations of high Carthage, and buildest up a fair city in dalliance? ah, forgetful of thine own kingdom and state! From bright Olympus I descend to thee at express command of heaven's sovereign, whose deity sways sky and earth; expressly he bids me carry this charge through the fleet air: with what device or in what hope dost thou loiter idly on Libyan lands? if such glories kindle thee in nowise, yet cast an eye on growing Ascanius, on Iülus thine hope and heir, to whom the kingdom of Italy and the Roman land is due." As these words left his lips the Cyllenian, yet speaking, quitted mortal sight and vanished into thin air away out of his eyes.

But Æneas in truth gazed in dumb amazement, his hair thrilled up, and the voice choked in his throat. He burns to flee away and leave the pleasant land, aghast at the high warning and divine ordinance. Alas, what shall he do? how venture now to smooth the tale to the frenzied queen? what prologue shall he find? and this way and that he rapidly throws his mind, and turns it on all hands in swift change of thought. In his perplexity this seemed the better counsel; he calls Mnestheus and Sergestus, and brave Seretus, and bids them silently equip the fleet, gather their crews to the shore, and prepare their armament, keeping the cause of the commotion hid; himself meanwhile, since Dido in her kindness knows not and looks not for severance to so strong a love, will essay to approach her when she may be told most gently, and the way for it be fair. All at once gladly do as bidden, and obey his command.

But the Queen—who may delude a lover? foreknew his devices, and at once caught the presaging stir, fearing even where no fear was. To her likewise had evil Rumour borne the maddening news of the fleet in equipment and the voyage prepared. Helpless at heart, she reels aflame with rage throughout the city, even as the scared Thyiad in her frenzied triennial orgies, when the holy vessels move forth and the cry of Bacchus re-echoes, and Cithæron calls her with nightlong din. Thus at last she breaks out upon Æneas:

"And thou didst hope, traitor, to mask such infamy, and slip away silently from my land? Our love holds thee not, nor the hand thou once gavest, nor the bitter death that is left for Dido's portion? Nay, even in winter weather thou labourest on thy fleet, and hastenest to launch into the deep amid northern gales; ah, cruel! Why, were thy quest not of alien fields and unknown dwellings, did thine ancient Troy remain, should Troy be sought in voyages over tempestuous seas? Fliest thou from me? me who by these tears and thine own hand beseech thee, since naught else, alas! have I kept mine own—by our union and the marriage rites begun; if I have done thee any grace, or aught of mine was once sweet to thee,—pity our sinking house, and if there yet be room for prayers, put off this purpose of thine. For thy sake Libyan tribes and Nomad kings are hostile; my Tyrians are estranged; for thy sake, thine, is mine honour perished, and the former fame, my one title to the skies. How leavest thou me to die, O my guest? since of the name of husband all that is left is this. For what do I wait? till Pygmalion overthrow his sister's city, or Gaetulian Iarbas lead me to captivity? At least if before thy flight a child of thine had been clasped in my arms, if a tiny Æneas were playing in my hall, whose face might yet image thine, I would not think myself ensnared and deserted utterly."

She ended; he by counsel of Jove held his gaze unstirred, and kept his anguish hard down in his heart. At last he briefly answers:

"Never, O Queen, will I deny that thy goodness has gone high as thy words can swell the reckoning; nor will I grudge a memory to Elissa while I remember myself, and breath sways this body. Little will I say where little is to be said. I never hoped to slip away in stealthy flight; fancy not that; nor did I ever hold out the marriage torch or enter thus into alliance. Did fate allow me to guide my life by mine own government, and calm my sorrows as I would, my first duty were to the Trojan city and the dear remnant of my kindred; the high house of Priam should abide, and my hand had set up Troy towers anew for a conquered people. But now for broad Italy has Apollo of Grynos bidden me steer, for Italy the oracles of Lycia. Here is my desire; this is my native country. If thy Phœnician eyes are stayed on the fortress of Carthage and thy Libyan city, what wrong is it, I pray, that we Trojans should find rest on Ausonian land? We too may seek a foreign realm unforbidden. In my sleep, often as the dank shades of night veil the earth, often as the stars lift their fires, the troubled phantom of my father Anchises comes in warning and dread;

my boy Ascanius comes and the wrong done to one so dear in cheating him of an Hesperian kingdom and destined fields. Now even the gods' interpreter sent straight from Jove—I call both to witness—has borne down his commands through the fleet air. Myself in broad daylight I saw the deity passing within the walls, and these ears drank his utterance. Cease to madden me and thyself alike with plaints. Not of my will do I follow Italy..."

Long ere he ended she gazes on him askance, turning her eyes from side to side and perusing him with silent glances; then thus wrathfully speaks:

"No goddess was thy mother, nor Dardanus founder of thy line, traitor! but rough Caucasus bore thee on his iron crags, and Hyrcanian tigresses gave thee suck. For why do I conceal it? For what further outrage do I wait? Has our weeping cost him a sigh, or a lowered glance? Has he broken into tears, or had pity on his lovers? Where, where shall I begin? Now neither doth Queen Juno nor our Saturnian lord regard us with righteous eyes. Nowhere is trust safe. Cast ashore and destitute I welcomed him, and madly gave him place and portion in my kingdom; I found him his lost fleet and drew his comrades from death. Alas, the fire of madness speeds me on. Now prophetic Apollo, now oracles of Lycia, now the very gods' interpreter sent straight from Jove through the air carries these rude commands! Truly that is work for the gods, that a care to vex their peace! I detain thee not, nor gainsay thy words: go, follow thine Italy down the wind; seek thy realm overseas. Yet midway my hope is, if righteous gods can do aught at all, thou wilt drain the cup of vengeance on the rocks, and re-echo calls on Dido's name. In murky fires I will follow far away, and when chill death has severed body from soul, my ghost will haunt thee in every region. Wretch, thou shalt repay! I will hear; and the rumour of it shall reach me deep in the under world."

Even on these words she breaks off her speech unfinished, and, sick at heart, escapes out of the air and sweeps round and away out of sight, leaving him in fear and much hesitance, and with much on his mind to say. Her women catch her in their arms, and carry her swooning limbs to her marble chamber and lay her on her bed.

But good Æneas, though he would fain soothe and comfort her grief, and quell her passion by speech, with many a sigh, and melted in soul by his great love, yet fulfils the divine commands and returns to his fleet. Then indeed the Teucrians set to work, and haul down their tall ships all along the shore. The hulls are oiled and afloat; they carry from the woodland green boughs for oars and massy logs unhewn, in hot haste to go.... One might descry them shifting their quarters and pouring out of all the town: even as ants, mindful of winter, plunder a great heap of wheat and store it in their house; a black column advances on the plain as they carry home their spoil on a narrow track through the grass. Some shove and strain with their shoulders at big grains, some marshal the ranks and chastise delay; all the path is as warm with work. What then were thy thoughts, O Dido, as thou sawest it? What sighs didst thou utter, viewing from the fortress roof the broad beach aswarm, and seeing before thine eyes the whole sea stirred with their noisy din? Injurious Love, to what dost thou not compel mortal hearts! Again she must needs break into tears, again essay entreaty, and bow her spirit down to love, not to leave aught untried and go to death in vain.

"Anna, thou seest the bustle that fills the circle of the shore. They have gathered from every quarter; already their canvas woos the breezes, and the joyous sailors have garlanded the sterns. This great pain, my sister, I shall have strength to bear, as I have had strength to foresee. Yet this one thing, Anna, for love and pity's sake—for of thee alone was the traitor fain, to thee even his secret thoughts were confided, alone thou knewest his moods and tender fits—go, my sister, and humbly accost the haughty stranger: I did not take the Grecian oath in Aulis to root out the race of Troy; I sent no fleet against her fortresses, neither have I disentombed his father Anchises' ashes and ghost. Why does he refuse my words entrance to his stubborn ears? Whither does he run? let him grant this grace—alas, the last!—to his lover, and await fair winds and an easy passage. No more do I pray for the old delusive marriage, nor that he give up fair Latium and abandon a kingdom. A breathing-space I ask, to give my madness rest and room, till my very fortune teach my grief submission. This last grace I implore—sister, be pitiful—let him but grant me this and I will repay it weighted with my death."

So she pleaded, and so her sister carries and recarries the piteous tale of weeping. But by no weeping is he stirred, and no words that he hears may bend him. Fate withstands, and lays divine bars on unmoved mortal ears. Even as when the eddying blasts of northern Alpine winds are emulous to uproot the secular strength of a mighty oak, it wails on, and the trunk quivers and the high foliage strews the ground; the tree clings fast on the rocks, and high as her top soars into the aery sky, so deep strike her roots to hell; even thus is the hero buffeted with changeful perpetual accents, and distress thrills his mighty breast, while his purpose stays unstirred, and her tears are shed in vain.

Then indeed, hapless and dismayed by doom, Dido prays for death, and is weary of looking on the arch of heaven. The more to make her fulfil her purpose and quit the light, she saw, when she laid her gifts on the altars alight with incense, awful to tell, the holy streams blacken, and the wine turn as it poured into ghastly blood. Of this sight she spoke to none—no, not to her sister. Likewise there was within the house a marble temple of her ancient lord, kept of her in marvellous honour, and fastened with snowy fleeces and festal boughs. Forth of it she seemed to hear her husband's voice crying and calling when night was dim upon earth, and alone on the house-tops the screech-owl often made moan with funeral note and long-drawn sobbing cry. Therewithal many a warning of wizards of old terrifies her with appalling presage. In her sleep fierce Æneas drives her wildly, and ever she seems being left by herself alone, ever going uncompanioned on a weary way, and seeking her Tyrians in a solitary land: even as frantic Pentheus sees the arrayed Furies and a double sun, and Thebes shows herself twofold to his eyes: or Agamemnonian Orestes driven over the stage, when his mother pursues him armed with torches and dark serpents, and the Fatal Sisters crouch avenging in the doorway.

So when, overcome by her pangs, she has caught the madness and resolved to die, she works out secretly the time and fashion, and accosts her sorrowing sister with mien hiding her design and hope calm on her brow.

"I have found a way, mine own—wish me joy, sisterlike—to restore him to me or release me of my love for him. Hard by the ocean limit and the set of sun is the extreme Æthiopian land, where ancient Atlas turns on his shoulders the starred burning axletree of heaven. Out of it has been shown to me a priestess of Massylian race warder of the temple of the Hesperides, even she who gave the dragon his food, and kept the holy boughs on the tree, sprinkling clammy honey and slumberous poppyseed. She vouches with her spells to relax the purposes of whom she will, but on others to bring passion and pain; to stay the river-waters and turn the stars backward: she calls up ghosts by night; thou shalt see earth moaning under foot and mountain-ashes descending from the hills. I take heaven, sweet, to witness, and thee, mine own darling sister, I do not willingly arm myself with the arts of magic. Do thou secretly raise a pyre in the inner court, and lay upon it the arms of the man that he cruelly left hanging in our chamber, and all the dress he wore, and the bridal bed where I fell. It is good to wipe out all traces of the accursed one, and the priestess orders thus." So speaks she, and is silent, while pallor overruns her face. Yet Anna deems not her sister drapes death in these strange rites, and grasps not her wild purpose, nor fears aught deeper than at Sychæus' death. So she makes ready as bidden....

But the Queen, when the pyre is built up of piled faggots and cleft ilex in the inmost of her dwelling, hangs the room with chaplets and garlands

it with funeral boughs: on the pillow she lays the dress he wore, the sword
he left, and an image of him, knowing what was to come. Altars are reared
around, and the priestess, with hair undone, thrice peals from her lips the
hundred gods of Erebus and Chaos, and the triform Hecate, the triple-
faced maidenhood of Diana. Likewise she had sprinkled pretended waters
of Avernus' spring, and rank herbs are sought mown by moonlight with
brazen sickles, dark with milky venom, and sought is the talisman torn
from a horse's forehead at birth ere the dam could snatch it. ... Herself,
the holy cake in her pure hands, hard by the altars, with one foot unshod
and garments flowing loose, she invokes the gods ere she die, and the stars
that know of doom; then prays to whatsoever deity looks in righteousness
and remembrance on lovers ill allied.

Night fell; weary creatures took quiet slumber all over earth, and woodland and wild waters had sunk to rest; now the stars wheel midway on
their gliding path, now all the country is silent, and beasts and gay birds
that haunt liquid levels of lake or thorny rustic thicket lay couched asleep
under the still night. But not so the distressed Phoenician, nor does she
ever sink asleep or take the night upon eyes or breast; her pain redoubles,
and her love swells to renewed madness, as she tosses on the strong tide
of wrath. Even so she begins, and thus revolves with her heart alone:

"Lo, what do I? Shall I again make trial of mine old wooers that will
scorn me? and stoop to sue for a Numidian marriage among those whom
already over and over I have disdained for husbands? Then shall I follow
the Ilian fleets and the uttermost bidding of the Teucrians? because they
are glad to have been once raised up by my succour, or the grace of mine
old kindness is fresh in their remembrance? And who will permit me, if
I would? or take a hated woman on their proud fleet? art thou ignorant,
ah me, even in ruin, and knowest not yet the forsworn race of Laomedon?
And then? shall I accompany the triumphant sailors, a lonely fugitive?
or plunge forth girt with all my Tyrian train? so hardly severed from Sidon
city, shall I again drive them seaward, and bid them spread their sails to
the tempest? Nay die thou, as thou deservest, and let the steel end thy
pain. With thee it began; overborne by my tears, thou, O my sister, dost
load me with this madness and agony, and cast me to the enemy. It was
not mine to spend a wild life without stain, far from a bridal chamber, and
untouched by this passion. O faith ill kept, that was plighted to Sychæus'
ashes!" Thus her heart broke in long lamentation.

Now Æneas was fixed to go, and now, with all set duly in order, was
taking hasty sleep on his high quarterdeck. To him as he slept the god
appeared once again in the same fashion of countenance, and thus seemed

to renew his warning, in all points like to Mercury, voice and hue and golden hair and limbs gracious in youth. "Goddess-born, canst thou sleep on in such danger? and seest not the coming perils that hem thee in, madman! nor hearest the breezes blowing fair? She, fixed on death, is revolving craft and crime grimly in her bosom, and swells the changing surge of wrath. Fliest thou not hence headlong, while headlong flight is yet possible? Even now wilt thou see ocean weltering with broken timbers see the fierce glare of torches and the beach in a riot of flame, if dawn break on thee yet dallying in this land. Up ho! linger no more! Woman is ever a fickle and changing thing." So spoke he, and melted in the black night.

Then indeed Æneas, startled by the sudden phantom, leaps out of slumber and bestirs his crew to headlong haste. "Awake, O men, and sit down to the thwarts; shake out sail speedily. A god sent from high heaven, lo! again spurs us to speed our flight and cut the twisted cables. We follow thee, holy one of heaven, whoso thou art, and again joyfully obey thy command. O be favourable; give gracious aid and bring fair sky and weather." He spoke, and snatching his sword like lightning from the sheath, strikes at the hawser with the drawn steel. The same zeal catches all at once; rushing and tearing they quit the shore; the sea is hidden under their fleets; strongly they toss up the foam and sweep the blue water.

And now Dawn broke, and leaving the saffron bed of Tithonus, shed her radiance anew over the world; when the Queen saw from her watch-tower the first light whitening, and the fleet standing out under squared sail, and discerned shore and haven empty of all their oarsmen. Thrice and four times she struck her hand on her lovely breast and rent her yellow hair: "God!" she cries, "shall he go? shall an alien make mock of our realm? Will they not issue in armed pursuit from all the city, and some launch ships from the dockyards? Go; bring fire in haste, serve out weapons, ply the oars! What do I talk? or where am I, what mad change is on my purpose? Alas, Dido! now evil deeds touch thee; that had been fitting once, when thou gavest away thy crown. Behold the faith and hand of him! who, they say, carries his household's ancestral gods about with him! who stooped his shoulders to a father outworn with age! Could I not have riven his body in sunder and strewn it on the waves? and slain with the sword his comrades and his dear Ascanius, and served him for the banquet at his father's table? But the chance of battle had been dubious. If it had! whom did I fear in the death agony? I should have borne firebrands into his camp and filled his decks with flame, blotted out father and son and race together, and flung myself atop of all. Sun, whose fires lighten all the works of the world, and thou, Juno, mediatress and witness of these my distresses, and Hecate, cried on by night in crossways of cities, and you, fatal avenging sisters and gods of dying Elissa, hear me now; bend your just deity to my woes, and listen to our prayers. If it must needs be that the accursed one touch his haven and float up to land, if thus Jove's decrees demand, and this is the appointed term,—yet, distressed in war by an armed and gallant nation, driven homeless from his borders, rent from Iülus' embrace, let him sue for succour and see death on death untimely on his people; nor when he has yielded him to the terms of a harsh peace, may he have joy of his kingdom or the pleasant light; but let him fall before his day and without burial amid its soil. This I pray; this and my blood with it I pour for the last utterance. Then do you, O Tyrians, pursue his seed with your hatred for all ages to come; send this guerdon to our ashes. Let no kindness nor truce be between the nations. Arise, some avenger, out of our dust, to follow the Dardanian settlers with firebrand and steel. Now, then, whensoever strength shall be given, I invoke the enmity of shore to shore, wave to water, sword to sword; let their battles go down to their children's children."

So speaks she as she kept turning her mind round about, seeking how soonest to break away from the hateful light. Thereon she speaks briefly to Barce, nurse of Sychæus; for a heap of dusky ashes held her own, in her country of long ago:

"Sweet nurse, bring Anna my sister hither to me. Bid her haste and sprinkle river water over her body, and bring with her the beasts ordained for expiation: so let her come: and thou likewise veil thy brows with a pure chaplet. I would fulfil the rites of Stygian Jove that I have fitly ordered and begun, so to set the limit to my distresses and give over to flame the pyre of the Dardanian chief."

So speaks she; the old woman went eagerly with quickened pace. But Dido, panting and fierce in her awful purpose, with bloodshot restless gaze, and spots on her quivering cheeks burning through the pallor of imminent death, bursts into the inner courts of the house, and mounts in madness the lofty stairs, and unsheathes the sword of Dardania, a gift sought for other use than this. Then after her eyes fell on the Ilian raiment and the bed she knew, dallying a little with her purpose through her tears, she sank on the pillow and spoke the last words of all:

"Dress he wore, sweet while doom and deity allowed! receive my spirit now, and release me from my distresses. I have lived and fulfilled Fortune's allotted course; and now shall I go a queenly phantom under the earth. I have built a renowned city; I have seen my ramparts rise; by my brother's punishment I have avenged my husband of his enemy; happy, ah me! and overhappy, had but the keels of Dardania never touched our shores!" She spoke; and burying her face in the pillow, "Death it will be," she cries. "and unavenged; but death be it. Thus, thus is it good to pass into the dark. Let the pitiless Dardanian's gaze drink in this fire out at sea, and my death be the omen he carries on his way."

She ceased; and even as she spoke her people see her sunk on the steel, and blood reeking on the sword and spattered on her hands. A cry rises in the high halls; Rumour riots down the quaking city. The house resounds with lamentation and sobbing and bitter crying of women; heaven echoes their loud wails; even as though all Carthage or ancient Tyre went down as the foe poured in, and the flames rolled furious over the roofs of house and temple. Death-stricken her sister heard, and in swift hurrying dismay, with torn face and smitten bosom, darts through them all, and calls the dying woman by her name. "Was it this, mine own? Was my summons a snare? Was it this thy pyre, ah me, this thine altar fires meant? How shall I begin my desolate moan? Didst thou disdain a sister's company in death? Thou shouldst have called me to share thy doom; in the self-same hour, the self-same pang of steel had been our portion. Did these very hands build it, did my voice call on our father's gods, that with thee lying thus I should be away, O merciless? Thou hast destroyed thyself and me together, O my sister, and the Sidonian lords and people, and this thy city. Give her wounds water: I will bathe them and catch on my lips the last breath that haply yet lingers." So speaking she had climbed the high steps, and, wailing, clasped and caressed her half-lifeless sister in her bosom, and stanched the dark streams of blood with her gown. She, essaying to lift her heavy eyes, swoons back; the deep-driven wound gurgles in her breast. Thrice she rose, and strained to lift herself on her elbow; thrice she rolled back on the pillow, and with wandering eyes sought the light of high heaven, and moaned as she found it.

Then Juno omnipotent, pitying her long pain and difficult decease, sent Iris down from heaven to unloose the struggling life from the body where it clung. For since neither by fate did she perish, nor as one who had earned her death, but woefully before her day, and fired by sudden madness, not yet had Proserpine taken her tress from the golden head, nor sentenced her to the nether Stygian world. So Iris on dewy saffron pinions flits down through the sky athwart the sun in a trail of a thousand changing dyes, and stopping over her head: "This lock, sacred to Dis, I take as bidden, and release thee from that body of thine." So speaks she, and cuts it with her hand. And therewith all the warmth ebbed forth from her and the life passed away upon the winds.